Saul Bellow's
Novels 1944–1953
is published with support from the

J. ARON CHARITABLE FOUNDATION, INC.

SAUL BELLOW

SAUL BELLOW

NOVELS 1944–1953

Dangling Man
The Victim
The Adventures of Augie March

THE LIBRARY OF AMERICA

First Printing
The Library of America—141

JAMES WOOD
WROTE THE NOTES FOR THIS VOLUME

Contents

DANGLING MAN

To Anita

THERE was a time when people were in the habit of
addressing themselves frequently and felt no shame at
making a record of their inward transactions. But to keep a
journal nowadays is considered a kind of self-indulgence, a
weakness, and in poor taste. For this is an era of hardboiled-
dom. Today, the code of the athlete, of the tough boy—an
American inheritance, I believe, from the English gentleman
—that curious mixture of striving, asceticism, and rigor, the
origins of which some trace back to Alexander the Great—is
stronger than ever. Do you have feelings? There are correct
and incorrect ways of indicating them. Do you have an inner
life? It is nobody's business but your own. Do you have emotions? Strangle them. To a degree, everyone obeys this code.
And it does admit of a limited kind of candor, a closemouthed
straightforwardness. But on the truest candor, it has an in-
hibitory effect. Most serious matters are closed to the hard-
boiled. They are unpracticed in introspection, and therefore
badly equipped to deal with opponents whom they cannot
shoot like big game or outdo in daring.

If you have difficulties, grapple with them silently, goes one
of their commandments. To hell with that! I intend to talk
about mine, and if I had as many mouths as Siva has arms and
kept them going all the time, I still could not do myself justice. In my present state of demoralization, it has become
necessary for me to keep a journal—that is, to talk to myself
—and I do not feel guilty of self-indulgence in the least. The
hard-boiled are compensated for their silence: they fly planes
or fight bulls or catch tarpon, whereas I rarely leave my room.

In a city where one has lived nearly all his life, it is not likely
that he will ever be solitary; and yet, in a very real sense, I am
just that. I am alone ten hours a day in a single room. As such
places go, it is not bad, though there are the standard rooming-
house annoyances: cooking odors, roaches, and peculiar neighbors. But over the years I have become accustomed to all three.

I am well supplied with books. My wife is always bringing
new ones in the hope that I will use them. I only wish I

could. In the old days, when we had a flat of our own, I read constantly. I was forever buying new books, faster, admittedly, than I could read them. But as long as they surrounded me they stood as guarantors of an extended life, far more precious and necessary than the one I was forced to lead daily. If it was impossible to sustain this superior life at all times, I could at least keep its signs within reach. When it became tenuous I could see them and touch them. Now, however, now that I have leisure and should be able to devote myself to the studies I once began, I find myself unable to read. Books do not hold me. After two or three pages or, as it sometimes happens, paragraphs, I simply cannot go on.

Nearly seven months have gone by since I resigned my job at the Inter-American Travel Bureau to answer the Army's call for induction. I am still waiting. It is a trivial-seeming thing, a sort of bureaucratic comedy trimmed out in red tape. At first, I took that attitude toward it myself. It began as a holiday, a short reprieve, last May, when I was sent home because my papers were not in order. I have lived here eighteen years, but I am still Canadian, a British subject, and although a friendly alien I could not be drafted without an investigation. I waited five weeks and then I asked Mr. Mallender at Inter-American to take me back temporarily, but business had so fallen off, he told me, that he had been obliged to lay off Mr. Trager and Mr. Bishop, in spite of their long years of service, and could not possibly help me. At the end of September I was informed by letter that I had been investigated and approved and again, in accordance with the regulations, I was instructed to present myself for a second blood test. A month later I was notified that I was in 1A and was told to hold myself ready. Again I waited. Finally, when November came, I began to inquire and found that through a new clause affecting married men my induction had been postponed. I asked for reclassification, pleading that I had been prevented from working. After three weeks of explaining, I was transferred to 3A. But before I could act (in a week, to be accurate), I was summoned for a new blood test (each holds good for only sixty days). And so I was shifted back. This tedious business has not ended yet, I am sure. It will drag on for another two, three, four months.

Meanwhile, Iva, my wife, has been supporting me. She claims that it is no burden and that she wants me to enjoy this liberty, to read and to do all the delightful things I will be unable to do in the Army. About a year ago, I ambitiously began several essays, mainly biographical, on the philosophers of the Enlightenment. I was in the midst of one on Diderot when I stopped. But it was vaguely understood, when I began to dangle, that I was to continue with them. Iva did not want me to get a job. As a 1A I could not get a suitable one anyhow.

Iva is a quiet girl. She has a way about her that discourages talk. We no longer confide in each other; in fact, there are many things I could not mention to her. We have friends, but we no longer see them. A few live in distant parts of the city. Some are in Washington, and some in the Army; one is abroad. My Chicago friends and I have been growing steadily apart. I have not been too eager to meet them. Possibly some of our differences could be mended. But, as I see it, the main bolt that held us together has given way, and so far I have had no incentive to replace it. And so I am very much alone. I sit idle in my room, anticipating the minor crises of the day, the maid's knock, the appearance of the postman, programs on the radio, and the sure, cyclical distress of certain thoughts.

I have thought of going to work, but I am unwilling to admit that I do not know how to use my freedom and have to embrace the flunkydom of a job because I have no resources —in a word, no character. I made an attempt to enlist in the Navy last time I was reclassified, but induction, it seems, is the only channel for aliens. There is nothing to do but wait, or dangle, and grow more and more dispirited. It is perfectly clear to me that I am deteriorating, storing bitterness and spite which eat like acids at my endowment of generosity and good will. But the seven months' delay is only one of the sources of my harassment. Again, I sometimes think of it as the backdrop against which I can be seen swinging. It is still more. Before I can properly estimate the damage it has done me I shall have to be cut down.

December 16

I have begun to notice that the more active the rest of the
world becomes, the more slowly I move, and that my solitude
increases in the same proportion as its racket and frenzy. This
morning Tad's wife in Washington writes that he has flown to
North Africa. In all my life I have never felt so stock-still. I
can't even bring myself to go to the store for tobacco, though
I would enjoy a smoke. I will wait. And simply because Tad is
now landing in Algiers or Oran or already taking his first walk
in the *Casbah*—we saw *Pepé le Moko* together last year. I am
honestly pleased for his sake, not envious. But the feeling per-
sists that while he rockets to Africa and our friend Stillman
travels in Brazil, I grow rooted to my chair. It is a real, a bodily feeling. I will not even try to rise. It may be that I could
get up and walk around the room or even go to the store, but
to make the effort would put me in a disagreeable state. This
will pass if I ignore it. I have always been subject to such hallucinations. In the middle of winter, isolating a wall with sunlight on it, I have been able to persuade myself, despite the
surrounding ice, that the month was July, not February. Similarly, I have reversed the summer and made myself shiver in
the heat. And so, also, with the time of the day. It is a common trick, I suppose. It can be carried too far, perhaps, and
damage the sense of reality. When Marie comes to make the
bed, I shall get to my feet, button on my coat, and go to the
store, and that will be the end of this feeling.

As a rule I am only too anxious to find a reason to leave my
room. No sooner am I in it than I begin to cast around for
one. When I do go, I do not go far. My average radius is
three blocks. I am always afraid of running into an acquaintance who will express surprise at seeing me and ask questions. I avoid going downtown and, when I must go, I
carefully stay away from certain streets. And I think I have
carried over from my schooldays the feeling that there is
something unlawful in being abroad, idle, in the middle of
the day.

However, I am poor at finding reasons. I seldom go out
more than four times a day, three times for meals and the
fourth on a contrived errand or on some aimless impulse. I
rarely take long walks. For lack of exercise, I am growing

heavy. When Iva objects, I point out that I shall lose weight quickly enough in the Army. The streets at this time of year are forbidding, and then, too, I have no overshoes. Occasionally I do take a longer excursion, to the laundry or to the barber shop, to Woolworth's for envelopes, or even farther, at Iva's request, to pay a bill; or, without her knowledge, to see Kitty Daumler. And then there are obligatory visits to the family.

I have fallen into the habit of changing restaurants regularly. I do not want to become too familiar a sight in any of them, friendly with sandwich men, waitresses, and cashiers, and compelled to invent lies for their benefit.

At half-past eight I eat breakfast. Afterward I walk home and settle down to read the paper in the rocker by the window. I cover it from end to end, ritualistically, missing not a word. First come the comic strips (I follow them because I have done so since childhood, and I compel myself to read even the newest, most unpalatable ones), then I read the serious news and the columnists, and, finally, the gossip, the family page, the recipes, the obituaries, the society news, the ads, the children's puzzles, everything. Reluctant to put it aside, I even reread the comics to see if I have missed anything.

Re-entering waking life after the regeneration (when it is that) of sleep, I go in the body from nakedness to clothing and in the mind from relative purity to pollution. Raising the window, I test the weather; opening the paper, I admit the world.

I am now full of the world, and wide awake. It is nearly noon, time for lunch. Since eleven I have been growing restless, imagining that I am hungry again. Into the silence of the house there fall accentuating sounds, the closing of a door in another room, the ticking of drops from a faucet, the rustling of the steam in the radiator, the thrum of a sewing machine upstairs. The unmade bed, the walls, are brightly striped. The maid knocks and pushes open the door. She has a cigarette in her mouth. I think I am the only one before whom she dares smoke; she recognizes that I am of no importance.

At the restaurant I discover that I am not hungry at all, but now I have no alternative and so I eat. The stairs are a little more difficult this time. I come into the room breathing hard, and turn on the radio. I smoke. I listen to half an hour of symphonic music, disturbed when I fail to catch the announcer before he begins to advertise someone's credit-clothing. By one o'clock the day has changed, has taken on a new kind of restlessness. I make my effort to read but cannot key my mind to the sentences on the page or the references in the words. My mind redoubles its efforts, but thoughts of doubtful relevance are straggling in and out of it, the trivial and the major together. And suddenly I shut it off. It is as vacant as the street. I get up and turn on the radio again. Three o'clock, and nothing has happened to me; three o'clock, and the dark is already setting in; three o'clock, and the postman has bobbed by for the last time and left nothing in my box. I have read the paper and looked into a book, I have had a few random thoughts. . . .

> "Mr. Five-by-five,
>   He's five feet high
>   An' he's five feet wide . . ."

and now, like any housewife, I am listening to the radio.

The landlady's daughter has cautioned us not to play it too loudly; her mother has been bedridden for more than three months. The old woman is not expected to live long. She is blind and very nearly bald; she must be close to ninety. I see her at times, between the curtains, as I go upstairs. The daughter has been managing the house since September. She and her husband, Captain Briggs, live in the third-floor apartment. He is in the Quartermaster Division. A man of about fifty (much older than his wife), he is solid, neat, gray, and quiet-spoken. We often see him walking outside the fence, smoking a last cigarette before retiring.

At four-thirty I hear Mr. Vanaker next door, coughing and growling. Iva, for some reason of her own, has named him the "werewolf." He is a queer, annoying creature. His coughing, I am convinced, is partly alcoholic and partly nervous. And it is also a sort of social activity. Iva does not agree. But I know that he coughs to draw attention to himself. I have lived in rooming houses so long that I have acquired an eye for the type. Years ago, on Dorchester Avenue, there was an old man who refused to shut his door but sat or lay facing the hall and watched everyone, day and night. And there was another on Schiller Street in whose washbasin you could always hear the water running. That was his manner of making himself known to us. Mr. Vanaker coughs. Not only that, but when he goes to the toilet he leaves the door ajar. He tramps down the hall, and a moment later you hear him splashing. Iva lately complained about this to Mrs. Briggs, who thereupon tacked a notice on the wall: *Occupant please close door when using and wear bathrobes to and fro.* So far it hasn't helped.

Through Mrs. Briggs we have learned a number of interesting facts about Vanaker. Before the old woman took to bed he was continually urging her to go to the movies with him. "When it should be plain to anybody Mamma can't see a thing." He was formerly in the habit of running down to answer the phone in his pajama trousers only—the reason for the bathrobe warning. The Captain had to step in and put an end to that. Marie has found half-smoked cigars ground out on the floors of unoccupied rooms. She suspects Vanaker of snooping through the house. He is no gentleman. She cleans his room, and she knows. Marie has high standards for white conduct, and her nostrils grow wider when she speaks of him. The old woman, Mrs. Kiefer, once threatened to put him out, she claims.

Vanaker is energetic. Hatless, he hurries in his black moleskin jacket up the street and between the snowy bushes. He slams the street door and kicks the snow from his boots on the first step. Then, coughing wildly, he runs up.

At six, I meet Iva at Fallon's for supper. We eat there quite regularly. Sometimes we go to the "Merit" or to a cafeteria on Fifty-third Street. Our evenings are generally short. We turn in before midnight.

December 17

It is a narcotic dullness. There are times when I am not even aware that there is anything wrong with this existence. But, on the other hand, there are times when I rouse myself in bewilderment and vexation, and then I think of myself as a moral casualty of the war. I have changed. Two incidents in the past week have shown me how greatly. The first can hardly be called an incident. I was leafing through Goethe's *Poetry and Life* and I came upon the following phrase: "This loathing of life has both physical and moral causes. . . ." I was sufficiently stirred by this to read on. "All comfort in life is based upon a regular occurrence of external phenomena. The changes of the day and night, of the seasons, of flowers and fruits, and all other recurring pleasures that come to us, that we may and should enjoy them—these are the main-springs of our earthly life. The more open we are to these enjoyments, the happier we are; but if these changing phenomena unfold themselves and we take no interest in them, if we are insensible to such fair solicitations, then comes on the sorest evil, the heaviest disease—we regard life as a loathsome burden. It is said of an Englishman that he hanged himself that he might no longer have to dress and undress himself every day." I read on and on with unaccustomed feeling. Goethe's heading on the next page was "Weariness of Life." Exactly. *Radix malorum est* weariness of life. Then came the statement: "Nothing occasions this weariness more than the recurrence of the passion of love." Deeply disappointed, I put the book down.

Nevertheless, I could not help seeing how differently this would have affected me a year ago, and how much I had altered. Then, I might have found it true but not especially noteworthy. I might have been amused by that Englishman but not moved. But his boredom threw that "passion of love" in the shadow and he instantly took his place for me beside that murderer Barnardine in *Measure for Measure* whose contempt for life equaled his contempt for death, so that he would not come out of his cell to be executed. To be so drawn to those two was proof that I had indeed changed.

And now the second incident.

My father-in-law, old Almstadt, came down with a bad cold, and Iva, knowing how inept her mother is, asked me to go there and help out.

The Almstadts live on the Northwest Side, a dreary hour's ride on the El. I found the house in great disorder. Mrs. Almstadt was trying to make the beds, cook, attend her husband,

and answer the telephone all at the same time. The telephone was never idle for more than five minutes. Her friends kept calling, and to each she repeated the full story of her troubles. I have always disliked my mother-in-law. She is a short, fair, rather maidenish woman. Her natural color, when visible, is healthy. Her eyes are large, and they wear a knowing look, but since there is nothing to be knowing about they only convey her foolishness. She powders herself thickly, and her lips are painted in the shape that has become the universal device of sensuality for all women, from the barely mature to the very old. Mrs. Almstadt, nearing fifty, is already quite wrinkled, much to her concern, and she is forever on the watch for new packs and face lotions.

When I came in, she was busy talking over the telephone to someone, and I went to my father-in-law's room. He was lying with his knees drawn up and his shoulders raised, so that his head seemed joined without a neck directly to his body. Through an opening in his pajamas his flesh showed white and fatty under graying hair. He looked unfamiliar in the high-buttoned tunic with the crest on the pocket, and a little ludicrous. This was Mrs. Almstadt's doing. She bought his clothes, and she had dressed him for bed like a mandarin or a Romanoff prince. His broad knuckles were joined on the silken quilt. He greeted me with a not wholly ungrudged smile, and also as though it might be considered unmanly or unfatherly to fall sick. At the same time, however, he tried to make it plain that he could afford to spend a few days in bed; he was far enough ahead of the game; the business (this he told me with conflicting nonchalance and defiance) was in good hands.

The phone rang again, and Mrs. Almstadt once more began to tell her story to one of her innumerable connections (who knows who they are?). Her husband had come down yesterday, and they had had the doctor in, and the doctor had said there was a regular epidemic of grippe this winter. She was worn out, just worn out, trying to keep house and take care of Mr. Almstadt. You couldn't leave a sick person alone . . . and what could you do without a maid? Her words showered down upon us like little glass pellets. Old Almstadt gave no indication that he heard; at times he seemed automatically deaf to her. But, of course, it was impossible not to

hear her; she has a high, atonal voice which penetrates everywhere. And what I now became curious to know was whether
he was unaffected or whether she was a nuisance to him. In
the five years that I had been his son-in-law I had heard neither criticism nor defense of her from him, save on two occasions when he said, "Katy's still a child; she never grew up."

Before I was aware of it I was saying, "How did you ever
manage to stick it out so long, Mr. Almstadt?"

"Stick out? What?" he said.

"With her," I plunged on. "It would get me, I know it
would."

"What are you talking about?" the old man asked, perplexed and angry. I suppose he thought it dishonorable to
allow anyone to say such things to his face. But I could not
help myself. It seemed, at the moment, not an error but a
very natural inquiry. I was suddenly in a state of mind that required directness for its satisfaction. Nothing else would do.
"I don't know what you mean; what are you talking about?"
he said again.

"Well, listen to her."

"Oh," he said, "you mean the telephone."

"Yes, the telephone."

He appeared somewhat relieved. "I don't pay any attention
to it. All women are talkers. Maybe Katy talks more than
most, but you got to allow for that. She . . ."

"Never grew up?" I said.

I doubt that this was what he intended to say, but since the
phrase was his he could not dissent. With lips tightly drawn
together, he nodded. "Yes, that's right. Some people just turn
out different than others. Everybody isn't alike." He spoke
stiffly; he was still angry. He had to make allowances for me,
too, once in a while. My behavior was not always what it
should be, he thus, indirectly, gave me to understand. His
color had thickened furiously; it was slow to recede. Harsh
and red his face shone under the branched brass fixture whose
light had a singular hue, like tea. Was he deliberately covering
up an opinion which, it must be conceded, he had every right
to hold privately, or did he believe what he said? The latter
was the more likely explanation. Babble, tedium, and all the
rest were to be expected; they came with every marriage.

There was still another possibility to consider, and that was that he was not resigned and that he did not ignore her as he pretended but—and there was every likelihood that he was unaware of this—heard and delighted in her, wanted her slovenly, garrulous, foolish, and coy, took pleasure in enduring her. His face, as we looked at each other, took on a doglike aspect. I was perturbed, and rebuked my imagination.

The doctor had left a prescription which the old man asked me to take to the drugstore. As I went out I heard Mrs. Almstadt saying, "My Iva's husband Joseph is here to lend a hand. He isn't working now, he's waiting for the Army, so he has all the time in the world." I started and turned, full of indignation, but she, pressing the black, kidney-shaped instrument to her cheek, smiled at me all oblivious. I wondered whether it was possible that she should not have said it intentionally, that she should be blameless; whether her thoughts were as smooth and contentless as counters or blank dominoes; whether she was half guile and half innocence; or whether there worked through her a malice she herself knew nothing about.

There was a sharp wind outside; the sun, low and raw in a field of coarse clouds, ruddied the bricks and windows. The street had been blown dry (it had rained the day before), and it presented itself in one of its winter aspects, creased and with thin sidelocks of snow, all but deserted. A block-long gap lay between me and the nearest walker—out on some unfathomable business—a man in a long, soldierly coat which the sun had converted to its own color. And then the pharmacy where I waited, sipping a cup of coffee under the crepe-paper lattice till my parcel, wrapped in green Christmas paper, was handed to me.

As I was going back, an exhibit in a barbershop attracted me: "*Fancy articles from kitchen odds and ends by Mrs. J. Kowalski, 3538 Pierce Avenue.*" And there were laid out mosaic pictures, bits of matchstick on mats of leaf from old cigar butts, ash trays cut from tin cans and shellacked grapefruit rind, a braided cellophane belt, a letter opener inlaid with bits of glass, and two hand-painted religious pictures. In its glass case the striped pole turned smoothly, the Lucky Tiger watched from a thicket of bottles, the barber read a magazine.

Turning with my parcel, I went on and, through the gray pillars and the ungainly door which clanked on the mailboxes, entered the sad cavern of the hall.

Upstairs, I worked energetically on the old man. I had Mrs. Almstadt make a pitcher of orange juice, dosed him with the medicine, and rubbed him down with alcohol. He grunted with pleasure during the massage and said that I was stronger than I looked. We were on better terms by this time. But I would not be drawn into a conversation. If I kept silent, I could not make another mistake. If I began to talk I would soon find myself explaining my position and defending my idleness. Old Almstadt did not bring up the subject. My own father, I must say, treats me less considerately in that respect. He would have asked me, but Almstadt said nothing about it.

I rolled down my sleeves and was preparing to go when my mother-in-law reminded me that she had poured a glass of orange juice for me in the kitchen. That was not lunch, but it was better than nothing. I went to get it and found on the kitchen sink a half-cleaned chicken, its yellow claws rigid, its head bent as though to examine its entrails which raveled over the sopping draining board and splattered the enamel with blood. Beside it stood the orange juice, a brown feather floating in it. I poured it down the drain. Wearing my hat and scarf, I wandered to the living room where I had left my coat. Mr. and Mrs. Almstadt were conversing in the bedroom. I looked out of the window.

The sun had been covered up; snow was beginning to fall. It was sprinkled over the black pores of the gravel and was lying in thin slips on the slanting roofs. I could see a long way from this third-floor height. Not far off there were chimneys, their smoke a lighter gray than the gray of the sky; and, straight before me, ranges of poor dwellings, warehouses, billboards, culverts, electric signs blankly burning, parked cars and moving cars, and the occasional bare plan of a tree. These I surveyed, pressing my forehead on the glass. It was my painful obligation to look and to submit to myself the invariable question: Where was there a particle of what, elsewhere, or in the past, had spoken in man's favor? There could be no doubt that these billboards, streets, tracks, houses, ugly and blind, were related to interior life. And yet, I told myself, there had to be a doubt. There were human lives organized around these ways and houses, and that they, the houses, say, were the analogue, that what men created they also were, through some transcendent means, I could not bring myself to concede. There must be a difference, a quality that eluded me, somehow, a difference between things and persons and even between acts and persons. Otherwise the people who lived here were actually a reflection of the things they lived among. I had always striven to avoid blaming them. Was that not in effect behind my daily reading of the paper? In their businesses and politics, their taverns, movies, assaults, divorces, murders, I tried continually to find clear signs of their common humanity.

It was undeniably to my interest to do this. Because I was involved with them; because, whether I liked it or not, they were my generation, my society, my world. We were figures in the same plot, eternally fixed together. I was aware, also, that their existence, just as it was, made mine possible. And if, as was often said, this part of the century was approaching the nether curve in a cycle, then I, too, would remain on the bottom and there, extinct, merely add my body, my life, to the base of a coming time. This would probably be a condemned age. But . . . it might be a mistake to think of it in that way. Mists faded and spread and faded on the pane as I breathed. Perhaps a mistake. And when I thought of the condemned ages and those unnamed, lying in their obscurity, I wondered. . . . How did we know how it was? In all principal ways the human spirit must have been the same. Good apparently left fewer traces. And we were coming to know that we had misjudged whole epochs. Besides, the giants of the last century had their Liverpools and Londons, their Lilles and Hamburgs to contend against, as we have our Chicagos and Detroits. And there might be a chance that I was misled, even with these ruins before my eyes, sodden, themselves the color of the fateful paper that I read daily. . . . The worlds we sought were never those we saw; the worlds we bargained for were never the worlds we got.

I have spoken of an "invariable question." But the fact is that it had for many months been not in the least invariable. These were things I would have thought last winter, and now, in their troubled density, they served only to remind me of the sort of person I had been. For a long time "common humanity" and "bring myself to concede" had been completely absent from my mind. And all at once I saw how I had lapsed from that older self to whom they had been so natural.

December 18

For legal purposes, I am that older self, and if a question of my identity were to arise I could do nothing but point to my attributes of yesterday. I have not tried to bring myself up to date, either from indifference or from fear. Very little about the Joseph of a year ago pleases me. I cannot help laughing at him, at some of his traits and sayings.

Joseph, aged twenty-seven, an employee of the Inter-American Travel Bureau, a tall, already slightly flabby but, nevertheless, handsome young man, a graduate of the University of Wisconsin—major, History—married five years, amiable, generally takes himself to be well-liked. But on close examination he proves to be somewhat peculiar.

Peculiar? In what way? Well, to begin with, there is something about his appearance, something wrong. His is a long, straight-nosed, firm face. He wears a little mustache, which makes him look older than he really is. His eyes are dark and full, rather too full, a little prominent, in fact. His hair is black. He does not have what people call an "open" look, but is restrained—at times, despite his amiability, forbidding. He is a person greatly concerned with keeping intact and free from encumbrance a sense of his own being, its importance. Yet he is not abnormally cold, nor is he egotistic. He keeps a tight hold because, as he himself explains, he is keenly intent on knowing what is happening to him. He wants to miss nothing.

His wife does not remember him without a mustache, and he had just turned seventeen when they met. On his first visit to the Almstadts, he had smoked a cigar and talked loudly and fairly expertly (he was then a Communist) about the German Social Democracy and the slogan "United Front from Below." Her father had taken him for twenty-five and had angrily ordered her not to invite grown men to the house. It amuses Mr. Almstadt to tell this story, now a family joke. He says: "I thought he was going to carry her away to Russia."

To turn now to Joseph's dress (I am wearing his cast-off clothes), it adds to his appearance of maturity. His suits are dark and conservative. His shoes, it is true, are pointed and rather dandyish, but that is possibly intended as a counterbalance. A broader toe would give you a man in his middle thirties. As he is in most things, Joseph is conscious of a motive in his choice of clothes. It is his answer to those whose defiant principle it is to dress badly, to whom a crumpled suit is a badge of freedom. He wants to avoid the small conflicts of nonconformity so that he can give all his attention to defending his inner differences, the ones that really matter. Furthermore, he takes a sad or negative satisfaction in wearing what he calls "the uniform of the times." In short, the less noteworthy the better, for his purposes. All the same, he manages to stand out.

In things of this sort his friends sometimes find him ridiculous. And, yes, he says, he admits he is on "the funny side" in many ways. But that can't be helped. The appearance and behavior of reflective men is seldom comparable to that of the less reflective, who unhesitatingly entrust all they stand for to their looks and gestures. What he is trying to do is not easy, and it is not unlikely that the more he succeeds, the more odd he may seem. Besides, he says, there is an element of the comic or fantastic in everyone. You can never bring that altogether under control.

"An element of the comic or fantastic . . ." Such phrases have a queer ring; and people who have begun by taking him for a clerk at Inter-American, a fairly nice chap, begin to look at him with changed eyes. But even his oldest friends, those who like John Pearl and Morris Abt have been close to him since boyhood, often find it hard to make him out. And, despite his anxiety to be understood, he cannot always help them.

Joseph, since leaving school, has not stopped thinking of himself as a scholar, and he surrounds himself with books. Before he interested himself in the Enlightenment he made a study of the early ascetics and, earlier, of Romanticism and the child prodigy. Of course, he has to earn his living, but he tries to strike a balance between what he wants and what he is compelled to do, between the necessity and the wish. A compromise exists, but then men's lives abound in such compromises. He is proud of the skill with which he manages both sides and—albeit somewhat mistakenly—likes to refer to himself as a Machiavellian. He keeps his roles successfully distinct and even goes out of his way to be an excellent employee, simply to prove that "visionaries" can be hardheaded.

Everyone admits, however, that Joseph has a close grasp on himself, that he knows what he wants and how to go about getting it. In the last seven or eight years he has worked everything out in accordance with a general plan. Into this plan have gone his friends, his family, and his wife. He has taken a great deal of trouble with his wife, urging her to read books of his choosing, teaching her to admire what he believes admirable. To what degree he has succeeded he does not know.

It should not be thought that Joseph, when he speaks of the "less reflective" or of his "element of the comic," is being harsh. He is not severe toward the world. He calls himself a sworn upholder of *tout comprendre c'est tout pardonner*. Theories of a wholly good or a wholly malevolent world strike him as foolish. Of those who believe in a wholly good world he says that they do not understand depravity. As for pessimists, the question he asks of them is, "Is that all they see, such people?" For him, the world is both, and therefore it is neither. Merely to make a judgment of that kind is, to representatives of either position, a satisfaction. Whereas, to him, judgment is second to wonder, to speculation on men, drugged and clear, jealous, ambitious, good, tempted, curious, each in his own time and with his customs and motives, and bearing the imprint of strangeness in the world. In a sense, everything is good because it exists. Or, good or not good, it exists, it is ineffable, and, for that reason, marvelous.

But for all that, Joseph suffers from a feeling of strangeness, of not quite belonging to the world, of lying under a cloud and looking up at it. Now, he says, all human beings share this to some extent. The child feels that his parents are pretenders; his real father is elsewhere and will some day come to claim him. And for others the real world is not here at all and what is at hand is spurious and copied. Joseph's feeling of strangeness sometimes takes the form almost of a conspiracy: not a conspiracy of evil, but one which contains the diversified splendors, the shifts, excitements, and also the common, neutral matter of an existence. Living from day to day under the shadow of such a conspiracy is trying. If it makes for wonder, it makes even more for uneasiness, and one clings to the nearest passers-by, to brothers, parents, friends, and wives.

December 20

Preparations for the holiday. I went out yesterday to do some shopping for Iva. Downtown there were bell ringers on every corner, in beards of soiled cotton and red Santa Claus costumes. For love of the poor, for dear charity, clang-clanging away in the din. Immense wreaths were mounted on buildings in the green, menacing air; the thousands upon thousands of shoppers ground through the stores and the streets under the smoky red façades and in the amplified roar of carols. The holly berries flashed on the tarred poles in thick drops. The jukeboxes in the taverns were playing "I'm Dreaming of a White Christmas." Everyone prays for snow, and the thought of rain or sleet brings panic.

Vanaker is restless these days. He keeps moving the furniture around his room. Marie complains more than ever. By changing the position of the bed he makes it hard for her to clean the room. The door is blocked. She doesn't like to go in anyway. He doesn't keep himself clean, she claims. Instead of sending his linen to the laundry, he airs it at the window. He hangs up his underwear at night and forgets to take it down in the morning. Mrs. Briggs tells me that he is engaged to marry a lady of sixty who insists that he be converted to the Catholic faith and that he goes every evening to the church of St. Thomas the Apostle for indoctrination. At the same time, I notice that he receives large quantities of mail from the Masonic Scottish Rite. It may be this conflict of principle that drives him to get up at two in the morning to change the position of his bed.

We have two invitations to Christmas dinner, one from the Almstadts and another from my brother Amos. I am for refusing both.

December 22

An unusual explosion of temper this afternoon, when I was with Myron Adler. I behaved unaccountably, greatly surprising myself and, of course, bewildering Myron altogether. He had phoned me about a temporary job which would consist of asking people questions for a poll he is conducting. I hurried down to meet him at the Arrow for lunch. I arrived first, took a table toward the back, and immediately fell victim to depression. I had not visited the Arrow for a number of years. It was at one time a hangout for earnest eccentrics where, at almost any hour of the afternoon or evening, you could hear discussions of socialism, psychopathology, or the fate of European Man. It was I who had suggested that we eat there; for some reason it had been the first place that came to my mind. Now it depressed me. Then, as I looked around at the steam tables and the posters of foundering ships and faces of Japanese, I suddenly saw Jimmy Burns sitting at a table with a man I did not know. Since the days when we had been Comrade Joe and Comrade Jim, we had seen each other no more than two, perhaps three, times. He looked changed; his forehead had grown higher and his expression more severe. I nodded to him, but got no recognition for my pains; he looked through me in the way which is, I suppose, officially prescribed for "renegades."

When Myron came in a few minutes later and started at once to talk about the job, I said impatiently, "Wait a second, now. Just hold on."

"What's the matter?"

"Something very special," I said. "Wait till I tell you. You see that man in the brown suit over there? That's Jimmy Burns. Ten years ago I was privileged to call him Comrade Jimmy."

"Well?" said Myron.

"I said hello to him, and he acted as if I simply wasn't there."

"What of it?" said Myron.

"Does that seem natural? I was once a close friend."

"Well?" said Myron.

"Stop saying that, will you!" I said in exasperation.

"I mean, do you want him to throw his arms around you?" asked Myron.

"You don't get the point. I despise him."

"Then I don't get the point. I confess I don't get it."

"No. Listen. He has no business ignoring me. This is always happening to me. You don't understand it because you're a person of no political experience. But I know what this means, and I'm going to go up to him and say hello whether he likes it or not."

"Don't be a fool. What do you want to make trouble for?" said Myron.

"Because I feel like making trouble. Does he know me or doesn't he? He knows me perfectly well." I was growing angrier by the minute. "I'm surprised that you shouldn't be able to see it."

"I came here to talk to you about a job, not to see you throw a fit," he said.

"Oh, a fit. Do you think I care about *him*? It's the principle of the thing. It seems to escape you. Simply because I am no longer a member of their party they have instructed him and boobs like him not to talk to me. Don't you see what's involved?"

"No," Myron said carelessly.

"I'll tell you what's involved. I have a right to be spoken to. It's the most elementary thing in the world. Simply that. I insist on it."

"Oh, Joseph," said Myron.

"No, really, listen to me. Forbid one man to talk to another, forbid him to communicate with someone else, and you've forbidden him to think, because, as a great many writers will tell you, thought is a kind of communication. And his party doesn't want him to think, but to follow its discipline. So there you are. Because it's supposed to be a revolutionary party. That's what's offending me. When a man obeys an order like that he's helping to abolish freedom and begin tyranny."

"Come, come," said Myron. "You're making too much fuss over it."

"I should be making twice as much fuss," I said. "It's very important."

"But you've been through with them for years, haven't you?" Myron asked. "Do you mean to say you've just discovered this now?"

"I haven't forgotten, that's all. You see, I thought those people were different. I haven't forgotten that I believed they were devoted to the service of some grand flapdoodle, the Race, *le genre humain*. Oh, yes, they were! By the time I got out, I realized that any hospital nurse did more with one bedpan for *le genre humain* than they did with their entire organization. It's odd to think that there was a time when to hear that would have filled me with horror. What? Reformism?"

"I've heard of that," said Myron.

"I should think so. Reformism! A terrible thing. About a month after we parted company, I sat down and wrote Jane Addams a letter of apology. She was still alive."

"Did you?" he said, looking at me curiously.

"I never mailed it," I said. "Maybe I should have. Don't you believe me?"

"Why shouldn't I?"

"I changed my mind about redoing the world from top to bottom à la Karl Marx and decided in favor of bandaging a few sores at a time. Of course, that was temporary too. . . ."

"Was it?" he said.

"Oh, for heaven's sake! You know that, Mike," I said loudly.

The man who was sitting with Burns turned around, but the latter still pretended not to see me. "That's right," I said. "Look the other way. Go on. That boy is mad, Myron. He's never been sane. Everything has changed, he's been left far behind, but he thinks it's as it used to be. He still wears that proletarian bang on his earnest forehead and dreams of becoming an American Robespierre. The rest have compromised themselves to the ears, but *he* still believes in the revolution. Blood will run, the power will change hands, and then the state will wither away according to the in-ex-or-able logic of history. I'd gamble my shirt on it. I know his mind.

Let me tell you something about him. Do you know what he used to have in his room? I went up with him one day, and there was a large-scale map of the city, with pins in it. So I said, 'What's this for, Jim?' And then—I swear this is true— he started to explain that he was preparing a guide for street-fighting, the day of the insurrection. He had all the critical streets marked in code for cellars and roofs, the paving material, the number of newsstands at each corner that could be thrown into barricades (the Parisian kiosks, you remember). Even abandoned sewers for hiding arms. He traced them through City Hall records. At that time I didn't know how crazy it was. The things we used to accept as natural—why, it's unbelievable! And he's still in that. I'll bet he still has the map. He's an addict. They're all addicted people, Mike. Hey, Burns! Hey!" I called out.

"Shut up, Joseph! For God's sake. What are you doing? Everybody's looking at you."

Burns glanced briefly in my direction and then resumed his conversation with the other man, who, however, turned again to examine me.

"What do you know about that! Burns won't give me a tumble. I can't arouse him. I'm just gone. Like that." I snapped my fingers. "I'm a contemptible petty-bourgeois renegade; could anything be worse? That idiot! Hey, addict!" I shouted.

"Have you gone mad? Come on." Myron pushed back the table. "I'm going to get you out of here before you start a fight. I think you would start a fight. Where's your coat, which is it? Why, you're a madman! Come back here!" But I was already out of his reach. I halted squarely before Burns.

"I said hello to you before, didn't you notice?"

He made no reply.

"Don't you know me? It seems to me that I know you very well. Answer me, don't you know who I am?"

"Yes, I know you," Burns said in a low voice.

"That's what I wanted to hear," I said. "I just wanted to be sure. I'm coming, Myron." I pulled my arm away from him and we strode out.

I was aware that this had made a bad impression on Myron, but cared to do little to rectify it beyond explaining in a few short words that I had not been myself lately. But I did not say this until we had come to our second course in another restaurant. I became very quiet. I did not, and still do not, know where this outbreak came from. I suspect that it originated in sheer dishevelment of mind. But how could I explain this to Myron without becoming entangled in a long description of the state I was in and its causes? I would make him squirm and I myself would squander my feelings in self-pity.

We talked about the job, and he promised to recommend me to his superiors. He hoped, he said (he had sounded more positive on the phone), that I would get it. Myron likes me, I know he does. But he has worked hard to reach his present position and, realist that he is, it cannot have taken him long to decide that he could not afford to be responsible for me. I might prove unreliable, raise a cry about "the principle of the thing," and with one quirk or impulse, undo him. I could not blame him after what had just happened.

But still, I could not condemn myself altogether for it. It was wrong to make a scene but, after all, it was not so wrong to be indignant at Burns. To have invented a letter to Jane Addams was, however, clearly wrong. Why on earth had I done that? I had a point to make, yes; but I should have thought of a better way. For a moment, in the interest of elementary honesty, I thought of confessing. But if I told him that and no more (and I did not want to say more), he would become even more confused and distrustful. And why bother?

And so I said, as we were about to separate, "Mike, if you have anyone else in mind for that job, feel free to suggest him. I can't tell how long I'll be around. They may notify me any day, and then I'd be forced to walk out in the middle of things. That wouldn't do. But thanks for thinking of me. . . ."

"Oh, now, Joseph, look. . . ."

"Never mind, Mike. And I really do mean that."

"I'll put your name up. And, Joseph, we ought to get together. I want to talk to you. One of these days."

"Well, all right. But the fact is, I'm not fit company. I'm all up in the air. And forget about the job." And I walked away quickly, certain that I had lifted a burden from him and, by so doing, had acquitted myself decently.

Later, thinking these incidents over, I felt less inclined to shoulder all the blame. It seemed to me that Myron might have been somewhat less worried about the spectacle I had made of myself and the attention I had drawn to him and more concerned about the cause of my outburst. If he had thought about it, he would have seen that there were reasons for my behavior, reasons that might well prove disquieting to a friend. And, moreover, he might have found that what I was driving at was not without importance. For the insolence of Burns figured the whole betrayal of an undertaking to which I had once devoted myself, and my chagrin—though it seemed to find its object in Burns—was actually aimed at those who had perverted it.

But then, I may be expecting too much from Myron. He has the pride of what he has become: a successful young man, comfortable, respected, safe for the present from those craters of the spirit which I have lately looked into. Worst of all, Myron has learned, like so many others, to prize convenience. He has learned to be accommodating. That is not a private vice; it has ramified consequences—terrible ones.

For months I have been angry with my friends. I have thought of them as "failing" me. Since the Servatius party, last March, I have been brooding over this failure. I have made it look like a major catastrophe, whereas it was nothing of the sort, and have made an obsessional grievance of betrayal where, in fact, only my shortsightedness was at fault—that and the inflationary, grandiose, tasteless attitudes I dissociate myself from by pinning them on Joseph. In reality, the Servatius party merely forced on my attention certain defects in the people around me which, if I had been as astute as I should have been, I would have recognized long before, and of which I think I must have been partly aware all the time.

Partly, I say. And here I feel it necessary to revive Joseph, that creature of plans. He had asked himself a question I still would like answered, namely, "How should a good man live; what ought he to do?" Hence the plans. Unfortunately, most of them were foolish. Also, they led him to be untrue to himself. He made mistakes of the sort people make who see things as they wish to see them or, for the sake of their plans, *must* see them. There might be some justice in the view that man was born the slayer of his father and of his brother, full of instinctive bloody rages, licentious and unruly from his earliest days, an animal who had to be tamed. But, he protested, he could find in himself no such history of hate overcome. He could not. He believed in his own mildness, believed in it piously. He allowed this belief to interfere with his natural shrewdness and did both himself and his friends a disservice. They could not give him what he wanted.

What he wanted was a "colony of the spirit," or a group whose covenants forbade spite, bloodiness, and cruelty. To hack, to tear, to murder was for those in whom the sense of the temporariness of life had shrunk. The world was crude and it was dangerous and, if no measures were taken, existence could indeed become—in Hobbes' phrase, which had long ago lodged in Joseph's mind—"nasty, brutish, short." It need not become so if a number of others would combine to defend themselves against danger and crudity.

He thought he had found those others, but even before the Servatius party he (or rather I) had begun to have misgivings about the progress that was being made. I was beginning to see that a difficult plan or program like mine had to take into account all that was natural, including corruptness. I had to be faithful to the facts, and corruptness was one of them.

But the party shocked me.

I did not want to go. It was Iva who insisted, out of loyalty to Minna Servatius and because she knew what it was to be a disappointed hostess. It was a long time since a party, any party, had given me pleasure. I liked nothing better than to see my friends singly or in pairs, but when they came together in a large group they disheartened me. You knew what to expect beforehand. If there were jokes, you knew how they would be told; if there were exhibitions, you knew who would make them and who would be hurt or shamed or gratified by them. You knew what Stillman would do, you knew what George Hayza would do, you knew that Abt would make fun of everyone and that Minna would have difficulties with her husband. You knew there was bound to be mischief, distortion, and strain, and yet you went. And why? Because Minna had prepared a party; because your friends were going to be there. And they were coming because you were going to be there, and on no account must anyone be let down.

When the heat and stridency of the party burst upon us through the open door, I began to regret that I had not been more firm in refusing, this once. Minna met us in the entry hall. She was wearing a black dress with a high, silver-trimmed collar; her legs were bare, and she had on high-heeled, red sandals. It was not immediately apparent how drunk she was. She appeared, at first, self-possessed and grave; her face was white, her forehead full of creases. Then we noticed how she was perspiring and how unsteady her eyes were. She looked first at Iva and then at me, saying nothing. We did not know what to expect. Then, with alarming suddenness, she cried, "Sound the gong; they're here."

"Who?" said Jack Brill, putting his head out of the door.

"Joseph and Iva. Always last to show up. They come when everybody's high so they can stand around and watch us make fools of ourselves."

"It's my fault," Iva murmured. We were both taken aback by Minna's outcry. "I have such a cold, and . . ."

"Darling," said Minna. "I was only joking. Come in."

She led us into the living room. There, both doors of the phonograph were open, but the guests talked; no one seemed to listen to the music. And here was the scene, predictable to the last detail, hours, days, weeks before—the light furniture in the popular Swedish style, the brown carpet, the Chagall and Gris prints, the vines trailing from the mantelpiece, the bowl of Cohasset punch. Minna had invited a number of "strangers"—acquaintances, that is, who did not belong to the inner circle. There was a young woman to whom I had once been introduced. I remembered her because of her downy, slightly protuberant lip. She was quite pretty, however. Her name escaped me. Did she work in Minna's office? Was she married to the fat man in the steel-rimmed glasses? Had I also met him? I would never know. And in this noise I could not help being indifferent about it. So it was with these strangers. Some, like Jack Brill, you came to know well, in time. The others remained grouped together indistinctly and were recalled, if the need arose, as "that fellow with the glasses" or "that pasty-looking couple."

One by one, the friends came forward—Abt, George Hayza, Myron, Robbie Stillman. They were the center of the party; they performed. The others looked on, and who could tell whether they were amused or resentful at their exclusion, or even if they were aware of being excluded? The party went on around them. If they were aware of what was happening, they made the best of it.

And so did you. Your first tour of the room done, you moved aside with a glass and a cigarette. You sat—if you could find a place—and watched the performers and the dancers. You heard Robbie Stillman tell a story he had told any number of times about the mishaps of a stuttering girl, or about a hobo with a new portable radio he had met one day on the steps of the Aquarium. You did not like him less for telling it. You felt, somehow, that he, too, was forced to endure it, that he began unwillingly and was under a compulsion to finish what no one wanted to hear finished. You could not blame him.

Minna went around the living room from group to group, unsteadily, as if in danger of falling from her high heels.

Finally she stopped before George Hayza. We heard them arguing. It turned out that she wanted him to record on the machine a poem he had made popular years ago when he had played at being a surrealist. To his credit, he refused. That is, he tried to refuse, reddening and smiling anxiously. He wanted to live it down. Everybody was tired of it, he most of all. Others came to his support. Abt said, with an edge of impatience in his voice, that George ought to be allowed to judge whether or not he should recite it. And since everyone had heard it—a dozen times . . .

"Everyone has not heard it," said Minna. "Besides, I want to make a record of it. It's clever."

"It used to be considered clever."

"It still is. It's very clever."

Abt gave up the argument, for a sense of a special situation was arising. Abt had once been engaged to Minna, but for reasons none of us knew, she had suddenly decided to marry Harry Servatius. There was, therefore, a complex history of injured feelings between Abt and Minna, and, in a gathering atmosphere of embarrassment, Abt withdrew, and Minna had her way. The poem was recorded. George's voice came out strangely high and unsteady.

"I am alone
And eat my hair as a calendar of regrets—"

George, with a grimace of apology, backed away from the phonograph. Only Minna was satisfied; she played the record again.

"What's wrong tonight?" I asked Myron.

"Oh—it's Harry, I guess. He's in the study with Gilda Hillman. They've been there all evening. Talking."

"Joseph," said Iva from her chair near by, "will you get me some more?" She held out her glass.

"Iva," said Jack Brill, with a warning laugh. "Go slow."

"With what? The punch?"

"It tastes mild, but it isn't mild at all."

"Maybe you shouldn't drink any more of it," I said, "since you're not feeling well."

"I don't know why I'm so thirsty. I haven't eaten anything salty."

"I'll bring you some water if you like."

"Water." She drew back the glass contemptuously.

"I wish you wouldn't drink tonight. It's a strong punch," I said. My tone was unmistakable. I did not mean to be disobeyed. Yet a little later I saw her at the bowl and frowned at the quick motion with which she raised her arm and drank. I was irritated enough to consider, for a moment, striding up and snatching the glass away.

Instead I started a conversation with Abt on the first subject that came to hand, the war in Libya. We wandered into the kitchen, talking.

Abt is one of my oldest and best friends. I have always been much attached to him and have valued him perhaps more than he has valued me. That does not make much difference; he certainly has great affection for me, and some respect. At college we roomed together for a while. We were temporarily estranged because of a political matter. When we returned to Chicago we resumed our friendship, and while he worked for his doctorate—until last June he was an instructor in political science—he practically lived with us.

"We owe a lot to the Italians," Abt was saying. "They have a sensible attitude toward the war. They want to go home. And that isn't our only indebtedness. Capitalism never made them the victims of addition and subtraction. They remained a thoughtful people." (He spoke slowly, so that I knew he was improvising, an old habit of his.) "And they never became swashbucklers. They have better taste and less false pride than the heirs of Arminius. Of course, that was an Italian mistake. Tacitus inflated the Germans. . . ."

My irritation with Iva faded. I found myself listening, amused, to his praise of the Italians. "So that's our debt," I said, smiling. "Do you think they're going to save us?"

"They won't do us any harm. It begins to look as though civilization may start its comeback from the Mediterranean, where it was born."

"Have you tried that on Dr. Rood?"

"He'd take me seriously and try to steal the idea."

Dr. Arnold Rood, or Mary Baker Rood, as Abt liked to call him, was the head of his department and a dean of the college.

"How is the old man?"

"Still oily, still the highest-paid Reader in the city, and just as ignorant as ever. I have become his favorite problem in conversion and I have to see him twice a week to discuss *Science and Health*. Some fine afternoon I'll stick a knife into him and say, 'Pray yourself out of that, you bastard.' That's a vulgar refutation, like Johnson's kicking the stone to triumph over Berkeley. But I can't think of any other way to deal with him."

I laughed, and at the same moment another, shriller laugh, almost an outcry, came from the front of the house. I stared down the hall.

"Minna," Abt said.

"I wish something could be done. . . ." It appalled me to hear that cry and to recall the look on her face when she had greeted us in the entry hall. The party blared on inside, and I began to think what a gathering of this sort meant. And it came to me all at once that the human purpose of these occasions had always been to free the charge of feeling in the pent heart; and that, as animals instinctively sought salt or lime, we, too, flew together at this need as we had at Eleusis,

with rites and dances, and at other high festivals and cor-
roborees to witness pains and tortures, to give our scorn,
hatred, and desire temporary liberty and play. Only we did
these things without grace or mystery, lacking the forms for
them and, relying on drunkenness, assassinated the Gods in
one another and shrieked in vengefulness and hurt. I frowned
at this dreadful picture.

"Oh, yes," said Abt, "she's having a bad time."

It reassured me to hear him say this; he felt as I did about it.

"But she shouldn't allow herself. . . ." Rapid footsteps
came toward the kitchen. "There's such a thing as. . . ." But
again he did not finish. Minna came in accompanied by
George.

"What's such a thing?" Minna said.

"Was that you yelling?" said Abt.

"I wasn't yelling. Stand aside from the refrigerator. George
and I have come for ice cubes. Say, what are you hiding in the
kitchen for, anyway? There's a party on. These two," she said
to George, "are always in a corner together. Him in his undertaker's suit, and this one . . . with rings under his eyes.
Like a couple of plotters." She walked out unsteadily. George,
with a set and disapproving face, carried the ice-filled bowl.

"Having a wonderful night, isn't she?" said Abt.

"Is Harry drunk, too? What's the matter with them?"

"He may be a little soused. I think he knows what he's doing," said Abt. "But it's really not our business. . . ."

"I thought they were getting along."

"There's trouble of some sort. But, ah!" he made a grimace. "It's very unlovely."

"It certainly is," I said.

"I've had my share, too, tonight. That business of George's
damned poem."

"Oh, I know."

"I'm going to keep my nose clean."

I felt increasingly disturbed. Abt looked and sounded ex-
ceptionally unhappy. Not that it was unusual for him to be
unhappy; he was seldom otherwise. But tonight there was a
much larger degree of harshness in his customary mixture of
levity and harshness. I had noticed that and, though I had
laughed, I had also winced a little when he spoke of stabbing

Dr. Rood. I sighed. Of course he was still in love with Minna. Or would it be better to say that he had never recovered from his disappointment in her? But there was more to it than that, I knew—a fundamental discontent which would not yield its meaning to such easy formulations as "love" and "disappointment." Still more, I was disturbed at myself because I knew that at heart I was tired of Abt's unhappiness and of seeing him rise to it like a jaded but skillful boxer. I did not want to admit that. I urged my sympathies to work for him. He *was* unhappy, after all, wasn't he?

We came back to the living room. Iva was sitting beside Stillman on the piano bench. Servatius and Gilda Hillman had appeared at last; they were dancing. Her face was lowered against his chest; they hung together, moving slowly.

"Nice-looking couple, aren't they?" Minna said. She was standing behind us. We turned uneasily.

"Well, they are," she said. "Harry dances well. She's not bad, either." We did not reply. "Oh, you're a couple of fish." She started to walk away but thought better of it. "You needn't have such high opinions of yourselves. You're not the man Harry is, and you're not, either."

"Minna," I said.

"Minna yourself!"

We turned from her. "She's getting worse and worse," I said awkwardly. "We ought to leave." Abt answered nothing.

I told Iva that I was going to get her coat. "What for?" she said. "I don't want to go yet." She regarded the matter as settled. She looked around calmly; she was mildly drunk.

I persisted. "It's getting late."

"Oh, don't break up the party," said Stillman. "Stay a while."

Red-faced and smiling broadly, Jack Brill came up to us a few minutes later, saying, "Minna's looking for you, Morris."

"For me? What does she want?" said Abt.

"Search me. But I'm pretty sure she'll get it."

"Morris!"

"Morris!"

"I told you. Here she comes," said Brill.

"Morris," said Minna, putting her hand on his shoulder, "I want you to do something for the party. It's got to be livened up, it's going dead."

"I'm afraid I can't help you," said Abt.

"Yes you can. I have a marvelous idea."

No one asked what this idea was. Jack Brill, after smiling at everyone's discomfiture, said, "What's your idea, Minna?"

"Morris is going to hypnotize somebody."

"You're mistaken," said Abt. "I've given up amateur hypnotism. You'll have to ask someone else to liven up your party." He spoke coldly and without looking at her.

"It's not a good idea, Minna," I put it.

"You're wrong; it's a wonderful idea. Keep out of this."

"Oh, drop it, Minna," said George Hayza. "Nobody wants to see it done."

"You shut up, too, George. Morris," she said beseechingly, "I know you're mad at me. But, please, this once. The party'll break up if something doesn't happen soon."

"I've forgotten how. I can't hypnotize anyone any longer. I haven't done it for years."

"Ah, you haven't forgotten. You can do it. You have a strong mind."

"Go away, Minna," I said.

"She'll get her way," Jack Brill chuckled. "Wait and see."

"You encourage her," I said severely.

"She does everything without encouragement. Don't blame me." He still smiled, but back of his smile there was a resentful and inimical coldness. "I just like to see how she goes about getting her way."

"Morris, please do it."

"Get someone else to do tricks. Get Myron, here."

"He's too stiff for tricks. He doesn't know any."

"Thank God for that," Myron said.

"Now, to get you a subject," said Minna.

"I don't want a subject."

She rapped for attention on the piano. "Announcement," she called out. Servatius and Gilda did not interrupt their dancing. "We need someone for Morris, here, to hypnotize. Judy, how about you?" Judy was the girl with the man in the steel-rimmed glasses. "No? Afraid you'll give yourself away? This takes a little courage. Stillman? These people are against it. Does anybody want to volunteer?" There were no volunteers. "Oh, what a lot of wet blankets."

"There," I said, "nobody's really interested. So you see. . . ."

"Then I'll be your subject myself," Minna said, turning to Abt.

"That's the silliest proposal yet," said George.

"Why shouldn't I be his subject?"

We waited to hear what Abt would say. He had so far given no indication of what he thought of her proposal. He regarded her with raised brows like a doctor who is considering how fully to answer a layman's question while, with quizzical, concealing eyes, he keeps him waiting. The indirect ceiling light gave the side of his face the look of a sheet of thick paper, artfully folded at the eye and pierced, high on the forehead, by straight, black hairs.

"I'll be damned," Jack Brill said softly to me. "He'll take her up on it, too."

"Oh, impossible," I said.

Abt hesitated.

"Well?" Minna said.

"All right," he said. "Why not?"

"Morris."

He disregarded me.

And the others also protested. "She's drunk," said Stillman. And George said, "Are you sure you know what you're up to?" But he disregarded them, too, and made no attempt to explain or justify himself. He and Minna started off toward the study.

"We'll call you. I mean, Morris will call you," Minna said. "Then you can all come in."

When they left, the rest of us fell silent. The dancing had stopped. Jack Brill, leaning one shoulder against the wall, smoked his pipe and seemed to relish watching us. Harry Servatius and Gilda were together on a narrow seat in the corner. They were the only ones talking; no words, however, were audible, only his heavy burring voice and her occasional choppy laughter. What on earth could he be saying that she found so funny? He was making an idiot of himself, and if Abt were correct in saying that he was not too drunk, then he was doubly idiotic. Iva still kept her glass on the piano ledge and took a small sip every so often. I did not like the aimless absorption with which she smoothed out the paper napkin on her knee, nor the rapid yet vague way her eyes moved around the room.

She remained behind with Harry and Gilda when Abt called us. The rest of us crowded into the study and, in embarrassed silence, stood looking down at Minna on the couch. I could not believe at first that she was not pretending; the change seemed too great. I was soon convinced that this was real enough. She lay loosely outstretched, a strong light behind her turned against the wall. One of her sandals had come unfastened and swung away from her heel. Her hands lay open at her sides. One noticed how narrow and bony her wrists were and the mole between two branches of a vein on her forearm. But, for all the width of her hips, and the feminine prominences, her knees under the dress, her bosom, the meeting of her throat and collarbones, she looked less specifically like a woman than a more generalized human being— and a sad one, at that. This view of her affected me greatly. I was even more prejudiced against Abt's performance.

He sat beside her and talked to her soothingly. Her breathing was regular, but touched with hoarseness; her upper lip was drawn away slightly from her teeth.

He began by making her feel cold. "Someone must have turned off the heat. I'm chilled. Don't you feel cold, too? You look cold. It is cold here; it's almost freezing." And she gasped a little and drew up her legs. He went on to tell her that when he pinched her hand she would feel no pain, and so she felt none, though the skin, where he had twisted it, remained white long afterwards. He deprived her of the power to move her arm and then ordered her to raise it. She struggled until he released her. The rest of us, half-tranced ourselves, eager to see and yet afraid of what we were seeing, concentrated on her face with its lifted lip and creased eyes. He let her rest, but only for a moment. Then he asked her to recall how many glasses of punch she had drunk. He would give a series of numbers and she was to make a sign at the right one. At this, her eyes moved or flinched under her lids, as though in protest. He began counting.

I was standing at a corner of the couch in such a position that her bare heel, the one from which the sandal hung, grazed my trouser-leg. I had an impulse to touch the mole on her arm with my finger. All at once, looking at her face and her closed lids, my impatience with Abt turned into anger. Yes, I thought, he *likes* this. I tried to think what I could do to stop it. Meanwhile he was counting. "Six? Seven?" She tried, but was unable to answer. Perhaps she was aware of the insult. "So you can't remember?" said Abt. "No?" She rolled her head. "Maybe you've forgotten how to count? Let's see if you have. I'm going to tap your cheek a few times. You count and tell me how many. Ready?"

"Bring her out of it, Morris, we've all had enough," I said.

He did not seem to hear me. "Now I'm beginning," he said. He struck her lightly four times. Minna's lips began to form the first "f" but dropped away, and the next instant she was sitting up, open-eyed, exclaiming, "Harry! Oh Harry!" Then she began to cry, her face fixed and bewildered.

"I told you you were going too far," I said. Abt reached his hand out to her in surprise.

"Let her alone!" someone said.

"Oh Harry, Harry, Harry!"

"Do something, Morris!" Robbie Stillman shouted. "Slap her, she's having a fit!"

"Don't touch her. I'll get Servatius," said Jack Brill. He ran, but her husband was already at the door, staring in.

"Harry, Harry, Harry!"

"Get out of the way, she doesn't see him," George said.

"Let's clear the room." Jack Brill began herding us out. "Go on, don't stand there." Abt pushed Brill's hand away and muttered something to me which I did not hear.

Iva was no longer in the living room. I went looking for her and found her on the porch off the kitchen.

"What are you doing here?" I said roughly.

"Why, it was warm. I wanted to cool off."

I pulled her inside. "What's the matter with you tonight?" I said. "What's got into you?"

I left her in the kitchen and strode back to the study. I found Brill guarding the door.

"How is she now?" I asked.

"She'll come out of it," said Brill. "George and Harry are in there with her. What a wow of a finish."

"My wife's gone and made herself drunk, too."

"Your wife. You mean Iva."

"Yes, Iva." He was right. I was still treating him like a semi-stranger and he resented it. He had irritated me before when I had thought that he was goading Minna on; but I saw now that, after all, he was no worse than any of the others.

"Well, the party turned into a terrible mess, didn't it?"

"Yes," I agreed.

"Do you ever wonder what's the matter with these people?"

"I've been wondering," I said. "What do you think?"

"So you want my opinion," Brill said, smiling. "You want to see this as an outsider sees it?"

"You're not exactly an outsider, Jack."

"I've only been around five or six years. Well, if you want to know how I feel about it. . . ."

"You're being a little hard on me," I murmured.

"That's right. I am. This is a tight little bunch. I like some of the people in it. I like Minna a lot. Others lean to the snob side. They're not very agreeable. They're cold. Even you, if you don't mind my saying so."

"I don't. . . ."

"You're all fenced around. It took me some time to find out you weren't such a bad guy. At first I thought you wanted people to come up and sniff you, as if you were a tree. You're a little better than that. Not Abt, though, he's a bad case."

"Maybe he needs more study."

"I wish I could give him what he needs more of. No, there's something wrong. And then you people all seem satisfied to settle down to a long life of taking in each other's laundry. Everybody else is shut out. It's offensive to people like me."

"What makes you come around then?" I said.

"I don't know," said Brill. "I guess it interests me to watch you carry on."

"Oh, I see."

"You asked."

"It's perfectly all right. So long, Jack." I offered him my hand; after a moment of surprise (perhaps it was an ironic surprise), he took it.

"So long, Joseph."

*

Iva was in no condition to walk. I got a cab, helped her in, and held her head on my shoulder all the way home. When we stopped at an intersection I looked down at her shadowed face. The yellow traffic light fell on her temple, where I saw a single vein near the surface of the skin, crooking with the slight groove of the bone. I responded to this almost as I had to Minna on the couch. The cab continued down the black street, which was streaked with the remnants of that afternoon's snowfall waning under the changed warm wind.

What could I say to all this? I asked myself fitfully and as though I, too, were a little drunk. I thought that with one leap "nasty, brutish, and short" had landed in our midst. All my feelings, what I had felt in looking at Minna, what I had felt at Jack Brill's words and at Iva's disobedience, now attacked me together. What could I say? I repeated, but in the midst of the question perceived my purpose in asking it. I was looking for a way to clear Abt or protect him, and, through him, what was left of the "colony of the spirit." But then, how much was he to be blamed?

For let us admit the truth. One was constantly threatened, shouldered, and, sometimes invaded by "nasty, brutish, and short," lost fights to it in unexpected corners. In the colony? Even in oneself. Was anyone immune altogether? In times like these? There were so many treasons; they were a medium, like air, like water; they passed in and out of you, they made themselves your accomplices; nothing was impenetrable to them.

The cab stopped. I helped Iva into the house, undressed her and put her to bed. She lay on the blankets, naked, shielding her eyes from the light with her wrist. I turned off the switch and in the dark took off my own clothes.

What sort of barrier could one put up against them, these treasons? If, in Abt, cruelty and the desire for revenge were reduced to pinching a woman's hand, what would my own mind give up if one examined its tiniest gaps and runnels? And what about Iva?—and the others, what about the others?

But suddenly I felt that none of this excused Abt and that I had only cunningly maneuvered to achieve the very end I had begun by rejecting. No, I could not justify him. I had been revolted by the way he had pinched her. I could find no excuse for him, none whatsoever. I was beginning to under-

stand what it was that I felt toward him. Yes, I had been revolted by the rage and spite which emerged in the "game"; it
had been so savage because its object could not resist. It was
some time before I could bring myself to fall asleep. I would
think of this more sanely tomorrow, I promised myself, wiping my forehead on the edge of the sheet. But I already knew
that I had hit upon the truth and that I could not easily dis-
pel it tomorrow or any other day. I had an uneasy, dream-
ridden night.

This was only the beginning. In the months that followed
I began to discover one weakness after another in all I had
built up around me. I saw what Jack Brill had seen, but,
knowing it better, saw it more keenly and severely. It would
be difficult for anyone else to know how this affected me,
since no one could understand as well as I the nature of my
plan, its rigidity, the extent to which I depended on it. Foolish or not, it had answered my need. The plan could be despised; my need could not be.

I have not visited Minna or Harry since the party. I do not
know what sort of aftermath there was; I suppose their troubles were eventually ironed out. Abt has gone to Washington.
He writes occasionally, usually to ask why he so seldom hears
from me. He is doing well as an administrator, one of the
"bright young men," though I understand he is not satisfied.
I don't think he ever will be satisfied. I should perhaps write
oftener; he is, after all, an old friend. It isn't his fault that I am
disappointed in him.

December 23

Slept until eleven o'clock; sat around all afternoon and
thought of nothing in particular. We are going to have Christmas dinner with Amos. Iva accepted his invitation.

December 24

Myron Adler phoned to say that his agency had decided to
hire women to make the survey; there is less possibility of
their being taken away, leaving things in mid-air. But he did

try to get me in, Myron says. He has kept a copy of the memorandum he sent recommending me and he is sending it on as proof that he kept his word. I told him it wasn't necessary to send it; I believed him. He is sending it anyway. He wants to have a talk with me in the near future. We have agreed tentatively to meet during the holiday. He feels, I daresay, that I need to be taken in hand by someone and straightened out. It's good of him, but I don't think I could allow him to do much for me.

We got "Season's Greetings" cards from John Pearl and from Abt. One of these days I'll have to get around to the dime store to buy envelopes. Iva put in a supply of cards a week ago but she forgot to buy envelopes. Can't convince myself that it's worth the bother. But I suppose we ought to keep up our end of the amenities.

Vanaker is drinking heavily these days. He disposes of his empty pints by throwing them into the neighboring yards. This morning I counted eighteen in the snow.

Iva insists that we keep our door locked. Some of her things are missing. Ethel Pearl sent her five small bottles of perfume for her birthday; two of these are gone from the basket on the dresser, and Iva says in her positive way: "He's a kleptomaniac." She means Vanaker, of course. She is indignant about the loss of her perfume and means to talk to Mrs. Briggs about it. I shall have to start wearing my room key on a chain.

December 26

I seem to be unable to stay out of trouble. Disgraced myself at my brother's house last night. I can take it lightly, but Iva feels it very keenly.

My brother Amos, who is my senior by twelve years, is a wealthy man. He began his career as a messenger on the Exchange and before he was twenty-five had become a member of that body, with a seat of his own. The family is very proud of him, and he, in turn, has been a reliable son, very much alive to his duties. Toward me he took a protective attitude at first, but he soon gave up, confessing that he did not know what I was after. He was hurt when I became a radical, re-lieved when he assured himself I was one no longer. He was disappointed when I married Iva. His own wife, Dolly, had a rich father. He had urged me to follow his example and marry a wealthy woman. He was even more disappointed when, in-stead of accepting the position he offered me in his business, I took what to him seemed a menial job at Inter American. He called me a fool, and for nearly a year we did not see each other. Then he and Iva arranged a reconciliation. We have been on fairly good terms since, however strange he thinks my choice of occupation and my ways. He tries not to disap-prove of me too openly; but he has never learned that I resent his way of questioning me when we meet. He is often tactless and sometimes rude. For some reason he has not been able to accept the fact that it is possible for a member of his family to live on so little.

"Haven't they given you a raise yet? How much are you making? Well, do you need money?" I have never accepted any.

Now that I have been out of work since May, he has be-come more pressing. Several times he has sent me checks for large amounts, which I have returned immediately. The last time this happened he said, "*I'd* take it, by golly. *I* wouldn't be so proud and stiff-necked. Oh, no, not Brother Amos. Some day you just try offering me money, and see if I pass it up."

A month ago when we visited him (he invites us for meals frequently, thinking, presumably, that we do not get enough to eat), he made such a scene when I refused to take some clothes he was thrusting on me that Iva at last whispered pleadingly, "Take it, Joseph, take the stuff!" and I gave in.

Dolly, my sister-in-law, is a pretty woman, still slender, large-bosomed, but attractively so, dark, with fine hair combed upward in a way designed to make the most of her neck. She has a very graceful neck; I have always admired it. It is one of the traits my fifteen-year-old niece Etta has inher-ited. To me it has always been one of the exquisite character-istics of femininity; I can well understand why it provoked the prophet Isaiah to utter the words: "Because the daughters of Zion are haughty, and walk with stretched forth necks and

wanton eyes, walking and mincing as they go, and making a
tinkling with their feet: therefore the Lord will smite with a
scab the crown of the head of the daughters of Zion, and the
Lord will discover their secret parts."

It astonishes me that the same association should be in
both our minds, though with a different cast. Certainly it is
the "stretched forth necks," or delicacy in conjunction with
the rugged ancient machinery of procreation, that has for a
long time been identified in my imagination with feminine
nature. Here the parallel ends, for I am the very opposite of
vindictive in regard to this duality and have, indeed, found
pleasure in recognizing it.

My niece and I are not on good terms; there is a long-
standing antagonism between us. Ours was not a rich family.
Amos tells frequently how he struggled, how badly he was
dressed as a boy, how little my father could give him. And he
and Dolly have brought up Etta to identify poverty not so
much with evil as with unimportance, to feel that she, the
daughter of a wealthy man, is worlds apart from those who
live drably, in ill-furnished flats, without servants, who wear
inferior clothing and have so little pride as to be debtors. She
prefers her mother's people. Her cousins have automobiles
and summer homes. I am in no way a credit to her.

In spite of our antagonism, I had until lately tried to influence the girl, sending her books and, on her birthday, record
albums. I knew I could have little effect on her. But when she
was twelve I undertook to tutor her in French as a means of
broaching other subjects. (Her father, naturally, wanted her to
be accomplished.) I was unsuccessful. My missionary eagerness betrayed itself too soon, before I had her confidence. She
told her mother that I was teaching her "bad things." And
how was I to explain to Dolly that I was trying to "save"
Etta? It would have been insulting. Etta hated the lessons, by
simple extension she hated me, and if I had not given her an
excuse for discontinuing them, she would soon have found
one.

Etta is a vain girl. I am sure she spends a great many hours
before the mirror. I am sure, also, that she must be aware of
the resemblance she bears to me. It goes beyond the obvious
similarities pointed out by the family. Our eyes are exactly

alike, and so are our mouths and even the shape of our ears, sharp and small—Dolly's are altogether different. And there are other similarities, less easily definable, which she cannot help recognizing and which—our enmity being what it is— must be painful to her.

At dinner the talk, in which I scarcely took part at first, was of the hardships of rationing. Dolly and Amos are coffee drinkers but, as patriots, they tempered their complaints with resignation. They turned next to shoes and clothing. Dolly's brother, Loren, who represents a large Eastern shoe firm, had warned them that the government intended to limit the sale of leather goods.

"We couldn't get along on four pairs a year," said Dolly.

But that was unpatriotic, wasn't it? The contradiction was too plain to be unnoticed.

"You have to take into account what people are accustomed to," said Amos; "their standard of living. The government overlooks that. Why, even charities don't give the same amounts to any two families. It would cause too much hardship."

"Yes, that's what I meant," said Dolly. "You couldn't call it hoarding."

"No," I replied. She had addressed herself to me.

"Later on there'll be a run on clothes, too," asserted Amos. "That's the way the consumer market is when people are earning."

"Of course, Joseph won't have to worry. The Army will take care of him. But we poor civilians. . . ."

"Joseph would be indifferent, anyway," said Iva. "It wouldn't affect him. He never buys more than one pair of shoes a year."

"He isn't on his feet much," said Etta. Her mother gave her a sharp look.

"I do lead a sedentary life," I said.

"That was all I meant, Mother," said Etta.

"He doesn't worry about any of those things too much, was what I meant," Iva continued, speaking quickly. "He doesn't particularly care what he eats, either, just so it's food. It was no problem pleasing him when I used to cook."

"It's a blessing to be that way. Amos is so hard to suit. You wouldn't think they were brought up by the same mother."

"He wasn't so easy to raise in all respects," Amos said with a smile across the table.

"When are you going into the Army, Joseph?" asked Etta.

"Now, Etta," said Amos reprovingly.

"*Uncle* Joseph, I'm sorry. When are you going?"

"I don't know. Whenever God wills."

This amused them.

"He's certainly taking His time about it," said Dolly.

"There's no hurry," Iva interposed. "The longer the better."

"Oh, of course," Dolly said, "I know how you feel."

"But Joseph doesn't feel that way about it, do you, Joseph?" Amos looked pleasantly at me. "I'm sure he'd like to find out how to hurry Him up. It isn't only the waiting, but he'll miss out on his chances for advancement. He ought to get in there and become an Officer Candidate."

"I don't think I want to try to make an officer of myself."

"Well, I don't see why not," said Amos. "Why not?"

"As I see it, the whole war's a misfortune. I don't want to raise myself through it."

"But there have to be officers. Do you want to sit back and let some cluck do what you can do a thousand times better?"

"I'm used to that," I said, shrugging. "That's the case in many departments of life already. The Army's no exception."

"Iva, do you intend to let him go in with that attitude? A fine Army we'd have."

"It's my conviction," I said. "Iva couldn't change it, and I'm inclined to think she wouldn't want to. Many men carry their ambitions over from civilian life and don't mind climbing upon the backs of the dead, so to speak. It's no disgrace to be a private, you know. Socrates was a plain foot soldier, a hoplite."

"Socrates, eh?" said Amos. "Well, that's a good and sufficient reason."

A little later in the evening, Amos, calling me aside, led me up to his bedroom and there, producing a hundred-dollar bill, thrust it like a handkerchief into my breast pocket, saying, "This is our Christmas present to you."

"Thank you," I said, pulling it out and laying it on the dresser; "but I can't take it."

"Why can't you take it? Nonsense, you can't refuse it. I tell you, it's a present." He picked up the bill impatiently. "Be a little more hardheaded, will you? You're always up in the air. Do you know what I paid in income taxes alone last year? No? Well, this isn't a drop in that bucket. I'm not depriving myself of anything to give it to you."

"But what will I do with it, Amos? I don't need it."

"You are the most obstinate jackass I've ever seen. You can't stand being helped even a little, by anyone."

"Why, this is your shirt I'm wearing, and these are your socks. I appreciate them, but I don't want anything else."

"Joseph!" he exclaimed. "I don't know what to do with you. I'm beginning to think you're not all there, with your convictions and your hop—! I wish I knew how it was going to turn out with you. You'll ruin yourself in the end. Think of Iva sometimes. What's her future going to be like?"

"Oh, the future."

"That's what I said."

"Well, who the devil has one?"

"Everybody," Amos said. "I have."

"Well, you're in luck. I'd think about it a little if I were you. There are many people, hundreds of thousands, who have had to give up all thought of future. There is no personal future any more. That's why I can only laugh at you when you tell me to look out for my future in the Army, in that tragedy. I wouldn't stake a pin on my future. And maybe I wouldn't have yours. . . ." Toward the end my voice had begun to shake.

Amos faced me quietly for a while. Then he said, "Take the money, Joseph," and left. I heard him going downstairs.

I sat on the bed groggily, holding my head. There was a weak lamp burning in one corner; from its copper slot one band of light crossed the curtain; the rest of the room was nearly dark. The ceiling had become a screen for the accidental motions of the greenish street beyond, and across half its width was thrown intact a reflection of the Venetian blind, like the ribs of some immemorial fish. What sort of impression had my words made on Amos? It was impossible to tell.

What could he think? Perhaps he considered me more hopeless than ever. But what did *I* think? Was what I had said half
as true as it was impetuous? His neat vision of personal safety
I disowned, but not a future of another kind. Still, how could
I reason with him? He was a distance beyond reckoning from
the craters of the spirit, so that they were no more than small
pits on his horizon. But in time they would draw closer. Yes,
everyone came to face them when those horizons shrank, as
they could not fail to shrink. I went to the bathroom and
washed. The crammed feeling at my heart began to wear off,
and when I hung the towel back on its glass rod I was less
confused. I picked up the hundred-dollar bill from the dusk
of the carpet where it had fallen. If I tried to hand it back
now there would be a scene; I knew better than to try. I
searched the top of Amos's dresser for a pin or clasp of some
kind. Not finding one there, I opened one drawer after another until, in Dolly's dressing table, I came upon a pin-
cushion. I went to the bed and stuck the bill to the counterpane
over the pillow. Then, in the hall, I stood for a while, hearing
the husky voice of the radio speaker below and the laughter
and comment of the others. I decided not to join them.

Instead, though I knew it meant working a hardship on Iva
to leave her to Dolly, Etta, and Amos, I climbed to the third
floor. There, in what had once been an attic, Dolly had furnished a music room. One entire side of it was taken up by a
broad monster of a piano which crouched on bowed legs,
awaiting use. It was, however, seldom touched, for it had
been replaced downstairs by a more jaunty and stylish instrument that showed its teeth like a darky entertainer. On the
opposite side of the room was a phonograph with a shelf of
records above it. I began to look for a record I had bought
Etta a year ago, a Haydn divertimento for the cello, played by
Piatigorsky. To find it, I had to hunt through a dozen albums.
Here Dolly and Etta, for all their sense of property, were careless; there were numerous broken records. But I found mine
whole and, thankfully—my dejection would have doubled if it
had been cracked or missing—I started it, and sat down facing the piano.

It was the first movement, the adagio, that I cared most
about. Its sober opening notes, preliminaries to a thoughtful

confession, showed me that I was still an apprentice in suffering and humiliation. I had not even begun. I had, furthermore, no right to expect to avoid them. So much was immediately clear. Surely no one could plead for exception; that was not a human privilege. What I should do with them, how to meet them, was answered in the second declaration: with grace, without meanness. And though I could not as yet apply that answer to myself, I recognized its rightness and was vehemently moved by it. Not until I was a whole man could it be my answer, too. And was I to become this whole man alone, without aid? I was too weak for it, I did not command the will. Then in what quarter should I look for help, where was the power? Grace by what law, under what order, by whom required? Personal, human, or universal, was it? The music named only one source, the universal one, God. But what a miserable surrender that would be, born out of disheartenment and chaos; and out of fear, bodily and imperious, that like a disease asked for a remedy and did not care how it was supplied. The record came to an end; I began it again. No, not God, not any divinity. That was anterior, not of my own deriving. I was not so full of pride that I could not accept the existence of something greater than myself, something, perhaps, of which I was an idea, or merely a fraction of an idea. That was not it. But I did not want to catch at any contrivance in panic. In my eyes, that was a great crime. Granted that the answer I was hearing, that went so easily to the least penetrable part of me, the seldom-disturbed thickets around the heart, was made by a religious man. But was there no way to attain that answer except to sacrifice the mind that sought to be satisfied? From the antidote itself another disease would spring. It was not a new matter, it was one I had frequently considered. But not with such a desperate emotion or such a crucial need for an answer. Or such a feeling of loneliness. Out of my own strength it was necessary for me to return the verdict for reason, in its partial inadequacy, and against the advantages of its surrender.

As I began to play the record for the third time, Etta came into the room. Without speaking to me, she went to the shelf and, taking down a bright-colored album, waited, an impatient frown on that fresher and somewhat harder or unworked version of my own face. I now scarcely heard the music. I was already braced for a struggle, the inevitability of which I recognized at once. I groped inside the cabinet of the phonograph for the lever.

"Just a minute. What are you doing?" she said, coming forward a step.

I turned with an aggressive movement. "What?" I said.

"I want to use the machine, Joseph."

"I'm not finished with it yet."

"I don't care," she insisted. "You've had it to yourself all this time. It's my turn. You've been playing that thing over and over."

"You snooped, didn't you?" I said accusingly.

"I did not. It was so loud everybody heard it downstairs."

"You'll have to wait, Etta."

"I will not," she said. "I want to play these Cugat records Mama gave me. I've been wanting to hear them all day."

I did not step aside. At my back the turntable whirred, the needle making a dull scrape among the last grooves. "As soon as I play the second part of this I'll go."

"But you've had the phonograph since dinner. It's my turn."

"And I say no," I replied.

"You have no business saying no to me," she said.

"No business!" I exclaimed with an abrupt, raw jerk of anger.

"It's my phonograph; you're keeping me from my phonograph!"

"Well, if that isn't small!" I said.

"What you call me or think about me doesn't matter." Her voice rose above the *tac-a-tac* of the machine. "I want to listen to Cugat. I don't care."

"Look," I said, making a strong effort to control myself. "I came up here with a purpose. What purpose it isn't necessary to tell you. But you couldn't stand to think that I was here alone, no matter why. Maybe you thought I was enjoying myself, ah? Or hiding away? So you hurried to see if you could spoil it for me. Isn't that true?"

"You're such a clever man, Uncle!"

"Clever man!" I said, mimicking. "Movie talk. You don't

even know what you're saying. This is absurd, quarreling with
a stupid child. It's a waste of time. But I know how you feel
toward me. I know how much and how genuinely you hate
me. I thank God, child that you are, that you have no power
over me."

"You're crazy, Uncle," she said.

"All right, that's said and over, there won't be any more of
it," I said, and believed that I was succeeding in checking myself. "You can listen to the conga, or whatever it is, when I
leave. Now, will you go or sit down and let me play this to the
end?"

"Why should I? You can listen to this. Beggars can't be
choosers!" She uttered this with such triumph that I could see
she had prepared it long in advance.

"You're a little animal," I said. "As rotten and spoiled as
they come. What you need is a whipping."

"Oh!" she gasped. "You dirty . . . dirty no-account. You
crook!" I caught her wrist and wrenched her toward me.

"Damn you, Joseph, let go! Let me go!" The album went
crashing. With the fingers of her free hand she tried to reach
my face. Seizing her by the hair fiercely, I snapped her head
back; her outcry never left her throat; her nails missed me
narrowly. Her eyes shut tightly, in horror.

"Here's something from a beggar you won't forget in a
hurry," I muttered. I dragged her to the piano bench, still
gripping her hair.

"Don't!" she screamed, recovering her voice. "Joseph! You
bastard!"

I pulled her over my knee, trapping both her legs in mine.
I could hear the others running upstairs as the first blows descended and I hurried my task, determined that she should be
punished in spite of everything, in spite of the consequences;
no, more severely because of the consequences. "Don't you
struggle," I cried, pressing down her neck. "Or curse me. It
won't help you."

Amos pounded up the last flight of stairs and burst in. Behind, breathless, came Dolly and Iva.

"Joseph," Amos panted, "let her go. Let the girl go!"

I did not release her at once. She no longer fought against
me but, with her long hair reaching nearly to the floor and

her round, nubile thighs bare, lay in my lap. Whether this was meant to be an admission of complicity and an attempt to lighten my guilt, or whether she wished them to see and savor it fully, I did not know at first.

"Stand up, Etta," Dolly said curtly. "Straighten your skirt."

Slowly, she got to her feet. I wonder if any of them were capable of observing how exactly alike we looked at that moment. "And now, if you can, Joseph," said Dolly, turning her dilated eyes on me, "explain what you were doing."

"Mother," Etta suddenly began to sob. "I didn't do anything to him. He attacked me."

"*What!* In the name of God, what are you talking about?" I exclaimed. "I spanked you because you had a spanking coming."

What unspeakable inference or accusation was that in Dolly's widened eyes? I returned her look steadily.

"Nobody has ever laid a hand on Etta for any reason whatsoever, Joseph."

"Whatsoever! Is calling her uncle a beggar a sufficient 'whatsoever'? There's something ambiguous in your mind. Why don't you speak out?"

She turned to Amos as though to say, "Your brother is going insane. Now he's springing at me."

"I put her over my knee and gave her a hiding, and it wasn't half of what she deserved. She swore at me like a poolroom bum. A mighty fine job you've done with her."

"He pulled me by the hair, that's what he did," Etta cried. "He nearly twisted my head off."

Iva, after turning off the phonograph, had seated herself near it in the background and did her best to efface herself. Which signified to me that she was acknowledging my shame. But there was no "shame." She, too, now came into the sphere of my anger.

"What else did he do?" Dolly demanded.

"Oh, so you think she's covering something up! I spanked her. What else are you fishing for? What are you hoping she'll say? What sort of vulgarity. . . ."

"Stop acting like a wild man!" Amos said peremptorily.

"It's your fault, too," I retorted. "Look how you've brought her up. It's mighty fine, isn't it. You've taught her to hate the class and, yes, the very family you come from. There's a whatsoever for you. Are people to be null because they wear one pair of shoes a year, not a dozen? Try your teeth on that whatsoever!"

"You had no right to raise your hand to the child," said Dolly.

"Why doesn't he tell you what he was doing in your room?" said Etta.

I could see Iva sit up in her chair rigidly.

"What?" said Dolly.

"He was in your room."

"I went there with Amos. Ask him," I said.

"Daddy wasn't there when I saw you. You were looking in Mama's dressing table."

"You little spy!" I shouted, glaring at her. "You hear?" I said to the others. "She accuses me of being a thief."

"What were you doing?" Etta said.

"I was looking for something. You can go down and see if anything's missing. There's nothing missing. Or you can search me. I'll let myself be searched."

"Tell us, what was it? Nobody says you're a thief."

"It's what you're thinking. It's clear enough to me."

"Well, tell us," Dolly insisted.

"It was only a pin. I needed one."

In the darkened corner near the phonograph Iva lowered her head into her hands. "Hey! what are you acting up for back there?" I called out to her.

"A pin, is that all?" Dolly said. She allowed herself, despite the seriousness of the moment, to smile.

"Yes. And it happens to be true." They did not answer. I said: "This, I suppose, makes my shame complete. I'm not only rash and stiff-necked, a beggar" (I bowed to Etta, who scornfully turned away her tear-smeared face) "and" (to Amos) "a jackass, but really an idiot." Iva left the room without looking at me. "You, Amos," I continued, "can begin living me down. You, too, Etta. Dolly is not a blood relative so she's absolved, of course. Unless I bring disgrace on the whole family. Convicted of theft, or assault, or worse. . . ." Neither Dolly nor Amos undertook to reply.

I followed Iva downstairs.

She did not speak to me on the streetcar and, when we got off, she hurried home ahead of me. I reached the door of our room in time to see her drop to the edge of the bed and burst into tears.

"Dearest," I shouted. "It's so nice to know that you at least have faith in me!"

December 27

Amos called us up this morning; I sent Iva down to talk to him. She returned and wanted to know why I hadn't spoken out, why I had wanted to give my brother's family a wrong impression. I replied that as long as they were satisfied with the impression they had of themselves I didn't care what impression they had of me. Iva rubbed mercuric oxide into her red lids before leaving for work. Her crying had continued for several hours.

I felt relieved on one score; I had been uneasy about the money, believing that Etta was not above taking it. But she went away without waiting to see what I was doing in Dolly's dressing table. She did not know about the money. She might have stolen it to spite me.

But I have been wondering, now, what it can mean to Etta that she so closely resembles me. And why should I, furthermore, have assumed that our physical resemblance was the basis for an affinity of another kind? The search for an answer takes me far into my earlier history, a field I do not always find agreeable but which yields a great deal of essential information. And there I discover that the face, all faces, had a significance for me duplicated in no other object. A similarity of faces must mean a similarity of nature and presumably of fate.

We were a handsome family. I was brought up to think myself handsome, though not by any direct process that I can recall. It was conveyed to me by the atmosphere of the household.

Now I recall an incident from my fourth year, a quarrel between my mother and my aunt over the way in which she (my mother) dressed my hair. My aunt, Aunt Dina, claimed it was high time my curls were cut; my mother refused to hear of it.

Aunt Dina was a self-willed woman; she had arbitrary ways. She took me to the barber and had him cut my hair after the fashion of the time, in what was called a Buster Brown. She brought the curls back in an envelope and gave them to my mother, who thereupon began to cry. I bring this up not simply to recall how the importance of my appearance was magnified in my eyes, but also because during adolescence I was to remember this in another connection.

In a drawer of the parlor table where the family pictures were kept, there was one to which I was attracted from earliest childhood. It was a study of my grandfather, my mother's father, made shortly before his death. It showed him supporting his head on a withered fist, his streaming beard yellow, sulphurous, his eyes staring and his clothing shroudlike. I had grown up with it. And then, one day, when I was about fourteen, I happened to take it out of the drawer together with the envelope in which my curls had been preserved. Then, studying the picture, it occurred to me that this skull of my grandfather's would in time overtake me, curls, Buster Brown, and all. Still later I came to believe (and this was no longer an impression but a dogma) that the picture was a proof of my mortality. I was upright on my grandfather's bones and the bones of those before him in a temporary loan. But he himself, not the further past, hung over me. Through the years he would reclaim me bit by bit, till my own fists withered and my eyes stared. This was a somber but not a frightening thought. And it had a corrective effect on my vanity.

Only by this time it was not so simple as that, it was not merely vanity. By this time my face was to me the whole embodiment of my meaning. It was a register of my ancestors, a part of the world and, simultaneously, the way I received the world, clutched at it, and the way, moreover, in which I announced myself to it. All of this was private and never spoken of.

But, still more, while I was conscious of being handsome I was not a little suspicious of it. Mortality, I've explained, played its part, making inroads on my vanity. Suspicion undermined it further. For I kept thinking, "There's something wrong." I meant that there was a falseness about it. And then this incident occurred:

In high school I became friendly with a boy named Will
Harscha, a German. I used to visit him at home and I knew
his sister and his younger brother, as well as his mother. But
I had never met his father, who kept a store in a distant
neighborhood. However, when I came to call one Sunday
morning, the father happened to be at home, and Will took
me in to meet him. He was a fat man, black-haired and swart,
but kindly-looking.

"So this is Joseph," he said as he shook hands with me.
"Well. *Er ist schön*," he said to his wife.

"*Mephisto war auch schön*," Mrs. Harscha answered.

Mephisto! Mephistopheles? I understood what she had said.
I stood frozen there. Mr. Harscha, observing me, must have
grasped that I knew what she had referred to, for he began
glaring at his wife, who, with her lips pressed together, continued to look at me.

I never saw them again. I avoided Will at school. And I
spent sleepless hours thinking of what Mrs. Harscha had said.
She had seen through me—by some instinct, I thought then
—and, where others saw nothing wrong, she had discovered
evil. For a long time I believed there was a diabolic part to
me. Later, I gave that up. It was "poor devil," if any devil.
Not me, specifically, just the general, poor, human devil. But
meanwhile I had the confirmation of people like Mrs.
Harscha for my suspicion that I was not like others but (and
I now know that it is an old belief and at the heart of what we
call "Romantic") that I concealed something rotten. And perhaps it is world-wide, such a conviction, and arises because we
know ourselves too well to accept the good but, rather, embrace the bad opinions others have of us. Mrs. Harscha may
have disliked me because I was too "well-behaved," or because of a way of mine in boyhood of making, or attempting
to make, a compact with the adult relatives of my friends, particularly mothers, over the heads of their sons. She may have
thought I had no business being unboyish. Many people resented that.

I have long ago freed myself from this morbidity. It is because of Etta that I undertook to trace it back. But there is no
reason to believe that there is any parallel between us. It may
be that grandfather's head hangs over both of us, but if and

when it devours us it will be devouring two people who have nothing else in common.

I have also been considering Dolly. Of course, I knew that she was no saint; but now, reviewing her part in last night's affair, I find her farther on the hellward side than ever. Here I have additional proof of my inability to read people properly, to recognize the likelihood of baseness in them—as natural in some as a blink, a nod, a flip of the hand. I make theoretical, that is, unreal, allowances for it. I shall have to begin schooling myself in shrewdness.

December 28

What would Goethe say to the view from this window, the wintry, ill-lit street, he with his recurring pleasures, fruits, and flowers?

December 29

Slept until one o'clock. Out at four for a walk, I lasted ten minutes and then retreated.

December 31

I shaved in honor of the holiday. But we are not going out. Iva has some sewing to do.

January 2, 1943

Mr. Vanaker observed the birth of the new year with large quantities of whisky, with coughing, pelting the yard with bottles, with frequent, noisy trips to the lavatory, and ended his revels with a fire. At about ten o'clock I heard his growls, unusually thick, and repeated thumps in the corridor and looked out to see him shambling through the smoke, feeling his way along the wall. Iva ran to summon Captain Briggs while I thrust open Vanaker's door. The armchair was burning. He hurried in with a cup of water, which he poured over it. He was wearing sleeveless pajamas, and his bare arms were marked with sooty fingerprints. His large, fleshy, somewhat concave face, with its high forehead overarched with gray curls in a manner that suggested a bonnet, was red and distressed. He did not speak; he ran to fetch another cupful.

By this time other roomers were on the scene, for the smoke had spread through the house: Mrs. Bartlett, the middle-aged practical nurse from the large room in the rear; Mrs. Fessman, the pretty Austrian refugee; and Mr. Ringholm, who shares the third floor with Captain and Mrs. Briggs.

"Tell him to carry out that chair," Mrs. Bartlett said to me.

"He's trying to put the fire out," I replied.

Hasty slapping sounds came from Vanaker's room.

"With his hands."

"He'd better take it out. This is a frame house. It's dangerous." Mrs. Bartlett came closer to me in the smoke, a tall figure in a kimono; her head was bound in a handkerchief, a black cotton sleeping mask hung around her neck. "Someone should tell him to. Take it out, mister." But the smoke was too much for her. She retreated to the stairs. I, too, was coughing and rubbing my eyes. I stepped back into our room to recover. Throwing open the window, I cleared my head in the frigid air. Loud knocks began outside. Iva looked in.

"He locked himself inside. He must be afraid of the Captain," she said.

I joined her in the hall. "Damn," said the Captain, amused and vexed. "What'd he start running for? How'm I going to get at the fire?" He doubled the tempo of his knocks. "Open up, Mr. Vanaker. Come on, now."

"It's a wonder you don't lose your temper, Sir," said Mrs. Bartlett.

"Mr. Vanaker!"

"I'm awright," Vanaker said.

"He's ashamed, that's what it is," Mrs. Bartlett explained to us.

"Well, I want you to let me in," the Captain said. "I have to see if the fire's out."

The key turned, and Vanaker, with streaming eyes, stood in

the doorway; the Captain passed by him into the ragged smoke. Mr. Ringholm, touching his head, complained that this was doing his hang-over no good.

"We're lucky not to be in ashes," said Mrs. Bartlett.

And now the Captain, also coughing, reappeared, dragging the chair. He and Mr. Ringholm together carried it down. The carpet had caught fire in several places. I brought a double handful of snow from the window sill, and Mrs. Briggs joined me in stamping out the sparks and wetting down the burned spots. Vanaker had fled to the bathroom, where we heard him washing, splashing in the sink.

A little later we heard Vanaker explaining: "It was a cigarette, Cap-tain. See? I put ah on the saucer. Then ah rolled off. . . ."

"You must be careful, old-timer," the Captain said. "With cigarettes you must be careful. They're dangerous; cigarettes are dangerous."

"Awright, Captain."

That was our only New Year's Day diversion and a rather poor substitute for observing the holiday. It did give us a feeling of being set aside to let the entire day slip by. Children ran past in the morning blowing horns; in the afternoon, families in their Sunday clothes went promenading. The Captain and his wife drove off in their car early in the day and had just returned when the fire broke out.

But what such a life as this incurs is the derangement of days, the leveling of occasions. I can't answer for Iva, but for me it is certainly true that days have lost their distinctiveness. There were formerly baking days, washing days, days that began events and days that ended them. But now they are undistinguished, all equal, and it is difficult to tell Tuesday from Saturday. When I neglect to look carefully at the newspaper I do not know what day it is. If I guess Friday and then learn that it is actually Thursday, I do not experience any great pleasure in having won twenty-four hours.

It is possible that that is one reason why I have been creating agitation. I am not sure. The circumstances at the Arrow and at Amos's house were provoking enough, but I could have avoided making scenes if I had wished. It may be that I am tired of having to identify a day as "the day I asked for a second cup of coffee," or "the day the waitress refused to take back the burned toast," and so want to blaze it more sharply, regardless of the consequences. Perhaps, eager for consequences. Trouble, like physical pain, makes us actively aware that we are living, and when there is little in the life we lead to hold and draw and stir us, we seek and cherish it, preferring embarrassment or pain to indifference.

January 3

A Jefferson Forman is listed as having crashed in the Pacific. His home is given as St. Louis. The Jeff Forman I knew came from Kansas City, but his family may have moved in the last few years. The name is not common; it must be the same Forman. I had heard that he was in the merchant marine. Probably he had himself transferred when the war broke out. I heard a rumor that he had been arrested in Genoa about four years ago for shouting *A basso* in a public place. No name, simply *A basso*. According to Tad, the consulate had great difficulty in getting him released, though nobody claimed that he had added anything to his *A basso*. Jeff was in love with excitement. He was expelled from the University for some misdemeanor or other. I never learned the facts about it. It is surprising that he was not thrown out during his first year. One night he knocked George Colin down on the street; he never tried to explain why, merely apologized to Colin before the Dean. And his inspiration for waking me early one winter morning was to throw snowballs mixed with ashes into my bed.

His rank was given in the paper as ensign; his ship was a Catalina. I suppose the submarine danger was not enough for him. I always suspected of him that he had in some fashion discovered there were some ways in which to be human was to be unutterably dismal, and that all his life was given over to avoiding those ways.

January 4

With all the respect we seem to have for perishable stuff, we have easily accustomed ourselves to slaughter. We are all, after some fashion, the beneficiaries of that slaughter and yet we have small pity for the victims. This has not come with the war, we were ready before the war ever started; it only seems more apparent now. We do not flinch at seeing all these lives struck out; nor would those who were killed have suffered any more for us, if we, not they, had been the victims. I do not like to think what we are governed by. I do not like to think about it. It is not easy work, and it is not safe. Its kindest revelation is that our senses and our imaginations are somehow incompetent. The old Joseph who, in view of the temporariness of life, was opposed to hacking and tearing, said that he regretted that with the best will in the world one must deal out his share of bruises. . . . Bruises! What a piece of innocence! Yes, he recognized that even those who meant to be gentle could not hope to escape whipping. And that was modest enough.

Yet we are, as a people, greatly concerned with perishability; an empire of iceboxes. And pet cats are flown hundreds of miles to be saved by rare serums; and country neighbors in Arkansas keep a month's vigil night and day to save the life of a man stricken at ninety.

Jeff Forman dies; brother Amos lays up a store of shoes for the future. Amos is kind. Amos is no cannibal. He cannot bear to think that I should be unsuccessful, lack money, refuse to be concerned about my future. Jeff, under the water, is beyond virtue, value, glamor, money, or future. I say these things unable to see or think straight, and what I feel is less injustice or inhumanity than bewilderment.

Myself, I would rather die in the war than consume its benefits. When I am called I shall go and make no protest. And, of course, I hope to survive. But I would rather be a victim than a beneficiary. I support the war, though perhaps it is gratuitous to say so; we have the habit of making these things issues of personal morality and private will, which they are not at all. The equivalent would be to say, if God really existed, yes, God does exist. He would exist whether we recognized him or not. But as between their imperialism and ours, if a full choice were possible, I would take ours. Alternatives, and particularly desirable alternatives, grow only on imaginary trees.

Yes, I shall shoot, I shall take lives; I shall be shot at, and my life may be taken. Certain blood will be given for half-certain reasons, as in all wars. Somehow I cannot regard it as a wrong against myself.

This afternoon I emptied the closet of all its shoes and sat on the floor polishing them. Surrounded by rags, saddle soap, and brushes—the brown light of the street pressing in at the windows, and the sparrows bickering in the dead twigs—I felt tranquil for a while and, as I set Iva's shoes out in a row, I grew deeply satisfied. It was a borrowed satisfaction; it was doing something I had done as a child. In Montreal, on such afternoons as this, I often asked permission to spread a paper on the sitting-room floor and shine all the shoes in the house, including Aunt Dina's with their long tongues and scores of eyelets. When I thrust my arm into one of her shoes it reached well above the elbow and I could feel the brush against my arm through the soft leather. The brown fog lay in St. Dominique Street; in the sitting room, however, the stove shone on the davenport and on the oilcloth and on my forehead, drawing the skin pleasantly. I did not clean shoes because I was praised for it, but because of the work and the sensations of the room, closed off from the wet and fog of the street, with its locked shutters and the faint green of the metal pipes along the copings of its houses. Nothing could have tempted me out of the house.

I have never found another street that resembled St. Dominique. It was in a slum between a market and a hospital. I was generally intensely preoccupied with what went on in it and watched from the stairs and the windows. Little since then has worked upon me with such force as, say, the sight of a driver trying to raise his fallen horse, of a funeral passing through the snow, or of a cripple who taunted his brother. And the pungency and staleness of its stores and cellars, the dogs, the boys, the French and immigrant women, the beggars with sores and deformities whose like I was not to meet again until I was old enough to read of Villon's Paris, the very breezes in the narrow course of that street, have remained so clear to me that I sometimes think it is the only place where I was ever allowed to encounter reality. My father blamed himself bitterly for the poverty that forced him to bring us up in a slum and worried lest I see too much. And I did see, in a curtainless room near the market, a man rearing over someone on a bed, and, on another occasion, a Negro with a blond woman on his lap. But less easily forgotten were a cage with a rat in it thrown on a bonfire, and two quarreling drunkards, one of whom walked away bleeding, drops falling from his head like the first slow drops of a heavy rain in summer, a crooked line of drops left on the pavement as he walked.

January 6

Abt has sent me a copy of a pamphlet he wrote on the government of the Territories. He expects a flattering comment, no doubt, and I shall have to rig one up. He will want me to tell him that no one else could have written such a pamphlet. Suppose I were to try to tell him what I thought of him. He would reply coldly, "I don't know what you're talking about." He was a way of turning aside everything he has no desire to understand.

Abt, more than anyone I have known, has lived continually in need of being consequential. Early in life he discovered that he was quicker, abler, than the rest of us, and that he could easily outstrip us in learning and in skills. He felt he could be great in anything he chose. We roomed together in Madison as freshmen. He was very busy that first year keeping up all his accomplishments, his music, his politics, his class work. Living with him had a bad effect on me, for I withdrew from any field he entered. People came from other campuses to consult him on doctrinal matters; no one had as much out-of-the-way information as he; he read foreign political journals the rest of us had never heard of, and reports of party congresses, those dun, mimeographed sheets on international decisions in France and Spain. No one was so subtle with opponents. Nor did many students get as much attention as he got from his teachers. A few were afraid of him and learned to avoid challenging him publicly. Late afternoons, he played the piano. I would often stop by for him at the music building on the way to dinner and spend half an hour listening. He did not waste time maturing, he did not make any of the obvious mistakes. His hold was too good. That winter he was Lenin, Mozart, and Locke all rolled into one. But there was unfortunately not enough time to be all three. And so, in the spring, he passed through a crisis. It was necessary to make a choice. But, whatever it was he chose, *that* would be the most important. How could it be otherwise? He gave up attending meetings and practicing the piano, he banished the party reports as trash, and decided to become a political philosopher. There was a general purge. Everything else went. *Anti-Duhring* and *The Critique of the Gotha Program* sank to the rear of the bottom shelf of his bookcase and were supplanted at the top by Bentham and Locke. Now he had decided, and in dead earnestness he followed greatness. Inevitably, he fell short of his models. He would never admit that he wanted to become another Locke, but there he was, wearing himself thin with the effort of emulation, increasingly angry at himself, and unable to admit that the scale of his ambition was defeating him.

He is stubborn. Just as, in the old days, it disgraced him to confess that he was not familiar with a book or a statement that came under his jurisdiction, he now cannot acknowledge that his plan has miscarried. But then, it bothers him to be found guilty even of small errors. He does not like to forget a date or a name or the proper form of a foreign verb. He cannot be wrong, that is his difficulty. If you warn him that there is a fissure at his feet, he answers, "no, you must be mistaken." But when it can no longer be ignored he says, "Do you see it?" as though he had discovered it.

Of course, we suffer from bottomless avidity. Our lives are so precious to us, we are so watchful of waste. Or perhaps a better name for it would be the Sense of Personal Destiny. Yes, I think that is better than avidity. Shall my life by one-thousandth of an inch fall short of its ultimate possibility? It is a different thing to value oneself, and to prize oneself crazily. And then there are our plans, idealizations. These are dangerous, too. They can consume us like parasites, eat us, drink us, and leave us lifelessly prostrate. And yet we are always inviting the parasite, as if we were eager to be drained and eaten.

It is because we have been taught there is no limit to what a man can be. Six hundred years ago, a man was what he was born to be. Satan and the Church, representing God, did battle over him. He, by reason of his choice, partially decided the outcome. But whether, after life, he went to hell or to heaven, his place among other men was given. It could not be contested. But, since, the stage has been reset and human beings only walk on it, and, under this revision, we have, instead, history to answer to. We were important enough then for our souls to be fought over. Now, each of us is responsible for his own salvation, which is in his greatness. And that, that greatness, is the rock our hearts are abraded on. Great minds, great beauties, great lovers and criminals surround us. From the great sadness and desperation of Werthers and Don Juans we went to the great ruling images of Napoleons; from these to murderers who had that right over victims because they were greater than the victims; to men who felt privileged to approach others with a whip; to schoolboys and clerks who roared like revolutionary lions; to those pimps and subway creatures, debaters in midnight cafeterias who believed they could be great in treachery and catch the throats of those they felt were sound and well in the lassos of their morbidity; to dreams of greatly beautiful shadows embracing on a flawless screen. Because of these things we hate immoderately and punish ourselves and one another immoderately. The fear of lagging pursues and maddens us. The fear lies in us like a cloud. It makes an inner climate of darkness. And occasionally there is a storm and hate and wounding rain out of us.

January 7

Adler's bureau is sending him to San Francisco for two weeks. He is leaving tomorrow. Our talk will have to be put off.

January 8

John Pearl writes of an exhibit of his pictures at a women's club in New York. It was not a success. For want of space they crowded his things into the dining room, then held so many Red Cross luncheons that no one could get in. He sold nothing. A lady who admired a still life wanted to order a flower painting for her daughter's bedroom—three flowers in a blue vase. "Only three? A fourth flower will cost you twenty-five dollars more. It'll fill the picture out. That's very reasonable." She pondered this but in the end she decided three would be enough. Her husband grew peonies; she would have the flowers and a vase sent over. "I'm sorry," Johnny said. "I thought we were talking about roses. Peonies are too big for the price. I'll have to charge ten dollars extra for each flower. It's the standard rate for flowers with a three-inch diameter. A lemon will be ten dollars more, unpeeled. Half-peeled, fifteen dollars."

"Are there rates for everything?" she said. She had become suspicious.

"In a manner of speaking, there are. They're a little lower than the ones I quoted you. The Jones Street Convention of 1930 set them lower. But, with inflation. . . ." Here she fled.

"Ethel said it was nasty of me, but the woman was so serious I could not resist joking. I didn't think it would lose me the commission."

He still has his job with the advertising agency, drawing "cartoon faces of bilious men and headachy office girls." And that, he goes on, serious all at once, "is the adult, common-sense, wise world. I am exhilarated by the tremendous unimportance of my work. It is nonsense. My employers are nonsensical. The job therefore leaves me free. There's nothing to it. In a way it's like getting a piece of bread from a child in return for wiggling your ears. It is childish. I am the only one in this fifty-three-story building who knows how childish it is. Everybody else takes it seriously. Because this is a fifty-three-story building, they think it must be serious. 'This is life!' I say, this is pish, nonsense, nothing! The real world is the world of art and of thought. There is only one worth-while sort of work, that of the imagination."

It is an attractive idea, it confers a sort of life on him, sets him off from the debased dullness of those fifty-three stories. He is not making this up. I know him. He has no reason to lie to me. He is telling me what he feels: that he has escaped a trap. That really is a victory to celebrate. I am fascinated by it, and a little jealous. He can maintain himself. Is it because he is an artist? I believe it is. Those acts of the imagination save him. But what about me? I have no talent for that sort of thing. My talent, if I have one at all, is for being a citizen, or what is to-day called, most apologetically, a good man. Is there some sort of personal effort I can substitute for the imagination?

That, I am unable to answer. But certainly he is better off. There he is in New York, painting; and in spite of the calamity, the lies and moral buggery, the odium, the detritus of wrong and sorrow dropped on every heart, in spite of these, he can keep a measure of cleanliness and freedom. Besides, those acts of the imagination are in the strictest sense not personal. Through them he is connected with the best part of mankind. He feels this and he can never be isolated, left aside. He has a community. I have this six-sided box. And goodness is achieved not in a vacuum, but in the company of other men, attended by love. I, in this room, separate, alienated, distrustful, find in my purpose not an open world, but a closed, hopeless jail. My perspectives end in the walls. Nothing of the future comes to me. Only the past, in its shabbiness and innocence. Some men seem to know exactly where their opportunities lie; they break prisons and cross whole Siberias to pursue them. One room holds me.

When the Italian General Bergonzoli (I think it was Bergonzoli) was captured in Libya, he would not discuss military matters or the strategy that led to his defeat, but said, "Please! I am not a soldier. I am primarily a poet!" Who does not recognize the advantage of the artist, these days?

January 11

The other night Iva was searching through the shelves for a book she had put away months before and was musing aloud about its disappearance.

I was trimming my nails, listening absently, guiding the tiny crescent shears away from the quick, and was, as I can become in small matters, preoccupied with the gathering up of the clippings, when suddenly I remembered that I had lent Kitty Daumler a book.

"What did you say you were looking for?"

"Didn't you hear me before? A small, blue book, *Dubliners*. Have you seen it?"

"It must be around."

"Help me look."

"It's probably buried among the others. Why don't you read another book? There're plenty."

But Iva would not be so easily dissuaded. She went on searching, piling books on the floor near my chair.

"You won't find it," I said after a time.

"Why not?"

"These things have a way of dropping out of sight and turning up months later. It may have fallen behind the case."

"Let's move it."

"Not I. Next time Marie holds a general cleaning." I picked up the clippings in pinches and threw them into the wastebasket. "I ought to bury them, by rights."

"Those? Why?" She stood up, in her blue figured wrap, to ease her back against the wall. "I can't stay bent over very long. Old age."

"Nails, hair, all cuttings and waste from the body. Fear of sorcery."

"The door's been locked for days; *he* couldn't have taken it. Anyhow, what would he do with *Dubliners*?"

"Vanaker?"

"Yes." Iva was still sure he was responsible for the disappearance of her perfume bottles.

"I'll dig the book up tomorrow," I said.

"But it *should* be here."

"Very well, it should. But if it's not, it won't appear, no matter how determined you are."

"You mean it isn't in the room?"

"I'm not saying that."

"Then what do you mean?"

"I mean you'd rather waste an evening looking for it than read another book."

She said indignantly: "You told me to read it yourself. You insisted."

"But that was long ago, months and months ago. You should have read it in a few hours."

"Yes," she said. "And it's months and months since you took an interest in me. Lately, for all you care, I might just as well not be here. You pay no attention to what I say. If I didn't come home for a week you wouldn't miss me."

I received this charge in silence.

"Well?" she said aggressively.

"Ah, that's all foolishness."

"That's no sort of answer."

"Iva, it's this situation we're in. It's changed us both. But it isn't permanent."

"You mean you'll go away soon, and that'll be the end of it."

"Oh," I said, irritated, "don't nag. It is the situation. You know it is."

"It certainly has changed you."

"Of course it has; it would change anyone."

Rising, I took my coat from the hanger and went to the door.

"Where are you going?"

"To get some air. It's stuffy here."

"Can't you see it's raining? But I suppose even that's better than spending the evening with a nagging wife."

"Right, it is better!" I exclaimed. I had no more patience. "For ten cents they'll bunk me in a flophouse, no questions asked. You needn't expect me back tonight."

"That's right, advertise to the entire house. . . ."

"It's just like you to worry about the house. Damn the house. It's more shameful to act this way than that the house should know. I don't give a bloody damn about the house!"

"Joseph!" she said.

I shut the door with a crash, already aware, under my anger, that this was beneath me and altogether out of proportion to the provocation. I pulled my hat down against the rain. Our windows, with their glowing shades, set two orange rectangles, trade-marks of warmth and comfort, against the downpour and the dark, the glitter of the trees, the armor of ice on the street. The intense cold of the past week had lifted. Fog had succeeded it, rising in spongy gray blooms from the soaked walks, hovering in the yards and over the hollows blinking with rain and changes of color from the muffled signal lights—green, amber, red, amber, green, shuttering down the street. Mr. Vanaker's window went up. He threw a bottle, using the neck as a hilt. It landed softly into the clay, beside the others; there were dozens of bottles among the bushes, their high shoulders streaming as though drops of mercury were falling on them from the withes. The window was run down hastily.

My shoes, their once neat points scuffed and turned up, squashed, as I walked, through half-a-dozen leaks. I moved toward the corner, inhaling the odors of wet clothes and of wet coal, wet paper, wet earth, drifting with the puffs of fog. Low, far out, a horn uttered a dull cry, subsided; again. The street lamp bent over the curb like a woman who cannot turn homeward until she has found the ring or the coin she dropped in the ice and gutter silt. I heard behind me the clicking of a feminine stride and, for a moment, thought that Iva had come after me, but it was a stranger who passed at the awning of the corner store, her face made bleary by the woolly light and the shadowy fur-piece at her throat. The awning heaved; twists of water ran through its rents. Once more the horn bawled over the water, warning the lake tugs from the headlands. It was not hard to imagine that there was no city here at all, and not even a lake but, instead, a swamp and that despairing bawl crossing it; wasting trees instead of dwellings, and runners of vine instead of telephone wires. The bell of an approaching streetcar drove this vision off. I hailed it and, paying my fare, remained on the platform. It was not far to Kitty's. If my shoes had been watertight, I would have walked.

My purpose was not to retrieve the book—though, of course, I might as well ask her to return it while I was there —but to see Kitty.

I don't recall how she came to ask me for the book, nor how it was that I volunteered to give it to her. She would not have heard of it, and I cannot conceive in what connection I mentioned it. Here was one more conflux I could not trace or interpret. Kitty—but I do not say this in dispraise—is not an intelligent or even clever girl. She is simple, warm, uncomplicated, and matter-of-fact. Two years ago I had mapped out a Caribbean tour for her, and she had come in later to tell me what a good time she had had and to ask me to appraise some of the things she had bought. For that purpose I went to her apartment. She accepted my verdict of her tourist stuff so casually and treated me with such marked friendliness that I began to think—not without a touch of pleased excitement—that she was less interested in the appraisal than in me. At the first opportunity, I mentioned Iva, but it was apparent from her reaction or lack of reaction that she had taken my being married for granted. For her, she said, marriage as such did not exist. There were only people. Then began a conversation on marriage and love which I don't care to remember in detail. I made it abundantly plain that while I would talk of such matters I would not venture beyond talk. I was, however, flattered that such a handsome woman should be drawn to me. She was saying that some of the others on the cruise had made themselves absurd with the guides and beach boys. She could not stand that kind of looseness, and the pretty, characterless romantic Latin faces filled her with aversion. They were such vapid-looking men.

As I was leaving, her friendly hand somehow finished a gesture on my shoulder. She hoped I would come again for a talk. Next time I should do the talking. She was also a good listener.

I did not see her again for a month. Then one day she walked up to me at Inter-American and, without preliminaries, asked why I had not visited her. I answered that we had been busy.

"But you can break away one evening, can't you?"

"I can, certainly, if I want to."

"Why not come Thursday, then? We can have supper together."

Iva and I had not been getting along well. I don't think the fault was entirely hers. I had dominated her for years; she was now capable of rebelling (as, for example, at the Servatius party). I did not at first understand the character of her rebellion. Was it possible that she should not want to be

guided, formed by me? I expected some opposition. No one,
I would have said then, no one came simply and of his own
accord, effortlessly, to prize the most truly human traditions,
the heavenly cities. You had to be taught to struggle your way
toward them. Inclination was not enough. Before you could
set your screws revolving, you had to be towed out of the
shallows. But it was now evident that Iva did not want to be
towed. Those dreams inspired by Burckhardt's great ladies of
the Renaissance and the no less profound Augustan women
were in my head, not hers. Eventually I learned that Iva could
not live in my infatuations. There are such things as clothes,
appearances, furniture, light entertainment, mystery stories,
the attractions of fashion magazines, the radio, the enjoyable
evening. What could one say to them? Women—thus I reasoned—were not equipped by training to resist such things.
You might force them to read Jacob Boehme for ten years
without diminishing their appetite for them; you might teach
them to admire *Walden* but never convert them to wearing
old clothes. Iva was formed at fifteen, when I met her, with
likes and dislikes of her own which (because, for some strange
reason, I opposed them) she set aside until the time when she
could defend or simply assert them. Hence our difficulty.
There were nervous quarrels. She, in brave, shaky, new defiance, started to enjoy her independence. I let her alone, pretending indifference.

Now I began to visit Kitty Daumler frequently. She lived in
a rooming house similar to the one where Iva and I had
stayed the first two years of our marriage, before we could afford a flat. I partly blamed the flat for the change in Iva and
so took some pleasure in Kitty's rooms. Her furniture was
soiled, the wallpaper next to the mirror was smeared with lipstick, clothes were flung about, the bed was always unmade,
and she was careless about herself, trying to rule her hair with
a single comb, pulling it back constantly from her solid face
with its large brows and large mouth. An affectionate,
worldly, impudent, generous face.

We talked about all kinds of ordinary things. My friends
were leaving the city, one by one. I found no comfort in them
anyway. I would not have held these conversations with anyone but Kitty. But I had learned to discern the real Kitty, the

lively, plump, high-colored, scented, gross girl, behind the talk. I liked her. Beyond talk, however, Kitty and I did not go. She freely admitted that she "liked being with men" if they were the kind that interested her. I did interest her. We were amiable toward each other and were continually smiling. And the burden of the amiability and the smiles, as we both understood, was twofold: the intention and its check; the smiles checked us. I continued to smile.

Until, one wet and prematurely cold evening in early fall, I came in to find her in bed, drinking rum and tea. She had been caught in the rain and chilled. I sat by the bedside, holding a cup of whisky that was daubed along the rim with lipstick (her mark: towels, pillowcases, spoons, napkins, forks, all bore it). The room, in its usual state—the bronze-leafed lamp, the tissue paper of shoe boxes, the doll with the telephone concealed in its petticoat, the framed Venetian scene, the drying slip hung from an elbow of the steampipe—was no longer, for some reason, the usual comfortable anchorage. I was not smiling. I had not smiled since entering. She sipped her drink, her head raised between the cleft of the raised pillows; her chin, when she lowered the cup, nestled above the other cleft, the world's most beautiful illustration of number, tender division of the flesh beginning high above the lace line of her nightgown. The blood charged quickly to my face. I was overcome when she spoke to me, stammered my answer. I had not heard. "What?"

"I said, will you bring my bag? It's in the next room."

I got up, gracelessly.

"I want to powder."

"Oh, sure."

My shoes had made a large gray stain on the round rug.

"Tracked your mat up. I'm sorry," I said.

She shifted and looked, balancing the cup.

"I should have asked you to take your shoes off."

"My fault. You have it cleaned; I'll pay," I said. My flush grew deeper.

"Why, that isn't what I meant at all. You poor thing, you must be drenched. Pull them off this minute and let me see your socks."

I bent to unlace my shoes, my head suddenly gorged with

blood. "Wet through and through," she said. "Give them here, and I'll hang them up for you." I saw my socks appear beside the slip. She was standing before me, holding out a towel. "Dry yourself. Do you want to catch pneumonia?" As I lowered myself to the chair, her hand passed over my head and grasped the chain of the lamp, yanking it rudely. I could hear it in the darkness, beating against the shell of the bulb. I waited for the sound to subside, then reached upward. She intercepted my fingers. "It would only be putting it off, Joey," she said. Withdrawing my hand, I hurriedly began to undress. She groped her way around the chair and sat on the bed. "I knew you'd see it my way sooner or later."

"Darling!"

I "saw it her way" for two months, or until she began hinting at my leaving Iva. She claimed that Iva did not treat me well and that we were not suited to each other. I had never given her cause to think so, but she said she could tell. I have no real appetite for guile; the strain of living in both camps was too much. And I was unlike myself. I was out of character. It did not take me long to see that at the root of it all was my unwillingness to miss anything. A compact with one woman puts beyond reach what others might give us to enjoy; the soft blondes and the dark, aphrodisiacal women of our imaginations are set aside. Shall we leave life not knowing them? Must we? Avidity again. As soon as I recognized it, I began to bring the affair with Kitty to a close. It died in the course of a long conversation, in which I made it clear that a man must accept limits and cannot give in to the wild desire to be everything and everyone and everything to everyone. She was disappointed but also pleased by my earnestness, the tone I took, and felt honored to have her mind, her superior nature, thus addressed. We agreed that I was to continue visiting her on a friendly basis. There was nothing wrong in that, was there? Why not be sensible? She liked me, liked listening to me; she had already learned a great deal. Did she understand, I asked, that my motives had nothing to do with her, personally? In many ways I was reluctant . . . I . . . was not the kind who could keep too many irons in the fire, she finished for me good-naturedly.

It was a great relief. But the matter was not ended. I felt obliged to visit her, at first, as though to assure her that I valued her as much as ever. Had she thought my interest in her was at an end, she would have been deeply offended. But my visits were not long obligatory and one-sided, for with the onset of the dangling days it was a positive relief to drop in now and then to smoke a few cigarettes and drink a glass of rum. I was comfortable with Kitty.

The missing book reminded me that I had not seen her for some weeks, and I thought I would spend the rest of the evening with her and avoid bickering with Iva and going to sleep in raw temper.

The transom over Kitty's door appeared dark, but the room was not unoccupied. I heard her voice before I knocked. There was a brief silence. I took off my glove and knocked again. Kitty's transom has been lacquered over because, from the staircase, one can easily peer into her apartment. It was not easy to tell, therefore, whether the lights were out. And even if they were, it was still possible that she might be in the adjoining room, the kitchen. But at my third knock light suddenly shone through the scratches and uneven brush strokes in the transom. I could hear her conferring with someone, and then the knob turned and Kitty appeared, tying the cord of her dressing gown. She was not, of course, delighted to see me and I, too, was somewhat put out. I said that I was passing by and had decided to drop in for my book. She did not ask me in, though I mentioned with inappropriate irony that my feet were wet.

"I—ah, can't look for it now. The place is such a mess. Suppose you stop by again tomorrow?"

"I don't know whether I can tomorrow," I replied.

"Busy?"

"Yes."

It was her turn to look ironical. She began to relish the situation and, her arm casually stretched across the door, smiled at me and now did not seem at all displeased at having been found out.

"Are you working?"

"No."

"Then what keeps you busy?"

"Oh, something's come up. I can't come. But I have to have the book. It isn't mine, you see. . . ."

"It's Iva's?"

I nodded. Glancing into the room, I caught sight of a man's shirt hanging on the back of a chair. Had I edged over a few inches, I know I would have seen a man's arm on the coverlet. The room was always kept overheated and, through the haze, the thick, comfortable yet stirring scent I had come to associate with her was diffused. It reached me here in the hall, arousing nostalgia and envy in me, and I could not resist feeling that, like a fool, I had irrevocably thrown away the comfort and pleasure she had offered me in an existence barren of both. She looked behind, and then turned to me with a smile, but half in contempt, as much as to say, "It isn't my fault that that isn't your shirt hanging on the chair."

I said angrily: "When can I get it?"

"The book?"

"It's important that I get it back," I said. "Can't you locate it now? I'll wait."

She seemed surprised. "I'm afraid not. Suppose I mail it tomorrow, will that be all right?"

"It'll have to be, from the looks of it."

"Well, good night then, Joseph." She closed the door.

I stood looking up at the transom. The streaks of light flashed out. It was left a tarnished dull brown. I started down the stairs, breathing the staleness of cabbage and bacon and of the dust sifting behind the wallpaper. As I approached the second floor, I saw in the apartment below, through the open bar of the doorway, a woman in a slip, sitting before the mirror with a razor, her arm crooked backward, a cigarette on the ledge of the radio beside her, and from it two curling prongs of smoke rising. The sight of her held me momentarily; then, possibly because the sound of my steps had ceased, or sensing that she was being watched, she looked up, startled —a broad, angry face. I hurried down the remaining stairs into the vestibule, with its ageless, nameless, rooming-house hangings, its plush chairs, high, varnished, sliding doors, and, on the grained oak board, the brass nipples of call bells. From various parts of the house there were sounds: of splashing and

frying, of voices raised in argument or lowered in appease-
ment or persuasion, singing popular songs:

> Dinner in the diner
> Nothing could be finer
> Chattanooga choochoo. . . .

of chiming telephones, of the janitor's booming radio one
floor below. On a pedestal a bronze Laocoön held in his suffering hands a huge, barbarically furred headpiece of a lampshade with fringes of blackened lace. Buttoning my gloves, I
passed into the outer hall, thinking, as I did so, that by this
time Kitty had slipped back into bed and that she and her
companion had (I sought a way to say it) fallen together
again, his appetite increased by the intrusion. And, while I
could objectively find no reason why she should not do as she
pleased, I found myself nevertheless ambiguously resentful
and insulted.

Fog and rain had gone, abolished by a high wind, and, in
place of that imagined swamp where death waited in the
thickened water, his lizard jaws open, there was a clean path
of street and thrashing trees. Through the clouds the wind
had sunk a hole in which a few stars dipped. I ran to the corner, jumping over puddles. A streetcar was in sight, crashing
forward, rocking on its trucks from side to side and nicking
sparks from the waving cable. I caught it while it was in motion and stood on the platform, panting; the conductor was
saying that it was bad business to flip a car in the wet, you
wanted to be careful about such tricks. We were swept off
with quaking windows, blinking through floods of air, the
noise of the gong drowning under the horn of the wind.

"Reg'lar gale," said the conductor, gripping the hand rail.

A young soldier and a girl got on, both drunk; an elderly
woman with a pointed, wolfish face; a seedy policeman, who
stood with his hands buried in his pockets so that he seemed
to be holding his belly, his chin lowered on the flaps of his
collar; a woman in a short skirt and fur chubby, her stockings
wrinkling over her knees, her eyes watering, and her teeth set.

"You'd think," said the conductor pityingly as she worked
her way through the car, "that a woman like that, who ain't
no youngster, would stay home close to the steam on a night

like this, instead of knockin' around on late cars. Unless," he added to the policeman and me, "she's out on business," and showed his yellow teeth in a smile.

"Do'ch'ster next. Do'ch'ster!"

I jumped off and struggled homeward against the wind, stopping for a while under the corner awning to catch my breath. The clouds were sheared back from a mass of stars chattering in the hemispheric blackness—the universe, this windy midnight, out on its eternal business.

I found Iva waiting up for me. She did not ask where I had been, taking it for granted, I suppose, that I had followed my custom after quarrels, of walking along the lake shore. In the morning we had a short talk and were reconciled.

January 13

A dark, burdensome day. I stormed up from sleep this morning, not knowing what to do first—whether to reach for my slippers or begin immediately to dress, turn on the radio for the news, comb my hair, prepare to shave. I fell back into bed and spent an hour or so collecting myself, watching the dark beams from the slats of the blind wheeling on the upper wall. Then I rose. There were low clouds; the windows streamed. The surrounding roofs—green, raw red blackened brass—shone like potlids in a darkened kitchen.

At eleven I had a haircut. I went as far as Sixty-third Street for lunch and ate at a white counter amid smells of frying fish, looking out on the iron piers in the street and the huge paving bricks like the plates of the boiler-room floor in a huge liner. Above the restaurant, on the other corner, a hamburger with arms and legs balanced on a fiery wire, leaned toward a jar of mustard. I wiped up the sweet sediment in my cup with a piece of bread and went out to walk through large melting flakes. I wandered through a ten-cent store, examining the comic valentines, thought of buying envelopes, and bought instead a bag of chocolate creams. I ate them hungrily. Next, I was drawn into a shooting gallery. I paid for twenty shots and fired less than half, hitting none of the targets. Back in the street, I warmed myself at a salamander flaming in an oil drum near a newsstand with its wall of magazines erected under the shelter of the El. Scenes of love and horror. Afterward, I went into a Christian Science reading room and picked up the *Monitor*. I did not read it. I sat holding it, trying to think of the name of the company whose gas stoves used to be advertised on the front page of the *Manchester Guardian*. A little later I was in the street again, in front of Coulon's gymnasium, looking at photographs of boxers. "Young Salemi, now with the Rangers in the South Pacific." What beautiful shoulders!

I started back, choosing unfamiliar streets. They turned out to be no different from the ones I knew. Two men were sawing a tree. A dog sprang from behind a fence without warning, yapping. I hate such dogs. A man in a mackinaw and red boots stood in the center of a lot, throwing boxes into a fire. At the high window of a stone house, a child, a blond boy, was playing king in a paper crown. He wore a blanket over his shoulders and, for a scepter, he held a thin green stick in his thin fingers. Catching sight of me, he suddenly converted his scepter into a rifle. He drew a bead on me and fired, his lips moving as he said, "Bang!" He smiled when I took off my hat and pointed in dismay to an imaginary hole.

The book arrived in the noon mail. I will find it tonight. I hope that will be the last deception imposed on me.

January 14

I met Sam Pearson, Iva's cousin, on Fifty-seventh Street today. He said, "Well, I didn't expect to see you, are you still among us?" He knew I was.

I said, glumly, "I'm not in Alaska."

"What are you doing with yourself?"

"Nothing."

He smiled, allowing me my joke. "Who was it that told me you were taking a course in a trade school . . . ?"

A: "That's just a rumor."

Q: "What are you doing, then?"

A: "Just living off Iva."

Again he smiled, but he was no longer sure of himself.

Q: "I heard you were studying, or something."

A: "No, I just sit at home all day and do nothing."

Q: "Nothing?"

A: "Absolutely nothing."

Q: "Oh, well, I suppose we'll all be going soon, won't we?" (Sam has three half-grown children).

A: "If the man power shortage becomes any more acute."

It's time I was uncivil to Sam. He has always, by his questions, exercised a social or family tyranny over me, checking on my suitability for Iva. No doubt he will report this to the Almstadts.

January 15

Look out for yourself, and the world will be best served.

Yesterday I had a talk with Mr. Fanzel, the tailor, an Alsatian gentleman. Last spring he bought some Lille thread, about two hundred spools, at a bargain. He paid twenty-five cents a spool; today the price is seventy-five cents. He does not intend to sell any of it. The increase goes into the garments he sews, and he is busier now than he was in his best year, 1928. One of his customers has just ordered six new suits and two sport jackets. "Pretty soon I maybe won't have material. I got to look ahead. So I make higher the price," says Mr. Fanzel. Which is his kind of wisdom, business wisdom. If everybody takes care of number one, the general welfare is assured. A year ago Mr. Fanzel sewed a button to my coat gratis; this year he charged fifteen cents. Perhaps he used precious Lille thread, or perhaps the value of his time has increased, now that he has so many customers. Mr. Franzel is frightened. He makes an outward show of confidence and of riding the wave but in many ways manifests his terror. The tenants of his building who were on relief four years ago now have become highly paid defense workers, and one of them, to his consternation, last week came down and ordered a suit costing eighty dollars. Heretofore Mr. Fanzel's customers have been the rich of the Kenwood district. He could not

stop talking about his tenant whom he was once on the verge
of evicting, and who now earns a hundred and ten dollars a
week. Mr. Fanzel is master only of his scissors and needles,
not of the greater fate that makes such changes, and, in his
fear, with wars and transformed tenants and, it may be, even
the shadow of Jeff Forman's falling plane crossing his security,
he resolves to protect himself by charging eighty dollars for
suits worth forty and fifteen cents for a button he formerly
sewed out of kindness. Mr. Fanzel is innocent. I blame the
spiritual climate. In it we enjoy our gobber of Jeff Forman
without a thought for him, let alone a word of gratitude. Supply is supply, and demand is demand. They will be satisfied,
be it with combs, fifes, rubber, whisky, tainted meat, canned
peas, sex, or tobacco. For every need there is an entrepreneur,
by a marvelous providence. You can find a man to bury your
dog, rub your back, teach you Swahili, read your horoscope,
murder your competitor. In the megapolis, all this is possible.
There was a Parisian cripple in the days of John Law, the
Scottish speculator, who stood in the streets renting out his
hump for a writing desk to people who had no convenient
place to take their transactions.

What can poor Mr. Fanzel do? He must make money while
he can; he is one of the little people. He barely managed to
hold on to his property during the crash. Though he knows
I am not working, he must charge fifteen cents for sewing
the button. Otherwise, through his very kindness, he may
find himself among the hindmost, where the devil, who is so
far among the foremost he has doubled his trail, can snatch
him up. And then who, if he keeps down his prices and al-
lows himself impulses of charity, will furnish Mr. Fanzel his
roast, his cabbage, his roll and coffee, his bed, his roof, his
morning *Tribune*, the price of his movie, and his Prince Albert tobacco?

He showed me an article by former President Hoover
which advocated the abolition of all control over prices, thus
encouraging manufacturing initiative in the interests of increased armament production.

"What do you think?" he said.

"What do *you* think of it, Mr. Fanzel?"

"Such a plan would save the country."

"But should we pay them to save the country? Have they no other reason to manufacture these things?"

"They are in business."

"Aren't they making lots of money now?"

"More will be better for everybody. It's business. Ah," he laughed, waving his hand at me, "you don't understand it. They will work harder and we will win the war faster."

"But the prices will go up, and then more money will be like less money."

"Oh, oh, you don't understand it," he said, snuffing with laughter through the ginger-colored hairs of his nose and mustache.

"Mr. Fanzel, when you sew a dress for your wife, do you charge her for it?"

"I make only men's garments, not ladies'."

I laid three nickels on the counter and picked up the coat.

"You think it over," he called to me. "They don't make a man the president for nothing."

I walked away, fingering the button which had been threatening for weeks to drop off, weighing the value of its stability against that of the fifteen cents, representing three cups of coffee, or three cigars, or a glass-and-a-half of beer, or five morning papers, or something less than a package of cigarettes, or three telephone calls, or one breakfast. Iva's check at the library having been held up, I went without breakfast. Money has been scarce this week. But it does not disturb me to miss a meal now and then. I do not use as many calories as an active man and I have fat to spare. Mr. Fanzel, I am sure, would have been appalled to learn that he had deprived me of my toast and coffee, despite the fact that he has every theoretical right to a clear conscience. I should be taking care of myself. He can't be responsible for me. I recall the words of the suitor Luzhin in *Crime and Punishment*. He has been reading the English economists, or claims he has. "If I were to tear my coat in half," he says, "in order to share it with some wretch, no one would be benefited. Both of us would shiver in the cold." And why should both shiver? Is it not better that one should be warm? An unimpeachable conclusion. If I were to tell this to Mr. Fanzel (without mentioning breakfast), he would certainly agree. Life is hard. *Vae victis!* The wretched must suffer.

January 16

Fairly quiet day.

January 18

I sat watching Marie this morning as she changed the sheets
and dusted and washed the windows. To see her at the windows fascinated me especially. It was merely her work, but
even she seemed to derive a sober pleasure from it, following
the rag over the glitter with her eyes, pulling the frames back
and forth on their resonant cords, moving the curved water
line further and further across the spotted glass.

To make a dirty surface clean—a very simple, very human
matter. I, while shining shoes, grew partly aware of it. In
those moments at the window, how different Marie was, how
purely human as she rubbed the glass. I sometimes wonder if
it can be entirely a source of pleasure to clean. There is too
much urgency in it; sometimes it becomes a preoccupation
of body and heart. "Ah, in anxiety I lie, thinking, what surface tomorrow?" But it has its importance as a notion of center, of balance, of order. A woman learns it in the kitchens of
her childhood, and it branches out from sinks, windows,
table tops, to the faces and hands of children, and then it
may become, as it does for some women, part of the nature
of God.

January 19

Susie Farson came over in tears to ask Iva what to do about
her husband. I withdrew and left them to talk. Susie and her
husband wage an endless fight. He, Walter, is a ruddy, big-
jawed, blond Dakota boy of the kind city girls are often attracted to. Susie, who was a schoolmate of Iva's, is six years
older than he. He resents this difference in their ages, he resents having been trapped into marriage, and, most of all, he
resents the baby, Barbara. Recently Iva indignantly wanted
me to punch his head for gagging the child with a handkerchief
because she disturbed his sleep. Last week he pressed her jaws

together for the same reason, almost suffocating her. This week he bruised Susie's face. Iva advised Susie to leave him, and Susie says she intends to.

January 20

Iva and I met downtown at six. The occasion was our sixth wedding anniversary. She had decided that we deserved a celebration. We had had none New Year's Eve. It had been a bad year—all the more reason for a good dinner and a bottle of French wine. She was determined that this was not to be just another evening.

I came down on the El, getting off at the Randolph and Wabash station. There were crooked streaks of red at one end of the street and, at the other, a band of black, soft as a stroke of charcoal; into it were hooked the tiny lights of the lake front. On the platform the rush-hour crowds were melting under the beams of oncoming trains. Each train was followed by an interval of darkness, when the twin colored lamps of the rear car hobbled around the curve. Sparks from the street below were caught and blanked in the heavy, flat ladder of ties. The pigeons under the sooty, sheet-iron eaves were already asleep; their wadded shadows fell on the billboards and, with every train, fluttered as though a prowler had sprung from the roof into their roost.

I walked along East Randolph Street, stopping to look at the rich cakes and the tropical fruits. When I came to the smoky alley alongside the library where the southbound cars emerge, I saw a man sprawl out in front of me, and at once I was in the center of a large crowd and, from a distance that could not have been as great as it seemed, a mounted policeman standing before a Cottage Grove car was gazing down.

The fallen man was well dressed and above middle age. His hat lay crushed under his large bald head, his tongue had come forward between his lips, his lips seemed swollen. I stooped and tore at his collar. A button sprang away. By this time the policeman had pushed his way forward. I drew back, wiping my hands on a piece of paper. Together, we stared at the fallen man's face. Then my attention was drawn to the policeman's own face. It was long and as narrow as a boot. His features were sharp, red, wind-scarred, his jaws muscular, his sideburns whitish, intersected by the straps of his stiff blue cap. He blew his steel whistle. The signal was not necessary. Other uniformed men were already coming toward us. The first to arrive was elderly himself. He bent and reached into the fallen man's pockets and produced an old-fashioned strap-fastened wallet like my father's. He held up a card and spelled the name. The victim's broad coat was hitched up behind, his chest and belly rose hugely together as he labored, snoring, for breath. A path was cleared for the approaching ambulance. Its bell beat rapidly; the onlookers moved away, reluctant to disengage themselves. Would the red face go gray, the dabbled hands stop their rowing, the jaw drop? Perhaps it was only an epileptic fit.

As I withdrew with the others, I touched my forehead; it had begun to smart. My finger tips searched for the scratch Aunt Dina had left on it the night of my mother's death. The nurse had called us. From all parts of the house we came running. My mother may still have been alive, though her eyes were shut, for when Aunt Dina threw herself upon her, her lips seemed to move crookedly in a last effort to speak or kiss. Aunt Dina screamed. I tried to pull her from the body, and she lashed at me, clawing with enraged fingers. In the next blurred moment, my mother was dead. I was looking at her, my hand pressed to my face, hearing Aunt Dina cry, "She wanted to say something! She wanted to talk to me!"

To many in the fascinated crowd the figure of the man on the ground must have been what it was to me—a pre-vision. Without warning, down. A stone, a girder, a bullet flashes against the head, the bone gives like glass from a cheap kiln; or a subtler enemy escapes the bonds of years; the blackness comes down; we lie, a great weight on our faces, straining toward the last breath which comes like the gritting of gravel under a heavy tread.

I mounted the library stairs and from there saw the tall blue ambulance slip from the narrow passageway, the calm horse stepping away from the car.

I mentioned nothing of this to Iva; I wanted to spare her.

But I could not spare myself, and several times during dinner the image of the fallen man came between me and my food, and I laid down my fork. We did not enjoy our celebration. She thought I was ill.

January 21

Susie Farson came by in great excitement and said that she and her husband were going to Detroit. He has been offered a radio training course by the War Department. She hopes to be admitted to the same school. They are leaving the baby with Farson's sister, who is a "twenty-six" girl in a downtown restaurant. "She'll look after her; Janey adores the kid. I'll write and tell you how we're getting along. And, Iva, you'll stop by once in a while and see how she's getting along. I'll give you Janey's address."

"Of course," said Iva, but coldly. And after Susie had rushed away, she said, "That fool! What if something should happen to the baby?"

"She doesn't want to lose her husband," I said.

"Lose him? I would have shot him by now. Besides, she's only making things worse. He'll blame her if anything goes wrong. And she believes she's doing it for love. Oh, be quiet, you!"

Mr. Vanaker was raking his throat, coughing, halting with a fleshy catch and coughing again. Any disturbance in our room sets him off. He did not stop until Iva, with a show of temper unusual for her, banged on the wall with her slipper.

January 22

I ate a large breakfast, intending to go without lunch. But at one o'clock, intensely hungry, I tossed aside Abt's pamphlet and went out for lunch. On the way back I bought several oranges and a large bar of chocolate. By four o'clock I had eaten them. Later, at Fallon's, I had a large dinner. And a few hours later, in the movies, I added to all this a whole package of caramels and most of a bag of mints. Now, at eleven, I am still hungry.

We had supper with the Almstadts yesterday. Cousin Sam has
not reported me. I had prepared Iva by telling her of our conversation, but nothing was mentioned. Old Almstadt dominated the conversation, telling of the profits he could make if
there were no shortage of supplies. My mother-in-law also is
kept busy these days. Last week she baked a cake for the Russian Relief Bazaar. This week all the ladies of her club are contributing blood to the Red Cross. She knits a muffler a week.
She tried gloves but had no success with them. She could not
do the fingers. And the girls, Alma and Rose, complained that
all the young men were disappearing into the Army and that
only high-school boys were left. Mrs. Almstadt again mentioned that she would like to have Iva with her when I was
drafted. I said there was time enough to decide. I love Iva too
much to turn her over to them.

Next week we are going to my father's. We have been declining my stepmother's invitations for weeks; she is becoming offended.

In bed with a cold. Marie made tea for me in the morning.
Iva came home after lunch to nurse me. She brought a box of
Louisiana strawberries and, as a treat, rolled them in powdered sugar. The coverlet was starred with the green stems.
She was at her most ample and generous best. She read to me
for an hour, and then we dozed off together. I awoke in the
middle of the afternoon; she still slept. I gazed up at the comfortable room and heard the slight, mixed rhythm of her
breathing and mine. This endeared her to me more than any
favor could. The icicles and frost patterns on the window
turned brilliant; the trees, like instruments, opened all their
sounds into the wind, and the bold, icy colors of sky and
snow and clouds burned strongly. A day for a world without
deformity or threat of damage, and my pleasure in the
weather was all the greater because it held its own beauty and
was engaged with nothing but itself. The light gave an air of
innocence to some of the common objects in the room, lib-
erating them from ugliness. I lost the aversion I had hitherto

felt for the red oblong of rug at the foot of the bed, the scrap of tapestry on the radiator seat, the bubbles of paint on the white lintel, the six knobs on the dresser I had formerly compared to the ugly noses of as many dwarf brothers. In the middle of the floor, like an accidental device of serenity, lay a piece of red string.

Great pressure is brought to bear to make us undervalue ourselves. On the other hand, civilization teaches that each of us is an inestimable prize. There are, then, these two preparations: one for life and the other for death. Therefore we value and are ashamed to value ourselves, are hard-boiled. We are schooled in quietness and, if one of us takes his measure occasionally, he does so coolly, as if he were examining his fingernails, not his soul, frowning at the imperfections he finds as one would at a chip or a bit of dirt. Because, of course, we are called upon to accept the imposition of all kinds of wrongs, to wait in ranks under a hot sun, to run up a clattering beach, to be sentries, scouts or workingmen, to be those in the train when it is blown up, or those at the gates when they are locked, to be of no significance, to die. The result is that we learn to be unfeeling toward ourselves and incurious. Who can be the earnest huntsman of himself when he knows he is in turn a quarry? Or nothing so distinctive as quarry, but one of a shoal, driven toward the weirs.

But I must know what I myself am.

It was good to lie in bed, awake, not dreaming. Hemmed in all day, inactive, I lie down at night in enervation and, as a result, I sleep badly. I have never known dreamless sleep. In the past, my dreams annoyed me by their prolixity. I went on foolish errands, and held even more foolish debates, and settled and arranged the most humdrum affairs. But now my dreams are more bare and ominous. Some of them are fearful. A few nights ago I found myself in a low chamber with rows of large cribs or wicker bassinets in which the dead of a massacre were lying. I am sure they were victims of a massacre, because my mission was to reclaim one for a particular family. My guide picked up a tag and said, "This one was found near. . . ." I do not remember the name; it ended in *Tanza*. It must have been Constanza. It was either there or in

Bucharest that those slain by the Iron Guard were slung from hooks in a slaughterhouse. I have seen the pictures. I looked at the reclining face and murmured that I was not personally acquainted with the deceased. I had merely been asked, as an outsider. . . . I did not even know the family well. At which my guide turned, smiling, and I guessed that he meant— there was not enough light in the vault to make his meaning unambiguous, but I thought I understood—"It's well to put oneself in the clear in something like this." This was his warning to me. He approved of my neutrality. As long as I took the part of the humane emissary, no harm would come to me. But it offended me to have an understanding with this man and to receive a smile of complicity from his pointed face. Could I be such a hypocrite? "Do you think he can be found?" I said. "Would he be here?" I showed my distrust. We continued up the aisle; it was more like the path of a gray draught than anything so substantial as a floor. The bodies, as I have said, were lying in cribs, and looked remarkably infantile, their faces pinched and wounded. I do not remember much more. I can picture only the low-pitched, long room much like some of the rooms in the Industrial Museum in Jackson Park; the childlike bodies with pierced heads and limbs; my guide, brisk as a rat among his charges; an atmosphere of terror such as my father many years ago could conjure for me, describing Gehenna and the damned until I shrieked and begged him to stop; and the syllables *Tanza*.

Some of the other dreams have been only slightly less dreadful. In one I was a sapper with the Army in North Africa. We had arrived in a town, and my task was to render harmless the grenade traps in one of the houses. I crawled through the window, dropped from the clay sill and saw a grenade wired to the door, ridged and ugly. But I did not know where to begin, which wire to touch first. My time was limited; I had other work before me. I began to tremble and perspire and, going to the far end of the room, I aimed my pistol long and carefully at the ridges and fired. When the din subsided, I realized that if I had hit the mark I would have killed myself. But I had scarcely a moment to feel relieved. Pincers in hand, I went forward to cut the first wire.

*

I recognize in the guide of the first dream an ancient figure, temporarily disguised only to make my dread greater
when he revealed himself.

Our first encounter was in a muddy back lane. By day it was
a wagon thoroughfare, but at this evening hour only a goat
wandered over the cold ruts that had become as hard as the
steel rims that made them. Suddenly I heard another set of
footsteps added to mine, heavier and grittier, and my premo-
nitions leaped into one fear even before I felt a touch on my
back and turned. Then that swollen face that came rapidly toward mine until I felt its bristles and the cold pressure of its
nose; the lips kissed me on the temple with a laugh and a
groan. Blindly I ran, hearing again the gritting boots. The
roused dogs behind the snaggled boards of the fences abandoned themselves to the wildest rage of barking. I ran, stumbling through drifts of ashes, into the street.

Could the fallen man of last week have seen, had he
chanced to open his eyes, his death in the face of that policeman who bent over him? We know we are sought and expect
to be found. How many forms he takes, the murderer. Frank,
or simple, or a man of depth and cultivation, or perhaps pro-
saic, without distinction. Yet he is *the* murderer, the stranger
who, one day, will drop the smile of courtesy or custom to
show you the weapon in his hand, the means of your death.
Who does not know him, the one who takes your measure in
the street or on the stairs, he whose presence you must ignore
in the darkened room if you are to close your eyes and fall
asleep, the agent who takes you, in the last unforgiving act,
into inexistence? Who does not expect him with the opening
of the door; and who, after childhood, thinks of flight or resistance or of laying any but ironic, yes, even welcoming
hands on his shoulders when he comes? The moment is for
him to choose. He may come at a climax of satisfaction or of
evil; he may come as one comes to repair a radio or a faucet;
mutely, or to pass the time of day, play a game of cards; or,
with no preliminary, colored with horrible anger, reaching
out a muffling hand; or, in a mask of calm, hurry you to your
last breath, drawn with a stuttering sigh out of his shadow.

How will it be? How? Falling a mile into the wrinkled sea?
Or, as I have dreamed, cutting a wire? Or strafed in a river

among chopped reeds and turning water, blood leaking through the cloth of the sleeves and shoulders?

I can safely think of such things on a bright afternoon such as this. When they come at night, the heart, like a toad, exudes its fear with a repulsive puff. But toward morning I have a way, also, of holding court on myself, and that is even more intolerable. Half-conscious, I call in a variety of testimony on my case and am confronted by the wrongs, errors, lies, disgraces, and fears of a lifetime. I am forced to pass judgment on myself and to ask questions I would far rather not ask: "What is this for?" and "What am I for?" and "Am I made for this?" My beliefs are inadequate, they do not guard me. I think invariably of the awning of the store on the corner. It gives as much protection against rain and wind as my beliefs give against the chaos I am forced to face. "God does not love those who are unable to sleep soundly," runs an old saying. In the morning I dress and go about my "business." I pass one more day no different from the others. Night comes, and I have to face another session of sleep—that "sinister adventure" Baudelaire calls it—and be brought to wakefulness by degrees through a nightmare of reckoning or inventory, my mind flapping like a rag on a clothesline in cold wind.

We had an enormous sunset, a smashing of gaudy colors, apocalyptic reds and purples such as must have appeared on the punished bodies of great saints, blues heavy and rich. I woke Iva, and we watched it, hand in hand. Her hand was cool and sweet. I had a slight fever.

January 28

We did not have a bad time at my father's house. My stepmother was cordial; my father did not pry. We left at ten o'clock. Iva did not tell me until today that, as she was preparing to go, my stepmother gave her an envelope containing a card congratulating us on our anniversary and a check.

"Now, Joseph, don't be angry," Iva said. "We can use the money. We both need things."

"I'm not angry."

"They wanted to give us a present. It was nice of them. You

need a new shirt. And some shorts. I can't keep darning them." She laughed. "There's no place for another patch."

"Whatever you like," I said, putting a strand of hair behind her ear.

I was glad enough to have escaped the usual interview with my father, which begins, as a rule, with his taking me aside and saying, "Have I told you about Gartner's boy, the youngest, the one who was studying chemistry? They've taken him out of school. He has an excellent job in a war plant. You remember him."

Indeed I do.

This means that I, too, should have been a chemist or physicist or engineer. A nonprofessional education is something the middle classes can ill afford. It is an investment bound to fail. And, in the strictest sense, it is not necessary, for any intelligent man can pick up all he needs to know. My father, for instance, never went to college, and yet he can keep up his end of a conversation with a quotation from Shakespeare—"Pause, now, and weigh thy values with an equal hand," "A loan oft loses both itself and friend," the passage beginning, "Yes, young boy," from *King John*.

My accomplishments, he acknowledges, are wider than his; my opportunities were greater. But bread and butter come first. Besides, professional men are also sometimes cultured. Take George Sachs, now (our family doctor in Montreal), who was a scholar and even wrote a book in his spare time. (A pamphlet for the Quebec Musical Society: *The Medical Facts about Beethoven's Deafness.*) My father's justification is, however, that I have prepared myself for the kind of life I shall never be able to lead. And, where my abiding obsession formerly was to carry out my plans, I know now that I shall have to settle for very, very little. That is, I shall have to accept very little, for there is no question of settling. Personal choice does not count for much these days.

January 29

As I was passing Vanaker's favorite dumping yard, I saw on a bush, amid the bottles, a pair of socks that had a familiar look. I took one of them off and examined it. It was mine. There could be no doubt about it; I had bought several pairs in this pattern about a year ago. To make doubly sure, I took one of the socks home and compared it with the others. It was the same in every detail. Perhaps he did steal Iva's perfume. I had been unwilling to believe it before. Vanaker, Mrs. Briggs tells me, has a good job in a garage. Sunday mornings, when we see him leaving for church, he is well dressed. What can have inspired this theft of my worn socks? I said nothing about it to Iva, but wrapped the evidence in a piece of paper and threw it away.

January 30

I wrote to Abt without mentioning his pamphlet. He is sure to be angry.

January 31

Slight letup in the cold. The fury of cleanliness. One of my shirts came back from the laundry without a single button. I must complain.

February 1

Near Sixty-third and Stony Island I ran into Alf Steidler, whom I hadn't seen in years. He had heard that I had been drafted, and I had heard the same news about him. "They turned me down," he said. "Bad teeth, bad heart, and emotionally unsuitable. Mostly the last. Jack Brill was bait, though."

"Did they take him?"

"In December. He's going to be a bombardier."

"What are you doing so far from Huron Street?"

"I've been up to see my brother in the hospital. He smashed his cab last Thursday."

"Too bad. Is he hurt much?"

"Oh, no, he damaged his looks a little, that's all."

I said I was sorry to hear it.

"That's the way the breaks run," said Steidler. "Doesn't

make much difference, now that he's married. It won't interfere with his wolfing around."

"I didn't know he was married."

"How would you? It didn't make the front pages."

"I'm trying to say that I'm surprised. Who . . . ?"

"Wilma. He married the kid."

"The girl I saw him with at the Paxton?"

"That's the one."

Whenever I meet Steidler, I think of Rameau's nephew, described by Diderot as ". . . *un (personnage) composé de hau-
teur et de bassesse, de bon sens et de déraison.*" But, less
emphatic, more sentimental (after his own fashion), and not
nearly as shrewd.

He carried a match to the stump of his cigar, sucking. His
black hair, freshly cut, was combed back in the usual way, as
though painted on, flush against the rising hump of his head.
It gave his face, with its contrasting long cheeks, jutting
bones and fleshy nose and lips, a curious bareness. He looked
very pale, almost limy in the dusty sunlight under the El pillars. He was shaved and powdered, and he wore a new striped
tie. But his once natty coat was frayed, the brown belt looked
greenish.

"How's our old school chum Morris?" he asked.

"Abt? He's doing very well; he's in Washington."

"And what about you?"

"I'm waiting for the Army call. What are you doing, Alf?"

"Oh, the same. Still trying to lead a genteel life. WPA
folded, you know. It was good going for a couple of years. I
was an honored artist of the republic. First I was in the theater, you remember. Then I organized a water ballet for the
parks system, and after that I led a chorus in a settlement
house. Say, but I started at the bottom. My first job was digging up a street. I had to explain to the people who asked me
what I was working at that I was a geologist. Ha, ha! Then I
was a smoke watcher."

"I don't understand."

"Up in the West Side factory district I sat on a roof with a
chart of six shades of smoke and watched the chimneys eight
hours a day. Then the theater project. Anyway, the whole
business folded up, and I went out to the Coast. Say, there's

a Thompson's down the way. How about a cup of coffee? Good. It's been years since I saw you. The gay old Coast. I went out with some ideas and tried to get in to see Lubitsch, but I couldn't find anyone to introduce me. Christ, it's mad out there. It's the world's greatest loony-bin. Ever been on the Coast?"

"Never."

"Christ, stay away from it, it's murder. But then, if you want to see what the life of the country can wash up, take the trip. I've been around a little bit. But in L.A. they conned me for my fifty bucks as though I'd been a baby. Of course, I'm drawn into different circles than you. Well, I was broke, so I wired my mother and got twenty bucks and a note about how slow the beauty-parlor business was. That was a tricky week. I had to go to work for a while, to raise some money." He looked at me somberly, a decayed Spanish prince with a splayed nose and a long upper lip covered with bristles. His blue eyes grew darker. "I didn't have it easy.

"One nice thing about the Coast, though," he added, brightening, "the nooky situation is awfully good where there aren't too many soldiers. You whistle for it. Did you read about that silly trial? Now, there was something really funny. If we were more civilized we'd put it on the stage. This Canadian officer kept that girl in a hotel. But it was just brotherly, she said. He called her his little strumpet. 'Crumpet, you mean,' said the prosecutor. Right then and there he must have known his case was gone. 'No,' she insists, 'strumpet. It's a kind of biscuit the British like.'" Alf laughed, holding the sugar shaker and spoon suspended over his cup. "Well, they wouldn't convict anybody on *that* sort of evidence." He reached forward to hand me the sugar, revealing a rolled copy of *Variety* in his coat pocket. He was lulled by the joke; musing, smiling, he stirred and sipped, and then wet a fresh cigar along his underlip.

At twenty-eight, he was old-fashioned. He had all the ways of a theatrical generation that was already at the point of death when, in his high-school days, he had cut classes to admire its aging comedians in the mangy splendor of the Oriental. He grew up behind his mother's beauty shop. When I knew him well, at sixteen, he was already a stage gentleman, and rose at two every day to breakfast on tea and sardines. He spent his evenings at the Arrow, amid amateur talk of *Magda* and *Desire Under the Elms*. He played in all the local productions, was Joxur in *Juno and the Paycock* and did *Cyrano* for a triumphant week (which he never forgot) at the school auditorium.

"I wouldn't have come back from the Coast," he said. "But my number came up; the board called me. It's a good sign for the country that I was rejected. They'd deserve to lose if they put me in their Army. The psychiatrist asked me what I did, and I replied, 'To be perfectly frank, I've been a deadbeat all my life.' He said, 'How do you think you'll get along in the Army?' and I answered, 'Now, what do you think, doctor?'"

"You said that?"

"Sure, I was being honest. I'd never be any damned good to them. I'd set an all-time record for gold-bricking. It's up to you normal bastards to do the fighting. I said, 'What do you think?' and he took another look at my papers and said, 'They've got you down for a bad heart, here. Well, this will make it final.' And he wrote down, 'Schizoid Type.' That would mean I was in the split-pea soup, wouldn't it? I looked it up. You think a guy can tell by looking at you? Or because you tell him you're a deadbeat? That isn't enough, is it?"

"No," I said, "they need more evidence than that; it isn't enough. Don't worry about it."

"Oh, I'm not worried, don't kid yourself." His glasses duplicated the triangular flame of another match. "They wouldn't know what to make of me, because I'm not your average guy. I know that. Why, I couldn't fight. It isn't my line. My line is getting by."

"How do you get by, Alf?"

"It's a wonder to me. But every January swings around, somehow, and there I am; I've come through. But I don't know how. I work a little, sponge a little, gamble a little. I suppose I am a deadbeat. Or will be till I am what I want to become. Well, I entertain the people I sponge from. That's something, anyhow."

"You expect me to pay for your coffee?" I said.

"*You*, Joseph? This is Dutch treat. What a corny joke!" He looked offended.

"I was referring to the entertainment."

"Oh. One of these days I expect an opening. . . ."

"I didn't mean anything by that," I said.

"Forget it. Who holds your bad jokes against you? Did you see me in any of the Federal productions?

"I wasn't bad. A big improvement over the old days. *Roxanne!* Remember? Ha, ha! Well, it's in the family. Have you ever heard my old lady sing, were you ever around when that happened? Oh, you've missed something. My brother writes songs, too. He just wrote one for the United Nations. It's called 'Let's Link Hands Across the Ocean.' He keeps bothering me to do something about it. He's sure it would make the Hit Parade. Now he wants me to go to New York on the insurance money. Wilma's against it."

"Do you intend to go?"

"A year ago I would have gone like a shot. But since Wilma's against it . . . I owe the girl a good turn. I got her into trouble a few years ago. Phil hung a shiner on her when they were living together for taking twenty dollars out of his pocket. Only she didn't take it. I took it."

"Did you confess?"

"Confess! It would spoil my credit with him forever. I was sure they'd make it up by and by. He gave her an awful pasting. She cried. . . ."

"Were you there when it happened?"

"Right in the room. I couldn't butt in."

"What about the money?"

"I pinned it on a false hope. I suppose you think that's terrible, huh? Well, this may sound hard, and you may not believe it, but they're more human when they're fighting. Besides, it was like a movie. He suffered remorse, she forgave him because he was her man, and so on. They got a big kick out of it. I know. I was their go-between. But now she says she's the one who should take the song to New York, if anyone goes. I guess she sees herself in Tin-Pan Alley, her face streaked with tears. . . ."

"Oh, it can't be that bad."

"Can't it, though? You don't know the type. Let me show you. She hides overnight in a publisher's broom closet and surprises Mr. Snaith-Hawkins himself in the morning. 'What

are you doing here?' 'Oh, for my sake, Sir, listen to this. My
husband wrote it.' As he sternly refuses, she throws herself at
his feet, and he says, 'Come now, my girl.' Not a bad man,
you see. 'It's not only for my sake, but for Democracy
and . . .'; as she goes on, he relents. 'You shouldn't be lying
on the floor, my dear. Here, take this chair. I'll have Mr. Trubshevsky run through it' (the score)—Just wait" (I had tried to
interrupt)—"Trubshevsky plays; Snaith-Hawkins frowns,
strokes his beard. His expression changes. Trubshevsky
pounds in ecstasy. They sing together, 'Let's link hands,' et
cetera. 'This is great, positively!' exclaims Snaith-Hawkins.
And Trubshevsky, enthusiastically, his eyes shining, 'Your husband is a genius, Madam, positively.' 'There, don't cry, my
dear,' says Snaith-Hawkins. 'Oh, Sir, you can't understand. All
those years of struggle, driving a cab, working at his music
after supper.' They're overcome. You see?" said Steidler.
"That's how they think. She'll probably go. It's money
thrown away. Well, he won't be satisfied otherwise."

"What a shame."

"It's not a shame at all. It's just as well. Just think what the
world would be like if their dreams came true."

Or if yours came true, I was tempted to say.

I had a full day of this. He walked home with me and
stayed until five o'clock, talking incessantly and smoking so
many cigars I had to ventilate the room when he left. I was as
tired as though I had spent the day in dissipations of a particularly degrading sort with Steidler as my accomplice. I did
not tell Iva of the visit. She disapproves of him.

February 2

Still no fruits and flowers. I have been too lazy to stir out. But
I know I am not lazy. Here is an incalculable deception. Lazy
we are not. When we seem so, our cyclonic wishes are baffled,
and pride requires us to be indifferent.

The Egyptians were right to make one of their gods a cat.
They, the worshipers, knew that only a cat's eyes could see
into their interior darkness.

*

The papers say no husbands have been drafted from Illinois since last summer. But now the supply of men is lower, and married men without dependents will soon be called up. Steidler asked me how I was using my liberty. I answered that I was preparing myself spiritually, that I was willing to be a member of the Army, but not a *part* of it. He thought this a very witty answer. He believes I am a natural comedian and laughs at everything I say. The more serious I become, the harder he laughs.

He now reveals that he lived in the County Hospital for three months, last year, in the internes' quarters. The officials knew nothing about it. His friend Shailer, who was then in residence, took him in, and the other internes agreed to keep his secret. He ate in the cafeteria, and his clothes were washed in the hospital laundry. He made his pocket money at cards; there were escapades and jokes; he was introduced to patients as a specialist; he gave advice. The internes were genial and admiring; he was hilarious. Shailer's room was crowded all night long. He was given a party right in the hospital before he left for California. And I suppose it is all true. He exaggerates, but he does not lie.

February 3

An Hour with the Spirit of Alternatives.

"Let's have a talk, shall we, Joseph?"

"Glad to."

"We'll make ourselves comfortable."

"You can't be very comfortable here."

"Perfectly all right. I thrive on small hardships."

"You'll find all you need."

"Don't worry about me. You're the one who's uneasy."

"Well, the fact is, though I'm glad to have this opportunity, I can't quite place you."

"By name?"

"That doesn't matter."

"Of course not. I go by several."

"Such as?"

"Oh—'*But on the Other Hand*,' or '*Tu As Raison Aussi*.' I always know who I am; that's the important thing."

"An enviable position."

"I often think so."

"Have an orange."

"Oh, thanks, no."

"Take one, go on."

"They're so expensive now."

"To please me."

"Oh, well. . . ."

"I've grown fond of you. I like your manner."

"We'll each take half."

"Good enough."

"So you like me, Joseph?"

"Oh, yes."

"That's flattering."

"No, really I do. I appreciate you."

"Do you take quick likes and dislikes?"

"I try to be reasonable."

"I know you do."

"Is that wrong?"

"To Understand?"

"You want me to trust Unreason?"

"I want nothing; I suggest. . . ."

"Feelings?"

"You have them, Joseph."

"Instincts?"

"And instincts."

"I know the argument. I see what you're after."

"What?"

"That human might is too small to pit against the unsolvables. Our nature, mind's nature, is weak, and only the heart can be relied on."

"What a rush you're in, Joseph. I didn't say that."

"But you must have meant it. Reason has to conquer itself. Then what are we given reason for? To discover the blessedness of unreason? That's a very poor argument."

"You're inventing a case against me. You're to be congratulated on your conclusions, but they're off the point. However, you've had a hard time."

"Am having."

"Quite so."

"And will continue to have."

"Of course. You must be prepared for it."

"I am. I am."

"It's sensible of you to expect so little."

"But it's sad, you must admit."

"It's a matter of knowing how much to ask for."

"How much?"

"I'm talking about happiness."

"I'm talking about asking to be human. We're not worse than the others."

"What others?"

"Those who proved it possible to be human."

"Ah, in the past."

"Listen, *Tu As Raison Aussi*. We abuse the present too much, don't you think so?"

"You're not so fond of it."

"Fond! What a word!"

"Alienated, then."

"That's bad, too."

"It's popular."

"There's a lot of talk about alienation. It's a fool's plea."

"Is it?"

"You can divorce your wife or abandon your child, but what can you do with yourself?"

"You can't banish the world by decree if it's in you. Is that it, Joseph?"

"How can you? You have gone to its schools and seen its movies, listened to its radios, read its magazines. What if you declare you are alienated, you *say* you reject the Hollywood dream, the soap opera, the cheap thriller? The very denial implicates you."

"You can decide that you want to forget these things."

"The world comes after you. It presents you with a gun or a mechanic's tool, it singles you out for this part or that, brings you ringing news of disasters and victories, shunts you back and forth, abridges your rights, cuts off your future, is clumsy or crafty, oppressive, treacherous, murderous, black, whorish, venal, inadvertently naive or funny. Whatever you do, you cannot dismiss it."

"What then?"

"The failing may be in us, in me. A weakness of vision."

"Aren't you asking too much of yourself?"

"I'm serious."

"Where shall I put these pips?"

"I'm sorry; have you been holding them? Here, in this ash tray. I'm telling you. It's too easy to abjure it or detest it. Too narrow. Too cowardly."

"If you could see, what do you think you would see?"

"I'm not sure. Perhaps that we were the feeble-minded children of angels."

"Now you're just amusing yourself, Joseph."

"Very well, I would see where those capacities have gone to which we once owed our greatness."

"That would be tragic."

"I don't say it wouldn't be. Have you any tobacco?"

"No."

"Or paper? If I had paper I could roll a cigarette out of these butts."

"I'm sorry I came empty-handed. If you're not alienated, why do you quarrel with so many people? I know you're not a misanthrope. Is it because they force you to recognize that you belong to their world?"

"I was wrong, or else put it badly. I didn't say there was no feeling of alienation, but that we should not make a doctrine of our feeling."

"Is that a public or a private belief?"

"I don't understand you."

"What about politics?"

"Do you want to discuss politics with me? With *me*? Now?"

"Since you refuse to subscribe to alienation, perhaps you might be interested in changing existence."

"Ha, ha, ha! Have you any ideas?"

"It's really not my place, you know. . . ."

"I know, but you started it."

"My position. You don't understand."

"Oh, I do."

"So, about changing existence. . . ."

"I never enjoyed being a revolutionary."

"No? Didn't you hate anyone?"

"I hated, but I didn't enjoy. As a matter of fact—"

"Yes—"

"You're so attentive—. I regarded politics as an inferior activity. Plato tells us that if everything were as it should be, the best men would avoid office, not vie for it."

"They did once vie for it."

"They did. Public life is disagreeable. It's forced on one."

"I often hear that complaint. But all this is neither here nor there as far as measures to be taken are concerned."

"But with whom, under what circumstances, how, toward what ends?"

"Ah, that's it, isn't it? With whom."

"You don't believe in the historic roles of classes, do you?"

"You keep forgetting. My province is . . ."

"Alternatives. Excuse me. With whom, to go on. A terrible, unanswerable question. With men dispersed into separate corners, incommunicado? One of their few remaining liberties is the liberty to wonder what will happen next."

"Still, if you had the power to see. . . . Here you are willing to say that it is weakness of imagination that leads to alienation but not, it seems, that a similar weakness is impairing you politically. If you could see it over-all. . . . Where are you going?"

"Just to look in my coat for a cigarette; I may have left one there."

"If you could see it that way."

"There isn't a smoke in the house."

"Over-all. . . ."

"You mean, if I were a political genius. I'm not. Now what do you face?"

"What to do under the circumstances."

"Try to live."

"How?"

"*Tu As Raison Aussi*, you're not giving much help. By a plan, a program, perhaps an obsession."

"An ideal construction."

"A German phrase. And you with a French name."

"I have to be above such prejudices."

"Well, it's a lovely phrase. An ideal construction, an obsessive device. There have been innumerable varieties: for study, for wisdom, bravery, war, the benefits of cruelty, for art; the

God-man of the ancient cultures, the Humanistic full man, the courtly lover, the knight, the ecclesiastic, the despot, the ascetic, the millionaire, the manager. I could name hundreds of these ideal constructions, each with its assertions and symbols, each finding—in conduct, in God, in art, in money—its particular answer and each proclaiming: 'This is the only possible way to meet chaos.' Even someone like my friend Steidler is under the influence of an ideal construction of an inferior kind. It is inferior because it is loosely made and little thought has gone into it. Nevertheless it is real. He would willingly let go everything in his life that is not dramatic. Only he has, I am afraid, a shallow idea of drama. Simple, inevitable things are not dramatic enough for him. He has a notion of the admirable style. It is poor stuff. Nobility of gesture is what he wants. And, for all his boasted laziness, he is willing to pursue his ideal until his eyes burst from his head and his feet from his shoes."

"Do you want one of those constructions, Joseph?"

"Doesn't it seem that we need them?"

"I don't know."

"Can't get along without them?"

"If you see it that way."

"Apparently we need to give ourselves some exclusive focus, passionate and engulfing."

"One might say that."

"But what of the gap between the ideal construction and the real world, the truth?"

"Yes. . . ."

"How are they related?"

"An interesting problem."

"Then there's this: the obsession exhausts the man. It can become his enemy. It often does."

"H'm."

"What do you say to all this?"

"What do I say?"

"Yes, what do you think? You just sit there, looking at the ceiling and giving equivocal answers."

"I haven't answered. I'm not supposed to give answers."

"No. What an inoffensive career you've chosen."

"You're forgetting to be reasonable."

"Reasonable! Go on, you make me sick. The sight of you makes me sick. You make me queasy at the stomach with your suave little, false little looks."

"Joseph, look here . . . !"

"Oh, get out. Get out of here. You're two-faced. You're not to be trusted, you damned diplomat, you cheat!" Furious, I flung a handful of orange peel at him, and he fled the room.

February 4

The landlady, Mrs. Kiefer, had another stroke yesterday that paralyzed her legs. According to Mrs. Bartlett, whom Mrs. Briggs has engaged as a nurse, she can't live more than a few weeks. The windows are kept darkened; the halls and stairways smell of disinfectant, so that, going up to the landing with its stained-glass window, one imagines oneself in the hospital of a religious order. Except when Vanaker comes or goes, the house is quiet. He still is noisy; he has not learned to close the door when he goes down the hall. To stop him, I have to come out and march threateningly toward the bathroom. Thereupon he slams it shut. I have several times made general but loud and menacing remarks about decency and politeness. But he is either too drunk or too witless to change. When I do these things, I make myself ill. When I step out of the door to reprimand and stop him I am merely a nervous or irascible young man and I feel the force on me of a bad, harsh mood which I despise in others—the nastiness of a customer to a waiter or of a parent to a child. Iva is the same way. She gasps, "Oh, the fool!" when I go into the hall with a cross pull at the door. I suppose she means Vanaker; but may she not also mean me?

February 5

My present ill temper first manifested itself last winter. Before we moved out of our flat I had a disgraceful fist fight with the landlord, Mr. Gesell.

That fight had been on the horizon a long time. Throughout the summer we had been on good terms. We exerted ourselves to be courteous to Gesell and to Mrs. Gesell, who made a daily racket in her shop downstairs with a machine-powered chisel. She was an amateur sculptress. Often the house trembled. Then she borrowed our books, and brought them back with stone dust on the pages. We did not complain.

But, when the frosts began, the house was underheated. We could not bathe at night; in December we had to go to bed at nine, when the radiators turned cold. Then, during one week in January, the furnace broke down. Mr. Gesell was an electrician himself; to save money, he undertook the repairs. But he had his job to attend to, so he worked at the furnace evenings and Sundays. The fireplace stifled us when we tried to use it, it was blocked with bricks. Below, Mrs. Gesell, surrounded by heat lamps, worked away at the figure of a sand hog she was designing for the new subway—she was going to enter a competition. When we went down to complain, she did not answer the bell. We ate supper with our sweaters on.

The gas stove in the kitchen, which was now our only source of heat, began to give us headaches. We lived with Myron for a week, the three of us in one bed. I caught Mr. Gesell at last, when he was airing the dog. He joked about the cold, and said I was so strapping I could bear it. He pounded my arms playfully, exciting the dog, from whom I shrank. Gesell said, "You'll do. You're pretty husky for a guy that leads such a soft life. Even though you couldn't stand up a day in my line." He was a strongly built man, about forty years old. He dressed in old trousers and flannel shirts. His wife wore the same costume—jeans, shirt, and neckcloth. He began to relate how near the two of them had come to freezing, during the depression, in a bare studio on Lake Park Avenue. They burned orange crates while waiting for the Relief to deliver coal. They took down the curtains and stuffed them in cracks against the wind. "The depression's over," I said. He laughed so hard he had to take hold of my arm to keep himself up. "Say, you're all right, you are." The dog, with rueful red eyes, watched the snow wreathing back and forth over the street. "We'll see what we can do about you," said Gesell.

A little heat began to seep up, but the house was not really warm. Iva hit upon the plan of holding up the rent. On the fifth of the month, Gesell made belligerent representations.

Iva retorted angrily. She didn't expect an artist to make a good landlord. "But *you*, Mr. Gesell!" "An artist!" I snorted, thinking of that poor sand hog with his nose and thick legs. Gesell probably carried this back to Beth Gesell, for she stopped speaking to me. There were hard feelings.

But in February things took a turn for the better. In our encounters, as we went in and out of the house, we began to greet one another once more. The rent was paid, the heat rose, the hot water returned. I entered one day, with a check, to find the Gesells having breakfast at a table you might expect to find in a log cabin. The Dalmatian came and rubbed himself against me embarrassingly—poor animal, he was an adjunct and had no life of his own. Gesell took the check with thanks and began to write out a receipt. Beth, resting her chin on the back of her hand, was looking out of the window, watching the snow. She was a fat woman, with red hair cut in square, boxlike, masculine fashion. I began to think she was still angry and did not want to speak to me, but she was watching the fall of soft, heavy flakes, and all at once she said:

"When we were kids in Montana, we used to say they were plucking geese in heaven. I wonder if they still say that."

"I never heard it before," I said, entirely willing to make peace.

"Maybe the saying's gone out. It was long ago."

"Couldn't be so long," I said generously, and won a saddened smile.

"Oh, yes, long enough."

Gesell wrote on, also smiling, thinking, perhaps, of his wife's girlhood or of similar myths of his own early days. The yawning dog closed his jaws with a snap.

"Then there was rain," said Beth.

"I know," said Gesell. "Angels?"

"Oh, get along, Peter." She laughed, and the color from her hair seemed to spread along her cheeks. "Placer mining."

"I never heard of that, either," I said.

"And here you are," said Gesell, fluttering the receipt.

We were smiling broadly, all three.

Not long afterward, however, on a Sunday afternoon, the house began to go cold, and at two o'clock the electricity was shut off. It was a mild day; we might easily have borne the chill. But we had been listening to a Brahms concerto. I hurried downstairs and rang at Gesell's door. The Dalmatian threw himself in a rage against it, clawing the glass. I ran around to the basement entrance and, without knocking, went in. Gesell stood at his workbench, a length of pipe in his hand. A pistol would not have deterred me. I strode toward him, kicking rods, board-ends, pieces of wire, out of my way.

"Why did you turn off the current?" I said.

"I had to work on this stoker, that's why."

"Why the devil do you wait until Sunday? And why couldn't you tell us beforehand?"

"I don't have to get your permission to work on this stoker," he said.

"How long are you going to keep it off?"

Ignoring this question, he turned sullenly back to his bench.

"Well, how long?" I repeated. And, when I saw that he was not going to reply, I took him by the shoulder and, forcing him round, pushed aside the pipe and struck him. He fell, the pipe clattering under him on the cement. But instantly he was up again, brandishing his fists, shouting, "If that's what you want!" He could not reach me. I carried him to the wall, hitting repeatedly into his chest and belly and cutting my knuckles on his open, panting mouth. After the first few blows, my anger vanished. In weariness and self-disgust I pinned him against the bricks. Hearing his thick, rasping shouts, I said pacifyingly, "Don't get excited, Mr. Gesell. I'm sorry about this. Don't get excited!"

"You damned fool!" he cried. "You'll get yours! You damned crazy fool!" His voice quivered with terror and anger. "Beth, Be-eth! You wait!" Twisting him away from the wall, I shoved him from me. "I'll get out a warrant. Be-eth!"

"You'd better not," I said. But I felt the emptiness of my threat and, more ashamed than ever, I went upstairs where I bandaged my hand and sat down to wait for the police. Iva laughed at my fears and said I would have a long wait. She was right, though I was prepared all week to go to court and pay a fine for disorderly conduct. Iva guessed that Beth was unwilling to invest in a warrant. We moved a month later. Iva and Beth made all the arrangements. We forfeited several weeks' rent to make our escape.

This was "not like" me; it was an early symptom. The old Joseph was inclined to be even-tempered. Of course, I have known for a long time that we have inherited a mad fear of being slighted or scorned, an exacerbated "honor." It is not quite the duelist's madness of a hundred years ago. But we are a people of tantrums, nevertheless; a word exchanged in a movie or in some other crowd, and we are ready to fly at one another. Only, in my opinion, our rages are deceptive; we are too ignorant and spiritually poor to know that we fall on the "enemy" from confused motives of love and loneliness. Perhaps, also, self-contempt. But for the most part, loneliness.

Iva, though she concealed it at the time, was surprised; she later told me so. This was a rebellion against my own principle. It alarmed me; and the treasons I saw at the Servatius party were partly mine, as I was forced at the time to acknowledge.

February 8

The thermometer still wavers around zero. The cold is part of the general malignancy. I think of its fitness, as the war news comes in. You are bound to respect such a winter for its unmitigated wintriness. "I tax not you, you elements, with unkindness," Lear yells. He invites their "horrible pleasure." He is quite right, too.

February 9

I feel I am a sort of human grenade whose pin has been withdrawn. I know I am going to explode and I am continually anticipating the time, with a prayerful despair crying "Boom!" but always prematurely.

The sense in which Goethe was right: Continued life means expectation. Death is the abolition of choice. The more choice is limited, the closer we are to death. The greatest cruelty is to curtail expectations without taking away life completely. A life term in prison is like that. So is citizenship in some countries. The best solution would be to live as if the ordinary expectations had not been removed, not from day to day, blindly. But that requires immense self-mastery.

February 10

Steidler has been here twice in the past week. He seems to find me congenial. Which means, I venture to say, that he assumes we are in the same boat. I would not mind the visits nor the assumption if it were not for the fact that I still feel, at the end of a few hours, that we are practicing some terrible vice together. We smoke and talk. He tells me about his adventures on the Coast, in the hospital, and about his present affairs. I have learned that he receives ten dollars a week from his mother and five more from his brother. Budgeting himself strictly, he manages to live on twelve, and the rest he spends on horses. Occasionally he wins, but he estimates that he has lost four or five thousand dollars in the last ten years.

He does not care to speak of such things. He mentions them only in passing. He is not at all blind to their meanness. He simply takes it for granted that they are bound to be mean. There is no dignity anywhere, nothing but absurd falsehood. It is no use trying to bury this falsehood. It would only rise again, to laugh at you. He says this in so many words. When you ask him about the details of his life, he gives you a look of surprise. He is not offended; but that such admittedly shabby things should interest you surprises him genuinely. He would rather tell you the story of a bet lost or won, a fraud, a clever reply, an interesting reprisal, an insulting letter he sent a creditor, a love affair.

Last time, he told me a tortuous, long story about his attempts to conquer a Norwegian girl who lives in his hotel— Laird Towers. He had met her on Thanksgiving Day, in the lobby. Hartly, the night clerk, had given him the wink, and so he set about the siege. She didn't like him, of course. It always started that way. Around Christmas she started to look at him more encouragingly. Unfortunately he was pinched, had no money. It came to his notice that other men in the hotel were making headway with her. Hartly kept him only too well informed. "He didn't have to tell me. I could see from the beginning she was dynamite."

During the holiday he made a killing on a little pony called Spotted Cow; it romped home two lengths ahead of the field. He asked the Norwegian out to the Fiorenza for a spaghetti dinner.

"I thought we were getting along pretty well, and when she excused herself for a few minutes at eleven o'clock I sucked tranquilly at my Perfecto Queen and said to myself, 'It's in the bag.' She had been drinking Pink Ladies, and she was running over. She went away unevenly. I waited. At eleven-fifteen there was no sign of her, so I thought, 'Maybe she's sick in the powder room?' And I went to get the matron to have a look. But I got as far as the orchestra, and there was the girl sitting in some guy's lap. Well, I tried not to seem injured, and I suggested that it was getting late, we ought to start for home. But she wouldn't get up, and I didn't want to make a fool of myself. So I beat it."

He sent her letters for two weeks. She did not answer. When he had almost spent the last of his winnings, he met her in the Loop. It was her birthday, she said. He offered to buy her a drink. They went to the Blackhawk and had four. By-and-by a few handsome, well-dressed fellows came up to the bar, one in a naval uniform. Alf rose, paid for the drinks, put the rest of his change on the table, and said, "I know when I'm outclassed." Without a cent in his pocket, he walked back to the hotel.

The story wandered to its inevitable conclusion—the conquest, with the Norwegian learning at last to distinguish between his superior worth and his appearance, giving in to him jokingly and condescendingly while drunk, and then finding that she had more than she had bargained for, et cetera. It would have shocked Alf to know that he was boring me, for he considers himself a first-class entertainer. Any night club would be lucky to have him. He can be original in several dialects. But I would rather not be entertained. I welcomed him at first, and I still rather like him. But I wish he would not come so often.

February 11

Myron Adler is back; he called this morning and said he was coming to visit me as soon as he could break away. Robbie Stillman has come in after six months in Officers' School. He has become an engineer. His business will be to construct airfields. Army life, he says, is not hard when you accustom yourself to discipline. You have to learn to submit.

His brother Ben is somewhere in the interior of Brazil. He hasn't been heard from since October.

February 14

No sign of Myron or of anyone else. Even Steidler seems to have deserted me. Two days without visitors, talk, interest. Nothing. A pair of perfect blanks punched out of the calendar. It's enough to make one pray for change, merely change, *any* change, to make one worship experience-in-itself. If I were a little less obstinate, I would confess failure and say that I do not know what to do with my freedom.

February 15

Letter from Abt, rich in Washington gossip and explanations of current policy. Why we act as we do in North Africa and toward Spain, De Gaulle, Martinique. It amuses me to catch the subtle pride with which he mentions his familiarity with important figures. (I assume they are important in official circles; I have never heard of them.)

February 16

Old Mrs. Kiefer is, as Mrs. Bartlett puts it, "sinking PDQ. She can drag along for a week or two weeks, but this"—in dumb show she sank a needle into her arm—"can't keep her going forever." We walk through the house gingerly. Captain Briggs no longer goes out for his evening smoke. It is too cold.

February 17

Iva and I have grown closer. Lately she has been remarkably free from the things I once disliked so greatly. She does not protest against this rooming-house life; she seems less taken up with clothes; she does not criticize my appearance or seem disturbed because my underwear is in such a state that in dressing I often put my leg through the wrong hole. And the rest: the cheap restaurant food we eat, our lack of pocket money. Yet she is as far as ever from what I once desired to make her. I am afraid she has no capacity for that. But now I am struck by the arrogance with which I set people apart into two groups: those with worth-while ideas and those without them.

February 18

Yesterday, passing the bush on which I found the stolen socks, I saw a second pair. Vanaker must have taken several. I pointed them out to Iva as we passed this evening. She, too, recognized them. She says we should find a way of showing that we are aware of the theft.

February 19

Another letter from John Pearl, asking for news of Chicago. As if I had any to give him. I know no more about it than he does. He wanted to go to New York but now sounds nostalgic and writes with deep distaste about his "peeling environment."

"Peeling furniture, peeling walls, posters, bridges, everything is peeling and scaling in South Brooklyn. We moved here to save money, but I'm afraid we'd better start saving ourselves and move out again. It's the treelessness, as much as anything, that hurts me. The unnatural, too-human deadness."

I'm sorry for him. I know what he feels, the kind of terror, and the danger he sees of the lack of the human in the too-human. We find it, as others before us have found it in the last two hundred years, and we bolt for "Nature." It happens in all cities. And cities are "natural," too. He thinks he would be safer in Chicago, where he grew up. Sentimentality! He doesn't mean Chicago. It is no less inhuman. He means his father's house and the few blocks adjacent. Away from these and a few other islands, he would be just as unsafe.

But even such a letter buoys me up. It gives me a sense of

someone else's recognition of the difficult, the sorrowful, in what to others is merely neutral, the environment.

If I had *Tu As Raison Aussi* with me today, I could tell him that the highest "ideal construction" is the one that unlocks the imprisoning self.

We struggle perpetually to free ourselves. Or, to put it somewhat differently, while we seem so intently and even desperately to be holding on to ourselves, we would far rather give ourselves away. We do not know how. So, at times, we throw ourselves away. When what we really want is to stop living so exclusively and vainly for our own sake, impure and unknowing, turning inward and self-fastened.

The quest, I am beginning to think, whether it be for money, for notoriety, reputation, increase of pride, whether it leads us to thievery, slaughter, sacrifice, the quest is one and the same. All the striving is for one end. I do not entirely understand this impulse. But it seems to me that its final end is the desire for pure freedom. We are all drawn toward the same craters of the spirit—to know what we are and what we are for, to know our purpose, to seek grace. And, if the quest is the same, the differences in our personal histories, which hitherto meant so much to us, become of minor importance.

Heavy snowfall last night. I skipped lunch, to avoid wetting my feet three times in one day.

Only twenty-two days until spring. I swear that on the twenty-first I will change from my winter clothes and, no matter what the weather is like, even if there is a blizzard, I will walk through Jackson Park hatless and gloveless.

March 1

Adler showed up, at last. He came in the middle of the afternoon, when I was not expecting him. Mrs. Bartlett had let him in and, I gathered, cautioned him against making noise, for when I saw him on the landing he was walking on tiptoe.

"Who's sick, Joseph?" he asked with a look back at Mrs. Bartlett, who was softly monitoring the street door. The pneumatic arm that shut it was out of commission.

"The landlady. She's very old."

"Oh-oh! And I rang twice," he said guiltily. I motioned him into the room. He was much disturbed. "Do you think I shouldn't have?"

"Everybody rings the bell. How do you suppose people get in here? Don't worry about it."

Adler was very spruce, in a wide-shouldered coat and a tweed suit, new style, without cuffs. He looked fresh and healthy. His hat with its blunt crown was new also, and very stiff. It had cut a red line into his forehead.

"Sit down, Mike," I said, clearing a chair for him. "You've never been here before, have you."

"No," he said, and he inspected the room, hardly able to conceal his surprise. "I thought you had an apartment."

"Our old apartment? We gave that up long ago."

"I know. But I thought you were living in one of those furnished flats."

"It's snug here."

It's true, the room did not look its best. Marie had cleaned it, after a fashion, but the coverlet was wrinkled, the towels on the rack looked as though they had not been changed for weeks, Iva's shoes under the bed showed a crooked line of heels. The day, too, was not altogether favorable. The sky hung low, loose, with blemished clouds that spotted the street from curb to horizon with shadows. And the weather intruded into the room. The walls above the radiator were as dirty as the snow in the yard, and the linen—the dresser scarf and the towels—seemed spun out of the same material as the sky.

"You've been here since last fall, haven't you?" he said.

"Since June," I corrected. "Nearly nine months."

"Is it that long?" he said unbelievingly.

"Almost the tenth."

"And there's nothing new?"

"Do I look as if I were concealing something new?" I exclaimed. This startled him. I relented and said, "Nothing's been changed."

"You don't have to take my head off because I ask."

"Well, you see, everybody asks the same question. You get tired of answering. I have this routine to do, over and over and over. Questions are fired at me, and I'm supposed to scramble like a retriever, fetching answers. Why? Well, if I don't I won't get a certificate of politeness. Hell!"

Adler's color changed, so that the dent the hat had made above his eyes showed white.

"You're not very generous, Joseph."

I did not reply. I looked down at the street, the yards, at the masses of snow like dirty suds.

"You've changed a lot. Everybody says so," he went on more calmly.

"Who?"

"Why, people who know you."

"I haven't seen anyone. You mean that business in the Arrow."

"No, no, that was only one case."

"I wasn't all wrong in the Arrow."

"You're becoming bad-tempered."

"Good! I am. Now, what do you want me to do? Did you come to tell me that I was bad-tempered?"

"I came to see you."

"That's mighty handsome of you."

In rising anger, he stared at me, his mouth pursing. I began to laugh, and at that he rose and made for the door. I pulled him back.

"Here, don't go, Mike. Don't be a fool. Sit down. I wasn't laughing at you. I just happened to think that I'm always hoping a visitor will come. When he does come, I insult him."

"I'm glad you see it," he muttered.

"I do see it. Certainly I see it."

"Why jump on people? Good Lord. . . ."

"It just turns out that way. As the French say, '*c'est plus fort que moi.*' Does that prove that I'm not happy to see you? Not at all. It's not really a contradiction. It's natural. Almost a welcome, one might say."

"What a welcome," he said; but he seemed somewhat mollified.

"I see people so seldom, I've forgotten how to act. I don't want to be bad-tempered. But, on the other hand, the people who accuse me of that haven't exactly been beating the woods in searching parties. Things have changed, Mike. You're busy and prosperous—best of luck to you. But we may as well be honest about this."

"Now what's coming?"

"We're temporarily in different classes, and it has an effect on us. Oh, yes, it does. For instance, the way you took in this room, the way you looked around . . ."

"I don't get what you're driving at," he said in perplexity.

"You get it. You're not stupid. Don't act like Abt, saying, 'I can't follow you.' We *are* in different classes. The very difference in our clothes shows it."

"What a change," he said. "What a difference." He shook his head in regret and reminiscence. "You used to be an absolutely reasonable guy."

"I was sociable."

"Now you sound so wild."

The subject would bear no more discussion. "How was your trip?" I asked.

He stayed all afternoon and tried to make an old-time visit of it. But, after such a start, that was impossible. He was hale and businesslike, wanting no further trouble with me. So, haltingly, we covered a variety of subjects—public opinion, the war, our friends, and again the war. Minna Servatius was about to have a baby. I had heard something about that. George Hayza was expecting a naval commission. I had heard about that, also. There was a rumor that Abt was to be sent to Puerto Rico. Adler said he would find out definitely next week. He was going East.

"You see, Joseph," he said at four o'clock, "there's nothing we'd rather do than come and chat with you as we used to. But that's all gone now. We're busy. You'll be busy yourself, one of these days, busier than you'd ever care to be."

"Yes, things change. *C'est la guerre. C'est la vie.* Good old punch lines."

"What a Frenchman you've become."

"Say, do you remember Jeff Forman?"

"I read about him. He got a posthumous medal. Poor Jeff."

"*C'est la vie.*"

"That's not funny," said Adler disapprovingly.

"I was just quoting from the last war. I didn't mean to be funny. We can't do anything for Jeff, anyway, by pulling a long face. Can we?"

"I guess not."

And, in this manner, the visit drew to a close.

"When you're in the East," I said, "look up John Pearl. He needs a breath of Chicago. You ought to stop in and see him, I think." I added, with a laugh, "You might run into another Chicagoan in New York. Steidler. He hasn't been here for a long time. My guess is he took his brother's money."

"Alf?"

"His brother wrote a song and wanted Alf to take it to New York for him. He's looking for a publisher."

"If I thought there was a chance of running into Steidler, I wouldn't see Pearl. Why isn't he in the Army?"

"He's leaving the war to us normal bastards, he says."

"You've been seeing him. I wouldn't. He's not your kind. Stay away from him."

"Oh, oh, now! He can't hurt me. Besides, beggars can't be choosers. I'm quoting my niece. Lines addressed to me."

"Really? Amos's girl?"

"Oh, yes," I said. "She's quite grown-up."

And so Myron left, plainly dissatisfied with the results of his call. I went down with him into the street. We tramped to the corner over the discolored snow. While we waited to cross to the car stop, Myron offered to lend me money.

"No," I said, and gently moved his hand away. "We have enough. We get along very well." He put the money back in his purse. "Here comes the Fifty-five car. Better run for it." He gave me a final pat on the shoulder and sprinted across, whipping off his hat as he went, to hail the motorman.

March 3

Dolly phoned to ask us to dinner next Sunday. I said we had already accepted another invitation.

The Farsons have returned from Detroit, their training over. Susie dropped in to see Iva at the library. The baby had grippe; not a serious case. They have decided to send her to Farson's parents in Dakota, while they themselves go to California to work in an aircraft factory. Susie is in good spirits and is delighted at going to California. Walter missed the child more than she did. They intend to send for her as soon as they settle down.

March 5

There is a woman who goes through the neighborhood with a shopping bag full of Christian Science literature. She stops young men and talks to them. Since we cover the same streets, I encounter her often, but she keeps forgetting me, and it is not always possible to avoid her. For her part, she has no understanding of the art of stopping people. She rushes to block you with her body clumsily, almost despairingly. If she misses, she is incapable of following up, and if you succeed in eluding her—if you want to elude her, if you have the heart to continue doing so time after time—she can only stand, defeated, staring after you. If you do stop, she takes out her tracts and begins to speak.

She must be nearly fifty, a tall and rather heavy woman. But she has a sickly face—thin chapped lips, square yellow teeth, recessed brown eyes which you vainly read and reread for a meaning. The skin under her eyes reveals tiny, purple, intersecting vessels. Her hair is grizzled, her forehead is broad and blazed with a scar that resembles an old bullet wound. She speaks in a rapid whisper. I listen and wait for an opportunity to disengage myself.

Her speech is memorized. I watch her chapped lips through which the words come, so dry and rapid, often pronounced as though she did not understand them. The words, the words trip her fervor. She says she has talked to many young men who are about to go to war, who are going to

face destruction. Her duty is to tell them that the means of
saving themselves is at hand if they want it. Nothing but belief can save them. She has spoken to many others who have
come back from the jungles and the fox holes, surviving the
maiming fire only because of their faith. The doctrines of the
science are not superstitions but true science, as has been
proved. She has a pamphlet of testimonials, written by soldiers who know how to believe.

Meanwhile her face and the hard brown shells of her eyes
do not change. She writes on a pad while she is talking. When
she is done, she hands you the paper. It contains the names
and addresses of the various churches and Reading Rooms in
the neighborhood. And that is all. She is now at your mercy.
She waits. Her lips come together like the seams of a badly
sewn baseball. Her face burns and wastes under your eyes; the
very hairs at the corners of her mouth seem already to have
shriveled. When, after a long pause, you do not offer to buy
one of the tracts, she walks away, her run-down shoes knocking on the pavement, her load swinging as heavily as a bag of
sand.

Yesterday she was sicker than ever. Her skin was the color
of brick dust; her breath was sour. In her old tam that half-
covered the scar, and her rough, blackened coat buttoned to
the neck, she suggested the figure of a minor political leader
in exile, unwelcome, shabby, burning with a double fever.

She addressed me in the usual whisper.

"You spoke to me two weeks ago," I said.

"Oh. Well . . . I have a pamphlet here about the beliefs of
Science. And testimony by . . ." She groped. Then I felt sure
it had taken her these extra minutes to hear what I had said.
I was about to ask, "Don't you feel well?" but, from fear of
offending her, I held back. Her lips were more badly chapped
than I had ever seen them. On the protruding point of the
upper, a scab had formed.

"The men from Bataan," I said. "The one you told me
about last time."

"Yes. Five cents."

"Which would you rather sell me, this or the other?"

She held out the one with the veterans' testimony.

"You're going to the Army, too? This is the one." She took

the coin and slid it into her pocket, which was edged with a sort of charred fur. Then she said, "You're going to read it."

I don't know what prevented me from saying yes.

"I'll try to find time for it," I said.

"No, then you aren't going to. I'll take it back."

"I want to keep it."

"You can have your nickel. Here it is back."

I refused it. She shook her lowered head as a child might, sorrowing.

"I'm going to read this," I said. I thrust the pamphlet into my coat.

"You mustn't be proud," she said. She misunderstood my smile. At that moment she looked very grimly sick; though her eyes retained their hard brown centers, the whites had lost their moisture and, in each, a dry streak of vein had appeared.

"I give you my word, I'll read it."

She had held out her hand with a stiff movement of her arm to receive the pamphlet back. Now her hand went back to her side. For a while, as I watched her face with its small chin and large, marred forehead, I thought she had lost all sense of her whereabouts. But she soon picked up her bag and walked away.

March 10

Rain, yesterday, that turned into snow overnight. Cold again.

March 12

Received a note from Kitty, asking why I hadn't stopped by lately. I tore it up before Iva could see it. I haven't thought about Kitty lately. I can't be missing her much.

March 15

Sunday was warm, hinting at spring. We visited the Almstadts. In the evening I walked in Humboldt Park, around the lagoon, across the bridge to the boathouse where we used to discuss *Man and Superman* and where, even earlier, with John Pearl, I pelted the lovers on the benches below the balcony with crab apples. The air had a brackish smell of wet twigs and moldering brown seed pods, but it was soft, and through it rose, with indistinct but thrilling reality, meadows and masses of trees, blue and rufous stone and reflecting puddles. After dark, as I was returning, a warm, thick rain began falling with no more warning than a gasp. I ran.

March 16

Another Talk with the Spirit of Alternatives.

"I can't tell you how much I appreciate your coming back."

"Yes?"

"And I'd like to apologize."

"That's not necessary."

"And explain."

"I'm used to abuse. It's in the line of duty."

"But I want to say—I'm a chopped and shredded man."

"Easily exasperated."

"You know how it is. I'm harried, pushed, badgered, worried, nagged, heckled. . . ."

"By what? Conscience?"

"Well, it's a kind of conscience. I don't respect it as I do my own. It's the public part of me. It goes deep. It's the world internalized, in short."

"What does it want?"

"It wants me to stop living this way. It's prodding me to the point where I shall no longer care what happens to me."

"When you will give up?"

"Yes, that's it."

"Well, why don't you do that? Here you are preparing yourself for further life. . . ."

"And you think I should quit."

"The vastest experience of your time doesn't have much to do with living. Have you thought of preparing yourself for that?"

"Dying? You're angry because I threw the orange peel."

"I mean it."

"What's there to prepare for? You can't prepare for anything but living. You don't have to know anything to be dead. You have merely to learn that you will one day be dead. I learned that long ago. No, we're both joking. I know you didn't mean that."

"Whatever I mean, you get it twisted up."

"No. But I'm half-serious. You want me to worship the anti-life. I'm saying that there are no values outside life. There is nothing outside life."

"We're not going to argue about that. But you have impossible aims. Everybody else is dangling, too. When and if you survive you can start setting yourself straight."

"But, *Tu As Raison Aussi*, this is important. And what's the rush? There are important questions here. There's the whole question of my real and not superficial business as a man."

"Oh, now, really. What makes you think you can handle these things by yourself?"

"With whom can I start but myself?"

"Nah, foolishness!"

"No, but the questions have to be answered."

"Aren't you tired of this room?"

"Weary of it."

"Wouldn't you rather be in motion, outside, somewhere?"

"Sometimes I think nothing could be better."

"Do you really think you can handle all your own questions?"

"I'm not always sure."

"Then your position is weak indeed."

"Look, there are moments when I feel it would be wisest to go to my draft board and ask to have my number called at once."

"Well?"

"I would be denying my inmost feelings if I said I wanted to be by-passed and spared from knowing what the rest of my generation is undergoing. I don't want to be humped protectively over my life. I am neither so corrupt nor so hard-boiled that I can savor my life only when it is in danger of extinction. But, on the other hand, its value here in this room is decreasing day by day. Soon it may become distasteful to me."

"There, you see it yourself."

"Wait, I'm collecting all my feelings and my misgivings. I am somewhat afraid of the vanity of thinking that I can make my own way toward clarity. But it is even more important to know whether I can claim the right to preserve myself in this flood of death that has carried off so many like me, muffling them and bearing them down and down, minds untried and sinews useless—so much debris. It is appropriate to ask whether I have any business withholding myself from the same fate."

"And the answer?"

"I recall Spinoza's having written that no virtue could be considered greater than that of trying to preserve oneself."

"At all costs, oneself?"

"You don't get it. *Oneself.* He didn't say one's life. He said oneself. You see the difference?"

"No."

"He knew that everyone must die. He does not instruct us to graft new glands or to eat carp's intestine in order to live three hundred years. We cannot make ourselves immortal. We can decide only what is for us to decide. The rest is beyond our power. In short, he did not mean preservation of the animal."

"He was speaking of the soul, the spirit?"

"The mind. Anyway, the self that we must govern. Chance must not govern it, incident must not govern it. It is our humanity that we are responsible for it, our dignity, our freedom. Now, in a case like mine, I can't ask to be immune from the war. I have to take my risks for survival as I did, formerly, against childhood diseases and all the dangers and accidents through which I nevertheless managed to become Joseph. Do you follow that?"

"It's impossible, every bit of it."

"We are afraid to govern ourselves. Of course. It is so hard. We soon want to give up our freedom. It is not even real freedom, because it is not accompanied by comprehension. It is only a preliminary condition of freedom. But we hate it. And soon we run out, we choose a master, roll over on our backs and ask for the leash."

"Ah," said *Tu As Raison Aussi*.

"That's what happens. It isn't love that gives us weariness of life. It's our inability to be free."

"And you're afraid it may happen to you?"

"I am."

"Ideally, how would you like to regard the war, then?"

"I would like to see it as an incident."

"Only an incident?"

"A very important one; perhaps the most important that has ever occurred. But, still, an incident. Is the real nature of the world changed by it? No. Will it decide, ultimately, the major issues of existence? No. Will it rescue us spiritually? Still no. Will it set us free in the crudest sense, that is, merely to be allowed to breathe and eat? I hope so, but I can't be sure that it will. In no *essential* way is it crucial—if you accept my meaning of essential. Suppose I had a complete vision of life. I would not then be affected essentially. The war can destroy me physically. That it can do. But so can bacteria. I must be concerned with them, naturally. I must take account of them. They can obliterate me. But as long as I am alive, I must follow my destiny in spite of them."

"Then only one question remains."

"What?"

"Whether you have a separate destiny. Oh, you're a shrewd wiggler," said *Tu As Raison Aussi*. "But I've been waiting for you to cross my corner. Well, what do you say?"

I think I must have grown pale.

"I'm not ready to answer. I have nothing to say to that now."

"How seriously you take this," cried *Tu As Raison Aussi*. "It's only a discussion. The boy's teeth are chattering. Do you have a chill?" He ran to get a blanket from the bed.

I said faintly, "I'm all right." He tucked the blanket round me and, in great concern, wiped my forehead and sat by me until nightfall.

March 17

Washed and shaved and rode downtown to meet Iva. I walked from Van Buren to Randolph Street on the park side of Michigan Boulevard, past the Art Institute lions and the types enjoying cigarettes in the watery sunlight and the shimmering exhaust gas, after a long winter in the interior. The leached grass is beginning to take on a weak yellow in some spots, and there are a few green stubs of iris showing, nearly provoking me into saying: "Go back, you don't know what you're getting into."

March 18

No mail in the box. Except for the paper that lies scrambled over the bed and the passing of an occasional soldier or military truck in the street, we are insulated here from the war. If we chose, we could pull the blinds and fling the paper into the hall for Marie to gather up, casting it out utterly.

March 19

Nevertheless, spring begins on Sunday. I always experience a rush of feeling on the twenty-first of March. "Thank heavens, I've made it again!"

March 22

I carried out my threat and walked in the park in my spring coat, and suffered for it. It was a slaty, windy day with specks of snow sliding through the trees. I stopped at a tavern on the way back and treated myself to a glass of rye.

Because of Mrs. Kiefer, we could not listen to the Philharmonic in the afternoon, so, after lolling on the bed eating oranges and reading the magazines and the Sunday features, we set out at four o'clock for the movies. As we stood buttoning our coats in the hall, in came Vanaker in his bowler and polka-dot muffler, carrying a bag in which bottles rattled.

"*Sacre du Vin Temps*," I smiled.

We had a late dinner and turned in at eleven. Vanaker coughed boozily all through the night and awakened me near dawn, banging doors and making his customary splash.

March 23

Mr. Ringholm moved out last week. His room has been rented by a Chinese girl. Her trunk came from International House this morning. I read the tag—Miss Olive Ling.

March 24

A picture postcard of Times Square from Steidler on the hall table this morning, with the message: "I am thinking of stopping here indefinitely." Probably he has already run through his brother's money.

Mrs. Barlett was beckoning to me as I was going upstairs; she asked if I would help her carry up a cot from the storeroom. She was going to sleep downstairs with Mrs. Kiefer henceforward. I descended with her. She had already pulled the folding bed from the musty wood closet across half the length of the cellar. In the hot light of the furnace grating, her face, the face of an overgrown country girl, with large, slightly protruding front teeth that lent it a kind of innocence, was rather prepossessing. I was glad she had asked me to help her. "Take it from the bottom, that's it. Now. Up. I'll go first." She puffed out her instructions. "Lord, they should make these contraptions of wood." We struggled up with it and carried it into the room where the old woman lay, her white hair arranged in a fringe that nearly met her brow. Kitty wore hers that way. Mrs. Kiefer's cheeks were collapsed and her face was moist. It reminded me of a loaf, before the baker puts it in the oven, smeared with white of egg. I went into the hall quickly.

"Thanks," Mrs. Bartlett whispered loudly from the dark square inlet of the lower hall. "Thanks loads." And her teeth shone up at me good-naturedly.

March 25

Morning began dull and numb, then brightened miraculously. I tramped the neighborhood. It was warm in earnest at one o'clock, with a tide of summer odors from the stockyards

and the sewers (odors so old in the city-bred memory they are
no longer repugnant).

In the upper light there were small fair heads of cloud turning. The streets, in contrast, looked burnt out; the chimneys
pointed heavenward in openmouthed exhaustion. The turf,
intersected by sidewalk, was bedraggled with the whole winter's deposit of deadwood, match cards, cigarettes, dogmire,
rubble. The grass behind the palings and wrought-iron frills
was still yellow, although in many places the sun had already
succeeded in shaking it into livelier green. And the houses,
their doors and windows open, drawing in the freshness, were
like old drunkards or consumptives taking a cure. Indeed, the
atmosphere of the houses, the brick and plaster and wood, the
asphalt, the pipes and gratings and hydrants outside, and the
interiors—curtains and bedding, furniture, striped wallpaper
and horny ceilings, the ravaged throats of entry halls and the
smeary blind eyes of windows—this atmosphere, I say, was one
of an impossible hope, the hope of an impossible rejuvenation.

Nevertheless, a few large birds, robins and grackles, appeared in the trees, and some of the trees themselves were beginning to bud. The large rough cases cracked at the tip,
showing sticky green within, and one tree was erupting in
crude red along its higher branches. I even saw in a brick passageway an untimely butterfly, out of place both in the season
and the heart of the city, and somehow alien to the whole
condition of the century.

And there were children, on skates and bicycles, or scouting along the curbs for salvage, playing ball or hopping after
bits of glass in chalk squares. There was a showing of ice-
cream cones, despite the inroads of rationing, and a sprinkling
of spring articles, though infants still wore wool leggings and
the elderly were fully buttoned and somberly hatted. Sound
was magnified and vision enlarged, red was rough and bloody,
yellow clear but thin, blue increasingly warm. All but the
sun's own yellow that ripped up the middle of each street,
making two of everything that stood—object and shadow.

The room, when I returned to it, was as full of this yellow
as an egg is of yolk. In honor of the transformation in the
weather, I decided to clean up for supper and, as I stood
changing my shirt in the unaccustomed brilliance of the

mirror, I observed new folds near my mouth and, around my eyes and the root of my nose, marks that had not been there a year before. It is not pleasant to find such changes. But, tying my tie, I shrugged them off as inevitable, the price of experience, an outlay that had better be made ungrudgingly, since it was bound in any case to be collected.

March 26

We had been short of funds for several days. Iva received her check on Thursday but, instead of cashing it, brought it home and left it in my bureau drawer with instructions to take it to the bank. The reason she gave for not taking it to the currency exchange downtown, as usual, was that this week she was working evenings in the reference room and did not want to risk carrying such a sum home. She had heard rumors of holdups.

But I refused to go to the near-by bank with it.

I had had several experiences there with Iva's checks. I had been turned down twice last fall; once because I had insufficient identification and, again, when the vice president, looking from my cards to me and from me to my cards, once more said, "How do I know you're this person?"

I replied, "You can take my word for it."

He did not smile; I did not rate a smile. But the indications were that under different circumstances—say, if I had been clean-shaven and my shirt had not been frayed, or if bits of torn lining had not shown from my coat sleeve—my words would have evoked one. He sat back seriously and considered the check. He was a plump man, about thirty years old. *Mr. Frink* stood in brass letters on the wooden block at his finger tips; his clean sandy hair was already fading back in two broad freckled arches. He would be bald within a few years, his bare head spotted with those blackish freckles.

"That's a city check, Mr. . . . Frink, is it?" He acknowledged the name. "Certainly there isn't much risk in accepting a city check."

"If you know who the endorser is," said Mr. Frink, unclasping his pen and shuffling professionally through my cards with one hand. "Now, where do you work, Joseph?"

In such cases I generally answer that I am working at Inter-American; it is an impressive reference and not a wholly false one; Mr. Mallender would stand behind me, I am sure. But because he addressed me by my first name, as though I were an immigrant or a young boy or a Negro, I said—dismissing diplomacy without a second thought—"I'm not working anywhere now. I'm waiting for my draft call."

Of course, that finished my prospects. He immediately said, reassembling his pen, that the bank did not make a practice of cashing the checks of nondepositors. He was sorry.

I gathered up my cards.

"Here, you'll notice that I have a surname, Frink," I said, holding one of the cards up. "I realize it's difficult to deal with the public efficiently and still politely. All the same, people don't like to be treated like suspicious characters and patronized at the same time." I made an effort to control myself as I said this, but when I ended I saw that several bystanders were looking at me. Frink seemed more alarmed by my tone than by my words. I am not sure he understood them, but he faced me as if to show that in him I menaced a courageous man. It was a foolish incident. A year ago I would have accepted his explanation politely and have moved away.

Too late, I stuffed the check into my pocket and, without another glance at Frink, I walked off.

Naturally, when I came to explain my reasons for not going back to the bank I could not tell Iva all of the story. I said merely that I had been turned down twice and did not want it to happen a third time.

"Oh, now, Joseph, why should there be any trouble about it? I've cashed hundreds of checks."

"But they turned me down. And it's as embarrassing as anything can be."

"I'll give you my identification disk. All you have to do is show it."

"I won't do it," I said.

"Then go somewhere else. Go to the currency exchange, the one near Lake-Park Avenue."

"Before they do business with you there, they make you fill out a long, long form. They want to know everything . . . where you're employed. If I say I'm not working, they'll laugh me out of the place. 'What? Not working? Anybody can get a job these days.' No, I won't go. Why don't you cash it downtown?"

"I'm not going to carry all that money late at night. It's out of the question. If I'm held up, we'll have to borrow from your father or mine, or from Amos."

"Have you ever been held up?"

"You know I haven't been."

"Then why have you suddenly begun to worry about it?"

"You read two papers a day, from front to back. You ought to know. There've been holdups."

"Pooh! Two people. And not near here, either, but miles away, up on Sixtieth Street."

"Joseph, are you or are you not going to cash this check?"

"No," I said.

Perhaps I should have told her about my experience with Mr. Frink. Then, at any rate, the reason for my refusal would have been clear. But she would have been just as angry. She would have been in the right, hence very severe. And, although she would have excused me from returning to the bank, it is likely that she would have made things hard for me in other ways. Therefore I said nothing about it.

"All right," she said. "The check will stay in the drawer. We won't eat."

"I can stand it if you can."

"I'm quite sure you can stand it. You'd have to be as weak as . . . as Gandhi before you'd give in. You're mulish."

"I don't think you have much right to call *me* mulish. As if you weren't twice as stubborn. I don't feel like fighting about it, Iva. That's the truth. I can't go. I have my reasons."

"You always have reasons, and with principles. Capital *P*," she said, tracing the letter on the air with her finger.

"Don't be a fool. Do you think it's pleasant to walk up to a bank window and be turned away?"

"Are you sure you didn't get into a fight of some kind over there?" she asked shrewdly. "I have a suspicion. . . ."

"Your suspicion is wrong. You always jump to the worst conclusion you can think of. If I wanted to do that . . . well."

"Well?"

"I'd say plenty."

"For example."

"You want me to do all kinds of things I was never expected to do before. Now, why this sudden fear of being robbed? I could say you trumped it up. You've been carrying money for years, and larger amounts, too. Suddenly it frightens you. Well, the reason is that you want me to run errands."

"Errands?"

"Yes."

"Let's have the whole thing. You must have a principle hidden somewhere."

"Don't make fun of me, Iva. Things have changed. You've become the breadwinner, and whether you know it or not you resent the fact that I stay at home while you go to work every morning. So you think up things for me to do. You want me to earn my keep."

"Of all the things to say." Iva grew white. "I never know what you're going to do. You go along quietly and all of a sudden you come out with something, something . . . it's a terrible thing to say."

"It happens to be true."

"It isn't."

"You aren't aware of it yourself, Iva. I'm not blaming you. But you are the provider. After all, it's bound to have an effect on you. . . ."

"*You're* having an effect on me. You're making me sick."

"No, listen to me, Iva," I persisted. "I'm not making this up. I see it and feel it constantly. I know you don't want it to be true, but it is, nevertheless. You take it for granted that I have nothing to do. Every morning you leave half a dozen orders for me. And just a while ago you mentioned that I read the papers."

"How you twist everything around," Iva said bitterly.

"Not as much as you think."

She reached for her handkerchief.

"Just as soon as I take up a subject you don't like, you begin to cry. Don't you want me to say anything about this?"

"I can depend on you not to keep quiet when you think you're being wronged. You think everybody's trying to take advantage of you. Even I . . ." and she could not continue.

"This is what happens whenever I bring up a disagreeable subject. I'm just trying to point out something I don't think you're aware of. I thought you wanted me to tell you such things. You never used to object."

"You never used to be so mean and ugly-tempered. You . . ." Now she broke off and began to cry.

"Jesus, Jesus! Can we never have a talk without a flood of tears? It's easy for you to cry. But what can I do? I'm getting out. I should get out for good. This is no sort of life. Stop that crying!" She did try to stop; her efforts ended in a grotesque sound brought up from her throat. She rolled over on the bed and concealed her face from me.

Up to this point in our quarrel, Vanaker had given several protesting coughs, and now I heard his footsteps in the hall as he went to the bathroom and then, just as I had expected, the sound through the open door, of his splash, growing louder as he trained his stream to the center where the water was deepest. Shuffling off my slippers, I stepped out stealthily and advanced on his silhouette. When he turned, hearing me, my foot was already in the door. He had neglected to turn on the light, but I could see perfectly clearly by the small bulb outside. In the semidark, a look of panic sprang to his moist, drunken eyes, and he pushed against me, but I was solidly planted on the threshold.

"Took you in it at last, didn't I!" I exclaimed. "You damned old whisky-head. By God, I've had more than I can stand. There's a dying woman downstairs, and you slam around here all boozed up, raising as much hell as you please."

"Joseph," Iva called in a strained voice. She had come into the hall. "Joseph!"

"It's about time I told him off. I'm fed up. Completely. Do you think you can get away with it forever?" I shouted at him. "Kicking up a racket in the middle of the night, hoicking, forcing us to listen when you make your business, you crow-bait? Didn't you ever learn to shut the door when you went to the toilet? By God, you kept it shut tight enough the night you set the house on fire!"

"Mister!" I heard Mrs. Bartlett cry from the stairs. A door closed. Iva had gone back into the room, and similar sounds told me that either Mrs. Fessman or Miss Ling had come out to listen and then had quickly retreated. There were further noises from Captain Briggs' apartment. I heard a man's tread in the passage above.

"And stealing, besides," I went on.

"Steal?" he said weakly.

"Stealing," I repeated. "Then going before the priest at St. Thomas the Apostle and standing in my socks and stinking of my wife's perfume. I've got a good mind to go and tell them about it there. How would you like that?" He stared dumbly, his head a long blob of shadow in the pewter gleam of the mirror on the medicine chest. Then he came forward a pace, hopefully, for the Captain was behind me in his dressing gown.

"What are you doing?" he said sternly. Mrs. Briggs appeared at his side. "Fasten yourself up," he ordered Vanaker, who thereupon took shelter behind the door.

"Either he moves, or my wife and I. . . . We refuse to put up with him," I said.

"Now," said the Captain. "You've done enough shouting. Calm down. They can hear you all over the house."

"It's an outrage," his wife breathed. "With my mother downstairs."

"I'm sorry, Mrs. Briggs," I said in a lower voice. "But I had as much as I could stand from him. I admit I lost myself."

"I should say."

"Just a minute, Mil," the Captain interrupted. And then to me: "We can't allow behavior of that sort here, and . . ."

"What about his behavior?" I said excitedly. "It seems he can do as he pleases, but if I protest I am the one who's blamed. Why don't you ask him about it? What's he skulking in there for?"

"If you had complaints, you should have brought them to me or to my wife instead of making a row. This is not a tavern. . . ."

"I put up with his indecency. I don't care. It's that kind of inconsiderateness," I said disconnectedly.

"This is terrible, shameful," said Mrs. Briggs.

"We can't have this," said the Captain, "we can't have it. It's the worst kind of rowdyism!"

"Howard," remonstrated Mrs. Briggs.

"You're the one that's shouting now, Captain," I said.

"Don't tell *me* how to talk," the Captain exploded.

"I'm not your subordinate. I'm a civilian. I don't have to take this from you."

"By Jesus, I'll take a swing at you in about a minute!"

"Try it!" I said, stepping back and tightening my fists.

"Howard, please. Howard," said Mrs. Briggs.

"Joseph," said Iva, appearing in the doorway. "Come here. Come into the room." I edged by them, guardedly. "Get in," commanded Iva.

"If he touched me, I'd murder him, soldier suit or no soldier suit," I growled as I went in.

"Oh, keep quiet," said Iva. "Mrs. Briggs, please, just a moment." She hurried toward them.

I put on my shoes, snatched my street clothes from the closet, and flung out of the house. I walked rapidly through the drizzle. It was not late, certainly not more than ten o'clock. The air was dense and black and pressed close on the hourglass figures the street lamps made. I could not have slowed my walk; I was not sure of my legs. So I went on for some time, until I came to an open place, a lot with a wire backstop for baseball games. The ground was flooded, a wind-blown sheet of water, utterly dark. Behind the backstop was a white drinking fountain and water from it flurring into the warm air. I drank and then I went on, not so fast as before but just as aimlessly, toward the static shower of lights in the street ahead, a spray of them hanging in the middle distance over the shine of the pavement. Then I turned back.

I could not even imagine what Iva's misery must be, nor the state of the house. Iva must be trying to explain; Mrs. Briggs, if she was listening at all, was listening frostily; while Vanaker was making his way to his room, meek but vindicated, and probably wondering what had happened. Once more he seemed to me, as in the early days, simple-minded, perhaps subnormal.

I walked over the cinders of a schoolyard and came into an alley approaching our windows. I looked for Iva's shadow on the blind. She was not there. I had halted near a fence against which a tree leaned, freshly budding and seething under the rain. I made an effort to dry my face. Then it occurred to me that the reason I could not see her was that she was lying on the bed again. My skin was suddenly as wet with perspiration as it had been a moment ago with rain. I turned and started back along the schoolyard fence. A steel ring on a rope whipped loudly against the flagpole. Then, for a moment, a car caught me in its lights. I stood aside for it and followed its red blur. It was gone. Something ran among the cans and papers. A rat, I thought and, sickened, I went even more quickly, skirting a pool at the foot of the street where a torn umbrella lay stogged in water and ashes. I took a deep breath of warm air.

I believe I had known for some time that the moment I had been waiting for had come, and that it was impossible to resist any longer. I must give myself up. And I recognized that the breath of warm air was simultaneously a breath of relief at my decision to surrender. I was done. But it was not painful to acknowledge that, it was not painful in the least. Not even when I tested myself, whispering "the leash," reproachfully, did I feel pained or humiliated. I could have chosen a harsher symbol than that for my surrender. It would not have hurt me, for I could feel nothing but gratification and a desire to make my decision effective at once.

It couldn't be later than half-past ten now. The draft board often held late sessions. I set out for its office in the Sevier Hotel. As I was walking across the old-fashioned lobby, trying to remember on which side the office was, the clerk called me over. He guessed what I wanted.

"If it's the board you're after," he said, "everybody's gone home."

"Can I leave a note? Oh, never mind, I'll mail it."

I sat down at a desk in a corner, near one of the portieres, and wrote on a sheet of stationery:

> "I hereby request to be taken at
> the earliest possible moment into
> the armed services."

To this I added my full name and call number, and across the bottom:

"I am available at any time."

After I had posted this, I stopped at a tavern and spent my last forty cents on a drink.

"I'm off to the wars," I said to the bartender. His hand hovered over the money. He picked it up and turned to the cash register. The place, after all, was full of soldiers and sailors.

March 27

This morning I told Iva what I had done. She made only one comment, namely, that I should have consulted her. But I said, "I'm doing myself no good here." There was no answer to that. She took the check downtown to cash. I waited for her on the library steps, sitting among the pigeons, reading the paper. She came down at noon, and we had lunch together. She did not look well. There was a blemish on her face that always shows up when she is disturbed. I felt weak myself, standing in the sunlight.

Mrs. Briggs had asked both parties to yesterday's disgrace to move.

"You can stay on alone," I said to Iva. "She won't object."

"I'll see about it. When do you think you'll be called?"

"I'm not sure. I think in about a week."

"I don't think you ought to spend your last week moving," she said. "We'll stay on for a while. I'm sure Mrs. Briggs will let us."

About her own plans she said nothing.

March 29

Mrs. Kiefer died during the night. When I went out to breakfast I saw her door thrown open, her bed empty, the curtains in the room pinned back, the window open. Later, Mrs. Briggs appeared in black. In the afternoon other mourners came, gathering in the parlor. At five o'clock they began to pour out of the house. They went up the still street to the undertaker. The odor of coffee drifted up from the kitchen.

That evening, as we came out of the restaurant, we saw Mrs. Bartlett across the way. She had changed her white uniform for a silk dress and a short fur coat. Her hat was a strange affair with a flat top and a curtain or wimple that fell about her neck—a fashion that disappeared many years ago. We guessed that she was on her way to the movies after her long confinement with Mrs. Kiefer. Her shiny, long, black pocketbook was clasped under her doubled arm; she walked in a heavy-hipped, energetic stride toward the brightly lit avenue.

March 31

Today, the funeral. The Captain drove up with a wreath in his car; to him came a woman in a blue cape and feathers and short legs in ribbed hose. Her foot was set on the running board as though she were standing at a bar. Then she sprang in, and they drove off together. Telegraph messengers kept coming all morning. I don't know how many children the old woman had. There was a son in California, Marie had once said. The family gathered on the porch. The women's faces were mottled with crying; the men looked morose. They returned from the funeral at noon and had lunch at a long table in the parlor. I saw them when I went down for the midday mail. The Captain caught me looking in, and frowned. I withdrew quickly.

The postman was putting a letter in the box next door and he pointed vigorously at me and drew his finger across his throat. I had received my notice. "A committee of your neighbors. . . ." I was summoned for the ninth. My blood test was to be on Monday. I took the papers out of the envelope and propped them up on the dresser where Iva could see them when she came in.

Later in the day, as I sat reading, Marie came to the door with fresh towels. She, too, was dressed in black. She went about the house somber and unapproachable, as though she shared with Mrs. Kiefer and the mourners some unusual secret about death. I took this opportunity to tell her that I was going away.

"Your wife going to stay?" she said.

"I don't know."

"Uh-huh. Well, good luck." She gloomily wiped her cheeks with a black-edged handkerchief.

"Thanks," I said.

She took the soiled towels and shut the door.

April 2

Universal relief. As old Almstadt put it, since I had to go, it was better to go and get it over with. And my father, too, said, "Well, at least you don't have to wait any more." Amos, when I spoke to him yesterday, asked me to have lunch with him at his club. I told him I was going to be busy. I know he would have introduced me to his friends as "my brother who is going into the Army," and would thereafter be known as a man who was "in it."

April 4

Vanaker moved this morning. I heard Marie in his room after he had gone and went in. She had found two empty perfume bottles in his wastebasket. I was right. He left an interesting lot of goods behind, lying in the stale closet. Bottles, of course—those he had not seen fit, for some reason, to throw into the yard—picture magazines with photos of nudes, gloves, soiled underwear, the bowl of a pipe, a grease-stained handkerchief, a copy of *Pilgrim's Progress* and a school edition of *One Hundred Great Narrative Poems*, a carton of matches, a felt hat, a necktie with some matter dried into it. The whole collection went into a box which Marie carried down to the basement.

Spent several hours putting my things away in the trunk.

April 5

While it was still dark, I left the house this morning to go for my blood test. I had not been out so early for many months. The cars were jammed with factory workers. When I asked the conductor about my destination, a small park which I had never heard of, he said, "Stick around, I'll fix you up." We plunged up the broad street for a mile or two, and then he nudged me and said, "Here y'are; comin' up." And with a sort of playfulness he pushed me toward the door, while the others looked on gloomily, sleepy and dark-faced.

I waited in line at the field house, under the thin trees. In the gymnasium I took off my clothes, marched naked around the floor with the others, examining their scars and blemishes as they did mine. There were few boys; most of the men were in their thirties. The cripples were swiftly weeded out. A doctor felt us in the groin; another, an aging man with a cigar, said perfunctorily, wielding the needle, "Clench your hand; open; that's it." Holding a swab to your arm, looking curiously at your blood in the tube, you filed out and were dismissed.

It was eight o'clock, morning, full and brilliant; my usual hour for rising. I stopped at a cafeteria for breakfast, went home, and read all day.

April 6

Iva has put together a few things she thinks I'll need in the Army—my razor, a few handkerchiefs, a fountain pen and a block of note paper, my shaving brush. I am not going to take the usual ten-day furlough. I would rather save the time and use it later, if that is possible. Iva, of course, thinks it a sign of coldness on my part. It is merely that I do not want any more delays. She is going back to the Almstadts'. Her father is coming on the tenth to move her things.

April 8

When I visited my father yesterday, I went upstairs to my old room. For a time after my marriage the maid had occupied it. It was unused now, and I found in it many of the objects I had kept around me ten years ago, before I left for school. There was a Persian print over the bed, of a woman dropping a flower on her interred lover—visible in his burial gown under the stones; a bookcase my mother had bought me; a

crude water color of a pitcher and glass done by Bertha, some
nearly forgotten girl. I sat in the rocking chair, feeling that my
life was already long enough to contain nearly forgotten periods, a loose group of undifferentiated years. Recently, I had
begun to feel old, and it occurred to me that I might be concerned with age merely because I might never attain any great
age, and that there might be a mechanism in us that tried to
give us all of life when there was danger of being cut off. And
while I knew it was absurd for me to think of my "age," I had
apparently come to a point where the perspectives of time appeared far more contracted than they had a short while ago: I
was beginning to grasp the meaning of "irretrievable." This
rather ordinary and, in some ways mean, room, had for
twelve years been a standard site, the bearded Persian under
the round stones and the water color, fixtures of my youth.
Ten years ago I was at school; and before that. . . . It was
suddenly given me to experience one of those consummating
glimpses that come to all of us periodically. The room, delu-
sively, dwindled and became a tiny square, swiftly drawn back,
myself and all the objects in it growing smaller. This was not
a mere visual trick. I understood it to be a revelation of the
ephemeral agreements by which we live and pace ourselves. I
looked around at the restored walls. This place which I
avoided ordinarily, had great personal significance for me. But
it was not here thirty years ago. Birds flew through this space.
It may be gone fifty years hence. Such reality, I thought, is actually very dangerous, very treacherous. It should not be
trusted. And I rose rather unsteadily from the rocker, feeling
that there was an element of treason to common sense in the
very objects of common sense. Or that there was no trusting
them, save through wide agreement, and that my separation
from such agreement had brought me perilously far from the
necessary trust, auxiliary to all sanity. I had not done well
alone. I doubted whether anyone could. To be pushed upon
oneself entirely put the very facts of simple existence in
doubt. Perhaps the war could teach me, by violence, what I
had been unable to learn during those months in the room.
Perhaps I could sound creation through other means. Perhaps. But things were now out of my hands. The next move
was the world's. I could not bring myself to regret it.

Amos and Dolly and Etta and Iva were at the table when I came in to dinner. My father presented me with a watch. Amos gave me a suitcase which, he said, would be handy for overnight trips when I came back. From Etta and Dolly I got a leather sewing kit, complete with scissors and buttons.

April 9

This is my last civilian day. Iva has packed my things. It is plain that she would like to see me show a little more grief at leaving. For her sake, I would like to. And I am sorry to leave her, but I am not at all sorry to part with the rest of it. I am no longer to be held accountable for myself; I am grateful for that. I am in other hands, relieved of self-determination, freedom canceled.

Hurray for regular hours!

And for the supervision of the spirit!

Long live regimentation!

THE VICTIM

To my friend
Paolo Milano

It is related, O auspicious King, that there was a merchant of the merchants who had much wealth, and business in various cities. Now on a day he mounted horse and went forth to recover monies in certain towns, and the heat oppressed him; so he sat beneath a tree and, putting his hand into his saddle-bags, he took thence some broken bread and dried dates and began to break fast. When he had ended eating the dates he threw away the stones with force and lo! an Ifrit appeared, huge of stature and brandishing a drawn sword, wherewith he approached the merchant and said, "Stand up that I may slay thee even as thou slewest my son!" Asked the merchant, "How have I slain thy son?" and he answered, "When thou atest dates and threwest away the stones they struck my son full in the breast as he was walking by, so that he died forthwith."

"The Tale of the Trader and the Jinni"
from *Thousand and One Nights*

Be that as it may, now it was that upon the rocking waters of the ocean the human face began to reveal itself; the sea appeared paved with innumerable faces, upturned to the heavens; faces, imploring, wrathful, despairing; faces that surged upward by thousands, by myriads, by generations. . . .

DE QUINCEY, *The Pains of Opium*

1

ON SOME NIGHTS New York is as hot as Bangkok. The whole continent seems to have moved from its place and slid nearer the equator, the bitter gray Atlantic to have become green and tropical, and the people, thronging the streets, barbaric fellahin among the stupendous monuments of their mystery, the lights of which, a dazing profusion, climb upward endlessly into the heat of the sky.

On such a night, Asa Leventhal alighted hurriedly from a Third Avenue train. In his preoccupation he had almost gone past his stop. When he recognized it, he jumped up, shouting to the conductor, "Hey, hold it, wait a minute!" The black door of the ancient car was already sliding shut; he struggled with it, forcing it back with his shoulder, and squeezed through. The train fled, and Leventhal, breathing hard, stared after it, cursing, and then turned and descended to the street.

He was bitterly irritated. He had spent the afternoon with his sister-in-law, his brother's wife, in Staten Island. Or, rather, he had wasted it because of her. Soon after lunch she had phoned him at the office—he was an editor of a small trade magazine in lower Manhattan—and immediately, with terrible cries, she implored him to come out, to come at once. One of the children was sick.

"Elena," he said as soon as he was able to make himself heard, "I'm busy. So I want you to control yourself now and tell me: is it really serious?"

"Come right away! Asa, please! Right away!"

He pressed the tip of his ear as if to protect himself from her shrillness and muttered something about Italian excitability. Then the connection was broken. He hung up, expecting her to ring again, but the phone remained silent. He did not know how to reach her; his brother was not listed in the Staten Island directory. She was calling either from a store or from a neighbor's house. For a long time, Leventhal had had very little to do with his brother and his brother's family. Only a few weeks ago he had received a card from him postmarked Galveston. He was working in a shipyard. At the

time, Leventhal had said to his wife, "First Norfolk, now
Texas. Anything is better than home." It was the old story;
Max had married young and now he was after novelty, adven-
ture. There were plenty of shipyards and jobs in Brooklyn and
Jersey. Meanwhile Elena was burdened with the care of the
children.

Leventhal had told her the truth. He was busy. A pile of
unchecked proofs lay before him. He moved away the phone
after waiting a few minutes and, making an impatient noise in
his throat, picked up a piece of copy. No doubt the child was
sick, probably seriously sick, or she wouldn't have carried on
so. And, since his brother was away, it was somewhat in the
nature of a duty to go. He would go this evening. It couldn't
be so urgent. It was just beyond Elena's power to speak
calmly about anything. He told himself this several times;
nevertheless her cries continued to sound in his ears together
with the windy thrum of the long-stemmed electric fans and
the tick of typewriters. What if it were really critical? And suddenly, impulsively, meanwhile condemning himself for it, he
got up, pulled his jacket from the back of the chair, went to
the girl at the switchboard, and said, "I'm going in to see
Beard. Buzz him for me, will you?"

With his hands in his hind pockets, pressing against his
chief's desk, bending toward him slightly, Leventhal announced quietly that he had to go out.

Mr. Beard's face, a face enlarged by baldness, with a fierce
bony nose and a veined forehead, took on an incredulous,
sharp look.

"With an issue to get ready?" he said.

"It's a family emergency," said Leventhal.

"Can't it wait a few hours?"

"I wouldn't go if I thought it could."

Mr. Beard made a short, unpleasant answer to this. He
slapped his metal ruler on the pages of the type-book. "Use
your own judgment," he said. There was nothing further to
be said, but Leventhal lingered beside the desk hoping for
something more. Mr. Beard covered his blemished forehead
with a trembling hand and studied an article silently.

"Goddammed fish!" said Leventhal to himself.

A thundershower began when he approached the outside

door. He watched it for a while. The air was suddenly as blue as siphon glass. The blind side wall of the warehouse on the corner was streaked black, and the washed paving stones and tar seams shone in the curved street. Leventhal returned to the office to get his raincoat, and as he was going down the hall he heard Mr. Beard saying in that nagging, prosecuting voice of his, "Walks out right in the middle of everything. Right in a pinch. With everybody else swamped."

Another voice which he identified as that of Mr. Fay, the business manager, answered, "It's funny that he should just pick up and go. There must be something up."

"Takes unfair advantage," Mr. Beard continued. "Like the rest of his brethren. I've never known one who wouldn't. Always please themselves first. Why didn't he offer to come back later, at least?"

Mr. Fay said nothing.

Expressionless, Leventhal put on his raincoat. His arm caught in the sleeve, and he pushed it through violently. He walked out of the office with his rather hulking stride, halting in the anteroom to draw a drink from the glass cooler. While waiting for the elevator, he discovered that he was still holding the paper cup. Crumpling it, he threw it with an energetic swing between the bars into the shaft.

The trip to the ferry was short, and Leventhal did not take off his rubber coat in the subway. The air was muggy; his face grew damp. The blades of the fan turned so slowly in the gloomy yellow light that he could count the revolutions. The shower was over by the time he reached the street, and when the boat rode out of the slip over the slight swell, the sun came out again. Leventhal stood in the open, his coat slung over his shoulder, the folds gathered in his hand. There was a slow heave about the painted and rusted hulls in the harbor. The rain had gone out to the horizon, a dark band far overreaching the faint marks of the shore. On the water the air was cooler, but on the Staten Island side the great tarnished green sheds were sweltering, the acres of cement widely spattered with sunlight. The disembarking crowd spread through them, going toward the line of busses that waited at the curb with threshing motors, in a shimmer of fumes.

Max lived in a large apartment building. His flat, like Leventhal's own on Irving Place, was a high walk-up. Children were running noisily through the foyer; the walls were covered with childish writing. A Negro janitor in a garrison cap was washing the stairs and looked angry at Leventhal's tracks. In the court, the wash swung stiff and yellow in the strong sun; the pulleys were creaking. Elena had not answered Leventhal's ring. The elder of his nephews came to the door when he knocked. The boy did not know him. Of course, Leventhal reflected, how should he? He glanced up at the stranger, raising his arm to his eyes to screen them in the sunny, dusty, desolate white corridor. Behind him the flat was dark; the shades were drawn and a lamp was burning amid the clutter of the dining-room table.

"Where's your mother?"

"She's in here. Who are you?"

"Your uncle," said Leventhal. Coming into the hall he unavoidably pushed against the boy.

His sister-in-law hurried toward him from the kitchen. She had changed; she was heavier than when he had last seen her.

"Well, Elena?" he said.

"Oh, Asa, you're here?" She reached for his hand.

"Sure I'm here. You asked me to come, didn't you?"

"I tried to call you again, but they told me you were gone."

"Why again?"

"Phillie, take Uncle's coat," said Elena.

"Doesn't the bell work?"

"We disconnected it because of the baby."

Leventhal dropped his raincoat into the boy's arms and followed her into the dining room where she busied herself with clearing a chair for him.

"Oh, look at the house," she said. "I haven't had time to clean up. My mind is just miles away. It's already three weeks that I took down the curtains and I haven't got them back yet. And look at me." She put down the clothes she had lifted from the chair and showed herself to him with outspread arms. Her black hair was in disorder, she was wearing a nightgown under her cotton dress, her feet were bare. She smiled mournfully. Leventhal, impassive as usual, merely nodded. He observed that her eyes were anxious, altogether too bright and too liquid; there was a superfluous energy in her move-ments, a suggestion of distraction or even of madness not very securely held in check. But he was too susceptible to such suggestions. He was aware of that, and he warned him-self not to be hasty. He looked at her again. Her face, once florid and dark, was softer, fuller, and more pale, a little yel-low. He was able to picture her as she had once been when he glanced at his nephew. He resembled her strongly. Only his slightly outcurving nose belonged to the Leventhals.

"Now, tell me, what's the matter, Elena?"

"Oh, Mickey is sick, he's terribly sick," said Elena.

"What's he got?"

"The doctor says he doesn't know what it is. He can't do anything with him. He runs high fevers all the time. It started a couple of weeks ago. I give him to eat and he doesn't keep it down. I try everything. I don't know what I should do with him. And today I got such a scare. I went into the room and I couldn't hear him breathe."

"No, what do you mean?" said Leventhal.

"Just what I'm telling you. I couldn't hear him breathe," she said with intensity. "He wasn't breathing. I put my head on the pillow by his. I couldn't hear a thing. I put my hand over his nose. I couldn't feel anything. I got cold all over. I thought I was going to die myself. I ran out to call the doc-tor. I couldn't get him. I called his office and everywhere. I couldn't find him. So then I called you. When I got back he was breathing. He was all right. Then I tried to phone you."

Elena's hand was resting on her bosom; the long, pointed fingers were dirty; beneath them her skin was white and very smooth.

So that was the crisis. He might have guessed it was some-thing like that.

"He was breathing all the time," he said somewhat roughly. "How could he stop and start again?"

"No, no," she insisted. "He wasn't."

Leventhal's composure was not perfect; it was tinged with fear. He thought, looking away from her toward a corner of the ceiling, "What superstition! Just like in the old country. The dead can come back to life, too, I suppose, and all the rest of it."

"Why didn't you feel his heart?" he said to her.

"I should have, probably . . ."

"You certainly should."

"You were busy, weren't you?"

"Well, sure, I had work. . . ."

She expressed such contrition at this that he told himself to be kinder. He might as well be; he was here, the harm was done. He assured her that he had an afternoon coming. He had been with the firm six years, and if he couldn't take a few hours off on a personal matter after six years, he might as well give up. He could go away every afternoon for a month without coming close to the number of hours of overtime without pay that he had put in. After he stopped talking his mind ran on in the same strain. In the civil service it was different. There you had your sick leave and you went home with a headache. And you had tenure. . . . But he did not want to dwell on this. He got up and turned his chair, as if to change the subject of his thoughts by changing his position.

"You should raise the shades," he said to Elena. "Why do you keep them down?"

"It makes the room cooler."

"It cuts off the air. . . . And you have to keep the lamp on. That gives off heat."

She had moved the clothing from his chair to the table, pushing back dishes, bread, milk cartons, magazines. He guessed that she kept the shades down for no other reason than to hide her slovenliness from the neighbors across the court. He looked at the room with displeasure. And Max drifted around from Norfolk to Galveston to God knows where. Perhaps he preferred living in rooming houses and hotels.

Elena gave Philip a dollar and sent him down for beer. She took the money from her dress pocket, which was filled with change. When he had gone, Leventhal asked to see Mickey.

He was lying in Elena's hot, shadowy, close room, dozing in the large bed that stood against the wall, the sheet pulled down to his waist. His short black hair seemed damp; his mouth was open. He was wearing a sleeveless undershirt. Leventhal carefully put the back of his hand to his cheek; it was burning. In withdrawing he knocked his ring against the bedpost. The look Elena shot him startled him. He found himself raising the same hand apologetically and felt his face flush. She, however, was no longer looking at him; she was drawing the sheet over the child's shoulder. Leventhal withdrew to the hall and waited for her. She shut the door slowly, with such care that it seemed to him whole minutes passed. He gazed into the room; it grew darker about the figure on the bed partly hidden from him by the bulge of the chiffonier. At last she released the knob and they returned to the dining room.

He sat down, depressed and gloomy. He began at once to argue that Mickey should be taken to a hospital. "Who is this doctor of yours?" he said. "What's wrong with him that he lets you keep the boy at home? The hospital is the place for him." But he soon realized that Elena, not the doctor was to blame. She said, with great obstinacy, that he was better off at home, where she could take care of him herself. She showed such a dread of hospitals that at last he exclaimed, "Don't be such a peasant, Elena!" She was silent, though she appeared more distressed than offended and probably did not understand him. He was annoyed with himself for being so vehement, but everything here oppressed him—the house, his sister-in-law, the sick child. How could the boy get well in such a place, in that room? "Well, for goodness sake, Elena," he argued in a different tone, "a hospital is nothing to be afraid of." She shut her eyes and shook her head; he began to shape another sentence but stopped and lay back in the mohair armchair.

Suddenly she said brightly, almost happily, "Here's Philip and the beer." She rose to bring glasses. There was a hunt for the bottle opener; it was not found, and Philip pried off the caps on the handle of a metal cabinet in the kitchen. Elena wanted to make sandwiches, but Leventhal said he was not hungry. "Oh, it'll be dinnertime soon. Your missis won't like it if your appetite is spoiled. How is she? She's such a pretty girl." Elena smiled warmly. She did not even know his wife's name. They had met only once or twice. He hesitated to tell her that Mary had gone South for a few weeks to be with her mother. Elena would have insisted that he stay.

To change the subject, he asked about his brother. Max had been in Galveston since February. He wanted the family to join him, but the city was so crowded it was impossible to find a flat. He looked for one whenever he had time to spare.

"Why doesn't he come back to New York where he's got a flat?" said Leventhal.

"Oh, he makes good money down there; he works fifty, sixty hours a week. He sends me plenty." She did not appear to feel abandoned or even greatly concerned about Max's absence.

Hurriedly drinking down his beer, Leventhal rose, saying that he might still go back to the office for an hour to clear up some things. Elena gave him a neighbor's phone number; he copied it into his book and told her to ring in a day or two if Mickey did not get better. At the door, he called Philip and gave him a quarter for a soda. The boy took it, muttering "Thanks," but with a look that refused obligation. Probably a quarter did not mean much to Philip. Elena's pocket was full of change; she must be free with it. Leventhal drew his finger along the boy's cheek. Philip dropped his head, and, somewhat disappointed and dissatisfied with himself, Leventhal left the house.

He had to wait long for a bus, and it was dusk when he reached Manhattan. Too late to be useful at the office, he nevertheless debated at South Ferry, in the tenebrous brown heat, whether to return. "Ah, they'll get along without me today," he finally decided. Beard would interpret his coming in now as an admission that he was in the wrong. Moreover, it might seem that he was trying to establish himself as one of the "brethren" who was different. No, not even a hint of that, thought Leventhal. He would have an early dinner and go home. He felt dry, rather than hungry, but he must eat. He made an abrupt start and walked toward the train.

2

LEVENTHAL'S FIGURE was burly, his head large; his nose, too, was large. He had black hair, coarse waves of it, and his eyes under their intergrown brows were intensely black and of a size unusual in adult faces. But though childishly large they were not childlike in expression. They seemed to disclose an intelligence not greatly interested in its own powers, as if preferring not to be bothered by them, indifferent; and this indifference appeared to be extended to others. He did not look sullen but rather unaccommodating, impassive. Tonight, because of the heat, he was disheveled, and he was even ordinarily not neat. His tie was pulled to the side and did not close with the collar; his shirt cuffs came out beyond his coatsleeves and covered his thick brown wrists; his trousers sagged loose at the knees.

Leventhal came originally from Hartford. He had gone through high school there and after that had left home. His father, who had owned a small drygoods store, was a turbulent man, harsh and selfish toward his sons. Their mother had died in an insane asylum when Leventhal was eight and his brother six. At the time of her disappearance from the house, the elder Leventhal had answered their questions about her with an embittered "gone away," suggestive of desertion. They were nearly full grown before they learned what had happened to her.

Max did not finish high school; he left in his second year. Leventhal graduated and then went to New York, where for a time he worked for an auctioneer named Harkavy, a friend of his Uncle Schacter. Harkavy took Leventhal under his protection; he encouraged him to go to college at night and even lent him money. Leventhal took a prelegal course, but he did not do well. Perhaps the consciousness that he was attempting to do something difficult overweighed him. And the school itself—its atmosphere, especially on blue winter nights, the grimness of some of the students, many of them over fifty, world-beaten but persistent—that disturbed him. He could not study; he had never learned how, in the room behind his father's store. He finished the course, but without distinguishing himself, and he was not encouraged to go on to law school. He would have been satisfied to remain Harkavy's assistant, but the old man caught pneumonia and died. His son Daniel, then a junior at Cornell, left school to take over the business. Leventhal still remembered how he had come into the shop after the funeral in a bearskin coat, tall, blond, serious, saying emotionally to each of the clerks, "Let's dig in and hold the line!" Leventhal, virtually the old man's ward, was too dispirited by his death and trusted himself far too little to be of much use to Daniel. The shop was soon shut down. Going back to Hartford was out of the question (his father had remarried), and Leventhal, beginning to drift, was in a short time, a few months after Harkavy's death, living in a dirty hall bedroom on the East Side, starved and thin. For a while he sold shoes on Saturdays in the basement of a department store. Later he found steady work as a fur dyer, and after that, for about a year, he clerked in a hotel for transients on lower Broadway. Then his turn came on a civil-service list and he put himself down for "assignment anywhere in the United States." He was sent to the Baltimore customhouse.

The life he led in Baltimore was considerably different; it was not so solitary. It came to him slowly that in New York he had taken being alone so much for granted that he was scarcely aware how miserable it made him. During his first winter in the customhouse he was invited to join a party that went to the opera in Washington on Saturdays. He sat through five or six performances with a kind of alien, skeptical interest. But he began to go out regularly. He learned to like seafood. He bought himself two suits and a topcoat—he who from October to April had sweated in a heavy camel's-hair coat old Harkavy had given him.

At a picnic on the Chesapeake shore one Fourth of July, he fell in love with a sister of one of his friends. She was a tall, heavy-moving, handsome girl. With his eyes, he followed her in the steady, fiery sparkle of the bay when she climbed to the dock from the excursion boat and started arm in arm with her brother toward the grove and the spicy smoke of the barbecue clouding in the trees. Later he saw her running in the women's race, her arms close to her sides. She was among the stragglers and stopped and walked off the field, laughing and wiping her face and throat with a handkerchief of the same material as her silk summer dress. Leventhal was standing near her brother. She came up to them and said, "Well, I *used* to be able to run when I was smaller." That she was still not accustomed to thinking of herself as a woman, and a beautiful woman, made Leventhal feel very tender toward her. She was in his mind when he watched the contestants in the three-legged race hobbling over the meadow. He noticed one in particular, a man with red hair who struggled forward, angry with his partner, as though the race were a pain and a humiliation which he could wipe out only by winning. "What a difference," Leventhal said to himself. "What a difference in people."

He ran in the egg race, he swam, he felt his spirits thawed out that day. He was with Mary most of the afternoon. They took their sandwiches to the beach, walking half-shoe over in the white sand to find a place to themselves. From sundown, when they started back, till they came into the heat of the sluggish harbor among the heels of tankers, and through the yellow film spread over the water and in the air by the mills and piers, they sat together on the fantail of the little steamer. Her brother was waiting for her in the crowd at the gangplank, and they said good night in the noise of the steam plunging loosely skyward.

By autumn they were engaged, and Leventhal's success amazed him. He felt that the harshness of his life had disfigured him, and that this disfigurement would be apparent to a girl like Mary and would repel her. He was not entirely sure of her, and, in fact, something terrible did happen a month after the engagement. Mary confessed that she found herself unable to break off an old attachment to another man, a married man. In the pain of the moment, Leventhal almost lost his power to speak. He looked at her—they were in a restaurant. Then he asked if she had gone on seeing this man during the engagement. She said that she had and only at that moment seemed to realize how serious the matter was. He started to leave, and when she tried to hold him back, he pushed her, and she lost her footing in the booth and fell. He helped her rise; her mouth had gone white, and she averted her eyes from him. They left the restaurant together—she even waited while he paid the check—but outside they instantly separated without speaking.

About two years later she sent him a friendly letter. He did not know how to reply. It stood on his dresser for more than a month, confronting him nightly and overriding all his other concerns. He was still deliberating when he received a second letter from her. In it she asked him directly to consider how harassed she had been; she admitted that she had tried to end her infatuation by becoming engaged to him but that that was not the only reason; she had not chosen him indiscriminately. Leventhal found this letter easier to answer. They began to correspond. At Christmas he went down to visit her, and they were married by a justice of the peace in Wilmington.

He had meanwhile moved back to New York, having left Baltimore a few weeks after the engagement was broken. Daniel Harkavy had somehow landed on a trade paper. Leventhal, who had been editing a book of departmental regulations, thought that he, too, could handle that kind of job. He got in touch with Harkavy, and Harkavy wrote back that he was sure he could place him on a paper if he wanted to come to New York. Harkavy had many connections. Leventhal packed his trunk one week end and sent it to Harkavy's rooming house. He could not bear to stay in Baltimore; he was too wretched. He could not think of it later without flushing and wincing. A man brought up on hardships should have known better than to cut himself adrift. Even then he had realized that it was foolhardy to throw up his job and worse than that to put faith in Harkavy, and he told his chief that he was resigning to take another position. He was ashamed to tell him the truth.

He found Harkavy looking a little different. He was losing his hair and he had grown a red mustache. There was a certain swagger about him; he had taken to wearing large bow ties and black suede shoes. But he was essentially the same. He had written about his connections, but he could think of only one man to call on. This was a middle-aged Kentuckian by the name of Williston, short and ruddy, with a broad head across which his brown hair was brushed with a sort of backwoodsman's Sunday care. He was one of those people who keep their regional traits after twenty years in New York. It was a cold fall day, and he had an electric heater beside his desk. He sat back in his swivel chair, occasionally raising a foot to warm it over the coils.

No, he said, there was no vacancy in his office. An experienced man might find something even now, in bad times. An inexperienced one didn't have a chance. Unless by a freak—his shoe shone over the burnished heater—unless he knew someone very influential.

"We don't," Harkavy said. "We have no pull. And how will he get experience?"

He wouldn't suggest, said Williston, that Leventhal try to get a job running copy with a pack of boys at six bucks a week. Even such jobs were scarce. He would suggest that he stick to his trade. Leventhal's face grew dark, more with self-condemnation than with resentment. He might have asked for a transfer instead of quitting the civil service outright and waited it out, no matter how long it took. He imagined that Williston partly divined what had happened. It stupefied him, what he had done. But, Harkavy was saying, speaking of himself, he had gotten his job by luck, without experience. Oh, no, Williston answered, his father's name counted for something in the antiques field—Harkavy worked on a paper for auctioneers and antique dealers. "Leventhal was with my father and me for a long time," Harkavy told him. And Williston lifted his shoulders and gazed into the face of the heater as if to say, "In that case, nothing's too good for him." He seemed to regret this when he saw Leventhal's pained, lowering look. Of course he would do what he could, he said, but he didn't want them to believe that much could be done. He would phone some people, and meanwhile Leventhal could begin making the rounds.

He began in a spirit of utter hopelessness. The smaller trade papers simply turned him away. The larger gave him applications to fill out; occasionally he spent a few minutes with a personnel manager and had the opportunity to shake someone's hand. Gradually he became peculiarly aggressive and, avoiding the receptionists, he would make his way into an inner office, stop anyone who appeared to have authority, and introduce himself. He was met with astonishment, with coldness, and with anger. He often grew angry himself. They were frightened, he observed to Harkavy, when you got out of line, out of the proper channel. But the channel led out of the door. How could they expect you to stay in it? He discussed it reasonably enough with Harkavy, but the provocations and near-quarrels continued, and in the heat of these provocations he frequently lost sight of his real object. He might remind himself while shaving or when he entered the bank to draw on his savings that he was after all defeating his own purpose, that anyone who, on an outside chance, had a job to give would not give it to him. But he did not change.

This queer condition lasted for about two months. Then, since Harkavy was becoming increasingly difficult to live with (several nights a week he entertained a woman friend and Leventhal, turned out of the room, went to a movie or sat in a cafeteria), and since his money was running low, Leventhal decided to take any job at all, the next that came his way—he was thinking of trying his old hotel on lower Broadway—when he received a note from Williston asking him to come in. One of his men was sick and had to go to Arizona for the winter, and Leventhal could fill his place till he came back.

So it was through Williston that Leventhal got his start in the profession. He was grateful and worked hard for him, and he discovered he had a knack for the job. From June until the end of summer he was idle again—that, too, was a difficult period. But now he had a season's experience and he found a place at last with Burke-Beard and Company. Apart from his occasional trouble with Beard, he was satisfied. He was really better off than in the civil service.

He said occasionally to Mary, revealing his deepest feelings, "I was lucky. I got away with it." He meant that his bad start, his mistakes, the things that might have wrecked him, had somehow combined to establish him. He had almost fallen in with that part of humanity of which he was frequently mindful (he never forgot the hotel on lower Broadway), the part that did not get away with it—the lost, the outcast, the overcome, the effaced, the ruined.

3

LEVENTHAL'S FATHER-IN-LAW had recently died, and his
mother-in-law had been persuaded by the family to give
up her house in Baltimore and to live in Charleston with her
son. Mary had gone to help her move.

In her absence Leventhal had been eating in an Italian
restaurant in the neighborhood. It was in the basement of an
old tenement. The stucco walls were almost black. It had a
damp, woody smell from the sawdust sprinkled over the plank
floor. But it suited him; the meals were cheap, and he generally
did not have to wait for a table. Tonight, however, there was
only one available. The waiter led him to it. It was in the corner
behind a projecting wall which cut off the breeze of the fan. He
was about to protest and opened his mouth impatiently, but
the waiter, a dark man with thin hair curved over his perspiring
forehead, anticipated him with a tired and rather insincere
shrug, indicating with a motion of his toweled arm that the
place was filled. Leventhal tossed his hat down, moved aside the
dishes, and leaned forward on his elbows. Near the kitchen
step, the proprietor and his wife were finishing their dinner. She
gave Leventhal a look of recognition which he acknowledged,
making a stir in his chair. The waiter brought his meal, an
omelet in a chipped, blackened enamel dish with tomato sauce
hardened on the rim, a salad, and some canned apricots. He
ate, and his mood gradually improved. The coffee was sweet
and thick; he swallowed even the sediment and put the cup
down with a sigh. He lit a cigar. There was no one waiting for
the table and he sat awhile, bent backward and puffing, clasping his hands on the densely growing hair on the back of his
neck. From the tavern across the way came the slow notes of a
guitar, the lighter carried away, the deeper repeated tranquilly.

Presently he shoved a tip under the saucer and went out.

There was still a redness in the sky, like the flame at the
back of a vast baker's oven; the day hung on, gaping fierily
over the black of the Jersey shore. The Hudson had a low luster, and the sea was probably no more numbing in its cold,
Leventhal imagined, than the subway under his feet was in its

heat; the trains rushing by under the gratings and along the slanting brown rock walls seemed to set off charges of metal dust. He passed through a small park where the double circle of benches were jammed. There were lines before each drinking fountain, the warm water limping and jetting into the stone basins. On all sides of the green square, the traffic of cars and cabs whipped endlessly, and the cumbersome busses crawled groaning, steering down from the tall blue oblong of light at the summit of the street through a bluish pallor. In the bushy, tree-grown corners, children played and screamed, and a revivalist band sang and drummed and trumpeted on one of the sidewalks. Leventhal did not stay long in the park. He strolled homeward. He thought he would mix a cold drink and lie down beside an open window.

Leventhal's apartment was spacious. In a better neighborhood, or three stories lower, it would have rented for twice the amount he paid. But the staircase was narrow and stifling and full of turns. Though he went up slowly, he was out of breath when he reached the fourth floor, and his heart beat thickly. He rested before unlocking the door. Entering, he threw down his raincoat and flung himself on the tapestry-covered low bed in the front room. Mary had moved some of the chairs into the corners and covered them with sheets. She could not depend on him to keep the windows shut and the shades and curtains drawn during the day. This afternoon the cleaning woman had been in and there was a pervasive odor of soap powder. He got up and opened a window. The curtains waved once and then were as motionless as before. There was a movie house strung with lights across the street; on its roof a water tank sat heavily uneven on its timbers; the cowls of the chimneys, which rattled in the slightest stir of air, were still.

The motor of the refrigerator began to run. The ice trays were empty and rattled. Wilma, the cleaning woman, had defrosted the machine and forgotten to refill them. He looked for a bottle of beer he had noticed yesterday; it was gone. There was nothing inside except a few lemons and some milk. He drank a glass of milk and it refreshed him. He had already taken off his shirt and was sitting on the bed unlacing his shoes when there was a short ring of the bell. Eagerly he

pulled open the door and shouted, "Who is it?" The flat was
unbearably empty. He hoped someone had remembered that
Mary was away and had come to keep him company. There
was no response below. He called out again, impatiently. It
was very probable that someone had pushed the wrong button, but he heard no other doors opening. Could it be a
prank? This was not the season for it. Nothing moved in the
stair well, and it only added to his depression to discover how
he longed for a visitor. He stretched out on the bed, pulling
a pillow from beneath the spread and doubling it up. He
thought he would doze off. But a little later he found himself
standing at the window, holding the curtains with both
hands. He was under the impression that he had slept. It was
only eight-thirty by the whirring electric clock on the night
table, however. Only five minutes had passed.

"No, I shouldn't have gone," he said to himself. He was
suddenly full of misgivings. It was a mistake to run out of the
office like that. If he had considered the thing sensibly, he
would have waited till evening. Five minutes more and Elena
would have called him again. Then why hadn't he waited?
Did he actually want to stand Beard up for once, was that
why he had left the office? No, and Beard's remark was disgusting, besides. It did not come as a surprise. He had known
all along that he was capable of making it. If a man disliked
you, he would dislike you for all the reasons he could think
of. It was not important, merely disgusting. All the same, he
shouldn't have gone. He washed his face, put on his shirt,
and left the apartment. His difficulty, he reflected, was that
when he didn't have time to consider, when pressure was put
on him, he behaved like a fool. That, mainly, was what troubled him. For instance, last week at the press Dunhill, the
linotyper, sold him a ticket he didn't want. He protested that
he didn't care for shows and had no use for one ticket—this
was before Mary left. But because Dunhill had insisted, he
bought the ticket. He gave it to one of the girls at the office.
Now if only he had been able to say at the outset, "I will not
buy your ticket. . . ." He muttered, "Well, what do I do it
for?" frowning. One of his neighbors appeared, bare-chested
and in tennis shorts, and deposited a clinking bag of bottles
to be removed by the janitor.

The Porto Rican superintendent, Mr. Nunez, in a straw hat, his dark feet in Chinese straw slippers, was sitting on the stoop. Leventhal asked him whether he had noticed anyone ringing his bell, and he answered that he had been on the stoop for half an hour and that no one had gone out in the last fifteen minutes or come in. "Maybe you heard the radio," he suggested. "Sometimes I think somebody is in the house talking to me, but it's the radio somewhere."

"No, the bell rang," Leventhal said positively; he looked seriously at the superintendent. "Was it the dumb-waiter bell, you think?"

"If somebody was fooling around the basement. I didn't touch it tonight."

Leventhal set out for the park. Perhaps it was a radio, though he did not think so. Perhaps something in the wiring, affected by the heat—he did not know much about electricity —or the dumb-waiter. What really concerned him was that perhaps his nerves were to blame and that he had imagined the ring just as he had imagined that he had slept. Since Mary's departure his nerves had been unsteady. He kept the bathroom light burning all night. Somewhat ashamed of himself, he had yesterday closed the bathroom door before getting into bed, but he had left the light on. This was absurd, this feeling that he was threatened by something while he slept. And that was not all. He imagined that he saw mice darting along the walls. There actually were mice in the apartment. The building was old; there were bound to be some nesting under the floors. He had no dread of them, and yet he had begun to jerk his head around at the suspicion of a movement. And now he had been unable to fall asleep. Heat had never hitherto interfered with his sleep. He was sure he was unwell.

The park was even more crowded than before, and noisy. There was another revivalist band on the corner, and the blare of the two joined confusingly above the other sounds. The lamps were yellowed, covered with flies and moths. On one of the paths an old man, sunburned, sinewy, in a linen cap, was shining shoes. The fountain ran with a green, leaden glint. Children in their underclothing waded and rolled in the spray, the parents looking on. Eyes seemed softer than by day, and larger, and gazed at one longer, as though in the dark heat some interspace of reserve had been crossed and strangers might approach one another with a kind of recognition. You looked and thought, at least, that you knew whom you had seen.

Some such vague thing was in Leventhal's mind while he waited his turn at the drinking spout, when suddenly he had a feeling that he was not merely looked at but watched. Unless he was greatly mistaken a man was scrutinizing him, pacing slowly with him as the line moved. "He seems to know me," he thought. Or was the man merely lounging there, was he only a bystander? Instantly Leventhal became reserved, partly as a rebuff to his nerves, his busy imagination. But it was not imagination. When he stepped forward, the man moved, too, lowering his head as if to hide a grin at the thin-lipped formality of Leventhal's expression. There was no hint of amusement, however, in his eyes—he was now very close; they were derisive and harsh.

"Who's this customer?" Leventhal said to himself. "An actor if I ever saw one. My God, my God, what kind of a fish is this? One of those guys who want you to think they can see to the bottom of your soul." He tried to stare him down, only now realizing how insolent he was. But the man did not go. He was taller than Leventhal but not nearly so burly; large-framed but not robust. "If he starts something," Leventhal thought, "I'll grab his right arm and pull him off balance. . . . No, his left arm and pull towards my left; that's my stronger side. And when he's going down I'll give him a rabbit punch. But why should he start anything? There's no reason."

He was squared and resolute; nevertheless there was a tremor in his arms, and during all of it he felt that he himself was the cause of his agitation and suspicion, with his unreliable nerves. Then in astonishment he heard the stranger utter his name.

"What, do you know me?" he asked loudly.

"Do I? You're Leventhal, aren't you? Why shouldn't I know you? I thought you might not recognize me, though. We met only a few times, and I suppose I look a little different than I used to."

"Oh, Allbee, isn't it? Allbee?" Leventhal said slowly, with gradual recognition.

"Kirby Allbee. So you do recognize me?"

"Well, I'll be damned," said Leventhal, but he said it rather indifferently. What if it were Kirby Allbee? And he certainly looked changed, but what of that?

Just then several people in the line pushed against him. It was his turn at the spout and, as he took a swallow of the warm water, he looked sidewise at Allbee. The woman who had preceded him—she was painted heavily and looked like a chorus girl who had slipped out of the theater for a breath of air—was in Allbee's way, and while he was trying to step aside, caught in the circle around the spout, Leventhal walked off.

He had never liked this Allbee, but he had never really thought much about him. How was it, then, that his name came to him so readily? He had a poor memory for names; still he saw the man and recognized him in a moment. "What a box, the mind," Leventhal thought with something approaching a smile. "You'd just as soon expect hair to grow in your hand as some of the things that come out of it."

"Hey, wait!"

Allbee was dodging through the crowd after him. "What does he want?" Leventhal irritably asked himself.

"Wait, where are you going?"

Leventhal did not answer. What business was it of his?

"Are you going home?"

"Yes, by and by," he said distantly.

"Well, now you've found out that I still exist and you're going home, is that it?" He had a curious smile.

"Why should I doubt that you exist?" Leventhal was smiling also, but without much mirth. "Is there any reason why you shouldn't? I'm afraid I don't get it."

"I mean that you just wanted to have a look at me."

"Pardon?" said Leventhal. He drew up his brows. "To have a look?"

"Yes, I think you did want to, to see how I've made out. The results."

"I came out to cool off a little." He was beginning to be really annoyed. "What makes you think you've got anything to do with it?"

"Well, I didn't expect this," Allbee said. "Of course, I didn't know what to expect. I wondered what line you were going to take with me." He brought his lips together as if to hold back laughter, slightly jeering, presumptuous, and drew his hand down his cheek over the blond bristles, and all the while his deeply ringed eyes looked angrily into Leventhal's. He appeared to be saying that he knew perfectly well what he was saying and that it was effrontery and bad acting to deny it. "Just like a bad actor to accuse everyone of bad acting," thought Leventhal, but he was troubled nevertheless. What was he after? He studied Allbee more closely; until now he had not noticed how seedy he looked, like one of those men you saw sleeping off their whisky on Third Avenue, lying in the doorways or on the cellar hatches, dead to the cold or the racket or the straight blaze of the sun in their faces. He drank, too; that was certain. His voice was thick. He had fair hair parted in the center over his large forehead, moist in the lamplight. He wore a flimsy shirt of material that must have been imitation silk; it opened on the chest on the dirty hem of an undershirt; his light cotton suit was soiled.

"The fact remains that you wanted to see me," he resumed.

"You're mistaken."

"Well, you got my letter, didn't you? And I asked you to meet me here tonight . . . ?"

"You wrote me a letter? What in the world for? I never got a letter from you. I don't understand this."

"Neither do I; if you didn't get it, this would be quite a co-incidence. But," he went on, smiling, "of course you're pretending you didn't get the letter."

"Why should I pretend?" said Leventhal excitedly. "What reason have I got to pretend? I don't know what letter you're talking about. You haven't got anything to write me for. I haven't thought about you in years, frankly, and I don't know why you think I care whether you exist or not. What, are we related?"

"By blood? No, no . . . heavens!" Allbee laughed.

Leventhal stared into his laughing face and then began to walk away, whereupon Allbee thrust his arm straight before him and held him back. Leventhal grasped it, but he did not jerk according to his plan. He felt no resistance to his grip. It was he rather than Allbee who was off balance, and he removed his hand; he appeared to scowl—in reality he was clearing his throat—and he said, not at all loudly, "What do you want?"

"Oh, that's more sensible." Allbee straightened his shoulders and pulled down his cuffs. "I don't want to wrestle. I'm probably no match for you. I wanted to talk. I didn't think there would be any physical violence. That's not how you people go about things. Not with violence."

"What people are you talking about?" asked Leventhal.

Allbee did not reply to this. "I wanted to take up a few things with you, which is why I wrote," he said.

"I tell you again, I never got a letter from you."

"So you're sticking to that." Allbee smiled deprecatingly as though wondering why Leventhal refused every opportunity to get rid of this clumsy pretense. "Then why are you here? You wanted to see but not be seen, and you're mad because you got caught."

"I'm here because I live down the street a way. Why don't you own up instead that you wanted to catch me. God only knows what for and what you've got to say."

Allbee moved his large face from side to side in denial. "It's the other way around. You knew I was here . . . well, it's immaterial. As for what I have to say to you, I've got plenty to say. But you know that."

"That's news to me, too."

Allbee grinned at him with an intimation of a shared secret that aroused and vexed Leventhal, and sickened him.

"Let's sit down," Allbee proposed.

"Damn him, he's got me, he's got hold of me," Leventhal thought. "He's become some kind of a crank. I shouldn't have gone out. I should have tried to sleep, after the day I've had."

They found a place on a bench.

"I haven't got much time. I get up early. What do you want?"

Allbee regarded him. "You've become stouter," he said. "Darker, too. How much do you weigh?"

"About two hundred and ten."

"That's too much. It's bad for your heart to carry so much

weight. Don't you feel it in this weather? I'll bet your heart takes a beating from it. You have a lot of stairs to climb."

"How do you know that?"

"Oh, I happen to know that you live on the fourth floor."

"*How* do you know?" Leventhal insisted.

"I just happen to. Is it some kind of a secret? Isn't anybody allowed to know that you live on the fourth floor?"

"What else do you know about me?"

"You work for the Burke-Beard people. You put out one of their sheets."

"Any more?"

"Your wife is away. She is . . ." he glanced over as though to see if he was entirely right, "down South. Went a few days ago. These things aren't hard to find out."

"Did you ring my bell before?"

"Did I ring it? No, why should I?"

Leventhal grimly looked at him in the light that came through the leaves. He had been spying on him, and the mystery was why! How long had he been keeping watch on him and for what reason—what grotesque reason? Allbee returned his look, examining him as he was examined, in concentration and seriousness, his lower jaw slipped to one side, his glum, contemplative eyes filled with a green and leaden color. And in the loom of these eyes and with the warmth of the man's breath on his face, for they were crowded together on the bench, Leventhal suddenly felt that he had been singled out to be the object of some freakish, insane process, and for an instant he was filled with dread. Then he recovered and told himself there was nothing to be afraid of. The man was a crank and irritating, and certainly it was creepy to think of being observed secretly. But there was nothing so alarming about this Allbee. He had become a bum and a drunk and he seemed to have an idea or a twist about him, a delusion; perhaps it was even invented. How could you tell about these drunks? There must be reasons, but they were beyond anybody's ability to find out—smoky, cloudy, alcoholic. Allbee had taken him by surprise. It was surprising. And in his present state of mind he was, moreover, easily carried away by things. He felt unwell, and that didn't help. He gave a steadying, wary pull to his shoulders.

Still looking at him, Allbee said, "It's hard to know what kind of a man you are, personally."

"Oh, it's me you want to talk about?"

"Now, you see? There's an example. You're outspoken, but are you leading away from the main thing? You are. It's a maneuver. I don't know whether you're smart or crude. Maybe you don't even care much about the main thing."

"What don't I care about?"

"Ah, come on, drop it, Leventhal, drop it! You know what it is."

"I don't."

There was a pause; then Allbee said with an effort at patience, "Well, if that's the way it's got to be—I guess you want me to go over the whole business. I thought it wouldn't be necessary, but all right. *Dill's Weekly.* You remember *Dill's Weekly?* Mr. Rudiger?"

"Of course I do. Sure. Rudiger. I have it written down in an old appointment book I've been hoping to run across; his name keeps getting away from me. Oh, Rudiger," he said reminiscently and began to smile, but with a line of constraint about his mouth.

"So you do remember?"

"Naturally."

"Now what about the rest of it? No, you won't go on to the rest of it. You'll make me do it. Okay, I will. It was through Rudiger that you got at me."

"Got at you?" said Leventhal, astonished. He turned his hot face to Allbee, and his scalp seemed to descend toward his brows.

"Got back at me. Got even with me," Allbee said with great distinctness. His lower lip came forward, it was dry and cracked; his nose looked swollen, all at once. His eyes were open to the full.

"No, no," Leventhal muttered. "You're mistaken. I never did."

Allbee passed his hand before him in a movement of denial and shook his head slowly. "I couldn't be mistaken about this."

"No? Well, you are."

"Did I get you an appointment with Rudiger? I fixed you up with an interview, didn't I?"

"Yes, you did. Yes. . . ."

"Then you went in and deliberately insulted Rudiger, put on some act with him, called him filthy names, deliberately insulted him to get me in bad. Rudiger is hot blooded and he turned on me for it. You knew he would. It was calculated. It worked out just as you thought it would. You were clever as hell. He didn't even give me a week's notice. He turned me out."

"That's all wrong. I heard you weren't with Dill's any more. Harkavy told me. But it couldn't have been my fault. I'm sure you're mistaken. Rudiger wouldn't blame you for the run-in we had. It was his fault, too."

"Rudiger did," said Allbee. "He was plenty clear about it. He almost killed himself blowing his top at me. And that was what you wanted."

"All I wanted was a job," Leventhal declared, "and Rudiger was tough and nasty. There's something wrong with that man. Hot blood isn't the word for it. He's vicious. I didn't exactly keep my temper down. I admit that. Well, if that's the reason I may be to blame in a way, indirectly. But you say. . . ."

"I say you're entirely to blame, Leventhal." He opened his mouth and appeared to hold his breath an instant as he smiled. Leventhal's attempt to keep a clear head came to nothing; he felt himself slipping into confusion.

"And why did I do it, do you say?"

"For revenge. Damn! You want to go over the whole thing to make sure that I'm really on. I really am on, Leventhal. Jesus, do you think I still haven't figured it out? Give me a little more credit than that; I was on a long time ago. But if you want me to pull it all out, I'm willing. I'll start farther back: Williston's house. There was a party."

"Yes, that's where we met, at Williston's."

"Ah, well, you recall it. I thought you'd balk all along the line and refuse to remember. Fine. Your friend was there too, another Jewish fellow—you mentioned his name before."

"Harkavy."

"That's the one, Harkavy. We're making headway." He laughed aloud. "Well, that's the key. A Jewish fellow. Lord, you want to draw the whole business out. Does it have to be drawn out? I suppose it has to. You were sore at something I said about Jews. Does that come back to you?"

"No. Yes, it does. It does, too," he corrected himself, frowning. "I also remember that you were drunk."

"Wrong. I was liquored up but not drunk. Positively not. You Jews have funny ideas about drinking. Especially the one that all Gentiles are born drunkards. You have a song about it —'Drunk he is, drink he must, because he is a Goy . . . *Schicker*.'" He had ceased laughing; he looked morose.

"Bah!" Leventhal said contemptuously. He pushed at the bar of the bench and got to his feet.

"Where are you going?"

"I had nothing to do with your losing that job. It was probably your own fault. You must have given Rudiger a plenty good reason to fire you, and I can imagine what it was. I'm not the sort of man who carries grudges. It's all in your mind. I remember all about that night at Williston's, but you were drunk and I didn't hold it against you. Besides it was a long time ago, and I don't see your object in looking me up just to remind me of it. Good night!"

He walked away. Allbee stood up and shouted after him, "You wanted to get even. You did plan it. You did it on purpose!" People turned to look at them, and Leventhal increased his pace.

"If he follows me now I'll punch him in the jaw. I'll knock him down," he thought. "I swear, I'll throw him down and smash his ribs for him!"

He opened the mailbox when he got home and found the note. It was signed "Sincerely, Kirby A." and said that he would be in the park at nine. Why the park? Well, why such an accusation? What an idea! The one made about as much sense as the other. There was no stamp on the envelope; Allbee must have delivered it himself. Chances were it was he who had rung the bell.

"Some judge of time, that Nunez," Leventhal growled, starting up the stairs.

4

H E FELL ASLEEP without difficulty and slept deeply. The
alarm clock on the night table awoke him, and he
seized it and clapped down the catch. Then he crouched
down at the window—he was naked—and looked over the sill.
Already, at half-past seven, the street looked deadened with
heat and light. The clouds were heavily suspended and slow.
To the south and east, the air was brassy, the factories were
beginning to smolder and faced massively, India red, brown,
into the sun and across the hot green netting of the bridges.
There was a hard encircling rumble of trucks and subterranean trains. Nunez was out in front, cleaning the sidewalk
with a bucket of water and the stub of a broom. His wife was
busy at the window boxes. New white strings stretched up to
the lintel; she was leaning out, training vines on them.

Leventhal washed and shaved. Allbee's note was lying on
the kitchen table. He reread it and threw it into the pail beside
the sink. He was about to slam down the lid but checked himself—he was behaving as he would have yesterday when he was
at the end of his patience—and, almost smiling at himself, he
set it in place lightly and pushed the pail toward the wall with
his foot. Well, he could have been forgiven yesterday for losing
his patience or even his head. What a day! With all that he had
weighing on him already, this Allbee shows up to add his little
bit. He must have brooded over the affair for years, until he
convinced himself that Rudiger had fired him because of that
interview. Of course, it was true enough that Rudiger had a
rotten bad temper, probably was born bad-tempered, but not
even he would fire an employee, not for what the man himself
had done but because of someone he had recommended.
"How could he?" Leventhal asked himself. "Not a good
worker; never." It was absurd. Allbee must have been fired for
drunkenness. When could you get a drinking man to acknowledge that he had gotten into trouble through drinking? Especially when he was far gone? And this Allbee was far gone.

He put on the wrinkled brown summer flannels he had
thrown over the foot of the bed last night, and a pair of white

shoes. He remembered to shut the windows and draw the drapes. The room was darkened. He took a handkerchief from the dresser and came across a statement on tax deductions for the year, a gloomy reminder of Mr. Beard and the office. Instead of keeping such things in the desk where they belonged, Mary had the habit of putting them under the linens. Irritated, he buried the paper deeper and roughly shoved the drawer shut. He went out with a frown. Beard would probably send for him and call him down, ostensibly for some mistake which he would dig up. Or he would delegate someone—he had done that before; perhaps that pinch-nosed, knob-faced little Millikan, his son-in-law. "If he sicks him on me . . ." he thought. But he did not know what threat to make. And now it seemed to him that he had rested badly. His legs were tired, his head ached, and his eyes—he examined them in the long mirror in the pillar before the coffeeshop—were bloodshot; he looked drawn. He shook his head in concern. The corners of the glass were flaming with the blue and red of the spectrum.

For a while he was so preoccupied with what awaited him at the office that he forgot about Allbee. He did not think of him again until he was on the subway. He was even less amused than before. From a sober person—that is, from a normal person, someone you would have to reckon with—such an accusation would be no trifle. With Allbee it came out like a stunt: the note, the bell ringing, the acting. And not quite a stunt, for a stunt was done deliberately, whereas it was questionable whether this queer, beaten, probably suffering Allbee was in control of his actions. Suffering? Of course, suffering, Leventhal told himself gravely: down and out, living in a moldy hotel somewhere, hanging out in bars, sleeping whole days, picked up off the streets by the paddywagon or the ambulance, haunted in his mind by wrongs or faults of his own which he turned into wrongs against himself; and that stirring around of the thoughts and feelings, that churning—everybody experienced it, but for a man like that it must be ugly, terrible, those thoughts wheeling around. It was something like this that Leventhal was thinking of when he occasionally said that he had gotten away with it. But (without taking credit for it; he might have fallen in another way) his character was different. Some men behaved as though they had a horse under them and went through life at a gallop. Or thought they could, at any rate. He was not that way.

He had met Allbee several times at Williston's house. In those unsettled days when he was jobhunting, the Willistons used to give parties frequently. Perhaps they still did; he had not seen them in several years. Because they were roommates, he and Harkavy were usually invited together. Allbee had shown an antipathy toward Harkavy, and Leventhal recalled that he, as a matter of fact, had been offended by several of Allbee's remarks and by his attitude generally. Mrs. Allbee was a quiet blonde. He wondered what had become of her; had she left him, divorced him? He found that he retained a distinct image of her, of the firmness of her face and the form of her eyes, gray eyes. He had thought her much too good for the husband lounging beside her with a glass, staring at the other guests and smiling. He might have been asked by Williston to classify them, he eyed them so, spread out there on the sofa, large-limbed, his face swelling with smiles. From time to time he made a comment to his wife, fixing his look on someone so that it was uncomfortably evident whom he was talking about. He frequently picked out Harkavy, which Leventhal resented, Harkavy himself seemingly unaware that he was being stared at.

It had to be admitted that Harkavy attracted stares. He liked to talk and at these parties he was easily kindled, for some reason. Any trifle made him enthusiastic, and when he spoke his hands flew and his brows slanted up, sharpening the line of his nose. His eyes were light, round, and depthless, his fair hair was fading back, the curls thinning. Allbee studied him, grinning and curious; Harkavy appeared to delight him. He must have had some witty things to say about him for he sometimes made his wife smile, and as a rule she did not respond to his remarks. Harkavy may have noticed this. Leventhal had never asked him about it, but perhaps it did light on his consciousness, for all his traits, the Jewish especially, became accentuated. He carried on, giving imitations of auctioneers, in reality burlesquing his father. Leventhal watched, unsmiling and even forbidding. The laughter and the somewhat ambiguous applause, sometimes led by Allbee, seemed to excite Harkavy, and he would start again, working up the bid. The Willistons laughed with the guests, though more moderately and with a trace of anxiety about Allbee. Leventhal himself, at times, could not help joining in. But he was annoyed.

The incident Allbee had referred to occurred one night when Harkavy and a girl he had brought to the party were singing spirituals and old ballads. It was late, and everyone else was silent, rather tired. That evening Harkavy had been a little more restrained than usual. He sang poorly, but at least he did not provoke laughter and was not trying to. Nor did the girl sing well; she hesitated over words. It was pleasant, however. Halfway through a ballad Allbee interrupted; regardless of his denial, he was drunk.

"Why do you sing such songs?" he said. "*You* can't sing them."

"Why not, I'd like to know?" said the girl.

"Oh, you, too," said Allbee with his one-cornered smile. "It isn't right for you to sing them. You have to be born to them. If you're not born to them, it's no use trying to sing them."

His wife spoke up. "Don't pay any attention to him," she said. "You sing it very nicely."

"Aaah, yes he does," he said contemptuously.

"Why, thank you, Mrs. Allbee," said Harkavy. "It's a lovely song."

"Go on, Dan, go on with it," Phoebe Williston urged him. And Leventhal said, "Sing the rest of it."

"I'm going to," Harkavy replied, and began over.

"No, no, no!" Allbee broke in again. "You shouldn't sing those old songs. You have to be bred to them."

His wife colored and said, "Kirby, don't be like that."

"Oh, I don't mind, ma'am." Harkavy drew in his chin and crossed his arms, his round eyes glimmering.

"Sing, Dan," said Leventhal.

"Sing a psalm. I don't object to your singing. Sing one of the psalms. I'd love to hear it. Go ahead, I would," said Allbee.

"I don't know any psalms."

"Then any Jewish song. Something you've really got feeling for. Sing us the one about the mother." And with a drunken look of expectancy he bent forward, leaning on his knees, and pretended to prepare to listen. It was apparent to everyone that he was deeply pleased; he smiled at Harkavy and the girl, and he had a glance for Leventhal, too. His wife seemed quietly to dissociate herself from him. The Willistons were embarrassed. Allbee was not merely an acquaintance but a friend, and Williston later tried to make excuses for him and explain away the insult.

That was what had happened. Leventhal had naturally been angry, but not for long. He had shrugged it off. Did Allbee think something like that would make him go to such lengths for revenge? He was an idiot if he did. He overestimated the magnitude of the insult and his power to be insulting. Or did he think that on that night he had revealed something that was not plain before? Then he was twice as idiotic. "And if I were mad, is that what I would do?" thought Leventhal. "He gives himself an awful lot of credit for nothing. Who does he think he is?"

That he had afterwards asked Allbee for an introduction to Rudiger should have shown how much importance he attached to the incident. At that time, Williston's man had returned from Arizona and Leventhal was looking for another place. Williston gave him a very good reference letter which made it easier to get interviews. However, several months went by before Leventhal was hired by Burke-Beard and Company, and during those months he was despondent and became quarrelsome once again, difficult, touchy, exaggerating, illogical, overly familiar. Reports of this reached Williston, who called him in and lectured him. Leventhal was bitter and suspicious of him and he offered to return the letter—foolishly, he now realized. But he thought that Williston regretted writing it.

It was his own idea to approach Allbee about a job at *Dill's*. Williston endorsed it and may have been instrumental in getting Allbee to introduce him to Rudiger. Or perhaps Allbee agreed in order to make up for his unpleasantness. Williston tried continually to explain it away. You had to know Allbee when he was sober, he said; he was intelligent and decent. His New England upbringing was behind his drinking; there were ministers in his family, influences to throw off, and once he

threw them off he would be another man. Leventhal indifferently acknowledged that that might be so; he had no particular grudge against him. "I'll be much obliged to him if he
gets me the introduction. What a break if I could land a job
with an outfit like that."

The interview at *Dill's* still troubled him.

Rudiger kept him waiting for nearly an hour in the reception
room and for a few minutes more in his office. He was watching several tugs shouldering a huge liner up the river and his
back was turned. But as soon as he faced about, Leventhal knew
at once that he had nothing to hope for; he saw even before
Rudiger uttered his first word that he did not want him. He was
a short man, broad featured and red; his hair was intensely red.
He had a mustache of short golden hairs overspread by a powerful nose with the cartilages widely separated at the tip. He
spoke energetically, peremptorily, quickly, in a husky tone. At
the outset Leventhal thought, "I've hit him at a bad time."
Later he could not decide whether he had come upon him in an
unusual mood of great stress and aroused cruelty or whether
Rudiger had only treated him as he generally did people whom
he didn't want to hire and who were wasting his time. In telling
Harkavy about it that same afternoon, Leventhal said, "He was
burning like a boiler. I never saw anything like it."

"Well?" Rudiger said, putting his hands on the desk. He
might have been arresting momentarily a swing back to the
window. Leventhal began to speak, and he cut him off with,
"No vacancies, no vacancies here. We're filled. Go somewhere
else."

Leventhal said stumblingly, "I thought there might be an
opening here. I didn't know. . . . Didn't Mr. Allbee say what
I wanted?"

Rudiger looked at him awhile. They were on the sixtieth
floor of the Dill Building. The sun was far behind the dull,
black, tarnished spikes and pinnacles of the skyscrapers below.

"What's your experience?" he said.

Leventhal told him.

"No, never mind that stuff. What newspapers have you
been on?"

"No papers," Leventhal said rather nervously.

Rudiger burst out, inflamed, "Then what in the name of

hell are you taking up my time for? What are you doing here? Get out. By Jesus, you come pestering around here when I'm busy without a goddam thing to offer."

"I'm sorry to bother you." Leventhal spoke stiffly, not to reveal his alarm.

"This is a news magazine. If you have no news experience, you've got no business here. Do you think we run a vocational school?"

"I thought I could do the work. I've read your magazine, and I thought I could." He labored at the words, stalling, and bent his head.

"Oh, did you? Did you?"

"Yes. . . ." He was beginning to recover his presence of mind. "I didn't know my experience wasn't the right kind for you. I have a letter from Mr. Williston. He says he knows you." Leventhal reached into his pocket.

But Rudiger exclaimed, "I don't want to see it."

"Well, Mr. Williston said he didn't see why I shouldn't be able to handle a job here. . . ."

"Nobody asked him. I don't care what he said."

"I think he knows what he's talking about. I respect his opinion."

"I know my own business. Never mind about Williston. I ought to know what I need here. You're not it."

"You probably know your business," Leventhal said stolidly, evenly, hunching his head forward. "I'm not saying you don't. But there's nothing so special about your magazine. I've read it, as I said." He put a cigarette in his mouth and, without asking Rudiger's permission, reached for a packet of matches on his desk, tore out one, struck it, and threw it into a tray. Angry and tense, he managed to present a surface of dry, uncaring calm. "Anybody who can write English can write for it. If you gave a man a try and then thought he couldn't make the grade, I'd say you knew your business a lot better. That's a prejudice, Mr. Rudiger, about newspaper experience."

Rudiger shouted, "Oh, is it?" Leventhal saw that he was not invulnerable, and by now a spell had been created, an atmosphere of infliction and injury from which neither could withdraw.

"Sure it is," said Leventhal rather easily. "It's a guild. Any outsider hasn't got a chance. But as a matter of fact you ought to think of your paper first and hire people because they can do the work. It wouldn't hurt."

"You think you could improve the paper?"

Leventhal replied that not his only but any fresh point of view wouldn't hurt. His confidence was enormous, so radically unusual that, despite his calm, it was like a seizure or possession, and he said things which his memory, limited by what was habitual, could not retain. So he did not know now exactly what followed. He recalled something like, "Well, you buy an article in the grocery and you know what you're getting when you buy a standard brand. You open up the can and the product is inside. You're not disappointed and you're not overjoyed. It's standard." He shrank from the recollection as from a moment of insanity and he flushed roughly; he surmised that he might be making it worse than it had been, but even one tenth of the reality was calamitous.

Then, glaring at him crazily, Rudiger said, "What did you want to be here for if it's so bad!"

And he answered, "I need a job, it so happens."

The air between them must have shaken, it was so charged with insult and rage. Under no circumstances could he imagine doing now what he had done then. But he had determined not to let his nose be pulled. That was what he told himself. "He thinks everybody who comes to him will let his nose be pulled." Too many people looking for work were ready to allow anything. The habit of agreement was strong, terribly strong. Say anything you like to them, call them fools and they smiled, turn their beliefs inside out and they smiled, despise them and they might grow red, but they went on smiling because they could not let themselves disagree. And that was what Rudiger was used to.

"Get out!" Rudiger cried. His face was aflame. He rose with a thrust of his stocky arm while Leventhal, evincing neither anger nor satisfaction, though he felt both, rose, smoothed the groove of his green velours hat, and said, "I guess you can't take it when people stand up to you, Mr. Rudiger."

"Out, out, out!" Rudiger repeated, pushing over his desk

with both arms. "Out, you case, you nut, you belong in the asylum! Out! You ought to be committed!"

And Leventhal, sauntering toward the door, turned and retorted, made a remark about two-bit big shots and empty wagons. He didn't believe he had said more than that—notwithstanding Allbee's charge that he swore. He had said something about empty wagons being noisy. His present mortification would not be greater if he had sworn. He did remember, and very clearly, too, that he was elated. He congratulated himself. Rudiger had not pulled his nose.

He went at once to see Harkavy and, over a cup of coffee in a corner cafeteria, told him the whole story. It delighted him.

"You said that to Rudiger? Oh, golly, that must have been something. Really something, Asa my boy. He's a bull, that man. I've heard stories about him. A regular bull!"

"Yes. Well, you've got to remember one thing, Dan." Leventhal's spirits dropped suddenly. "Someone like that can make trouble for me. He can have me black-listed. You've got to realize . . . Eh, can he?"

"Never, Asa," Harkavy said.

"You don't think so?"

"Never. Who do you think he is?" Harkavy looked at him severely with his round, clear eyes.

"He's a big shot."

"There isn't a thing he can do to you. Whatever you do, don't get ideas like that into your head. He can't persecute you. Now be careful. You have that tendency, boy, do you know that? He got what was coming to him and he can't do anything. Maybe that Allabee, what-do-you-call-him, put him up to it, wanted to play you a dirty trick. You know how it goes: 'There's a fellow bothering me. Do me a favor and give him the works when he comes around.' So he does it. Well, he fouled his own nest. You follow me, boy? He fouled his own nest. So by now he realizes it was his own fault and he had it coming. How do you know it wasn't rimmed?"

"You really think they did? I don't know. And I didn't bother that Allbee. I only asked him once."

"Maybe he didn't put him up to it. But he might have. It's a possibility. Something like that happened to another friend of mine—Fabin. You know him. They gave him the works, and it was a put-up job. Only he didn't talk back the way you did. He just let them fling it at him. No, you did right and you haven't got a thing to worry about."

Nevertheless, Leventhal was not reassured. And on afterthought he had misgivings about Harkavy's reference to persecution. Harkavy used such words whether they fitted or not. Rudiger's anger was not imaginary, and he was a man to fear. There were black lists; that was well known. Of course, he had not actually worked for Rudiger and Rudiger could not black-list him as a former employee. In the nature of it, it must be a secret process, passing through many connections, private and professional. After all, Rudiger was influential, powerful. And who knew how these things were done, through what channels? It was downright silly of Harkavy to speak of imaginary persecution.

Leventhal suspected, in the days that followed, that the black list was real enough, for firm after firm turned him down. It was only when he found his present job that his suspicions faded and he ceased to fear Rudiger.

Beard did not send for him; Leventhal's apprehensions were unfounded. The old man, when they met in the lavatory in the afternoon, was not affable, but he was not so disagreeable as Leventhal had anticipated. He even asked about the family troubles. It was Leventhal himself that was distant.

"Was it as urgent as you thought?" said Beard.

"Oh, absolutely," Leventhal replied. "And my brother is away. I have to look out for his family."

"Yes, I see. Naturally. Your brother is a family man, is he?"

"He has two children. He's married to an Italian woman."

Mr. Beard said with a look of mild inquiry, "Oh, a mixed marriage."

Leventhal nodded slightly. Mr. Beard shook his dripping hands and dried them on the towel he carried over his shoulder. He did not use the paper towels in the tin box. In words hardly above a whisper, he made some comment about the heat, wiped his wan forehead, and went out, tightening his belt, pulling down his white vest, a round-shouldered figure with bald head and large elbows. The old man's mildness made him feel easier. They had met the deadline without him. It hadn't been so catastrophic; Fay and Millikan stayed an hour overtime. He would have done the same in a similar emergency. Had done it. And what if he himself had been sick? A man wasn't made of metal parts. Damn him, old Beard might have let him off a little more pleasantly. It gratified Leventhal, however, to have made that remark about Elena. Mixed marriage! It had come out instantaneously. He wondered how to hint to the old man that he had heard him yesterday, or that he was under no illusions, at any rate. He wanted him to know.

On the way to his desk he met Millikan, nervous, narrow-faced, sallow, with his scrap of mustache. He carried a towel, too, and approached, signaling with it. How he aped his father-in-law!

"Telephone, Leventhal. Miss Ashmun's been looking for you. Some party on your line."

"Who?" Leventhal was filled with anxiety, suddenly. He went rapidly to his desk.

"Asa?" It was Elena.

"Yes, what's the matter? Anything wrong?"

"The baby is worse. Mickey . . ." he heard her say. Her voice shot up and she became incoherent.

"Slower, slower Elena, please. I can't follow you. What's happening over there?" He guessed, his heart sinking, that she, too, was growing worse. "Now tell me slowly what's the matter."

"I want to get a specialist."

"Why don't you send the boy to the hospital?"

"I want a specialist to come to the house."

"What does your doctor say?"

"He didn't come today. Let him stay away. What good does he do him anyway? He doesn't do any good. He doesn't come even when he knows Mickey is so sick. Asa, do you hear me? I want a big man."

"All right. But if you took my advice about the hospital . . ."

Again she cried out incoherently, piercingly. He made out phrases of exclamation and question but scarcely any words except the persistent "No! No, no, no!" He attempted to interrupt. It was the operator, depositing the coin with a mechanical whirr, who put a stop to it. Elena, in fear, shrieked, "Asa!"

"Here. We haven't been cut off yet. I'm still on the wire. Listen, I'll get another doctor and be out myself after work."

"A specialist . . . I don't want anybody else."

Twice the operator demanded another coin. "Shut up!" Leventhal at last said, exasperated. "Can't you wait another second." But he was already talking on a dead line. He banged the instrument and jolted it aside with his elbow. Miss Ashmun seemed astonished. He gazed at her gloomily and presently picked up the phone again. He called the Harkavys. Harkavy's sister Julia had a child and should be able to recommend a good doctor. Harkavy's mother answered the phone. She was extremely fond of Leventhal and spoke to him cordially, asking about his wife. "But I guess it's Dan'l you want to talk to. 'Dan'l!'" she called. "He's home today."

Leventhal at once explained it was Julia he wanted. Afterward he regretted that he had not taken the opportunity to ask Harkavy about Kirby Allbee. But what a time it was to have thought of him!

5

A FTER a hurried supper of a sandwich and a bottle of soda at a stand near the ferry, Leventhal crossed to Staten Island. He walked onto the deck with his hands in the pockets of his fully buttoned, wrinkled jacket. His white shoes were soiled. Posted beside a life ring, his dark forehead shining faintly under his ill-combed, thick hair, he gazed out on the water with an appearance of composure; he did not look as burdened as he felt. The formless, working, yellowish-green water was dull, the gulls steered back and forth, the boat crept forward into the glare. A barge was spraying orange paint over the hull of a freighter, which pointed high, lifting its bow out of the slow, thick cloud. Surely the sun was no hotter in any Singapore or Surabaya, on the chains, plates, and rails of ships anchored there. A tanker, seabound, went across the ferry's course, and Leventhal stared after it, picturing the engine room; it was terrible, he imagined, on a day like this, the men nearly naked in the shaft alley as the huge thing rolled in a sweat of oil, the engines laboring. Each turn must be like a repeated strain on the hearts and ribs of the wipers, there near the keel, beneath the water. The towers on the shore rose up in huge blocks, scorched, smoky, gray, and bare white where the sun was direct upon them. The notion brushed Leventhal's mind that the light over them and over the water was akin to the yellow revealed in the slit of the eye of a wild animal, say a lion, something inhuman that didn't care about anything human and yet was implanted in every human being too, one speck of it, and formed a part of him that responded to the heat and the glare, exhausting as these were, or even to freezing, salty things, harsh things, all things difficult to stand. The Jersey shore, yellow, tawny, and flat, appeared on the right. The Statue of Liberty rose and traveled backwards again; in the trembling air, it was black, a twist of black that stood up like smoke. Stray planks and waterlogged, foundering crates washed back in the boat's swell.

The specialist was coming. But what he could do depended on Elena. Contagious cases were hospitalized; the health authorities were called in. But the first doctor seemed to have given up the struggle with Elena, and presumably he knew the law. With unconscious grimness, Leventhal prepared himself to struggle with her. As long as she held out, all the specialists in the world were futile. The prospect of interfering, rushing in to rescue the boy, was repugnant to him; it made him feel, more than ever, that he was an outsider. But what could you do with Elena? To begin with, ordinary good care might have kept the child from falling sick, and judging from what he had seen . . . well, her fear of the hospital was an indication of her fitness to bring up children. Some people would say that she loved them and that her love made up for her shortcomings—not to look too closely at those shortcomings. Love, by all means. But because the mother and the child were tied together in that way, if the child died through her ignorance, was she still a good mother? Should someone else—he thought of it seriously—have the right to take the child away? Or should the fate of the two of them be considered one and the same, and the child's death said to be the mother's affair only because she would suffer most by its death? In that case the child was not regarded as a person, and was that fair? Well, that was the meaning of helplessness; that was what they meant when they said it. Now with that in mind you could understand why little children sometimes cried the way they did. It was as if it were in them to know. Unfair, thought Leventhal, not to say tragic.

He began to consider his own unfortunate mother whose large features and black hair he could summon up very faintly. Invariably he saw her wearing an abstracted look, but he was not in fact sure that her look was abstracted. Perhaps he attributed it to her. And when he examined his idea of her more closely he realized that what he really meant by abstracted was mad-looking; a familiar face and yet without anything in it directed toward him. He dreaded it; he dreaded the manifestation of anything resembling it in himself. A period of coolness toward Harkavy had followed the latter's remark about persecution. Knowing his history, how could Harkavy say that to him? But eventually he satisfied himself that Harkavy was merely thoughtless and didn't sufficiently understand what he was saying. Until he spoke, he himself didn't know what was coming. So he had forgiven Harkavy, but he was left more conscious of his susceptibility to remarks of that kind. He was afraid the truth about him was so apparent that even Harkavy might see it.

He had spoken of his fears to Mary late one night in bed. She laughed at him. Why did he accept his father's explanation of his mother's illness? And he had never really learned the facts about it, it was true. He had only his father's word for it that she died insane. Many of the things that terrified people lost their horror when a doctor explained them. Years ago everyone spoke of brain fever; now it was known that there was no such sickness. "For my own peace of mind," Mary said, "I would try to find out what she had." But, although Leventhal then promised that he would go into the matter soon, make a real inquiry, so far he had done nothing about it. As for his fears, he was too ready, Mary told him, to believe anything and everything about himself. "That's because you're not sure of yourself. If you were a little more sure you wouldn't let yourself be bothered," she said with all the firmness of her own confident strength. And she was probably right. But, my God, how could anyone say that he was sure? How could he know all that he needed to know in order to say it? It wasn't right. Leventhal felt the presumption of it without, however, blaming Mary; he knew she expressed truthfully what she felt.

"The only proof there is of anything wrong with your mother is that she married that father of yours," Mary had ended. This remark brought tears into Leventhal's eyes as he sat in the dark, cross-legged, bending away from the pillow at his back. Nevertheless Mary's words were beneficial on the whole. Till he had better evidence, his fears were the fears of hypochondria. The word was helpful; it gave them an amusing aspect. Still the fact remained that when he called up his mother's face at some moment it was, for all of that, abstracted.

He gazed down at the dented deck brass. For the present he preferred to be cautious about Elena and assume that her nerves were overworked. She gave way without control to what any parent with a sick child was liable to feel. But when he allowed himself to go further, to think of more than over-worked nerves and Italian emotions, he saw the parallel between her and his mother and, for that matter, between himself and Max and the two children. The last was not so important. But it gave him a clearer view of each of the women to consider that they were perhaps alike. At least you could say of them that they were both extraordinary when they were disturbed (he had not forgotten his mother's screaming)—whatever the right word for it was.

The winches began to rattle, a gate dropped resoundingly in the green wooden cove of the slip. The water turned yellow and white under the bows like stale city snow. The boat started back and then, with shut engines, glided in, bumping the weedy timbers. On the long hill beyond the arches of the sheds, the house fronts were suddenly present, and Leventhal, moving ashore in the crowd, heard the busses throbbing before the station.

Philip again let him in. Recognizing his uncle he stood aside for him.

"Where's Elena. Is she here?" Leventhal said, striding into the dining room. "How's the boy?"

"He's sleeping. Ma's downstairs using Villani's telephone. She said she'd be up right away." He turned to the kitchen, explaining from the doorway, "I was eating supper."

"Go ahead, finish," said Leventhal. He walked restlessly round the room. Mickey was asleep; the second alarm seemed to be like the first. Touching the hall door, he debated whether to go into the child's room alone. No, it would be wiser not to; there was no telling how Elena would take it.

It was shortly before sundown, and there were lights in the flats giving on the airshaft where the walls, for a short distance below the black cornice, were reddened by the sky. Leventhal went into the kitchen where Philip sat beside the table on a high stepstool. He had a bowl of dry cereal before him and he poured milk over it, digging up the flap of the milk carton with his thumbnail; he peeled and sliced a banana, sprinkled sugar over it, and flipped the skin into the sink with its pans and dishes. The paper frills along the shelves of the cupboard crackled in the current of the fan. It ran on the cabinet, sooty, with insectlike swiftness and a thrumming of its soft rubber blades; it suggested a fly hovering below the tarnish and heat of the ceiling and beside the scaling, many-jointed, curved pipes on which Elena hung rags to dry. The boy's knees were level with the tabletop, and he bent almost double as he ate, spreading his legs. Leventhal reflected that he had taken the stool instead of a chair because he felt the need to do something extreme in his presence. "I used to do stunts, too, when there was a visitor," he reminded himself. "And that is what I am here, a visitor."

"Is this your whole supper?" he asked.

"When it's hot like this, I never eat a lot." The boy had a rather precise way of speaking.

"You ought to have bread and butter, and so on, and greens," said Leventhal.

Philip interrupted his eating to look at his uncle briefly. "We don't cook much during the heat wave," he said. He set his feet on a higher rung and bent even lower. His hair had been newly cut, roughly clipped on top and shaved high up the back of his neck to a line above his large but delicately white ears.

"What kind of a barber do you have?"

Philip looked up again. "Oh, Jack McCaul on the block. We all go to him; Dad too, when he's home. I told him to cut it this way. I asked for a summer haircut."

"They ought to take away the man's license for giving you one like that." He said this too forcefully and overshot his intended joke, and he paused and made an effort to find the right tone.

"Oh, McCaul's all right," said Philip. "He takes care of us. I was waiting for the kid to get better so's we could go together. But Ma said I should go and have a trim before she had to buy me a fiddle to go with my hair. This haircut is all right for the weather. Last summer I got a baldie—all off."

"Well, it's really okay." Leventhal watched him eat, penetrated with sympathy for him. "An independent little boy," he thought. "But how they treat him."

He sat down by the window, unbuttoning his creased jacket, and glanced at the sky through the airshaft's black square. In one of the other flats, a girl in a parlor chair was brushing a dog that yawned and tried to lick her hand. She pushed its muzzle down. A woman in a chemise passed through the room, back and forth from kitchen to hall. Mickey's window gave on the shaft; it was on the corner, and if he were awake now he might be able to see his brother and his uncle.

"The doctor's going to be here any minute." Leventhal was suddenly impatient. "I thought Elena was in such a hurry for him to come. What's keeping her?"

"I'll go and see." Philip sprang from the stool.

"Don't leave your supper. Tell me where she is and I'll find her." But Philip was already in the corridor. Leventhal, however, instead of footsteps, heard voices through the open doors. Had he met Elena coming up the stairs? The light went on in the dining room, under the green glass panes of the shade, and Leventhal had a glimpse of a woman in a black dress moving beside the table.

"Boy?" he called out. "Say, Phil?"

"Here. Come on in."

"Who is it?" he inquired in a low voice. He tried to see beyond the lamp to the other end of the room.

"My grandmother."

"The old woman?" said Leventhal in surprise. He had heard something about her from Max but had never seen her. He started from the doorway and, looking confused, went toward her around the dining-room table, changing his direction when she turned and sat down in the mohair armchair.

"This is Dad's brother," Philip said to her. Leventhal was conscious of prolonging his nod almost into a bow; he wanted to be prepossessing. The old lady gave him only a brief sharp glance. Taller than Elena, she was gaunt and straight-backed, and the carriage of her head was tense. She wore large gold earrings. The hair came out short and white at her temples; toward the back of her head it was black and tightly knotted. Her dress also was black, a black silk, and despite the heat she wore a shawl on her shoulders.

Since she remained silent, Leventhal stood undecided; it seemed inadvisable to say more; to sit down without being answered would embarrass him. But, also, it might be impolite to return to the kitchen. Maybe he misunderstood her taciturnity. However, she seemed to avert her head from him, and he had to struggle with an angry urge to compel her to face him. Nevertheless she had not spoken, and he could not be sure. It was possible that he was mistaken.

"I thought you were going to fetch your mother," he said

to Philip somewhat impatiently. And when Philip started to leave, he said hastily, "I'll go with you." He had decided that the grandmother's look was unfriendly, though in the dusty green-tinged light that came through the lampshade it was difficult to get a definite impression. But he felt her antagonism. In a shambling gait—the heat made him heavy—he followed Philip down several turns of the stairs to the neighbor's flat. Philip knocked, and in a few seconds Elena came hurrying out to them, eager and fearful.

"Oh, Asa, you," she said. "And the specialist? Did you bring him?"

"He said between seven and eight. He ought to be here soon."

The neighbor, Mr. Villani, smoking a twisted stogie, appeared in the hallway and cried out to her, "You let us know right away what he says about the boy up there." He looked at Leventhal, perfectly unconstrained in his curiosity. "How do?" he said to him.

"This is my husband's brother," said Elena.

"Yes, sure," said Villani taking the cigar out of his mouth. Leventhal impassively looked back at him, his eyes solemn and uncommunicative, only a little formally inquiring. A drop of sweat ran down his cheek. Villani, one hand in his pocket, spread his trousers wide. "You look like Mr. Leventhal, all right," he said. He turned to Elena. "And what the doctor tells you, you do it, missis, you hear? We're gonna pull that boy through, so don't worry. What I think is he's only got summer fever," he said to Leventhal. "It ain't serious. My kids had it. But this missis is the worrying kind."

"It's plenty serious," said Elena. She spoke quietly, but Leventhal, watching her closely and paying particular attention to the expression of her eyes, felt a pang of his peculiar dread at their sudden widening.

"Ah, ah, how do you know? Are you a doctor? Wait a while."

"The man is right, I think, Elena," said Leventhal.

"Sure I am. You got to have confidence in the doctor." An impassioned, sharp sound caught in his throat and he flung his arm out in a short, stiff, eloquent curve. "What's the matter! Sure! You listen to me. That boy is all right." The cigar glowed in his fingers.

"She'll have confidence," Leventhal assured him.

They started upstairs. On the fourth floor Elena stopped and with an excited escape of breath, "Phillie, what did you tell me—Grandma's here?"

"She just came."

"Oh my!" She turned with anxious abruptness to Leventhal. "What did she say to you, anything?"

"Not a single word."

"Oh, Asa, if she does. . . . Oh, I hope to God she doesn't. Let her say what she wants. Just let it pass."

"Oh, sure," he said.

"She's a very peculiar type of person, my mother. She acted terrible when Max and I got married. She wanted to throw me out of the house because I was going with him. I couldn't bring him in. I had to meet him outside."

"Max mentioned once or twice. . . ."

"She's an awfully strict Catholic. She said if I married anybody but a Catholic she wouldn't have any more to do with me. She would curse me. So when I left the house she did. I didn't even see her until Phillie was born. I still don't see her much, but since Mickey is sick she's here pretty often. If Max is home she won't even come in. She's very superstitious, my mother. She has all the old-country ways. She thinks she's still in Sicily." Elena spoke in a near-whisper, covering the side of her face with her hand.

"Don't worry, I'll know how to take her."

"She just is that way," Elena explained, smiling helplessly.

"You can stop worrying."

The old woman met them in the hallway and she began immediately to speak to her daughter, her eyes occasionally moving to Leventhal's face. Her voice had what to him was a characteristic Italian hoarseness. Her long head was drawn back rigidly on her black shoulders. He observed how she turned down her underlip, exposing her teeth as she lingered on a syllable. Elena, dejected, shook her head and answered in short phrases. Leventhal tried to seize a word here and there. He understood nothing. Suddenly Elena interrupted her mother, crying out, "Where? Why didn't you say so right away, Mamma? Where is he? The man is here!" she exclaimed to Leventhal. "The specialist!" She ran in. Leventhal, walking behind the grandmother in the hall leading to the bedroom, contorted his face in an unusual release of feeling. Ugly old witch! To make her daughter wait and listen to her complaints before telling her the doctor had arrived. "Parents!" he muttered. "Oh, yes, parents! My eye, parents!" He was tempted to jostle her.

They entered the bedroom. The doctor had pulled up Mickey's shirt and was listening to his heart. The child seemed scarcely awake; he was dull and submitted to the examination, listless with the fever, lifting his eyes only to his mother, identifying rather than appealing to her. Philip leaned on the bedpost to see him.

"Phil, don't shake, stay off it," Elena said.

The doctor turned a glance over his shoulder. He was a young man with a long, rosy face and thin, gold-rimmed lenses over his close-set eyes. While he pressed the stethoscope on the child's chest and shoulders, he looked steadily at Leventhal, evidently taking him for the father. At first Leventhal was bothered by this error. Soon, however, he grasped the fact that the doctor was trying to tell him the illness was serious. Unobserved by Elena, who was folding back the counterpane, he gave him a gloomy nod to show that he understood. The doctor let the earpieces of the instrument fall around his neck and felt the boy's arms with his clean red fingers. In the yellowish, stiff web over the blackness of the window, the ferns and the immense moths were shot with holes and gaps. The kitchen air and the noises of the court entered the room. The boy was raised and his pillow turned over.

"You should sponge him every few hours," said the doctor.

"I did it this afternoon. I'll do it again soon," said Elena.

She had been whispering to him from time to time and now she spoke up eagerly, almost joyfully. She seemed to feel there was nothing to fear any longer. "I trust him so much," she said to Leventhal, gazing at the doctor. Leventhal's hands were damp and chill. He was beginning to feel ill from the sudden doubling of his tension. He wiped his face, passing the handkerchief over the bristles on his cheek and leaving a piece of lint on them. He was sure he had interpreted the doctor's silent communication correctly. Elena's hopefulness stunned him. He turned, careworn, looking at her and at the

children, and a few moments passed before it came to him
that this burden after all belonged to his brother. At once he
was furious with Max for being away. He had no right to go
in the first place. Leventhal felt for his wallet; he had put
Max's card in it. He would wire him tonight. Or no, a night
letter was better, he could put more into it. He began to form
the message in his mind. "Dear Max, if you can tear yourself
away from what you're doing . . . if you can manage to get
away for a while . . ." He would not spare him. The harsher
the better. Just look at what he left behind him: this house, a
tenement; Elena, who might herself need taking care of; the
children they had brought into the world. Leventhal returned
to the composition of the night letter. "You are needed here.
Imperative." That it was he, almost a stranger to the family,
who was sending the message, should show Max how serious
the matter was. Ah, what a business! And the grandmother? If
anything happened to the boy she would consider it in the
nature of a judgment on the marriage. The marriage was impure to her. Yes, he understood how she felt about it. A Jew,
a man of wrong blood, of bad blood, had given her daughter
two children, and that was why this was happening. No one
could have persuaded Leventhal that he was wrong. Hardly
hearing what was being said in the room, he contemplated
her grimly, her grizzled temples, the thin straight line of her
nose, the severity of her head pressed back on her shoulders,
the baring of her teeth as she opened her lips to make a remark to her daughter. No, he was not wrong. From her
standpoint it was inevitable punishment—that was how she
would see it, a punishment. Whatever else she might feel—
and after all the boy was her grandson—she would feel this
first.

He just then observed great agitation in Elena and began
to pay attention to the conversation. He heard the doctor
speaking of the hospital and he thought, "She can't keep the
kid here any more. She'll have to give in."

"I told her yesterday she ought to send him to the hospital," he said.

Elena still resisted. "But why isn't it just as good for him at
home? Better. I can look after him better than a nurse."

"He's got to go if you want me to take the case."

"But what's the matter here?" she pleaded.

"Has to be done," said the doctor knocking up the clips of his bag.

"Should I go for a cab?" Philip softly asked his uncle.

Leventhal nodded. Philip ran from the room.

6

THE DOCTOR told Leventhal on the way back to Manhattan that he thought—though he needed more evidence to confirm the diagnosis—Mickey had a bronchial infection of a rare kind. He named it two or three times, and Leventhal tried to fix it in his mind but failed. Such cases were serious; not necessarily fatal, however. "You think you'll be able to help him, doctor?" he asked in great eagerness, and the doctor's word of hope raised his spirits. The boat moved out; the immense golden crowns of light above the sheds now had space to play on the water between the stern and the shore. "I was going to wire my brother to come," said Leventhal—he had already explained that he was not the father. The doctor answered that he didn't think it was necessary at present. It was enough to tell him to stand by. Leventhal accepted this as sensible advice. Why create a scare now? It wasn't so critical after all. He would send Max a night letter and let him decide for himself whether to come or wait. The ferry crawled in the heat and blackness of the harbor. The mass of passengers on the open deck was still, like a crowd of souls, each concentrating on its destination. The thin discs of the doctor's spectacles were turned to the sky, both illumined in the same degree by the bulb over his head. Leventhal wanted to ask him more about the disease. It was rare. Well, did medicine have any idea how a thing like that singled out a child in Staten Island rather than, say, St. Louis or Denver? One child in thousands. How did they account for it? Did everyone have it dormant? Could it be hereditary? Or, on the other hand, was it even more strange that people, so different, no two with the same fingerprints, did not have more individual diseases? Freed from his depression by the doctor's encouragement, he had a great desire to talk. He would have liked to discuss this but he had already asked the name of the disease several times and failed to retain it, and so the doctor must have a poor opinion of him. And maybe he would be condescending to a layman. Accordingly, Leventhal was silent and thought, "Well, let it ride." But he continued to wonder about it. They said that God was no respecter of persons, meaning that there were the same rules for everybody. Where was that? He tried to remember.

They were in the middle of the harbor when the heat was suddenly lifted by a breeze. High and low between the shores, the lights of ships, signals, and bridges drifted and ran, curved, and stood riding on the swell, and the sonorous, rather desolate bells rang from the water when the buoys were stirred. The breeze blew a spray to the deck, and the boat now and then seemed to tremble to the pull of the ocean beyond the islands. As they neared the Manhattan side, people began to get up from the benches in the salon; there was a great press when the chains were dropped. Leventhal was separated from the doctor.

He went home on the subway, pushing through the revolving steel gate at his station and breathing the cooler air of the street with deep relief.

He was expecting a letter from Mary—one was about due —and he opened the mailbox swiftly while Nunez' dog sniffed at his legs. Instead of a letter, Mary had sent two post cards closely covered with writing. She and her mother were starting for Charleston on Friday. The house was sold. They were both well and she hoped he was, too, in spite of the heat. It was fine old Baltimore summer weather—it simply drugged you. The second card was different; there were intimate references on it. Only Mary could write such things on cards for everybody in the world to read. Amused, proud, pleased with her, pleased rather than embarrassed at the possibility that postal clerks had read the cards, he put them in his pocket. "Do I pass inspection?" he demanded of Nunez' dog. "Blow now." Stooping he caught the dog's head and rubbed it. He started up stairs and the animal came after him. "Blow now, I say." He barred the way with his leg, then whirled inside and slammed the hall-door. "Go home!" he yelled, and laughed uproariously. "Go on home!" He pounded the glass, and the dog barked raucously and leaped at the pane. Leventhal told one of the neighbors, whom he hardly knew, "The super's dog is having a fit. Hear him?" An elderly, guarded, pale face gave him an uncertain smile and seemed to listen in awe to the racket in the foyer. Leventhal hurried up with thumping steps, whipping his hat on the banister and entering his flat with a commotion. Dear Mary! If she were only here now to put his arms around and kiss. He flung away his hat and his jacket, pulled off his shoes, and went to open the windows and push aside the curtains. It had turned into a beautiful night. The air was trembling and splendid. The moon had come out; there were wide-spaced stars, and small clouds pausing and then spinning as the cool gusts broke through the heat.

He lit the lamp on the secretary and began to write to his wife. Gnats fell and rose again from the illuminated green blotter. He gave her an account of himself, forgetting that he had felt nervous, restive, and unwell. He said nothing about what had happened at the office. It did not seem worth saying. He wrote swiftly and exuberantly; he discussed the weather, he mentioned that Wilma had drunk the beer, that the parks were terribly crowded. Then he found himself telling her about his nephew, writing with sudden emotion, the words beginning to sprawl as his hand raced. In a changed tone he described Elena. He had been afraid to look at her, he confessed, when she got into the cab and he laid the bundled-up child—she had him in two blankets although the temperature must have been over ninety—on her lap. All the impressions of the moment returned to him—the boy's eyes with the light of the meter on them, the leathery closeness of the back seat, the driver's undershot jaw and the long peak of his black cap, Philip's crying, Villani keeping back the children on the sidewalk. The beating of Leventhal's heart rose and his tongue became dry. As for his brother . . . But when he had written Max's name he stood up and leaned over the paper. He had meant to send the night letter before coming up. The pen was staining his fingers. He dropped it and began looking for his shoes outside the circle of lamplight. He had just found them and was forcing his feet into them without bothering about the laces when his bell rang, piercingly and long. Leventhal straightened up with a grunt of annoyance and surprise. "Now who in the name of hell would ring like that?" he said. But he already knew who it was. It was Allbee. It must be. He opened the door and listened to the regular sibilance and knocking of the footsteps in the hollow stair well. It occurred to him that he could escape Allbee by going to the roof. If he went out stealthily he could still get away. And if he were followed, the next rooftop was only a matter of six inches away, an easy step over. Then he could get into the street and good-by. He could go even now. Even *now*. Yet he stood firm and strangely enough he felt that he had proved something by doing so. "I won't give ground," he thought. "Let him. Why should I?" He promptly went back to his letter, leaving the door open. He finished it abruptly with a few perfunctory sentences and read it over. He wrote "All my love," signed his name, addressed the envelope, and by that time Allbee was in the room. He knew that he had come in; nevertheless he controlled his desire to turn. He stamped the envelope first, sealed it, momentarily guessed at its weight, and only then did he appear to take notice of his visitor, who smiled at him without parting his lips. To enter without a knock or invitation was an intrusion. Of course the door was open, but it was taking too much for granted all the same not to knock. Leventhal thought there was a trace of delight in the defiance of Allbee's look. "I *owe* him hospitality, that's how he behaves," passed through his mind.

"Yes," he said tonelessly, indifferently polite.

"You're well fixed up here," said Allbee taking in the room. He might have been comparing it with his own place. Leventhal could imagine what that was like.

"As long as you're here, sit down," Leventhal said. "What's the use of standing?" He would not get rid of him without hearing him out, and it might as well be now as another time.

"Much obliged," said Allbee. His head came forward courteously and he seemed to read Leventhal's face. "It's a long pull up those stairs. I'm not used to these high walk-ups." He drew a chair close to the desk, crossed his legs, and clasped his knee with somewhat rigid fingers. His cuffs were frayed, the threads raveled on the blond hairs of his wrist. His hands were dirty. His fair hair, unevenly divided on his scalp, was damp. It was apparently true that the climb had been hard for him. "It's quite a height, this," he smiled. "And for me, well . . ." he caught his breath, "I'm used to low places." He pointed his finger at the floor and worked it as though pulling a trigger.

"Are you here to give me the same song and dance as the last time? Because if you are let me tell you once and for all . . ."

"Oh, hold on," said Allbee. "Let's be sensible and open. I didn't come to complain to you. Why should I? I only said what's obvious. Nothing to wrangle about. I'm on the bottom. You don't want to deny that, do you?" He extended his arms as if to offer himself for examination, and although he did it wryly Leventhal saw that he was really in earnest. "Whereas you . . ."

He indicated the flat. Leventhal said, "Oh, please," and shook his head. "Don't give me that stuff."

"It's a fact, a hard fact," said Allbee. "I'm the best judge of the facts. I know them intimately. This isn't just theoretical with me. The distance between you and me is greater than between you and the greatest millionaire in America. When I compare myself with you, why you're in the empyrean, as they used to say at school, and I'm in the pit. And I have been in your position but you have never been in mine."

"What do you mean? I've been down and out."

Allbee gave him a tolerant smile.

"Stony broke, without a nickel for the automat," Leventhal said.

"Ah, go on. You don't know anything about it, I can tell by your talk. You've never been in my place. Nickels for the automat . . . temporary embarrassment. That . . ." and he ended with his head to one side nearly touching his shoulder, and with his outstretched arm and open hand he made a gesture of passing the comparison away. There rose immediately to Leventhal's mind the most horrible images of men wearily sitting on mission benches waiting for their coffee in a smeared and bleary winter sun; of flophouse sheets and filthy pillows; hideous cardboard cubicles painted to resemble wood, even the tungsten in the bulb like little burning worms that seemed to eat up rather than give light. Better to be in the dark. He had seen such places. He could still smell the carbolic disinfectant. And if it were *his* flesh on those sheets, *his* lips drinking that coffee, *his* back and thighs in that winter sun, *his* eyes looking at the boards of the floor. . . ? Allbee was right to smile at him; he had never been in such a plight. "So I'm mistaken," he reflected. "Why do I have to match him in that? Is it necessary? Anyway, what does he want?" For a time he forgot about the night letter. He waited for Allbee to reveal what he had come for. He did not know just what to expect, but he considered it very likely that he would repeat his charge despite his saying that he was not here to complain.

"Well," he said, prefacing his remark with a short laugh. "It's a peculiar statement to begin a visit with."

"Why, no. What could be better. It's the height of politeness to admire your host's house. And the contrast between us should please you very much. It should give you a lot of satisfaction to have done it all yourself."

"Done what myself?" said Leventhal suspiciously.

"Raised yourself up, I mean," said Allbee quickly. "You were just telling me you were once broke, which is to say that you're a self-made man. There's a lot of satisfaction in that, isn't there? And when you see somebody that hasn't made out so well it adds something to your satisfaction. It's only human. Even if you know better."

"I didn't say I was a self-made man or any such thing. That's a lot of nonsense."

"I'm glad to be corrected then," Allbee replied. "I must have had the wrong impression. Because, you know, the more I think about it the more I feel it's bunk, this self-made business. The day of succeeding by your own efforts is past. Now it's all blind movement, vast movement, and the individual is shuttled back and forth. He only thinks he's the works. But that isn't the way it is. Groups, organizations succeed or fail, but not individuals any longer. Don't you agree?"

"Oh, it's not that way, exactly," Leventhal said. "No, I don't."

"You don't agree that people have a destiny forced on them? Well, that's ridiculous, because they do. And that's all the destiny they get, so they'd better not assume they're running their own show. That's the kind of mistake I wouldn't care to make. There's nothing worse than being confused, too, in addition to being unlucky. But you find people who have their luck and take the credit for it, too—all brains and personality, when all that happened was that they were handed a bucket when it rained."

"Let's have this cleared up right now, if you please," said Leventhal coldly. "We might as well be open and aboveboard. What does all this lead up to?"

"Oh, it doesn't lead to anything. It's just discussion, talk. Talk, talk, talk, talk, talk!" he exclaimed grinning, flinging up his hands. His eyes began to shine.

Leventhal impassively looked at him. "And what's that for?" he asked.

Allbee now appeared to be very depressed, perhaps at his own unsteadiness, and Leventhal was a little sorry for him. His alternation of moods, however, affected him unpleasantly. It was clear that the man was no fool. But what was the use of not being a fool if you acted like this? For instance, there was his language, did he have to speak like that, make himself sound so grand? Because he needed something to brace himself on? Oh, there was a smashup somewhere, certainly, a smashup and a tragic one, you could be sure of that. Something crushing, a real smash. But the question that remained uppermost with Leventhal was, "What does he want?" And notwithstanding his insistence on being aboveboard, he was unable to ask it.

"Is that your wife?" Allbee looked over Leventhal's head at a framed photograph on the secretary.

"Yes, that's Mary."

"Oh, say, she's charming. Ah, you're lucky, you know?" He stood up and bent over him, turning the photograph to the light. "She is charming."

"It's a good picture of her," said Leventhal, not liking his enthusiasm.

"She has that proud look that's proud without being hard. You know what I mean. It's a serious look. You see it in Asiatic sculpture."

"Oh—Asiatic!" said Leventhal scoffing.

"Certainly, Asiatic. Look at the eyes, and those cheekbones. You're married to a woman and don't know she has slant eyes?" He made a descriptive turn of his thumb. "She's positively Asiatic."

"She comes from Baltimore."

"First generation?"

"Her mother is native-born, too. Further back than that I don't know."

"I'm willing to bet they came from Eastern Europe, originally," said Allbee.

"Why, that's not so stupendous. You wouldn't get any takers."

"I know I wouldn't get any takers in your case."

"No? Maybe since you investigated me and found out so much about me, you took the trouble to find out what part of Europe my parents came from."

"It's apparent enough; it doesn't need any investigating. Russia, Poland . . . I can see at a glance."

"You can, ah?"

"Well, of course. I've lived in New York for a long time. It's a very Jewish city, and a person would have to be a pretty sloppy observer not to learn a lot about Jews here. You know yourself how many Jewish dishes there are in the cafeterias, how much of the stage—how many Jewish comedians and jokes, and stores, and so on, and Jews in public life, and so on. You know that. It's no revelation."

Leventhal refrained from answering. It was, after all, no revelation.

Allbee once more turned his attention to Mary's picture. As he studied it and nodded, his eyes, to Leventhal's amazement, filled with tears, and he took on an expression of suppressed grief and injury.

"*Your* wife . . . ?" Leventhal ventured in a low voice.

"She's dead," replied Allbee.

Leventhal's tone fell even lower as he said, with a resonance of horror, "Dead? Oh, too bad. I'm sorry. . . ."

"So you should be. So you should." The words seemed to have been brought up from Allbee's chest as if they had been stored there and were now dislodged and uttered irregularly before he could hold them back.

Leventhal concentrated on them, averting his face—a characteristic of his when he was puzzling something out. He did not understand what Allbee meant.

"Of course I should be," he murmured, not quite aware that he was acknowledging a charge. The things that had happened to him in the last two days had made him acutely responsive, quick to feel. "What a shame!" he said in deep emotion, recalling the woman's face. "She was much too good for him, much too good," he thought. "But why should I say that? He was her husband, so that doesn't enter in now. He has to be considered. She's dead, but he's alive and feels. That's what brought him down. He wouldn't be like this otherwise."

"So you're alone, now," he said.

"Yes, I'm a widower, have been for over four years. Four years and about three weeks."

"And how did it happen?"

"I don't know exactly. I wasn't with her. Her family wrote the news. She was hurt in an automobile accident. They thought she would recover, but she died suddenly. That's all I know. She was buried before I had a chance to get to Louisville."

"They didn't wait till you came?"

"Well, to tell you the truth I didn't want to be there. It would have been a terrible business. The family would have relieved itself by being angry with me. I would have tried to relieve myself by sneaking out to a bar, probably sat in the bar and missed the whole thing. That would have made it ten times worse for everybody. I was in that condition. And it was hot then. Louisville in hot weather. For *that*! Oh no, brother, I holed up where I was. It would have been brutal. She was dead. I wouldn't have been going to see *her* but *them*, her people. Dead is dead. Finished. No more. You long for your wife when she goes, if you love her. And maybe sometimes if you don't love her so much. I wouldn't know. But you're together, she bends to you and you bend to her in everything, and when she dies there you stand, bent, and look senseless, fit nothing. That's my personal feeling. Of course, I'm the first kind. I loved her. Well, I say, you long for her . . . but everything inanimate is the same to me. I'm not sentimental."

He was acting, lying, Leventhal decided. His moment of genuineness had passed and once more he had taken up his poise, mystifyingly off center and precarious. When he had announced his wife's death, he had sounded wrathful, but Leventhal had felt himself come nearer to him or to something clear, familiar, and truthful in him. Now he was repelled again. He wondered whether Allbee was not actually a little drunk.

"But," said Allbee, "that's not all there is to it."

"No? There's more, eh?"

"Somewhat. We were separated before she died. That's why my relations with her family weren't good. Naturally, from their standpoint . . ." He paused to rub his eyelid and when he stopped it was red and appeared to have gone lower than the other. "They were prejudiced against me, wanted to shove the whole blame on me. I could blame them, if I wanted to. Her brother was driving the car; got off with scratches and a few bangs. The way those Southerners drive. Pickett's charge over and over again. Well . . . we were separated. Do you know why?"

"Why?"

"Because after Rudiger fired me, I couldn't get a job."

"What do you mean? You couldn't find any jobs? No jobs at all?"

"Not in my line. What could I have earned at any job? Not enough to keep going. After a man spends years in one line he doesn't want to change. He isn't in a position to do much. In something else he has to start at the bottom. What was I going to do, become a peddler? Salesman? Besides, I'd have to stop looking for what I wanted by taking any job."

"I would have taken anything before I let my wife go."

"We're made of different stuff, you and I." Allbee grinned. "And I didn't let her go. She left me. I didn't want her to go. She was the one."

"You're not telling me all there is to tell."

"No, no," he said, almost delightedly. "I'm not. And what's the rest? You tell me."

"Didn't your boozing have something to do with it?"

"Oh, there you go, there you go," said Allbee, smiling at the floor and swaying his large frame slightly. "My vice, my terrible vice. She left me because of my drinking. That's the ticket."

"A woman doesn't leave her husband for anything—just for a trifle."

"That's perfectly true, she doesn't. You're a true Jew, Leventhal. You have the true horror of drink. We're the sons of Belial to you, we smell of whisky worse than of sulphur. When

Noah lies drunk—you remember that story?—his gentile-minded sons have a laugh at the old man, but his Jewish son is horrified. There's truth in that story. It's a true story."

"Watch your talk," said Leventhal stiffly. "You sound like a fool. I don't know what you're after, but you're not doing yourself any good with talk like that. I tell you that straight."

"Well . . ." he began; but he arrested himself. "All right, never mind. But it's unfair to try to put the blame for my wife's death on me. It's worse than unfair; it's cruel when you consider what she was to me and what I've been through. I don't know how you look at it, but I take it for granted that we're not gods, we're only creatures, and the things we some-times think are permanent, they aren't permanent. So one day we're like full bundles and the next we're wrapping-paper, blowing around the streets."

"But I warn you I won't stand for such talk. Get that!" Leventhal spoke curtly, and Allbee seemed to lose his pres-ence of mind and lowered his head, grieved and incapable of answering. It was hard to tell whether he was looking for the strength to continue, conniving something new, or disclosing his true state without pretense. Leventhal saw the side of his face, deeply indented at the lid and mouth, his cheek and chin covered with golden bristles, the blue of his eye fixed in brooding. The skin of his forehead, even-grained by the light of the lamp, was wet, and that of his jaw and throat was creased in a way that made Leventhal think of gills. Allbee's remark about creatures had touched his imagination in a sin-gular way, and for an instant he was no more human to him than a fish or crab or any fleshy thing in the water. But only for an instant, fleetingly, until Allbee moved and looked at him. He appeared discouraged and tired.

"You'll excuse me," said Leventhal with somewhat provocative politeness, "but I have a wire to send. I was about to go send it when you came." Did that sound like an inven-tion? Allbee might think so and interpret it as a maneuver to get rid of him. However, he had seen him writing when he entered, so why shouldn't it be true? He might have been drafting the message. Anyhow, why should he care? And be-sides, it was absolutely a fact that he was going to wire Max. Allbee could come along and check up on him if he wanted to. He studied his face to see how he was taking it. Allbee had risen. Suddenly Leventhal twisted about and his heart sprang. He thought he had seen a mouse dart into the corner and he hurried after it, lit a match, and examined the molding. There was no hole. "Ran away!" he thought. Or was it his fancy? "We have mice here," he explained to Allbee, who was at the door in the dark vestibule. He seemed to turn his head away, unresponding.

When they reached the lower hall, Allbee stopped and said, "You try to put all the blame on me, but you know it's true that you're to blame. You and you only. For everything. You ruined me. Ruined! Because that's what I am, ruined! You're the one that's responsible. You did it to me deliberately, out of hate. Out of pure hate!"

He had clutched Leventhal's shirt and he twisted it as he spoke.

"You're crazy!" Leventhal shouted in his face. "You're a crazy stumblebum, that's what you are. The booze is eating your brain up. Take your hands off me. Off, I say!" He pushed Allbee with all the force of his powerful arms. He fell against the wall with an impact that sickened Leventhal. Allbee stood up, wiped his mouth, and stared at his hand.

"No blood. Too bad. Then you could say I spilled your blood, too," Leventhal cried.

Allbee answered nothing. He dusted his clothes unskillfully, stiff-handedly, as though beating his arms. Then he went. Leventhal watched his hasty, unsteady progress down the street.

Mr. Nunez, who had seen the incident, started up astride the striped canvas of his beach chair, and his wife, who lay on the bed near the window in a white slip, whispered, "*Que pasa?*" Leventhal looked at her in bewilderment.

THE NERVE of him, that damned clown!" said Leventhal fiercely. His high, thick chest felt intolerably bound and compressed, and he lifted his shoulders in an effort to ease his breathing. "Ruined! I'll ruin him if he comes near me. What a gall!"

The letter to Mary was crumpled in his hand. It was impossible to send it like this. He would have to get another envelope and stamp, and for a moment this inconvenience grew overwhelmingly into the worst consequence of the scuffle. He tore the letter open, crushed the envelope, and threw it over the balustrade. Nunez had gone into the house and he was alone on the stoop. His glance seemed to cover the street; in reality he saw almost nothing but was only aware of the featureless darkness and the equally featureless shine of bulbs the length of the block.

Then his anger began to sink. He drew in his cheeks, somberly enlarging his eyes. The skin about them felt dry and tight. To think up such a thing! The senselessness of it perturbed him most of all. "Why me?" he thought, frowning. "Of course, he has to have someone to blame; that's how it starts. But when he goes over everybody he knows, in that brain of his, how does he wind up with me?" That was what was puzzling. No doubt the Rudiger business had a bearing on it; for some reason it caught on, and worked on a deeper cause. But that alone, out of hundreds of alternatives, had snagged.

In a general way, anyone could see that there was great unfairness in one man's having all the comforts of life while another had nothing. But between man and man, how was this to be dealt with? Any derelict panhandler or bum might buttonhole you on the street and say, "The world wasn't made for you any more than it was for me, was it?" The error in this was to forget that neither man had made the arrangements, and so it was perfectly right to say, "Why pick on me? I didn't set this up any more than you did." Admittedly there was a wrong, a general wrong. Allbee, on the other hand, came along and said "*You!*" and that was what was so meaningless. For you might feel that something was owing to the pan-handler, but to be directly blamed was entirely different.

People met you once or twice and they hated you. What was the reason; what inspired it? This Allbee illustrated it well because he was too degenerate a drunk to hide his feelings. You had only to be yourself to provoke them. Why? A sigh of helplessness escaped Leventhal. If they still believed it would work, they would make little dolls of wax and stick pins into them. And why do they pick out this, that, or the other person to hate—Tom, Dick or Harry? No one can say. They hate your smile or the way you blow your nose or use a napkin. Anything will do for an excuse. And meanwhile this Harry, the object of it, doesn't even suspect. How should he know someone is carrying around an image of him (just as a woman may paste a lover's picture on the mirror of her vanity case or a man his wife's snapshot in his wallet), carrying it around to look at and hate? It doesn't even have to be a reproduction of poor Harry. It might as well be the king of diamonds with his embroidery, his whiskers, his sword, and all. It doesn't make a bit of difference. Leventhal had to confess that he himself had occasionally sinned in this respect, and he was not ordi-narily a malicious person. But certain people did call out this feeling. He saw Cohen, let us say, once or twice, and then, when his name was mentioned in company, let fall an un-complimentary remark about him. Not that this Cohen had ever offended him. But what were all the codes and rules, Leventhal reflected, except an answer to our own nature. Would we have to be told "Love!" if we loved as we breathed? No, obviously. Which was not to say that we didn't love but had to be assisted whenever the motor started miss-ing. The peculiar thing struck him that everything else in na-ture was bounded; trees, dogs, and ants didn't grow beyond a certain size. "But we," he thought, "we go in all directions without any limit."

He had put the letter in his pocket and he now took it out and debated whether to climb up to the flat for a stamp and envelope, or to try to buy them in a drugstore. He might not be able to obtain a single envelope. He did not want to buy a box of stationery.

Then he heard his name called and recognized Harkavy's voice.

"Is that you, Dan?" he said looking down the stairs at the dim, tall figure on the sidewalk. The shifting of the theater lights across the way made his vision uncertain. It was Harkavy. There were two women with him, one holding a child by the hand.

"Come down out of the clouds," said Harkavy. "Are you asleep, or something, on your feet?"

Nunez returned to his deck chair. His wife was in the window, resting her head on the sash.

"Do you go into a trance when the little woman is away?"

Harkavy's companions laughed.

"Dan, how are you?" said Leventhal, descending. "Oh, Mrs. Harkavy, so that's you?"

"Julia, Julia, too." Harkavy pointed at his sister with his cigarette holder.

"Julia, Mrs. Harkavy, glad to see you both."

"And my granddaughter Libbie," said Mrs. Harkavy.

"Oh, this is your girl, Julia?"

"Yes."

Leventhal tried to make out the child's features; he saw only the vivid pallor of her face and the reddish darkness of her hair.

"Very active, Libbie," said Harkavy. "A little too energetic, at times."

"Oh, she runs me ragged," Julia said. "I can't keep up with her."

"It's the food you give her. No child should have so much protein," said Mrs. Harkavy.

"Mother, she doesn't get more than others do. It's just her nature."

"We came to call on you," Harkavy said to Leventhal. "But it looks as if you're stepping out."

"I have a couple of errands," said Leventhal. "I was going to send a wire."

"We'll walk you to Western Union, then. Are you wiring Mary? I suppose you want her back already." Harkavy smiled.

"Daniel, it's not a thing to joke about, if a couple is devoted," his mother said. "It's nothing to ridicule. These days when marriages are so flimsy it's a real pleasure to see devotion. Couples go to City Hall like I might go to the five-and-dime to buy a hinge. Two boards on a hinge, and clap, clap, clap, that's a marriage. Wire your wife, Asa, it's the right thing and it's sweet. Never mind."

"It's my brother I've got to send the wire to, not Mary."

"Libbie, come here to me, here!" Julia furiously exclaimed, pulling the child's arm. "I'll tie you in the middle with strings!"

"Oh, your brother?" said Mrs. Harkavy.

Leventhal flushed, inexplicably. "Yes, it was his boy I called Julia about. My nephew."

"Did you get hold of the doctor?" Julia asked. "Doctor Denisart, mother."

"Oh, he's a fine doctor, Asa; his mother is a lodge sister of mine and I've known him since he was a boy. You can have confidence in him. They gave him the very best education. He studied in Holland."

"Austria, mother."

"Abroad, anyway. His uncle put him through. He was in jail afterwards, the uncle, for income taxes, but that wasn't the Denisarts' fault. They used to send him pheasant to Sing Sing and they say he was allowed to have card parties in his cell. But they really learn in Europe, you know. That's because their slums are worse; they get complicated cases in their clinics. Our standard of living is so high, it's bad for the education of our doctors."

"Why, who says so?" said Harkavy, looking at his mother with interest.

"Everybody. Why, all the medical books Papa used to bring home from the salesroom were full of European cases—Fraülein J. and Fraülein K. and Mademoiselle so and so. The best medical education is foreign."

"And how is your nephew?" Harkavy said.

"They took him to the hospital today."

"Oh, very sick, does that mean? I'm sorry to hear it," said Julia.

"Very."

"But you can depend on Doctor Denisart. He's a fine young man—brilliant. I'll talk to his mother tomorrow. He'll take more interest in the case."

"I'm sure he'd do his best without being spoken to," said Julia. They were walking, and she pressed her daughter's head to her side.

"Influence is a good thing," Mrs. Harkavy said. "You mustn't forget it. If you don't use it, you're left behind in the race of the swift. Everything depends on it. Of course, the doctor would do his best because of his ethics and so on, but if I talk to his mother he'll pay special attention to the case and do his very best. People are bound not to take things too much to heart, for their own protection. You've got to use influence on them."

"Take it up with Mrs. Denisart, then. It can't hurt," said Harkavy.

"I will."

"Dan," said Leventhal, drawing his friend behind, "do you remember a fellow called Allbee?"

"Allbee? Who? What's his last name?"

"Allbee is his last name. Kirby Allbee. We met him at Williston's. A big man. Blond."

"I suppose I could remember him if I put my mind to it. I have a pretty good memory."

They had come to the telegraph office, and Leventhal, standing at the yellow pine counter, wrote out a message to his brother entirely forgetting the sharp words he had intended to use. When he came out, he took Harkavy aside.

"Dan, could we have a private conversation for a few minutes?" he said.

"Why, I should say so. What's the matter, old fellow? Wait a minute. Let's ditch the women."

Mrs. Harkavy, Julia, and Libbie were waiting at the corner.

"Ladies, excuse us," said Harkavy with a pleased smile, fitting a cigarette into his holder. "Asa wants to talk over something with me."

"I'll see Mrs. Denisart for you tomorrow. Don't you worry," Mrs. Harkavy said.

Leventhal thanked her, and he and Harkavy crossed the street.

"Now what's the trouble, did you get into a scrape?" asked Harkavy. "You know you can trust me. It's safe to tell me anything. You can bank on it. Anything you confide in me will never come back to you through a third party, not any more than if you whispered it in the confession box. So let's have it."

"There's no secret to keep. It's nothing like that." Glancing at his friend, he hesitated, dissatisfied. Would it be worthwhile to explain the whole matter to Harkavy? He was warmhearted and a sincere friend, but he frequently put emphasis on the wrong things. He was already on the wrong track, suspecting a scrape. He probably meant an intrigue, a scrape with a woman. "It's this Allbee," Leventhal said. "He's been giving me a headache. You must remember him. He made fun of your singing one night at Williston's. You and that girl. Sure you can recall him. He worked at Dill's. . . ."

"Oh, *him*. That bird." It seemed to Leventhal that Harkavy listened more gravely, though perhaps it was his own wish to have something so troubling to him taken seriously that was behind this impression. He described his first meeting with Allbee in the park. When he told him how amazed he was at Allbee's spying, Harkavy murmured, "Well, isn't that the limit? Isn't that disagreeable? Nervy. Disagreeable."

"I thought you wouldn't forget how he went for you over that song."

"Oh, no, I have him definitely placed now. So that's the man?" He drew his head back with a restrained rearing motion and, from the stretching of his clear eyes, Leventhal saw that a connection of the utmost importance had been established in his mind.

"Dan, do you know any facts about him that I don't?"

"What do you call facts? It depends. I think so. I mean, I've heard. But was he around again? Let's have the rest of it."

"What have you heard?"

"You tell me first. Let's see if it's all one piece. Maybe it isn't. It may not be worth bothering about—loony all of it, and we ought to tie a can to it?"

He would not speak, and Leventhal hurriedly set forth all that Allbee had done and said, and, despite his haste and his eagerness to find out what Harkavy knew, he interrupted himself from time to time to make scornful, almost laughing comments which in his heart he recognized to be appeals to Harkavy to confirm the absurdity, the madness of the accusations. Harkavy, however, did not respond to these appeals. He was sober. He continued to say, "Disagreeable, disagreeable," but his manner did not give Leventhal much comfort.

"He makes out a whole case that I'm responsible for his wife and everything . . . !" said Leventhal, his voice rising nearly to a cry.

"His wife? That's far-fetched, far-fetched," said Harkavy. "I wouldn't listen to stuff like that."

"You think I do? I'd have to be crazy too. How could anybody? Could you?"

"No, no, I say it's far-fetched. He's overstraining the imagination. He must have a loose screw." Harkavy twisted a finger near his head and sighed. "But the story went round that he was canned, and then I heard that he couldn't get another job. They canned him at quite a few places before."

"Because of drinking. . . ."

Harkavy shrugged. His face was wrinkled and he was half turned away from Leventhal. "Maybe. He wasn't in good anywhere, as I heard it, and he was just about running out of breaks when he got the job with Dill's."

"Who told you that?"

"Offhand I don't recollect."

"Do you think there's a black list, Dan? When I talked over that Rudiger thing with you, you laughed at the idea."

"Did I? Well, I don't believe in such stuff in general."

"All right, here's proof. You see? There is a black list."

"I'm not convinced. This man of yours wasn't steady, and the word got around. It just got to be known he wasn't reliable."

"Why did he lose the job at Dill's? It was because he boozed, wasn't it?"

"Why, I can't say," Harkavy replied, and Leventhal thought that he looked at him anxiously. "I haven't got the inside information on it. As it came to me, the reason was different. In these cases, though, you get all kinds of rumors. Who knows? The truth is hard to get at. If your life depended on getting it, you'd probably hang. I don't have to tell you how it is. This one says this, and that one says that. Y says oats, and Z says hay, and chances are . . . it's buckwheat. Nobody can tell you except the fellow that harvested it. To the rest it's all theory.

Why? He was skating on thin ice and he had to skate fast, faster and faster. But he slowed up . . . and he fell through. As I see it . . ." Harkavy himself was discontented with this explanation; it was obviously makeshift. He faltered and his glance wandered. He had, unmistakably, information that he was trying to hold back.

"Why did he lose the job? What do they say?"

"There's no 'they'."

"Dan, don't try to give me the runaround. This is something I won't rest easy about till I know. It's no trifle. You must tell me what they say."

"If you don't mind, Asa, there's one thing I have to point out that you haven't learned. We're not children. We're men of the world. It's almost a sin to be so innocent. Get next to yourself, boy, will you? You want the whole world to like you. There're bound to be some people who don't think well of you. As I do, for instance. Why, isn't it enough for you that some do? Why can't you accept the fact that others never will? Figure it on a percentile basis. Is it a life and death matter? I happen to have found out that a young lady I always liked said I was conceited. Perhaps she didn't think it would get to me, but it did. Too bad people everywhere don't know what I'm really like. Or you. It would be a different universe. Things are too subtle for me; I have to knock along on common sense. What about this girl? I know she has reasons that she doesn't understand herself. All I can say is, 'Lady, God bless you, we all have our faults and are what we are. I have to take myself as I am or push off. I am all I have in this world. And with all my shortcomings my life is precious to me.' My heart doesn't sink. Experience has taught me to expect this once in a while. But you're so upset when somebody doesn't like you, or says this or that about you. A little independence, boy; it's a weakness, positively."

"I want you to tell me," Leventhal persisted. "I'll stick to you till you do. Considering what I'm being blamed for, it's natural that I should want to find out."

Harkavy gave in to him. "Williston thought you made trouble for this fellow when you went to Dill's and you acted up. He kind of hinted that it was intentional."

"What? Williston says that? Did he say that?"

"Well, something like it."

"How could he? Is he such an idiot?" Pale, his lips tight, making a great effort to hold back his anger and the unaccountable fear that filled him, Leventhal put his hand to his throat and stared frowningly at Harkavy. He said loudly, "And did you stand up for me?"

"Naturally I said he was mistaken and did all I could. I told him he was wrong."

"You ought to have said that I came to you immediately with the whole story about Rudiger. You even thought that it might be rigged up, that Allbee and Rudiger wanted to make a fool of me and it was hatched out by the two of them. Did you bring that up?"

"No, I didn't take the trouble."

"Why not!" He swiftly clenched his fist as though catching at something in the air. "Why not!" he demanded. "It was your duty if you're a friend of mine. Even if you didn't know the facts you should have defended me. And you did know the facts. I told them to you. You should have said it was a slander and a lie. If anybody repeated such a lie to me about you, you'd see how fast I'd take him up on it. It's not only loyalty but fairness. And how did he know what I did at Dill's? Why were you such a stick? Were you afraid to hurt his feelings by contradicting him?"

"I was not," said Harkavy. His marveling eyes took Leventhal in, but he answered quietly. "I didn't think it would benefit you if I argued with Williston. I just said that he was wrong."

"My friend!"

"Yes, if you ever had one. I am your friend."

"He might have asked me, before he said a thing like that, given me a chance to defend myself. He'd rather take that drunk Allbee's word for it. Where's their Anglo-Saxon fairness . . . fair play?"

"It's hard for me to understand Williston's side of it. I had an idea he was pretty level."

"Is it so hard?" Leventhal said bitterly. "I told you why Allbee said I was out for revenge. And if Williston believes that I went to Dill's to make trouble, he must think what Allbee does, all around."

"Who, Williston? Oh, you're way off, boy, way off."

"Oh, am I? Well, you don't know what it's all about, I can see that. Williston is too nice a fellow, you mean. Talk about being innocent! Talk about a man of the world! Any child knows more about these things than you do, Dan. If he has it in him to think it was that insult . . . the insult to you, too, Dan, come to think of it. If that's what he believes . . ."

"Williston *is* a nice fellow," said Harkavy. "Remember, he was nice to you."

"I do remember. What makes you think I don't? That's exactly it. That's what makes it so bad, horrible. That's the evil part of it. Of course he helped me. So now if he wants to believe this about me he has the right? Can't you see how it stacks up?" He groped. "Certainly he helped me."

"You can be sure he doesn't know what your Mr. Allbee is up to and wouldn't like it if he did. Regardless. I mean that he couldn't believe that he says . . . that you ruined him. The man is off his trolley, sleuthing after you like that. He's disturbed in his mind. Haven't you ever seen such a case before? It's very pitiful. It happened in the family. My father's sister got strange during the change of life—said all the clocks were warning her to look out, look out, look out. Oh, she was just off. It was a calamity. She claimed that somebody was stealing out of her mailbox, taking letters. Oh, all kinds of things. I couldn't begin to tell you. Well, obviously that's the kind of case you're up against. It's disagreeable, but it's nothing to be alarmed about. She started telling people that she was Krueger the match king's widow, though my uncle was still living. Sometimes she said Cecil Rhodes, not Krueger. My grandfather fought in the Boer War. Where else could she have gotten that? She went to an institution, poor thing. How those ideas get into their heads only Heaven knows."

Leventhal nodded inattentively. He could only brood over Williston. How could Williston believe that of him? Was it possible to know him and yet think him capable of deliberately injuring someone? For a reason like that? For any reason, even strict self-defense? He could not have imagined and carried out such a plan. Leventhal was deeply roused. He turned away from Harkavy, wrinkling up his eyes. Williston had helped him. He was indebted to him. Would he deny it? Harkavy had in his way rebuked him for seeming to forget it.

He had not forgotten. But it was only natural to ask how much he owed Williston and how far gratitude should be expected to stretch. He had used the word "evil" a while ago, and what had given rise to it was a feeling that Williston had made the accusation under an influence against which he could not help himself. If he was ready to believe that he was such and such a person—why avoid saying it?—that he would carry out a scheme like that because he was a Jew, then the turn he always feared had come and all good luck was canceled and all favors melted away. He looked hopelessly before him. Williston, like himself, like everybody else, was carried on currents, this way and that. The currents had taken a new twist, and he was being hurried, hurried. His heart shrank and he felt faint for a moment and shut his eyes.

"I'll get it from him straight," he muttered, recovering himself a little. "I won't take somebody else's word for it. That would be doing what he did." He pulled out his handkerchief and mopped his face.

8

BUT THE WEEK passed and Leventhal made no move to get in touch with Williston, though he promised himself every day to clear up the whole business. Allbee did not appear, and Leventhal hoped that he had seen the last of him without really believing that he had. But at least matters in Staten Island were going better. Mickey was by no means out of danger; still he was improving, and Leventhal felt less worried about him. Max had wired back that he was ready to leave as soon as the doctor gave the word, and Leventhal wrote to say that while he thought Max ought to come home where he was needed, the decision was his own to make.

On Friday night Leventhal felt Mary's absence keenly. Before going to bed, he was tempted to put in a call to Charleston. He even went to the telephone, lifted it, and turned it, untangling the cord, but he set it down and went on undressing. He put on a white cotton robe she had given him on his last birthday, smoothing the lapels lightly and glancing down. She would be sure to feel if he called her now, at the beginning of the week-end, that he found being alone unendurable and was appealing to her to come home. And that would be unfair, since she could not come as long as her mother needed her. Also, when he hung up and she was inaccessible again, he would miss her even more than he did now. And she him.

There were several glasses on the sink. He washed them and turned them upside down to dry. Then he went into the dining room which had been shut since her departure. He left all the doors in the flat standing open; it made him feel easier.

He did not sleep well. Most of the night he could hear the motor of the refrigerator shuddering and rocking as it started and stopped. Several times he opened his eyes because of it. The light was burning in the bathroom. There was a short downpour and mist floated at the window. Toward morning he was aware that someone was speaking loudly in the street and he listened, breathing heavily. There was enough light to see by. He had gone to bed in the cotton robe and he lay, both pillows under his head, his hands joined on his chest; his feet and outspread legs were visible beside the deep shadow of the wall. The air was gray and soft in the long defile of the street.

A woman's voice cried out, and he flung himself up, brushing aside the curtains with a clatter of rings. There was a commotion at the corner. He saw a man start a crazy rush at one of two women; another threw himself in his way, shrieking, and held him off. Across the street two soldiers stood watching. They had been with the women, it was clear enough, and then the man had caught them—perhaps a husband, a brother, probably the former—and they drew off. The man circled with short, sidling steps, and the woman hung back dumbly, with horrible attentiveness, ready to run. Her high heels knocked on the pavement. He had reached her once, her dress was ripped from neck to waist. She shook her head and pulled back her hair. He darted in again, grabbing at her, and the friend, uttering her begging, agonized cries, caught his arms and was swung round by him. The soldiers had an air of being present at an entertainment especially arranged for them, and seemed to laugh to themselves from time to time. The husband's soles scraped on the pavement as he pushed toward his wife, and this time she ran away. She ran up the street awkwardly but swiftly, her soft figure shaking, and the soldiers started off at once in the same direction. The husband did not chase her; he stood still. The other woman with her hands on his arm spoke to him urgently, thrusting forward her face. The rain was rapidly, unevenly drying from the street. Leventhal growled under his breath and wound the robe around himself more tightly. There was a gleam, as if a naked copper cable was lifted from the water and rose quickly, passing over masonry and windows. The sun was forcing its way through a corner of the gray air. The woman was still speaking to the man, imploring, pulling him the other way. She wanted him to go with her. Leventhal drew the shade and dropped into bed.

He was up at ten o'clock with a free week-end before him. The day had changed its look since dawn; it was warm, singularly beautiful. The color of the sky was strong; the clouds were as white as leghorn feathers rolling before a breeze that blew into the curtains and hauled at the strings of Mrs. Nunez' flower boxes. Leventhal bathed, dressed, and went down for breakfast. In the restaurant he took a booth instead of sitting at the counter as he did on weekdays. He found a copy of the *Tribune* on the seat and read, propping the paper on the sugar shaker while he drank his coffee. Afterward he took a walk uptown, enjoying the weather and looking into shopwindows.

The scene on the corner remained with him, however, and he returned to it every now and then with the feeling that he really did not know what went on about him, what strange things, savage things. They hung near him all the time in trembling drops, invisible, usually, or seen from a distance. But that did not mean that there was always to be a distance, or that sooner or later one or two of the drops might not fall on him. As a matter of fact he was thinking of Allbee—he was not sure that he had stopped spying on him—and with the thought came a faint sick qualm. Once more he reminded himself that he had to call Williston. But gradually the qualm passed, and his intention slipped to the back of his mind. And later, when he took some nickels out of his pocket to pay for a drink and saw an empty phone booth at the rear of the store, he reconsidered and decided, for the time being, not to make the call. He had not seen Williston for three years or more, and to ask him, out of a clear sky, about something so difficult and obscure, perhaps forgotten, might appear strange. Besides, if Williston was capable of believing he had injured Allbee on purpose, he would be cold to him. And perhaps Harkavy was right. Perhaps he would be trying to get Williston to assure him that he still liked him, to demand that assurance of him more than fairness. He pictured Williston sitting before him in a habitual pose, at ease in his chair, his fingers in the pockets of his vest, red-cheeked, his blue eyes seeming to say, "So much frankness and no more," the exact amount remaining in doubt. In all likelihood Williston had made up his mind that he was responsible for what had happened to Allbee and while he would listen—if Leventhal knew him—with an appearance of courtesy and willingness to suspend judgment, he would already be convinced. To imagine himself pleading with him filled Leventhal with shame. Didn't he know, he himself, that he had never consciously wanted to harm Allbee? Of course he did. It was for Williston, even if he was his benefactor, to explain why he was ready to believe such a thing. And when you said that someone was your benefactor, what did it actually mean? You might help a man because he was a bother to you and you wanted to get rid of him. You might do it because you disliked him unfairly and wanted to pay for your prejudice and then, feeling that you had paid, you were free and even entitled to detest him. He did not say that it was so in Williston's case, but in a question like this you couldn't be blamed for examining every possibility, or accused of being cold-blooded or heartless. It was better to think well of people—there was a kind of command that you should. And on the whole it was Leventhal's opinion that he had an unsuspicious character and preferred to be taken advantage of rather than regard everyone with distrust. It was better to be genuinely unsuspicious; it was what they called Christian. But it was foolish and miserable to refuse to acknowledge the suspicions that came into your mind in an affair like this. Because if you had them you should not put on an innocent front with yourself and deny that you did.

At the same time Leventhal was reasonable enough to admit that he might be trying to release himself from a sense of obligation to Williston by finding fault with him. He had never been able to repay him. Was he looking for a chance to cancel the debt? He did not think so. He wished he could be sure. Ah, he told himself, he was sure. He had never felt anything but gratitude. Again and again he had said—Mary could testify—that Williston had saved him.

But then, as he dwelt on it, the whole affair began to lose much of its importance. It was, after all, something he could either take seriously or dismiss as an annoyance. It was up to him. He had only to insist that he wasn't responsible and it disappeared altogether. It was his conviction against an accusation nobody could expect him to take at face value. And what more was there for him to say than that his part in it was accidental? At worst, an accident, unintentional.

The morning, with its brilliance and its simple contrasts, white and blue, shining and darkened, had a balancing effect on him of which he was conscious. He looked up, and a slight smile appeared on his face, swarthy in the sunlight. His clean white shirt was crookedly buttoned and tight at the neck; he put his fingers inside the band and tugged at it, drawing his chin up, and he straightened his shirt front clumsily, his gold wedding ring clicking on the buttons.

At noon he was in the west Forties. He ate a bowl of chili in a place opposite a music shop where a man in shirt sleeves, standing at one of the broad-swung windows on the second floor, blurted out an occasional note, testing a horn, one arm embracing the shining roundness of the brass. He was blowing erratically rich impatient notes and deep snores whose resonance Leventhal felt somehow entering his very blood as he gazed into the sun and dust of the peaceful street. He broke a cigar out of its wrapper, making a ball of the cellophane small enough to squeeze into the band. He felt along his thigh for matches and, when he had blown out his first puff, he walked into a booth and phoned Elena. One of the Villani children was sent to fetch her. Leventhal's eyes remained fixed on the horn player during the conversation.

Elena sounded quieter than usual. She was going to visit Mickey at three o'clock. He asked her about Philip and while Elena, after she had said, "Oh, Phillie? He's upstairs," went on talking about the hospital, Leventhal conceived the idea of spending the day with him and interrupted her to propose that Philip come over to Manhattan.

"I'll meet him at South Ferry. If you want me to, I'll come for him."

"Oh, I'll send him," said Elena. "That's fine. He'll like it. No, he can go on the ferry himself. What's there to it?"

Already full of plans, Leventhal hurried into the street. They would take a ride along the Drive on an open bus. The boy might enjoy that. Perhaps he would prefer Times Square, the shooting galleries, the penny arcades and pinball games. He congratulated himself on having thought of Philip; he was delighted. He would have passed the time tolerably well, he reflected, until some time toward evening when he realized he had not spoken three words to a living soul and the blues descended on him. And Philip, too, would have been left alone when his mother went to the hospital. Leventhal took the train downtown and sat in the small square on a bench commanding the ferry gates.

He kept his swarthy, unimpassioned face turned to the exit. The strain of waiting made him almost tremble, yet it was pleasurable, a pleasurable excitement. He wondered why it was that lately he was more susceptible than he had ever been before to certain kinds of feeling. With everybody except Mary he was inclined to be short and neutral, outwardly a little like his father, and this shortness of his was, when you came right down to it, merely neglectfulness. When you didn't want to take trouble with people, you found the means to turn them aside. Well, the world was a busy place—he scanned the buildings, the banks and offices in their Saturday stillness, the pillars ribbed with soot, and the changeable color of the windows in which the more absolute color of the sky was darkened, dilated, and darkened again. You couldn't find a place in your feelings for everything, or give at every touch like a swinging door, the same for everyone, with people going in and out as they pleased. On the other hand, if you shut yourself up, not wanting to be bothered, then you were like a bear in a winter hole, or like a mirror wrapped in a piece of flannel. And like such a mirror you were in less danger of being broken, but you didn't flash, either. But you had to flash. That was the peculiar thing. Everybody wanted to be what he was to the limit. When you looked around, that was what you saw most distinctly. In great achievements as well as in crimes and vices. When that woman faced her husband this morning after he had most likely tracked her all night from joint to joint and finally caught her catting, too red-handed to defend herself; when she faced him, wasn't she saying, silently, "I'm being up to the limit just what I am"? In this case, a whore. She may have been mistaken in herself. You couldn't expect people to be right, but only try to do what they must. Therefore hideous things were done, cannibalistic things. Good things as well, of course. But even there, nothing really good was safe.

There was something in people against sleep and dullness, together with the caution that led to sleep and dullness. Both were there, Leventhal thought. We were all the time taking care of ourselves, laying up, storing up, watching out on this side and on that side, and at the same time running, running desperately, running as if in an egg race with the egg in a spoon. And sometimes we were fed up with the egg, sick of it, and at such a time would rather sign on with the devil and what they called the powers of darkness than run with the spoon, watching the egg, fearing for the egg. Man is weak and breakable, has to have just the right amounts of everything—water, air, food; can't eat twigs and stones; has to keep his bones from breaking and his fat from melting. This and that. Hoards sugar and potatoes, hides money in his mattress, spares his feelings whenever he can, and takes pains and precautions. That, you might say, was for the sake of the egg. Dying is spoiling, then? Addling? And the last judgment, candling? Leventhal chuckled and rubbed his cheek. There was also the opposite, playing catch with the egg, threatening the egg.

Boats from the island were arriving every few minutes, and, after the crowds had several times poured out and dispersed, Leventhal saw Philip standing at the gates. He got up and beckoned him, grunting, "Here, this way," and, waving his arm, advanced to the curb. The noise of the busses made shouting useless. "Here, here!" He motioned, and at last the boy saw him and came over.

"Well, was it nice crossing?" were Leventhal's first words.

"It's a swell day. You can smell the sea here." He breathed deeply. "Fish and clams."

He observed approvingly that Philip's short hair was wetted and brushed, and that his shirt collar, which lay over the collar of his coat, was fresh and clean. He himself was wearing a seersucker suit that had just come back from the laundry; it made him feel set for the holiday.

"Now, how will we go uptown? On the bus?" He touched the boy on the shoulder. "There isn't much to look at on a Saturday from the Broadway bus."

"Oh, I get over to Manhattan," said Philip. "I know what it looks like. Let's take the subway."

They walked down, Leventhal guiding him through the turnstile and the gloom of the curved platform. A distant, rapid concussion of cars, like hammer blows, came to them in the tunnel.

It was fortunate that Philip was talkative, for, if he had been shy, Leventhal would have thought he was being reproached for his past neglect, not to be made up for in a single afternoon. He had read such a reproach into his silence last week, when he gave him the quarter. But there was no cause for misgiving. Philip talked on fluently, and Leventhal, though his mind sometimes appeared to be elsewhere, was secretly minutely attentive. The emotions Philip raised in him deepened his ordinary stolidity. But he glanced frequently at the slope of his cropped, handsome long head and into his face, and he thought that Elena's blood might show in his features but not in his nature. There they had something in common. The boy seemed to see it, too, Leventhal told himself.

Philip put his hand on a chocolate slot machine on one of the pillars, and Leventhal hastily went through his pockets for pennies and put in five or six, turning the knobs. The train rolled in while he was getting the chocolate out of the metal trough, and they abandoned the machine and ran.

"What do you say we walk a little?" Leventhal suggested at Pennsylvania Station. They go out and started up toward Times Square.

The air was stiller here in midtown, and they walked, Leventhal listening to Philip's chatter, often a little puzzled by it. Philip was curious about the foundations of the skyscrapers. Was it true that they had to have shock absorbers? They must have something to ride out the vibrations of the subway and to take in the play at the top, the swaying. They all swayed. Max had told him that in a ship the plates were arranged in parts of the deck to give when there was bad weather to ride out.

"It sounds reasonable," said Leventhal. "Of course, I'm no engineer."

Philip went on, speculating about what there was under the street in addition to foundations: the pipes, water pipes and sewage, gas mains, the electrical system for the subway, telephone and telegraph wires, and the cable for the Broadway trolley.

"I suppose they have maps and charts at City Hall." Leventhal stopped. "What about a drink?"

They had a glass of orangeade at a bamboo stand where the

paper grass bristled on the walls. The woman at the tank clapped down the pull with her wrist, holding her fingers with their cameo rings rigid. The drink was slightly bitter with ground rinds.

Coming out of the stand they walked into a crowd that had formed around a man selling toy dogs that skittered and barked. The peddler, in a flecked sweat shirt and broken shoes, a band with Indian figures on his forehead, pushed them with his wide toe whenever they slowed down. "Run three minutes, guarantee," he said. To wind them he clasped them by the head; his fingers were too big to get at the key easily. "Three minutes. Two bits. They cost me eighteen. That's the con." He made his joke sullenly. His cheeks were heavy, his gaze unconciliating. "Three minutes. Don't pester, don't *shtup*. Buy or beat it."

There was laughter among the bystanders. "What's he saying?" Philip wanted to know.

"He's telling them in Yiddish not to push," Leventhal replied. He was reminded of what Allbee had said about Jews and New York. "Come on, Phil," he said.

On Forty-second Street the boy stopped often to look at the stills outside theaters, and Leventhal reluctantly—he did not care for movies—asked whether he wanted to take in a show. "I'd certainly like to," Philip said. Leventhal surmised that Mickey's illness had probably interfered with his Saturday movie-going.

"Any one you want," he said.

Philip chose a horror picture, and they bought tickets and passed over the brown rugs of the sunless lobby, between the nebulous lamps in their shattered, dust-eaten silk shades, and the long brocaded chairs, into the stifling darkness. They sat down in the leather seats.

On the screen an old scientist was seen haunting the dressing room of a theater where he had murdered his mistress many years ago. He had hallucinations about a young star who resembled her and he attempted to strangle the girl. The flaring lights hurt Leventhal's eyes, the music was strident, and, after half an hour of it, his nerves jarred, he went down to the lavatory. He found an old man there, leaning against a yellow sink, picking clean the end of a rolled cigarette.

"The stuff they put Karloff in," he said. "A man of his ability."

"You like him?" said Leventhal.

"In his line, he's a genius." He offered Leventhal a light, holding the match vertically pinched between limy white nails; his fingers were raw; he must be a dishwasher. "Here he's horsing around. It's an inferior vehicle. Even so, he shines. He really understands what a mastermind is, a law unto himself. That's what he's got my admiration for."

Leventhal threw away his cigarette; the smell of disinfectants interfered with the taste of it. He rejoined Philip, sliding into the seat. He shortly fell asleep. The efforts of the man next to him to push out of the row woke him up. He rose suddenly and heard the music of the newsreel.

"Phil, let's go. There's no air in the place," said Leventhal. "It's a wonder anybody stays awake."

The street was glaring when they emerged. The lights in the marquee were wan. There was a hot, overrich smell of roasting peanuts and caramel corn. A metallic clapping sound came to them from a shooting gallery. And for a time Leventhal felt empty and unstable. The sun was too strong, the swirling traffic too loud, too swift.

"Well, where next?" he asked. "What about the park? We can take in the zoo. A little fresh air wouldn't be bad, would it? Out in the open? We'll have a sandwich first and then walk down."

Philip agreed, and Leventhal could only guess whether the idea pleased him, or whether, having had his way about the movies, he felt obliged to acquiesce. "I'm out of touch with kids," he thought. "Maybe he's too sophisticated for the zoo. But I don't know why he should be." His earlier confidence in the understanding between them was fading.

"Is there anything you'd rather do instead?" he said to the boy. "You don't have to be afraid to speak up."

"The only thing I can think of is the Dodgers against Boston. But it must be about the fifth inning by now. I'm not afraid to speak up."

"Good. We'll get the ball game another time. When you've got something on your mind, I want you to tell me. Meanwhile let's have a bite."

The restaurant they went into was an immense place, choked with people. There were several lines before each counter. Leventhal sent Philip to buy soft drinks; he himself went for sandwiches. They found a table and Leventhal began to eat, but Philip went in search of a mustard jar. Leventhal sat sipping out of his bottle. Suddenly there was a stir in the crowd at the front of the restaurant; voices rose sharply. Several people stood up on chairs to see what was happening. Leventhal, too, lifted himself up and looked around for Philip, frowning, beginning to feel troubled. He entered the crowd and pushed forward.

"Here's my uncle. Uncle!" shouted Philip, catching sight of him. His arm was held by a man whose back was turned but whose blond head and cotton jacket Leventhal immediately recognized.

"What are you doing?" he said. In his astonishment he spoke neither to Philip nor to Allbee, but, as it were, to them both.

"I took the mustard from the table and this man grabbed me," Philip cried.

"That's right, I did. You put it back."

Leventhal flushed and pulled Philip away from Allbee.

"Oh, so this is your uncle?" Allbee smiled, but his eyes did not rest long on Leventhal. He was playing to the crowd and, standing there, his head hung awkwardly forward, he could hardly keep from laughing at the sensation he was making. And yet there was the usual false note, the note of impersonation in what he did.

"I asked if I could have the mustard. I asked a lady and she said it was all right," said Philip. "Where is she?"

"That's right, mister." Leventhal met the distressed eyes of a young girl. White-faced, she pressed her pocketbook to her breast.

"What did I tell you?"

"You sneaked the mustard jar away. It doesn't belong to this young woman. It belongs to the table."

"I didn't see you at the table," she cried.

"You keep on following me around," said Leventhal in a low voice, tensely, "you keep it up and see what happens. I'll get out a warrant. I'm not joking."

"Oh, I could get a warrant out for you on a battery charge. Very easily. There was a witness."

"I should have broken your neck," Leventhal muttered. His large head twitched. Because of the boy he dissembled his anger.

"Oh, you should have. I wish it was broken." Allbee moistened his lips and stared at him.

"Come on, Phil." Leventhal led him out of the crowd.

"Who is he?" asked Philip.

"He's a nuisance. I used to know him years ago. Don't pay any attention to him. He's just a nuisance."

They sat down. Philip smeared mustard on his sandwich and looked silently at his uncle.

"It didn't upset you, did it?"

"Well, I jumped when he grabbed me, but I wasn't afraid of him."

"He's nothing to be afraid of." He pushed his plate across the table. "Here, eat this half of mine, Phil." His heart was pounding. He gazed at the entrance. Allbee was out of sight for the moment.

"I won't stand it," he thought. "He'd better stay away from me."

9

I N THE THRONGED ZOO, Leventhal kept an eye out for Allbee. Defiant and alert at first, he soon became depressed.
For if Allbee wanted to trail him how could he prevent it?
Among so many people he could come close without being
seen. Frequently Leventhal felt that he was watched and he
endured it passively. Half out of fear of being mistaken, he
made no effort to catch Allbee. He tried to put him out of his
thoughts and give all his attention to Philip, forcing himself
to behave naturally. But now and then, moving from cage to
cage, gazing at the animals, Leventhal, in speaking to Philip,
or smoking, or smiling, was so conscious of Allbee, so certain
he was being scrutinized, that he was able to see himself as if
through a strange pair of eyes: the side of his face, the palpi-
tation in his throat, the seams of his skin, the shape of his
body and of his feet in their white shoes. Changed in this way
into his own observer, he was able to see Allbee, too, and
imagined himself standing so near behind him that he could
see the weave of his coat, his raggedly overgrown neck, the
bulge of his cheek, the color of the blood in his ear; he could
even evoke the odor of his hair and skin. The acuteness and
intimacy of it astounded him, oppressed and intoxicated him.
The heat was climbing again, and the pungency of the animals and the dry hay, dust, and manure filled his head; the
sun, overflowing above the topmost twigs and bent back from
bars and cages, white and glowing in long shapes, deprived
him for a moment of his sense of the usual look of things, and
he was afraid, too, that his strength was leaving him. But he
felt normal again when he forced himself to walk on.

Leaving the zoo, he and Philip went into the park. Philip
wanted to rest and went toward a bench. But Leventhal said,
"We'll find a place with more shade," because this was at a
crossing of two paths and exposed to all directions. They sat
down on a slope where no one could approach unseen. At the
crossing, about fifty yards distant, there was a knot of people,
one of whom might have been Allbee. Evening was coming
on, and a new tide of heat with it, thickening the air, sinking

grass and bushes under its weight. Leventhal watched. He even thought of turning the tables on Allbee, lying in wait for him somewhere. But what if he did trap him, what use was it? Would he embarrass him? He was beyond being embarrassed. Beat him? With pleasure. But he felt that he ought to beware, for his own sake, of countering absurdity with absurdity and madness with madness. And of course he did not want to make another scene while Philip was with him. He did not know what effect Allbee had had on him in the restaurant. He believed that Philip realized how much the incident had disconcerted him and therefore tactfully hid his feelings. He had a mind to talk to him about it. But he did not want to betray his anxiety; furthermore, he was afraid to begin a conversation without knowing in advance where it would lead. And maybe he was giving the boy credit for too much discernment. But the mood of the outing had changed. Philip looked pensive; he had nothing to say; and it would have been natural for him to mention the incident once, at least. Certainly he hadn't forgotten it.

"What's up, Phil," he said.

"Nothing. My feet are tired," he answered, and Leventhal remained in the dark as to what Philip really felt.

He decided to take a taxi to the ferry and he stood up, saying, "Let's go, Phil. Time to get you back." He set a rapid pace toward Fifth Avenue. Philip appeared to be somewhat puzzled by his haste but he enjoyed the ride in the open-roofed cab. Leventhal accompanied him to Staten Island and put him on the bus. Then he returned to Manhattan.

About nine o'clock, after a seafood dinner he barely tasted, he was on his way home without a thought of going elsewhere. He wandered into a cigar store, glanced round at the shelves beyond the flame on the counter, and bought a package of cigarettes. He took the change absent-mindedly, but, instead of putting it in his pocket, he began to look through it to find a nickel with which to phone Williston. For all at once he had a consuming need to get an explanation from him, tonight, immediately. He could not understand why he had put it off all week. He leafed through the directory quickly, copied the number out, and went into the booth.

Phoebe Williston answered, and the sound of her voice

gave him an unexpected stab; he was reminded of the many times he had called to ask a favor of Williston, to get advice from him, or an introduction. The Willistons had been patient with him, usually, and he had often rather helplessly and dumbly put his difficulties in their hands and waited, sat in their parlor or hung on the telephone, waiting while his problems were weighed, conscious that he was contributing nothing to their solution, wishing he could withdraw them but powerless to do so. Inevitably there had been times when his calls were unwelcome and the Willistons' patience overdrawn. Whenever he rang their bell, or dropped a nickel in the slot and heard the dial tone, the question in his heart was, "How will it be this time?" And now, too, it was present, despite the fact that the circumstances were altogether different.

"This is Leventhal," he said. "How are you?"

"Leventhal? Oh, Asa Leventhal. How are you, Asa?" He thought she didn't sound unfriendly. It was too much to ask that she should be positively cordial, considering that this was his first call in three or four years.

"I'm good enough."

"You want to talk to Stan, I suppose."

"Yes."

He heard the instrument being laid on the table with a knock and then, for several minutes, the sound of a conversation carried on at a distance. "He doesn't want to talk to me," thought Leventhal. "He must be telling her that she should have said he was out." Presently the phone was picked up.

"Hello, there."

"Yes, hello. Is that you, Asa?"

Leventhal said without preliminaries, "Say, Stan, I want to see you. Can you give me a little time tonight?"

"Oh, tonight? That's pretty short notice."

"Yes, I know it is. I should have asked if you were going out."

"Well, we were planning to later, as a matter of fact."

"I won't stay. About fifteen minutes is all I want."

"Where are you now?"

"Not far. I'll grab a taxi."

It seemed to him that Williston did not conceal his reluctance. But when he said, "All right," Leventhal did not even

bother to say good-by. He did not care how Williston consented to see him, just so he consented. He went into the
middle of the street and flagged a cab. Of course, he observed
to himself getting in, Williston was displeased by his phoning
and blurting out his request, dispensing with the usual for-
malities. But there was much more than that to be concerned
about, assuming that Williston really did side with Allbee.
There was fairness, a man's reputation, honor. And there were
other considerations as well.

The cab raced uptown, and Leventhal suddenly felt his face
burning, for he had just recalled a verse his father had liked to
repeat:

> *Ruf mir Yoshke, ruf mir Moshke,*
> *Aber gib mir die groschke.*

"Call me Ikey, call me Moe, but give me the dough. What's
it to me if you despise me? What do you think equality with
you means to me? What do you have that I care about except
the *groschen*?" That was his father's view. But not his. He rejected it and recoiled from it. Anyway, his father had lived
poor and died poor, that stern, proud old fool with his savage
looks, to whom nothing mattered save his advantage and to
be freed by money from the power of his enemies. And who
were the enemies? The world, everyone. They were imaginary. There was no advantage. He carried on like a merchant
prince among his bolts and remnants, and was willing to be a
pack rat in order to become a lion. There was no advantage;
he never became a lion. It gave Leventhal pain to think about
his father's sense of these things. He roused himself to tell the
driver to hurry. But the cab was already in Williston's block,
and he grasped the handle of the door.

He recognized the elderly Negro who took him up in the
elevator. Short, broad-shouldered, and slow, he stooped over
the lever, handling it with the utmost deliberateness. They
rose and stopped smoothly on the fourth floor. The knocker
on Williston's door was also familiar—a woman's head cast in
copper that surprised you by its heaviness.

Phoebe Williston let him in. Leventhal shook hands with
her and she preceded him along the high-walled gray corridor
into the living room. Williston stood up from his chair in the

bay window, a newspaper falling from his lap and spreading around the base of the lamp. He was in his shirt sleeves, the cuffs turned back on his smooth, reddish forearms. He hadn't lost any of his ruddy color. His brown hair was brushed sideways and his dark green satin tie hung unknotted from his buttoned collar.

"Pretty much the same, eh?" he said in his pleasant, deep voice.

"Yes, just about. You, too, I see."

"A couple of years older all around," Phoebe remarked.

"Well, it goes without saying."

Williston brought another chair forward in the bay window and the two men sat down. Phoebe remained standing, resting her weight on one foot, her arms folded, and Leventhal thought that her look was fixed on him longer than it need have been. He submitted to this prolonged look with an air of allowing her the right, under the circumstances, to inspect him.

"You seem to be all right, filled out," she said. "How's your wife?"

"Oh, she's out of town for a while, down South with her mother and family. She's fine."

"Lord! South in this weather? And are you still in the same place?"

"Address or job? Both the same. The same job, Burke and Beard; same people. I guess Stan knows."

The maid came in to ask Phoebe a question. She was a pale, slow-spoken girl. Phoebe listened, inclining her head and twisting her necklace in her fingers. She went back with her to the kitchen. Williston explained, "That's a new girl learning her way around." Leventhal, as in the past, felt conscious of a household that had more of the atmosphere of established habit than any he had ever known. Williston lay loosely in his chair, crossing his feet, his fingers pushed under his belt. Within the metal guard of the semicircular window were several flowerpots with blossoms coarse as bits of red ore. Looking at them, Leventhal considered how he should begin. He was unprepared. It had seemed simple enough; he came with a grievance and he wanted an explanation. Perhaps he had counted on finding Williston roused against him; he certainly had not expected him to sit back and wait while minute after minute of the time he had requested ran out. He had not foreseen the effect Williston was having on him; he had forgotten what he was like. More than once, in the old days, he had mistrusted him. He had been full of rancor toward him when he thought Williston was uneasy about the reference letter. But on that occasion and others he had changed his opinion; he invariably did when he was face to face with Williston. He came to him complaining, but soon, without quite knowing how it happened, he began to feel unsure of his ground. So it was now, and he was unable to start. He sat in the bay window looking down, over the heads of the flowers, at the sprinting headlights in the depth of the park below the net of trees, as they turned on a curve and illuminated the boulders and trailing bushes of a steep hillside, one beam after another passing through an immobility of black and green.

"I wanted to talk to you about your friend Allbee," he said at last. "Maybe you understand what he's up to."

Williston was immediately interested; he lifted himself up in his chair. "Allbee? Have you seen him?"

"I sure have."

"I lost track of him years ago. What's he doing? Where did you see him?"

But Leventhal would answer no questions till he knew where he stood with Williston. "What was he doing last time you saw him?" he said.

"Nothing. He was living on insurance money. His wife was killed, you know."

"I heard."

"It hit him hard. He loved her."

"All right, he loved her. He didn't go to her funeral. And why did she leave him?"

Williston raised his eyes to him curiously. "Why," he said with a certain reserve, "I can't say for sure. That was something between them."

Leventhal was quick to feel the rebuke in this and he changed his tone somewhat. "Yes, I guess a third party never really gets the true story. I thought maybe you knew." He sensed that he ought to explain himself further. "I'm not trying to find out something that's none of my business. I have a good reason. Maybe you have an idea what it is . . . ?"

"Well, I think I do," Williston replied.

Leventhal's heart ran hot. "I understand that you take his side," he said. "You know what about. You think I'm responsible for everything, just as he does."

"Everything takes in a lot of territory," said Williston. "What are you driving at? I'd be more specific about something I was going to land on a man for." He was not quite so composed and genial, now; his voice was beginning to sound taut, and Leventhal thought, "Better, much better. Maybe we'll get somewhere." He bent his heavy, dark face forward.

"I didn't come to accuse you of anything, Stan. I'm not landing on you. I came to ask why you said certain things about me without hearing my side of the case?"

"Unless you tell me exactly what you're talking about, I can't answer."

"You want me to believe that you don't know? You know . . ." He made an ill-defined pushing gesture. "I want you to tell me right out if you think it's my fault that Allbee was fired from *Dill's Weekly*."

"You do? You want to?" Williston asked this grimly, as if offering him the opportunity to reconsider or withdraw the question.

"Yes."

"Well, I think it is."

A hard stroke of disappointment and anger went through Leventhal and drove the breath from his body. His limbs were empty; his thighs felt hollow and rigid as brass, and he could not stir his hands from them. He hardly knew what expressions were crossing his face.

"It is . . . It is?" he said, struggling. "I don't see why."

"For definite reasons."

Leventhal, his glance bitter and uncertain, said stumblingly, "I wanted to know. . . ."

Williston did not treat this as needing an answer.

Leventhal continued more surely, "I asked you, so you were bound to give me your opinion. If it's right, fair enough. But what if it's wrong? It might be wrong."

"I'm not infallible."

"No. When you say it's my fault, you're as good as telling me that I set out to make trouble for Allbee because of the way he acted toward Harkavy that night at your house, here. It must mean that I wanted to get even with him because of what he said about Jews." Williston's frown told him that this was something he didn't want to hear. Ah, but he would hear it, Leventhal said to himself fiercely. "That's what Allbee claims, that I wasn't going to let him get away with it and I made a plan to get him kicked out of his job. So, now, do you think that too?"

"I didn't say so."

"But if you blame me you must have the same idea. I don't see any difference. And what if it is wrong? Isn't it awful if you're wrong? Doesn't it make me out to be terrible without giving me a chance to tell my side of it? Is that fair? You may think you have a different slant on it than Allbee has, but it comes out the same. If you believe I did it on purpose, to get even, then it's not only because I'm terrible personally but because I'm a Jew."

Williston's face had flamed up harshly. At either corner of his mouth there was a white spot of compression. He looked at Leventhal as though to warn him of the dangerous strain on his self-control. "I shouldn't have to tell you, Asa, that that wouldn't enter into it with me," he said. "You misunderstand me. I hope Allbee didn't tell you that I agree with him about that. I don't."

"That sounds fine, Stan. But it adds up to the same thing, as far as I'm concerned. You think that he burned me up and I wanted to get him in bad. Why? Because I'm a Jew; Jews are touchy, and if you hurt them they won't forgive you. That's the pound of flesh. Oh, I know you think there isn't any room in you for that; it's superstition. But you don't change anything by calling it superstition. Every once in a while you'll hear people say, 'That's from the Middle Ages.' My God! We have a name for everything except what we really think and feel."

"Looks like you're pretty sure of what I feel and think," Williston said stingingly, and then he shut his teeth and seemed to fight off his exasperation. "The Jewish part of it is your own invention. You take it for granted that I think you got Allbee in trouble purposely. I didn't say that. Maybe you aimed to hurt him and maybe you didn't. My opinion is that you didn't. But the effect was the same. You lost him his job. He might have lost it anyway, eventually. He was shaky at *Dill's*; they had him on probation."

"How do you know?"

"I knew it then and I had a talk with Rudiger about it later. He told me so himself."

Leventhal's black eyes went vacant. "Go on!" he said.

"That's the story. I would have told you right away but you wanted to jump all over me first. Rudiger claimed that Allbee brought you up to Dill's on purpose and that he either gave you instructions or knew you would act as you did. They had it in for each other. I guess Rudiger isn't an easy person to please. He was giving Allbee a last chance but he was more than likely hankering for him to make a false step so that he could land on him. He must have been on his tail all the time and he knew best whether Allbee had reasons for wanting to get a lick in at him."

"The whole thing is crazy. You can't answer for everybody you recommend. You know that. . . . But that's what Rudiger told you?"

Williston nodded.

"And didn't Allbee's boozing have anything to do with it?"

"He lost quite a few jobs because he drank. I won't deny it. His reputation wasn't good."

"Was he on a black list?" Leventhal said, intensely curious.

Williston was not looking at him. His face was directed reflectively toward the flowers, rough and crumbling in the warm night air.

"Well, as I say, he was on probation at *Dill's*. I asked Rudiger about the drinking. He had to admit Allbee had stayed on the wagon. He wasn't fired because he drank."

"So . . ." Leventhal said blankly. "In a way it really seems to be my fault, doesn't it?" He paused and gazed abstractedly at Williston, his hands still motionless on his knees. "In one way. Of course I didn't mean to get him in trouble. I didn't know what this man Rudiger was like. . . ."

"No, you didn't."

There was something more than agreement in this reply. Leventhal waited for Williston to make it explicit but he waited in vain.

"How was I supposed to know what I was walking into?" he said. "This Rudiger . . . I don't see how anybody works for him. He's vicious. He started right away to tear at me like a dog."

"Rudiger said that never in all his experience had he had such an interview."

"Nobody ever talked back to him. He's used to doing whatever he likes. He . . ."

Williston whose color had deepened again to a hard red interrupted. "Don't let yourself off so easily. You were fighting everybody, those days. You were worst with Rudiger, but I heard of others. You came to ask him for a job and he wouldn't give you one. He didn't have to, did he? You should have had better judgment than to blow up."

"What, wipe the spit off my face and leave like a gentleman? I wouldn't think much of myself if I did."

"That's just it."

"What is? What I think of myself? Well . . ." He checked himself, sighed, and gave a slightly submissive shrug. "I don't know. You go to see a man about work. It isn't only the job but your right to live. Say it isn't his lookout; he's got his own interests. But you think you've got something he can use. You're there to sell yourself to him. Well, he tells you you haven't got a goddam thing. Not only what he wants, but nothing. Christ, nobody wants to be cut down like that." He suddenly felt weak-headed and confused; his face was wet. He changed the position of his feet uneasily on the soft circle of the carpet.

"You were wrong."

"Maybe," Leventhal said, drooping. "My nerves were shot. And I never was any good at rubbing people the right way. I don't know how to please them."

"You're not long on tact, that's perfectly true," said Williston. He seemed somewhat appeased.

"I never intended to hurt Allbee. That's my word of honor."

"I believe you."

"Do you? Thanks. You'd do me a favor if you'd tell Allbee that."

"I don't see him. I told you before that I haven't seen him for years."

Allbee was ashamed to show himself to his old friends, Leventhal thought. Of course it was only natural.

"He thinks I'm his worst enemy."

"Where did you run into him? What's he doing? I didn't even know he was still in New York. He sank out of sight."

"He's been following me around," Leventhal said. And he told Williston about his three encounters with Allbee. Williston listened with a gravely examining expression and a modified but noticeable disapproving tightness at the corners of his mouth. Leventhal concluded, "I don't see what he's after. I can't find out what he wants."

"You ought to," said Williston. "You certainly ought."

"Does he mean that I ought to do something for him?" said Leventhal to himself. That, unmistakably, was what he implied. But what and how? It was not at all clear. He felt that he had not said everything he had come to say. The really important things, the deepest issues, had not been touched. But he saw that it was necessary for him to accept some of the blame for Allbee's comedown. He had contributed to it, though he had yet to decide to what extent he was to blame. Allbee had been making a last great effort to hold on to his job. . . . However, it was time to go. He had taken up much more than his fifteen minutes. He stood up.

Williston said at the door that he expected to hear from him about the matter; he was very much interested in what was happening to Allbee.

Leventhal pressed the button for the elevator. It started up with a subdued meshing and locking of the metal doors and rose with measured slowness.

In bed later, lying near the wall, his knees pulled up and his face resting on the striped ticking of the mattress, Leventhal went over his mistakes. Some of them made him wince; others caught at his heart too savagely for wincing, and he stifled his emotion altogether and all expression, merely moving his lids downward. He did not try to spare himself; he recalled them all, from his attack on Williston tonight to the original scene in Rudiger's office. When he came to this, he turned on his back and crossed his bare arms over his eyes.

But even as he did so, he recognized one of those deeper

issues that he had failed to reach before. He was ready to accept the blame for losing his head at *Dill's*. But why had he lost it? Only because of Rudiger's abuse? No, he, he himself had begun to fear that the lowest price he put on himself was too high and he could scarcely understand why anyone should want to pay for his services. And under Rudiger's influence he had felt this. "He made me believe what I was afraid of," Leventhal thought, and he doubted whether Williston could have understood this. For he belonged to the professional world and was loyal to it. There was always a place for someone like him, there or elsewhere. And another man's words and looks could never convert him into his own worst enemy. He did not have to worry about that.

Williston had not tried to justify Rudiger, true, but to Leventhal it was apparent that he himself was considered the greater offender. And looking at the incident from Rudiger's standpoint and taking Allbee's character into account, too, it was, after all, plausible that he, Leventhal, had been sent with instructions to make a scene. Harkavy had suspected Allbee and Rudiger of rigging it up in the first place. It had seemed reasonable to him and it seemed reasonable also to Rudiger. Only to Rudiger the suspicion was instantly true, true because it occurred to him, probably. That was the kind of man he was.

There was still another consideration—he ran his hand down his throat and through the hair of his chest which began with the shaven line above his collarbone. Had he unknowingly, that is, unconsciously, wanted to get back at Allbee? He was sure he hadn't. The night of the party he was angry, of course. But since then, no. Truthfully, no. Williston had said that he believed him; he wondered, however, whether he really did. It was hard to tell where you stood with Williston.

10

L EVENTHAL ran into Harkavy early Sunday afternoon in a
cafeteria on Fourteenth Street.

He had come in as much to escape the hot wind as to eat.
The glass door shut on the dusty rush behind him, and he advanced a few steps over the green tile floor and paused, opening his mouth a little to take in the coolness of the place. The
trays were on a stand nearby, and he picked one up and started
toward the counter. The cashier called him back. He had forgotten to pull a check from the machine. She smiled. "Sunday
hangover, or what?" But Leventhal did not respond. He turned
from the machine and found Harkavy standing in his path.

"Are you hard of hearing this morning? Man, I called you
three, four times."

"Hello. Oh, the cashier was yelling too. I can't hear everything at once."

"You're not very alert today, are you? Anyway, come sit
with us. I'm here with some people. My brother-in-law—you
know Julia's husband, Goldstone—and some of his friends."

"Do I know them?"

"I think you do," said Harkavy. "Shifcart's one of them."

"That musician? The trumpeter?"

"Not any longer. Give the woman your order or you'll
never get waited on. No, he's not in that line any more. He's
with a big Hollywood outfit, Persevalli and Company, the im-
presarios and talent farmers, or whatever you call them. And
you remember Schlossberg."

"Do I?"

"Oh, sure you do. The journalist. He writes for the Jewish
papers."

"What does he write?"

"Whatever comes to hand, I think. Nowadays, theater rem-
iniscences—he used to be a theatrical man. But science, too,
I hear. You know, I can't read Yiddish."

"Let me have a Swiss on rye," said Leventhal over the
counter. "Elderly man, isn't he? Didn't I meet him at your
house with someone else?"

"That's right; his son, whom he still supports at thirty-five."

"Is he sick?"

"No, just looking around; hasn't made up his mind about a vocation. There are daughters, too. Worse yet."

"Loose?"

"Here's your sandwich," said Harkavy. The woman sent the plate across the counter with a spin and a rattle, and Harkavy hurried Leventhal to his table. The three men shifted their chairs to make room.

"This is an old friend of mine, Leventhal."

"I think I used to know Mr. Shifcart," said Leventhal. "—How are you?—When I roomed with Dan, we met."

"In the bachelor days," Harkavy said. "Goldstone—no introduction needed. And this is Mr. Schlossberg."

Shifcart was bald and high-colored, his neck was thick and his lips small but fleshy. He said amicably, "Yes, I think I place you," and with a spanning hand pressed on the round gold rims of his glasses. Schlossberg repeated his name sonorously but obviously did not remember him. He spoke in deep tones, not always distinctly because of his heavy breathing. He was a large old man with a sturdy gray head, hulking shoulders, and a wide, worn face; his eyes were blue and disproportionately small, and even their gaze was rather worn. But he was vigorous and he must once have been (some of his remarks evoked him, for Leventhal, as a younger man) sensual, powerful, flashy, a dandy—as his double-breasted vest and pointed shoes attested. He wore a knitted tie which had lost its shape with pulling and was made up with a bold, broad knot. Leventhal felt himself strongly drawn to him.

"We were just talking about an actress Shifcart sent out West a few years ago," said Goldstone bringing his long, bony, hairy hand to the back of his head. "Wanda Waters."

"Persevalli is the one that makes them," Shifcart said. "He's a great showman."

"But you picked the girl."

"I didn't know she was your discovery, Jack," said Harkavy.

"Yes, I saw her singing with a band one night."

"You don't say."

"At the shore in New Jersey. I was on vacation."

"She's very appealing," said Goldstone.

"You might not like her much, in person."

"Why, she certainly looks like a gingery piece in the pictures," said Harkavy.

"Yes, she has magnetic eyes. But you'd pass her on the street any day and not notice her."

"Oh, I don't know," Harkavy said. "You have a professional attitude in this, seeing so many beauties. I'm still unspoiled. I suppose you can do a lot with paint and cameras, but there has to be something to start with. You can't fake those gorgeous sex machines, can you? Or is it the gullible public again? They look genuine to me."

"Some really are. And if the rest take you in, that's what they're supposed to do."

"It must be quite a knack to pick them," Goldstone remarked.

"It isn't all guesswork. You can't go and run a screen test for every girl you see. But I myself, personally, don't care for some of the best successes I sent into Hollywood."

"Which do you like?" asked Goldstone.

"Oh," he said slowly, thinking, "there's Nola Hook."

"You don't mean it," said Schlossberg. "A little cactus plant . . . skinny, dry. . . ."

"I think she has a kind of charm. Or what's the matter with Livia Hall?"

"Such a discovery!"

"She is. I'll stand up for her."

"Oh, a firebrand." The old man's countenance was too large for fine degrees of irony. Only Shifcart, his lips open to begin his reply, did not join in the laughter.

"What's the matter; hasn't she got anything?"

"She's got!" Schlossberg waved him down. "God made her a woman, so who are we to say? But she isn't an actress. I saw your firebrand last week in a picture. What is it? She poisons her husband."

"In *The Tigress*."

"What a lameness!"

"I don't know what your standards are. A perfect piece of casting. Who else could have done it?"

"Wood, so help me. She poisons her husband and she

watches him die. She wants the insurance money. He loses his voice and he tries to appeal to her she should help him. You don't hear any words. What is she supposed to show in her face? Fear, hate, a hard heart, cruelness, fascination." He shut his eyes tightly and proudly for a moment, and they saw the veins in his lids. Then he slowly raised them, turning his face away, and a tremor went through his cheeks as he posed.

"Oh, say, that's fine!" Harkavy cried, smiling.

"That's the old Russian style," said Shifcart. "That doesn't go any more."

"No? Where's the improvement? What does she do? She sucks in her cheeks and stares. A man is dying at her feet and all she can do is pop out her eyes."

"I think she was marvelous in that show," said Shifcart. "Nobody could have been better."

"She is not an actress because she is not a woman, and she is not a woman because a man doesn't mean anything to her. I don't know what she is. Don't ask me. I saw once Nazimova in *The Three Sisters*. She's the one whose soldier gets killed in a duel over a nothing, foolishness. They tell her about it. She looks away from the audience and just with her head and neck —what a force! But this girl . . . !"

"Terrible, ah?" Shifcart said sardonically.

"No, isn't it? And this is a success? This is your success, these days. You said you could pass this Waters on the street and not recognize her. Imagine!" the old man said, making them all feel his weighty astonishment. "Not to recognize an actress, or that a man shouldn't notice a beautiful woman. It used to be an actress was a woman. She had a mouth, she had flesh on her, she carried herself. When she whispered tears came in your eyes, and when she said a word your legs melted. And it didn't make any difference; on the stage or off the stage you knew she was an actress."

He stopped. They considered his words gravely.

"Say," began Harkavy. "My father used to tell a story about Lily Langtry, the English actress, when she was presented at court by Edward the Seventh. Old Victoria was still alive, and he was the Prince of Wales."

"That's the one they call the Jersey Lily, isn't it?" said Shifcart.

"I've heard this." Goldstone got up and took Leventhal's tray. "Does anyone want coffee? I'm going to the counter."

"Is it good, Monty?"

"My late father-in-law's favorite." He strode off to the steam table.

"Pop told me this one after I was old enough to vote. He saved up all his best stories till I was of age. Before that . . . But of course you pick up everything yourself and they know it. It's only off the record. Well, you know that Edward was a sport. And when he fell in love with Langtry he wanted to present her at court. They say people in love want to be seen together in public. Proud to have it known. I suppose it has a dangerous outcome, sometimes. Well, he wanted to present her. Everybody was scandalized. What was Lily going to say to the old woman, and wouldn't Victoria be angry at having her son's mistress in St. James or Windsor or wherever? All the reporters were waiting after the ceremony. She came out, and they asked her, 'Lily, what did you say to Her Majesty?' 'I was worried that I would say the wrong thing,' said Lily. 'But the last moment the right one came to me. I kissed the hem of her dress and said, *"Ich dien"!"*'"

A smile went around the table. Goldstone, carrying the tray, pulled his chair aside with his foot.

"The motto of the King of Bohemia in the Hundred Years War," Harkavy explained, his round eyes shining at them. "They found it on his helmet after the Battle of Poitiers."

"I doubt very much if she would kiss the queen's dress," said Leventhal. "Is that a part of the ceremony?"

"Curtsy," Goldstone laughed, pulling his napkin open to demonstrate."

"All right, I tell it as my father did. I haven't changed a word."

"The old woman being a German, she figured she'd understand her," Schlossberg said.

"What? No, that's the Hanoverian motto," Goldstone said.

"That was a deal. A German queen, a British Empire, and an Italian Jew for prime minister."

"Disraeli an Italian?" said Goldstone. "Wasn't he English born?"

"But his father."

"Not even his father. His grandfather. He was an authentic Englishman, if citizenship stands for anything."

"He wasn't an Englishman to the English," Leventhal said.

"Why, they loved him," said Goldstone.

"Then who said he was the monkey on John Bull's chest?"

"He had enemies, naturally."

"I understand they never took him in," Leventhal declared.

"Wrong!" Harkavy cried. "He was a credit to them and to us."

"I don't see that," Leventhal slowly shook his head. "It didn't make any difference to them that Victoria was a German. But Disraeli . . . ?"

"He showed Europe that a Jew could be a national leader," said Goldstone.

"That's Leventhal all over for you," exclaimed Harkavy. "That shows you where he stands."

"Jews and empires? Suez and India and so on? It never seemed right to me."

"To teach the world a lesson with empty hands—I know that stuff by heart." Harkavy stared at him with shocked, reprimanding eyes. "The Empire was certainly his business. He was an Englishman and a great one. Bismarck admired him. *Der alter Jude, das ist der Mann!*"

"Is there such a difference between an empire and a department store?" asked Shifcart. "You're managing a business."

"And he was managing the firm?" said Goldstone. "Bull and Company. The sun never sets on our stores. B. Disraeli, chief buyer."

Leventhal at the outset had been a little reluctant to speak and had a fleeting feeling that it was a mistake to be drawn or lured out of his taciturnity. Nor had he thought, with his first remark, that he had much to say on this subject. But now, to his surprise, he was unable to hold back his opinions—they were his, of course, but he had never before expressed them, and they sounded queer to him.

"You bring up Bismarck," he said. "Why did he say *Jude* instead of Englishman? Disraeli was a bargainer, so he was a Jew to him, naturally."

"Don't misrepresent Bismarck on the Jews," warned Harkavy. "Be careful, boy. He lightened their load."

"Yes, he had something to say about making a great race. What was it, now? 'A German stallion and a Jewish mare.'"

"A regular Kentucky Derby," said Schlossberg. "Hay for everybody."

"Don't be down on a man for a figure of speech," said Goldstone. "He was an old cavalryman. That was just his way of talking about the best qualities of both."

"Who needs his compliments?" Schlossberg said. "Who wants them?"

"Does it sound like flattery to you?" Leventhal raised his hand from the top of his head questioningly.

"I see what's on your mind," Goldstone answered. "You're blaming him for the Germans of today."

"I don't," cried Leventhal. "But why are you so glad to have one word of praise from Bismarck, and cockeyed praise too?"

"Why do you have it in for Disraeli?" demanded Harkavy.

"I don't have it in for him. But he wanted to lead England. In spite of the fact that he was a Jew, not because he cared about empires so much. People laughed at his nose, so he took up boxing; they laughed at his poetic silk clothes, so he put on black; and they laughed at his books, so he showed them. He got into politics and became the prime minister. He did it all on nerve."

"Oh, come on," Harkavy said.

"On nerve," Leventhal insisted. "That's great, I'll give you that. But I don't admire it. It's all right to overcome a weakness, but it depends how and it depends what you call a weakness. . . . Julius Caesar was sick with epilepsy. He learned to ride with his hands behind his back and slept on the bare ground like a common soldier. What was the reason? His disease. Why should we admire people like that? Things that are life and death to others are only a test to them. What's the good of such greatness?"

"Why, you're succumbing yourself to all the things that are said against us," Harkavy began in an upbraiding tone.

"No, I don't think I am," said Leventhal. He declined to argue further. He had already said too much and he gave notice by the drop of his voice that he intended to say no more.

A Filipino busboy came to clear the table. He was an old

man and frail looking, and his hands and forearms were whitened by immersions in hot water. The cart loaded, he bent his back low over it, receiving the handlebar in his chest, and pushed away slowly. Behind the steam tables, one set of white-lettered menu boards was hauled down and another sent up in the steel frame with a clash.

"I have seen only one actor do Disraeli," said Goldstone. "That was George Arliss."

"Made for the part, that man," Shifcart asserted.

"Him I liked in that," said Schlossberg. "You're right, Jack, he was made for it. He had the right face to play it, with his thin lips and long nose."

"Somehow I've passed up all the Victorias," remarked Goldstone. "I haven't seen a single one."

"So what have you missed?" said Schlossberg. "A successful Victoria I have yet to see."

It was a slow hour in the restaurant. On all sides there were long perspectives of black-topped tables turned on an angle to appear diamond-shaped, each with its symmetrical cluster of sugar, salt, pepper, and napkin box. From end to end their symmetry put a kind of motion into the almost empty place. At the rear, under the scene of groves painted on the wall, some of the employees sat smoking, looking toward the sunlight and the street.

"I have seen good ones," Shifcart contended. "Don't you like any of them?"

"No. One thing is why there should be so many Victorias. Maybe it's because she was so plain. An ordinary-looking queen has a lot of appeal these days. Everything has to be pulled down a little. Isn't it so? Why is she so popular?" He held out his hands to them as though soliciting a better answer. "She loved Albert; she was stubborn; she was a good housekeeper. It goes over."

"I thought Eunice Sherbarth was a good Victoria," said Harkavy.

"She's a healthy, beautiful lady; it's a pleasure to look at her," said Schlossberg.

"So what's the matter?" asked Shifcart. "She can't act? You only wish you had her contract, Schlossberg."

"Why not?" Schlossberg admitted. "As long as I'm wishing,

I'd like to be thirty years old today with death a little farther off than it is. Besides, my pants are shiny. And who can't use money? She must make plenty, I can imagine. And partly she has it coming because she's good to look at. But act? I could play a better Victoria myself." And indeed he could, thought Leventhal with more respect than amusement, if his voice weren't so deep.

"Yes, in skirts you could be a hit," said Shifcart.

"Anybody could be a hit today," Schlossberg replied. "With the public so crazy to be pleased. It's a regular carnival. Everybody is on the same side with illusion. Tell me, Jack, do you think you have ever discovered a good actress?"

"You mean an artist, I suppose, not a little type like Waters."

"I mean an actress."

"Then I say Livia Hall."

"You mean that?"

"Yes, I do."

"Impossible," said Schlossberg. "A pair of chopsticks."

Shifcart's stout neck grew red in patches and he said, a shade away from anger, "She is not a cheap success. Not everybody is so hard to satisfy, Schlossberg. It looks like it's a big job to entertain you and maybe nobody does."

"You are a tough critic, Marcus," Goldstone said.

"Do I make up the specifications?" said Schlossberg. "*Narischer mensch!* I'm speaking for you, too. This is not the public. Between ourselves we can tell the truth, can't we? What's the matter with the truth? Everything comes in packages. If it's in a package, you can bring the devil in the house. People rely on packages. If you will wrap it up, they will take it."

"I didn't claim the woman was Ellen Terry. I only said she was a good actress. You have to admit, Schlossberg, she's got some ability."

"For some things, maybe. Not too much."

"But some?"

"Yes, some," Schlossberg carelessly granted.

"*Something* at last pleases him, thank God!" Shifcart said.

"I try to give everybody credit," declared the old man. "I am not a knocker. I am not too good for this world."

No one contradicted him.

"Well," he said. "And what am I kicking for?" He checked their smiles, holding them all with his serious, worn, blue gaze. "I'll tell you. It's bad to be less than human and it's bad to be more than human. What's more than human? Our friend—" he meant Leventhal, "was talking about it before. Caesar, if you remember, in the play wanted to be like a god. Can a god have diseases? So this is a sick man's idea of God. Does a statue have wax in its ears? Naturally not. It doesn't sweat, either, except maybe blood on holidays. If I can talk myself into it that I never sweat and make everybody else act as if it was true, maybe I can fix it up about dying, too. We only know what it is to die because some people die and, if we make ourselves different from them, maybe we don't have to? Less than human is the other side of it. I'll come to it. So here is the whole thing, then. Good acting is what is exactly human. And if you say I am a tough critic, you mean I have a high opinion of what is human. This is my whole idea. More than human, can you have any use for life? Less than human, you don't either."

He made a pause—it was not one that invited interruption —and went on.

"This girl Livia in *The Tigress*. What's the matter with her? She commits a murder. What are her feelings? No love, no hate, no fear, no lungs, no heart. I'm ashamed to mention what else is missing. Nothing! The poor husband. Nothing is killing him, less than human. A blank. And it should be so awful the whole audience should be afraid positively to look in her face. But I don't know if she's too pretty or what to have feelings. You see right away she has no idea what is human because her husband's death doesn't mean to her a thing. It's all in packages, and first the package is breathing and then it isn't breathing, and you insured the package so you can marry another package and go to Florida for the winter. Now maybe somebody will answer me, 'This sounds very interesting. You say less than human, more than human. Tell me, please, what is human?' And really we study people so much now that after we look and look at human nature—I write science articles myself—after you look at it and weigh it and turn it over and put it under a microscope, you might say, 'What is all the shouting about? A man is nothing, his life is nothing. Or it is even lousy and cheap. But this your royal highness doesn't like, so he hokes it up. With what? With greatness and beauty. Beauty and greatness? Black and white I know; I didn't make it up. But greatness and beauty?' But I say, 'What do you know? No, tell me, what do you know? You shut one eye and look at a thing, and it is one way to you. You shut the other one and it is different. I am as sure about greatness and beauty as you are about black and white. If a human life is a great thing to me, it *is* a great thing. Do you know better? I'm entitled as much as you. And why be measly? Do you have to be? Is somebody holding you by the neck? Have dignity, you understand me? Choose dignity. Nobody knows enough to turn it down.' Now to whom should this mean something if not to an actor? If he isn't for dignity, then I tell you there is a great mistake somewhere."

"Bravo!" said Harkavy.

"Amen and amen!" Shifcart laughed. He drew a card out of his wallet and threw it toward him. "Come and see me; I'll fix you up with a test."

The card fell near Leventhal, who seemed to be the only one to disapprove of the joke. Even Schlossberg himself smiled. The sunlight fell through the large window over their heads. It seemed to Leventhal that Shifcart, though he was laughing, looked at him with peculiar disfavor. Still he did not join in. He picked up the card. The others were rising.

"Don't forget your hats, gentlemen," called Harkavy.

The musical crash of the check machine filled their ears as they waited their turn at the cashier's dazzling cage.

11

I saw Williston last night," Leventhal mentioned to Harkavy outside.

"How is Stan? Oh, yes, about that thing you were telling me." Harkavy would perhaps have said more, but the others were waiting for him. "Say, one of these days let me know how you're making out with it, will you?"

"Sure," Leventhal said. And Harkavy loitered off eastward on Fourteenth Street with Goldstone and his friends. He was the tallest among them. His yellow hair drifted flimsily, silkily over his bald spot. Leventhal watched him go. He would not admit to himself that he felt deserted. "Maybe it's a good thing he isn't interested," he thought. "I don't know if I could explain it anyhow. It's getting too complicated. And he'd give me all kinds of useless advice—the usual. Anyhow I'm glad. I don't think I really wanted to talk about it." He remained aimlessly in the same place for a while and then walked off, pressing the bulky Sunday paper under his arm. He did not have a conscious destination and was distantly under the dread of being the only person in the city without one.

In the next block he remembered that he had neglected to call Elena to make sure Philip had gotten home safely and to ask about Mickey. He stopped at a cigar store and dialed Villani's number. He sat in the booth, one leg stretched out of the door. No one answered. Leaning out, he looked at the clock cut squarely into the patterned tin of the wall. It was half-past two, and Elena had probably left to visit Mickey. He phoned the hospital, though he understood well enough that the information given about patients wasn't reliable. He heard that Mickey was doing nicely, which was what he had expected to hear. There were upward of three thousand beds in the hospital. How could the girls at the switchboard be expected to know anything but the bare facts about each patient —whether he was alive or dead, that is? The word "dead," dissociated from what he had thought, accompanied him ominously out of the store, and he made haste to get rid of it, simultaneously realizing, in another part of his mind, how superstitious he was becoming. All he had meant was that the hospital was too vast, and suddenly he had to erase an incidental word. Why, everyone born was sick at one time or another. Nobody grew up without sickness. He had had pneumonia himself and an ear infection, and Max had been down, too—he couldn't recall with what.

He began to wonder how long Max was going to put off coming home. "Maybe he's afraid of being tricked into returning," he thought. "I'll have a thing or two to say to him when I see him. For once in our lives. It's time somebody called him down. Elena won't, so he's used to doing whatever he wants." And what would Max have to say for himself? Something simple minded and foolish, he was certain. Because he was foolish. Philip already had more common sense than his father. Leventhal visualized his brother's strongly excited face and imagined his incoherencies. "He sends them money and that makes him a father. That's the end of his responsibilities. That's fatherhood," he repeated to himself. "That's his idea of duty."

From the dark staircase and hall, he entered the brilliantly sunlit front room. He sat on the edge of the bed and pushed off his shoes. The sheets were warm to his touch. The heavy folds of the curtain, the brown door, the fine red flowers in the carpet slowly consumed into a light smoke of dust, gave him a feeling of suspension and quietness. There was a long spider's thread on the screen, quivering red, blue, and deeper blue against the wires like the last pliant, changeable thing in the stiffening, fixative heat. With one stockinged foot set on the other, his shoulders drooping, Leventhal sat watching, his face somnolent, his hands looking as if it would require a great effort to unclasp them.

Presently he went into the kitchen. He absent-mindedly rinsed a few dishes under the rumbling tap and, returning to the front room, unbuckled his belt, drew the curtains, and with the Sunday paper unheeded under his legs, went to sleep.

A deep rolling noise awakened him. He thought at first that it came from below, out of the subway. But there was no accompanying tremor through the building. He soon placed the sound outside and above him. It was thunder. He looked out. There had been a storm. The screen was still clogged with raindrops. The street was softly darkened by the clouds and the wet brownstone. In one of the rooms across the way a two-branched green lamp was shining. A woman lay on a sofa, one arm bent over her eyes. At the next sound of the re-treating thunder she moved her legs.

Leventhal glanced again into the mist and water of the street and then went to the phone and tried Villani's number. There was still no answer. Apparently they were out some-where, making a day of it. He poised the receiver over the hook, aimed it, and let it fall into place.

He worked his feet into his shoes, treading down the heels, and went down to the restaurant for an early dinner. The waiter, the same bald, lean man who last week had anticipated his protest about the bad table with a gesture of insincere helplessness, appeared to be occupied with thoughts of his own. His black suit looked damp, and his leather bow tie was not fastened but hung on its elastic from a buttonhole. He brought Leventhal a veal cutlet and a bottle of beer and hur-ried away with a muscular swing, softly—his soles were padded with sawdust—to wait on a long table of *boccie* play-ers whose game had been rained out and who were drinking wine and coffee. The odor of wet wood was very noticeable. Leventhal did not linger over his meal. He was soon outside again. The air was dimmer than before, and hotter. He turned west on Eighteenth Street and saw Allbee waiting for him on the corner. He had to look twice in the wavering, longitudinal grays and shadows of the watery street to iden-tify him.

Leventhal did not halt until Allbee detained him, stepping in his way. He dropped his head diffidently and clumsily, as though asking Leventhal to understand that he was com-pelled to do this.

"Well?" Leventhal said after a moment's silence.

"Why didn't you stop? You saw me. . . ."

"And if I did? I'm not looking for you. You're the one. You follow me around."

"You're mad about yesterday, aren't you? That was a co-incidence."

"Oh, it was for sure."

"I wanted to talk to you yesterday, it so happens. You won't hunt me up. If I want to talk to you, I have to find opportunities."

"Is that the way you describe it?"

"But when I remembered it was Saturday—you people don't do business on Saturday—I postponed it." The saying of this appeared to delight him. But then his expression changed. He seemed to recognize and even to be depressed by the poorness of his joke. He looked somberly and earnestly at Leventhal, who understood that Allbee wanted him to know of the feelings that gave rise to it, and to know also that since those feelings were dire and powerful the joke dissembling them was actually a courtesy.

"I don't observe the holiday," said Leventhal deliberately and dryly.

"Oh, of course not," said Allbee, and he again began to smile. He added, a second later, "As far as 'following' is concerned, that's not the way to put it. I have a perfect right to see you. You act as if I had some kind of game, whereas you're the one that's playing a game."

"How do you figure that?"

Allbee raised his hand. "You pretend that I haven't got a grievance against you. That's playing." His fingers brushed over his chest, and then he covered his mouth and cleared his throat.

"Say . . . with the kid—stuff like that has got to stop."

"I didn't know he was with you."

"Not much! Well, I'm telling you. Besides, I told you the first time, I never wanted to do you any harm."

"We differ about that. And there was a second time, too." He gave an illustrative push that stopped short of Leventhal's shoulders. "That was a little too much game for me. Or were you trying to scare me off?"

"If I was, you mean that I can't, huh?"

"Well," Allbee suggested, "you might have sent me to the hospital and gotten rid of me that way for a while." He grinned. "You said you should have broken my neck."

Leventhal said contemptuously, "But otherwise . . . to scare you? It's impossible to scare you, isn't it?"

"A year ago I wouldn't have come to you. But now that I've done it, made up my mind, it is impossible."

"What was different a year ago?" asked Leventhal.

"Then I was getting by, somehow, and I wouldn't have thought of coming near you," he said quite seriously.

"And now?"

"My wife left me some money. It wasn't a lot, but I stretched it. As long as it lasted—why, if I were still getting by you'd never hear from me. I'll say it again. But maybe I don't have a real sense of honor or I wouldn't put myself in such a position. I mean real honor. There's no getting away from it, I suppose, honor is honor. Either you've got it up to here," he drew a line across his throat, "or you haven't got it. It doesn't make you any happier to tell yourself you ought to have it. It's like anything else that counts. You have to make sacrifices to it. You know, I'm from an old New England family. As far as honor's concerned, I'm not keeping up standards very well, I admit. Still, if I was born with my full share of it, in New York I'd have an even worse handicap. Oh, boy!— New York. Honor sure got started before New York did. You won't see it at night, hereabouts, in letters of fire up in the sky. You'll see other words. Such things just get swallowed up in these conditions—modern life. So I'm lucky I didn't inherit more of a sense of it. I'd be competing with Don Quixote. Now with you it's different, altogether. You're right at home in this, like those what-do-call-'ems that live in the flames— salamanders. If somebody hurts you, you hit back in any way and anything goes. That's how it is here. It's rugged. And I can appreciate it. Of course, the kind of honor I'm familiar with doesn't allow that. Mine tells me not to ask for damages, and so on. But I have it in diluted form; that's obvious."

Allbee said this conversationally, in a factual manner; nevertheless Leventhal heard the spiteful ring in it. But he evinced no feeling and made no comment.

"I have an idea that it's one of those things that's bound to go."

"You went through the money," Leventhal said, disregarding the rest. "Why didn't you get a job?"

"What did I want to work for? What sort of a job could I get anyhow? Nobody would give me what I wanted. And do you think I could take a leg job, like a high-school kid? An errand boy? Besides, I was in no hurry. Why should I be?"

"Were you black-listed?" Leventhal was unable to conceal his concern. "Is that the reason?"

Allbee did not reply to this directly. "Why, Rudiger wouldn't have taken me back even to empty his ash trays."

After this they were both silent for a while. Under its flat rim the ball of the lamp nearby began to shine in the gray and blue depth of the air, revealing suddenly the perspiration on Allbee's face. The rings under his eyes gave him an aspect of suffering anger and hate. Yet he seemed unaware of any exposure and spoke evenly.

"No, I didn't want to work," he said. "I had a hell of a time after my wife was killed and I decided to take myself off the market for a while. I lived like a gentleman."

Leventhal said grimly to himself, "Oh, gentleman. It looks like it. A marvelous gentleman."

"Well, what do you want from me?" he asked Allbee. "You lived like a gentleman. I guess that means getting up at eleven or twelve every day. I get up at seven and go to my job. You've had a long vacation. Still you want me to do something for you. I don't know what you want. What do you want?"

"I could use some help. The vacation's lasted a little too long."

"What sort of help?"

"I don't know what sort. I wanted to take that up with you. You could help me if you wanted to. You must have connections. I'd like to get away from my old line, something new, a complete change."

"For example?"

"Do you think you can get something for me in a bank?"

"Oh, you want to go straight where they keep it, where the money is," said Leventhal.

"Or a brokerage firm?"

"Stop your joking," Leventhal said somewhat sharply. "I don't care for the sort of jokes you make. I'm not under an obligation to you. I'll do something for you if I can. And just remember, it doesn't mean I admit anything. I think you're crazy. But Stan Williston thinks I ought to help you, and out of respect for him I'll try."

"What!" exclaimed Allbee. "You discussed me with Williston? What did you tell him about me?"

"Oh, you don't like that? No, I see you don't," said Leventhal. "I didn't make anything up."

"What did you tell him?" he said again, in agitation.

"What do you think I could tell him? Are you afraid I blackened your character? Are you touchy about your reputation? I thought you had lost your sense of honor?"

"You had no business—no damned business!" Allbee cried out in a flash of hatred and with an intensity of shame that disturbed Leventhal in spite of himself.

"Well, you're a crazy, queer bastard," he said. "What's the matter with you? You come to me with this hokum about being too down and out to have any pride left—you can even come to me, and this and that. I knew it was all fake. One minute you're on the bottom, couldn't be any lower, and the next you're a regular Lord Byron."

There was an interval of silence during which Allbee appeared to be struggling for control over himself. Then he said in a low voice, "Williston is an old friend of mine. I just happen to have special feelings about him and Phoebe. But I guess it really doesn't make much difference." He gradually recovered his smile and he remarked, withdrawing his eyes from Leventhal and beginning a protracted, glittering study of the street behind him, "I should have expected you not to miss still another chance to get at me."

"Are you in your right mind?" Leventhal demanded. "Are you straight in the head? Is it the booze or what? God almighty! Every day I see new twists." He looked heavenward and gave way to a short laugh. "So help me, it's like a menagerie. They say you go to the zoo to see yourself in the animals. There aren't enough animals in the world to see ourselves in. There would have to be a million new feathers and tails. There's no end to the twists."

Allbee, preoccupied with the dwindling violets and grays of twilight and the swarms of light, seemed also to find this comical.

"Well, you've got nothing on me," he said.

"You think not?"

"You're just as much of a monster to me."

"I am?"

"Hell, yes. Well, you look like Caliban in the first place," Allbee said, more serious than not. "But that's not all I mean. You personally, you're just one out of many. Many kinds. You wouldn't be able to see that. Sometimes I feel—and I'm saying this seriously—I feel as if I were in a sort of Egyptian darkness. You know, Moses punished the Egyptians with darkness. And that's how I often think of this. When I was born, when I was a boy, everything was different. We thought it would be daylight forever. Do you know, one of my ancestors was Governor Winthrop. Governor Winthrop!" His voice vibrated fiercely; there was a repressed laugh in it. "I'm a fine one to be talking about tradition, you must be saying. But still I was born into it. And try to imagine how New York affects me. Isn't it preposterous? It's really as if the children of Caliban were running everything. You go down in the subway and Caliban gives you two nickels for your dime. You go home and he has a candy store in the street where you were born. The old breeds are out. The streets are named after them. But what are they themselves? Just remnants."

"I see how it is; you're actually an aristocrat," said Leventhal.

"It may not strike you as it struck me," said Allbee. "But I go into the library once in a while, to look around, and last week I saw a book about Thoreau and Emerson by a man named Lipschitz. . . ."

"What of it?"

"A name like that?" Allbee said this with great earnestness. "After all, it seems to me that people of such background simply couldn't understand. . . ."

"Of all the goddamned nonsense!" shouted Leventhal. "Look, I've got things to attend to. I have a phone call to make. It's important. Tell me what in the name of hell you want and make it snappy."

"I assure you, I wasn't trying to be malicious. I was only discussing this. . . ."

"I assure you, you were trying, I assure you!" Leventhal flung out. "Now what are you after? Probably a few bucks for whisky."

Allbee laughed aloud. "They say drinking is only another

kind of disease," he said. "Like heart disease or syphilis. You wouldn't be so hard on anyone with heart disease, would you? You'd be more sympathetic. They even say crime is only a sort of disease and if you had more hospitals you'd need fewer prisons. Look how many murderers are let off and get treatment instead of execution. If they're sick it's not their fault. Why can't you take that attitude?"

"Why?" Leventhal involuntarily repeated. He was bewildered.

"Because you've got to blame me, that's why," said Allbee. "You won't assume that it isn't entirely my fault. It's necessary for you to believe that I deserve what I get. It doesn't enter your mind, does it—that a man might not be able to help being hammered down? What do you say? Maybe he can't help himself? No, if a man is down, a man like me, it's his fault. If he suffers, he's being punished. There's no evil in life itself. And do you know what? It's a Jewish point of view. You'll find it all over the Bible. God doesn't make mistakes. He's the department of weights and measures. If you're okay, he's okay, too. That's what Job's friends come and say to him. But I'll tell you something. We do get it in the neck for nothing and suffer for nothing, and there's no denying that evil is as real as sunshine. Take it from me, I know what I'm talking about. To you the whole thing is that I must deserve what I get. That leaves your hands clean and it's unnecessary for you to bother yourself. Not that I'm asking you to feel sorry for me, but you sure can't understand what makes a man drink."

"All right, so I can't. What then? What did you stop me for, to tell me that?"

"No, you never could and I'll tell you why. Because you people take care of yourselves before everything. You keep your spirit under lock and key. That's the way you're brought up. You make it your business assistant, and it's safe and tame and never leads you toward anything risky. Nothing dangerous and nothing glorious. Nothing ever tempts you to dissolve yourself. What for? What's in it? No percentage."

Leventhal's expression was uncomprehending and horrified. His forehead was wrinkled. His heart beat agonizingly, and he faltered out, "I don't see how you can talk that way.

That's just talk. Millions of us have been killed. What about that?"

He seemed to be waiting for a reply, but before it could be given he turned and walked away rapidly, leaving Allbee alone under the lamp.

12

LEVENTHAL strode home blindly and rapidly, his stout body shaken by the unaccustomed gait. Perspiration ran from his bushy, lusterless hair over his dark skin. He was thinking that he should have done something, slammed Allbee on the head, not let him off. He felt he had answered stupidly, although he did not know what he should have told him; he was unable to remember all that had been said. But as the first throbs of anger began to pass into soreness, it began to appear to him that he had known all along, all through the conversation, what to do and had failed to do it, that he had been unequal to what was plain, clear, and necessary. "I ought to have done it," he thought, "even if it meant murdering him."

Just then, the blink of a yellow light in the middle of the street started him into a trot. An eddy of exhaust gas caught him in the face. He was behind the bus. A tearing of gears carried it forward, and he came up on the curb, breathless. He rested a moment and then went on, gradually slowing to his ordinary pace. His head ached. There was a spot between his eyes that was particularly painful; the skin itself was tender. He pressed it. It seemed to have been the dead center of all his staring and concentration. He felt that his nerves were worse than ever and that his rage had done him harm, affected his very blood. He had an impression of bad blood as something black, thick, briny, caused by sickness or lust or excessive anger. His heart quickened again. He cast a glance behind. Several people were going in the other direction. "Let him better not come near me," he muttered. His brain was clearer, and the single thought of murder that had risen in it was gone. However, he regretted not having hit Allbee and would almost have welcomed another chance. What was the use of wasting words on such people? Hit them! That was all they understood. A woman in the movies whom Mary had asked to remove her hat, two or three years ago, had turned around and uttered some insult about "the gall of Jews." Woman or no, Leventhal had had a powerful desire to drive his fist into her head, tear the hat off. He had afterwards argued with Mary that there were times when that should be done. "Where would it get you?" was Mary's answer. Practically, she was right, no doubt; she knew the value of staying cool. But he regretted it. Oh, how he sometimes regretted not slapping off that hat. With his father it had at least been "*gib mir die groschke*," a potentially real compensation. "But what about me?" Leventhal asked with an arrested upward glance of his large meditative eyes. There was a murky redness in the clouds, absorbed from the neon lights and the clock tower on Fifth Avenue. His father had believed in getting his due, at any rate. And there was a certain wisdom in that. You couldn't say you were master of yourself when there were so many people by whom you could be humiliated. As for Mary, she must have been thinking, in answering, of the night he had pushed her, years ago in Baltimore. Perhaps she wanted to remind him of it. Of course, there was no excuse for that. But he still felt that the woman's hat should have been snatched off and hurled away.

And he uttered a low, unwilling laugh when he recalled how he had stood, just stood, without the presence of mind to realize that he was being insulted. It did have to do with presence of mind, exactly as in the case of Dunhill, the linotyper who sold him the unwanted ticket. With Allbee there was the added confusion that he brought off his insults with an air of discussion. When he started out, even though he made a crooked joke here and there, he seemed to be speaking impersonally. But all at once he said something in earnest that was terrible. Of course, he was sick. He himself had brought up the subject of disease, so he must be aware of it. But did his sickness, whatever it was, account for what he said, or would good health only have given him the strength to keep it to himself? Some people, gentle to begin with, were kind when they were sick. Leventhal said to himself, impatiently, "There are two billion people or so in the world and *he's* miserable. What's he so special?"

Mrs. Nunez was standing on the brownstone stoop. She and her husband had just returned from a Sunday outing. She carried gloves and a red patent-leather bag. Her hat was a white straw with cherries on the brim. Her Indian face was small, but she had an ungainly, full-hipped figure. She wore a close-fitting striped suit, her shoulders were raised, her bosom was high, and her lips were parted as if at the end of a long breath. Mary, whom nothing escaped, had once said about Mrs. Nunez' suits, "I don't see why she wears them. She could look very pretty in silk prints." Till then Leventhal had scarcely noticed her. Now, when she said good evening and he nodded to her, he remembered this and had a moment of intense longing for his wife.

"Were you caught in the rain?" said Mrs. Nunez.

"No, I slept through the whole storm."

"We were in Prospect Park to see the flowers. My brother works in the hothouse. My, it was terrible. A tree fell down. The lightning hit it."

"That must have been frightening."

"Terrible. We were inside. But I was scared. Oh, awful," she said with a release of breath. "Your missis coming back already?"

"Not yet."

She drew the gloves out and worked them with her long brown fingers whose size and strength he noted in absent-minded surprise.

"Coming soon?"

"I don't think so."

"Oh, too bad, too bad," she said in her light, flat, rapid way. Leventhal had often paused at the Nunez' door to listen, entertained, to their quick-running Spanish, not a word of which he understood. "Too bad," she repeated, and Leventhal, with a glance of surmise at her small face under the white brim, wondered what hint her sympathy might contain. There was a burst of music above them; a window was thrown open.

"I'll be a bachelor for a month or so yet," he said.

"Oh, maybe you enjoy yourself anyhow; makes you a change for a while."

"No," he said bluntly.

He went into the foyer where Nunez' dog scampered at him, jumping up. He bent and clasped the animal, and rubbed its head. It licked his face and pushed its muzzle into his coat under his sleeve.

"She's crazy about you," said Nunez from the doorway. "I

think she smells you coming." He was polishing his glasses with a flowered handkerchief of his wife's. Beside the bed, in his room, there were beer cans and newspapers.

"That's a friendly dog. I have a soft spot for dogs myself."

"Up, Smoke," said Nunez. "Do hounds ever faint, Mr. Leventhal? Sometimes I think this one is going to faint when you rub her belly."

"I don't know. Do animals faint? Does anyone faint from pleasure?"

"Somebody," Nunez joked. "A lady with a weak heart, maybe. Look a' that, on her back. Look a' that chest on her." He put on his glasses and held the edge of the door. The red of the foyer and the yellow of his flat were drawn on its black panels. His sport shirt was open, and a religious medal swung over the twist of hair between the muscles of his dark, reddish breast.

"Come in and have a beer," he said.

"I can't, thanks, I have something to do." Leventhal remembered that he had not yet reached Elena. It occurred to him, moreover, that Nunez had been a witness to his scuffle with Allbee in the hall. He looked at him uncomfortably and moved toward the stairs.

For the third time he got no answer at Villani's and he began to be anxious. The Villanis had young children, and young children had to be put to bed. It was already after eight. "Maybe I'd better go out and see Elena and Phil," he said to himself. "I don't have anything to do tonight." But his concealed thought was that Villani's absence was a bad sign. He set out again, nodding to Mrs. Nunez on the stoop as though he saw her for the first time.

He found Villani and the old woman sitting with Philip and Elena in the parlor. They had just returned from the hospital, and he gathered that Mickey was worse. He appeared to be losing weight. Villani betrayed his misgivings by the pitch of his optimism. He cried, "Don't worry about them, out there. They make them eat. There's no such thing in a hospital, not eating. They see to it. They can handle the kids; they got experience." Elena was coldly silent. Evidently she had accused the hospital of not feeding the child. Her look was waxen. Everything—her black hair, dark nostrils, and white lips; her lack of stir at his arrival; even the fact that she was dressed for the street and not in her gingham with the nightgown under it—made Leventhal uneasy.

"Give them time," said Villani. "He ain't been there long. What do you say?"

Leventhal gave out a sound of confirmation and glanced from Elena to the old woman in her dark colors. Her lean wrists, marked with raised, dull blue veins, rested in her lap. He observed that her ankles, above her unfashionable black shoes, were swollen—probably from walking the long hospital corridors. Her mouth was thin, the underlip not quite matching the expressionless upper because her chin was sunk. The tilt of her body in the Morris chair, her crossed feet, suggested rest, and yet rest was what she seemed to be resisting, drawing off her shoulders from the cushion behind her. Her eyes, whenever her lids went up, disclosed a fierceness as piercing as a rooster's. Leventhal, in spite of himself, was arrested by her face. Other people might change themselves still; it was hard, it might not work, but they could try. This woman, as she was, was finished forever.

He took the first opportunity to whisper to Villani that perhaps Max ought to be sent for now, and Villani shut his eyes in agreement. It was serious, then. He would phone the doctor in the morning and get a report. Denisart had promised to tell him when to send for Max.

He got away to the kitchen for a while, ostensibly for a glass of water. Actually he was afraid that if he sat opposite Elena much longer he might lose control of himself. His face might twitch, perhaps, or his voice crack. Worst of all, he might ask her why she thought he was to blame, and that would be utterly wrong and possibly dangerous. She did hold him responsible, plainly. He had urged her to send the boy to the hospital. But the doctor had done that, too. And what could he look for later, if she blamed him now? This was only the beginning, judging from the signs Villani gave; there was more to expect. They themselves, the parents, were responsible insofar as anyone was. Especially Max. Why did he postpone coming home? Because he thought he could get by? He could get by, though, only if Mickey, hanging on in the hospital, got by. Not that Max's being at home now could make a real difference to the child, but at all events he might not seem so given up to that enormous hospital, and on Max's side an acknowledgment would be made. After all, you married and had children and there was a chain of consequences. It was impossible to tell, in starting out, what was going to happen. And it was unfair, perhaps, to have to account at forty for what was done at twenty. But unless one was more than human or less than human, as Mr. Schlossberg put it, the payments had to be met. Leventhal disagreed about "less than human." Since it was done by so many, what was it but human? "More than human" was for a much smaller number. But most people had fear in them—fear of life, fear of death, of life more than of death, perhaps. But it was a fact that they were afraid, and when the fear was uppermost they didn't want any more burdens. At twenty they had vigor and so were careless, and later they felt too weak to be accountable. They said, "Just let me alone, that's all I ask." But either they found the strength to meet the costs or they refused and gave way to dizziness—dizziness altogether, the dizziness of pleasures before catastrophes. Maybe you could call it "less than human" to refuse; he liked to think "human" meant accountable in spite of many weaknesses—at the last moment, tough enough to hold. But to go by what happened in the majority of cases, it was the last dizziness that was most typical and had the best claim to the name.

He went back to the parlor for a while. When he announced that he was leaving, Elena looked at him but did not say good night.

Philip, heavy eyed and dejected, sat outside the circle of adults, his arms wound around the back of the chair. His shirt was pulled out at the sides and his shoes untied.

"Tired from trotting after them all day," Leventhal observed to himself. He was filled with tenderness toward him. "Go to sleep, Phil," he said.

"I will."

"Did you have a good time yesterday?"

"Yes, swell."

"When the kid gets out we'll take one of those boat excursions around the island. I understand they're really beautiful."

Philip laid his cheek on the top rung of the chair in a way

that fatigue alone could not have explained. Leventhal passed his hand over his short hair, saying, "All right, boy." But beyond that he could bring nothing out. He foundered, the thread of reassurance lost, the very breath with which to make reassurances driven out of him by his pity for the children. He hurried down the dirty tile stairs. A bus loomed up, half a block away, and he ran across the street. Though there were empty seats around him he stood up, supporting himself on the shining pole, hardly hearing the escape of air from the brakes and the pneumatic doors, and seeing only chaotically shapeless colors with his brimming eyes. Philip must have noticed him whispering to Villani. But probably he had begun to understand earlier. He knew, Leventhal was convinced. And perhaps even little Mickey in the hospital comprehended it all, after a fashion, affected as a candle flame is by varying amounts of air, as all that wants to be what it was made responds to whatever feeds or endangers it.

Looping and swerving the bus reached the waterfront. The smell of the harbor and the flash of the arcades came to Leventhal. He made his way through the dim space of the shed to the bow of the boat and looked out on the water, the sharp stars, and the crimson and yellow spots hung from the cranes and hulls swinging between the slip and the incandescent low crust of the shore.

13

T HE WEEK that followed was a miserable one for him. Dr.
Denisart was not optimistic on Monday, and, since he
had proved before that he was anything but an alarmist, Leventhal saw that in his professional way he was giving notice
that there was very little hope. On Tuesday he said he
thought it advisable that Max should come home. Leventhal
cried into the phone, "What do you mean? Is this it?" The
doctor answered, "The father ought to be on hand." "It's the
showdown, in other words," Leventhal said. He sent the wire,
and that evening and the next he went out to the hospital,
making every effort to avoid meeting Elena. Mickey was now
unconscious, and they fed him intravenously. Hot and grimy
after his long trip, Leventhal bent over the bed. The boy's
face was darkened with fever; the needle was taped to his arm
with strips broad enough for a grown man. The level of the
liquid in the flask held by a clamp on the long stand did not
seem to change. Leventhal moved to the window and lifted
the edge of the shade an inch or two with his forefinger, peering down at the stone jars of vines and geraniums, too massive for the small sunken court. Then he went out, with a
hesitation at the foot of the bed. He traveled two hours in
order to spend ten minutes in Mickey's room.

He kept telling himself, "The showdown is coming"—
guiltily, for at heart he had no hope. The word itself was an
evasion, and he, not the doctor, had introduced it. But it was
a comprehensive word; it embraced more than Mickey's crisis,
or Elena's, or his own trouble with Allbee. These were included; what had been going on with Allbee, for example,
could not be allowed to continue indefinitely. But what he
meant by this preoccupying "showdown" was a crisis which
would bring an end of his resistance to something he had no
right to resist. Illness, madness, and death were forcing him
to confront his fault. He had used every means, and principally indifference and neglect, to avoid acknowledging it and
he still did not know what it was. But that was owing to the
way he had arranged not to know. He had done a great deal

to make things easier for himself, toning down, softening, looking aside. But the more he tried to subdue whatever it was that he resisted, the more it raged, and the moment was coming when his strength to resist would be at an end. He was nearly exhausted now.

It was nearly midnight when he came home on Wednesday. Even before he unlocked the door, he heard the refrigerator panting as though it were trying to keep up a charge of energy in the air of the empty flat. He turned on the lights in the front room and in the bathroom where he undressed and put on pajamas. Opening the medicine chest, he stared like someone who has forgotten what he is looking for; in reality, his mind was empty. His hand touched his razor and, unthinkingly, he changed the blade and set it back in the red velvet groove of the case. Barefooted he walked into the front room. There was paper on the desk, and it occurred to him to send a note to Mary. He sat down, twisting his legs around the legs of the chair, wrote a few words, and stopped to consider what he ought or ought not to say. There was plenty to choose from. That he missed her? That it was still hot? He put down the pen and leaned on the desk, pressing his chest against the edge of the leaf. Dumb and motionless in the silent room, he heard the slamming of car doors and the racing of motors outside. Suddenly there was a prolonged, tearing peal of the bell. A finger screwed the pusher mercilessly in the socket. Hurrying to the door he shouted, "Yes?" He heard his name pronounced several times and called back, "Who is it?" Stooping over the banister, he caught sight of Allbee on the landing below and he withdrew into the vestibule and shut the door. Presently the handle was turned, turned again quietly, and then shaken.

"Yes, yes, what do you want now? What do you want?" he said.

Allbee knocked. Leventhal jerked the door open and saw him with his knuckles raised, ready to knock again.

"Well?"

"I want to see you," said Allbee.

"Well, you're seeing me." He made as if to close the door, and Allbee brought his head forward quickly in a movement of melancholy protest, looking at Leventhal without rancor, however.

"That isn't fair," he said. "I work up my courage to come and see you. It takes me nearly a day to do it."

"To cook up something new."

Allbee's expression was serious. The insane element usually manifested in his smiles was absent.

"The other night—last week—I was getting around to something," he said. "There was something I wanted to say to you."

"I don't want any more discussions. I won't stand for any. Anyhow, it's after midnight."

"Yes, I know it's late," Allbee conceded. "But there was something important to say. We were sidetracked."

"You were," Leventhal said heavily. "I wasn't even in it."

"I guess I know what you're referring to. But whatever I did say, I didn't intend to be personal. You shouldn't consider . . ."

"What? It was all theory, theoretical?" he said sarcastically.

"Well, partly. It was partly joking," Allbee explained painfully. "That's an ingrained habit with me. I know it's bad."

"I'm sorry, but I don't understand you. Maybe I don't understand Emerson either. It goes together."

"Please . . ." he said despondently.

There was a hush in the hall under the dull spokes of the skylight and the filmy glass.

"You take it all in the wrong spirit," he went on.

"How should I take it?"

"You ought to realize that I'm not entirely . . ." he stumbled, "that I'm not entirely under control." The slant of the shadows on his pale, fleshy face made it look infirm. The marks beneath his eyes brought to Leventhal's mind the bruises under the skin of an apple. "Things get away from me. I'm not trying to excuse myself. But you wouldn't believe how much . . ."

"Say, nowadays you can believe almost anything," Leventhal said, and he laughed a little but without relish.

With a grave look, Allbee appealed to him not to persist in this. His brows went up, he pushed his fingers through his dirtyish blond hair, and Leventhal remarked to himself that there was an element of performance in all that he was doing.

But suddenly he had a strange, close consciousness of Allbee, of his face and body, a feeling of intimate nearness such as he had experienced in the zoo when he had imagined himself at Allbee's back, seeing with microscopic fineness the lines in his skin, and the smallest of his hairs, and breathing in his odor. The same sensations were repeated; he could nearly feel the weight of his body and the contact of his clothes. Even more, the actuality of his face, loose in the cheeks, firm in the forehead and jaws, struck him, the distinctness of it; and the look of recognition Allbee bent on him duplicated the look in his own. He was sure of that. Nevertheless he kept alive in his mind the thought that Allbee hated him, and his judgment, although it was numbed by his curious emotion of closeness —for it was an emotion—did not desert him. His burly, keen-set figure did not budge from the doorway any more than the spokes in the skylight moved.

"Will you let me in?" Allbee said at last.

"What for?"

"I want to talk to you."

"I told you, it's late."

"It's late for you, but it's all the same to me what time it is. You said you'd help me."

"I don't want to start discussing your future now. Go away."

"It's the present, not the future."

Leventhal felt inexplicably weak against him. "Am I forgetting all the things he said to me, how mad I was, all that ugly stuff?" he asked himself. And it was true that his sense of injury had not remained sharp; his self-reproach did not make it any sharper. The hall was airless, just as Mickey's room had been. He was starved for a free breath of air. His eyes were hot and tired, and the feeling of closeness seemed to have superseded and made faint all other feelings.

"What, the present?" he said.

"Well, you can go in, turn off the lights, and go to sleep," said Allbee. "It's nothing you have to think about. But I have nowhere to go. Not for the last few nights. I was put out."

Leventhal studied him silently. Then he moved aside and said, "All right. Come on." He let Allbee precede him into the front room and pointed to a chair. He himself went to the

window and put his head out, getting a glimpse of the reddened and darkened heavy forms of the street as he drew a
long breath. He sat down on the creaking bed. It had not
been made for a week, and papers and cardboard crescents
the laundry put inside his collars were scattered over it. In
crossing his legs, Allbee gave a twitch to his stained, loose-
hanging trousers. His manner in some things was persistently
gentlemanly. He knit his fingers around his knee.

"Now let's have it again. What happened, you were thrown
out? Where were you, in a hotel, a room?"

"A furnished room. My landlord confiscated my stuff. Not
that there was much of it." Allbee's smile crept for a moment
into the corners of his mouth and then was gone. "But such
as there was."

"For back rent?"

"Yes."

"Was it much?"

"I have no idea what I owed him. Or them. There's a landlady, too. In fact she's the whole works. The Punts. They're a
couple of Germans. She's a fat old woman with snag teeth.
The nephew's a longshoreman. He's not so bad. It's that
smelly old woman's fault. She kept after him. Old people, especially old women, are the hardest customers. They've made
it, so to hell with everybody."

"Made what? What are you talking about?"

"Lived so long. Pulled through. A long life," said Allbee.
"All the hardships. The rich are rough on the poor for the
same reason. The veteran is rough on the tenderfoot. All the
way down the line. You know that yourself. . . ."

"How much do you owe them? Ten dollars, twenty . . . ?"
said Leventhal stopping him impatiently.

"More like forty or fifty. To be honest with you, I can't
even make an estimate. I gave them a little on account, now
and then. I don't know. Less than they say, you can be sure of
that."

"Didn't they say?"

"I don't remember."

"Don't tell me!"

Allbee did not speak.

"Don't you want to go back there, pay them a little? If it's forty dollars, I haven't got that kind of money on hand, but if you give them something . . . ?"

"No, thanks, the whole house smells. Pardon me, but that old Mrs. Punt—I can't stand uncleanliness like that."

"I'll bet you're a model roomer, too."

"I'm not the worst."

"Excuse me, but I forgot you were an aristocrat," Leventhal muttered with a short laugh. Allbee looked at him simply, without a touch of reproof.

"Well, where have you been staying?"

"Fortunately the weather's been nice. I slept out. In the open. I could have gone to a shelter or a mission. I thought if the weather turned bad that I would. I'd go religious for a while. But it's been beautiful."

"I don't know how you could let things get that bad. If you're telling me the truth."

"If I told you the whole truth, it wouldn't sound plausible, so I'm only telling you part of it. I'm cutting it short. I suppose I shouldn't have let things get out of hand like this. Last week I kept warning myself to hurry up and do something, but I didn't pull myself together for some reason, and then Punt threw me out and there I was." He turned his hand inward in a gesture of self-presentation. "The way I look, pearl diving is about the only work I could get."

"How much money did your wife leave you?" Leventhal asked suddenly.

Allbee colored. "What business is it of yours?" he said.

"Why, man, you should have done something with it instead of just living it up."

"You can't bring the world to its knees with a little insurance money. . . ." He hesitated and added, "I don't owe you any explanation, do I?"

"You don't owe me anything. I don't owe you anything, either."

Allbee did not accept this, but he confined his disagreement to a shrug. Then he examined Leventhal at length. "I had my reasons for doing what I did," he said. "I was in a peculiar state of mind and I wanted to get off the merry-go-round. Your wife is away, now. What if she were killed in an accident? Then you'd have the right to ask me such a question."

"You're an idiot!" said Leventhal.

"I'm only saying that we're not in the same boat. Wait till we're in the same boat."

"God forbid!"

"Of course. Who wants to see harm come to anyone? But accidents happen. You ought to realize that."

"Look," said Leventhal, "it's as I say. I don't owe you anything. But I'll give you a few bucks. Go to your rooming house or to a hotel."

"I can't go back. It's impossible. I can't ring Punt's bell at this time of the night. Besides, they have somebody else in the room. That's why they threw me out. And what sort of hotel would take me in? Like this? Without a bag? Unless you're suggesting a flophouse?"

"Well," said Leventhal. "Why beat around the bush? I see you've got your heart set on sleeping here tonight. I could see that all along."

"Can you suggest a place for me to go?"

"You're just inviting yourself in. It's after one, do you know that?"

Allbee did not answer.

"After the way you've acted I should throw you out. And if you really believe half the things you said to me, you shouldn't want to stay under the same roof. You're a lousy counterfeit."

"Why, you have the whole place to yourself. You can put me up," Allbee said quietly smiling. "I wouldn't be inconveniencing you. But if you want me to do this in the right spirit . . ." And to Leventhal's astonishment—he was too confounded when it happened to utter a sound—Allbee sank out of his chair and went to his knees.

Then he shouted, "Get up!"

Allbee pulled himself to his feet.

"For Christ's sake, stop this damned clowning! What do you think this is?"

With a look of amusement, his eyes appearing fixed and large, Allbee seemed to taste first one lip and then the other.

"I warn you," said Leventhal, "I won't stand for your monkeyshines. Your jokes!" His disgust was passionate. "You know they're not jokes; they're not supposed to be funny.

You're trying to work something on me. You think you'll throw me off and I won't know what's happening."

"You don't understand. I only wanted to do what was appropriate."

"That's all right," said Leventhal grimly, refusing to hear. "I want you to get this—as far as I'm concerned, I'm letting you sleep here tonight to return a favor, and that's all. Do you hear me?"

"Oh, you *do* owe me something."

"Am I the only one that does? Haven't you ever done anybody else a favor? It looks as if I'm the only one. And what do I owe you? You've pestered enough out of me already. I could shove you out in the hall and shut the door in your face with a clear conscience."

"In your position—if I were in it, and I don't say that I could be—my conscience wouldn't be clear."

"All right, conscience! I don't want to discuss my conscience with you," said Leventhal. "It's late."

He took some bedding from the cupboard and, going into the dining room, flung it onto the day bed.

"It's soft," Allbee remarked feeling the mattress.

"Now what else do you need—you want to wash? There's the bathroom."

"I'd like a shower," said Allbee. "It's been a long time since I had one."

Leventhal gave him a towel and found an old bathrobe for him in the closet. He sat down on the bed in his crumpled pajamas and listened disquieted to the water pelting the shower curtain and streaming in the tub. Soon Allbee came out, carrying his clothes. Wet and combed, his yellow hair gave him quite a different look. Leventhal observed his feet with a queer feeling of aversion. The insteps were red, coarse, and swollen, his toes long and misshapen, with heavy nails.

"Amazing, what a shower can do for you," said Allbee.

"I'm going to sleep," Leventhal said. He switched off the bed lamp.

"Good night," said Allbee. "I'm really grateful for this hospitality."

"Okay. There's milk in the refrigerator, if you want something."

"Thanks, I may have a glass." He went toward the dining room. Leventhal covered himself and pulled the pillow into position. The door of the refrigerator clicked open and he thought, "He is taking some." He was already falling asleep when he heard it shut.

14

H E SLEPT but he did not rest. His heart beat swiftly and the emotions of the day still filled him. He had an unclear dream in which he held himself off like an unwilling spectator; yet it was he that did everything. He was in a railroad station, carrying a heavy suitcase, forcing his way with it through a crowd the sound of whose shuffling rose toward the flags hanging by the hundreds in the arches. He had missed his train, but the loud-speaker announced that a second section of it was leaving in three minutes. The gate was barely in sight; he could never reach it in time. There was a recoil of the crowd—the guards must have been pushing it back—and he found himself in a corridor which was freshly paved and plastered. It seemed to lead down to the tracks. "Maybe they've just opened this and I'm the first to find it," he thought. He began to run and suddenly came to a barrier, a movable frame resembling a sawhorse. Holding the suitcase before him, he pushed it aside. Two men stopped him. "You can't go through, I've got people working here," one of them said. He wore a business suit and a fedora, and he looked like a contractor. The other man was in overalls. "I must, I've got to get to the tracks," Leventhal said. "There's a gate upstairs. This isn't open to the public. Didn't you see the sign on the door? What door did you come through?" "I didn't come through any door," said Leventhal angrily. "This is an emergency; the train's leaving." The second man appeared to be a thoughtful, sympathetic person, but he was an employee and couldn't interfere. "You can't go back the way you came, either," the contractor told him. "There's a sign up there. You'll have to leave through here." Leventhal turned and a push on the shoulder sent him into an alley. His face was covered with tears. A few people noticed this, but he did not care about them.

He found himself not awake, precisely, but so nearly awake as to be conscious that he lay in the dark. He had a sense of marvelous relief at the end of the dream. He was, it seemed to him, in a state of great lucidity, and he experienced a rare, pure feeling of happiness. He was convinced that he knew the truth, and he said to himself with satisfaction, "Yes, I do know it, positively. Will I know it in the morning? I do now." For what he thought would have been very strange to his waking mind, difficult to accept if not downright foolish. But why was that? "Why?" he reflected. "Dear God, am I so lazy, so weak, is my soul fat like my body?" His heart was jolting painfully; nevertheless he felt confident and happy. What was it? What did he and others do? Admittedly, like others, he had been in the wrong. That was not so important, either. Everybody committed errors and offenses. But it was supremely plain to him that everything, everything without exception, took place as if within a single soul or person. And still—here he was almost tempted to smile at himself—still he suspected, more than suspected, knew, that tomorrow this would be untenable. "I won't be able to hold onto it," he thought. Something would prevent it.

He had a particularly vivid recollection of the explicit recognition in Allbee's eyes which he could not doubt was the double of something in his own. Where did it come from? "Speak of black and white," he mused. Black and white were Mr. Schlossberg's words, to which he frequently returned. Either the truth was simple or we had to accept the fact that we could not know it, and if we could not know it there was nothing to go by. "There's just so much that we can do. What's the use of wearing yourself out for nothing?" Leventhal said to himself. No, the truth must be something we understand at once, without an introduction or explanation, but so common and familiar that we don't always realize it's around us.

Gripping the pillow, he turned over and shut his eyes. He was too stirred to sleep, however. He could hear Allbee's breathing, and he got up and closed the connecting door.

He had forgotten to set the alarm and he woke up late. The day was gray and hot. Irritated at oversleeping, he dressed and shaved hastily. After he washed off the lather he still looked unshaven. He shook some powder onto a towel, rubbed it on his chin, and slipped a shirt over his head. He had no time to stop for breakfast. In the kitchen he picked up an orange to eat on the way to the subway.

He went into the dining room where Allbee lay face down,

closely wrapped in the sheet. His broad calves were bare, his arms thrown forward, one hand touching the chair on which his clothes were heaped. Leventhal pulled at the mattress, but Allbee did not stir, and he was about to shake him but hesitated, nervously and angrily, and decided it would be unwise. For if he got him up now he was liable to lose half the morning in getting him out of the house. Leventhal did not know what to do about him. However—he looked at his watch—there was no time to deliberate now. Full of misgivings, he started for the office.

He almost welcomed his green metal desk with its hundreds of papers. The great, cloud-filled gray space his windows opened on seemed stationary. The activity around him, the swinging of the gates as the girls strode through them, the tremor and shimmer of the long-stemmed fans, had a settling effect on him. He worked hard. By eleven o'clock he had finished a complete set of galleys and he went in to Mr. Beard to discuss a lead article for the next number. Millikan, the son-in-law, was there, sitting beside the old man. He took no part in the conversation. Beard made a few remarks of tentative opposition, merely, Leventhal felt, for the sake of his authority, because he wanted to avoid agreeing at once, not because he had countersuggestions. His eyeshade, dividing his forehead with its white blots from the rest of his face, hid his expression somewhat, but there were indications that he was pretty well satisfied. His mouth and jaw showed it. "Well, can I handle your goddamned job?" Leventhal wanted to ask. He did not say this, he looked casual. Nevertheless a deep quiver of vindication went through him. "Everything is going smoothly," he remarked. Neither of them answered. Leventhal prolonged the silence for nearly a minute, until he forced a nod from Beard, and then he stalked out. He didn't claim to be indispensable; on the other hand, they might admit occasionally, without killing themselves, that he was valuable to them. With all his troubles and distractions, he was still finishing his work well within the deadlines. And Beard realized how efficient he was, that was why he had said that unpleasant thing to Mr. Fay. "What really bothers him," Leventhal thought, "is having to admit that he needs anyone for his business. He wants to be the one, the only, and the all-important. That's not the way a modern concern is run. He'll always be small potatoes."

On the way back to his desk, he encountered Mr. Fay. The fact that Fay had made an effort that day to defend him had led Leventhal to hope for more, a hint as to what had happened, an attempt to warn or advise him. One sign was all that was necessary. It wouldn't hurt to have a friend in the office. Moreover he wanted to thank Fay for putting in a word for him. "Maybe he will talk, one of these days," Leventhal told himself. Fay stopped him and mentioned an advertiser who was finishing a new plant that ought to be written up. He had spoken of it before. This time Leventhal was attentive, asked for more of the details, made notes on his pad, and said, "That's easy to fix up." He looked at Fay so expectantly that the latter seemed to think he was going to say more and paused, his dark eyes actively questioning under his graying, short brows and behind the shining circles of his glasses. "Yes," said Leventhal, "I'll get the story for you," and, with a mixture of impressions and, principally, the feeling that Fay was going to disappoint him, he turned away.

The ringing of the phone, reminding him of his sick nephew and of Allbee whom he had left sleeping, brought the blood to his face. He jerked his neck awkwardly as he fixed the receiver between his shoulder and his ear, praying that it might be a business call. With one hand he feverishly worked at the tangled wires.

At first he heard no one and he tried to signal the operator. Presently she broke in casually with, "Somebody by the name of Williston, for you." To restore his self-command, he stopped his breath for an instant. Then he said, "Put him on." He swung slowly back in the leather-backed chair, pulling a drawer open with the tip of his shoe and throwing his leg over it.

"Hello," Williston said.

"Hello, Stan, how've you been?"

"Pretty fair."

"You calling about Allbee?" Leventhal knew perfectly well that this directness was what Williston least wanted; Williston preferred to be roundabout. But why should he permit it?

He did not answer immediately.

"Well, aren't you?"

"I suppose I am. Yes, I am," Williston said, sounding reluctant. "I was wondering if you had seen him."

"Oh, I've seen him. He's been coming around. As a matter of fact, he showed up last night; said he was kicked out of his rooming house. I put him up. He stayed over."

"Kicked out?" Williston doubtfully said.

"What's the matter, you think I'm exaggerating? You haven't seen him. One look at him and it wouldn't sound so impossible."

"What does he aim to do?"

"I wish I could tell, but he probably couldn't say himself. If you want to know, I think he's probably sick. There must be something wrong with him."

Williston seemed to consider this; there was no reply for a while. Then he said, "Hasn't he given you any clue as to what he wants?"

"Too many clues. I can't get any single thing out of him, that's the trouble." He slipped his leg from the drawer and bent over the desk, cradling the phone in both hands. "You should hear him; you'd find out in a hurry there was something wrong."

Williston's voice came back in a drawling laugh. "He's trying to calm me down," thought Leventhal, feeling discouraged. "He thinks I'm overdoing the complaining and wants to kid me out of it."

"Oh, it isn't that bad, is it?" said Williston.

"It's plenty bad. You don't know how bad it is. I tell you, you haven't seen him or heard what he's got to say, what his line is. I did go wrong with Rudiger, I know, and that whole business was unfortunate. I won't try to duck out of it, although I could if I wanted to. But listen, you have no idea what he's like. Probably the thing to do is to get him a job. Whether he'll take it or not is another story. Maybe he doesn't want to work. I can't tell you. He wants everything, and I don't think he wants to do anything. He keeps play acting with me." He stopped and grumbled to himself, "I'll put him straight whether he wants to be put straight or not."

"Oh, now, that's just boyishness," said Williston. Leventhal was unable to decide to which of them the boyishness was attributed. He hunted for words, bluntly bracing his face against the difficulty of carrying on this conversation. It was purposeless, an added burden.

"Well, maybe you can make a useful suggestion, Stan."

"I said I'd do whatever I could." Williston appeared to feel himself accused.

"After all, I'm supposed to be his enemy. You're his friend."

He did not hear all of his answer. He only caught a reference to a "practical step" and understood that Williston was impatient with the way the conversation was going.

"Sure I'm in favor of something practical," he replied. But as soon as the words were out he was aware that he and Williston had swung farther than ever, hopelessly far, from the real issues. Over the telephone the "practical step" was vague enough and when he tried to apply it to Allbee it dissolved into irrelevance. For himself, the practical step was to get rid of the man, and this was not what Williston had in mind. "You think of something," he urged. "You know him. Maybe you can figure out what would satisfy him."

"He must have a definite object. If I could talk to him I might find out."

"How would you get to talk to him? He doesn't want you to know anything about him. He was mad when he found out I talked to you about him. But I'll suggest it to him and see what happens."

"I'll expect to hear from you, then," said Williston. "You won't forget to call, will you?"

"I'll call you," Leventhal promised. He hung up and, setting the phone on some of his papers as a weight, he made an abstracted survey of his desk, slipped his jacket from the back of the chair, and started out to lunch.

He went down in the elevator amid a crowd of girls from the commercial school upstairs, largely unconscious of the pleasure that he took in their smooth arms and smooth faces. The elevator sank slowly in the musty shaft with a buzz of signals and a sparking of tiny arrowheads. On the street Leventhal bought a paper and glanced through it in the cafeteria. After lunch, he walked toward the river, passing through the sidewalk markets, between the sacks of coffee beans. The roasting odor was mixed with the smell of gas. The occasional piping of a tug or the low blurt of a steamer came through the trample and jamming of trucks, and booms bristled like the spikes of a maguey, dividing the white of the sky as the piers did that of the water.

He was the first to return to the office; the place was empty. A breeze passed over the papers on the desk or left rolled in the typewriters, and shadowed the green linen blinds on the crosspieces of the windows. He stepped out onto the fire escape to finish his cigar, and had just ground it out on the rail and tossed it into the air when one of the phones began to ring. In the violence of his turn, he struck his shoulder on the doorframe and for an instant he could not see—the interior of the office seemed black. The ringing filled the air wildly, coming from all four corners of the room simultaneously. He felt a clutch of horror at his heart, and the thrilling, piercing run of the bell was infinitely faster than the flow of his blood. He reached his desk. The call was for him.

"Yes? Who wants me?" he cried to the operator.

It was Villani.

Leventhal closed his eyes. It was what he had been expecting. Mickey was dead. He listened awhile to Villani and then roared out, "Where is my damned brother!"

"He came in last night," said Villani. "He went straight out to the hospital. It was too late already. Poor little boy."

Leventhal put the phone down. He could not restrain the play of muscles in his throat. He held himself off from the edge of the desk, as if about to stand up, and with the sick drop of fuller realization his broad face lost all color and his features grew thick.

After a time he picked up a pad and, printing Mr. Beard's name in large crayon strokes, wrote under it, "Death in the family" and, rising, went to lay it on his desk.

He walked with angry energy to the toilet and began to bathe his head. He had a crushing headache. Over the sink, when his face was wet, he began to cry. He snatched a paper towel from the box and covered his eyes. Then he heard someone approaching and turned blunderingly into a stall. He shut the door and, with his back against it, gradually, with silent effort, brought himself under control.

15

ON THE FERRY there was only a current of brackish air instead of the usual fresh breeze. The boat took the water with a sullen thudding beneath the broad lip of its bow. The air was chalky and the afternoon sun looked pale. One of the deck hands sat with his naked back touching the pilothouse, his head lying on his knees, his big forearms locked about his legs. At the slip, he dragged himself down the ladder to take down the chain, and Leventhal sprang past him and hurried through the shed. His bus was just pulling away from the curb, and he ran alongside and slammed at the door with his open hand. The bus stopped, the door folded open, and he squeezed in among the passengers on the lower step. The driver raised himself in his seat and called out something, stridently. His throat was taut and angry, his gray collar blackened with sweat. No one answered and, after a delay, he ground down the gearshift and they started again. Leventhal was panting. He did not heed the streaming of his face or the stinging of his hand. He was thinking, as he had thought on the boat, that he must expect to be blamed. Elena was bound to blame him and her mother sure to egg her on. He had argued for the hospital, he had brought the specialist; he had meddled. The old lady did not matter, but his dread of Elena was intense. Probably the disease was already in the fatal stage when Denisart took the case. In the hospital Mickey had at least had a chance, and if she had listened to the first doctor's advice he might have been saved. So it was her fault, if anyone's. But it was precisely because of the unreasonableness of the blame that he feared her. Nevertheless he was obliged to face her. He could not stay away now.

He hunted among the rows of bells, found his brother's, rang, and climbed up. The door of the flat was open a few inches. He pushed it and was startled to feel a resisting weight on the inside. Letting the knob go, he retreated a step. It ran swiftly through his mind that it was not a child behind that door, not Philip. And why should Max try to keep him out? Could it be Elena? A hot wave of fright passed over him at the thought that the energy of madness had held back his push.

"Who's there?" he said hoarsely. "Who is it?" He went up to the door again. This time, merely at his touch, the door swung open. Elena's mother was in the hallway. He understood at once what had happened. Standing at the hinge to see who was coming she had been caught against the wall in the narrow vestibule.

"What are you doing?" His tone was harsh.

She was silent, and he was baffled by her look; behind its vindictiveness there was something crazily resembling amusement.

"Where is everybody?"

"Go out. I alone," she said in her rough voice. He had never before heard her speak English. It surprised him. As for the amusement, he must have been mistaken about that. It was the concentration of her look that had suggested it. The boy was, after all, her grandson.

"Where did they go?"

Either she did not know or was unable to explain. She uttered a few sounds. Steam was coming from the kitchen; he saw it behind her. Was she cooking dinner?

"Where are they, at the chapel? Is the funeral today?"

She merely shrugged; she refused to answer, and she gave him another of those frightful glances of spite and exultation, as though he were the devil.

"They're going to come home to eat, aren't they—*mangare*? When?"

It was a waste of time. She only wanted to get rid of him. He turned from her and went downstairs.

No one responded to his knock at Villani's. His headache was becoming severer. He frowned and hit at the door despairingly. Then it occurred to him to try the superintendent. He found him in the court, reading the paper in the shade of the furnace room stairs.

"Do you know where I can find my people?" he said. "I'm Max Leventhal's brother."

The superintendent got up. Old and slow, he rested his weight on bent, swollen knuckles.

"Why, the boy's being buried out of Boldi's parlors."

"The old mother-in-law is upstairs, but she wouldn't tell me. Where is this Boldi place?"

"Two blocks down. Turn left when you leave the building. Same side as this. There's a church on the corner." He bent to gather up the paper which had unfolded over his brown felt slippers.

The sun had come round to a clearer portion of the sky and its glare was overpowering. Leventhal took off his jacket. The heat of the pavement penetrated his soles and he felt it in the very bones of his feet. In a long, black peninsular yard a row of scratchy bushes grew, dead green. The walls were flaming coarsely, and each thing—the moping bushes, the face of a woman appearing at a screen, a heap of melons before a grocery—came to him as though raised to a new power and given another quality by the air; and the colors, granular and bloody, black, green, blue, quivered like gases over the steady baselines of shadow. The open door of the grocery was like the entrance to a cave or mine; the cans shone like embedded rocks. He had a momentary impression of being in a foreign city when he saw the church the superintendent had mentioned—the ponderousness, the gorgeousness, the decay of it, the fenced parish house, the garden, and the small fountain thick with white lead and flimsily curtained with water.

He passed through Boldi's office and entered the lounge. There he saw Philip sitting in a wicker chair. His legs were crossed on a footstool and his head rested on his raised shoulder.

"How are you, boy?" Leventhal said quietly.

"Hello, uncle," said Philip. He looked listless.

"I hear your father's back."

"Yes, he came in."

Leventhal caught the flush of candles through the oval windows of the studded leather door. He went into the chapel. It was cool. A master fan murmured somewhere in the building. Beyond the heaped-up, fiery glasses of the altar hung a Christ of human size. Taking off his hat, Leventhal walked up to the coffin. He was struck by the softness of the boy's face, the absence of signs of recoil or fright. He noted the curve of his nose, the texture of his brushed-up hair, the ends of which touched the folds of the satin, the poise of his small chin over his breast and decided, "He was going to turn out like Max and me. A Leventhal." Reflectively he fingered the smooth copper rail with its knot of dark plush and glanced upward. The chapel displeased him. Elena had undoubtedly insisted on a Catholic funeral. That was her right. But from the Leventhals' side, and the boy was one of them, too, it was peculiar, after so many generations, to have this. Prompted by an indistinct feeling, he thought to himself, "Never mind, thanks, we'll manage by ourselves. . . ."

He turned from the rail and encountered his brother.

The sight of him hit Leventhal with a terrible force. He had been prepared to meet him in anger; his very first word was to have been a rebuke. But now, instead of speaking, he took in his brother's appearance, the darkness and soreness of his swollen face, the scar at the corner of his mouth from a cut received in a street fight years ago in Hartford. Outdoor work had weathered him; the loss of several teeth made his jaw longer. His suit—it was a suit such as laborers used to buy in his father's store. His new black shoes were dusty.

"I didn't make it in time," he said.

"I heard, Max."

"I left as soon as the telegram came. I got in about ten minutes late."

"When's the funeral?"

"Four o'clock." Max motioned him to come aside. In the aisle near the wall, clasping Leventhal's hand and stooping over it, he burst into tears. He whispered, but occasionally one of his sobs or half-articulated words broke out of key and reverberated through the place. Leventhal stiffened his arm and supported him. He heard him say, "He was covered up," and bit by bit, through many repetitions, he learned that Max had come into the room unaware that Mickey was dead and found the sheet drawn over his head.

"Awful," he said. "Awful."

He gazed at Max's burly back and his sunburnt neck, and, as his glance moved across the polished rows of benches, he saw Elena sitting between Villani and a priest. The look she gave him was one of bitter anger. Though the light was poor, there was no mistaking it. Her face was white and straining. "What have I done?" he thought; his panic was as great as if he had never foreseen this. He was afraid to let her catch his eye and did not return her look. Helping Max up the aisle, he sat down beside him, still holding his arm. What would he do if then and there—imagining the worst—she began to scream at him, accusing him? Once more she turned her face to him over her shoulder; it seemed to be blazing in its whiteness. She must be mad.

She was mad. He did not allow himself to use the word again. He held it back desperately like a man who is afraid to whisper lest he end by shouting.

He rode out to the cemetery with Villani and the priest, behind the limousine with Max, Elena, Philip, and Mrs. Villani. During the burial he sheltered himself under a tree, hanging back from the others at the graveside in the full blast of the sun. When the shoveling of the earth began he walked back to the car. The chauffeur was waiting on the running board at the edge of the stonedust driveway. The glow of the sun in the locust trees gave a yellowish shine to his uniform. He had white hair, his eyes were bloodshot and his long lips impatiently drawn as he endured the heat moment by moment and breath by breath. Soon Villani and the priest came up. The priest was a Pole, stout and pale. He gave a push to his black Homburg, lit up, drawing deeply, and let the smoke out between his small teeth. Pulling out a handkerchief, he wiped his face and neck and the back of his hands.

"You're a relative, huh?" he said, addressing Leventhal for the first time.

Villani answered for him. "He's the man's brother, Father."

"Ah, yeah, tough deal." His fingers, virtually nailless and curving at the tips, pinched the cigarette. He looked keenly into the sky, creasing the thick white skin of his forehead, and made a remark about the heat. The family were now approaching the cars and the chauffeurs started up the motors.

"Too hot back there for three," said Leventhal, and climbed into the front seat. He wanted to avoid the priest. Touching the heated metal of the handle, he said mentally, "So long, kid," and peered out of the moving window at the yellow and brown of the large-grained soil and at the two booted men working their shovels. He occasionally saw Max in the back seat of the Cadillac and tried to recall Elena, persistently picturing how she had looked on the way to the grave, walking between Max and Villani, the fullness of her figure in the black dress, the grip of her hands on each arm, the jerking of her head. Poor Max, what was he going to do with her? And what about Philip? "I'd take him in a minute," he thought.

He did not say good-by to the family. It was after sunset when he reached the ferry. The boat went slowly over the sluggish harbor. The splash of a larger vessel reached it and Leventhal caught a glimpse of the murky orange of a hull, like the apparition of a furnace on the water. The searchlight on the bridge passed over it and it was lost in a moment, put out. But its giant wading was still audible seaward in the hot, black air.

After getting off the subway he delayed going home. He stopped in the park. The crowd was extraordinarily thick tonight. The same band of revivalists was on the curb. A woman was singing. Her voice and the accompaniment of the organ were very dim, only a few notes emerging from the immense, interminable mutter. He searched for a long time before he found a seat near the pond where a few half-naked children were splashing. The trees were swathed in stifling dust, and the stars were faint and sparse through the pall. The benches formed a dense, double human wheel; the paths were thronged. There was an overwhelming human closeness and thickness, and Leventhal was penetrated by a sense not merely of the crowd in this park but of innumerable millions, crossing, touching, pressing. What was that story he had once read about Hell cracking open on account of the rage of the god of the sea, and all the souls, crammed together, looking out? But these were alive, this young couple with bare arms, this woman late in pregnancy, sauntering, this bootblack hauling his box by the long strap.

Leventhal fell to thinking that to his father what had happened in Staten Island today would be incomprehensible. In Hartford the old man used to point at the baskets of flowers in the doorways and remark how many foreign children, Italian or Irish, died. He was amazed at the size of the families, at the numbers born and dying. How strange if he could know that his own grandson was one of these, buried in a Catholic cemetery. With flowers, like the others. And baptized. It occurred to Leventhal for the first time that Elena must have had him baptized. And that a son of his was a workingman, indistinguishable from those who came to the store to buy socks, caps, and shirts. He would not have understood it.

Heartsick and tired, Leventhal started home at ten o'clock. He did not think of Allbee till he began to go up, and then quickened his step. Twisting the key, he threw the door back with a bang and turned on the lights. On the couch in the dining room, sheets, bathrobe, and towel were twisted together. There was half a glass of milk on the floor.

He went back to the front room and stretched out on the bed, intending to rest awhile before taking off his clothes and shutting off the lights. He put his hand to his face with a groan. Almost at once he fell asleep.

During the night he heard a noise and sat up. The lights were still burning. Someone was in the flat. He went softly into the dark kitchen. The dining-room door was open, and by the window he saw Allbee undressing. He stood in his underpants, pulling his shirt over his head. The fear that Leventhal felt, though deep, lasted only a second, a single thrust. His indignation, too, was short lived. He returned to the front room and took off his clothes. Switching off the lights, he went toward his bed through the dark, mumbling, "Go, stay—it's all the same to me." He was in a state of indifference akin to numbness, and he lay down more conscious of the heat than of any emotion in himself.

Mr. Millikan, who attended to make-up at the printer's, was representing the firm at an all-industry conference, and Leventhal, at midday, had to go to the shop in Brooklyn Heights to replace him.

He waited on the subway platform in the dead brown air, feeling spent. He did not know how he was going to get through the day. The train rolled up and he sat down spiritlessly under the slow-wheeling fan that stirred the heat. Again and again he thought about the child's death. So soon closed over, covered up. So soon. He repeated it involuntarily while his head rocked with the bucketing of the cars in the long pull under the river that ended below the St. George Hotel. He left the train and rode up to the street level in the elevator.

Millikan had made up four pages, leaving him four more. The work went slowly; he became drowsy and made mistakes and tedious recounts. Toward four o'clock, he began to drop off. "It's the machine," he thought. The presses were upstairs and they ran without interruption all day. He took time out for a walk. It was curious that he should feel so dull and heavy, and yet at the same time so apprehensive.

He went into a restaurant for a cup of coffee. The chairs were standing on the tables and a boy with a red, bluff head and freckled, rolling shoulders was mopping the tiles. The waitress made a detour of the advancing line of dirty water to ask Leventhal to move out of the way. He drank his coffee at the counter, wiped his mouth on the oblong of a paper napkin he did not bother to unfold, loitered through the lobby of the St. George, examining a few magazines, and returned to the shop. Contemplating the pages with their blank spaces, he sighed and picked up the scissors. The presses had stopped before he was done. At half-past six he pasted his last strip and rubbed his hands clean with a piece of wastepaper.

On his way to dinner, he stopped at his flat to look in the mailbox. There was a note from Mary saying that she was writing a long letter which she expected to mail in a day or two. Disappointed, he slipped the note into his shirt pocket.

He did not go upstairs. Near the corner he met Nunez, in his dungarees and straw hat, carrying a webbed market bag full of groceries.

"Eh, eh, hey! How are you, Mr. Leventhal? I see you got yourself some company while your wife is away."

"How do you know?" said Leventhal.

"Us supers, we keep track of everything around a building. We're supposed to be nosey. That's not what it is, you find out even if you don't care. You can't help it. The tenants get surprised. *Brujo*, I see through the wall. They don't know, eh?" He described a spiral with his fingers, enjoying himself greatly. "No. You go out in the morning and then I hear your radio play. This afternoon the dumb-waiter goes up to the fourth floor. Later on, what's in it?—A empty soup can and rye bottle."

"So that's what he's doing?" thought Leventhal. "Guzzling all day. That's what I let him in for." He said to Nunez, "I've got a friend staying with me."

"Oh, I don't care who you got." Nunez gave a suggestive laugh and wrinkled his nose with pleasure, the veins on his forehead puffing out.

"Who do you think I've got?"

"That's okay. The way the dumb-waiter went up, there was no lady pulling on the rope, I know that. Don't worry." He swung the bag with his big-jointed, muscular arm tattooed with a bleeding heart. Leventhal continued toward the restaurant. "No money for rent," he said going down the stairs and bending under the awning. "But for hooch he has it. For hooch he can raise it. Where?" It occurred to him that Allbee had stolen some article from the house and pawned it. But what valuables were there? Mary's sealskin coat was in storage. Spoons? The silver was not worth stealing. Clothing? But a pawnbroker would be running a great risk, seeing how Allbee was dressed, to deal with him. No, hockshops had to think of their licenses. Leventhal did not really fear for his clothes. He had a tweed suit sealed in a mothproof bag in his closet; the rest was not worth pawning. And the suit was a small enough price to pay for getting rid of Allbee. Allbee was certainly clever enough to realize that. Drunks, of course, when they were thirsty enough, desperate enough, turned reckless. "But it isn't the few bucks he's after," Leventhal reasoned. For he had already offered him money. Allbee must have some of his own, since he could afford to buy whisky. Then what about his being evicted, was that an invention? But what of his appearance, that filthy suit of his, his shirt, his long hair? Leventhal tentatively concluded that he kept a little money for whisky by economizing on rent and other things. "But I better lock up the valuables, meanwhile," he told himself.

He ate a small dinner of baked veal overseasoned with thyme, had a glass of iced tea with sandy, undissolved sugar, and lit a cigar. Max and the family had replaced Allbee in his mind. Should he phone? Not just now, not tonight—he busily supplied good excuses, flinching a little at the shadow of his own weakness which lay behind them. He knew it was there. But this was not really the time to call. Later, when things had settled down, Max would soon find out—assuming that Elena's last look in the chapel signified what he thought it did—what he had on his hands. Though perhaps there was nothing so unusual in that look under the circumstances. Perhaps—Leventhal studied the seam in the long ash of his cigar—he had let his imagination run away with him. Grief, overloading of the heart. . . . "Horror, you know," he silently explained. People crying when their faces were twisted might appear to be laughing, and so on. "Well, I hope to God I'm wrong," he said. "I hope I am. And if he can run the old woman out of the house, maybe they can come through." The boy's death ought to bring the family closer together, at least. The old woman's influence on Elena was bad; and now especially she could work round her. For Philip's sake, Max ought to show the old devil the door. With her cooking and housekeeping she might try, at a time like this, to make herself a power in the house. He must impress the danger of this on Max, who might be inclined to let her stay. "Throw her out, don't give her a chance!" Leventhal exclaimed. If Max came to rely on her, why. . . . And he might, if it freed him, go where he liked and leave Philip in her hands. No, she must be pitched out. He sat awhile at his gloomy corner table, his black eyes giving very little evidence of the gloomy anxiety that filled him.

At home he took off his jacket in the vestibule. Through

the window, in the clear depth over the wandering brown smoke and the low-lying red of twilight clouds, he saw the evening star. He went through the narrow kitchen into the dining room, which was empty. Coming back to the front room, he was not immediately aware of Allbee's presence. It was only after he had dropped into a chair beside the window that he discovered him sitting between the desk and the corner, and he cried out fiercely, "What's the big idea!"

He shot up and turned on the desk lamp. His hands were shaking.

"I was enjoying the evening."

"My foot, the evening," Leventhal grumbled. "Drunken bastard!"

He was stubbornly silent, after this, determined that Allbee should speak first. The electric clock whirred swiftly. Allbee's head lay on the back of the chair, his large legs were thrown wide apart, their weight supported on his heels. His hands, loose-wristed, were folded on his chest. After some time he moved a little and sighed, "This killing heat, it takes my energy away."

"It couldn't be something besides heat that takes it away, could it?"

"What—?"

"Whisky," Leventhal said. "You're supposed to be looking for work. What have you been doing? Sitting here, drinking? When you came I understood you were going to get something to do and find yourself a room."

Allbee brought his head forward.

"I don't want to rush into anything," he said beginning to smile. "In any deal—you know that, you must know it by instinct—the worst thing of all is to hurry. Before you make up your mind . . . if you settle for buttons, peanuts . . . You have to think things over," he ended with an unsteady, delighted, foolish look of self-congratulation. Was he drunk? Leventhal wondered.

"*You*, a deal," he said contemptuously. "What kind of a deal have you got?"

"Oh, I might have. I might have something."

"Furthermore, how do you get in and out of here? I locked the door last night. I'm sure I locked it."

"I hope you don't mind. There were some keys in the kitchen and one of them fitted."

Leventhal scowled. Had Mary forgotten her key? Or was this an extra? "Originally the agent gave us two," he thought, "and the mailbox keys and the key to the locker in the basement. Or were there three house keys?"

"I wasn't sure I was coming back," said Allbee. "But as long as there was a possibility of it, I thought it would be more convenient to have a key. I tried to call you at your office yesterday, but you weren't in."

"Don't start bothering me at the office," Leventhal said excitedly. "What did you want?"

"I wanted to ask permission about the key, for one thing. And then there was something else that occurred to me, that on an outside chance there was an opening for someone like me at Beard and Company, and I might apply. You're in a position to help me there."

"At Beard's?—It didn't just occur to you! I don't believe it."

"It did so," Allbee quickly began, but stopped. His large full lips were parted and his loud breathing suggested repressed laughter; he looked at him with comic curiosity. But, seeing him stare back, he started over again, more seriously. "No, it did, it struck me all of a sudden as I was eating breakfast. 'Why shouldn't Leventhal help me get a job at his place?' And it's fair enough, isn't it? I introduced you to Rudiger. We won't count what happened. We'll forget about it. Let's think of it only as a return courtesy. You make an appointment with Mr. Beard for me—does he do the hiring over there in person?—and we'll be square."

"They don't need anybody."

"Let me find that out for myself."

"Anyway, they couldn't give you the type of job you want."

"But you don't care what kind of job I want. It wouldn't make any difference to you, what," he said grinning. "Whether I became a dish washer or scavenger, or hired myself out as human bait."

"No, it wouldn't, that's true," Leventhal replied.

"Then why should you worry about the type of work they offer me at your place?"

"Didn't I hear you talking about a deal?" said Leventhal. He went to the mantel, fumbled for a cigarette in a jar, and, sitting down, slid his hand across the window sill toward the packet of matches lying in the ash tray. Allbee watched him.

"You know, when I see how your mind works, I actually feel sorry for you," he said finally.

Leventhal pulled deeply at the cigarette; it stuck to his lips and he plucked it away.

"Look, the answer is a straight no. Never mind the discussion. I have plenty of trouble as it is. Skip the discussions." His self-possession was temporary, like a reflection in water that may be wiped out at the first swell.

"I understand. You're afraid I'll turn around and do to you what you did to me at Dill's. You think I want to go there and retaliate by getting you fired. But your introduction isn't necessary. I can make trouble for you without it."

"Go ahead."

"You know I can."

"Well, do!" he began to be shaken by the swells. "You think the job is so valuable to me? I can live without it. So do your worst. Hell with it all!"

"I took Williston's word about you. He said you were all right, so I made the appointment for you with Rudiger. See? I wasn't suspicious. It's not in my make-up, I'm happy to say. I didn't even know who you were, except from seeing you a few times at his parties."

"I feel too low to horse around with you, Allbee. I'm willing to help you out. I told you so already. But as far as having you in the same office where I could see you every day— no! As it is, there are plenty of people over there I don't care to see every day. You'd fit in with them better than I do. I don't have any choice about them. But I do about you. So it's out of the question. No!—and finished. I couldn't stand it."

Allbee seemed to be considering something in Leventhal's words that pleased him, for his smile deepened.

"Yes," he admitted. "You don't have to have me around. And you're right. I think you really are right. You have a choice. I envy you, Leventhal. Because when it came to the important things in my life, I never had the chance to choose. I didn't want my wife to die. And if I could have chosen, she wouldn't have left me. I didn't choose to be stabbed in the back at *Dill's* either."

"Who! I stabbed you in the back?" Leventhal furiously said, making a fist.

"I didn't choose to be fired by Rudiger, do you like that better? Anyway, you're in an independent position and I'm not." He was already falling into that tone of speculative earnestness that Leventhal detested. "Now I believe that luck . . . there really is such a thing as luck and those who do and don't have it. In the long run, I don't know who's better off. It must make things very unreal to have luck all the time. But it's a blessing, in some things, and especially if it gives you the chance to make a choice. That doesn't come very often, does it? For most people? No, it doesn't. It's hard to accept that, but we have to accept it. We don't choose much. We don't choose to be born, for example, and unless we commit suicide we don't choose the time to die, either. But having a few choices in between makes you seem less of an accident to yourself. It makes you feel your life is necessary. The world's a crowded place, damned if it isn't. It's an overcrowded place. There's room enough for the dead. Even they get buried in layers, I hear. There's room enough for them because they don't want anything. But the living. . . . Do you want anything? Is there anything you want? There are a hundred million others who want that very same damn thing. I don't care whether it's a sandwich or a seat in the subway or what. I don't know exactly how you feel about it, but I'll say, speaking for myself, it's hard to believe that my life is necessary. I guess you wouldn't be familiar with the Catholic catechism where it asks, 'For whom was the world made?' Something along that line. And the answer is, 'For man.' For every man? Yes, for every last mother's son. Every man. Precious to God, if you please, and made for His greater glory and given the whole blessed earth. Like Adam. He called the beasts by their names and they obeyed him. I wish I could do that. Now that's clever. For everybody who repeats 'For man' it means 'For me.' 'The world was created for me, and I am absolutely required, not only now, but forever. And it's all for me, forever.' Does that make sense?"

He put the question with an unfinished flourish and

Leventhal looked at his sweating face and only now realized how drunk he was.

"Who wants all these people to be here, especially forever? Where're you going to put them all? Who has any use for them all? Look at all the lousy *me's* the world was made for and I share it with. Love thy neighbor as thyself? Who the devil is my neighbor? I want to find out. Yes, sir, who and what? Even if I wanted to hate him as myself, who is he? Like myself? God help me if I'm like what I see around. And as for eternal life, I'm not letting you in on any secret when I say most people count on dying. . . ."

Leventhal had an impulse to laugh. "Don't be so noisy," he said. "I can't help it if the world is too crowded for you, but pipe down."

Allbee also laughed, strenuously, with a staring expression; his entire face was distended. He cried out thickly, "Hot stars and cold hearts, that's your universe!"

"Stop yelling. That's plenty, now. You'd better go to sleep. Go and sleep it off."

"Oh, good old Leventhal! Kindhearted Leventhal, you deep Hebrew. . . ."

"Enough, stop it!" Leventhal interrupted.

Allbee obeyed, though he went on grinning. From time to time he released a pent-up breath and he sank deeper into the armchair.

"Are you really going to do something for me?" he said.

"You've got to stop the tricks, first of all."

"Oh, I don't want to see old man Beard," Allbee assured him. "I won't bother you up there, if that's what you mean."

"You've got to try to do something about yourself."

"But will you really try? You know, use your connections for me?"

"For the love of Mike, I can't do much. And as long as you behave the way you do. . . ."

"Yes, you're right. I've got to get next to myself. I have to change. I intend to. I mean it."

"You see that yourself, don't you?"

"Of course I do. Don't you think I've got any sense at all? I must take myself in hand before everything wriggles away from me . . . get back to what I was when Flora was alive. I feel worthless. I know what I am. Worthless." Delirious tears came to his eyes. "There were good things in me." He struggled and fumbled, half revolting in the fervor of his self-abasement, but half—ah, half you could not help feeling sorry. "Williston will tell you. Flora would if she was here to speak and forgive me. I think she would. She loved me. You can see how I've come down if I talk to you like this. If she were alive, it wouldn't hurt me so much to be a failure."

"Ah, quit—!"

"I'd still be ashamed, but at least I wouldn't have so much to blame myself for."

"You? You hypocrite, you'd never blame yourself in a thousand years. I know your type."

"I am to blame. I know it. My darling!" He put the heel of his hand to his wet forehead, spread his mouth open crudely, and wept.

Leventhal regarded him with a kind of dismayed pity. He rose and stood wondering what to do.

"The thing to do is to make him coffee, I suppose," he decided. He hurried to fill the pot and, striking a match, held it to the burner. The flames spurted up in the star-shaped rows. He tapped the jar with the spoon and measured out the coffee.

When he came back to the front room, Allbee was asleep. He shouted, "Wake up, I'm fixing coffee for you." He clapped his hands and shook him. Finally he lifted one of his lids and looked at his eye. "Passed out," he said. And he thought with grim distaste, "Can I let him stay here like this? He may slide out of the chair and lie on the floor all night." The idea of spending the night like that, with Allbee on the floor and perhaps waking up, frightened him somewhat. Besides, he was beginning to be aware of the disgusting smell of alcohol that came from him. He hauled Allbee from the chair and began to drag him from the room. At the kitchen door he lifted him onto his back, holding him by the wrists, and he carried him to the dining room and dropped him onto the day bed.

17

Labor Day was approaching; the coming week was short-ened. Press time had been moved back and all copy had to be ready by Friday. Beard called a meeting of the editors to announce this. He was in a talkative mood and he swiveled back and forth, catching the red threads of the carpet in the casters of his chair. At every other sentence he lifted his hand and let it fall slackly. He made it an official occasion because of the holiday. He wouldn't keep them long. They had their work and brevity was the soul of wit. But this had been a good year for the firm, and he wanted the personnel to know how much he appreciated their loyalty and hard work. When you said work you said decency. They went together. So he wasn't thanking his people so much as complimenting them. It was better to wear out than to rust out, as was often quoted. He was a hard worker himself. He lived five miles as the crow flies from the office and he always allowed himself enough time so that if the subway broke down he could still walk the distance before nine o'clock. If a job was worth holding it was worth being loyal to. Life without loyalty was like—Shakespeare said it—a flat tamed piece. Leventhal in his white shirt, his face concealing his somber, weary annoyance, knew this was aimed at him. He kept his eyes on the image of the light striped window shade filling like a sail in the glass of the desk which was already cleared for the holiday.

"*Grosser philosoph.*" Leventhal, walking through the office, repeated his father's phrase with all his father's satire. Of all days to waste time. He got back to work even before the lamp over his papers had come to its full blue radiance. He had promised himself to take a breather today in order to think things over. But he was not really sorry to be too busy.

Mr. Millikan, his face pale and his nostrils widened, strode through the office carrying galley sheets in each hand. Mr. Fay stopped by to remind Leventhal about his manufacturer who wanted a spread.

"First thing next week, I'll take care of it," Leventhal said. "On Tuesday."

"Say, I'm sorry to hear you had such bad luck in your family—bereavement." Mr. Fay's lips thinned, his tone was formal, and the skin began to gather on his forehead. "Who was it?"

"My brother's kid."

"Oh, a child."

"A little boy."

"That's awfully tough. Beard mentioned it to me." The severity of his lips gave him a look of coldness bordering on suffering. Leventhal understood what caused it.

"Any other children?"

"They have another son."

"That makes it a little easier."

"Yes," Leventhal said.

He let his work drift briefly while he gazed after Mr. Fay. He at least was decent. Beard might have taken a moment off to say something. And Millikan rushed by and didn't even have time to nod. It showed the low quality of the people, their inferiority and meanness. Not that it made any difference to him. This Millikan, when he finally did get around to ask a personal question, never listened to the answer, only seemed to. He was like a shellfish down in the wet sand, and you were the noise of the water to him. Leventhal glanced over his desk—the papers, the glassful of colored pencils, the thick inkstand, the wire letter tray. There were several messages on his spindle and he tore them off. One, dated yesterday, was from Williston; he wanted him to call. Leventhal held the slip of paper in his palm, against his chest, and looked down at it. He thought, "I'll call him when the pressure's off me. It couldn't be so urgent or he would have tried to reach me at the shop or at home, last night."

At noon the receptionist rang to say that there was a man in the waiting room looking for him.

"What's his name?"

"He didn't give any."

"Well, ask him, will you?" The phone went silent. There was no response when he tried to signal her a few minutes later. He walked into the aisle to look at the switchboard. Her place was vacant. He took his straw hat from the hook and put it on. It had been his first guess that the visitor was Max. Max, however, would have given his name. It was probably Allbee. So much for his promise not to bother him at work. The waiting room was deserted. Leventhal, trying to force open the opaque glass slide to see whether she had returned to her switchboard by another entrance, heard her behind him. She was coming through the office door.

"Well, did you locate him?"

"Yes, he's in the corridor, but he doesn't want to give his name or come in." She was laughing, perplexed, and her small eyes seemed to ask Leventhal what was up. He stepped into the corridor.

Allbee was watching the cables and the rising weight at the back of the elevator shaft. He was carrying his jacket wrapped around his arm; his face was yellow and unshaven, his soiled shirt open; he stood loose-hipped, one hand bent against his chest. His shoes were untied. He appeared to have dragged on his clothes as soon as he got out of bed and set out, without losing a second, to see him. No wonder the girl had laughed. But Leventhal was not really disturbed either by her laughing or by Allbee himself. The lower half of the red globe above the doors lit up and the elevator sprang to a soft stop. He and Allbee crowded in among the girls from the commercial school upstairs.

"Nice," Allbee whispered. They were forced to stand close. Leventhal could scarcely move his arms. "Nice little tender things. Soon you and I, we'll be too old to take notice." Leventhal was silent. "Last night he was crying for his wife," he was thinking as they sank slowly along the wall.

Allbee followed him through the lobby and into the street.

"I thought you said you weren't going to come around?" said Leventhal.

"You'll notice that I waited outside."

"Well, I don't want you around. I told you that."

Allbee's eyes shone at him with reproachful irony. They were quite clear, considering how drunk he had been. His voice was thick, however. "I promised you I wasn't going to make trouble for you here. Since things are like this between us, you ought to have a little faith in me."

"Yes?" said Leventhal. "How are things between us?"

"Besides, I had a look at the goings-on inside. That's not for me."

"Well, what's on your mind? Make it quick. I have to have lunch and get right back."

Allbee was slow to begin. Could it be, Leventhal wondered, that he was unprepared and improvising something? Or was it part of his game to appear awkward, like this?

"I know you're suspicious of me," he finally said.

"Come on, let's have it."

He wiped his hand over his eyes. There were lines of strain about the root of his nose.

"I've got to get myself in motion."

"What, are you going away?"

"No, I didn't say I was. Well, yes, as soon as I can. That's understood. I mostly wanted to say. . . ." He reflected. "I was in dead earnest last night; I want to do something about myself. But before I can start there are certain things I'll have to have . . . clean up, make myself look a little more respectable. I can't approach anybody this way."

Leventhal agreed.

"I should get a haircut. And this shirt," he plucked at it. "My suit should be cleaned. Pressed, at least. I need some money."

"You find money for whisky. You don't have any trouble about that."

Allbee's look was earnest and even somewhat impressive, despite the sullen sickliness of his face.

"I suppose you weren't drunk last night. What did you do it on, sink water?"

"That was absolutely the last of Flora's money, the last few dollars. The last connection with her," he uttered the words slowly, "in something tangible."

Leventhal raised his eyes to him skeptically. His gaze contained all the comment he thought necessary. He shrugged and turned his face away.

"I didn't expect you to approve of that or even sympathize. You people, by and large—and this is only an observation, nothing else, take it for what it's worth—you can only tolerate feelings like your own. But this was good-by to my wife. That wasn't sentimental. Just the opposite. To get a haircut or a new shirt with those last few dollars of hers would have been sentimental. Worse. That would have been hypocrisy." His large lips made a burst of disgust. "Hypocritical! The money had to go the way the rest did. It would have been cheap and dishonest to use the last dime differently from the first."

"In other words, it was all for your wife."

"It was. I wasn't going to use a single cent of it to advance myself with. I felt bound to do it that way no matter how much it hurt me. And it did hurt me." He put his hand to his breast. "But this way I've been decent, at least. I didn't become a success at her expense. I didn't become what I wasn't before she died. And consequently I can face myself today." He stood swaying over him, ungainly, his mouth beginning to swell out derisively. "You wouldn't have done that, Leventhal."

"Maybe I wouldn't have to," Leventhal said disgustedly.

"It's easy for you to say. You haven't been touched. Wait till you're touched."

"Pardon?"

"Wait till something happens to your wife."

Leventhal blazed up. "You stop that harping on something happening . . . and that hinting. You've done it before. Damn you, you stop!"

"I don't want anything to happen," Allbee said. "All I've been trying to show is that you've been luckier than I. But you shouldn't forget that luck cuts both ways and be prepared, and when you're in my position—*if* you ever are. That's the whole thing, that *if*." He had recovered his favorite key and he brightened. "*If* swings us around by the ears like rabbits. But *if*. . . ! And you have to square it with yourself, every mistake you ever made, all your sins against her, then maybe you'll admit it isn't so simple. That's all I want to say."

"Oh, now we're on my sins."

"I'm not talking about cheating on your wife. I don't know how it stands, but that's a very unimportant part of it—your cheating on her, or her cheating on you. What I'm talking about holds good regardless. You mustn't forget you're an animal. There's where a lot of unnecessary trouble begins. Not that I'm in favor of infidelity. You know how I feel about marriage. But you see a lot of marriages where one partner takes too much from the other. When a woman takes too much from a man, he tries to recover what he can from another woman. Likewise the wife. Everybody tries to work out a balance. Nature is too violent for human ideals, sometimes, and ideals ought to leave it plenty of room. However, we're not monkeys, either, and it's the ideals we ought to live for, not nature. That brings us back to sins and mistakes. I heard of a case. . . ."

Leventhal cried, "Do you think I'm going to stand here and listen to your cases?"

"I thought you might be interested," Allbee said pacifyingly.

"Well, I'm not."

"All right."

Leventhal started toward the restaurant and Allbee walked beside him. The slanting parallels of shadow from the elevated tracks passed over them. The windows and window metals trembled and flashed.

"Where do you eat around here?"

"Down a way."

They came to a corner. "No use going on with you," said Allbee. "I had my coffee before getting on the subway."

"Good-by," Leventhal said indifferently, hardly pausing; he glanced at the traffic light. Allbee hung on, a little to the rear.

"I wanted to ask you—will you lend me a few dollars? Five or so . . . ?"

"To start life over?" said Leventhal, still looking away.

"You offered me some, awhile back."

"Tell me why I should give you anything." Leventhal turned squarely to him.

Allbee met this with an uncertain, puzzled smile while Leventhal, on the other hand, felt more steadily balanced and confident.

"You tell me," he said again.

"You offered it. You'll get it back." Allbee dropped his glance, and there was a curious flicker not only in his lowered lids, over the fullness of his eyeballs, but over his temples.

"Yes, naturally I will," Leventhal said. "You're a man of honor."

"I want to borrow ten bucks or so."

"You raised it. You said five, before, and five is what I'll let you have. But I'll give you notice now that if you show up drunk. . . ."

"Don't worry about that."

"Worry? It's not my lookout."

"I'm not a drunkard. Not a real one."

Leventhal had half a mind to ask what he was, really, what he genuinely thought he was. But he said instead, with casual irony, "And here I believed you when you said you were so reckless." He opened his wallet and took out five singles.

"I appreciate it," said Allbee, folding the money and buttoning it up in his shirt pocket. "You'll get every penny back."

"Okay," Leventhal replied dryly.

Allbee turned away, and Leventhal thought, "If he takes one shot—and he probably thinks he'll have one and quit—he'll take two and then a dozen. That's the way they are."

There was a letter from Mary waiting for him that evening. He pulled it out of the mailbox thankfully. Allbee's hints had bothered him more than he knew. He had brushed them aside. What reason did he have to be anxious about her? Nevertheless there were coincidences; things were mentioned and then they occurred. He worked his finger under the flap and tore open the envelope. The letter was thick. He sat down on the stairs and read it in absorption and deep pleasure. It was dated Tuesday night; she had just come back from dinner at her uncle's. She asked for news of Mickey—Leventhal had put off writing about him—and she complained mildly about her mother. It was comical and strange that her mother treated her like a child. She didn't make coffee enough for two in the morning, assuming that her daughter still drank milk, unable to grasp the fact that she was not merely a grown woman but a woman no longer so young. This morning a few gray hairs had showed up. Old! Leventhal smiled, but his smile was touched with solicitude. He turned the page. She had so much time on her hands and so little to do that she had bought yardgoods and was sewing herself some slips, trimming them with lace from old blouses of her mother's, "still in good condition and very pretty as you'll see when I get home." The rest of the letter was about her brother's children. He put it to his mouth as though to cover a cough and touched the paper with his lips.

If she were still in Baltimore, he would have gone down for the holiday. But unless he flew, he could not get back from Charleston by Tuesday. And besides there was her mother in Charleston, recently widowed and no doubt difficult. He would wait and have Mary to himself in a few weeks, when things were quieter. She would make them quieter. He had great faith in her ability to restore normalcy.

The thought of reunion made entering the house all the harder. He listened at the door before going in. He wanted to avoid being taken by surprise again. There were no sounds. "Let him just come back drunk," Leventhal said to himself. "That's all I ask."

Within a few days the flat had become dirty. The sink was full of dishes and garbage, newspapers were scattered over the front-room floor, the ash trays were spilling over, and the air stank. Depressed, Leventhal opened the windows. Where was Wilma? Didn't she generally come on Wednesdays? Perhaps Mary had forgotten to ask her to continue in her absence. He decided to ask Mrs. Nunez tomorrow to clean the place. Picking up an ash tray, he took it to the toilet to empty. The tiles were slippery. He grasped the shower curtains for support; they were wet. In the dark his foot encountered something sodden and, setting the ash tray in the sink, he bent to the floor and picked up his cotton bathrobe. He took a quick, angry step into the front room and spread the dripping robe to the light. There were shoeprints on it and, around the pocket, pale blue stains that looked like inkstains. He emptied it and found several ads torn from the paper, Jack Shifcart's business card, the one jokingly intended for Schlossberg, and, bent and smeared, the two postcards he had received from Mary a few weeks ago. He hurled the robe furiously into the tub. His face was drawn, his mouth gaping with rage. "The . . . . sucking bitch!" he brought out, almost inarticulate and struggling ferociously against a stifling pressure in his throat. He flung aside the chair before his desk, threw the writing leaf down, tore papers out of the pigeonholes and drawers, and began to go through them—as if, in his numbness and blindness, he could tell what was missing. Awkwardly, his hands stiff, he spread them out: letters, bills, certificates, bundles of canceled checks, old bankbooks, recipes that Mary had pasted on cards and put away. Heaping them together again he picked up the blotter, banged up the leaf with his knee, and pushed them, blotter and all, into a drawer. He locked it, put the key in his watch pocket, and sat down on the bed. He still retained the cards and the clippings he had taken from the pocket of the robe. "I'll kill him!" he cried, bringing his fist down heavily on the mattress between his knees; and then he was silent and his large eyes stared as though he were trying to force open an inward blindness with the sharp edge of something actual. He rubbed his fingers thickly on his forehead. Presently he began to read Mary's cards, the words of intimacy meant only for him. There were a few private references and abbreviations that no one else could understand; the drift of the rest was hard to miss. "To carry them around like that, to keep them to look at!" he thought. He felt a drench of shame like a hot liquid over his neck and shoulders. "If that isn't nasty, twisted, bitching dirty!" It sickened him. If Allbee had seen them accidentally . . . that too would have been hateful to him. But it was not accidental; Allbee had gone into his things, his desk—Shifcart's card proved that, for Leventhal was certain he had put it away—and snooped over his correspondence and kept these cards to amuse himself with. And perhaps he had seen Mary's earliest letters, the letters of reconciliation after the engagement was broken. They were in the desk, somewhere. Was that the reason he had made those remarks today about marriage and the rest? He might have made them without knowing, on the chance that he was susceptible. Nearly everyone was, Leventhal thought with a stab of that incident before his marriage and Mary's behavior, which he still did not understand. How could she have done that? But he had long ago decided to accept the fact and stop puzzling about the cause. To Allbee, who might have read the letters, it must have seemed a wonderful opportunity: Mary away, and so why not drop a hint? What he did not know was that Leventhal's old rival was dead. He had died of heart-failure two years ago. Mary's brother had brought the news on his last visit North. It wasn't to be found in a letter.

To himself he said, "A lot a dirty drunk like that would know about a woman like Mary."

18

THE DARK came on. He did not light the bed lamp but sat, still with the cards in his hand, waiting for Allbee, listening for footsteps and hearing instead a variety of sounds from below, the booming of radio music through the floor, mixed voices, the rasping of the ropes in the dumb-waiter; the cries of boys scudding down the street rose above the rest, as distinct as sparks from fire. With the setting of the sun, the colored, brilliant combers of cloud rolled more and more quickly into gray and blue, while red lights appeared on the peaks of buildings, pilot warnings, like shore signals along a coast. The imperfections of the pane through which Leventhal gazed suggested the thickening of water at a great depth when one looks up toward the surface. The air had a salt smell. A breeze had begun to blow; it swayed the curtains and rattled among the papers on the floor.

After a time, Leventhal held his wrist up to the faint, gold bits of light under the window and studied his watch. It was well past eight; he had been sitting for more than an hour. He looked meditatively into the street. His first anger had passed over. From waiting to confront Allbee, he had lapsed gradually into a state of inert rest and now he felt hungry and got up to go to dinner. No use waiting for Allbee, who was probably drinking up the last of the five dollars in some bar and was in that case disposing of himself the quickest way. It was just as well, he reflected, that Allbee had not showed up, for what he obviously wanted was to be taken seriously. Once he had succeeded in this he could work him, Leventhal, as he liked. And that, quite plainly, was his object.

The restaurant was full; there was a crowd around the small bar. He moved to the rear in search of a table. "I got customers next at the bar," the bony, dark waiter said, "but I'll see what I can do for you." He had a cup of coffee in either hand and he hurried away. Leventhal was undecided whether to wait with the others or stand at the kitchen door. It was not very likely that the waiter would give him a table out of turn if he got into the crowd. He continued toward the leaning wall of the kitchen passage. Through the arch he saw one of the cooks beside the brick oven wiping the flour from his arms and waving his apron to cool his face. Leventhal brushed against someone who seemed to have stretched an arm into his path accidentally. Without looking, he said, "Beg your pardon." A man said laughingly, "Why don't you watch?" And though it was peculiar that this should be said with a laugh, he did not turn but merely nodded, and he was going on when he felt his jacket being pulled. It was Williston. Phoebe was with him.

"Well, hello," she said. "Don't you talk to people any more?" It came over Leventhal that she was accusing him of deliberately avoiding them.

"My mind was somewhere else," he said, his cheeks darkening coarsely.

"Sit down. Are you alone?"

"Yes, I am. They promised me a table, so don't let me. . . ."

"Oh, come ahead. Here." Williston pushed back a chair.

Leventhal hesitated, and Phoebe said, "What's the matter, Asa?" in a manner that indicated it was impossible to show reluctance for another moment without offending her.

"Oh, Mary's out of town," he said, "and I don't bother too much about meals. I just run out and grab something. And you're almost through."

"Now sit down, will you?" said Williston.

"What does your wife's being away have to do with it? My Lord!"

Leventhal looked at her dead-white complexion, her thick level eyebrows, and the short, even teeth her smile revealed. The noise of the place cut off their conversation for a moment. He accepted the chair, massively crowding the table as the waiter passed behind him. With an anxious face he struggled up again to catch his attention. He sat down again, telling himself not to be so nervous. Why should they rattle him? He read the menu with his hand to his forehead, feeling the heat and moisture under his fingers, and putting his swarming emotions in order. "What's the matter; can't I stand up to them?" he asked himself. The challenge strengthened him. When he closed the menu he was surer of himself. The waiter came up.

"What's special?" he said.

"Soup, you want bean soup? *Lasagna*, we got tonight."

"I see mussels." He pointed to the shells.

"Very good," said Phoebe.

"*A la possilopo*." The waiter wrote.

"And a bottle of beer; a plate of soup to start."

"Right up."

"I've been trying to reach you," Williston said.

"Oh?" Leventhal turned to him. "Anything in particular?"

"The same matter."

"I got your message. I was going to call back, but I've been tied up."

"By what?" said Phoebe.

Leventhal considered his answer. He was unwilling to speak of his family; he did not want to appear to be soliciting sympathy, and besides he was incapable of mentioning Mickey's death conversationally. The thought was repugnant to him.

"Oh, things," he said.

"Labor Day pile-up, eh?" said Williston.

"That and some private things. Mostly work."

"What are you doing with yourself over the week end?" Phoebe asked him. "Planning to go somewhere? We're invited to Fire Island."

"No, I'm not going anywhere."

"Are you facing three days in town alone? You poor man."

"I'm not what you might call alone, exactly." Leventhal glanced at her, speaking quietly. "I have a friend of yours staying with me."

"Of ours?" she cried. He saw that he had her off balance. "You mean Kirby Allbee?"

"Yes, Allbee."

"I wanted to ask you about that," said Williston. "Is he still with you?"

"Still."

"Tell me, how is he?" Phoebe said. "I didn't know you came about him, the other night. I wouldn't have stayed in the kitchen."

"I didn't realize you were so interested."

"Well, now I'd like to know how he is," she said. Leventhal wondered how much of his description Williston had repeated.

"Didn't Stan tell you?"

"Yes, but I want to hear more from you." Her habitual cool, good temper was missing. A faint color appeared below her eyes, and he commented to himself, "Out in the open, for a change." He delayed, thinking that Williston might intervene. The waiter put the black and green mussels before him, and he said, taking up the fork as if to weigh it, "Oh, he's getting around." He began to eat.

"Is he very broken up about Flora?"

"His wife? Yes, he's broken up."

"It must have been terrible for him. I never thought they'd separate. They started out so brilliantly."

"Brilliant?" Leventhal thought. He paused, letting them see that the word had struck him. "What does she mean? That's only the way women talk about marriage. What could be brilliant? He, Allbee, brilliant?" He made an indifferent movement of concession.

"I attended the wedding, if you want to know why it interests me," she said.

"Phoebe and Flora were roommates at school."

"Were they?" said Leventhal, somewhat curious. He poured the beer. "I met her a few times at your house."

"Yes, you must have," Williston said.

Phoebe for a brief moment regained her usual manner. "At the church I remember they were going to have a singer and they didn't on account of his mother. They didn't want to hurt her feelings. Everybody humored her about her singing. She studied in Boston for years and years. She was about sixty, and she might have had a voice once, but she certainly didn't have one then. She sang anyway. She was bound to, at her son's wedding. They couldn't stop her. Poor Kirby. But the old lady was very nice. She told me she had beautiful legs when she was a girl and was so proud of them, wasn't it a shame she had to wear long skirts? She said she was born too soon."

"Excuse me for asking," put in Leventhal, "but was this marriage supposed to be a good thing from his wife's point of view?"

"What do you mean?"

"Did her family like him?"

"They were suspicious. But I thought he was very promising. Intelligent and charming. So did lots of other people. I always believed he'd outdistance all our friends."

Williston corroborated her. "Yes, he's brainy and well read, too. He used to read an awful lot."

"And suddenly the bottom falls out. I wonder whom you could blame for that." Phoebe sighed and turned her long, handsome, pensive face with its marked, level brows to her husband first and then to Leventhal.

"Why, she wasn't to blame, was she?" said Leventhal. "His wife?"

"No. . . ." Phoebe appeared to be disconcerted. "Why should she be? She loved him."

"Well, if she wasn't to blame, who's left?" asked Leventhal. "She left him, didn't she?"

"Yes, she did. We never learned why. She didn't take it up with me. We saw it from the outside, mostly. It was hard to understand because he was so charming."

"Charming!" Leventhal scornfully repeated to himself. "—Brilliant start!" What could this woman actually have seen with those two eyes of hers? What did she allow herself to see? Could anything that started so well, so promisingly, have ended so badly? There must have been a flaw in the beginning, visible to anyone who wanted to see. But Phoebe did not want to see. And as for Allbee, no wonder he stayed away from the Willistons, they had such a high opinion of him.

He said reservedly, "They say that drinking people usually make a good impression. They're supposed to be likeable."

"Still drinking, eh?" Williston asked in an undertone.

"Still?" Leventhal shrugged, as if to say, "What's the use of asking?"

"No, he was just what I say. Ask Stan. Even before he started drinking. But you haven't told me how he's making out and what he's doing."

"He's doing nothing. And he hasn't told me what he's going to do, either."

"Well, ask him to come over and see us, will you?" Her face was tremulous with hidden resentment.

"With pleasure." Leventhal sounded rather sharp. Williston was turning over a spoon in his short fingers. He had spoken very little realizing, perhaps, that Phoebe was in the wrong, and was afraid to make matters worse by interfering. Leventhal hid his annoyance. They wanted to see Allbee—they could have him altogether, as far as he was concerned—but they didn't say they wanted him to stay with them, only to visit. And why, Leventhal wanted to know, didn't it occur to Phoebe to ask why Allbee was with him rather than with his friends? Logically, they were the ones for him to go to. But it struck him, in examining her white face, that there were certain logical questions she didn't want to ask. She did not want the facts; she warded them off. In a general way she understood them well enough, he was sure. She only wanted to insist that Allbee be taken care of. And chances were that she no more wanted to see him in his present condition than he wanted to see her. She probably knew what he was like. Oh, of course she knew. But she wanted him changed back to what he had been. "My dear lady," Leventhal protested in thought, "I don't ask you to look at things my way, but just to look. That would be enough. Have a look!" However, and he always returned to this, the Willistons had been kind to him; he was indebted to them.—Although what Williston had done for him was nothing compared to what he was being told implicitly to do for Allbee.

Williston roused himself, or so it appeared to Leventhal. "I don't think Kirby wants to see us now, dear," he said. "He would have come before."

"Too bad he hasn't," said Leventhal. He showed more feeling than he had intended, and Phoebe quickly took him up.

"I don't think I understand that, Asa," she said.

"You ought to see him. From the way you're talking about him, I don't think you'd recognize him. I know I don't recognize the same man."

"Well, that may not be my fault." She stopped with a short release of breath. The red began to come out again under her eyes.

"I suppose he has changed," said Williston slowly.

"Believe me, he's not what Phoebe says. I'm telling you." Leventhal tenaciously limited himself to this in order to control his mounting sense of wrong.

"You ought to be more charitable," Phoebe said.

At this he almost lost his head, staring at her while the color spread to her cheeks. He pushed away his plate, muttering, "I can't change myself over to suit you."

"What?" said Williston.

"I said, if I'm not, I'm not!"

"I don't think Phoebe meant what she said, exactly. Phoebe? I think Asa got the wrong impression."

"I see that you misunderstood me," she grudgingly said.

"Well, it doesn't make any difference."

"I didn't mean anything except that Kirby *was* promising, and so on. I wasn't saying anything but that."

What did she know about him? Leventhal thought bitterly. But he was silent.

"I phoned because I wanted to know if I could help out with a little money," said Williston. "I haven't been able to think of a job for him, but he must need things. I guess he can use a few dollars."

"That's right," Leventhal said.

"I want to give you ten or so. You don't have to tell him where it comes from. He might not want to accept money from me."

"I'll give it to him," said Leventhal. "It's very nice of you."

The Willistons left. Leventhal watched them in the blue mirror of the bar above the massed forms of the bottles. Stan waited while Phoebe stopped to give a touch to her hat and they went up the stairs together, passing under the awning.

19

FROM THE FOYER he saw Mrs. Nunez sitting cross-legged on the divan, putting up her freshly washed hair. She held her chin against her breast, and there were pins in her mouth and others strewn on the brown and white squares of her skirt. He rapped, and she drew her hair back from her eyes but did not change her position or cover her unsymmetrically gartered legs.

"I don't want to disturb you," he said, looking at them. "I was thinking—the flat's pretty dirty. Could you give me a lead about a cleaning woman? Ours hasn't been around."

"Clean? I don't know anybody. If it's straighten, I'll do it for you. I don't do the heavy work."

"Nothing heavy, I just want the place to look a little neater."

"Sure, I'll straighten it for you."

"I'll be much obliged. It's getting to be too much for me."

The look of his front room by lamplight disgusted him. It would have done Phoebe good to see it. He half regretted that he had not invited the Willistons home with him. He set to work gathering up the papers from the floor and spread clean sheets on his bed and laid out a pair of pajamas. In the bathroom he soaked and rinsed the robe and rubbed out the inkstains with a brush and soap powder. Taking it to the roof he wrung it out and spread it on a line. There was a smell of approaching fall in the breeze. Leventhal walked over the pebbles and tar to the parapet. To the east the lights of the two shores joined in a long seam in midriver. Summer would end soon after the holiday and with the start of fall everything would change; Leventhal felt inexplicably convinced of this. The sky was overcast. He looked out awhile and then returned to the staircase, careful of lines and wires in the dark. He touched the robe in passing. It was drying rapidly in the breeze.

On the landing he heard someone coming and glanced below. It was Allbee. Regularly his hand clasped and released the banister as he made his way up. Catching sight of Leventhal at the last turn, he paused and raised his head and seemed to examine him. The low light crossed his face up to the brows and eyes and gave it an expression, most likely accidental, of naked malice. A stir of uneasiness went over Leventhal. He remembered immediately, however, that there were a few things Allbee had to answer to him for. And, to begin with, was he drunk? But he was already quite sure, he could sense that he was sober.

"Well?" he said.

Reaching the landing, Allbee gave him a restrained nod. His hair had been trimmed. Along the sides of his head and down his cheeks there was a conspicuous margin of shaven whiteness. His face shone. He had on a new shirt and a black tie and he carried a paper bag. When he saw Leventhal inspecting him he said, "I picked these up on Second Avenue, in a bargain store."

"I didn't ask you."

"I owe you an accounting," he said matter-of-factly. Leventhal listened for a provocative note in his answer; there was none. He looked at him suspiciously.

"I haven't had a drink today," said Allbee.

"Come in here. There's something I want to find out."

"What is it?"

"Not here; in the house."

Allbee held back. "What's the trouble?" he asked.

Leventhal seized his coat and pulled him forward. Allbee resisted, and he lay hold of him with both hands, and, with a sullen look of determination, his anger rekindled, dragged him into the house and flung the door shut with his foot. He twisted him around. Allbee tried to free himself anew, and Leventhal shouted, "What the hell do you think I'll stand for!"

"What are you talking about?"

"You'll answer me. You won't duck out of it."

He tore his coat out of Leventhal's grasp and swung away. "What's the idea?" he said with a trembling, short laugh, wonderingly. "Have you decided to beat me up?"

"How much do you think I'll take from you!" Leventhal was panting. "Do you think you can get away with everything?"

"Don't lose your head, now." His laugh was gone and he

looked at him gravely. "After all, I expect to be treated fairly. I'm in your house, and you have certain advantages over me. . . . Anyway, you ought to tell me what this is all about."

"This is what it's about." Leventhal snatched out the cards. "Going through my desk like a damned crook and black-mailer. That's what it's about."

"Oh, is *that* it?" He swung his hand loosely toward them.

Leventhal's voice broke as he cried, "*That*? Isn't that anything? You followed me around and snooped, before. I let you in here and you get your dirty hands all over my things, my private business, my letters."

"Well, now, that's not true. I haven't touched your letters. I'm not interested in your business."

"Where did I find these!" Leventhal threw the cards down. "In my bathrobe that you were wearing."

"That's where I found them. I don't like to defend myself against such accusations. They're not fair. This is the kind of thing that gets people in trouble."

"Isn't this yours?" Leventhal picked up a clipping from the classified ads.

"Oh, I know what was in that pocket. But some of it was there when I put the robe on. Maybe you object to the fact that I used the robe. I'm sorry, I. . . ."

Leventhal refused to be deflected. "You mean to say that you didn't go through my desk?"

Allbee made a movement of sincere, straightforward denial.

"How about this? Where did you get this?" Leventhal pointed to Shifcart's card.

"I found it on the floor. Now, there I'll admit . . . if I did anything really wrong it was to take that card. It was on the floor near your bed. I had no right to keep it. Perhaps you needed it. I should have asked. But I didn't think of that. I was interested in it. In fact, I was going to bring it up in connection with something I've been thinking about but kept forgetting."

"You're lying."

Allbee was silent. He stood looking at him.

"I didn't put the postcards in the bathrobe," said Leventhal, "and this card of Shifcart's was in the desk."

Allbee answered simply, "If you didn't put them there, then a third party must have. I know I didn't."

"But you read them!" He said this violently, but he wanted to sink away.

"Yes, I did," Allbee dropped his eyes as if to spare him.

"Damn you to hell!" Leventhal shouted in anguish and outrage. "That's not all you read. What else!"

"Nothing."

"You did!"

"No, that was all. I couldn't avoid looking them over. It wasn't intentional. But I took them out of the pocket and so I had to see what they were. It's mostly your wife's fault. She should have put them in an envelope—things like that. I never would have pulled a letter out of an envelope. But I read this before I realized what it was. It's not so serious, is it? What's so special about your cards? Any wife might write like that to a husband, or a husband to a wife. And an old married man like me . . . it's not the same as if a young person, say a young girl, got hold of them. And even then, I wonder if anybody is innocent. And last of all, I don't think it would matter to your wife. This is not the kind of thing for postcards. If she cared, she'd have written it in a letter."

"I still think you're lying."

"Well, if you do, I can't change your mind. But I'm not. Why not keep your desk locked, as long as you don't trust me?"

"It is now."

"You should have locked it sooner. Nobody likes to be jumped on like this. Keep it locked. You have a right to lose your temper when there's definite proof that somebody is monkeying with your private things. It's not very nice. But neither are such accusations. Suppose I did look in your desk, and I absolutely deny it, why should I want to carry the cards around?"

"Why should you? Search me!"

"Like a mental case? Not me, you've got the wrong party."

Leventhal did not know what more to say. Perhaps he was wrong. Except when Allbee spoke of young girls he made sense and even that, fully explained, might not be irrelevant. Besides, the haircut, the shirt and tie, and the fact that he was sober made a difference. It was the haircut, mainly; it gave him a new aspect. His face appeared more solid. Leventhal all at once felt nothing very strongly; he only had a certain curiosity about Allbee. He sat down beside the desk. Allbee sank into the easy chair and stretched his legs out.

After a few minutes of silence he said, "Did you see this morning's paper?"

"Why, what's in the paper?"

"There was an item in it I thought you might have picked up. It's about Rudiger. Really about Rudiger's son, but he was mentioned too. The son's in the army and he was promoted, yesterday. To the rank of major."

"What about it?"

"I just happened to notice. I was in the barber shop looking at the paper and saw the boy's picture. He worked in the office for a while. He's a very ordinary boy. Nice . . . I can't criticize him. Just a college boy; very ordinary, no special spark. It's no business of mine; that is, it can't do me any good or harm. But I'm always interested in the way things work themselves out. Now somebody without influence spends twenty years in the service, first in this hole of a garrison and then in that one, lives with native girls because he can't afford to marry. Maybe he gets a little rank in the end, becomes a second lieutenant. You can't tell me it isn't a matter of influence."

"It probably is," said Leventhal idly.

"Yes. Not that I have anything against him because he happens to be his father's son. Why shouldn't he take advantage of the old man's position? And what else can the old man do for him?" He suddenly changed the subject with a quick laugh. "Notice my haircut?"

"I see."

"I didn't drink, either. That's not what you expected, is it?"

"Go ahead, surprise me."

"No, you thought I'd get looped again."

"Maybe."

"I told you I wasn't that far gone."

"I'm glad to see it."

"Are you?" There was a break of excitement in his hilarity.

"Sure," said Leventhal. He felt a responsive laugh forming

in his chest and he held it down. "What do you want, a basket of roses?"

"Why not?"

"A medal?" Leventhal began to smile.

"Yes, a medal." He coughed thickly. "I ought to have one."

"You ought to get one."

"Well, I wasn't even tempted, to be honest about it. I didn't have to fight a yen; not a bit of trouble."

Allbee bent forward and laid his hand on the arm of Leventhal's chair, and for a short space the two men looked at each other and Leventhal felt himself singularly drawn with a kind of affection. It oppressed him, it was repellent. He did not know what to make of it. Still he welcomed it, too. He was remotely disturbed to see himself so changeable. However, it did not seem just then to be a serious fault.

"I had clippers on the sides." Allbee brought the tips of his fingers to his head. "I got into the habit. It's cleaner that way, I've learned. Because of nits. You wouldn't know anything about that, would you?"

Leventhal shrugged.

"Oh, if you got them in your hair, hair like that. . . . Your hair amazes me. Whenever I see you, I have to study it. With some people you sometimes doubt if it's real and you want to see if your man is wearing a wig. But your hair; I've often tried to imagine how it would be to have hair like that. Is it hard to comb?"

"What do you mean, is it hard?"

"I mean, does it tangle. It must break the teeth out of combs. Say, let me touch it once, will you?"

"Don't be a fool. It's hair. What's hair?" he said.

"No, it's not ordinary hair."

"Ah, get out," Leventhal said, drawing back.

Allbee stood up. "Just to satisfy my curiosity," he said, smiling. He fingered Leventhal's hair, and Leventhal found himself caught under his touch and felt incapable of doing anything. But then he pushed his hand away, crying, "Lay off!"

"It's astonishing. It's like an animal's hair. You must have a terrific constitution."

Leventhal jerked his chair away, wrinkling his forehead in confusion and incipient anger. Then he bawled, "Sit down, you lunatic!" and Allbee went back to his place. He sat forward, ungainly, his hands under his thighs, his jaw slipped to one side, exactly as on the night when he had first confronted Leventhal in the park. The white of his trimmed temples and his shaven face made the blue of his eyes conspicuous.

No further word was spoken for a while. Leventhal was trying to settle his feelings and to determine how to recover the ground he had lost through this last piece of insanity.

"It's hard to have the right mixture of everything," Allbee suddenly began.

"What are you driving at now?" said Leventhal.

"Oh, this about your calling me a lunatic when I give in to an impulse. Nobody can be sure he has the right mixture. Just to give you an example. Lately, a couple of weeks ago, there was a man in the subway, on the tracks. I don't understand how he got there. But he was on the tracks and a train came along and pinned him against the wall. He was bleeding to death. A policeman came down and right away forbid anyone to touch this man until the ambulance arrived. That was because he had instructions about accidents. Now that's too much of one thing—playing it safe. The impulse is to save the man, but the policy is to stick to rules. The ambulance came and the man was dragged out and died right away. I'm not a doctor and I can't say whether he had a chance at any time. But suppose he could have been saved? That's what I mean by the mixture."

"Was he yelling for help? What line was that?" Leventhal said with a frown of pain.

"East-side line. Well, of course, when a man is spread-eagled like that. He was filling the tunnel with his noise. And the crowd! The trains were held up and the station was jammed. They kept coming down. People should have pushed the cop out of the way and taken the fellow down. But everybody stood and listened to him. Those are the real trimmers."

"Trimmers?"

"They're not for God and they're not for the Old Scratch. They think they're for themselves but they're not that either."

"What does he tell me this for?" thought Leventhal. "Does he want to work on my feelings? Maybe he doesn't know why himself."

Allbee began to smile. "You should have seen how surprised you looked when I showed up dead sober. You're going to be even more surprised, you know."

"By what?"

"You were joking with me this morning about a new start. You wouldn't take me seriously."

"Do you believe it yourself?"

"Don't you worry," he said confidently. "I know what really goes on inside me. I'll let you in on something. There isn't a man living who doesn't. All this business, 'Know thyself'! Everybody knows but nobody wants to admit. That's the thing. Some swimmers can hold their breath a long time —those Greek sponge divers—and that's interesting. But the way we keep our eyes shut is a stunt too, because they're made to be open."

"So. You're off again. You can do it without whisky. I thought it was the whisky."

"All right," cried Allbee. "Now let me explain something to you. It's a Christian idea but I don't see why you shouldn't be able to understand it. 'Repent!' That's John the Baptist coming out of the desert. Change yourself, that's what he's saying, and be another man. You must be and the reason for that is that you can be, and when your time comes here you will be. There's another thing behind that 'repent'; it's that we know what to repent. How?" His unsmiling face compelled Leventhal's attention. "*I* know. Everybody knows. But you've got to take away the fear of admitting by a still greater fear. I understand that doctors are beginning to give their patients electric shocks. They tear all hell out of them, and then they won't trifle. You see, you have to get yourself so that you can't stand to keep on in the old way. When you reach that stage—" he knotted his hands and the sinews rose up on his wrists. "It takes a long time before you're ready to quit dodging. Meanwhile, the pain is horrible." He blinked blindly several times as if to clear his eyes of an obstruction. "We're mulish; that's why we have to take such a beating. When we can't stand another lick without dying of it, then we change.

And some people never do. They stand there until the last lick falls and die like animals. Others have the strength to change long before. But repent means *now*, this minute and forever, without wasting any more time."

"And this minute has arrived for you already?"

"Yes."

"I don't know whom you're stringing, me or yourself."

"Every word is sincere—sin-cere!" said Allbee inclining his head and gazing at him. He hesitated, his large lips remained parted, the upper, with its long groove, moving a little.

"Go on!" Leventhal abruptly laughed.

"Well, I thought I would *try* to explain it to you." He turned slightly in his chair, resting one shoulder on the cushion, and slowly rubbed the side of his extended leg. "I'm not religious or anything like that, but I know that I don't have to be next year what I was last year. I've been at one end and I can get to the other. There's no limit to what I can be. And even if I should miss being so dazzling, I know the idea of it is genuine."

"We'll see what you are next year."

"You'll be the same, I know. You people. . . ." He shook his head and his cheek brushed his collar.

"If you start that again, you'll be on the steps in a minute." Leventhal began menacingly to rise.

"All right, all right, let's drop it. Only when a man says something serious about himself he likes to be believed," said Allbee. "It makes sense to me that a man can be born again. —I'll take a rain check on the kingdom of heaven, but if I'm tired of being this way I can become a new man. That's all I'm saying." Straightening himself in his chair he was silent and lightly held his big hands together. By the curve of his mouth Leventhal saw that he was very pleased with himself. Indeed the position of his hands spoke of applause rather than rest. The hump of shadow behind him was occasionally extended by the slight stirring of his head. The lamp in its green, watered-silk shade made a second, softer center of brightness in the polish of the desk. A rush of low sounds came up from the street, and a gust of air swelled and separated the curtains; they drifted together again.

At this moment Leventhal felt Allbee's presence, all that

concerned him, like a great tiring weight, and looked at him with dead fatigue, his fingers motionless on his thighs. Something would have to happen, something that he could not foresee. Whatever it was, he would be too muddled and fatigued to deal with it. He was played out. His old weakness, his nerves, had never been so bad; he could not concentrate long enough to settle any of his difficulties, and had to wait for the occasion to bring this or that to his attention, and was slow and fitful in his thinking. He ought to have thought of what was going on in Staten Island, if only for Philip's sake, and he should have phoned Max at least once. Max had hung on to him in the chapel; he had no one else to hang on to. And by now he must have decided that he had no one at all. But the reason Leventhal shrank from calling was that he was unable to clarify his thoughts or bring them into focus, and he lacked the energy to continue the effort. And anyway the sparks, the clear spark of Mickey's life, the spark of Elena's sanity, the sparks of thought and courage, even courage as confident as Mary's—how such sparks were chased and overtaken, drowned, put out. Then what good was thinking? His dark, poring face with its full cheeks and high-rising dull hair was hung toward his chest. He drew a deep, irregular breath and raised his hands from his lap in a gesture of exorcism against the spell of confusion and despair. "God will help me out," passed through his mind, and he did not stop to ask himself exactly what he meant by this.

"About the card I picked up," said Allbee. "The business card: is that man a moving-picture agent of some kind? I want to explain why I picked it up. I suppose you know him."

"A little."

"What does he do? What's his line?"

"I think he looks for talent."

"Is he influential? I mean, is he. . . ." But Allbee canceled this question as if it were a mark of his persistent innocence or unworldliness.

"Is he what?"

"Oh . . . on the inside." His lip began to curl; his eyes were distended and humorlessly direct. "I've come to the conclusion that if you want to get along nowadays you have to go along with the powers. It's no use trying to buck them."

"Who told you Shifcart was a power?"

Allbee declined to answer. He lifted his shoulders and looked away disdainfully.

"Who?" Leventhal repeated.

"Let's say he can help me, then, and leave out other considerations."

"Do you want to become an actor?"

"Wouldn't I make a good one?"

"You?"

"Is that so funny?"

A faint smile crossed Leventhal's shadowed face. "I understand your mother thought she was a singer," he said. "And you think you are an actor."

"Oh, you've heard about my mother. Who told you about her, Phoebe?"

"Yes. She sang at your wedding, didn't she?"

"Sensationally," said Allbee in an indeterminate tone; and, after a pause, "No, of course I don't want to act. But I thought with all my experience on magazines that I might be able to get into movie work. I once heard about somebody—an acquaintance of an acquaintance—who was doing some preliminary scenario job, looking up stories, and making digests of them, and if I could get into that. . . . Well, maybe your friend can tell me how to do it."

"He's no special friend of mine. How long ago did you hear about this?"

"I don't remember, now. A few years ago."

"Then how do you know you can still get such a job? Why don't you find out from this acquaintance of yours? What have you got to go on? Ask him about it."

Allbee answered quickly, "I couldn't. I wouldn't know where to find him or how to start looking. Besides, he doesn't owe me anything, Leventhal. Why should I go to him?"

"Why? Well, why to me? It makes just as much sense."

His reply tremendously aroused Allbee.

"Why? For good reasons; the best in the world!" He shocked Leventhal by clenching his fists before his breast as if passionately threatening to tear loose from all restraint. "I'm giving you a chance to be fair, Leventhal, and to do what's right. And I want what's right from you. Don't drag anybody else in. This is just between the two of us."

"Don't be crazy."

"Just you and I. Just the two of us."

"I never . . . I never. . . ." Leventhal stammered.

"I can't afford to fool around. The fooling has been kicked out of me. I've been put straight the hard way, the way you pay for with years of your life." He lowered his head and stared at him before continuing. There was a noticeable pulsation in the sides of his face beside his eyes, and in his eyes there was a glint that astounded Leventhal; it resembled nothing in his experience. "Look," said Allbee firmly in a lower voice. "You know that when I say I want an introduction to this man Shifcart it means I am ready to play ball. I'm offering a settlement. I'm offering to haul down my flag. If he helps me. Do you understand?"

"No, I don't understand," Leventhal said. "I don't even begin to get it. And as long as you keep on talking about settling, I won't lift a finger for you."

"Listen," said Allbee. "I know you want to settle. And so do I. And I know what I'm talking about when I say I'll play ball. The world's changed hands. I'm like the Indian who sees a train running over the prairie where the buffalo used to roam. Well, now that the buffalo have disappeared, I want to get off the pony and be a conductor on that train. I'm not asking to be a stockholder in the company. I know that's impossible. Lots of things are impossible that didn't use to be. When I was younger I had my whole life laid out in my mind. I planned what it was going to be like on the assumption that I came out of the lords of the earth. I had all kinds of expectations. But God disposes. There's no use kidding."

Leventhal, his eyes raised to the ceiling, seemed to ask, "You follow? I don't."

There was a knock at the door.

20

I T WAS MAX. He stood before Leventhal with a rolled news-paper under his arm, his shirt open at the throat, the black hair of his chest coming out, and his soft collar pulled over the collar of his coat, the same way Philip's had been on the day of the outing. The suit was the double-breasted one he had worn at the funeral. When the door opened, he seemed to hesitate on the landing, and Leventhal cried out in a cracked voice, "Max! Come in, for heaven's sake."

"You folks in?" Max asked huskily, still hesitant.

It struck Leventhal that his brother was behaving as if he were about to enter a stranger's house. He had never been here before.

"Well, I am, that's sure. I didn't get a chance to tell you the other day. Mary's out of town. But come on in." And he led him over the threshold and turned to the front room, filled with anxiety at his new difficulty. He did not know what to expect from Allbee, what he would say when he learned who Max was. He was already leaning forward inquisitively. Leventhal stood arrested for an instant, incapable of speaking or moving forward. Glancing into the room and seeing Allbee, Max said, apologetically, "Say, you're busy. I'll come back later."

"I'm not," Leventhal whispered. "Come on."

"I should have called up first."

But Leventhal held him by the arm and forced him in.

"This is my brother Max. This is Kirby Allbee."

"Your brother? I didn't know you had one."

"Only one."

Reticent and somber, Max looked down, perhaps partly to acknowledge his share in their estrangement.

"I don't know what made me think you were an only child, like me." Allbee was conversational and bright, and Leventhal wondered what he was preparing and hid his dread in impassivity. He brought up a chair and Max sat down. The points of his dusty shoes were turned inward. The side of his lowered face and his large neck formed one surface, from the curve of his nose to the padded thickness of his shoulder.

"I often used to wish there were two of us," said Allbee.

"How are things at home, Max?" asked Leventhal.

"Oh," Max said. "You know . . ." Leventhal expected him to finish the sentence, but it tailed off.

Allbee seemed to be commenting to himself smilingly on something in the appearance of the two brothers. Leventhal covertly indicated the door with his head. Allbee's brows curved up questioningly. His whole air said, "Why should I?" Leventhal bent close to him and muttered, "I want to talk to my brother."

"What's the matter?" Allbee spoke out loudly.

Sternly Leventhal made the same sign with his head.

But Max had heard. "Did you ask me what was the matter?" he said.

Allbee looked at Leventhal and shrugged, to confess his slip. He did not reply.

"I guess it must show on me," said Max.

"We had a death in the family recently," Leventhal said. "My youngest son."

An expression went over Allbee's face that Leventhal could not interpret, a cold wrinkling. "Oh, sorry to hear it. When?"

"Four days ago."

"You didn't mention it to me," Allbee said to Leventhal.

"No," Leventhal answered flatly, gazing at his brother.

Allbee came forward swiftly in his chair. "Say, was that the boy . . . the other day?"

"No, not the one that was with me. He means Phil," Leventhal explained to Max. "I took him to the movies awhile back, and we ran into Mr. Allbee."

"Oh, Phil. Knock wood. That's my other son you saw."

"Oh, I see, two children. . . ."

"Are you going?" Leventhal said to him, aside.

"Will you fix it up for me with Shifcart?"

Leventhal fastened his hand on his arm. "Will you go?"

"You said you'd help me."

"We'll take it up later." Leventhal was growing savage with impatience. "Don't think you can hold me up."

"I don't want to interfere with business," said Max.

"What business! There's no business."

Allbee rose and Leventhal went into the hall with him.

"I'll be back for your answer," Allbee said. He looked into Leventhal's face as though he saw something new there. "I'm really surprised. Here this happens to you—your nephew. I'm in the same house and you don't even say a word about it."

"What do I want to talk to you about it for?" Before Allbee could speak again, he had shut the door.

"Who is he?" said Max, when Leventhal came back. "A friend?"

"No, just a guy who keeps coming around."

"He's peculiar looking. . . ." Max checked himself and then said, "I hope I didn't butt in on anything."

"Oh, hell no. I was going to call you up, Max. But I thought I'd better wait awhile."

"I was kind of expecting you to, since you took an interest and came to the funeral, and all."

Max addressed him diffidently, a little formally, feeling his way with a queer politeness, almost the politeness of a stranger. Subdued, worn, and plainly, to Leventhal's eyes, tormented, he was making an effort, nevertheless, to find an appropriate tone, one not too familiar. The blood crowded to Leventhal's heart guiltily. He wanted to say something to Max about it. He did not know how and he was afraid of creating a still greater difficulty. How should they talk when they had never, since childhood, spent an hour together? And he surmised also that the flat, the contrast between his upholstered chairs and good rugs and the borax furniture in Staten Island, shabby before half the installments were paid, made Max deferential.

"So how are things going?" he said. He thought Max would speak about Elena. He was in fact certain that the main object of his visit was to discuss her with him.

"I guess as good as I can expect."

"Phil all right?"

"Well, when one kid passes on it's pretty hard on the other one."

"He'll come around."

Max said nothing to this, and Leventhal began to think he was debating whether to mention Elena at all, undecided at the last moment, and struggling with himself.

"Yes, kids come around," Leventhal repeated.

"I wanted to ask you," said Max. "I want to straighten it up with you about the specialist. He says you gave him ten dollars the first visit." His hand dropped inside his coat.

"Oh, no."

But Max opened his wallet and, half rising, laid a ten dollar bill beside the lamp on the desk.

"That's not necessary."

"I want to pay you back. Thanks."

"Now he takes over," was Leventhal's unspoken comment. His original vexation with Max revived and he said, a shade coldly, "You're welcome."

"Not just for the money," said Max. "The rest, too."

Leventhal's temper got the better of him.

"For doing a small part of what you should have been here to do."

Max reflected, raising his rough-skinned, large-jawed face with its high-ridged, freckled nose. "Yes," he said. "I should have been here." He was submissive, seeming to find nothing in himself with which to resist.

Leventhal could not hold back his next question.

"What does Elena say?"

"About what?"

"About me?"

Max appeared surprised.

"What should she say? All she said was that she wondered why you didn't come to the house after the funeral. But she doesn't say much. She's in bed most of the time, crying."

Leventhal had edged forward. The lamplight shone into his hair and over his shoulders.

"Does she give you a lot of trouble, Max?"

"Trouble? You've got to consider. It's a rough deal. She cries. That's pretty natural."

"You might as well be open with me."

Max's surprise grew.

"What's there not to be open about?"

"If you don't know, I don't either. But you've got a chance to talk it out, if you want to. I realize we're not so close. But do you have anyone else to talk to? Maybe you have friends. I didn't notice many at the funeral."

Max said uncertainly, "I don't catch your drift, exactly."

"I asked if Elena gives you trouble."

The blood rose darkly in Max's face under the full mask of his ill-shaven beard. There was a show of fear and bewilderment in his eyes and, reluctantly, he began a motion of denial with his black-nailed hands; he did not finish; he gave it up.

"She's calming down."

"What does she say?"

"All kinds of things," Max said with obvious difficulty, still shunning a direct answer.

But Leventhal did not need a direct answer. He could picture Elena in the brass bed where Mickey had lain, in that terrible room, crying and raging; and Max sitting just as he saw him sitting now, abjectly listening. For what could he do? And Philip had to listen, too. The thought struck into him. But how could the boy be protected? He would have to hear and learn. Leventhal believed what he had said to Max about children coming through. They were mauled in birth and they straightened as they grew because their bones were soft. Mauled again later, they could recover again. She was his mother, so let him see and hear. Was that a cruel view of it? He was full of love for the boy. But it did not do to be soft. Be soft when things were harsh? Not that softness was to be condemned, but there were times when it was only another name for weakness. Softness? Out of the whole creation only man was like that, and he was half harsh.

"Have you had a doctor for her?" he asked.

"What makes you think she needs one?"

"Remember Mamma!"

Max started. "What are you talking about?" he said with a sudden flash of indignation.

"I don't blame you for not wanting it brought up."

"Why do you bring Ma into this? Does she remind you of Ma?"

Leventhal hesitated. "Once in a while, she does. . . . But you admit you have trouble with her."

"What do you expect? She carries on. Sure she carries on. It's a kid, after all. That hits. But she'll be all right. She's getting better already."

"Max, I don't think you understand. People go overboard easily. I guess they're not as strong that way as they used to be and when things get rough they give in. There's more and more of that all the time. Everybody feels it. I do myself, often. Elena was very queer about the kid and the hospital. —That's what she yells about, isn't it? The hospital?" He grew increasingly unsure of himself. "And I thought . . ."

"I remember Ma pretty often, too, and Hartford, and all. You're not the only one."

"No?" Leventhal said. He looked at him searchingly.

"And you're wrong about Elena."

"You don't think I want to be right, do you?"

"The main trouble I'm having with her is that I want to move the family down south. I was looking for a place in Galveston. That was what took so long. I found one and I have a deposit on it. I was going to bring them all down there."

"That's good. The best thing you could do. Take Philip out of New York. It's no place to bring him up."

"But I can't talk Elena into it."

"Why?"

"Maybe I started in too soon after the funeral. But she says she doesn't want to go."

"Tell me, is the old woman around much—her mother?"

"Oh, she's in and out all the time."

"For God's sake, throw her out!"

His vehemence astonished Max.

"She doesn't have anything to do with it."

"Don't let her get a hold. Protect yourself against her."

Max for the first time began to smile.

"She won't hurt me."

"I'll bet she's telling Elena not to go. How do you know what she tells her? You don't understand what they're saying."

Max's look changed; he became grave again and his mouth sank at the corners. "I understand a little," he said. "I guess you think I should have married a Jewish girl."

"You never heard me say so," Leventhal answered vigorously. "Never."

"No."

"You never will. I'm talking about her mother, not Elena. You told me yourself that the old woman hated you, years ago. She'll do you all the harm she can. Maybe you're used to the old devil and don't notice what she's like any more. But I've watched her. It's as clear as day to me that she thinks the baby's death was God's punishment because Elena married you."

Max started and then his lips stiffened, and there was a submerged flaming of indignation beneath his natural darkness and the added darkness of care. "What kind of talk is that!" he said. "I never heard anything so peculiar in all my life. First you've got ideas about Elena and now the old woman."

"You've been away," said Leventhal. "You don't know how she's been acting. She's poison."

"Well, you've sure turned into a suspicious character." Max's face began to soften and he sighed.

"She's full of hate," Leventhal insisted.

"Go on, she's a harmless old woman."

If he were wrong about Elena, thought Leventhal, if he had overshot the mark and misinterpreted that last look of hers in the chapel, the mistake was a terrible and damaging one; the confusion in himself out of which it had risen was even more terrible. Eventually he had to have a reckoning with himself, when he was calmer and stronger. It was impossible now. But he was right about the old woman, he was sure. "You must get rid of your mother-in-law, Max!" he said with savage earnestness.

"Ah, what are you talking about?" he said rather wearily. "She's just an old widow, old and cranky. Elena is her only daughter. I can't tell her to stay away. This week she helped, she kept house and cooked for us. I know she doesn't like me. So what? A worn-out old woman. I feel sad, sometimes, when I look at her. No, we'll go to Galveston. Phil will start school there in the fall. He wants to go, and so does Elena. I can talk her into it. She wants to leave New York, only she's still mixed up. But she'll come. I've got to get back to my job, and we don't want to be separated again. I don't see why you're so disturbed about the old woman. If she's the worst I'm ever up against . . ." The large fold of his jacket reached kiltwise almost to his knees on which his hands were set. His unshapely fingers thickened where they should taper and the creases at the joints resembled the threads of flattened screws. "You don't know Elena when there's a tight spot," he resumed. "She's excitable all in pieces before something happens, but usually when it happens she's stronger than I am. During the depression when I was laid up, she went out and peddled stuff from door to door."

"I never heard that you were laid up."

"Well, I was. And then when we were on relief, she has a brother who's a hood and he wanted to take me into a kind of racket he had out in Astoria. I could've seen a little money, but she said no and went all the way out against it, so it was 'No' and we stayed on relief. Another woman would have said, 'Go ahead.'"

"I see."

"Afterwards things started to pick up and we thought we could add on to the family. Mickey wasn't ever a healthy kid like Phil. And then we must have made mistakes, too. But what can you do? It's not like with God, you know, in the Bible, where he blows his breath into Adam, or whoever. I think I told you that I asked a nurse what room he was in, when I got to the hospital. I went in there and he was lying covered up already. I pulled the sheet off and had a look at him."

"Those fools!" Leventhal exclaimed. "Not to have somebody posted there."

Max excused them with a downward wave of the hand. "All the nurses didn't know. It's a big place." He added, consecutively, "I'm going south with the idea of a new start. I paid a deposit and so on. But to tell the truth, I don't expect much. I feel half burned out already."

Leventhal felt his heart shaken. "Half burned?" he said. "I'm older than you and I don't say that."

Max did not reply. His large trunk was ungainly in the double-breasted jacket.

"There have been times when I felt like that, too," Leventhal went on. "That's a feeling that comes and goes." His brother turned his crude, dark face up to him and his voice died.

They sat together in silence and at last Max stirred and got up. Leventhal went with him to the subway. A heavy mist lay over the street. At the turnstile he dropped two nickels into the slot and Max said over his shoulder, "You don't have to wait with me."

But Leventhal pushed through. They stood at the edge of the platform till the grind of the approaching train reached them.

"If you need me for anything . . ." Leventhal said.

"Thanks."

"I mean it."

"Thank you." He extended his hand. Leventhal clumsily spread his arms wide and clasped him. They felt the concussion of the train, and the streaked face of the lead car with its beam shot toward them in a smolder of dust; the windows ran by. Max returned his embrace. "Call me," Leventhal said hoarsely in Max's ear. The crowd swirled around them at the doors. When the train started, he saw Max gripping a strap and bending over the heads of passengers, peering out.

Pulling out a handkerchief, Leventhal wiped his sweat. He began to labor up the long, steel-striped concrete flights, opening his mouth to assist his breathing. Halfway up he stopped, squeezing against the wall to let others past, looking as if the lack of air maddened him. He felt faint with the expansion of his heart.

Then he continued. The mist had gathered to a light rain. At the top of the stairs he saw an umbrella flung open, like a bat in the chill current of air. The bars of the revolving door raced and clinked. Buttoning his coat, he raised the collar, and his eyes moved from the glare of the cars flowing up in the street to the towering lights that stood far ahead, not quite steady in the immense blackness.

21

I N THE Saturday mail there was an invitation from Mrs.
Harkavy to a party that same evening in honor of her
granddaughter's seventh birthday. The postman whom Leventhal encountered in the fog on the outer stairs handed it to
him. There was nothing from Mary and he was secretly glad
of it, for the truth was that he felt he was stealing away and
leaving Allbee in possession of the house. Ostensibly he was
going out for coffee. He had risen to find the flat cold, and
the windows dripping and gray as tin. Allbee was still asleep
in the dining room, his naked arms locked around the narrow
mattress, sprawling, uncouth. His clothes lay on the floor and
the air was stifling. Leventhal had gone into the kitchen and
put on the coffee but, when he pictured himself sitting down
in the cheerless front room to drink it, he made a face, shut
off the gas, and went down to eat at the Greek's. But he had
no intention of coming back after breakfast.

Around Mrs. Harkavy's invitation he half unconsciously
and in a complicatedly indirect fashion made out a schedule.
He was at first uncertain about attending the party. Should he
go so soon after Mickey's death? But, having decided that it
would be a good thing for him to be among people, he rode
uptown to buy the girl a present. And finding himself near the
library at noon, he spent a few hours glancing over some of
the trade papers to see what others were doing. So it was
nearly evening and he was coming out of a newsreel theatre
in Times Square before he realized that behind everything he
had contrived to fill this weary day was his unwillingness and
inability to deal with Allbee. He had set off purposefully
down Broadway, and now something seemed to hinder the
steady action of his legs and he faltered and began to go
slower.

"All right, I'll send him to Shifcart," Leventhal decided.
"What do I care? I'll do it, and if that isn't enough for him,
we'll see. Only what will Shifcart think?" But he was already
in disfavor with Shifcart, who had looked at him peevishly in
the cafeteria when he failed to laugh at his joke. "It would be

better to come in cold than with a recommendation from me. But as long as he believes so much in connections let him go and find out for himself."

He stopped at home before dinner to put on a clean shirt. Allbee was out. The dirt and disorder of the place sickened Leventhal. There was rubbish on the kitchen floor and the remains of a meal on the table. "He'd behave better in a flophouse. He's just trying to show me," thought Leventhal. He swept out the kitchen. Bending down with the dust pan, he experienced a curious tightness in the skin of his face. He threw the broom into the corner, washed his hands, and left.

Mrs. Harkavy met him in the entry and she disconcerted him by saying, "I was awfully upset to hear about your nephew." For he had just then, in the elevator, been thinking about Mickey. "Doctor Denisart told me about it. I'm sure he did his best."

Leventhal muttered that he thought so too. Because he was disturbed, he was more conscious than usual of the bracing process he went through on meeting one of the Harkavys. He was fond of them, they were kind, but he had never been able to work out a satisfactory balance with them. Mrs. Harkavy's expression was like her son's, lively and erratic. Yet there was a durable, underlying melancholy in her animation, and occasionally it came uppermost and took him by surprise.

"Someday science will conquer death," she said. "Last Sunday there was a symposium in the *Times* about it."

Leventhal pulled himself together sufficiently to reply, "I hope. . . ."

"Oh, it looks definite. Then the size of the population will have to be controlled. But science will figure that out, too. There are brains enough for everything. This man discovered something to make the tissues live forever. I don't think we can expect much in our lifetime. It's for future generations. Meanwhile, we have to make the best of it. I think Mr. Banting's father died of diabetes about a year before insulin was discovered. And this Mr. Bogomolets couldn't use his own serum on account of a bad heart, and he died. Asa, how old was the child?"

"Three and a half, four. . . ."

The freakishness seemed to leave her. Only her eyes moved, meeting his own with a familiar, instantaneous significance.

"That's the brother who lives in Queens?"

"Staten Island."

"Asa, sometimes I feel wicked still to be here at my age while children die."

He was at a loss for an answer.

"But I'm not taking it away from anybody," she said, falling back into her eccentricity; it quivered at the corners of her green-ringed eyes.

"Mamma," Julia called.

"The men are in the dining room, Asa. There's wine and liquor on the sideboard." Her face was flushed and she turned away, wide-hipped in her blue dress with its ornamented shoulders.

The guests, none of whom he knew, were playing pinochle. He was disappointed. He had hoped to see Schlossberg or Shifcart.

"Take a hand," said Harkavy.

"No, I don't think I will. Is anybody else coming, Dan?"

"We're expecting a few more people," said Harkavy. He was engrossed in his cards.

Leventhal poured himself a glass of wine and took a diamond-shaped biscuit sprinkled with sugar. Suddenly he remembered the present he had brought and he drank down the wine, tugged the package out of his pocket, and went into the kitchen. There was a cloud over the range. Julia was raising a colander of fried potatoes from the oil, averting her face from the sputter and crying nervously, "Mother, Mother, keep Libbie back."

"Stay away, honey. Julia, don't rush those potatoes. They'll be raw."

Leventhal came forward with his package.

"I brought something for the girl."

"Oh, how thoughtful of you," said Mrs. Harkavy. "With all your own troubles."

Leventhal was impassive.

"Here," he said. "Happy birthday."

There was a gold seal pasted on the tissue paper and Libbie, after one quick glance at him, began picking it off.

"Not even 'thank you, Uncle Leventhal.'" Julia looked furious.

"Julia, it's only shyness, nervousness."

"Say thanks, you little animal."

The girl ran into the hall and Leventhal returned to the dining room. He had a second glass of the sweet wine, and a third.

"Come, sit in," Goldstone said to him.

He shook his head and slouched against the sideboard, leaning on his elbow and sipping. This was his fourth glass and he was beginning to feel a heavy, solvent, milky warmth. He was conscious of being extremely clear-eyed, of seeing everything, catching every movement as if under extraordinary illumination. As the cards slapped and flicked over the red leather pad, he diverted himself by observing the hands, shuffling, dealing, manipulating the money, the variety of knuckles and fingers. Harkavy's were white, pointed, and simple looking. The hands of the man next to him were strung with veins and overgrown with hair, his thumb was turned back and blackened, perhaps by lead—he might be a printer. The flesh of his palm was red and brutally cross-hatched. "Used hard," reflected Leventhal. Yet these hands were limber with coins, and counted and tossed them with the ease of deep familiarity.

Leaving the sideboard he strolled into the dark living room and lit a cigar. He felt the blood at his heart and brain to be a very rich and powerful mixture, for the most part pleasurable. A little painful also. The slight distress, however, was part of the pleasure. He took a sip of wine, licked the base of the glass and wiped it on his wrist to prevent a ring, and set it on a little table. Mrs. Harkavy's voice came down the hall. "Future generations!" he grinned. "My Lord!" He sat down, lame and heavy limbed.

After some time he saw Harkavy come in to the room apparently looking for him. He spoke up from his corner.

"Hey, here!"

"Oh, hiding out, having a quiet cigar. The house is filling up. Mamma and Julia are starting to serve." Leventhal heard the scrape of chairs on the parquet floor of the dining room.

"Say, do you expect Shifcart tonight?"

"I don't think he was asked. What do you want him for?"

"Do you think I made a bad impression on him that day?"

"I know you did on me. I've never seen such an exhibition of ghetto psychology. The attitude you took toward Disraeli amazed me."

"No, I don't mean that. Did he say anything to you?"

"Nothing. Is this an attack of your old weakness—worrying whether people like you?"

"I wanted to sound him out about something. . . . To see what he'd say. If he'd help me out with someone."

"Who's the favor for?"

"It doesn't matter who, does it?" Leventhal said.

"No, it doesn't. You don't have to tell me." There was already a ring of exasperation in his voice.

"It doesn't make any difference who."

"I asked to be helpful. But I won't play button-button with you. Especially since you have an edge on. I saw you drinking."

"Ah, you could have had a lot of opportunities to be helpful," said Leventhal.

"Why, it must be that what's-his-name that's been bothering you," said Harkavy with a sudden nicker of amused discovery. "That's who, isn't it?"

Leventhal dumbly nodded.

"Then what's the mystery?"

"No mystery," Leventhal muttered.

"Why do you need help with him? What does he want? I don't understand how Shifcart comes into the picture."

"Well, Dan, this Allbee is interested in scenario work and since he once got me an introduction at Dill's he wants me to do the same for him with Shifcart, seeing he's in the movie line. It's mostly for the record that I'm doing it."

"You know Shifcart has nothing to do with scenario. He deals with actors, talent."

"Allbee thought he might have a connection somewhere. I didn't think so, but he asked me, and I thought . . . Well, to tell you the truth, Dan, I didn't know what to think. I had my doubts. But he did get me the interview with Rudiger. So I thought, 'Well, let him go and see Shifcart. Why should I answer for Shifcart? I'll show my good intentions and return the favor,' and so on. That's the story."

"I don't believe it. It seems to me that he's got you on the merry-go-round."

One of Mrs. Harkavy's plants stood behind Leventhal. He felt a leaf graze his hair as he shut his eyes and leaned backwards.

"How did he ever sell you such a bill of goods?" said Harkavy. "Where did he hear of Shifcart?"

"He happened to be at the house and saw a card of Shifcart's."

"So he keeps coming around. You must be encouraging him. I thought we came to the conclusion he was off his nut."

"*You* did!" Blindly roused, Leventhal flung out his arm. "You were the one. That was what you said. You compared him to your aunt."

"Well, you're impetuous tonight. Both of us came to the same conclusion."

"No, no!" Leventhal refused to hear him. "I absolutely deny it. Absolutely!"

"Where did I get it from, if you didn't say it? I can't understand you. I haven't seen the man. Anyhow, what's the odds? Why should that be an issue? I can see you're losing your bearings. Of course, you've got quite a little wine in your system; maybe that partly accounts for your funny behavior. Yes, it is very funny. I always thought you didn't know how to take care of yourself. I can see this man has you eating out of his hand. He comes around, you get excited when you talk about him, you're going to send him to Shifcart. . . ."

"I'd send him anywhere to get rid of him," said Leventhal.

"There, you wouldn't say anything like that unless you were in pretty deep. I can tell that you're keeping back information; don't have to be much of a mindreader to see that. I can't help you any more than to remind you that you're playing for keeps. You're not a boy, any more."

"Dan, you know Shifcart. This has to be done. Tell me . . ." He caught Harkavy's hand.

"Take it up with him yourself."

"Yes, I will, but I want to ask you . . ."

"We'd better go in. They must be waiting for us. We'll discuss this tomorrow when your head is clearer and if you want to be open with me."

The guests, all men, had taken off their jackets and were sitting in the high-backed chairs. In the kitchen door, talking with Mrs. Harkavy, was Mr. Schlossberg who had just arrived and was still wearing his brown topcoat. Leventhal said good evening to him and Schlossberg answered, "How are you?" He did not seem, however, to remember him. "Fourteenth Street a couple of weeks ago," said Leventhal.

"His memory is bad," Harkavy whispered. He drew Leventhal into the row of chairs along the buffet.

Across the table, Leventhal recognized the possessor of the red hands he had watched during the card game. His name was Kaplan and his face, like his hands, was red and creased. He had a sharp blue squint, as though—Leventhal thought—he had made an effort to pierce heaven and distorted his eyes. Just now he was holding up a glass of brandy and saying, "Here's to all."

"Drink up," someone said. "Next year in Jerusalem."

Leventhal heard Julia say, "We had a children's party last year. It was too nerve racking. This time we decided we would have older people."

"Shall we begin eating?" asked Goldstone.

"We ought to have the cake brought in first," Mrs. Harkavy said. She explained to the company. "They weren't very careful with it at the bakery. Some of the frosting came off with the wax paper. We did our best to repair it."

Julia put the cake with its seven candles on the table. Libbie stood staring into the flames. Her eyes were much like her grandmother's and her uncle's.

"Blow, kiddie," said Harkavy. "Once, that's luckiest."

But Libbie reached out and tried to capture a drop of the melting wax.

"Libbie, dear. . . ." her father urged.

"People are waiting," Julia cried impatiently. "Would you rather be hanging upside down in the closet?"

The child lowered her face to the clear ring of candles. Leventhal saw the liquid image of them in her eyes and on her white forehead. She blew, and the whitish, odorous wax smoke drifted over the table. The guests clapped and cried out.

"Sweet little kid," said Harkavy to Leventhal, who nodded and still gazed heavy eyed at the candles. Julia and her grandmother kissed the girl.

The supper began. Leventhal's clothing, especially his shirt, bound and chafed him, and he opened his collar, grumbling to Harkavy, "It's cutting my neck." But Harkavy had resumed an argument begun earlier in the evening with a Mr. Benjamin who sat between Goldstone and Julia. Leventhal had noticed him in the hall before, clumping on a specially built shoe. He had the complexion of a Hindu, a head of grizzled short curls, and scornful brown-freckled lips; there was a drop of yellow in his wide-set black eyes. Benjamin sold life insurance, and Harkavy had assailed the insurance companies. "It's all in the Cardozo investigation. Does any more have to be said? The same money that's taken from the customers is used against them." "I don't see, Harkavy," said Mr. Benjamin, "why one business has to be run down more than another. You ought to be against them all. And against government. You're an amateur, Harkavy, an amateur. I've heard your argument from experts. You have to pay for regulation and for order. It's one kind of harness or another. Men need a harness. This is light harness compared to some." "Oh, my dear man, you're as reactionary as they come," said Harkavy. "Are you against all banks and business?" asked Benjamin. "Damn it, certainly I am." Harkavy's voice rose. "Let's hear what kind of a system you're thinking about?" Mr. Benjamin's acerbity almost wiped out his smile.

"Stop the wrangling, Dan, for God's sake," said Goldstone.

"I'll make it easier for you," said Benjamin. "Don't you want to provide for the people you love? Let's not argue about the best system. This one is standing yet."

"It may not be for long. You never know when everything will be swept away overnight." "But meantime . . ." Mrs. Harkavy interrupted. "Daniel, you're just being sensational. I don't like to hear such talk from you." "Mamma, what I say is perfectly true. There have been big organizations before and people who thought they would last forever." "You mean Insull?" said the man on his left. "I mean Rome, Persia, the great Chinese empires!"

Mr. Benjamin shrugged his shoulders. "We have to live today," he said. "If you had a son, Harkavy, you'd want him to have a college education. Who's going to wait for the Messiah? They tell a story about a little town in the old country.

It was out of the way, in a valley, so the Jews were afraid the Messiah would come and miss them, and they built a high tower and hired one of the town beggars to sit in it all day long. A friend of his meets this beggar and he says, 'How do you like your job, Baruch?' So he says, 'It doesn't pay much, but I think it's steady work.'" There was an uproar at the table. "There's a moral, for you!" cried Benjamin in a suddenly strengthened voice. Leventhal felt himself beginning to smile. "It is!" shouted Mr. Kaplan, laying his hand on Benjamin's shoulder. Mrs. Harkavy, flushing, raised her delighted brows and covered her mouth with her handkerchief.

"Anyway, I don't think it's right," said Harkavy, "to go frightening people the way you do." "Oh? What now?" Harkavy knitted his brows. "I know how you insurance gentlemen work," he said. "You go in to see a prospect. There he is, behind his desk or his counter, still in pretty fair shape, you may say. He has his aches and his troubles, but in general everything is satisfactory. Suddenly you're there to say, 'Have you considered your family's future?' Well and good, every man dies, but you're playing it unfair and hitting where you know it hurts. He thinks about these things alone at night. Most of us do. But now you're undermining him in the daytime. When you've frightened him good he says, 'What'll I do?' And you're ready with the contract and the fountain pen." "Now, Dan," said Goldstone restrainingly. Benjamin glanced at him with his yellow and black eyes as though to say that he needed no defender. "So what," he said. "I do them a favor. Shouldn't they be prepared?"

"Oh, Death!" someone quoted at the far end of the table. "Thou comest when I had thee least in mind." "Yes, that's the thing," Benjamin said lifting himself with a scuff of his heel and pointing. "That's it." "My heavens," said Mrs. Harkavy. "What a morbid thing for a birthday party. With all this food on the table. Can't we find something lighter to talk about?" "The funeral baked meats did furnish forth the marriage feast." "Where the blazes is this poetry coming from?" said Goldstone. "It's Brimberg. His father died and he was able to go to college." Goldstone smiled. "Be serious, down there," he said. "Cousins of mine," he explained to Leventhal, happening to catch his glance. "My mother sewed her own shroud," said Kaplan, raising his distorted shining blue eyes to them. "That's right, it was the custom," said Benjamin. "All the old people used to do it. And a good custom, too, don't you think so, Mr. Schlossberg?" "There's a lot to say for it," Schlossberg replied. "At least they knew where they stood and who they were, in those days. Now they don't know who they are but they don't want to give themselves up. The last funeral I went to, they had paper grass in the grave to cover up the dirt." "So you're on Benjamin's side?" said Harkavy. "No, not exactly," said the old man. "Sure, Benjamin's business is to scare people." "So you're on my side, then?" Mr. Schlossberg looked impatient. "It's not a question of people's feelings," he said. "You don't have to remind them of anything. They don't forget. But they're too busy and too smart to die. It's easy to understand. Here I'm sitting here, and my mind can go around the world. Is there any limit to what I can think? But in another minute I can be dead, on this spot. There's a limit to me. But I have to be myself in full. Which is somebody who dies, isn't it? That's what I was from the beginning. I'm not three people, four people. I was born once and I will die once. You want to be two people? More than human? Maybe it's because you don't know how to be one. Everybody is busy. Every man turns himself into a whole corporation to handle the business. So one stockholder is riding in the elevator, and another one is on the roof looking through a telescope, one is eating candy, and one is in the movies looking at a pretty face. Who is left? And how can a corporation die? One stockholder dies. The corporation lives and goes on eating and riding in the elevator and looking at the pretty face. But it stands to reason, paper grass in the grave makes all the grass paper. . . ." "There's always something new with Schlossberg," said Kaplan. He strangely altered his squint by raising his brows. "What's on his lung is on his tongue."

"Really," Julia broke in. "Mamma is right. What kind of talk is this for a birthday?"

"Never out of place," said Benjamin.

"Out of place?" said Brimberg at the foot of the table. "It depends on your taste. I heard about a French lady of easy virtue who dressed in a bridal veil for her clients."

"Sammy!" came Mrs. Harkavy's scolding scream. And there was more laughter and a hubbub out of which grew a new conversation to which Leventhal, however, did not listen. Harkavy was not watching and he poured himself another glass of wine.

22

B EFORE HE was fully awake, Leventhal, on Harkavy's couch where he had spent the night, realized that his head was aching, and, when he opened his eyes, even the gray light of the overcast day was too strong for him and he turned his face to the cushions and hitched the quilt over his shoulder. He was in his undershirt and his feet were bare but he had not taken off his trousers. His belt was tight and he loosened it, and brought his hand out, pressing and kneading the skin of his forehead. Over the arm of the couch he gazed at the period furniture, the ferns, the looped and gathered silk of the unmodish lamps, and the dragons, flowers, and eyes of the rug. He knew the rug. Old Harkavy had gotten it from the estate of a broker who committed suicide on Black Friday.

Occasionally the windows were slammed by a high wind, and when this occurred the curtained French doors shook a little. Steam hissed in the pipes and there was a fall smell of heating radiators. Leventhal's nose was dry. The mohair was rough against his cheek. He did not change his position. Shutting his eyes, he tried to doze away the oppressiveness of his headache.

At a stir behind the French doors he said loudly, "Come!" No one entered, however, and he pushed away the covers. The strap of his watch was loose and it had worked round to the wrong side of his wrist. The lateness of the hour made him frown—it was nearly half-past one. He sat up and leaned forward, his undershirt hanging shapeless over his fat chest. He was about to reach for his shoes and stockings, but his hands remained on his knees and he was suddenly powerless to move and fearfully hampered in his breathing. He had the strange feeling that there was not a single part of him on which the whole world did not press with full weight, on his body, on his soul, pushing upward in his breast and downward in his bowels. He concentrated, moving his lips like someone about to speak, and blew a tormented breath through his nose. What he meanwhile sensed was that this interruption of the customary motions he went through un-

thinkingly on rising, despite the pain it was causing, was a disguised opportunity to discover something of great importance. He tried to seize the opportunity. He put out all his
strength to collect himself, beginning with the primary cer-
tainty that the world pressed on him and passed through him.
Beyond this he could not go, hard though he drove himself.
He was bewilderingly moved. He sat in the same posture,
massively, his murky face trained on the ferns standing softly
against the gray glass. His nostrils twitched. It came into his
head that he was like a man in a mine who could smell smoke
and feel heat but never see the flames. And then the cramp
and the enigmatic opportunity ended together. His legs quivered as he worked his feet back and forth on the carpet. He
walked over to the window and he heard the loud crack of the
wind. It was pumping the trees in the small wedge of park six
stories below, tearing at the wires on rooftops, fanning the
smoke out under the clouds, scattering it like soot on paraffin.

He dressed, feeling a little easier. His shirt cuffs were
soiled; he turned them underside up and transferred the
links. He stuffed his tie into his pocket; he would put it on
after washing. Stripping the couch, he folded up the sheets
and the silk quilt and laid them on a chair. When he opened
the French doors, he expected to meet Mrs. Harkavy or one
of the family in the hall and he wondered why the house
was so silent. Harkavy's dark room was open, the bed empty.
Leventhal switched on the light and saw trousers hung
neatly from the top drawer of the dresser and the suspenders
coiled on the floor. An open magazine covered the lamp.

Harkavy was sitting alone in the kitchen. At his elbow the
toaster was ticking, and a pot of coffee was warming on the
electric heater. He was wearing a corduroy jacket over his pajamas, a belted jacket with large leather buttons. His bare feet
were crossed on a chair. His green slippers had fallen to the
floor.

"Good morning," Harkavy's look was amused. "The reveler."

"Good morning. Where's the family?"

"Gone to Shifcart senior's for the birthday dinner."

"Why didn't you go?"

"To Long Island City when I have a chance to sleep late?
They left at nine."

"I hope you didn't stay here because of me."

"You? No, I wanted to sleep. Holidays are poison if I have to get up early." He stroked the golden-green jacket. "I like a late, peaceful breakfast. Bachelor habits. As long as I'm not married, I've got to stand pat on my advantages."

The kitchen light, reflecting from the tiles and the white refrigerator, was too sharp for Leventhal. He winced away from it slightly.

"How do you feel—not very well?"

"Headache."

"You're not used to drinking."

"No," said Leventhal. The banter annoyed him.

"You were bright-eyed, last night."

He looked rather sullenly at him. "What if I was?"

"Nothing. I'm not blaming you, you understand, for getting a little tight. You probably have good reasons."

"Where's your aspirin?"

"In the bathroom. I'll bring you some." Harkavy started to rise.

"Stay put; I'll find it."

"Have a cup of coffee. It'll do you more good." He removed his feet from the chair. They were very long and white, with toes as slender as fingers.

Leventhal poured himself a cup of black coffee. It was bitter and coated his tongue with a sediment, but he felt it would do him good.

Harkavy sighed. "I'm a little under the weather myself. Not from drinking; the excitement, the arguing, and such. Mamma, though, she was up at seven and got everything in order. What vitality she's got! Her mother—there was another dry old fire for you. She lived to be ninety-four. Do you remember her? Down on Joralemon Street?"

"No." Leventhal, trying to recapture the feeling that had interrupted his dressing, found he retained almost nothing of it.

"I'm a different type," Harkavy said. "The sword that wears out the sheath. But some of these old people. . . . Take Schlossberg, for example, still supporting his family, his good-for-nothing son and his daughters. The old man is a blowhard, sometimes, but you have to hand it to him. With him it's a case of 'touch me and you touch a man,' and these days you can't always be sure what you're touching. I set myself up against him, now and then, because I like a good argument. I don't trust people who won't argue."

Gradually Harkavy's manner underwent a change. He was slouching in his chair, his heels were set wide apart on the linoleum and his arms were hanging over the back of the chair; his hands with their whitish hairs were full veined. Beneath the clear water lines, his lids suddenly appeared flushed and irritated, and when he began again to speak it was with a nervous dodge of the head, as if he were already putting aside an objection.

"Why don't you come clean now on this business we were talking about last night?" he said.

"What's there to come clean about?"

"It baffles me. I've been giving it some thought. After what you said about him, that you should be trying to arrange this. . . ."

Leventhal did not stir his face from the cup. "We went over that yesterday. I told you about *Dill's*."

"He must have you by the tail."

Leventhal reflected, "This is just curiosity on his part. Why should I satisfy it? That Sunday when he could have helped me out he went away with Goldstone and his friends, and now, because he's itching to know, *I* should talk." He resolved to give him no satisfaction. Nevertheless, the saucer shook in his hand and he held it against his chest, bending his head until folds of skin appeared under his chin and along his jaw. He meditated on his weakness. How weak he was becoming. Even Harkavy could make him tremble.

"How come you changed your mind about him? You said he was loony."

"No, you did."

"On your information. What you told me was all I had to go by. It looks as if he really did a job on you, sold you a bill of goods."

Leventhal doggedly refrained from answering. He kept his head down with a look of worn endurance.

Harkavy persisted. "Didn't he?"

Leventhal drew his lips against his teeth as he wiped his mouth. "I must have wanted to buy," he said.

"It's beyond me. When you came to talk to me about him, you were mad enough to hang him. He was accusing you of some crime and blaming you for what happened to his wife and what not. Now you want to send him to Shifcart with a reference. And unless I'm mistaken you were fishing for me to help you. I couldn't believe my ears when you asked me about Shifcart. What kind of impression will a man like that make on him? And why do you let him hang around? Didn't you tell me he picked up Shifcart's card at your house? Besides, you know Shifcart can't do anything for him."

"I suppose not."

"And where does he get the idea that Shifcart can help him?"

Though he knew he was making a mistake, Leventhal said, and to some extent it was involuntary, "I think he believes it's all a Jewish setup and Shifcart can pull strings for him. . . . Jews have influence with other Jews."

"No!" Harkavy cried. "No!" His hands flew to his head. "And you're trying to do something for him? You're willing, regardless? Boy, do you know what this does to my opinion of you? Are you in your right mind?"

His horror shook Leventhal.

"Look, Dan, I don't want to go into this any further. Don't push me. I asked you about Shifcart. You told me what you think. . . . Let that be the end of it."

"But how does he do it?" Harkavy's voice rang. "What's he got on you? Is it blackmail? Have you done something?"

"No, nothing. . . . I've been having a lot of trouble. My family—you heard about that. And Mary's away, that's been hard on me, too. My nerves aren't in very good shape. I feel I've been trying to throw something off. You aren't being very helpful. Just let me alone to handle this in my own way." This was a great deal for him to say; it was exorbitant, like a plea. His hands were less steady than ever. He set down the coffee, splashing some of it into the saucer.

"What's between you? How does he work you? First you come to complain about him. Next thing I know he sounds like the Protocols, but it's all right with you." He furiously pounded the metal table, his face and his elongated throat flaming. "Influence with Jews!" he shouted.

Leventhal silently reproached himself. "That was a real mistake. I shouldn't have said that. Why did I let it slip out? I'm not even sure Allbee means that."

To Harkavy, he said, "Don't fly off the handle. I realize it seems bad, but you don't know the facts. I can judge this better than you." He kept his voice low in order to control it.

"The facts? What are you letting this man do to you? Are you going off your rocker?"

"Don't be foolish, Dan," he cried. "I know you mean well, but you're being carried away. And please remember my mother before you say a thing like that. You know about my mother. I told you about her as friend to friend. The meaning of it hasn't sunk in."

This silenced Harkavy briefly. He seemed to scowl. In reality he was clearing his throat. After considering him for a while he said, "Well, you *are* a privileged character. You're the only man living whose mother lost her mind and died." Immediately he changed his tone, clapping his hands sharply. "As friend to friend, what are the facts? This thing about Shifcart is such nonsense it isn't even worth talking about. But you, you must be in a trance. Tell me, what's going on. Just look at you!"

"What's the matter?"

"You look like the devil."

"Do I? Well, I told you. There was the kid's death, first of all."

"You were more honest when you were drunk, last night. You admitted that you wanted to get the man off your neck. Don't hide behind the child. That's not good. It's dishonest. Wake up! What's life? Metabolism? That's what it is for the bugs. Jesus Christ, no! What's life? Consciousness, that's what it is. That's what you're short on. For God's sake, give yourself a push and a shake. It's dangerous stuff, Asa, this stuff."

Leventhal looked at Harkavy in blank perplexity.

"Well, I'm damned if I can see it," he finally said. "In the first place, when I came to you, you were the one who told me about Williston. . . ."

"And?"

But Leventhal would not continue.

"And? What next?" said Harkavy, sitting forward.

There was a short pause and then Leventhal said, "Say, I've got to have that aspirin." He rose.

"All right, you don't want my help. I can't make you take it. God bless you. You had a chance to unburden yourself and get some advice. How many friends have you got?" He put a slice of bread in the toaster and rammed down the lever.

Among the bottles of lotion and cologne and the powder boxes in Mrs. Harkavy's medicine chest, Leventhal found the aspirin and swallowed a tablet with a sip from the tap. He filled the sink with warm water and pushed back his sleeves; the light green color gave him a kind of pleasure. He dipped in his hands and then glanced at the tub with its thick nickled spout. The linen closet stood open, giving out a dry perfume of soap. Leventhal took a towel and let the metal stopper fall. "I'm going to take a bath, if you don't mind," he called to Harkavy.

"Go ahead."

The faucet ran loudly and Leventhal shut the door and began to undress. The room grew hot. He sat on the edge of the tub in the roar of the steaming water and lathered his hairy dark body, energetic and all absorbed. The tumult of the faucet relieved him, for some reason. As he lay back in the charge and sway of the water, he observed to himself, as if in compliment, "He didn't get anything out of me." He stroked his chest, releasing tiny bubbles from the hairs. "I'll be better off taking care of things by myself," he thought. He turned off the cold tap and the hot water ran on, green with a white inner shape and a thread of vapor.

He wondered what success Max was having with Elena. He was concerned for him, of course, but he worried mainly about Philip whom, if it turned out that Max was wrong about Elena, he would go to any lengths to save. He postponed thinking about himself. Eventually he would have to— provided that Max was right about Elena and he wrong. The reason for a mistake like that could not be neglected; it had to be dug out. But dug out when he had the strength for the operation, not now. A ring of soap, melting from the bar in his hand, spread over the water.

While he dried himself, his heart beat rapidly. However, his headache was almost gone, and he felt freshened and almost cheerful. He went into the kitchen. Harkavy had set out plates and was scrambling some eggs.

It was not until the meal was nearly over that he suffered a recoil, a raw, painful current through his overtried nerves. He could not continue this way with Allbee. It was enough. It had to be ended. Any day he expected to hear that Mary was coming back. What if she should come back before it was ended? He freed himself from this fear much as one might brush away a clinging insect from one's face. And Allbee might think, because he had not slept at home last night— what might he think, that he was afraid of him? It would give him the confidence to make new demands. He could have the introduction to Shifcart. More than that, no. And he would have to get out of the house. "Enough!" he silently decided. "Enough, enough!" He dropped his fork noisily. Under Harkavy's questioning eyes he looked, as usual, unperturbed; moping somewhat, but steady and calm. He recovered the fork and touched his food with it. But he was unable to swallow another bite.

23

H E STARTED home at half-past four. The wind had
dropped, the sky was cold and darkening rapidly. In
the little park the turned-up rusty shells of leaves scraped in
the path and cracked underfoot. Very little green remained
in those that streamed raggedly in the trees. A damp
warmth, smelling of stone, rose from the subway, and
through the gratings Leventhal caught a glimpse of the inert
light on the roadbed and of the rails, hard and gray in their
simultaneous strike. The close brownstone houses looked au-
tumnal and so did the foot-burnished, steel manhole lids;
they were glinting sharply. Summer seemed to have ended
prematurely in chill and darkness. The people who had gone
out of town for the holiday would be building fires on the
beaches, those who were not already crowding the trains
into the city.

Leventhal halted on the sidewalk opposite his flat. All the
windows in the building were dark. The tiny red lamp in the
foyer appeared to be embedded in the fanlight and sent its
bloody color into the corners and as far as the polished, florid
head of the banister at the rear. Mrs. Nunez' vines, spreading
thickly upwards, swayed in a mass on the taut strings. "He's
out," said Leventhal to himself. He was exasperated, almost as
if Allbee had gone away to thwart him. But actually it was to
his advantage to be the first one home, for so far he had not
decided how to deal with Allbee. And now, while going up
the stairs, he occasionally touched the dust-hung concave of
the wall and thought, "What will I do?" He was, however, far
too agitated to make any plans. He climbed rapidly, rather
struck by the number of landings and, until he recognized a
fire bucket with cigarettes buried in the sand, wondering why
the place did not look more familiar. Reaching the fourth
floor, he put his back against the wall while he felt in both
pockets for his key. He brought out a handful of change and
keys, and began to pick it over under the weak light. Then it
seemed to him that someone was moving in the flat. It could
be that Allbee had been sleeping and had just gotten up. That

would explain the dark windows. He rapped and put his ear to the panel. He was sure that he heard steps.

He was far from calm when he turned the key in the lock. The door yielded a few inches, and then bumped and held with a rattle. He thrust his hand into the opening and felt the chain. Were there thieves in the house? He was on the point of running down to fetch Nunez or to phone the police when he heard Allbee say, "Is that you?"

"What's the chain up for?" he demanded.

"I'll explain to you later."

"No, you won't, you'll explain it right now."

But the chain remained in place. Leventhal urged himself not to lose his head and an instant later he punched at the door so that it shook and waited, staring at its ancient black trickles and tears of enamel. Then he began to pound again, enraged, shouting, "You! Open!" When he stopped he heard a low sound and, peering into the crack, he saw Allbee's face or rather a segment of his face, his nose, his full lip, and, with the lingering effect of a trance, his eye and the familiar stain beneath it.

"Come on!" he said to him.

"I can't," Allbee whispered. "Come back a little later, will you? Give me about fifteen minutes."

"I'll give you nothing."

"Ten minutes. Be decent."

Leventhal threw himself at the door, whirling around and striking it with the side of his body and his lowered shoulder, his feet gritting on the tiles. He gripped the door posts and pushed. He now heard two voices inside. Again, more desperately, he lunged. The chain broke and he was thrown against the wall of the vestibule. He recovered and rushed into the front room. There Allbee, naked and ungainly, stood beside a woman who was dressing in great haste. He was helping her, handing her stockings and underwear from the heap on the chair beside the bed. She had on her skirt but from the waist up she was bare. Brushing aside his hand with the proffered stockings, she bent to squeeze her foot into a shoe, digging her finger in beside the heel. Her hair covered her face; nevertheless Leventhal thought he recognized her. Mrs. Nunez! Was it Mrs. Nunez? The horror of it bristled on him, and the outcry he had been about to make was choked down.

She stooped toward the light—only the bed lamp was lit and it cast a limited circle over the twisted sheets and the rug —and turned her blouse right side out. Her scared eyes glimmered at him and her breasts hung down heavily as she thrust her arm through the sleeve. Meanwhile, Allbee had hurried to the door and closed it. He came back and put on his shirt, the new shirt he had bought on Second Avenue. The stiff loop of the collar stood off from his neck. Next he drew on his pants, nearly losing his balance as he shifted from foot to foot. Breathing heavily, he looked down and, while he buttoned himself, he said quietly to Leventhal, "At least, go into another room for a while, till she leaves."

"You get out, too."

He dropped his head, and Leventhal could not tell from his expression whether he was entreating or ordering him. He looked at him with anger and contempt, and began to walk toward the kitchen. The woman turned and he saw her plainly. She was straightening her hair, her elbows working quickly above her head. She was a stranger, not Mrs. Nunez; simply a woman. He felt enormously lightened, but at the same time it gave him a pang to think of his suspicion. She was a big woman, large hipped; her shoulders were high and the straight lines of her blouse made them appear square. She was tall and her hair was black, and that was all there was to the resemblance. There was an irregularity in the shape of her eyes; one was smaller than the other. It was with the larger, more brilliant eye that she returned his stare. Her smile was unsteady and resentful. He hovered near her a moment, inhaling the strong odor of powder or perfume that emanated from her in the heat of the room. She pushed a white comb into her hair and moved away from him.

He banged the kitchen door and, in the dark, beside the throbbing refrigerator, he waited and heard the low sounds of a conversation. He did not try to follow it. There were footsteps; the tread was the woman's, she was going toward the door. It was for her sake primarily that he had withdrawn, in order to spare her. It wasn't her fault. Probably Allbee had not told her the flat was someone else's. The nerve of him, the nerve! Leventhal nearly cried aloud in revulsion. He distorted his face wildly, stretching his mouth. The nastiness of it! The refrigerator faltered and quivered but always recovered and ran, chaotically and interminably, ran and ran. Its white crown was on a level with his eyes; he could see blue sparks within. The only other thing visible in the room was the pilot light, also blue, a much deeper blue, in the black hollows and spidery bars of the gas range.

The woman's look remained with him. So did her scent; it seemed to cling to the rooms. The voices continued in the vestibule. Leventhal went into the dining room. On the daybed's crumpled sheets, the pillow gray, almost black, there were newspapers, underclothes, and socks. Between the curtains, on the sill, he discovered a cup of coffee in which drops of mold floated, and crumbs and scraps of food.

The outer door shut and he strode into the front room.

"Look here," said Allbee, as soon as he came through the kitchen door. "I thought you were out of town for the week end. You didn't come home last night. I thought . . ."

"You thought you'd bring a tramp in from the street."

"No . . . now wait." He gave a hasty, somewhat breathless laugh. "I know I have a fallen nature. I never pretended to be anything I wasn't. Why all the excitement? You might have given me a few minutes." He spoke placatingly, with humorous chagrin. He looked sallow and his lips were dry. His smile persisted at the corners covertly, it was boastful.

Leventhal flushed thickly. "In my bed!"

"Well, the day bed is so narrow. No place to take a lady. . . . I wanted a little more space. . . ." He was by no means sure of himself and his voice wavered as he made the joke. "I fail to see what there is to fuss about."

"Oh, you don't see! It gave you a bang to put your whore where I sleep."

The vehemence of his loathing gave a different turn to Allbee's smile; it became jeering, and a yellowish hot tinge came over his bloodshot eyes. Leventhal heard him murmur something about "fastidiousness."

"You hypocrite! I thought you couldn't get over your wife."

"Don't you mention my wife!" Allbee cried.

"Why not, you're always crying about her, aren't you?"

"I say don't! Leave things alone that you can't understand."

"What can't I understand?"

"Not that, for sure!" Allbee said harshly. His face was inflamed; his cheekbones looked as if they had been branded. But he checked himself and slowly the color retreated. Only a few refractory spots remained. He seemed to force himself to make a gesture of retraction. "I mean," he said, "she's dead. What does she have to do with it? I have needs, naturally, the same as anybody else."

"What did she have to do with the other things? You mealymouth, you were using her to work on my feelings. All right, what do I care? Go to hell. But you weren't satisfied that you made this place so filthy I can't stand to come in; you had to bring this woman into my bed."

"But what's there to be so upset about? Where else, if not in bed . . . ?" He looked amused again and blinked his bloodshot eyes. "What do you do? Maybe you have some other way, more refined, different? Don't you people claim that you're the same as everybody else? That's your way of saying that you're above everybody else. I know."

"Go get your stuff in the dining room and clear out. I don't want any more of you."

"You don't care about the woman. You're just using her to make an issue and break your promise to me. Well, and I thought I had seen everything in the way of cynicism. By God, you could give lessons! I never met anyone who could touch you. I guess there's an example in the world of everything a man can imagine, no matter how great or how gruesome. You certainly are not the same as everybody else." He looked at him, keenly, brilliantly, triumphantly insolent. "What do you care about my wife! But your instinct told you where to jab, in the way that insects know where they'll find the most sap."

"You dirty phoney!" Leventhal cried huskily. "You ugly bastard counterfeit. I said it because you're such a liar, with your phoney tears and your wife's name in your mouth, every second word. The poor woman, a fine life she must have had with you, a freak like you, out of a carnival. You don't care what you say. You'll say anything that comes into your head.

You're not even human, if you ask me. No wonder she left you."

"It's very interesting that you should take her part. She was like me. What do you think of that? We were alike," he shouted.

"Well, get out! Beat it! I told you to leave when the woman did."

"What about your promise?"

Leventhal pushed him toward the door. Allbee fell back a few steps and, seizing a heavy glass ash tray, he aimed it menacingly and cried, "Keep off me!" Leventhal made a rush at him and knocked the ash tray down. Pinning his arms, he wheeled him around and ran him into the vestibule.

"Let go. I'll leave," he panted.

The door, as Leventhal jerked it open, hit Allbee in the face. He did not resist when Leventhal thrust him out on the landing and, without looking back, he started down the stairs.

Winded, Leventhal stumbled into a chair, pulled at his collar. The sweat ran into his eyes and a pain, starting at his shoulders, passed downward through his chest. Suddenly he thought, "Maybe he's still hanging around. I'd better look." He forced himself up and went to the stairs. Holding the rail, he started into the shaft. It was silent. He thought as he returned to the flat, "He didn't even have the courage to fight back. As much as he hates me. And he's bigger; he could have killed me." He wondered whether Allbee was stunned by the door when it struck him in the face. The sound of that did not leave him.

He stopped to examine the chain. The staple was only loosened and might have been hammered in. But one of the links had given. He tossed the severed half away. Over the furrows of the rug in the front room there was a long, curving trail of ashes. He wiped his sweat with his sleeve and took in the room, angry, but exultant also; he felt dimly that this disorder and upheaval was part of the price he was obliged to pay for his release.

The radiators were spitting and the room was unendurably hot. He flung up the window and bent out. Instantly he heard the tumultuous swoop of the Third Avenue train rising above the continuous, tidal noise of the street. People were walking among the stripes of light on the pavement, light that came from windows opening on carpeted floors and the shapes of furniture; they passed through the radiance of the glass cage that bulged before the theater and into shadows, tributaries that led into deeper shadows and led, still further on, into mighty holes filled with light and stifled roaring. "Is he around somewhere?" Leventhal asked himself. He doubted that Allbee was near. Certainly he knew he had nothing more to hope for here after tonight. And what he had hoped for in the first place remained a mystery. The idea of an introduction to Shifcart lost all its substance; it was a makeshift demand, improvised. That he was able to see this gave Leventhal the feeling that he was becoming himself again after a long lapse.

The breeze was cooling him too rapidly. He drew his head in, shivering, and sat down, wiping the grit of the sill from his palms. His throat was bitter and raw, and there was a deadening weight in his side. But he sat and rested briefly and soon felt better. When he rose, he began unsystematically to set the flat in order, going slowly and desultorily from task to task.

He stripped the linen from the beds and threw it in the laundry hamper. Then, without taking the trouble to clean out the scraps in the drain, he spilled soap powder over the dishes in the kitchen sink and let the hot water run until the foam boiled up and covered them. He made up his bed with clean sheets, awkwardly shaking the pillows into pillow cases and dragging the bed away from the wall in order to tuck in the blankets. In the dining room, he turned over the mattress of the day bed and forced up the seldom-opened windows. On one of the chairs he found a glossy haberdasher's bag with a Second Avenue address. It contained Allbee's old shirt and a few other articles that he did not examine. He threw the bag into the dumb-waiter, together with the socks and undershirts and the newspapers Allbee had accumulated. Next, in the bathroom, he took down the towels, turned on the shower to rinse the tub, and made an effort to clean the basin. After a few strokes he gave this up and returned the rag to its pipe beneath the sink.

He was moving chairs into place when he saw a comb on

the carpet. It must have been the mate to the one the woman had fastened in her hair. Studying it, he could not help breathing its odor. It was a white comb, white bone, its teeth darkened yellow in an uneven fringe. On one side it was decorated with a diamond-shaped piece of glass; on the other, the bit of glass had fallen out of its setting. He did not linger over the comb very long; he let it fall into the wastebasket. He recalled the women in the wrangle he had watched on the corner several weeks back and even reflected that she might have been one of them. She might, easily. After all, where had Allbee picked her up? Probably in a tavern in the neighborhood.

A breeze blew through the flat while he swept the ashes from the rug. It brought the cold and vacancy of the outside into the room. Nevertheless, the smell of the comb occasionally returned, coming over him with some fragment of what had occurred that evening in its wake, like a qualm. It must have been frightening, sickening for her to hear the crash of the door and then to run out of bed—still another bed. And even granting that she could endure roughness better than another (many a woman would have cried from terror or sheer mortification), he was sorry to have subjected her to it. He found himself regretting the whole incident because of her and almost wished that he had listened to Allbee and gone away. He could have attended to him later. A few impressions of her remained vividly with Leventhal—the heaviness of her figure in the skirt, the way she had crouched to work her foot into the shoe, the look he had received from her queerly shaped eyes. It now struck him that there was more amusement in it than fear, and he could see, too, how with a grain of detachment it was possible for her to find the incident amusing. He began to remember how Allbee had stumbled in pulling up his pants and how comically he had held out the woman's stockings to her. It was low, it was painful, but it was funny. He grinned, his eyes dilated and shone; he gave way explosively to laughter, driving the broom at the floor. "The stockings! Those damn stockings! Standing there without a stitch and passing those stockings!" He broke suddenly into a cough. When he was done laughing and coughing, his face remained unusually expressive. Yes, and he ought not to leave himself out of the picture, glaring at them both. Meanwhile, Allbee was burning, yet trying to keep his head. The woman must have grasped that he did not dare say what he felt. Perhaps he had been boasting to her, telling lies about himself, and that was why his predicament amused her.

But when he sat down for a moment on the bed, all the comedy of it was snatched away and torn to pieces. He was wrong about the woman's expression; he was trying to transform it into something he could bear. The truth was probably far different. He had started out to see what had happened with her eyes and had ended by substituting his own, thus contriving to put her on his side. Whereas, the fact was that she was nearer to Allbee. Both of them, Allbee and the woman, moved or swam toward him out of a depth of life in which he himself would be lost, choked, ended. There lay horror, evil, all that he had kept himself from. In the days when he was clerking in the hotel on the East Side, he had been as near to it as he could ever bear to be. He had seen it face on then. And since, he had learned more about it out of the corner of his eye. Why not say heart, rather than eye? His heart was what caught it, with awful pain and dread, in heavy blows. Then, since the fear and pain were so great, what drew him on?

He picked up the broom and returned to his tasks. As he bent on trembling legs to brush up the ashes, he was thinking, "Maybe I didn't do the right thing. I didn't know what it was. I don't yet. And there had to be a showdown sooner or later. What was I going to do with him? He hated me. He hated me enough to cut my throat. He didn't do it because he was too much of a coward. That's why he was pulling all those stunts instead. He was pulling them on himself as much as on me, and the reason for that was that he hated himself for not having enough nerve, but by clowning he could pass off his own feelings.—All that stuff, the mustard and going on his knees and all that talk. That's what it was for. I had to do something with him. I suppose I handled it badly. Still, it's over; that's the main thing. . . ."

The chairs did not look quite as they did when Mary arranged them; the bed was unevenly made. A swath of ashes still remained on the rug. However, things began to right themselves and it soothed him to be busy. He opened a can of vegetable soup and set it on the stove. While it was heating, he washed the dishes and, for the first time in weeks, turned on the radio simply to hear a voice. The phone rang. It was Max, calling, he said, from a drugstore on Fourteenth Street. He did not want to come unannounced a second time. A good thing, too, Leventhal thought; he would not have answered the doorbell.

He was finishing his soup ten minutes later, when Max arrived. Elena had agreed at last to leave New York. That was his news. He was coming from Pennsylvania Station where he had picked up the reservations. Villani's brother, a second-hand dealer on Bleecker Street, was buying the furniture.

"It'll cost us twice what we're getting to buy new things down there," he said.

"Ah, you don't want this stuff."

"What's the matter with it? Shipping is too high, that's all." Then he smiled at Leventhal. "So . . . ?" he said.

"You mean I was mistaken about Elena."

"I sure do. And about the old lady."

"Oh. Well, you caught me in a bad mood the other night, Max. I'm not always like that. I hope I didn't hurt your feelings."

The lines radiating out from Max's eyes deepened. "Oh, I got a kind of a kick out of the way you built up the old woman," he said.

"I'm glad you finally got Elena to come around. It's going to be all to the good. I'm glad for Phil's sake, especially. When you're settled we'll come down and visit."

"Sure, you'll be welcome. Anytime. Is she going to be back soon?"

Leventhal noticed that Max did not mention Mary by name. Like Elena, he probably did not know what her name was.

"Mary? Just as soon as I can get her to come. I'm going to phone her tonight."

"Your radio's on pretty loud. Got a drive on against spooks?"

They smiled together.

"I guess I really don't know where I'm at when she's away."

Max poured himself a glass of water, declining to sit down

for coffee. "Too many things to take care of," he said. He pulled his hat down. His sideburns were long and ill-trimmed, overgrowing his ears.

"I'll see you off," said Leventhal. "When are you leaving?"

"Friday, four o'clock on the Natchez Prince."

"I'll be on hand."

After talking to his wife, Leventhal prepared for bed in a kind of intoxication. He walked up and down the room, undressing, and stopped before her picture on the desk and caressed her face with his thumb over the glass. Under the arch of his chest, he felt a thick, distinct stroke that seemed to him much slower than the actual, remote, jubilant speeding of his heart. His legs were melting with excitement. Mary was probably packing her bags, for she had promised to leave on the earliest train tomorrow. From the way she spoke, he realized that she had been waiting for him to make this call. When he said, "Can you come soon?" she replied, "Tomorrow," with an eagerness that astonished him. She would arrive very early on Tuesday, if the Labor Day crowd did not delay her too much. Meanwhile, he had to attend to the flat; she had to find it as she had left it. Half an hour ago he had thought it passable. Now it looked appallingly dirty. He slipped a coat over his pajamas and was about to go down to see Mrs. Nunez. But he remembered in time that the Nunez' had a telephone and turned back. As usual, he chided himself; the easiest, sensible way came to him last. He found the number in Mary's alphabetized book and dialed it. In a moment he heard her aspirated Spanish "'Allo?" The thing was quickly arranged: she would be up in the morning. After hanging up, he silently apologized to her for his suspicion. But there was no place in his present mood for penitence or even for thought.

He locked the front door. He ought to have spoken to Nunez about the broken chain while he was on the wire. And for that matter Allbee still had a key; the lock should be changed. He had not retained the number, and he picked up the book again and then decided to let the thing go until morning. Explanations were necessary. Why was the chain broken? Why did a perfectly good lock have to be taken out? He had to have time; he could not invent reasons on the telephone.

He got into bed, piled the pillows against the wall, and sat with a magazine in his lap. He did not read; he had no desire to, and besides nothing took shape before his eyes. Restlessly, he turned the pages and heard the interminable sleepy sigh of the steam in the radiators and the intermittent shock of the subway beneath the house. Finally he threw down the magazine and turned face down on the pillow. His impatience made him groan. He could hardly bear to lie still. Over and over again he saw the station platform, the cars in the tunnel, and made out Mary's face in the crowd of passengers—her hat, her light hair, and last of all her face. He embraced and kissed her, and asked, "Did you have a good trip?" Would that do? He struggled over a choice of greetings. Then once more he imagined himself running on the platform. It was unendurable. He resolved to go to sleep and he turned off the lamp. But as soon as he had done this, he rose—the room was not entirely dark because the light was burning in the bathroom—and dragged the heavy desk chair to the door. He fixed the back of it tightly under the knob and returned to bed. "For God's sake," he muttered, "let me get a night's rest." There was a pallor on the windows; the moon had risen. Standing on the bed, he drew the curtains and dropped down. He pulled the blanket over his head and soon he was asleep.

At first he slept deeply, but after a time he began to stir. He was too warm; he threw some of his covers off; his legs moved as if unwilling to be relaxed, and once or twice he was on the point of jumping up and turning on the lamp. But he held his head down between the pillows obstinately and presently he began to dream.

He was on a boardwalk in broad, open, blue summer weather. The sea was flaring on his right and the shore blackened with bathers. On his left, there was an amusement park with ticket booths, and he saw round yellow and red cars whipping around and bumping together. He entered a place that resembled a hotel—there was a circular veranda where people sat looking at the bay—but proved to be a department store. He was here to buy some rouge for Mary. The salesgirl demonstrated various shades on her own face, wiping off each in turn with a soiled hand towel and bending to the round mirror on the counter to draw a new spot. There was a great, empty glitter of glass and metal around them. What could this possibly be about? Leventhal wondered. For he was perfectly sure he had once seen a chart with all the colors. This work was unnecessary. Nevertheless, he watched her smearing the rouge on her sharp face and did not interrupt her. The odor of the towel had from the beginning seemed familiar. He made so strong an effort to identify it that he half roused himself, aware, all at once, that the odor came from his bed. His eyes were open and his unshaven chin rustled on the pillow. Could the woman's scent have penetrated the slip and the ticking? He raised his head, feeling stifled, and saw the dazzling wall of the bathroom, the yawning clothes hamper, the black fin of the scale. He thought he could hear the steam in the pipes, and yet the room was not warm. He shivered and lit the lamp. His heart nearly burst with fear, for the chair was down and the front door gaping. There were movements in the kitchen. He hunched forward in the gathered bedclothes, listening, and the wires of the spring sang out. His terror, like a cold fluid, like brine, seemed to have been released by the breaking open of something within him. "My God!" he cried to himself. His mouth was parched and the taste of his lips was like that of dried blood. But what if the chair had slid down and the door opened by itself? And what if the kitchen were empty? His nerves again, his sick imagination. But why nerves—as an excuse for his cowardice? So that he would not have to go to the kitchen to investigate? Had he locked the door? He was ready to swear to it. And if it was open now, it was because Allbee, who had a key, had opened it. Leventhal's legs were braced to spring, but he held back, feeling that to be deceived now through his nerves would crush him. But suddenly he rushed from bed, dragging the sheets in which his foot had caught. He kicked free and ran into the kitchen. He collided with someone who crouched there, and a cry came out of him. The air was foul and hard to breathe. Gas was pouring from the oven. "I have to kill him now," he thought as they grappled. He caught the cloth of his coat in his teeth while he swiftly changed his grip, clutching at Allbee's face. He tore away convulsively, but Leventhal crushed him with his weight in the corner. Allbee's fist came down heavily on his neck, beside the shoulder. "You want to murder me? Murder?" Leventhal gasped. The sibilance of the pouring gas was almost deafening.

"Me, myself!" Allbee whispered despairingly, as if with his last breath. "Me . . . !"

Then his head shot up, catching Leventhal on the mouth. The pain made him drop his hands, and Allbee pushed him away and flung out of the kitchen. He stumbled after him down a flight of stairs, trying to shout and bruising his naked feet on the metal edges of the treads. He heard Allbee jump and saw him running into the foyer. Seizing a milk bottle from a neighbor's sill, he threw it. It smashed on the tiles.

He raced back to turn off the gas. He feared an explosion. By the wildly swinging light, he saw a chair placed before the open oven from which Allbee apparently had risen when he ran in.

Leventhal threw open the front-room window and bent out, tears running down his face in the cold air. The long lines of lamps hung down their yellow grains in the gray and blue of the street. He saw no one, not a living thing.

When he had had enough air, he limped to the bathroom. He had bitten his tongue and he rinsed his mouth with peroxide. In spite of the struggle, the revolting sweetness of the gas like the acrid sweetness of sewage, the numbness in his neck, and, now, the sight of blood, he did not seem greatly disturbed. He looked impassive, under the cloud of his hair. He rinsed and spat, washed out the sink, wiped the stains from the mouth of the peroxide bottle, and went to pick up the sheets he had dragged to the floor. By the time he had remade the bed, the flat was nearly free of gas. Though he scarcely thought that Allbee would be back again, he shut the door and barricaded it with the dresser. He would sleep undisturbed; he cared about nothing else. Drowsily, he went to check the stove again, to make sure no more gas was escaping. Then he dropped onto the bed. He was still sleeping at eleven o'clock when Mrs. Nunez arrived to start the cleaning. Her repeated knocks woke him.

24

T HAT FALL, one of the editors of Harkavy's paper, *Antique Horizons,* went to a national magazine and, through Harkavy, Leventhal got the vacancy. Characteristically, Beard at first declined to meet the offer and then went two hundred dollars higher, but Leventhal left him.

Things went well for him in the next few years. The consciousness of an unremitting daily fight, though still present, was fainter and less troubling. His health was better, and there were changes in his appearance. Something recalcitrant seemed to have left him; he was not exactly affable, but his obstinately unrevealing expression had softened. His face was paler and there were some gray areas in his hair, in spite of which he looked years younger.

And, as time went on, he lost the feeling that he had, as he used to say, "got away with it," his guilty relief, and the accompanying sense of infringement. He was thankful for his job at *Antique Horizons;* he didn't underestimate it; there weren't many better jobs in the trade field. He was lucky, of course. It was understandable that a man suffered when he did not have a place. On the other hand, it was pitiful that he should envy the man who had one. In Leventhal's mind, this was not even a true injustice, for how could you call anything so haphazard an injustice? It was a shuffle, all, all accidental and haphazard. And somewhere, besides, there was a wrong emphasis. As though a man really could be made for, say, Burke-Beard and Company, as though that were true work instead of a delaying maze to be gone through daily in a misery so habitual that one became absentminded about it. This was wrong. But the error rose out of something very mysterious, namely, a conviction or illusion that at the start of life, and perhaps even before, a promise had been made. In thinking of this promise, Leventhal compared it to a ticket, a theater ticket. And with his ticket, a man entitled to an average seat might feel too shabby for the dress circle or sit in it defiantly and arrogantly; another, entitled to the best in the house, might cry out in rage to the usher who led him to the third balcony. And how many more stood disconsolately in the rain and snow, in the long line of those who could only expect to be turned away? But no, this was incorrect. The reality was different. For why should tickets, mere tickets, be promised if promises were being made—tickets to desirable and undesirable places? There were more important things to be promised. Possibly there was a promise, since so many felt it. He himself was almost ready to affirm that there was. But it was misunderstood.

Occasionally he thought about Allbee and wondered whether Williston knew what had happened to him. But he had written to Williston, returning the ten dollars which, for one reason and another, he had failed to give Allbee. In his letter he made a special effort to explain his position, and, realizing that Williston believed he had a tendency to exaggerate, he gave a very careful and moderate account of what had taken place. Allbee, he said, "tried a kind of suicide pact without getting my permission first." He might have added, fairly, "without intending to die himself." For there were reasonable grounds to suspect this. But no reply came from Williston, and Leventhal was too proud to write a second letter; that would be too much like pleading. Perhaps Williston felt that he had kept the money from Allbee out of malice. Leventhal made it as clear as he could that he had had no opportunity to pass it on to him. "Does he think I'm that cheap?" he asked himself resentfully. Repeatedly, he went over all that he had done during those confusing weeks. Hadn't he tried to be fair? Didn't he intend to help him? He considered that he and Allbee were even, by any honest standards. Much difference ten dollars would have made! At first he was deeply annoyed; later he prepared some things to say to Williston if they should meet. But the opportunity never came.

From time to time he heard rumors about Allbee. Invariably, however, he heard them from people who did not know him personally, and he could never be sure that the man to whom they referred actually was Allbee. "Some journalist, from New England, originally, who hit the bottle," etcetera. In three years a dozen or so stories reached him, no two of which agreed. He did not attempt to follow up any of them. Although they always interested him, the truth was that he did not want to know precisely where he was and what he was doing. He believed that he had continued to go down. By now he was in an institution, perhaps, in some hospital, or even already lying in Potter's Field. Leventhal did not care to think too much or too literally about it.

But one night he saw Allbee again.

It happened that a dealer who had furnished some of the antiques for a play that was running on Broadway gave Leventhal two passes. He was reluctant to go; Mary, however, insisted. Mary was pregnant; she was expecting the baby in a month, and she would be tied down, she argued, for a long time to come. Leventhal said that the theater would be very warm—this was early June and prematurely hot—but offered no real opposition. The evening of the play he came home early. (They had moved to the uptown end of Central Park West, closer to the Porto Rican slum than to the blazoned canopies of the Sixties and Seventies.) During dinner he was heavy eyed. But before he had finished his dessert, Mary was clearing the table. He washed, shaved for the second time that day, and put on a Palm Beach suit, breaking it out of the brown paper wrapper in which the cleaner had sealed it eight months ago. The trousers were a little tight and short, for during the preceding winter he had put on weight.

The subway was hot enough; the theater was suffocating. Leventhal sat and endured the play. He had no taste for plays in general, and this was sentimental and untrue—a complicated love affair in a Renaissance palace. He held Mary's hand. In the refulgence of the stage, he saw drops of moisture on her forehead, under the thick loop of her braid, and on her nose. Her skin looked very pure, and his heart rose as he watched her, intent on the play. Presently he brought his eyes back to the stage. His own dark face was damp, and his tight suit was already crumpled; his collar was soaked with sweat.

At the first curtain he quickly got to his feet and guided Mary through the crowd to the lobby. An usher opened the doors to the sidewalk, and they walked out. The tavern adjoining the theater was filling up. Leventhal and Mary lit cigarettes and gazed into the street and upward at the glow of yellow glass that passed into the haze. The afternoon had been almost tropical. A few large drops of rain had fallen; the air was moist, odorous, and black; one felt it like a soft weight. There were night clubs and restaurants in the block, and the traffic was heavy. Suddenly a taxi cut a dangerous curve from the far side of the street and made an abrupt, pitching stop in front of the theater. There was a terrific croaking of horns behind it. The door flung open and a woman was handed out. Something about the queerness of existence, always haunting Leventhal at a short distance, came very close to him when he saw her escort's face over her shoulder in the faint light. The glass slide in the roof of the cab was drawn aside, and the top of a straw hat circled and shone in the opening. The woman left the running board with a little bound, holding her silk scarf to her throat with one hand and gathering her skirt up with the other. Slender and long-legged, she walked with a somewhat free stride, elegant and yet slightly awkward. There were jewels beneath the scarf and on her fingers. Her painted nails looked purple under the frosted light of the marquee. She stood with her back to the street, irritated, holding a small, heavy, glittering bag. The man lingered, for some reason, in the cab.

Mary touched Leventhal's arm.

"Do you recognize her?" she whispered.

But Leventhal was trying to see her companion.

"Isn't that Yvonne Crane?"

"Who?"

"The actress."

"I don't know," he said, looking blankly. "Is it?"

"She's still perfectly beautiful," said Mary with admiration. "How do they stay looking so young?"

The woman, after waiting awhile, turned and said in a low, harsh tone, "Come on. Will you come out of there?"

The man inside shouted quarrelsomely, "He took us the long way around. Does he think I don't know the city? I'm no greenhorn here."

They did not catch the woman's next words, but they heard the driver, laconic and confident, and then the escort, crying out laughingly, "Don't give me that. . . . That's for the visiting fat boys."

The woman opened her purse and threw a bill to the driver.

Leventhal, when he heard the voice, was certain that the

man was Allbee, and, with a rigid face and a look approaching horror in his eyes, he waited for him to appear.

Then Allbee stepped to the curb, saying, "You shouldn't have done that." The cab started away with its open door flapping; the driver, without slowing up, reached back and slammed it.

Leventhal had a close view of Allbee as the two walked into the theater. He was wearing a white dinner jacket. A flower, pinned erratically, swung from his lapel; he pressed his hat under his arm and strode forward, his large shoulders stiffly raised, swaggering and gallant. His cheeks were red and shining. He was laughing into his companion's pretty but nervously severe face. He seemed to be pushing her playfully, and it was evident from the set of her arms that she did not wish to be pushed.

"I don't recognize him," said Mary. "But I'm sure she's Yvonne Crane. I've seen her picture a hundred times. Don't you remember her?"

Throughout the second act, Leventhal peered round at the boxes. He could see no more than the color of a face in the radiance thrown back from the stage, or, occasionally, the black shape of a head rising near the red ball of an exit light, or moving its shadow across the obscure shine of the rails. He thought that they must be sitting in a box. The woman might or might not be Yvonne Crane, though Mary was probably right. She was, in any case, a wealthy woman; and Allbee looked more than moderately prosperous in the dinner jacket and the silk-seamed formal trousers. To say nothing of the flower. The flower struck Leventhal in a very curious way as a mark of something extraordinary, barbaric, rich, even decadent. "Yes, he's gone places," Leventhal mused. "And that woman, whoever she is, he's got that woman under his thumb." None of the rumors had described him as so well off. "And here I had him dead and buried in Potter's Field. Dead. But imagine!" He tugged a handkerchief from his breast pocket and wiped his neck and chin. The lights came to life in the arches, causing him to squint and frown. The curtain was swooping down. There was applause. He had not noticed that the act was ending. The orchestra began a march and, more hurriedly than the first time, he helped Mary rise.

He was lighting her cigarette, looking everywhere for Allbee, when, over her head, he caught sight of him on the stairs. He was alone, and, widening his eyes, he smiled at Leventhal and raised his hand with stiffly spread fingers in a gesture he did not understand. Mary spoke to him. Utterly confused, he answered something. She repeated what she had said. She was asking for her compact, which he had in his pocket. She was going to the ladies' lounge. He hastily got it out and gave it to her. His expression seemed to puzzle her, and she glanced at him sharply before turning away.

As she passed Allbee on the stairs, he gave her pregnant figure an appraising look. Leventhal walked out of the lobby. He was aware that Allbee was coming up to him, but he did not raise his eyes until he heard him speak.

"Hello, Leventhal."

The low, thick voice with its old tone of complicity, the big, obtrusive figure in the white jacket, disturbed him.

"Hello," he answered nervously.

"I saw you when we were coming in."

"I didn't think you did."

"I knew it would be all right with you if I acted like a total stranger, so it's up to me, and I'd feel like a terrible fool if I didn't speak to you. . . . You saw me, didn't you?"

"Yes."

"And who I was with?"

"The actress? My wife recognized her."

"Oh, your wife," he said politely. "Very handsome. Very fetching, even in her condition." He began to smile broadly, displaying his teeth. With his hands on his hips, he bent forward slightly. "Congratulations. I see you're following orders. 'Increase and multiply.'"

Leventhal answered him with a dull, short nod. It seemed to him that Allbee had no real desire to be malicious; he was merely obedient to habit. He might have been smiling at himself and making an appeal of a sort for understanding. On nearer sight, Allbee did not look good. His color was an unhealthy one. Leventhal had the feeling that it was the decay of something that had gone into his appearance of well-being, something intimate. There was very little play in the deepened wrinkles around his eyes. They had a fabric quality, crumpled and blank. A smell of whisky came from him.

"You haven't changed much," said Allbee.

"I wasn't the one that was going to change so much."

"Ah, that. Well, do I still look the same to you?"

"You still drink."

"Ever since I saw you, I've been wondering whether you'd mention that. You're true to form." He grinned, but he was somewhat hurt. "No, I only take it socially because everybody else does."

"You look successful."

"Oh," he said lightly. "Success is a big word. You ought to be careful how you use it."

"What do you do?"

"Just now I'm squiring Miss Crane around. The columnists say we're friends, when they bother to mention her. She's not the drawing card she used to be. You probably know. Well, she doesn't want much public attention now, or she'd be seen with someone more celebrated. But she doesn't care. She's glad all that professional business is over for her and she can live more quietly. She's actually a very intelligent person. We're both a little lost, out there on the Coast."

Leventhal nodded again.

"Oh, yes. She's real nobility. She's really fine. Queenly, if you know what I mean. Some of those women become loathsome when their popularity dies down. They live like criminals. They want to make up for all those years under the public eye, I guess."

"So . . . I congratulate you too," Leventhal murmured.

"She's not Flora, of course. . . . My wife." His continued smile gave a touch of cynicism to the sensational, terrible look of pain that rose to his eyes. Leventhal saw that he could not help himself and pitied him. "She has qualities. . . ."

His last words were lost in the braying of the taxis. Leventhal found nothing to say.

"I want you to know one thing," said Allbee. "That night . . . I wanted to put an end to myself. I wasn't thinking of hurting you. I suppose you would have been. . . . But I wasn't thinking of you. You weren't even in my mind."

Leventhal laughed outright at this.

"You could have jumped in the river. That's a funny lie. Why tell it? Did you have to use my kitchen?"

Allbee glanced around restlessly. The bays that rose into his loose blond hair became crimson. "No," he said miserably. "Well, anyhow, I don't remember how it was. I must have been demented. When you turn against yourself, nobody else means anything to you either." Bitterly shamefaced and self-mocking, he took Leventhal's hand and pressed it. "But I want to say that I owe you something. I was trying to get around it when I talked about trying to kill myself only." He spoke with great difficulty. "I don't want to exaggerate, but I don't want to play it down either. I know I owe you something. I knew it that night when I was standing in your shower. . . ."

Leventhal pulled his hand away.

"What do you do out there, are you an actor?"

"An actor? No, I'm in radio. Advertising. It's a middle-sized job. So you see? I've made my peace with things as they are. I've gotten off the pony—you remember, I said that to you once? I'm on the train."

"A conductor?"

"Conductor, hell! I'm just a passenger." His laugh was short and faint. "Not even first class. I'm not the type that runs things. I never could be, I realized that long ago. I'm the type that comes to terms with whoever runs things. What do I care? The world wasn't made exactly for me. What am I going to do about it?"

"What?" Leventhal smiled at him.

"Approximately made for me will have to be good enough. All that stiffness of once upon a time, that's gone, that's gone."

The crowd was beginning to return. The curtain bell had rung.

"Anyway, I'm enjoying life." Suddenly he looked around and said, "Say, I've got to run. Yvonne will send them out looking for me."

"Wait a minute, what's your idea of who runs things?" said Leventhal. But he heard Mary's voice at his back. Allbee ran in and sprang up the stairs. The bell continued its dinning, and Leventhal and Mary were still in the aisle when the houselights went off. An usher showed them to their seats.

THE ADVENTURES OF
AUGIE MARCH

To my Father

Chapter I

I AM an American, Chicago born—Chicago, that somber city —and go at things as I have taught myself, free-style, and will make the record in my own way: first to knock, first admitted; sometimes an innocent knock, sometimes a not so innocent. But a man's character is his fate, says Heraclitus, and in the end there isn't any way to disguise the nature of the knocks by acoustical work on the door or gloving the knuckles.

Everybody knows there is no fineness or accuracy of suppression; if you hold down one thing you hold down the adjoining.

My own parents were not much to me, though I cared for my mother. She was simple-minded, and what I learned from her was not what she taught, but on the order of object lessons. She didn't have much to teach, poor woman. My brothers and I loved her. I speak for them both; for the elder it is safe enough; for the younger one, Georgie, I have to answer—he was born an idiot—but I'm in no need to guess, for he had a song he sang as he ran dragfooted with his stiff idiot's trot, up and down along the curl-wired fence in the backyard:

> Georgie Mahchy, Augie, Simey
> Winnie Mahchy, evwy, evwy love Mama.

He was right about everyone save Winnie, Grandma Lausch's poodle, a pursy old overfed dog. Mama was Winnie's servant, as she was Grandma Lausch's. Loud-breathing and windbreaking, she lay near the old lady's stool on a cushion embroidered with a Berber aiming a rifle at a lion. She was personally Grandma's, belonged to her suite; the rest of us were the governed, and especially Mama. Mama passed the dog's dish to Grandma, and Winnie received her food at the old lady's feet from the old lady's hands. These hands and feet were small; she wore a shriveled sort of lisle on her legs and her slippers were gray—ah, the gray of that felt, the gray despotic to souls—with pink ribbons. Mama, however, had large feet, and around the house she wore men's shoes, usually without strings, and a dusting or mobcap like somebody's fanciful cotton effigy of the form of the brain. She was meek and long, round-eyed like Georgie—gentle green round eyes and a gentle freshness of color in her long face. Her hands were work-reddened, she had very few of her teeth left—to heed the knocks as they come—and she and Simon wore the same ravelly coat-sweaters. Besides having round eyes, Mama had circular glasses that I went with her to the free dispensary on Harrison Street to get. Coached by Grandma Lausch, I went to do the lying. Now I know it wasn't so necessary to lie, but then everyone thought so, and Grandma Lausch especially, who was one of those Machiavellis of small street and neighborhood that my young years were full of. So Grandma, who had it all ready before we left the house and must have put in hours plotting it out in thought and phrase, lying small in her chilly small room under the featherbed, gave it to me at breakfast. The idea was that Mama wasn't keen enough to do it right. That maybe one didn't need to be keen didn't occur to us; it was a contest. The dispensary would want to know why the Charities didn't pay for the glasses. So you must say nothing about the Charities, but that sometimes money from my father came and sometimes it didn't, and that Mama took boarders. This was, in a delicate and choosy way, by ignoring and omitting certain large facts, true. It was true enough for *them*, and at the age of nine I could appreciate this perfectly. Better than my brother Simon, who was too blunt for this kind of maneuver and, anyway, from books, had gotten hold of some English schoolboy notions of honor. *Tom Brown's Schooldays* for many years had an influence we were not in a position to afford.

Simon was a blond boy with big cheekbones and wide gray eyes and had the arms of a cricketer—I go by the illustrations; we never played anything but softball. Opposed to his British style was his patriotic anger at George III. The mayor was at that time ordering the schoolboard to get history books that dealt more harshly with the king, and Simon was very hot at Cornwallis. I admired this patriotic flash, his terrific personal wrath at the general, and his satisfaction over his surrender at Yorktown, which would often come over him at lunch while we ate our bologna sandwiches. Grandma had a piece of boiled chicken at noon, and sometimes there was the gizzard for bristleheaded little Georgie, who loved it and blew at the ridgy thing more to cherish than to cool it. But this martial true-blood pride of Simon's disqualified him for the crafty task to be done at the dispensary; he was too disdainful to lie and might denounce everybody instead. I could be counted on to do the job, because I enjoyed it. I loved a piece of strategy. I had enthusiasms too; I had Simon's, though there was never much meat in Cornwallis for me, and I had Grandma Lausch's as well. As for the truth of these statements I was instructed to make—well, it was a fact that we had a boarder. Grandma Lausch was our boarder, not a relation at all. She was supported by two sons, one from Cincinnati and one from Racine, Wisconsin. The daughters-in-law did not want her, and she, the widow of a powerful Odessa businessman—a divinity over us, bald, whiskery, with a fat nose, greatly armored in a cutaway, a double-breasted vest, powerfully buttoned (his blue photo, enlarged and retouched by Mr. Lulov, hung in the parlor, doubled back between the portico columns of the full-length mirror, the dome of the stove beginning where his trunk ended)—she preferred to live with us, because for so many years she was used to direct a house, to command, to govern, to manage, scheme, devise, and intrigue in all her languages. She boasted French and German besides Russian, Polish, and Yiddish; and who but Mr. Lulov, the retouch artist from Division Street, could have tested her claim to French? And he was a serene bogus too, that triple-backboned gallant tea-drinker. Except that he had been a hackie in Paris, once, and if he told the truth about that might have known French among other things, like playing tunes on his teeth with a pencil or singing and keeping time with a handful of coins that he rattled by jigging his thumb along the table, and how to play chess.

Grandma Lausch played like Timur, whether chess or klabyasch, with palatal catty harshness and sharp gold in her eyes. Klabyasch she played with Mr. Kreindl, a neighbor of ours who had taught her the game. A powerful stub-handed man with a large belly, he swatted the table with those hard hands of his, flinging down his cards and shouting "*Shtoch! Yasch! Menél! Klabyasch!*" Grandma looked sardonically at him. She often said, after he left, "If you've got a Hungarian friend you don't need an enemy." But there was nothing of the enemy about Mr. Kreindl. He merely, sometimes, sounded menacing because of his drill-sergeant's bark. He was an old-time Austro-Hungarian conscript, and there was something soldierly about him: a neck that had strained with pushing artillery wheels, a campaigner's red in the face, a powerful bite in his jaw and gold-crowned teeth, green cock-eyes and soft short hair, altogether Napoleonic. His feet slanted out on the ideal of Frederick the Great, but he was about a foot under the required height for guardsmen. He had a masterly look of independence. He and his wife—a woman quiet and modest to the neighbors and violently quar-relsome at home—and his son, a dental student, lived in what was called the English basement at the front of the house. The son, Kotzie, worked evenings in the corner drugstore and went to school in the neighborhood of County Hospital, and it was he who told Grandma about the free dispensary. Or rather, the old woman sent for him to find out what one could get from those state and county places. She was always sending for people, the butcher, the grocer, the fruit peddler, and received them in the kitchen to explain that the Marches had to have discounts. Mama usually had to stand by. The old woman would tell them, "You see how it is—do I have to say more? There's no man in the house and children to bring up." This was her most frequent argument. When Lubin, the caseworker, came around and sat in the kitchen, familiar, bald-headed, in his gold glasses, his weight comfortable, his mouth patient, she shot it at him: "How do you expect chil-dren to be brought up?" While he listened, trying to remain comfortable but gradually becoming like a man determined not to let a grasshopper escape from his hand. "Well, my dear, Mrs. March could raise your rent," he said. She must often have answered—for there were times when she sent us all out to be alone with him—"Do you know what things would be like without me? You ought to be grateful for the way I hold them together." I'm sure she even said, "And when I die, Mr. Lubin, you'll see what you've got on your hands." I'm one hundred per cent sure of it. To us nothing was ever said that might weaken her rule by suggesting it would ever end. Be-sides, it would have shocked us to hear it, and she, in her miraculous knowledge of us, able to be extremely close to our thoughts—she was one sovereign who knew exactly the proportions of love, respect, and fear of power in her subjects—understood how we would have been shocked. But to Lubin, for reasons of policy and also because she had to express feelings she certainly had, she must have said it. He had a harassed patience with her of "deliver me from such clients," though he tried to appear master of the situation. He held his derby between his thighs (his suits, always too scanty in the pants, exposed white socks and bulldog shoes, crinkled, black, and bulging with toes), and he looked into the hat as though debating whether it was wise to release his grasshopper on the lining for a while.

"I pay as much as I can afford," she would say.

She took her cigarette case out from under her shawl, she cut a Murad in half with her sewing scissors and picked up the holder. This was still at a time when women did not smoke. Save the intelligentsia—the term she applied to herself. With the holder in her dark little gums between which all her guile, malice, and command issued, she had her best inspirations of strategy. She was as wrinkled as an old paper bag, an autocrat, hard-shelled and jesuitical, a pouncy old hawk of a Bolshevik, her small ribboned gray feet immobile on the shoekit and stool Simon had made in the manual-training class, dingy old wool Winnie whose bad smell filled the flat on the cushion beside her. If wit and discontent don't necessarily go together, it wasn't from the old woman that I learned it. She was impossible to satisfy. Kreindl, for example, on whom we could depend, Kreindl who carried up the coal when Mama was sick and who instructed Kotzie to make up our prescriptions for nothing, she called "that trashy Hungarian," or "Hungarian pig." She called Kotzie "the baked apple"; she called Mrs. Kreindl "the secret goose," Lubin "the shoemaker's son," the dentist "the butcher," the butcher "the timid swindler." She detested the dentist, who had several times unsuccessfully tried to fit her with false teeth. She accused him of burning her gums when taking the impressions. But then she tried to pull his hands away from her mouth. I saw that happen: the stolid, square-framed Dr. Wernick, whose compact forearms could have held off a bear, painfully

careful with her, determined, concerned at her choked
screams, and enduring her scratches. To see her struggle like
that was no easy thing for me, and Dr. Wernick was sorry to
see me there too, I know, but either Simon or I had to squire
her wherever she went. Here particularly she needed a witness
to Wernick's cruelty and clumsiness as well as a shoulder to
lean on when she went weakly home. Already at ten I was
only a little shorter than she and big enough to hold her small
weight.

"You saw how he put his paws over my face so I couldn't
breathe?" she said. "God made him to be a butcher. Why did
he become a dentist? His hands are too heavy. The touch is
everything to a dentist. If his hands aren't right he shouldn't
be let practice. But his wife worked hard to send him through
school and make a dentist of him. And I must go to him and
be burned because of it."

The rest of us had to go to the dispensary—which was like
the dream of a multitude of dentists' chairs, hundreds of them
in a space as enormous as an armory, and green bowls with
designs of glass grapes, drills lifted zigzag as insects' legs, and
gas flames on the porcelain swivel trays—a thundery gloom in
Harrison Street of limestone county buildings and cumbersome red streetcars with metal grillwork on their windows
and monarchical iron whiskers of cowcatchers front and rear.
They lumbered and clanged, and their brake tanks panted in
the slushy brown of a winter afternoon or the bare stone
brown of a summer's, salted with ash, smoke, and prairie
dust, with long stops at the clinics to let off clumpers, cripples, hunchbacks, brace-legs, crutch-wielders, tooth and eye
sufferers, and all the rest.

So before going with my mother for the glasses I was always instructed by the old woman and had to sit and listen
with profound care. My mother too had to be present, for
there must be no slip-up. She must be coached to say nothing. "Remember, Rebecca," Grandma would re-repeat, "let
him answer everything." To which Mama was too obedient
even to say yes, but only sat and kept her long hands folded
on the bottle-fly iridescence of the dress the old woman had
picked for her to wear. Very healthy and smooth, her color;
none of us inherited this high a color from her, or the form

of her nose with nostrils turned back and showing a little of the partition. "You keep out of it. If they ask you something, you look at Augie like this." And she illustrated how Mama was to turn to me, terribly exact, if she had only been able to drop her habitual grandeur. "Don't tell anything. Only answer questions," she said to me. My mother was anxious that I should be worthy and faithful. Simon and I were her miracles or accidents; Georgie was her own true work in which she returned to her fate after blessed and undeserved success. "Augie, listen to Grandma. Hear what she says," was all she ever dared when the old woman unfolded her plan.

"When they ask you, 'Where is your father?' you say, 'I don't know where, miss.' No matter how old she is, you shouldn't forget to say 'miss.' If she wants to know where he was the last time you heard from him, you must tell her that the last time he sent a money order was about two years ago from Buffalo, New York. Never say a word about the Charity. The Charity you should never mention, you hear that? Never. When she asks you how much the rent is, tell her eighteen dollars. When she asks where the money comes from, say you have boarders. How many? Two boarders. Now, say to me, how much rent?"

"Eighteen dollars."

"And how many boarders?"

"Two."

"And how much do they pay?"

"How much should I say?"

"Eight dollars each a week."

"Eight dollars."

"So you can't go to a private doctor, if you get sixty-four dollars a month. The eyedrops alone cost me five when I went, and he scalded my eyes. And these specs"—she tapped the case—"cost ten dollars the frames and fifteen the glasses."

Never but at such times, by necessity, was my father mentioned. I claimed to remember him; Simon denied that I did, and Simon was right. I liked to imagine it.

"He wore a uniform," I said. "Sure I remember. He was a soldier."

"Like hell he was. You don't know anything about it."

"Maybe a sailor."

"Like hell. He drove a truck for Hall Brothers laundry on Marshfield, that's what he did. *I* said he used to wear a uniform. Monkey sees, monkey does; monkey hears, monkey says." Monkey was the basis of much thought with us. On the sideboard, on the Turkestan runner, with their eyes, ears, and mouth covered, we had see-no-evil, speak-no-evil, hear-no-evil, a lower trinity of the house. The advantage of lesser gods is that you can take their names any way you like. "Silence in the courthouse, monkey wants to speak; speak, monkey, speak." "The monkey and the bamboo were playing in the grass . . ." Still the monkeys could be potent, and awesome besides, and deep social critics when the old woman, like a great lama—for she is Eastern to me, in the end—would point to the squatting brown three, whose mouths and nostrils were drawn in sharp blood-red, and with profound wit, her unkindness finally touching greatness, say, "Nobody asks you to love the whole world, only to be honest, *ehrlich.* Don't have a loud mouth. The more you love people the more they'll mix you up. A child loves, a person respects. Respect is better than love. And that's respect, the middle monkey." It never occurred to us that she sinned mischievously herself against that convulsed speak-no-evil who hugged his lips with his hands; but no criticism of her came near our minds at any time, much less when the resonance of a great principle filled the whole kitchen.

She used to read us lessons off poor Georgie's head. He would kiss the dog. This bickering handmaiden of the old lady, at one time. Now a dozy, long-sighing crank and proper object of respect for her years of right-minded but not exactly lovable busyness. But Georgie loved her—and Grandma, whom he would kiss on the sleeve, on the knee, taking knee or arm in both hands and putting his underlip forward, chaste, lummoxy, caressing, gentle and diligent when he bent his narrow back, blouse bagging all over it, whitish hair pointy and close as a burr or sunflower when the seeds have been picked out of it. The old lady let him embrace her and spoke to him in the following way: "Hey, you, boy, clever *junge,* you like the old Grandma, my minister, my *cavalyer*? That's-a-boy. You know who's good to you, who gives you gizzards and necks? Who? Who makes noodles for you? Yes.

Noodles are slippery, hard to pick up with a fork and hard to pick up with the fingers. You see how the little bird pulls the worm? The little worm wants to stay in the ground. The little worm doesn't want to come out. Enough, you're making my dress wet." And she'd sharply push his forehead off with her old prim hand, having fired off for Simon and me, mindful always of her duty to wise us up, one more animadversion on the trustful, loving, and simple surrounded by the cunning-hearted and tough, a fighting nature of birds and worms, and a desperate mankind without feelings. Illustrated by Georgie. But the principal illustration was not Georgie but Mama, in her love-originated servitude, simple-minded, abandoned with three children. This was what old lady Lausch was driving at, now, in the later wisdom of her life, that she had a second family to lead.

And what must Mama have thought when in any necessary connection my father was brought into the conversation? She sat docile. I conceive that she thought of some detail about him—a dish he liked, perhaps meat and potatoes, perhaps cabbage or cranberry sauce; perhaps that he disliked a starched collar, or a soft collar; that he brought home the *Evening American* or the *Journal*. She thought this because her thoughts were always simple; but she felt abandonment, and greater pains than conscious mental ones put a dark streak to her simplicity. I don't know how she made out before, when we were alone after the desertion, but Grandma came and put a regulating hand on the family life. Mama surrendered powers to her that maybe she had never known she had and took her punishment in drudgery; occupied a place, I suppose, among women conquered by a superior force of love, like those women whom Zeus got the better of in animal form and who next had to take cover from his furious wife. Not that I can see my big, gentle, dilapidated, scrubbing, and lugging mother as a fugitive of immense beauty from such classy wrath, or our father as a marble-legged Olympian. She had sewed buttonholes in a coat factory in a Wells Street loft and he was a laundry driver—there wasn't even so much as a picture of him left when he blew. But she does have a place among such women by the deeper right of continual payment. And as for vengeance from a woman,

Grandma Lausch was there to administer the penalties under the standards of legitimacy, representing the main body of married womankind.

Still the old lady had a heart. I don't mean to say she didn't. She was tyrannical and a snob about her Odessa luster and her servants and governesses, but though she had been a success herself she knew what it was to fall through susceptibility. I began to realize this when I afterward read some of the novels she used to send me to the library for. She taught me the Russian alphabet so that I could make out the titles. Once a year she read *Anna Karenina* and *Eugene Onegin*. Occasionally I got into hot water by bringing a book she didn't want. "How many times do I have to tell you if it doesn't say *roman* I don't want it? You didn't look inside. Are your fingers too weak to open the book? Then they should be too weak to play ball or pick your nose. For that you've got strength! *Bozhe moy!* God in Heaven! You haven't got the brains of a cat, to walk two miles and bring me a book about religion because it says Tolstoi on the cover."

The old *grande dame*, I don't want to be misrepresenting her. She was suspicious of what could have been, given one wrong stitch of heredity, a family vice by which we could have been exploited. She didn't want to read Tolstoi on religion. She didn't trust him as a family man because the countess had had such trouble with him. But although she never went to the synagogue, ate bread on Passover, sent Mama to the pork butcher where meat was cheaper, loved canned lobster and other forbidden food, she was not an atheist and free-thinker. Mr. Anticol, the old junky she called (search me why) "Rameses"—after the city named with Pithom in the Scriptures maybe; no telling what her inspirations were—was that. A real rebel to God. Icy and canny, she would listen to what he had to say and wouldn't declare herself. He was ruddy, and gloomy; his leathery serge cap made him flat-headed, and his alley calls for rags, old iron—"recks aline," he sung it—made him gravel-voiced and gruff. He had tough hair and brows and despising brown eyes; he was a studious, shaggy, meaty old man. Grandma bought a set of the *Encyclopedia Americana*—edition of 1892, I think—from him and saw to it that Simon and I read it; and he too, whenever he met us, asked,

"How's the set?" believing, I reckon, that it taught irreverence to religion. What had made him an atheist was a massacre of Jews in his town. From the cellar where he was hidden he saw a laborer pissing on the body of his wife's younger brother, just killed. "So don't talk to me about God," he said. But it was he that talked about God, all the time. And while Mrs. Anticol stayed pious, it was his idea of grand apostasy to drive to the reform synagogue on the high holidays and park his pink-eye nag among the luxurious, whirl-wired touring cars of the rich Jews who bared their heads inside as if they were attending a theater, a kind of abjectness in them that gave him grim entertainment to the end of his life. He caught a cold in the rain and died of pneumonia.

Grandma, all the same, burned a candle on the anniversary of Mr. Lausch's death, threw a lump of dough on the coals when she was baking, as a kind of offering, had incantations over baby teeth and stunts against the evil eye. It was kitchen religion and had nothing to do with the giant God of the Creation who turned back the waters and exploded Gomorrah, but it was on the side of religion at that. And while we're on that side I'll mention the Poles—we were just a handful of Jews among them in the neighborhood—and the swollen, bleeding hearts on every kitchen wall, the pictures of saints, baskets of death flowers tied at the door, communions, Easters, and Christmases. And sometimes we were chased, stoned, bitten, and beat up for Christ-killers, all of us, even Georgie, articled, whether we liked it or not, to this mysterious trade. But I never had any special grief from it, or brooded, being by and large too larky and boisterous to take it to heart, and looked at it as needing no more special explanation than the stone-and-bat wars of the street gangs or the swarming on a fall evening of parish punks to rip up fences, screech and bawl at girls, and beat up strangers. It wasn't in my nature to fatigue myself with worry over being born to this occult work, even though some of my friends and playmates would turn up in the middle of these mobs to trap you between houses from both ends of a passageway. Simon had less truck with them. School absorbed him more, and he had his sentiments anyway, a mixed extract from Natty Bumppo, Quentin Durward, Tom Brown, Clark at Kaskaskia, the messenger who brought the good news from Ratisbon, and so on, that kept him more to himself. I was just a slow understudy to this, just as he never got me to put in hours on his Sandow muscle builder and the gimmick for developing the sinews of the wrist. I was an easy touch for friendships, and most of the time they were cut short by older loyalties. I was pals longest with Stashu Kopecs, whose mother was a midwife graduated from the Aesculapian School of Midwifery on Milwaukee Avenue. Well to do, the Kopecses had an electric player piano and linoleums in all the rooms, but Stashu was a thief, and to run with him I stole too: coal off the cars, clothes from the lines, rubber balls from the dime store, and pennies off the news-stands. Mostly for the satisfaction of dexterity, though Stashu invented the game of stripping in the cellar and putting on girls' things swiped from the clotheslines. Then he too showed up in a gang that caught me one cold afternoon of very little snow while I was sitting on a crate frozen into the mud, eating Nabisco wafers, my throat full of the sweet dust. Foremost, there was a thug of a kid, about thirteen but un-dersized, hard and grieved-looking. He came up to accuse me, and big Moonya Staplanski, just out of the St. Charles Reformatory and headed next for the one at Pontiac, backed him up.

"You little Jew bastard, you hit my brother," Moonya said.

"I never did. I never even saw him before."

"You took away a nickel from him. How did you buy them biscuits else, you?"

"I got them at home."

Then I caught sight of Stashu, hayheaded and jeering, pleased to sickness with his deceit and his new-revealed broth-erhood with the others, and I said, "Hey, you lousy bed-wetter, Stashu, you know Moon ain't even got a brother."

Here the kid hit me and the gang jumped me, Stashu with the rest, tearing the buckles from my sheepskin coat and bloodying my nose.

"Who is to blame?" said Grandma Lausch when I came home. "You know who? You are, Augie, because that's all the brains you have to go with that piss-in-bed *accoucherka*'s son. Does Simon hang around with them? Not Simon. He has too much sense." I thanked God she didn't know about the stealing. And in a way, because that was her schooling temperament, I suspect she was pleased that I should see where it led to give your affections too easily. But Mama, the prime example of this weakness, was horrified. Against the old lady's authority she didn't dare to introduce her feelings during the hearing, but when she took me into the kitchen to put a compress on me she nearsightedly pored over my scratches, whispering and sighing to me, while Georgie tottered around behind her, long and white, and Winnie lapped water under the sink.

Chapter II

AFTER THE AGE of twelve we were farmed out in the summer by the old woman to get a taste of life and the rudi-
ments of earning. Even before, she had found something for
me to do. There was a morning class for feeble-minded children, and when I had left Georgie in school I reported to
Sylvester's Star Theatre to distribute handbills. Grandma had
arranged this with Sylvester's father, whom she knew from the
old people's arbor in the park.

If it got to our rear flat that the weather was excellent—
warm and still, she liked it—she would go to her room and
put on her corset, relic of when she was fuller, and her black
dress. Mama would fix her a bottle of tea. Then in a chapeau
of flowers and a furpiece of tails locked on her shoulder with
badger claws she went to the park. With a book she never intended to read. There was too much talk in the arbor for that.
It was a place where marriages were made. A year or so after
the old atheist's death, Mrs. Anticol found herself a second
husband there. This widower traveled down from Iowa City
for just the purpose of marriage, and after they were married
the news came back that he kept her locked a prisoner in his
house and made her sign away all rights of legacy. Grandma
did not pretend to be sorry; she said, "Poor Bertha," but she
said it with the humor she was a crackerjack at, as thin and full
of play as fiddle wire, and she took much credit for not going
in for that kind of second marriage. I quit thinking long ago
that all old people came to rest from the things they were out
for in their younger years. But that was what she wanted us to
believe—"an old *baba* like me"—and accordingly we took her
at her word to be old disinterested wisdom who had put by
her vanity. But if she never got a marriage offer, I'm not prepared to say it made no difference to her. She couldn't have
been so sold on *Anna Karenina* for nothing, or another favorite of hers I ought to mention, *Manon Lescaut*, and when
she was feeling right she bragged about her waist and hips, so,
since she never gave up any glory or influence that I know of,
I can see it wasn't only from settled habit that she went into

her bedroom to lace on her corset and wind up her hair but
to take the eye of a septuagenarian Vronsky or Des Grieux. I
sometimes induced myself to see, beyond her spotty yellow-
ness and her wrinkles and dry bangs, a younger and resentful
woman in her eyes.

But whatever she was after for herself, in the arbor, she
wasn't forgetting us, and she got me the handbill job through
old Sylvester, called "the Baker" because he wore white ducks
and white golfer's cap. He had palsy, this the joke of his making rolls, but he was clean, brief-spoken, serious in the aim of
his bloodshot eyes, reconciled, with an effort of nerve that
was copied straight into the curve of his white horse-shoe of
mustache, to the shortness of his days. I suppose her pitch
with him was as usual, about the family she was protecting,
and Sylvester took me to see his son, a young fellow whom
money or family anxiety always seemed to keep in a sweat.
Something, his shadow business and the emptiness of the
seats at two o'clock, the violinist playing just for him and the
operator in the projection box, made it awful for him and misery to come across with my two bits. It made him act tough.
He said, "I've had kids who shoved the bills down the sewer.
Too bad if I ever find out about it, and I have ways to check
up." So I knew that he might follow me along a block of the
route, and I kept watch in the streets for his head with the
weak hair of baldness and his worry-wounded eyes, as brown
as a bear's. "I've got a couple of tricks myself for any punk
who thinks he's going to pull a fast one," he warned me. But
when he believed I was trustworthy, and at first I was, following his directions about rolling the bills and sticking them
into the brass mouthpieces over the bells, not fouling up the
mailboxes and getting him in dutch with the post office, he
treated me to seltzer and Turkish Delight and said he was
going to make a ticket-taker of me when I grew a little taller,
or put me in charge of the popcorn machine he was thinking
of getting; and one of these years he was going to hire a manager while he went back to Armour Institute to finish his engineering degree. He had only a couple of years to go, and his
wife was after him to do it. He took me for my senior, I suppose, to tell me this, as the people at the dispensary did, and
as often happened. I didn't understand all that he told me.

Anyway, he was just a little deceived in me, for when he said his other boys had dumped bills down the sewer I felt I couldn't do less either and watched for my chance. Or gave out wads to the kids in George's dummy-room when I came at noon to fetch him at the penal-looking school built in the identical brick with the icehouse and the casket factory which were its biggest neighbors. It had the great gloom inside of clinks the world over, with ceilings the eye had to try for and wood floors trailed with marching. Summers, one corner of it was kept open for the feeble-minded, and, coming in, you traded the spray of the icehouse for the snipping, cooing hubbub of paper-chain making and the commands of teachers. I sat on the stairs and divided the remaining bills, and when class let out Georgie helped me get rid of them. Then I took him by the hand and led him home.

Much as he loved Winnie, he was scared of strange dogs, and as he carried her scent he drew them. They were always sniffing his legs, and I carried stones to pitch at them.

This was the last idle summer. The next, as soon as the term was over, Simon was sent to work as a bellhop in a resort hotel in Michigan, and I went to the Coblins' on the North Side to help Coblin with his newspaper route. I had to move there, for the papers came into the shed at four in the morning and we lived better than half an hour away on the streetcar. But it wasn't exactly as though I were passing into strange hands, for Anna Coblin was my mother's cousin and I was accordingly treated as a relative. Hyman Coblin came for me in his Ford; George howled when I left the house; he had a way of demonstrating the feelings Mama could not show under ban of the old woman. George had to be shut up in the parlor. I sat him down by the stove and left. Cousin Anna wept enough for everybody and plastered me with kisses at the door of her house, seeing me dog-dumb with the heartbreak of leaving home—a very temporary kind of emotion for me and almost, as it were, borrowed from Mama, who saw her sons drafted untimely into hardships. But Anna Coblin, who had led the negotiations for me, cried the most. Her feet were bare, her hair enormous, and her black dress misbuttoned. "I'll treat you like my own boy," she promised, "my own Howard." She took my canvas laundry bag from me and put me in Howard's room, between the kitchen and the toilet.

Howard had run away. Together with Joe Kinsman, the undertaker's son, he had lied about his age and enlisted in the Marine Corps. Their families were trying to get them out, but in the meantime they had been shipped to Nicaragua and were fighting Sandino and the rebels. She grieved terribly, as if he were dead already. And as she had great size and terrific energy of constitution she produced all kinds of excesses. Even physical ones: moles, blebs, hairs, bumps in her forehead, huge concentration in her neck; she had spiraling reddish hair springing with no negligible beauty and definiteness from her scalp, tangling as it widened up and out, cut ducktail fashion in the back and scrawled out high above her ears. Originally strong, her voice was crippled by weeping and asthma, and the whites of her eyes coppery from the same causes, a burning, morose face, piteous, and her spirit untamed by thoughts or the remote considerations that can reconcile people to awfuler luck than she had. Because, said Grandma Lausch, cutting her case down to scale with her usual satisfaction in the essential, what did she want, a woman like that? Her brothers found her a husband, bought him a business, she had two children in her own house and a few pieces of real-state besides. She might still be in the millinery factory where she started out, over the Loop on Wabash Avenue. That was the observation we heard after Cousin Anna had come to talk to her—as one comes to a wise woman—amassed herself into a suit, hat, shoes, and sat at the kitchen table looking at herself in the mirror as she spoke, not casually, but steadily, sternly, with wrathful comment; even at the bitterest, even when her mouth was at the widest stretch of tears, she went on watching. Mama, her head wrapped in a bandanna, was singeing a chicken at the gas plate.

"*Daragaya*, nothing will happen to your son; he'll come back," said the old woman while Anna sobbed. "Other mothers have their sons there."

"I *told* him to stop going with the undertaker's. What kind of friend was that for him? He dragged him into it."

She had the Kinsmans down for death-breeders, and I found out that she made a detour of blocks when shopping to avoid Kinsman's parlors, though she had always boasted before that Mrs. Kinsman, a big, fresh, leery-looking woman, was a lodge sister and friend of hers—the rich Kinsmans. Coblin's uncle, a bank officer, was buried out of Kinsman's, and Friedl Coblin and Kinsman's daughter went to the same elocution teacher. She had the impediment of Moses whose hand the watching angel guided to the coal, Friedl, and she carried her stuttering into fluency later. Years after, at a football game where I was selling hotdogs, I heard her; she didn't recognize me in the white hat of the day, but I remembered coaching her in "When the Frost Is on the Punkin'." And recalled also Cousin Anna's oath that I should marry Friedl when I was grown. It was in her tears of welcome when she pressed me, on the porch of the house that day. "Hear, Owgie, you'll be my son, my daughter's husband, *mein kind!*" At this moment she had once more given Howard up for dead.

She kept this project of marriage going all the time. When I cut my hand while sharpening the lawn-mower she said, "It'll heal before your wedding day," and then, "It's better to marry somebody you've known all your life, I swear. Nothing worse than strangers. You hear me? Hear!" So she had the future mapped because little Friedl so resembled her that she lived with foreknowledge of her difficulty; she herself had had to be swept over it by the rude Providence of her brother. No mother to help her. And probably she felt that if a husband had not been found for her she would have been destroyed by the choked power of her instincts, deprived of children. And the tears to shed for them would have drowned her as sure as the water of Ophelia's brook. The sooner married the better. Where Anna came from there was no encouragement of childhood anyhow. Her own mother had been married at thirteen or fourteen, and Friedl therefore had only four or five years to go. Anna herself had exceeded this age limit by fifteen years at least, the last few, I imagine, of fearful grief, before Coblin married her. Accordingly she was already on campaign, every young boy a prospect, for I assume I was not the only one but, for the time being, the most available. And Friedl was being groomed with music and dancing lessons as well as elocution and going into the best society in the neighborhood. No reason but this would have made Anna belong to a lodge; she was too gloomy and house-haunting a woman, and it needed a great purpose to send her out to benefits and bazaars.

To anybody who snubbed her child she was a bad enemy and spread damaging rumors. "The piano teacher told me herself. Every Saturday it was the same story. When she went to give Minnie Carson her lesson, Mister tried to pull her behind the door with him." Whether true or not, it soon became her conviction. It made no difference who confronted her or whether the teacher came to plead with her to stop. But the Carsons had not invited Friedl to a birthday party and got themselves an enemy of Corsican rigor and pure absorption.

And now that Howard had run away all her enemies were somehow implicated as hell's agents and deputies, and she lay in bed, crying and cursing them: "O God, Master of the Universe, may their hands and feet wither and their heads dry out," and other grandiose things, everyday language to her. As she lay in the summer light, tempered by the shades and the catalpa of the front yard, flat on her back with compresses, towels, rags, she had a considerable altitude of trunk, the soles of her feet shining from the sheets like graphite rubbings, feet of war disasters in the ruined villages of Napoleon's Spanish campaign; flies riding in echelon on the long string of the light switch. While she panted and butchered on herself with pains and fears. She had the will of a martyr to carry a mangled head in Paradise till doomsday, in the suffering mothers' band led by Eve and Hannah. For Anna was terribly religious and had her own ideas of time and place, so that Heaven and eternity were not too far; she had things segmented, flattened down, and telescoped like the stages and floors of the Leaning Tower, while Nicaragua was at a distance double the circumference of the world, where the bantam Sandino—and who *he* was to her is outside my power to imagine—was killing her son.

The filth of the house, meantime, and particularly of the kitchen, was stupendous. Nevertheless, swollen and fire-eyed, slow on her feet, shouting incomprehensibly on the telephone, and her face as if lit by that gorgeous hair which finally advanced her into royalty, she somehow kept up with her duties. She had meals on time for the men, she saw to it that Friedl practiced and rehearsed, that the money collected was checked, counted, sorted and the coins rolled when Coblin wasn't on hand to do it himself, that the new orders were attended to.

"*Der . . . jener . . .* Owgie, the telephone ringt. Hear! Don't forget to tell them it's now extra the Saturday afternoon paper!"

And when I tried to blow on Howard's saxophone I learned how quickly she could get out of bed and cover the house. She tore into the room and snatched it from me, yelling, "Already they're taking his things away from him!" in a way that made the skin gather down my head and the whole length of my neck. And I saw where a son-in-law—granted, only a prospective one—ranked with respect to her son. She did not forgive me that day, though she knew she had scared me. But I guess I looked less wounded than I felt, and she assumed I had no sense of penitence. What really is more like it is that I had no grudge-bearing power, unlike Simon with his Old South honor and his *code-duello* dangerous easiness that was his specialty of the time. Besides, how could you keep a grudge against anyone so terrific? And even while she pulled the saxophone out of my hands she was hunting her reflection in the small mirror on top of the long chest of drawers. I went down to the cellar where the storm windows and the tools were, and there, after I decided I couldn't cut out for home just yet only to be sent back by Grandma Lausch, I became interested in why the toilet trickled, took the lid off the waterbox, and passed my time below there, tinkering while the floor of the kitchen bowed and crunched.

That would be Five Properties shambling through the cottage, Anna's immense brother, long armed and humped, his head grown off the thick band of muscle as original as a bole on his back, hair tender and greenish brown, eyes completely green, clear, estimating, primitive, and sardonic, an Eskimo smile of primitive simplicity opening on Eskimo teeth buried in high gums, kidding, gleeful, and unfrank; a big-footed contender for wealth. He drove a dairy truck, one of those electric jobs where the driver stood up like a helmsman, the bottles and wood-and-wire cases clashing like mad. He took me around his route a few times and paid me half a buck for helping him hustle empties. When I tried to handle a full case he felt me up, ribs, thighs, and arms—this was something he loved to do —and said, "Not yet, you got to wait yet," lugging it off himself and crashing it down beside the icebox. He was the life of the quiet little lard-smelly Polish groceries that were his stops, punching it out or grappling in fun with the owners, head to head, or swearing in Italian at the Italians, "*Fungoo!*" and measuring off a chunk of stiff arm at them. He gave himself an awful lot of delight. And he was very shrewd, his sister said. It wasn't so long ago he had done a small part in the ruin of empires, driving wagons of Russian and German corpses to burial on Polish farms; and now he had money in the bank, he had stock in the dairy, and he had picked up in the Yiddish theater the fat swagger of the suitor everybody hated: "Five prope'ties. Plente money."

Of a Sunday morning, when the balloon peddlers were tootling in the sweetness and calm of the leafy street and blue sky, he came down to breakfast in a white suit, picking his teeth finely, Scythian hair stroked down under a straw katie. Nonetheless he had not cast off his weekday milk smell. But how fine he was this morning, windburned and hearty-blooded, teeth, gums, and cheeks involved in a bursting grin. He pinched his copper-eyed sister who was sullen with tears.

"Annitchka."

"Go, breakfast is ready."

"Five prope'ties, plente money."

A smile stole over her face which she morosely resisted. But she loved her brother.

"Annitchka."

"Go! My child is missing. The world is chaos."

"Five prope'ties."

"Don't be a fool. You'll have a child yourself, and then you'll know what *wehtig* is."

Five Properties cared absolutely nothing about the absent or the dead and freely said so. Hell with them. He had worn their boots and caps while the stiffs were bouncing in his wagon through shot and explosion. What he had to say was usually on the Spartan or proconsular model, quick and hard.

"You can't go to war without smelling powder." "If granny had wheels she'd be a cart." "Sleep with dogs and wake with fleas." "Don't shit where you eat." One simple moral in all, amounting to, "You have no one to blame but yourself" or, Frenchy-wise—for I have put in my time in the capital of the world—"*Tu l'as voulu, Georges Dandin.*"

Thus you see what views Five Properties must have had on his nephew's enlistment. But he partly spared his sister.

"What do you want? He wrote you last week."

"Last week!" said Anna. "And what about meanwhile?"

"Meanwhile he's got a little Indian girl to tickle and squeeze him."

"Not *my* son," she said, turning her eyes to the kitchen mirror.

But in fact it appeared the boys had found someone to shack up with. Joe Kinsman sent his dad a snapshot of two straight-haired native girls in short skirts and hand in hand, without comment. Kinsman had shown it to Coblin. The fathers weren't exactly displeased; at least they didn't see fit to show displeasure to each other. On the contrary. But Cousin Anna didn't hear of the picture.

Coblin had fatherly fears of his own, but not Anna's rage against Kinsman, and he kept up the necessary liaison with him at his office, for of course the undertaker couldn't enter the house. Generally speaking, Coblin's main lines were outside anyway, and he led a life of movement, steady and square-paced. By comparison with Anna and her brother he appeared small, but he was really a good size himself, sturdy, and bald in a clean sweep of all his hair, his features also big, rounded and flattened, puffy at the eyes which were given to blinking just about to the point of caricature. If you took this tic of his with the standard interpretation of meekness—well, there are types and habits that develop to beguile the experience of mankind. He was not beaten down by Anna or Five Properties or other members of the family. He was something of a sport, he had his own motives and he had established his own right of way with the determination of a man who is liable to be dangerous when he makes a fight. And Anna gave in. Therefore his shirts were always laid away in the drawer with strips of whalebone in the collar, and the second break-

fast he took when he came back from morning deliveries had
to include cornflakes and hard-boiled eggs.

The meals were of amazing character altogether and of
huge quantity—Anna was a strong believer in eating. Bowls
of macaroni without salt or pepper or butter or sauce, brain
stews and lung stews, calves'-foot jelly with bits of calves' hair
and sliced egg, cold pickled fish, crumb-stuffed tripes, canned
corn chowder, and big bottles of orange pop. All this went
well with Five Properties, who spread the butter on his bread
with his fingers. Coblin, who ate with better manners, didn't
complain either and seemed to consider it natural. But I know
that when he went downtown to a carriers' meeting he fed
differently.

To begin with, he changed from the old check suit in which
he did his route with a bagful of papers, like Millet's "Sower,"
for a new check suit. In his snap-brim detective's felt and
large-toed shoes, carrying accounts and a copy of the *Tribune*
for the Gumps, the sports results, and the stock quotations—
he was speculating—and also for the gang-war news, keeping
up with what was happening around Colossimo and Capone in
Cicero and the North Side O'Bannions, that being about the
time when O'Bannion was knocked off among his flowers by
somebody who kept his gun-hand in a friendly grip—with this,
Coblin got on the Ashland car. For lunch he went to a good
restaurant, or to Reicke's for Boston beans and brown bread.
Then to the meeting, where the circulation manager gave his
talk. Afterward, pie à la mode and coffee at the south end of
the Loop, followed by a burlesque show at the Haymarket or
Rialto, or one of the cheaper places where farm or Negro girls
did the grinds, the more single-purposed, less playful houses.

Again, it's impossible to know what Anna's idea was of his
downtown program. She was, you might say, in a desert, pastoral condition of development and not up to the fancy stage
of Belshazzar's Feast of barbaric later days. For that matter,
Coblin wasn't really up to it either. He was a solid man of relatively low current in his thoughts; he took the best care of
his business and wouldn't overstay downtown to an hour that
would make it difficult for him to get up at his regular time,
four o'clock. He played the stock market, but that was business. He played poker, but never for more than he carried in

his change-heavy pockets. He didn't have the long-distance burrowing vices of people who take you in by mildness and then turn out to have been digging and tunneling all the while—as skeptical judges are proud to point out when they see well-thought-of heads breaking through the earth in dark places. He was by and large okay with me, although he had his sullen times when he would badger me to get on faster with filling in the Sunday supplement. That was usually Anna's effect, when she obtained the widest influence on him and got him on war-footing with her in the smoke of her trenches. But on his own he had an entirely different spirit of private gayness, as exemplified by the time I walked in on him when he was in the bathtub, lying in the manly state, erect, and dripping himself with the sponge in the steamy, cramped steerage space of the small windowless bathroom. It might have been more troublesome to ponder that the father of a Marine and of a young daughter, and the husband of Cousin Anna, should be found in so little dignity—much more troublesome, I see now, than it actually was. But my thoughts on this topic were never of any great severity; I could not see a debauchee where I had always seen Cousin Hyman, largely a considerate and merciful man, generous to me.

In fact they were all generous. Cousin Anna was a saving woman, she sang poor and did not spend much on herself, but she bought me a pair of winter hightops with a jack-knife on the side. And Five Properties loved to bring treats, cases of chocolate milk and flouncy giant boxes of candy, bricks of ice-cream and layer cakes. Both Coblin and he were hipped on superabundance. Whether it was striped silk shirts or sleeve garters or stockings with clocks, dixies in the movies or cracker-jacks in the park when they took Friedl and me rowing, they seldom bought less than a dozen, Five Properties with bills, Cousin Hyman with his heaps of coins, just as flush. There was always much money in sight, in cups, glasses, and jars and spread on Coblin's desk. They seemed sure I wouldn't take any, and probably because everything was so lavish I never did. I was easily appealed to in this way, provided that I was given credit for understanding what the setup was, as when Grandma sent me on a mission. I could put my heart into a counterfeit too, just as easily. So don't think I'm trying to put over that, if handled right, a Cato could have been made of me, or a young Lincoln who tramped four miles in a frontier zero gale to refund three cents to a customer. I don't want to pass for having such legendary presidential stuff. Only those four miles wouldn't have been a hindrance if the right feelings were kindled. It depended on which way I was drawn.

Home made a neat and polished contrast on my half-days off. At Anna's the floors were washed on Friday afternoon, when she got down from bed and waded barefoot after the strokes of the mop, going forward, and afterward spread clean papers that soaked and dried and weren't taken up again till the week was over. Here you smelled the daily cleaning wax, and everything was in place on a studious plan—veneer shining, doilies spread, dime-store cut-glass, elkhorn, clock set in place—as regular as a convent parlor or any place where the love of God is made ready for on a base of domestic neatness and things kept well separated from the sea-composition of brutal and noisy trouble that heaves over every undefended wall. The bed that Simon and I slept in bulged up in full dress with pieces of embroidery on the pillow; books (Simon's hero's library) stacked; college pennants nailed in line; the women knitting by the clear, wall-browned summer air of the kitchen window; Georgie among the sunflowers and green washline poles of the yard, stumbling after slow Winnie, who went to smell where sparrows had lighted.

I guess it troubled me to see how absent Simon and I could be from the house and how smooth it went without us. Mama must have felt this and fussed over me as much as was allowable; she'd bake a cake, and I was something of a guest, with the table spread and jam dishes filled. That way my wage-earning was recognized, and it gave me pride to dig the folded dollars out of my watch pocket. Yet when any joke of the old woman's made me laugh harder than usual a noise came out of me which was the echo of the whooping cough —I was only that much ahead of childhood, and although I was already getting rangy and my head was as big as it would ever grow, I was still kept in short pants and Eton collar.

"Well, they must be teaching you great things over there," said Grandma. "This is your chance to learn culture and refinement." She meant to boast that she had already formed me and we had nothing to fear from common influences. But a little ridicule was indicated, just in case there should be any danger.

"Is Anna still crying?"

"Yes."

"All day long. And what does he do?—he looks at her and blinks with his eyes. And the kid stammers. It must be lively. And Five Properties, that Apollo—still looking for an American girl to marry?"

That was her deft, scuttling way. With the small yellow bone of her hand, the hand that had been truly married in Odessa to a man of real weight, she threw the switch, the water rushed in and the clumsy sank—money, strength, fat, silks, and candy boxes, and all—and left the witty and superb smiling to contemplate the ripples. You had to know, to get this as I did, that on Armistice Day of 1922, when Grandma turned her ankle coming down the stairs at eleven o'clock while the factories brewed up their solemn celebrating noise and she should have been standing still, Five Properties picked her up while she was spitting and wincing and rushed her to the kitchen. But her memory specialized in misdemeanors and offenses, which were as ineradicable from her brain as the patrician wrinkle was between her eyes, and her dissatisfaction was an element and a part of nature.

Five Properties was keen on getting married. He took the question up with everybody and naturally had been to see Grandma Lausch about it, and she masked herself up as usual and looked considerate and polite while in secret she checked off and collected what she wanted for her file. But also she saw a piece of change in it for her, a matchmakers's fee. She watched for business opportunities. Once she had masterminded the smuggling of some immigrants from Canada. And I happen to know that she had made an agreement with Kreindl about a niece of his wife, that Kreindl was to act as go-between while the old woman encouraged Five Properties from her side. The scheme fell through, although Five Properties went into it eagerly at first, arriving to present himself brushed and burnished, flaming from his shave up to the Eskimo angle of his eyes, at Kreindl's basement where the meeting was to be. But the girl was thin and pale and didn't satisfy him. He had in mind a bouncing, black-haired, large-lipped, party-going peach. He was gentlemanly about his refusal and took the thin girl out once or twice; she got a kewpie doll from him and one of those cartwheel crimson Bunte candy boxes, and he was done. The old woman then said she gave him up. However, I believe her arrangement with Kreindl stood for some time after, and Kreindl didn't quit. He still went to the Coblins' on Sundays, and he did a double errand, as he had Hebrew New Year's cards to sell on commission for a printer. It was one of his regular lines, like buying job-lots and auction goods and taking people from the neighborhood to the Halsted Street furniture stores when he got wind of their needing a suite.

He worked on Five Properties craftily, and I would see them confabbing in the shed, Kreindl with his rolled legs and his conscript's history pasted on his eager, humiliated back, his beef-eater's face inflated to the height of his forehead with the fine points of the young lady of that day: of good family, nourished from her mother's hand with the purest and whitest food, brought up without rudeness or collision, producing breasts on time, no evil thoughts as yet, giving nothing but the clearest broth, you might say—and I can put myself in Five Properties' thoughts as he listened, crossed his arms, grinned, and appeared to scoff. Was she really so gentle, swell, and white? And if she overflowered into coarseness and grossness, after a little marriage, and lay in the luxury of bed eating fig newtons, corrupt and lazy, sending messages by window shade to sleek young boys? Or if her father was a grafter, her brothers bums and cardsharks, her mother loose or a spendthrift? Five Properties wanted to be awfully careful, and he didn't lack warnings and cautions from his sister, who, by ten years of seniority, could tip him off to American dangers and those of American women for green, old-country boys especially. She was comical when she did it, but grimly comical, for it was time taken from mourning.

"It'll be something different than with me, somebody that understands life. If she wants a fur coat, like her swell friends, you'll have to buy a fur coat, and she won't care if it takes your last drop of blood to do it, a fresh young thing."

"Not me," said Five Properties, in somewhat the way Anna

had said, "Not *my* son." He was rolling bread pills in his broad fingers and smoking a cigar, his green eyes awake and cold.

Busy at his accounts in his BVDs—the afternoon was hot— Coblin blinked me an extra smile, observing how I neglected my book to listen to this conversation. He never had it in for me because I broke in on his privacy in the bathroom; just the contrary.

As for the book, it was Simon's copy of the *Iliad*, and I had been reading how the fair Briseis was dragged around from tent to tent and Achilles racked up his spear and hung away his mail.

Early risers, the Coblins went to bed soon after supper, like a farm family. Five Properties was the first up, at half-past three, and waked Coblin. Coblin took me out with him to have breakfast at a joint on Belmont Avenue, a night-crowd hangout of truckers, conductors, postal clerks, and scrub-women from Loop offices. Bismarcks and coffee for him, flap-jacks and milk for me. He was in a big mood of sociability here, with the other steady patrons and with the Greek, Christopher, and the waitresses. He had no repartee but laughed at everything. At the convict hour between four and five when even those with the least to fear are darkened and sober, and back away from waking. It wasn't so for him; in the summer, at least, he loved to get out of the house and have the coffee before him and the bulldog edition under his arm.

We would go back to the shed to meet the paper trucks that came booming down the alley, tearing off leaves, with punks on the tail gate (to be on newspaper trucks was as sure a stage in their advancement to hoodlums as a hitch in Bridewell or joy-riding in stolen cars), booting off bundles of *Tribune*s or *Examiner*s. Then the crew of delivery boys showed up with bicycles and coasters, and the route was covered by eight o'clock, Coblin and his older hands taking the steep back porches where you needed the knack of pitching the paper up to the third floor over the beams and clothes-lines. Meanwhile Cousin Anna was awake and back at her specialties—as if the charge of them in the cottage had run down overnight—tears, speeches, lamentations, and bothering the morning mirrors with her looks. But also second breakfast was on the table, and Coblin ate before setting out on collections and the light banging of screen doors, in polite panama hat, blinking rapid-fire. He had morning gossamers on his trousers from being the first one through the yards, and he was ready for any conversation with up-to-the-minute gang news of the bloody nights of the beer barons and the last curb quotations—everybody was playing the stock market, led by Insull.

And I was at home with Anna and the kid. Usually Anna went to Northern Wisconsin to escape the pollen in August, but this year, because of Howard's running away, Friedl was deprived of her vacation. Anna often signed off with the complaint that Friedl was the only one of the better-class children to have no holiday. To make up for it she fed her more than ever, and the child had the color of too much nourishment in her face, a hectic, touchy, barbarous face. She couldn't be got to close the door when she went to the can, as even Georgie had been taught to do.

I hadn't forgotten that Friedl had been promised to me when I kept out of sight at the football game that day—the players bucking and thudding on the white lines of the frozen field. She was a young lady then, corrected of all such habits, I'm sure, grown big like her mother, and with her uncle's winesap complexion, and wearing a raccoon coat, eagerly laughing and flagging a Michigan banner. She was studying to be a dietitian at Ann Arbor. This was about ten years removed from the Saturdays when I was given the money by Coblin to take her to the movies.

Anna did not object to our going, but she herself wouldn't touch money on holy days. She observed them all, including the new moons, from a little Hebrew calendar, covering her head, lighting candles, and whispering prayers, with her eyes dilated and determined, going after religious terrors with the fear and nerve of a Jonah driven to enter frightful Nineveh. She thought it was her duty while I was in her house to give me some religious instruction, and it was a queer account I got from her of the Creation and Fall, the building of Babel, the Flood, the visit of the angels to Lot, the punishment of his wife and the lewdness of his daughters, in a spout of Hebrew, Yiddish, and English, powered by piety and anger, little flowers and bloody fires supplied from her own memory and fancy. She didn't abridge much in stories like the one about Isaac sporting with Rebecca in Abimelech's gardens, or the rape of Dinah by Shechem.

"He tortured her," she said.

"How?"

"*Tortured!*"

She didn't think more was necessary and she was right. I have to hand it to her that she knew her listener. There wasn't going to be any fooling about it. She was directing me out of her deep chest to the great eternal things.

Chapter III

E VEN AT THAT TIME I couldn't imagine that I would marry into the Coblin family. And when Anna snatched Howard's saxophone, my thought was, "Go on, take it. What do I want it for! I'll do better than that." My mind was already dwelling on a good enough fate.

While the old lady, following her own idea of what that fate would be, continued to find various jobs for me.

Saying "various jobs," I give out the Rosetta stone, so to speak, to my entire life.

These earliest jobs, though, that she chose for us, they weren't generally of the callousing kind. If hard, they were temporary and supposed to lead to something better. She didn't intend us to be common laborers. No, we were to wear suits, not overalls, and she was going to set us on the way to becoming gentlemen despite our being born to have no natural hope of it, unlike her own sons with the German governesses and tutors and *gymnasium* uniforms they had had. It was not her fault that they couldn't do better than to become small-town businessmen, for they had been brought up to give the world a harder shake. Not that she ever complained of them, and they behaved with decent respect toward her, two sizable broad men in belted overcoats and spats, Stiva driving a Studebaker and Alexander a Stanley Steamer. Both were inclined to be silent and bored. Addressed in Russian, they answered in English, and apparently they weren't so enormously grateful for all she had done. Perhaps she worked so hard over Simon and me to show them what she could do even with such handicaps as ours; and maybe she sermonized us both about love because of her sons. Although she had a quick way of capturing their heads when they bent down to give her the kiss of duty.

Anyway, she had us under hard control. We had to brush our teeth with salt and wash our hair with Castile, bring home our report cards, and sleeping in skivvies was outlawed; we had to wear pajamas.

What did Danton lose his head for, or why was there a

Napoleon, if it wasn't to make a nobility of us all? And this universal eligibility to be noble, taught everywhere, was what gave Simon airs of honor, Iroquois posture and eagle bearing, the lithe step that didn't crack a twig, the grace of Chevalier Bayard and the hand of Cincinnatus at the plow, the industry of the Nassau Street match-boy who became the king of corporations. Without a special gift of vision, maybe you wouldn't have seen it in most of us, lining up in the school-yard on a red fall morning, standing on the gravel in black sheepskins and twisted black stockings, mittens, Western gauntlets, and peeling shoes, while the drum and bugle corps blasted and pounded and the glassy tides of wind drove weeds, leaves, and smoke around, struck the flag stiff and clanked the buckle of the rope on the steel pole. But Simon must have stood out, at the head of the school police patrol, in starched linen Sam Browne belt ironed the night before and serge cap. He had a handsome, bold, blond face; even the short scar on his brow was handsome and assertive. In the school windows Thanksgiving cut-outs were hanging, black and orange Pilgrims and turkeys, strung cranberries, and the polished glass showed the blue and the red chill of the sky, the electric lights and the blackboards inside. A red and dark building; an abbey, a mill by the Fall River or the Susquehanna, a county jail—it resembled each somewhat.

Simon had a distinguished record here. President of the Loyal League, he wore the shield on his sweater, and was valedictorian. I didn't have his singleness of purpose but was more diffuse, and anybody who offered entertainment could get me to skip and do the alleys for junk, or prowl the boathouse and climb in the ironwork under the lagoon bridge. My marks showed it, and the old lady would give me a going-over when I brought them in, calling me "cat-head" and, in her French, "*meshant*," threatening that I'd go to work at fourteen. "I'll get you a certificate from the Board and you can go like a Polack and work in the stockyards," she'd say.

Other times she'd take a different tone with me. "It isn't that you don't have a brain, you're just as smart as anybody else. If Kreindl's son can be a dentist you can be governor of Illinois. Only you're too easy to tickle. Promise you a joke, a laugh, a piece of candy, or a lick of ice-cream, and you'll leave everything and run. In short, you're a fool," she said, taking her shawl of woolen knitted spider-circles in her hands and drawing it down as a man draws on his lapels. "You don't know what's coming if you think you can get by with laughing and eating peach pie." Coblin had given me a taste for pie; she scorned and despised it. "Paper and glue," she said with hatred and her Jehovah jealousy of outside influences. "What else did he teach you?" she menacingly asked.

"Nothing."

"Nothing is right!" And she would make me stand and endure a punitive silence, a comment on myself and my foolishness, overgrown and long-legged in my short pants, large-headed, with black mass of hair and cleft chin—a source of jokes. And also a healthy complexion, wasted on me evidently, for she would say, "Look, look, look at his face! Look at it!" grinning and gripping the holder in her gums, smoke trickling up from her cigarette.

She once caught me in the street, which was being paved, chewing tar from one of the seething tar-pots, with my friend Jimmy Klein whose family she didn't approve of anyhow, and I was in her bad books for a longer time than ever. These periods kept increasing, my misdemeanors growing worse. From taking my punishments very hard, consulting Mama as to how to be forgiven and asking her to approach the old lady for me, and shedding tears when I was pardoned, I got to the stage of feeling more resistant, through worldly comparisons that made me see my crimes more tolerantly. That isn't to say that I stopped connecting her with the highest and the best— taking her at her own word—with the courts of Europe, the Congress of Vienna, the splendor of family, and all kinds of profound and cultured things as hinted in her conduct and advertised in her speech—she'd call up connotations of the utmost importance, the imperial brown of Kaisers and rotogravures of capitals, the gloominess of deepest thought. And I wasn't unaffected by her nagging. I didn't want to go out at fourteen with a certificate and work in the packing plants, so occasionally, for a spell, I'd pick up; I'd do my homework and almost climb out of my seat, wagging my arm with zeal to answer questions. Then Grandma would swear that I'd not only go to high school but, if she lived and had strength, to college. "Just so you *want*! Heaven and earth will be moved." And she spoke of her cousin Dasha who had rolled on the floor nights to stay awake, studying for her medical exam.

When Simon graduated and gave the commencement address I was skipped a grade, and the principal mentioned us in his speech, both March brothers. The whole family was present —Mama at the back where she had placed herself with George, in case he should act up. She wasn't going to leave him at home today, and they were in the last row, where the floor and the bottom of the gallery came the closest. I was sitting up in front, in the feather-trailed air, with the old lady, who was dressed up in dark silk and multiply-wound gold chains with the heart of a locket that one of her teething children had dented; she was narrow-nosed with pride, and distinguished, in a kind of fury of silent trying, from the other immigrant relatives, her double spray of feathers busy hanging in two directions. This was what she had been attempting to get over to us, that if we did as she said we could expect plenty of results like this public homage.

"Now I want to see you up there next year," she said to me.

But she wasn't going to. It was already too late, notwithstanding that I had applied myself enough to skip; my past record was against me, and anyhow I didn't take permanent inspiration from this success. I wasn't cut out for it.

And besides, Simon didn't keep it up himself. He remained more attentive to school than I, but he went through a change the summer he waited on tables in Benton Harbor, and came back with some different aims from his original ones and new ideas about conduct.

A sign of his change, and of great importance for me, was that he returned in the fall brawnier and golden-colored but with an upper-front tooth broken, sharp and a little discolored among the whole and white ones, and his face, laughter and all, altered by it. He wouldn't say how it had happened. Was it in a fight that someone had cracked it?

"Kissing a statue," he said to me. "No, I was biting a dime in a crap game."

Six months before such an answer would have been unthinkable. Also, there was money not accounted for to Grandma's satisfaction.

"Don't tell me all you made in tips was thirty dollars! I know that Reimann's is a first-class resort, and they have people all the way from Cleveland and St. Louis. I expected you to spend something on yourself when you were away the whole summer, but—"

"Well, sure, and I did spend about fifteen dollars."

"You always have been honest, Simon. Now Augie brought us home every cent."

"*Have* been? I am!" he said, mounting up on his pride and tallest falsehood-spurning dignity. "I brought you my wages for twelve weeks, and thirty bucks besides."

She let the matter drop with a silent, piercing glitter from the flat of her gold-wired goggles and a warning-off from a false course in her grayness and wrinkles and a quick suck of her cheek. She indicated she could strike a blow when the moment came. But for the first time I felt from Simon that he was thinking you didn't *have* to worry about that. Not that he was ready to jump off into rebellion. But he had some ideas, and by and by we were saying to each other things that couldn't be said before the women.

At first we often worked in the same places. We went to Coblin's sometimes when he needed us for his crew, and down in Woolworth's cellar we unpacked crockery from barrels so enormous that you could walk into them; we scooped out stale straw and threw it in the furnace. Or we loaded paper into the giant press and baled it. It was foul down there from the spoiled food and mustard cans, old candy, and the straw and paper. For lunch we went upstairs. Simon refused to take sandwiches from home; he said we needed a hot meal when we were working. For twenty-five cents we got two hotdogs, a mug of root beer, and pie, the dogs in cotton-quality rolls, dripping with the same mustard that made the air bad below. But it was the figure you cut as an employee, on an employee's footing with the girls, in work clothes, and being of that tin-tough, creaking, jazzy bazaar of hardware, glassware, chocolate, chickenfeed, jewelry, drygoods, oilcloth, and song hits—that was the big thing; and even being the Atlases of it, under the floor, hearing how the floor bore up under the ambling weight of hundreds, with the fanning, breathing movie organ next door and the rumble descending from the trolleys on Chicago Avenue—the bloody-rinded Saturday gloom of wind-borne ash, and blackened forms of five-story buildings rising up to a blind Northern dimness from the Christmas blaze of shops.

Simon moved on soon to a better job with the Federal News Company, which had a concession of the stands in the railroad stations and the candy and paper sales on trains. The family had to lay out the deposit on a uniform, and he began to keep midnight hours, downtown and on the trains, smart and cadet-like in the spanty new uniform. Sunday mornings he rose late and came out in his bathrobe, sitting down to breakfast big and easy, emboldened by his new earning power. He was shorter than before with Mama and George, and occasionally he was difficult with me.

"Lay off that *Tribune* before I get to it. Christ, I bring it home at night, and in the morning it's all in pieces before I can look at it!"

On the other hand he gave Mama some of his pay without Grandma's knowledge, to spend on herself, and saw to it that I had pocket money and that even George got pennies for soldier-caramels. There was never anything mean about Simon where money was concerned. He had kind of an oriental, bestowing temperament; he had no peace or rest if he ever lacked dough and would sooner beat a check altogether than go out of a lunchwagon without leaving a good tip. He banged me on the head once for taking up one of the two dimes he put under our plates in a coffee shop. Ten cents seemed to me enough.

"Don't let me catch you doing such piker things again," he said to me, and I was afraid of him and didn't dare talk back.

Those Sunday mornings in the kitchen, then, with his uniform seen inside the bedroom, hung with care from the foot of the bed, and comfortable tears of mist running on the windows, he felt the strength of his position as the one getting ready to take the control of the family into his own hands. For he sometimes spoke to me of Grandma as of a stranger.

"She's really nothing to us, you know that, don't you, Aug?"

It wasn't so much rebellion as it was repudiation she had to fear, not being heeded, when he spread his paper over the entire table and read with his hand to his forehead and the darkening blond hair falling over it. Still, he didn't have any plan for deposing her and didn't interfere with her power over the rest of us—especially over Mama, who remained as much a slavey as before. And with her eyes deteriorating, so that the glasses fitted the year before were no longer strong enough. We went back to the dispensary for a new pair and cleared another inquisition; we only just cleared it. They had Simon's age on the record and asked whether he wasn't working. I thought I didn't need Grandma's rehearsing any more and could invent answers myself; and even Mama didn't obey as usual by being silent, but lifted up her odd clear voice and said, "My boys are still in school, and after school I need them to help me out."

Then we were nearly caught by the clerk in the making out of the budget and were terrified, but we were favored by the crowd that day and got the slip to the optical department. We were not ready yet to do without the old woman's coaching.

Simon's news became the chief interest of the house now, when he was shifted from the trains to a stand in the La Salle Street Station and then to the central stand that carried books and novelties, just where the most rushing and significant business was done, in the main path of travel. There he was able to see the celebrities in their furs or stetsons and alpacunas, going free in the midst of their toted luggage, always more proud or more melancholy or more affable or more lined than they were represented. They arrived from California or from Oregon on the Portland Rose in the snow whirled from the inhuman heights of La Salle Street or cleaving hard in the speed lines of the trains; they took off for New York on the Twentieth Century, in their flower-garnished, dark polished parlor-like compartments upholstered in deep green, washing in silver sinks, sipping coffee out of china, smoking cigars.

Simon reported, "I saw John Gilbert today in a big velour hat," or, "Senator Borah left me the change of a dime from his *Daily News*," or, "If you saw Rockefeller you'd believe that he has a rubber stomach, as they say."

When he gave these accounts at the table he set off the hope that somehow greatness might gather him into its circle since it touched him already, that he might appeal to somebody, that Insull's eye might be taken by him and he would give him his card and tell him to report at his office next morning. I have a feeling that soon Grandma began to blame Simon in her secret thought for not making the grade. Maybe he didn't care enough to seem distinguished, maybe his manner wasn't right, impudent, perhaps. Because Grandma believed in the stroke or inspiration that brought you to the notice of eminent men. She collected stories about this, and she had a scheme for writing to Julius Rosenwald whenever she read that he was making a new endowment. It was always to Negroes, never to Jews, that he gave his money, she said, and it angered her enormously, and she cried, "That German *Yehuda*!" At a cry like that the age-crippled old white dog would stand up and try to trot to her.

"That *Deutsch*!"

Still, she admired Julius Rosenwald; he belonged to the inside ring of her equals; where *they* sat, with a different understanding from ours, and owned and supervised everything.

Simon, meanwhile, was trying to find a Saturday place for me in the La Salle Street Station and rescue me from the dime-store cellar, where Jimmy Klein had taken his place. Grandma and even Mama were after him to do something.

"Simon, you *must* pull Augie in."

"Well, I ask Borg every time I see him. Holy Jesus, folks, everybody has relatives there!"

"What's the matter, won't he take a bribe?" said Grandma. "Believe me, he's waiting for you to offer him one. Ask him for dinner and I'll show you. A couple of dollar bills in a napkin."

She'd show us how to practice in the world. Short of brushing the throat of a rival or hindrance with a poison feather at the dinner table, of course, as Nero had done. Simon said he couldn't invite Borg. He didn't know him well since he was only an extra, and he didn't want to look like a toady and be despised.

"Well, my dear Graf Potocki," Grandma said, narrowing down her look, cold and dry, while he in his impatience was already out of breath. "So you'd rather leave your brother working at Woolworth's with that foolish Klein boy in the basement!"

After months of this Simon at last got me on downtown, proving that her power over him wasn't ended yet.

He brought me in to Borg one morning. "Remember now," he warned me on the streetcar, "no funny stuff. You'll be working for old foxy grandpa himself, and he isn't going to put up with any fooling. On this job you handle a lot of dough and it comes at you fast. Anything you're short at the end of the day Borg will take out of your little envelope. You're on probation. I've seen some dopes go out on their ear."

He was particularly severe with me that morning. It was stiff cold weather, the ground hard, the weeds standing broken in the frost, the river giving off vapor and the trains leghorn shots of steam into the broad blue Wisconsin-humored sky, the brass handgrip of the straw seats finger-polished, the crusty straw golden, the olive and brown of coats in their folds gold too, and the hairs of Simon's sizable wrists a greater brightness of the same; also the down of his face, now shaved more often than before. He had a new tough manner of pulling down breath and hawking into the street. And whatever the changes were that he had undergone and was undergoing, still he hadn't lost his fine-framed independent look that he controlled me with. I was afraid of him, though I was nearly his size. Except for the face, we had the same bones.

I wasn't fated to do well at the station. Maybe Simon's threats had something to do with this, and his disgust with me when I had to be docked the first day. But I was a flop, and nearly as much as a dollar short each time, even by the third week. Since I was allowed only two bits above my carfare—forty cents to the penny—I couldn't cover my shortages, and Simon, grim and brief, told me on the way to the car one night that Borg had given me the boot.

"I couldn't *run* after people who short-changed me," I kept defending myself. "They throw the money down and grab a paper; you can't leave the stand to shag them."

At last he answered me coldly, with a cold lick of fire in his eyes, on the stationary wintriness of the black steel harness of the bridge over the dragging unnamable mixture of the river flowing backwards with its waste. "You couldn't get that money out of somebody else's change, could you!"

"What?"

"You heard me, you dumbhead!"

"Why didn't you tell me before?" I cried back.

"Tell you?" he said, pushing angrily by me. "Tell you to keep your barn buttoned, as if you didn't have any more brains than George!"

And he let the old woman yell at me, saying nothing in my defense. Before this he had always stood up for me when it was any serious matter. Now he kept aside in the low lights of the kitchen, his fist on his hip and his coat slung over his shoulder, once in a while lifting the lid on the stove where our supper stood warming, and prodding the coals. I took it hard that he was disloyal to me, but also I knew I had let him down with Borg, whom he sold a bright brother that turned out stupid. But I had been at a small stand under a pillar, where I seemed to get merely stragglers, and Borg gave me only the coat of a uniform, gone in the lining, with ragged cuffs and the braid shot. Alone, I had nobody to point out celebrities to me if any came that way, and I passed the time mooning and waiting for lunch relief and the three o'clock break, when I would watch Simon at the main stand and admire the business there—where the receipts were something to see—the pour of money and the black molecular circulation of travelers knowing what they wanted in gum, fruit, cigarettes, the thick bulwarks of papers and magazines, the power of the space and the span of the main chandelier. I thought that if Borg had started me here instead of in my marble corner, off on the edge where I heard only echoes and couldn't even see the trains, I would have made out better.

So I had the ignominy of being canned and was read the riot act in the kitchen. Seemingly the old lady had been waiting for just this to happen and had it ready to tell me that there were faults I couldn't afford to have, situated where I was in life, a child of an abandoned family with no father to keep me out of trouble, nobody but two women, feeble-handed, who couldn't forever hold a cover over us from hunger, misery, crime, and the wrath of the world. Maybe if we had been sent to an orphanage, as Mama at one time thought of doing, it would have been better. For me, at least, in lessons of hardness, since I had the kind of character that looked for ease and places where I could lie down. She shook the crabbed unit of her hand at me with the fierceness of the words, till now spoken only to herself, bitterly, and with them there came out an oceanic lightning of prophecy that had gathered in her skull by the stove-side through days not otherwise very lighted.

"Remember when I am in my grave, Augie, when I will be dead!"

And the falling hand landed on my arm; it was accidental, but the effect was frightful, for I yelled as if this tap had tenfold hit my soul. Maybe I was yelling about my character, made to feel the worst of it, that I'd go to the grave myself with never the hope of another and better; no power to relieve me of it, purify and redeem me from it; and she was putting herself already beyond life to make her verdict on me binding beyond recall.

"*Gedenk, Augie, wenn ich bin todt!*"

But she couldn't stand to dwell long on her death. Heretofore she hadn't ever mentioned her mortality to us, so it was a sort of lapse; and even now she was like a Pharaoh or Caesar promising to pass into a God—except that she would have no pyramids or monuments to make good the promise and was that much inferior to them. However, her painful, dreadful, toothless, gape-gummed crying the cry of judgment in the lock of death worked hard on me. She had the power to make a threat like this more than the threat of ordinary people, but she also had to pay the price of her own terror at it.

Now she switched back to our fatherlessness. It was a bad moment, and I had brought it on Mama. Simon kept silent by the nickel and bitumen black of the stove, fiddling with the poker-handled steel coil of the lid lever. In the other corner sat Mama, sober and guilty, the easy mark of whoever was our father. The old lady was out to burn me to small ash that night, and everyone was going to get scorched.

I couldn't go back to my old Woolworth job. And so Jimmy Klein and I went together to look for work, despite Grandma's warnings against him. He was highly sociable and spirited, slight and dark-faced, narrow-eyed, witty-looking, largely willing to be honest but not overstrapped by conscience—the old lady was right about that. He couldn't come to the house; she wouldn't encourage me to keep bad company, she said. But I was welcome at the Kleins', and even Georgie was. Afternoons, when I had to take him out, I could leave him there playing with the little chicks they raised, or tried to raise, in the dark, clay areaway between buildings, and Mrs. Klein could keep an eye on him from the cellar kitchen, where she sat at the table, handy to the range, paring, peeling, slicing, cutting meat for stew, and molding meatballs.

Weighing more than two hundred pounds, and with one leg shorter than the other, she couldn't keep long on her feet. Unworried and regular-looking, brow bent to brow, nose curving and short, she dyed her hair black with a liquid ordered by mail from Altoona; she applied it with old toothbrushes she kept in a glass on the bathroom window; this gave her braids a peculiar Indian luster. They fell along her cheeks down to the multiform work of her chins. Her black eyes were small but merciful to confusion; she was popelike and liberal with pardons and indulgences. Jimmy had four brothers and three sisters, some of them occupied mysteriously, but all were genial and glad-handing, even the married elder daughters and the middle-aged sons. Two of her children were divorced and one daughter was a widow, so that Mrs. Klein had grandchildren in her kitchen at all times, some coming from school for lunch and after school for cocoa, others creeping on the floor or lying in buggies. Everyone in those prosperous days was earning money, and yet all had trouble. Gilbert had to pay alimony; the divorced sister, Velma, was not getting hers regularly. Her husband had knocked out one of her teeth in a brawl, and now he often came to beg her mother to plead with her to come back. I saw him lay his red head on the table and cry while his sons and daughters were playing in the seats of his taxi. He made good dough, still he wouldn't give Velma enough, figuring she'd come back to him if he kept her needy. She borrowed, however, from her family. I've never seen such people for borrowing and lending; there was dough changing hands in all directions, and nobody grudged anyone.

But the Kleins seemed to need a great many things and bought them all on the installment plan. Jimmy was sent out —and I with him—the money put inside the earflaps of his cap, to make payments. On the phonograph, on the Singer machine, on the mohair suite with pellet-filled ashtrays that couldn't be overturned, on buggies and bicycles, linoleums, on dental and obstetrical work, on the funeral of Mr. Klein's father, on back-supporting corsets and special shoes for Mrs. Klein, on family photos taken for a wedding anniversary. We covered the city on these errands. Mrs. Klein didn't mind our going to shows, as we often did, to hear Sophie Tucker whack herself on the behind and sing "Red Hot Mama," or see Rose La Rose swagger and strip in the indolent rhythm that made Coblin her admirer. "That girl is not just a beautiful girl," he said. "There are a lot of beautiful girls, but this girl feels men's hearts. She doesn't drop off her dress the way others do, she pulls it over her head. That's why she's the top of her profession today."

We were in the Loop much more than we ought to have been and were continually running into Coblin standing in theater lines during school hours. He never told on me. He only said, like a sport, "What's today, Augie? The mayor closed up the school?" Cheerful as usual, grinning and happy in the limy and red lights of the marquee, like the old king of the Scotch mists who had half a face of emerald and half of red jewel.

"What's the feature?"

"*Bardelys the Magnificent* plus Dave Apollon and his Komarinsky dancers. Come along and keep me company."

We had a reason, at that time, for keeping away from school. Steve the Sailor Bulba, my lockermate, brute-nosed and red, with the careful long-haired barbering and toutish sideburns that gave notice that he was dangerous; bearish, heavy-bottomed in his many-buttoned, ground-scuffing sailor pants and his menacing rat-peaked shoes; a house-breaker who stole plumbing fixtures and knocked open telephone coin boxes in recently vacated flats—this Bulba had taken my science notebook and turned it in as his own. Since there was nothing I could do with Bulba, Jimmy lent me his notes, and I carelessly erased his name and wrote my own over it. We were caught, and Simon had to be called in. Simon didn't want Mama to be brought to school any more than I did. He was able to get around Wigler, the science teacher, eventually.

But all the while Bulba, small-eyed and looking mild, his forehead peaceful and blind, wrinkled to the gentle winter light of the classroom, was trying to make his clasp-knife stand up on its blades, like a horny insect.

After this it wasn't hard for Jimmy to induce me to go downtown with him, especially on science afternoons, to ride, if there was nothing better to do, in the City Hall elevator with his brother Tom, from the gilded lobby to the Municipal Courts. In the cage we rose and dropped, rubbing elbows with bigshots and operators, commissioners, grabbers, heelers, tipsters, hoodlums, wolves, fixers, plaintiffs, flatfeet, men in Western hats and women in lizard shoes and fur coats, hothouse and arctic drafts mixed up, brute things and airs of sex, evidence of heavy feeding and systematic shaving, of calculations, grief, not-caring, and hopes of tremendous millions in concrete to be poured or whole Mississippis of bootleg whisky and beer.

Tommy sent us to his bucket-shop stockbroker on Lake Street, back of the panels of a cigar-store front, later a handbook. Tommy was in a good position to get leads. But even in those money-minting days he never did more than break even. If you didn't count the gains that went into his wardrobe and the gifts he gave his family. The Kleins were all gift-givers. Gift robes and wrappers, venetian mirrors and chateaux-in-the-moonlight tapestries, teacarts, end tables, onyx-based lamps, percolators and electric toasters, and novels—boxes of things stacked up in the closets and under the beds, awaiting their time of usefulness. And yet, except on Sundays when they dolled up, the Kleins looked poor. Old Klein wore his vest over his long-sleeved undershirt and rolled his cigarettes in a little machine.

The one unmarried daughter, Eleanor, had a gypsy style and got herself up in flaming, bursting flowers and Japanese dyes. Fat and pale, with an intelligent Circassian bow to her eyes, very humane, overreconciled to a bad lot, taking it for granted that she was too fat to get a husband and forgiving her married sisters and mobile brothers their better luck, she had a genial cry, almost male and fraternal. She was especially kind to me, called me "lover" and "little brother" and "heartbreaker," told my fortune in cards and knitted me a three-peaked skating cap in yellow and green so that I would look like a Norwegian champion on the pond. When she was well enough—she suffered from rheumatism and had female disorders—she worked in the wrapping department of a soap factory on the North Branch; and when she was at home sat with her mother in the kitchen, wrapped in a flamboyant floral material, heavy black hair slipping back loose and tuberous from a topknot, drinking coffee, knitting, reading, shaving her legs, playing operettas on the gramophone, painting her nails, and, doing these necessary or half-necessary or superfluous things, invisibly paid herself out farther and farther into the mood of a long-seated woman.

The Kleins respected and admired Grandma Lausch for the task she undertook with us. However, Grandma heard, from one of her Pinkerton sources, that Georgie was seen with the chicks between the buildings—they never reached full size, these animals, from lack of sunlight and good feed, but moulted and died scraggly and in a queer state of growth—and she called the Kleins some ugly names.

She didn't come down to give them a piece of her mind because it was no use fighting; they were sometimes able to get me some small job or other, through the influence of Jimmy's uncle Tambow, who delivered the vote of his relatives in the ward and was a pretty big wheel in Republican ward politics. We had a very good month before elections, passing out campaign literature. Tambow often had use for us when someone put a piece of business in his way, like lost articles in the post office or distressed goods in a bankruptcy. It had to be something worth while to pull him away from his card game, but when he had made his buy of razors, leather straps, or doll dishes, toy xylophones, glass-cutters, hotel soap, or first-aid kits, being exempt from licenses, he'd set up a stand on Milwaukee Avenue and hire us to run it. His own sons refused to work for him.

He was divorced and lived in a single room. He had a huge nose, and a countenance loose in the skin, with the eye-bags of a fishing bird, seamy, greenish, and gray. Patient, diligent-looking, and gross, on his chair like a *vaquero* deep sunk in the saddle, he whistled when he breathed from his burden of weight and the bite on his cigar; hair grew from his nose and about the various rings on his knuckles. All times of the year were alike to him. May or November, he had his eleven o'clock breakfast of tea with milk and lump sugar and sweet rolls, dinner of steak and baked potatoes, he smoked ten or twelve Ben Beys, wore the same pants of aldermanic stripe, a hat of dark convention drawing the sphere of social power over his original potent face while he considered what to meld and when to play jack or ace, or whether he could give his son Clementi the two bucks he often came in to ask for. Clementi was the younger son who lived with his mother and stepfather back of their infants'-wear store. "Mine boy, with pleasure," or, "Tomorrow, with pleasure," Tambow said. Tambow didn't say no to sons who had a stepfather. And, a good five rinds inside his old Adam, in the grease, tea, and onion blaze of his restaurant headquarters, crumbling ashes on his lap and picking up his cards with one hand, he wasn't, with his other sins, worried over money; he was grand-ducal with it, like the Kleins. And Clem was an easy spender too, and stood treat. But he wouldn't work, not for his father or for anyone else. So old Tambow set us up in the Milwaukee Avenue throng with, usually, Sylvester in charge, put in a fix with the cops so we wouldn't be bothered, and went back to his card game.

It was a bad time for Sylvester. He had lost the lease on his movie, which had been failing anyway—it was now a wallpaper and paint shop—and he was living with his father, for his wife had left him and, he told us himself, threw stones at him when he tried to come through the backyard to see her. He had given her up for crazy and sent a letter agreeing to an annulment. To raise the money for his fees at Armour Tech, where he was trying to finish his work for an engineer's degree, he had sold his furniture and movie equipment, and now he said that he had been away from school too long to sit in a classroom. Eyes tearing in the November wind as he stood with us on Milwaukee Avenue, thick hands in his overcoat pocket, neck sunk, foot knocking foot, he made depressed jokes. The difference in our ages was no consideration with him. He told all his thoughts. When he finished his degree he was off to see the total globe. Foreign governments were crying for American engineers, and he could write his own ticket. He'd go to Kimberley, where he understood it was true that the natives tried to hide the diamonds in their guts. Or to Soviet Russia—now giving us the whole story, that he sympathized with the Reds and admired Lenin, and especially Trotsky, who had won the civil war, traveling in a tank and reading French novels, while czar, priests, barons, generals, and landlords were being smoked out of the palaces.

Meantime, Jimmy and I were sitting on Tambow's two big suitcases, and we called, "Get ya blades here!" and tended to business. Sylvester collected the money.

Chapter IV

A LL THE INFLUENCES were lined up waiting for me. I was born, and there they were to form me, which is why I tell you more of them than of myself.

At this time, and later too, I had a very weak sense of consequences, and the old lady never succeeded in opening much of a way into my imagination with her warnings and predictions of what was preparing for me—work certificates, stockyards, shovel labor, penitentiary rockpiles, bread and water, and lifelong ignorance and degradation. She invoked all these, hotter and hotter, especially from the time I began to go with Jimmy Klein, and she tried to tighten house discipline, inspected my nails and shirt collar before school, governed my table conduct more sharply, and threatened to lock me out nights if I stayed in the streets after ten. "You can go to the Kleins, if they'll take you in. Listen to me, Augie, I'm trying to make something of you. But I can't send Mama out to follow you and see what you do. I want you to be a *mensch*. You have less time to change than you think. The Klein boy is going to get you into trouble. He has thievish eyes. The truth now—is he a crook or not? Aha! He doesn't answer. True," she said, pushing sharply. "Say!"

I answered emptily, "No," and wondered what she knew and who had told her. For Jimmy, like Stashu Kopecs, did take what he wanted in stores and from stands. And at this very time we were engaged in a swindle in Deever's neighborhood department store, where we were Christmas extras in the toy department, Santa Claus's helpers, in elves' costumes, with painted faces.

High-school sophomores, we were getting too big for this sort of thing, but Santa Claus himself was enormous, a Swedish stoker and handyman, from the alley side of the store, a former iron-boat fireman from Duluth, with trelliswinding muscles and Neanderthal eye-sockets, hootch-shining lumps in his forehead and his beard-hidden lip packed with Copenhagen Seal snuff. Over an undershirt full of holes, he strapped pillows for girth, wadded up his pants, for his legs were long and thin, and we helped pull on his coat. Painted and rouged with theater greasepaint and dusted with mica snow, Jimmy and I marched around the store with tambourines and curl-tongued noisemakers, turning somersaults in our billiard-felt jester's suit, and we gathered a gang of kids to lead to the third floor where the Swede Santa Claus sat in his sleigh, with reindeer artfully hung from the ceiling, the toy trains snicking and money baskets mousing swift and mechanical on the cables to the cashier's cage. Here we were in charge of a surprise-package barrel done up in red and green paper, hollies and diamond powder and coils of silver bristles. These Christmas packages sold for two bits, and Jimmy decided that no inventory of them was possible and began to pocket every tenth quarter. For several days he didn't tell me this, only stood me to lunch. Then he let me into his secret as the volume of business got heavier. We were supposed to carry the money to the cashier when we had accumulated ten dollars. "She dumps it straight in the sack with the rest of the change," he said. "She doesn't mark down where it comes from because she's too busy raking it in, so why shouldn't we take a cut?" We had many discussions about it and raised the percentage to two quarters in every ten. There was a great thriving noise and glitter; all minds were dispersed into this Christmas tinkling, whirring, carols, and signal chimes, and what we were doing in secret with our hands wasn't observable. We stole considerable money. Jimmy was ahead of me. Not only had he started earlier, but I was out several days from the effect of butterscotch cream pie and other rich stuff we treated ourselves to. Or perhaps from a heightening of nerves through the brilliance and success of the wrong we were doing and the problem of how to spend the money. Jimmy spent a lot on presents—elegant slippers and string-feathered mules for everyone, smoking jackets, jazzy ties, rag rugs, and Wearever aluminum. From me, Mama got a bathrobe, the old woman a cameo pin, Georgie plaid stockings, and Simon a shirt. I gave presents to Mrs. Klein and Eleanor too, and to some girls at school.

Days when we weren't working I stayed by preference at the Kleins', where the window sills were level with the sidewalk, and got a taste of what it was to be sitting on parlor furniture while outside something was shaping up from our misdeeds, as for a Roger Touhy, Tommy O'Connor, Basil Banghart, or Dillinger, who had had surgery on their faces, acid on their fingertips, who played solitaire, followed the sports results, sent out for hamburgers and milkshakes, and were trapped at last going to the movies or on a roof. Sometimes we lettered on Jimmy's genealogical chart, it being a belief of the Kleins that they went back to a Spanish family called Avila, in the thirteenth century. They had a cousin in Mexico City who manufactured leather jackets, and he was the author of this theory. Me, I was perfectly willing to believe in such lucky breaks of descent. I worked with Jimmy on the sheet of mechanical-drawing paper, lettering out his family tree in red and india inks. I was uneasy.

At the end of the Christmas holiday Deever's caught up with us. The department manager came and had a talk with Grandma. There had been an inventory of the packages. We didn't attempt to deny the theft, and I at any rate didn't argue the figure of seventy dollars that the manager gave, though the amount we took was actually less. The old lady at first refused to see me through. Icy, she told Simon he had better call in Lubin, the caseworker, for she didn't have the strength to give and had only undertaken to help bring up children, not to handle criminals. Simon brought her around because, he said, the Charities would want to know how long we had been working and why they weren't told. Of course the old lady never had the slightest intention of letting me be sent to reform school, as was threatened. But the threat was made, and I was prepared to go to Juvenile Court and pass on to the house of correction with a practically Chinese acquiescence in their right to punish that foretold what I'd let be done with me. It partly showed I felt people were right because they were angry. On the other hand, I lacked the true sense of being a criminal, the sense that I was on the wrong side of the universal wide line with the worse or weaker part of humankind, carrying brow marks or mutilated thumbs and slit ears and noses.

There wasn't just threatening and scolding this time but absolute abasement. After the first giant crash, in full brass, Grandma put me on cold treatment. Simon was distant to me. I couldn't throw it up to him that he had given me advice about short-change; he'd only say curtly that I was a chump and act as though he didn't know what I was talking about. Mama must have felt she was in one of her star-crossed hours, and that the result of her unlucky capitulation to our father was beginning to show its final retributive shape. Even she said a few sharp things to me. I suffered like a beaver. However, they couldn't get me to beg and entreat—though I wasn't unmoved by the thought of a jail sentence, head shaven, fed on slumgullion, mustered in the mud, buffaloed and bossed. If they decided I had it coming, why, I didn't see how I could argue it.

But I was never in real danger of the house of correction. The robe, cameo, and other things were given back. Enough money was saved out of my wages at Coblin's to pay up. Jimmy's family got him off too. He was clobbered by his father, his mother cried, and the whole thing was done with long before my disgrace was lifted a single degree. We had it much austerer at our house. Nor did the Kleins remain angry with me; in their eyes it wasn't a great subject for anger nor thought of as a disfigurement of my soul. In a few days I was as welcome as ever, and Eleanor was calling me "lover" and knitting a muffler for me to replace one I had to return.

When Jimmy came out of his scare, having carried himself unmoved and cynical all along and taken his father's sharp, erratic wallops, given by his undershirted arm, without shrinking, he was indignant that Deever's had made a profit on us. They had, too. He had some ideas about revenge and went as far as speaking of setting a fire, but I had had as much trouble as I wanted with Deever's, and, really, so had he, but it took some of the sting out of it for him to plot at least.

Clem Tambow, Jimmy's cousin, had a healthy laugh on us for the debate on burning down the store and the other desperado proposals. He suggested that if we wanted to make up some of the money we had lost we could get into the Charleston contest at the Webber and try to earn an honest dollar. He wasn't kidding. He wanted to be an actor and had already tried amateur night, imitating a Britisher who tried to tell a long story about an incident in the Khyber Pass. The Poles and Swedes booed him, and the master of ceremonies sent out the hook. His brother Donald had actually won five dollars, singing "Marquita" and doing a tap dance. Donald was the handsome one, black and curly—the mother's son. She too was handsome and dignified, and wore black dresses and pince nez in her shop. Her special subject was her brother the industrialist, who had died in Warsaw of typhus during the war. Clem had his father's looks, high color, bony head and beak, low-grown point of hair, large lips, everything but the weight; his legs were nervous and long. He would have had a chance to win the city half-mile if he hadn't hurt his wind with cigars and—he bragged about it—what the health manuals called self-abuse and depletion of manhood. He jeered at his wickedness and at all the things that make the admonitory world groan. He strutted on the track, his thighs as skinny as his calves and covered with straight black hairs, nifty and supercilious toward his competitors, the squares who were prancing and bracing. But he was all the same a little dubious and haunted, his black eyes in the long joke-austerity of his head often very melancholy. He could be as melancholy as dirt. He said there was nothing I couldn't do better than he, if I wanted to try. "Oh yes," he said, "you could make broads who wouldn't even look at me." It was this, mainly, that he gave me credit for. "With teeth like yours. They're perfect. My mother let me ruin mine. If I ever do get into big-time I'll have to wear a plate." I laughed at nearly everything he said, and he often told me I was dim-witted. "Poor March, anything can make him laugh."

On the whole we got on very well. He was lenient about my greenness, and I had some support from him and Jimmy when I took sick with love, with classic symptoms of choked appetite and utter absorption, hankering, great refinements of respect in looks, incompetent, and full of movie-born ideas and phrases of popular songs. The girl's name was Hilda Novinson, and she was fairly tall but small-faced, with pallor and other signs of weakness of the chest, light-voiced, hasty-spoken, and shy. I never said a word to her, but came by with a miserable counterfeit of merely passing, secretly pumped with raptures and streaming painfully. I clumped by, looking unfeeling and as if I was thinking about other things. With her Russian facial angle and pale eyes, placed low and denying you a direct glance, she had the look of an older woman. She wore a green jacket, she smoked, she walked with a raft of schoolbooks held to the breast and in open galoshes, the clasps clinking. The spread of those open, high-heeled galoshes and their quick clink acted on my love-galled spirit like little fever-feeding darts and made me bristle with an idiot desire to fall before her. Later, when I wised up and was debeatified, I was more sensual. Those first times I was in the state of courtliness, craving pure feeling, and I was well stocked, probably by inheritance, in all the materials of love.

I had no idea that Hilda might be flattered by my following her and was astonished when Clem and Jimmy said it was so. I trailed her in the corridors and maneuvered myself behind her at basketball games, joined the Bonheur Club so that I might be in the same room with her one hour a week, after school, and, suffering badly, stood on the rear platform of her streetcar when she went home. She descended at the front end, and I jumped down from the rear into the high-piled sooty snow and gray, soaked boards of the West Side street. Her father was a tailor, and the family lived behind the shop. Hilda went through the curtain and—what did she do? Take off her gloves? The galoshes? Drink a cup of cocoa? Smoke? I didn't smoke myself. Fiddle with her books? Complain of a headache? Confide to her mother that I was hunkering around in the glints of the dark street on a winter afternoon, heavy-stepping and in a sheepskin coat? I didn't think she'd do that. And her tailor father didn't seem to know of my being there, this lean, unshaved, back-bent man, and I could gaze at him as much as I liked while he pinned, sponged, and pressed, fatigued-looking and oblivious. Anyhow, once she had gone in Hilda didn't come out again; she sunk into the house and seemed to have no business whatever out of doors.

"With all the babes there are to fall for!" said Clem Tambow, scornful and ugly-nosed. "Let me once take you to a whore, and you'll forget all about her," he said. Of course I didn't answer. "Then I'll write her a letter for you," he offered, "and ask for a date. As soon as you've taken one single walk with her and kissed her you'll be washed up. You'll see how beanbrained she is, and she's not pretty; she has lousy teeth." I declined this too. "All right, I'll talk to her then. I'll tell her to grab you while you're still blind. She'll never get anybody handsomer, and she must know it. What gets you about her? That she smokes, I bet." Finally Jimmy said, "Don't bother him, he wants to carry the torch," and they grabbed their genitals obscenely and threw themselves around on the furniture of the Kleins' living room, which was our club. But I didn't stop this sadhearted, worshipful blundering around or standing like painted wood across the street from the tailor shop in the bluey afternoon. Her scraggy father labored with his needle, bent over, and presumably thinking nothing of his appearance to the street in the lighted glass; her chicken-thin little sister in black gym bloomers cut paper with the big shears.

It took several weeks before the acute part of this passed, and meanwhile I was still in the doghouse at home. It didn't improve things that during this love-struck time I brought in very little money. Simon now had strange hours for coming and going, and he couldn't be questioned about them, since he was working. We no longer came home for lunch; consequently Mama had the chores we used to do at noon, lugging up the coal, airing Winnie, fetching George from school, and doing all the hard wringing of sheets by herself on washdays, growing leaner and more haggard from the extra work. Anyhow, there was a tone and air of anarchy and unruliness around, and of powers thickening with age and delays, planning the stroke that would make the palace ring as in old times and knock the courtiers' noggins on the walls when they were least dreaming of it.

"Well, Augie? What? Are you through working?" Grandma said to me. "Finished work, eh? You want to live on the Charities all your life?"

I did have a sort of job at the time, in a flowershop. Only, on the afternoons when I was attending the meetings of the Bonheur Club or trailing Hilda Novinson in her heart-trap galoshes through the slush, I could easily say that Bluegren had no deliveries for me.

Bluegren gave me what he felt like giving on any particular afternoon; and that, usually, was more for helping him shake down and wire the straw cores of wreaths (he had a big gangster clientele) than for deliveries, when he reckoned I would get tips, which by and large turned out pretty fair. I didn't like traveling on streetcars with large wreaths or floral door-pieces for funerals, because early in the evening I struck the home-going traffic and had to fight for space and hold a corner against conductors and winter-moody passengers, covering the flowers with my body, and was pretty harassed. And then if it was an undertaker's I was bound for, swinging my package overhead like a bass fiddler and making slow way through the beeping, grinding, and the throng, there hardly ever was anyone in the quilted, silent plush and rose glow of mahogany in the parlor to give me a tip, but only some flunky received me in my pointed skating cap and with my runny nose kept just decent by an occasional touch of my wool glove. Once in a while I'd strike on a wake where there was a jar of bootleg red-eye passing around, in one of those offside green bungalows approached by a boardwalk over the long marsh of the yard, a room of friends and mourners. When you came into one of those whisky-smelling mourning rooms with your flowers, why, nobody was so absorbed that you were ignored, as in other sorts of grieving that I've seen, and you were sure to come out with a buck or so in change weighing down your cap. But anyway I preferred to be in the shop—in that Elysian Fields' drift of flowers piled around the loam boxes of the back room or stacked behind the thick panes of the icebox, the roses, carnations, and chrysanthemums. Especially as I was in love.

Bluegren was an imposing man too, fair, smooth, and big, with considerable healthy flesh—a friend of gangsters and rum-runners, very thick with people like Jake the Barber and, in his time, the chief of the North Siders, Dion O'Bannion, who was a florist himself after a fashion and was knocked off in his own shop by three men said to have been sent by Johnny Torrio and who got away in a blue Jewett sedan. Bluegren used gloves to protect himself from thorns when he whipped out a rose to treat it to the shears. He had blue, cold eyes, prepared for any kind of findings, and a big fleshy nose, a little sick of things. I suppose the confusion will happen of having sharp thoughts and a broad face, or broad thoughts and a sharp face. Bluegren's was the first kind, from, I reckon, the connection he had with gangsters, and the effects of fear or temporariness. This was what made him that way. He could be rude and bitter, very shrewish sometimes, especially after an important murder of a Genna or Aiello. And a lot of guys were shot that winter.

It was a bad winter for everyone—not just for notables but for people oblivious of anything except their own ups and downs and busy with the limited traffic of their hearts and minds. Kreindl, say, or Eleanor Klein, or my mother. These days Kreindl had operatic nerves and made bitching scenes in his English-basement flat; he threw dishes on the floor and stamped his feet. And Eleanor was in a slump of spirits and often wept in her room over the general drift of her life. There was plenty of such impulse, enough to reach and move all, just in the tone of days. I might have felt this more myself if it hadn't been for Hilda Novinson.

Mama also was very nervous; it was something you had to know how to detect since she didn't give any of the usual signs. I noticed it from the grimness that showed through her docility, and the longer rest of her weak green eyes on things around her, and sometimes the high-breasted breathing that didn't arise from any exertion at her work. She had a dizzy watchfulness from the buzzing of some omen or other.

Presently we all knew what was up; the old woman was ready to deliver her stroke. She waited for an evening when we were all at supper. I came in from delivering death-flowers; Simon was off from the station. The old woman hit out in her abrupt way and declared it was time we did something about Georgie, who was growing up. There was beef stew on the table, and everybody, the kid included, continued to eat meat and wipe up gravy. But I never assumed, like the old woman, that he was an unwitting topic; not even the poodle was entirely that but knew even when she became deaf before her death that she was spoken of. And sometimes Georgie had the Gioconda's own look and smile when he was being discussed, I declare he did, a subtle look that passed down his white lashes and cheeks, a sort of reflex from wisdom kept prisoner by incapacity, something full of comment on the life of all of us. This wasn't the first time Grandma had spoken of Georgie's future, but now it was not just another observation but getting down to cases. I assume Mama already knew

about it, from the look of waiting that came on her face.
Sooner or later something had to be done about him, said the
old woman. He was hard to manage, now he was growing so
tall and beginning to look like a man. What would we do if
he got it in his head to take hold of some girl, she said, and
we had to deal with the police? This was her rebuke in full for
all our difficulty, disobedience, waywardness, and unmindful-
ness of our actual condition, and I was the main cause of it,
as I realized very well. She said Georgie should go to an institution. It was common sense anyhow that he couldn't stay
with us all his life, and we hadn't shown much ability to carry
burdens so far. Besides, Georgie had to learn to do something
and be trained in basketry or brush-making or what it was
they could teach the feeble-minded, some trade that would
help pay his keep. She finished strong, with the threat that
neighbors with little daughters already were angry, seeing him
roam around the yards, ready to put on long pants. Not making her distaste any too fine, she said he had reached his development of a man. As something lewd that had, however,
to be faced. She got this across, in her granny grimace of re-
pugnance, and left us with her horror.

Ah, it was great for her to make us take a long swig of her
mixture of reality and to watch the effect come up sober in
our eyes. Finishing her speech, she had a terrific look of
shrewd pleasure. Her brows were standing up. I maintain that
Georgie had an idea of the topic, while he went on and wiped
up the beef gravy. I don't want to make out that her position
was all wicked evil while his was nothing but sublimity. That
couldn't be true. She had a difficult practical burden, that of
suggesting this shocking thing by which supposedly we would
benefit. We wouldn't have had the strength or wisdom to
propose it. Like so many loving, humane people who, however, have to live, just like everyone else, and count on
tougher souls to carry them along. But I am allowing Grandma her best excuse. Because there still remains the satisfaction
this gave her. She breathed that tense "Aha!" to herself with
which she closed a trap in chess. It was always this same thing;
we refused to see where our mistakes were leading, and then
the terrible consequences came on. Similar to Elisha's bear
that rushed on the children who were taunting him; or the

divine blow that cracked down that Jew so thoughtless as to put out a hand to keep the ark of the covenant from falling off the wagon. It was punishment for mistakes there would be no time now to correct, that was what it was. She was happy when she could act in behalf of this inexorability she was all the time warning us about.

George sat there with one foot stepping on the other and ate the gravy in that unconscious, mind-crippled seraph's way of his by contrast to this worldly reasoning. Mama in her hurt, high voice tried to answer but only spoke confusion. She was anyway incapable of saying much that was clear, and when she was excited or in pain you couldn't understand her at all. Then Georgie stopped eating and began to moan.

"You! Quiet!" said the old woman.

I spoke up on his side and Mama's. I said that George hadn't done wrong yet and that we wanted to keep him with us.

She had counted on this from me and was prepared. "*Kopfmensch meiner*," she said with powerful irony. "Genius! Do you want to wait until he gets in trouble? Are you here to take care of him when you're needed? You're in the streets and alleys with Klein, that hoodlum, learning to steal and every kind of dirt. Maybe you'd enjoy being an uncle to a bastard by your brother from a Polish girl with white hair, and explain to her stockyards father that he would be a fine son-in-law to him? He'd murder you with a sledgehammer, like an ox, and burn down the house."

"Well," Simon said, "if Augie really wants to take charge of him—"

"Even if Augie were better than he is," she answered quickly, "what would be the good of it? When Augie works once in a while, there's more trouble than money. But if he didn't work at all, imagine how fine it would be! He'd leave the boy at the Kleins' anyhow, and bum with his friend. Oh, I know your brother, my dear boy; he has a big heart if it costs him no trouble, pure gold, and he can promise you anything when his heart is touched. But how reliable he is I don't have to tell you. But even if he were as good as his word, could you afford for him to stop bringing in the little he makes? What? Did you inherit a fortune? Can you have servants, *gouvernantkes*, tutors, such as Lausch laid down his life to give our sons? I have done as much as I could to give you a little education and an honest upbringing, even tried to make gentlemen of you. But you must know who you are, what you are, and not get unreal ideas. So I tell you that you better do for yourself, first, what the world will do anyway for you without kindness. I've seen a little more than you; I know how mistakes are corrected, and how many ways there are to die just from foolishness alone, not to say other things. I tried to explain something about this to your brother, but his thoughts are about as steady as the way a drunkard pees."

Thus she went on with this ominous crying and prophecy. She didn't have to win Simon over; in this one matter of Georgie he was with her. He wasn't openly going to join her because of his feeling for Mama, but when we were alone in the bedroom he let me make all my accusations and arguments, waiting me out with a superior face, taking it easy full-length on the sheets—sewed together of Ceresota sacks—and when he thought I was ready to hear him he said, "Tell it to the Marines, kid. Whyn't you use your brains once in a while before they turn to powder and blow away? The old woman is right and you know it. And don't think you're the only one that cares about George either, but something has got to be done with him. How do you know what he might pick up and do? He's not just a sprout any more, and we can't be watching him all his life."

Simon had been rough on me since I had lost the job at the station and during my trials with Wigler and Sailor Bulba and my crookedness at Deever's. Nor did he think much of Clem and Jimmy, and I had made the mistake of telling him how I felt about Hilda and laid myself open to ridicule. "Why," he said, "Friedl Coblin'll be better looking than that when she grows up. She'll probably have tits anyhow." Of course Simon knew I wasn't a real grudge-bearing character but the type that comes down as fast as he boils up. And he considered that he had the right to treat me like this, because he was making progress while I was making a fool of myself, and he intended to carry me along with him, when it was time, the way Napoleon did his brothers. During my worst difficulties with the old lady he'd be stiff and keep a distance, but then he'd also tell me that I could expect him to help me out of real trouble as long as I was reasonably deserving. He didn't like to see my bubble-headed friends get me in dutch. Yes, he had a sense of duty toward me, and toward George too. I couldn't say he was being hypocritical about George.

"I was sore as hell there for a while when you just let Mama talk and didn't say anything," I told him. "You know damn well I can't do much about the kid unless I quit school and take care of him. But if Mama wants him home you should leave that up to her. And you shouldn't have sat there and let her make a holy show of herself."

"Ma might as well get it all at once as in installments." Simon lay on the dark iron bedstead, brawny and blond. He spoke out strongly. Then he paused and took a calm touch of his broken tooth with his tongue. He seemed to have expected that I would light into him harder than I did, and when I had said my sharpest words he went on to let me hear what I pretty well knew without being told. "She got you dead to rights, Augie. You know you've been pretty damn sloppy. But anyway we wouldn't have had the kid with us more than another year. Even if you were in there pitching, which you're not."

"Well, she thinks she's boss now."

"Let her think," he said. He cleared the passages of his head with the loud, short pull that had got to be the mark of his soberest moments and tripped the light switch with his foot. He began to read.

So there wasn't much I could do after that. I couldn't any longer acknowledge Grandma to be the head of the family, and it was to Simon that some of the old authority became attached. I stayed in the room with him rather than go out and face Mama, who, when the dishes were done and the crumbs shaken off the cloth, would be more lying than sitting in her chair with the Prussian-spiked bulb emitting its glossy villain light through the head on the squashlike wens and bubbles and hard-grained paint of the walls. When she had a grief she didn't play it with any arts; she took straight off from her spirit. She made no fuss or noise nor was seen weeping, but in an extreme and terrible way seemed to be watching out the kitchen window, until you came close and saw the tear-strengthened color of her green eyes and of her pink face, her gap-toothed mouth; she laid her head on the wing of the chair sideways, never direct. When sick she was that way also. She climbed into bed in her gown, twisted her hair into braids to keep it from tangling, and had nothing to do with anyone until she felt able to stay on her feet. It was useless for us to come with the thermometer, for she refused to have it; she lay herself dumbly on the outcome of forces, without any work of mind, of which she was incapable. She had some original view on doom or recovery.

Well, it was now decided about George, and, not reproaching anyone, she did her work while Grandma Lausch made speed to carry out her project. The old lady went down to the drugstore herself to phone Lubin, the caseworker. That in itself was significant, because she scarcely ever set foot in the street when snow had fallen after that icy Armistice Day when she had twisted her ankle. Old people often suffered out their days with broken bones that couldn't mend, she observed. Besides, even if it were only for a block, she couldn't go in a housedress. It wasn't right. She had to get herself up and change from worsted stockings—actually golf hose held with snarled elastics—to silk, to black dress, put up her triple-circle coif and, looking mean, powder her face. Not caring how ungentle she looked to us, she mounted her air-sweeping feathers with hat pins and, got up in the condition of ceremony, she went out with an aged quickness of anger, but as she walked down she still had to set both feet on each tread of the stairs.

It was an election day, and crossed flags were hung over the polling places, burly party men were in the snow, breathing steam and flapping long sample ballots. School was closed, and I was available to accompany her, but she wouldn't have me. And half an hour later when I went out with the ash drawer of the stove I saw her on one knee in the snowy passageway. Fallen. It was hurtful to see her. She never before had gone out without protection. I flung away the tin drawer and ran to her, and she fastened on my thin-shirted arm with the snow-wet gloves. Once on her feet, though, she wanted no support from me, either because of a big, swollen consciousness of sacrifice or maybe a superstitious thought of retribution. She got up the stairs alone and limped straight through the house to her room, where she further laid out precedent by locking the door. Till then I had never even known there was a key; she must have kept it hidden from the earliest days, with her jewels and family papers. Mama and I stood outside, astonished, and asked if she was hurt, until we got the answer of firm rage to go away and let her alone, and I was enough shaken up by having seen her snow-spitten face to tremble now at the cat-intensity of her voice. And *there* was a change in the main established order: that a door less to be thought of locked than the door of a church, and always accessible, should have a key, and that that key should be used! The significance of this election-day fall was all the deeper since usually all her cuts and kitchen burns were treated with great seriousness and much business, with downright melancholy and the haunting of the ultimate threat. After applying the iodine or oil and bandages she would take a cigarette for her nerves. But the Murads were in her sewing basket in the kitchen and she didn't come out of her room.

Lunchtime passed, and it was well on in the afternoon before she came out. She was wearing a thick bandage on her leg. She came along the old paths of the house, the parrot colors of the rug worn down to fiber on a line skirting the parlor stove and entering the short hall that gave on the kitchen, where the trail changed to brown in the linoleum, a good part of this the work of her own feet and flint-colored slippers going steadily along this fox run for the better part of ten years. She wore her everyday clothes and shawl again, so that everything was to be presumed back to normal or almost so; whereas it was actually nerve-silent, and her face, attempting to be steady and calm, was blenched as if she really had lost blood, or else her longtime female composure at the sight of blood. She had to have been horribly moved and scared to lock her door, but apparently she had decided that she had to come back and, moony-pale as she was, turn on her influence. But there was something missing. Even the frazzled, pursy old bitch whose white wool had gone brown around her eyes, took a slow walk with clickety claws, as if she sensed that new days were pushing out the last of an old regime, the time when counselors and ministers see the finish of their glory, and Switzers and Praetorian Guards get restless.

I now began to spend full time with Georgie, in the last

month, pulling him around on the sled, walking him in the park, and taking him to the Garfield Park conservatory to see the lemons bloom. The administrative wheels were already going; eleventh-hour efforts did no good. Lubin, who had always said that Georgie would be better off in an institution, brought the commitment papers, and Mama, without Simon's support against the old lady (and probably even that would not have stopped her, since Grandma was in a decisive action and was carried along with the impulse of a doom), had to sign. No, Grandma Lausch couldn't have been withstood, I'm convinced. Not now, not in this. Everything considered, it was, no matter how sad, wiser to commit the kid. As Simon said, we would later have had to do it ourselves. But the old lady made of it something it didn't necessarily have to be, a test of strength, tactless, a piece of sultanism; it originated in things we little understood: disappointment, angry giddiness from self-imposed, prideful struggle, weak nearness to death that impaired her judgment, maybe a sharp utterance of stubborn animal spirit, or bubble from human enterprise, sinking and discharging blindly from a depth.

Do I know? But sending Georgie away could have been done differently.

At last notice arrived that there was place for him in the Home. I had to go and buy him a valise at the Army-Navy store—a tan, bulldog gladstone, the best I could get. The thing would be his for life, and I wanted it to be right. I taught him how to work the clasps and the key. Where he was going there would always be people of course to help him, but my idea was that he should be master of a little of his own, when he went from place to place. We also bought him a hat in the drygoods store.

It was sunless but snow-melting weather at the late start of spring, and the trees and roofs dripped. In that grown man's hat and the coat he didn't wear intelligently—not appearing to feel the need to settle it right on his shoulders—he looked grown up and like a traveler. In fact, beautiful, and the picture of a far traveler, with his pale, mind-crippled, impotent handsomeness. It was enough to make you break down and cry, to see him. But nobody did cry; neither of us, I mean, for by then there were only my mother and I—Simon had given him a kiss on the head when leaving in the morning and said, "Good-by, old socks, I'll come and see you." As for Grandma Lausch, she stayed in her room.

Mama said, "Go and tell Gramma we're ready to go."

"It's Augie," I said at Grandma's door. "Everything is set."

She answered, "Well? Go, then." This she said in her one-time decisive and impatient way, but without the brightness or what you might call the sea ring of real command. The door was locked, and I suppose she was lying on the feather-bed in her apron, shawl, and pointing slippers, with the bric-à-brac of her Odessa existence on her vanity table, dresser top, and on the walls.

"I think Mama wants you to say good-by."

"What is there to say good-by? I'll come and visit him later on."

She didn't have the strength to go and look at the results she had worked hard to get and then still keep on trying to hold power in her hands. And how was I supposed to interpret this refusal if not as feebleness and a cracking of organization?

Mama showed at last the trembling anger of weak people that it takes much to bring on. She seemed determined that Georgie should get the treatment of a child from the old woman. But in a few minutes she returned alone from the bedroom and said with harshness not intended for me, "Pick up the satchel, Augie." I took hold of Georgie's arm through the wide sleeve and we left by the door of the front room, where Winnie was snoozing under the ferns. Georgie softly chewed at a corner of his mouth as we went. It was a slow trip on the cars; we changed three times, and the last stretch on the West Side took us by Mr. Novinson's shop.

We were about an hour getting to the Home—wired windows, dog-proof cyclone fence, asphalt yard, great gloom. In the tiny below-stairs office a moody-looking matron took the papers and signed him into the ledger. We were allowed to go up to the dormitory with him, where other kids stood around under the radiator high on the wall and watched us. Mama took off George's coat and the manly hat, and in his shirt of large buttons, with whitish head and big white, chill fingers— it was troubling that they were so man-sized—he kept by me beside the bed while I again showed him the simple little stunt of the satchel lock. But I failed to distract him from the terror of the place and of boys like himself around—he had never met such before. And now he realized that we would leave him and he began to do with his soul, that is, to let out his moan, worse for us than tears, though many grades below the pitch of weeping. Then Mama slumped down and gave in utterly. It was when she had the bristles of his special head between her hands and was kissing him that she began to cry. When I started after a while to draw her away he tried to follow. I cried also. I took him back to the bed and said, "Sit here." So he sat and moaned. We went down to the car stop and stood waiting by the black, humming pole for the trolley to come back from city limits.

After that we had a diminished family life, as though it were care of Georgie that had been the main basis of household union and now everything was disturbed. We looked in different directions, and the old woman had outsmarted herself. Well, we were a disappointment to her too. Maybe she had started out by dreaming she might have a prodigy in one of us to manage to fame. Perhaps. The force that directs these things in us higher beings and brings together lovers to bear the genius that will lead the world a step or two of the slow march toward its perfection, or find the note that will reach the ear of the banded multitude and encourage it to take that step, had come across with a Georgie instead, and with us. We were far from having the stuff in us that she must have wanted. Our parentage needn't have mattered so much, and it wasn't just a question of high or even legal birth. Fouché got as far as Talleyrand. What counted was natural endowment, and on that score she formed the opinion bitterly that we were not born with talents. Nonetheless we could be trained to be decent and gentlemanly, to wear white collars and have clean nails, brushed teeth, table manners, be brought up to fairly good pattern no matter what office we worked in, store we clerked in, teller's cage we reliably counted in—courteous in an elevator, prefatory in asking directions, courtly to ladies, grim and unanswering to streetwalkers, considerate in conveyances, and walking in the paths of a grayer, dimmer Castiglione.

Instead we were getting to be more common and rude, deeper-voiced, hairy. In our underpants, mornings while getting dressed, we punched and grappled in play, banging to the springs, to the floor, knocking over chairs. Passing then into the hall to wash, there, often, we saw the old woman's small figure and her eyes whitely contemptuous, with a terrible little naked yawn of her gums, suck-cheeked with unspoken comment. But power-robbed. Done for. Simon would say sometimes, "Wha'che know, Gram?"—even, occasionally, "Mrs. Lausch." I never repudiated her that much or tried to strike the old influence, such as it had become, out of her hands. Presently Simon too took a less disrespectful tone. By now, however, it didn't matter much. She had seen what we were and what we were capable of.

The house was changed also for us; dinkier, darker, smaller; once shiny and venerated things losing their attraction and richness and importance. Tin showed, cracks, black spots where enamel was hit off, threadbarer, design scuffed out of the center of the rug, all the glamour, lacquer, massiveness, florescence, wiped out. The old-paste odor of Winnie in her last days apparently wasn't noticed by the house-dwelling women; it was by us, coming in fresh from outdoors.

Winnie died in May of that year, and I laid her in a shoe box and buried her in the yard.

Chapter V

WILLIAM EINHORN was the first superior man I knew. He had a brain and many enterprises, real directing power, philosophical capacity, and if I were methodical enough to take thought before an important and practical decision and also (*N.B.*) if I were really his disciple and not what I am, I'd ask myself, "What would Caesar suffer in this case? What would Machiavelli advise or Ulysses do? What would Einhorn think?" I'm not kidding when I enter Einhorn in this eminent list. It was him that I knew, and what I understand of them in him. Unless you want to say that we're at the dwarf end of all times and mere children whose only share in grandeur is like a boy's share in fairy-tale kings, beings of a different kind from times better and stronger than ours. But if we're comparing men and men, not men and children or men and demigods, which is just what would please Caesar among us teeming democrats, and if we don't have any special wish to abdicate into some different, lower form of existence out of shame for our defects before the golden faces of these and other old-time men, then I have the right to praise Einhorn and not care about smiles of derogation from those who think the race no longer has in any important degree the traits we honor in these fabulous names. But I don't want to be pushed into exaggeration by such opinion, which is the opinion of students who, at all ages, feel their boyishness when they confront the past.

I went to work for Einhorn while I was a high-school junior, not long before the great crash, during the Hoover administration, when Einhorn was still a wealthy man, though I don't believe he was ever so rich as he later claimed, and I stayed on with him after he had lost most of his property. Then, actually, was when I became essential to him, not just metaphorical right hand but virtually arms and legs. Einhorn was a cripple who didn't have the use of either, not even partial; only his hands still functioned, and they weren't strong enough to drive a wheel chair. He had to be rolled and drawn around the house by his wife, brother, relations, or one of the people he usually had on call, either employed by or connected with him. Whether they worked for him or were merely around his house or office, he had a talent for making supernumeraries of them, and there were always plenty of people hoping to become rich, or more rich if already well-to-do, through the Einhorns. They were the most important real-estate brokers in the district and owned and controlled much property, including the enormous forty-flat building where they lived. The poolroom in the corner store of it was owned outright by them and called Einhorn's Billiards. There were six other stores—hardware, fruit, a tin shop, a restaurant, barbershop, and a funeral parlor belonging to Kinsman, whose son it was that ran away with my cousin Howard Coblin to join the Marines against Sandino. The restaurant was the one in which Tambow, the Republican vote-getter, played cards. The Einhorns were his ex-wife's relatives; they, however, had never taken sides in the divorce. It wouldn't have become Einhorn Senior, the old Commissioner, who had had four wives himself, two getting alimony still, to be strict with somebody on that account. The Commissioner had never held office, that was just people's fun. He was still an old galliard, with white Buffalo Bill vandyke, and he swanked around, still healthy of flesh, in white suits, looking things over with big sex-amused eyes. He had a lot of respect from everyone for his shrewdness, and when he opened his grand old mouth to say something about a chattel mortgage or the location of a lot, in his laconic, single-syllabled way, the whole hefty, serious crowd of businessmen in the office stopped their talk. He gave out considerable advice, and Coblin and Five Properties got him to invest some of their money. Kreindl, who did a job for him once in a while, thought he was as wise as a god. "The son is smart," he said, "but the Commissioner—that's really a man you have to give way to on earth." I disagreed then and do still, though when the Commissioner was up to something he stole the show. One of my responsibilities in summer was to go with him to the beach, where he swam daily until the second week in September. I was supposed to see that he didn't go out too far, and also I handed him lighted cigarettes while he floated near the pier in the pillow striping of his suit with large belly, large old man's sex, and yellow, bald knees; his white back-hair spread on the water, yellowish, like polar bear's pelt, his vigorous foreskull, tanned and red, turned up; while his big lips uttered and his nose drove out smoke, clever and pleasurable in the warm, heavy blue of Michigan; while wood-bracketed trawlers, tarred on the sides, chuffed and vapored outside the water reserved for the bawling, splashing, many-actioned, brilliant-colored crowd; waterside structures and towers, and skyscrapers beyond in a vast right angle to the evading bend of the shore.

Einhorn was the Commissioner's son by his first wife. By the second or third he had another son who was called Shep or, by his poolroom friends, Dingbat, for John Dingbat O'Berta, the candy kid of city politics and friend of Polack Sam Zincowicz. Since he didn't either know or resemble O'Berta and wasn't connected with Thirteenth Ward politics or any other, I couldn't exactly say how he came by the name. But without being a hoodlum himself he was taken up with gang events and crime, a kind of amateur of the lore and done up in the gangster taste so you might take him for somebody tied in with the dangerous Druccis or Big Hayes Hubacek: sharp financial hat, body-clasping suit, the shirt Andalusian style buttoned up to the collar and worn without a necktie, trick shoes, pointed and pimpy, polished like a tango dancer's; he clumped hard on the leather heels. Dingbat's hair was violent, brilliant, black, treated, ripple-marked. Bantam, thin-muscled, swift, almost frail, he had an absolutely unreasonable face. To be distinguished from brutal—it wasn't that, there was all kind of sentiment in it. But wild, down-twisting, squint-eyed, unchangeably firm and wrong in thoughts, with the prickles coming black through his unmethodical after-shave talcum: the puss of an executioner's subject, provided we understand the prototype not as a murderer (he attacked with his fists and had a killer's swing but not the real intention) but as somebody intractable. As far as that goes, he was beaten all the time and wore a mishealed scar where his cheek had been caught between his teeth by a ring, but he went on springing and boxing, rushing out from the poolroom on a fresh challenge to spin around on his tango shoes and throw his tense, weightless punches. The beatings didn't squelch him. I was by one Sunday when he picked a fight with that huge Five Properties and thrust him on the chest with his hands, failing to move him; Five Properties picked him up and threw him down on the floor. When Dingbat came back punching, Five Properties grinned but was frightened and shied back against the cue rack. Somebody in the crowd began to shout that Five Properties was yellow, and it was thought the right thing to hold Dingbat back, by the arms, struggling with a blinded, drawn face of rage. A pal of his said what a shame that a veteran of Château Thierry should be shoved around by a greenhorn. Five Properties took it to heart and thereafter stayed away from the poolroom.

Dingbat had had charge of the poolroom at one time, but he was unreliable and the Commissioner had replaced him with a manager. Now he was around as the owner's son—racked up balls, once in a while changed color like a coal when a green table felt was ripped—and in the capacity of key-man and bravo, referee, bet-holder, sports expert, and gang-war historian, on the watch for a small deal, a fighter to manage, or a game of rotation at ten cents a ball. Between times he was his father's chauffeur. The Commissioner couldn't drive the big red Blackhawk-Stutz he owned—the Einhorns never could see anything in a small car—and Dingbat took him to the beach when it was too hot to walk. After all, the old man was pushing seventy-five and couldn't be allowed to risk a stroke. I'd ride with him in the back seat while Dingbat sat with mauled, crazy neck and a short grip on the wheel, ukelele and bathing suit on the cushion beside him; he was particularly sex-goaded when he drove, shouting, whistling, and honking after quiff, to the entertainment of his father. Sometimes we had the company of Clem or Jimmy, or of Sylvester, the movie bankrupt, who was now flunking out of his engineer's course at Armour Tech and talking about moving away to New York altogether. On the beach Dingbat, athletically braced up with belt and wrist-bands, a bandanna to keep the sand out of his hair when he stood on his head, streaked down with suntan oil, was with a crowd of girls and other beach athletes, dancing and striking into his ukelele with:

Ani-ka, hula wicki-wicki
Sweet brown maiden said to me,
And she taught me hula-hula
On the beach at Waikiki . . .

Kindled enough, he made it suggestive, his black voice cracking, and his little roosterish flame licked up clear, queer, and
crabbed. His old sire, gruff and mocking, deeply tickled, lay
like the Buffalo Bill of the Etruscans in the beach chair and
bath towel drawn up burnoose-wise to keep the dazzle from
his eyes—additionally shaded by his soft, flesh-heavy arm—his
bushy mouth open with laughter.

"Ee-*dyot*!" he said to his son.

If the party began after the main heat of the day William
Einhorn might come down too, wheel chair brought on the
baggage rack of the Stutz, and his wife carrying an umbrella
to shade them both. He was taken pick-a-back by his brother,
or by me, from the office into the car, from the car to the
right site on the lakeshore; all as distinguished, observing,
white, untouched and nobiliary as a margrave. Quickeyes.
Originally a big man, of the Commissioner's stature, well
formed, well favored, he had more delicacy of spirit than the
Commissioner, and of course Dingbat wasn't a patch on him.
Einhorn was very pale, a little flabby in the face; considerable
curvature of the nose, small lips, and graying hair let grow
thickly so that it touched on the ears; and continually watchful, his look going forward uninterruptedly to fasten on
subject matters. His heavy, attractive wife sat by him with the
parasol, languorous, partly in smiles, with her free, soft brown
fist on her lap and strong hair bobbed with that declivity that
you see in pictures of the Egyptian coif, the flat base forming
a black brush about the back of the neck. Entertained by the
summer breeziness and the little boats on the waves and the
cavorting and minstrelsy.

If you want to know what she thought, it was that back
home was locked. There were two pounds of hotdogs on the
shelf of the gas range, two pounds of cold potatoes for salad,
mustard, a rye bread already sliced. If she ran out, she could
send me for more. Mrs. Einhorn liked to feel that things were
ready. The old man would want tea. He needed to be pleased,

and she was willing, asking only in return that he stop spitting on the floor, and that not of him directly, being too shy, but through her husband, to him it was merely a joking matter. The rest of us would have Coca-Cola, Einhorn's favorite drink. One of my daily chores was to fetch him Cokes, in bottles from the poolroom or glasses from the drugstore, depending on which he judged to have the better mixture that day.

My brother Simon, seeing me carry a glass on a tray through the gathering on the sidewalk—there was always an overflow of businessmen in front of Einhorn's, mixing with the mourners from Kinsman's chapel and the poolroom characters—gave a big laugh of surprise and said, "So this is your job! You're the butler."

But it was only one function of hundreds, some even more menial, more personal, others calling for cleverness and training—secretary, deputy, agent, companion. He was a man who needed someone beside him continually; the things that had to be done for him made him autocratic. At Versailles or in Paris the Sun King had one nobleman to hand him his stockings, another his shirt, in his morning levee. Einhorn had to be lifted up in bed and dressed. Now and then it was I who had to do it. The room was dark and unfresh, for he and his wife slept with the windows shut. So it was sleep rank from nights of both bodies. I see I had no sense of criticism about such things; I got used to it quickly. Einhorn slept in his underwear because changing to pajamas was a task, and he and his wife kept late hours. Thus, the light switched on, there was Einhorn in his BVDs, wasted arms freckled, grizzled hair afly from his face that was inclined to flatness, the shrewd curved nose and clipped mustache. If peevish, and sometimes he was, my cue was to be quiet until he got back his spirits. It was against policy to be out of temper in the morning. He preferred to be jocular. Birdy, teasing, often corny or lewd, he guyed his wife about the noise and bother she made getting breakfast. In dressing him, my experience with George came in handy, but there was more style about Einhorn than I was used to. His socks were of grand silk, trousers with a banker's stripe; he had several pairs of shoes, fine Walkovers that of course never wrinkled below the instep, much less wore out, a belt with a gothic monogram. Dressed to the waist, he was lifted into his black leather chair and pulled on quaky wheels to the bathroom. At times the first settling in the chair drew a frown from him, sometimes a more oblique look of empoisoned acceptance; but mostly it was a stoical operation. I eased him down and took him, traveling backwards, to the toilet, a sunny room with an east window to the yard. The Commissioner and Einhorn, both rather careless in their habits, made this a difficult place to keep clean. But for people of some nobility allowances have always been made in this regard. I understand that British aristocrats are still legally entitled to piss, if they should care to, on the hind wheels of carriages.

There wasn't anything Mrs. Einhorn could do about the wet floor. Once in a while when Bavatsky the handyman was gone too long in Polack Town or drunk in the cellar, she asked me to clean up. She said she didn't like to impose on me because I was a student. Nevertheless I was getting paid. For unspecified work of a mixed character. I accepted it as such; the mixed character of it was one of the things I liked. I was just as varietistic and unfit for discipline and regularity as my friend Clem Tambow; only I differed from Clem in being a beaver, once my heart was attached to a work or a cause. Naturally, when Einhorn found this out, and he quickly did, he kept me going steadily; it suited him perfectly because of the great number of things he had to be done. Should he run out, my standing by made him invent more. So I didn't often get the toilet detail; he had too many important tasks for me. And when I did get it, why, what I had had under Grandma Lausch made an inconsiderable thing of it to be porter for an hour.

But now in the toilet with Einhorn: he kept me by him to read the morning headlines from the *Examiner*, the financial news, closing quotations from Wall Street and La Salle Street. Local news next, something about Big Bill Thompson, that he had hired the Cort Theatre, for instance, and presented himself on the stage with two caged giant rats from the stockyards whom he addressed by the names of Republican renegades—I came to know what items Einhorn would want first. "Yes, it's just as Thompson says. He's a big gasbag, but this time it's true. He rushed back from Honolulu to save what's-his-name from the penitentiary." He was long and well-nigh perfect of memory, a close and detailed reader of the news, and kept a file on matters of interest to him, for he was highly systematic, and one of my jobs was to keep his files in order in the long steel and wood cases he surrounded himself with, being masterful, often fussy for reasons hard to understand when I placed something before him, proposing to throw it away. The stuff had to be where he could lay his hands on it at once, his clippings and pieces of paper, in folders labeled Commerce, Invention, Major Local Transactions, Crime and Gang, Democrats, Republicans, Archaeology, Literature, League of Nations. Search me, why the League of Nations, but he lived by Baconian ideas of what makes the man this and that, and had a weakness for complete information. Everything was going to be properly done, with Einhorn, and was thoroughly organized on his desk and around it—Shakespeare, Bible, Plutarch, dictionary and thesaurus, *Commercial Law for Laymen*, real-estate and insurance guides, almanacs and directories; then typewriter in black hood, dictaphone, telephones on bracket arms and a little screwdriver to hand for touching off the part of the telephone mechanism that registered the drop of the nickel—for even at his most prosperous Einhorn was not going to pay for every call he made; the company was raking in a fortune from the coinboxes used by the other businessmen who came to the office—wire trays labeled Incoming and Outgoing, molten Aetna weights, notary's seal on a chain, staplers, flap-moistening sponges, keys to money, confidential papers, notes, condoms, personal correspondence and poems and essays. When all this was arranged and in place, all proper, he could begin to operate, back of his polished barrier approached by two office gates, where he was one of the chiefs of life, a white-faced executive, much aware of himself and even of the freakish, willful shrewdness that sometimes spoiled his dignity and proud, plaque-like good looks.

He had his father to keep up with, whose business ideas were perhaps less imaginative but broader, based on his connections with his rich old-time cronies. The old Commissioner had made the Einhorn money and still kept the greater part of the titles in his name, not because he didn't trust his son, but only for the reason that to the business community he was *the* Einhorn, the one who was approached first with offers. William was the heir and was also to be trustee of the shares of his son Arthur, who was a sophomore at the University of Illinois, and of Dingbat. Sometimes Einhorn was unhappy about the Commissioner's habit of making private loans, some of them sizable, from the bankroll he carried pinned inside the pocket of his Mark Twain suit. More often he bragged about him as a pioneer builder on the Northwest Side and had dynastic ideas about the Einhorns—the organizer coming after the conqueror, the poet and philosopher succeeding the organizer, and the whole development typically American, the work of intelligence and strength in an open field, a world of possibilities. But really, with all respect for the Commissioner, Einhorn, while still fresh and palmy, had his father's overriding powers plus something else, statesmanship, fineness of line, Parsee sense, deep-dug intrigue, the scorn of Pope Alexander VI for custom. One morning while I was reading from a column on the misconduct of an American heiress with an Italian prince at Cannes, he stopped me to quote, "'Dear Kate, you and I cannot be confined within the weak list of a country's fashion. We are the makers of manners, Kate, and the liberty that follows our places stops the mouth of all find-faults. . . .' That's Henry Fifth for you. Meaning that there's one way for people at large and another for those that have something special to do. Which those at large have to have in front of them. It braces them up that there's a privilege they can't enjoy, as long as they know it's there. Besides, there's law, and then there's Nature. There's opinion, and then there's Nature. Somebody has to get outside of law and opinion and speak for Nature. It's even a public duty, so customs won't have us all by the windpipe." Einhorn had a teaching turn similar to Grandma Lausch's, both believing they could show what could be done with the world, where it gave or resisted, where you could be confident and run or where you could only feel your way and were forced to blunder. And with his son at the university I was the only student he had to hand.

He put on a judicious head, and things, no matter how they ran, had to be collared and brought to a standstill when he was ready to give out. He raised his unusable arms to the desk by a neat trick that went through several stages, tugging the sleeve of the right with the fingers of the left, helping on the left with the right. There wasn't any appeal to feelings as he accomplished this; it was only an operation. But it had immense importance. As a robust, full-blooded man might mount up to a pulpit and then confess his weakness before God, Einhorn, with his feebleness demonstrated for a preliminary, got himself situated to speak of strength, with strength. It was plenty queer to hear him on this note, especially in view of the daily drift of life here.

But let's take it back to the toilet, where Einhorn got himself ready in the morning. At one time he used to have the barber in to shave him. But this reminded him too much of the hospital, he said, where he had put in a total of two and one-half years. Besides he preferred to do things for himself as much as possible; he had to rely on too many people as it was. So now he used a safety razor stropped in a gadget a Czech inventor had personally sold him; he swore by it. To shave took better than half an hour, chin on the edge of the sink and hands in the water, working round his face. He fished out the washrag, muffled himself in it; I could hear him breathe through its papillae. He soaped, he rubbed and played, scraped, explored with fingers for patches of bristle, and I sat on the cover of the pot and read. The vapor woke up old smells, and there was something astringent in the shaving cream he used that cut into my breath. Then he pomaded his wet hair and slipped on a little cap made of an end of woman's hose. Dried and powdered, he had to be helped into his shirt, his tie put on, the knot inspected many times by his fingers and warped exactly into place with some nervousness about the top button. The jacket next, finished off with the dry noise of the whiskbroom. Fly re-examined, shoes wiped of water drops, we were all set and I got the nod to draw him into the kitchen for breakfast.

His appetite was sharp and he crowded his food. A stranger with a head on him, unaware that Einhorn was paralyzed, would have guessed he was not a well man from seeing him suck a pierced egg, for it was something humanly foxy, paw-handled, hungry above average need. Then he had this cap of a woman's stocking, like a trophy from another field of appetites, if you'll excuse a sporting reference, or martial one, on his head. He was conscious of this himself, for pretty much everything was thought of, and his mind in its way performed admirable work with many of the things he did; or did not care to stop himself from doing; or was not able to stop; or thought it only creaturely human nature to do; or enjoyed, indulged; was proud his disease had not killed his capacity for but rather left him with more capacity than many normal men. Much that's nameless to many people through disgust or shame he didn't mind naming to himself or to a full confidant (or pretty nearly so) like me, and caught, used, and worked all feelings freely. There was plenty to be in on; he was a very busy man.

There was a short executive period, after coffee, when Einhorn threw his weight around about household matters. Wrinkled, gloomy Tiny Bavatsky, string-muscled, was fetched up from the basement and told what he must do, warned to lay off the bottle till night. He went away, hitch-gaited, talking to himself in words of menace, to start his tasks. Mrs. Einhorn was not really a good housekeeper even though she complained about the floor of the toilet and the old man's spitting. But Einhorn was a thoughtful proprietor and saw to it that everything was kept humming, running, flushing, and constantly improved—rats killed, cement laid in the backyard, machines cleaned and oiled, porches re-timbered, tenants sanitary, garbage cans covered, screens patched, flies sprayed. He was able to tell you how fast pests multiplied, how much putty to buy for a piece of glazing, the right prices of nails or clothesline or fuses and many such things; as much as any ancient senator knew of husbandry before such concerns came to be thought wrong. Then, when everything was under control, he had himself taken into his office on the specially constructed chair with cackly casters. I had to dust the desk and get him a Coke to drink with his second cigarette, and he was already on his mail when I got back with it. His mail was large—he had to have it so, and from many kinds of correspondents in all parts of the country.

Let it be hot—for I'm reporting on summers, during vacations, when I spent full time with him—and he was wearing his vest in the office. The morning, this early, was often gentle prairie weather, long before the rugged grind—like the naïveté you get to expect in the hardest and toughest-used when you've been with them long enough—I refer to business and heat of a Chicago summer afternoon. But it was breathing time. The Commissioner wasn't finished dressing yet; he went into the mild sun of the street in his slippers, his galluses hung down, and the smoke of his Claro passed up and back above his white hair, while his hand was sunk comfortable and deep below his waistband. And Einhorn, away back, the length of the office, slit open his letters, made notes for replies, dipped into his files or passed things on for me to check on—me, the often stumped aide, trying to get straight what he was up to in his numerous small swindles. In this respect there was hardly anything he didn't get into, like ordering things on approval he didn't intend to pay for—stamps, little tubes of lilac perfume, packages of linen sachet, Japanese paper roses that opened in water, and all the sort of items advertised in the back pages of the Sunday supplement. He had me write for them in my hand and give fictitious names, and he threw away the dunning letters, of course, and said all of these people calculated losses into what they charged. He sent away for everything that was free: samples of food, soaps, medicine, the literature of all causes, reports of the Bureau of American Ethnology and publications of the Smithsonian Institution, the Bishop Museum in Hawaii, the *Congressional Record*, laws, pamphlets, prospectuses, college catalogues, quack hygiene books, advice on bust-development, on getting rid of pimples, on longevity and Couéism, pamphlets on Fletcherism, Yoga, spirit-rapping, anti-vivisection; he was on the mailing list of the Henry George Institute and the Rudolf Steiner Foundation in London, the local bar association, the American Legion. He had to be in touch with everything. And all this material he kept; the overflow went down to the basement. Bavatsky or I or Lollie Fewter, who came in three days a week to do the ironing, carried it below. Some of it, when it went out of print, he sold to bookstores or libraries, and some he remailed to his clients with the Einhorn stamp on it, for good will. He had much to do also with contests and entered every competition he got wind of, suggesting names for new products, slogans; he made up bright sayings and most embarrassing moments, most delightful dreams, omens he should have heeded, telepathic experiences, and jingles:

> When radio first appeared, I did rave,
> And all my pennies I did save,
> Even neglected to shave.
> I'll take my dear Dynamic to the grave.

He won the *Evening American*'s first prize of five dollars with this, and one of my jobs was to see that what was sent out to contests, anagrams on the names of presidents or on the capitals of states, or elephants composed of tiny numbers (making what sum?), that these entries were neat, mounted right, inside ruled borders, accompanied by the necessary coupons, boxtops, and labels. Furthermore, I had to do reference work for him in his study or at the library downtown, one of his projects being to put out an edition of Shakespeare indexed as the Gideon Bible was: Slack Business, Bad Weather, Difficult Customers, Stuck with Big Inventory of Last Year's Models, Woman, Marriage, Partners. One thousand and one catchpenny deals, no order too big, no sum too small. And, all the time, talkative, clowning, classical, philosophical, homiletic, corny, passing around French poses and imitation turds from the Clark Street novelty stores, pornographic Katzenjammers and Somebody's Stenog; teasing with young Lollie Fewter who was fresh up from the coal fields, that girl with her green eyes from which she didn't try to keep the hotness, and her freckled bust presented to the gathering of men she came among with her waxing rags and the soft shake of her gait. Yea, Einhorn, careful of his perch, with dead legs, and yet denying in your teeth he was different from other men. He never minded talking about his paralysis; on the contrary, sometimes he would boast of it as a thing he had overcome, in the manner of a successful businessman who tells you of the farm poverty of his boyhood. Nor did he overlook any chance to exploit it. To a mailing list he got together from houses that sold wheel chairs, braces, and appliances, he sent out a mimeographed paper called "The Shut-In." Two pages of notices and essays, sentimental bits cribbed from *Elbert Hubbard's Scrapbook*, tags from "Thanatopsis." "Not like the slave scourged to his quarry" but like a noble, stoical Greek; or from Whittier: "Prince thou art, the grown up man/Only is Republican," and other such sources. "Build thee more stately mansions, O my soul!" The third page was reserved for readers' letters. This thing—I put it out on the mimeograph and stapled and carried it to the post office—gave me the creeps once in a while, uneasy flesh around the neck. But he spoke of it as a service to shut-ins. It was a help to him as well; it brought in considerable insurance business, for he signed himself, "William Einhorn, a neighborhood broker," and various companies paid the costs. Like Grandma Lausch again, he knew how to use large institutions. He had an important bearing with their representatives—clabber-faced, with his intelligent bit of mustache and shrewd action of his dark eyes, chicken-winged arms at rest. He wore sleeve garters—another piece of feminine apparel. He tried to maneuver various insurance companies into competitive bidding to increase his commissions.

Many repeated pressures with the same effect as one strong blow, that was his method, he said, and it was his special pride that he knew how to use the means contributed by the age to connive as ably as anyone else; when in a not so advanced time he'd have been mummy-handled in a hut or somebody might have had to help him be a beggar in front of a church, the next thing to a *memento mori* or, more awful, a reminder of what difficulties there were before you could even become dead. Whereas now—well, it was probably no accident that it was the cripple Hephaestus who made ingenious machines; a normal man didn't have to hoist or jack himself over hindrances by means of cranks, chains, and metal parts. Then it was in the line of human advance that Einhorn could do so much; especially since the whole race was so hepped-up about appliances, he was not a hell of a lot more dependent than others who couldn't make do without this or that commodity, engine, gizmo, sliding door, public service, and this being relieved of small toils made mind the chief center of trial. Find Einhorn in a serious mood when his fatty, beaky, noble Bourbon face was thoughtful, and he'd give you the lowdown on the mechanical age, and on strength and frailty, and piece it out with little digressions on the history of cripples—the dumbness of the Spartans, the fact that Oedipus was lame, that gods were often maimed, that Moses had faltering speech and Dmitri the Sorcerer a withered arm, Caesar and Mahomet epilepsy, Lord Nelson a pinned sleeve—but especially on the machine age and the kind of advantage that had to be taken of it; with me like a man-at-arms receiving a lecture from the learned *signor* who felt like passing out discourse.

I was a listener by upbringing. And Einhorn with his graces, learning, oratory, and register of effects was not out to influence me practically. He was not like Grandma, with her educational seventy-fives trained on us. He wanted to flow along, be admirable and eloquent. Not fatherly. I wasn't ever to get it into my head that I was part of the family. There was small chance that I would, the way Arthur, the only son, figured in their references, and I was sent out when any big family deal began to throb around. To make absolutely sure I wouldn't get any such notions, Einhorn would now and then ask me some question about my people, as if he hadn't informed himself through Coblin, Kreindl, Clem, and Jimmy. Pretty clever, he was, to place me this way. If Grandma had ideas about a wealthy man who might take a fancy to us and make our fortune, Simon's and mine, Einhorn had the reverse. I wasn't to think because we were intimately connected and because he liked me that I was going to get into the will. The things that had to be done for him were such that anybody who worked for him was necessarily intimate with him. It sometimes got my goat, he and Mrs. Einhorn made so sure I knew my place. But maybe they were right; the old woman had implanted the thought, though I never entertained it in earnest. However, there was such a thought, and it bulged somewhat into my indignation. Einhorn and his wife were selfish. They weren't mean, I admitted in fairness, and generally I could be fair about it; merely selfish, like two people enjoying their lunch on the grass and not asking you to join them. If you weren't dying for a sandwich yourself it could even make a pleasant picture, smacking on the mustard, cutting cake, peeling eggs and cucumbers. Selfish, Einhorn was, nevertheless; his nose in constant action smelled, and smelled out everything, sometimes austerely, or again without manners, covert, half an eye out for observers but not to be deterred if there were any, either.

I don't think I would have considered myself even remotely as a legatee of the Commissioner if they hadn't, for one thing, underlined my remoteness from inheritance, and, for another, discussed inheritances all the time.

Well, they were steeped and soaked necessarily in insurance and property, lawsuits and legal miscarriages, sour partnerships and welshings and contested wills. This was what you heard when the connoisseurs' club of weighty cronies met, who all showed by established marks—rings, cigars, quality of socks, newness of panamas—where they were situated; they were classified, too, in grades of luck and wisdom, darkness by birth or vexations, power over or subjection to wives, women, sons and daughters, grades of disfigurement; or by the roles they played in comedies, tragedies, sex farces; whether they screwed or were screwed, whether they themselves did the manipulating or were roughly handled, tugged, and bobbled by their fates; their frauds, their smart bankruptcies, the fires they had set; what were their prospects of life, how far death stood from them. Also their merits: which heavy character of fifty was a good boy, a donor, a friend, a compassionate man, a man of balls, a lucid percentage calculator, a fellow willing to make a loan of charity though he couldn't sign his name, a giver of scrolls to the synagogue, a protector of Polish relatives. It was known; Einhorn had it all noted. And apparently everybody knew everything. There was a good circulation of frankness and a lot of respect going back and forth. Also a lot of despicable things. Be this as it might, the topic inside the railed space of benches or at the pinochle game in the side-office annex was mostly business—receiverships, amortizations, wills, and practically nothing else. As rigor is the theme of Labrador, breathing of the summits of the Andes, space to the Cornish miner who lies in a seam under the sea. And, on the walls, insurance posters of people in the despair of fire-traps and the undermining of rats in the beams, housewives bringing down the pantry shelves in their fall. Which all goes to show how you couldn't avoid the question of inheritance. Was the old Commissioner fond of me? While Mrs. Einhorn was a kindly woman ordinarily, now and again she gave me a glance that suggested Sarah and the son of Hagar. Notwithstanding that there was nothing to worry about. Nothing. I wasn't of the blood, and the old man had dynastic ideas too. And I wasn't trying to worm my way into any legacy and get any part of what was coming to her elegant and cultivated son Arthur. Sure the Commissioner was fond of me, stroked my shoulder, gave me tips; and he thought of me no further.

But he and Einhorn were an enigma to Tillie. Her pharaoh-bobbed hair grew out of a head mostly physically endowed; she couldn't ever tell what they might take it into their minds to do. And especially her husband, he was so supple, fertile, and changeable. She worshipfully obeyed him and did his biddings and errands just as the rest of us did. He'd send her to City Hall with requests for information from the Recorder's Office of the License Bureau; he wrote notes, because she could never explain what he wanted, and she brought back the information written out by a clerk. To get her out of the way when he was up to something he sent her to visit her cousin on the South Side, an all-day junket on the streetcars. To be sure she'd be good and gone; and what's more, she knew it.

But now suppose we're at lunchtime, in Einhorn's specimen day. Mrs. Einhorn didn't like to bother in the kitchen and favored ready-made or easy meals, delicatessen, canned salmon with onion and vinegar, or hamburger and fried potatoes. And these hamburgers weren't the flat lunch-wagon jobs, eked out with cornmeal, but big pieces of meat souped up with plenty of garlic and fried to blackness. Covered with horseradish and chili sauce, they didn't go down so hard. This was the food of the house, in the system of its normalcy like its odors and furnishings, and if you were the visiting albatross come to light, you'd eat the food you ne'er had eat and offer no gripe. The Commissioner, Einhorn, and Dingbat asked no questions about it but ate a great deal, with tea or Coca-Cola as usual. Then Einhorn took a white spoonful of Bisodol and a glass of Waukesha water for his gas. He made a joke of it, but he never forgot to take them and heeded all his processes with much seriousness, careful that his tongue was not too coated and his machinery smooth. Very grave, he was sometimes, when he acted as his own physician. He liked to say that he was fatal to doctors, especially to those who had never given him much hope. "I buried two of them," he said.

"Each one told me I'd be gone in a year, and before the year was out he croaked." It made him feel good to tell other doctors of this. Still, he was zealous about taking care of himself; and with this zeal he had a brat's self-mockery about the object of his cares, bottomless self-ribbing; he let his tongue droop over his lip, comic and stupid, and made dizzy crosses with his eyes. Nevertheless he was always thinking about his health and took his powders and iron and liver pills. You might almost say he followed assimilation with his thoughts; all through his body that death had already moved in on, to the Washington of his brain, to his sex and to his studying eyes. Ah, sure, he was still a going concern, very much so, but he had to take thought more than others did about himself, since if *he* went wrong he was a total loss, nowise justified, a dead account, a basket case, an encumbrance, zero. I knew this because he expressed everything, and though he wouldn't talk openly about the money he had in the bank or the property he owned, he was absolutely outspoken about vital things, and he'd open his mind to me, especially when we were together in his study and busy with one of his projects that got more fanciful and muddled the more notions he had about being systematic, so that in the end there'd be a super-monstrous apparatus you couldn't set in motion either by push or crank.

"Augie, you know another man in my position might be out of life for good. There's a view of man anyhow that he's only a sack of craving guts; you find it in *Hamlet*, as much as you want of it. What a piece of work is a man, and the firmament frotted with gold—but the whole *gescheft* bores him. Look at me, I'm not even express and admirable in action. You could say a man like me ought to be expected to lie down and quit the picture. Instead, I'm running a big business today"—that was not the pure truth; it was the Commissioner who was still the main wheel, but it wasn't uninteresting all the same—"while nobody would blame me for rotting in the back room under a blanket or for crabbing and blabbing my bitter heart out, with fresh and healthy people going around me, so as not to look. A kid like you, for instance, strong as a bronco and rosy as an apple. An Alcibiades beloved-of-man, by Jesus. I don't know what brain power you've got; you're too frisky yet, and even if you turn out to be smart you'll never be in the class of my son Arthur. You shouldn't be angry for hearing the truth, if you're lucky enough to find somebody to hear it from. Anyhow, you're not bad off, being an Alcibiades. That's already way and above your fellow creatures. And don't think they didn't hate the original either. All but Socrates himself, ugly as an old dog, they tell us. Nor just because that the young fellow knocked the dongs of the holy figures off, either, before he shipped for Sicily. But to get back to the subject, it's one thing to be buried with all your pleasures, like Sardanapalus; it's another to be buried right plunk in front of them, where you can see them. Ain't it so? You need a genius to raise you above it . . ."

Quiet, quiet, quiet afternoon in the back-room study, with an oilcloth on the library table, busts on the wall, invisible cars snoring and trembling toward the park, the sun shining into the yard outside the window barred against house-breakers, billiard balls kissing and bounding on the felt and sponge rubber, and the undertaker's back door still and stiller, cats sitting on the paths in the Lutheran gardens over the alley that were swept and garnished and scarcely ever trod by the chin-tied Danish deaconesses who'd come out on the cradle-ribbed and always fresh-painted porches of their home.

Somewhat it stung me, the way in which he compared me with his son. But I didn't mind being Alcibiades, and let him be in the same bracket with Socrates in the bargain, since that was what he was driving at. We had title just as good as the chain-mail English kings had to Brutus. If you want to pick your own ideal creature in the mirror coastal air and sharp leaves of ancient perfections and be at home where a great mankind was at home, I've never seen any reason why not. Though unable to go along one hundred per cent with a man like the Reverend Beecher telling his congregation, "Ye are Gods, you are crystalline, your faces are radiant!" I'm not an optimist of that degree, from the actual faces, congregated or separate, that I've seen; always admitting that the true vision of things is a gift, particularly in times of special disfigurement and world-wide Babylonishness, when plug-ugly macadam and volcanic peperino look commoner than crystal—to eyes with an ordinary amount of grace, anyhow—and when it appears like a good sensible policy to settle for medium-grade quartz. I wonder where in the creation there would be much of a double-take at the cry "*Homo sum!*" But I was and have always been ready to venture as far as possible; even though I was never as much imposed on by Einhorn as he wanted me to be in his big moments, with his banker's trousers and chancellor's cravat, and his unemployable squiggle feet on the barber-chairlike mount of his wheeled contraption made to his specifications. And I never could decide whether he meant that he was a genius or had one, and I suppose he wanted there should be some doubt about the meaning. He wasn't the man to come out and declare that he wasn't a genius while there was the chance he might be one, a thing like that coming about *nolens volens.* To some, like his half-brother Dingbat, he was one. Dingbat swore up and down, "Willie is a wizard. Give him two bits' worth of telephone slugs and he'll parlay it into big dough." His wife agreed too, without reservations, that Einhorn was a wizard. Anything he did— and that covers a lot of territory—was all right with her. There wasn't any higher authority, not even her cousin Karas, who ran the Holloway Enterprises and Management Co. and was a demon moneymaker himself. Karas, that bad, rank character, cinder-crawed, wise to all angles, dressed to kill, with a kitty-cornered little smile and extortionist's eyes, she was in awe of him also, but he wasn't presumed to be in Einhorn's class.

But Einhorn wasn't exactly buried in front of his pleasures. He carried on with one woman or another, and in particular he had a great need of girls like Lollie Fewter. His explanation was that he took after his father. The Commissioner, in a kindly, sleepy, warm-aired, fascinated way, petted and admired all women and put his hands wherever he liked. I imagine women weren't very angry when he saluted them in this style because he picked out whatever each of them herself prized most—color, breasts, hair, hips, and all the little secrets and connivances with which she emphasized her own good things. You couldn't rightly say it was a common letch he had; it was a sort of Solomonic regard of an old chief or aged sea lion. With his spotty big old male hands, he felt up the married and the unmarried ones, and even the little girls for what they promised, and nobody ever was offended by it or by the names he invented, names like "the Tangerines," or "the Little Sled," "Madame Yesteryear," "the Six-Foot Dove." The grand old gentleman. Satisfied and gratified. You could feel from the net pleasantness he carried what there had been between him and women now old or dead, whom he recognized, probably, and greeted in this nose or that bosom.

His sons didn't share this quality. Of course you don't expect younger men to have this kind of evening-Mississippi serenity, but there wasn't much disinterestedness or contemplation in either of them. There was perhaps more of it in Dingbat than in his brother. There scarcely was a time when Dingbat wasn't engaged to a nice girl. He scrubbed himself and dressed himself to go to see her in a desperate, cracked rage of earnest respect. Sometimes he would look ready to cry from devotion, and in his preparations he ran out of the perfumed bathroom, clean starched shirt open on his skinny hairiness, to remind me to fetch the corsage from Bluegren's. He could never do enough for these girls and never thought himself good enough for them. And the more he respected them the more he ran with tramps between times, whom he picked up at Guyon's Paradise and took to the Forest Preserves in the Stutz, or to a little Wilson Avenue hotel that Karas-Holloway owned. But Friday evenings, at family dinner, there was often a fiancée, now a piano teacher, now a dress designer or bookkeeper, or simply a home girl, wearing an engagement ring and other presents; and Dingbat with a necktie, tense and daffy, homagefully calling her "Honey," "Isabel, hon," "Janice dear," in his hoarse, thin black voice.

Einhorn, however, didn't have such sentiments at all, whatever sentiments he entertained on other scores. He took the joking liberties his father did, but his jokes didn't have the same ring; which isn't to say that they weren't funny but that he cast himself forward on them toward a goal—seduction. What the laugh was about was his disability; he was after a fashion laughing about it, and he was not so secretly saying to women that if they'd look further they'd find to their surprise that there was the real thing, not disabled. He promised. So that when he worked his wicked, lustful charm, apparently so safe, like a worldly priest or elderly gentleman from whom it's safe to accept a little complimentary badinage or tickle, he was really singlemindedly and grimly fixed on the one thing, ultimately *the* thing, for which men and women came together. And he was the same with them all; not, of course, foreseeing any great success, but hoping all the same that one of them—beautiful, forward, intrigued with him, wishing to play a secret game, maybe a trifle perverse (he suggested), would see, would grasp, would crave, burn for him. He looked and hoped for this in every woman.

He wouldn't stay a cripple, Einhorn; he couldn't hold his soul in it. Sometimes it was dreadful, this; he'd lose everything he'd thought through uncountable times to reconcile himself to it, and be like the wolf in the pit in the zoo who keeps putting his muzzle to the corners of the walls, back and forth, in his exhibition jail. It didn't happen often; probably not oftener than ordinary people get a shove of the demon. But it happened. Touch him when he was off his feed, or had a cold and a little fever, or when there was a rift in the organization, or his position didn't feel so eminent and he wasn't getting the volume of homage and mail he needed—or when it was the turn of a feared truth to come up unseen through the multitude of elements out of which he composed his life, and then he'd say, "I used to think I'd either walk or swallow iodine, and I'd have massages and exercises, and drills when I'd concentrate on a single muscle and think I was building it up by my will, and it was all the bunk, Augie, the Coué theory, etcetera. For the birds. And *It Can Be Done* and the sort of stuff that bigshot Teddy Roosevelt wrote in his books. Nobody'll ever know all the things I tried before I finally decided it was no go. I couldn't take it, and I took it. And I *can't* take it, yet I do take it. But how! You can get along twenty-nine days with your trouble, but there's always that thirtieth day when goddammit you can't, when you feel like the stinking fly in the first cold snap, when you look about and think you're the Old Man of the Sea locked around Sinbad's neck; and why should anybody carry an envious piece of human junk? If society had any sense they'd give me euthanasia or leave me the way the Eskimos do their old folks in an igloo with food for two days. Don't you look so miserable. Go on away. See if Tillie wants you for something."

But this was on the thirtieth day, or more seldom, because in general he enjoyed good health and looked on himself as a useful citizen and even an extraordinary one, and he bragged that there was hardly anything he couldn't bring off if he put his mind to it. And he certainly did some bang-up things. He'd clear us all out of the way to be alone with Lollie Fewter; he'd arrange for the whole lot of us to drive out to Niles Center and show the Commissioner a piece of property. Ostensibly getting ready to occupy himself with a piece of work while we were away—the files and information were laid out for him—he was unhurried, engaging, and smooth-tempered in his tortoiseshells, answering every last question in full and even detaining the excursion to have some last words with his father about frontages or improvements. "Wait till I show you on the map just where the feeder-bus comes through. Bring the map, Augie." He'd have me fetch it and kept the Commissioner till he became impatient, with Dingbat grinding the klaxon and Mrs. Einhorn already settled with bags of fruit in the back seat, calling, "Come, it's hot. I'm fainting here." And Lollie in the passage between the flat and the offices sauntered up and down with the dustmop in the polished dimness, big and soft, comfortable for the heat in a thin blouse and straw sandals, like an overgrown girl walking a doll and keeping a smile to herself about this maternal, matrimonial game, lazy and careless and, you could say, saving force for the game to follow. Clem Tambow had tried to tell me what the score was but hadn't convinced me, not just because of the oddness of the idea, and that I had a boyish respect for Einhorn, but also because I had made a start with Lollie myself. I found excuses to be with her in the kitchen while she was ironing. She told me of her family in the Franklin County coal fields, and then about the men there, and what they tried and did. She rolled me in feelings. From suggestion alone, I didn't have the strength to keep my feet. We soon were kissing and feeling; she now held off my hands and now led them inside her dress, alleging instruction, boisterous that I was still cherry, and at last, from kindness, she one day said that if I'd come back in the evening I could take

her home. She left me so horny I was scarcely able to walk. I
hid out in the poolroom, dreading that Einhorn would send
for me. But Clem came with a message from her that she had
changed her mind. I was bitter about that but I reckon I felt
freed, too, from a crisis. "Didn't I tell you?" said Clem, "You
both work for the same boss, and she's his little nooky. His
and a couple of other guys'. But not for you. You don't know
anything and you don't have any money."

"Why, damn her soul!"

"Well, Einhorn would give her anything. He's nuts about
her."

I couldn't conceive that. It wouldn't be like Einhorn to
settle his important feelings on a tramp. But that exactly was
what he had done. He was mad for her. Einhorn knew, too,
that he shared her with a few hoodlums from the poolroom.
Of course he knew. It wasn't in his life to be without information; he had the stowage of an anthill for it, with weaving
black lines of approvisioners creeping into the crest from
every direction. They told him what would be the next turn
in the Lingle case, or what the public-auction schedule would
be, or about Appellate Court decisions before they were in
print, or where there was hot goods, from furs to school supplies; so he had a line on Lollie from the beginning to the
end.

Eleanor Klein asked me sentimental questions. Did I have a
sweetheart yet? It was a thing I appeared ripe for. Our old
neighbor, Kreindl, asked me too, but in a different way, on
the q.t. He judged I was no longer a kid and he could reveal
himself, his cockeyes turning fierce and gay. "*Schmeist du
schon*, Augie? You've got friends? Not my son. He comes
home from the store and reads the paper. *S'interesiert ihm
nisht.* You're not too young, are you? I was younger than you
and *gefärlich.* I couldn't get enough. Kotzie doesn't take after
me." He much needed to pronounce himself the better, and
in fact the only, man in his house; and he did look very sturdy
when he massed up his teeth and creased his out-of-doors,
rugged face to smile. He saw a lot of weather, for he went
through the entire West Side on foot with his satchel of samples. Because he had to count every nickel. And he had the
patience and hardness of steady pavement going, passing the

same lead-whited windows of a factory twenty times a month and knowing to the last dent every empty lot between him and a destination. Arriving, he could hang around hours for a six-bit commission or a piece of information. "Kotzie takes after my missis. He is *kaltblutig*." Sure I knew it was he himself that did all the trumpeting, screaming, and stamping down in his flat, throwing things on the floor.

"And how is your brother?" he said intriguingly. "I understand the little *maidelech* wet their pants for him. What is he doing?"

As a matter of fact I didn't know what Simon was up to these days. He didn't tell me, nor did he seem curious as to what was happening to me, having decided in his mind that I was nothing but a handyman at Einhorn's.

Once I went with Dingbat to a party one of his fiancées was giving, and I met my brother with a Polish girl in a fur-trimmed orange dress; he wore a big, smooth, check suit and looked handsome and sufficient to himself. He didn't stay long, and I had a feeling that he didn't want to spend his evenings where I did. Or maybe it was the kind of evening Dingbat made of it that didn't please him, Dingbat's recitations and hoarse parodies, his turkey girding and obscene cackles that made the girls scream. There were several months when Dingbat and I were very thick. At parties I horsed around with him, goofy, his straight man; or I hugged and pitched on the porches and in the backyards with girls, exactly as he did. He took me under his protection in the poolroom, and we did some friendly boxing, at which I was never much good, and played snooker—a little better—and hung about there with the hoods and loudmouths. So that Grandma Lausch would have thought that the very worst she had ever said about me let me off too light, seeing me in the shoeshine seat above the green tables, in a hat with diamond airholes cut in it and decorated with brass kiss-me pins and Al Smith buttons, in sneakers and Mohawk sweatshirt, there in the frying jazz and the buzz of baseball broadcasts, the click of markers, butt thumping of cues, spat-down pollyseed shells and blue chalk crushed underfoot and dust of hand-slickening talcum hanging in the air. Along with the blood-smelling swaggeroos, recruits for mobs, automobile thieves, stick-up men, sluggers and bouncers, punks with ambition to become tor-pedoes, neighborhood cowboys with Jack Holt sideburns down to the jawbone, collegiates, tinhorns and small-time racketeers and pugs, ex-servicemen, home-evading husbands, hackies, truckers and bush-league athletes. Whenever some-one had a notion to work out on me—and there were plenty of touchy characters here to catch your eye in a misconstrued way—Dingbat flew around to protect me.

"This kid is a buddy of mine and he works for my bro. Monkey with him and you'll get something broke on your head. What's the matter, you tough or hungry!"

He was never anything but through and through earnest when the subject was loyalty or honor; his bony dukes were ready and his Cuban heels dug down sharply; his furrowed chin was already feeling toward its fighting position on the shoulder of his starched shirt, prepared to go into his stamp-ing dance and start slugging.

But there weren't any fights over me. If there was one doc-trine of Grandma Lausch's that went home, it was the one of the soft answer, though with her this was of tactical not mer-ciful origin, the dust-off for heathen, stupes, and bruteheads. So I don't claim it was a trained spirit turning aside wrath, or *integer vitae* (how could I?) making the wolves respect me; but I didn't have any taste for the perpetual danger-sign, eye-narrowing, tricky Tybalt all coiled up to stab, for that code, and was without curiosity for what it was like to hit and so I refused all the bids to outface or be outfaced.

On this I had Einhorn's views also, whose favorite example was his sitting in the driver's seat of the Stutz—as he some-times did, having been moved over to watch tennis matches or sandlot games—and a coal heaver running up with a tire tool because he had honked once or twice for the Stutz to move and Dingbat wasn't there to move it. "What could I do," said Einhorn, "if he asked me no questions but started to swing or punch me in the face? With my hands on the wheel, he'd think I was the driver. I'd have to talk fast. Could I talk fast enough? What could make an impression on an an-imal like that? Would I pretend to faint or play dead? Oh my God! Even before I was sick, and I was a pretty husky young fellow, I'd do anything possible before I started to trade punches with any sonofabitch, muscle-minded ape or bad character looking for trouble. This city is one place where a person who goes out for a peaceful walk is liable to come home with a shiner or bloody nose, and he's almost as likely to get it from a cop's nightstick as from a couple of square-heads who haven't got the few dimes to chase pussy on the high rides in Riverview and so hang around the alley and plot to jump someone. Because you know it's not the city salary the cops live on now, not with all the syndicate money there is to pick up. There isn't a single bootleg alky truck that goes a mile without being convoyed by a squad car. So they don't care what they do. I've heard of them almost killing guys who didn't know enough English to answer their questions." And now, with eager shrewdness of nose and baggy eyes, he began to increase his range; sometimes, with that white hair bunched over his ears and his head lifted back, he looked grand, suffering more *for* than *from* something, relaxing his tense care of himself. "But there is some kind of advantage in the roughness of a place like Chicago, of not having any illusions either. Whereas in all the great capitals of the world there's some reason to think humanity is very different. All that ancient culture and those beautiful works of art right out in public, by Michelangelo and Christopher Wren, and those ceremonies, like trooping the color at the Horse Guards' parade or burying a great man in the Pantheon over in Paris. You see those marvelous things and you think that everything savage belongs to the past. So you think. And then you have another think, and you see that after they rescued women from the coal mines, or pulled down the Bastille and got rid of Star Chambers and *lettres de cachet*, ran out the Jesuits, increased education, and built hospitals and spread courtesy and politeness, they have five or six years of war and revolutions and kill off twenty million people. And do they think there's less danger to life than here? That's a riot. Let them say rather that they blast better specimens, but not try to put it over that the only human beings who live by blood are away down on the Orinoco where they hunt heads, or out in Cicero. But the best specimens always have been maltreated or killed. I've seen a picture of Aristotle mounted and ridden like a horse by some nasty whore. There was Pythagoras who got killed over a diagram; there was Seneca who had to cut his wrists; there were the teachers and the saints who became martyrs.

"But I sometimes think," he said, "what if a guy came in here with a gun and saw me at this desk? If he said 'Stick 'em up!' do you think he'd wait until I explained to him that my arms were paralyzed? He'd let me have it. He'd think I was reaching in a drawer or pushing a signal button, and that would be the finish of Einhorn. Just have a look at the hold-up statistics and then tell me I'm dreaming up trouble. What I ought to do is have a sign put up above my head saying 'Cripple.' But I wouldn't like to be seeing that on the wall all the time. I just hope the Brink's Express and Pinkerton Protective labels all over the place will keep them away."

He often abandoned himself to ideas of death, and notwithstanding that he was advanced in so many ways, his Death was still the old one in shriveling mummy longjohns; the same Death that beautiful maidens failed to see in their mirrors because the mirrors were filled with their white breasts, with the blue light of old German rivers, with cities beyond the window checkered like their own floors. A cheating old rascal with bones showing in his buckskin fringes, not a gentle Sir Cedric greeting young boys from the branches of an apple tree. Einhorn had no kind familiar thoughts of him, but superstitions about this frightful snatcher, and he only played the Thanatopsis stoic but maneuvered to beat this other, who had already gained so much on him. Who maybe was the only real god he had.

Often I thought that in his heart Einhorn had completely surrendered to this fear. But when you believed you had tracked Einhorn through his acts and doings and were about to capture him, you found yourself not in the center of a labyrinth but on a wide boulevard; and here he came from a new direction—a governor in a limousine, with state troopers around him, dominant and necessary, everybody's lover, whose death was only one element, and a remote one, of his privacy.

Chapter VI

WHAT DID I, out of all this, want for myself? I couldn't have told you. My brother Simon wasn't much my senior, and he and others at our age already had got the idea there was a life to lead and had chosen their directions, while I was circling yet. And Einhorn, what services he needed of me he pretty well knew, but what I was to get from him wasn't at all clear. I know I longed very much, but I didn't understand for what.

Before vice and shortcoming, admitted in the weariness of maturity, common enough and boring to make an extended showing of, there are, or are supposed to be, silken, unconscious, nature-painted times, like the pastoral of Sicilian shepherd lovers, or lions you can chase away with stones and golden snakes who scatter from their knots into the fissures of Eryx. Early scenes of life, I mean; for each separate person too, everyone beginning with Eden and passing through trammels, pains, distortions, and death into the darkness out of which, it is hinted, we may hope to enter permanently into the beginning again. There is horror of grayness, of the death-forerunning pinch, of scandalous mouth or of fear-eyes, and of whatever is caused by no recollection of happiness and no expectation of it either. But when there is no shepherd-Sicily, no free-hand nature-painting, but deep city vexation instead, and you are forced early into deep city aims, not sent in your ephod before Eli to start service in the temple, nor set on a horse by your weeping sisters to go and study Greek in Bogotá, but land in a poolroom—what can that lead to of the highest? And what happiness or misery-antidote can it offer instead of pipes and sheep or musical, milk-drinking innocence, or even merely nature walks with a pasty instructor in goggles, or fiddle lessons? Friends, human pals, men and brethren, there is no brief, digest, or shorthand way to say where it leads. Crusoe, alone with nature, under heaven, had a busy, complicated time of it with the unhuman itself, and I am in a crowd that yields results with much more difficulty and reluctance and am part of it myself.

*

Dingbat, too, for a short while, had his effect on me, speaking of deep city aims. He thought there was a lot he could teach me that even his brother couldn't. I learned about Dingbat that he was full of the thought of justifying himself before the Commissioner and Einhorn and aimed to produce a success, one that was characteristic of him. He swore he would, that it was in him to make a fortune and a reputation, and he wanted to glitter as a promoter, announced on the radio among the personalities that pass through the ring before the main event, his specs like diamonds. Now and then he got a fighter to manage, somebody mesmerizable. And at this time he became the manager of a heavyweight. At last, he said, he had a good one. Nails Nagel. Dingbat had had middles and welters, but a good heavyweight fighter was the biggest dough of all, provided he was championship material, which, Dingbat declared—cried out in his sincerest ready-for-battle assertion—Nails was. Nails sometimes allowed himself to think so too; at heart probably not, or he would have thrown himself full time into it and stopped going back to his job in the auto-wrecking yard. He was both slow and spasmodic in the way he used the grime-crowned hands that ended his rugged white arms, lashed with extra reinforcements of sinew at the joints. His dull and black jaw was similarly reinforced, and it backed stiffly down on his shaven throat to shelter from punches; the top of his head was surrounded by a cap and the visor stuck forward over lair-hidden eyes. Hurt, decent manhood, meaning no wrong or harm, a horsehair coil or ragged ball of slob virility, that was what he made you feel. He was very strong and an angel about taking punishment; also his big white flanky body moved fast enough, for a heavy's. What he didn't have was ring wit. He depended on Dingbat to tell him what to do, suffered himself to be run, and he couldn't differ effectively because his tongue, among missing teeth, was very slow, and the poolroom wisecrackers said, "Change to light oil; she won't turn over in this weather." He was miscast as a fighter, the chicken-woman's son. His mother had worked for years in a poultry-shop back, plucking hens and geese, a burlap-dressed woman who couldn't close her mouth over her teeth. She made good dough, and Nails still took more from her than he ever earned. He was in a racket he only had a strong apparent capacity for.

However, he was cuckoo about being admired as a fighter, and he was unbelievably happy one time when Dingbat brought him along to stand by while he, Dingbat, gave a talk to a boys' club in a basement on Division Street, invited by a poolroom buddy who was sponsor. It went something like this: both Dingbat and Nails in their best clothes, black suede shoes and wearing spotless, eye-cramming fedoras and key chains. "Boys, the first thing you got to understand is how important it is to live clean, train hard, get plenty of milk and vegetables, and sleep with open windows. Take a fighter like my boy here"—happily grinning Nails, toughly sending them his blessings—"on the road, makes no difference where, Nagel works up a full sweat at least once a day. Then, hot shower, cold shower, and a fast rub. He gets the body poisons out of his pores, and the only time he gets to smoke is when I give him a cigar after a vict'ry. I was reading where Tex Rickard wrote the other day in the *Post*, that before the Willard fight, when it was a hundred in the shade out there in Ohio, Dempsey was trained so fine that when he took a nap before the event, in his underwear, they were crisp and there wasn't a drop of sweat on him. Boys, I want to tell you, that's wonderful! That's one of the worth-while ways to be. So take my advice and don't play with your dummy. I can't tell you how important that is. Leave it alone. Not just if you want to be an athlete, and there's few things that's finer, but even if you got other ambitions, that's the first way to go wrong. So hands off; it'll make your brains fuzzy. And don't play gidgy with your little girl friends. It don't do you or them any good. Take it from me, I'm giving it to you straight because I don't believe in shady stuff and hanky-panky. The hot little punks I see around the street—just pass them by. If you got to have a girl friend, and I don't see why not, there's plenty of honest kids to choose from, the kind who'd never grab you by the fly or let you stick around till one a.m. mushing with them on the steps"—and on and on, with his glare of sincerity to the membership on camp chairs.

Being a manager was perfect for Dingbat. And it was just what he needed, to make speeches (his brother was a lodge and banquet orator), and to drag Nails out of his room in the morning for road work in the park, and to coax, coach, neigh, and brandish around and dispute the use of equipment in Trafton's gym, always angrily on his rights over tapes and punching bags in the liniment-groggy, flickety-rope-time, tin-locker-clashing, Loop-darkened rooms and the Polish, Italian, Negro thump-muscled, sweat-glittering training-labor, where the smart crowd of owners and percentage-figurers was. When he had gotten Nails into condition he took him on the road, out West by bus, with money borrowed from Einhorn, but wired from Salt Lake City where they landed broke, and they came back hungry and white. Nails had won two fights in six, and it was hard going among the gibes in the poolroom.

But Dingbat was out of the fight racket for a while; it was at the time of the great jailbreak at Joliet, and he was a corporal in the National Guard called in by the governor. He was around at once in his khakis and corded campaign hat, not hiding the worry that he might be in the patrol that cornered Tommy O'Connor or Larry the Aviator or Bugsy Gonzalez whom he admired.

"Fall in a ditch, stupid, and stay there," Einhorn said to him. "But the state troopers will have them rounded up before you're on the train, and the worst you'll have is a crowded ride and beans to eat."

The Commissioner, whose health hadn't been good lately, called from bed, "Let's see you, Cholly Chaplin, before you leave," and when Dingbat, looking wronged, and leg-bound in the deforming breeches, stood up to him, he said, colossally amused, "Ee-*dyot*!"—Dingbat drawn up in a consumption of misunderstood feelings. Mrs. Einhorn was frightened by the uniform and wept, hanging on Lollie Fewter's neck. Dingbat was bivouacked around Joliet in rainy weather for a few days and came back leaner, blacker, ground into tiredness, with provoked eyes squinty from fatigue. But he took up with Nails immediately. He had gotten him a match in Muskegon, Michigan. Einhorn sent me along to get the lowdown on what happened to Dingbat and Nagel in the sticks. He said, "Augie, I owe you a holiday. If your friend Klein, whom I don't trust too much, will pinch-hit for you here a couple of afternoons, you can go and have an excursion. Maybe it'll give Nagel confidence to have somebody in his corner. Dingbat cracks the whip over him too much and gets him down. Maybe a cheerful third party—*sursum corda*. How good's your Latin, kid?" Einhorn was happy as the devil with his idea; when what he wanted coincided with a good deed, it made his emotions warm. He called his father and said, "Dad, give Augie here ten bucks. He's going on a trip for me"— thus to show that his generosity had an obstacle to pass. The Commissioner gladly gave, being openhanded and bland about any amount; in parting with dough he was exemplary.

Dingbat was glad I was coming, and he made a speech to all, with that animal effrontery of his whenever he was in charge. "All right, fellas; we've got to click this time . . ." Poor Nails, he didn't look good in the Wasps AC mulberry jacket bagging over his muscles, and his togs in the bag hung down to his bowed giant gams as heavy as plumber's tools. An immense face like raked garden soil in need of water. And in this porous dryness, a pair of whity eyes fearing the worst, and a punch-formed nose.

The worst, for that day, had already happened to somebody else; one of the Aiello brothers had been found shot to death in his roadster. There was a big spread on it in the *Examiner;* we read it in the pier-bound trolley, and Nails thought he had played softball once against this Aiello. He was downcast. But it was still very early, right after dawn, when the slum distances of the morning streets were hollow, with only a white drop of sun on the brinks of buildings. When we walked down the pier to the *City of Saugatuck* and came out of the shed, suddenly the town gloom ended in a flaming blue teeter of fresh water, from the black shore-ends down into the golden whiteness eastward. The white-leaded decks had just been washed down and were sparkling with colors of water in a Gulf of Mexico warmth, and the gulls let the air currents carry them around. Dingbat was finally happy. He got Nails to do his road work around the ship before the decks became too crowded. Eight hours on the water without exercise and he'd be too stiff to fight that night. So Nails threw himself into a trot, smiling; he was a changed man in this swift-water sunshine and the gulls dropping almost from a standstill to the surface for pieces of bread. He unpacked a few jabs from the top of his chest, ginger, technical, and dangerous, and Dingbat, in stripes like a locust's leg, advised him to put more shoulder into them. They were pretty convinced they were sailing to a victory. The two of them went into the rosy carpeting of the lounge for coffee. I stayed on deck in joy of the sun, the colors, up in the hay odors from the hatch where there were the horses of a yokel-circuit circus; it sent my blood happy to sit there in the blue and warm, with the slow air coming up against me from my feet in pretty much frazzled gym shoes, large-sized, lettered in india ink, up my jeans, and my head with plenty of hair to cushion it against the bulkhead.

When we were well out on the warm, unsalty water Dingbat walked out of the salon with two young women, friends of Isabel or Janice, whom he had met there, both in tennis whites and ribboned-up hair, starting on vacation, to run and straight-arm high-bounders on the tennis lawn of a Saugatuck resort and canoe their nice busts on the idle shore water. He pointed out the departing sights with his hat, his outstanding hair getting a chance to live in the sun and evaporate its perfumes—what was there better for a rising young fight manager than to stroll in his white shoes and with yachtsman's furl to his pants on a sweet morning indulgent to human hopes and be the cavalier to girls? Nails stayed in the salon, trying to win a prize on a machine called the Claw, a little derrick in a glass case filled with cameras, fountain pens, and flashlights embedded in a hill of chickenfeed candy. For a nickel you could maneuver it by two gadgets, one that aimed and another that gripped the claw. He had nothing to show for fifty cents except a handful of waxy candy. He wanted a camera for his mother.

So he shared the candy with me, on deck, and then declared that he had strained his eyes at the machine and felt dizzy, but it was the motion and the water bursting smoothly at the bow that got him, and when we were in close to the Michigan shore and its groundswell he turned death-nosed, white as a polyp, even in his deepest wrinkles. While he vomited, Dingbat supported him fiercely from the back—his boy, he'd see him through hell—and pleaded with an unhidable bitterness of disappointment, "Oh, man, hold up, for Chrissakes!" But Nails went on heaving and tearing air into his chest, his hair lapping down over his cold face and land-longing eyes. When we touched Saugatuck we didn't dare tell him that we were hours yet from Muskegon. Dingbat took him below to lie down. Nails could feel secure only in a few streets of all the world.

At Muskegon we led him off, yellow and flabby, down the planks of the pier where there wasn't enough motion over the sand of the bottom to camouflage the perch from the afternoon anglers. We went to the YMCA and washed him, got a meal of roast beef, and then went to the gym. Though he complained of a headache and wanted to lie down, Dingbat forced him through his paces. "If I let you, you'll only lie there and feel sorry for yourself, and you won't be able to fight worth a damn tonight. I know what you need. Augie'll go over and get a pack of aspirins. You go on and start running off the meal." I got back with the pills, and Nails, white and crampy from his ten laps of the blind, airless room, sat and panted under the basketball standards, and Dingbat rubbed his chest and tried to pump him with confidence but only gave him more anguish, not knowing how to raise hopes without threats. "Man, where's your will power, where's your reserves!"

It was no use. Already sunset, and the bout an hour away, we sat out in the square, but there was a fresh-water depth smell there, and Nails was queasy and sagged with a hinging head on the bench. "Well, come on," Dingbat said. "We'll do the best we can."

The fight was in the Lions' Club. Nails was in the second event against a man named Prince Jaworski, a drill-operator from the Brunswick plant who got all the encouragement of the crowd, especially as Nails shambled and covered from him or held him in clinches, looking frightened to death in the dry borax sparkle of the ring and gawping out into the ringside faces and the strident blood yells. Jaworski padded after him with wider swings. He had both height and reach on poor Nails, and, I estimate, was about five years younger. Dingbat was frantic with anger at the boos and shouted at Nails when he came to the corner, "If you don't hit him at least once this round I'm gonna walk out and leave you here alone." "I told you we shoulda taken the train," said Nails, "but you were going to save four bucks." He listened, however, to the noise against him, startled in the eyes, and plunged out with more spirit the second round, carrying the fight to Jaworski, reckless, with slum motions of deadliness in his giant white knots. But in the third round he was hit where he could least stand a blow, in the belly, and he went deadweight flat, counted out in a terror of roars and barks, accusations of dive-taking and fixed fight, with Dingbat mounted on the first rope and flapping his hat at the referee, who made a headstall of his hands and covered his ears. Nails came doubled out of the ring, dead-eyed in the white electric brilliance and with a wet moss of whiskers on the stony sponge of his cheeks. I helped him dress and took him back to the YMCA, where I got him into bed and locked him in the room, then waited in the street for Dingbat so that he wouldn't go and kick at his door. But he was too glum and droopy for that. He and I took a walk together and bought lard-fried potatoes at a street wagon, and then turned in.

In the morning we had to cash in our return tickets to pay the hotel bill, for Dingbat had counted on a purse and was flat broke. We hitched rides toward Chicago and spent a night on the beach at Harbert, a little way out of St. Joe, Nails wrapped in his robe and Dingbat and I sharing a slicker. We went through Gary and Hammond that day, on a trailer from Flint, by docks and dumps of sulphur and coal, and flames seen by their heat, not light, in the space of noon air among the black, huge Pasiphaë cows and other columnar animals, headless, rolling a rust of smoke and connected in an enormous statuary of hearths and mills—here and there an old boiler or a hill of cinders in the bulrush spawning-holes of frogs. If you've seen a winter London open thundering mouth in its awful last minutes of river light or have come with cold clanks from the Alps into Torino in December white steam then you've known like greatness of place. Thirty crowded miles on oil-spotted road, where the furnace, gas, and machine volcanoes cooked the Empedocles fundamentals into pig iron, girders, and rails; another ten miles of loose city, five of tight—the tenements—and we got off the trailer not far from the Loop and went into Thompson's for a stew and spaghetti meal, near the Detective Bureau and in the midst of the movie-distributors' district of great posters.

There was nobody much interested in our return. For there had been a fire at Einhorn's meanwhile. It destroyed the living room—big reeking black holes in the mohair, the oriental rug ruined, and the mahogany library table and the set of Harvard Classics on it scorched and soaked by the extinguishers. Einhorn had filed claim for two thousand dollars; the inspector didn't agree that the cause of the fire was a short-circuit but hinted it had been set, and there was opinion heard that he wanted to be paid off. Bavatsky wasn't around; I had to take on part of his duties for a while but had better sense than to ask about him, knowing he must be in hiding. The day the fire broke out Tillie Einhorn had been visiting her cousin-in-law and Jimmy Klein had taken the sick Commissioner to the park. The Commissioner looked vexed about it. His bedroom was off the parlor, where the smell lasted for weeks, and he lay with silent frowns, condemning his son's way of doing business. Tillie had been asking for a new suite, so he had it in for her too —furniture-insatiable women and their nest-winding thoughts.

"Wouldn't I give you the five, six hundred dollars you'll chisel out of the company," the Commissioner said to his son, "so I wouldn't have to smell this *ipisch* in my last days? Willie, you knew I was sick." This was certainly true. Beaky, white, and solemn, Einhorn took the rebuke as deserved, filially, from the Commissioner risen out of bed, in his long underwear and his open, brocaded, heel-touching dressing gown, standing enfeebled in the kitchen and refusing the natural support of the back of a chair, independent. "Yes, Dad," Einhorn answered, the sense of a bad piece of work settled about his neck in two or three loose rings; and without humor but strenuously and almost fiercely he looked at me. Now I had come to know definitely that he was the author of the fire, and probably it was in his thoughts that I was getting to learn all his secrets. They were safe with me, but it injured his pride that they should get out. I made myself inconspicuous and didn't remind him when he forgot my pay that week. Maybe that was too much delicacy, but I was at an exaggerating age.

Summer passed, school reopened, and the insurance company still wasn't satisfied. I heard from Clem that Einhorn was after Tambow Senior to get somebody in City Hall to approach a vice-president about the claim, and I know he got off quite a few letters himself, complaining that one of the biggest brokers couldn't get a small fire settled. How did they expect him to convince clients that their losses would be covered promptly? As you'd expect, he had insured himself with the company that got most of his business. Holloway Enterprises alone paid premiums on a quarter of a million dollars' worth of property, so that there must have been pretty clear proof of arson, for I'm sure the company wanted to be obliging. The reeking, charred furniture, covered with canvas, remained until the Commissioner wouldn't have it around any more, and it was moved into the yard where the kids played King of the Hill on it and the junkmen came offering to take it away, sweating around the office humbly till Einhorn would see them and say, no, he was thinking of donating it to the Salvation Army when the claim was settled.

Really, he had already promised to sell it to Kreindl, who was going to have it re-covered. Especially because of the inconvenience, Einhorn was set on getting full value out of it. And because of the scorn of the Commissioner. But on the whole he thought he had been right; that this was the way you answered your wife's request for a new living-room suite. He made me a present of the Harvard Classics with the covers ruined by the carbonic spray. I kept the volumes in a crate under my bed and started on Plutarch, Luther's letters to the German nobility, and *The Voyage of the Beagle*, in which I got as far as the crabs who stole the eggs of stupid shorebirds.

I couldn't read more because I didn't have much studious peace at night. The old lady had become loose in the wires and very troublesome, with the great weaknesses of old age. Although she had always claimed she hadn't taught Mama anything if not to be a great cook, she now wanted to cook for herself and set aside pots and pans for her own use, and groceries and little jars in the icebox covered with paper and bound with elastic, forgot them till mold set in, and then was scratching mad when they were thrown out, accused Mama of stealing. She said two women could not share a kitchen—forgetting how long it had been shared—especially if one was dishonest and dirty. Both trembled, Mama from the scare more than from the injustice; she tried to locate the old woman with her eyes, which were deteriorating very fast. To Simon and me Grandma scarcely ever spoke any more, and when the puppy her son Stiva gave her—she couldn't really accept a successor to Winnie but anyway demanded a dog—when it ran to us she cried, "*Beich du! Beich!*" But the tawny little bitch wanted to play and wouldn't lie at her feet as the old dog had done. She wasn't even named or housebroken properly, such was the condition the women were in now. Simon and I agreed to take turns cleaning; Mama couldn't any longer keep up with it. But Simon worked downtown, so there was no way to make a fair division. And there wasn't any longer enough character in the house even to give a name to and domesticate this pup. I couldn't go on crawling under Grandma Lausch's bed, one of the dirtiest places, while she, glaring into a book, refused to say a single word, blind and dumb toward me unless her *beich* yipped around my cuffs, when she would shriek. This was where much of my time was going.

And, furthermore, since Mama couldn't go alone to visit Georgie, because of her eyesight, we had to take her to the far West Side. George was bigger than I now, and sometimes a little surly and offended with us, though still with the same mind-crippled handsomeness, a giant moving with slow-pants, mature heaviness in the dragfoot gait of his undeveloped legs. He wore my hand-me-downs and Simon's, and it was singular to see the clothes worn so differently. At the school they had taught him broom-making and weaving and showed us the thistle-flower neckties he made with wool on a frame. But he was growing too old for this boys' Home; in a year or so he'd have to move on to Manteno or one of the other downstate institutions. Mama took this very badly. "There maybe once or twice a year we'll be able to visit him," she said. Going to see this soft-faced man of a George wasn't easy on me either. So, afterward, on these trips, as I had money in my pockets these days, I'd take Mama into a fancy Greek place on Crawford Avenue for ice-cream and cakes, to try to raise her out of her rock-depth of heavy trouble, where, I guess, the greater part of human beings have always spent most of their silent time. She let me divert her somewhat,

even if rattled by the fancy prices, and protesting in high
tones of a person unaware of what a sound she is making. To
which I'd say calmingly, "It's okay, Ma. Don't worry." Because Simon and I were still at school we were still on charity,
and with both of us working and George in the institution,
we had more dough than we'd ever had. Only it was Simon
who took care of the surplus, and no longer Grandma, as in
the old administration.

Sometimes I had glimpses of Grandma in the parlor, at the
light end of the dark hallway, in her disconnection from us,
waiting by herself beside the Crystal-Palace turret of the
stove, in dipping bloomers and starched dress with hem as
stiff as a line of Euclid. She had too many wrongs against us
now to forgive us, and they couldn't be discussed. From
weakness of mind of the very old. She that we always had
thought so powerful and shock-proof.

Simon said, "She's on her last legs," and we accepted her
decline and dying. But that was because we were already out
in the world, whereas Mama didn't have any such perspective.
Grandma had laid most of her strength on Mama as boss-
woman, governing band, queen mother, empress, and even
her banishment of George and near-senile kitchen scandals
couldn't shake the respect and liege feeling so long established. Mama wept to Simon and me about Grandma's
strange alteration but couldn't answer her according to her
new folly.

But Simon said, "It's too much for Ma. Why should the
Lausches get away with sloughing the old woman off on us?
Ma's been her servant long enough. She's getting older herself and her eyes are bad; she can't even see the pooch when
it's under her feet."

"Well, this is something we ought to leave up to Ma herself."

"For Chrissake, Augie," said Simon, blunt—his broken
tooth showed to much effect when he was scornful—"don't
be a mushhead all your life, will you! Honest to God, you
make me think I was the only one of us born with a full set
of brains. What good is it to let Mama decide?" I usually
didn't find much to offer when it was a question of theory or
reality with regard to Mama. We treated her alike but thought
about her differently. All I had to say was that Mama wasn't

used to being alone and, as a fact, my feelings took a bad drop when I imagined it. She was already nearly blind. What would she do but sit by herself? She had no friends, and had always shambled around on her errands in her man's shoes and her black tam, thick glasses on her rosy, lean face, as a kind of curiosity in the neighborhood, some queer woman, not all there.

"What kind of company is Grandma though?" said Simon.

"Oh, maybe she'll come around a little. And they still talk sometimes, I guess."

"When did she ever? Bawls her out, you mean, and makes her cry. The only thing you're saying is that we should let things ride. That's only laziness, even though you probably tell yourself you're just an easygoing guy and don't want to be ungrateful to the old dame for what she's done. We did things for her too, don't forget. She's been riding Ma for years and put on the ritz at our expense. Well, Ma can't do it any more. If the Lausches want to hire a housekeeper, that's a fair way to settle it, but if they don't they're going to have to take her out of here."

He wrote a letter to her son in Racine. I don't know what things were like with these two Quaker-favored men in their respective towns. I've never gone through a place like Racine without thinking which house with the rubber-tire swing for kids and piano-practicing inside was like Stiva Lausch's, who had two daughters brought up with every refinement, including piano lessons, and how such little-speaking Odessa-bred sons had gotten on a track like this through the multiverse. What did they go for, that they were so regular and unexcitable of appearance? Well, there was at least a hint of what in the note that Stiva sent, pretty calmly saying that he and his brother didn't feel a housekeeper was the solution and that they were making arrangements for their mother to live in the Nelson Home for the Aged and Infirm, and would consider it a great service if we would move her there. Which, considering our long association with their mother (a dig at our ingratitude), they didn't hesitate to request.

"This is it then," said Simon, and even he looked as if we had gone too far. But the thing was done, and there were only last details to attend to. Grandma had received a letter in

Russian at the same time, and took it with considerable coolness, as you expect from somebody with that degree of pride,
boasting even, "Ha! How well Stiva writes Russian! In the
gymnasium, when you learned, you *learned* something." We
heard from Mama also what Grandma said about the Home,
that it was a very fine old place, just about a palace, built by
a millionaire, and had a greenhouse and garden, was near the
university and therefore most of the people retired professors.
Going to a better place. And she was glad of rescue from us
by her sons; where she would be among equals and exchange
intelligent views. Mama was confounded, aghast at the thing,
and not even she was so simple-minded as to believe that
Grandma, so many years bound to us, would have thought it
up herself, as she now apparently claimed.

The packing went on for two weeks. Pictures came off the
walls, the monkeys with scarlet nose holes, the runner from
Tashkent, egg cups, salves and medicines, her eiderdown from
the closet shelf. I brought up her wood trunk from the shed,
a yellow old pioneer piece with labels from Yalta, Hamburg
Line, American Express, old Russian journals in its papered
interior of blue forest flowers, smelly from the cellar. She
wrapped with caution each of her things of great value, the
crushable and breakable on top, and covered all with the
harsh snow of mothflakes. On the final day she watched the
trunk wag down the front stairs, on the back of the mover,
with an amazing, terrible look of presidency, and supervised
everything, every last box, in this fashion, gruesomely and violently white so that her mouth's corner hairs were minutely
apparent, but in rigid-backed aristocracy, full face to the important transfer to something better, from this (now that she
turned from it) disgracefully shabby flat of a deserted woman
and her sons whom she had preserved while a temporary
guest. Ah, regardless how decrepit of superstructure, she was
splendid. You forgot how loony she'd become, and her can-
tankerousness of the past year. What was a year like that when
now her shakiness of mind dropped off in this moment of
emergency and she put on the strictness and power of her
most *grande-dame* days? My heart went soft for her, and I felt
admiration that she didn't want from me. Yes, she made retirement out of banishment, and the newly created republi-

cans, the wax not cool yet on their constitution, had the last pang of loyalty to the deposed, when mobs, silent, see off the limousine, and the prince and princely family have the last word in the history of wrongs.

"Be well, Rebecca," said the old woman. She didn't exactly decline Mama's weeping kiss on the side of the face, but was objective-bound primarily. We helped her into the panting car, borrowed from Einhorn. Tensely, with impatience, she said good-by, and we started—me managing around with the big, awkward apparatus of the hostile tomato-burst red machine and its fire-marshal's brass. Dingbat had just taught me how to drive.

Not a word passed between us. I don't count what she said in the Michigan Boulevard crush, because that was just a comment about the traffic. Out of Washington Park we turned east on Sixtieth Street, and, sure enough, there was the university, looking strange but restful in its Indian summer rustle of ivy. I located Greenwood Avenue and the Home. In front was a fence of four-by-fours, sharp angles up, surrounding two plots of earth and flower beds growing asters that leaned on supports of sticks and rags; on the path to the sidewalk black benches made of planks; and on the benches on the limestone porch, on chairs in the vestibule for those who found the sun too strong, in the parlor on more benches, old men and women watched Grandma back down from the car. We came up the walk, between the slow, thought-brewing, beat-up old heads, liver-spotted, of choked old blood salts and wastes, hard and bone-bare domes, or swollen, the elevens of sinews up on collarless necks crazy with the assaults of Kansas heats and Wyoming freezes, and with the strains of kitchen toil, Far West digging, Cincinnati retailing, Omaha slaughtering, peddling, harvesting, laborious or pegging enterprise from whale-sized to infusorial that collect into the labor of the nation. And even somebody here, in old slippers and suspenders or in corset and cottons, might have been a cellar of the hidden salt which preserves the world, but it would take the talent of Origen himself to find it among the terrible appearances of white hair and rashy, vessel-busted hands holding canes, fans, newspapers in all languages and alphabets, faces gone in the under-surface flues and in the eyes, of these people sitting in the sunshine and leaf-burning outside or in the mealy moldiness and gravy acids in the house. Which wasn't a millionaire-built residence at all, only a onetime apartment house, and no lovely garden in the back but corn and sunflowers.

The truck arrived with the rest of Grandma's luggage; she wasn't allowed to have the trunk in her bedroom, for she shared it with three others. She had to go down to the basement where she picked out what she would need—too many things, in the opinion of the stout brown lady superintendent. But I carried the stuff up and helped her to stow and hang it. I then went to the back of the Stutz to search, on her orders, for anything that might have been forgotten. She didn't discuss the place with me, and of course she would have praised it if she had found anything to praise to show what an advantageous change she had made. But neither did she let me see her looking downcast. She ignored the matron's suggestion that she get into a housedress and sat down in the rocker with a view of the corn, sunflower, cabbage lot in the back, in her Odessa black dress. I asked her if she would care for a cigarette, but she wasn't having anything from anyone and especially not from me—the way she felt Simon and I were repaying her years of effort. I knew she needed to be angry and dry if she was to avoid weeping. She must have cried as soon as I left, for she wasn't so rattlebrained by old age that she didn't realize what her sons had done to her.

"I have to bring back the car, Grandma," I said at last, "so I'll have to go now, if there isn't anything else you want done."

"What else? Nothing."

I started to leave.

She said, "There's my shoebag I forgot to take. The chintz one inside the clothescloset door."

"I'll bring it out soon."

"Mama can keep it. And for your trouble, Augie, here's something." She opened her purse of dull large silver antennae and with short gesture she gave me an angry quarter—the payoff—which I couldn't refuse, couldn't pocket, could scarcely close my hand on.

Things were in a queer way at Einhorns' too, where the

Commissioner was dying in the big back room, while up front, in the office, deeds were changing hands with more thousands and greater prosperity than ever. A few times a day Einhorn had himself wheeled to his father's bedside to ask advice and get information, now everything was in his hands, grave and brow-drawn as he began to feel the unruliness of what he had to manage, and all the social chirping of the office became the dangerous hints of the desert. Now you could see how much he had been protected by the Commissioner. After all, he became a cripple at a young age. Whether before or after marriage I never did find out—Einhorn said after marriage, but I heard it told here and there that the Commissioner had paid off Mrs. Einhorn's cousin Karas (Holloway) and bought his paralytic son a bride. That she loved Einhorn wasn't any evidence against this, for it'd be constitutional with her to adore her husband. Anyhow, regardless of what he bragged, he was a son who had lived under his father's protection. That's something that *I* wouldn't have failed to see. And his world-gypping letters and operations, and all his poetical schemes, even if he had a son at the university himself, were doings of a boy. And, indulged so long, into middle age, how was he going to get over it? He thought, by being fierce and serious. He stopped his old projects; "The Shut-In" wasn't published any more and the on-approval packages no longer opened—I toted them down to the storeroom with the pamphlets and the rest of the daily prizes of the mail; and he got himself consumed by business and closed and opened the deals on the Commissioner's calendar, began or dissolved partnerships in lots or groceries in the suburbs, and, on his own—the kind of thing he loved—cheaply bought up second mortgages from people who needed ready money. He insisted on kickbacks from plumbing, heating, or painting contractors with whom the Commissioner had always been cronies, and so made enemies. That didn't bother him, to whom the first thing was that the fainéants shouldn't be coming after Charlemagne—as long as people understood that. And furthermore, the more difficulty and tortuousness there were, the more he felt safe. So there were quarrels about broken agreements; he'd never pay bills till the last day of grace; and most people who put up with this did it for the Commissioner's sake. He grabbed command very toughly. "I can argue all day the runner didn't touch base," he said, "even if I know damn well he did. The idea shouldn't get started that you can be made to back down."

This was the way the lessons and theories of power were taught to me in the intervals of quiet that became fewer and fewer; and these lessons were self-addressed mostly, explanations of what he was doing, that it was right.

At this time all his needs were very keen, and he wanted things in the house he hadn't cared much about before—a special kind of coffee that only one place in town carried, and he ordered several bottles of bootleg rum from Kreindl, which was one of Kreindl's sidelines; he brought them in a straw satchel from the South Side, where he was in second- or third-hand touch with all kinds of demon, dangerous elements. But Kreindl had an instinct to get people what they had a craving for—of a steward or batman or fag or a Leporello or pimp. He hadn't quit on Five Properties. And now that the Commissioner was dying, and Dingbat, who would inherit a lot of money, was still unmarried, Kreindl hung out at Einhorn's, keeping the Commissioner company in the bedroom, talking to Dingbat, and having long conversations privately with Einhorn, who made use of him in various ways.

One of their subjects was Lollie Fewter, who had quit in September and was working downtown. Einhorn suffered over her no longer being in the house, impossible as it would have been during his father's sickness and his increased work to put the blocks to her as in the leisurely summer. There were always people in the flat and office. But it was now that he wanted her and kept sending her notes and messages and harping about it. And at such a time! It hurt him too. Nevertheless he kept thinking how, in spite of the time, he could carry it off, and didn't merely brood, but discussed, obstinately, how it could be done. I heard him with Kreindl. And still he was the family leader, the chief, the man of administration and thought, responsible custodian, remarkable son of a remarkable father. Awfully damn remarkable. Even the rising of his brows toward his whitening hair was that. And what if, together with this, he had his inner and personal growths of vice, passion, even prurience, unbecoming obscenity? Was it unbecoming because he was a cripple? And then if you satisfy that difficult question by saying it's not up to us to declare what a man should renounce because he is crippled or otherwise cursed, there's still the fact that Einhorn could be ugly and malicious. You can know a man by his devils and the way he gives hurts. But I believe he has to run a chance of injuring himself too. In this way you can judge, if he does it safely for himself, that he is wrong. Or if he has no spur gear to something not himself. And Einhorn? Jesus, he could be winsome—the world's charm-boy. And that was distracting. You can grumble at it; you can say it's a ruse of feint of gifted people to sidetrack you from the viper's tangle and ugly knottedness of their desires, but if the art of it is deep enough and carried far enough into great play, it gets above its origin. Providing it's festive, which sometimes it was with Einhorn, when he was not merely after something but was gay. He could be simple-hearted. Nevertheless I was down on him occasionally, and I said to myself he was nothing—nothing. Selfish, jealous, autocratic, carp-mouth, and hypocritical. However, in the end, I every time had high regard for him. For one thing, there was always the fight he had made on his sickness to consider. No doubt smiting the sledded Polack on the ice was more, or being a Belisarius, and Grail-seeking was higher, but weighing it all up, the field he was put into and the weapons he was handed, he had made an imposing showing and, through mind, he connected with the spur gear that I mentioned. He knew what retributions your devils are liable to bring for the way you treat wife and women or behave while your father is on his deathbed, what you ought to think of your pleasure, of acting like a cockroach; he had the intelligence for the comparison. He had the intelligence to be sublime. But sublimity can't exist only as a special gift of a few, due to an accident of origin, like being born an albino. If it were, what interest could we have in it? No, it has to survive the worst and find itself a dry corner of retreat from the mad, bloody wet, and mud-splashing of spike-brains, marshals, Marlboroughs, gold-watch-consulting Plugsons, child-ruiners, human barbecuers, as well as from the world-wide livery service of the horsemen of St. John. So why be down on poor

Einhorn, afflicted with mummy legs and his cripple-irritated longings?

Anyway, I stood by him, and he said to me, "Oh, that bitch! That lousy freckle-faced common coal-mine whore!" And he sent messages by Kreindl to her, downtown, with lunatic offers. But also he said, "I know I'm no goddam good to have pussy on the brain at a time like this. It'll be my downfall." Lollie answered his notes but didn't come back. She had other ideas for herself.

And meantime the Commissioner was passing out of the picture. At first he had lots of friends coming to see him in the onetime sumptuous bedroom, furnished by his third wife, who had left him ten years ago, with an Empire four-poster bed and gilded mirrors, Cupid with his head inside a bow. Spittoons on the floor, cigars on the dresser, check stubs and pinochle decks, it had become an old businessman's room. He seemed to enjoy himself, when old-country and synagogue buddies and former partners were there, telling them he was done for. It wasn't a habit he could check, joking, having joked all his life. Coblin came often, on Sunday afternoons, and Five Properties in the milk truck during the week—for a young man, he had considerable orthodoxy; respectful form, anyhow. I can't say I believe he cared a whole lot, but his presence was not a bad thing and showed he knew at least where the right place for the heart was. And probably he approved of the way the Commissioner was making his death, his first-class stoicism. Kinsman the undertaker, the Einhorns' tenant, was very disturbed that he could not visit and stopped me in the street to ask after the Commissioner, begging me not to mention it. "Those are my worst times," he said. "When a friend is passing I'm about as welcome as old Granum who works for me." Old Granum was the deathbed watcher and Psalm reciter, feeble and ruination-faced, in Chinatown black alpaca and minute, slippered feet. "If *I* come," said Kinsman, "you know what people think."

As the old man made deeper progress toward death fewer visitors were allowed, and the *klatch* ruled by his deep wise-cracking tones ended. Now Dingbat was with him most, and he didn't need to be urged by Einhorn to come out of the poolroom to tend his father but was much affected; he had been the last to accept the doctor's forecast and said confidently, "That's the way all croakers talk when an old fellow is sick. Why, the Commissioner is really built, he's powerful!" But now he hastened in and out of the room on his noisy and clumping tango-master's heels, fed the Commissioner and rubbed him down and shagged away the kids who played on the furniture in the backyard. "Beat it, you little jag-offs, there's a sick person here. Damn snots, where's your upbringing!" He kept the sickroom dark and camped on a hassock, reading *Captain Fury, Doc Savage,* and other pulp sports stories by the vigil light. I saw the Commissioner afoot only once, at this stage, when Einhorn sent me to his study to fetch some papers, and in the darkness of the living room the Commissioner was rambling slowly in his underclothes, looking for Mrs. Einhorn, to demand an explanation for missing buttons, annoyed that from neck to bottom there were only two and he was exposed and naked between. "That's no way!" he said. "*Lig a naketter.*" He was angry still about the fire.

At last Dingbat surrendered his place in the bedroom to Kinsman's Granum, when the Commissioner seldom roused and, awake, didn't easily recognize anyone. But he did recognize the bricky, open sponge-ball cheeks of the old watcher in the towel-looped twelve-watt light, and said, "*Du?* Then I slept longer than I thought." Which Einhorn repeated scores of times, mentioning Cato and Brutus and others noted for the calm of their last moments; he was a collector of facts like these, and shook down all he read, Sunday supplements, Monday reports of sermons, Haldeman-Julius blue books, all collections of sayings, for favorable comparisons. Things that didn't always fit. Not that this old lover the Commissioner doesn't deserve citation for having no alarm and dying undisgusted, without last minute revision of lifetime habits.

He was laid out that night in a colossal coffin, at Kinsman's. When I came in the morning the office was shut, with the shades in green and black wrinkles against the cold sunshine and dry fall weather, and I went round the back. The mirrors had been covered by Mrs. Einhorn, in whom superstition was very strong, and a candle burned down in a pale white ecclesiastical glass in the dark dining room by a photo of the Commissioner taken when his Bill Cody whiskers were still full and glossy. Arthur Einhorn had come from Champaign for his grandfather's funeral and sat at the table in detached college elegance, hand in his woolly intellectual hair, taking it easy in the expected family folly of such an occasion; he was engaging and witty, though not youthful in appearance—he had lines in his cheeks already—despite his raccoon coat that was lying on the buffet with a beret dropped on it. Einhorn and Dingbat had razor slits in their vests, symbolizing rent clothes. The ex-Mrs. Tambow was there, in duenna hairdress and arched pince-nez, along with her son Donald, who sang at receptions and weddings; and, also on family duty, Karas-Holloway and his wife, she with poodle tuft on the front of her head and her usual concentrated unrest or dislike. She had a lot of flesh, and her face was red, resentful, criticizing. I was aware that she was always after her cousin-in-law to protect herself from the Einhorns. She didn't trust them. She didn't trust her husband either, who gave her everything, a large super-decorated flat on the South Side, Haviland china, venetian blinds, Persian rugs, French tapestry, Majestic radio with twelve tubes. That was Karas, in a sharkskin, double-breasted suit and presenting a look of difficulties in shaving and combing terrifically outwitted, the knars of his face gotten-around and his hair flattened. His smoothness was a huge satisfaction to him, as, also, his extraordinary English that hadn't hampered him in making a fortune, plus his insignificance in the old country—people gave way before his supple wrinkles and small eyes and, comparably, the onslaught of his six-cylinder car, a yellow Packard.

Long afterward I had a queer ten minutes with Mrs. Karas, in a bakery near Jackson Park where I came in with a Greek girl she assumed to be my wife because we were arm in arm, in summer flannels, intimate early in the morning. She recognized me on the spot, with a coloring of extreme pleasure, but with errors of memory there was no stopping or correcting, they were so singular. She told the girl I had been practically a relative to her, she had loved me as much as Arthur, and received me in her own house like kin—all joy and happy reunion, she was, embracing me by the shoulders to say how fine and handsome I had become, but then my complexion had always been the envy of girls (as if I had been Achilles among the maidens, in the office and poolroom). I must say I was stumped by such major will to do over the past with affection and goodness. People have been adoptive toward me, as if I were really an orphan, but she had never been like that, but only morose with her riches, and mad at her mystifying, dapper husband, and critical of the Einhorns. I had been in her flat only as Einhorn's chauffeur and sat in another room while they visited. Tillie Einhorn, not the hostess, brought me sandwiches and coffee from the table. And now Mrs. Karas, who had come out to buy rolls for breakfast, fell into a lucky chance to adorn the past with imaginary flowers grown in worried secret. I didn't deny anything; I said it was all true, and allowed her her enthusiasm. She even chided me for not coming to visit her. But I remembered her off-with-their-heads stony-facedness and the breakfast before the funeral when I helped out in the kitchen. Bavatsky made the coffee.

Einhorn, weary but not crushed, had his black homburg on the back of his head as he smoked—no word to spare for me but an occasional one of command. Dingbat insisted with dry, roughened voice that he was going to wheel his brother into Kinsman's parlors. After that it was I who carried Einhorn, not Arthur, who walked alongside with his mother. On my back, I took him in and out of the limousine, in the autumn park of the cemetery, low-grown with shrubs and slabs; back again to the cold-cuts dinner for the mourners, and afterward, at nightfall, to the synagogue in his black duds, his feet riding stirrupless and weak by sides and his cheek on my back.

Einhorn wasn't religious, but to go to the synagogue was due form and, regardless of what he thought, he knew how to conduct himself. The Coblins belonged to this congregation too, and I had strung along with Cousin Anna in the oriental, modified purdah of the gallery while she wept for Howard amid the coorooing and smelling salts of the women in finery, sobbing at who would be doomed the coming year by fire or water—as the English text translated it. This was different, however, from the times of crowds praying below in shawls and business hats, and the jinking of the bells on the velvet dresses of the two-legged scrolls. It was dark, and a small group, the shaggy evening regulars, various old faces and voices, gruff, whispered, wheezy, heart-grumbled, noisily swarm-toned, singing off the Hebrew of the evening prayers. Dingbat and Einhorn had to be prompted when it came their turn to recite the orphans' *Kaddish.*

We went back in Karas's Packard, with Kreindl. Einhorn whispered to me to tell Kreindl to go home. Dingbat turned in. Karas was off to the South Side. Arthur had gone to visit friends; he was leaving for Champaign in the morning. I got Einhorn into more comfortable clothes and slippers. There was a cold wind pouring and moonlight in the backyard.

Einhorn kept me with him that evening; he didn't want to be alone. While I sat by he wrote his father's obituary in the form of an editorial for the neighborhood paper. "The return of the hearse from the newly covered grave leaves a man to pass through the last changes of nature who found Chicago a swamp and left it a great city. He came after the Great Fire, said to be caused by Mrs. O'Leary's cow, in flight from the conscription of the Hapsburg tyrant, and in his life as a builder proved that great places do not have to be founded on the bones of slaves, like the pyramids of Pharaohs or the capital of Peter the Great on the banks of the Neva, where thousands were trampled in the Russian marshes. The lesson of an American life like my father's, in contrast to that of the murderer of the Strelitzes and of his own son, is that achievements are compatible with decency. My father was not familiar with the observation of Plato that philosophy is the study of death, but he died nevertheless like a philosopher, saying to the ancient man who watched by his bedside in the last moments . . . ." This was the vein of it, and he composed it energetically in half an hour, printing on sheets of paper at his desk, the tip of his tongue forward, scrunched up in his bathrobe and wearing his stocking cap.

We then went to his father's room with an empty cardboard file, locked the doors and turned on the lights, and began to go through the Commissioner's papers. He handed me things with instructions. "Tear this. This is for the fire, I don't want anyone to see it. Be sure you remember where you put this note—I'll ask for it tomorrow. Open the drawers and turn them over. Where are the keys? Shake his pants out.

Put his clothes on the bed and go through the pockets. So this was the deal he had with Fineberg? What a shrewd old bastard, my dad, a real phenomenon. Let's keep things in order now—that's the main thing. Clear the table so we can sort stuff out. Lots of these clothes can be sold, what I won't be able to wear myself, except it's pretty old-fashioned. Don't throw any little scraps of paper away. He used to write important things down that way. The old guy, he thought he'd live forever, that was one of his secrets. I suppose all powerful old people do. I guess I really do myself, even on the day of his death. We never learn anything, never in the world, and in spite of all the history books written. They're just the way we plead or argue with ourselves about it, but it's only light from the outside that we're supposed to take inside. If we can. There's a regular warehouse of fine suggestions, and if we're not better it isn't because there aren't plenty of marvelous and true ideas to draw on, but because our vanity weighs more than all of them put together," said Einhorn. "Here's a thing about Margolis, who lied yesterday when he said he didn't owe Dad anything. '*Crooked Feet, two hundred dollars!*' He'll pay me or I'll eat his liver, that two-faced sonofabitch confidence man!"

At midnight we had a pile of torn papers, like the ballots of the cardinals whose smoke announces a new pontiff. But Einhorn was dissatisfied with the state of things. Most of his father's debtors were indicated as Margolis had been—"Farty Teeth," "Rusty Head," "Crawler," "Constant Laughter," "Alderman Sam," "Achtung," "The King of Bashan," "Soup Ladle." He had made loans to these men and had no notes, only these memoranda of debts amounting to several thousand dollars. Einhorn knew who they were, but those who didn't want to pay didn't actually have to. It was the opening indication that the Commissioner had not left him as strong as he believed, but subject to the honor of lots of men he hadn't always treated well. He became worried and thoughtful.

"Is Arthur in yet?" he nervously said. "He's got an early train to make." In the demolition of the once gorgeous room where the old man had been camped ruggedly in female luxury, he reflected with the round eyes of a bird about his son, and then, more easily, he observed, "Well, this stuff isn't for him, anyway; he's with poets and intelligent people, having conversation." He always spoke this way of Arthur, and it gave him first-rate solace.

Chapter VII

I'M THINKING of the old tale of Croesus, with Einhorn in the unhappy part. First the proud rich man, huffy at Solon, who, right or wrong in their argument over happiness, must have been the visiting Parisian of his day, and condescending to a rich island provincial. I try to think why didn't the warmth of wisdom make Solon softer than I believe he was to the gold- and jewel-owning semibarbarian. But anyway he was right. And Croesus, who was wrong, taught his lesson with tears to Cyrus, who spared him from the pyre. This old man, through misfortune, became a thinker and mystic and advice-giver. Then Cyrus lost his head to the revengeful queen who ducked it in a skinful of blood and cried, "You wanted blood? Here, drink!" And his crazy son Cambyses inherited Croesus and tried to kill him in Egypt as he had put his own brother to death and wounded the poor bull-calf Apis and made the head-and-body-shaved priests grim. The Crash was Einhorn's Cyrus and the bank failures his pyre, the poolroom his exile from Lydia and the hoodlums Cambyses, whose menace he managed, somehow, to get round.

The Commissioner died before the general bust, and wasn't very long in his grave when the suicides by skyscraper leaps began to take place in La Salle Street and downtown New York. Einhorn was among the first to be wiped out, partly because of the golden trust system of the Commissioner and partly because of his own mismanagement. Thousands of his dough were lost in Insull's watered and pyramided utilities—Coblin too dropped lots of money on them—and he lost his legacy, and Dingbat's and Arthur's inheritance as well, by throwing it into buildings that in the end he couldn't hold. And at the finish he had nothing but vacant lots in the barren Clearing and around the airport, and of these several went for taxes; and when I sometimes took him for a ride he'd say, "We used to have that block of stores, over there," or, of a space full of weeds between two shanties, "Dad got that in a trade eight years ago and wanted to build

a garage on it. Just as well he never did." So it was a melancholy thing to drive him, although he didn't make a heavy
grouse; his observations were casual and dry.

Even the building in which he lived, constructed by the
Commissioner with a cash outlay of a hundred thousand dollars, was finally lost as the shops closed and the tenants in the
flats upstairs stopped paying rent.

"No rent, no heat," he said in the winter, resolving to be
tough. "A landlord ought to act like one or give up his property. I'll stick by economic laws, good times, bad times, and
be consistent." This was how he defended his action. He was
taken to court, however, and lost, legal costs and all. He then
rented the empty stores as flats, one to a Negro family and
another to a gypsy fortuneteller, who hung a painted hand
and giant, labeled brain in the window. There were fights in
the building and thefts of pipes and toilet fixtures. By now the
tenants were his enemies, led by the red-headed Polish barber
Betzhevski, who had given mandolin concerts on the sidewalk
in affable days, and now glared with raw winter eyes when he
passed in front of Einhorn's plate glass. Einhorn started evic-
tion proceedings against him and several others, and for this
he was picketed by a Communist organization.

"As if I didn't know more about communism than they
do," he said with bitter humor. "What do *they* know about it,
those ignorant bastards? What does even Sylvester know
about revolution?" Sylvester was now a busy member of the
Communist party. So Einhorn sat at the Commissioner's
front desk where the pickets could see him, to await action by
the sheriff's office. He had his windows smeared with candle
wax, and a paper sack of excrement was flung into the
kitchen. Whereupon Dingbat organized a flying squad from
the poolroom to guard the building; Dingbat was in a killing
rage against Betzhevski and wanted to raid his shop and
smash his mirrors. It wasn't much of a shop Betzhevski had
moved into at this point of the Depression, a single chair in a
basement, where he also kept canaries in a sad Flemish gloom.
Clem Tambow still went to him to be shaved, saying that the
red-headed barber was the only one who understood his
beard. Dingbat was annoyed with him for it. But Betzhevski
was evicted, and his wife stood on the sidewalk and cursed

Einhorn for a stinking Jew cripple. There was nothing Dingbat could do to her. Anyhow, Einhorn had commanded, "No
rough stuff unless I say so." He didn't rule it out, but he was
going to control it, and Dingbat was obedient, even though
Einhorn had lost him every cent of his legacy. "It didn't hit
only just us," Dingbat said, "it hit everybody. If Hoover and
J.P. Morgan didn't know it was coming, how should Willie?
But he'll bring us back. I leave it to him."

The reason for the evictions was that Einhorn had had an
offer from a raincoat manufacturer for the space upstairs.
Walls were torn out in several apartments before City Hall
came down on him for violating fire and zoning ordinances
and trying to get industrial current into a residential block.
By that time some of the machinery had already been installed, and the manufacturer—a shoestring operator himself
—was after him to foot the bill for removal. There was another suit about this when Einhorn tried to claim, throwing
away all principle, that the machinery was bolted to the
floor, hence real property belonging to him. He lost this case
too, and the manufacturer found it handier to break out
windows and lower his equipment by pulley than to disas-
semble it, and he got a court order to do so. Einhorn's
huge, chain-hung sign was damaged. Only this didn't matter
any more because he lost the building, his last large property, and was out of business. The office was shut down and
most of the furniture sold. Desks were piled on desks in the
dining room and files by his bed, so that it could be approached only from one side. Against better times, he
wanted to keep as much furniture as he could. There were
swivel chairs in the living room, where the burned furniture
(the insurance company was kaput and had never paid his
claim), cheaply reupholstered and smelling of fire, was
brought back.

He still owned the poolroom, and personally took over the
management of it; he had a sort of office installed in the front
corner, around the cash register, and still, after a fashion, did
business. Dropped down into this inferior place, he was slow
to get over it. But in time he became chief here too, and had
reorganizing ideas for which he began to accumulate money.
First, a lunch counter. The pool tables were shifted to make

room. Then a Twenty-Six green diceboard. He had remained a notary public and insurance agent, and he got himself accredited by the gas, electric, and telephone companies to take payment of bills. All this slowly, for things had low action these mortified times, and even his ingenuity was numb from the speed and depth of the fall, and much of his thought went into tracing back the steps he should have taken to save at least Arthur's money—and Dingbat's. Besides, there was the environment, narrowed down to a single street and place now that he had lost all other property, the thickened and caked machine-halted silence from everywhere lying over this particular sparseness and desolation, plus the abasement from dollars to nickels. And he, a crippled and aging man, scaled down from large plans to mere connivances. In his own eyes, the general disaster didn't excuse him sufficiently—it was that momentum he had which often blurred out others—and it appeared that as soon as he inherited the Commissioner's fortune it darted and wriggled away like a collection of little gold animals that had obeyed only the old man's voice.

"Of course," he explained sometimes, "it isn't personally so terrible to me. I was a cripple before and am now. Prosperity didn't make me walk, and if anybody knew what a person is liable to have happen to him, it's William Einhorn. You can believe that."

Well, yes, I both could and couldn't. I knew this assurance was a growth of weak light, more pale than green, and what a time of creeping days he had had when he lost the big building and the remaining few thousands of Arthur's legacy in the final spurt to save it, inspired by pride instead of business sense. He officially let me go then, saying weakly, "You're a luxury to me, Augie. I'll have to cut you out." Dingbat and Mrs. Einhorn took care of him during that bad period when he kept to his study, hard hit; overcome, in his black thought, many days unshaved—and he a man who depended for the whole tone of life on regularity in habit—before he left the drab, bookish room and declared he was taking over in the pool hall. An Adams, beaten for the presidency, going back to the capital as a humble congressman. Unless he took Arthur out of the university and sent him to work—provided Arthur would have agreed—he had to do something, for there was nothing to fall back on; he had even turned his insurance policies in to raise cash for the building.

And Arthur had no profession; he had been—unlike Kreindl's son Kotzie, the dentist, who now supported his family—given a liberal education in literature, languages, and philosophy. Suddenly what the sons had been up to became exceedingly important. Howard Coblin earned money with his saxophone. And Kreindl didn't any longer scoff to me about his son's unnatural coolness with women. Instead he advised me to ask him for a job in the pharmacy below his office. Kotzie got me a relief spot behind the counter as apprentice soda jerk. I was thankful, for Simon had graduated from high school and was cut off from Charity. Also, he had lost some of his days at the La Salle Street Station. Borg was putting in his own jobless brothers-in-law and giving others the shove, left and right.

As for the savings, the family money Simon had handled as Grandma's successor, they were gone. The bank had closed in the first run, and the pillared building was now a fish store—Einhorn had a view of it from his poolroom corner. Still, Simon graduated pretty well—I can't understand how he managed—and was elected class treasurer, in charge of buying rings and school pins. It was his rigorous-looking honesty, I suppose. He had to account to the principal for the money, but that didn't keep him from fixing a deal with the jeweler and making a clear fifty dollars for himself.

He was up to much; so was I. We kept it from each other. But I, because I watched him by long habit, knew somewhat what he was up to, whereas he didn't pause to look back over my doings. He signed up at the municipal college, with the idea that everyone had then of preparing for one of the Civil-Service examinations. There was a rush on for Weather Bureau, Geological Survey, and post-office jobs, from the heavy-print announcements in layers of paper on the school and library bulletin boards.

Simon had forefront ability. Maybe his reading was related to it, and the governor's clear-eyed gaze he had developed. Of John Sevier. Or of Jackson in the moment when the duelist's bullet glanced off the large button of his cloak and he made ready to fire—a lifted look of unforgiving, cosmological captaincy; that look where honesty had the strength of a prejudice, and foresight appeared as the noble cramp of impersonal worry in the forehead. My opinion is that at one time it was genuine in Simon. And if it was once genuine, how could you say definitely that the genuineness was ever all gone. But he used these things. He employed them, I know damned well. And when they're used consciously, do they turn spurious? Well, in a fight, who can lay off his advantages?

Maybe Grandma Lausch had gotten her original dream scheme of Rosenwald or Carnegie favors from appreciation of this gift of Simon's. Standing at a corner brawl, he would be asked by a cop, from among a dozen volunteer witnesses, what had happened. Or when the coach came out of the gym-supply room with a new basketball, tens of arms waving around, beseeching, it would be Simon, appearing passive, that he flung it to. He expected it and was never surprised.

And now he was on soggy ground and forced to cut down the speed he had been making toward the mark he secretly aimed at. I didn't know at the time which mark or exactly understand why there needed to be a mark; it was over my head. But he was getting in, all the time, a big variety of information and arts, like dancing, conversation with women, courtship, gift-giving, romantic letter-writing, the ins and outs of restaurants and night clubs, dance halls, the knotting of four-in-hands and bow ties, what was correct and incorrect in tucking a handkerchief in the breast pocket, how to choose clothes, how to take care of himself in a tough crowd. Or in a respectable household. This last was a poser for me, who had not assimilated the old woman's conduct lessons. But Simon, without apparently paying attention, had got the essential of it. I name these things, negligible to many people, because we were totally unfamiliar with them. I watched him study the skill of how to put on a hat, smoke a cigarette, fold a pair of gloves and put them in an inner pocket, and I admired and wondered where it came from, and learned some of it myself. But I never got the sense of luxury he had in doing it.

In passing through the lobbies of swank places, the Palmer Houses and portiered dining rooms, tassels, tapers, string ensembles, making the staid bouncety tram-tram of Vienna waltzes, Simon had absorbed this. It made his nostrils open. He was cynical of it but it got him. I ought to have known, therefore, how ugly it was for him to be in the flatness of the neighborhood, spiritless winter afternoons, passing time in his long coat and two days unshaven, in a drugstore, or with the Communist Sylvester in Zechman's pamphlet shop; sometimes even in the poolroom. He was working only Saturdays at the station, and that, he said, because Borg liked him.

We had a little time for palaver, in the slowness of the undeveloping winter, sitting at the lunch counter of the poolroom by the window that showed out on horse-dropped, coal-dropped, soot-sponged snow and brown circulation of mist in the four o'clock lamplight. When we had done the necessary at home for Mama, set up the stoves, got in groceries, taken out the garbage and ashes, we didn't stay there with her—I less than Simon, who sometimes did his college assignments on the kitchen table, and she kept a percolator going for him on the stove. I didn't pass on to him the question that Jimmy Klein and Clem asked of me, namely, whether Sylvester was converting him to his politics. I had confidence in the answer I gave, which was that Simon was hard up for ways to kill time, and that he went to meetings, bull sessions and forums, socials and rent parties, from boredom, and in order to meet girls, not because he took Sylvester for one of the children of morning, but he went for the big babes in leather jackets, low heels, berets, and chambray workshirts. The literature he brought home with him kept coffee rings off the table the morning after, or he tore the mimeographed pages with his large blond hands to start the stove. I read more of it than he did, with puzzled curiosity. No, I knew Simon and his idea of the right of things. He had Mama and me for extra weight, he believed, and wasn't going to pick up the whole of a class besides, and he wouldn't have Sylvester's moral sentiments any more than he would buy a suit that didn't fit. But he sat in Zechman's shop, calm, smoking sponged cigarettes, under the inciting proletarian posters, hearing Latinistic, Germanic, exotic conversation, with large young side of jaw at rest on his collar in the yellow smoke of cold air, mentally blackballing it all.

That he showed up in the poolroom was a surprise to me

too, in view of what he had formerly said about my tie-in with the Einhorns. But the explanation was the same—because it was a dull time, because he was broke; he soon kept company with bear-eyes Sylvester in his pamphlet-armed war with the bourgeoisie and took lessons in pool from Dingbat. He became good enough at it to win some in rotation at a nickel a ball, staying away from the deadeyes who made their career in the parlor. Occasionally he played craps in the back room, and his luck at this was pretty fair, too. He kept clear of the hoodlums, torpedoes, and thieves on their professional side. In that regard he was smarter than I, for I somehow got to be party to a robbery.

I ran with Jimmy Klein and Clem Tambow much of the time. Toward the last high-school terms I hadn't been seeing a lot of them either. Jimmy's family was hard hit by the unemployment—Tommy lost his job at City Hall when the Republicans were pushed out by Cermak—and Jimmy was working a great deal; he was also studying bookkeeping at night, or trying to, for he was no good at figures or at any head work for that matter. Only he had much determination to get ahead for the sake of his family. His sister Eleanor had gone to Mexico, by bus the entire journey, to see whether she could make a go of it with the cousin there, the one that had started Jimmy's interest in genealogy.

As for Clem Tambow, his contempt of school was extreme, and he passed as much time as he could get away with in bed, reading screen news, going over scratch sheets. He was developing into a superior bum. Through his mother, he carried on a long-term argument with her second husband, who didn't have a job either, about his habits. A neighbor's son was working as a pin boy in a downtown alley for thirty cents an hour; why, therefore, did *he* refuse to look for work? They were all four living in the back rooms of the infants'-wear shop that the ex-Mrs. Tambow ran by herself. Bald, with harsh back-hair, Clem's stepfather, in his undershirt, read the *Jewish Courier* by the stove and prepared lunch of sardines, crackers, and tea for them all. There were always two or three King Oscar cans on the table, rolled open, and also canned milk and oysterettes. He was not a fast-thinking man and didn't have many subjects. When I visited and saw him in the cirrus-cloud weave of his wool undershirt, the subject was always what was I earning.

"Do stoop labor?" said Clem to his mother when she took it up with him. "If I can't find anything better I'll swallow cyanide." And the thought of swallowing cyanide made him laugh enormously, with a great "haw, haw, haw!" bigmouthed, and shake his quills of hair. "Anyhow," he said, "I'd rather stay in bed and play with myself. Ma"—his mother in her skirts and with feet of a dancer of Spanish numbers— "you're not too old to know what I mean. You're in the room next to mine, remember, you and your husband." He made her gasp, unable to answer because of me, but staring at him with furious repudiation. "Put on with me, that's okay—what should I suppose you got married for?"

"You oughtn't talk to your old lady like that," I said privately to him.

He laughed at me. "You should spend a couple of days and nights around here—you'd say I was going easy on her. Her pince-nez takes you in, and you don't know what a letch she's got. Let's face the facts." And of course he told me these facts, and it seemed even I figured in them, that she had made sly inquiries about me and said how strong I looked.

In the afternoon Clem took a walk; he carried a cane and had British swagger. He read the autobiographies of lords from the library and guffawed over them and played the Piccadilly gentleman with Polack storekeepers, and he was almost always ready to burst out haw-hawing with happy violence, decompression, big thermal wrinkles of ugly happiness in his red face. When he could cadge a few bucks from his father he bet on the horses; if he won he'd stand me to a steak dinner and cigars.

I was around people of other kinds too. In one direction, a few who read whopping books in German or French and knew their physics and botany manuals backwards, readers of Nietzsche and Spengler. In another direction, the criminals. Except that I never thought of them as such, but as the boys I knew in the poolroom and saw also at school, dancing the double-toddle in the gym at lunch hour, or in the hot-dog parlors. I touched all sides, and nobody knew where I belonged. I had no good idea of that myself. Whether I'd have been around the poolroom if I hadn't known and worked for Einhorn I can't say. I wasn't a grind certainly, or a memorizing eccentric; I wasn't against the grinds and eccentrics either. But it was easier for the gangsters to take me for one of them. And a thief named Joe Gorman began to talk to me about a robbery.

I didn't say no to him.

Gorman was very bright, handsome and slim, clever at basketball. His father, who owned a tire shop, was well off, and there was no apparent reason for him to steal. But he had a considerable record as a car thief and was in St. Charles twice. Now he intended to rob a leather-goods shop on Lincoln Avenue, not very far from the Coblins', and there were three of us for the job. The third was Sailor Bulba, my old lockermate who had stolen my science notebook. He knew I wasn't a squealer.

Gorman would get his father's car for the getaway. We'd break into the shop by the cellar window at the rear and clean out the handbags. Bulba would hide them, and there was a fence in the poolroom named Jonas who would sell them for us.

On one o'clock of an April night we drove to the North Side, parked beside an alley, and one by one slipped into the backyard. Sailor had cased the place; the half-size basement window had no bars. Gorman tried to open it, first with a jimmy and then with bicycle tape, a technique he had heard of in the poolroom but never tried. It didn't work. Then Sailor rolled a brick in his cap and pounded out the pane. After the noise we scattered into the alley, but crept back when no one came. I was sick with the thing by now, but there was no getting out of it. Sailor and Gorman went in and left me as lookout. Which didn't make much sense, for the window was the only way of escape, and if I had been caught by a squad car in the alley they'd never have gotten away either. Nevertheless, Gorman was the experienced one, and we took his orders. There was nothing to hear but rats or paper scuttling. Finally there was a noise from the cellar, and Gorman's sharp, pale face came up below; he started handing out the bags to me, soft things in tissue paper, which I stuffed into a duffel bag I had carried under my trench coat. Bulba and I ran through backyards into the next street with the stuff, while Gorman drove the car around. We dropped Bulba at the rear of his house; he tossed the bag over the fence and vaulted after, swinging up with a wide flutter of his sailor pants and landing in cans and gravel. I walked home by a short cut, over lots, got the key out of the tin mailbox, and went into the sleeping house.

Simon knew I had come in very late and said that at midnight Mama had come in to ask where I was. He didn't appear to care what I had been up to, or notice that I was, behind my casualness, miserable. I had stayed awake hours trying to figure out how I was to explain the twenty or thirty dollars my cut probably would amount to. I thought to ask Clem to say that we had won together on a horse, but that didn't appear feasible. And it really wasn't a difficulty at all, since I could give it to my mother bit by bit over a period of weeks, and besides, nobody, as in Grandma's days, watched closely what I was doing. It was a while before I could think straight about it, having the shakes.

But I wasn't afflicted long. From reasons of temperament. I went to school, missing only one period; I showed up for glee-club rehearsal, and at four o'clock went to the poolroom, and Sailor Bulba was sitting up in a shoeshine chair in his bell-bottomed pants, observing a snooker game. It was all right. Everything was already arranged with Jonas, the fence, who would take the stuff that night. I put the whole thing out of mind, and in this had the help of perfect spring, when the trees were beginning to bud. Einhorn said to me, "They're having bicycle races over in the park. Let's take them in," and I willingly carried him out to the car and we went.

I had decided there wasn't going to be any more robbery for me, now that I knew what it was like, and I told Joe Gorman that he wasn't to count on me for future jobs. I was prepared to be called yellow. But he didn't take on and wasn't scornful. He said quietly, "Well, if you think it isn't your dish."

"That's just the way it is—it isn't my dish."

And he said thoughtfully, "Okay. Bulba is a jerk, but I could get along swell with you."

"No use doing it if it isn't in me."

"What the hell for then? Sure."

He was very mild and independent. He combed his hair in the gum-machine mirror, fixed up his streaming tie, and went away. Thereafter he didn't have much to say to me.

I took Clem out, and we blew in the money together. But I wasn't done with this matter by a long shot. Einhorn found out about it through Kreindl, who was approached by the fence to peddle some of the bags. Probably Kreindl and Einhorn decided that I should get a going-over for it. So Einhorn called me to sit by him, one afternoon in the poolroom. I saw from his stiffness that he was getting up an angry blow against me, and of course I knew why.

"I'm not going to sit by and let you turn into jailbait," he said. "I partly consider myself responsible that you're in this environment. You're not even of age to be here, you're still a minor"—so, by the way, were Bulba and Gorman and dozens of others, but nothing was ever made of it—"though you're overgrown. But I won't have you doing this, Augie. Even Dingbat, and he's no mental giant, knows better than to get into robbery. I have to put up with all kinds of elements around here, unfortunately. I know who's a thief or gunman or whoremaster. I can't help it. It's a poolroom. But, Augie, you know what better is; you've been with me in other times, and if I hear of you on another job I'm going to have you thrown out of here. You'll never see the inside of this place or Tillie and me again. If your brother knew about this, by Jesus Christ! he'd beat you. I know he would."

I admitted that it was so. Einhorn must have seen the horror and fear in me as through a narrow opening. My hand lay where he could reach it; he put his fingers on it. "This is where a young fellow starts to decay and stink, and his health and beauty go. By the first things he does when he's not a boy any longer, but does what a man does. A boy steals apples, watermelons. If he's a wildcat in college he writes a bad check or two. But to go out as an armed bandit—"

"We weren't."

"I'll open this drawer," he said with intensity, "and give you fifty bucks if you'll swear Joe Gorman didn't have a gun. I tell you he had one."

I was hot in the face but faint. It could be true; it was plausible.

"And if the cops had come he'd have tried to shoot his way out. That was what you let yourself in for. Yes, that's right, Augie, a dead cop or two. You know what cop-killers get, from the station onward—their faces beaten off, their hands smashed, and worse; and that would be your start in life. You can't tell me there's nothing but boyish high-jinks spirits in that. What did you do it for?"

I didn't know.

"Are you a real crook? Have you got the calling? I don't think I ever saw a stranger case of deceiving appearances then. I had you in my house and left stuff in the open. Were you tempted to steal, ever?"

"Hey, Mr. Einhorn!" I said, violent and excited.

"You don't have to tell me. I know you didn't. I only asked if you have the real impulses from the bottom, and I don't believe you do. Now, for God's sake, Augie, stay away from those thieves. I'd give you twenty bucks for your widowed mother if you asked me. Did you need it so badly?"

"No."

It was kindness itself of him to call Mama a widow when he knew she really wasn't.

"Or were you looking for a thrill? Is this a time to be looking for a thrill, when everybody else is covering up? You could take it out on the roller coasters, the bobs, the chute-the-chutes. Go to Riverview Park. But wait. All of a sudden I catch on to something about you. You've got *opposition* in you. You don't slide through everything. You just make it look so."

This was the first time that anyone had told me anything like the truth about myself. I felt it powerfully. That, as he said, I did have opposition in me, and great desire to offer resistance and to say "*No!*" which was as clear as could be, as definite a feeling as a pang of hunger.

The discoverer of this, who had taken pains to think of me —to *think* of me—I was full of love of him for it. But I was also wearing the discovered attribute, my opposition. I was clothed in it. So I couldn't make any sign of argument or indicate how I felt.

"Don't be a sap, Augie, and fall into the first trap life digs for you. Young fellows brought up in bad luck, like you, are naturals to keep the jails filled—the reformatories, all the institutions. What the state orders bread and beans long in advance for. It knows there's an element that can be depended on to come behind bars to eat it. Or it knows how much broken rock for macadam it can expect, and whom it can count on to break it, and whom it can expect for chancre treatments at the Public Health Institute. From around here and similar parts of the city, and the same in other places throughout the country. It's practically determined. And if you're going to let it be determined for you too, you're a sucker. Just what's predicted. Those sad and tragic things are waiting to take you in —the clinks and clinics and soup lines know who's the natural to be beat up and squashed, made old, pooped, farted away, no-purposed away. If it should happen to you, who'd be surprised? You're a setup for it."

Then he added, "But I think I'd be surprised." And also, "I don't ask you to take me for your model either," too well realizing the contradiction, that I knew about his multifarious swindles.

Einhorn had his experts who tinkered with the gas meters; he got around the electric company by splicing into the main cables; he fixed tickets and taxes; and his cleverness was unlimited in these respects. His mind was continually full of schemes. "But I'm not a lowlife when I think, and *really* think," he said. "In the end you can't save your soul and life by thought. But if you *think*, the least of the consolation prizes is the world."

He continued, but my thoughts took their own direction. No, I didn't want to be what he called determined. I never had accepted determination and wouldn't become what other people wanted to make of me. I had said "No" to Joe Gorman too. To Grandma. To Jimmy. To lots of people. Einhorn had seen this in me. Because he too wanted to exert influence.

To keep me out of trouble and also because he was accustomed to have a delegate, messenger, or trusted hand, he hired me again for less money. "Don't forget, old man, I've got my eye on you." Didn't he always have his eye on as many things and people as he could get in range? Conversely, however, I had my eye on him. I took closer interest in his swindles than when I had been not much more than houseboy and the Einhorn business was too vast for me to understand.

One of the first things I helped with was a very dangerous piece of work—taking in a gangster, Nosey Mutchnik. A few years before, Nosey Mutchnik, nothing but a punk, had worked for the North Side gang, throwing acid on clothes in dry-cleaning shops that wouldn't buy protection and doing similar things. Now he had reached a higher stage, when he had money and was looking for investments, particularly in real estate. For, he said seriously to Einhorn, on a summer evening, "I know what happens to guys who stay in the rackets. In the end they get blasted. I seen it happen enough."

Einhorn told him he knew of a fine vacant lot that they could buy as partners. "If I'm going into it with you myself, you don't have to worry that it's not on the up and up. I stand to lose if you do," he said with sincere heart to Mutchnik. The asking price for the property was six hundred dollars. He could get it down to five. This was a perfectly just assurance, because Einhorn himself owned the lot, having acquired it from a buddy of his father's for seventy-five dollars; and he now became its half-owner at a further profit. All this was done by means of various tricks, and very coolly. It ended well, with Mutchnik finding a buyer for it, delighted to make a hundred dollars in a piece of legitimate business. But if he had found out he would have shot Einhorn or had him shot. Nothing simpler to do, or more natural in his eyes, in defense of his pride. I was in terror that Mutchnik might have taken a notion to investigate in the Recorder's Office and find out that a relation of Mrs. Einhorn had nominally owned the lot. But Einhorn said, "What are you bothering your head about, Augie? I've got this man figured out. He's terribly stupid. I keep suggesting angles to him for his protection."

Thus, without risking a cent, Einhorn made more than four hundred dollars in this particular deal. He was proud, gleeful with me; this was what he really dug. It was a specimen triumph of the kind—only bigger and bigger—he wanted his whole history to consist of. While he sat still at his Twenty-Six baize board, the leather dice cup there, and the green reflected up to his face, his white skin and underpainted eyes.

He kept the valuable ivory cue balls by him in a box, inside the nickel-candy case, and his attention to what went on in the establishment was keen and close. He ran it his own way entirely.

I never knew another poolroom where there was a woman permanently, like Tillie Einhorn, behind the lunch counter. She served very good chili con, omelettes, navy bean soup, and learned to operate the big coffee urn, even the exact moment to throw in salt and raw egg to make the coffee clear. She took to this change in her life energetically, and physically she appeared to become broader and stronger. She flourished, and the male crowd made her tranquil. There was a lot said or shouted that she didn't know the meaning of, which was to the good. She didn't soften things in the poolroom, or put a limit, like a British barmaid or bistro proprietress; here things were too harsh and ornery to be influenced; the clamor and fights and the obscene yelling and banging weren't going to stop, and didn't stop. Only she somehow became part of the place. By limiting herself to the chili, wieners and beans, coffee and pie.

The Depression had altered Einhorn too. Retrospectively, he was rather green in the Commissioner's lifetime, and some ways, for his years, unformed. Now he was no longer second-to-last, but the last and end-term of his family; there was nobody expected to die before he did, and, you could say, troubles came directly to his face, and he showed the test of them. No more willowiness; he had to get thicker and harder, and so he did. But toward women he didn't change at all. He saw fewer of them, naturally, than in past days. What women entered a poolroom? Lollie Fewter didn't come back to him. And for him—well, I suppose that souls not in the very best state have to have organizing acts, devices that brace them, must shave or must dress. To Einhorn, the enjoyment of a woman not his wife was such an organizing act. And Lollie must have been important to him, for he kept track of her to the last, for better than ten years, that is, when she was shot by a teamster-lover, the father of several children, whom she got involved in black marketing. He was caught, and there was prison coming to him, and no rap for her. Therefore he killed her, he said, "So another guy wouldn't live rich with her off my troubles." Einhorn saved the clippings from the papers. "You see what he says—'live rich'? Living rich was what it was with her. I can tell you." He wanted me to know he could. He could tell me indeed, and there were few people better placed than I to hear it from him.

"Poor Lollie!"

"Ah, poor, poor kid!" he said. "But I think she was bound to die like that, Augie. She had a Frankie-and-Johnny mentality. And when I knew her she was beautiful. Yes, she was rich." All white-headed, and shrunken some from his former size, he told me about her with fervor. "They say she was getting sloppy toward the end, and greedy about money. That was bad. There's trouble enough from fucking. She was made to have a violent thing happen to her. The world doesn't let hot blood off easy."

Wrapped and planted in this was an appeal to me to remember his hot blood. My services to him had put me in some striking positions—he wanted to know what thought I had of them, maybe; or, humanly enough, whether I would celebrate them with him. Oh, the places where pride won't make a stand!

What I was particularly bidden to recall in this talk was the night of my graduation from high school. The Einhorns had been extremely kind to me. A wallet with ten dollars in it was my present from the three of them, and Mrs. Einhorn came to the graduation exercises with Mama and the Kleins and Tambows that February night. Afterward there was a party at the Kleins', where I was expected. I drove Mama home from the assembly—I didn't have my name in the evening program, like Simon, but Mama was pleased and smoothed my hand as I was leading her upstairs.

Tillie Einhorn waited below in the car. "You go to your party," she said as I was taking her back to the poolroom. My having finished high school was of immense importance in her eyes, and she honored me extraordinarily, in the tone she took. She was a warm woman, in most matters very simple, she wanted to give me some sort of blessing, and my "education" had, I think, suddenly made her timid of me. So we drove in the black and wet cold to the poolroom, and she said several times over, "Willie says you got a good head. You'll be a teacher yourself." And then she crushed up against me in her sealskin coat, belonging to the good days, to kiss me on the cheek, and had the happy tears of terribly deep feeling to wipe from her face before we went into the poolroom. Behind this, probably, was my "orphancy," and the occasion woke it up. We were dressed in our best; Mrs. Einhorn even gave off a perfume, in the car, from her silk scarf and dress established with silver buttons on her breast. We crossed the wide sidewalk to the poolroom. Below, the windows, as required by law, were curtained, and above, the rods of the signs writhed in their colors in the wet. The crowd in the poolroom was small tonight because of graduation. So you could hear the kissing of the balls from the farthest cavelike lights and soft roaring of green tables, and the fat of wieners on the grill. Dingbat came from the back, holding the wooden triangular ball rack, to shake hands.

"Augie is going to a party by Klein," said Mrs. Einhorn.

"Congratulations, son," said Einhorn with state manners. "He's going, Tillie, but not right away. I have a treat for him first. I'm taking him to a show."

"Willie," she said, disturbed, "let him go. Tonight it's his night."

"Not just a neighborhood movie, but to McVicker's, a stage show with little girls, trained animals, and a Frenchman from the Bal Tabarin who stands on his head on a pop bottle. How does that sound to you, Augie? Like a good thing? I planned it out a week ago."

"Sure, that's all right. Jimmy said the party would run late, and I can go after midnight."

"But Dingbat can take you, Willie. Augie wants to be with young people tonight, not with you."

"If I'm going out Dingbat is needed here and will stay here," said Einhorn and shook off her arguments.

I wasn't so intoxicated with its being *my* night that I couldn't see a reason for Einhorn's insistence, a small darkness of a reason no bigger than a field mouse yet and very swift.

Mrs. Einhorn dropped her hands to her sides. "Willie, when he *wants*—" she apologized to me. But I was practically one of the family, now that no inheritances were in the way. I tied on his cloak and carried him to the car. My face was red in the night air, and I was annoyed. For it was a chore to take Einhorn to the theater, and there were many steps and negotiations necessary. First to park the car, and then to find the manager and explain that two seats had to be found near the exit; next to arrange to have the steel firedoors opened, to drive down the alley, tote Einhorn into the theater, back out of the alley, and find another parking space. And at that, once in the theater, you sat at a bad angle to the stage. He had to be right next to the emergency exit. "Imagine me in the middle of a stampede in case of fire," he said. Hence we saw things to the side of the main confrontation of the big dramatic shell, powder and paint on the faces, and voices muffled, then loud, or glenny silver, and frequently didn't know what made the audience laugh.

"Don't speed," said Einhorn to me on Washington Boulevard. "Take it slow here." I suddenly observed that he had an address in his hand.

"It's near Sacramento. You didn't think I really was going to drag you to McVicker's tonight, did you, Augie? No, we're not going downtown. This place I'm taking you to, I've never been in before. It's a back entrance, I understand, and on the third floor."

I stopped the car and went out to scout, came back when I had found the joint, and got him on my back. He used to talk about himself as the Old Man of the Sea riding Sinbad. But there was Aeneas too, who carried his old dad Anchises in the burning of Troy, and *that* old man had been picked by Venus to be her lover; which strikes me as the better comparison. Except that there was no fire or war cry around us, but dead-of-night silence on the boulevard, and ice. I went down the narrow cement walk, below sleeping windows, with Einhorn telling me, clear and loud, to watch my step. Luckily I had cleared out my locker that day and was wearing the rubbers that had lain at the bottom of it the better part of a year, and so my feet didn't slip. But it was difficult work all the same, up the wooden stairs and under the short clotheslines on the porches. "This better be it," he said when I rang the bell on the third floor, "or they'll be asking me what the hell I'm doing." It always was he who was principally present in a place.

But we hadn't rung the wrong bell. A woman opened the door, and I said, "Where?" out of wind. "Go on, go on," said Einhorn. "This is only the kitchen." Which it was; a beery place. I walked with him carefully into the parlor and put him down before the astonished people there, on the couch. Seated, he felt equal to them all and looked at all the women. I stood beside him and looked too, in great eagerness and excitement. I always felt, in taking him somewhere, a great sense of responsibility; and here, far more than ever, I sensed how heavy his dependence on me was. And I didn't want to have to worry about it now. Though he didn't look at a disadvantage, only imperious and imperturbable, with no uneasy flinch of disgrace at being a man of importance seen helpless before terrible needs. "I heard the girls were nice here," he said, "and they are nice. Pick one out."

"Me?"

"Of course you. Which one of you girls is going to entertain this handsome boy who graduated from high school tonight? Look around, kid, and keep your head," he said to me.

The madam came to the parlor from one of the rooms. Her peculiarity was in the paint of her face, the insect dust or lampblack of colors and moth's wing red of the cheek pigment.

"Mister," she began to say.

But it was all right. Einhorn had a card from someone, and it had been prearranged, as she recalled. Only she hadn't been told, I could see, that Einhorn would be carried in. He wouldn't have trusted himself here without an introduction.

Nevertheless there was embarrassment, and Einhorn sat shoe to shoe and in the banker's trousers covering his immovable legs. When I think of it with a collected mind, Einhorn, asking who would entertain me, might well have been voicing anticipation of the aversion of the girl *he* chose. Even here, where he was paying. But perhaps it wasn't so. My head was a long way from being clear in this lionish place, the paltry, ritzy den of a parlor, and he maybe was not as bold and easy as he sounded.

At last Einhorn said to the girl he had called over to chat with, "Which is your room, kid?" and with perfect calm, ignoring the effect of it, had me carry him there. A pink coverlet was on the bed (this was a better-class place as I was later to know by contrast), and she skimmed it off. I laid him down. As the girl, in a corner of the room, began to take off her clothes, he beckoned me to bend to him again and whispered, "Take my wallet," and I took out the heavy leather article and put it in my pocket. "Hang on to it," he said. The look of his eye was bold, full, even resentful. Resentful of this posture, I think, not of me. There was a pressure in his face, and his hair spread on the pillow. He began to talk to the woman in a tone of instruction. "Take off my shoes," he said. She did. He watched in that active way; along the line of his entire body his glance went, to the woman in her wrapper who bent over his feet, this woman of strong neck and red fingernails, standing in a pair of felt slippers by the bed. "Just a thing or two more I have to tell you," he said. "There's my back; I have to go easy till I'm set right, miss, and take everything step by step."

"Haven't you gone yet?" He saw me by the door. "Go on, do you have to be told what to do? I'll send them for you after."

I didn't have to be told, but as long as he didn't send me from him I'd have delayed.

I went back to the parlor, where there was someone waiting for me; the rest had gone, so the choice had been made for me. As always with strangers, I behaved as if I knew exactly what I was doing and from an idea that at a critical time it was best and most decent to have my own momentum. She did not take this away from me. She whose business or burden it was to be calm in the primal thing, where no one else is, and have an advantage of the strong. She wasn't young—the women had made the right choice for me—and she had sort of a crude face; but she encouraged me to treat her lover-like. Undressing, she had playful frills or point edges on her underthings—these gewgaws that go with the imposing female fact, the brilliant, profound thing. My clothes were off and I waited. She approached and took me round the body. She even set me on the bed. As if, it being her bed, she'd show me how to use it. And she pressed up her breasts against me, she curved her shoulders back, she closed her eyes and held me by the sides. So that I didn't lack kindness of person and wasn't pushed off when done. I knew later I had been lucky with her, that she had tried not to be dry with me, or satirical, and done it mercifully.

Yet when the thrill went off, like lightning smashed and dispersed into the ground, I knew it was basically only a transaction. But that didn't matter so much. Nor did the bed; nor did the room; nor the thought that the woman would have been amused—with as much amusement as could make headway against other considerations—at Einhorn and me, the great sensationalist riding into the place on my back with bloodshot eyes and voracious in heart but looking perfectly calm and superior. Paying didn't matter. Nor using what other people used. That's what city life is. And so it *didn't* have the luster it should have had, and there *wasn't* any epithalamium of gentle lovers. . . .

I had to wait for Einhorn in the kitchen, and to think of him, close by, having this violence done to him for his pleasure. The madam didn't look pleased about it. Other men were coming in, and she was mixing drinks in the kitchen, and I came in for peevish glances until Einhorn's girl came in dressed again to have me fetch him. The madam went along with me for the money, and Einhorn paid with finesse and gave tips, and as I carried him through the parlor where my partner was with another man, smoking a cigarette. Einhorn said to me for my private ear, "Don't look at anybody, understand?" Was he afraid to be recognized, or was this order simply about the best composure for passing through the parlor again with him clinging to my back in his dark garments?

"You'll have to be careful as hell about the way you go down," he said on the porch. "It was stupid not to bring a flashlight. All we need now is a spill." And he laughed; with irony, but laughed. The house was thoughtful though, and a whore came out, in a coat like any ordinary woman, to light our way down to the yard, where we thanked her and all politely said good night.

I brought him home and took him into the house, though the poolroom was still open, and he said, "Never mind putting me to bed. Go on to your party. You can take the car, but don't go getting drunk and joy-riding, that's all I ask.

Chapter VIII

FROM HERE a new course was set—by us, for us: I'm not going to try to unravel all the causes.

When I face back I can recognize myself as of this time in intimate undress, with my own and family traits of hands and feet, greenness and grayness of the eyes and up-springing hair; but at myself fully clothed and at my new social passes I have to look twice. I don't know how it all at once came to me to talk a lot, tell jokes, kick up, and suddenly have views. When it was time to have them, there was no telling how I picked them from the air.

The city college Simon and I attended wasn't a seminary in charge of priests who taught Aristotle and casuistry and prepared you for European games and vices and all the things, true or not true, actual or not actual, nevertheless insisted on as true and actual. Considering how much world there was to catch up with—Asurbanipal, Euclid, Alaric, Metternich, Madison, Blackhawk—if you didn't devote your whole life to it, how were you ever going to do it? And the students were children of immigrants from all parts, coming up from Hell's Kitchen, Little Sicily, the Black Belt, the mass of Polonia, the Jewish streets of Humboldt Park, put through the coarse sifters of curriculum, and also bringing wisdom of their own. They filled the factory-length corridors and giant classrooms with every human character and germ, to undergo consolidation and become, the idea was, American. In the mixture there was beauty—a good proportion—and pimple-insolence, and parricide faces, gum-chew innocence, labor fodder and secretarial forces, Danish stability, Dago inspiration, catarrh-hampered mathematical genius; there were waxed-eared shovelers' children, sex-promising businessmen's daughters—an immense sampling of a tremendous host, the multitudes of holy writ, begotten by West-moving, factor-shoved parents. Or me, the by-blow of a traveling man.

Normally Simon and I would have gone to work after high school, but jobs weren't to be had anyway, and the public college was full of students in our condition, because of the unemployment, getting a city-sponsored introduction to higher notions and an accidental break into Shakespeare and other great masters along with the science and math leveled at the Civil-Service exams. In the nature of the case it couldn't be avoided; and if you were going to prepare impoverished young folks for difficult functions, or if merely you were going to keep them out of trouble by having them read books, there were going to be some remarkable results begotten out of the mass. I knew a skinny, sickly Mexican too poor for socks and spotted and stained all over, body and clothes, who could crack any equation on the board; and also Bohunk wizards at the Greeks, demon-brained physicists, historians bred under pushcarts, and many hard-grain poor boys who were going to starve and work themselves bitterly eight years or so to become doctors, engineers, scholars, and experts. I had no special eagerness of this kind and never had been led to think I should have, nor gave myself anxious cares about being revealed a profession. I didn't feel moved to take it seriously. Nevertheless I turned in a fairly good performance in French and History. In things like Botany, my drawings were cockeyed and smudgy and I was behind the class. Though I had been Einhorn's office clerk I hadn't learned much of neatness. And besides I was working five afternoons a week and all day on Saturday.

This was not at Einhorn's any longer, but in women's shoes, in the basement of the downtown clothing shop where Simon was upstairs in men's suits. His situation had gotten better, and he was excited by the change. It was a fashionable store where the management wanted you to be well dressed. But he went beyond anything demanded of a salesman and was not just natty but hot stuff, in a double-breasted striped suit, with a tape measure around his neck. I hardly knew him there, among mirrors, rugs, racks of clothes, eight stories above the Loop; he was big, fast and busy, heavy in his body, and his blood evident in him, in his face.

Below, I was in a bargain department under the sidewalk, seeing and hearing the shoppers pass over the green circles of glass set in concrete, skirts of heavy coats flying as shadows through these lenses, but the weight of bodies actual enough, the glass creaking and soles going every which way. This vault was for the poorer class of customers or for solitary-hornet shoppers, girls with outfits to match, hats and accessories; women with three or four little daughters to buy shoes for on the same day. The goods were heaped up on tables by sizes, and then there were cardboard-cell walls of boxes and fitting stools in a circle under the honeycomb of the sidewalk.

A few weeks of apprenticeship here and the buyer had me up to the main floor. Only to help out, in the beginning, and run stock for the salesmen or return boxes to the shelves. And then I became a shoe-dog myself, only having to be told by the buyer to cut my hair shorter. He was a worried guy and his stomach was bad. From shaving twice a day his skin was tender, and, on a Saturday morning when he got the salesmen together before opening to give them a speech, his mouth would bleed a little at the corners. He hoped to be more severe than he could be, and I expect his trouble was that he was really not the man to direct a snazzy operation. For the place was a salon, with Frenchy torches held by human-arm brackets out from the walls, furled drapes, and Chinese furniture—such corners as are softened, sheltered from the outside air, even from the air of the Rue de Rivoli, by oriental rugs that swallow sounds in their nap, and hangings that make whispers and protocol unavoidable. Differences of inside and outside hard to reconcile; for up to the threshold of a salon like this there was a tremendous high tension and antagonistic energy asked to lie still that couldn't lie still; and trying to contain it caused worry and shivers, the kind of thing that could erupt in raging, bloody Gordon or Chartist riots and shoot up fire like the burning of a mountain of egg crates. This unknown, superfluous free power streaming around a cold, wet, blackened Chicago day, from things laid out to be still, incapable, however, of being still.

Financially Simon and I were doing first rate; he was getting fifteen dollars a week before commissions, and I was pulling down thirteen-fifty. Therefore it didn't matter that we were disqualified from Charity. Practically blind, Mama couldn't do the housework any longer. Simon hired a mulatto named Molly Simms, a strong lean woman, about thirty-five, who slept in the kitchen—on George's old cot, in fact—and whispered or sang out to us when we came home late. We never had gotten the habit of using the front entrance, forbidden to us in the old lady's time.

"She means you, sport," Simon said.

"Bushwah, you're the one she looks at all the time."

On New Year's Day she didn't show up, and I kept things running and fixed the meals. Simon was away too. He had gone to a New Year's Eve party, leaving the house in his best: bowler hat, polka-dot muffler, spats on his two-tone shoes, pigskin gloves. And he didn't get back till early evening the next day, out of a rapid, sparkling snow. He was filthy, scowling, with blood in his eyes and scratches through his blond stubble. A first good look at his violent and lavish nature, it was, to see him heaving in from the quiet snowfall of the back porch, kicking his shoes clean on the bricks and bristling over them with broom, next showing his face, streaky, as if he had been shagged through brambles, and putting his hard hat, with a puncture in it, on the chair. It was lucky Mama couldn't see him; at that she knew something was wrong and asked in her high cry.

"Why, there's nothing the matter, Ma," we said to her.

Slangily, so that she wouldn't understand, he told me a cock-and-bull story about a scrap on a Well Street El platform with a couple of drunk jokers, ferocious Irishmen, of one catching his arms in his coat by yanking down the collar while the other pushed his face into those guard wires on the banister and threw him down the stairs. None of that convinced me. It didn't explain where he had been a day and a night.

I said, "You know, Molly Simms didn't show up, and she said she was going to."

He didn't try to deny he had been with her, but sat heavy in his wet, foul best, brute-exhausted. He had me heat the boiler for his bath, and when he stripped his shirt revealed more skin torn from his back. He didn't trouble himself as to what I thought. And, neither boasting nor complaining, he told me that he had gone to Molly Simm's room early in the morning. It was true he had fought with two micks; he was drunk, after the party; but she had given him the scratches. Furthermore, she hadn't let him go till good and dark, and then he blundered in the Black Belt streets, in the snow. Lifting the covers to climb into bed, he said to me that we would have to get rid of Molly Simms.

"Where do you get that 'we' stuff?"

"Or she'll think she's boss of the place, and the woman's a wildcat."

We were in our ancient little room, where the stiff wallpaper of many layers bulged out in bubbles and the comfortable snow raced dry on the window and mounted on the sill.

"She'll want to build it up to something. She told me already."

"What did she tell you?"

"That she loves me," he said, grinning but somber. "She's a crazy bitch."

"What? She's close on forty."

"What difference does that make? She's a woman. And I went to see her. I didn't ask her age before getting on her."

He sent her away that week. I noticed how she observed his scratched face at breakfast. She was a thin, gypsyish woman, and her face was very keen; she could put on a manner when she felt like it, but she didn't care a damn who saw her when she didn't, and she gave her sharp, greenish-eyed grin. He wasn't rattled by her; he had decided she was going to be a nuisance, and she caught on at once that he was bent on giving her the shove-ho. She was an experienced woman, rough from being so much on the losing side and from having knocked around from town to town, Washington to Brooklyn to Detroit, with what other stops you'd never know, getting gold teeth here and a slash in the cheek there. But she was an independent and never appealed for any sympathy; was never offered any either. Simon bounced her and hired Sablonka, an old Polish woman who disliked us, a slow-climbing, muttering, mob-faced, fat, mean, pious widow who was a bad cook besides. But we were neither of us around much. Within a few weeks after she began I was not even living at home, but had dropped from school and was living and working in Evanston. And I was on a peculiar circuit, for a while, of the millionaire suburbs—Highland Park, Kenilworth, and Winnetka—selling things, a specialized salesman in luxury lines and dealing with aristocrats. It was the shoe buyer who put me onto this when asked by a business acquaintance in Evanston to recommend someone; he brought me forward, where Mr. Renling, this Evanstonian sporting-goods man, could get a load of me as I crossed the floor.

"Where does he come from?" he asked, this frosty, dry, self-commenting, neutral-eyed man, long-legged and stylish. He looked like a Scotsman.

"From the Northwest Side," said the buyer. "His brother works upstairs. They're clever boys, both of them."

"*Jehudim?*" said Mr. Renling, still looking neutrally at the buyer.

"Jew?" the buyer said to me. He well knew the answer; he merely passed the question on.

"Yes. I guess."

"Ah," said Renling, this time to me. "Well, out there on the North Shore they don't like Jews. But," he said, brimming frostily with a smile, "*who* makes them happy? They like hardly anybody. Anyway, they'll probably never know." And to the buyer again he said, "Well, do you think this is a kid who can be glamorized?"

"He's done all right here."

"It's a little more high-pressure on the North Shore."

Prospective house slaves from the shacks got the same kind of going-over, I suppose, or girls brought to an old *cocotte* by their mothers for training. He had me strip my jacket so he could see my shoulders and my fanny, so that I was just about to tell him what he could do with his job when he said I was built right for his purpose, and my vanity was more influential than my self-respect. He then said to me, "I want to put you in my saddle shop—riding habits, boots, dude-ranch stuff, fancy articles. I'll pay twenty bucks a week while you're learning, and when you're broken in I'll pay you twenty-five plus commission."

Naturally I took the job. I'd be earning more money than Simon.

I moved into a student loft in Evanston, where soon the most distinguished thing was my wardrobe. Maybe I ought to say my livery, since Mr. and Mrs. Renling saw to it that I was appropriately dressed, in fact made a clotheshorse of me, advancing the money and picking out the tweeds and flannels, plaids, foulards, sport shoes, woven shoes Mexican style, and shirts and handkerchiefs—in the right taste for waiting on a smooth trade of mostly British inclination. When I had sounded the place out good I didn't go for it, but I was too stirred up at first, and enthusiastic, to see it well. I was dressed with splendor and working back of the most thrilling plate glass I had ever seen, on a leafy street, in a fashionable store three steps under a western timber from the main part of Renling's shop, which sold fishing, hunting, camping, golf and tennis equipment, canoes and outboard motors. You see now what I meant by saying that I have to marvel at my social passes, that I was suddenly sure and efficacious in this business, could talk firmly and knowingly to rich young girls, to country-club sports and university students, presenting things with one hand and carrying a cigarette in a long holder in the other. So that Renling had to grant that I had beat all the foreseen handicaps. I had to take riding lessons—not too many, they were expensive. Renling didn't want me to become an accomplished horseman. "What for?" he said. "I sell these fancy guns and never shot an animal in my life."

But Mrs. Renling wanted me to become a rider and to refine and school me every way. She had me register for evening courses at Northwestern. Of the four men who worked in the store—I was the youngest—two were college graduates. "And you," she said, "with *your* appearance, and *your* personality, if *you* have a college degree . . ." Why, she showed me the result, as if it already lay in my hands.

She played terribly on my vanity. "I'll make you perfect," she said, "completely perfect."

Mrs. Renling was pushing fifty-five, light-haired, only a little gray, small, her throat whiter than her face. She had tiny, dry red freckles and eyes of light color, but not gentle. Her accent was foreign; she came from Luxembourg, and it was a great pride of hers that she was connected with names in the Almanach de Gotha for that part of the world. Once in a while she assured me, "It is all nonsense; I am a democrat; I am a citizen of this country. I voted for Cox, I voted for Al Smith, and I voted for Roosevelt. I do not care for aristocrats. They hunted on my father's estate. Queen Carlotta used to go to chapel near us, and she never forgave the French, because of Napoleon the Third. I was going to school in Brussels when she died." She corresponded with ladies of the nobility in different places. She exchanged recipes with a German woman who lived in Doorn and had something to do with the Kaiser's household. "I was in Europe a few years ago and I saw this baroness. I knew her long. Of course they can never really accept you. I told her, 'I am really an American.' I brought some of my pickled watermelon. There is nothing like that over there, Augie. She taught me how to make veal kidneys with cognac. One of the rare dishes of the world. There's a restaurant now in New York that makes them. People have to make reservations, even now, in Depression time. She sold the recipe to a caterer for five hundred dollars. I would never do that. I go and cook it for my friends, but I would consider it beneath me to sell an old family secret."

She could cook all right, she had all the cooking arcana. She was known all over for the dinners she threw. Or for those she cooked at other places, because she might decide to make one anywhere, for friends. Her social set were the hotel manager's wife at the Symington, the jewelers, Vletold, who sold to the carriage trade—the heaviest, crested, cymbal-sized fruit dishes and Argonaut gravy boats. There also was the widow of a man involved in the Teapot Dome Scandal, who bred coach dogs. Any number of people like this. For new friends who didn't know her veal kidneys she'd prepare everything at home and cook it in at their table. She was an ardent feeder of people, and often cooked for the salesmen; she hated to see us go to restaurants, where everything, she said, in her impersonator's foreign voice that nothing could interrupt, was so cheap and sticky.

That was just it, with Mrs. Renling—she couldn't be interrupted or stopped, in her pale-fire concentration. She would cook for you if she wanted to, feed you, coach you, instruct you, play mah-jongg with you, and there was scarcely anything you could do about it, she had so much more force than anybody else around; with her light eyes and the pale, fox stain of her freckles lying in the dust of powder or on the back of her hands, with long hard rays of the tendons. She told me I would study advertising in the School of Journalism at the university, and she paid my fees, and so I did. She also chose for me the other courses I needed for a degree, stressing that a cultured man could have anything he wanted in America for the asking, standing out, she said, like a candle in a coal mine.

I had a busy life. In my new person of which, at the time, I was ungodly proud. With my class evenings, evenings in the library reading history and the cunning books for creating discontent in the consumer; attending Mrs. Renling's bridge or mah-jongg soirées in her silk, penthouse parlor, something of a footman, something of a nephew, passing around candy dishes, opening ginger ale in the pantry, with my cigarette holder in my mouth, knowing, obliging, with hints of dalliance behind me, Sta-comb shining on my hair, flower blooming out of my lapel, smelling of heather lotion, snitching tips on what was what in behavior and protocol; till I found that much of this last was off the cuff and that many looked to *you* to know what tone to take. The real touchstone was Mrs. Renling, who couldn't be denied leadership. Mr. Renling didn't seem to care and played his cards or ivories, truly detached and passionless. He didn't speak much, and Mrs. Renling said what she was going to say without hearing other opinion. This other opinion, what was said about servants, or about unemployment or the government, was monstrous, no two ways about it. Renling knew this but he didn't care. These were his friends of the business community; a man in business had to have such, and he visited and entertained but neither touched nor was touched, ever.

He had a personality strictly relative to his business. Once in a while he'd take off to show his skill with a piece of rope in knot tying, or he'd sing:

> "So this, so this, is Wenice
> And where do we park the car?"

His upper lip had a pretty big perch on the other one, and he looked gloomy and patient. He was a wintry, slick guy, like many people who have to do service but save something for their own—like a headwaiter or chief of bellhops—individuals who are mixed up in a peculiar life-game where they sign on to lose and then anyhow put up a kind of underneath battle.

He was a fight fan and took me to the matches now and then, at a ring near the Montrose Cemetery. Saying, at about ten o'clock, in a gathering, "Augie and I have a pair of duckets it would be a shame to waste altogether. We can still make the main event if we leave now." Since there were things men found it necessary to do, Mrs. Renling said, "Well, by all means."

During the bouts Renling didn't holler or carry on, but he ate them up. Anything that took stamina got him—six-day bike races, dance marathons, walkathons, flagpole sitting, continuous and world flights, long fasts by Gandhi or striking prisoners, people camping underground, buried alive and fed and breathing through a shaft—any miracles of endurance and effort, as if out of competition with cylinder walls or other machine materials that withstand steam, gases, and all inhuman pressure. Such exhibitions he'd drive any distance in his powerful Packard to get a load of, and, driving, he raced. But he did not appear to be going fast. For there was his stability in the green leather seat, plus his unshaking, high-placed knees beside the jade onion of the gear knob, his hands trimmed with sandy hairs on the wheel, the hyper-smoothness of the motor that made you feel deceived in the speedometer that stood at eighty. Until you noticed how a mile of trees cracked open like a shadow inch of tape, that the birds resembled flies and the sheep birds, and how swift the blue, yellow, and red little bloods of bugs spattered on the glass. He liked me to go with him. And what his idea of company was was perplexing, since, as we came and went like a twister, there was no warmth of conversation to counteract the scene-ignoring cold rush, the thin thresh of the radio antenna and yacking of broadcasts through the gold-mesh mouth in the panel. But what was mostly touched on, now and again, was the performance of the car and gas and oil statistics. We'd stop for barbecue chicken in some piny place, on warm sand, like a couple of earth-visiting Plutonians, and sip beer in the perfect clothes we wore, of sporting hound's-tooth or brown Harris tweed, carrying field glasses in cases from the shop: a gloomy, rich gentleman and his gilded nephew or young snob cousin, we must have looked. I was too much engaged with feeling this raiment on me, the closeness of good cloth to my body, or with thoughts of the cock-green Tyrolean brush in my hat and splendor of British shoes, to be able to see Renling as I did see him later. He was an obstacle-eater. He rushed over roads. He loved feats and worshiped endurance, and he took between his teeth all objections, difficulties, hindrances, and chewed and swallowed them down.

Sometimes he'd tell something of himself in the form of a short remark, as when we passed under a North Shore viaduct once and he said, "I helped build that. I wasn't any older than you then, and helped pass cement to the mixer. Must have been the year the Panama Canal was opened. Thought the job would knock me out in the stomach muscles. Buck and a quarter was pretty good dough in those days."

This was how he borrowed me for company. It probably gave him some amusement, how I took to this sort of life.

There was a spell in which I mainly wished to own dinner clothes and be invited to formal parties and thought considerably about how to get into the Junior Chamber of Commerce. Not that I had any business ideas. I was better than fair in the shop, but I had no wider inventiveness about money. It was social enthusiasm that moved in me, smartness, clotheshorseyness. The way a pair of tight Argyle socks showed in the crossing of legs, a match to the bow tie settled on a Princeton collar, took me in the heart with enormous power and hunger. I was given over to it.

Briefly I ran with a waitress from the Symington, Willa Steiner. I took her dancing at the Merry Garden and went to the beach with her at night. She kindly let me get by most of the time with putting on the dog and pompousness, being a warm girl. She was nowise shy herself, making no bones about what we were together for. She had a home-town lover too, whom she talked about marrying—I'm certain without any hinder-thought of making me jealous. For she had a number of things against me about which she was probably in the right, my dandy gab and conceit and my care about clothes. Soon informed, Mrs. Renling came down hard on me for getting mixed up with her. Einhorn didn't know more of what went on around him than she did about everything in her territory. "Augie, I'm astonished at you," she said. "She's not even a pretty girl. She has a nose like a little Indian"—I had especially petted Willa Steiner with this pretty nose for my theme; it wasn't courageous of me not to defend it—"and she's covered with freckles. I have freckles too, but mine are different, and anyhow, it's only as an older person that I'm talking to you. Besides, the girl is a little prostitute, and not an honest prostitute, because an honest prostitute, all *she* wants is your money. And if you have to do this, if you come to me and tell me you have to—and don't be ashamed of that —I'll give you money to go somewhere on Sheridan Road near Wilson, where such places are." Another instance of people offering to contribute money to keep me out of trouble; as Einhorn had, when he lectured me about the robbery. "Augie, don't you see this little tramp wants you to get her in trouble so that you'll have to marry her? That's all you need now, to have a baby with her right at the start of your career. I would think that *you* would know what this is about."

Sometimes I thought it was clever and free of her to talk as she did, and again that it was terribly stupid. I had an impression that, glancing out from the partitions where she observed, with her dotty, smarting, all-interfering face, she was bent on pulling whom she wanted to her, to infuse and instill. It was the kind of talk gilded dumb young men have heard from protectresses, generals' and statesmen's wives, in all the duchies, villas, and capital cities of the world.

"But you don't really know anything about Willa, Mrs. Renling," I said clumsily. "She doesn't—" I didn't go on, because of all the scorn in her face. "My dear boy, you talk like a nitwit. Go on with her if you want. I'm not your mother. But you'll see," she said in her impersonator's voice, "when she has you roped. D'you think all she wants out of life is to wait on tables and work to feed herself just to keep in shape for you, so you'll have nothing to do but enjoy her? You know nothing about girls; girls want to marry. And it's not in the modest old times when they sat on it till somebody would have mercy." She spoke disgustedly; she had disgust to burn.

It didn't occur to me, when Mrs. Renling had me drive her to Benton Harbor where she took mineral baths for her arthritis, that she was getting me away from Willa. She said she couldn't think of going out to Michigan alone, and that I would drive and keep her company in the hotel. Afterward I understood.

Benton Harbor was plenty different for me from what it had been last time, when I had hitch-hiked back from Muskegon with Nails and Dingbat, with sweat shirt tied on my neck by the sleeves and my feet road-sore. Actually we stayed in St. Joe, next to Lake Michigan, at the Merritt Hotel, right in front of the water and the deep, fresh smell of sea volume in the glossy pink walls of the rooms. The hotel was vast, and it was brick construction, but went after the tone of old Saratoga Springs establishments, greenery and wicker-work, braid cord on the portieres, menus in French, white hall runners and deep fat of money, limousines in the washed gravel, lavish culture of flowers bigger than life, and triple-decker turf on which the grass lived rich. Everywhere else, in the blaze of July, it was scanty.

I had the long bath hours to myself to see what the territory round about was like. It was mostly fruit country, farmed by Germans, the men like farmers anywhere, but the older women in bonnets, going barefoot in long dresses under the giant oaks of their yards. The peach branches shone with seams of gum, leaves milky from the spray of insecticides. Also, on the roads, on bicycles and in Ford trucks, were the bearded and long-haired House of David Israelites, a meat-renouncing sect of peaceful, businesslike, pious people, who had a big estate or principality of their own, and farmhouse palaces. They spoke of Shiloh and Armageddon as familiarly as of eggs and harnesses, and were a millionaire concern many times over, owning farms and springs and a vast amusement park in a big Bavarian dell, with a miniature railway, a baseball team, and a jazz band that sent music up clear to the road from the nightly dances in the pavilion. Two bands, in fact, one of each sex.

I brought Mrs. Renling here a few times to dance and drink spring water; the mosquitoes, though, were too active for her. Afterward I sometimes went alone; she didn't see why I should want to. Nor did she see what I strayed into town for in the morning, or why I took pleasure in sitting in the still green bake of the Civil War courthouse square after my thick breakfast of griddle cakes and eggs and coffee. But I did, and warmed my belly and shins while the little locust trolley clinked and crept to the harbor and over the trestles of the bog-spanning bridge where the green beasts and bulrush-rocking birds kept up their hot, small-time uproar. I brought along a book, but there was too much brown stain on the pages from the sun. The benches were white iron, roomy enough for three or four old gaffers to snooze on in the swamp-tasting sweet warmth that made the redwing black-birds fierce and quick, and the flowers frill, but other living things slow and lazy-blooded. I soaked in the heavy nourishing air and this befriending atmosphere like rich life-cake, the kind that encourages love and brings on a mild pain of emotions. A state that lets you rest in your own specific gravity, and where you are not a subject matter but sit in your own nature, tasting original tastes as good as the first man, and are outside of the busy human tamper, left free even of your own habits. Which only lie on you illusory in the sunshine, in the usual relation of your feet or fingers or the knot of your shoe-strings and are without power. No more than the comb or shadow of your hair has power on your brain.

Mrs. Renling did not like to be alone at meals, not even at breakfast. I had to eat with her in her room. Each morning she took sugarless tea, with milk, and a few pieces of zwieback. I had the works, the bottom half of the menu, from grapefruit to rice pudding, and ate at a little table by the open window, in the lake airs that lapped the dotted Swiss curtains. In bed, and talking all the while, Mrs. Renling took off the gauze chin band she slept in and began to treat her face with lotions and creams, plucked her eyebrows. Her usual subject of conversation was the other guests. She got them down and polished them off, but good. In the leisure of the early hour, when she bravely rode fence on her face. She would die a well-tended lady who had kept up fiercely all civilized duties, as developed before Phidias and through Botticelli—all that great masters and women of illustrious courts had prescribed and followed for perfection, the kind of intelligence to wear in the eyes and the molds of sweetness and authority. But she had a wrath-ruled mind. Giving herself these feminine cares in the brightness of her suite in the soft-blown-open summer beauty, she was not satisfied without social digging and the toil of grievances and antipathies.

"Did you notice the old couple on my left, last night at the Bunco party, the Zeelands? Marvelous old Dutch family. Isn't he a beautiful old man? Why, he was one of the greatest corporation lawyers in Chicago, and he's a trustee for the Robinson Foundation, the glass people. The university gave him an honorary degree, and when he has a birthday the newspapers write editorials. And still his wife is stupid as her own feet, and she drinks, and the daughter is a drunkard too. If I knew *she* was going to be here I would have gone to Saratoga instead. I wish there was some way to get an advance guest list from these hotels. There ought to be a service like that. They have a suite for six hundred dollars a month in Chicago. And as soon as the chauffeur comes for the old man in the morning—this is something I *know*!—the bellhop goes out and buys them a bottle of bourbon and bets on a horse for them. Then they drink and wait for the results. But that *daughter*— she keeps herself a little old-fashioned. If you didn't notice her last night, look for a heavy-built woman who wears feathers. She threw a child out of the window and killed it. They used all their influence and got her free. A poor woman would have gotten the chair, like Ruth Snyder, with the matrons standing all around and picking up their skirts so the photographers couldn't get a picture of it. I wonder if she dresses like this now so as to feel nothing in common with that young flapper who did that thing."

You needed a strong constitution to stick to your splendor of morning in the face of these damnation chats. I had to struggle when she called out her whole force of frights, apocalypse death riders, church-porch devils who grabbed naked sinners from behind to lug them down to punishment, her infanticides, plagues, and incests.

I managed. But the situation was that I was enjoying what a rich young man enjoys and arranged my feelings accordingly, filling in and plastering over objections. Except that there were rotten moments, such as when she spoke of the Snyder execution and evoked this terrible protection of a woman's modesty who was writhing in thousands of volts. And though I was avoiding everything that didn't agree with what I wanted, the consistent painting of doomedness and evil she specialized in did get under my skin. What if it really was as she said? If, for instance, the woman had thrown her baby out of the window? It wasn't Medea, a good, safe long time ago, chasing her pitiful kids, but a woman I saw in the dining room, wearing feathers, sitting down with her white-haired father and mother.

But there were people at the table near theirs that soon were of more interest to me—two young girls, of beauty to put a stop to such thoughts or drive them to the dwindling point. There was a moment when I could have fallen for either one of them, and then everything bent to one side, toward the slenderer, slighter, younger one. I fell in love with her, and not in the way I had loved Hilda Novinson either, going like a satellite on the back of the streetcar or sticking around her father's tailor shop. This time I had a different kind of maniac energy and knew what sexual sting was. My expectations were greater; more corrupt too, maybe, owing to the influence of Mrs. Renling and her speaking always of lusts, no holds barred. So that I allowed suggestions in all veins to come to me. I never have learned to reproach myself for such things; and then my experience in curtailing them was limited. Why, I had accepted of Grandma Lausch's warning only the part about the danger of our blood and that, through Mama, we were susceptible to love; not the stigmatizing part that made us out the carriers of the germ of ruination. So I was dragged, entrained, over a barrel. And I had a special handicap, because of the way I presented myself—due to Mrs. Renling—as if God had not left out a single one of His gifts, and I was advertising His liberality with me: good looks, excellent wardrobe, mighty fine manners, social ease, wittiness, handsome-devil smiles, neat dancing and address with women—all in the freshest gold-leaf. And the trouble was that I had what you might call forged credentials. It was my worry that Esther Fenchel would find this out.

I worked, heart-choked, for the grandest success in these limits, as an impostor. I spent hours getting myself up to be a living petition. By dumb concentration and notice-wooing struggle. The only way I could conceive, in my blood-loaded, picturesque amorousness. But, the way a hint of plague is given in the mild wind of flags and beauty of a harbor—a scene of safe, busy peace—I could perhaps, for all of my sane look of easy, normal circumstances, have passed the note of my thoughts in the air—on the beach, on the flower-cultured lawn, in the big open of the white and gold dining room—and these thoughts were that I could submit to being hung in the girl's hair—of that order. I had heavy dreams about her lips, hands, breasts, legs, between legs. She could not stoop for a ball on the tennis court—I standing stiff in a foulard with brown horses on a green background that was ingeniously slipped through a handcarved wooden ring which Renling made popular that season in Evanston—I couldn't witness this, I say, without a push of love and worship in my bowels at the curve of her hips, and triumphant maiden shape behind, and soft, protected secret. Where, to be allowed with love, would be the endorsement of the world, that it was not the barren confusion distant dry fears hinted and whispered, but was necessary, justified, the justification proved by joy. That if she would have, approve, kiss, use her hands on me, allow me the clay dust of the court from her legs, the mild sweat, her intimate dirt and sweat, deliver me from suffering falsehood—show that there wasn't anything false, injurious, or empty-hearted that couldn't be corrected!

But in the evening, when nothing had come of my effort, a scoreless day, I lay on the floor of my room, all dressed up to go to dinner, with doomed patience, eaten with hankering and thinking futilely what brilliant thing to do—some floral, comet, star action, casting off stupidity and clumsiness. But I had marked carefully all that I could about Esther, in order to study what could induce her to see herself with me, in my light. That is, up there in sublimity. Asking only that she join me, let me, ride and row in love with me, with her fresh, great female wonders and beauties which would increase by my joy that she was exactly as she was, with her elbows, her nipples at her sweater. I watched how she chased a little awkwardly on the tennis court and made to protect her breasts and closed in her knees when a fast ball came over the net. My study of her didn't much support my hopes; which was why I lay on the floor with a desiring, sunburned face and lips open in thought. I realized that she knew she had a great value, and that she was not subject to urgent-heartedness. In short, that Esther Fenchel was not of my persuasion and wouldn't much care to hear about her perspiration and little personal dirts.

Nevertheless the world never had better color, to say it exactly as it strikes me, or finer and more reasonable articulation. Nor ever gave me better trouble. I felt I was in the real and the true as far as nature and pleasure went in forming the native place of human and all other existence.

And I behaved ingeniously too. I got into conversations with old Fenchel, not the girls' father but their uncle, who was in the mineral-water business. It wasn't easy, because he was a millionaire. He drove a Packard, the same model and color as the Renlings'; I parked behind him on the drive so that he had to look twice to see which was his, and then I had him. *Inter pares.* For how could he tell that I earned twenty-five dollars a week and didn't own the car? We talked. I offered him a Perfecto Queen. He smiled it away; he had his own tailor-made Havanas in a case big enough for a pistol, and he was so ponderously huge it didn't even bulge in his pocket. His face was fat and seamed, black-eyed—eyes black as the meat of Chinese litchi nuts—with gray, heinie hair, clipped to the fat of the scalp, back and sides. It was a little discouraging that the girls were his heiresses, as he right away told me, probably guessing that I wasn't bringing out the flower of my charm for his old cartilage-heavy Rembrandt of a squash nose with its white hairs and gunpowder speckles. To be sure not. And he wanted me to know in what league I was playing. I didn't give an inch. I've never backed down from male relatives, either calf or bull, or let father and guardians discomfit me.

Getting to Esther's aunt was harder, since she was sickly, timid, and silent, with the mood of rich people whose health lets them down. Her clothes and jewelry were fine, but the poor lady's face was full of private effort; she was a little deaf from it. I didn't have to put on friendly interest; I really (God knows from where) had it. And by instinct I knew that what would fetch her—as infirm, loaded with dough, and beaten a long way out of known channels by the banked spoon-oars of special silver as she was—was the charm of ordinary health. So I talked away to her and was pretty acceptable.

"My dear Augie, was that Mrs. Fenchel you were sitting with?" said Mrs. Renling. "She hasn't done anything but watch the sprinkler all month, so I thought she was screwloose. Did you speak to her first?"

"Well, I just happened to be sitting by her."

I got a good mark for this; she was pleased. But the next thing to be thought of was my purpose, and this she immediately and roughly found out. "It's the girls, isn't it! Well, they are very beautiful, aren't they? Especially the black-haired one. Gorgeous. And mischievous, full of the devil she looks. But remember, Augie, you're with me; I'm responsible for your behavior. And the girl is not a waitress, and you better not think you-know-what. My dear boy, you're very clever and good, and I want to see you get ahead. I'll see that you do. Naturally, with this girl, you haven't got a chance. Of course, rich girls can sometimes be little whores too, and have the same itch as common ones and sometimes even worse. But not these girls. You don't know what German upbringing is."

So to speak, reserved for the brass, the Fenchel heiresses. But Mrs. Renling wasn't infallible, and had already made one mistake, that of thinking it was Thea rather than Esther Fenchel I was in love with. Also, she had no notion how much in love I was, down to the poetic threat of death. I didn't want her to have any notion either, though I would have been happy to tell someone. I did not like what I foresaw Mrs. Renling would make of it, and so I was satisfied to let her think it was Thea, the kinky-haired but also glorious-looking sister I carried the torch for, and I used some deceit. It didn't take much, as it was pleasing to Mrs. Renling's pride to think she had guessed, quick and infallible, what was bothering me.

As a matter of fact Thea Fenchel was better than merely pleasant to me, and I was fishing after her uncle, who was in a bad mood, surly and difficult, one morning, when she asked me whether I played tennis. I had to say, and though it was a bad moment for me, smiling, that riding was my sport; and I desperately thought that I must get a racket and go at once to the public courts in Benton Harbor to learn. Not that I had been born to the saddle either; but it covered my origins somewhat to say that I was a horseman and had a pretty creditable clang.

"My partner hasn't come," said Thea, "and Esther's on the beach."

Within ten minutes I too was on the sand, notwithstanding that I had promised to play cards with Mrs. Renling after her mineral bath, when, she said, she felt too weakened to read. I lay hot and wandering-witted on my belly, watching Esther, and my notions were many-branched, high-seasoned, erotic, a good half painful, hoping for and afraid of notice as she bent down and rubbed sun-oil like brightness on her legs, and her head turned toward me, who was loony and drunk with assessing the weight of her breasts and the soft little heaviness of her belly, so elegantly banded in by the sheath of her swim suit, or her hair which she combed, it seemed to me, with great animal strength, taking off the close white rubber helmet.

The sand swallows burst out of their scupper holes in the bluffs and out over the transparent drown of the water, back again to the white, to the brown, to the black, from moving to stock-still sand waves and water-worked woods and roots that hugged and twisted in the sun.

Presently she went up; and so did I, a little later. Mrs. Renling gave me the icy treatment for being late. And, I thought, lying on the floor of my room with my heels upon the bedspread like an armored man fallen from his horse, spur-tangled and needing block and tackle to be raised, that it was time, seeing my inattention was making Mrs. Renling angry, to have some progress to show for it at least. I got up and brushed myself without particular heart or interest, using two military brushes she had given me. I went down in the slow, white elevator and, on the ground floor, moseyed around in the lobby.

It was sundown, near dinnertime, with brilliant darkening water, napkins and broad menus standing up in the dining room, and roses and ferns in long-necked vases, the orchestra tuning back of its curtain. I was alone in the corridor, troubled and rocky, and trod on slowly to the music room, where the phonograph was playing Caruso, stifled and then clear cries of operatic mother-longing, that ornate, at heart somber, son's appeal of the Italian taste. Resting her elbows on the closed cabinet, in a white suit and round white hat, next thing to a bishop's biretta, bead-embroidered, was Esther Fenchel; she stood with one foot set on its point.

I said, "Miss Fenchel, I wonder if you would like to go with me some evening to the House of David." Astonished, she looked up from the music. "They have dancing every night."

I saw nothing but failure, from the first word out, and felt smitten, pounded from all sides.

"With you? I should say not. I certainly won't."

The blood came down out of my head, neck, shoulders, and I fainted dead away.

I came out of it without help. There wasn't anyone to offer any, Esther not having spent an instant in seeing what had happened to me, evidently, because the singing rolled in on me in the splendor of its wind-up, at first with the noise of a seashell, then louder, with the climbing of the orchestra on the staircase of a magnificent hall, to the clear heartbreak of the very top where the drums severed and killed and gave a hammering burial to everything.

I don't know whether it was the refusal or the emotion of speaking and being spoken to that knocked me down, and I wasn't in any condition to touch around and feel for the trigger, where it was and why it was like a loose tooth. It was enough I had found out how strong the charge was, and that it was the kick of a false situation that went off. And meanwhile I was sucking breath and the air felt chilly to me because of my damp face. I got my back against a sofa, where I felt I had got trampled all over my body by a thing some way connected by weight with my mother and my brother George, who perhaps this very minute was working on a broom, or putting it down to shamble in to supper; or with Grandma Lausch in the Nelson Home—somehow as though run over by the beast that kept them steady company and that I thought I was safely away from.

Meantime Miss Zeeland was standing in the doorway, the daughter of the famous corporation lawyer, looking at me, in her evening feathers, and her body in the long drape of her dress making a single unbroken human roll. She had on golden shoes and white gloves to the elbow, and looked visionary, oriental, with her rich hair swept up in a kind of tower that was in equilibrium to her big bust. Her face was clear and cold, like a kind of weather, though the long clean groove of her upper lip was ready to go into motion, as if she were going to break her silence with something momentous and long-matured; explain love to me, perhaps. But no, her ideas remained closed to me, though she didn't leave until I got up to turn off the phonograph, and then she glided or fanned away.

I went to the men's toilet to wash my face with a little warm water and then went to dinner. I didn't do much with the food, not even the *pêche flambée*, as didn't escape Mrs. Renling, and she said, "Augie, when is this love nonsense going to stop? You'll hurt your system. Is it that important?" Then she used her most fondling words on me, to get me around by kidding, and, as a woman, tried to put a top on my imagination of women where she thought a top should be, explaining what there was and was not to women, and praised the male in all things as if she was working for Athena. It drove me a little crazy. I wasn't right on my rocker anyway, and hearing her run down the body of womankind in her metal, bristling way made me look at her with a streak of bad blood in the eye. And I waited almost with the shakes of malaria for Esther to appear in the dining room. The old Fenchels were already at their table. Then Thea came, but her sister wasn't having supper apparently.

"And you know," said Mrs. Renling after a time, "the girl hasn't had her eyes off you since she came in. Is there something between you already? Augie! Have you done something? Is that why you're low? What have you done?"

"I haven't done anything," I said.

"You better not!" She was on me, sharp and shrewd, just like a police matron. "You're too attractive to women for your own good, and you'll end up in trouble. So will she; she's got hot pants, that little miss."

She gave Thea stare for stare. The waiter set light to the Fenchel's *flambée*, and there were little fires here and there in the green of twilight.

I left the dining room without saying more. To walk around on the shore road and get the shameful twists out of my guts and digest my trouble. It was awful, the feelings I was having, the disgrace and anger over Esther and the desire to conk Mrs. Renling on the head. I went along the edge of the water, and then around the grounds, staying away from the porch where I knew Mrs. Renling would be waiting to pay me off for my rudeness, and then to the back, to the children's playground, and sat down on the slat seat of the garden swing.

Sitting here, I started to dream that Esther had thought it over and had come out of her room to look for me, so that I had to groan over the grip my stupidity had on me and was sloshed all over with corrupting feelings, worse than before. Then I heard someone light coming near, a woman stepping under the tree into the dusty rut worn beside the swing by the feet of kids. It was Esther's sister Thea, come to talk to me, the one Mrs. Renling warned me of. In her white dress and her shoes that came down like pointed shapes of birds in the vague whiteness of the furrow by the swing, with lace on her arms and warm opening and closing differences of the shade of leaves back of her head, she stood and looked at me.

"Disappointed that it isn't Esther, aren't you, Mr. March? I guess you must be having a terrible time. You looked pretty white in the dining room."

Wondering what she knew and what she was after, I didn't say anything.

"Have you recovered a little?"

"Recovered from what?"

"From fainting. Except Esther thought it might be an epileptic fit."

"Well, maybe it was one," I said, feeling heavy, sullen, and crumbling.

"I don't think so. You're just sore, and you don't want me to bother you."

That wasn't so; on the contrary, I wanted her to stay. So I said, "No," and she sat down beside my feet, touching them with her thigh. I made a move, but she touched my ankles and said, "Don't bother. You don't have to make yourself uncomfortable because of me. What happened anyway?"

"I asked your sister for a date."

"And when she said, 'No' you passed out."

I thought she was warm toward me and not merely curious.

"I'm all for you, Mr. March," she said, "so I'll tell you what Esther thinks. She thinks that you service the lady you're with."

"*What?*" I cried out and jumped from the seat and gave myself a crack on the head against the dowels of the swing.

"That you're her gigolo and lay her. Why don't you sit down? I thought I should explain this to you."

As if I had been carrying something with special sacred devotedness and it had spilled and scalded me, that was how I felt. And here I had all along thought that the worst that could occur in the minds of young girls, heiresses even, was innocent by the standards of Einhorn's poolroom.

"Who thought of that, you or your sister?"

"I don't want to throw all the blame on Esther. I thought it might be so too, even though she brought it up first. We knew you weren't related to Mrs. Renling because we heard her say once to Mrs. Zeeland that you were her husband's protégé. You never danced with anybody else, and you held hands with her, and she is a sexy-looking woman for her age. You ought to see the two of you together! And then she's a European, and *they* don't think it's so terrible for a woman to have a much younger lover. I don't see what's so terrible about it either. Just my deadhead of a sister does."

"But I'm not European. I come from Chicago. I work for her husband in Evanston. I'm a clerk in his store, and that's the only occupation I have."

"Now don't be upset, Mr. March. Please don't be. We get around and see a lot. Why do you think I came out here to talk to you? Not to trouble you more. If you did, you did, and if you didn't, you didn't."

"You don't know what you're saying. It's a lousy thing to think of me, and of Mrs. Renling too, who's been only kind to me." I was angry and sounded angry, and she held her answers back; she also was heated and tight with excitement. I felt as well as saw her eyes deeply studying me. Whereas till now she had smiled occasionally there was no longer the least bit of humor in her face, which I saw well in the whiteness and ground dust and orchard leaves. I began to understand that I was with someone extraordinary, for it was a hot, prompt, investigative, and nearly imploring face. It was delicate but also full of strong nerve, with the recklessness that gives you as much concern as admiration, seeing it in a young woman; as when you see birds battling, like two fierce spouts of blood; they could easily die from small harms and don't seem to realize it. Of course that's one of those innocent male ideas probably.

"You don't really believe I'm Mrs. Renling's gigolo, do you?"

"I've already told you I wouldn't care if you were."

"Sure, what difference should it make to you!"

"No, you don't get it. You've been in love with my sister and following her around, so you haven't noticed that I've done exactly the same to you."

"You've what?"

"I've fallen in love with you. I love you."

"Go away. You don't. It's just an idea. If it's even an idea. What are you trying to give me?"

"You couldn't love Esther if you knew her. You're like me. That's why you fell in love. She couldn't. Augie! Why don't you change to me?"

She took my hand and drew it to her, leaning toward me from the hips, which were graceful. Oh, Mrs. Renling over whom I thought I had triumphed because her suspicions were so misplaced!

"I don't care about Mrs. Renling," she said. "Suppose you did, once."

"Never!"

"A young person can do all sorts of things because he has more in him than he knows what to do with."

Did I say that the world had never had better color? I left something out of account, a limping, crippled consideration which seems to lose ground as you reach beauty and Orizaba flowers, but soon you find it has preceded you.

"Now, Miss Fenchel," I said, trying to keep her in her seat as I stood up. "You're lovely, but what do you think we're doing? I can't help it, I love Esther." And as she wouldn't stay put I had to escape from the swing and get away in the orchard.

"Mr. March—Augie," she called. But I wasn't going to talk to her now. I went into the hotel by the service entrance. When I was in the room, with the phone off the hook so that

Mrs. Renling couldn't reach me, I explained to myself, while taking off my good duds and dropping them on the floor, that this was merely something between sisters and I figured in it accidentally, not really personally. But my other thought was that, if it weren't so, there was no luck in these things; how everyone seemed to get drawn in the wrong direction. So for the same desires to meet was a freak occurrence. And to feel them so specific, settled on one person, maybe was an unallowable presumption, too pure, too special, and a misunderstanding of the real condition of things.

When I walked in to have breakfast with Mrs. Renling next morning I left the door open.

"What, were you born in the coal scuttle?" she said. "Close it. I'm lying here." And when I went, halfhearted, to do it, she observed how wrinkled I looked. "Go down to the tailor after breakfast and get pressed. You must have slept in your pants. I make allowance for you because you're in love, even the way you were so courteous to me last night. But you don't have to be a tramp."

After breakfast she took off for her mineral bath and I went down to the lobby. The Fenchels had checked out. There was a note at the desk for me from Thea. "Esther told uncle about you, and we are going to Waukesha for a few days and then East. You were foolish last night. Think about it. It's true I love you. You'll see me again."

Then I had a few rough days and got stretched out in melancholy. I thought, where did I get that way, putting in for the best there was in the departments of beauty and joy as if I were a count of happy youth, and like born to elegance and sweet love, with bones made of candy? And had to remember what very seldom mattered with me, namely, where I came from, parentage, and other history, things I had never much thought of as difficulties, being democratic in temperament, available to everybody and assuming about others what I assumed about myself.

And in the meantime, more and more, I had to carry what till now had carried me. This place, for instance, the Merritt, cream and gold, was now on my neck—the service, the dinner music, the dances; the hyperbolical flowers all of a sudden like painted iron; the chichi a millstone; and, on top of it,

Mrs. Renling and her foundry-cast weight. I couldn't take her now when she was difficult. There was bad luck even in the weather, which turned cool and rainy toward the last; and rather than stay in where she could lay hands on me and carry on and tyrannize, I stuck around the amusement park at Silver Beach, where the seats of the Ferris wheel were covered, getting blackened, and I got soaked through my raincoat (from the old times and not up to my recenter elegance). I sat in the hot-dog stands among the carnies, concessionaires, and shell-game operators, waiting for the course of baths to finish.

Near the end of the holiday Simon wrote that he was coming to St. Joe with a girl friend, and he had luck with the weather. I was on the pier when the white steamer tied up. All the blue and green was fresher from the rains, and the cold of the wet days was down to a pin core. As for the people debarking, the hard use of the city was on them; it had come off only a little during this four-hour excursion on the water. Families, single men, working girls in pairs bringing their beach and summer things, some not so visibly encumbered but heavily loaded all the same. Tough or injured, according to their lot or nature. Off the ship they tramped, over the motor-driven edge of water and into the peaceful swale of brightness, and here and there the light picked out a specialized or warily happy face; and also illuminated were silks, hairs, brows, straws, breasts come to breathe out charges of nerves or let rise the driven-down simplicities, bearers of things as old as the most ancient of cities and older; desires and avoidances bred into bellies, shoulders, legs, as long ago as Eden and the Fall.

Taller than most, blond and brown, there was my Germanic-looking brother. He was dolled up like a Fourth of July sport, and a little like a smart gypsy, smiling, his chipped tooth foremost, his double-breasted plaid jacket open wide, knuckles down on the handles of two grips. He gave off his fairness with a kind of heat in the blue color of his eyes, terrifically; it was also in his cheeks, down into his neck, rich and animal. He walked heavy in balance, in his pointed shoes over the gangplank, arms drawn down by the weight of the valises, searching for me in the shade of the pier. I never saw him looking better than there, in the sun, rolling in with the crowd in his glad rags. When he clapped his arm around me I was happy to feel and smell him, and we grinned, mugged, pushed faces, with man's bristles under each other's fingers, and went through a rough, teasing grip.

"Well, you jerk?"

"And you, money-man?"

There wasn't any sting in this, though Simon had for a while been acting quiet toward me because I was earning more than he and cruising in luxury.

"How's everybody—Mama?"

"Well, the eyes, you know. But she's okay."

And then he fetched up his girl—a big dark girl named Cissy Flexner. I had known her at school; she was from the neighborhood. Her father, before he went bust, had owned a drygoods store—overalls, laborers' canvas gloves and long-johns, galoshes, things like that; and he was a fleshy, diffident, pale, inside sort of man, back in his boxes. But she, although in a self-solicitous way, was a beautiful piece of tall work, on colossal but careful legs, hips forward; her mouth was big and would have been perfect if there hadn't been something self-tasting in it, eyes with complicated lids but magnificent in their slow heaviness, an erotic development. So that she had to cast down these eyes a little to be decent with her endowment, that height of the bosom and form of hips and other generic riches, smooth and soft, that may take the early person, the little girl, by surprise in their ampleness when they come on. She accused me somewhat of examining her too much, but could anybody help that? And it was excusable on the further score that she might become my sister-in-law, for Simon was powerfully in love. He already was husbandly toward her, and they hung on each other with fondling and kissing and intimacy, strolling by the steep colors of water and air, while I swam by myself in the lake a little distance away. Also on the sand, when Simon, after he had rubbed his fine shield of chest hair, dried her back, he kissed it, and it gave me a moment's ache in the roof of the mouth, as if I had got the warm odor and touch of skin myself. She had so much, gave out so much splendor. As stupendous quiff.

But personally I didn't care too much for her. Partly because I was gone on Esther. But also because what came across as her own, that is, apart from female brilliance, was slow. Maybe she herself was stupefied by what she had, her slaying weight. It must have pressed down on her thoughts, like any great vitality in nature. Like the aims that live in the blood of grizzly or tiger, bearing down on the mind of such beasts with square weight, a manifestation of one thing carried out completely, to the very stripes and claws. But what about the privilege over that of being in the clasp of nature, and in on the mission of a species? The ingredient of thought was weaker in Cissy's mixture than the other elements. But she was a sly girl, soft though she seemed.

And as she lay stretched on the sand, and the hot oil of popcorn and sharpness of mustard came in puffs, with crackling, from the stands of Silver Beach, she kept answering Simon, whom I couldn't hear—he was on his side next to her in his red trunks—"Oh, fooey, no. What bushwah! Love, shmuv!" But her pleasure was high. "I'm so glad you brought me, dear. So clean. It's heavenly here."

I didn't like Simon's struggle with her—for that was what it was—to convince her, sway her, work her around. Nearly everything he proposed she refused. "Let's not and say we did," and similar denials. It led him into crudenesses I hadn't ever seen him in before, the way he laid himself out, dug, campaigned, swashed, flattered her, was gross. His tongue hung out with the heat of work and infatuation; and there was a bottom ground where he was angry, his anger rising straight into his face in two flaming centers, under his eyes, on either side of his nose. I understood this, as we were covering the same field of difficulty and struggle in front of the identical Troy. This that happened to us would have given Grandma Lausch the satisfaction of a prophetess—the spirit, anyhow, of her; the actual was covered up in the dust of the Home, in the band of finalists for whom there was the little guessing game of which would next be taken out of play. So I recorded this seeming success of prediction for her. And as for Simon, all the places where he and I had once been joined while still young brothers, before there were differences and distances between us—these places began to act up, feeling attachment near again. The reattachment didn't actually take place, but I loved him nevertheless. When he was on his feet with the flowered cloth of her beach dress on his shoulders, it made something crass but brave, his standing up raw and sunburned, by the pure streak of the water, as if he were being playful about the wearing of this girl's favor.

I took them to the evening steamer, for she refused to stay overnight, and was on deck with them through the long working out of sunset, down to the last blue, devoid of other lights; fall weight and furrows in the clouds set cityward, let go from the power of the sun to sink down on the moundings and pilings of the water, gray and powerful.

"Well, sport, we may be married in the next few months," he said. "You envy me? I bet you do."

And he covered her up with his hands and arms, his chin on her shoulder and kissing her on the neck. The flamboyant way he had of making love to her was curious to me—his leg advanced between her legs and his fingers spread on her face. She didn't refuse anything he did, although in words never agreed; she had no kindness in speaking. With her hands up the sleeves of her white coat, hugging out the chill, she stood by a davit. He was still in his shirt, owing to sunburn, but wore his panama, the breeze molding the brim around.

Chapter IX

JUST WHEN Mrs. Renling's construction around me was nearly complete I shoved off. The leading and precipitating reason was that she proposed to adopt me. I was supposed to become Augie Renling, live with them, and inherit all their dough. To see what there was behind this more light is needed than probably I can turn on. But first of all there was something adoptional about me. No doubt this had something to do with the fact that we were in a fashion adopted by Grandma Lausch in our earliest days; to please and reward whom I had been pliable and grateful-seeming, an adoptee. If not really so docile and pliable, this was the hidden ball and surprise about me. Why had the Einhorns, protecting their son Arthur, had to underscore it that they didn't intend to take me into their family? Because something about me suggested adoption. And then there were some people who were especially adoption-minded. Some maybe wishing to complete their earthly work. Thus Mrs. Renling in her strenuous and hacked-up way, and the whiteness that came from her compression into her intense purposes. She too had her mission on earth.

There's one thing you couldn't easily find out from Mrs. Renling; I never knew what was her most deep desire, owing to her cranky manners and swift conversation. But she wanted to try being a mother. However, I was in a state of removal from all her intentions for me. Why should I turn into one of these people who didn't know who they themselves were? And the unvarnished truth is that it wasn't a fate good enough for me, because that was what came out clearly when it became a question of my joining up. As son. Otherwise I had nothing against them; just the opposite, I had a lot to thank them for. But all the same I was not going to be built into Mrs. Renling's world, to consolidate what she affirmed she was. And it isn't only she but a class of people who trust they will be justified, that their thoughts will be as substantial as the seven hills to build on, and by spreading their power they will have an eternal city for vindication on the day when other founders have gone down, bricks and planks, whose thoughts were not real and who built on soft swamp. What this means is not a single Tower of Babel plotted in common, but hundreds of thousands of separate beginnings, the length and breadth of America. Energetic people who build against pains and uncertainties, as weaker ones merely hope against them. And, even literally, Mrs. Renling was very strong, and as she didn't do any visible work it must have come, the development in her muscles, from her covert labor.

Mr. Renling also was willing to adopt me and said he would be happy to be my father. I knew it was more than he would say to anyone else. From his standpoint, for me, reared by poor women, it was a big break to be rescued from the rat race and saved by affection. God may save all, but human rescue is only for a few.

When I told Mrs. Renling that Simon was going to get married and that Cissie was the daughter of a busted dry-goods man, she began to work it out and do the sociology of it for me. She showed me the small flat and the diapers hanging in the kitchen, the installment troubles about furniture and clothes and my brother an old man at thirty from anxiety and cut-off spirit, the captive of the girl and babies. "While you at thirty, Augie, will just start thinking about getting married. You'll have money and culture and your pick of women. Even a girl like Thea Fenchel. An educated man with a business is a lord. Renling is very clever and has come far, but with science, literature, and history he would have been a real prince and not just average prosperous—"

She pressed in the right place when she mentioned the Fenchels. It opened up a temptation. But it was only one temptation and that was not enough. I didn't believe Esther Fenchel ever would have me. And, moreover, though I was still in love with her, my attitude toward her wasn't what it had been. I more and more believed what her sister had said. And then, when I told myself absolutely the truth, I conceded that I didn't have a chance.

Anyway, Mrs. Renling put tender weights on me. She called me "son," and she would introduce me to people as "our youngster," and she petted me on the head and so forth. And I was robust and in possession of my sex; I mean by that it wasn't stroking a boy of eight on his new glossy hair, and there was something more to be assumed than that I was a child.

That I didn't want to be adopted never spontaneously occurred to her, and she assumed, as if it were normal but not to be mentioned, something else: that, like everyone, I was self-seeking. So that if I had any objections in reserve, they'd be minor ones, and I'd keep them covered. Or if I had thoughts of helping my brothers or Mama, those thoughts would be bound up and kept in the back. She had never seen Mama and didn't intend to; and when I told her in St. Joe that Simon was coming she didn't ask to meet him. There was a little in it of Moses and the Pharaoh's daughter; only I wasn't a bulrush-hidden infant by any means. I had family enough to suit me and history to be loyal to, not as though I had been gotten off of a stockpile.

So I drew back; I turned down the hints, and when they became open offers I declined them. I said to Mr. Renling, "I appreciate your kindness, and you two are swell. I'll be grateful to you as long as I live. But I have folks, and I just have a feeling—"

"You fool!" said Mrs. Renling. "What folks? What folks?"

"Why, my mother, my brothers."

"What have they got to do with it? Baloney! Where's your father—tell me!"

I couldn't say.

"You don't know even who he is. Now, Augie, don't be a fool. A real family is somebody, and offers you something. Renling and I will be your parents because we will give you, and all the rest is bunk."

"Well, let him think about it," said Renling.

I think that Renling was out of sorts that day; he had a cowlick at the back of his hair and the loops of his suspenders showed from his vest. Which indicated that he suffered some, with a despair of his own, nothing to do with me, for as a usual thing he presented himself perfect.

"Oh, what's to think!" Mrs. Renling cried. "You see how he thinks! He has to learn *how* to think first, if he wants to be a dumbbell and work for other people all his life. If I let him, he'd be married already to the waitress next door, that Indian with the squashed nose, and waiting for a baby, so in two years he'd be ready to take gas. Offer him gold and he says, no, he chooses shit!"

She went on like that and worked ugly terror on me. Renling was disturbed. Not terribly disturbed, but in the manner a nightbird, that knows all about daylight, will beat through it if he must, a crude, big, brown-barred shape, but only if he must, and then he will fly toward the thick of the woods and get back to the darkness.

And I—I always heard from women that I didn't have the profounder knowledge of life, that I didn't know its damage or its suffering or its stupendous ecstasies and glories. Being not weak, nor with breasts where its dreads could hit me. Looking not so strong as to be capable of a superior match with it. Other people showed me their achievements, claims and patents, paradise and hell-evidence, their prospectors' samples—often in their faces, in lumps—and, especially women, told me of my ignorance. Here Mrs. Renling was menacing me, crying out that I was the child of fools, dead sure that I would be crushed in the gate, stamped out in the life struggle. For, listen to her, and I was made for easy conditions, and to rise from a good bed to the comfort of a plentiful breakfast, to dip my roll in yolk and smoke a cigar with coffee, in sunshine and comfort, free from melancholy or stains. Such the kind faction of the world wanted for me, and if I refused my chance there was oblivion waiting for me instead; the wicked would get hold of me. I tried not to reject the truth in what I was told, and I had a lot of regard for the power of women to know it.

But I asked for time to think the matter over, and I could have thought very successfully, for the weather favored it— the first and best of autumn, football weather, cold yellow asters in the fine air, and the full sounds of punting and horses stamping on the bridle path.

I took an afternoon off to consult Einhorn.

Einhorn's luck had begun to turn again and he had opened a new office, moving from the poolroom to a flat across the street where he could continue to keep an eye on it. The change made him somewhat egotistical, as also the fact that there was a woman in love with him. It gave him a big boost.

He had been putting out his paper for shut-ins again, on the mimeograph machine, and one of his readers, a crippled girl named Mildred Stark, had fallen for him. She wasn't in first youth any more; she was aged about thirty and heavy, but she had a vital if somewhat struggle-weakened head, hair and brows strong and black. She wrote answers in verse to his inspirational poems and at last she had her sister bring her to the office, where she made a scene and wouldn't go away until Einhorn had promised to let her work for him. She didn't ask for any salary, only that he should rescue her from home-boredom. Mildred's trouble was with her feet, and she wore orthopedic shoes. They made slow going, and, as I later had the chance to learn, Mildred was somebody for whom impulses came fast and in force, and these impulses ran onto non-conductors and were turned back, stored up until she got dark in the face. In her person, as I say, she was heavy, and her eyes were black, her skin was not well lit. To develop from crippled girl into crippled woman, in the family, in the house, such staleness and hardship—that's what it makes for, darkness, saturninity, oversat grievance. Being without what's needed to put a satisfied, not dissatisfied, face at the window.

But Mildred wouldn't accept lying down and dying, though she never recovered from looking near middle-aged and dark and sore, as a woman forced to sit, or someone who has missed out on children, or whom men have swindled. It could not be rubbed out, though it was arrested by her love for Einhorn, who permitted her to love him. In the beginning she came only two or three times a week to type some letters for him, and ended by becoming his full-time secretary, as well as other things—his servant and confidante. Someone who could literally say, biblically, "Thy handmaiden." Pushing his rolling chair for him, she needed its support in her limping and foot-dragging. He sat, well satisfied, well served. He looked severe and even impatient, but the truth was otherwise. The spirit I found him in was the Chanticleer spirit, by which I refer to male piercingness, sharpness, knotted hard muscle and blood in the comb, jerky, flaunty, haughty and bright, with luxurious slither of feathers.

Ah, but there are other facts that have to be satisfied too, after this comparison. It's too bad but it is so. Humankind does not have that sort of simplicity—not the single line that a stick draws on the ground but a vast harrow of countless disks. His spirit was piercing, but there has to be mentioned his poor color, age-impoverished and gray; plus the new flat's ugliness; dullness of certain hours, dryness of days, dreariness and shabbiness—mentioned that the street was bare, dim and low in life, bad; and that there were business thoughts and malformed growths of purpose, terrible, menacing, salt-patched with noises and news, and pimpled and dotted around with lies, both practical and gratuitous.

To Tillie Einhorn, as far as anybody could tell, Mildred was acceptable. The force of Einhorn on Tillie was such that to judge him wrong was too much of an operation for her. Besides, you have to think of a condition of people that gets into them like a cobbler's stretcher into a shoe; this stretcher for Tillie was Einhorn's special need as a cripple. She was used to making allowances.

Well, this was how Einhorn was situated when I came to ask him for advice; I found him too busy to give me his attention. He kept looking to the street as I talked, then asked me to push him to the toilet, which I did, on the gaggling casters that could, as always, stand an oiling. All he replied was, "Well, it's pretty unusual. It's quite an offer. You were born lucky." He gave it less than half his mind, thinking I was telling him the news that the Renlings wanted to adopt me, not that I considered refusing. Naturally he was wrapped up in his own affairs. And I could look at Mildred Stark if I wanted an example of how someone became attached to, and then absorbed into, a family.

I finished the afternoon downtown, and while I was eating a liver sandwich at Elfman's and watching the unemployed musicians on the Dearborn corner, I saw a guy named Clarence Ruber passing and knocked on the plate glass with my ring till he noticed me and came in to talk. I knew this Ruber from Crane College, where he had run a baseball pool at the Enark Café; he was quiet and dirty-spoken, smooth in the face, fat behind, with a slow, shiny Assyrian fringe on his head and a soft-bosomed fashion of clothes, silky shirts, yellow silk tie, and gray flannel suit. Looking me over, he saw that I was doing well too, in contrast to the Depression musicians and the other eaters, and we traded information. He had opened a small shop on the South Shore, in partnership with a cousin's widow who had a little money. They dealt in lamps, pictures, vases, piano scarves, ashtrays and such bric-a-brac, and since the cousin and his wife had been, before the Bust, interior decorators with big hotels for clients, they did a good trade. "There's dough in this. It's one of these rackets where people pay for being handled a particular way. Dazzle business. Because, if they knew it, they could buy a lot of this crap at the dime store, but they can't trust their judgment. It's a woman's line," he said, "and you have to understand how to tickle their bellies." I asked him what he was doing here among the musicians. "Musicians, my ass," he said. He had been seeing a man in the Burnham Building who had invented a rubberized paint for bathrooms, a waterproof product that, with the widow-cousin's contacts in hotels, ought to make him a fortune. It kept walls from rotting; the water didn't harm the plaster. The inventor was just beginning to go into production. Ruber himself was going to go out and sell it, for there was a lot of money in it. Therefore, he said, they would need a man to replace him in the shop. And since I had experience with rich customers, a ritzy clientele, I was just the man for the substitution. "I don't want any more fucking relatives around; they get in my hair. So if you're interested come out and have a look at the setup. If you like it we can talk terms."

Seeing that I could not stay with the Renlings unless I became their adopted son, which by now I knew would suffocate me, no other arrangement possible after I had turned them down, I closed a deal with Ruber. I made up a story to tell Renling about a marvelous business opportunity of a lifetime with a school chum, and I pulled out of Evanston in a cold air—Mrs. Renling iron with anger toward me, and Renling himself on the cool side of well-wishing, but saying anyway that I was to come to him if ever I needed help.

I took a room on the South Side, in a house on Blackstone Avenue, four flights up, three of mingy red carpet and one of thready wood, up in the clumsy dust, next door to the can. Here I wasn't far from the Nelson Home, and as it was a Sunday morning when I set myself up, and I had time, I went to visit Grandma Lausch. By now she was almost like everyone else in the joint, to my eyes, having lost her distinguishing independence, weakened, mole-ish, needing to look around for her old-time qualities when she greeted me, as if she had laid them down, forgetting where. She didn't seem to recall what grievances she had against me either, and when we sat down together on a bench in the parlor, between some silent old people, asked me, "And how is—is *jener*, the idiot?" She had forgotten Georgie's name, and it horrified me; yes, it sent me for a loop until I remembered to think how small a part of her life compared with the whole span she had spent with us, and how many bayous and deadwaters there must be to the sides of an old varicose channel. And as there is a strength or stubbornness about people that doesn't want the first fact about them spoken, also there is a time when that fact or truth can't any more be helpful—what can it do for the ruin of an old woman?—but it appears as a blot in the eyes over old expressions. What good can this fact be so near death? Except as a benefit to its witnesses, since we human creatures have many reasons to believe there's advantage and profit for someone in everything, even in the worst muds, wastes, and poison by-products; and a charm of chemical medicine or industry is how there are endless uses in cinders, slag, bone, and manure. But in reality we're a long way from being able to profit from everything. Yes, and besides even a truth can get cold from solitude and solitary confinement, and doesn't live long outside the Bastille; if the rescuing republican crowd is the power of death it doesn't live at all. This was how it was with Grandma Lausch, who had only a few months left of life. Whose Odessa black dress was greasy and whitening; who gave me an old cat's gape; who maybe didn't too well place me; who had this blob of original fact, of what had primarily counted with her, like a cast in the eye; weakly, even infant and lunatic. Her we always thought so powerful and shock-proof! It really threw me. Yet I also thought she did remember who I was and that old consciousness was not lost but in a phase of a turntable that turned too slowly. I even thought that she appreciated the visit and said I was her neighbor now and would come again. But I couldn't make it, and the same winter she died of pneumonia.

In my new job I had a downgrade from the start. Ruber's cousin's widow was a dissatisfied woman; she didn't trust me very much. This lady—she wore her fur coat in the style of a cloak in the store, with a hat of the same creature like a prickly crown, and a face always aware of its imperfections and suffering from them, wretched skin and meager lips—she had stomach troubles and a stiff clamp on bad temper. She cramped my style, the style learned with what I thought was anyway a better class of customers, and she wouldn't let me come near the important ones. And in the office she locked drawers; she didn't want me to know costs. What she wanted was to confine me to the work in the back, packing, wrapping, matting, framing, and winding cellophane on lampshades. So that, with being kept in the rear or out on errands to various little factories and potteries in lofts around Wabash Avenue, I quick caught on that she was pushing me toward the door. And as soon as the rubberized paint went into production I became a salesman for it, as I think Ruber too had all the time intended. He said that the shop didn't actually need me since I seemed satisfied to be errand boy and didn't take enough interest in the business. "I thought you'd have some ideas, not be just a salary man, but that ain't the way it's been," he told me.

"Well," I said, "Mrs. Ruber has ideas about me."

"Of course," said Ruber, "I seen she's been trying to make you suck hind titty. But the thing is why you let her."

Now he took me off salary and put me on a commission basis. There was nothing I saw to do but accept, and went around on the streetcars and El with a can of the paint, to hotels, hospitals, and such, trying to get orders. It was a flop. I couldn't land anything, money was so tight, and I was dealing with a peculiar sort of people. I had leads from Mrs. Ruber, into hotels, where she claimed to be better known than she actually was (or managers would not acknowledge her till they knew my business); and, moreover, these were not easy people to lay hold of, in the backstairs and workshops of the cream, noble marble, footmanned, razmataz, furnished-for-pontiffs lakeside joints. Also, many hotels had painting contractors or graft arrangements; controlled by receivers, appointed by the courts, the original corporations in bankruptcy; the receivers were themselves interested in the insurance, plumbing, catering, decorating, bars, concessions, and the rest of the interlocking system. To be sent by the manager to the painting contractor was to be given a runaround. They didn't want to see my rubber paint. I waited on enough of them in outside offices, which I don't say breeds the best thoughts, and soon this was clear.

It was now full winter, and barbarous how raw; so going around the city on the spidery cars, rides lasting hours, made you stupid as a stoveside cat because of the closeness inside; and there was something fuddling besides in the mass piled up of uniform things, the likeness of small parts, the type of newspaper columns and the bricks of buildings. To sit and be trundled, while you see: there's a danger in that of being a bobbin for endless thread or bolt for yard goods; if there's not much purpose anyway in the ride. And if there's some amount of sun in the dusty weep marks of the window, it can be even worse for the brain than those iron-deep clouds, just plain brutal and not mitigated. There haven't been civilizations without cities. But what about cities without civilizations? An inhuman thing, if possible, to have so many people together who beget nothing on one another. No, but it is not possible, and the dreary begets its own fire, and so this never happens.

I did make a few sales. Karas, Einhorn's cousin-in-law, in the Holloway Enterprises, gave me a break and bought a few gallons to try in a little Van Buren Street gray-bedding hotel, almost a bum's flop, near the railroad station, and he said he would never use it in any of his better establishments because it made a loud smell of rubber in the heat and moisture of the shower room. There was also a doctor at State and Lake, a buddy of Ruber's, an abortionist; he was doing over his suite and I got an order from him; and here Ruber tried to chisel from the commission; he didn't need me, he said, to make this sale. I would have quit him flat then and there if I hadn't gotten pretty familiar by then with the situations-wanted columns of the *Tribune*. I wasn't earning enough to give anything toward Mama's support any more, but at least I was making expenses and Simon didn't have to support me. Of course he beefed because I had quit Renling. How was he going to marry if he had to keep Mama by himself? I said,

"You and Cissy can move in with her." But this made him look black, and I understood that Cissy wasn't having any of that, the old flat and Mama to take care of. "Well, Simon, you know I don't want to stick you," I said, "and that I'll try my best." We were having coffee in Raklios's, and my pot of paint was on the table and my gloves on top of that. Open at the seams, the gloves showed how I had lost my grip on prosperity. And I was getting dirty, for a salesman, for whose appearance there are laws which are supposed to guarantee a certain firmness of personality. I had fallen below the standard, unable to afford cleaning and repairing, nor was able to spare much feeling for it.

The way I was living was becoming crude, and I was learning some squatter lessons. Up in my room the heat didn't reach, and I wore my coat and socks at night. In the morning I went down to the drugstore to warm up on a cup of coffee and lay out my route for the day. I carried my razor in my pocket and shaved downtown with the free hot water, liquid soap, and paper towels of public toilets, and I ate in YMCA cafeterias or one-arm joints and beat checks as often as I could. Vigorous at nine, my hope ran out by noon, and then one of my hardships was that I had no place of rest. I could try to pass the afternoon in Einhorn's new office; he was accustomed to people on his bench, outside the railing, who had no special tasks. But I who had worked for him had to be doing something, and he would send me on his business. So that I might as well have been on my own, once I was already on the streetcar. Besides I had an obligation to Simon that would not let me loaf, although simply to move around was in itself of no advantage. It was not only for me that being moored wasn't permitted; there was general motion, as of people driven from angles and corners into the open, by places being valueless and inhospitable to them. In the example of the Son of Man having no place to lay His head; or belonging to the world in general; except that the illuminated understanding of this was absent, nobody much guessing what was up on the face of the earth. I, with my can of paint, no more than others. And once I was under way, streetcars weren't sufficient, nor Chicago large enough to hold me.

Coming out of an El station one day, when the snow was running off, at the tail end of winter, I ran into Joe Gorman whom I hadn't seen since after the robbery. He was in a good blue coat of narrow style, and a freshly blocked fedora, dented like a soft bread by the fingers. He was buying magazines, out of the wall of them that hung by the stand. His nose was raised up and he looked ruddy and well, benefited by a good breakfast and the cold morning—although it would have been more like his habit of life to have come from an all-night poker game. Sizing me up, with my sample paint can, it was plain to him that I was having it bad. I had the face of someone pretty much beat.

"What's this racket you're in?" he asked me, and when I explained it he said, but not in a triumphing way, "Sucker!" He was certainly right, and I didn't put much force into defending myself. "It's a way of meeting people," I answered, "and something may open up one of these days."

"Yes," he said, "a deep hole. What if you do meet people—you think somebody is going to do something for you because you're a pretty boy? Give you a big break? These days they take care of their relatives first. And what have you got in the way of relatives?"

I didn't have much. Five Properties was still driving his milk truck, but I didn't mean to ask him for a job. Coblin had lost everything except his paper route in the crash. Anyway, I hadn't seen much of either of them since the Commissioner's funeral.

"Come and have some cheese and pie on me," he said, and we went into a restaurant.

"What's up with you?" I said, for I didn't want to ask explicitly; it was bad manners. "Do you ever see Sailor Bulba?"

"Not that dumbhead, he's no good to me. He's in an organization now, slugger for a union, and it's all he's good for. Besides, what I'm in now, I have no use for anybody like that. But I could do something for you if you wanted to earn a fast buck."

"Is it risky?"

"Nothing like what worried you last time. I don't go in for that any more myself. It's not legitimate, what I'm doing, but it's a lot easier and safer. And what do you think makes the buck so fast?"

"Well, what is it?"

"Running immigrants over the border from Canada, from around Rouse's Point over to Massena Springs, New York."

"No," I said, not having forgotten my conversation with Einhorn. "I can't do that."

"There's nothing to it."

"And if you're caught?"

"And if I'm caught? And if I'm not caught?" he said with savage humor, poking fun at me. "You want me to go around and peddle paint? I'd rather sit still, like the pilot light inside the gas; and I can't sit around or I'd go bats."

"This is federal."

"You don't have to tell me what it is. I only asked you because you look as if you needed a break. I make this trip two and three times a month, and I'm getting tired of doing all the driving. So if you want to come along and be my relief on the road as far as Massena Springs I'll give you fifty bucks and all expenses. Then if you decide to come the rest of the way I'll up it to a hundred. There'll still be time to think it over on the way, and we'll be back in three days."

I took him up on this and considered it a break. Fifty dollars, clear, would go a long way toward easing my mind about Simon. I was fed up with trying to peddle the rubberized paint, and my reckoning was that with a little dough to tide me over I could spend a week or two looking for something else, perhaps dope out a way to get back to college, for I had not altogether given up on that. All this was how I decided, in my outer mind, to go; with the other, the inner, I wanted a change of pressure, and to get out of the city. As for the immigrants, my thought about them was, Hell, why shouldn't they be here with the rest of us if they want to be? There's enough to go around of everything including hard luck.

I gave the paint to Tillie Einhorn, to decorate her bathroom, and early in the morning Joe Gorman picked me up in a black Buick; it was souped up, I could tell the first instant, from the hell-energy that gives you no time to consider. I wasn't even well settled, with spare shirt wrapped in a newspaper in the back seat and my coat straightened under me, before we were on the far South Side, passing the yards of Carnegie Steel; then the dunes, piled up like sulphur; in and out of Gary in two twists and on the road for Toledo, where the speed increased, and the mouth of the motor opened out like murder, not panting, but liberated to do what it was made for.

Slender, pressing down nervous on the wheel, with his long nose of broken form and the color running fast up his face and making a narrow crossing on his forehead, Gorman was like a jockey in his feeling toward the car. You could see what pleasure he got out of finding what he needed to wrap his nerves in. Outside Toledo I took the wheel, and occasionally found him looking sardonically sidewise from his narrow face, a long dark eye making a new measure of me from its splotch of discoloration by fatigue or by the trouble of a busy will; and he said—they seemed his first words to me, though they weren't literally—"Step it up!"

So I apologized that I didn't have the feel of the car yet and obeyed. But he didn't like my driving, particularly that I hesitated to pass trucks on the hills, and took the wheel from me before we had covered much of the ground to Cleveland.

It was beginning April, and the afternoon was short, so that it was getting dark when we approached Lackawanna. Some way beyond it we stopped for gas, and Gorman gave me a bill to buy some hamburgers at a joint next door. There I went to the can first, and from the window saw a state trooper by the pump, examining the car, and no sign of Gorman. I slipped into the filthy side hall and glanced into the kitchen, where an old Negro was washing dishes, and passed behind him without being noticed, over a bushel in the doorway, into the intervening yard, or lot, and I saw Gorman beating it along the wall of the garage, swiftly, toward the border of trees and bushes where the fields began. I ran parallel, having a start of ten yards or so, and met him back of these trees, and there was almost a disaster before he recognized me, for he had a pistol in his hand—the gun Einhorn had warned me he carried. I clapped my hand to the barrel and pushed it away.

"What've you got that out for?"

"Take your hands off, or I'll clobber you with it!"

"What's got into you? What're you running from the cops for? It's only for speeding."

"The car's hot. Speeding hell!"

"I thought it was your car!"

"No, it's stolen."

We started to run again, hearing the motorcycle in the lot, and threw ourselves down in plowed field. It was open country, but dusk. The trooper came as far as the trees and looked but did not come through. Luck was with us that he didn't, since Gorman had him covered with the gun on a sod for a rest, and was cowboy enough to shoot, so that I tasted puke in my throat from terror. But the trooper turned off, splitting the beams of his lamp on the evergreens, and we beat it over the plowland to a country road well back from the highway. This place, for sure, had a demon; it was blue, lump-earthed, oil-rank, and machinery was cooking in the dark, not far back of us, into heaven, from the Lackawanna chimneys.

"You weren't going to shoot, were you?" I said. He was reaching inside his sleeve with a lifted shoulder, almost like a woman pulling up an inside strap. He put away his gun. Each of us, I suppose, was thinking in his own fashion that we didn't make a pair—I of the vanity of being so leaping dangerous, and he, despisingly, that I must have shit in my blood, or such poolroom contempt.

"What did you run for?" he said.

"Because I saw you running."

"Because you were scared."

"That too."

"Did the guy in the garage notice two of us?"

"He must have. And if he didn't somebody in the hamburger joint must be wondering where I went."

"Then we'd better split up. We're not far outside of Buffalo, and I'll pick you up there tomorrow in front of the main post office at nine o'clock."

"Pick me up?"

"In a car. By then I'll have one. You've got the tenner I gave you for the chow—that'll take care of you. There must be a bus into town. You go up the road and take it; I'll go down. Let a couple of buses go by so we won't be getting on the same one."

So we split up, and I felt safer without him.

Narrow, tall, sharp in the way his shoulders, hat, and features broke, he seemed, as he watched me get started up the road, like a city specialist on this unfamiliar interurban ground. Then he turned swiftly too, going low on his legs downhill, fast, scraping on the stones.

I tramped a considerable distance to take the first crossroad back to the highway. Headlights on a barn approached around a curve and made me drop down. It was a state police car, and what would it be doing on a side lane like this if not looking to pick us up? Probably Gorman hadn't even bothered to change the license plates of the car. I got off the lane into the fields then, and made up my mind to take the shortest way back to Lackawanna and not to meet him in Buffalo. He was too inspired for me, and his kind of outlawry wasn't any idea of mine; therefore why should I be sprawling in the mud waiting for him to commit a hothead crime and get me in as a accessory for a stiff sentence? When I had left him to go up the road I had already begun to think of this and was actually on my way back to Chicago.

I began to run cross-country because I was tired of picking my way, and I came out to the highway near town, where the edge of Lake Erie approaches. And there I saw a crowd, forming up in old cars, with banners and signs, blocking the traffic. I think it was an organization of the unemployed, many veterans, wearing Legion caps; I was too hard pushed in the crude hard air of darkness to get it straight. But they were gathering for a march on Albany or Washington to ask for a relief increase and starting out to meet the Buffalo contingent. I came up slowly and saw that there were more troopers around, who were trying to keep traffic open, and also town cops, and I figured it to be safer to mingle than to try to go into town. By the lamps I was able to see how much mud had stuck to me, too wet to get off. There was such yelling and sheaving of old engines jockeying to form a line that I got to the tail gate of a jalopy, and, giving a man a hand putting in planks for benches and laying a tarpaulin over the top, I made myself a part of his outfit in the dusk. And now, though no distance at all from Lackawanna, I was about to start for Buffalo anyhow. I might have returned to the fields and gone around into town, but I calculated that, looking as I did, I might be picked up.

As I was tying down canvas behind the cab the crowd was

slowly forced back, and from the beam that was painting back and forth on the people, yellow and red, I knew that a squad car was forcing a path and saw the eye of it swiveling and rolling smoothly from the top. I twisted backward from the running board to look, and it was as fear had inspired me to suspect, Joe Gorman was sitting in the back seat between two troopers, with blood lines over his chin showing that he had probably tried to fight with them and they had opened up his lip, doing their cops' work. This was what he had come a long way to get, and got it, and looked not dazed but bright awake —which may have been an appearance, as the red of the blood appeared black. I felt powerfully heartsick to see him.

The squad car passed, and we started off in the truck at a slow sway, something like twenty men stowed in shank to shank behind the black open roar of the engine. There was nasty weather; rain, first thing, and the wet blowing in, which made a human steam like the steam of rinsing in a dairy, and while we were squelching and rocking over the swells of the road I was thinking of the misery of Joe Gorman's being picked up, how they must have nabbed him, and if he had a chance to pull his gun. Behind the canvas I didn't get to see the gas station and whether the car we had left was still there, or anything else. Until the truck got into the city I couldn't see a thing.

I dropped off the tail gate in the middle of town and found myself a hotel where I was dumb enough not to ask the price; but I was more concerned that the clerk shouldn't see the dirt on me and carried the coat on my arm. Besides, I was so sick over Joe Gorman I didn't think. Then, when they had beaten me out of two bucks in the morning, or about twice what a fleabag like that should have cost, and after I had paid for a big breakfast, which I had to have, there wasn't enough money for a bus ticket back to Chicago. I telegraphed Simon to wire me some money, and then I went to see the main drag, and I took the excursion to Niagara Falls where nobody seemed to have any business that day, only a few strays beside the crush of the water, like early sparrows in the cathedral square before Notre Dame has opened its doors; and then in the brute sad fog you know that at one time this sulphur coldness didn't paralyze everything, and there's the cathedral to prove it.

So I walked around the rails by the dripping black crags until it began to drizzle again, and I returned to see whether Simon's reply had come in yet. Till late afternoon I kept asking, and at last the girl in the cage looked tired of seeing me, and I recognized that I had the option of another night in Buffalo or hitting the road. And I was dim with the troubles I had got into, all this speeding and scattering, Gorman in the squad car pressing through the crowd, then the terrific emptying of Niagara waters, and also bobbling on the Buffalo cars, eating peanuts and hard rolls, my bowels like a screw of rubber, and the town unfriendly and wet—because if I hadn't been in such a dim state I'd have realized sooner that Simon wasn't going to send any money. But all of a sudden I realized that that was so. He might not even have it to spare, just after the first of the month when there was the rent to pay.

Thinking this, I told the telegraph girl to forget about the wire, I was leaving town.

Not to be picked up on the road in northern New York, I took a ticket to Erie at the Greyhound Station, and I was in the Pennsylvania corner that evening. To get off in Erie gave me no feeling that I had arrived somewhere, in a place that was a place in and for itself, but rather that it was one which waited on other places to give it life by occurring between them; the breath of it was thin, just materialized, waiting.

The flop I found was in a tall clapboard hotel, a kind of bone of a building, with more laths than plaster, with burns in the blanket, splits in the sheet opening on the mattress and its many stains. But I didn't care too much where I was; it would have been a nuisance to care; and I dropped off my shoes and climbed in. It sounded like a gale on the lake that night.

Nevertheless it was a serene warm morning when I went out on the road to start thumbing. I wasn't alone; people in great numbers were on the highways. Sometimes they traveled in pairs, but more usually alone, because it was easier to get rides alone. There was the CCC, draining swamps and planting trees in the distance, and on the road was this wanderer population without any special Jerusalem or Kiev in mind, or relics to kiss, or any idea of putting off sins, but only the hope their chances might be better in the next town. In this competition it was hard to get lifts. Appearances were against me too, for the Renling clothes were both smart and filthy. And then in my hurry to put distance between me and the stretch of road near Lackawanna where Joe Gorman had been picked up, I didn't have the patience to stand and flag for long but walked.

The traffic dived and quivered past me, and when I reached a place near Ashtabula, Ohio, where the Nickel Plate line approaches the highway, I saw a freight going toward Cleveland with men sitting on the boxcars, and in the flats, and in under-angles of gondolas, and eight or ten guys shagging after and flipping themselves up on the rungs. I ran too, down from the unlucky highway, up the rocky grade where I felt the thinness of my shoes, and took hold of a ladder. I wasn't agile, so ran with the red car, unable to swing from the ground until I was helped by a boost from behind. I never saw who it was that gave it—someone among the runners who didn't want me tearing my arms from their sockets or breaking the bones of my feet.

So I climbed to the roof. It was a high-backed cattle car topped with broad red planks. Ahead the slow bell was turning over and over, and I was in plenty of company, the rough-looking crowd of non-paying passengers the Nickel Plate was carrying. I felt the movement of the stock against the boards and sat in the beast smell. Until Cleveland, with the great yards and overbuilt hills and fume, chaff and grit flying at your face.

There was a hotshot or nonstop express to Toledo making up in the yards, the word came, which would be ready in a couple of hours. Meanwhile I went up to the city to get some food. Going back to the yards, I climbed down a steep path, like a cliff of Pisgah, below the foundations of factories, and emerged on rusty tracks by the Sherwin Williams paint factory—the vast field of rails and hummocky ground to the sides covered with weed stalks where people were waiting: catching a nap, reading old papers, mending.

This was both a boring and a tense afternoon, soon dark with oncoming rain, while we squatted in the weeds, waiting; brackish and yet nerve-touching. Therefore I rushed up when I saw by the rising and motion along the darkening line that the train was coming. In the sudden shift toward the open and the tracks it seemed that hundreds had risen, the most distant already closing in upon the train. The locomotive came slowly, like a bison, the iron shell of the boiler black.

The train crashed its boxes and went backwards a moment. It was picking up its last cars. In that moment I got under a gondola carrying coal, into the angle of it between the slope end and the wheels. When we rolled forward the wheels creaked and bit out sparks like grindstones, and the couplings played free and hooked tight in a mechanical game into which your observation and brain were forced. Having to recognize whose kingdom you were in, with tons of coal at the back and riding in the tiny blind gallery with the dashing dark rain at the sides. There were four of us sitting in this space; a lean, wolfy man, who stretched his legs clear over the wheels, on the bar, while the rest of us fetched ours up short. I saw his face when he lit a butt, grinning and somewhat sick, blues under his eyes like chain links. He held his fingers in his crotch. On the other side was a young boy. The fourth man, as I didn't know till we were chased off the train at Lorain, was a Negro. All I saw of him as we were running was his yellow raincoat, but when I caught up by a trackside shack he was leaning on the boards, his big eyes shut, a stumpy, heavy man getting his breath with much trouble and his beard sparkling about his mouth with sweat or drizzle.

The hotshot stopped at Lorain; it wasn't a hotshot at all. Or perhaps they stopped it because it carried too many free riders. These made a ragged line, like a section gang that draws aside at night back of the flares as a train comes through, only much more numerous. There were flashlights swinging from car to car as the cops emptied them, and then the train went off, cleared of riders, down into the semaphore lights and the oily blues of the track.

This stocky young boy—Stoney was his name—attached himself to me and we went into the town. The harbor with its artificial peaks and cones of sand and coal was visible from the muddy main stem. In the featureless electric faces of bulbs hung on the dredges, cranes, cables, the rain looked like nothing either and was nullified. I laid out some of my money for bread and peanut butter and a couple of bottles of milk and we had supper.

It was after ten and streaming rain. I wasn't going to chase another freight that night, I was too bushed. I said, "Let's find a place to flop," and he agreed.

On the sidings we found some boxcars retired from service, of great age, rotten and swollen, filled with old paper and straw, a cheesy old hogshead stink of cast-off things such as draws rats, a marly or fungus white on the walls. There we bedded down in the refuse. I buttoned up, for security as well as the cold, and stretched out. There was plenty of room at first. But till far into the night men kept arriving, rolling back the door, and passing back and forth over us, discussing where to sleep. I heard them coming, grating with the feet along the rows of cars, until our boxcar was so full that new-comers would look in and then pass on. It was no time to be awake, or half awake, with the groaning and sick coughing, the grumbles and gases of bad food, the rustling in paper and straw like sighs or the breath of dissatisfaction. And when I fell asleep I didn't sleep long, for the man next to me began to press up, and I thought it was only his unconscious habit of the night, that he was used to a bedmate, and I just drew away, but he drew after. Then he must have worked long in secret to open his pants and first to touch my hand as if by ac-cident and then to guide my fingers. I had trouble getting free because he finally held my wrist with both hands, and I knocked his head against the boards. That couldn't have hurt much, the wood was so rotten it was almost soft, but he let me go and said almost with laughter, "Don't raise a fuss." He rolled back from me a space. I sat up and I reasoned that if I didn't move he might think he wasn't unwelcome to me. As a matter of fact he was waiting and he began to talk, with a hard tremble, both cynical and hopeful, about the filth of women, and when I heard that I went away, helping myself up in back against the wall and stepping over bodies to where I had seen Stoney lie down. A bad night—the rain rattling hard first on one side and then on the other like someone nailing down a case, or a coop of birds, and my feelings were big, sad, comfortless, of a thinking animal, my heart acting like an orb filled too big for my chest, not from revulsion, which I have to say I didn't feel, but over-all general misery.

And I lay down by Stoney, who roused a little, recognized

me, and fell asleep. Only it was cold; toward morning, deathly cold; and now and then we'd find we were pressed close, rubbing faces and bristles, and we would separate. Until it was too freezing to take account of being strangers—we were trembling too hard—and had to clasp close. I took off my coat and spread it over the both of us to keep in the warmth a little, and even so we lay shivering.

There was a rooster some brakeman's family nearby owned, and he had the instinct or the temerariousness to crow in the wet and ashes of the backyard. This morning signal was good enough for us, and we got out of the car. Was it really day? The sky was dripping, and cloud was running as light as smoke; there was pink in it, but whether that was the reflection of the sun or of railroad fire how could you tell? We entered the station where there was a stove of which the bottom skirt was hot to transparency, and we steamed ourselves by it. The heat pushed into your face.

"Stand me a cup of coffee," said Stoney.

It took five such days of travel to get back to Chicago, for I got a train to Detroit by error. A brakeman told us there was a train for Toledo coming soon, and I went to catch it. Stoney came along. Our luck seemed good. Because of the hour this freight was practically empty. We had a car to ourselves. Furniture must have been hauled in it the last trip, for there was clean excelsior on the floor, and we made beds in this paper fleece and lay there sleeping.

I woke when the angle of the sun was very narrow in the door and guessed it must be noon. If it was that late we must already have gone through Toledo and be crossing Indiana. But these oak woods and the deep-lying farms and scarce cattle were not what I had seen in Indiana crossing it with Joe Gorman. We were going very fast, flying, the locomotive and the empty cars. Then I saw a Michigan license on a truck at a crossing.

"We must be bound for Detroit; we missed Toledo," I said.

As the sun went south it was back of us and not on the left hand; we were going north. There was no getting off either. I sat down, legs hanging at the open door, back-broken and dry, hungry furthermore, and my eyes followed the spin of the fields newly laid out for sowing, the oak woods with hard bronze survivor leaves, and a world of great size beyond, or fair clouds and then of abstraction, a tremendous Canada of light.

The short afternoon soon darkened; between the trees and stumps it turned blue. The towns became industrial, factories riding up and tank cars and reefers sitting on the spurs. Queer that I didn't worry more about being taken these hundreds of miles out of my way when there were only a few quarters and some thinner stuff in my pocket, about a buck in all. Riding in this dusk and semiwinter, it was the way paltry and immense were so mixed, perhaps, the jointed spine of train racing and swerving, the steels, rusts, bloodlike paints extended space after space in the sky, and then other existence, space after space.

Factory smoke was standing away with the wind, and we were in an industrial sub-town—battlefield, cemetery, garbage crater, violet welding scald, mountains of tires sagging, and ashes spuming like crests in front of a steamer, Hooverville crate camps, plague and war fires like the boiling pinnacle of all sackings and Napoleonic Moscow burnings. The freight stopped with a banging and concussion, and we jumped out and were getting over the tracks when someone got us by the shoulders from behind and gave us each a boot in the ass. It was a road dick. He wore a Stetson and a pistol hung on the front of his vest; his whisky face was red as a winter apple and a crazy saliva patch shone on his chin. He yelled, "Next time I'll shoot the shit out of you!" So we ran, and he threw rocks past us. I wished that I could lay for him till he came off duty and tear his windpipe out.

However, we were legging it over the rails on the lookout for anything swift that might come down on us out of the steel coldly laid out in the dark and the shrivels of steam and cyclops headlamps, a loose-rolling car. Also the coal rumbled in the hoppers and bounded grim to the ground. We ran, and I didn't feel angry any more.

A highway marker told us we were twenty miles from Detroit. As we stood there the fellow came up who had ridden out of Cleveland under the gondola with us, the wolf-looking one. Though it was dark, I spotted him coming in the road.

He didn't seem to have anything special in mind, only to hang around.

I said to this stocky boy Stoney, "I have a buck to take me back to Chicago, so let's get some chow."

"Hang on to it, we'll mooch something," he said. He tried a few stores along the highway and by and by turned up some stale jelly bismarcks.

A truck carrying sheet-metal took all three of us into town. We lay under the tarpaulin, for it was cold now. The truck dragged up the hills in low gear, and it took hours, with all the stops. Stoney slept. Looking capable of harm, Wolfy didn't seem to mean us any; he had only tied in with us to be carried along as we were. As we started again in the late night for the city he began to tell me what a rough town it was, that he had heard the cops were mean and everything rugged; he said he had never been here before himself.

While we penetrated more, by a series of funnels of light, into the city, he made me feel dejected, describing it as he did. Then the truck stopped and the driver let us off. I couldn't see where; it was empty and silent, past midnight. There was a small restaurant; all else was closed doors. So we went into this joint to ask where we were. It was narrow as a corridor, laid out with oilcloth. The short-order guy told us we were off the center of town, about a mile, if we followed the car line from the next intersection.

When we came out, there was a squad car waiting with open doors and a cop blocking the way who said, "Get in."

Two plainclothesmen were inside, and I had to hold Wolfy on my lap while Stoney lay on the floor. This Stoney was only a young boy. Nothing was said. They brought us into the station—concrete, and small openings everywhere, the bars beginning at the end of a short flight of stairs not far from the sergeant's desk.

The cops kept us to one side, for there was another matter being heard, and four or five faces of peculiar night-wildness by the electric globe of the desk, and the sergeant with his large flesh and white fatty face presiding. There was a woman, and it was hard to take in the fact that she had been in the middle of a brawl, she was so modest-looking and dressmakerish, with a green trout knot to her hat. Alongside her there were two men, one with a bloody beehive of bandages, totter-headed, and the other shut up with defiance and meanwhile his hands pressing all his concern to his chest. He was supposed to be the offender. I say supposed because it was the cop who did the explaining, the three principals being deaf-mutes. This guy attacked the other with a hammer, was what he said; he said that the woman was a lousy bitch and didn't care for whom she spread, and the bastard was the biggest cause of trouble in the deaf-mute community even if she did look like a schoolteacher. I report what the cop told the sergeant.

"What's my idea," he said, "is that this poor jerk thought he was engaged to her and then he caught her with this other joker."

"What doin'?"

"I wouldn't know. It depends on how much of a sorehead he is. But with the pants off, I wouldn't be surprised."

"I wonder what makes 'em so randy. They fight more about love than the dagoes," said the sergeant. His face had a one-eye emphasis, and his cheek was so much rough wall. The arm he had up his sleeve was very thick; I wouldn't have liked to see it used. "Why do they have t'be all the time hittin'? Maybe because they talk with their hands."

Stoney and Wolfy grinned, wishing to be of the same humor as the cops.

"Well, is anything broke under them bandages?"

"They took a couple of stitches on his dome."

The bloody-haired topple-bandage was pushed into the light where the sergeant could see.

"Well," he said when he had looked, "take an' lock 'em up till we can see if we can get an interpreter tomorrow, and if we can't, then just kick 'em out in the morning. What would they do with this cocky in the workhouse? Anyway, a night in the clink will show them they aren't alone by themselves in the world and can't be carryin' on as if they was."

We were next, and I had meantime been worrying about a connection between Joe Gorman's arrest and our being picked up, but there was no such connection. There was only that shirt in the back seat of the stolen Buick to trace me by. The laundry mark. That was far-fetched, but I didn't know what else to think. I was relieved when I heard what they had us in for: theft of automobile parts from wrecking yards.

"We've never been in Detroit before," I said. "We just arrived in town."

"Yeah, where from?"

"Cleveland. We're hitch-hiking."

"You're a sonofabitch liar. You belong to the Foley gang and you been stealing car parts. But we caught up with you. We'll get all you guys."

I said, "But we're not even from Detroit. I'm from Chicago."

"Where you goin'?"

"Home."

"That's a fine way to get to Chicago from Cleveland, by way of this town. Your story stinks." He started on Stoney. "Where're you gonna say you come from?"

"Pennsy."

"Where's that?"

"Near Wilkes-Barre."

"And where you headin' for?"

"Nebraska, to study to be a vet'narian."

"And what's that?"

"About dogs and horses."

"About Fords and Chevvies, you mean, you little asswipe hoodlum! And you, where's home for you, what's your story?" He started on Wolfy.

"I'm from Pennsylvania too."

"Whereabouts?"

"Around Scranton. It's a little town."

"How little is it?"

"About five hundred population or so."

"And what's the name of it?"

"It ain't much of a name."

"I bet. Well, tell me, what is it?"

He said, his eyes moving tensely, which was poison to his effort to smile easily. "The name of it is Drumtown."

"It must be a tough little hole to breed up rats like you. Okay, we'll see where it is on the map." He opened his drawer.

"It ain't on the map. It's too small."

"That's okay, if it has a name it'll be on my map. It's got them all."

"What I mean is it ain't really incorporated. It's just a little burg and hasn't got around to be incorporated yet."

"What do they do there?"

"Dig up a little coal. Nothin' much."

"Hard coal or soft coal?"

"Both," said Wolfy, sinking his head and still grinning a little; but his underlip was somewhat withdrawn from his teeth and his sinews were out.

"You belong to Foley's gang, friend," the sergeant said.

"No, I never been in this town before."

"Fetch me Jimmy," the sergeant instructed one of the cops.

Jimmy came, slow and old, from the narrow stairs of the lower cells; his flesh was like a stout old woman's; he was wearing cloth slippers and a front-buttoned sweater holding up his wide breasts; he seemed to die a little with every breath. But his eyes were as explicit as otherwise everything was vague about this gray, yellow, and white-haired head, bent with weakness. The eyes, however, trained so they were foreign to anything but their long-time function, they had no personal regard. This Jimmy gazed on Stoney and me and passed us and his look rested on Wolfy. To him he said, "You was in here three years ago. You rolled a guy, and you got six months. It won't be three years yet till May. One month more."

This great classifying organ of a police brain!

"Well, Bumhead, Pennsylvania?" said the sergeant.

"That's right, I did six months. But I don't know Foley, that's the truth, and never stole car parts. I don't know anything about cars."

"Lock 'em all up."

We had to empty our pockets; they were after knives and matches and such objects of harm. But for me that wasn't what it was for, but to have the bigger existence taking charge of your small things, and making you learn forfeits as a sign that you aren't any more your own man, in the street, with the contents of your pockets your own business: *that* was the purpose of it. So we gave over our stuff and were taken down, past cells and zoo-rustling straw where some prisoner got off his sack for a look through the bars. I saw the wounded deaf-mute like a magus holding his head, on a bunk. We were marched to the end of the row where the great memory-man sat sleeping, or perhaps he was only at dim rest all night, in a chair below a fish tail of ribbon tied into the grill of a ventilator. They stuck us in a large cell, a yell going up over us, "We got no room. We got no more room!" and obscene lip sounds and razzberries and flushing of the toilet, ape-wit and defiances. It really was a crowded cell, but they pushed us in anyway, and we did as well as we could, squatting on the floor. The other mute was in here, sitting by the feet of a drunk, crouched up as if in a steerage. An enormous light was on at all hours. There was something heavy about it, like the stone rolled in front of the tomb.

Then by the wall, at day, a big dull rolling began, choking, the tube-clunk of trucks and heavy machine fuss, and also the needle-mouth speed of trolleys, fast as dragonflies.

I must say I didn't get any great shock from this of personal injustice. I wanted to be out and on my way, and that was nearly all. I suffered over Joe Gorman, caught and beat.

However, as I felt on entering Erie, Pennsylvania, there is a darkness. It is for everyone. You don't, as perhaps some imagine, try it, one foot into it like a barbershop "September Morn." Nor are lowered into it with visitor's curiosity, as the old Eastern monarch was let down into the weeds inside a glass ball to observe the fishes. Nor are lifted straight out after an unlucky tumble, like a Napoleon from the mud of the Arcole where he had been standing up to his thoughtful nose while the Hungarian bullets broke the clay off the bank. Only some Greeks and admirers of theirs, in their liquid noon, where the friendship of beauty to human things was perfect, thought they were clearly divided from this darkness. And these Greeks too were in it. But still they are the admiration of the rest of the mud-sprung, famine-knifed, street-pounding, war-rattled, difficult, painstaking, kicked in the belly, grief and cartilage mankind, the multitude, some under a coal-sucking Vesuvius of chaos smoke, some inside a heaving Calcutta midnight, who very well know where they are.

In the dinky grayness and smell of morning, after giving us

coffee and bread, they let Stoney and me out; Wolfy was kept on suspicion.

The cops said to us, "Get out of town. We give you a flop last night, but next time you'll get a vagrancy hung on you." There was a dawn smokiness and scratchiness in the station as the patrolmen off the night beat were taking a load off themselves, unstrapping guns, lifting off hats, sitting down to write out reports. Was there a station next door to Tobit, the day the angel visited, it would have been no different.

We went along with the main traffic and ended in Campus Martius, which is not like the other Champs de Mars I know. Here all was brick, shaly with oil smoke and the shimmying gas of cars.

We started off to ride to city limits on the trolleys; and then it happened that the conductor shook my shoulder to warn me that we were at a transfer point, and I jumped out thinking that Stoney was back of me, but I saw him still asleep by the window as the car passed with air-shut doors, and pounding on the glass didn't wake him. Then I waited the better part of an hour before going on to the end of the line where the highway was. I stayed there till nearly noon. He maybe thought I had shaken him off, which wasn't so. I felt despondent that I had lost him.

At last I started to flag rides. First a truck took me to Jackson. I found a cheap flop there. Next afternoon a salesman for a film company picked me up. He was going to Chicago.

Chapter X

WHEN EVENING came on we were tearing out of Gary and toward South Chicago, the fire and smudge mouth of the city gorping to us. As the flamy bay shivers for homecoming Neapolitans. You enter your native water like a fish. And there sits the great fish god or Dagon. You then bear your soul like a minnow before Dagon, in your familiar water.

I knew I wasn't coming back to peace and an easy time. In rising order of difficulty, there'd be the Polish housekeeper, always crabbing about money; next Mama, certain to feel my unreliability; and Simon who'd have been storing up something for me. I was ready to hear hard words from him; I felt I deserved some for going off on this trip. I also had a few to answer with, about the telegram. But I wasn't approaching the usual kind of family fight with its hot feelings and wrangled-out points; it was something different and much worse.

A new, strange Polish woman who spoke no English came to the door. I thought the old housekeeper had quit and this one had replaced her, but it was odd how the new woman had filled the kitchen with bleeding hearts, crucifixes, and saints. Of course, if she had to have them in her place of work, Mama couldn't see them anyhow. But there were also little children, and I wondered if Simon had taken in an entire family; and then, from the way the woman kept me standing, I began to grasp that this was no longer our flat, and an older girl wearing the dress of St. Helen's parochial school came to tell me that her father had bought the furniture and taken over the flat from the man who owned it. That was Simon.

"But isn't my mother here any more? Where's my mother?"

"The blind lady? She's downstairs by the neighbors."

The Kreindls had put her in Kotzie's room, which had only a small window with bars on the passage where people ducked through the brick subterranean vault on a shortcut through the alley or stopped to take a leak. Since she could only just distinguish light from dark and didn't need a view, you couldn't say on that score it was an unkindness to have been put there. The deep kitchen cuts in her palms had never softened out, and I felt them when she took my hands and said in her cracky voice, queerer than ever just then, "Did you hear about Grandma?"

"No, what?"

"She died."

"Oh no!"

That was a shaft! It went straight and cold into my bowels, and I couldn't bring up my back or otherwise move, but sat bent over. Dead! Horrible, to imagine the old woman dead, in a casket, underground, with the face covered and weight thrown on her, silent. My heart shrunk before the idea of this violence. Because it would have had to be violent. She, who always tore off interferences as she did that dentist's hand, would have had to be smothered. For all her frailty she was a hard fighter. But she fought when clothed and standing up, alive. And now it was necessary to picture her captured and pulled down into the grave, and lying still. That was too much for me.

My grates couldn't hold it. I shed tears with my sleeve over my eyes.

"What did she die of, Ma, and when?"

She didn't know. A few days ago, before she had moved down, Kreindl had told her, and she had been in mourning ever since. According to her notions of how she should mourn.

All that she had in this vault of a room was a bed and chair. Well, I tried to find out from Mrs. Kreindl why Simon had done this. As it was suppertime, Mrs. Kreindl was at home. Usually she was away, afternoons, playing poker with other housewives; they played in earnest, for blood. How she had the repose of a big sheep, don't ask me, since she was always in a secret fever from gambling and from warring with her husband.

She couldn't tell me anything about Simon. Was it to get married that he had sold everything? He had been desperate, before I left, about marrying Cissy. But the furniture was old stuff, and how much would the Pole have paid for it? What would anyone give for that cripple kitchen stove? Or for the beds, even older; and the leatherette furniture we used to slide and rock on when we were kids? This stuff went back to the time of Rameses' *Americana* set, to the last century. Maybe my father had bought the furniture. All pain-causing reflections. Simon must have been in a terrible way for money to have sold off all of that veteran metal and leather and left Mama in this cell with the Kreindls.

I was empty with hunger as I questioned Mrs. Kreindl but couldn't apply to her for a meal, remembering her to be not very free about food. "Do you have any money, Mama?" I said. But all she had in her purse was a fifty-cent piece. "Well, it's a good idea for you to have some change," I told her, "in case you happen to want something, like gum drops or a Hershey bar." I'd have taken a buck from her if Simon had left her something, but I could make out a little longer without her last fifty-cent piece. To ask for it, I thought, would scare her, and that would be barbarous. Especially on top of Grandma's death. And she already was frightened, although, as when sick, she was upright in her posture and like waiting for the grief to come to a stop; as if this stop would be called by a conductor. She wouldn't discuss with me what Simon had done but clung rather to her own idea of it. To which she didn't wish me to add anything. I knew her.

I stayed a little longer because I sensed she wanted it, but then I had to leave, and when I scraped back my chair she said, "You going? Where do you go?" This was a question about my absence when the flat was sold up. I couldn't answer it.

"Why, I have that room on the South Side still that I told you about."

"Are you working? You have a job?"

"I always have something. Don't you know me? Don't worry, everything is going to be all right."

Answering, I shunned her face a little, though there was no reason to, and felt my own face bitten as though it were a key, notched and filed out, some dishonorable, ill-purpose key.

I headed for Einhorn's, and on the boulevard, where the trees had begun to bud in the favorite purple of Chicago April evening, instilled with carbon and with the smells of crocodile beds of guck from the cleaned sewers, by the lamps of the synagogue, people were coming out in new coats and business hats, with square velvet envelopes for their prayer things.

It was the first night of Passover, of the Angel of Death going through all doors not marked with blood to take away the life of the Egyptian first-born, and then the Jews trooping into the desert. I wasn't permitted to pass by; I was stopped by Coblin and Five Properties, who had seen me as I got into the street to walk around the crowd. They were on the curb, and Five Properties snatched me by the sleeve. "Look!" he said. "Who is in *shul* tonight!" Both were grinning, bathed-looking, in their best cleanliness and virile good condition.

"Hey, guess what?" said Coblin.

"What?"

"Doesn't he know?" said Five Properties.

"I don't know anything. I've been out of town and just got back."

"Five Properties's getting married," said Coblin. "At last. To a beauty. You ought to see the ring he's giving. Well, we're through with whores now, aren't we? Ah, boy, somebody's in for it!"

"True?"

"So help me the Uppermost," said Five Properties. "I invite you to my wedding, kid, a week from next Sunday at the Lion's Club Hall, North Avenue, four o'clock. Bring a girl. I don't want you should have anything against me."

"What is there to have against you?"

"Well, you shouldn't. We're cousins, and I want you to come."

"Happy days, man!" I said to him, doing my best, and thankful the murk was so deep they couldn't see me well.

Coblin began to draw me by the arm. He wanted me to come to the Seder dinner. "Come along. Come home."

While I stunk of jail and before I had begun to digest my misery? Before I found Simon? "No, some other time, thanks, Cob," I said, going backwards.

"But why not?"

"Leave him, he's got a date. Have you got a date?"

"As a matter of fact I do have to see somebody."

"He's starting his horny time of life. Bring your little pussy to the wedding."

Cousin Hyman still smiled, but he thought probably of his daughter and so didn't urge me more; he clammed up.

In Einhorn's door I met Bavatsky as he descended to re-place a fuse. Tillie had blown it with her curling iron, and up-stairs, one woman hobbled and the other just as slow from weight and uncertainty approached with candles and so re-called to me a second time it was the night of Exodus. But there was no dinner or ceremony here. Einhorn observed only one holy day, Yom Kippur, and only because Karas-Hol-loway, his wife's cousin, insisted.

"What happened to that drunken wart Bavatsky?"

"He couldn't get to the fuse box because the cellar was locked, so he went to fetch the key from the janitor's wife," said Mildred.

"If she has beer in the house we go to bed in the dark tonight."

Suddenly Tillie Einhorn, with candle in a saucer, saw me by the flame.

"Look, it's Augie," she said.

"Augie? Where?" said Einhorn, quickly glancing between the uneven sizes of light. "Augie, where are you? I want to see you."

I came forward and sat by him; he shifted his shoulder in token of wanting to shake hands.

"Tillie, go in the kitchen and make coffee. Mildred, you too." He sent them back into the dark kitchen. "And take the plug out of the curler. I go nuts with their electric appliances."

"It is out," said Mildred, with a voice tired of, but always ready for, the duty of these answers. Obedient in the smallest point, however, she shut the doors, and I was alone with him. In his night court. At least I thought he was grimacing with strictness at me. He had shaken hands only to give me a for-mal feel of his fingers and of the depth of his coldness. And the candles were now as genial to me as though they had been the ones stuck into loaves of bread by night and sailed on a black Indian lake to find the drowned body sunk to the bottom. Now the white middle way of his hair was down near the plate glass of his desk as he fixed to get and light a ciga-rette—as ever, the methodical struggle and pulling of the arms by the sleeves, that transport of flies by the ants. Then he began to blow smoke and prepared to speak. I decided I couldn't allow myself to be chided like a kid of ten for the Joe

Gorman deal, of which he by now certainly knew. I had to talk to him about Simon. But then it seemed he wasn't going to lecture me at all. I must have looked too sick—low, gaunt, pushed to an extreme, burned. Last time we met I had had my Evanston fat on me; I had come to consult him about the adoption.

"Well, you haven't been doing so well, it looks like."

"No."

"Gorman was caught. How did you get away?"

"By dumb luck."

"Dumb? In a hot car, without even changing the plates! Talk about brainlessness! Well, they brought him back. The picture was in the *Times*. You want to see?"

No, I didn't want to, for I knew what it would be like: between two hefty detectives and probably trying to tip his hat over his eyes as much as his held arms would allow, and spare his family direct eyes into the camera, or his plastered face. It was always like that.

"How come it took you so long to get back?" said Einhorn.

"I bummed, and I wasn't very lucky."

"But why did you have to bum? Your brother told me he was sending you the money to Buffalo."

"Why, did he come and tell you?" I creased my brow with effort. "You mean he tried to borrow from you?"

"He got it from me. I made him another loan too."

"What loan? I didn't get anything from him."

"That's no good. I was stupid. I should have sent it to you myself. Beh?" He let out his tongue and his eyes went bright, looking surprised. "He took me—well, so he took. But he shouldn't have let you down. Especially since I gave it to him over and above what I lent him personally. Even if he was in bad shape that's too much."

I was powerfully bitter and mad, but I felt an advance sway from a wave of something even worse, below the present depth.

"What do you mean—in bad shape? Why was he raising money? What did he want?"

"If he had told me for what I might have helped. I lent it to him because he is your brother; otherwise I hardly know the man. He went into a proposition with Nosey Mutchnik—

the one I had that deal with in the lot. Remember? Now I could hold my own with him, but your brother is green. He took an interest in a betting pool, and the first game the White Sox played this season they told him he lost his share and if he wanted to stay in he'd have to bring another hundred bucks—I have the whole story now. They took that from him too, and he got a sock in the teeth when he became hotheaded. Mutchnik's hooligans knocked him into the gutter. That's what happened. I suppose you know why he wanted to make a fast buck?"

"Yes, to get married."

"To get on top of Joe Flexner's daughter, who made him wild. He never will now."

"But why not? They're engaged."

"I begin to feel sorry for your brother, though he isn't very smart, and if I did drop seventy-eight bucks . . ." As I saw the anguishing thing of Simon knocked over and bloodied in the gutter, I only listened and didn't speak of Grandma's death, or the furniture, and Mama put out of the house. "Now she won't marry him," said Einhorn.

"She won't? Tell me!"

"Kreindl is the one I heard it from. He made a match for her with a relative of yours."

"Not Five Properties—with him?" I shouted.

"Your greenhorn cousin. It's going to be his hand that sets apart those fine legs."

"Oh hell! No! They couldn't do that to Simon!"

"They did."

"And by now I guess he knows."

"*Does* he! He went to Flexner's and started a riot, breaking chairs. The girl went and locked herself in the toilet, and then the old man had to send for the police. The squad car came and got him."

Arrested too! I suffered to myself for Simon. It was crazy, how. It crushed me to hear and picture.

"Cynical quiff, ah?" Einhorn said. He wanted to bring it all home to me with his queer stare of severity. "Cressida going over to the Greek camp—"

"And where's Simon, in jail still?"

"No, old Flexner let the charge drop when he promised no

more trouble. Flexner is a decent old man. He went broke owing nobody. He wouldn't have the heart. He's a sport too. They kept your brother one night and let him out this morning."

"He spent last night in jail?"

"One night, that's all," said Einhorn. "Now he's out."

"Where is he though? Do you know?"

"No. But I can tell you you won't find him at home." Kreindl had told him about Mama, and he was preparing to let me hear all; but I said I had already been home. I sat before him stripped; I knew of nowhere to turn and had no force to leave.

Till now, as a family, we had had some privacy, even if it was known that we were deserted as kids and on Charity. In Grandma's time nobody, not even the caseworker Lubin, was informed exactly about us. At the free dispensary I'd go and do my guile not just on account of the money but so we should have some power of guidance over ourselves. Now there were no secrets, so anybody interested could look. This maybe was the consideration which made me not say to Einhorn what was the cruelest thing of all, that Grandma was dead.

"I'm sorry for you; especially for your mother," Einhorn started out, trying to raise me up. "Your brother got ahead of himself. Too inspired by tail. What got him so hot?"

In part I thought this question came from envy that anyone should be subject to such inspirations and heat. But also, on this side, Einhorn couldn't be altogether unsympathetic.

Gradually, talking, he lost view of his first aim, which was to comfort me, and he got so bitter he tried to curl his fists inward and breasted the desk. "Why should you care if your brother gets a rupe up the behind!" he said. "He deserves it. He left you in a hole, he sold the flat, he got the money out of me because of you and you didn't smell a dime of it. If you were honest with yourself you'd be glad. You'd do yourself some good by saying so, and I'd respect you more for it."

"Say what? That it's all his fault and I'm glad of that? That falling in love made him not care what happened to Mama? Or just that he's miserable? What am I supposed to be glad about, Einhorn?"

"Don't you realize the advantage you have from now on? You'd better not be easy on him. He's got to make it right to you. The advantage has passed to you, and you've got him by the balls. Don't you understand that? And if there's only one thing you can get out of this right now it's to admit at least that you're happy he caught it in the neck. Jesus! if anybody did this to me I'd certainly have satisfaction knowing he was good and burned himself. If I didn't, I'd worry I wasn't clear in my head. Good for him! Good, good!"

I'm not sure why Einhorn worked over me with such savagery approaching waked-up despair. He even forgot to raise hell about Joe Gorman. I guess, back of it, that he thought of Dingbat's inheritance which he had run into the ground. Maybe he didn't want me to be despised as he somewhat despised Dingbat for not being angry. No, there was even more to the view he was driving so strongly, though sprawl-handed, against the desk. He intended that, as there were no more effective prescriptions in old ways, as we were in dreamed-out or finished visions, that therefore, in the naked form of the human jelly, one should choose or seize with force; one should make strength from disadvantages and make progress by having enemies, being wrathful or terrible; should hammer on the state of being a brother, not be oppressed by it; should have the strength of voice to make other voices fall silent— the same principle for persons as for peoples, parties, states. This, and not a man-chick, plucked and pinched, with scraggle behind and anxious face full of sorrow-wrinkles, human fowl chased by brooms.

Now the lights began to twitter as Bavatsky fiddled in the fuse box, and it was discovered that instead of considering this as I should have been, I was bawling. I think Einhorn was disappointed and maybe even shocked; shocked, I mean, by his misjudgment of my fitness to follow him in his shooting trajectory into what a soul should be. He gave me chilly gentleness such as he might have offered a girl. "Don't worry, we'll work something out for your mother," he said, for he seemed to think it was mainly that. He didn't know I was mourning Grandma too. "Blow out these candles. Tillie's bringing coffee and sandwiches. You can sleep with Dingbat tonight, and tomorrow we'll start on something."

Next day I hunted for Simon and couldn't locate him; he hadn't been back to see Mama. I did find Kreindl at home, however, as he sat at a late breakfast of smoked fish and rolls. He said to me, "Sit down and catch a bite."

"I see you finally found a bride for my cousin," said I to the cockeyed old artilleryman, observing how the short, sufficient muscles of his forearms were operating in the skinning of the golden little fish and how the scabbards of his jaw were moving.

"A beauty. Such *tsitskies*! But don't blame me, Augie. I don't force anybody. *Zwing keinem*. Especially a pair of proud *tsitskies* like that. Do you know anything about young ladies? I should hope! Well, when a girl has things like that nobody can tell her what to do. There's where your brother made his mistake, because he tried. I'm sorry for him." He whispered, mounting his eyes to make sure his wife was at a distance, "This girl makes my little one stand up. At my age. And salute! Anyways, she's too independent for a young fellow. She needs an older man, a cooler head who can say yes and do no. Otherwise she could ruin you. And maybe Simon is too young to marry. I've known you since you both was snot-noses. Pardon, but it's true. Now you're big, so you're hungry, and you think you're ready to marry, but what's the hurry? You got plenty of jig-jig ahead of you before you settle down. *Take* it! *Take, take* if they give you! Never refuse. To come together with a peepy little woman who sings in your ear. It's the life of the soul!" He argued this to me with a squeeze of his awkward eyes, the old pimp and egger-on; he even made me smile, and I was in no mood for smiling. "Besides," said he, "you can see what kind of a man your brother is, that when he gets it in his mind he can sell the goods of the house and put his mother out."

I expected him to mention this and pass from defense to the practical matter of Mama's support. In the past Kreindl had always been a kind enough neighbor, but we couldn't expect him to keep Mama. Especially as Simon now had him down as one of his chief enemies. Furthermore, I couldn't let her stay in that brick vault, and I told Kreindl I'd make other arrangements for her.

I went to appeal to Lubin, at the Charity, on gloomy Wells

Street. Lubin had always visited us as a sort of distant foster-uncle, formerly. In his office, to my maturer eyes, he came out differently. Something in his person argued what the community that contributed the money wanted us poor bastards to be: sober, dutiful, buttoned, clean, sad, moderate. The sadness and confusion of the field he was in made him sensible. Only a certain heaviness of breath that drew notice to the thickness of his nostrils gave you a sense of difficulty and, next, one of the labor of being patient. I made note in this broad man of the tame ape-nature promoted to pants and offices. This is the opposite of that disfigured image of God that falls away by its sin from Eden; or of the same bad copy excited and inflamed by promise of grace to recover its sacredness and golden stature. Lubin's belief was that he didn't fall from Paradise but rose from the caves. But he was a good man, and this is no slander of him, but merely his own view.

When I told him Simon and I had to find a home for Mama he doubtless thought we were getting rid of everyone —Georgie first, then Grandma, and now Mama. Therefore I said, "It's only temporary, till we get on our feet, and then we'll have another flat and housekeeper for her." But he took this very aridly, which wasn't to be wondered at, considering the tramp appearance I made, in the wrack of my good clothes, inflamed at the eyes, and looking garbage-nourished. However, he said he could get her into a Home for the blind on Arthington Street if we could pay part of the cost. It came to fifteen bucks a month.

That was as good as I could expect. Also he sent me with a note to an employment bureau, but there was nothing doing at the time. I went to my room on the South Side and took most of my clothes to hock, the tuxedo, sports clothes, and hound's-tooth coat. I pawned them and I got Mama established, and then started to hunt work. Being as they say up against it and *au pied du mur*, I took the first job that came, and I've never had one that was more curious.

Einhorn got it for me through Karas-Holloway, who had a financial interest in the business. It was a luxury dog service on North Clark Street, among the honkytonks and hock shops, antique stores and dreary beaneries.

In the morning I drove out in a station wagon along the

Gold Coast to pick up the dogs, at the back doors of mansions or up the service elevators of lakeshore apartment hotels, and I brought the animals back to this club joint—it was called a club.

The chief was a Frenchman, a dog-coiffeur or groom or *maître de chiens*; he was rank and rough, from Place Clichy near the foot of Montmartre, and from what he told me he had been a wrestler's shill in the carnivals there while studying this other profession. Some ways his face was short of humanity, by its energetic stiffness and abruptness of color, like an injection. His relation with the animals was a struggle. He was trying to wrest something from them. I don't know what. Perhaps that their conception of a dog should be what his was. He was on the footing of Xenophon's Ten Thousand in Persia, here in Chicago; for he washed and ironed his own shirts, did his own marketing, and cooked his own meals in his beaverboard quarters in a corner of this doggish place— his lab, kitchen, and bedroom. I realize much better now what it means to be a Frenchman abroad, how irregular everything must appear, and not simply abroad but on North Clark Street.

We were located in no mere firetrap but had two stories of a fairly new modern building just off the Gold Coast, not far from the scene of the St. Valentine's Day Massacre and, for that matter, from the Humane Society on Grand Avenue. It was the great feature of this outfit, I say, paid for by the subscribers, that it was a club for dogs, that the pets were entertained as well as steamed, massaged, manicured, clipped, that they were supposed to be taught manners and tricks. The fee was twenty dollars a month, and no shortage of dogs; more in fact than Guillaume could handle, and he had to fight the front office continually, which wanted to go beyond capacity. The club was already as hell-deep as dogs' throats could scrape it; the Cerberus slaver-choke turmoil was at the full when I came in from the last pick-up and changed from truck livery to rubber boots and ponchos; the racket made the skylight glass shiver. Organization was marvelous, however. Guillaume had real know-how; and let people go a little and they'll build you an Escurial. The enormous noise, as of Grand Central, was only the protest of chaos coming up against regulation—the trains got off on time; the dogs got their treatment.

Though Guillaume used the hypo more than I thought he should. He gave *piqûres* for everything, and charged it extra. He'd say, "*Cette chienne est galeuse*—this is a mangy bitch!" and in with the needle. Moreover, he'd give a drop of dope to the savage ones whenever organization was threatened, yelling, "Thees jag-off is goin' to get it!" Consequently I carried home some pretty wan dogs, and it wasn't easy to come up a flight of stairs with a sleeping boxer or shepherd and explain to the colored cook that he was only tuckered out from playing and pleasure. Dogs in heat Guillaume wouldn't tolerate either. "*Grue! En chasse!*" Then he'd say to me anxiously, "Did anything 'appen in the back?" But since I had been driving, how was I to know? He was furious with the owners, especially if the animal was a *chienne de race*, and its aristocracy was not respected, and he wanted the office to slap an extra charge on them for letting them into the club in this state. Any pedigree made a courtier of him, and he could call on a very high manner, if he wanted to, and get his lips into a tight suppressive line of dislike to baseness—the opposite to breeding. He had the staff come over, two Negro boys and me, to show us the fine points of the animal, and I will say for Guillaume that his idea was to run an *atelier* and to act like master in a guild, so that when he got a good poodle to trim it was down-tools for us while he demonstrated; there was then a spell of good feeling and regard for him and for the lamb-docile, witty, small animal. Oh, it wasn't always vexation or the snapping and bickering of little dogs to which Marcus Aurelius compares the daily carryings on of men, though I once in a while see what he was getting at. But there's a dog harmony also, and to be studied by dog eyes, many of them, has its illumination too.

Only the work fatigued me, and I stunk of dog. People would move from me on the streetcar, as they do from the hoof-and-hides stockyards' man, or give me round-eye glares and draw down their mouths on the mobbed Cottage Grove line. Furthermore, there was something Pompeian that I minded about the job—the opulence for dogs, and then their ways that reflected civilized mentality, spoiled temperaments of favorites, mirrors of neuroticism. Plus the often needling thought that their membership fee in the club was more than I had to pay for Mama in the Home. All this together once in a while got me down. From my neglected self-betterment I had additional pricks. I should be more ambitious. Often I looked for vocational hints in magazines, and I considered training at night school to become a court reporter, should I have the aptitude, and even going back to the university for something bigger. And then I not seldom had Esther Fenchel on my mind, since I moved around the dog-owning height of society. I never had a back-door glimpse of it without a twinge of the soul for her sake, and similar childishness. The sun of that childishness goes on shining even when the larger bodies of hotter stars have risen to smelt you and cover you with their influence. The recenter stars may be more critical, more in the eye, but that earlier sun still remains a long time.

I had some spells of adoring-sickness, and then I had deeper pangs of sex, later; from service with animals maybe. The street too was aphrodisiac, the honkytonks and titty photos, legs with sequins. Plus Guillaume's girl friend, who was a great work of ripple-assed luxury with an immense mozzarella bust, a middle-aged lady who'd go straight to bed and wait for him just as we started to close up shop in the evening, soughing in there like a white stout tree. But there wasn't much I could do about my needs. I was too strapped by money to chase. Though I risked running into the Renlings in that neighborhood, I went to Evanston to look for my friend Willa at the Symington, but she had quit to get married. As I returned on the El I was engrossed in thoughts of marriage bed, of Five Properties' behavior with Cissy, and of my brother's losing his head when he thought of their nuptials and honeymoon.

Simon meanwhile stayed away from me and didn't answer the messages I left with Mama and elsewhere. I knew he must be in a bad way. He wasn't giving any money to Mama, and folks who saw him told me how beat he looked. So his keeping to himself, in some hole of a room like mine, or worse, was understandable; he never before had had to approach me abashed, owing explanations and excuses, and wasn't going to do it now. With my last message to him I enclosed five bucks.

He took this fin all right, but I didn't hear from him till he was able to repay it, and that was some months later.

One possession of mine that was saved from the sale of the furniture was the damaged set of Dr. Eliot's Five-Foot Shelf that Einhorn gave me after his fire. I had it with me in my room and read at it when I could. And I was blasting out a paragraph of von Helmholtz one day, on a corner downtown, between cars, when a onetime classmate of mine, at Crane College, a Mexican named Padilla, took it out of my hand to see what I was reading and gave it back saying, "What are you on this stuff for? It's been left way far behind." He started to tell me the latest, and I had to say I couldn't keep up with him. He asked me how things were then, and we had a long conversation.

In my math section Padilla had been the great equation cracker. He sat at the back of the room, rubbing his narrow front peak and working over smoothed-out pieces of paper others had stuffed into the desk, since he couldn't afford to buy a notebook. Called to the board whenever everyone else was stumped, he came with haste in his filthy whitish or creamed-herring suit, of cloth used in the cheapest summer caps, and naked feet in a pair of Salvation Army rummage shoes, also white, and would start hanging up the answer, covering his scrappy chalkings with his skinny body, infinity symbols like broken ants, and blittering Greek letters aimed downward to the last equal sign. As far as I was concerned, it was godlike that relations should be so clear to anyone. Sometimes he'd get a hand for his performance when he went clacking back swiftly in his shoes, which were loose because he had no socks. But his face, with small beak and the pricked skin of smallpox, didn't stock anything in gratification as we understand it. Anyway, he didn't deal much in expression. He often seemed chilly. And I'm not speaking of his character now, but it was cold winter, and sometimes I'd see him flying down Madison Street in his white suit, across the snow, running from home to warm himself in the school building. He never did look warm enough, but chill and sickly and with primitive prohibition of anyone's approaching him. Smoking Mexican cigarettes, he went through the halls by himself, often with a comb, running it through his hair, which was beautiful, black and high.

Well, there had been some changes. He looked healthier, or at least didn't have that thistle-flower purple in his tinge, and he wore a better suit. Under his arm were heavy books.

"Are you at the university?" I said.

"I got a scholarship in math and physics. What about you?"

"I wash dogs. Can't you tell I spend my time with dogs?"

"No, I don't notice anything. But what are you doing?"

"That *is* what I'm doing."

It greatly bothered him that I had such a flunky job, washing cages and sweeping up dogs' hair; and also that I was no longer a college man but trying to keep up on Helmholtz who was a dead number to him; in other words, that I should be of the unformed darkened-out mass. It was often that way with me, that people would feel the world owed me distinctness.

"What would I do at the university? I'm not like you, Manny, with a special talent."

"Don't tear yourself down," he said. "You should see the snots there are on campus. What special have they got, except the dough? You should go and find out what you can do, and then after four years if you aren't any good at any special thing, you at least have this degree, and it won't be just any sonofabitch who can kick you around."

My aching back! I thought. There'd still be black forces waiting to give me the boot, and if I had a degree the indignity would be all the greater, and I'd have heartburn from it.

"You shouldn't waste your time," he further said. "Don't you see that to do any little thing you have to take an examination, you have to pay a fee and get a card or a diploma? You better get wise to this. If people don't know what you qualify in they'll never know where to place you, and that can be dangerous. You have to get in there and do something for yourself. Even if you're just waiting, you have to know what you're waiting for, you have to specialize. And don't wait too long or you'll be passed by."

It wasn't so much what he said that affected me, though that was interesting and probably full of truth; it was his friendship that I responded to. I didn't want to let go of him, and I clung to him. I was moved that he thought of me.

"How'm I supposed to go to school, Manny, if I'm broke?"

"How do you think I do it? The scholarship isn't enough, it's only a tuition scholarship. I get a little dough from the NYA and I'm in a racket swiping books."

"Books?"

"Like these. I stole them this afternoon. Technical books, texts. I take orders even. If I pick up twenty or thirty a month and get from two to five bucks apiece, I make out all right. Texts cost. What's the matter, are you honest?" he said, looking to see if he had queered himself with me.

"Not completely. I'm just surprised, Manny, because all I knew about you was that you were a wizard at math."

"Also I ate once a day and didn't own a coat. You know that. Well, I give myself a little more now. I want to have it a little better. I don't go stealing for the kicks. As soon as I can I'll quit."

"But what if you get nailed?"

He said, "I'll explain how I feel about it. You see, I don't have larceny in my heart; I'm not a real crook. I'm not interested in it, so nobody can make a fate of it for me. That's not my fate. I might get into a little trouble, but I never would let them make it *my* trouble, get it?"

I did get it, having been around Joe Gorman, who looked at the same question another way.

But Padilla was a gifted crook all the same and took pride in his technique. We made a date for Saturday, and he gave me an exhibition. When we walked out of a shop I couldn't tell whether or not he had taken anything, he was so good at maneuvering. Outside he'd show me a copy of Sinnott's *Botany* or Schlesinger's *Chemistry*. Valuable books only; he'd never take orders for cheaper ones. Handing me his list, he'd tell me to pick the next title and he'd swipe it even if it was kept back of the cash desk. He went in carrying an old book with which he covered the one he wanted. He never hid anything under his coat, so that if they were to stop him he could always plead he had set down his own book to look at something and then picked up his own and another, unawares. Since he delivered the books on the same day he stole them, there was nothing incriminating in his room. It was greatly in his favor that he didn't in the least look like a crook, but only a young Mexican, narrow-shouldered, quick in his movements, but somewhat beaten down and harmless, that entered the shop, put on specs, and got lost with crossed feet in thermodynamics or physical chemistry. That he was pure of all feeling of larceny contributed a lot to his success.

There's an old, singular, beautiful Netherlands picture I once saw in an Italian gallery, of a wise old man walking in empty fields, pensive, while a thief behind cuts the string of his purse. The old man, in black, thinking probably of God's City, nevertheless has a foolish length of nose and is much too satisfied with his dream. But the peculiarity of the thief is that he is enclosed in a glass ball, and on the glass ball there is a surmounting cross, and it looks like the emperor's symbol of rule. Meaning that it is earthly power that steals while the ridiculous wise are in a dream about this world and the next, and perhaps missing this one, they will have nothing, neither this nor the next, so there is a sharp pain of satire in this amusing thing, and even the painted field does not have too much charm; it is a flat place.

Well, Padilla in his thieving wasn't of this earthly-power class, and had no ideas such as involved the whole world. It wasn't his real calling. But he enjoyed being good at it and liked the whole subject. He had all kinds of information about crooks, about dips, wires, and their various tricks; about Spanish pickpockets who were so clever they got to the priest's money through the soutane, or about the crooks' school in Rome of such high tuition that the students signed a contract to pay half their take for five years after graduation. He knew a lot about Chicago clipjoints and rackets. It was a hobby with him, as other people go in for batting averages. What fascinated him was the little individual who tries to have a charge counter to the central magnetic one and dance his own dance on the periphery. He knew about B girls and how the hip-chicks operated in the big hotels; a book he read often was the autobiography of Chicago May, who used to throw her escorts' clothes out of the window to her accomplice in the alley, and was a very remarkable woman.

Padilla himself when he went to have a good time didn't stint; he spent everything he had. I was his guest at a flat on Lake Park Avenue that a couple of Negro girls kept together. First he shopped at Hillman's; he bought ham, chicken, beer, pickles, wine, coffee, and Dutch chocolate; then we went there and spent Saturday evening and Sunday in those two rooms, kitchen and bedroom. The only retiring space was the toilet, so everything was in common. This suited Padilla. Toward morning he started to say that we should make an exchange so no exclusive feelings would develop. The girls were glad and voted that this made sense. They appreciated Padilla and his spirit of the thing, so let themselves into the fun. Nothing was very serious nor much held back but in the very best sympathy. I liked best the girl I had first, as she was willing to be more personal with me and wished our cheeks to touch. The second was taller and less given to it; she seemed to have more of a private life to defend against us. There was more style to her. Also she was an older girl.

Anyway, it was Padilla's show. If he got out of bed to eat or dance he wanted me to do likewise, and on and off during the night he was sitting up on the pillows, talking of his life.

"I once was married," said Padilla when the subject came to that. "In Chihuahua when I was fifteen. I had a kid before I was a man myself."

I didn't approve of his boasting that he had left a wife and kid behind in Mexico, but then the tall girl said she had a child too, and maybe the other did also and just didn't say, and so I let the subject pass, since if so many do the same wrong there maybe is something to it that's not right away apparent.

We were lying in the two beds, all four, with only as much shape as there was light to reveal it proceeding from the curtains in the slow opening of Sunday, originating white in the east but falling gray upon the upright staggers of walls. Such a sight as the old Negro walls in these streets had a peculiar grandness, if dread too, where this external evidence was of a big humanity which you now couldn't see. It was like the Baths of Caracalla. The vast hidden population slept away into the morning of Sunday. The little girl I liked lay with saddle nose and her sleepy cheeks and big, sensitive, thoughtless mouth, smiling a little at Padilla's speeches. We lay and warmed ourselves by the girls, like kings, till nearly evening, then we left, kissing and fondling while dressing and then to the door, promising we'd be back.

Broke, Padilla and I had supper at his house, a more empty house than the one we had just left; that at least had old carpets, old soft chairs, and doodad girls' ingenuities, whereas Padilla lived with some aged female relatives in a big railroad flat off Madison Street. It was almost empty; in one room was a table with a few chairs and in another nothing but mattresses laid on the floor. The old women sat in the kitchen and cooked, fanning a charcoal fire, fat-burdened, slow, stone-inexpressive old creatures to whom he didn't even speak. We ate soup with ground meat at the bottom of the bowl and tortillas which came wrapped in a napkin. Finishing quickly, Padilla left me at the table, and when I went to see what had become of him found him already in bed, an army blanket drawn up to his face, with sharp nose and hair fallen back.

He said, "I have to get some sleep. I have a quiz first thing in the morning."

"Are you ready for it, Manny?"

He said, "Either this stuff comes easy or it doesn't come at all."

And that stayed with me. Therefore I was thinking on the streetcar. Of course! Easily or not at all. People were mad to be knocking themselves out over difficulties because they thought difficulty was a sign of the right thing. So I decided to try this out and, to begin with, to experiment with book stealing. If it went easily I'd leave the dog club. And if I made as much at it as Padilla did, that would be double what Guillaume paid me, and I could start saving toward the tuition fee at the university. I didn't mean to settle down to a career of stealing even if it were to come easy, but only to give myself a start at something better.

So I began; at first with more excitement than I could tolerate. I had nausea after, on the street, and sweated. It was a big Jowett's *Plato* that I took. But I was severe with myself to finish the experiment. I checked the book in a dime locker of the Illinois Central station as Padilla had told me to do and immediately went after another, and then I made good progress and became quite cool about it. The difficult moment wasn't that of walking out of the store; it came when I picked the books up and put them under my arm. But then I felt more casual, confident that if stopped I'd be able to explain myself, laugh it off as an error of thoughtlessness and charm my way out. In the store, Padilla told me, the dicks would never arrest you; it was when you stepped into the street that they nabbed you. However, in a department store, without glancing back, I'd drift into another section—men's shoes at Carson Pirie's, candy or rugs at Marshall Field's. It never entered my mind to branch out and steal other stuff as well.

Sooner than I had planned I quit the dog club, and it wasn't only confidence in my crook's competence that made me do it, but I was struck by the reading fever. I lay in my room and read, feeding on print and pages like a famished man. Sometimes I couldn't give a book up to a customer who had ordered it, and for a long time this was all that I could care about. The sense I had was of some live weight driven into tangles or nets of hungry feeling; I wanted to haul it in. Padilla was sore and fired up when he came to my room and saw stacks of books I should have gotten rid of long ago; it was dangerous to keep them. If he had restricted me to books on mathematics, thermodynamics, mechanics, things probably would have been different, for I didn't carry the germ of a Clerk Maxwell or Max Planck in me. But as he had turned over to me his orders for books on theology, literature, history, and philosophy, and I copped Ranke's *History of the Popes* and Sarpi's *Council of Trent* for the seminary students, or Burckhardt or Merz's *European Thought in the Nineteenth Century*, I sat reading. Padilla raised hob with me about the Merz because it took so long to finish and a man in the History department was after him for it. "You can use my card and get it out of the library," he said. But somehow that wasn't the same. As eating your own meal, I suppose, is different from a handout, even if calory for calory it's the same value; maybe the body even uses it differently.

Anyhow, I had found something out about an unknown privation, and I realized how a general love or craving, before it is explicit or before it sees its object, manifests itself as boredom or some other kind of suffering. And what did I think of myself in relation to the great occasions, the more sizable being of these books? Why, I *saw* them, first of all. So suppose I wasn't created to read a great declaration, or to boss a palatinate, or send off a message to Avignon, and so on, I could *see*, so there nevertheless was a share for me in all that had happened. How much of a share? Why, I knew there were things that would never, because they could never, come of my reading. But this knowledge was not so different from the remote but ever-present death that sits in the corner of the loving bedroom; though it doesn't budge from the corner, you wouldn't stop your loving. Then neither would I stop my reading. I sat and read. I had no eye, ear, or interest for anything else—that is, for usual, second-order, oatmeal, mere-phenomenal, snarled-shoelace-carfare-laundry-ticket plainness, unspecified dismalness, unknown captivities; the life of despair-harness, or the life of organization-habits which is meant to supplant accidents with calm abiding. Well, now, who can really expect the daily facts to go, toil or prisons to go, oatmeal and laundry tickets and all the rest, and insist that all moments be raised to the greatest importance, demand that everyone breathe the pointy, star-furnished air at its highest difficulty, abolish all brick, vaultlike rooms, all dreariness, and live like prophets or gods? Why, everybody knows this triumphant life can only be periodic. So there's a schism about it, some saying only this triumphant life is real and others that only the daily facts are. For me there was no debate, and I made speed into the former.

This was when I heard from Simon again. He said on the phone he was coming to repay the five bucks I had sent him. It meant that he felt ready to face me—otherwise he'd have mailed the money. Thus when he entered I sensed how he carried a load of lordly brass and effrontery; that's how he was ready; he was prepared to put me down, should I begin to holler and blame. But when he saw me surrounded by books, barefoot in an old gown, and noted, probably, the air puffs and yellow blisters of wallpaper and the poverty of light, he was more confident and easy. For he very likely felt that I was the same as before, that my wheels turned too freely, that I was hasty, too enthusiastic, or, in few words, something of a *schlemiel*. Suppose he touched on Grandma's death, I'd easy be led to cry, and then he'd have me. The question for him was always whether I was this way by character or choice. If by choice I could maybe be changed.

Me, on my side, I was glad he had come and eager to see him. I could never in the world have taken Einhorn's advice to be hard with him and keep him down. It's true he ought to have sent me that money when I wired from Buffalo, but he'd been in dutch and I could forgive him that. Then the loan from Einhorn wasn't too grievous either, since Einhorn himself had let lots of people down for far larger amounts; and he, Einhorn, was big enough and gentleman enough not to scream and moan about it. So far so good. But what about Mama and the flat? I confess that had gone down hard, and that if I had seen Simon when I was rushing downstairs to Kreindl's to look for Mama I'd have broken his head for him. But later when I had thought it through I conceded to myself that we couldn't have kept the old home going much longer and set up a gentle kind of retirement there for Mama, neither of us having that filial tabby dormancy that natural bachelors have. Something in us both consented to the busting up of the house. All Simon had to do was speak of this; if he didn't it was because he felt his blame too much to have a clear head.

I expected to see him haggard; instead he was fatter. However, it wasn't comfortable-looking fat but as if it came from not eating right. It took me a minute to get over my uneasiness about his creasing smile and the yellow and gold bristles on his chin—it wasn't like him not to shave; but then he was all right and sat down, big fingers knit on his chest.

It was summer, a late afternoon, and though I was on the top floor of this old frame house the shade tree was so huge it passed the roof, so all around it was green, as if in the woods, glossy; and underneath on the lawn this bird was, like a hammer tapping a waterpipe in the grass. It could have helped us to feel peaceful, but it didn't.

I believe people never knew how to observe one another so damagingly as they do now. Kin too, of course. I tried to avoid it with Simon, but we couldn't. So on each side, for a moment, the worst was thought. Then he said, "What are you doing out on the South Side with all these books, becoming a student?"

"I wish I could afford to."

"So you must be in the book business. It can't be much of

a business though, because I see you read them too. Leave it to you to find a business like this!" He said it scornfully, or meant to, but there was a dead place where the scorn should have rung; and he said reasonably, "But I suppose you could ask where my mastermind got me."

"I don't have to ask. I know. I can see."

"Are you sore, Augie?"

"No," I said, husky, and with one glance he could see how far from anger my feeling was. One glance was all he wanted, and he dropped his eyes. "I was sore when I found out. It came all together, including the news about Grandma."

"Yes, she's dead, isn't she? I guess she must have been very old. Did you ever find out how old? I guess we'd never . . ." And so he passed over it with irony, sadness, even awe. We'd always smile and attribute extraordinary things to her.

Then Simon put off the brass he had come in, and he said, "I was a damn fool to get mixed up with that mob. They took away the dough and beat me up. I knew they were dangerous, but I thought I could hold my own with them. I didn't think, I mean, because I was in love. Love! She let me go only so far. On the sun porch at night. I thought I'd bust out of my skin. I was dying for her, just to get a touch of it, and that's about all I got." He said it with coarse anger, despisingly. It gave me a shiver. "When I heard they were married I had dreams about them jazzing, like a woman with an ape. She wouldn't care. And you know what he's like. But it makes no difference, he can raise hell up there same as any other man. Besides he has dough. That's what she thinks is dough! All he owns is a few buildings. It's chickenfeed. It'll look like a lot to her until she gets to know better." Now his face was red, and with an emotion different from that despising anger. He said, "You know I hate to be like this and have such thoughts. I'm ashamed of it, I tell you honestly. Because she wasn't all that glorious and he's not all that bad. He wasn't bad to us when we were kids. You haven't forgotten that, have you? I don't want her to make me act like a damn Eskimo dog with his scruff up about a piece of fish. I used to have my sights set kind of high, as a kid. But after a while you find out what you've really got or haven't, and you wise up to the fact that first comes all the selfish and jealous stuff, that you don't care what happens to anybody else as long as you get yours; you start to think such things as how pleasant it would be if somebody close to you would die and leave you free. Then I thought it would be all the same to the some-bodies if *I* died."

"What do you mean, died?"

"By suicide. I came close to it in jail, there on North Avenue."

This reference to suicide was only factual. Simon didn't work me for pity; he never seemed to require it of me.

"I don't have much feeling against death, do you, Augie?" he said. In the change of leaves about him he was calmer, heavy in his seated position, with the crown of his felt hat tak-ing the side against variants, played by the green shadow and yellow of the leaves. "Well, say, do you?"

"I'm not so hot about dying."

This, after two or three thoughts had come in succession to his face, made him easier and more relaxed, softer with me. He laughed at last. He said, "You'll die like everybody else. But I have to admit that's not what you make people think of when they look at you. You're a pretty gay numero, I'll say that for you. But you're not much good at taking care of yourself. Any other brother but you would have sweated the money out of me. If you had pulled what I pulled I'd have made things rough for you. Or anyway I'd be glad to see you land on your ass the way I've done. I'd say, 'It serves you right. Good for you!' Well, since you won't look out for your interests I see I'm going to have to do it for you."

"My interests?"

"Sure," he said, a little angered by the question. "Don't you believe I ever think about you? We've both been running too much with the losers, and I'm tired of it."

"Where're you living now?" I said.

"On the Near North Side," he said, brushing this off, that I wanted to know definite things about him. He wasn't going to say whether there was a sink in his room, or carpet or linoleum, or whether he was on a car line or facing a wall. It's normal for me to have such curiosity about details. But he wasn't going to satisfy this curiosity, since to dwell on such things implied it would be hard to get away from them; for him they were things to pass quickly. "I'm not going to stay there," he said.

"What have you been living on?" I asked. "What are you doing?"

"What do you mean, living on?" He threw difficulties in my way by repeating questions. He stood too much on his pride to say how things were and show what a bad rip he had gotten in his stuff. A kind of gallantry of presentation he had always had in the quality of older brother he wouldn't give up. He had been a fool and done wrong, he showed up sallow and with the smaller disgrace that he was fat, as if overeating were his reply to being crushed—and with this all over him he wasn't going to tell me, he balked at telling, some small details. He took my asking as a blow at him while he was trying to climb out of the hole of mortification, and he warded it off with a stiff arm, saying, "What do you mean?" as if he'd remember later I had tried to hit him or at least goad him. Later he didn't mind telling me that he had washed floors in a beanery, but this was long afterward. But now he fought this off. Loaded on the hard black armchair—I put it that way because of his increased bulk—he passionately pulled together his nerves and energies—I could see him concentrate and do it—and he started to deal with me. He did it more strongly than was necessary, with pasha force. "I haven't been wasting my time," he said. "I've been working on something. I think I'm getting married soon," he said, and didn't allow himself to smile with the announcement or temper it in some pleasant way.

"When? To whom?"

"To a woman with money."

"A woman? An older woman?" That was how I interpreted it.

"Well, what's the matter with *you*? Yes, I'd marry an older woman. Why not?"

"I bet you wouldn't." He was still able to amaze me, as though we had remained kids.

"We don't have to argue about it because she's not old. She's about twenty-two, I'm told."

"By whom? And you haven't even seen her?"

"No, I haven't seen her. You remember the buyer, my old

boss? He's fixing me up. I have her picture. She's not bad. Heavy—but I'm getting heavy too. She's sort of pretty. Anyhow, even if she weren't pretty, and if the buyer isn't lying about the dough—her family is supposed to have a mountain of dough—I'd marry her."

"You've already made up your mind?"

"I'll say I have!"

"And suppose she doesn't want you?"

"I'll see that she does. Don't you think I can?"

"Maybe you can, but I don't like it. It's cold-blooded."

"Cold-blooded!" he said with sudden emotion. "What's cold-blooded about it? I'd be cold-blooded if I stayed as I am. I see around this marriage and beyond it. I'll never again go for all the nonsense about marriage. Everybody you lay eyes on, except perhaps a few like you and me, is born of marriage. Do you see anything so exceptional or wonderful about it that makes it such a big deal? Why be fooling around to make this perfect great marriage? What's it going to save you from? Has it saved anybody—the jerks, the fools, the morons, the *schleppers*, the jag-offs, the monkeys, rats, rabbits, or the decent unhappy people or what you call nice people? They're all married or are born of marriages, so how can you pretend to me that it makes a difference that Bob loves Mary who marries Jerry? That's for the movies. Don't you see people pondering how to marry for love and getting the blood gypped out of them? Because while they're looking for the best there is—and I figure that's what's wrong with you— everything else gets lost. It's sad, it's a pity, but it's that way."

I was all the same strongly against him; that he saw. Even if I couldn't just then consider myself on the active list of lovers and wasn't carrying a live torch any more for Esther Fenchel. I recognized his face as the face of a man in the wrong. I thought there was too much noise of life around him for a right decision to be made. Furthermore, the books I had been reading—I noticed that Simon was aware of their contribution to my opposition and his eye marked them as opponents, and there was a little bit of derision in his glance too. But I couldn't deny or be disloyal to, at the first hard blink of a challenger or because of derision, things I took seriously and consented to in my private soul as I sat reading.

"What do you want me to agree with you for? If you believe what you're saying, it shouldn't make any difference whether I agree or not."

"Oh hell!" he said, sitting forward and looking into me with widened eyes. "Don't flatter yourself, kid. If you really understood you'd agree. That would be nice, but I can certainly get along without if I have to. And besides, though this may not flatter either of us, we're the same and want the same. So you understand."

I wasn't of that opinion, and not from pride; only because of the facts. Seeing that he needed me to be similar, however, I kept quiet. And if he was talking about the mysterious part of parentage, that our organs could receive waves or quanta of the same length, I didn't know enough about it to differ with him.

"Well, maybe it's as you say. But what makes you think this girl and her family are going to want you?"

"What are my assets? Well, first of all we're all handsome men in our family. Even George, if he were normal, would have been. The old lady knew that and thought we'd capitalize on it. But besides, I'm not marrying a rich girl in order to live on her dough and have a good time. They'll get full value out of me, those people. They'll see that I won't lie down and take it easy. I can't. I have to make money. I'm not one of those guys that give up what they want as soon as they realize they want it. I want money, and I mean *want*, and I can handle it. Those are my assets. So I couldn't be more on the level with them."

You couldn't blame me for listening to this with some amount of skepticism. But then things like this are done by people with the specific ambition to do them. I didn't like the way he talked; for instance, the boast that we were handsome men—it made us sound like studs. However, I couldn't hope that he'd have another failure; he wasn't that rich in heart that he could make good use of it.

"Let's see the girl's picture."

He had it in his pants pocket. She seemed young enough, a big girl, with a pretty good face. I thought she was rather handsome, though not of an open or easy nature.

"She's attractive, I told you. A little too heavy maybe."

Her name was Charlotte Magnus.

"Magnus? Wasn't it a Magnus truck that delivered coal to the Einhorns?"

"That's her uncle, in the coal business. Four or five big yards. And her father owns property by the acre. Hotels. Also a few five-and-dime stores. It'll be the coal business for me. That's where I think the most dough is. I'll ask for a yard as a wedding present."

"You have it all pretty well figured out."

"Sure. I have something figured out for you too."

"What, am I supposed to get married also?"

"In time, yes, we'll fix you up. Meanwhile you have to help me out. I have to have some family. I've been told they're family-minded people. They wouldn't understand or like it, the way we are, and we have to make it look better. There'll be dinners and such things, and probably a big engagement party. You don't expect me to go downstate and fetch George here to show them, do you? No, I have to have you. We need clothes. Do you have any?"

"They're in hock."

"Get them out."

"And what am I going to use for money?"

"Don't you have any at all? I thought you were in some kind of book business here."

"Mama gets all the money I have to spare."

He said tightly, "All right, don't be wise. I'll take care of all that soon. I'll raise the dough."

I wondered where his credit might still be good. Perhaps his buyer friend lent him some money. Anyway, I got a postal order from Simon a few days later, and when I redeemed the clothes he came to borrow one of my Evanston suits. Soon he said that he had met Charlotte Magnus. He believed she was already in love with him.

Chapter XI

NOW THERE'S a dark Westminster of a time when a multitude of objects cannot be clear; they're too dense and there's an island rain, North Sea lightlessness, the vein of the Thames. That darkness in which resolutions have to be made —it isn't merely local; it's the same darkness that exists in the fiercest clearnesses of torrid Messina. And what about the coldness of the rain? That doesn't deheat foolishness in its residence of the human face, nor take away deception nor change defects, but this rain is an emblem of the shared condition of all. It maybe means that what is needed to mitigate the foolishness or dissolve the deception is always superabundantly about and insistently offered to us—a black offer in Charing Cross; a gray in Place Pereires where you see so many kinds and varieties of beings go to and fro in the liquid and fog; a brown in the straight unity of Wabash Avenue. With the dark, the solvent is in this way offered until the time when one thing is determined and the offers, mercies, and opportunities are finished.

The house where I was living on the South Side was a student house within range of the university chimes and chapel bell when the evenings were still, and it had a crowded medieval fullness, besides, of hosts inside the narrow walls, faces in every window, every inch occupied. I had some student book customers and even several friends here. In fact I really knew everybody through the circumstance that Owens, the old Welshman who operated the place, had me answering telephone calls and distributing the mail in the little varnished hole called the lobby. This I did in exchange for my rent. And as I sorted the letters I unavoidably read return addresses and postcards, and, signaling by bell to call people to the telephone, I had to hear their conversations since there was no booth. Owens too listened in, he and his spinster sister who was housekeeper; the door of their stale parlor was always open—the smell of the kitchen governed over all the other smells of the house—where I at my post in the wicker rocker two hours every evening could see their after-supper state, their square pillars of walnut, the madnesses of starched lace, the insects'-eye inspiration of cut-glass, the screwy detail of fern both fiddle-necked and expanded, the paintings of fruit, which were full of hardness against liberty, plus the wheels of blue dishes around the wainscoting. With such equipment making an arsenal of their views—I mustn't forget the big fixtures of buffalo glass hanging on three chains—they demonstrated how they were there to stay and endure. Their tenants were transient, hence the Owenses probably needed something like this to establish home for themselves, and it was made very heavy.

Clem Tambow took to visiting me. His father the old politician had died, and Clem and his brother, now a tap dancer on the Loew's circuit, had divided an insurance policy. Clem wouldn't say how much he had inherited, out of a queer personal niceness or privacy, or maybe from superstition. But he had registered at the university, in the psychology department, and was living in the neighborhood.

"What do you think of the old man leaving me money?" he said, laughing, shy of his big mouth and carious teeth—he still had the big clear whites of his eyes and his head furry at the back as when a boy; and he went on confessing the trouble of his ugliness to me, being somber about the grief of his nose, but interrupting his complaints with enormous laughs, suddenly and swiftly moving his hand to save his cigar from falling. Now that he had money he wore a row of Perfecto Queens in his coat.

"I didn't appreciate my old man enough. I was all-out for my mother. I *mean* out. I would be still, but now she's just plain too old. Can't kid myself about it any more, especially since I've read a few psychology books."

Speaking of psychology, he always laughed. He said, "I'm only on campus because of the pussy." And then, a little melancholy, "I have some dough now, so I may as well harvest. I wouldn't get anywhere otherwise, with this fish mouth and my nose. Educated girls, you can appeal to their minds, and they don't expect you to spend too much on them." He couldn't consider himself a student; he was a sort of fee-paying visitor; he played poker in the law-school basement and pool at the Reynolds Club and went to a handbook on

Fifty-third Street to bet on horses. If he attended a class he was apt to "haw-haw-haw" in the big lecture hall at Kent, the amphitheater, at any standard joke of the science, or from private fun, unpreventably.

"But," he would explain, "that dumbbell was trying to put over some behaviorist junk, that all thinking is in words and so it must take place partly in the throat, in the vocal cords—what he said was 'inhibited sub-vocalization.' So they got curious as to what happened with mutes, and got some and put dinguses on their necks and read them syllogisms. But all the stuff was escaping through the fingers, because of course they talk with their hands. Then they poured plaster casts on their hands. Well, when the guy got this far I started laughing—*haw-haw!* And he asked me to leave."

Clem said this with one of his convulsions of embarrassment and shyness which then was wiped out by further laughter. *Haw-haw-haw!* Then a big flush of delight. Then gloom again, as he recalled his troubles, his having been short-weighted as to gifts by nature. I tried to tell him that he was wrong and that he didn't need to make up for anything. It was his ramming time, and his appearance was strongly virile in spite of exaggerations, such as his mustache, the gambler's stripe of the $22.50 suits he bought on time—he had the money but he preferred to pay installments. He said, "Don't be nice to me, Augie. You don't have to." Sometimes he took the air toward me of an uncle with a nephew of nearly the same age. He sought middle-agedness. He had decided that he could appeal to women whose taste was for experience; a little worn, somewhat bitter, debauched uncle. And that was how he tried to play it.

"Well, what about you, Augie, what's the matter with you?" he said. "What are you slopping around here for? You've got more possibilities than you know what to do with. The trouble with you is that you're looking for a manager. Now you're in cahoots with this Mexican. What are you postponing everything for?"

"What's everything?"

"I don't know. But you lie here in a wicker chair, taking it easy, holding a book on your chest, and letting time go by when there are a thousand things you could do."

Clem had a vast idea of what things there were to be had, which was quite natural when you consider how it wounded and stung him to believe that they were out of his reach. He meant, I know, money, admiration, women made absolutely helpless before you by love. The goods of fortune. He was disturbed by these thousand things, and, sometimes, so was I. He insisted that I should be going somewhere, at least that I should be practicing how to go, that I should concentrate on how to be necessary, and not be backward but energetic, absolute, and so forth. And of course I had some restlessness to be taken up into something greater than myself. I could not shine the star of great individuality that, by absorbed stoking, became a sun of the world over a throng to whom it glitters —whom it doesn't necessarily warm but only showers down a Plutarch radiance. Being necessary, yes, that would be fine and wonderful; but being Phoebus's boy? I couldn't even dream of it. I never tried to exceed my constitution. In any case, when someone like Clem urged me and praised me, I didn't listen closely. I had my own counseling system. It wasn't infallible, but it made mistakes such as I could bear.

Clem wasn't fooling with me on this great topic, but it wasn't his main purpose to talk to me when he came to the house. He wasn't there to hop me up or tell me news about Jimmy Klein, who was already married, and the father of a child, and working in a department store; or about his brother's trying to get on Broadway big-time. He came because he was after a girl named Mimi Villars who lived in the house.

Mimi wasn't a student; she waited on tables in a student hash-house on Ellis Avenue. I had noted her with appreciation, maybe the more fit to judge because I had no thought of making her myself. She was very fair and ruddy, of a push-faced tough beauty, long brows continued in very thin pencil slightly upward, like the lash of the euglena, away from their natural line toward tight blond ears that had to be looked for amid her curls, and a large mouth, speaking for a soul of wild appetite, nothing barred; she'd say anything, and had no idea of what could hinder her. Her hips were long and narrow, her bust was large, and she wore close-fitting skirts and sweaters and high heels that gave a tight arch of impatience to the muscles of her calves; her step was small and pretty and her laughter violent, total, and critical. She didn't much remind me of Willa from the Symington, also a waitress. Willa, whom I preferred personally, this country girl—I think I could have been perfectly happy with Willa and lived all my life in a country town if the chance had ever presented itself. Or, anyhow, I sometimes tell myself that.

Mimi came from Los Angeles. Her father had been an actor in the silent movies. She'd speak of him when she wanted to say how she hated Englishmen. Originally she came to Chicago to study, but she was expelled from the university for going past the bounds of necking at Greene Hall, in the lounge. She was a natural for being bounced. You wouldn't doubt that she was capable of the offense, if it was one, and as for the penalty, it was a favorite subject of her ferocious humor.

I knew that Clem didn't stand a chance with her. The cause of her strong color was not sheer health or self-excitement: love also contributed to it. By a coincidence her lover was one of the customers Padilla had passed on to me, a man named Hooker Frazer who was a graduate assistant in Political Science. He was hard to deal with, for he ordered rare and out-of-print books. Two volumes of Nietzsche's *Will to Power* I had a hell of a time swiping, for they were in a closed case at the Economy Book Store; I also got him Hegel's *Philosophy of Right*, as well as the last volumes of *Capital* from the Communist bookshop on Division Street, Herzen's *Autobiography*, and some de Tocqueville. He bargained keenly, just as he spoke keenly, with unusual concision, and he was a man the university ought to have been pleased about, with his tall, free look of intelligence early crow-footed from the practice of consideration, a young Calhoun or statesman already, with clear blue spaces indicative of rigorous consistency and an untimely wrinkle, like the writing of a seismograph. He was not one of those tall men of whom you think that they must come in sections of different mechanical principle, but was not awkward although his posture was loose. The fact that he lived in Burton Court, so much like a new Christ Church or Magdalen, and in a don's state, that learned bachelorhood, itself fetched me. It didn't Padilla, with his stiff nose of Gizeh's mummy and livid eye-patches, his narrow vault of shoulders and back, and his hard, sharp step on the getting-to-be-venerable stones. Manny came from a high mountain slum and had a cultureless disposition. He didn't go in for the Old World much.

But Hooker Frazer was Mimi Villars' man, and, seeing them together on the stairs of Owens' house, I admired them, both made so well, she hard and spirited, editing her words for no one, and he so distinct-looking he might have been lineally direct from Cro-Magnon man—but of course with present-day differences, including the disorders. He had a temper that didn't go with the rest of him, with his composure and even toploftiness. His teeth were often set hard, and his straight nose ended in a nervous fancifulness that must have originated in character rather than inheritance. But even Padilla, who didn't like him much, said he was *muy hombre*, a considerable man. Padilla was, however, down on him for his condescension to us; to me more than to him, for Frazer was aware that Padilla was a genius at mathematical physics. But he called us both "mister," as though he were a West Pointer, and treated us like amusing thieves. As if he wasn't a receiver of stolen goods himself. He'd say, "Mr. March, will you take a trip downtown and expropriate from the expropriators a good copy of the *Esprit des Lois*? The other day I noticed one at the Argus." I'd laugh out loud at his mixture of pompousness and revolutionist's jargon and his amended Tennessee accent. At first he seemed to consider me an agreeable nitwit and joshed me about my color. "Anybody would say that you spent your days in the cow pasture, Mr. March, from your rosiness, instead of breathing the air of bookshops." Later he was more grave with me and offered me old copies of Communist and Trotskyist papers and magazines—he had them in stacks, sheaves, and bundles in his room, in various languages; he received all kinds of journals and bulletins. He even invited me once to hear him lecture, but that may have been because I was his cheap source of supply; I extended him credit, and he wanted to stay on good terms with me. Padilla threw fits when he heard that I gave him books on the cuff; I thought he would haul off and punch me with his skinny, long-fingered fist; he screamed at me, "*Bobo!*" and "you gringo dummy!" And I said I'd stop Frazer's credit at twenty-five dollars. It was a lie to calm him; he was already into me for nearer to forty. "Shit! I wouldn't give him a penny. This is just the way he shows he's better than you," Manny said. But I wasn't affected. Probably I too much enjoyed delivering a few books to Frazer for the chance of spending half an hour in the atmosphere of his rooms and hearing him talk. Often I stole two copies of what he ordered, from curiosity, to read one myself, and thus had some dull and difficult afternoons.

I never blamed myself for throwing aside such things as didn't let themselves be read with fervor, for they left nothing with me anyhow, and I took my cue from Padilla not to vex myself about what didn't come easy. After all, I wasn't yet in any special business, but merely trying various things on.

But I had to tell Clem that he wouldn't get anywhere with Mimi Villars.

"Why," he said, "because I'm so homely? I figure her for the kind that doesn't care about looks. She's a hot girl."

"Your looks have nothing to do with it. She has a man already."

"What, and you think she'll never have another one? That's how much you know."

So he backed his belief about her stubbornly, and came to sit with me, washed and fresh-shaved, long black shoes gleaming, and acted with his depressed gallantry, practicing it even on me, lacking only laces and swords to be a follower of decayed Stuarts in exile—his heavy drama of boredom. Only his unlicked electric fur of boyish back-hair and the soft glossiness of his eye whites and his *haw-haw!* told a different story about him. I was glad of his company. But of course I couldn't tell him all I knew about Mimi. It wasn't only that I read postcards and couldn't help listening to telephone conversations; it was that Mimi didn't care about secrecy. She led a proclaimed life, and once she got talking she held back nothing. Frazer would occasionally send her a card breaking a date, and she would go into a temper, flinging it away, and say to me furiously, tearing open the clasp of her purse, "Sell me a slug"; and to him on the phone she'd say, "You yellow bastard, can't you call me and tell me why you won't come? Don't give me any of that old crap about working on your thesis! What were you doing on Fifty-seventh Street the other night with those fat goofs when you were supposed to be working on it? Who are they? One of them was an English fairy, I could spot him a mile away. Don't tell me I don't understand. I'm tired of your bullshit, you preacher!"

In her breathers, I could hear his voice going on measuredly as I sprawled and listened in the rocker. And then Owens' beefy wrist would come out to fetch the door and slam it. He didn't care what tenants did in their rooms, but he didn't like her swearing to reach his parlor—he was sitting in there on his leather, crunching like dry snow; his main sounds were, at close range, breathing, and, at a distance, turning his weight. "You'll never live to hear me beg for anything," were Mimi's last words to Frazer, and when she slammed phone and hook together with cruelty it was as a musician might shut the piano after he had finished storming chords of mightiest difficulty without a single flinch or error.

To rip off a piece of lover's temper was pleasure in her deepest vein of enjoyment. She said to me then, "If that bastard calls back, tell him I ran out of the house swearing." However, she would be waiting for his next call.

What made me sure, though, that she would have no interest in Clem, at least for the time being, was that lately Frazer had been phoning with regularity, and she took her time about descending when I buzzed her. He, knowing it was I that answered the phone, said, "Can't you get her to make it a little faster, Mr. March?" To which I said, "I can try, but I'm not King Canute, you know," and let the big club of the receiver hang from the cord.

"What do you want?" were her first words when she laid her burning cigarette on the instrument box. "I can't talk to you. I'm stymied. If you want to find out how I am you can come over in person and ask." And then in her joyful, reckless way of welcoming her anger, "All right, if you don't care, I don't care either. No, I haven't come around yet, but don't worry, you won't have to marry me. I wouldn't marry a man who doesn't know what love is. You don't want a wife, you want a looking glass. What! What do you mean, money! You still owe *me* forty-seven dollars. That's okay. I don't care what it was spent for. If I'm up the stump I'll take care of it myself. Sure you owe everybody. Don't give *me* that kind of stuff. Tell it to your wife. She seems to swallow everything."

Frazer was not yet divorced from his first wife, from whom Mimi, in her version of it, had rescued him. "Do you remember a picture called *The Island of Dr. Moreau*? This mad scientist made men and women out of animals? And they called the laboratory 'The House of Pain'? Well, with his wife he was living like one of those animals," she once told me, speaking of how she had first found him. "This girl had a flat —you wouldn't believe a man like Hooker could live in it; no matter what I think of his personality, he's intelligent, he has ideas; when he was a Communist he was chosen to go study at the Lenin Institute, where they train national leaders like Cachin and Mao; he didn't make it because he was expelled over the German question. Well, in this flat there were chenille rugs in the toilet so you felt you were doing wrong, going in your shoes. A man can't do anything while putting up with that. Women really are no good, Augie," she declared with her characteristic and favorite humorous rage. "They're no fucking good. They want a man in the house. Just there, in the house. Sitting in his chair. They pretend to take what he thinks and says seriously. Is it about government? Is it about astronomy? So they play along and make believe they care about parties and stars. They baby men, and they don't care what game they play, just so there's a man in the house. If the husband is a Socialist, she's a Socialist, hotter than he, and if he changes into a Technocrat she beats him to it—she makes him think so. All she really cares about is to have a man in the house and doesn't give a hoot in hell what she says she is. And it isn't even hypocritical, it's deeper than that. It's having the man." With things like this—and it was one of many—Mimi tried to pierce you through. Sufficiently *said*, I suppose, the thing was true for her. She believed in words, in speaking, and if she convinced you, then she herself could believe what her inspiration told her. And when it came to speaking, she had borrowed some from Frazer—that private forensic method that didn't always seem quite right in personal conversation: he with his long knees spread and elbows resting on them, hands clasped, perfect earnestness of eyes, and, as a further warrant of plain talk, the straight white middle part of his sandy hair. Mimi followed his manner as much as she might, and she had more knottedness in her and passion, and the speed you can get from narrow gauge and high compression.

She was, as Einhorn had rightly said that I was, in opposition; only she named names and wrongs, and was an attacker where I had other ways, temperamentally, and she didn't persuade me. I didn't believe she was right because emphatic. "Well," she said, "if you don't agree with me, why are you quiet? Why don't you say what you think instead of turning down what I say by grinning? You try to look more simple than you are, and it isn't honest. But if you know better, come on and speak up."

"No," I said, "I don't know. But I don't like low opinions, and when you speak them out it commits you and you become a slave of them. Talk will lead people on until they convince their minds of things they can't feel true."

She took this as a harder criticism of her than I had meant it to be, and answered me nastily with a kind of cat's electric friction and meanness of her face.

"Why, you're a lousy bonehead! If you don't even know how to be indignant—why, Christ, even a cow gets indignant! And what do you mean, *low*! You want to have high opinions of garbage? What do you want to become, a sewage plant? Hell, I say no! If a thing is bad it's bad, and if you don't hate it you kiss it on the sly."

She shot it off in my face that I wasn't mad enough about abominations or aware enough of them, didn't know how many graves were underneath my feet, was lacking in disgust, wasn't hard enough against horrors or wrathful about swindles. The worst of which swindles was in getting terrible payment for what should be a loving exchange of bodies and the foundation of all the true things of life. The women to blame for this were far worse than whores. And I guess that she exploded against me in this conversation because I wasn't enough of an enemy of such things but smiled at such ruining wives too for their female softnesses. I was too indulgent about them, about the beds that would be first stale and then poisonous because their manageresses' thoughts were on the conquering power of chenille and dimity and the suffocation

of light by curtains, and the bourgeois ambering of adventur-
ing man in parlor upholstery. These things not appearing so
threatening to me as they ought to appear, I was, on this
topic anyhow, a fool to her, one who also could be stuck, leg-
bent, in that white spiders' secretion and paralyzed inside
women's edifices of safety. She had torn Frazer out of that.
He was worth saving.

And here I could see what a value she set on the intelligence of men. If they didn't breathe the most difficult air of
effort and nobility, then she wished for them the common-
place death in the gas cloud of settled existence, office
bondage, quiet-store-festering, unrecognized despair of marriage without hope, or the commonness of resentment that
grows unknown boils in one's heart or bulbs of snarling flowers. She had a high, absolute standard, and she preferred people to miss it from suffering, vice, being criminal or perverted,
or of loony impulse. I learned about her when I knew her
better that she was a thief too; she stole her clothes from department stores, stole a good deal, since she liked to dress
well, and had even been arrested but got off on suspended
sentence. Her method was to put on layers of dresses in the
fitting booths, also underpants and slips; and the way she had
gotten out of the rap was to convince the court psychiatrist
that she had money and could pay but was afflicted with klep-
tomania. She was proud of this and urged me to do the same
should I be caught—she knew of course that I was lifting
books. There was another thing of which she was not so
proud. About a year before, late one night as she was passing
an alley on Kimbark Avenue, a stickup man had tried to take
her pocketbook, and she had kicked him in the groin,
snatched the gun when he dropped it, and shot him through
the thigh. It made her wretched to remember this, and when
she talked about it her hands became nervous and worked inward at her waist—which was small: she drew notice to its
smallness by wearing broad belts—and her color got rough
enough to be a symptom of scarlatina. She tried to get into
Bridewell Hospital to see him, and wasn't allowed.

"The poor guy," she said, and this was remorse over her
savage speed and rashness as well as pity for this boy, haunting the mouth of an alley with that toy of swift decisions. For

the robbery money can shrink mighty small, and you can soon handle the satisfaction out of it, but having someone do precisely what you say is a thing of a different order. And a woman too. She didn't interpret this as cowardice of the assailant but as special mark of crude love appeal, that a city-tutored rough child struggled for his instinct and was less cared about, providentially speaking, than the animal in the woods who was at least in the keeping of nature. Well, she had to go to court and testify, to explain why she had shot him. She didn't, however, want to bring charges, and she tried to speak a piece to the judge and was prevented. So the boy was given five years for armed robbery, and now she sent him packages and letters. Not because she feared harm from him when he got out, but out of remorse.

This time she wasn't up the stump, as she spoke of it. Eventually she was able to give Frazer better news. But she made him wait for it. She wanted him to worry, or to give him practice in learning to worry about her and not about himself. She was not easy toward him. She knew it was unequal, that she loved him more than he could her or anyone. But neither was love his calling, as it was hers. And she was very severe and exalted about this. She too could have lived in desert wilderness for the sake of it, and have eaten locusts.

The thing I began to learn from her was of the utmost importance; namely, that everyone sees to it his fate is shared. Or tries to see to it. You may say that I should have known this before. I should have, and in a way I did, or else Grandma Lausch or Einhorn or the Renlings would have had more success with me. But it was never so clear in anyone as in Mimi Villars, whose actual body was her recruiting place and who more conspicuously issued her own warrant, license, diploma, asserting what she was, and she had no usual place of legitimate activity, like a store, office, or family, or membership anywhere, but banked all on her clinching will, her hard reason, and her obstinate voice. I think she must have recognized—and how could it fail to give her sharp pain?—the contradiction of harsh persuasion to such a love belief as hers. But the thick rind of world-organized resistance made that inevitable. Well, that too was a fate to be shared and another underlying bitterness.

By the end of summer we were already close friends and under suspicion by Tambow of being more. But there was nothing to that except his envious although not grudging imagination, backed by such slight apparent proof as that she came into my room in her petticoat. This was only because we lived on the same floor. She went into Kayo Obermark's the same way—we had the attic between the three of us; it just was proximity; even if provocation was never far away it came simply from unremitting practice, like that of the fiddler who has a rubber ball in the pocket of his great alpacuna as he rides the train to a concert and is never far from, for him, the greatest thing, along the accidentals and slides of landscape and steel rail. No, she came to borrow a cigarette or to use the closet where she kept the overflow of her dresses. Or to talk.

We now had something more to talk about, for by and by we found we had another connection. It was through that swarthy Sylvester for whom I used to pass out movie handbills and who had tried to make a Communist of Simon. He had never finished his degree at Armour Tech. He said it was from lack of dough and hinted also his political assignment elsewhere, but it was everybody's thought that he had washed out. Be that as it might, he was living in New York and working for the subway at a technical job. Under Forty-second Street. He seemed bound to have occupations in the darkness, and by now this had laid a peculiar coloring on him, his face darkened sallow and slack-cheeked and his eyes, injured by worry, now more Turkish from a thickening of the skin by the continual effort and wrinkling his eyes, probably, at the ruby and green cut buttons of his burrow office—there where he sat at a drawing board and copied blueprints and read pamphlets in his leisure time. He had been expelled, like Frazer, from the Communist party. On charges of Infantile Leftism and Trotskyist Deviationism—the terms were queer to me, and just as queer was his assuming that I understood them. He belonged to another party now, the Trotskyites, and was still a Bolshevik, and disclosed that he was never free from duty, never unassigned, never went anywhere without permission from party chiefs. Even returning to Chicago, ostensibly to visit his father, the old man called by Grandma "the Baker," he had a mission, which was to contact Frazer.

So I inferred that Frazer was being recruited to the new party. I happened to walk behind them on Fifty-seventh Street one day. Sylvester was toting a fat briefcase and looking up at Frazer and talking with special slowness in a kind of political accent while Frazer was looking past and over him with aloof gravity and had his hands clasped at his back.

I also saw Sylvester on the stairs of the rooming house, with Mimi. He was, or had been, Mimi's brother-in-law, married in New York to her sister Annie, who had now left him and was getting a divorce. I recalled how his first wife threw stones at him when he tried to come through her father's backyard to talk to her, and I even remembered the surroundings in which I had heard about this from him, the grim air of cold Milwaukee Avenue when we peddled razorblades and glasscutters with Jimmy Klein. Sylvester wanted Mimi to plead with her sister for him. "Hell," Mimi told me, as much for my private ear as any of her opinions were, "if I had known him before they were married I would have told Annie not to do it. He leaks misery all over. I wonder how she could stand two full years of him. Young girls do the goddamnedest things. Can you imagine being in bed with him, and that mud face and those lips? Why, he looks like the frog prince. I hope now she'll get under the sheets with a young strong stevedore." If somebody fell against Mimi's lines she had no mercy, and as she listened to Sylvester she kept in mind her sister bolt upright in a huskier man's clasp and struggling her arms with pleasure, and it made me for a minute dislike her for her cruelty that she held her eyes open for Sylvester so that he might look in and see this. What was to make it an acceptable joke was the supposition that he couldn't see. No, he probably couldn't.

It needs to be explained that in Mimi's hard view all that you inherited from the mixing peoples of the past and the chance of parents' encountering like Texas cattle was your earthy material, which it was your own job to make into admirable flesh. In other words, applied to Sylvester, he was in large measure to blame for how he looked; his spirit was a bad kiln. And also it was his fault that he couldn't keep his wives and girls. "I hear his first one was a dizzy bitch. And Annie has something of a slut about her too. What makes them go for him at the start? That really interests me," said Mimi. And she supposed that they must take his little gloom for real devilishness and expect him to visit their places with prickles and fire, like a genuine demon; when he failed to, turning out to be mere uncompleted mud, they threw stones at him, real or figurative. She was savage-minded, Mimi, and prized her savagery as proof that there was no monkey business about her; she punished and took blows as the real thing.

That humiliated, bandy-legged, weak-haired, and injured-in-the-eyes Sylvester, however, the subterranean draftsman and comedy commissar of a Soviet-America-to-be, teaching himself the manner and even the winner's smile and confidence, why, he was going to blast off the old travertine and let the gold and marble shine for a fresh humanity. He tried to impress me with the command he had over Marxian coal and cotton, plenary dates, factional history, texts of Lenin and Plekhanov; what he had really was the long-distance dreaming gaze of the eyes into the future and the pick of phrase, which he smiled and smelled like a perfume, heavy-lidded. He condescended to me and dutch-uncled me because he knew that I liked him and wasn't aware how much I knew about him. Which I was bound to spare him. Anyway, his defects weren't as serious to me as they were to Mimi.

With me he could be fully confident, and some of his charm couldn't live except in the presence of confidence. "How's tricks, kid?" he said with a rejoicing smile—but darkness and bitterness could never wholly leave it any more—and while he gentled his palms on his double-breasted joint belly and chest. "What are you up to? Getting by? What are you here, a student? No. A *macher*? A proletarian?" This word, even jesting, he pronounced with veneration.

"Well, a sort of student."

"Our boys," he replied, more deeply smiling. "Anything but honest labor. And how's your brother Simon? What's he doing? I thought I could recruit him once. He'd have made a good revolutionary. Where are they going to come from if not from your kind of background? But I guess I couldn't make him see it. He's very intelligent though. One day he'll see it himself."

*

In the peculiar fate of people that makes them fat and rich, when this happens very swiftly there is the menace of the dreamy state that plunders their reality. Let's say that anyway old age and death would come, so why shouldn't the passage be comfortable? But this proposal doesn't make a firm mind, in the strange area where things swim too fast. Against this trouble thought may be a remedy; force of person is another one, and money and big-scale lavishness, unpierceable concreteness, organizational deeds. So there are these various remedies and many more, older ones, but you don't actually have full choice among all the varieties, especially those older ones of the invisible world. Most people make do with what they have, and labor in their given visible world, and this has its own stubborn merit.

Not only did Simon make what he had do, but he went the limit. It astonished me how he took his objectives and did exactly what he had projected. It was well-nigh unfair to have called the turns so accurately and to do to people what he planned while he was still a stranger to them. Charlotte was in love with him. Not only that, but they were already married, and it wasn't only he who had hastened and pushed the thing, but she too was in a hurry. Partly because he was too broke to court her long. He told her that, and she and her parents agreed they shouldn't waste time. Only, the ceremony was performed out of town to keep the news out of the papers, and for the rest of the family there had to be an engagement and a wedding. So Charlotte and her mother had worked it out, and while Simon paid rent in a good bachelor's club downtown he was actually living with the Magnuses in their huge old West Side flat.

He came to see me after the one-day honeymoon which was all the secrecy of the marriage gave them time for. They had been in Wisconsin. Already he had more new attributes than I could keep track of, draped in comfortable flannel, owning a new lighter, and effects in his pockets he didn't yet have the hang of. He said, "The Magnuses have been wonderful to me." There was a new gray Pontiac at the curb—he showed it to me from the window; and he was learning the coal business at one of the Magnuses' yards.

"And what about your own yard? Didn't you say—"

"Certainly, I said. They've promised me that as soon as I can run a place myself. It won't take long. No, it hasn't been so hard," he said further, understanding my unasked question. "They'd rather have a poor young man. A poor young man gets up more steam and pressure. They were like that themselves, and they know."

Already he didn't look like such a poor young man in the high quality gray flannel, and shoes with new stitching; his shirt smelled of the store; it hadn't been to the laundry yet.

"Get dressed, I'm taking you to dinner there," he said. When we were outside, walking down the path to the car, he took a stiff shot of breath and hawked, exactly as on the day I went with him to the La Salle Street Station where apparently I was too dumb to sell papers. Except that this time he had gloomy big rings round his eyes; and we sat down in the car, which had that sour spice of new rubber and car upholstery. It was the first time I had seen him drive. He swung it round like a veteran, even somewhat recklessly.

So I was taken into that hot interior of lamps and rugs, to the Magnuses'. Everything was ungainly there, roomy and oversized. The very parrots painted on the lampshades were as big as Rhode Island Reds. The Magnuses too were big; they had a Netherlandish breadth of bone. My sister-in-law was of that size also, and was aware or shy of it as indelicacy, giving me the touch of her hand as though it were a smaller one. She needn't have. It's difficult when outsized people worry about their presentation, and women especially, who have secret dismay of grossness. She had remarkably handsome eyes, soft, with occasional lights of distaste though, shrewd, and expressing immense power of management; but also they were warm. So was her bosom, which was abundant, and she had large hips. She was on her guard with me, as if afraid of my criticism, of what I would say to Simon the first time we were alone. She must have convinced herself that he had done her a great favor by marrying her, he was so obviously smart and good-looking, and at the same time she was swept with resentment lest she shouldn't be thought good enough or the money be too much remembered. The issue most alive was whether he would have married her without money. It was much too troubling not to be spoken of, so it was spoken of in a kind of fun and terrible persiflage. Simon did it with the kind of coarseness that has to be laughed at because to take it seriously would be murder—his saying, for instance, when the three of us were left alone in the parlor to become acquainted, "Nobody's ever been laid better at any price." It was so ambiguous and inside-out as to who had paid the price that it had to be taken as amusing, and she hurried and came down from a romantic, sentimental position and denied it all by pretending that this randy talk was the joke of sincerity and deep underlying agreement, a more realistic sort of love. But leaning above him like a kind of flounced Pisan tower construction—she dressed with luxury and daring—keeping a hand on his hair, she had instants of great difficulty before me.

She had difficulty only for a while, until she absorbed from Simon the attitude that I was a featherhead, affectionate but not long on good sense. She soon enough learned to deal with me. But it was painful until she found confidence, and I suppose that at the time she hadn't recovered from the honeymoon, which, Simon had been frank to tell me, was awful. He didn't specify in which way, but he expressed enough to make it profoundly believable; he had some notes in the end of the scale that I would rather not have heard played for the consents to death that rang in them, but I was forced to listen to all he had, struck right on the key and sounded from top to bottom. I could be sure these said-in-jest things were the weirdest of their kind ever to be laughed at and spoken in that carpeted peace and brown-gravy velour. It was all supposed to pass for fun and bridegroom's lustiness, energy, and play-wickedness, and it came through to me that he was being tortured by thought of suicide, stronger than a mere hint, but simultaneously he could dive to clasp his compensations, such as his pride in audaciousness and strength of nerve and body or the luxury he was coming into, and furthermore, a certain recklessness in demands: the sense of what he could do and what he could exact without caring what anybody thought was much to him.

Then the family came in, wondering what type of person I

might be. I wondered at them no less. They were so big you
thought what could prevent them from handling even Simon
and me like children, though we were by no means midgety
—Simon was nearly six feet tall and I only an inch shorter
than he. It was their width that made the difference, and even
now that he was getting stout Simon didn't begin to approach them. They were substantial in their lives as in girth;
they made their old people respected—there was a grandmother there that evening—and they bought the best of
everything, clothes, furniture, or machinery. Also they were
grateful for entertainment and admired speed of wit, which
they didn't have themselves, and dramatic self-presentation,
which Simon gave them. He more than pleased them and
more than made a big hit. He went both deep and far into
the place of star and sovereign. They had patriarchs and ma-
triarchs but they had no prince before him. To make this of
himself, the prince, he went through a metamorphosis. That
was the next of my astonishments. Elsewhere I've said that he
had always, even when silent, been noticeable. But he wasn't
silent any more, and his old reserve was gone to pieces; he
was boisterous, capricious, haughty, critical, arbitrary, mimicking and deviling, and he crowed, croaked, made faces and
had the table all but spinning in this dining room of stable
and upright wealth. I saw Grandma's satire in him, across the
plaited white bread and the sprigged fish and candles—yes,
the old woman's hardness of invention and travestying savagery, even certain Russian screams. I didn't know Simon had
gotten so much from her. I could draw my mind back over
some six or seven hundred Friday nights and see his uncom-
menting eyes follow a performance of the old woman's. And
how deep that had sunk in, without even appearing to. At the
shrieks he caused I nearly heard her comment of disdain, a
disdain of which Simon was not all innocent either. He both
borrowed from her and burlesqued her. His appearance was
new in more than one way; more was new than the shirt, or
the jewel on his finger and minor gems in his cuffs, or even
the fat, and the haggardness from unwanted thought that lit
on him in instants between the turns of his performance. The
task of doing bold things with an unhappy gut, that was it. In
a way he made them meet the expense of this too, as when he

imitated his good queen mother-in-law's accent. But it was just the opposite of offensive to her and to them all; it was grand and uproarious.

However, he wasn't just their entertainer; when he turned grave and stopped the vaudeville with a pair of somber eyes he got earnest silence for the speech he was going to make, and a full weight of respect.

He spoke to me, but of course his words were in large part for them. "Augie," he said, putting his arm around Charlotte —she laid her painted nails on his hand—"you can see how unlucky we were not to have this kind of close and loyal family. There isn't anything these people won't do for one another. We don't even understand what that is because we never experienced it, we missed it all our lives. We had no luck. Now they've taken me in and made me one of them, as if I were their own child. I never understood what a real family was till now, and you ought to know how grateful I am. They may seem a little slow-witted to you"—Mr. and Mrs. Magnus didn't quite get this, Simon's tone being enough for them and the fine satisfaction they took in him, but Charlotte was seized with a laugh in the throat at this mischief interrupting his seriousness—"but they have something you'll have to learn to appreciate, and that's their kindness and the way they stick by their own."

When he scrawled this on me, I had a fit of hate for the fat person he was becoming, and I wanted to say, "This is crummy, to boost them and tear down your own. What's the matter with Mama or even Grandma?" But then what he said of the Magnuses had its truth, you couldn't miss it. I was a sucker for it too, family love. And though Simon did this thing in a bad gross way I doubt that he could have been absolutely insincere and putting on. Finding yourself amongst warm faces, why, there're many objections that recede, as when enemy women may kiss. Many common lies and hypocrisies are like that, just out of the harmony of the moment. And with Simon there was also a revulsion from his gnawing trouble and his need to get some breath on his Valley of Ezekiel slain. Therefore he was building up his causes for gratitude. And therefore, also, I answered nothing.

As he had said this to me, however, they were watching and

were suspicious because I didn't grab a piece of this love feast. I had consented to play his game, but I wasn't fast enough to do everything. I had a sea of feeling of my own which I was straining under. And then I think all their unresolved suspicions about Simon came to gather on me. They seemed to expect me to clear myself—all, in their ruddiness and size, including the granny who was dissolving from both, losing color and getting small, an old creature in black, wearing pious wig and amulets, who looked to have metaphysical judgmental powers. Well, they owned stores; maybe they smelled a thief in me. Anyway, they looked at me so acutely that I could perceive myself with their eyes, just about, my sizable head and uncommitted smile, my untrained and anti-disciplinary hair. Instead of asking, "Who are they?" about both Simon and me, they could demand of themselves, "Who is *he*?" Indeed, who *was* I to be sharing their gold soup of supper light and putting their good spoons in my mouth?

Observing this difficulty, Simon quickly came up with a remedy, saying, "Augie is a good kid, he just doesn't know his own mind yet." They were glad to be reassured about me; all they asked was that I should be regular, that I should speak up more, make a few jokes, laugh when all laughed. I ought not to be so different from Simon. Of course there was an obstacle to being like him, which was that I hadn't yet grasped him in his new character. But I soon caught on a little and made myself more acceptable, even welcome, by joining in the fun and dancing in the parlor after dinner. The only nearly serious hitch, with Mr. Magnus, was that I didn't know how to play pinochle. How was it that a decently brought-up young fellow didn't know how? Otherwise an indulgent easygoing character, Mr. Magnus was dissatisfied about this. Like Talleyrand making a tight mouth about the man who didn't play whist. Simon could play pinochle. (Where had he learned? Well, where, for that matter, had all his new accomplishments come from?) "Oh, Augie is a sort of studious type and he doesn't go in for such things." he said. This wasn't good enough for Mr. Magnus, with the long gray threads of baldness on his robust head. "I don't like a young man should gamble either," he said. "But he should play a friendly game." I felt he wasn't unjustified. "I'll play if you teach me,"

I said, which went a long way toward improving the situation and making me one of the house. I sat in a corner with some of the younger children to study pinochle.

More relatives came; the vast apartment filled. It was family custom on Friday night, and, moreover, the word was out that Charlotte was engaged. People wanted to see Simon. He already knew most of them, the giant uncles and heavy-pelted aunts in their Siberian furs who came up from their Cadillacs and Packards: Uncle Charlie Magnus who owned the coal yards; Uncle Artie who owned a big mattress factory; Uncle Robby who was a commission merchant in South Water Street, ponderous, white, and caracul-haired—like Stiva Lausch—and with a hearing-aid plugged in. There were sons in uniform, from military academy, and others with football letters, and daughters, and little children. Simon was ready for the uncles and aunts, very familiar and even already overbearing to some. He had a natural hang of their whole system of fellowship and contempt—how not to be caught under any circumstances in a position where to be looked down on was unavoidable, so that you could read in a back, bearishly turned, that you were a *schmuck*.

I have to say that Simon's confidence was superb, and it was he who was getting them under, though he was deferential with a few of the women. Toward these, heartiness or brazening wasn't indicated, but what was necessary was to prove that in addition to everything he was also a lover. I must say also that he had no embarrassment because of me; he assumed my complicity and was teaching and leading me. So I followed him around, because there was nobody else for me to stand close to comfortably. It lacked white stockings and fans to resemble the Directorate—I'm thinking of commoners suddenly in the palaces of power. But the Magnuses seemed less to know what to do. However, in all the world there was no one who had more than they of anything except money—a gap that could perhaps be closed.

Over this tumultuousness and family heat, melding yells at the pinochle table, the racing of the kids, pitchers of cocoa and tea and masses of coffee cake carried in, political booming and the sharper neighing of women and all this grand vital discord, there was the supervision of Uncle Charlie standing, or rather rearing, beside his wigged mother in her black dress. If it strikes me as advisable to add "rearing" it is because of the tightness of his belly and the great weight supported by his feet, and possibly also because the old woman wore a collar of things in gold shaped like grizzly-teeth, and that reminds me of creatures. He was white, thick, and peevish, and had the kind of insolence that sometimes affects the eyes like snowblindness, making you think there's something arctic about having a million bucks. At least an immigrant who during the Depression was a millionaire had this dazzle. Not that Uncle Charlie was formidable in all respects; I'm taking him at a posed moment, during a family occasion, a niece to be married off and new kin to be added.

Through Simon I had got to be a candidate too. If he worked out well then I might also be considered as a husband, for there wasn't any lack of daughters to marry, some of them pretty and all with money. So far Simon had had nothing but successes. For several weeks he had been working under Uncle Charlie's eye, first as weighmaster and cashier and then learning to buy, meeting brokers and salesmen and learning about freight rates and the different coal fields. Uncle Charlie certified that he was *fehig*, or apt, a naturally good businesshead, and all were very pleased. Simon was already looking for a yard of his own, hoping to find one with an overhead track that would reduce unloading costs. In short, Uncle Charlie was extremely indulgent with him as an up-and-comer, and he received all the marks of the old boy's favor, the simple cordial obscenities and hand on the shoulder; he wagged his head near Simon's face and opened up all bounties. His humor made everybody laugh with pleasure. Nobody thought to remonstrate about children and young girls when Uncle Charlie said, "Sonofabitch, you're fo-kay, my boy, fo-kay. You got the goods. I think you can put it down between the sheets too, eh?" because this was just his usual manner of speaking.

"What do you think?" said Simon. "Leave it to me."

"Yes, I think. I leave it to you. You think I'm goin' to take it myself? Wouldn't be fun for Charlotte. Look how she's built. Nothing was left out. She has to have a young husk."

Here I came in for my share of the notice. Kelly Weintraub,

one of the distant cousins by marriage and a trucker who worked for Uncle Robby, said, "Look at his brother. The girls are popping their eyes out at him. Your daughter Lucy the worst. You got no shame, kid? In this family the girls can't hardly wait."

There were shrieks about this. Through them Lucy Magnus continued to smile at me though her color deeply changed. She was slighter than most of her family; she wasn't shy to make a declaration of honest sensuality under the scrutiny of the whole clan. None of the Magnuses took the trouble to conceal such things; it wasn't necessary. The young ones could tell their parents exactly what they wanted, which I found admirable. I could look at Lucy with pleasure too. She was plain but had a healthy face, very clear skin, and pretty breasts that she swung where she pleased. Only her nose might have been finer; it was a little broad, as was her mouth, but her black eyes were strong and declarative, and her hair black and delicate. It made me think of her maiden hair and there were suggestions I didn't try at all to evade. But these were lover's not husbandly thoughts. I had no special mind to get married. I saw Simon's difficulties too clearly for that.

"Come here," said her father to me, and I had to stand close inspection. "What do you do?" he said, winking with the full snowblindness.

Simon answered for me, "He's in the book business. Until he saves enough to go back to the university and finish his degree."

"Shut up!" he said. "C—sucker! I asked *him*, not you, budinski! What do you do?"

I said, "I'm in the book business, as Simon told you." I thought the old man must be able to pierce by strength of suspicion my crookery, all the oddity of Owens' house and my friends there. What a book business could signify to him but starving Pentateuch peddlers with beards full of Polish lice and feet wrapped in sacking, I couldn't fathom.

"Goddammit the schools. There's schoolboys now until gray hair. So what are you studying for, a lawyer? Fo-kay! I guess we got to have them, the crooks. My sons don't go to school. My daughters go, so long it keeps them out of trouble."

"Augie was thinking of going to law school," Simon said to Lucy's mother.

"Yes, that's right," I too said.

"Fine, fine, fine, fine," said Uncle Charlie, my hearing done and his face of thick white hide turned in dismissal from us all; he threatened with his intensest care his daughter Lucy, who answered him with one of her smiles. I saw that she promised him obedience and he promised back the satisfaction of all legitimate needs as long as she obeyed him.

There was another special glance on me, that of my sister-in-law Charlotte, with her investigative, warm, and to some extent despairing eyes. I don't doubt that she already knew some displeasing things about Simon, and perhaps she was trying to see them in me also. I presume she was thinking what risks her cousin Lucy ran with me.

Meanwhile Kelly Weintraub was saying, "He has a pair of bedroom eyes, Augie." But I was the only one of the principals to hear and I took a good look at him to see how much harm he really meant me and to what extent he was kidding, the handsome teameo, slick-haired, with certainly horny eyes of his own and a suggestive pad of a chin.

"I know you guys," he said to me.

Then I recognized him, not greatly different, really, from what he had been in the schoolyard, in his sweaters.

"You had a little brother, George."

"We still have him. He's not little any more," I said. "He's big and he's living downstate."

"Where, in Manteno?"

"No, it's in another town, a little place down near Pinckneyville. You know that part of the state?" I didn't know it myself. Simon was the only one of us who had ever gone down there, the Renlings having been unable at that time to spare me.

"No, I don't. But I remember George," he said.

"I remember you too, skitching rides on the ice wagons." I shrugged, smiling. It was foolish of him to be suggesting a menace. He thought he could put a stick in Simon's spokes; Simon was way ahead of him.

"Of course Charlotte knows," said Simon when I told him

about Kelly Weintraub. "Why should we make a secret of it? She even wants to put George into a private institution. Don't worry, nobody pays any attention to this guy. He doesn't count around here. Anyhow, I recognized him first and got the jump on him. Leave it to me, I have them all eating out of my hand." He added, "You'll be doing the same if you'll listen to me. You made a good first impression."

I quickly learned what power he really had with them. For he had absolutely meant it when he said he had plans for me, and he came for me several times a week to take me on his rounds. We had lunch with uncles and cousins in the rich businessmen's restaurants and clubs, fancy steakhouses. Simon was hard with them and didn't yield ground whether it was a joke or an argument that came up, while in an undertone he gave me the lowdown on them, contemptuously. I saw him developing some terrible abilities in quarrelsomeness; he differed with all their opinions no matter on what subject. It might be about tailors, or entertainers, or heavyweight fighters, or politics—things on which he informed himself as he went along. He was impatient even in his jokes; he made waiters fear him, sending dishes back to the kitchen, but then he gave large tips also. He seemed to have no regard for money—he always carried a big bankroll now—but actually, by the way he handled wallet and the bills, he convinced me that he knew what he was doing.

He said to me, "With these people you've got to spend. If they see you cautious with a buck, you lose your standing with them. And I have to stand in good. They know everybody, and I'm going out for myself soon and I need them. Just these bull-session lunches and going to the Chez Paree and the Glass Derby, proving I can keep up their speed, you see, that's the first thing. They're not going to deal with anybody that's not one of them. Now you understand why a slob like Kelly Weintraub doesn't count. He can't afford to eat lunch in joints like these, he can't take a check at the Chez Paree without everybody being uncomfortable and reckoning he can't afford it, because they know exactly what he's pulling down a week. You see, he's a negligible factor and nobody will listen to him. I'll remember him though," he said with dangerous promise. I knew he kept a file of accounts to settle. Did Cissy and Five Properties have a folder in it to themselves? I thought they must.

"Ah!" he said. "Come downtown with me. Let's get our hair cut."

We drove to the Palmer House and went below into the big radiance of the barbershop. Simon would have let his fine English coat fall to the ground if the Negro attendant hadn't run in time to gather it in his arms. We sat before the huge mirrors in those episcopal machines, the big chairs, and were groomed and shampooed. Simon had himself steamed and singed, manicured, had everything lavished on himself, and not simply urged me but forced me to do as he did. He wanted to try all they knew how to do.

It was getting so that I had to undergo an examination of almost brass-hat severity when I appeared before him. My heels must not be turned over by so much as an eighth of an inch, my cuffs had to strike my shoes right, he supplied me with ties, taking mine away and leaving a dozen of his own choice on the rack. He yelled and bullied if he thought I didn't wear my clothes exactly as he thought I should. And these were things I had lost interest in since Evanston. I had to expect ridicule from Mimi for having polished nails. I let it be done. I didn't consider my fingers much. It was probably an asset to me as a book thief. Looking at my hands and at my ties, who would suspect me? For I hadn't, of course, stopped stealing. I didn't any longer have to support Mama; Simon took care of that. But while he paid for me wherever we went, it was still expensive to go with him. Occasionally there were tips or drinks or cigars or corsages for Charlotte that slipped his mind, and I had larger cleaning and laundry bills than ever before. Once in a while I went, moreover, with Padilla for a Saturday night with our friends on Lake Park Avenue. And besides, I was trying to get together the university entrance fee. Shrewdly, Simon gave me little money; mostly he gave me things. He wanted me to learn to have expensive needs, and the desire for dough would come of itself. Then if I were to begin to ask him for more, he could hook me.

From the barbershop we'd go to Field's to buy him a dozen or so shirts, imported Italian underclothes or slacks or shoes, all things of which he already had a surplus; he showed me drawers, closets, shelves full, and still kept buying. Some part of this was due to his having been on the wrong side of the counter, or the servile back on the shoe-fitting stool, and in part this was his way of tempting me. But also I knew that in the barbershop and on the shopping trips he was aiming to refresh himself; he slept badly and was looking flabby and ill, and one morning when he came to fetch me he locked himself in the toilet and cried. After that day he wouldn't come upstairs; he honked his horn for me in the street. He said, "I can't stand the joint you live in; they don't keep it clean. Are you sure they don't have bed animals? And the can is filthy. I don't see how you can go into it." Soon he took to saying this with the same inspection glare he had for my appearance. "When are you going to move out of this rat nest! Jesus, it's the sort of place plagues and epidemics start in!" Eventually he stopped calling for me. He'd phone when he wanted me; sometimes he'd send wires. At first, however, he wanted me with him constantly. So, then, we were in the gleaming lanes and warm indoor puffing of the department store, but after when he started back to the West Side, wearing one of his new ties and temporarily in a better state, suddenly he would lose it all, it seemed, and, pressing on the gas pedal, he must have seen himself speeding across the last boundary of his strength. But just as the car, squealing around corners, righted itself, he too kept balance. However, it was evident that his feelings were suicidal from the way he drove and the way he leaped forward in arguments, hit him who would; he kept a tire tool under the driver's seat for his weapon in traffic arguments, and he cursed everybody in the street, running through lights and scattering pedestrians. The truth back of all this was that he had his pockets full of money as an advance on his promised ability to make a rich man of himself and now had to deliver.

In spring he leased a yard, at the end of the coal season. It had no overhead track, only a long spur of siding, and the first rains made a marsh of the whole place. It had to be drained. The first coal was unloaded in the wet. The office itself was a shack; the scale needed expensive repairs. His first few thousand dollars ran out and he had to ask for more; he had a credit to establish with the brokers, and it was important that he meet his bills on time. Uncle Charlie made that easier. Nevertheless, there was Uncle Charlie himself to satisfy.

There was, besides, a substantial wage to pay his yard manager and weighmaster, Happy Kellerman, whom he had lured away from a large old West Side company. He'd have hired me instead (at perhaps a little less) if I'd been able to handle the job, and he insisted on my coming to learn the ropes from Happy, so that presently I was spending a good amount of time at the office; for when he grabbed my wrist and told me, almost drunkenly, with the grime and chapping of the mouth that comes of long nervous talking, saying low, huskily, viciously, "There's got to be somebody here I can trust. *Got* to be!" I couldn't refuse. However, there was not much that Happy could be dishonest about. He was a beer *saufer*, droopy, small, a humorist, wry, drawn, weak, his tone nosy and quinchy, his pants in creases under his paunch; his nose curved up and presented offended and timorous nostrils, and he had round, disingenuous eyes in which he showed he was strongly defended. He was a *tío listo*, a carnival type, a whorehouse visitor. His style was that of a hoofer in the lowest circuit, doing a little cane-swinging and heel-and-toe routine, singing, "I went to school with Maggie Murphy," and telling smokehouse stories while the goofy audience waited for the naked star to come out and begin the grinds. He had a repertory of harmless little jokes, dog yipes, mock farts; his best prank was to come up behind and seize you by the leg with a Pekinese snarl. By Simon's wish I had to spend afternoons with him studying the business. Especially since I had heard him weeping in the can Simon wasn't easy for me to turn down.

Often I relieved Happy at lunch. He hopped a car down to Halsted Street because he detested walking. Coming back at two, he would shuffle off at the stop by the driveway, carrying his coat and straw skimmer, vest stuffed with cigarettes, pencils, and cards—he had his own business card: "Happy Kellerman representing March's Coal and Coke": a rooster chasing a frantic hen, with the line beneath, "*I mean business.*" Walking in, he tested the beam of the scale, put the *Times* in the stove, walked around the yard, and then, these being the dog days, great heat, we would sit where the coolness rose from the concrete pit of the scale. The office had the appearance of a squatter's shack or end house of a Western street. Over the way was a stockyards siding, dusty animals bawling in the waiting cars, putting red muzzles to the slats; truck wheels sucked through the melting tar, the coal split and tarnished on the piles, the burdocks died on the stalk. There were rats in a corner of the yard who did not stir or go away for anyone, whole families, nursing, creeping, feeding there. I had never seen them so domestic, going whither they list, walking by your feet without fear. Simon bought a pistol —"We need one anyhow," he said—and shot at them, but they only scattered to come back. They didn't even bother to dig holes, only scooped out shallow nesting places.

There were a few sales. Happy entered them on the big yellow sheets; an elegant penman, boastful of his hand, he sat up on the high stool in his flat straw, feathering out the wide and thin strokes. This old-fashioned bookkeeping desk of a scratched yellow brought the writer's face to a tiny square of window over the scale, and at times I saw Simon there, making out checks in the wide triple checkbook. Writing checks had fascinated him at first. He had wormed out of me that I owed Padilla two bucks for the satisfaction of paying one of my debts with his signature. There was no such satisfaction now, as the figures of the balance took fewer spaces, and he thought of his last audaciousness in money when he had tried to grab a fast buck in order to marry Cissy. This time he believed his whole life was staked. He had not merely been shooting his mouth off the day he had come to tell me he was getting married about how earnest he was over money; it was now proved by the mental wounds of his face, the death of its color, and the near-insanity of his behavior. The misery of his look at this black Sargasso of a yard in its summer stagnation and stifling would sometimes make my blood crawl in me with horror. If I took so much time from my own enterprises of theft and reading to walk around this yard with him, hands in pockets, it wouldn't be enough to say it was from solicitude, it was downright fright. The loose way he handled the pistol shooting at the rats was ominous to me. And that he complained of seething in his head, saying, "My brains are going to boil out of my ears."

I had to keep him from clouting Happy once when he misjudged the moment to grab Simon's leg with his yiping-dog prank. It was a near thing. And just a while ago he had been laughing with Happy at his stories of being a shill during the Florida land boom; and about his love affair with a Turkish woman who wouldn't let him out of the house; and his account of his first dose, when he said, "It was like getting into a can of hot angleworms." This change from great laughter to savagery made Happy ready to quit, his big, skillful, poachy eyes morose, warning, filling up, as I tried to iron things out. For it was up to me to bring back the peace. "I never took no shit in bigger concerns," said Happy from the corner of his mouth to me, but that Simon should hear. I knew that Simon had a strongly beating heart by the way his head hung downward, his mouth open on that still unmended front tooth, and that his craving which he would of necessity fight off was to take Happy by the seat of the pants and throw him into the street.

At last Simon said, "Okay, I want to say I'm sorry. I'm kind of nervous today. You ought to realize, Happy . . ." Thought of the Magnuses had overcome him, and a horror of so far forgetting that he was a young man in business and Happy merely a drip as to get himself towering about this nonsense. Simon's patience and swallowing were worse to me than his wrath or flamboyance—that shabby compulsory physical patience. Another such hard thing was his speaking low and with an air of difficult endurance to Charlotte on the telephone and answering her questions with subdued repetitiousness, near the surrender point.

"Well," he said to Happy and me, "why don't you two take the car and go see some of the dealers? Try to drum up some trade. Here's five bucks for beer money. I'll stay here with Coxie and try to get that back fence in shape. They'll steal us blind of we don't do something about it." Cox was the handyman, an old wino in a slap-happy painter's cap that looked like an Italian officer's lid. He sent him scouting along the fence of the Westinghouse plant for old planks. Coxie worked for hamburgers and a bottle of California K. Arakelian's sherry or of yocky-dock. He was watchman too, and slept on rags back of the green lattice before the seldom used front door. Off he limped—he carried a bullet, he claimed, from San Juan Hill—by the mile-long big meshed fence of the corporation in which such needs as fences were met by sub-officers' inviting contractors' bids and a tight steel net permitted all to look in at the vast remote shimmer, the brick steeples, the long power-buildings and the Vesuvian soft coal under the scarcely smeared summer sky and gaudiness.

I went with Happy, who drove. His fear in the Bohunk streets was that he would run over a kid and a crowd would tear him to pieces in its rage. "If it's their kids anything happens to, then look out, even if it's not your fault, the way they chase around." So he was always somewhat in this terror and wouldn't let me have the wheel, who didn't dread this enough to be vigilant. We took the coal-and-ice dealers into taverns and drank beer and swapped talk, in those sleepy and dark with heat joints where the very flies crept rather than flew, seeming doped by the urinal camphors and malt sourness, and from the heated emptiness and woodblock-knocking of the baseball broadcast that gave only more constriction to the unlocatable, undiagnosed wrong. If you thought toward something outside, it might be Padilla theorizing on the size of the universe; his scientific interest kept the subject from being grim. But in such places the slow hairy fly-crawl from drop to drop and star to star, you could pray the non-human universe was not entered from here, and this was no sack-end of it that happened to touch Cook County and Northern Illinois.

Such a consideration never would trouble Simon. Whatever the place was, he would make it pay off, the only relation with it that concerned him; it had dollars, as the rock water, as the waste-looking mountain is made to spit its oil or iron, where otherwise human beings would have no wish to go, the barrens, the Newfoundlands, the scaly earths and the Antarctic snow blackened with the smoke of fuel tapped in Texas or Persia.

Hrapek, Drodz, Matuczynski these dealers were called; we found them in their sheds, by the church, by the funeral home, or on a moving job. They sold coal by the ton and by the bag; they had stake trucks or dump trucks; they had to be convinced and sold, entertained, offered special deals, flattered, bantered, told secrets about the veins of the mines, made up with specious technical information about BTU's and ash percentages. Happy was crafty with them, an excellent dealer's man with talents comparable to those of a ship's chandler; he drank as much *piva* as they did, glass for glass, and he got results. Enticed by undercut prices and the pick of the coal, they began to come in.

Also, Simon ran some sales, just to get things moving. He had me pass out handbills in Chinatown, advertising coke which the laundry Chinese favored above other fuel, and slowly he accumulated customers. He also covered the city and hit his new relatives for orders; Charlie Magnus threw business his way, and little by little things began to stir.

Simon was wised up as to how to do things politically—to be in a position to bid on municipal business—and he saw wardheelers and was kissing-cousins with the police; he took up with lieutenants and captains, with lawyers, with real-estate men, with gamblers and bookies, the important ones who owned legitimate businesses on the side and had property. During the chauffeurs' and hikers' strike he had squad cars to protect his two trucks from strikers who were dumping coal in the streets. I had to wait for his calls in the police station to tell the cops when a load was setting out from the yard, my first lawful sitting in such a place, moving from dark to lighter inside the great social protoplasm. But the dark of this West Side station! It was very dark. It was spoiled, diseased, sore and running. And as the mis-minted and wrong-struck figures and faces stooped, shambled, strode, gazed, dreaded, surrendered, didn't care—unfailing, the surplus and superabundance of human material—you wondered that all was stuff that was born human and shaped human, and over the indiscriminateness and lack of choice. And don't forget the dirt-hardness, the dough fats and raw meats, of those on the official side. And this wasn't even the big Newgate of headquarters downtown but merely a neighborhood tributary.

As a son-in-law of the Magnuses, and also because he wanted to be, Simon was on very good terms with Lieutenant Nuzzo, than whom few were more smooth and regular-looking. I am not sure how the lieutenant managed. A cop, who even in the friendliness of a joke must take you by the shoulder as if in an arrest, with hands whose only practice is to be iron. In some manner Lieutenant Nuzzo had stayed a Valentino, even though his flesh was heavy and his face kept imprints long, like sleep creasings and the marks of fingers. We had dates to go to the Chez Paree with him—a party of five until I began to take Lucy Magnus, making it six—and had spaghetti and chicken livers with sparkling burgundy or champagne; the lieutenant, he looked around like a master of ceremonies on a visit from a much better night club. His wife seemed like a woman on probation; as everybody is, after a fashion, with a police lieutenant. Even a wife. He was an Italian, he brought the style of ancient kingdoms with him. A lot of them do. Authority must have death behind it. To cut off Masaniello's head; to hang great admirals themselves, as Lord Nelson did in Naples harbor. This I believe was how to read the lieutenant's smooth face while he sat in the enjoyable noise of the Chez Paree, viewing Veloz and Yolanda or the near-naked chicks who didn't altogether know what they were doing but suggested the motions of busy people bringing their private pleasures to a head. Anyway, while this night club remained tops, Simon and Charlotte were great ones for it, as much, shrewdly, for the lowdown to be gotten there and contacts and public life and business, as to have their pictures taken by flashbulbs, laughing and in shenanigan embraces with paper caps and streamers, an important face at their table, a singer in strapless gown appealing with her lifted chin and fine teeth, or the chairman of a board finishing a drink.

Simon grasped very soon the importance for business of such close contact. Didn't the Chief Executive pass sleepless nights at Yalta because Stalin for the first two days did not smile? He couldn't deal with a man who wouldn't yield to charm or trade on the basis of love. There had to be sport and amiability to temper decisions that could not all be pleasant, and at least the flash of personality helped. This was something Simon well understood, how to be liked, and how to reach an accord on the basis of secret thoughts with people similarly placed.

But I'm still in the middle of the summer with him, at the worst of his trouble when he was envenomed with the fear that he'd go bankrupt, and he had to confess to himself, I'm sure, that he was really afraid of the Magnuses, and terrified by what he had taken on himself. So I spent most of these months with him. I won't say we were never closer—he kept his ultimate thoughts stubbornly to himself—but we were never more together. From the fresh of morning to the grime and horn color of late afternoon I rode in the car with him and made all his stops—downtown, the union hall, the bank, the South Water market office Charlotte was managing for her Uncle Robby, the kitchen at Magnuses' where we stopped to get sandwiches from the black cook, or the back room where they had put the marriage bed—the marriage still the secret of the immediate family. Here the door opened on what supported the weight of this heaped-up life. The room had been refurnished for him and Charlotte with silk-shaded reading lamps, bedside fleeces, drapes against the alley view and its barbarity—as in a palazzo against the smell of the canals—a satin cover on the bed, and auxiliary pillows on the roll of the bolster.

To save steps to the dresser Simon walked on the bed. He changed clothes, letting things lie where they were dropped or flung, kicking his shoes into the corner and drying the sweat from his naked body with an undershirt. There were days when he changed three times, or four, and others when he might sit listless and indifferent, and get up from his office chair heavy after hours of silence, saying, "Let's get out of here."

Instead of going home to change, sometimes he'd drive to the lake.

We'd go swimming at the North Avenue point the late Commissioner had loved. In whose mouth, as he floated by, I used to place cigarettes. The loose spread of Simon's legs as he plunged and the embracing awkwardness of his arms to the water gave me the worry that he threw himself in with a thought of never coming back to the surface alive, as if he went to take a blind taste of the benefits of staying down. He came up haggard and with a slack gasp of his mouth and rough blood in his face. I knew it made a strong appeal to him to go down and not come up again. Even if he didn't make a display of this half-a-desire and swam up and down, sullen, with flattened coarse hair, making master passes at the water; the water turned around on the shore and its crowd and carried black spools in its horizon, the cool paving of one of the imaginary series of worlds, clear into the flaming ether.

My brother down there, as if Alexander in the harmful Cydnus whose cold made him sick when he leaped in after battle, I stood in striped trunks with toes bent over the wood of a pile, ready to jump after if need be. I didn't go in when he did. He came up the ladder shivering, the big flies bit nastily, the hullabaloo waterside carnival turned your head. I'd help him dry; he'd lie down on the stone like a sick man. But when he'd warm and get his comfort back, he'd start to make bullish approaches to women and girls, his eyes big and red, and as if someone who bent over to choose a plum from her lunch bag was making the offer of a Pasiphaë. And then he'd start to blare like brass and he'd hit me on the arm and say to me, "Look at the spread on that broad!" forgetting that he was not only married but also engaged—the engagement had taken place before the eyes of the world, in a reception at a hotel. He didn't think of that. Instead he thought of the powerful possibility in a new Pontiac standing near Lincoln Park, and the money he had; also the things to be done in one street, building, room that need have no bearing on what came later in the day elsewhere. So he got violent and lustful, with step and sidle, and protrusion of his head that made a kind of wall of his neck, charged and hard like that of a fighter who has been hit but not damaged, only roused.

There wasn't anything in his new class or of his speed at the North Avenue beach (called a beach, it was merely a stone slab waterfront); the place was rough and hard, the young fellows were tough and the girls battlesome, factory hands, salesgirls, with some Clark Street sluts and dance-hall chicks. Therefore Simon said and proposed without sorting or choosing words. "You look good to me. You interested?" Direct, without game, not even nickel phrases of circumlocution. That very fact maybe made it no indecency; instead it created awe and fear, that brute charge that gave the veins too much to bear and seemed to endanger his underjaw by crowding, his eyeballs darkening with currents of heat violet and darker, to near black. The girls were not always frightened of him; he had a smell of power, he was handsome, and I don't know what floors his bare feet left in shade-drawn hot rooms. Only a year ago he would not have given a second glance at such bims.

Now, where he went, he had information unavailable to me, but he had to have advantages and prerogatives, I reckon, in exchange for sacrifices. Yes, principals like that practice an anger not everyone is allowed. They come playing the god like bloody Commodus before the Senate, or run with jockeys and wrestlers like Caracalla, while knowing that somewhere the instrument of their downfall is beginning to gather thought to thought about them, like loops on the knitting needle. That was how it was with Simon, as I had had the chance to see before, when he put on a lady's hat at the Chez Paree and pranced around, or when he had brought me along to a bachelor's stag where two naked acrobatic girls did stunts with false tools. From circus games to private dissoluteness, then, and only doing as many others did—except that from the force of his personality he was prominent and played a leading part.

"And you? *Do* you?" said Simon to me. "What a question! Who's that babe who lives on your floor? Is that why you don't want to move? Mimi, isn't that her name? She looks like an easy broad."

I denied it, and he didn't believe me.

On her side Mimi was interested in Simon. "What's eating him?" she asked me. "It was him I heard crying in the can, wasn't it? What's he want to be such a sharp dresser for? What's the matter? He has a woman on his neck, huh?" She was prepared to approve of him despite the satire, noting something extravagant and outlaw about him that she approved of.

He wasn't all brashness, however, and headlong despair, Simon. No, he was also making a prize showing. It was summer, and slow, and naturally he was losing money. Charlotte, an excellent businesswoman, and highly important as backer, counselor, consultant, gave him just what united them closer than common conjugality. Though he fought with her and even from the very first roared and cursed her, saying astonishing things, she held on steady. A close watcher could see her recoil and then come back to the great, the all-important thing, which was that he was one of those anointed to be rich and mighty. His very outrageousness when he yelled "You goofy cow!" was proof. She took it with a nervous laugh that recalled him to his better judgment and reminded him that such things were supposed to come out as comedy. Whereat he almost never failed to add the laughter drop of the entertainer, even while the glare of his eyes might remain savage. And he was made to do that even when feelings on both sides had burst out so close to injury that it was too much to try to kid them back into something that could pass for affectionate roughness. But Charlotte's first aim and the reason for her striving was to make the union serious by constructing a fortune on it. She said to me, "Simon has real business ability. This stuff now"—he was already, at the time she spoke, making money—"is just nothing." When she said this, sometimes, it was in the territory of seriousness where distinctions of sex do not exist; the power invoked is too great for that. It is of neither man nor woman. As when Macbeth's wife made that prayer, "Unsex me here!" A call so hard, to what is so hard, that it makes the soul neuter.

Neither her ladies' trimming and gewgawing, the detail of her tailored person, nor the decorating of the flat when they furnished one, nor his way of carrying on was of real consequence. But in what related to the bank, the stock, the taxes, head approached to head discussing these, the great clear and critical calculations and confidences made in the key to which real dominion was set, that was what wedlock really rested on. Even though she was continually singing and whistling songs to herself like "My Blue Heaven" and "A Faded Summer's Love," doing her nails, revising her hair, she didn't live in these vanities. Which indeed were hopeless. She gave them all their due, and more. High heels, sheer hose, beautiful suits, hats, earrings, feathers, and the colors of pancake maquillage, plus electrolysis, sweet-sweats, and the hidden pinnings where adoration could come to roost. She neglected nothing in this respect, she had a lot of dignity, she could be monumentally handsome. But her ultimate disbelief in this was unmistakable in the real mouth, unconforming to the painted one, impatient, discounting less important things. She wouldn't have chosen a young man to marry from the pictures on the sheet music of her piano any more than she'd have chosen a schoolboy; she bore her ambition tight and was prepared to see, without being moved in her purpose, any limits of coarseness, rashness, harshness, scandal. She knew this in advance by consulting with herself, and she didn't have to wait to see a great part in actuality; it first arose in her mind and there was where she dealt with it.

Simon, in the odd way of these things, was all for her. He said, "She's got more brain and ability than six women. She's a hundred per cent straight, no faking. She's as goodhearted as they come"—there was a considerable element of truth in this—"and she likes you too, Augie." He said this with a view to my beginning to court Lucy Magnus, as I presently agreed to do. "She keeps sending Mama stuff. She wants to board her with a private family. Her idea. Mama never has complained about the Home. The company there is good for her. What do you think?"

While driving around the city we sometimes stopped to see Mama. Most often we simply passed the building. But you never knew with Simon what your destination was. Saying, "Hop in," he'd perhaps himself not know where he was off to, answering a need he didn't understand yet. Perhaps it was food he was after, perhaps a fight, perhaps disaster, perhaps a woman beckoning from behind, or a business order, a game of billiards, a lawyer's office, a steam bath at the athletic club. So then among these possible stops was the Home on Arthington Street.

It was of gray stone, the porch just a widening before the doorway on which there were two benches. There were benches inside too. It was furnished like a meeting hall or public forum, all the common space of it bare; only the bad state of the windows kept the outsider from looking in; the panes were full of glassy gnarls and dirty, probably from the hands of people who had touched them to discover that this was not wall but window. Everything that could have made a hazard in the old house had been taken away; thus there were a bar of plaster where the mantelpiece had been and a cork grade at the doorsills. But the blind did not go around very much. They sat, and didn't seem to have any conversation, and soon you were aware of leisure gone bad. I had learned something of this during Einhorn's days of dirty mental weather. Or of the soul, not the mind, the sick evil of not even knowing why anything should ail you since you're resigned to accept all conditions.

The director and his wife boasted that they fed their people well; it was a fact that you knew the next menu in advance by the smell of the kitchen.

In general I considered it a blessing that Mama was simple. I thought that if there were any characters here that were intriguing or quarrelsome—and how would there fail to be?—there must be some awful events in the innermost privacy of the house. But Mama had put in many years of appeasing tempestuousness or staying out of its way, and she very likely had more trouble as a result of one of Simon's visits than she ever did with her companions. For he came to check on how she was treated, and he had a harsh way of inquiring. He was tough with the director, who hoped to get mattresses wholesale from Arthur Magnus through him. Simon had promised him this favor. But he threw his weight around, full of menace, pleased with nothing. He objected to Mama's having roommates, and when he obtained a private room for her it was next to the kitchen and all its noise and smell, and that was nothing to thank him for. And then, one summer afternoon, we found her sitting on her bed at the task of fitting pins into Roosevelt campaign buttons; she was getting ten cents a hundred and earning a few dollars a week by the goodheartedness of the precinct captain. Seeing her with her unskillful hands of rough housework at the brass pins, feeling the two objects together in her lap, Simon went into a rage that made her flinch, and knowing that I was with him she turned her face and tried to find me and get me to intercede; she was frightened, too, to discover that she had been doing wrong unawares.

"Stop roaring," I said, "for God's sake!"

But he couldn't be stopped. "What do they mean! Look what they've got her doing! Where's that sonofabitch?"

It was the director's wife who came, in her house dress. She meant to remain respectful but not be servile; she was white, and she already had a fighting face and quivered, but spoke up, practical and proud.

"Are you responsible for this?" he shouted at her.

She said, "Mrs. March wasn't made to do anything she didn't want. She was asked and she wanted to. It's good for her to have something to keep her occupied."

"Asked? I know how people are asked so they're afraid to say no. I'll have you know that my mother isn't going to do any piecework for ten, twenty, thirty cents, or a dollar an hour. She gets all the money she needs from me."

"You don't have to yell like this. These are all very sensitive people and easy disturbed."

In the passage I saw many of the blind stop and a group gathered, while in the kitchen the big sloven-haired cook turned with her knife from the meatblock.

"Simon, *I* wanted, *I* asked," said Mama. She was unable to put weight in her tones; she had never been able; she lacked experience.

"Calm down," I said to him with some effect at last.

It appeared that he could no longer take out the first intention of his heart without touching the inflamed place of self-distinction. Wrongly blessing and cursing like Balaam, but without any outside power to reverse him, only his own arbitrariness doubling back on him. So he could not speak for Mama without commanding how he himself was to be looked upon.

Next he went to the closet to see whether the things were there that Charlotte had given her, the shoes, handbag, dresses, and he missed at once a light coat, handed down by a more robust person, that didn't fit her anyway.

"Where is it—what have they done with that coat?"

"I sent it to the cleaners. She spilled coffee on it," the director's wife explained.

"I did," said Mama in her clear, tuneless voice.

And the woman, "I'll take it in for her when it comes back, it's too big in the shoulders."

Simon wore a look of anger and detestation, silent, still regarding the closet. "She can afford a good tailor if she needs alterations. I want her to look right."

He left her money each time, single dollars so that she could not be cheated in the changing. Not that he really distrusted the director and his wife; he wanted them, however, to realize that he did not have to depend on their honesty.

"I want her to go for a walk every day."

"It's the rule, Mr. March."

"I know rules. You keep them when you want to." I spoke to him in a low tone, and he said, "That's all right. Be quiet. I want her to go to the hairdresser at least once a week."

"My husband takes all the ladies in the car together. He can't be taking one at a time."

"Then hire a girl. Isn't there a high-school girl you can get to go with her once a week? I'll pay for it. I want her to be taken care of. I'm getting married soon."

"We'll try to accommodate you, sir," she said, and he, not missing her derision though all she looked was steadfast and unintimidated, stared, spoke to himself, and took up his hat.

"Good-by, Ma."

"Good-by, good-by, boys."

"And take away this junk," said Simon, scattering the pins with a tug of the bedcover.

He left, and the woman tartly said to me, "I hope at least FDR is good enough for him personally."

Chapter XII

WHEN the cold weather came Simon started to make money and everything went well. His spirits rose. The wedding was a great affair in the main ballroom of a big hotel, the bridal party getting organized in the governor's suite where Simon and Charlotte also spent the first night. I was an usher, Lucy Magnus the bridesmaid opposite me. Simon went along with me to rent a tuxedo, and then liked the fit of it so well he bought it outright. On the wedding day Mimi helped me with the studs of the boiled shirt and the tie. My neighbor Kayo Obermark sat in to observe, on my bed, fat feet bare, and laughed over Mimi's digs at marriage.

"Now you look like the groom himself," said Mimi. "You probably aim to become one soon, don't you?"

I snatched up my coat and ran, for I had to pick up Mama. I had the Pontiac for the purpose. She was my charge; I was supposed to see her through. Simon ordered me to have her wear dark glasses. The day was frosty, windy, clear, the waves piled up, from the slugging green water, white over the rocks of the Outer Drive. And then we came to the proud class of the hotel and its Jupiter's heaviness and restless marble detail, seeking to be more and more, introducing another pot too huge for flowers, another carved figure, another white work of iron; and inside luxuriously warm—even the subterranean garage where I parked had this silky warmth. And coming out of the white elevator, you were in an Alhambra of roses and cellular ceilings, gilt and ivory, Florida feathering of plants and muffling of carpets, immense distances, and everywhere the pure purpose of supporting and encompassing the human creature in conveniences. Of doing unto the body; holding it precious; bathing, drying, powdering, preparing satin rest, conveying, feeding. I've been at Schönbrunn and in the Bourbon establishment in Madrid and seen all that embellishment as the setting of power. But luxury as the power itself is different—luxury without anything ulterior. Except insofar as all yearning, for no matter what, just so its scope is vast, is of one cluster of mysteries and always ulterior. And what will this power do to you? I know that I in, say, an ancient place like Venice or in Rome, passing along the side of majestic walls where great men once sat, experienced what it was to be simply a dot, a speck that scans across the cornea, a corpuscle, almost white, almost nothing but air: I to these *ottimati* in their thought. And this spectacular ancient aggrandizement with its remains of art and many noble signs I could appreciate even if I didn't want to be just borne down by the grandeur of it. But in this modern power of luxury, with its battalions of service workers and engineers, it's the things themselves, the products that are distinguished, and the individual man isn't nearly equal to their great sum. Finally they are what becomes great—the multitude of baths with never-failing hot water, the enormous air-conditioning units and the elaborate machinery. No opposing greatness is allowed, and the disturbing person is the one who won't serve by using or denies by not wishing to enjoy.

I didn't yet know what view I had of all this. It still wasn't clear to me whether I would be for or against it. But then how does anybody form a decision to be against and persist against? When does he choose and when is he chosen instead? This one hears voices; that one is a saint, a chieftain, an orator, a Horatius, a kamikazi; one says *Ich kann nicht anders—so help me God!* And why is it *I* who cannot do otherwise? Is there a secret assignment from mankind to some unfortunate person who can't refuse? As if the great majority turned away from a thing it couldn't permanently forsake and so named some person to remain faithful to it? With great difficulty somebody becomes exemplary, anyhow.

Conceivably Simon felt that I was this kind of influenceable person and looked liable to become an example. For God knows there are abandoned and hungry principles enough flowing free and looking for attachment. So he wanted to get to me first.

Simon's idea was that I should marry Lucy Magnus, who had more money even than Charlotte. This was how he outlined the future to me. I could finish my pre-legal course and go to John Marshall law school at night while I worked for him. He'd pay my tuition and give me eighteen dollars a week. Eventually I could become his partner. Or if his business didn't suit me, we could go into real estate with our joint capital. Or perhaps into manufacturing. Or, if I chose to be a lawyer, I wouldn't need to be a mere ambulance chaser, shyster, or birdseed wiseguy and conniver in two-bit cases. Not with the money I'd have to play with as Lucy Magnus's husband. She was a juicy piece besides, even if he didn't care for the way her collarbones stood out when she wore a formal, and she was full of willingness. He would back me while I courted her. I didn't need to worry about the expenses; he'd give me the use of the Pontiac for taking her out, build me up with the family, remove the obstacles. All I had to do was play along, make myself desired, interpret, as I could do, the role of the son-in-law her parents wanted. It was a lead-pipe cinch.

We were alone in his room in the governor's suite, a room of white walls and gold paneling, heavy mirrors hung on silk hawsers, a Louis XIV bed. Having come out of the glass stall of the shower, dried in a thick Turkish mantle, put on black socks and a stiff shirt, he was now lying on the bed, smoking a cigar, while he explained this to me, practical and severe. He sprawled out with his big body, the mid-part of it nude. This comfort and luxury were not what he preached at me, but the thing to do: not to dissolve in bewilderment of choices but make myself hard, like himself, and learn how to stay with the necessary, undistracted by the trimmings. This was what he thought, and to some extent I thought it too. Why shouldn't I marry a rich man's daughter? If I didn't want to do as Simon did in every respect, couldn't I arrange my life somewhat differently? Wasn't there any other way to ride this gorgeous train? Provided Lucy was different from her cousin, why shouldn't there be? I wasn't unwilling to look into this and profit by Simon's offers. I was already taking so many of his orders, putting in so much time, that I might as well accept wages too, go the whole way and make it official. And I may as well say that I had a desire to go along with him out of the love I felt for him and enthusiasm for his outlook. In which I didn't fundamentally believe. However, that I shouldn't be too good to do as he was doing was of enormous importance to him, and the obstinacy that had always made me hold out against him for unspoken or anyway insufficient reasons seemed at last over. I didn't oppose him, so he spoke to me with unusual affection.

He rolled from the bed to finish dressing, saying, "Now we begin going places, you and me. I wondered when you'd start to show some sense, if ever, and worried you wouldn't be anything but a punk. Here, fix this stud for me in back. My mother-in-law got this set for me. Christ! how'm I going to find my dress shoes? All this tissue paper. You can't find anything. Get rid of it. Leave it in the can for the governor," he said, spirited and nervous in his laugh. "The world hasn't set too tight yet. There's room, if you find the openings to it. If you study it out you can find them. Horner is a Jew too, after all, and probably didn't have a better start than we did, and is governor."

"Are you thinking of giving politics a try?"

"Maybe. Why not? It depends on how things shape up. Uncle Artie knows a guy who was made ambassador by contributing often enough to campaign drives. Twenty, thirty, even forty thousand bucks, and what's that to a man who has it?"

This being an ambassador couldn't be envisioned as in the old days—a Guicciardini arriving from Florence with his clever face, or a Russian coming to Venice, or an Adams—such grandeurs have sunk down as the imagination has been transferred from the bearer of his country's power walking on rugs to his blowing shellac through the waterpipes of Lima to stop the rust.

Simon, when he put on his tails and walked from mirror to mirror, doubling back his fingers to tug down the white cuffs and pulling up his chin to make his strong neck freer in the band of the butterfly collar, had the vigor to make the place live up to him; more—the thought lay in the open—than the governors for whom it was reserved. And having gotten in without ever having been a candidate he could perhaps get far beyond them without running or going through the tiresome part of politics. He had come into a view of mutability, and I too could see that one is only ostensibly born to remain in specified limits. That's what you'll be told in the ranks. I don't say that I exactly shared his feelings, or spirits of the dauphin's horse, almost tearing down hangings and shouldering into mirrors with that bucking pride, but with him now I certainly felt less boxed than I ever before had, nothing that others did so inconceivable for me.

However, people were waiting below and Simon was holding things up, taking his time. Charlotte came in herself, like a big bridal edifice in her veil and other lace, carrying long-stemmed flowers. With her there wasn't much hiding of the behind-the-scenes of life to keep a man in the bonds of love, as Lucretius advises when he tells you to make allowances for mortality. You only had to see her practical mouth to know everything about mortality was admitted in advance, though she did for form's sake all that other women do. Her frankness gave her a kind of nobility. But here when she came into the room was the visible means to governors' suites and ambassadorships, and the best that Simon could do brought him back to her.

"Everybody else is ready. What are you doing?"

She spoke to me, for she wouldn't blame him in any circumstances where she could blame me instead, his stand-in.

"I've been dressing and shmoosing," said Simon. "There's plenty of time—what's the big rush? Anyhow, you didn't have to come, you could have phoned. Now, honey, don't be nervous; you look beautiful and everything is going to be fine."

"It will be if I see to it. Now will you go and talk to the guests?" she said in her bidding tone.

She sat on the bed to call the caterer, the musicians, the florist, the management, the photographer, for she kept all under close control and had made every arrangement herself, relying on no one; and with her white shoes on a chair and a pad on her knees she made figures and dickered with the photographer, at the last moment still trying to beat down his price. "Listen, Schultz, if you try to hold me up you'll get no business out of any of the Magnuses ever again, and there're plenty of us."

"Augie," said Simon when we went out, "you can have the car to take Lucy out. You'll probably need some dough, so here's ten bucks. I'll send Mama home in a cab. I want you at the office at eight though. Is she wearing those glasses I told you to get her?"

Mama had obediently put on the glasses, but it displeased

him to see that she carried her white cane. She was sitting with Anna Coblin in the lounge, the cane between her knees, and he tried to take it away from her, but she wouldn't yield it up.

"Ma, give me that stick, for Chrissake! How will it look? They're going to take a picture."

"No, Simon, people will bump into me."

"They won't bump into you—you'll be with Cousin Anna."

"Hear, let her keep it," said Anna.

"Ma, give that cane to Augie and he'll check it for you."

"I don't want to, Simon."

"Mama, don't you want everything to look nice?" He tried to loosen her fingers.

"Cut it out!" I said to him, and Cousin Anna with her burning morose face muttered something to him.

"You shut up, you cow!" he said to her. He went, but left me instructions. "You get it away from her. What a turnout from our side!"

I let her keep the cane, and had to pacify Cousin Anna and beg her to stay for Mama's sake.

"Money makes you *meshuggah*," she said, sitting heavy and tall in her corset, glaring maddened into the luxurious lounge.

I approved of Mama's exhibition of will, wondering at the surprises the meek will pull. Anyway, Simon dropped the matter; he was too busy to fight every fight through, and he was somewhere off the ballroom where the ceremony was shaping up. I went around looking among the guests for some I knew. He had invited the Einhorns, including Arthur. Arthur, who had graduated from the University of Illinois, was in Chicago, where he was doing nothing in particular. Occasionally I saw him on the South Side and knew that he was friendly with Frazer's set and that he was supposed to be translating poems from the French. Einhorn would always back him in any intellectual pursuit. There were the Einhorns then, in the ballroom, the old man with a sort of military cloak, gray, looking like the former possessor of a splendor just as good as this who, without special rancor but understanding how it all comes about, watches it change hands. He said to me, "You look very fine in your tuxedo, Augie." Tillie kissed me, taking my face in her dark hands, Arthur smiling. He could behave with exceptional charm, but this was absent-mindedly conferred on you.

I went on to welcome Happy Kellerman and his wife, a thin blond rattle of a woman who bore out her belly and was wound high and low with beads and pearls. Next I saw Five Properties and Cissy. Simon had asked them from motives not hard to understand, partly to show Cissy what he had gone on to do and also to subject Five Properties to a cruel comparison. Cissy defeated all, though, with that sly provoking decency about her female gifts, breast touching breast in the low opening of her dress. She showed her tongue softly in the few words that she spoke. Five Properties had come for a reconciliation of cousins. She had taught him to comb his Scythian hair differently; it now came lower on the rugged forehead without modifying the skeptical grinning of his eyes; that savage green would always express everything that Five Properties thought. He too was dressed in a tuxedo, wore it on his enormous trunk to be equal to the opulence Simon had invited him to see. And so he grinned all around with his gum-buried teeth and green eyes. It was evident that Cissy steered him, taught him civilized behavior—him who had loaded and driven the wagon of jolting corpses the Russians and Germans had made of one another in the Polish mud. She coached him. All the same she couldn't prevent him by her smile and slow murmured word from feeling her on the back and fondling her. "So what's wrong, babe?" he said.

Well, the wedding music began. I went to see that Mama was taken to a plush bench, her place inside the flower cage beside the altar—the Coblins were with her—and then into rehearsed position in the procession, with Lucy Magnus, along the white carpet down which the principals came: Charlotte and her father with rose-scattering children before, Mrs. Magnus and Uncle Charlie, and then Simon with Lucy's brother Sam, first-string guard on the Michigan team, a hulky walker. Throughout the ceremony Lucy looked at me in her unambiguously declarative way, and when the ring was on and Simon swung Charlotte back before all to kiss her, and all clapped and cried out, Lucy came and took my arm. We went in to the banquet; ten dollars a plate, it was—for that day a staggering price. But I couldn't sit through the meal in peace. An usher came to tell me I was wanted and rushed me to the back of the hall. Five Properties, angry, was walking out because he and Cissy had been put at a little table apart behind a pillar. Whether it was Charlotte who was responsible for this, or Simon himself, I never found out. One was as capable of it as the other. Whoever had done it, Five Properties was powerfully offended.

"'S okay, Augie. Against you I got nothing. He asked me? I came. I wish him all. But what way is it to treat a cousin? Okay. Eat I can where I want. I don't, God forbid, need his meal. Babe, come on."

I went to get her fur, knowing it was useless to argue, and I saw them to the garage elevator with some dawning thought about rudeness as the measure of achievement and the systems of storing up injury. As Cissy passed into the elevator she said, "Tell your brother congratulations. His wife is awfully pretty."

But this was one game in which I wasn't going to play intermediary, and when Simon asked me eagerly about their leaving I said casually, "Oh, they just didn't have the time to stay. They came only for the ceremony." I gave no satisfaction.

But as for that other more important game into which he had gotten me, I played it to the full, going to night clubs, sorority dances, and shows and night-football games at which Lucy and I pitched and necked. She was, up to the last thing of all, unrestrained and exploratory; and where she stopped I stopped. You never know what forms self-respect will take, especially with people whose rules of life are few. But I enjoyed all that was allowed and to that extent I remained myself. But I wasn't much myself in other ways, and it was very disturbing, and sometimes pressed on my head with very heavy weight, and I realized I was in the end zone of my adaptability. It was my pride to make it seem easy though. So that if you took me at Uncle Charlie's house on a Sunday afternoon, after dinner, by the fire, among the family, with Mrs. Magnus knitting a shawl that rose out of a tapestry carpetbag; with Sam, Lucy's brother, standing by, his chin picked up to make way for the foulard beneath it and his dressing gown swelling over his behind while every now and then he treated his plastered hair with affection; with Uncle Charlie listening to Father Coughlin who hadn't yet begun to shag out the money-changers but had that boring fervor of the high-powered and misleading who won't let you be but have to make you feel all the trembling vacancy of winter space between Detroit and Chicago—if you took me there, by the firelight, facing Uncle Charlie who had one leg thrown forward and his fingers inside the crevice of his shirt drawing at the mat of his chest, I wasn't the success envy might have believed me to be. My own envy went out with, I don't doubt, sick eyes through the clear gray panes where the kids were warring and shooting snowballs that splatted on the black trunks and soared in the elegant scheme of twigs. Not that Lucy, in dark wool dress that just covered the tops of stockings she had helped me loosen the night before so that I could stroke her skin, didn't make up for much. In some way, not the deepest nor yet trivially, I was gone on her and as far as I was allowed gave her a real embrace that she returned, licking my ear and praising and promising me; she already called me husband.

The deep consideration women give, as seen privately in their thoughtful eye, to demands for the most part outlawed out of fear for everything that has been done to make a reasonable, continuous life, the burden that made Phedra cry she wanted to throw off her harmful clothes, you could find that in Lucy too. It took her as far as to choose me. It was evident I was less desirable than Simon from her family's standpoint. Their main investigation was conducted on my willingness to be as they were in everything. They never were too sure, and were forever asking to have another look at my credentials, and, so to speak, would come in without knocking, as if I were at West Point, to see whether all was dusted and the hospital corners satisfied regulations. Lucy stood up for me; it was her only disobedience so far as I, a wayward but close student of the situation, could see. When I suggested that we run away and get married at Crown Point she refused flat, and I could see the difference between her and Charlotte. I probably shouldn't forget the difference between Simon and me; he had been able to talk Charlotte into eloping. And if Lucy already called me "husband," Mimi Villars would have said, no compliment intended, that she was a wife, wanting the whole wifely racket. In other words, minor sensuality and no trouble. Unless she was flirting with trouble by having detected a source of it in me.

But I was, as at the Renlings', under an influence and not the carrier of it. I had to get around; I had a figure to cut, the car to drive, the money to spend, the clothes to wear, and served before I had it clear whether I wanted or liked the doing of it at all. Even if her father stole in on us at two in the morning as we were loving-up, he stole through a mansion, and it was hard to think him wrong when the lights went on and he prowled peevish toward us. I suppose I saw nothing very wrong anywhere, and it took me longer than it should have taken to discover that he didn't like me, because everything flashed so, all was rich, was heavy, velvet, lepidopterous.

The circuit I was in, at the Glass Derby and Chez Paree and the dances at Medinah Club, kept me very busy. Here what had to be established was whether I was qualified in pocket to mix with the sons of established fathers. I had to mind my step, for Simon kept me on a minimum budget; he somehow thought that I could do what he had done on just a little less. It was true that I could make money go farther, but Lucy thought less about economics than Charlotte. And I had to notice cover charges, tips, the cost of a parking lot, and slip out to the store for Camels instead of buying them from the cigarette girl. I got through examination by Lucy's set, not hearing what I didn't want to hear, or forcing others to give ground, and even if it did strengthen the hypocrite's muscle in my face and harden my stomach I thought it did me credit to bluff it through.

These weren't our only company. We went to visit Simon and Charlotte in their flat—they had, for a beginning, only three rooms—and to eat off the trousseau linen and the wedding china. The Magnuses went to exceptional lengths to procure anything for one of their own, and these plates and cups had been baked in an English kiln, as the rug was really from Bokhara and the silver by Tiffany. If we stayed after dinner we played bridge or rummy, and at ten o'clock Charlotte phoned the drugstore to send peppermint ice-cream and hot fudge. So we licked spoons and I was in general sociable, helpful, debonair, and thought of the two colors of my silk suspenders and the fit of my shirt, Simon's gifts. Obedient to him, Charlotte treated Lucy and me like an engaged pair, but with wariness and reserve camouflaged from him. With the instinct of her family she knew that I didn't have Simon's qualities, that I really didn't intend to follow in his steps, his difficulties perhaps too much for me to undertake.

This he was becoming aware of too. He was pleased at first by my willingness and fluency and spoon-lickery and obliging and niceness that continued while I moved before the regard of the Magnuses and made the most that could be made of the appeal of their seductions—all that opulence, the strength of cars in the great rout of cars in the cold-lit darkness of the North Side Drive, and that mobile heraldry on soft tires rushing toward the floating balls and moons of the Drake Hotel and the towers around it; the thick meat, solid eating, excitement of dancing. Following the lake shore, you left the dry wood and grayed brick of the thick-built, jammed, labor-and-poverty Chicago standing apart, speedily passed to the side. Ah no! but the two halves of the prophecy were there together, the Chaldee beauties and the wild beasts and doleful creatures shared the same houses together.

Being in the yard daily, the beginning of this winter, I was not in a position to forget even if my evenings and Sundays were in another sphere. And my Sundays themselves were divided. Simon had me open the gates Sunday morning to catch what trade there was in the very cold weather. He drove me hard, bound to discipline me. Some mornings he checked on the time I arrived. If once in a while I overslept it wasn't to be wondered at, since, after taking Lucy home and leaving his car in the garage, I had to ride home on the trolley and so rarely got into the sack before one in the morning. He wouldn't, however, take any excuses from me. He said, "Well, why don't you make your time with her a little faster? Marry her and you'll get more rest." This, at first, was half a joke, but later, when he began more to doubt me, he was surly and before long fierce toward me. He grudged me the extra money, thinking it was merely thrown away. "What the hell are you waiting for, goddam you, Augie! She ought to be a pushover. If it was me I'd show you how, but fast." He was more violent as the resistance of her family began to shape up, though this I didn't understand for a while.

But should I come in at eight-fifteen instead of eight I might find him at the scale, glaring at me. "What's the matter, did that Mimi keep you?" He was convinced that I had carried on and continued still with Mimi.

We had other difficulties too. As I was assistant bookkeeper as well as weighmaster, he expected me to take from the pay-envelopes of the Negro hikers installments on the cast-off clothing he had sold them, and on a few occasions there was bad feeling between us. As in December, once, a lushed-up dealer named Guzynski tore onto the scale out of the slushy yard with white steam gushing from his busted radiator. He was buying a ton of coal and was overweight by several hundred pounds; when I told him he was heavy he cursed me, and he came down from the truck to force his way into the office and break my arm for cheating. I met him at the door and threw him out, and when he picked himself up from the snow, instead of pushing me again, he dumped his coal on the scale. There was now a jam of trucks and wagons in the street as well as in the yard. I told a hiker to clear the scale, but Guzynski was standing over his coal with a shovel and swung on him when he came near. Happy Kellerman was phoning for a squad car when Simon arrived. Simon went for the gun at once, and as he was running from the office with it I caught him by the arm and swung him back, and in his rage he drove a punch at me and hit me in the chest. I yelled at him as he got away, "Don't be an idiot! Don't shoot!" and then saw him stagger for his balance in the coaly slush as he turned the corner. Guzynski was not too drunk to see the gun and he threw himself, burly in his short filthy coat and seaman's watch cap, to the side of his truck, trying to get to the cab. Here, in the narrow space between the truck and the office wall, Simon caught him, had him by the throat, and hit him in the face with the side of the gun. This happened right below Happy and me; we were standing at the scale window, and we saw Guzynski, trapped, square teeth and hideous eyes, foul blue, and his hands hooked, not daring to snatch the gun with which Simon hit him again. He laid open Guzynski's cheek. My heart went back on me when the cuts were torn, and I thought, Does it make him think he knows what he's doing if the guy bleeds? Now he let him go and with the pistol signed to the hikers to clear the scale platform, and their shovels began to scrape or gouge the dirty silence of Guzynski looking with loathing at his blood. He sprang into his truck, and I feared he would crash it into the gates, but he skidded into the snow mash of the street and the tracks caught his wheels and straightened him out in the traffic that took him up with it toward the sunless, faint direction.

"Any odds he's going to the station to swear out a warrant?" said Happy.

Simon, who had put down the gun, listened to him, and with a heavy breath he said, "Get me Nuzzo on the phone." He spoke to me, and it was in a fashion I had made up my mind to get used to and generally obeyed. He no longer looked up a number himself or did the dialing but took the instrument only when his party was already waiting. This time, however, I didn't stir. My arms were crossed and I held my place by the scale. He marked me down for this, grimly. Happy got the number for him.

"Nuzzo!" said Simon. "This is March. How y'doin'? What? No, it's cold enough, I can't kick. Now listen, Nuzzo, we just had a little trouble down here from a squarehead dealer who hit one of my men with a shovel. What? No, he was drunk as a lord, dumped his load on my scale and tied me up for an hour. Look, he's probably on his way to make a complaint because I roughed him up. Take care of him for me, will you? Keep him in the clink till he cools off. Sure I will, I got witnesses. You tell him if he's thinking of laying for me after, you'll fix his clock good. What? He does bushel business down by that church on Twenty-eighth. Do that for me, will you?"

He did, and Guzynski was in the lockup several days. Next time I saw him he wasn't plotting any revenge. His scars were crusty yet when he came back still a customer, quiet, and I know that Simon was watching his eyes and would have acted on the least hint. But there was no trouble to hint. Nuzzo, or Nuzzo's people, had put a deep fright in him in their cellar below cellar, and gave him a Saturn's bite in the shoulder to show him how he could be picked up whole and eaten. He must even come back a customer. And Simon, too, knew how to put home the clincher, and at Christmas gave Guzynski a bottle of Gordon's Dry Gin and his wife a box of New Orleans pecan pralines in the form of a cotton bale. She said to him that it had done Guzynski good.

"Of course," said Simon. "He's satisfied now. Because he knows where he stands. When he swung that shovel he didn't know and was trying to find out. Now he knows."

For Simon wanted to show me how justly he handled such crises, and how badly, by contrast—because of chicken-heartedness—I did. I should have quelled Guzynski's riot as soon as it broke. But I wasn't prompt, wasn't brave, didn't understand that Guzynski had to be pistol-whipped and thrown in jail if he wasn't to become a Steelkilt mutineer to buffalo all captains. The inference was clear that if I didn't make time with Lucy Magnus it was from these same shortcomings. If I became her husband in two-armed fact, the rest was merely a formality. But I didn't mount the step of power. I could have done so from love, but not to get to the objective.

Thus things became more tough for me at the yard; Simon increased my hardships both for my good and because it didn't displease him to do it. At this time he couldn't say how many high things were suitable for him and was trying on guises. His last thoughts at breakfast sometimes were the next new policy, and this might be to devote himself absolutely to the bottom-most detail or fistful in a business that reckoned by tons; or, again, to skim in the big space of principle only and leave the details to subordinates—as he could do if they, and mainly I, were trustworthy; or to be a Jesuit of money; or to be self-made: that was one of his weakest ideas but it was also persistent. I said, "Oh, but you're not a Henry Ford. After all, you married a rich girl." "The question is," he said, "what you have to suffer to get money, how much effort there is in it. Not that you start with a nickel, like the Alger story"—I here remembered what a reader Simon had been— "and run it into a fortune. But if you get a stake, what you do with it, whether you plunge or not." But this was the discussion of theory, which became rarer between us. Mostly I had to see in his disgusted eyes what his theory was and how disadvantageously I fitted into it, where I trailed, lagged, and missed the mark.

So those were evil days for me, in that particular field of feeling that had the shape of the yard, the forms of the fence, coal heaps, machinery, the window of the scale, and that long, brass, black-graduated beam where I weighed. These things: and also the guys that worked, the guys that bought, the cops that came for theirs, the mechanics and the railroad agents, the salesmen, got into me. My head was full of things to remember; I must not quote a wrong price and stumble in arithmetic or any dealing. Mimi Villars heard me talking in my sleep one night about prices and came in and asked me questions, as though in a telephone conversation. She quoted the prices back to me in the morning, all correctly. "Brother! things must be bad for you," she said, "if that's all you can dream." I might have confessed even worse, if I'd cared to, since Simon had decided on the roughest treatment for me and sent me on errands not exactly for Hesperides apples. I had to fight with janitors about clinkers, soothe and bribe them, sweeten dealers with beer, wrangle with claims agents about shrinkage, make complicated deposits in the pushing, barking crowd at the bank, everybody in a hurry and temper; I had furthermore to hunt up shovelers in flophouses and court them in the Madison Street gutter when we were suddenly shorthanded. I had to go to the morgue to identify one found shot with our pay envelope empty in his shirt pocket. They lifted the bristling, creased wrap from him and I recognized him, his black body rigid, as if he died in a fit of royal temper, making fists, feet out of shape, and crying something from the roof of his mouth, which I saw.

"You know him?"

"That's Ulace Padgett. He worked for us. What happened to him?"

"Girl friend shot him, they say." He pointed out the wound in his breast.

"Have they caught her?"

"Naw, they won't even look for her. They never do."

Simon had given me this mission because, he said, I was driving the car anyway, to take Lucy out, and might as well attend to it on the way home. I had to hurry and change, and

I didn't have the time to wash off any but the exposed dirt of face, neck, and ears. All over the rest of me was grit from the yard, up my heels and legs. Even in the corners of the eyes there were shadowed places I didn't get into. They widened out my look by darkness. I had no time to eat, even if I had enjoyed an appetite, for the morgue had taken long and Lucy was waiting. I drove faster than I had any business to, and had a near thing at Western Avenue and Diversey, a long, down-hill skid that turned the Pontiac round so that I finished back-wards, against a streetcar. The motorman had a good forty yards to see me and was standing on a grade, under the rail-road bridge. So I didn't hit hard. I smashed the rear lights but couldn't see much other damage, and was congratulated by that sudden gathering that always collects on such an oc-casion. I was told how lucky I was and laughed it all off, hopped back of the wheel again and continued. I got to the Magnuses' in marvelous spirits, in the black night of the drive and the snow head of the portico, confident and whistling, the keys melodious in the coat I tossed down on the bench in the hall. However, when Lucy's brother Sam gave me a drink I went back, infinitely quicker than the speed at which I had come, to the morgue—the smell of the whisky on an empty stomach did that for me—and to the accident, which now made my work-filthy legs too weak to hold me. I sank down in a chair. Lucy said, "Why are you so white?" And Sam came near, like the host of a B movie, concerned after all lest his sis-ter, huggable, press-bosom dolly, get herself engaged to a weakling. With more of this interest than mercy he bent to me, the stripes of his dressing gown stretched tight over his can.

"Am I white?" I struggled to say and picked up my head. "Maybe because I haven't eaten."

"Oh, how silly. Since when? Why, it's after nine." She sent Sam to the kitchen to get a sandwich and a glass of milk from the cook.

"I also had an accident—almost," I said to her when he had gone, and described what had happened.

I'm not sure which most came through, her concern, or the sudden thought at the rear of her mind that I was a Jonah —I, the happy lover of the present moment. Trained fine in foresight, when, as now, she wanted to make use of it, she must have been seeing a drift of hard luck if not downright misery in the horizon. "Did you damage the car badly?" she said.

"It's banged up a little."

She didn't like my vagueness about it.

"The trunk?"

"I don't know exactly. I broke the tail lights, that I know. About the rest it's hard to tell in the dark, but it probably isn't much."

"We'll go in my car tonight," she said, "and I'll drive. You must be shaky from the accident."

So we went out in her roadster, a new one her father had recently given her, to our party on the North Shore, and afterward parked in one of the big sectors of shadow around the Bahai temple to stroke, struggle, and shiver at the base of that cold religious knoll and its broken-up moonlight. Things seemed as usual but were not, either for her or for me. When we got back she wanted to have another look at the damage, afraid for me. I wouldn't go bend over the back of the car with her and put my finger in the dents. I turned off her headlights, under which the examination was taking place. And in the front hall afterward, when I was in coat and hat, fondling her and being assured she loved me, I knew there was an obstruction of sympathy. She foresaw that Simon would raise hell about the damage—as he did—and what's more, no point of view but his seemed possible to her, and she was somewhat frightened at me, feeling that I had one. And I might smell her shoulder and lift up her breast, but it wasn't the same intimacy any more in that riches-cluttered hall partly inventoried by the moon, the old man snuffing upstairs, vigilant whether asleep or not.

I was therefore worn out in advance of the dripping yellow morning and its sick cold and the close filthy heat of the oil-squirting stove indoors. There is a way, I don't doubt, to carry all such things like little sticks in the bulge of the flood water, if you determine your energy to flow that way, and the weight of morgues and cars depends on the hydraulic lifting power you dispose of. Napoleon when he escaped in the old box of a sledge from wintry Russia, the troops of his dead lying like so many flocks covered in snow, talked three days to

Caulaincourt who probably couldn't hear very well because his ears were bandaged—his master couldn't practice his old trick of pulling them—but he must have seen in his boss's swollen face the depth that kept floating a whole Europe of details.

Yes, these business people have great energy. There's a question as to what's burned to produce it and what things we can and can't burn. There's the burning of an atom. Wild northern forests go like so many punk sticks. Where's the competitor-fire kindling, and what will its strength be?

And another thing is that while for the sake of another vigor is lacking, for the sake of the taste of egg in one's mouth there's all-out effort, and that's how love is lavished.

I couldn't hold up all of these different elements. Simon came in and bawled me out over the car and I was too broken-down to give any back talk or even feel he was doing me wrong. All I did reply was, "What are you fussing about? It wasn't much of an accident, and you're insured."

This was just where the error was; it was that I *had* to feel bad about the back shell of the car and those crustacean eyes that were dragging by the wires, and it wasn't so much the accident as my failure to care as I should that he minded. That was why he burned me with his eyes and showed his broken-edged tooth while his head settled downward with menace. I was too despondent to stand up to him. Nothing visible backed me, as it did him, to see and trust, but all was vague on my side and yet it was also very stubborn.

I stayed in that evening to read. According to our agreement I was to start at the university in the spring, when business would let up a little and Simon could spare me. I still had the craving that I had given in to all summer long when I had lived on books, to have the reach to grasp both ends of the frame and turn the big image-taking glass to any scene of the world. By now Padilla had sold most of my books for me—he himself had given up stealing lately since he had taken a part-time job calculating the speed of nerve impulses in a biophysics lab—and I had only a few things left. However, there was Einhorn's fire-damaged set of classics in a box under the bed, and I picked out Schiller's *Thirty Years' War* and was lying in my socks reading when Mimi Villars came in.

Often she came and went without talking to me, only for her things in the closet. But she had something to say tonight, and didn't spar, but told me, "Frazer knocked me up."

"Gosh, are you sure?"

"Of course I'm sure. Come out with me. I want to talk to you and I don't want Kayo to be in on it. He listens through the wall."

It was black weather, not too cold but very windy, and the street light was hacked and banged like a cymbal.

"But where's Frazer?" I said, having been out of touch with the house lately.

"He had to leave. He has to read a damn paper at a convention in Louisiana, Christmas, and so he went to see his folks first, because he can't be with them for the holiday. But what difference is it where he is—what's the good of him?"

"Well, honestly now, Mimi, wouldn't you like it if you could get married?"

She gave me enough silence in which to take it back, looking at me. "You must think I lose my head easily," she said when I didn't retract. We hadn't gone down into the wind yet; we were on the porch. She had one foot pointed to the side and her hand coming from her deep sleeve held the back of her neck while her round face of tough happiness was turned close under mine. Tough happiness? Yes, or hard amusement, or something spiritual and gymnastic, with pain done to the brows to make them point finely. "If I wouldn't marry him before, why should I now because of an accident? I see you've been under good influences. Let's go get a cup of coffee."

She took my arm, and we got as far as the corner, where we stopped again and were talking when a little dog came up, followed by his mistress in a Persian lamb coat and astrakhan hat, and an astonishing thing happened of the sort that made me see how believable it was that Mimi should have grabbed the gun from a stickup man and shot him; for the dog, somehow misoriented, perhaps because of the strong weather, wet on Mimi's ankle, and she shouted at the woman, who seemed incapable of looking to see what was happening, "Take away your dog!" And then she tore off the woman's high fur hat to dry herself with it and left her like that, her hairdress beginning to be destroyed by the wind as she cried out, "My hat!" The hat was on the street where Mimi had flung it.

That lack of respect in occurrences for the difficulties that there already are! But then proofs always flocked to Mimi to help her make her case. Anyway, in the drugstore, when she had stripped off and rolled her stocking and put it in her bag, it only made her laugh. A real and pure chance for temper tickled her heart.

But what she wanted to discuss over coffee was a new method of abortion she had heard about. She had already tried drugs like ergoapiol, with walking, climbing stairs, and hot baths, and now one of the waitresses at the co-op told her of a doctor near Logan Square who brought on miscarriages by injection.

"I never heard of such a thing before, but it's worth a try, and I'm going to try."

"What is it that he uses?"

"How should I know? I'm not a scientist."

"And if it has a bad effect you'll have to go to the hospital, and then what?"

"Oh, they have to take you in if you're in danger of your life. Only they'd never get out of me how it happened."

"It sounds risky. Maybe you'd better not try at all."

"And have a baby? Me? Can you see me with a kid? You don't care how the world gets populated, do you! Maybe you're thinking about your mother"—I thus knew that either Sylvester or Clem Tambow had talked to her about me—"and that you wouldn't be here if your mother had ideas like mine. Nor your brothers either. But even if I could be sure I'd have a son like you," she said, with her usual comment of laughter, "not that I don't think the world of you, pal, even with all your faults—why should I get into this routine? So the souls of these things shouldn't get after me when I die and accuse me of not letting them be born? I'd tell them, 'Listen, stop haunting me. What do you think you ever were? Why, a kind of little scallop, that's all. You don't know how lucky you are. What makes you think you would have liked it? Take it from me, you're indignant because you don't know.'"

We were sitting near the counter, and all the help stopped and listened to this speech. Among them was a man who said, "What a crazy broad!"

She heard him, he caught her eye, and she laughed at him and said, "Here's a guy who'll live and die trying to look like Cesar Romero."

"First thing, she comes in, she has to take off her stockings and show her gams . . ."

This argument had to run its course, and then we couldn't stay; we finished our conversation in the street.

"No," I said, "I can't complain about having been born."

"Yes, sure, you'd even feel grateful if you knew to whom, and for what was only an accident."

"It couldn't have been all an accident. On my mother's side at least I can be sure there was love in it."

"Is it love that saves it from being an accident?"

"I mean the desire that there should be more life; from gratitude."

"Show me where that is! Why don't you go down to the Fulton egg market and think it over there. Find me the gratitude—"

"I can't argue with you that way. But if you ask me whether obliviousness would have been better for me, then I'd be a liar if I answered 'yes' or even 'maybe,' because the facts are against it. I couldn't even swear that I knew what obliviousness was, but I could tell you a lot about how pleasant my life has been."

"That's hunky-dory for you; maybe you like the way you are, but most people suffer from it. They suffer from what they are, such as they are; this woman because she's getting wrinkled and her husband won't love her; and that one because she wants her sister to die and leave her her Buick; and still another who is willing to devote her whole life to keep her fanny in the right shape; or getting money out of somebody; or thinking about getting a better man than her husband. Do you want me to give you a list on men too? I could go on as long as you like. They'll never change, one beautiful morning. They can't change. So maybe you're lucky. But others are stuck; they have what they have; and if that's their truth, where are we?"

Me, I couldn't think all was so poured in concrete and that there weren't occasions for happiness that weren't illusions of people still permitted to be forgetful of permanent disappointment, more or less permanent pain, death of children, lovers, friends, ends of causes, old age, loathsome breath, fallen faces, white hair, retreated breasts, dropped teeth; and maybe most intolerable the hardening of detestable character, like bone, similar to a second skeleton and creaking loudest before the end. But she, who had to make up her mind practically, couldn't be expected to make it up by my feelings. She let you know, but quick, that you, a man, could talk, but she was the one for whom it was the flesh and blood trouble, and she even had a pride about it that made her cheeks shine, that in her was something ultimate.

I didn't keep up these arguments with her. And although not convinced by her, I wasn't utterly horrified for the unborn either. To be completely consistent in that kind of economy of souls you would have to have great uneasiness and remorse that wombs should ever be unoccupied; likewise, that hospitals, prisons, and madhouses and graves should ever be full. That wide a spread is too much. The decision was really up to her, whether to have a child by Frazer who wasn't free to marry her now, even if she wanted to marry him. And, by the way, I didn't take at face value all that she said about him.

However, I wasn't any too sure about the injection. I wanted to ask Padilla about it, who was my scientific authority, and I tried to get him at his laboratory. If he didn't know the answer himself he could ask one of his biological buddies in that semi-skyscraper of a building where there were always dogs barking with abnormal strain, which made me flinch a little when I heard it. Padilla didn't seem to mind this; he only went there to do calculations in that slip-slop queer swift way, standing on an eccentric point, a hand in his pocket and an untouched cigarette burning with forked smoke. But I couldn't find him before Mimi's appointment with the doctor. To which I took her.

This doctor was a man made dolorous, or anyhow heavy of mood, by the bad times, and he looked very unprofessional. There was a careless office of old equipment, and he sat in rolled sleeves and smoked cigars at a desk where my book-accustomed eyes spotted a Spinoza and a Hegel and other things odd for a doctor, and especially one in his line. Under him there was a music shop. My memory gives me back the name: Stracciatella. In the window there was the entire family, playing guitars to a microphone—the young girls and barelegged boys whose feet didn't yet touch the floor, and the sounds covering the street, cold that night, after a snowfall, with a noise of wires stronger even than the competition of the streetcars, old on that line and passing with a ruckus.

The doctor didn't misrepresent what he had to offer—he was too careless even for that. He wasn't hardhearted maybe, but he appeared to ask, "What could I accomplish by caring?" Perhaps there was a disdain about him for the double powerlessness of creatures, first to oppose love and then to be free of the consequences. Naturally he took me for the lover. I suppose Mimi wanted him to; as for me, that wasn't what I cared about. Therefore, this was how we were, in the office, the stout doctor explaining his injection for our lay understanding, fat-faced, dry, unarduous, heavy of breath, his arms hairy, the office stinking of cigars and of his sedentary career in old black leather. He was not actually unkind, in his goggles, and partly a man of thought—just as far as the difficulties that purify, and no farther. Then the guitars breaking their step, a wiry woe and clatter. And Mimi with fair face and hair, red cheeks, a cloth rose laying down its folds front and center of her hat, assisted by white and less serious flowers. O that red! of summer walls and yet of fabric and the counters of stores. Also her demonish or ciliary eyebrows, so hard-set and yet she was also so confused. But the time was one of the highest opportunity, if I understood her spirit, having to do with that same powerlessness the doctor observed—the powerlessness of women waiting for what will be done to them, and that way and none other to buy glory.

"This injection causes contractions," said the doctor, "and it may expel your trouble. Nobody can promise that it will, and sometimes even if it works you still need a dilation and curettage. The thing actresses in Hollywood describe in the paper as appendicitis."

"I'd appreciate it if you wouldn't make any jokes. I'm only interested in your medical services," Mimi told him right off, and he saw he wasn't dealing with a timid little knocked-up factory girl who was grateful, he'd think, for his wit and signal back to him dimly with a smile over the vast separating distances of real grief and danger. Some poor body in trouble from tenderness. But Mimi—her tenderness didn't have an easy visibility. You wondered what it would be, and after what terrific manifestations it would appear.

"Let's just keep everything professional," she said.

He said, with offended dark nose holes, "Okay, do you want the injection or not?"

"Well, what the hell do you think I came all this way for, a cold night!"

He got up and put an enamel pot on the gas ring—a grizzly-claw collar of fires giving hot scratches. His handling of the pot was suggestive of the laziness and sloppiness of his morning egg in the kitchen; he dropped the hypo in, fished it up again with tongs, and was ready.

"And suppose I need other help, if this only works halfway, will I get it from you?"

He shrugged.

Her voice began to ring. "Well, you're one hell of a doctor! Don't discuss it before you start? Or don't you give a damn what happens to people after they take your injection? You think they're so desperate you don't have to give a damn and they're only fooling with their lives, is that the way it is?"

"If I had to, I might be able to do something for you."

I said, "You mean you do if you get paid. How much do you soak for it?"

"A hundred bucks."

"You wouldn't settle for fifty?" she said.

"You might find somebody who would." He meant to show—and I thought it was genuine—that he didn't care. *Non curo!* That was what came easiest to him. He would just as soon have put away the hypo and gone back to picking his nose and to his ideas.

I counseled her not to talk money with him. I said to her, "That part of it isn't important."

"You want to go ahead with it? Look, to me it's just the same."

"Mimi, you can still change your mind," I said for her own ear.

"And where will I be if I change it? On the same spot still."

I helped her off with her fur-collared coat, and she took me by the hand as if it were I that had to be led to the needle. At the moment of my putting my arm around her—feeling her need and wanting greatly to do all I could to meet it—she broke into sobs. The thing affected me too; I caught it from her. So we held together like what we were not, a pair of lovers.

However, the doctor would not let us forget he was waiting. Sorrowful or tiresome, was this for him? Something between the two, and he watched how I would comfort her. Whatever there was to envy before, taking me as her lover, this was not enviable to him now. Well, he didn't know.

But Mimi had decided, and she wasn't wavering; these tears didn't mean that. She gave him her arm, and he sank the needle in it; the hard-looking fluid went down. He told her she would have pains like birth pangs and had better go to bed. The bite for this was fifteen bucks, which she was able to pay; she didn't want any money from me at the moment. Not that I had a lot of it. Going with Lucy kept me broke. Frazer owed me something, but if he had been able to pay he would also have been able to send money to Mimi. She didn't want him to be bothered about it. He was still raising money for his divorce. Besides, it was part of Frazer's style not to know about such things. There was always something superior to what was happening in the immediate view, more eminent. This was a part of him that Mimi's satire was always aimed at, and yet she encouraged it as something precious as well as foolish. It wasn't that he was specially ungenerous but that he put things off to give his generosity a longer and more significant route.

Anyway, Mimi went to bed, cursing the doctor, for the action had already set in. However, it was "dry," she said, and the cramps weren't going to effect anything. She shuddered and sweated, her bare shoulders thin and square above the quilt, and the childish form of her forehead painfully determined with lines, eyes greatly widened, strongly lighted blue.

"Oh, that dirty, bloody gypper!"

"Mimi, but he said nothing might happen. Wait—"

"What in the name of hell can I do now but wait when I'm shot full of this terrible poison? I must be caught strong, for it's squeezing my guts out. That lousy clumsy cow doctor! Oh!"

Intermittently the spasms passed off and she found the spirit for a relieving joke. "It's sitting tight, won't budge; stubborn thing. While some women have to stay on their backs nine months to keep theirs. Listen to the radio. But"— increasing in seriousness—"I can't let it alone now and be born, with all the stuff I've taken. It might be hurt. Groggy. If not, it might be dangerous because it's so obstinate, and be a criminal. I think if he'd be wild enough and kick the world around I might let him come. Why do I say 'he' though? It might be a girl, and what would I do to a daughter, poor child? Still women—women. They do themselves more credit, there's more reality in women. They live closer to their nature. They have to. It's more with them. They have the breasts. They see their blood, and it does them good, while men are let to be vainer. Oh! give me your hand, will you, Augie, for Chrissake?" It was the return of the gripes, making her sit stiffly and squeeze and bear down on my hand. With shut eyes she let the spasm pass through and then lay back, and I helped her cover up.

Little by little the effect of the drug ended and left her tired in the muscles and belly, furious with the doctor and angry also with me.

"But you know he didn't make any promises."

"Don't be stupid," she said, ugly. "How do you know he gave me a big enough dose? Or if he didn't want me to come back and have it done the other way, so he'd get more? And that's what it will have to be. Only I'm not going to him."

Seeing how she was, fiery and sullen, though weakened, and wanting nobody near, I let her be and went to my room.

Kayo Obermark had the room between us, and of course he was on to what was happening; in spite of Mimi's efforts to keep him out, how could he miss? He was young, about my own age of twenty-two, but ponderous already, a big, important, impatient face, irritable, smoky with thought that went out far. He was gloomy and rough. His life was rugged in there, that room; he didn't like classes, his notion being that he could do all his own learning; the room was foul from the moldering of old things and smelled of bottles he used for urine, because he didn't like to make trips to the toilet when he was working. He lived half-naked in his bed, which all the rest of the room approached, heaped up with commodities and dirt. He was melancholy and brilliant. He thought the greatest purity was outside human relations, that those only begot lies and cabbage-familiarity, and he told me, "I prefer stones any time. I could be a geologist. I'm not even disappointed in humankind, I just don't care about it, and if there's one thing that's sure, it's that this world is certainly not enough, and if there isn't any more they can have it all back."

Kayo wanted to know about Mimi although she always baited him.

"What's the matter, she having it rough? She has hard luck."

"Yes, it's bad."

"But nah! it's not all luck," he said—one of the things he couldn't stand was that you should agree with him. "You notice people have the same kind of thing happen to them, over and over and over."

His attitude to her had something in common with the doctor's; it was woman's trouble she had, and neither of them could place it very high. Kayo, however, was a much more intelligent man than the doctor, and though as he stood in my room on bare weight-flattened feet in undershirt, the hair in tufts on his shoulders, and that large face from which everyone was reproached for letting him down and coming short of the mark—though, in other words, he was the hard figure of prejudice, there was still in him an extra effort of justice, a channel kept open.

"Well—you understand. Everyone has bitterness in his chosen thing. Bitterness in his chosen thing. That's what Christ was for, that even God had to have bitterness in his chosen thing if he was really going to be man's God, a god who was human. She also goes in for it." He gave a heave of terrible impatience. "That was Christ. Other gods poured on the success, knocked you down with their splendor. Those that didn't give a damn. Real success, you see, is terrifying. Can't face that. Rather ruin everything first. Everything would have to be changed. You can't find a pure desire except the one that everything should be mixed. We run away from what can be conceived pure, and everyone acts out this disappointment in his own way as if to prove that the mixed and impure will and must win."

I was always impressed by him and his big horse's eyes startled by wisdom or the shadow of it, as a horse may shy at a ridiculous thing the same as at an important one. I felt what he was saying. I knew there was truth in it, and had respect for him as the source of illumination; even while himself he was in dark colors, some of smudge, and green and blue by the eyes, but some of radiance; and, hands on his fat hips, he looked at me with a face in which some original beauty was turned down as a false lead. That this fact that all had to give in was acted out I could see, and the accompanying warning that to hope too much was a killing disease. Yes, pestilential hope that passes under the evils and leaves them standing. I had enough of a dose of it to recognize it. So I was both drawn to Kayo's view and resistant to it. No painted sky of the human theater for him, but always on the outside toward the diamond-drop true sky by means of the long, star-crawling clear fog of the medulla and brain, a copy of the Milky Way.

But I had the idea also that you don't take so wide a stand that it makes a human life impossible, nor try to bring together irreconcilables that destroy you, but try out what of human you can live with first. And if the highest should come in that empty overheated tavern with its flies and the hot radio buzzing between the plays and plugged beer from Sox Park, what are you supposed to do but take the mixture and say imperfection is always the condition as found; all great beauty too, my scratched eyeballs will always see scratched. And there may gods turn up anywhere.

"If you go into reasons," I said to Kayo, "there may be reasons for these mixed things too."

"Not real," he answered. "You wouldn't try to live on a movie screen. When you understand that, you'll be on your way to something. You can be too, if I'm not wrong about

your character. You wouldn't be afraid to believe in something. What I don't get is why you want to make a dude of
yourself. It won't keep up though."

Mimi heard that we were talking and she called me. I went
back to her.

"What does he want?" she said.

"Kayo?"

"Yes, Kayo."

"We were just talking."

"You were talking about me. If you tell him anything I'll
murder you. All he ever looks for is proof he's right, and he'd
walk on my chest with his big feet if he could."

"It's you yourself that don't keep your own secrets," I said,
trying to be easy about it, however. It wasn't the time to talk
back in any fashion, and she stared at me, harsh, from the
bent-metal bed with its so many cast-iron nuclei and iron ribbon bows.

"What I say, I say, but I can tell you not to."

"Just take it easy, Mimi, I won't."

Nevertheless I had to ask Kayo to keep an eye on her next
day, not knowing what might come up and worrying through
it at the office and at the supper meeting of the Magnus
Cousins Club that took place once a month in an oak room
downtown. I tried phoning the house and couldn't get anyone but Owens himself, who when peeved, and he was with
Mimi, put on a Welsh accent I couldn't penetrate, so that it
was just wasting nickels to continue phoning. Lucy wanted to
go dancing after the meeting; I got out of that by alleging
tiredness, which I didn't have to counterfeit, and cut out for
home.

Mimi was there, and she had happy news. Dressed in a
black and white suit, a black ribbon in her hair, she was sitting
in my room.

"I used my head today," she said. "I started by saying to
myself, 'Are there any ways to get this done legally?' Well,
there are a few. One is if you go to an alienist and get him to
say you're nuts. They don't want madwomen to be having
kids. I once got off a rap that way so it's on a court record. But
I don't feel like doing it now. You can go too far. So I decided,
to hell with that stuff of putting on a wacky act. The other

thing is that if your heart is weak or your life in danger they'll do it for you. So I went to the clinic today and said I thought I was pregnant but not normally, and kept having trouble. There was a guy who examined me and thought he was pretty sure I had a tube pregnancy. So I have to be examined again, and if they still think so they might have to operate."

This was what overjoyed her. She already was banking on it.

I said to her, "What did you do, bone up in a book on what a tube pregnancy was like and then go down and describe the symptoms to them?"

"Baby, what an idea! Do you think I'm such a daredevil? And do you think you can walk in there, tell them any old thing, and take them in?"

"They can be fooled about some things at a clinic. That I can tell you. But watch what you're getting into, Mimi. Don't try to put it over on them."

"It isn't all my idea; they think so too, and I have some of the symptoms. But I won't go back, I'll go to that veterinarian."

I couldn't keep watch over her the next few days, having a full calendar of suppers and gatherings, and the times I looked in on her, late at night or at half-past six in the morning when I had to turn out, she was too sleepy to talk to me. When I went to wake her she seemed to know at once whose hand was on her shoulder and what the question was, and answered as though out of sleep, "No, nothing, no soap."

Winter was pouring on, late December, smoky and dark. Clobbering down the steps in my galoshes these mornings of mist and smoke, usually running late, I made for the car line in the seeping-back of night from the bad filters of low sky. Nine o'clock, after the first rush of business, I could catch up with breakfast at Marie's greasy-spoon, walled with decorative tin panels, one-arm chairs by the walls, no great amount of light because of the height of the fixtures.

On a Saturday afternoon I was taking a break at Marie's. She had the opera on the radio, tuned in from New York, and that eloquence turned loose didn't reach me but went on in my ears. There you have a service formerly paid for, as when a Burgundian duke in prison in Bruges sent for a painter to alleviate the dark shutters with gold faces and devotional decoration. This kind of aid to people in trouble now diffused practically free, as in magazines or on the air. However, I didn't hear it well, except as powerful and formal voices.

Sent by Happy Kellerman, a shoveler came to say that I was wanted on the phone by a lady.

It was a nurse from a South Side hospital, calling with a message from Mimi.

"Hospital? What's the matter? Since when has she been there?"

"Since yesterday," the woman said, "and perfectly all right, but says she wants to see you."

I told Simon, who listened to me with suspicion, irony, reprimand, already hard and waiting to spurn my explanation that I had to get off early to see a friend in the hospital.

"Which friend? You mean that broad of yours, the roughneck blonde? Pal, you have too many irons in the fire. How are you mixed up with her? I think you're going a little too fast, aren't you, trying to keep up with two dames? That's why you look so dug-up lately. If one of them didn't haul your ashes you might make faster time with the other. Or is it more than an ash-haul job? Ah, that would be just like you, to fall in love too! You can't hold your load of love, can you! What do you have to give for a piece of tail? You can't climb in bed with a girl without feeling that you have to take care of her for life?"

"You don't have to say all this, Simon, it doesn't have any bearing. Mimi's sick and wants me to come see her."

"As long as the boy is getting laid, I don't see what's such a rush to marry," said Happy.

"If this gets around to *them*," said Simon, out of Happy's hearing; and, strangely, his look got hung up on something that resembled satisfaction and pleasure more than anything else, and I saw that he had already handled the consequences of this to himself; he'd repudiate me, and it would do him no harm. As for his notions, the wedding night, of what we two would be able to combine and achieve, he had no doubt changed them, deciding that all should be the work of a single mind and authority.

But I was not thinking of this much, but rather of Mimi in the hospital. I was sure she had gone through with her plan to trick the doctors.

Late afternoon I saw her, in a ward; I was in the door, and she was snapping her fingers from the distance and trying to sit up in bed.

"You went through with it?"

"Oh, sure! Didn't you know I would?"

"Well? At least, is it over?"

"Augie, I've had an operation for nothing. It's all normal. I still have the thing to go through with."

I didn't get it at first; I felt block-headed and stupid.

She said with devilish towering humor and plunging bitterness, "Augie, they all come in to congratulate me that I'm going to have a normal baby. It's not a fallopian pregnancy. The doctor, the internes, the nurses, they think I should be wild with happiness, and I can't even yell at them. I've been crying. I'm so crossed up."

"But why did you go through with it? Didn't *you* know? You invented the symptoms."

"No, I wasn't sure. I didn't invent everything, I had some. Maybe it was that injection. And when they thought it might be in the tube I was afraid not to have the operation. Then I thought when they had me on the operating table they'd do it for me. But they didn't."

"Of course they didn't, they're not allowed to. That's what it was all about in the first place."

"I realize. I realize. I thought I could crash the gate, I suppose. One of my bright schemes." She wasn't crying now, though in her eyes there were the crimson threads that tear salts bring out, and her nose was stung with them too, but she was not less but more, as was clear on her push-faced beauty, an aristocrat in her idea of the energy you should devote to love.

"How long are you supposed to stay in bed, Mimi?"

"I'm not going to stay as long as they think. I can't."

"But you have to."

"Oh no. It's getting late. A little more and I won't be able to. You call that man and get an appointment for me for late next week. By that time I'll be able to take it."

This touched me very wrong, and I couldn't help it, I showed my horror at such nerve to practice on one's own body. "Oh, you think a woman should be more fragile than that," she said. "I keep forgetting you're just about engaged to be married."

"But shouldn't you wait at least until they let you out?"

"They say ten days, and it'll only weaken me to stay in bed that long. Anyhow, I can't stand the ward. And the nurses' being so pleased about the blessed event. I can't put up with it. And I'm beginning to be nervous. Do you have any dough?"

"Not much. Do you?"

"Not even half of what I need, and can't raise much. He won't touch me for a buck under the price, I know. Frazer hasn't got anything either."

"If I could get into his room I could take some of his books and sell them. There are things there worth good money."

"He wouldn't like that. Anyhow, you can't get in." She broke her preoccupation to give me a look for my own sake, straight, and said with a laugh that didn't last, "You take my side, don't you?" I saw no necessity to answer. "You can see the point of love, I mean." She kissed me feelingly, and with some pride in me. All the rest, the women, wan, visiting or gazing around.

"Well," I said, "we can raise this money. How much short of the hundred are you?"

"I'll need at least fifty more."

"We'll get it."

The easiest way I knew to raise extra dough—so easy I was rather proud of it—was to steal books. I needed to ask no one, and Simon least of all.

I headed downtown right away. It was still early in the evening, glittering with electric, with ice; and trembling in the factories, those nearly all windows, over the prairies that had returned over demolitions with winter grass pricking the snow and thrashed and frozen together into beards by the wind. The cold simmer of the lake also, blue; the steady skating of rails too, down to the dark.

I went to Carson's on Wabash Avenue, the book section on the ground floor, warm and busy with a late crowd of shoppers under the Christmas bells and silvery ivies. I didn't as a rule loiter long, thus drawing attention. I knew what books I was after, a rare Plotinus, an English edition of *The Enneads* worth a whole lot of money, more than it was priced. I took the volumes down, leafed them, looked over the bindings, put them under my arm, and with fair ease made my way to the Wabash Avenue door. It was spinning slowly. I got into the quadrant that opened up for me and was half through when the door stuck and caught me, inches from the street. I turned to see whether the cause of the jamming was the worst that could be, having in my mind already police, court, and prison, up to a terrible year in Bridewell. But behind me was Jimmy Klein, practically a stranger to me since the old days, but not a stranger nevertheless. It was he who had me caught in the brass barrel that the doors turned within, and he signaled me that he would release me, that I was to wait in the street. There was a good deal of practice in his regard, under the felt brim, and the hook of the forefinger downward, meaning precisely, "Stop outside."

By these signs I knew him to have become a store dick. Hadn't Clem Tambow told me that he was working at Carson's? I wasn't going to make a break. The first thing was to get free of the trap, and I surrendered the books to him in the street. He said quickly, "By the stoplight on the corner. I'll be there right away."

I saw his hasty back and hat as he ran in the circle of the door. His behavior was not angry, but he appeared to deal with what he had foreseen and been ready for. By the stoplight, in the crowd, I sweated in the cold air, weak and grateful after the passed danger. Grandma's warning against Jimmy, that he was a crook, came back to me. He dealt, anyway, with lawbreaking.

"Okay," he said, returning. "You dropped the books and beat it when I hollered. I didn't see your face, but I'm out looking if I can spot you, you understand? Now you just go to Thompson's on Monroe. I'll be right behind."

I set off, drying my face with my silk muffler. In the cafeteria I carried my cup from the counter to a table. Presently he came too, and sat down.

He considered me for a while; he had gotten to be wrinkled at the eyes, sallow, shrewd, stillish, a commentator. Yet on both sides, as much as the circumstances let it be, there was happiness at meeting again.

"Was you scared in the door?" he finally said.

"Jesus, yes—what do you think?" I said, smiling.

"Same jerk as you always were. A train could hit you and you'd think it was just swell and get up with smiles, like knee-deep in June. What's all the happy joy this time?"

"Well, I'm glad it was you, not a real dick."

"I am a real dick, only not for you, you fool. I had to chase you. I was standing with the buyer and you came right smack in our sights, two yards' range. So what could I do but go for you? But what are you swiping books for? I thought they beat it out of us both at the same time when we worked that Santa Claus deal. My old man almost killed me. He almost killed me."

"And he made a detective of you?"

"He? Shit! I go where they put me and do what they tell me."

I knew his mother was dead; that, limping and corpulent, she had sunk into coffin and gone down to grave. But what had happened to the others?

"What about your dad now?"

"Putzin' on. He got married again after Ma died. It turned out he had a romance from the old country lasting about forty years. Isn't that something? While he had eight kids by Ma and the woman had four by her husband, both eating their hearts out with love. She became a widow, so they went and got married. What's the matter, you surprised?"

"Why, yes. I remember your father always being at home."

"Well, he had to go to the West Side sometimes, and when he did he had a transfer good for the Sixteenth-Street Kenton streetcar, so he used it."

"Don't be so rough on him, Jimmy."

"I'm not against him. I'd be happy if it did him good, but he stayed the same. He's the same now."

"And how's Eleanor? She went to Mexico, I heard."

"Oh, you're out of date. That was a long time ago. She's been back a good while. You should visit her. You was her favorite in the old days, and she still talks about you. Eleanor has a big heart. I wish she was better."

"She sick?"

"She was. She's working again, at Zarropick's on Chicago

Avenue where they make the suckers they sell in the stores next-door to schools. She shouldn't be working though. She got sick in Mexico."

"I thought she was going there to marry."

"Oh, you remember?"

"Your Spanish relative."

He smiled downward. "Yeah. Well, he runs a sweatshop of leather goods, and he had Eleanor working in it for about a year while they were supposed to be engaged. But he was laying the other broads working there too, and he wasn't really thinking of getting married. Finally she got sick and came home. She's not heartbroken; it was great to see another country."

"I'm sorry for Eleanor."

"Yeah, she hoped to be in love. She banked a lot on it."

He was contemptuous beyond measure, not toward Eleanor for whom he happened to care a lot. No, perhaps for her sake, toward love, as to something that had undermined and debilitated her.

"You're kind of hard on it."

"I don't think *anything* of it."

"But you're married, Clem told me."

This innocence of mine pleased him. "That's right, and have a son. He's a winner."

"And your wife?"

"Oh, she's a good kid. She has sort of a hard life. We live with her folks, we have to. And there's another married sister and brother-in-law. Well, what do you think it's like, with fights about who's going to use the toilet or take down the wash, or cook, or yell at the kid? There's still another sister who's a tramp and spreads on the stairs, so you can step on her in the dark coming home from the show, so there's brawls all the time. What I get out of it is space in a double bed. Don't you know how it is by now? It's all that you want from life comes to you as one single thing—fucking; so you and some nice kid get together, and after a while you have more misery than before, only now it's more permanent. You're married and have a kid."

"Is that how it happened to you?"

"I fooled around with her, I got her in the family way, and I married her."

The path of wretchedness as Mrs. Renling had drawn it for me when she predicted what would happen if Simon married Cissy.

"You're set up like the July fourth rocket," said Jimmy. "Just charge enough to explode you. Up. Then the stick falls down after the flash. You live to bring up the kid and oblige your wife."

"Is that what you do?"

"Well, it's not much to me; I give up on that. I don't think I give her much of a bang. But what are we talking about me for? You're the wonder boy. And what the hell are you doing, or think you're doing? I died when I saw you glom onto those books. That's a fine way to meet again. Augie, a crook!"

It was not all dismay; in part he seemed glad of it.

"Not a full-time crook, Jim."

"But even part-time it doesn't go with what I've heard about you and Simon, that you're so successful."

"He's doing fine—married and in business."

"That's what I heard from Kreindl. And you was going to the university. Is that why you were copping books? We catch a lot of students. Most of them don't make a good impression."

I explained to him my need for money, letting him assume that I was Mimi's lover, for otherwise it would have been difficult to make him understand; and though it was curious to meet Jimmy as the cop that caught me, and I felt light with relief and one foot on paradox and all the spirited melancholy that came of that, I had to get on with my money-raising and the other things there were to attend to. However, Jimmy was aroused by what I told him, and his eyes and all the skin of his face expanded with concern and with the immediate determination he took.

"How far gone is she?"

"Over two months."

"Listen, Augie, I'll help you as much as I can."

"No, Jimmy," said I, surprised, "I couldn't tap you. I know you have it hard."

"Don't be a dummy. Compare a few bucks to a life of grief. Say it's for my own sake—me not wanting to see it happen to anybody I used to be buddies with. How much do you need?"

"About fifty bucks."

"Easy. Between me and Eleanor it won't be anything. She has some dough put aside. I won't tell her what it's for. She wouldn't ask, but anyway why should she know? You don't have to tell me why you don't put the bee on your brother. You wouldn't be stealing it if he'd be willing to give it to you."

"If push came to shove I might ask him, but there're special reasons why I can't. Well, Jim—thanks. It's great of you. Thanks, Jimmy!"

The extent of my gratitude made him laugh at me. "Don't exaggerate. I'll see you here Monday, this same time, and give you the fifty bucks."

Jimmy had no confidence that he could keep company with kind motives; he was abashed by them. And I understood well that he wanted to defeat a mechanism as much as he wanted to help a onetime friend.

However that was, he gave me the money, and I made the appointment with the doctor for the end of Christmas week. Things were difficult to arrange. I had a date with Lucy that same night and couldn't break it with Simon's knowledge because I needed the car. Therefore, when I had left Mimi with the doctor I went down in great nervousness and phoned Lucy from a drugstore.

"Honey, I'll have to be very late tonight," I told her. "Something's come up. It'll be ten o'clock before I can get to your place."

She, however, had not much thought of me tonight. She whispered on the phone, "Darling, I ran into a fence and bent my fender. I haven't told Daddy. He's downstairs, so I'm stymied."

"Oh, he won't be so angry."

"But, Augie, I've had the car less than a month. He said he'd sell it if I didn't take good care of it. I had to promise there wouldn't be any trouble for six months."

"Maybe we can have it fixed without his knowing."

"Do you think I could?"

"Oh, probably. I'll dope out something. I'll be around late."

"Not too late."

"Well, then, if I'm not there by ten, don't expect me."

"In that case maybe I ought to get some sleep before New Year's Eve. You'll be on time tomorrow, won't you? And don't forget it's formal."

"Tomorrow at nine, in my tuxedo, and maybe even this evening. But I promised to help out a friend who's having a little trouble. Don't worry about the car."

"I do though. You don't know Daddy."

Empty, I left the booth; feeling stiff, and the soldier of my fears, and all that I didn't know had power over me.

Stracciatella was closed, and in the gaunt glass curled saxophones and guitars shrunk in their sides. Deeper, cracks of goblin light out of the spaghetti-feasting kitchen where the family sat.

I waited upstairs in the corridor by the door, which, in time, I heard unlocked. Mimi passed through it alone, handed out, and it shut before I could see the doctor to question him. I couldn't now, having to support Mimi, who tottered. She was only two days out of the hospital, and the variety of decisions she had made alone, not counting pain and blood loss, was enough to have taken away her strength. She was faint to such a degree that for the first time I saw her without expression, like a kid asleep on the excursion train, fatigued at night from picnicking. Except that when her head rolled on my shoulder and approached my neck, she drew on the skin of it with her lips, weakly, a reflex of sensuality. For the moment perhaps I was Frazer and she was confirming that no matter what complication, injury, foulness, she didn't back down from her belief that all rested on the gentleness in privacy of man and woman—they did in willing desire what in the rock and water universe, the green universe, the bestial universe, was done from ignorant necessity.

As we stood at the head of the stairs, her lips at my neck while I clasped her and whispered, "Easy now, let's start down easy," a man came up from the street and I nervously thought I saw something familiar about him. Mimi too was aware that someone was approaching and took several steps. So it happened that we were in the shadow, not in the main light of the corridor, when he came up. Nevertheless we recognized each other. It was Kelly Weintraub, the Magnuses' cousin by marriage who came from my neighborhood, the one who had threatened me about Georgie. By the slow increase of his smile when he saw me, and what there was in the flesh of his mouth more jubilant than mere smiling, also by the setting of his eyes, more clear to me than the eyes themselves in this obscurity, I realized that he had me. He knew.

"Why, Mr. March, what a hell of a surprise this is! You been to see my cousin?"

"Who's your cousin?"

"The doctor is."

"That makes sense."

"What does?"

"That you're his cousin."

I could never run so far or plunge so deep that this man, this Weintraub, wouldn't have enough erotic line to pay out after me, so he was telling me with his full, handsome teameo's look, fleshy and brow-bent, while he swaggered a little at the knees.

"I have other cousins also," he said.

I felt like hitting him, since I probably would never be seeing him after he had blabbed, but I couldn't do it because I was supporting Mimi. It may have been the dilation of the senses by rage that made me think I smelled blood, raw, but the result in horror is what counted. I said to him, "Get out of the way!"

To take Mimi home and get her into bed was all I cared about now.

"He's not my boy friend," said Mimi to Kelly. "He's only going out of his way to help me out of trouble."

"That makes sense too," he answered.

"Oh, you dirty bastard!" she said. She was too weakened to put in all the power of savagery she felt.

Shaking, I carried her to the car and drove off fast.

"Kid, I'm sorry. I loused things up for you. Who is he?"

"Just a guy—he doesn't amount to anything. Nobody ever listens to him. Never mind about that, Mimi. Was it all right?"

"He was rough," she said. "First he took the money."

"But it's over?"

"It's all gone now, if that's what you mean."

The drive was clear of snow, and I went fast over the endless varieties of black and smooth, along the tracks, through tunnels, lights streaming as if wind had gotten into a church and flown over the candles, sucking out breath, so much the speed fused things down.

We arrived. I lifted her up the four flights, and while she was getting under the covers ran down to get an icebag from Miss Owens, who fussed with me about the ice.

"What!" I yelled. "It's the middle of winter."

"Go out and chop some then. Ours is made in the refrigerator and takes electricity."

I stopped yelling, seeing that I had snagged a spinsterish trouble upsetting her by rushing in wildly, not thinking how I showed anguish. Calming down, I reasoned with her, turning on what charm I had on reserve. There can't have been much, the low charge in my trembling wires there was at this moment.

I said, "Miss Villars has had a tooth pulled and it's very bad."

"A tooth! You young people get so excited." She gave me the ice tray and I scooted back with it.

Ice, however, didn't help much. She bled very swift, and she tried to keep it secret, but presently she had to tell me, as she herself, astonished, with open eyes, tried to keep track of it. She began to soak the bed. I was for taking her to the hospital at once, but she said, "It'll get better soon. I think it has to be like this at first."

Going below, I phoned the doctor, who told me to watch and he'd tell me what to do if it didn't slacken. He'd stand by. There was fright in his tone.

When I pulled off her sheets and made up her bed with my sheets her hands came up to oppose me, but I said, "Look, Mimi, this has to be done"; she shut her eyes and let me make the change, laying her cheek down to the hollow of her shoulder.

There have great things been done to mitigate the worst human sights and teach you something different from revulsion at them. All the Golgothas have been painted with this aim. But since probably very few people are now helped by these things and lessons, each falls back on whatever he has.

I flung the bloody bedclothes into the closet, and she noticed the energy of the swing and said, "Don't be panicky, Augie."

I sat down by her, trying to be calmer. "Did you realize it might be like this?"

"Or even tougher," she said; and as her eyes were yellowish and lacking in moisture and her mouth was pale, it occurred to me that possibly she couldn't grasp just how tough it already was. "But . . ."

"But what?" I said.

"You can't let your life be decided for you by any old thing that comes up."

"A champion way to be independent," I said, intending the words for myself, but she heard me.

"It makes a difference what you go down from, don't fool yourself. It does to me, now. Though," she said, face frowning and then growing smooth while she made the concession, "probably that is only if I come up again. If you're dead, does it make a difference for what?"

I couldn't bear to talk now, and sat quiet, watching. And as she had thought it would, the hemorrhaging gradually let up; she was less braced and stiff-spread on the bed, and I was less benumbed in the muscles. My thoughts were crumbled, for I had been having fancies about how I was going to get her into a hospital, knowing how tough it was in such cases, and I imagined pleading and being refused, and official highhandedness and being driven mad.

"Well," she said, "it looks as if even he couldn't croak me."

"You beginning to feel better?"

"I'd like a drink."

"Shall I bring you something soft? I don't think you ought to drink whisky tonight."

"I mean whisky. I think you could use some yourself."

I took Simon's car to the garage and came back in a cab with a bottle. She took a good-sized slug, and I drank the rest, for now that I felt reassured about Mimi my own trouble came forward; as I was crawling naked into my sheetless bed in the dark it gave me an enormous squeeze, and I took a last swig at the bottle for the sake of stupefaction and sleep. But I woke in the small hours, earlier than my usual rising time. Kelly Weintraub would never let me get by but would nail me. And what I felt about this more definite than general darkness and fear, like the unlighted gathered cloud that hung outside, I didn't know.

I dressed in my yard clothes. The whisky was still working in me; I was not used to drink. In the grimness and mess of her room Mimi seemed to be very hot but normally asleep. When I went to have coffee I arranged at the drugstore to have breakfast sent up to her.

Watchfulness and care made me rocky that morning. The weather stayed black, undispersed soot sitting on the snow. Like the interior of something that should be closed. It was much more awful than sad, even to me, a native who didn't have much else to know. Out of this middle-of-Asia darkness, as flat in humanity as the original is in space, to the yard, on business, came trucks and wagons, dying nags inquiring through the window with their grenadiers' decorations of velvet green or red, looking at us under the brilliant bulbs making out receipts and laying the dollars in the cash drawer. The dollar bills felt snotty and smelled perfumed.

Simon kept examining me, so that I wondered whether Kelly had already reached him. But no, he was only keeping me under his severity, stout and red in the eye. And I wasn't doing too well.

It was, however, a short day, the last of the year. We were passing out little single-snort bottles of bourbon and gin and the joint got merry and jumping, peppered with these empties on the floor. Even Simon loosened up by and by. With the scrapping of the calendar and the old twelvemonth sagging off with his scythe and Diogenes lantern, Simon was after all on a new beginning. His summer troubles were well behind him.

He said to me, "I understand you and Lucy are going formal tonight. Well, how can you put on a tux with a head of hair as wild as that? Go and see a barber. In fact, get some rest. You been balling it somewhere? Take the car and go on. Uncle Artie is coming for me. Who tired you out like that? It probably wasn't Lucy. It must be that other snatch. Well, go —Christ, I can't tell if you look more tired or more dumb." Simon could only vouch for himself alone as being safe from the touched mentality of our family; when he was irritated his suspicion fell on me.

I lit out for home, wasting no time, and upstairs ran into Kayo Obermark coming out of the toilet with a wet towel for Mimi's head. He looked badly worried; his eyes, a big enough size in themselves, a few times enlarged by his specs, and his lips stuck out anxiously. His face was dark with bristle or dirt.

"I think she's bad," he said.

"Bleeding?"

"I don't know—but she's burning up."

To accept any help from Kayo she must, I thought, be in bad condition; and so she was, though talkative and of false alertness and sharpness—false because it didn't correspond to the expression of her eyes. The little room was overhot and gamy, everything about it felt stale and sickly, of swampy rottenness commencing to be dangerous.

I got hold of Padilla, and he came over from his laboratory with pills for her fever, having consulted with some Physiology grad students. We waited for results, which were slow to come, and wanting not to lose my head I agreed to play rummy. He, always alert in numbers, took every game. Until I couldn't any longer hold the cards. Toward night—I go by the hour and not by darkness, which was the same that day at six as it had been at three, fuming and slow—her fever went down somewhat. Then Lucy phoned to ask me to come an hour earlier than arranged. I felt that there was trouble at that end too and said, "What's up?"

"Nothing; only please try to be here at eight," she said, sounding a little stifled.

It was already well past six and I was unshaved. I did the job quickly and started getting into my tuxedo, meanwhile consulting with Padilla and Kayo.

"The big risk," said Padilla, "is if he gave her a septicemia. Suppose she has puerperal fever. That's too dangerous to keep her here with. You have to take her to the hospital."

Without waiting to hear more, in the boiled shirt, I crossed the hall and said to her, "Mimi, we have to try to get you in a hospital."

"They won't take me in anywhere."

"We'll make them take you."

"Call up and ask, you'll see."

"We won't call," said Padilla. "We'll just go."

"What's he doing?" she said to me. "How many people have to be in on this?"

"Padilla is a good friend of mine, don't worry about this now."

"You know what they'll do there, don't you? They'll try to get me to tell on the doctor. What do you think, will I keep my mouth shut?" This was a way of boasting that they could not make her squeal, even on him.

Padilla muttered, "What do you waste time with her for? Get going."

I dressed her in hat and coat, packed a little case with nightgown, toothbrush, and comb, and Padilla and I took her down to the car covered with a blanket.

As I opened the gray car door Owens called from the porch, "Eh March!" He had come out in his shirt and was giant and shrunk-shouldered, knees together, in the cold of this bad death of the year. "Important, on the telephone."

I ran up. It was Simon.

"Augie!"

"Talk fast. What's up? I'm in a hurry!"

"It's you who'd better talk fast," he said, furious. "I just had a call from Charlotte, and Kelly Weintraub is spreading a story about you that you took a bim to have an abortion."

"So? What about it, Simon?"

"That's the dame, isn't it, that one from your house? So you went and fixed yourself, you jazzed yourself right out into the cold. This is where I shake you, Augie, before you do worse to me. I can't carry you along any more. I'm going to have a tough time explaining this, how you were fucking this girl all the time you were engaged to Lucy. I'll say you're no damned good, which is no lie since you're too dumb to live."

"Aren't you even going to ask me if Kelly's story is true?"

Contemptuous that I should be so simple as to think him foolish enough to believe what I would feed him, he said in an almost amused voice, "All right—what? You were doing another guy a favor, huh? You've never been between this doll's legs? You've been living next door to her without touching her? Listen, we're no more ten years old, kid. I've seen that tramp. She wouldn't let you alone even if you wanted to be let alone. And you didn't. Don't try to tell me you're not horny. We all are, in our family. What do you think started us out in the first place—all three of us? Someone found he could come ring the bell whenever he wanted. Do you think I care if you were laying that girl? But you had to get tied up this way too—in dutch good and solid; that's the way it has to be to feel right. You must really be like Ma. Well, that's nothing to me if you have to do it that way. But I won't let you get me in trouble with the Magnuses."

"There isn't any reason why you should be in trouble with the Magnuses. Listen, I'll tell you about this tomorrow."

"No, you won't. Not after tomorrow either. You're not with me from here on. Just bring back the car."

"I'll come by and tell you what this really is—"

"Stay away, that's the last and only thing I'll ever ask you."

"You sonofabitch!" I yelled with tears. "You shit! I hope to see you dead!"

Padilla came running for me and called into the sitting room, "Hurry, cut out the gabbing."

Bawling, I shoved and kicked past the wicker or paper furniture and plunged out.

"What's the matter? What's the tears for? This too much for you?"

I answered when able, "No, I had a scrap."

"Let's go. You want me to drive?"

"No, I can."

We drove first to the hospital where she had had her operation. Soberer in the cold air, she said she would go in herself. We led her up to the emergency entrance and let her walk in, then sat in the car, hoping she would not come out. But presently, through the gilded, frosted drops of the windshield, I saw her appear in the door and I rushed to get her.

"I *said*—"

"Why didn't they take you in?"

"There's this guy. When I told him he said, 'We got no room in a place like this for people like you. Why didn't you have the kid? Go home and wait for the undertaker.'"

"*Chinga su madre!*"

Padilla helped me lead her back to the car. "I think I know

a guy in a hospital on the North Side working in a lab, if he's still there. I'll call him."

I drove him to a cigar store and he went in to phone.

"We should try it," he said when he returned. "We should say she did it to herself. Lots of women do. He told me who to ask for. If this other guy is on duty. He's supposed to be a good guy." In lower tones he said, "We may have to dump her there and beat it. She's just about passing out. What will they do? They can't put her in the street."

"No, we won't dump her."

"Why not? They see you and throw her right back at you because they don't want her on their hands. They pick what troubles they want to help. But let's use our heads. I'll go in first and case the doctor."

However, we all entered together. I couldn't wait in the car with her and was determined anyhow that they would take her in or I'd smash everything in sight. So we went through the near-empty first rooms; I made a one-handed grab at a guy in an orderly's gray coat who advanced in the way. He ducked and Padilla said to me, "What the Jesus are you doing! You're going to queer everything. Now take her over there and sit down till I find out if this buddy of mine is on duty."

Mimi drooped on me, and I felt her heat in the cheek. She could no longer sit; I held her propped until a stretcher was brought for her.

Padilla had gone, and they had me, at first, as if in arrest. There was a cop on duty. Together with the orderly he came out of a side door with a cup of coffee, in blue shirt, even holding a club.

"Now what's the story?" said a doctor.

"Instead of asking, why don't you take care of her?"

"Did you smack this guy?" said the cop. "Did he swing on you?"

"He swung, but he didn't hit."

Conceivably the cop now observed that I wore a tuxedo, because he wasn't quite so deadly packed in the flesh of the neck and small-eyed when he spoke to me. I was in the clothes of a gentleman, and therefore why should he take chances?

"What's the matter with this woman? What are you, the husband? She doesn't wear a wedding band. Are you related, or just friends?"

"Mimi? Has she passed out?"

"No, she's just not answering. She moves her eyes."

Padilla returned, the doctor hurrying before him. "Just bring her here and we'll see what gives," said the doctor.

Manny gave me a great look of success. We got rid of the whole ugly sniff-nosed crowd wanting to be in on trouble and went with the doctor. As we followed Manny gave him a story.

"She did it to herself. She's a working girl and couldn't have a kid."

"How did she do it?"

"With something, I guess. Don't women make a study of these things all their life long?"

"I've seen some dandies. But also I've heard pretty stinking stories made up. Well, if the women live we don't look for the abortionist, because what good does it do the profession?"

"How does she look offhand?"

"A lot of blood lost is all I can tell until I look it over. Who's this second fellow who's so worried?"

"Her friend."

"All he had to do was really smack that orderly and he'd have had New Year's fun in the calaboose with the drunks. Why is he in the monkey suit?"

"Hey what about your date?" said Padilla as he put his hand to his long face with shock. It was after eight by the smooth-pulled electric clock in the brilliant room we entered.

"When I find out what's up with Mimi."

"Go on. You better. I'll be here. I have no date tonight and was staying in anyway. The doctor doesn't think it's so bad. What do you have on?"

"A ball at the Edgewater."

I stood waiting until the doctor returned.

"It's mostly blood loss and infection from the belly surgery, I think," he said. "Where did she get that done?"

"She'll answer your questions herself if she wants to," I told him. "I don't know."

"What do you know? Do you know, for instance, who can be billed?"

Padilla said, "There's money. Can't you see how good her clothes are?" And he said to me, for it worried him deeply, "Are you blowing or not? This guy's engaged to a millionaire's daughter and on New Year's Eve he keeps her waiting."

"Write me a pass so I can get back tonight to see Mimi," I said to the doctor. He made a perplexed face to Padilla about me and I said further, "For Chrissake, Doc, don't fiddle around with me, but write the thing out. What's it to you if I come back? I'd tell you my whole hard luck story but don't have the time."

"Ah, go on, it's no skin off your nose," said Padilla to him.

"A pass from me wouldn't do you any good in front. I'm on now till morning, so just come and ask for me, Castleman."

"I may be back before long," I said. For I was sure that Kelly Weintraub, since he was talking, had already gotten to Uncle Charlie Magnus. But I reckoned also that he and his wife had not told Lucy, not on New Year's Eve, when she was going to a dance. Later they'd throw me out on my prat. But why had she asked me to come an hour sooner? The dance didn't really begin until ten o'clock. I phoned her once more and asked, "Are you waiting?"

"Of course I'm waiting. Where are you?"

"Not far."

"What are you doing?"

"I had to stop at a place. I'll hurry now."

"Please!"

About that last word of hers I thought as I drove that it was not like lovers' impatience, but neither soft nor hard. Turning too wide at the driveway, with a last-minute twist I put my wheels through mud and bushes and scraped back under the portico. Inside, on the turned-over heels of the yard shoes I hadn't remembered to change, I walked to the mirror to knot my black tie and saw backward, by the drape in the living room, the tense belly of Uncle Charlie, his sharp feet prepared, and sitting waiting in the oriental mix-up of brass, silk, wool, and all that gave the place so much power, Lucy, her mother, and Sam, observing me. I felt there was a big machine set against me. But I had come in order not to disappoint Lucy, toward whom, given their chance, my feelings could have shone and warmed again. I expected poisoned looks, against which I was coated and immune; at least, my greater trouble made such looks seem negligible; and I wasn't willing to be tagged for lascivious crime and false pretenses or whatever the counts were that they thought they had against me. By no means nervous, therefore, I judged that I had to do only with Lucy, no fortune hunting now involved, for I could go any distance independent of brothers, relations, and all, provided that her impulse was a true one and she was, as she had always said, in love. This was the thing, for I saw that she had been worked on, though I didn't know how much she had been told. The large-mouthed smile she gave me, staying at her seated distance instead of coming to kiss me, was curious—that pretty sketch of charm, in lipstick, widening, the relative of the awful cleft, running the other way, of the schismatics in the sixth bulge of hell, hit open from the bottom and split through the face. Ah, dear face! treasured as the representative of all the body which, though, dies away from this top delegate when it becomes too gorged and valuable. She, now so unearnest with me through her worked-up countenance, I saw she had been gotten to by her parents and that decisions had been made. My only cue was to leave. But not a single word had been spoken yet in this oriental assembly, and I had no pretext. I was still the escort, dolled up, if you didn't scrutinize me too close, like a chorus boy, in a boiled shirt, and thinking of nothing but courtship and dances.

"Why don't you sit down?" said Mrs. Magnus.

"I thought we were leaving right away."

"Well, Lucy!" said her father.

And on this signal she told me, "I'm not going with you, Augie."

"Now or ever," he directed.

"Never again."

"You'll go to the dance with Sam."

"But I came to take her, Mr. Magnus."

"No, these things when you decide to break them, it's better to break at once," said Mrs. Magnus. "I'm sorry, Augie. I personally don't wish you any bad luck. But I advise you to control yourself. It's not too late. You're a handsome and intelligent young man. There's nothing against your family; I respect your brother. But you're not what we had in mind for Lucy."

"What about what Lucy had in mind?" I said with a rising throatful of rage.

The old man was impatient with Mrs. Magnus's effort toward queenly dignity and wisdom. "No dough if she marries you!" he said.

"Well, Lucy, to whom does that make the difference, to you or to me?"

Her smile spread wider and lost all other intentions in the single suggestion that it was she who had inflamed me and when hot I had discharged it all upon someone else but that it really didn't matter since she wasn't so little her father's child, though a girl, that all that ardor in the car and in the parlor and with the lips and tongues and fingertips and the rest could make her really lose her head and be unwise.

I couldn't be sure just what the deal was. Something was said about the damage to her car. Now she confessed it. Her father said of course it would be fixed. As long as nothing else was broken, this being his delicacy about the hymen. But it was worth a laugh to him; this way a threat and groan also escaping in his fatherly joy that she had remained intact.

There was nothing further to stay for. I was threatened by her brother Sam, whom I found near me when I picked up my coat in the hall, that he would break my back if I bothered his sister; but with all his thickset hairiness and spreading keister, he couldn't make it mean anything to me.

I started the car, to which I also felt commitment ending, and drove to the hospital.

Padilla had given Mimi blood, and he was lying down after the transfusion in the room where I had left him, sucking an orange; his skimpy arm with its one curious ball of muscle taped, and his eyes, below surface indifference, black and active toward what I couldn't readily see.

"How is Mimi?"

"They took her upstairs. She's still off her head, but this Castleman says he gives her a good chance."

"I'm going up to see her. How is it with you?"

"Well, I don't think I'll be sticking around now. I'll be going home soon. Are you staying?"

I gave him the cab fare, for I didn't want him to bang all that long way to Hyde Park in a streetcar on a crowded holiday night.

"Thanks, Manny."

He put the money in the pocket of his shirt, and suddenly he asked, surprised, "Say, what are you doing back from the dance already?"

I didn't stand and answer but went out.

Mimi was in one of the maternity wards. Castleman said that there had been no other place to put her, and I thought that she more or less belonged there. So I went up. It was a tall, big chamber, and in the middle on a table was a little Christmas fir with lit bulbs and under it a box with cotton wool and nativity dolls.

Castleman told me, "You can stick around, but don't make yourself noticed or you'll be thrown out. I think she's going to pull out of it though she did everything she could not to except cut her wrists and take poison."

There I sat by her bed, it being half-darkness. Nurses coming to bring infants for the breast now and then, there were whispers and crimped cries and sounds of turning in bed, and of coaxing and sucking. I was open to feelings that had no obstacle in coming to cover me, as I was, in darkness and to the side, scorched, bitter, foul, and violent; and these feelings receding by and by, I was aware of others full of great suggestion and of this place where I was cast up. I began to breathe by my own normal measure and grew much calmer. When the midnight noise exploded, the tooting, sirens, horns, all that jubilation, it came in rather faint, all the windows being shut, and the nursery squalling continued just the same.

At about one o'clock, alert enough to hear me stirring, Mimi whispered, "What are you doing here?"

"I don't have any place special to go."

She knew where she was, hearing the infants cry. Her comment to me was melancholy, about whether she had outwitted a fate or met it. That was perhaps according as she was weak or strong toward what she had chosen and done, and in the truth of her feeling at the present moment, hearing the suckling and crying, and the night-time business of mothering.

"Anyhow, I think you're in good hands," I told her.

I went out to take a stroll, looking at the infant faces through the glass, and then, no one interfering, the nurses probably in a New Year's gathering of their own to snatch a moment's celebration, I passed through to another division where the labor rooms were, separate cubicles, and in them saw women struggling, outlandish pain and huge bellied distortion, one powerful face that bore down into its creases and issued a voice great and songlike in which she cursed her husband obscenely for his pleasure that had got her into this; and others, calling on saints and mothers, incontinent, dragging at the bars of their beds, weeping, or with faces of terror or narcotized eyes. It all stunned me. So that when a nurse hurried up to investigate who I was and what business I had to be there, she made me falter. And just then, in the elevator shaft nearby, there were screams. I stopped and waited for the rising light I saw coming steadily through the glass panels. The door opened; a woman sat before me in a wheel chair, and in her lap, just born in a cab or paddy wagon or in the lobby of the hospital, covered with blood and screaming so you could see sinews, square of chest and shoulders from the strain, this bald kid, red and covering her with the red. She too, with lost nerve, was sobbing, each hand squeezing up on itself, eyes wildly frightened; and she and the baby appeared like enemies forced to have each other, like figures of a war. They were pushed out, passing me close by so that the mother's arm grazed me.

"What are you doing here?" said the nurse with angry looks. I had no right to be there.

I found my way back, and when I saw Mimi resting, much cooler, I cleared out of the hospital by the stairs Castleman had shown me and went to the car, new snow floating at my feet over the gray plating of ice.

I didn't exactly know where I was when I started. I went slowly in the increasing snow, through side streets, hoping to come out on a main drag, and at last I did hit Diversey Boulevard in a deserted factory part, not far from the North Branch of the river. And here, as the thought of soon sacking in began to seem agreeable, I had a flat, at the rear. The tire sunk, and I dragged to the curb on the wheel rim and killed the motor. I had to thaw the lock of the trunk with matches, and when I got out the tools I didn't understand the working of the bumper jack. It was new that year, and I was used to the axle type that Einhorn had had. For a while I tried, though the boiled shirt cut me and the cold gripped my feet and fingers, and then I flung the pieces back, locked up, and started to look for a place where I could get warm. But everything was shut, and now that I had my bearings I knew that I was not far from the Coblins'. Knowing Coblin's hours, I didn't hesitate to go there and wake him.

When the yellow lamp flashed in the black cottage hall and he discovered who was ringing he blinked his eyes, astonished.

"The car broke down on Diversey and I thought I could come by because you get up around this time for the route."

"No, not today. It's New Year's; no presses working. But I wasn't sleeping. I just before heard Howard and Friedl when they got in from a party. Come inside, for God's sake, and stay. I'll give you a blanket on the couch."

I went in gratefully, took off the tormenting shirt, and covered my feet with cushions.

Coblin was delighted. "What a surprise they'll have in the morning when they see Cousin Augie! Boy, that's great! Anna will be in seventh heaven."

Because of the brightness of the morning and also the kitchen noise, I was up early. Cousin Anna, no less slovenly than in other days, had pancakes and coffee going and a big spread on the table. Her hair was becoming white, her face with its blebs and hairs darker; her eyes were gloomy. But this gloom was the form of her emotion and not any radical pessimism. Weeping and catching me in her arms, she said, "Happy New Year, my dearest boy. You should know only happiness, as you deserve. I always loved you." I kissed her and shook hands with Coblin, and we sat down to breakfast.

"Whose car broke down, Augie?"

"Simon's."

"Your bigshot brother."

"It didn't break down. It's a flat, and I was too cold to change it."

"Howard will help you when he gets up."

"Don't have to bother—" I thought I might mail Simon

the keys and let him come after his damned car himself. This angry idea was momentary, however. I drank coffee and looked out into the brilliant first morning of the year. There was a Greek church in the next street of which the onion dome stood in the snow-polished and purified blue, cross and crown together, the united powers of earth and heaven, snow in all the clefts, a snow like the sand of sugar. I passed over the church too and rested only on the great profound blue. The days have not changed, though the times have. The sailors who first saw America, that sweet the sight, where the belly of the ocean had brought them, didn't see more beautiful color than this.

"Augie, it was too bad Friedl couldn't come down from Ann Arbor for your brother's wedding; she had exams. You haven't seen her since a child, and you should. She's so beautiful. I don't say because she is my child—God is my witness. You'll see her soon for herself. But here, look, this is a picture from the school. And this one was in the paper when she was chairlady of the junior benefit. And not only beautiful, Augie—"

"I know she's very pretty, Cousin Anna."

"And why do you want to get mixed up with your brother's new relatives, those coarse people? Look how developed she is on this picture. She was your little sweetheart when you were kids. You used to say you were engaged."

I almost corrected her, "No, *you* used to say it." Instead I laughed, and she thought I was laughing over those pleasant memories and joined in, clasping her hands and closing her eyes. Slowly I realized that she was shedding tears as well as laughing.

"I ask one thing only, that before I die I should see my child happy with a husband."

"And children."

"And children—"

"For the love of mike, let's have pancakes. There's nothing on the plate," said Coblin.

She hurried to the stove, leaving the pictures spread before me, album and clippings; at which I stared. Only to turn my eyes at last again to the weather.

Chapter XIII

I WAS no child now, neither in age nor in protectedness, and I was thrown for fair on the free spinning of the world. If you think, and some do, that continual intimacy, familiarity, and love can result in falsehood, this being thrown on the world may be a very desirable even if sad thing. What Christ meant when he called his mother "Woman." That after all she was like any woman. That in any true life you must go and be exposed outside the small circle that encompasses two or three heads in the same history of love. Try and stay, though, inside. See how long you can.

I remember I was in fishmarket square in Naples (and the Neapolitans are people who don't give up easily on consanguinity)—this fishmarket where the mussels were done up in bouquets with colored string and slices of lemon, squids rotting out their sunk speckles from their flabbiness, steely fish bleeding and others with peculiar coins of scales—and I saw an old beggar with his eyes closed sitting in the shells who had had written on his chest in mercurochrome: *Profit by my imminent death to send a greeting to your loved ones in Purgatory: 50 lire.*

Dying or not, this witty old man was sassing everybody about the circle of love that protects you. His skinny chest went up and down with the respiration of the deep-sea stink of the hot shore and its smell of explosions and fires. The war had gone north not so long before. The Neapolitan passersby grinned and smarted, longing and ironical as they read this ingenious challenge.

You do all you can to humanize and familiarize the world, and suddenly it becomes more strange than ever. The living are not what they were, the dead die again and again, and at last for good.

I see this now. At that time not.

Well, I went back to books, to reading not stealing them, while I lived on the money Mimi repaid, and on what she loaned me when she was on her feet and working once more. Through with Frazer, Mimi had met Arthur Einhorn and had taken up with him. She was still waiting on tables. I got my meals at the joint where she worked. And I lay down and finished the Five-Foot Shelf Einhorn had given me, fire- and water-spotted books I had kept in the original cardboard box. They had a somewhat choky smell. So if Ulysses went down to hell or there were conflagrations in Rome or London or men and women lusted as they did in St. Paul, I could breathe an odor that supplemented the reading. Kayo Obermark lent me volumes of poets and took me to lectures now and then. This improved his attendance. He didn't like to go alone.

I can't be sure it isn't sour grapes that the university didn't move me much—I say that because according to the agreement I had made with Simon I was to have gone back in the spring—but it didn't. I wasn't convinced about the stony solemnity, that you couldn't get into the higher branches of thought without it or had to sit down inside these old-world-imitated walls. I felt they were too idolatrous and monumental. After all, when the breeze turned south and west and blew from the stockyards with dust from the fertilizer plants through the handsome ivy some of the stages from the brute creation to the sublime mind seemed to have been bypassed, and it was too much of a detour.

That winter I had a spell of the WPA. Mimi urged me to go and be certified. She said it would be simple, which it certainly was. I had the two requirements, being indigent and a citizen.

The trouble was that I didn't care to be put on one of the street details I'd see picking up bricks and laying them down, and with that shame of purposelessness you smelled as the gang moved a little, just enough to satisfy the minimum demand of the job. However, she said I could always quit if too proud to be assigned to this; she thought it wasn't a good sign in me that I had to have a clerical job; I'd be in better shape in the open air among simpler people. It wasn't the people that I complained of, but the clinking on a brick and that melancholy percussion of fifty hammers at a time. But I went to apply because she felt obliged to take care of me, making me her responsibility, giving me money, and as we weren't lovers this would be unfair.

Anyhow, I was certified and got a strolling kind of job that was about as good as I could expect. I was with a housing survey, checking on rooms and plumbing back-of-the-yards. I could fix up my own time card and soldier considerably, as everyone expected me to do; in bitter weather I could pass the time in the back booth of a coffeepot until the check-out hour. Also, the going into houses satisfied my curiosity. It was finding ten people to a room and the toilets in excavations under the street, or the rat-bitten kids. That was what I didn't like too much. The stockyard reek clung to me worse than the smell of the dogs at Guillaume's. And even to me, as accustomed to slums as Indians are to elephants, it was terra incognita. The different smells of flesh in all degrees from desire to sickness followed me. And all the imagination, passion, or even murder you could conceive were wrapped up in apparent simplicity or staleness, with elementary coarseness of a housewife feeling cabbages in a Polack store, or a guy who lifted a glass of beer to his white, flat-appearing face, or a merchant hanging ladies' bloomers and elastics in the drygoods window.

I stayed with this deal until the end of winter, and then Mimi, who was always up on these things, had an idea that there might be something for me in the CIO drive that had just started. This was soon after the first sitdown strikes. Mimi was an early member of the restaurant workers' union CIO. Not that she had any special grievance where she worked, but she believed in unions and she was on fine terms with her organizer, a man named Grammick. She brought us together.

This Grammick was no rough-and-tumble type but had points of similarity with Frazer and also Sylvester. He was a college man, soft-spoken, somewhat of a settlement-house minister doing his best, meek with the punks but used to them, and causing you a sense of regret. He had a long chest but his legs were relatively short; he walked quickly, toes in, slovenly in his double-breasted long jacket, a densely hairy, mild, even delicate person. But he wasn't an easy man for opponents to deal with. He couldn't be caught off balance, he clung hard, he was clever, and he knew a thing or two about deceit himself, Grammick did.

I produced a pretty favorable impression, and he agreed I might make an organizer. In fact his behavior toward me was very sweet. I had an idea that my good impression wasn't all my doing, but that he was trying to make time with Mimi.

But I got to value Grammick for various reasons. Though he was so inconspicuous that he could come and go, not specially noticed around hotel lobbies and service passages, still when a matter came to a head he could act with authority and not be frightened by a situation he had created. I appreciated his consciousness in advance of rights and wrongs that hadn't risen to view yet.

"Yes, they're hiring organizers. They want experienced people, but where are they going to find them? The problems are piling up too fast."

"Augie is the kind of person you ought to have," said Mimi, "somebody who can speak the workers' language."

"Oh, really, does he?" said Grammick, looking at me. It made me laugh to hear this advertised of me, and I said I didn't know whose language I spoke.

It couldn't have made less difference I soon learned when I began to work at the job. People were rushing to join up, and it was a haste that practically belonged to nature, like a change of hives, and, bent on their ends, they had that touchiness from being immersed in the sense of their own motion that causes striking and stinging. It must have resembled a migration, land race, or Klondike. Except that this time the idea was about justice. The big strikes had set it off, those people sitting down by their machines and holding parties, but grim parties. That was in the automobile and rubber industries, and of this I saw the far-reaching result, down to the most negligible pearldiver on skid row.

I started out at a table of the union hall—which wasn't the kind of rugged place you might picture but as solid as a bank building, on Ashland Avenue; it even had a restaurant of its own as well as a pool parlor—just a toy, for the members' recreation, nothing like Einhorn's—in the basement. I was supposed to be Grammick's inside man and take care of the telephone and office part of things. It was anticipated I wouldn't be busy above what was average and could gradually pick up what I needed to know. Instead there was a rush on me of people having to have immediate action; some hand-hacked old kitchen stiff as thickened with grease as a miner or sandhog would be with clay, wanting me to go and see his boss, *subito*; or an Indian would bring his grievances written in a poem on a paper bag soaked with doughnut oil. There wasn't an empty chair in my room, which was a room well apart from the main offices reserved for workers in the big industries. It made no difference how hidden I was. I'd have been found had I been in a steel vault by the feeblest signal of possible redress, or as faint a trace as makes the night moth scamper ten miles through clueless fields.

There were Greek and Negro chambermaids from all the hotels, porters, doormen, checkroom attendants, waitresses, specialists like the director of the *garde-manger* from flossy Gold Coast joints, places where I had gone with the dog-wagon and so understood a little. All kinds were coming. The humanity of the under-galleries of pipes, storage, and coal made an appearance, maintenance men, short-order grovelers; or a ducal Frenchman, in homburg, like a singer, calling himself "the beauty cook," who wrote down on his card without taking off his gloves. And then old snowbirds and white hound-looking faces, guys with Wobbly cards from an earlier time, old Bohunk women with letters explaining what was wanted, and all varieties of assaulted kissers, infirmity, drunkenness, dazedness, innocence, limping, crawling, insanity, prejudice, and from downright leprosy the whole way again to the most vigorous straight-backed beauty. So if this collection of people has nothing in common with what would have brought up the back of a Xerxes' army or a Constantine's, new things have been formed; but what struck me in them was a feeling of antiquity and thick crust. But I expect happiness and gladness have always been the same, so how much variation should there be in their opposite?

Dealing with them, signing them into the organization and explaining what to expect, wasn't all generous kindness. In large part it was rough, when I wanted to get out of the way. The demand was that fierce, the idea having gotten around that it was a judgment hour, that they wanted to pull you from your clerical side of the desk to go with them. Instead I had to promise to investigate.

"When?"

"Soon. As soon as possible. We have a big backlog. But soon."

"Sonsofbitches! Those guys! We're just waiting there to give it to them. You should see that kitchen!"

"There'll be an organizer out to contact you."

"When?"

"Well, I'll tell you the truth, we're shorthanded because there's such a rush; we haven't got enough men. But what you must do meanwhile is get ready, have your people sign the cards, and prepare your demands and grievances."

"Yeah, yeah. But, mister, when is the man going to come? The boss is gonna call in the AFL and sign a contract with them, that's some outfit."

I tried to discuss this danger with my higher-ups. Just then hotels and restaurants were a sideline with them, however; they lacked time to deal with them, busy with retail clerks who were out on a big strike and with runaway dress shops in Chicago Heights and so forth, but they couldn't bring themselves to turn down new memberships and aimed to keep them until they were prepared to devote the necessary time and money. In short, Grammick and I were intended to hold the line. I learned to do somewhat as he did. He would work sixteen hours daily for ten or twelve days at a stretch and then for two whole days he couldn't be found by anyone. He spent that time in his mother's flat, sleeping and eating steaks and ice-cream, taking the old lady to the movies or reading. Once in a while he slipped away to a lecture. He was studying law too. Grammick wasn't going to be sucked away from all private existence.

I went along with this rush, really needing some such thing now because of my blowout with Simon. After office hours I was out on the streetcars, traveling to see cooks and dish-washers or hotel clerks on night duty—those leafy nights of the beginning green in streets of the lower North Side where the car seemed to blunder as if without tracks, off Fullerton or Belmont, when the white catalpa bells were opening and even the dust could have a sweet odor. Many clerks especially asked you to come at night, when they could speak freely. The conspiratorial part of it was fine; and with the radical ideas then going, these people who were placed in a position to be thoughtful, since they were up all night, wanted the chance to say those self-rehearsed things that sometimes had been on their hearts too long. True and false light was distributed just about as usual, is my opinion. But it wasn't my place to judge that, but only to advance the work. Some of these guys just plain meant business. I suspect they wanted me to be more dangerous than I appeared to be. I know I seemed too fresh and well in color, not enough smoked and yellowed to appreciate what they were up against. My manner was both slipshod and peppy. They were looking for some fire-fed secret personality that would prepare the moment when they could stand up yelling rebellion. And here instead I would breeze in—I knew sometimes that my color and the height of my hair, my relaxed way, would give offense. But there wasn't any help for that.

Occasionally they'd even ask for my credentials.

"Did they send *you* from headquarters?"

"You Eddie Dawson?"

"That's right."

"I'm March. You talked to me on the telephone."

"You?" said Dawson. And I knew he had expected to see some sandy, suck-cheeked devil, veteran of coal fields or oil or New Jersey textile strikes. Yes, that at least—someone on whom it was evident that his first strength had been drawn out of him in the Paterson jail.

"You don't have to worry. I'm reliable."

Then he resigned himself; he had been taken in by my telephone voice. I could be at least a messenger to the higher-ups who'd be busy Guy-Fawkesing the Drake Hotel or the Palmer House—because it was that to Eddie Dawson, hauling up gunpowder in the tunnels.

He would tell me, then, what he wanted my superiors to know and give me directives.

"I want you to arrange a meeting with your top man down there—"

"Mr. Ackey, you mean?"

"You tell him I can get the employees together, but before we go out on strike we want to talk to him, all of us. That's to give my people confidence."

"Why are you sure you'll have to go out? Maybe you'll get your demands."

"Do you know who runs this bedbug palace?"

"What, some bank? Is it a receivership? Most of these small joints—"

"It's an outfit called Holloway Enterprises."

"Karas?"

"You know him?"

"Yes, I do, it so happens. I used to work for the insurance man Einhorn who is his cousin-in-law."

"He writes the policies for this place. You know what kind of a joint this is, don't you? For quickies."

"Is that so?" I said, observing that the big forehead, flushed and deeply vein-fed in the light cloud of fair hair, was covered with a sweat and that he wiped his hands the nails of which were manicured nails on his pink-striped shirt with an unconscious clutch. "If that's a problem it's a police problem. You don't want the CIO to start a union of *them*, do you?"

"Don't talk foolish. I mean I get the brunt of the trouble because I'm night clerk. Anyhow, if you know Karas you can tell me how easy it'll be to get our demands."

"He's a pretty tough character."

"Now when I have the shop ready to go, you ask Mr. Ackey for a few minutes so we can talk to him."

"We can arrange it," I said, who didn't know Ackey well enough to say good day when passing in and out of the toilet. But I represented him.

The situation was different in the hash-houses. I was more trusted and highly regarded. In the kitchens were old men— flophouse, County Hospital, and mission attendance inscribed all over them big and bold, and there was nothing like the resentment of a fellow like Dawson in that striped shirt, who was close enough to Karas's condition to figure how he made profit, to hate and envy, and also to wish to be nifty at the track, to wear hound's-tooth checks, to have a case and binoculars and be seen with a proud-cheeked fine big broad.

But take one of these old guys from a Van Buren Street greasy-spoon—I'd be requested by him to come around by the alley, the large paving stones breathing fumes of piss, and signal him through the window. Whereupon he'd go tight with caution and make me an oblique response with his head that might be taken by other eyes as a random motion. At last, by the door, we'd have a shushing conversation that we could have had just as well after hours. Except that he would want me to have a look at his place of work probably. The angry skin of his dish-plunging arms and his twist horse-gauntness, long teeth and spread liquidness of eyes in the starry alley evening; also that terrible state of food when you suspect it of approaching garbage that he brought out in his clothes and on all his person, his breath and the hair of his head just below me. Under the fragile shell of his skull he leakily was reasoning. And did it matter to him as it did to Dawson whether I looked like the organizer of his dreams? He wanted to make his dim contribution to the righting of wrongs, so that it was enough for him that he could locate me in an office or that I would come down this reeking alley to talk to him and accept the lists he slipped me of other stiffs who wanted to belong to the union. I was supposed to hunt them up in their moldy rooms. Where I had been on altogether different errands while I worked for Simon, recruiting coal hikers. No use assuming that I had reversed all and was now entering these flophouse doors from the side of light, formerly from that of darkness. Those times that I thought clearly of my duties I decided that I couldn't consider persons so much but rather the one degree of advancement in which everybody could be included.

Having a call in the old neighborhood one morning, I dropped in on Einhorn and found him in his sunny parlor office, in that peculiar, familiar staleness of coffee and bed, papers, his own shaving lotions and the powders of the two women. Mildred with her orthopedic shoes—she was polite but didn't like me—was already at her machine, heated and lit on the back of the neck, which had just been shaved up to the border where her potent hair began. Over the way, empty, were the windows of the old place of great days and *grands circonstances.* I didn't find Einhorn in a good state though I wasn't supposed to know it from his weighty face. For a while I thought he wanted to sit me out silently, until I went away. He breathed and felt of himself, looked out in the morning, smoked, nibbled, croaked off some shallow gas. He appeared melancholy and even savage.

"How's the pay at this new job of yours?" he asked me, deciding to speak. "Fair?"

"It's liberal."

"Then there's good coming out of it," he said with his dry decisiveness.

I laughed at him. "Is that all you think?"

"At least that anyway. Kid, I don't want to take away your zeal if you think you're doing something. And remember, I'm no conservative. Just because I sit here in a chair. This is no rich guy's club. In fact I have less to lose than other men, so I don't shrink from thinking to the extreme. I do a little business with Karas, but it doesn't follow that my ideas have to be where my interests are. What interests! Some interests! He's a *knacker*, Karas, he just bought a big new place in San Antonio."

I was now convinced that something was wrong. "Then you think it's a waste of time, what I'm doing?"

"Oh, it seems to me on both sides the ideas are the same. What's the use of the same old ideas? On both sides. To take some from one side and give it to the other, the same old economics."

He hadn't wanted to talk to me in the first place, but since I didn't go away he drove himself into the subject at first by irritation and then summoning up what he really thought. I wasn't zealous, not as he implied, but I did feel called on to say, "Well, people get up every morning to go to work; it isn't right that it should be an illusion, or that they should be so grateful for being allowed to continue in their habit that they shouldn't ask for anything more."

"You think that with a closed shop you're going to make men out of slobs? If they have a steward to gripe for them? Fooey!"

"So," I said, "is it better to leave it to Karas or a gorilla of a business agent who takes graft from him?"

"Look here, because they were born you think they have to turn out to be men? That's just an old-fashioned idea. And who tells them that? A big organization. One more big organization. A big organization makes dough or it doesn't last. If it makes dough it's *for* dough."

"If there can't be much sense in these big organizations

that's all the more reason why they should stand for a variety of things," said I. "There ought to be all kinds."

Meanwhile, ignoring, Mildred went on typing out statements. Einhorn didn't reply; I thought it was the appearance of Arthur from the kitchen half of the house that stopped him, for Arthur's brainy authority made his dad occasionally hesitate to sound off. But this time it wasn't that. He came forward only briefly, but it was evident that all the nervousness and difficulty were because of him. In a black sweater, narrow-shouldered, his hands in his back pockets, he sauntered, an elderly wrinkle on him that surprised me, and his eyes retreated with gradations of dark into a very somber color of trouble. He put his head to the side, his bushy hair touched the doorframe, and the smoke of his cigarette escaped to the sun where it became silky. Though he wasn't quite sure who I was at first, his smile was all the same suave, but also sick or fatigued. I was aware that Einhorn, to the very cloth of his coat, was stiff to him and prepared to be curt, within a degree of telling him to beat it, and I realized also that this was why Mildred had been so cold to me and hitting her machine as though it were a way to get me to leave.

Then a little kid came running from the kitchen, and Arthur held it with the clasp of a father, unmistakably, the kid swaying from his fingers. Behind, Tillie stood but didn't come forward. If I'm not mistaken they hadn't yet decided whether they could keep this a secret, for I realized it was recent news to the Einhorns too, and it was touch and go about acknowledging the baby, a little boy. He, while Arthur turned back into the kitchen, came running to Mildred and secured himself on her knee. She picked him up eagerly, and his booties catching in her skirt, it rode up on her thighs with their little dark hairs. About which she was calm. Thither I followed Einhorn's look. She kissed the boy with almost adult kisses and sought the hem to straighten her dress.

"What do you say to our news!" Einhorn spoke harshly and turned to me with a stiff curve in the back of his neck, partly with intention to bully but also greatly bowed by trouble, and that great representative of him, his face, twitched with an impulse that darted in from a little-explored place.

"That Arthur is married?" I didn't know what to say.

"Already divorced. It went through last week, and we didn't know anything about it. The girl was from Champaign."

"So you have a grandson. Congratulations!"

He looked strained, his eyes gemmy with the determination to sustain all, but his nosy face flat and with a light of pale unhappiness.

"And this is his first visit?" I said.

"Visit? She dumped him on us. She put him inside the door with a note and beat it, and then we had to wait for Arthur to come home and explain."

"Oh, he's dear and sweet," Mildred said with great spirit, the child on her breast cruelly clasping her neck. "I'll take him any time."

At this from his second wife, which in effect she was, Einhorn had all his cares come around to his first source: himself; his sensuality. And he looked angrily struck by this thought for all his Bourbon pride of profile and reflected it to the very depth of his black eyes. Like the roof-crouched goblin of an old church, he looked, his hands covered with pale spots placed at the sides of his often purposeless-appearing pants. His hair had the wave of unstranded rope, and from the set of his head there was the sense of ruins forming up behind him. With no motion in his arms, he might have been a man in a cape or a bound prisoner. Poor Einhorn! At any hour of his decline he could formerly have taken out the gilt bond representing Arthur, and now the spite had come upon him that the value had gone, like that of Grandma's picture-watered czarist money. The gleaming vault where he had kept this reserve wealth now let out the smell of squalor. Einhorn didn't even look at the kid, which was a jolly little kid that trod in Mildred's lap. Tillie stayed out of sight altogether.

I hesitated to show sympathy; he'd have thrown it back, though I was one of the few remaining people, I imagine, who'd give him full credit on his old-time greatness. I served a purpose that way for him, that I was prepared to testify that it was true noble and regal greatness. But he himself now started out weakly, saying, "It's not a good situation. Augie— you have some idea what capacities Arthur has. And before he can begin to use them, he gets into this—"

"I don't see what's so wrong," said Mildred. "You have a cute grandson."

"Keep out of this, please, will you, Mildred? A child isn't a toy."

"Oh," she said, "they grow up. Time does it more than fathers and mothers. The parents take too much credit."

Einhorn said to me in a lower voice, wanting no conversation with her, "I think Arthur hangs around your part of the woods. And there's a girl named Mimi he's interested in. You know her?"

"She's a good friend of mine."

Quick his brows rose, and I interpreted the hope that she was my mistress and therefore Arthur couldn't get into further trouble.

"Not that kind of friend."

"You don't lay her?" he said secretly.

"No."

I disappointed him; there was also a very fine salt of condescension or mockery, only a glitter on the surface of his look, but I saw it.

"Don't forget I was practically engaged until New Year's Day," I told him.

"Well, what kind of girl is this Mimi? He brought her around a couple of weeks ago, and Tillie and I thought she was pretty tough, and with somebody like Arthur whose thoughts always have an intellectual or poetic direction, she could give him a pretty rough time of it. But maybe she's goodhearted. I don't want to tear her down needlessly."

"Why, is Arthur thinking of remarrying already? Well, I'm an admirer of Mimi."

"Platonic?"

I laughed but felt sullen too, for it seemed to me that Einhorn didn't want his son to succeed me as Mimi's lover, or any girl's. I said, "The best person to ask about Mimi is Mimi herself. But I was going to say that I don't think she would be interested in a marriage proposal."

"That's good."

I expressed no agreement.

"Augie," he said with a rich preliminary of the face which I knew belonged to business, "it occurs to me that maybe my son could fit into your organization somewhere."

"Is he looking for a job?"

"No, I am for him."

"I could try." It was a discouraging favor to be asked. I could see Arthur stooping his weight on a desk in the union hall, one finger between the covers of his Valéry, or whatever he was interested in. "Mimi could help him if she wanted to," I said. "I got the job because she knew someone."

"Who knew someone, your friend?" He hoped still, slyly, to trap me into confessing intimacy with Mimi, but he drew a blank. "Well," he said, "you don't mean to tell me you keep that bursting health without the cooperation of a dear friend?" He was so pleased to have said this that his own troubles for a moment slipped his mind. But then the kid crowed on Mildred's neck and he changed again from a sensual to a sad or austere face.

It was a true guess that I had a friend. She was a Greek girl whose name was Sophie Geratis and she was chambermaid in a luxury hotel. She spoke for a delegation that came to me to apply for membership. They were earning twenty cents an hour, and when they went to their local to ask one of the head guys to put in for a raise he was playing poker and wouldn't be bothered. They knew he was in cahoots with the management. This small Greek girl was shapely every which way, in legs, mouth, and face; her lips went a little forward and their expression was sweetened a lot by the clear look of her eyes. She had a set of hard-worked hands and she lived with her beauty on rough terms. I couldn't for even a minute pretend that I didn't go for her. As soon as I saw her I thought that in the form of her eye-corners there was a personal hope of tenderness, and it got me. What I felt was tender too, rather than that heat that makes Nile mud of you, as like to crack as to be fertile.

As soon as the women signed there was a wild excitement and uprush of indignation and they began to call out, as if it was a working woman's Thesmophoria of these pale people. They wanted to be led into a strike right away. But I explained, and felt as usual the creep over me of legalistic hypocrisy, that it was a case of dual unionism. Legally they were represented by the AFL and therefore another union couldn't bargain for them. But when a majority of the employees was on the CIO side an election could be held. They didn't understand this, and as I couldn't talk against their noise I asked Sophie to come out with me and I would make the position clear. The corridor being empty for the moment, we kissed at once, riskily. Our legs were shaking. She said under her breath that I could explain the whole thing to her later; she would take the women away and come back. I locked up the office, and when she returned I took her home with me. We couldn't go to her room. She lived with her sister and the two were engaged to a pair of brothers. They were going to be married in June, six weeks' time. I saw the photo of her fiancé; he was a calm, responsible-looking gink. She thought she was being sensible, storing up pleasure so she wouldn't have any unfaithful craving once married. She was made very finely, all her little formations intricate and close and everything smooth. That was the happiness Einhorn took notice of, that I enjoyed in Sophie.

Kayo Obermark had too much masculine respect to ask me about her utterances and noises, laughing and otherwise. But Mimi said, "What kind of dame do you have who carries on like that?" She took a kidding tone, but I felt her nose was somewhat out of joint. "She brings her own cheering section."

I had no answer ready because I had never expected to be asked.

"There was someone else looking for you the other day," she went on. "I forgot to tell you. It's getting to be like a shrine up here."

"Who was it?"

"A young lady and a very pretty one, prettier than the noisy girl."

I wondered if it could be that Lucy had changed her mind. "She didn't leave a note?"

"No, she said she had to talk to you, and I thought she was very agitated, but maybe she wasn't used to climbing stairs and was winded."

It didn't especially stir me to think that it had been Lucy. I had no further interest in her; I was only rather curious about her visit.

I took up Einhorn's suggestion about Arthur with Mimi. If Einhorn had found fault with her, she was violent against him.

"Why, that old stinker!" she said. "As soon as I was close to him for a minute he had his hand on my leg. I don't like these old men who think they're all sex."

"Oh, you have to understand him," I said. "That's just his form of salute or chivalry."

"Hell! Who says an old cripple has to be so randy?"

"He's really a grand old guy. I've known him from a kid, and he means a lot to me."

"To me he means exactly nothing, and he's terrible to Arthur."

"Why, I think he loves Arthur more than anything in the world."

"That's how much *you* know! He takes it out on him all the time. In fact I have to help him get out of there because the old man is riding him to death on account of the kid."

"Isn't the mother coming back for it?"

"I can't make out from Arthur whether she's a nice girl or a tramp. He's terribly vague unless discussing ideas. What kind of bitch would ditch a kid—when she's already had it? Unless she's sick. In the head, you understand."

"Doesn't Arthur tell you what she's like?"

"You can't keep Arthur on a subject like this. His mind won't stick to it."

I said, "I wonder if you've got him straight about what his father does to him. This has been hard for Einhorn to take. He banked on Arthur. So did Tillie. Now it's just part of the Depression picture. Children coming back with their kids to live with the old folks in their flat."

"Why should it be any different for Einhorn than for the Poles or sausage-eaters on his street? It would be bad if it were different and helped the old fool to put it over that he was entitled to a better fate than anybody around. But when the things that happen pour over everyone alike, then we can *really* see who is better and who's worse. And then what's so awful about what happened to Arthur? Anyhow, he's better than Frazer. Frazer's back with his wife, they tell me, and he probably won't pay me the money I lent him because he would be admitting that he once nearly did wrong, and he's not the guy to admit that anything past, present, or future could be wrong. A girl was laughing over something in a book yesterday and showed me—you know, I hardly even read novels. It said, 'Error has never approached my mind.' That was Prince Metternich. Well, it could be Frazer. I don't think he would ever in his life forget himself. He'd never miss a train. Jesus, your Mr. Einhorn would love a son like that who always keeps his head and has a word ready to say and would never miss a train. But Arthur is a poet, and that old romancer really didn't want that to happen to him and be the father of a Villon or a Rimbaud."

"Oh, is *that* it!" I said. "Well, what is Einhorn doing to Arthur that makes him so cruel?"

"He nags him night and day and looks for chances to insult him. Yesterday it was that the old man was feeding the baby candy and when Arthur said it wasn't good for it he told him, 'This is *my* house, he's *my* grandson, and you can get the hell out if you don't like it.'"

"Oh, that's rough. He ought to blow then. Why does he take that?"

"He can't leave. He hasn't got any money. And besides he's sick. He's got a dose."

"Holy smokes! He's got everything. Did he tell you?"

"Well, don't be stupid. How do you think I found out? Of course he told me."

She smiled, and it was with the shine of real excitement. If I hadn't known it before I would now have realized that she had decided about him. She was for him.

"I'll see him out of the woods," she said. "He's going to a doctor now, and when this thing is dried up he's going to leave his father's house."

"With the kid?"

"No. Somebody will take care of the kid. What do you think! Should he become a housewife because of that crazy girl?"

"If he had given her some money maybe she'd have kept the baby."

"How do you know? Well, perhaps that would have been best. Old people shouldn't bring up a child."

"Einhorn wanted me to get Arthur an organizer's job."

She was too astonished at this even to smile but stared at me firmly, as if she wanted me to admit there was no limit to how grotesque people could make themselves, and then she went about her business, washing out stockings and underwear. She wouldn't answer.

Of course Arthur couldn't anyway try to work while he had the clap, and I reckoned it was best to invent a pleasant reason for Einhorn, and I did, saying there was no opening just then on Arthur's level. Even though it mustn't have been so pleasant for the old man to be referred back to his onetime vanity about Arthur's superiority. But it did sound reasonable that they couldn't offer someone like Arthur simply any old job that happened to be lying around.

As for Lucy Magnus, and I couldn't imagine who else it might be, I was merely, in the flattest way, curious, but I didn't give her supposed call much thought until a few nights later when there was a feminine knock at the door. It came at an awkward time, when Sophie Geratis was sitting on the bed in her slip and we were talking away. Seeing her startled, I said, "Don't worry, honey, nobody's going to bother us." She liked my saying this, so that it led to our starting to kiss, and the hooked links of the spring made that sound which goes in such a queer way with love, and which would have sent away anyone but this particular knocker. She said, "Augie—Mr. March!" and not in the voice of Lucy Magnus but that of Thea Fenchel. For some reason I remembered it and placed it immediately. I got out of bed.

"Hey, put on a robe," said Sophie. She was disappointed at the kissing ending when another woman spoke at the door.

I put my head out and blocked the door with my shoulder and naked foot. It was Thea. She had said in that note I hadn't seen the last of her, and here she was.

"I'm sorry," she said, "but I've already come a couple of times and I want to see you."

"Only once, I thought. How did you find me?"

"I hired a detective. Then that girl didn't tell you about both times. Is she in there with you? Ask her."

"No, that's not the same one. You actually went to a detective agency?"

"I'm glad it's not that girl," she said.

I didn't answer, only looked.

She wasn't keeping her composure very well. That prompt face, different from what I remembered, delicate but not so firm in nerve, wide-cheeked and pale, her nostrils open wide. I recalled that Mimi had told me she was breathing heavily from the climb, but it must also have been from determination not to give in to disappointment at not finding me alone. She was dressed in a brown silk suit, kind of strikingly water-marked; in spite of all, she wanted me to notice it. But at the same time, by her gloved hands and the unsteadiness of her hat of flowers, I was aware she was trembling; and as the rustling in mid-ocean against the bulwarks is the slight sign of very great miles of depth and extent, the stiffness of the silk gave a small sound of continual tremor.

"It's nothing," she said. "How could you tell that I was coming? I don't expect . . ."

I felt no need to be pardoned, as if I should have been waiting for her, and would have been within my rights in smiling but I wasn't able to do that. I had thought back on her as an erratic rich girl with whom the main thing was to be rivals with her sister; I couldn't continue to think so, for no matter how it had started it was now clearly something else. What sets you off not being good enough, you find the better reason once you have got going. This might have happened to her; but I couldn't tell which was uppermost, nobility or illness, whether she was struggling with personal objections of pride or the social ones about what is due a young woman from herself—those spiked things that press with such ugly sharpness on the greater social weakness of women. Whether she fought against or went out to look for a torturing occasion, I mean. But that was not all I thought of or felt by any means. Otherwise I'd have shooed her away, for I liked Sophie Geratis too well to give her up because I was merely interested or flattered. Or because I saw a chance to get back at Esther Fenchel through her sister, for, as I've said before, I haven't any grudge-bearing ability to speak of. But all at once Sophie wasn't even in it.

"What are you doing?" I said, turning to her. She had put on her shoes. I saw her hold up her arms and the black dress fell on her shoulders. She softly battled her body into it, pulled it into place across her breasts and over her hips, and shook her face free of her hair.

"Honey, if this is somebody you want to see . . ."

"But, Sophie, I'm with you tonight."

"You and me are just having a fling before I'm married, aren't we? Maybe you want to get married too. It's just an affair, isn't it?"

"You're not going," I said. But she didn't listen, and when she went on to tie her laces covered the underside of her thigh from me as she lifted her knee. Because I didn't sound firm enough. And through this act of covering her bare leg—not sore, but with a resigned sort of drop of her head—she drew back those vital degrees from lover's heat. To have her again I realized I'd have to pass a large number of tests and perhaps last of all I'd have to ask her to marry me. So I admitted in my private mind she was right to go since I couldn't any longer honestly furnish that gay interest that had brought us together.

A piece of paper slid under the door, and we heard Thea going away.

"At least she's not so brassy as to stand and look at me come out," said Sophie. "Anyway, she had plenty of brass to knock when she could tell you had company. Are you engaged to her or something? Go ahead and read your note."

Sophie took her congé and kissed me on the face but wouldn't let me return the kiss or accompany her down to the door. So, undressed still, I sat on the cot in the May night air of the high window and opened the piece of paper. It gave her address and number and said, "Please call me tomorrow, and don't be angry because of what I can't help."

When I thought how she had been ashamed for the jealousy rising to her face, and how rich in trouble the moment had been for her to hold fast while I came to the door naked and talked to her, I wasn't inclined to feel angry at all. In fact I couldn't help but be glad. Even though it was high-handed to go and proceed against Sophie as she did and assume that only she had the right grade of love. And then I had a lot of other notions, such as whether I was in danger of falling in love to oblige. Why? Because love was so rare that if one had it the other should capitulate to it? If, for the time, he had nothing more important on? In this thought there was a good measure of poking fun, with, however, the fact that I was stirred in all kinds of ways, including the soft shuffle in the treetop of leaves just broken out of the thick red beaks. I thought the business of a woman must be only love. Or, at another time, only a child. And I let this be an amusement and an objection in my light mind. And this lightness of mind —I could have benefited from the wisdom about it that the heavy is the root of the light. First, that is, that the graceful comes out of what is buried at great depth. But as wisdom has to spread and knot out in all directions, this can also refer to the slight laugh which is only a little of what is sent upward by great heaviness of heart, or also to the gravity which passes off by performer's flutter or pitch for laughs. Even the man who wants to believe, you sometimes note kidding his way to Jesus.

That night I fell deeply asleep, any old way, in and out of the sheets. They still smelled of Sophie's powder, or whatever she had imparted to them, so I slept wrapped in her banners, after a fashion. When I waked I thought it had been a peaceful sleep, and the early day was radiant. But I was mistaken. I remembered nightmares I had had of the jackals trying to get over the walls of Harar, Abyssinia, to eat the plague dead— from a book Arthur had left lying around, about one of his favorite poets. I heard Mimi below bitching and yelling at the telephone, though it was just some ordinary conversation. It was a fresh day, of beauty nearly material enough to pick up, with corners of the yard full of the heat of flowers grown in old iron and adapted cast-off boilers. That red which in the greater strength of the day would make you giddy and attack your heart with a power almost like a sickness, some sickness causing spat blood, spasm, and rot just as much and as rich as pleasure. My face prickled as if I had been hit sharp enough to cause nosebleed. I looked and felt puffy and sullen, and as if I had a surplus of blood and foresaw trouble from it, that it would have to be let. Also my hands and feet were that ominous way. I went out half stone, but even the pavement chafed me through the leather; my veins seemed slowed up with lead. I couldn't bear being in the confinement of the drugstore even for the minute of time it took to swallow a cup of coffee. I dragged myself to the office in the poky cars, and when I had fallen into my chair with my legs spread out, I felt the toil of all my processes, down to the arteries of the feet as they sprung and shot with regularity, and I prayed I wouldn't have to get up. The door and window were open, the fustiness of the hard-trod place having its brief chance to clear out in the courthouse-hung tranquillity before the resumption of hostilities, the meadow hour before the ashcan barrage of Flanders tears the skies. And the lark, who doesn't need to spit or clear his throat, goes up.

But then the business of the day got under way, and in my harassed inability to keep up, it was like a double-quick-time stamping or dancing; angry grim waltz in which the clutched partners were out to wear one another down; or solo clog or tarantella of the hopping mad; or the limper sway of the almost gone from consciousness; the decorous *sevillanas* of the stiff whose faces didn't betray how their heels were slamming; the epidemic kick of German serfdom; the squatting *kazatsky*; the hesitation-step of adolescence; the Charleston. I confronted all the varieties, and as far as I could I avoided rising. Except when I had to go to the biffy to take a leak, or when I thought I was hungry and ducked below to the billiard room and lunch counter, where the green of the felt went to my head. However, I had no appetite. It was another kind of gnawing, not emptiness of gut that was the matter.

When I went back there was a fresh crowd waiting to do their stuff. Me the weary booking agent or impresario, watched by them with wrath and avidity, with tics, with dignity by some and booby-hatch glares by others. And what was I going to accomplish for them in the way of redress and throwing open princedoms by explaining how they must fill out a card? Holy Lord and God! I know man's labor must be one of those deals figured out by Providence that saves him by preserving him, or he would be hungry, he would freeze, or his brittle neck would be broke. But what curious and strange forms he ends up surviving in, becoming them in the process.

It was in my unusual state of feeling that I reflected about this, and meantime when I would remember the rustle of

Thea's brown silk it made me shiver. Along with the strange outcomes of the history of toil.

Every chance I got I phoned her. There wasn't any answer, and Grammick reached me before I could talk to her. He had to have my help in South Chicago that night in a gauze and bandage factory he had organized more or less in passing. For it was like a band of Jesuits landing where a heathen people thirsted for baptism in the dense thousands, thronging out of their brick towns. I had to fill a bag with literature and blanks and race over to the Illinois Central to get the electric train and meet Grammick at his headquarters in a tavern, a rough place but with a ladies' and family entrance, for many of the gauze-winders were women. I can't say how they kept bandages clean in that sooty, plug-ugly town built as though so many fool amateur projects for the Tower of Babel that had got crippled at the second story a few dozen times and then all hands had quit and gone in for working in them instead. Grammick was in the middle of this show and busy organizing. He was as firm as a Stonewall Jackson, but he was also as perfectly pacific as a woodshop instructor in a high school or some personage of the Congress party, somebody from that white-flutter India setting out to conquer the whole place flat. By the power of meekness.

Most of the night we were up and were ready in the morning with everything necessary, committees on their mark, demands drawn up, negotiation machinery all set and the factions in agreement. At nine o'clock Grammick picked up the phone to talk to management. At eleven the negotiations were already under way, and late that night the strike was won and we went out to a wiener and sauerkraut shindy with the glad union members. It was all a matter of course to Grammick, though I was hopped up about it and full of congratulation.

I went to the booth in the back with my glass of beer and tried Thea's number again. This time I got through. I said, "Listen, I'm calling from out of town where I had to go on business, otherwise you would have heard from me before. But I expect to be back tomorrow."

"When?"

"Afternoon, I think."

"Can't you come sooner? Where are you now?"

"Out in the sticks, and I'm coming as soon as I can."

"But I don't have long to stay in Chicago."

"Do you have to go? But where?"

"Honey, I'll explain it when I see you. I'll wait in all day tomorrow. If you can't phone first, ring the doorbell three times."

Like a strong brush the excitement went over me, and I stood up to it with shut eyes of pleasure, heat snarls at the ears and thrills descending my legs. I was dying to get to her. But I wasn't able to leave yet. There were loose ends to tie up. It was important how even victors said au revoir. Grammick couldn't leave until he had arranged the bookkeeping and everything was in order. Then, when we got back to the city, I had to go with him to headquarters to report our success. This was to advance me too, and was to get a knockdown to Mr. Ackey and be a little thicker with the officials, not stay a supernumerary.

Ackey was waiting for us, not to congratulate us but with a redeployment order on his spindle. "Grammick," he said, asking him instead of me, "is this your protégé March? March," he went on, still not finding me with his eyes, as if the time wasn't just ripe, "you're going to have to do some serious trouble-shooting today, and right this minute. It's one of those hot dual-union situations. They're murder. The Northumberland Hotel—that's a ritzy place—how many people do we have signed up there? Not enough. They must have upward of two hundred and fifty in a place like that."

I said, "I think we have about fifty cards from the Northumberland, and most of those from chambermaids. But why, what's going on?"

"They're getting ready to strike, that's what. This morning there have been about five calls for you from Sophie Geratis, one of the maids. There's a strike meeting on right now in the linen room, and you get over there and stop them. The AFL is in there, and the thing to aim for is an election."

"Then what am I supposed to do?"

"Hold the line. You sign them up and keep them from going out. Quick now, there must be hell broke loose."

I snatched up my pack of membership blanks and lit out for

the Northumberland; a huge building, it was, with florid galleries and Roman awnings fluttering up to the thirtieth story and looking down at the growth of the elms and flaglike greens of Lincoln Park.

I flashed up in a Checker cab. There wasn't any doorman on duty; the place glittered from the copper arms swelling on shields from either side and from the four glasses of the revolving door and their gold monograms. I didn't think I'd get far by way of the lobby, and I hurried back to the alley and found a service entrance. Up three flights of steel stairs, as nobody answered the bell of the freight elevator, I heard yelling and tracked it through the corridors, now velvet, now cement, to this place, the linen room.

The fight that was going on was between those who were loyal to the recognized union and the rebellious, mostly the underpaid women, who were scalding mad about the last refusal to raise them from twenty cents an hour. All were in uniform or livery. The room was white and hot, right in the path of the sun, the doors open to the laundry, and the women in their service blues and in white caps shouted and spoiled for war and struggle. They stood on the metal tables and soap barrels and screamed for the walkout. I looked for Sophie, who saw me first. She cried, "Here's the organizer. Here's the man. Here comes March!" She was on top of one of the hogsheads, with her gams wide apart in their black stockings. Hot, but grim and pale, and her black hair covered by the cap, her excitement of the eyes was all the blacker. She tried to express no familiarity in them toward me, so no scrutiny could have found out that our arms ever had crossed or hands ever stroked up and down.

I looked around and could see my friends and enemies in a minute, jeering or urging, distrustful, partisan, indignant, crying. There was one gaffer dressed up as white as any intern, and a face on him like Tecumseh, or one of the painted attackers of Schenectady; he wanted right away to explain a strategy to me, being very deliberate in that birdhouse of tropical screaming and laundry heat, to say nothing of the whiteness of the sun.

"Now wait," I called, taking Sophie's place on the hogshead.

Some began to yell, "We strike!"

"Now please listen. It won't be legal—"

"Oh, the hell! Cry-eye! What's legal, that we get a buck and a half a day? What's there after carfare and union dues? Do we eat? We're just going to walk out."

"No, you don't want to do that. It would be a wildcat strike. The Federation guys would send other people to take your place and it would be legal. The thing to do is sign with us so there can be an election, and when we win we can represent you."

"Or if you win. That's again a few months."

"But it's the best you can do."

I broke open a bundle of cards from my bag and was distributing them into the waving hands when suddenly a bulge started from the direction of the laundry; several men were fighting through the crowd; thrusting away the women, and the joint began to jump. Just as I realized that these were the enemy union guy and his goons I was grabbed from behind, off the barrel, and slugged as I landed, in the eye and on the nose. I burst into blood. My buddy with the Indian's beak stepped on me, but that was in his rush at the guy who hit me. As he pushed him back a Negro chambermaid raised me. Sophie thrust her hand into my pocket and pulled out my handkerchief.

"Dirty gangsters! Honey, don't worry. Throw your head back."

There was now a ring of women guarding me, formed around the overturned barrel. When one of the sluggers made a start for me there was a lunge of the women for that place. Some had picked up scissors, knives, soap scoops, so the union guy called off his gorillas, and they came to position around him, who was small by contrast but dangerous-looking, if a runt, in his snappy man-about-town suit and his Baltimore heater. He appeared like somebody from the sheriff's office who had changed to the other side of the law; or from cat meat to human flesh. He seemed as if he would smell at close quarters like a drinking man, but that was perhaps the color of rage and not of whisky in him. Of unpreventable meanness, able to harm as much as he threatened. I could somewhat show that with those bursts of blood on my noserag and shirt, and snorting out more, while my stinging eye swelled to a slit. However, he was the one who had the law on his side, being the representative under contract of these people.

"Now, ladies, get out of the way and let my men take over this punk who got no business here. He's breakin' Acts of Congress and I could swear a warrant against him. Besides the hotel could jug him for trespassin'."

The women screamed and showed their scissors and weapons, and the Negro woman, who sounded like a West Indian or some Empire Britisher, said, "Never, you bloody little peanut!" So, while scared, I was also astonished.

"That's okay, sister, we'll get him," said one of the goons. "He can't go everywhere with this nooky protection."

His boss told him, "Whyn't you shut your trap!" And he said to me, "What right you got to come here?"

"I was asked here."

"Damn right he was! You bet we asked him!" While the cooks in their long hats and others of the better-off faction hollered and scoffed and held noses and pulled the imaginary toilet chain at me.

"Listen, you-all. I'm your representative. When there's any beefs, what am I for?"

"To throw us out when we come to the hall to ask you something, while your feet are on the table and you're drinking from the bottle and pickin' horses!"

"There doesn't have to be any goddam mutiny, does there? Now I see a lot of cards this sonofabitch meddler passed around, and I want you all to tear 'em up and have no more truck with him and them."

I said, "Don't do it!"

The guy who had slugged me made a pass to push through the defense of women and they heaved against him. Sophie pulled me away, through the back and along service corridors. "There's a firedoor back here," she said. "You can get down the escape. Take care, honey, they'll be after you now."

"What about you?"

"What can they do me?"

"You'd better forget about striking for the time being."

Drawing strongly, her feet planted wide apart, she hauled

open the ponderous firedoor, and as I went out she said, "Augie, you and me will never get together again, will we?"

"I think not, Sophie. There is this other girl."

"Good-by, then."

I hustled down the hot black fire-escape frames and swung from the ladder, jumped, and when I made a choice of streets to run to I had no luck. One of the goons was there; he came for me, and I took off toward Broadway. I flinched from the shots he might have taken, that not being unknown in Chicago, that people should be knocked off in the street. But there was no noise of any gun, and I reckoned that his object was to work me over, finish the beating, break bones perhaps; and lay me up.

I had just enough of a lead on the slugger to get across Broadway before him. I saw him, waist up, stopped by traffic, his eyes still on me, and I breathed on the dry snot of fear in my blood-clotted nose. A streetcar making slow time came by, and I sprang to the platform. I was sure to be followed, because of the slow cumbersomeness of the car approaching the Loop. But I might be able to shake him in the crowds. Meanwhile I rode in the front with the motorman, where I could watch the length of the car and also had within reach the switch-iron that motormen lower through a hole in the floorboards. I could be sure the slugger was coming on behind in one of the taxis in the file of cars fluddering and shimmering off their blue gas stink in this dull hot brute shit of a street. I was harrowed by my hate for it, as well as for the creeping of the trolley. I was torn up and sick with it. But gradually the bridge approached and the towers, all series and the same from top to bottom, the river of washwater filth and the bone-nosed gulls. The car picked up speed over the clear of the bridge and came down the swoop with heavy liberty, but then crept again in the Loop and its crush of traffic. I waited until near Madison Street, and in the middle of the block I said to the motorman, "Off here!"

"This ain't the stop."

I said, raging, "Open it up or I'll bust your head open," and when he saw the ugliness of my face and the chink of my eye he let me get off and I ran for it, but ran only to turn the corner and lose myself. I took the chance of getting into a line moving rapidly at the McVickers where there was a Garbo picture, and inside the thick red cords that looped off in-going from departing crowds, and in the lobby, which was like an apartment Cagliostro and Seraphina had laid out to fuddle the court and royalty, I was out of danger for the time. I was anyway beginning to feel that if he trapped me now it might be dangerous for him too, as for the overseer killed by Moses. I went down to the can and vomited up my breakfast. Bathing off the blood, I dried at the electric blower. Then I went up and lay in one of the seats at the back of the house where I could watch who entered, and there I rested until the end of the show and next change of audience, when I went out too, straight to the middle of the street, which was roaring and flinging up hot midday dust.

I jumped into a taxi and drove to Thea's, which had been my real objective of days.

Chapter XIV

I WAS HURRYING to fulfill the prophecy Thea Fenchel had made on that swing in St. Joe. And while it was no minor thing to me that I was beat up and chased like this, I couldn't feel the importance of the cause much, or that it would benefit anyone for me to fight on in it. If I had felt this as such a matter of conscience I might have been out in front of Republic Steel at the hour of the Decoration Day Massacre, as Grammick was. He was clubbed on the head. But I was with Thea. It wasn't even in my power to be elsewhere, once we had started. No, I just didn't have the calling to be a union man or in politics, or any notion of my particle of will coming before the ranks of a mass that was about to march forward from misery. How would this will of mine have got there to lead the way? I couldn't just order myself to become one of those people who do go out before the rest, who stand and intercept the big social ray, or collect and concentrate it like burning glass, who glow and dazzle and make bursts of fire. It wasn't what I was meant to be.

As I ran into Thea's apartment house from the cab and rang the bell three times, fast, I didn't especially observe where I had come. It was a showy, heavily furnished lobby, no one in it, and as I was trying to find out which of the elegant doors belonged to the elevator, a square of light appeared in one of them. Thea had come down for me. The door opened. There was a velvet bench and we sank down on it, pressing and kissing as the smooth elevator rose. Not noticing the blood-stiffened shirt, she passed her hand over my chest and up to my shoulders. I opened her housecoat on her breasts. I was not in control of my head. I was unaware, nearly blind. If anyone else had been near neither of us would have known it. I can't for certain say I don't remember a face, maybe that of a maid when the door opened, and we went on embracing in the corridor and then in the apartment, by the door, on the carpet.

With Thea it wasn't at all as it had been with other women, those who gave you their permission, so to speak, to undo one thing at a time and admire it, the next thing guarded again, and the last thing most guarded of all. She didn't delay, or seem to hurry either. As if studying deeply from a surrendered mind, and with the lips, the hands and hair, the rising bosom and legs, without the use of any force, presently it seemed as if an exchange or transfer had happened of us both into still another person who hadn't existed before. There was a powerful feeling of love. And so finally, as if I had been on my bent knees in what's supposed to be an entirely opposite spirit, praying, with my fingers pressed together, I think it would have been no different from what I felt come over me with the fingers not together but touching her on the breasts instead. My bursting face with the swatted eye lay between, and her arms were around my neck.

Now the sun began to heat us by the door, on the rug where we were lying. It had the same filmy whiteness as it had in the linen room. It had shone dirtier on the Loop sidewalk where I jumped from the streetcar. Here it glowed white once more. Presently I wanted to pull the curtain because of the glare on my eye, and when I stood up she observed for the first time how I looked.

"Who did that to you?" she cried.

I explained the whole business to her, and she kept saying, "Is that why you didn't come? Is that what you were doing all that time?" The time lost was the most important thing of all to her. Although it gave her a tremor to look straight at my bruise, the specific reason for my being beaten didn't interest her and she wasn't very curious about it. Yes, she had heard of the big union drive, but that I was in it was sort of irrelevant. For while I was not with her, where I was intended to be, it didn't make much difference where I was. All intervening things and interferences were of the same unreal kind and belonged—out there. Gauze-winders, hotel workers on strike, errors like my illusion about her sister, that farce of being taken for Mrs. Renling's gigolo, all that Thea had herself done meanwhile, these were entirely "out there." The reality was now, and in here; she had followed it by instinct since St. Joe. So this was the reason for the cry of all that time lost and it made me feel what her fear was like of never succeeding in finding her way from the "out there" but blundering forever.

Of course I didn't grasp this right away. It came out during the next few days, during which we stayed in the apartment. We slept and woke, and we didn't really discuss my doings or hers. Suitcases were standing around the bed, but I didn't ask about them. It was just as well that I didn't go out, for the hoodlums were looking to make an object lesson of me. Grammick told me when I got around to phoning him.

Other women I had known—well, I didn't blame them that I loved them less than Thea. Only it was through her that I began to learn somewhat about the reasons behind my opinions. There were some people who were too slow in their life, because of fatigue, unwillingness, hardship, sorrow, mistrust; and some were too fast out of other trouble or desperation. But as far as I was concerned, Thea had perfect life. So that any no-account thing, such as her walking to the kitchen or bending to pick up an object from the floor, when I would see the shape of her back, her spine, or the soft departure of her breasts, or her brush, made my soul topple over. I loved her to the degree that anything she chanced to do was welcome to me. I was very happy. And when she was going about the room and I lay stretched and occupied so much of her bed with my body, I was about like a king, as to the pleasure of my face, looking on, watching her.

Her face was paler than I had remembered, but then I hadn't observed it so well before. Some pains of life were in it too, sure enough, when you looked close, though just at present her eyes were relatively clear of them. She had black hair. The roots came a little unevenly from her forehead, upward, beautiful at that. You had to look well to notice this eccentricity. Her eyes were most dark. She often applied rouge to her mouth from a little tube on the bed table as though feeling she had to stay adorned at least that way, with the carnation color, and a fire smudge came off on the pillows and on me.

Now, when I had called in from South Chicago, Thea had told me she didn't have much time, she would have to leave soon. And the first few days, as I've said, she didn't speak of it, but eventually the open suitcases brought up the subject and she told me that she had been, and legally still was, married, and she was on her way from Long Island to Mexico to get a divorce. Afraid to hurt my feelings, all she'd say at the

outset was that her husband was considerably older than either of us and was very rich. But gradually more came out.
He flew a Stinson plane, he had tons of ice dumped in his private lake when it became lukewarm in July, he went on Canadian hunting trips, he wore cufflinks worth fifteen hundred
dollars, he sent to Oregon for apples and they cost him forty
cents apiece, he cried because he was growing bald so quickly,
etcetera. Whatever she said was chosen to prove she didn't
love him. But I wasn't very jealous. I guess because he had
lost out there was no cause. Esther also was married and to a
man rich as all get-out, a lawyer in Washington, D.C. This
rung very foreign to me, as she didn't quite observe—the
planes, the hunting, and the colossal cliffs of dough. Thea too
traveled with sports equipment—breeches, boots, gun cases,
cameras; in the can I had by chance turned on an infra-red
bulb that she used for developing films, and in the bathtub
were pans with fluid and unfamiliar pipes and gizmos.

Well, during this talk it was evening beside the window. We
were at the table, having just eaten supper, which was ordered
by phone. There was a watermelon rind, chicken bones, and
so on. She was telling me about her husband, but all I could
think of was my luck, at this point and hour as she was leaning her head on the curtain, and on her own hands behind
her just by the open window and its shadow of blue which
cleared the trees and then got paler. The trees grew in the
little yard, which was covered with white gravel. Some big insect flew in and began walking on the table. I don't know
what insect it was, but it was brown, shining, and rich in
structures. In the city the big universal chain of insects gets
thin, but where there's a leaf or two it'll be represented. And
then beneath us the dinner dishwater was splashing in an
apartment; and over toward Hell's Kitchen, from a couple of
belfries like the twin points of the black leathery sand-shark
egg-cases you find on beaches, the sound of bells went out.
This Roman-twilight firing or mild shelling the targets
scarcely even heard for the sloshing of the tapwater and the
conk of china. I was wearing one of her bathrobes and my
legs were stretched under the table from a silk armchair, and
on an occasion like this, as glad as I was, what was I going to
do, be envious of her husband whom she had left?

Since I had come near being Lucy Magnus's husband, I understood why Thea had married at the same time as her sister and to the same sort of man. Though she could be ironical about them now, I found out later that she had a weakness for being successful in social circles like this man Smith's, or at least she liked to feel she outclassed the women from those Boston or Virginia families. Which was a department of rivalry I didn't know much about.

She assumed that I'd go to Mexico with her, and I never seriously thought of refusing. I knew I didn't have what it took, of pride, or of a strong feeling of duty, to ask her to come back another time when I was ready, or at least in better position, honorably quits with the union, or when I could at least pay my own way. I said I had no money, and she answered seriously, "Take what you need from the refrigerator." She was in the habit of leaving the dough she got in change from the delivery men and also checks and so forth in the refrigerator. The money was mixed up with rotting salad leaves and lying with saucers of bacon grease, which she didn't like to throw away. Anyway, the fives and tenners were there, and I was to pick up what I needed on the way out, as a man takes a handkerchief from his drawer on slight thought.

I had a conversation with Grammick to ask him to step into my place at the Northumberland. He already had done what he could. There was no wildcat strike. He said the union guy and his boys were really gunning for me, to lay low. When I told him I was quitting and leaving town he was surprised. However, I explained about Thea, that I absolutely had to go with her, and he appeared to take it better. He said it was a lousy deal anyway to be stuck in these dual-union situations, and the organization ought to put on a real drive in the hotel field or quit.

Thea outfitted me before the trip. In which connection, for some reason, I get the picture something like the Duke of Wellington stepping out in the dress of the Salisbury Hunt, blue coat, black cap, and buckskins. Maybe this is because Thea had such very exact ideas as to what I should put on. We went from shop to shop in the station wagon to try on clothes. When she thought a thing was right she kissed me and cried, "Oh, baby, you make me happy!" unmindful of all the stiffness in the salespeople and the other customers. When I picked something she didn't like she'd give a laughing start and say, "Oh, you *fool!* Take it off. That's like what the old lady in Evanston thought was so smart." The clothes Simon had given me she disliked too. She wanted me to look like a sportsman, and she got me a heavy leather jacket at Von Lengerke and Antoine's that required you to want to kill game or you couldn't wear it. It was a knockout, with a dozen different kinds of pockets and slits for cartridges and handline, knife, waterproof matches, compass. You could be thrown in the middle of Lake Huron in it and hope to live. Then for boots we crossed Wabash Avenue to Carson's, where I hadn't gone since Jimmy Klein trapped me that bad moment in the revolving doors.

In these joints it was she who did the talking. Mostly silent, feeling full of blood, I came up smiling to try on the things and walk inside the triple mirror to let her turn me by the shoulder and see. I was glad over her least peculiarity—that she spoke high, that she didn't care that her slip showed a loop from her brilliant green dress, or that there were hairs on her neck that had escaped the gathering of the comb, hairs of Japanese blackness. Her dresses were expensive, but, as I had noticed her hat trembling when she had come up to my room, there never lacked one piece of disorder caused by excitement, and where arrangement failed.

Going through this, being kissed in the stores and the purchases and gifts, my luck didn't make me hangdog, I'll say that for myself. If she had handed me titles and franchises like Elizabeth to Leicester it wouldn't have caused me awkwardness; nor would wearing feathers, instead of the deep Stetson that pleased her. So the checks, plaids, chamois, suedes, or high boots that made me come out on Wabash Avenue like a tall visitor or tourist were no embarrassment but made me laugh and even be somewhat vain, putting on like a stranger in my own home town.

She was cuckoo about dime stores, where she bought cosmetics and pins and combs. After we locked the expensive purchases in the station wagon we went into McCrory's or Kresge's and were there by the hour, up and down the aisles with the multitude, mostly of women, and in the loud-played love music. Some things Thea liked to buy cheaply; they maybe gave her the best sense of the innermost relations of pennies and nickels and expressed the real depth of money. I don't know. But I didn't think myself too good to be wandering in the dime store with her. I went where and as she said and did whatever she wanted because I was threaded to her as if through the skin. So that any trifling object she took pleasure in could become important to me at once; anything at all, a comb or hairpin or piece of line, a compass inside a tin ring that she bought with great satisfaction, or a green-billed baseball cap for the road, or the kitten she kept in the apartment—she would never be anywhere without an animal. This little striped and spike-tailed tom, like a cat of the sea in the wide darkness of the floors of those rooms of the suite that Thea never used. She rented a big place and then settled in a space-economizing style, gathering and piling things around her. There were plenty of closets and dressers but she was still living out of the suitcases, boxes, cases, and you had to approach the bed at the center of this confusion through spaces between. She used sheets as towels and towels as shoe rags or mats or to wipe the kitten's messes, for it wasn't housebroken. She gave the maids bribes of perfume and stockings to clean up, wash the dishes, underclothes, and do other extras; or maybe she did it so that they wouldn't criticize her disorderliness. She thought she was first-rate with clerks and servants. I, the ex-organizer, didn't say anything.

It didn't matter. I let a lot of things go past. Those days, whatever touched me had me entirely, and whatever didn't was like dead, my heart not giving it a tumble. I was never before so taken up with a single human being. I followed her sense wherever it went. As I wasn't yet old enough to be tired of confinement to my own sense, I didn't appreciate this enough.

What I did at times realize was how I was abandoning some mighty old protections which now stood empty. Hadn't I been warned enough because of my mother, and on my own account? With terrible warnings? Look out! Oh, you chump and weak fool, you are one of a humanity that can't be numbered and not more than the dust of metals scattered in a magnetic field and clinging to the lines of force, determined by laws, eating, sleeping, employed, conveyed, obedient, and subject. So why hunt for still more ways to lose liberty? Why go toward, and not instead run from, the huge drag that threatens to wear out your ribs, rub away your face, splinter your teeth? No, stay away! Be the wiser person who crawls, rides, runs, walks to his solitary ends used to solitary effort, who procures for himself and heeds the fears that are the kings of this world. Ah, they don't give you much of a break, these kings! Many a dead or dying face lies or drifts under them.

Here Thea appeared with her money, her decided mind set on love and great circumstances, her car, her guns and Leicas and boots, her talk about Mexico, her ideas. One of the chiefest of these ideas being that there must be something better than what people call reality. Oh, well and good. Very good and bravo! Let's have this better, nobler reality. Still, when such an assertion as this is backed by one person and maintained for a long time, obstinacy finally gets the upper hand. The beauty of it is harmed by what it suffers on the way to proof. I know that.

However, Thea had one superiority in her ideas. She was one of those people who are so certain of their convictions that they can fight for them in the body. If the threat to them goes against their very flesh and blood, as with people who are examined naked by police or with martyrs, you soon know which beliefs have strength and which do not. So that you don't speak air. For what you don't suffer in your person is mostly dreaminess, or like shots of light, sky-sprinkling fireworks and creamy wheels that scatter to a sad earth. Thea was prepared for the extremest test of her thoughts.

Not that she herself was always on her own highest standard. I had to accept her version of everything, this being the obstinacy of assertion I spoke of. Also it was evident that she was used to having what she wanted, including me. Her behavior was sometimes curious and crude. When certain long-distance calls came through she'd just about order me out of the room, and then I could hear her yelling and be startled, astonished that she could have a voice like that. I couldn't catch the words and could only speculate as to the reasons. Then how I'd criticize her if I weren't her lover would come to me.

She assumed she understood everything about me, and it was astonishing how much she did know; the remainder she made up with confidence and trusted to closed eyes and fast strokes. She therefore said some harsh and jealous things and her look occasionally was more brilliant than friendly. She was aware of her weakness in having come after me—in her confident moments she thought of it instead as strength and was proud of it.

"Did you like that Greek girl?"

"Yes, sure I did."

"Was it just the same with her as with me?"

"No."

"I can tell you're just lying, Augie. Of course it was the same for you."

"Don't you find it different with me? Am I like your husband?"

"Like him? Never!"

"Well, can it be so different for you and not also for me? You think I can put it on and not love you?"

"Oh, but I came to look for you, not you for me. I had no pride"—she was forgetting that I scarcely knew her in St. Joe. "You were getting tired of this little Greek chambermaid, and I happened to show up, and it flattered you so much you couldn't resist. You like to get bouquets like that." And now, to say this, made her breathe with labor; she was suffering. "You want people to pour love on you, and you soak it up and swallow it. You can't get enough. And when another woman runs after you, you'll go with her. You're so happy when somebody begs you to oblige. You can't stand up under flattery!"

Maybe so. But what I couldn't stand up under at the moment was this glare, when she went so hot and white in the face with its strong nerve and metaphysical reckless assertion. Although she painted her mouth with carnation lipstick she didn't make it sensual, nor did she have a sensual face, but any excitement, no matter what it was, took up her person, her entire being. It was the same whether she was angry or when she was loving and had her breasts against me, clasping hands, touching feet. So even if this jealousy made no sense, still it wasn't play-acting jealousy.

"If I'd been wise enough I'd have come for you," I said. "I just didn't have enough sense, so I'm grateful that you did. And you don't have to be afraid."

No, no, what did I want with the upper hand or pride contests? None of that stuff. When she heard me speak like this there was a tremor in her features of the strain passing off; she shrugged and smiled at herself and a more normal color began to appear.

Not only was she accustomed to independence struggles and to resistance, to going counter to the open direction of everyone else, which made her judgments severe, but she was in many ways suspicious. Her experience was, socially, much wider than mine, and so she suspected many things which at the time were out of my range. She must have remembered that when we met I seemed an old woman's hanger-on who sponged on her and maybe worse than that. Of course she knew better. What she knew of me by now, *really* knew, was plenty from information I gave freely. Because involuntarily. But so was her habitual shrewdness involuntary, the shrewd suspiciousness of a rich girl. And then, once you've irrevocably made up your mind, does that mean you don't sweat and fear you can be wrong? Even Thea with her convictions and confidence wasn't immune to occasional fits of doubt.

"What makes you say these things about me, Thea?" They bothered me. Certainly there was some truth in them; I felt it in my lining, somewhere, like an object that had slipped down out of the pocket.

"Aren't they right? Especially about your being so obliging?"

"Well, partly. I used to be much more so. But not so much now." I tried to tell her that I had looked all my life for the right thing to do, for a fate good enough, that I had opposed people in what they wanted to make of me, but now that I was in love with her I understood much better what I myself wanted.

But what she had to answer was this: "What makes me say these things is that I see how much you care about the way people look at you. It matters too much to you. And there are people who take advantage of that. They haven't got anything of their own and they'll leave you nothing for yourself. They want to put themselves in your thoughts and in your mind, and that you should care for them. It's a sickness. But they don't want you to care for them as they really are. No. That's the whole stunt. You have to be conscious of them, but not as they are, only as they love to be seen. They live through observation by the ones around them, and they want you to live like that too. Augie, darling, don't do it. They will make you suffer from what they are. And you don't really matter to them. You only matter when someone loves you. You matter to me. Otherwise you don't matter, you're only *dealt* with. So you shouldn't care how you seem to them. But you do, you care too much."

She went on like this. It was bitter sometimes, for usually her wisdom was against me. As if she foresaw that I'd do her wrong and was warning me. But then, too, I was eager to hear what she said and I understood it, I understood only too well.

These conversations we had more often on the road when we set out for Mexico.

She had several times tried to tell me what we would do in Mexico besides obtaining her divorce, and she seemed to assume that I knew intuitively what her plans were. I frequently was confused. I couldn't tell whether she owned or rented a house in the town of Acatla, and what she described of the country didn't make me altogether happy. It sounded like a risky place when she talked of the mountains, hunting, diseases, robbery, and the dangerous population. I wasn't clear for a long time about the hunting. I thought she intended to hunt eagles, and that seemed peculiar to me, but what I understood wasn't so peculiar as what she really meant. She wanted to hunt *with* an eagle trained in falconry, and as she had owned hawks she was eager to imitate a British captain and an American couple who had taught or "manned" golden and American eagles, some of the few since the Middle Ages. She had gotten the idea for this hunt from reading articles by Dan and Julie Mannix, who actually had gone to Taxco some years before with a trained bald eagle and used the bird to catch iguanas.

Near Texarkana there was a man who had eaglets to sell. He had offered one to George H. Somebody-or-other, an old friend of Thea's father, who kept a private zoo. This friend of her father, who by the accounts she gave seemed to me loony, like the mad King Ludwig of Bavaria, had built himself a copy of the Trianon in Indiana, only with cages inside, and had made Hagenbeck voyages everywhere to fill them with beasts of his own capture. He was in retirement now, too old to travel; but he had asked Thea to bring him some giant iguanas—or challenged her to—these huge furious lizards, mesozoic holdouts in the mountains south of Mexico City. As this information came out, which I didn't know how seriously to take, I thought this was like me and my life—I could not find myself in love without it should have some peculiarity.

I'm not going to say that she was more than I had bargained for, because it has to be absolutely understood that I didn't bargain. What I will say is that she was singular, unforeseen, and contradictory in her flightiness, steadiness, nervousness, or courage. When she tripped on the stairs in the dark she cried out, but she traveled with snake-catching equipment and she showed me snapshots of the outings of a rattler-collectors' club she had belonged to. I saw her holding a diamondback behind the head and milking the poison from him with a slice of rubber. She told me how she had crawled into a cave after him. In Renling's shop I had sold sports equipment, but the only hunting I had ever watched was in the movies, apart from having seen my brother Simon shooting at the rats in his yard with his pistol. My special memory was of one large one with humped back like a small boar but terrible, swift-clawed feet racing for the fence. I was, however, ready even to become a hunter. Thea took me out into the country before we left Chicago, and I practiced shooting at crows.

This was while we held over in Chicago a few days longer; she was waiting for a letter from Smitty's—her husband's—lawyer and used the time to give me lessons with the guns in the woods off toward the Wisconsin line. When we came home and she took off her breeches and sat in her out-of-doors shirt with bare legs, she might take up a piece of costume jewelry to fix the clasp and sit like a girl of ten, in a rapt way, her neck bent and knees up, her fingers kind of clumsy. Then we'd ride on the Lincoln Park bridle path, and there

was nothing clumsy about her there. I hadn't forgotten how
to manage a horse since my Evanston days. But that was what
it was, managing rather than riding. I followed her speed as
fast as I could, red in the face and hitting the saddle hard, using my weight against the animal. I managed to stay on, but
how I did it amused her.

I was amused, too, when I caught my breath and climbed
down from the saddle, but asked myself just how many new
adaptations I was going to have to try to make. Along with
the snapshots of the Rattlesnake Club I saw others; she had a
leather case full of them. Some were of that very summer in
St. Joe when I met her, of her uncle and aunt, her sister Esther and sports in white pants with tennis rackets and pad-
dling canoes. When she showed me Esther's picture it didn't
touch me except through her resemblance to Thea. There
were photos also of her parents. Her mother had been a lover
of the Pueblos, so there she was, sitting in a touring car in a
hat and furs, looking at the cliffs. One picture in particular
took my attention. It was of her father in a rikshaw. He wore
a white drill suit and a helmet with a nipple, his eyes also
whitish, the influence of the sun whose spottiness made the
wheels seem like tea-soaked lemon. He looked over the
shaved head of the Chinese human horse who stood with
thick wide calves between the shafts.

Then there were more pictures of hunting. Some of Thea
with different falcons on her gloved arm. Several of Smitty,
her husband. In riding pants. At play, wrangling with a dog.
Or again with Thea in a night club—she laughed with eyes
closed in the flash of the bulb and he covered his bald head
with slender fingers while an entertainer flung arms out over
the table. Many of these things troubled me. For instance, in
her laughter at the night club I saw the bosom, shoulder,
chin, with kind of a happy recognition, but the hands of
ridicule and squawk of limelight laughter—no, those were
foreign. There was no place for me, there, by the table. Nor
by her father in the rikshaw. Nor by the mother in the touring car with the fur about her neck. And then the hunting
troubled me. I didn't know how earnestly I was to take it.
Banging at crows, fine, that was okay. But when she bought
me a gauntlet so I could handle the eagle, and I put it on, a

strange sense came over me as if I were a fielder in a demons' game and would have to gallop here and there and catch burning stone in the air.

So I was very uncertain. Not as to whether I should go with her, which was no decision since I had to, but as to what to expect, what I'd have to go through or put up as my share, where we were headed. To explain it sensibly to anyone was more than I was capable of. I tried. Mimi, who should have been the one best able to sympathize, was just the friend with whom I had most awkwardness about it. She didn't like it a bit and said, "Now what are you trying to tell me?" unwilling to believe I was, as I said, in love, and the skin of her forehead thickened and drew along her upshot brows. As I explained in more detail she laughed in my face. "What, what, *what!* You have an eagle to pick up in Arkansas? An eagle? Don't you mean a buzzard?" From loyalty to Thea I didn't laugh; Mimi couldn't get me to, even if the queerness of the expedition worried me plenty. "Where did you find a babe like this?"

"Mimi, I love her."

This made her take another, nearer look at me, which showed me to be in earnest. And Mimi thought so much of the seriousness of love she doubted there were many who could get it right, and, soberer, she said, "Watch out you don't get in trouble. And why are you quitting your job? Grammick told me you had a future as an organizer."

"I don't want any more of that. Arthur can have it."

As if she thought I spoke of Arthur with disrespect she said, "Don't be silly. He has to finish those translations, and he's working very hard; he's in the middle of an essay on the poet and death," and she began to tell me how poets must be allowed to run funerals. Arthur was installed in my room, and he had discovered the fire-ruined set of Dr. Eliot's classics in the old box under the bed and asked to be allowed to take care of it for me. Since the books were stamped "W. Einhorn," it would have been hard to refuse even if I had wanted to. Meanwhile he was in a cure for his clap, and Mimi watched over him and could have only side concerns about anybody else.

It was easy to explain my going off to Mama. Of course I didn't have to tell her much, only that I was engaged to a young lady who had to go to Mexico, and that I was going too.

Though Mama no longer did kitchen work, the knife marks in her hands had stayed, and there probably always would be those dark lines; so, also, her color still was gentle, but her eyes increasingly cloudy and her lower lip expressed continually less sense. I suppose what I said was pretty well indifferent to her, as long as the tone of it didn't distress her. That was what she listened to. And why should it distress her, since I was riding high and in the best silks and colors? Say if the main bonds of attachment were death ropes, crazy, in the end, at least I felt them now as connections of joy, and if that was a deception it would never appear more substantial or marvelous. But I denied it would be a deception, unless nothing so vivid can be substantial. No, I wouldn't admit that.

"Is she a rich girl, like Simon's wife?"

I thought perhaps she believed Thea was Lucy Magnus.

"This isn't any of Charlotte's family, Ma."

"Well, then don't let her make you unhappy, Augie," she said. And what lay behind this, I believe, was that if Simon hadn't helped me to choose, if I had picked for myself, my mother thought me to be sufficiently like her to get myself in a bad fix. I said nothing of the hunting to her, but it did occur to me how it was inevitable for the son of a Hagar to go chase wild animals at one time or another.

I asked about Simon. The only recent news I had of him was from Clem Tambow, who had seen him in a fistfight with a Negro on Drexel Boulevard.

"He bought a new Cadillac car," said Mama, "and he came to give me a ride. Oh, it's wonderful! He's going to be a very rich fellow."

It didn't hurt me to hear of him in prosperity, and even if he was Duke of Burgundy, let him go ahead and be it. But I have to admit that I couldn't keep down the satisfaction of the thought that Thea was an heiress too. I don't want to pretend that I could.

I looked up Padilla too before I left, and found him in front of his institute. He was in a blood-spotted lab coat, although he was hired to do calculations, as far as I knew, not experiments, and he smoked one of his stinking dark-tobacco cigarettes while in his swift way he debated about two curves with a character who held open a big looseleaf notebook.

Padilla wasn't so terribly pleased that I was bound for Mexico, and he warned me not to go near Chihuahua, his province. He said that in Mexico City, where he himself had never been, he had a cousin, whose address I took. "If he'll rob you or help I can't predict, but look him up if you want somebody to look up," he said. "He was piss-poor fifteen years ago when he went away. He sent me a postcard last year when I got my M.A. Which maybe means that he wants me to send for him. Fat chance! Well, enjoy your trip, if they let you, but don't tell me afterward I didn't warn you to stay home." Suddenly he smiled in the sunshine and creased his short curved nose and forehead which sloped backward into his handsome Mexican hair. "Go easy with that wild native tail." I couldn't even grin at him to be sociable, it was such inappropriate advice to a man in love.

Nobody, then, gave the happy *bon voyage* I'd have liked. Everybody warned me, in some way, and I even thought of Eleanor Klein and what Jimmy had told me of her being rooked there in Mexico, and her mishaps. I argued back to myself that it was just the Rio Grande I had to cross, not the Acheron, but anyway it oppressed me from somewhere. Really, it was the strangeness of the state I was in and not so much that of the destination I was aware of. The great astonishment of this state was that the unit of humanity should maybe be not one but two. Not even the eagle falconry distressed me as much as that what happened to her had to happen to me too, necessarily. This was scary.

This trouble of course wasn't clear to me then. I put it all on Mexico and the hunting. And finally I said to Thea, on an evening while she was playing the guitar—with a rounded-back thumb on the hind string; she treated the instrument easily and it supplied its own strength—I said, "Do we have to go to Mexico?"

"Do we have to?" she said and shut off the strings with her hand.

"You can get a quick divorce in Reno and in other places."

"But why shouldn't we go to Mexico? I've been there several times, many times. What's wrong with it?"

"But what's wrong with other places?"

"There's a house down in Acatla, and we're going there to

catch some of those lizards and other animals. Besides, I've arranged with Smitty's lawyer to be divorced there. And there's still another reason why it's better for us to be there."

"What's that?"

"I won't have much money after the divorce."

I shut my eyes and put my palm on my forehead as if trying to help the sudden astonishment go through. "Well, Thea, excuse me if I don't follow you. I thought you and Esther had lots of money. What about the stuff in the ice-box?"

"Augie, our part of the family never did have very much. It's my uncle, my father's brother, who's rich, and Esther and I are the only kin, and we always had allowances and were brought up in the money, but we were supposed to make good. Esther did; she married a rich man."

"And so did you."

"But it's over, and I may as well tell you there was a scandal about it. It isn't anything you should mind, it was just foolishness, but I took off from a party with a naval cadet. He looked just like you. It didn't amount to anything. I was thinking of you all the time, but you weren't there."

"A substitute!"

"Well, that Greek girl wasn't even that for you."

"I never said I spent all the time since we were in St. Joseph thinking about you."

"Nor about Esther?"

"No."

"Do you want to argue, or do you want to hear? I'm only trying to explain what happened. My aunt was visiting us— you remember the old lady—and the party was at our house, at Smitty's house. And she saw how this kid and I were petting. Augie, you really don't have to mind that. It was thousands of miles away and I didn't realize that I was going to come to Chicago to look for you. But I couldn't take Smitty any more. I had to have somebody else. Even if it was only just another boy, like that Navy boy. After that my old aunt went home, and my uncle talked to me long-distance and told me I was on probation with him. And that's one more reason why I have to go to Mexico, to make some money."

"With the eagle?" I cried out. Many kinds of things were

disturbing me. "How do you expect to make anything with an eagle! Even if he catches those blasted lizards or whatever you mean. Holy smokes!"

"It isn't just the lizards. We're also going to make movies of hunting. I have to capitalize on the things I know how to do. We can sell articles about it to the *National Geographic.*"

"How do you know we can? And who can write them?"

"We'll have the material and find somebody to help us. There's always such a person wherever you go."

"But, darling, you can't count on that. What do you think! It's not so easy."

"It's not so terribly hard, I don't believe. I know lots of people everywhere who are crazy to do me a favor. I don't suppose it is going to be very easy to man that bird. But I'm thrilled to try. Besides, we can live cheaper in Mexico."

"But what about the money you're spending now? In this suite?"

"Smitty pays all the expenses until the divorce is final. That doesn't matter to you, does it?"

"No, but you ought to take it easier, not put out all this gold."

"Why?" she said, and genuinely didn't understand.

Any more than I could understand some of her notions about spending. She would pay thirty dollars for a pair of French sewing scissors in a silver shop on Michigan Boulevard —one big dead sizzle of trousseau silver—and those scissors would never cut a thread or snip a button, but disappear into the flow of articles in the bags and boxes, in the rear of the station wagon, and perhaps never show up again. Yet she could talk about being thrifty in Mexico.

"You don't mind spending Smitty's money, do you?"

"No," I said, and truthfully I scarcely cared. "But suppose I wasn't going to Mexico with you—would you have gone on alone? With the bird, and so on?"

"Of course. Don't you want to come with me, though?"

She knew, however, that I could no more stay here and let her go than I could put out my eyes. Even if it was African vultures, condors, rocs, or phoenixes. She had the initiative and carried me; if I had had a different, independent idea I might have tried to take the lead instead. But I had none.

So she asked me whether I didn't want to stay behind, and then seeing it all over my face how I loved her she took back her question and was silent; the only sound was the strike of the guitar as it was set down.

Then she said, "If the bird worries you, just forget about it till you see it. I'll show you what to do. Only don't think about it beforehand. Or think what a kick there may be in it when you get the animal trained, and how beautiful it is."

I tried to take her advice, but all the same my bottom skepticism of West-Side Chicago nagged after me and asked, "Nah, what is this!" And since we were only a short distance from the zoo I took a walk to see their eagle, who perched on a trunk inside a cage forty feet high and conical like the cage of a parlor parrot, in its smoke and sun colors dipped somewhat with green, and its biped stance and Turkish or Janissary pants of feathers—the pressed-down head, the killing eye, the deep life of its feathers. *Oy!* In the old-country park green of lawns and verdigris-covered ironwork, ordinary tree shade and garden sunlight, there seemed nothing a bird like this might want. I thought, How could anybody ever tame him? And also, We'd better make speed for Texarkana and start with this thing before it grows too big.

The letter from Smith's lawyer had arrived. The day we received it we loaded up the wagon and left the city, heading toward St. Louis. As we started late we didn't quite make it that far. We camped, sleeping on the ground under a shelter-half. I figured we weren't too far from the Mississippi, which I was eager to see. I was terribly excited.

We lay beside a huge tree. Such a centuries' old trunk still had such small-change of foliage—it was difficult to think this enormous thing should live merely by these tiny leaves. And soon you distinguished the sound of the leaves, moved by the air, from the insects' sound. First near and loud; then farther and mountainous. And then you realized that wherever it was dark there was this sound of insects, continental and hemispheric, again and again, like surf, and continuous and dense as stars.

Chapter XV

W HAT CLASS we started out in! We were risen up high
with pleasure. We had all the luck in love we could ask,
and it was maybe improved by the foreignness we found in
each other, for in some ways Danaë or Flora the Belle Ro-
maine couldn't have been stranger to me, while only God can
guess what sort of oddity out of barbarous Chicago I was to
her. But these differences I think reduced the weight of precious personality and the veteran burden that familiarity is always a part of.

The way we set out and all that we did or saw, what we ate,
under what trees we took off our clothes and what protocol
there was about kissing, from the face to the legs and back
again up to the breasts, what we agreed and disagreed about,
or what animals or people came our way I can always recall
when I want to. Some things I have an ability to see without
feeling much previous history, almost like birds or dogs that
have no human condition but are always living in the same age,
the same at Charlemagne's feet as on a Missouri scow or in a
Chicago junkyard. And often that is how the trees, water,
roads, grasses may come back in their green, white, blue,
steepness, spots, wrinkles, veins, or smell, so that I can fix my
memory down to an ant in the folds of bark or fat in a piece of
meat or colored thread on the collar of a blouse. Or such dis-
criminations as where, on a bush of roses, you see variations in
heats that make your breast and bowel draw at various places
from your trying to correspond; when even the rose of rot and
wrong makes you attempt to answer and want to stir. Which is
to say also that the human heat that circulates and warms,
when it's piled at any bar or break, burns inward or out with
typical embers or sores, and makes a track of fever or fire whose
corresponding part is darkness and cold gaps. So there are
burning roses, there are sores, and there are busted circuits.
It's rare to find us without these breaks and interferences.

Thea and I had our troubles. She kept me uncertain, as I
did her. I'd do it by looking, through long old habit, casual
and unattached; it was hard for me to change. And on her

side, she couldn't make me any promises. She just wouldn't. I knew that Smitty wouldn't have divorced her because of one single naval cadet. I figured in those high-up social circles a falling-off here and there was not of such importance. When I took it up with her she admitted it. "Of course," she said, "now and then. Because of Smitty. Well—also because of myself. But *we* don't have to think about that. Because nothing like you has ever happened to me. So what do I know about far in the future? I've never been this way before. Have you?"

"No."

"Why," she said, exactly right, "this makes you jealous! Why, Augie, the others would be jealous of you. They should be. Those just were incidents. You know, this can be one of the most unimportant things in the world. If it's good, why grudge anybody? And if it's bad you can only feel sorry. And can you blame me if I tried? And don't you want me to tell you the truth?"

"Oh! Yes, I do. No. I'm not sure. Maybe not."

"Suppose I hadn't looked—what would I know? And if I can't tell *you* the truth, and you can't tell me . . ."

Yes, yes, I knew the truth had to be appropriate somewhere, but was this the place for it?

She wanted to say and to know all. Pale as she was, she got paler at the approach of this desire to say and know, and often her seriousness was right on the border of panic. For of course she was jealous too. Yes, she was jealous. It did me good sometimes to realize it. She wanted to be hard about the truth, and when she was she shook and got frightened.

Sometimes I reckoned that mere jealousy of her sister had interested her in me in the first place. It wasn't a reassuring thought. But then it's actually very common that at the outset you desire a thing for the wrong reasons; there's an even more deep desire which will bring you out of such reasons. Otherwise there'd never be any human motives but miserable, green ones, and only the illusion of better and riper. Rather than as the history of the world shows, that inferior reasons are not the only leading ones. Because why have unhappy people persisted in thinking of the best, and the best only? You take that poor Rousseau, in the picture he leaves of himself, stubble-faced and milky, in a rope wig, while he wept at his own opera performed at court for the monarch, how he was encouraged by the weeping of the heart-touched ladies and fancied he'd like to gobble the tears from their cheeks— this sheer horse's ass of a Jean-Jacques who couldn't get on with a single human being, goes away to the woods of Montmorency in order to think and write of the *best* government or the *best* system of education. And similarly Marx, with his fierce carbuncles and his poverty and the death of children, whose thought was that the angel of history would try in vain to fly against the wind from the past. And I can mention many others, less great, but however worried, spoiled, or perverse, still wanting to set themselves apart for great ends, and believing in at least one worthiness. That's what the more deep desire is under the apparent ones.

Oh, jealousy, sure. But there were plenty of other defects and inferiorities. What I sometimes didn't think of myself, in the fine pants and the buckskins, boots, sheath knife, while I drove the station wagon as if from the court at Greenwich and along the Thames, just back from a Spanish raid, goofy flowers in my hat. This was how I'd note myself with satisfaction and glowing; I may ask a partial excuse, because of the swelling of my heart, that I was such a happy jerk. But she could be singular too, when she'd swagger or boast or vie against other women; or fish compliments, or force me to admire her hair or skin, which I didn't have to be forced to do. Or I would find her stuffing toilet paper into her brassiere. Toilet paper! What a strange idea of herself—complete failure to know what she had! What did she want with different breasts? I would look over into her blouse, where they seemed to me perfect, and perplex myself with this question.

I could enumerate more difficulties, like pangs, vexations, bellyaches, anxious nosebleeds and vomiting, continual alarms about pregnancy. Also she was snobbish now and then about her extraction and would brag about her musical ability. Actually, I heard her play the piano only once, in a roadhouse, in the afternoon. She went up on the bandstand, and the instrument may have been out of whack from use by jazz musicians; anyway, it began to crash from the energy she turned loose on the keys, chords overreached and elements spilled.

She abruptly quit and came back silent to the table, drops of sweat on her nose. She said, "This seems to be an off day." Well, I didn't care whether she could play or not, but to her it seemed important.

But these shortcomings, both in her and me, could have been corrected or changed. Whatever wasn't essential I thought might simply be rolled over. Like camp articles we rolled over that were in our way; we forgot to clear them aside—I am thinking of one particular day; there were some aluminum cups and lines and straps that happened to be on the blanket. It was afternoon; we were in the Ozark foothills, well off the road, in the woods near a pasture. Up from where we were there was a totter of small pines, and above them bigger trees, and subsiding land below. Because the water we had was poor we spiked it with rye for taste. The weather was hot, and the air was glossy, the clouds white and heavy, rich, dangerous, swagging, silk. The open ground glared and baked, the wheat looked like the glass of wheat, the cattle had their feet in the water. First the heat and then the rye made us take off our clothes, shirts, then trousers, finally all. I was startled to see those pinks of her breast, so heavy and forward, and despite everything I was still, at first, somewhat shy of them. When I put down my tin plate and began to kiss her, both kneeling, her hand passed over my belly hairs; it sometimes surprised me where she would put a kiss of gentleness, and I didn't know where the jump of happiness would come from. She gave me only the side of her face at first, and, when her lips, she would not let my mouth go for some time, until her arms locked in my head. I felt, when I was roofed and covered with heat, met all over and to the smallest hair, carried on her body, easily. She didn't shut her eyes, but they were not open in order to see me or anything; filled and slow, they made no effort but only received or showed. Very soon I didn't notice either, but knew I came out of my hidings and confinements, efforts, ends, observations, and I wanted nothing that was not for her and felt the same from her. We stayed a length of time as we were, easing and slowly lying apart on each other's arms, then once more nearer, kissing neck and breastbone and on the edge of the face and on the hair.

Meanwhile the clouds, birds, cattle in the water, things,

stayed at their distance, and there was no need to herd, account for, hold them in the head, but it was enough to be among them, released on the ground as they were in their brook or in their air. I meant something like this when I said occasionally I could look out like a creature. If I mentioned a Chicago junkyard as well as Charlemagne's estate, I had my reasons. For should I look into any air, I could recall the bees and gnats of dust in the heavily divided heat of a street of El pillars—such as Lake Street, where the junk and old bottle-yards are—like a terribly conceived church of madmen, and its stations, endless, where worshipers crawl their carts of rags and bones. And sometimes misery came over me to feel that I myself was the creation of such places. How is it that human beings will submit to the gyps of previous history while mere creatures look with their original eyes?

We had few such afternoons when we started to train the eagle. After all, love can be the calling of mythological characters around Mount Olympus or Troy, like Paris, Helen, or Palamons and Emilies, but we had to start to earn our own bread. And it couldn't be in any way other than this one that Thea had chosen, to send out a bird after another animal. And so the gilded and dallying part of the excursion ended in Texarkana.

Seeing that fierce animal in his cage, I felt darkness, and then a streaming on my legs as if I had wet myself: it wasn't so, it was only something to do with my veins. But I really felt dazed in all my nerves when I saw with what we would have to deal, and dark before the eyes. The bird looked to be close kin to the one that lit on Prometheus once a day. I had hoped this would be a smaller bird, brought up by us from a baby, he'd learn something about affection. But no—to my despair —here he was as big as the one in Chicago, with the same Turkish or paratroop knickers down to his merciless feet.

Thea was terribly excited and keen. "Oh, he's so beautiful! But how old is he? He's not an eaglet; he looks full grown and must weigh twelve pounds."

"Thirty," I said.

"Oh, honey, no."

Of course she knew more about it than I did.

"But you didn't get him from the nest, did you?" she asked the owner.

This old guy, who kept a roadside zoo of mountain lions and armadillos, a few rattlers, was an ancient-prospector or desert-rat-looking joker, with the sort of eyes that request you to believe their crookedness is only the freak of nature or effect of unfavorable light. But I hadn't served around Einhorn's poolroom or had Grandma Lausch's upbringing for nothing, and I recognized him for a crooked old bastard and prick in his heart.

"No, I didn't climb for him. Fellow brought him in when he was real tiny. They grow so durn fast."

"He looks older to me. My guess is he's in the prime of life."

Thea said, "I have to know if he was ever a haggard—ever hunted wild."

"He's never been outside that cage since practically from hatching. You know, miss, I've been shipping animals to your uncle for close on twenty years." He thought George H. Something-or-other was her uncle.

"Oh, of course we're going to take him," said Thea. "He's so magnificent. You can open the cage."

I rushed forward because I feared for her eyes. Falconry with those little peregrine hawks was all right in the tame meadows out East in the company of ladies and sporting gentlemen; but we were on the edge of Texas, within smell of deserts and mountains, and she had never touched an eagle before even if she was experienced with smaller birds and capable of the capture of poisonous snakes. However, she was very steady when it came to dealing with animals; she had no fear of them at all. With the gauntlet pulled on, she held a piece of meat inside the cage. The eagle struck it out of her hand and then took it. She tried another piece, and he mounted her arm with that almost inaudible whiff of his spread wings that's so fearful in itself, the raised shoulder with its forward power and the fan of the pinions with hidden rust and angel-of-death armpit or deepest hollow inside the wing. His talons held her arm steady while he tore up the meat. However, when she wanted to take him out he attacked and tore with his beak. I reached for him next, and he struck me above the gauntlet and cut gashes in my arm. I expected this, if not worse, and somehow I was relieved that it happened so quick, making me fear him a little less. As for Thea, fascinated, and whiter than ever in her cap with green bill, quick, strong, erect in the head with her purpose to get and tame him, the spurt of blood on my arm was, just now, only an incident, like the grate of gravel under our boots. In action, she was that way about accidents—spills and falls from horses and motorcycles, knife cuts or any hunting injuries.

Finally we got the bird transferred to the back of the station wagon. Thea was happy. I had things to do, such as bandaging my arm and stowing the boxes anew to give the bird more space, that allowed me to hide my gloom. While the old man, as Thea described her scheme, could hardly keep his grin in his whiskers. Like so many enthusiasts, Thea rarely got the number of anyone who pretended to listen seriously. Since the old man was getting a fancy price for his eagle, or, the way I felt about it, had found a place for this harsh client of his, he was very pleased and malicious. So we drove off, with the thing supervisor of the back of the wagon. I observed how glad and confident Thea was, and took note of the shotgun behind the seat.

I can remember a cousin of Grandma Lausch who recited "The Eagle," by Lermontov, in Russian; which I didn't dig, but the elocution was wonderful and romantic. She was dark, she had black eyes, her throat was ardent but her hands rather powerless. She was much younger than Grandma, and her husband was a furrier. I'm only trying to gather together what a city-bred man knew of eagles altogether, and it's curious: the eagle of money, the high-flying eagles of Bombay, the NRA eagle with its gear and lightnings, the bird of Jupiter and of nations, of republics as well as of Caesar, of legions and soothsayers, Colonel Julian the Black Eagle of Harlem; also the ravens of Noah and Elijah, which may well have been eagles; the lone eagle, animal president. And, as well, robber and carrion feeder.

Well, given time, we all catch up with legends, more or less.

The bird had looked to me to be in his prime, but the old man was approximately right, even though he probably lied by as much as eight months. American eagles are generally blackish until maturity; before they get the white part of their plumage they moult a good many times. Ours didn't yet have his, the full bad eye of the head when it whitens, and was still only Black Prince, not King. He was, however, powerfully handsome, with his onward-turned head and buff and white feathers among the darker, his eyes that were gruesome jewels and meant nothing in their little lines but cruelty, and that he was here for his own need; he was entirely a manifesto of that. I hated him beyond measure, at the start. In the night we had to be up because of him, and it was an interference with love. If we slept out-of-doors and I woke and missed her, I would find her by him; or she would shake and send me to check if all was well—the jesses around his legs, the swivel through the hole of the jesses, the leash through the swivel. If we had a hotel room he shared it. I'd hear his step; he crackled his feathers or hissed as if snow was sliding. He was right away her absorption and *idée fixe*, almost child, and he made her out of breath. She turned to him continually in her seat as we rode, or when we ate, and I wondered at other times whether he was on her mind.

Of course he had to be subdued, so that we didn't have a mighty and savage animal at our backs, antagonism constantly increasing between captive and masters. And since I had to, I got along with him. He didn't require that I should love him; he looked the other way from that. Meat was how you came to terms with him. Thea really did understand how to tame him, and naturally, since she had the know-how, she had to think of him more than I did. Soon he started to come to our fists for his beef. You had to get used to it. Under the gloves your skin was twisted by his talons, and he did do a whole lot of damage. I also had to accustom myself to the work he did with his beak when he ravened. But later when I saw vultures on carcasses I appreciated his prouder pull of a more noble bird.

So as we ran through Texas, and it was very hot. We stopped several times a day to work with the bird. By the time we got close to Laredo, where it was desert, he would come both to my fist and hers from the top of the station wagon. And this open shadow would shut out your heart with its smell and power—the Etna feathers and clasped beak opening. Often, then, without the preparatory move you observe in other animals, he ejected a straight, heavy squirt of excrement before he wound up to fly again to the top of the wagon. Thea was mad about him for his progress. I was that about her, and for lots of reasons, among them admiration, seeing how she succeeded with the bird.

Birds that hunt have to be hooded; Thea had this thing ready, a tufted cover with drawstrings that you struck or loosened before you released the animal to rise and wait on its game. But before the eagle would take the hood he had to be thoroughly mastered, and I carried him on my arm some forty hours without sleep. He wouldn't drop off, and Thea kept me awake. This was in Nuevo Laredo, just over the border. We put up in a hotel full of flies, a brown room with giant coarse cactus almost in the window. And there I paced at first, rested, at length, in the dark, with my arm on the table, overborne by him. After several hours a numbness grew over my entire side and into my shoulder as deep as the bone. The flies nipped me because I had only one hand free and anyhow didn't want to startle him. Thea had a kid bring up coffee for us, which she took from him at the door. I could see him stare as he tried to dope us out, for he knew we had the bird and perhaps even saw his shape on my victimized arm, or his wakeful eye.

There had been an amazing crowd when we drove up to the hotel and opened the back door of the station wagon. In a few minutes more than fifty men and children had gathered. The eagle came on my hand for his meat and the kids screamed, "*Ay! Mira, mira—el águila, el águila!*" Some sight, I guess, since I'm fairly tall and wore that height-increasing hat and whipcord breeches, and, moreover, obviously followed the lead of Thea's beauty and importance. And anyway the eagle has ancient respect in Mexico from the old religion and the great class of knights in those days of obsidian sword slaughter that Díaz del Castillo witnessed. The children, I said, were screaming, while he rocked on my fist, "*El águila, el águila!*" And because I heard Spanish for the first time, it was another word I made out, the Roman name of Caligula. I thought in my heart how suitable it was. Caligula!

"*El águila!*"

"*Si, Caligula,*" I said. That name was the first satisfaction I had in him.

Now he had my arm pinned to the table with torture, and my mouth and chest filled with moans I couldn't give out. I had to drag him with me everywhere, to the toilet too, and sitting or standing I had his eye on me and his comment to try to read and will to feel. From moody sunkenness, when I rose to go, he thrashed back, his neck began to swim and his eyes livened; his clutch grew more positive. I won't attempt to play down my fear when I had to take him into the toilet for the first time. I held him as far off as I had the strength to do, while he started to stretch his wings and change the stance of his thick legs.

O observation! We had our struggle on that very thing, it appears to me. The conversation with Thea about living in the eyes of others, I've reported. When has such damage been done by the gaze and so much awful despotism belonged to the eyes? Why, Cain was cursed between them so he would never be unaware of his look in the view of other men. And police accompany accused and suspects to the can, and jailers see their convicts at will through bars and peepholes. Chiefs and tyrants of the public give no relief from self-consciousness. Vanity is the same thing in private, and in any kind of oppression you are a subject and can't forget yourself; you are seen, you have to be aware. In the most personal acts of your life you carry the presence and power of another; you extend his being in your thoughts, where he inhabits. Death, with monuments, makes great men remembered like that. So I had to bear Caligula's gaze. And I did.

He resisted the hood for a long time. Several times we tried it on him, and I had my hand slashed badly and cursed him with all my might; but I continued to carry him. Occasionally Thea would spell me, but he was too much of a weight for her and after an hour or so I'd lure him back to my unrested arm. During the last groggy stretch I couldn't any longer stay in and went into the street with him where the cries about him made him restive. We brazened our way into a movie and sat in the back row; here the sound got him even worse, and I was afraid he'd blow his top. I took him back to the room and fed him chunks of meat to soothe him. Then, in the middle of the night, under the infrared bulb of Thea's photographic kit, I tried the hood once more, and he submitted to it at last. We continued to give him meat under it, and he was calm. Covered eyes made him much more docile. Henceforth he rode either my fist or Thea's and took the hood without using his beak on us.

When we had this victory and Caligula was standing on the dresser in his hood with tufts, we kissed and danced or tromped around the room. Thea went to get ready for bed and I fell asleep in my breeches and was out for ten hours. She pulled off my boots and let me lie.

Next afternoon, hot and bright, we started out for Monterrey; trees, bushes, stones, as explicit as glare and the spice of that heat could make them. The giant bird, when Thea brought him out, seemed to shoulder it with a kind of rise of sensuality. I felt dizzy from long sleep and the wires of radiant heat curling up from road and rock. Also the paws and pads, the tongues and jaws of cactus and their spines, the dust like resin, the squamous crumbly walls, were a trial to the sight and the skin. But as the wagon climbed and the day cooled we both revived.

We didn't stop over in Monterrey but only got a few supplies—more raw meat for Caligula than anything else. The curiosity of evening in this foreign city would have held me—it was so green, and the buildings red, the humanity so numerous in the flat open beside the railroad station and its length of low entrances and windows. But it was Thea's idea to drive on and beat the hot weather. It wasn't easy going, for the fields weren't fenced and there were cattle in the way; the road had no night markers and took foolish twists. For some time there was a mist although the moon was plain enough. The animals rose up in big shapes from this vague cover, and sometimes we came up with horsemen and left behind the slap of iron shoes and the loose change and slash of harness.

At a town well past Valles we stopped for what was left of the night and then because I insisted. The air was sharp, the stars pricking, the roosters sounding off, and the never-sleeping element of Mexican towns came to see us take out the eagle, with the same solemnness about it as at the Sunday promenade of a holy image, and, as everywhere, said to one another, astonished, "*Es un águila!*" I wanted to leave him in the station wagon where by now his excrement and fowlish smell were so thick, but he wouldn't stand for it. Left alone all night, he was vicious in the morning, and Thea was by now so wrapped up in his career that for the time very few considerations took precedence. Because she was making history. Those gallant young sons of financiers who flew planes in the twenties and took off to break records from New Orleans to Buenos Aires, over the jungles which sometimes collected both them and machines, their passions must have been on this order. She kept reminding me how few people since the Middle Ages had manned eagles. I agreed it was terrific and admired her without limit; I thanked God I was even her supernumerary or assistant. But I tried to tell her that the eagle in the room disconcerted me at love, which was awkward; and also that he was a beast after all, not a child in cradle for whom you had to have titty or bottle. Thea, however, couldn't see any arguments, only her objective with the bird, which she never doubted that I shared. She thought I disagreed as to how to manage him. The motive of power over her, the same as afflicted practically everyone I had ever known in some fashion, and which in my degree, though in a different place, I had too, carried and plunged us forward. Of course, when you had an eagle by the tail, so to speak, how could you quit? Having started, you had to follow up. But it wasn't being halfway in a course of difficulties that counted. No, what carried her was the passion for him to capture those huge lizards.

By the door of the *posada* two dirty lumps of kerosene light were burning, like persimmons streaked with black. The stones of the street were slippery, but neither from dew nor from rain, and the smells which I didn't yet know how to sort rose thickly mixed—smells of straw, clay, charcoal and ocote smoke, cookery, stone, shit and corn meal, boiled chicken, pepper, dog, pig, donkey. Nothing was as before; all was strange. In the barnyard, which gave a heave most likely of terror as Caligula in his hood was brought through; and in the bedroom where the perfumed air of the branchy mountainside washed over the white wall and on the stinks of community, as the long impulse from well out in ocean bobs the rotten oranges and other trash at the wharfside; and the Indian woman who turned down the counterpane of the iron bedstead which was in a form of fantasy, a white spider monkey.

It was not a long night's rest, for early in the morning washerwomen at their tank started slapping their clothes; corn was pounding; the animals were lively, especially the burros, penetrated with necessity; and the church clanged. However, Thea woke happy, and she was busy right away giving Caligula his pacifier of morning meat, while I set out through the damp rooms to find bread and coffee.

Because of the bird we traveled rather slowly. Now Thea wanted to teach him to fly after a lure. This was a horseshoe with chicken or turkey wings and heads tied to it; it was slung by a rawhide line, and when it was thrown he gave a great lurch of preparation and soared after it. Some of his problems were like those of an airline pilot, as to judging distances and the air currents. It wasn't, with him, the simple mechanics of any little bird that went and landed as impulse tickled him, but a task of massive administration. When he was high enough he could look as light as a bee, and later on I saw him at such altitudes that he appeared to tumble or turn somersaults like a mere pigeon—it must have been that he played the various air pockets of hot and cold. Anyway, it was glorious how he would mount away high and seem to sit up there, really as if over fires of atmosphere, as if he was governing from up there. If his motive was rapaciousness and everything based on the act of murder, he also had a nature that felt the triumph of beating his way up to the highest air to which flesh and bone could rise. And doing it by will, not as other forms of life were at that altitude, the spores and parachute seeds who weren't there as individuals but messengers of species.

The more south we were, the more deep a sky it seemed, till, in the Valley of Mexico, I thought it held back an element too strong for life, and that the flamy brilliance of blue stood off this menace and sometimes, like a sheath or silk membrane, showed the weight it held in sags. So when later he would fly high over the old craters on the plain, coaly bubbles of the underworld, dangerous red everywhere from the sun, and then coats of snow on the peak of the cones—gliding like a Satan—well, it was here the old priests, before the Spaniards, waited for Aldebaran to come into the middle of heaven to tell them whether or not life would go on for another cycle, and when they received their astronomical sign built their new fire inside the split and emptied chest of a human sacrifice. And also, hereabouts, worshipers disguised as gods and as gods in the disguise of birds, jumped from platforms fixed on long poles, and glided as they spun by the ropes—feathered serpents, and eagles too, the *voladores,* or fliers. There still are such plummeters, in market places, as there seem to be remnants or conversions or equivalents of all the old things. Instead of racks or pyramids of skulls still in their hair and raining down scraps of flesh there are corpses of dogs, rats, horses, asses, by the roads; the bones dug out of the rented graves are thrown on a pile when the lease is up, and there are the coffins looking like such a rough joke on the female form, sold in the open shops, black, white, gray, and in all sizes, with their heavy death fringes daubed in Sapolio silver on the black. Beggars in dog voices on the church steps enact the last feebleness for you with ancient Church Spanish, and show their old flails of stump and their sores. The burden carriers with the long lines, hemp lines they wind over their foreheads to hold the loads on their backs, lie in the garbage at siesta and give themselves the same exhibited neglect the dead are shown. Which is all to emphasize how openly death is received everywhere, in the beauty of the place, and how it is acknowledged that anyone may be roughly handled—the proudest—pinched, slapped, and set down, thrown down; for death throws even worse in men's faces and makes it horrible and absurd that one never touched should be roughly dumped under, dumped upon.

When Caligula soared under this sky I sometimes wondered what connection he made with this element of nearly too great strength that was dammed back of the old spouts of craters.

But he wasn't soaring yet. He was still cumbersomely flying after the lure and its slimy giblets spoiled by the sun. Again and again it was flung out, downslope, for that was the only way to get him going. Whenever Thea miscalculated the distance he made me stagger, since we were tied by a rope that passed under my arms. She ran to watch him devour the chicken and signaled when I was to pull at the leash. So gradually he learned to come back to the fist from the lure. No matter how isolated a mountain place we stopped in to practice, there was an audience soon of herdsmen and peasants in their sleeping-suit white costumes and sandals soled with pieces of rubber tire, little kids and the mountaineers with the creased impassivity that showed how gravely they took it.

As for Thea, sometimes she looked more barbarous than they did in spite of the civilized lipstick and conventional shape of the jodhpurs she wore. Her arm was held out to the eagle when he descended, braked with his wings and feet together, the stirred air showing on his breast. Her cap fluttered. I took a great pride in her. I thought it was the most splendid human act I would ever see. It went around my soul like fine ribbon. She'd call out to me too, when I poised myself forward to bring the bird in, admiring how gallant it looked. I was pleased, of course, though not groggy with glory.

After ten days we reached Mexico City. Thea had to see the representative of Smitty's lawyer and we therefore stayed awhile. Against her desire, which was to go on immediately to Acatla. We put up very cheaply in a hotel called La Regina, for only three pesos a day. They didn't appear to mind the eagle, and the place was quiet and modest-looking, unusually clean, with a skylight over the center and galleries onto which you came from rooms, showers, or toilets. The lobby was also very fine, and empty. From above it had a diagrammatic look. The chairs and writing tables were arranged with geometry, but no one was there to use them. And soon we found that the queen for whom the place was named was the licentious old Cyprian one. The closets were full of douche pans, the beds were heavily prepared with rubber under the sheets, which was an annoyance. During the day we were alone in the hotel with the maids, whom we amused. They thought it was fun that we lived in a house of assignation and they waited on us, did laundry and pressed pants, fetched coffee and fruit, because we were the only guests. Thea's Spanish entertained them—I had only begun to pick up a few words—as did her requests, that she summoned them when we were in bed and ordered mangos for us and meat for the bird. Encouraged to be free around the place, we covered with only a towel when we went to take a shower, and when I wanted to be without the eagle nobody minded if we went into one of the other rooms. It was only at night that there were drawbacks to the Regina; though the clients were probably respectable people they had no ideas whatever about quiet, and very few of the doors had glass in the transom. However, we were out to all hours ourselves, seeing the city, and we did a lot of a daytime sleeping. I rested my arm, of which the gashes were healing. Thea took me to the palaces and night clubs, zoo and churches. The rideresses in Chapultepec, those patrician ladies in hard hats and immense skirts and foot-conforming little black leather shoes, sitting sidesaddle, they impressed me. I thought the world was really much greater than I had ever fancied. I said to Thea, "I don't actually know much, I begin to see."

She laughed and answered, "You're welcome to all the side of things I can give information about. But how much are you obliged to know?"

"No, there actually is a lot," I said, for I was amazed and struck, it was so splendid. I wanted to stay, but there was our business with the bird, and Thea didn't like the city very much.

I couldn't question her judgment about Caligula—there I went along with her and had confidence by now, based on her proved ability with him. A creature like that, he'd have torn me to strips if I'd ever taken him on myself, assuming that I'd have had the nerve. No, where the eagle was concerned I did as she said, insofar as I backed the undertaking. When I knew more about it I trembled, thinking of the precautions we didn't take. We ought to have worn wire masks, especially at the time he was being taught to give up the lure for meat on the fist, since bald eagles are most dangerous when they have their quarry under them. She might have been struck in the eyes. But that never happened, and eventually she succeeded in teaching him to respond to our voices and come directly after the stoop for the hand-fed meat. We talked to him and used every gentleness on him. He liked to be stroked with a feather. He became pretty tame, but all the same my heart picked up a few beats when we hooded him or struck the hood.

At the Regina the scared maids were called in to be present

when we worked with him. Thea lined them up and said, "*Hablen, hablen ustedes!*" They had to chatter. For the thing was to accustom Caligula to close human presence and sound. So the Indian women, in smocks, frightened as well as amused by us—they stood in a row and watched Thea take the eagle down from the dresses on her hand. What I had imagined at the first sight of him actually happened to one of these young chicks, that she wet her pants when the hood came off from the unmerciful face and weapon beak with its breathing holes. But it did affect Caligula to be surrounded by these women; he ate and then at one moment he seemed to lean his head toward Thea and act like a cat who wants to wipe and wreathe and ply himself at a woman's legs.

"Oh, look at him," Thea cried. "Augie, see what he's doing, he wants to be petted!"

Then she was impatient with having to wait on in the city. "Now's the time to follow up. We ought to be in the country with him."

"Well, let's drive out away."

"No, we can't. I have to see the lawyer. But I can't bear to lose the time. Now, now, we could be getting home. We could start to enter him to his quarry."

By this she meant his first introduction to lizards. Not the giant variety with the high frill of which she had shown me pictures, the game we were after, but littler lizards. And furthermore Caligula had to become accustomed to a horse or burro; these giant lizards were in almost inaccessible parts of the mountain, far from roads, and we couldn't lug Caligula the whole long difficult way.

I felt Thea maybe ought not to hurry the divorce too much. She might not be getting a good deal. I didn't want to ask about the details, and I figured probably she had been an heiress long enough to look after things for herself. What could I tell her of that? Besides, I didn't care to find out in its entirety about the trouble between her and Smitty, and had I asked she would have told me. So I laid off the topic, and we used the spare time to take color pictures of Caligula on my arm in front of the cathedral; until mounted officers who appeared to gallop out of the gates of a ministry drove us off the plaza. They were tough with me. I understood them to say the bird was dangerous, and they shouted that they wanted to see my papers. They were more deferential to Thea, but with lady-killer smiles they anyway made us go. Thea still intended to sell illustrated articles about Caligula to the *National Geographic* or *Harper's*. She knew a writer in Acatla who would help us; and she kept notes in a little book which was a very classy affair of red leather with a gold pencil attached. At any time at all she'd take it out on her knees and write with bent neck, a few words to a page, while, as she paused to think or remember, she moved her hand like someone in the process of shading a drawing. I studied her so well I even noted that the creases at the joints of her fingers were much like my own.

"Darling, what town was that in Texas where he wanted to go after a jack rabbit?"

"Around Uvalde, wasn't it?"

"Honey, no. Could it have been?"

She took my thigh with her hand. Here in the city she had gilded her nails. They shone. And she had put on a velvet dress, this soft red one, which was heavy. The buttons were in the form of seashells. We sat under a tree on a wrought-iron chair. As I looked at the clear skin of her breast I felt its heat as actual as the heat of her hand through the thin cloth of my trousers. I assumed we'd get married when the divorce came through.

Chapter XVI

And strange it is
That nature must compel us to lament
Our most persisted deeds.
Antony and Cleopatra

WE FOUND Thea's house ready. If it was her house. Perhaps it was Smitty's. I thought I'd find out in due time. There was no rush about it.

The towers and roofs of town appeared and then were hid many times in knots of mountain and back of cliffs of thousands of feet before the descending road became a street and we arrived in the cathedral square, or *zócalo*. There we parked, and, the way to the villa being narrow, we had to walk. Even normally we'd have been met by a gang of kids, beggars, loafers, hotel-touts, and so forth, but the eagle on my fist brought out a mob from the shops and bars and from the awning-covered market just below the cathedral. A lot of people recognized Thea and sounded off with yells and yelps, whistles, picked-up sombreros, and in this turbulent escort that raised a dust around us we climbed a few hundred yards above the *zócalo* on the pointy stone terraces, to the gate of the villa. "Casa Descuitada," I read on a blue tile under the branches of pomegranate trees—Carefree House. We entered, and the cook and houseboy met us. Mother and son, they stood a good distance apart, both with bare feet on the red stone of the porch, she by the kitchen and he by the bedroom door. In her shawl she carried an infant, and at the sight of the bird, even in his hood, started to back into the kitchen. We took the bird away. The toilet became his mews; he perched on the waterbox or cistern where the sound of trickling seemed to please him. The boy, Jacinto, tagged after to see how we handled him. He was thrilled.

Sometimes I thought that if to earn money was the reason for this goofy undertaking I should devote myself to the money question and how to make a killing; then I'd set Caligula free or give him away. But I knew that to make money was not Thea's objective. I didn't overlook the nobility of her project, how ancient it was, the kind of ambition that was involved or the aspect of game or hazard; I even was aware of a link to earliest times in the great venture of domestication. Yes, for all my opposition and dread of the bird, wishing him a gargoyle of stone or praying he would drop dead, I saw the other side of it, and what was in it for her, that she was full of brilliant energy. But I thought, What was wrong with the enjoyment of love, and what did there have to be an eagle for? So then, if I had dough at least there couldn't be that pretext. Then I understood, next, how to think idly of money is terribly frivolous. Being unreasonable perhaps about the capture of the lizards, Thea nevertheless had a bird and had made a start, whereas my thought of money was only a flutter of imagination. What was I doing in breeches and campaign hat down here in Central Mexico if I wanted to be serious about it? In short, I saw anew how great a subject money is in itself. Here was vast humankind that meshed or dug, or carried, picked up, held, that served, returning every day to its occupations, and being honest or kidding or weeping or hypocritic or mesmeric, and money, if not the secret, was anyhow beside the secret, as the secret's relative, or associate or representative before the peoples.

Here we arrived, and lunch was served to us—soup, chicken with black molé sauce, tomato and avocados, coffee and guava jelly. And this strange, mouth-inflaming delicate food, as I was eating, was what brought my mind to this question of the dollar.

The house was handsome and wide, deeper than appeared from outside, because from the garden you descended to the rooms. The walls were reddish and floors darker red or green tile. There were two patios, one with a fountain and barrel-shaped oxhide chairs; the other was by the kitchen, a sort of old stable yard, and here we continued Caligula's training. He flew down to us from the tiles of the shed where Jacinto slept.

From the porch where we ate we had the town and the cliffs before us. Nearly immediately below was the *zócalo*, the dippy bandstand and its vines, the monstrous trees around. The cathedral had two towers and a blue-varied belly of dome, finely crusted and as if baked in a kiln, overheated, and in places with the mutilated spectrum that sometimes you split out of brick. It was settled uneven on the stones of the square, and occasionally in the midst of admiration gave you a heavy, squalid, gut-sick feeling, so much it incorporated all that was in the surroundings. The bells clung like two weak old animals, green and dull, and the doors opened on a big gloom in which stood dead white altars and images slashed and scratched with axes, thorns, raked with black wounds— some of these flashy with female underpants on their hips, nail-cloven and hacked as they were, and bleeding as far as their clothespin white fingers. Then on a hill to one side was the cemetery, white and spiky, and on another side and higher in a star of connecting gullies was a silver mine, and there you could see where the force of great investment had dented. The mountainside was eaten for some distance by machine. I was intrigued and climbed up there one day. It certainly was odd what mechanisms you saw all over Mexico, what old styles there gnawed and crawled, pit or tunnel makers, and machine scarabaeuses, British and Belgian doojiggers, Manchester trolleys or poodle locomotives at the head of sick cars covered with blanketed men and soldiers.

Within the town still, along the road to the mine, the garbage was thrown into a little valley, hummocky with soft old decays; the vultures hung over it all day. At one of the highest points you could see, in a cliff, there was a waterfall. Sometimes it was covered in a cloud, but there usually flew the slight smoke of water, paler than the air, above the treeline. A good deal below were pines, at the widows' peaks of wrinkled rock; and then more tropical trees and flowers, and the hot stone belt of snakes and wild pigs, the deer, and the giant iguanas we had come to catch. Where they hung out the light was very hot.

In a Paris or a London where the distinction of the sun isn't so great, in the grays and veilings, it isn't credited with its full power, and many southern people have envied those places the virtues it's possible to think of having in the cool or cold. I believe Mussolini was not kidding about blasting pieces out of his Alps and Apennines to let the cold foggy currents of Germany over the peninsula and make the Perugini and the Romans into fighters. That same Mussolini who was slung up dead by the legs with shirt tails drooped off his naked belly, and the flies, on whom he had also declared war, walked on his empty face relaxed of its wide-jawed grimace, upside down. Ay! And his girl friend with poor breasts bullet-punctured also hung by the feet. But what I want of the contrast of broadcast or exposing versus discreet light is to suggest what the claims are, or the illusions, the discreeter seems to allow. Now I've mentioned that Thea carried among other pictures one of her father, taken in the south of China, in a rikshaw. She put it on the dresser, tucked in the mirror frame, and I often found myself studying him, his white shoes of far manufacture off the ground being used by the dish-faced Cantonese. In his white suit. And I thought what there was to such being picked for special distinction. Maybe I looked at him with special regard as lover or future husband of his daughter. But anyway, he was sitting gentlemanly up in the human taxi. Around him spectators from the millions gowping at him, famine-marks, louse-vehicles, the supply of wars, the living fringe of a great number sunk in the ground, dead, and buzzing or jumping over Asia like diatoms of the vast bath of the ocean in the pins of the sun.

Well, in the hot light I saw the wild mountain, the semi-tropical band of it where the iguanas haunted in the big leaves and gorgeous flowers, the laborers and peasants, and I didn't realize right away how many visitors from the cool and cold were paying their good dough to be here. Very near us was a luxury hotel, the Carlos Quinto. Its swimming pool shone in the garden, blue and white like heavenly warmth and weather, and there were large foreign cars in the drive. Acatla was beginning to attract people who once went to Biarritz and San Remo but now wanted to be out of the way of politics. There were already some Spaniards here, from both sides of the disaster, and also some Frenchwomen, and Japanese and Russians, a family of Chinese who ran a bar and manufactured rope-soled *alpargatas*. The American colony was large, and so the place was boiling and booming. I knew little about that at first.

It entertained me to look into the gardens of the Carlos Quinto next door, the bar on the terrace, the swimmers in the pool, the riding parties setting out, the small deer kept in a wire pen. The manager was an Italian; he wore diplomatist's pants and a claw-hammer coat that accommodated his wide prat. His hair was smooth and his face confident for others, worried toward himself. I noticed how quick his fingers were, in and out of his vest pockets where many of his functions started. From our wall Thea introduced me to him; he was called da Fiori. There was a private end of the garden for his own family on which our bedroom window looked down. In the morning old da Fiori, his tiny father, came out in a cap and old English type of suit, dark green, fuzzy, with a belt on the jacket and chestnut buttons. He brushed the ends of his whiskers with hairy knuckles, and when he walked, his little feet didn't seem adequate to support him. We loved to sit up in bed, each by the other's nude waist, and watch him mouse around in the enormous flowers. Then came his son, already combed, pale, bored; his spats in the dew, he bent and kissed his father's hand. And then came two little daughters, like white birthday cake, and the soft mother. All carried the old geezer's tiny hand to their mouths. It gave us a lot of pleasure. They would sit down in the arbor and be served.

By now the eagle had learned Thea's voice and mine, and he'd come off the lure to eat out of our hands when called. It was time to introduce or enter him to lizards. Live ones were a trouble, because they'd run away, and they were so small. Dead ones didn't suit Thea. She worried about those Jacinto brought in; she suggested doping the larger ones a little with ether, just enough to make them sluggish. I was fond of them. Some soon became tame. You stroked them on the little head with a finger and they got affectionate, up your sleeve or on your shoulder, into your hair. At night, when we were at dinner, I'd stare at the ones that lay near the bug-attracting lights, with swift puff of the throat and their tongues which are supposed to have the power to hear. I wished we could leave them alone, thinking of that thunderous animal whose weight was on the toilet cistern, with his ripping feet and beak. About this Thea was both gay and sharp with me, and when she argued against my sympathy with these gilded Hyperion's kids made me laugh and also squirm. It wasn't as if she hadn't thought about it independently.

She said, "Oh, you screwball! You get human affection mixed up with everything, like a savage. Keep your silly feelings to yourself. Those lizards don't want them, and if they felt the way you do they wouldn't be lizards—they'd be too slow, and pretty soon they'd be extinct. And look, if you were lying dead the little lizard would run down your open mouth to catch beetles, as if you were a log."

"And Caligula would eat me."

"Could be."

"And you'd bury me?"

"Because you're my lover. Of course. Wouldn't you me?"

Unlike Lucy Magnus, she never called me husband, or by any domestic term. I sometimes believed her marriage views, except that they weren't polemical, were similar to Mimi's.

This conversation about lizards was one of several on the same general topic, and gradually Thea made me see what she was driving at with me. You couldn't get the admission out of me that a situation couldn't be helped and was inescapably bad, but I was eternally looking for a way out, and what was up for question was whether I was a man of hope or foolishness. But I suppose I felt the good I had must be connected with a law. While she, I guess, didn't care for my statue-yard of hopes. It seemed when somebody held me up an evil there had to be a remedy or I pulled my head and glance away, turned them in another direction. She had me dead to rights when she accused me of that; and she tried to teach me her view.

Nevertheless I hated to see the little lizards hit and squirt blood, and their tiny fine innards of painted delicacy come out under Caligula's talons while he glared and opened his beak.

On a Sunday morning, when the band boomed and spat in the *zócalo*, where it began at dawn, and the heat was dry in the kitchen patio after breakfast—we had sunnyside-up eggs —we were working with the bird. It was something to hear the exercise of his wings in the heated space of the air. Jacinto brought us a larger lizard. We tied him with short fishing line to a stake, which gave him no chance to dart away. Then the eagle came beating down with a sharp threat of pinions in the electrical dry air and its hurried dust and went to set his claws in the lizard. But there was enough play in the line for the quick animal to whip around, and it opened its mouth and

showed a tissue of rage to the big beast over it, then snapped
its jaws and hung from the bird's thigh, curved with the force
of its attack and bite. One of those thighs that made the bird
seem to ride like an Attila's horseman through the air.
Caligula made a noise. I don't believe he had ever in his life
been hurt and his astonishment was enormous. He tore off
the lizard, and when he had already squeezed and wounded it
past recovery he hopped off. I couldn't show it, but it did my
heart good to see Caligula so offended. He sorted among the
feathers with his beak to find the hurt place.

Thea was furious at him, her face red. She shouted, "Get
him! Go finish him!" But when he heard her voice he rose up
and flew to her for his usual meat. Since he came to her she
had to let him land and extended her arm. But she was very
angry. "Oh, the dirty bastard! We can't let him run away from
a little bit of an animal like that. What'll we do? Augie, don't
you grin about it!"

"I'm not, Thea, it's the sun making me squint."

"What should we try now?"

"I'll pick up the lizard and call Caligula back. The poor
thing is almost dead."

"Jacinto, kill the *lagarto*," Thea said.

With pleasure the boy ran from the shed on bare feet and
hit the creature on the head with a stone. I laid it, dead, on
my gauntlet, and Caligula didn't refuse to come but he
wouldn't eat. He shook the lizard with fury and let it drop to
the ground. When I offered it a second time, now a dusty
dead thing, he did the same.

"Oh, that damned crow! Get him out of my sight!"

"Now, Thea, wait a minute," I said. "This has never happened to him before."

"Wait? He only came out of an egg once. How many times
did he have to do that? He's supposed to have instincts. I'll
wring his neck. How is he going to fight the big ones if a
little nip does this to him?"

"Why, if you're hurt, what do you expect?"

But that was my humanizing again, and she shook her
head. She believed fierce nature shouldn't be like that.

I put the eagle on his waterbox, and gradually Thea let me
pacify her. I said, "You've done wonders with this bird al-

ready. You can't miss. We'll make it, sure. After all, he doesn't have to be as terrible as he looks. He's still a young bird."

At last, in the afternoon, she got over her anger and proposed for the first time that we go to Hilario's bar in the *zócalo* for a drink. While she was unpleasantly stirred against Caligula I felt a little condemned with him.

Though Thea was specially loving when we went into the room to change for Sunday p.m. in the *zócalo*. She took off her clothes. The outer were rugged, the inner silky. And when she was naked, smoking a cigarette, she looked at me differently as I sat shirtless and pulled off my boots in the heated shade and the radiated color of the tiles. I went and put my head on her breast. But I knew that, both in love, we were not quite the same in our purpose. She had the idea of an action for which love makes you ready and sets you free. This happened to be connected with Caligula. He meant that to her. But as she suspected now that he preferred brought meat to prey, perhaps she thought also, about me, whether I could make the move from love to the next necessary thing.

We rose from bed and dressed. In the lace blouse she wore, how soft she looked. Her hair fell long on her back. She took my arm, not because she needed its support on the sharp cobbles, but to keep close, and in the shade of the fruit trees she looked very much as she had in St. Joe on the swing, a young girl.

Since the Fenchels had owned the Acatla house for many years Thea was acquainted in the town. But at Hilario's bar we sat at a small table; she didn't want company. Nevertheless, people came over to greet her, to ask after her sister, her aunt and uncle, and Smitty, and of course to give me the once-over. Many of these remained. Thea continued to hold my arm.

To my Chicago eyes these others mostly looked far and odd. Now and then Thea explained who or what they were, and I didn't always understand her. So then this bald old German had been a dancer, and on this side was a jeweler, and the blonde, his wife, came from Kansas City; here was a woman of fifty who was a painter, and the man with her was a sort of cowhand, or Reno-cowhand; and coming up now was a rich fairy, once a queen. Here was a woman who opened a mouth of intelligence on you; she seemed to look at me severely; I thought, at first, because I had taken Smitty's place. Her name was Nettie Kilgore, and she turned out to be not bad at all, only sometimes impatient in look, and something of a lush. She didn't care a hang about Smitty. Well, I'd known plenty of grotesque people before, but none who had made it their life's specialty. The foreign colony of this town represented Greenwich Village, or Montparnasse, or the equivalent from a dozen countries. There was a Polish exile, there was an Austrian with a beard, there was Nettie Kilgore; there were a pair of writers from New York, one named Wiley Moulton, the other, his friend, simply called Iggy; there also was a young Mexican, Talavera, whose father owned the taxi service and rented out horses. A man who sat near Iggy turned out to be the second husband of Iggy's first wife. His name was Jepson and he was the grandson of an African explorer. Well, all this was new to me, and so it went. While Thea and I, fresh from bed, sat side by side. It was curious amusement and didn't much touch me. I was nearly as much entertained by the kinkajou Hilario had in a cage and I fed it potato chips. This large-eyed little animal.

I felt flattered when people assumed I was the eagle's master. Of course I said, "Oh, Thea is his real boss," but people seemed to feel that only a man could cope with a bird of that size. All except the handsome brown strong young chap, Talavera, who said he knew how good Thea was with animals. I didn't altogether care for his contribution to the conversation, though I have to admit he looked to be in a different class from the rest of this gang. I couldn't get over their queerness. The person who sat next to him seemed to have a kind of bony crest to the middle of his head, and the back of his hand was like the instep of another man's foot—white, thick, and dead-appearing. Then Nettie Kilgore. Then Iggy, red-eyed. Then a man I secretly named Ethelred the Unready —like Grandma Lausch or Commissioner Einhorn, I would sometimes do that, give a name. Then Wiley Moulton, the weird-story writer. He was big-bellied and long-haired; his face was sort of subtle, with brown lids; his teeth were small and tobacco dyed; his fingers seemed all back-bent at the last joint.

There was hard work in some of these people, that they made the most partial little good climb around in tremendous mountain ranges of opposition to prove itself.

"So you're going to catch these monsters with your bird?" said Moulton.

"Yes, we are," said Thea quite calmly. It was a great thing about her that she could not be swayed to make small changes of plan or views in order to get on with people. "I don't like monkey games," she always said.

"It has been done," I observed.

And now again the public band in the *zócalo*, just below, began to pound and smite, so the air quivered with the ragged march. It was nearly twilight. Young people promenaded, but in rapid time, so you felt flirtation and desperate flying, both. Firecrackers jumped in the air. A blind fiddler played and howled, with dance-of-death scrapes, serenading the tourists. Then the cathedral started to ring the bells, the deepest voice of that big, crusted sadness. So with this noise the conversational people were silenced for a time; they drank their beer or knocked off their shots of tequila with tastes of salt licked from the thumb in the stylish Mexican way and bites of lime.

Thea wanted Moulton's help with the articles; when you could hear your own voice again she asked him about that.

"I'm not in that line now," he said. "I make more by sticking to Nicolaides." Nicolaides was the editor of the pulp magazine Moulton contributed to. "I had a bid to go up and interview Trotsky last month and I let it go because I'd rather write for Nicolaides. Besides it takes all the strength I've got to turn out the installments."

I felt that Moulton had in store all kinds of words and in fact would say anything. Anything! He only waited for the conversation to give him the chance.

"But you did write magazine articles at one time," said Thea, "and you can show us how to do it."

"I take it Mr. March is not a writer."

"No." I answered for myself.

What he was fishing for was my calling. I suppose he knew that I didn't have one I could announce even to these worldly people—for I imagined they were of the great world, and they just about were. Moulton smiled at me, and not without kindness. With the deep creases of his eyes, he look on a powerful resemblance to a fat lady of the old neighborhood.

"Well, in a pinch maybe Iggy can help if I can't."

Moulton and Iggy were friends, but this recommendation everybody knew was a joke, because Iggy specialized in bloodcurdlers for *Doc Savage* and *Jungle Thrillers*. He couldn't write anything else.

I liked this Iggy Blaikie. His real handle was Gurevitch, but that didn't have the dash that went with the proud Anglo-Saxon names of his heroes. So as Gurevitch was abandoned and Blaikie had never been real in the first place he became entirely Iggy. He had a real poolroom look. The boy with the bucket in Nagel's corner, a little weavy and punchy himself. He wore an apache jersey and a pair of the rope-soled sandals from the Chinese shop; he was lean but his face was flushed and gross, with bloodshot green eyes and mouth of froggy width, the skin of his throat creased, dirty, half shaved; his voice was choky and his conversation only part coherent. Except by someone experienced in sizing up such people, who would have known he was innocent, he might have been taken for a dope peddler, a junk-pusher, or minor hoodlum. His was a case of a strongly misleading appearance.

As to young Talavera, I didn't know just what to make of him. It was obvious that he looked me over measuringly, and he made me conscious, from the outside, of how I seemed, with tanned face and freestyle hair. I felt foolish somewhat, but I had to grant after all that I had studied him too. I wasn't experienced enough to be suspicious of the young man and native of the place who attaches himself to the foreign visitors, especially to women. Such are the broke characters to whom ancient names belong, in Florence in front of Gilli's Café, or the young men in tight pants who wait around at the top of the funicular in Capri for Dutch or Danish girls to pick up. And if I had been that experienced I might not have been quite right about Talavera. He was a mixed type. Very handsome, he looked like Ramon Novarro of the movies, both soft and haughty, and was said to be a mining engineer by profession; that was never proved but he had no need of work, his father was rich, and Talavera was a sportsman.

I said to Thea, "I don't think that young fellow likes me much."

"Well, what about it?" she answered carelessly. "We're only renting horses from his father."

For Caligula we first tried a burro, but though he stood hooded on the saddle and was well secured, the burro was bowed with terror and its head bristled. We then tried horses, and they were shy of him. I couldn't keep my seat when Thea handed Caligula up to me. And she herself wasn't more successful. Finally Talavera Senior brought out an old horse who had been through the Zapatista rebellion and wounded in guerrilla battles. To be ridden by a picador was all this gray animal appeared fit for, and be gored in the ring. But he was first-rate with the eagle. I would have said myself there was more sorrow than anything else in his accepting the bird on his back. Old Bizcocho, that was what this horse was called; it was hard to make him go at more than a fast amble, though he still had a few bursts of speed in him.

We took him out of town to a flat place, first, to practice. Out beyond the cemetery and its bones that lay accidental on the ground, the reek of flowers along the white tomb walls: first I on the gray animal who clopped slow, the eagle braced on my arm; then Thea on another horse; and Jacinto in his white sleeping-suit garb and dark feet carried just above the ground riding a donkey. We would pass a funeral, often of a child, and the father himself with the casket on his head would step out of the road—so would the whole cortege, musicians included—and with his eyes, like the milk of blackness, a few Mongolian mustache hairs fine and long on the savage bulges of his mouth, even afflicted, and while inimical, would follow the eagle as he passed. There would be the same whisper, "*Mira, mira, mira—el águila, el águila!*" So we'd pass by the white stones and walls that scaled in the heat, the iron prickles, the bones of death, the sleepers' clothes flappy and humiliated at the back; and also the little fever-slain child that rode inside.

We got up to the plateau, from which the town lay half covered in a picturesque hole, and there practiced with Caligula to get him used to a take-off while in motion. When he learned that, Thea's confidence in him entirely came back.

In fact we did it well. He sat on my arm, I stirred old Biz-cocho to move faster, and the eagle took hold strongly with his feet and wrung me through the demon's glove. I struck the hood and then slipped the swivel—I had to drop the reins to do this and grip with my knees—and Caligula put forward his breast with a clap of the huge wings and started to take the air.

In a few days Bizcocho was ready, and in tremendous ex-citement, one morning, we went out for the giant lizards. Ja-cinto came with us to flush them out of the rocks, and we climbed down the mountainside to their tropical place. There the heat was thick; it collected stagnant in the rocks, which were soft and eaten by rain acids into grottos and Cambodian shapes. The lizards were really huge, with great frills or sails—those ancient membranes. The odor here was snaky, and we seemed in the age of snakes among the hot poisons of green and the livid gardenias. We waited, and the cautious kid went to poke under leaves with a long pole, for the iguanas were savage. Then on a ledge above us I saw one who looked on, but as I pointed him out we saw the Elizabethan top of him scoot away. These beasts were as fast and bold as anything I had ever seen, and they would jump anywhere and from any height, with a pyre writhe of their sides, like fish. They had great muscles, like fish, and their flying was monstrously beautiful. I was astonished that they didn't dash themselves into pellets, like slugs of quicksilver, but when they smashed down they continued without any pause to run. They were faster than the wild pigs.

I was anxious for Thea. I knew what a state she was in. The place was steep, there was no room to maneuver, and she wheeled and plunged her horse. I had the burden of the eagle, and the old Zapatista gray couldn't turn fast though he was game enough and understood taking chances. So I heard more than I saw most of the time.

"Thea," I shouted, "for Chrissake, don't do that!"

But she was crying something to Jacinto and at the same time waved to me to get into position. She wanted to get the lizards driven down a slope of stones where they had no cover. Sometimes silver, sometimes dusty, gray, statue-green they looked as they flew. Finally she signaled me to strike the eagle's hood and slip his leash. I took a lurch, Bizcocho started downslope on the loose rocks, Caligula gripped me; I slipped the drawstring and took off the hood, drew the swivel, and he went up, forward in the deep air of the mountainside, once again up toward the high vibrations of blue. Coming and going in stages, he went to a great height to wait on.

Thea sprang to the ground to seize the pole from the boy. He was just sweeping it through the thick growth and tore off magnificent flowers as red as meat that tumbled down in the wave of ferns, and he cried, "*Ya viene!*" An iguana fled down the rocks. Caligula saw him and made his pitch. Feathered and armored he looked in his black colors, and such menace falling swift from heaven. Down the iguana made his pure leap too, crashed, ran, doubled at Caligula's stoop, slithered from the snatch of the talons, rolled, fought over his belly from the shadow that haunted him so fast, flew again. I saw the two sharp fierce faces, and as Caligula put his foot on the monster it opened its angular mouth with strange snake rage and struck the eagle in the neck. Jacinto cried, and Thea even shriller, at this sight. Powerfully Caligula shook, but only to get free. The iguana dropped and fled, glittering its blood on the rocks. Thea yelled, "After him! Get him! There he goes!" But the eagle didn't pursue down the slope; he landed and stood beating his wings. When the thrashing of the lizard couldn't be heard any more he folded them. He didn't fly to me.

Thea shrieked at him. "You stinking coward! You crow!" She picked up a stone and flung it at him. Her aim was wide; Caligula only raised his head when it struck above him.

"Stop that, Thea! For the love of God, stop! He'll tear out your eyes!"

"Let him try to come at me, I'll kill him with my hands. Let him just come near!" She left her mind with fury, and there was no sense in her eyes. I felt my arms weak, seeing her like this. I tried to keep her from throwing another stone, and when I couldn't I ran to unstrap the shotgun for use, and also to keep it from her. Again she missed, but this time came close, and Caligula took off. As he rose I thought, Good-by bird! There he goes to Canada or to Brazil. She pulled at the breast of my shirt and with great pain and tears she cried,

"We wasted our time with him, Augie. Oh, Augie. He's no good. He's chicken!"

"Maybe the thing hurt him."

"No, he was the same with the little one. He's scared."

"Well, he's gone. He beat it."

"Where?" She tried to look, but I reckon couldn't see well for the tears. And I wasn't any longer sure, either, which of various spots in the sky he was.

"I hope he flies to hell!" she said with a shiver of anger. Her face burned. At his fraud, that he should look such a cruel machine, so piercing, such a chief, and have another spirit under it all. "Is he hurt if he flies like that?"

"But you threw rocks at him," I said. And once again I felt implicated, because he had been tamed on my arm.

Well, it was hard to take this from wild nature, that there should be humanity mixed with it; such as there was in the beasts that embraced Odysseus and his men and wept on them in Circe's yard.

At home, when we got there sadly, we sent the horses back to Talavera's with Jacinto. Thea wouldn't have had the spirit to walk back from the stables, and I didn't want to leave her now. Entering the patio, we heard cries from the cook, who ran into the kitchen with her baby because Caligula was going back and forth on the shed roof.

I said to Thea, "Here's the eagle, he's back. What do you want to do about him?"

She said, "I don't care. I don't want to do anything. He just came back for his meat, because he's too much of a coward to hunt for it."

"I disagree. He's back because he doesn't feel in the wrong. He simply isn't used to animals that fight when he grabs them."

"For all I care you can feed him to the cats."

I took some meat from a basket by the stove and went out to him; he came to my fist, and I hooded him and passed the swivel, then put him on the waterbox, his dark cool place.

About a week passed and I was his sole custodian. Thea interested herself in other things. She set up a darkroom and started to develop the films she had taken en route. The eagle was left to my care; I exercised and handled him alone in the patio, like one man who rows a large lifeboat by himself. And at this time also I had an uneasy gut, an attack of dysentery, and thus saw him more often than I ordinarily would have cared to. The doctor prescribed Carbosome and told me to stay off tequila and town water. I had perhaps been taking a little too much of that smoky tequila, which made you unreliable if you weren't used to it.

But the slump from nobility of pursuit harmed everybody. The house was dull while Thea was in her laboratory. Dull isn't perhaps the word when you consider what disappointment and wrath were kept down. And also I couldn't stay in bed while Caligula was being neglected, if only for the reason that he'd become dangerous through hunger, let alone the humane side of it.

Beneath some paper stored for kindling beside the fireplace I found a big volume, without covers and in fine type. It contained Campanella's *City of the Sun*, More's *Utopia*, Machiavelli's *Discourses* and *The Prince*, as well as long selections from St. Simon, Comte, Marx and Engels. I don't recall what ingenious person made this collection, but it certainly was a whopper. Two days it rained, and I was sunk in it while wet wood tried to burn and I tossed in whole bundles of resinous ocote to try to make a blaze. It was too wet to fly Caligula. I stood upon the toilet seat and fed him through the hood, pushed the meat on him in order to get back as quickly as possible to the book. Utterly fascinated I was, and forgot how I sat on my bones, getting up lamed, dazed by all that boldness of assumption and reckoning. I wanted to talk to Thea about this, but she was too preoccupied with other things.

I said, "Whose is this book?"

"Just a book. Somebody's."

"Well, this is some splendid stuff."

She was glad I had found something to interest myself in but didn't care about the topic. She laid her hand to one side of my face and kissed me on the other; however, that was only to send me on my way. I took a stretch in the rainy garden. From the wall I saw old da Fiori in the arbor as he picked his nose.

Then I went to get my rubber poncho, for I had a great craving for company. Thea had asked me to get some photographic paper, which gave me an errand. As I marched down the wide, terraced stony stages in the slow rain there was a shaggy long-legged pig who lay in the red mud of the ditch, and a chicken stood on him and pecked the lice. And the gramophone was playing at Hilario's through a loudspeaker,

Tres cosas hay en la vida
Salud dinero y amor

and next something winding and slow by Claudia Muzio or maybe Amelita Galli-Curci from *Jewels of the Madonna*. Eleanor Klein once had had that record. It made me feel sad, though not in a low state.

In my foul-weather gear I passed before the cathedral where the beggars soaked in their wool colors and showed their lopped puckered limb ends. I left some coins behind; after all, the dough originally was Smitty's; I thought some of it should pass on.

From Hilario's second-floor porch of flowers somebody called me and banged on the tin shield of Carta Blanca beer to get my attention. It was Wiley Moulton, who said, "Come on up." I was glad to.

Besides Iggy there were two other people at the table who at first seemed man and wife to me. He was pushing fifty but behaved younger, a dry, thin, tall person. But I looked first at the girl, introduced to me merely as Stella. I was happy to see her. She ranked everything in the house, man, beast, and plant, as far as beauty went. Her features rose very slightly from the surface of her face, full of sense; her eyes were, I guess I'd say, amorous. It was natural that I should be happy to see her; I think, the way revolutionists feel the hands of passersby to know whether they're common people or aristo-crats, when you're in love you also make identifications like that. Stella was this man Oliver's girl. And although when he looked at me he appeared to be at ease he was suspicious, and that's the irrationality of people, for he had arranged to make himself envied instead.

Moulton soon made it clear that I wasn't unattached. "Hah, Bolingbroke," he said.

"Who's that, me?"

"Of course you. You can't look like a personage and not expect to receive an illustrious name. Something clicked when

I saw you, and I said there's a man who ought to be Boling-broke if he isn't already. You don't mind, do you?"

"Could anyone mind being Bolingbroke?"

Each, according to his tendency, had a look of pleasantry, with malice or with sympathy.

"This is Mr. March. Bolingbroke, what's your first name?"

"Augie."

"How is Thea?"

"Fine."

"We haven't seen you two much. Must be that eagle that keeps you busy."

"He does, we are busy."

"I admired you like anything when you arrived in the sta-tion wagon and I saw you take out that bird. I was sitting up here and watching the whole thing. But I understand he's flunked."

"Who said so?"

"Oh, the word went around that he was a flop."

That little bastard Jacinto!

"Is it true, Bolingbroke—is that mighty bird funky? Is he yellow?"

"Why," I said, "that's a lot of nonsense! How's one eagle different from another? They're all more or less the same. An eagle is an eagle, a wolf a wolf, a bat a bat."

"You're right, Boling. I'd say in our species, even, we're pretty much alike. Just the same, the differences are interest-ing. So what about your eagle?"

"He's not ripe yet for this kind of hunting. But he will be soon. Thea's a great trainer."

"I wouldn't deny it. But if he's timid he must have been a lot easier to train than a real triple-threat, piss-and-vinegar ea-gle like the one that actually caught those lizards a while back."

"Caligula is a bald American, the strongest and most savage kind."

I had yet to find out how little people want you to succeed in an extraordinary project, and what comfort some have that the negligible is upheld and all other greater effort falls on its face. On behalf of the writers I had been reading I felt a grievance too.

"Oliver is editor of a magazine," said Iggy. "Maybe he wants the story on your eagle."

"Which magazine is that?"

"*Wilmot's Weekly.*"

"Yes, we drove down for a holiday," said this Oliver.

He looked rather silly, frail in the head, with thready lips, small mustache, and knobby cheekbones. Obviously he was a lush, and a very vain man. It was only recent, his coming up in the world. Moulton and Iggy had known him back in New York, and one of the first things Moulton told me about him was that only a couple of years before if you let this Oliver into your house you ran the risk that he would steal some of your clothes and hock them for whisky; and when last heard from he was in the booby-hatch for the insulin cure, with the screaming meemies. Yet here he was, dressed to kill, with a new convertible and this beauty who was supposed to be an actress. And he was really the editor of *Wilmot's Weekly.* Of which he now said, "We're interested mainly in political articles."

"Well, Christ, Johnny, don't try to tell me it's all so serious in your mag—all think-pieces. It never used to be."

"Under the new owners everything is different. You know," he said, and changed the subject in a way that soon became predictable. "I wrote my autobiography last week. Just before we started out. It took a week. Childhood one day, boyhood next, and the rest in five days flat. Ten thousand words a day. It's coming out next month." When he talked about himself it was with such satisfaction that for the moment he looked healthy and well, glossy. Then he had a relapse when the topic got away from him, and seemed very meager.

Stella said, "We're staying at the Carlos Quinto. Come and have a drink with us."

"Yes, why don't we," said Oliver. "We ought to take advantage of it; it's costing plenty. We can sit in the garden at least."

I went away, for I was really worked up about the eagle after Moulton's ribbing. I'd have thought, myself, that Caligula's flop would give me a sort of pleasure, but, curiously, that wasn't how it worked out. Before, he had interfered with love; but now that he had flopped he did even more harm. Suddenly Thea and I appeared to have lost the place, and I was bewildered. What was the matter that pureness of feeling couldn't be kept up? I see I met those writers in the big book of utopias at a peculiar time. In those utopias, set up by hopes and art, how could you overlook the part of nature or be sure you could keep the feelings up?

I went home determined that we would not back down but fly Caligula and catch those giant iguanas, just like that other American couple.

First I wanted to collar Jacinto for blabbing, but I couldn't find him. Nor was Thea in the house. The cook told me, "*Están cazando.*"

"*Que?*"

"*Culebras,*" said she, in that voice that was like a haywisp of antiquity, it was always so thin and distant.

I looked the word up in the dictionary. They had gone to hunt snakes. Caligula was in his closet.

At night they returned. A band of town kids tagged after them, some of Jacinto's gang, and yelled to one another by the fiery gate light of Casa Descuitada. In a box Jacinto carried two snakes.

"Where have you been, Thea?"

"We caught these pit vipers—fine ones."

"Who? All these kids weren't with you, were they?"

"Oh no. We picked them up on the way back when Jacinto told them what we had."

"Thea, you're marvelous to go out and catch them. It's great! But why didn't you wait for me? They're dangerous, aren't they, these things?"

"I didn't know when you were coming back. A charcoal burner showed up and told me he had seen vipers, so I went right out after them."

She put them in one of the cases we had made ready for the iguanas, and that was the start of her collection. In time the porch became a snake gallery, so that the cook wanted to quit, fearing for her kid.

The moment was right to mention the eagle, when Thea was freshened by her success. She listened and was reasonably ready to be swayed, agreeing that Caligula should have another try. I never thought I'd be pleading for him with her. Jacinto went to Talavera's for the horses next morning. At the gate of the villa I got the traps ready, the cages and the pole, and when Jacinto returned we were there with Caligula, who, as usual, looked great, dangerous. I frowned at Thea's occasional skeptical glance toward him. We set out. Now and then I talked to him and stroked him with a feather. I said, "Old man, this time you'd better do your stuff."

We came to the same place, the iguanas' haunt, and I took a higher position than the last time, to give Caligula a better view of that stony slope. We stood then. His grip was very sharp; I tried to transfer some of his weight to the thigh, not hold him continually on my raised arm. Bizcocho twitched off the ferocious flies of this place who pinned themselves sparkling on his gray ribs.

Thea rode below, and I saw her through a floor of ferns. I caught glimpses also of Jacinto climbing on the turrety white rocks and began to hear some of the giants scuttle and crash when they leaped and fled, and see the voluptuary flowers tremble heavily.

Suddenly I got the idea of what it was to hunt, not with a weapon but with a creature, a living creature you had known how to teach because you'd inferred that all intelligences from the weakest blink to the first-magnitude stars were essentially the same. I touched him and stroked him. As if to check up on me Bizcocho turned his head. And just then Thea whipped the bandanna from her hair, the prearranged signal. I found the cord of the hood and gave the galloping fall on the saddle, feeling called upon not to spare myself. Bizcocho started off very fast. I must have picked too abrupt a downcourse, for the old horse went faster than he ever had. I gripped with my thighs and I pulled the hood and swivel. I was shouting, "Go to it!" when I too suddenly began to go, over the head of the horse as he struck with his hoofs for balance on the sliding stone. He was falling and so was I. I felt the push of Caligula's spring as he left my arm, and then I saw the color of my own blood on the slope of stones. I struck and slid. I heard Bizcocho's crazy neigh and Jacinto's cry.

"Roll, go on rolling!" shouted Thea. "Augie, darling, roll! He's kicking! He's hurt!"

But one of Bizcocho's hoofs caught me square in the head, and I was out.

Chapter XVII

IT TAKES some of us a long time to find out what the price is of being in nature, and what the facts are about your tenure. How long it takes depends on how swiftly the social sugars dissolve. But when at last they do dissolve there's a different taste in your mouth, bringing different news which registers with dark astonishment and fills your eyes. And this different news is that from vast existence in some way you rise up and at any moment you may go back. Any moment; the very next, maybe.

Well, that poor Bizcocho, he cracked my skull, but he had broken a leg and Thea shot him. Unconscious, I didn't hear the explosion. She and Jacinto dragged me up on her horse. The boy mounted with me and held me up like a sack of meal. The blood was spilling from my head, and I had lost some teeth too, from the lower jaw. So, sagging in Jacinto's arms with the bandanna Thea had used for signaling so soaked it couldn't absorb more blood, I was carried to the doctor's house. When we were nearly there I gave myself a heave and said, "Where's the eagle?"

A hunting accident would never make Thea shed tears, even one as bad as this. She didn't cry at all. As I was deafened from faintness or from blood or hair or soil in my ears, I didn't hear but rather saw how she cursed Caligula. I felt a wave or divot of my scalp curl or wrinkle on my head. I glimpsed how her hand, which held my leg tight, was streaked with red. Her pallor was very hot. With that depth and hollow narrowness of sight that you have at such moments her face came before me with spots of light on it from the pattern of brass eyelets on her hat, a spatter of heat across the bridge of her nose and on her lips.

My hearing cleared; I heard the kids cry, "*Es el amo del águila!*" *El águila!* Who was doing loops somewhere in the heavens with great pinions, with Turkish feather pants and rending beak. The whole height of space appeared very great to me. I felt I crept along at the bottom of it. Thea said, "You've lost a tooth." I nodded. I knew where the gap was. But sooner or later you're bound to lose some teeth.

From the doctor's yard two women came for me with furled stretcher, and they laid me on it. I kept fading in and out, extremely weak. But as we went through the patio I was conscious and admired the day, which was notably beautiful. However, I thought next that it was because of me that Bizcocho was dead, that he had survived wild Zapatista night of guerrilla shooting and slithering and probably been present when men were crucified or their bellies filled with ants, that he had been whanged at by blasting shotguns, and it had to be me that killed him.

The doctor had a flower in his buttonhole when he came forward, and he was smiling. But basically he was gloomy. His room stunk of drugs and ether. I got a dose of ether that made me reek for days after. I kept puking. I was covered with bandages; my face was stiff with the crusts of scratches. I could eat only gruel and turkey soup, and I couldn't stand myself. Inside the turban of bandages I heard a hissing as if I had a faucet or jet there. From the pain and this hiss or trickle I suspected that gloomy smiler of doing a bad job and I worried about my skull because of the careless Mexican approach to slaughter, sickness, and burial; but the doctor turned out later to have done a good job. But then I suffered, I was low, eyes deep circled, cheeks drawn in, gap-toothed. In the bandages I seemed to myself to resemble my mother and at times my brother Georgie.

And even after the scratches healed and the headaches dimmed down I was gnawed and didn't know from what cause. Thea also became very restless. Caligula's washout and my being such a chump as to spur poor Bizcocho from the top of a bluff terribly disappointed her. With her eagerness and boldness, that she should be held back by my incompetence after having undertaken this, planned it out, mastered the animal, was very hard to take. Thea sent Caligula away to her father's friend in Indiana, for his Trianon zoo. I thought how the old desert rat in Texarkana would enjoy hearing about this. I hobbled out to see the eagle, caged and crated, loaded on the wagon. The white patch of maturity was beginning to show on his head; the eye wasn't a bit less imperial and his beak with its naked purposes of breathing and tearing just as awesome as before.

I said, "Good-by, Calig."

"Good-by and good riddance, you phony," said Thea. We were near tears, both of us, from the crackup of hopes and ridiculing of expectations. The gauntlets and hood lay for a long time in a corner and took on oblivion.

As Thea sat with me and minded and nursed me for a few weeks it became more and more clear that if she didn't show any unrest there were other expressions that didn't appear on her face either. When I started to recover I didn't want her to hang around for my sake and company, if she was going to look like this. We had one of those arguments of sacrifice; she didn't want to leave me alone and I insisted that she go out, though I didn't want it to be after snakes that she went. But somebody had tipped her off to some green and red vipers, and what didn't show in her looks, patient toward me as I lay deaf and gaunt in my turban, in the sequel of the great flop—what didn't show was how she sat and dreamed of catching these snakes. I recognized that she was bored and needed action.

At first she went after wild pigs and such creatures, to keep me satisfied, but later she brought home snakes from the mountains in a burlap sack. Because of the good it did her I didn't squawk about it. I could measure her improvement daily with the eye. Only I didn't want her to go hunting alone, and I urged her to get some of her friends to accompany her, not just Jacinto. There was a hunting set in town, and sometimes the doctor went out with her, sometimes young Talavera.

So I was alone and went around the villa in robe and bandages, into the garden, along the porch with the snakes who writhed in the straw and raced their tongues—I had a cold eye for them. I felt it was less from horror than from antagonism. After all, I had tamed an eagle and got somewhere with wildlife, so I could claim a certain amount of courage. I didn't have to be clothed in intrepidity all the time or love all creatures. There was a kind of snake smell, like the smell of spoiled mango or rotten hay, the same as where we had hunted the giant iguana.

When I wasn't too restless I sat in one of the bullhide chairs and read the utopia book. I still had the dysentery bug and in the morning often felt that heavy drape of the guts that made me run to the biffy, Caligula's old roost. There I kept the door open. It gave me a view of the entire town, which now, late fall, after the deepest heats had passed off, was very beautiful. There weren't real seasons here, but the shadows of harsher climates varied the months, from the north or from the south. Daily there was this sure blue, while the powerful forces of heaven took it easy over the mossy tiles. This blue beauty compensated me considerably, as did the book when I was in the right mood for it. Otherwise I schlepped around useless and melancholy, feeling like a slob. As my cheeks had fallen, their bones became large and my eyes appeared a little sleepy, from the uneasiness they'd have shown had they opened wider. I grew a kind of Indian mustache of fair hair by the sides of my mouth too.

Thea drank her coffee, told me to be well, put on her sombrero of brass eyelets, and went out to the horses. I would come and watch her mount. With just the slight heaviness of confident body she sat in the saddle. She no longer asked me whether I wanted her to stay with me, only recommended that I take a walk in the afternoon. I said I'd see about it.

Moulton and Iggy came to visit me, and Moulton said, "Boling, you look like hell," so I felt even more sad over myself and was in the dumps, with omens that moved around in my heart.

Stella too, Oliver's girl friend, regretted that I didn't look better when I talked to her from the garden wall. I observed there was a shadow over her also. These days I was drinking up a fair amount of tequila limonada, and I invited her to join me. She refused. Regretfully she said, "I wish I could. One of these days maybe I will. I'd like to talk to you. But you know we're supposed to move out of the Carlos Quinto." I didn't know, and before I could find out why, thin Oliver came lifting his feet over the flowers, his horsy ankles in gartered silk socks, his little red mouth sullen. He took her away from the wall, not even talking to me.

What was wrong with him?

Moulton said he was jealous.

"And she says they're moving out."

"Yes, Oliver rented that Jap's villa. The Jap has to go back to Nagasaki. Oliver says the biddies at the Carlos are giving

Stella the treatment. Because they know they aren't married. If I had a girl like that, a lot I'd care what some old bags were saying!"

"But why is he settling down here? Doesn't he have that magazine to take care of in New York?"

"He runs it from Mexico," said Iggy.

Moulton said, "Bushwah! He's here because he's in dutch."

"You think he embezzled money?" said Iggy, astonished.

Moulton looked as though he knew much more than he judged fit to tell. Satchel ass. His portly hard middle hung over with a shirt illustrated with pineapples. He even had a faint shame of the apparition he made in the sunlight. His lids were as dark in stain as his smoker's fingers, and he had the blinking habit.

"Jepson says he heard he wants to throw a big party on account of Stella in the villa, to show those old bitches at the Carlos," said Iggy.

"He's going to show everyone, and knock people down with his success. Whoever thought he was nothing but an international bum, and that's everybody in the world who ever laid eyes on him, now's going to be shown. Boy! People are right where he left them, and he's going to come back and wow them. He *has* been around the world too, but he didn't know it because he was drunk." As he said this, Oliver appeared to my thought in a shack of Outer Mongolia, where soldiers in quilted coats saw him lying in his vomit in a stupor. Moulton liked to show that ill, miserable things and rubbish supplied the unity of the world. Only amusement supposedly made this tolerable, and so he specialized in amusement. All these people, the whole colony, did that.

Well, they visited me at the villa. Then after half an hour Moulton ran out of talk. They had stamped out a dozen butts, and Moulton began to look terribly bored. He had exhausted this particular corner where we sat and so looked sick that he had to stay.

"Bolingbroke," he said, "you don't have to stick around the house because you wear that turban. Come down to the *zócalo*. We'll meet folks there or play on the fribble machine. Come along, Boling. To horse."

"Yes, come on, Boling."

"Not you, Iggy. Go home. Eunice raises hell with me because I keep you away from work."

"But I thought you were divorced, Iggy?" I said.

"He is, but his wife keeps him on a chain. She makes him stay with the kid while she and the new husband go out."

Down at Hilario's we sat amid the flowers of the porch, over the square. They were the simpler flowers of cooler weather. Except the red poinsettia, star of Christmas, with velvet thrust-out peaks, the leader in splendor. It said a lot to me that these flowers should have no power over their place of appearance, nor over the time, and yet be such a success of beauty and plaster the insignificant wall. I saw also the little kinkajou who roved over his square of cage in every dimension, upside down, backwards. In the depth of accident, you be supple—never sleepy but at sleeping time.

And Moulton sat and continued his satire on Iggy. Eunice took the checks from New York and kept Iggy on a budget. But Iggy didn't know how to handle dough. He'd only go to the *foco rojo* with it, and the girls would take it away. Iggy with his bloodshot green eyes and froggy kindly mouth felt praised, sort of, pictured among the whores of the *foco rojo*.

"Eunice needs the money for the kid. Or I'd lose it to you in poker. That's what gets Wiley, he can't win real jack off me."

"Hell, what would I care if I didn't see Jepson lush in here with your money, the money he gets out of Eunice?"

"Why, you're nuts! He's got his own. His grandfather had an expedition to Africa. No bunk."

To be near his daughter, an overpetted dark little kid, Iggy lived in the same villa as his ex-wife. It was mostly in order to protect her and the kid from Jepson. I think Iggy probably still loved Eunice.

I went around with him and with Moulton now. As the house was void, as there were more snakes on the porch, as I wasn't strong enough to go with Thea but wasn't too weak to be restless, as I was horse-shy and hunt-shy, as I was in reality in a fork about my course of life, I stalled and delayed. Besides, I was intrigued with Moulton and Iggy and others of the international colony. I couldn't deny their appeal. I learned their language fast. But also fatigue of them came fast.

And the strange thing was, you know, how you woke early in the morning and saw the air, a light gold, thin but strong before daily influences took it away from you. But you felt no reason why, as far as the air itself was concerned, these influences had to be such as they were, low, anxious, or laughable.

Under the pomegranate tree, on the wood bench, Iggy asked me to help him with his difficulties. His story was hung up and he had to have a plot angle. There is a busted ensign on the beach who becomes a rummy. A half-breed proposes to him to run coolies illegally into Hawaii. But among the plantation hands he discovers there are spies, so the old U.S. officer in him is stirred, and he's going to surrender the whole swatch of them to the authorities. But he has to fight it out with the lascar who now suspects him. Iggy worried out his story, and I went on bare feet for the tequila bottle.

Then Moulton came and we left. The cook had fixed lunch, but I didn't like to eat alone. I bought *tacos* in the market, which made my gut worse, or I got a sandwich at the Chinaman's.

So things shouldn't cram on his mind but be orderly, Bacon had music played in the next room when he thought out the *New Atlantis*. But down in the *zócalo* all day the machines played "Salud Dinero" or "Jalisco," and there was furious noise, the rapid dual hammer of the mariachis and the yockering of the lame-tongue blind fiddler and crazy scrapes, plus the bang of bus motors and bells, and this mingling was the bed of my disharmonies. So mostly I felt confusion, and dangers that were as terrible as the sky and mountain sights were gorgeous in their painting. The town whirled and howled as it hit the stride of its season.

While Iggy doped out how the American and the half-breed would fight it out over the signals to warn the coast guard we were on the way to Moulton's hotel. He coaxed me to stay while he ground out his installments of men from Mars. He hated his work; the solitude of it above all. I'd sit on the roof outside his room, droop-shouldered, hands hung large from my knees, and look toward the knotted mountains and wonder in my sun-dimmed mind where Thea might be.

Coming from the cigarette-gray room to think, Moulton paced in shorts that showed his concave knees and thick huge legs; he narrowed the eyes of his great face and looked at the town as though it were all a racket. He poured a drink, he was a chain-smoker; and in the business of mixing, lighting, dragging, flipping, blowing smoke through his satirical nose, there seemed to be contained about all he thought really worth effort. He was mighty bored. And he understood how to make me go through the long characteristic moment of his mood—this ash, ice, butts, lemon peel and sticky glass, panting space of empty time. He saw to it his lot was shared, like everybody else, and did something with you to compel you to feel what he felt. Moulton could even put it in words himself. He said, "Boredom is strength, Bolingbroke. The bored man gets his way sooner than the next guy. When you're bored you're respected." With small nose, gross thighs, and those back-bent smoke-dyed fingers, he obliged me with this explanation, and he thought to have more effect on me than he really ever could have. When I didn't argue he was satisfied that he had persuaded me, and was not the first to make that mistake. A conversation was something he could run well, so he liked the reality of his life to be that of conversations. I was on to this.

"Ah well, let's have a break and play blackjack." He carried a deck of cards in his shirt pocket. So he blew the cigarette dust from the table and cut for the deal, and when he saw my glances still going out to the mountains he said, to distract me, not roughly, "Yeah, she's up there. Come on, chum, deal me. Okay. Take yourself. Want a side bet? I bet I get the deal from you in ten minutes."

Moulton was a big boy for a game of cards, poker most of all. We played at Hilario's at first, and when Hilario kicked about these long sessions that lasted far into the night we moved over to the filthy Chinese restaurant. Very soon I began to put all my time into gambling. It seems the ancient Huron tribe thought gambling was a remedy for some illnesses. Maybe I had one of those illnesses. Moulton must have too. He had to be betting continually. I matched pesos with him, cut for high card, played fribble—which was what he called pin-ball—and even put-and-take, with a little top. I was lucky and also skillful at poker, which I had learned in a great school, Einhorn's poolroom. Moulton complained, "Brother, you must have studied with the Capablanca of poker. I can't tell when you're bluffing because you always look so innocent. Nobody can really be as innocent as all that." This was true, though I would have said I actually did intend to be as good as possible. That's how much I myself knew. But Jesus, Lord! Dissembling! Why, the master-dissemblers there are around! And if nature made us live and do as worms and beetles do, to escape the ichneumon fly and swindle other enemies by mimicry, and so forth—well, all right!! But that's not our problem.

With Thea too I behaved as though nothing was wrong, and yet I knew we were slipping. If I didn't show what despair this caused it was a lead-pipe cinch to bluff Moulton out with only a jack.

Why these snakes? Why did she have to hunt snakes? She came back with heaving sackfuls, which made my intestines go wrong with reaction; and then she gave them such loving treatment that I could see nothing in it but eccentricity. You had to be careful not to provoke them into striking the glass, because it gave them mouth sores hard to cure. And in addition they had parasites that got between the scales, and they had to be dusted or washed with mercurochrome; some had to be given inhalations of eucalyptus oil for their lung ailments, for snakes get tuberculosis. Toughest of all was the casting of the skins, which was like labor when they couldn't writhe out of the epidermis and even their eyes were clouded with a dirty milk. Thea sometimes took forceps to help them or covered them with damp rags to soften the skin, or she put the more restless ones in water and in the water set a block of wood afloat so the beast might rest its little head when fatigued with swimming. But then they would gleam out, one day, and their freshness and jewelry would give even me pleasure, their enemy, and I would like to look at the cast skin from which they were regenerated in green or dots of red like pomegranate seeds or varnished gold crust.

Meanwhile Thea and I were not satisfied with each other. I was resentful of the snakes and that she tended them. I felt myself between two peculiarities, hers and the peculiarity of the town in full stride of its season. But I didn't tell her. When she asked me how about coming out with her to hunt I said I wasn't well enough yet. So she looked at me, and the thought was very prominent that after all I was lushing and playing cards, so if I stood before her skinny, ill, and with secret thoughts smoldering, what remedy could we ever agree on?

"I don't like that gang you're with," she said.

"They're harmless," I casually answered, but it was not a harmless kind of answer.

"Why don't you come out with me tomorrow? Talavera has a safe horse for you. There are some places I want to show you, wonderful places."

"Well, that'll be swell," I said. "When I feel more ready."

I had tried to put Caligula over and that was enough of a trial; I had stretched myself as far as I could and had no more stretch. I'd be damned if I could get myself into Thea's excitement about catching snakes. It was too extreme a way of making out, with that vigor that couldn't be satisfied in ordinary pursuits. If she had to go and snatch these dangerous animals by the throat with a noose, and keep them and milk their venom from them, okay. But I knew at last that definitely there was one thing that was not for me.

She was gone for two days in the mountains. When she returned I heard of it but didn't go up to the house; I was in a game at Louie Fu's and couldn't leave. Next morning I saw her in the garden, in riding breeches and the heavy boots she wore for snaking, thick and sturdy so that fangs couldn't pierce. Her white skin showed she was unwell, sullen; she hadn't rested and she craved and smarted, she wanted to punish me. Under the eyes there was a thickening of trouble. From her head the black hair gave back the heat of the sun, and along those particular hairs of irregular departure from her forehead there burned the red thread that was part of the secret of the black.

She said fiercely, "Where were you!"

"I got in very late."

She was hot, shaky, and hasty, and heavy clear tears gave her eyes that crazy largeness of grievance that sometimes they would get. I thought she would sob, but she only shook.

"I kind of expected *you*, the night before last," I said, and she didn't answer me. We were both sore but not prepared really to fight. What she shook with was breaking and not increasing anger.

"What do you see in those people down there?" she demanded. "I think they must make you feel ashamed of me, ever since Caligula. They make fun of me."

"You think I'd let them do that?"

"I know them better than you do. That Moulton stinks."

She lit into Wiley Moulton and other residents. I listened, and in this way we ignored our real differences. We couldn't yet stand a fight.

Sometimes I almost convinced myself that I was ready to bat around the mountains with the snake nooses and cameras and guns. I could have used some action, because I was nervous and overcharged and because I longed that she and I should be back as we had been in Chicago. But I never could quite bring myself to go.

It seemed to me that I had to continue playing poker. I was ahead and couldn't quit. Moulton kept yelling how I had drawn blood on everybody; I had to give people their chance for revenge. So I had a deck of cards between my fingers as their most familiar object, and actually I became a very dexterous and fancy dealer. Soon people were looking for me who didn't even know me, and I seemed to be running a game at the Chinese restaurant. Louie Fu in his coat sweater was of that opinion even. I was Bolingbroke or the Eagle Man to tourist strangers who sat in the game, world-tour bums, Moulton called them. My pockets were full of different foreign currencies. I didn't know exactly what I had. But I did have money. It was mine, not Smitty's. There was no longer any refrigerator with bills in the greens and dishes; Thea never seemed to think to offer me an allowance. If I hadn't been sick I'd have felt well-off, prosperous, with my pounds, dollars, pesos, and Swiss francs. But it was only my superficial luck that was good; I was rattled, I was bandaged in an unclean bandage, gaunt, the town seemed to want to blow its silly self to pieces, Thea was collecting coral snakes and rattlers, I had to win a fight of patience with my anxious backside to sit at Louie's, or in somebody's hotel room, or even at the *foco rojo* where the game sometimes moved. There the whores were in the rear; in front there was a little bar which was a soldiers' hangout, before the tourists took over. The soldiers read comic books, ate beans, and drank pulque. Rats walked on the beams. The girls cooked, swept, or read too, or washed their hair in the yard. One half-naked kid with a garrison cap clonked on the marimba; the little black rubber balls on his sticks struck fast. I felt I had to do something well, so it shouldn't all be a total loss, and so I watched the cards.

I didn't convince Thea when I said that I'd go along with her just as soon as I felt up to it, nor did she convince me by her gestures toward me. She consented to keep me company in town some evenings, and it was good to see her legs in skirts, not covered by trousers. But it burned me up on the day her divorce papers came and I said, as I had figured to do, "Let's get married," and she simply shook her head. Then I remembered how once when afraid of pregnancy she let escape the fear of explaining to her family that I was the father. Where at first it had disappointed me, and later graveled me more, this now gave me a harsh sting. For sure enough I had a glimmer of things from her standpoint, of how it is one thing to have a young man for your happy friend in the rosy days of love, and quite different the faulty creature to face in practical weather. I knew how I'd seem to her uncle, the powerful millionaire with his squash white-haired nose and his tailor-made Havanas. It was true that Thea defied him and aimed to become financially independent; but as she couldn't count on me she wouldn't cut herself off from her family for my sake. Had I been as enthusiastic on birds, snakes, horses, guns, and photography as she we might have made the grade. But I wouldn't have read a light meter for gold, I didn't want to capture snakes, and I felt ornery about it all. I hoped Thea would tire of it; while she, I suppose, waited for me to get tired of Moulton and Co.

It was one fiesta after another meantime. The band plunged in the *zócalo*, clashed, drummed, and brayed; the fireworks bristled and ran off in strings, the processions swayed around with images. A woman died of a heart attack at a five-day drunk party, and there were scandals. Two young men, lovers, had an argument about a dog and one of them took an overdose of sleeping pills. Jepson forgot his jacket in the *foco rojo*; the madame herself, Negra, brought it to the house, Iggy's ex-wife locked Jepson out, so he begged to sleep on Moulton's porch. Moulton wouldn't let him stay because he tried to borrow money, he drank his whisky. Now Jepson was living in the street, but as the town was foaming his sorrow wasn't particularly noticeable in it. Wolves or wild swine or the giant iguanas themselves or stags wouldn't have been either if they had slipped in from the mountains.

A bright dust blew around and whitened the nights. The hotels and shops wanted there should be a hullabaloo and paid money for the music and shots and tolling, but to keep up these long fiestas cash wouldn't have been enough, and the energy for them must have come from the olden-time worship of those fire snakes and smoke mirrors and gruesome monster gods. Even the dogs ran and mumbled as if fresh back from their errand in the land of death, Mictlan. The old belief of the Indians was that dogs carried the souls of the dead there. There was an intestinal-amoeba epidemic which was hushed up, but funerals tangled with the other processions. There were big entertainments. A Cossack chorus sang in the cathedral; the priest had never had such a crowd inside, and it made him frantic; he scolded and clapped his hands at everyone, crying we were in *la casa de Dios*. It didn't do a bit of good with that crowd. I can't say those Russians looked out of place in the *zócalo* in their tunics, boots, and tucked-in pants, musing around at night, burning their long cigarettes. A Brazilian-Italian opera company did *La Forza del Destino*. They sang and throbbed powerfully, but as though they didn't believe any of it themselves. Therefore I was skeptical too. Thea didn't come back for the second act. Then there was an Indian circus that gave a grim performance. The equipment of the acrobats was as if ripped out of an old foundry; the horses were shabby; the performers were solemn Michoacán Indians, and they stunted without nets or any safety devices. The savage little girls who came out in their soiled trousers to juggle and walk the wires and perform other tasks never smiled or bowed.

Thus in this town I didn't see anything familiar, except in reminiscence—as when those Russians made me remember Grandma Lausch.

Until one day when it was fairly quiet and I was sitting on a bench in the *zócalo* petting a kitten that tried to get into my armpit, and several large cars drove up to the cathedral. They were old cars but powerful, with something cast-iron about them, the long hoods, the low sling of expensive European automobiles. Immediately I knew there was a personage in the middle car, for bodyguards emerged from the two others, and I wondered who it was that could be so important and yet so run-down. Among the rest were two Mexican policemen, grouchy and proud of their tunics, which they smoothed straight right away; but the guards were Europeans or Americans, in leather jackets and leggings. Their hands were on their holsters and they were jittery; it seemed to me they didn't know the first thing about their job. So I judged, having now and again, in Chicago, seen the real thing.

It was a cool day. I wore the thick jacket with many pockets that Thea had bought for me on Wabash Avenue, the one that could save you in the wilderness. But it was zipped open, as I sat in the sun. The kitty was nuzzling and kneading under my arm with her paws—I felt her little spine with satisfied amusement and I watched to see who would come out of the center limousine now that the arrangements were complete. An aide gave the nod and a guard started to work the handle of the door, who obviously didn't have the hang of it, and all stood helpless during this embarrassment till the opposite door impatiently was thrown back with iron bump from the extreme wads of old upholstery, and heads of a foreign comb, specs, beards bent forward within the beautifully polished glass. Here and there was a briefcase; I thought I recognized something political about these briefcases. One person was saying something, smiling and chatty, into the chauffeur's phone. And then the principal figure came out with a spring, he was very gingery and energetic, debonair, sharp, acute in the beard. He addressed himself without waste of attention to the study of the front of the cathedral. He wore a short coat with fur collar, large glasses, his cheek was somewhat soft but that didn't take away from an ascetic impression he gave. As I looked at him I decided with a real jolt that this must be Trotsky, down from Mexico City, the great Russian exile, and my eyes grew big. I always knew my entire life would not go by without my having seen a great man; and strangely enough my thought was of Einhorn, condemned to sit in a chair and study faces in the papers and limited to seeing only the people who chanced to come by. I was very enthusiastic and right away stood up. The beggars and loafers were already collecting in their Middle Ages style, the touts and schnorrers and the others uncovering their damages and stock-in-trade woes from bandages and rags. Head thrown back, Trotsky regarded and estimated the vast church, and with a jump in which hardly anything elderly appeared he went up the stairs and hastened in. There was a surge after him; the people with the briefcases—members of radical organizations I used to know in Chicago always had briefcases like those—and also a huge man with hair like a woman's, and some of those queer bodyguards, and quite a few crutch-hoppers and singsong *limosnita* beggars who true enough were near dead, as they claimed, went through the dark gap of the church door.

I too wanted to go in; I was excited by this famous figure, and I believe what it was about him that stirred me up was the instant impression he gave—no matter about the old heap he rode in or the peculiarity of his retinue—of navigation by the great stars, of the highest considerations, of being fit to speak the most important human words and universal terms. When you are as reduced to a different kind of navigation from this high starry kind as I was and are only sculling on the shallow bay, crawling from one clam-rake to the next, it's stirring to have a glimpse of deep-water greatness. And, even more than an established, an exiled greatness, because the exile was a sign to me of persistence at the highest things. So I was wild with enthusiasm; it bumped up inside my skull like the handle of a broom and made me recall that my head still was bandaged and I should go easy. I stood watching till he came out again.

But the reason for telling you all this is that one of the bodyguards turned out to be my old friend Sylvester, the one-time owner of the Star Theater, the engineering student from Armour Tech, the ex-husband of Mimi Villar's sister, the former subway employee. I recognized him in his Western-style rig. Ye gods! How severe, melancholy, duty-charged, and baffled he looked! Same as the others, he packed a pistol; the spread of his pants was wide at the back and his belly hung over the belt. I hollered at him, "Sylvester! You, Sylvester!" He looked sharply at me, as if I took a dangerous liberty; yet he was curious. I was full of glee, and my head was pounding. My face got very red with laughter and excitement, because I was so extremely happy to see him. "You damned fool, Sylvester, don't you know who it is? It's Augie March. You mean to stand there and not recognize me? I haven't changed that much, have I?"

"Augie?" he asked and smiled a little with dark bitter lips, incredulous. His question made an uncertain creak in his throat.

"Of course! It's me, you dope! Jesus, how did you get here? What are you doing with that hardware?"

"How did *you* land down here? Gosh, we sure get around. What's wrong with your head?"

"I fell off a horse," I said, and in spite of my joy at seeing him I quickly ran through in my mind a variety of reasonable, and not especially true, accounts. But he didn't ask, which astonished me. It now astonishes me less, for I know more about how people get preoccupied.

"Gee, it's swell to see you, Sylvester. How come you're doing this?"

"I got assigned to it—what do you mean? They wanted somebody with a technological background."

Technological background! As I was laughing still from pleasure at meeting him I could get away with a laugh over this too. Poor Sylvester, with this story about being a technician. Well, well, whatever we got out of this meeting it sure wasn't going to be the truth. I had prepared a story myself, should he ask me what I was up to. That's how it is. One day's ordinary falsehood if you could convert it into silt would choke the Amazon back a hundred miles over the banks. However, it never appears in this form but is distributed all over like the nitrogen in potatoes.

"So?" I said. "You're with Trotsky all the time, you know him well, I guess? It must be marvelous. I wish I could know him!"

"You?"

"Gosh, I suppose I wouldn't fit in. What's he like? Do you think I could at least meet him, Sylvester? You could introduce me."

"Yeah? Just like that?" said Sylvester, amused, with his

heavy eyes. "It couldn't be more complicated than you think, could it? You're a funny guy. But look, I have to go. When you get up to the city phone me. I'd like to see you; we'll have a beer. You remember Frazer from Chicago? He's one of the old man's secretaries. Don't forget now." Another guard was calling him, and he trotted away to the cars.

Oliver cursed the Japanese for the delay about the villa, but finally the Japanese sailed for Japan and Oliver moved in and prepared to throw a huge party and have the best society in town. That would poison his enemies at the Carlos Quinto. Moulton helped him make up a guest list and invitations were sent out to the old residents. Mostly a lot of riffraff turned up, however, in observance of his troubles, which were by then public and had been for some time. A Treasury agent came to town, and he didn't hide his identity but told everyone, with swell humor, what he was. He sat spread on one of Hilario's wire-harp chairs and drank beer as if on a holiday, or fed peanuts to the kinkajou. Oliver managed to look indifferent when he went through the square, he and Stella as usual dressed up to the eyes. The more he looked self-possessed, the more it was a disaster, and I was sorry for him. Stella was scared. She sometimes tried to make me understand that she'd like to talk to me about this. I never thought it unnatural that I should be the one she wanted to discuss her troubles with. However, there was no chance to do it. Oliver watched her very closely.

I said to Moulton, "What do they want Oliver for? It must be serious or they wouldn't have sent a man from Washington."

"The guy says income-tax evasion, but it must be worse than that. Oliver's a vain, silly type, but he wouldn't be so dumb as to get in that sort of trouble. It's worse."

"Poor Oliver!"

"He's a jerk."

"Maybe so. But fundamentally—I mean, as a man."

"Oh, fundamentally," he said thoughtfully. But then he seemed to shake himself out of it and said, "Maybe fundamentally too he's a jerk."

Meanwhile it was in a terrible way instructive to see how Oliver behaved, how unruffled he tried to appear. But he was always in small ways losing control. One afternoon he got into a fight with old Louie Fu. Louie, he was queer enough, with his Spanish-Chinese cackles, and in addition he was also a terribly economizing old man, and I suppose in famine China he may have known what it was to pick grains out of manure; so it was nothing much to him now to pour the drinks people didn't finish into a single pop bottle. With his unassertive chest covered with gray knots of a loopy sweater, at the zinc counter, he poured together what was left of orange pop one day and put it in the icebox; Oliver caught him and punched him in the face. This was terrible. Louie screamed. His family was infuriated and started to yell. All we foreigners started up from the card game. The police appeared and closed in from the front door. I took Stella by the hand through the curtain of beads into the other half of the shop, where they sold drygoods, and as we came into the street we saw a gang swirl out and follow the arrestees to city hall and the magistrate's court. Louie's eye was already covered by a large stain and his throat was full of cords as he shouted. Oliver got one of the Mexican guitar-playing fancy-boys to interpret for him. And the defense he made was that what Louie had done was very dangerous because of the amoeba. Oliver couldn't have done worse than to claim he was protecting public health. The magistrate slapped his hand down *en seguida* on this irresponsible rumor of dysentery. He was large and squat, a man who raised bulls for the ring, and he wore his hat in the court like a businessman-prince, this dark powerful person. He named a whopping fine which Oliver paid on the spot, looking sporting, if grim, and also entertained. Money was one thing he didn't seem to lack. And how did Stella take this—in her sleeveless lace dress and wearing a hat? She appealed to me with her large disturbed eyes to see for myself what she was up against. With so much going on in the town I hadn't given it the consideration it called for. Why, even, did she need to wear such an elegant dress to Louie Fu's afternoon poker game? It must have been that she had no dresses except elegant ones, and no places to visit except those Oliver took her to. It was very odd. She said, "I have to talk to you one of these days. Soon."

But this was not the time. Oliver was now with us and said

to Moulton and Iggy various peculiar things, such as, "I've been to courts the world over." And, "Now they can't go on pretending about the trots, that there isn't any amoeba." And, "That yellow old c—sucker, at least I taught him a lesson."

Listening, I felt quite queer myself, in my bandages, cards and currencies in my pockets, my heart tight in my breast and toes free in the huaraches. I felt like someone who might come into the vision of a theosophist, that kind of figure.

At dinner Thea said, "I hear there was a riot in town. Were you in it, too?"

I didn't care for that. Why must she put it like that? I told her the story, or rather gave her a version of what happened. Anyway, she frowned. As I spoke of Stella I realized that I wanted to represent her as in love with Oliver. Thea didn't believe me.

"Augie," she said, "why don't we get away from here? At least while the season lasts. Let's get away from these people."

"Where do you want to go?"

"I thought we'd drive to Chilpanzingo."

Chilpanzingo was down in the hot country. But I was willing to go. I would go. But what would I do there?

"There are some interesting animals down there," she said.

So I answered evasively, "Well, I think I may feel up to it soon."

"You look run-down," she said, "but how can you expect to look anything else when you lead such a life? You never touched a drop before you got down here."

"I never had much reason to. I don't get stinking drunk either."

"No," she said, bitter, "just enough to carry you through your mistakes."

"*Our* mistakes," I corrected her.

So we sat at the dinner table, full of trouble and under the shadow of disappointment and anger. Then, after long thought, I said to her, "I will go to Chilpanzingo with you. I'd rather be with you than with anyone in the world."

She looked at me more warmly than she had in a long time. I wondered if there was something we might do in Chilpanzingo instead of hunting snakes. But she didn't say there was.

Everyone tries to create a world he can live in, and what he can't use he often can't see. But the real world is already created, and if your fabrication doesn't correspond, then even if you feel noble and insist on there being something better than what people call reality, that better something needn't try to exceed what, in its actuality, since we know it so little, may be very surprising. If a happy state of things, surprising; if miserable or tragic, no worse than what we invent.

Chapter XVIII

So I agreed to go down to Chilpanzingo with Thea; there was an interval, extremely short, when we both showed gratitude. I appreciated it that she let up her severity, and she was happy that she was still my preference. So on the night of Oliver's house-warming party she said, "Let's go and see what it's like," and I understood that she wanted to do something for me, because I wanted to go. Did I! I was wild to go, having been in the house for two days straight in support of my good intentions. I looked carefully at her and saw how she sustained her smile to back up her suggestion, but I thought, Hell, let's!

I knew by this time what Thea thought of these people and in fact of most people, with their faulty humanity. She couldn't stand them. And what her eccentricity amounted to was that she proposed a different kind of humanity altogether. I guess nothing restrains people from demanding ideal conditions. Very little restrains them from anything. Thea's standard was high, but she wasn't exactly to blame as having arbitrarily set it high. For when she talked to me about some particular person she'd be more frightened than scornful. People with whom she had to struggle scared her, and what I'd call average hypocrisy, just the incidental little whiffs of the social machine, was terribly hard on her. As for greediness or envy, fat self-smelling of appreciation, hates and destructions, fraud, gnawing, she had a very poor tolerance of them, and I'd see her go out in the eyes in a really dangerous way at a gathering. So of course I knew she didn't want to go; but I did, badly, and my thought was, If I can stand her snakes, she can take this for one evening.

I changed into good clothes, therefore. I took off my turban and wore only a patch of bandage over the shaved place. Thea put on an evening dress with black silk *rebozo*. But there was nobody to take note how we arrived. I've never seen such a goons' rodeo as that party. When we got to the villa we found ourselves in the overflow of a mob that covered the street. I saw the most amazing male and female bums, master-molds of some of the leading turpitudes, fags, apes, goofs, and terminal and fringe types, lapping, lushing, gabbing, and celebrating notoriety. Because it was no secret that Oliver was wanted by the government and that this was a big last fling. Probably Thea was the only person in town who didn't know what was happening.

Some of the guests were lying in the garden with bottles, about to pass out or already looped in full; the Japanese flowers were trod down and tequila empties floated in the fish pond. Things had been taken out of the hands of the servants, and people poured for themselves, broke off chunks of ice with candlesticks, grabbed glasses from one another. In the patio the hired orchestra fiddled weakly and the soberer company danced. Thea wanted to leave immediately, but as she began to say so I saw Stella by an orange tree. She made me a small sign, and I had to go and talk to her; I was very eager. Annoyed that Thea tried to pull me away as soon as we had arrived, I didn't look at her. And when Moulton in a dinner jacket but still in short pants asked her for a dance I handed her over. I thought her dislike for him was exaggerated and it wouldn't do her any harm at all to go around the floor with him once or twice.

Since Oliver's trial when Stella said she had to talk to me I had been all worked up, I realized now. I didn't know what had got into me that I was so excited. But I was sure this was something I was bound to figure in; the play would go to me. So I got away from Thea on the dancing patio, aware how she appealed to me not to leave her, and how angry, also, she was. But it wouldn't really hurt her and I'd find out about this other thing. I could see another case much more clearly than my own, and because of that vagueness and incapacity that I felt about going to Chilpanzingo, or throwing myself more blind and deeper down into Chilpanzingo, I perhaps needed an opportunity to be definite and active and to believe that definiteness and action still existed. But in fact I also felt assailed by weakness when I saw Stella beckon. Not that I intended anything toward her. I thought merely I'd feel swayed, but nothing would happen. I'd be confidential with a beautiful woman. This was terribly pleasing to me, inasmuch as it followed, with self-appreciation, that such a woman would naturally turn for help to a man in her own class. I forgot that I had fallen from the horse on my face, and looked it. That's the kind of thing you're apt to forget. But it did occur to me that the last time I had been called aside like this for a discussion apart was with Sophie Geratis, when we had fallen into each other's arms. And what did I think of that? But some involutional, busy, dippy horsefly in me made such a mad fuss of love over this treasure of crystal-sugar esteem I didn't think much of that at all. Of course at the same time I was very serious; I knew she was in trouble. But that she chose me to consult with and to ask for help—for what else could she do but ask help?—was like a kindness she did me and I was under obligation to her before she spoke even a word.

She said, "Mr. March, I count on you to help me."

Immediately I was overwhelmed. I said, "Oh, sure, certainly. I'll do all I can." Down me went a shiver of willingness. My thought was fuzzy, yet my blood excited. "What can I do though?"

"I'd better tell you what the situation is. Just let's get out of this crowd first."

"Yes," I agreed, looking around. She assumed that I was watching out for Oliver and said, "He's not here. I don't expect him for half an hour yet." It was Thea, however, of whom the thought burdened me, just as much. But when Stella took my hand and led me deeper into the trees I felt her touch leap through my arm and further, and as I went along with her my sense of consequences was never weaker, not even when I committed robbery. I was full of curiosity to hear the truth about Oliver, yet I knew he was as light a being as I had ever weighed in my judgment.

"You must know about the government man who's here to get Oliver," she said. "Everybody knows. But do you know why he's here?"

"No, why?"

"*Wilmot's Weekly* was bought by money that came from the Italian government. There was a fellow in New York who did it. His name is Malfitano. He bought the magazine and made Oliver editor. All the important things that were printed were planned in Rome. Now this Malfitano was arrested a couple of months ago; that's why we didn't go back. I don't know what he was arrested for. Now they've sent this government man for Oliver."

"Why?"

"I don't know why. I know about the entertainment world. Ask me why something is in *Variety* and I can maybe explain it."

"They probably want him to give evidence against this Italian. I believe the smartest thing would be for him to go back. Oliver is just one of those old-time journalists who don't see any difference between one government and the next."

She misunderstood me. "He's not so terribly old."

"He should make a deal and go back to testify."

"That's not what he aims to do," she said.

"No? Don't tell me he's going to try to run away? Where to?"

"I can't tell. It wouldn't be fair."

"To South America? He's wacky if he thinks he can. And that will make the thing serious, if they have to chase him. Why, he's small fry."

"No, he thinks it was a very serious thing."

"And what do you think?"

"I think I've had about enough," she said. She looked with her wide swimming eye-surfaces in which the lanterns from the garden were changed entirely into the lights of her meaning. "He wants me to come with him."

"No! Down to Guatemala, Venezuela. Where—?"

"That's one thing I don't want to say, even though I trust you."

"But on what? Does he have money socked away? No, he wouldn't have. You'd be on the beach with him somewhere. He probably hopes you love him that much. Do you?"

"Oh—not that much, no," she said as if it was something she hoped to find the degree of. I suppose she had to say she loved him somewhat to give herself character. Why, that poor, bony, dopey skull and romantic jumping-jack of an Oliver! I saw his imaginary luck of money and car and love collapsing, and was bitter for him in a kind of fleeting way. I caught a glimpse of her ingratitude too, but I couldn't for long see anything to her discredit. Before her, hid in the trees from the crackling party, I felt something happen to me that drew upon my character in the most vital part, where I couldn't prevent.

"The party is supposed to be just a cover-up," she said. "He went out to take the car down the road and hide it, and then he's coming back for me. He says the cops are ready to arrest us."

"Oh, he *is* loony," I said with fresh conviction. "How far does he expect to get in that red convertible?"

"In the morning he's going to ditch it. He's really serious. He's carrying a gun. And he has gone a little crazy. He was pointing it at me this afternoon. He says I want to two-time him."

"That poor fool! He thinks he's a big-league fugitive. You'll have to get away from him. How did you ever get into a fix like this?"

I knew this was a foolish question to put to her. She couldn't tell me. About some paths of life either you guess or you never know because you can't be told. Yes, it was very foolish; but then I was aware of many wrong things said and done which I nevertheless couldn't stop.

"Well, I've known him for quite a while. He was likable, and he had lots of money."

"Oh, all right, you don't have to tell me."

She said, "Didn't you come to Mexico in something like the way I did?"

So that was what she thought we had in common. "I came because I was in love."

"Well, she is so lovely that of course that's a difference. But all the same," she said with a sudden shrewdness and frankness—and I might have known it was there—"it's her house, isn't it, and all the things are hers? What have you got of your own?"

"What have I got?"

"You don't have anything, do you?"

Of course I wasn't going to be such a hypocrite as to argue with her and put on a face, as though I had never in all the world given a momentary thought, not even a one, to the matter of money. For what was that stuff in my pockets, that assorted dough, my winnings, the rainbow foreign currencies I had raked in at the Chinaman's? Even czarist rubles had been thrown in the pot, for which I blamed those Cossack singers. Don't worry, I had been mindful of money, all right, so I knew what she was talking about.

"I do have something," I said. "I can lend you enough to get away on. Don't you have any money at all?" At this moment of our conversation we were very close together in understanding.

"I have a bank account in New York. But what good does that do me now? I can give you a check for the pesos you lend me. There's no money I can lay my hands on right away. I'd have to go to Mexico City and wire from Wells Fargo to the bank."

"No, I don't want a check."

"It won't bounce—you don't have to worry about that!"

"No, no. I'll just take your word for it. I meant that you don't have to give me any check at all."

"What I thought of asking was whether you'd take me to Mexico City," she said.

This I had been expecting, though I don't think I ever intended to do anything about it. Now, when it came, it did something to me. I shivered, as if my fate had brushed me. Admitted that I always tried to elicit what I hoped for; how did people, however, seldom fail to supply it so mysteriously?

"Why—why, where does that suddenly fit?" I said, treating it not merely as a plan for her safety but as a proposal involving me. The holleration and screeches of the party were loud and the narrow grove of oranges where we were seemed like the last strip of field the harvesters are cutting. Any minute I awaited some drunk interrupter or a blazing couple crashing in. I knew I had to get out and start looking for Thea. But first this had to be attended to. "You don't have to put it to me that way," I said. "I'll help you anyway."

"You're getting ahead of yourself. I don't blame you, but you are. Maybe I'd even feel bad if you didn't, but . . . I can't be as vain as to think I deserve the very best way of escaping from my trouble. You don't even know me. And all I should think about now is getting away from this poor guy who's lost his mind."

"I'm very sorry. I apologize. I talked out of turn."

"Oh, you don't have to apologize. We know what the score is here, pretty much. I admit I was often looking, and I have thought of you. But one of the things I thought is that you and I are the kind of people other people are always trying to fit into their schemes. So suppose we didn't play along, then what? But we don't have the time to go into it now."

To these words that she spoke I responded tremendously, I melted toward her. I was grateful for her plain way of naming a truth that had been hanging around me anonymously for many long years. I did fit into people's schemes. It was an emotion of truth that I had, hearing this. Mainly of truth. For I will admit that among other things I considered that here was a woman who wouldn't put me on trial for my short-comings or judge me. Because I was tired of being socked on the head and banged by judgments. But that was all.

However, we had no time to go into this further. Oliver would be coming back right away. He had packed her things and taken them away, all but a few articles she had hidden from him.

"Listen," said I, "I can't take you to Mexico City, but what I can do is take you a good way out of town, where you'll be safe. Meet me by the station wagon in the *zócalo*. Which way was he going? You can trust me. I don't especially want to see him get caught. I have no reason to."

"He was going toward Acapulco."

"Okay, that's fine. We'll go the other way."

So he wanted to catch a ship at Acapulco, did he, the poor jerk! Or was he plotting to escape through the jungle into Guatemala, as brain-softened as that? Why, if the Indians didn't murder him for his black and white sports shoes he'd die of exhaustion.

I hurried to find Thea. She had gone, Iggy told me, leaving Moulton in the middle of the floor. "She was quite in a mood," said Iggy. "We looked for you. Then she said for me to tell you she was pulling out for Chilpanzingo first thing in the morning. She was all nervous and shaking, Bolingbroke. Where did you disappear?"

"I'll tell you some other time."

I ran down to the *zócalo* and opened the station wagon. Soon Stella arrived and slipped in. I threw off the brake and twisted the ignition key. From disuse the battery was low; and the starter chattered but the motor failed to turn. Not to run the battery any lower I nervously took to the crank. As I began to turn it I right away had a crowd to watch me, that unfailing bunch of a Mexican square that comes to maintain its secret view of life. Sweating with the crank, I was in a furious rage, and I said to a few of them, "Beat it! Scat, goddam you!" But this fetched only jeers and scorn, and I heard my old title, *el gringo del águila*. My heart was full of murder toward them, as toward the motorman that day on the State Street line when the slugger was in pursuit of me. But I put my breast against the radiator and heaved. Stella hadn't had the sense to duck down—I suppose she had to see what was happening and be ready for flight. Now she had been recognized by the bystanders, and it was too late.

"Augie, what are you doing?"

I had prayed that Thea had gone straight back to Casa Descuitada to pack for Chilpanzingo, but she was here, and the crowd around me at the station wagon had brought her over. She stared at Stella through the windshield.

"Where are you going with her? Isn't she the hostess? Why did you dump me at that horrible party?"

"Oh, I didn't dump you."

"With that terrible Moulton. No? Well, I couldn't find you."

I couldn't pretend that it was an extremely serious thing to have left her alone at that party. "It was just for a few minutes," I said.

"And now where are you going?"

"Listen, Thea, this girl is in a lot of trouble."

"Is she?"

"I'm telling you she is."

Stella didn't come out, or change her position behind the spotted dust of the glass.

"And are you getting her out of trouble?" said Thea, angry, ironic, and sad.

"You can think what you want about me," I said, "but it's because you don't understand how urgent it is, and that she's in danger."

I was full of the frantic hurry of escape, and in true fact I already felt caught.

As for Thea, enfolded in the *rebozo*, she stared at me—hard, begging, firm and infirm, all together. There was something about Thea of a nervousness, and she was a kind of universalist, believing that where she stood the principal laws were underfoot. And this made her tremble, but also she was daring. So at a time like this I didn't know what to expect from her.

One thing more: she was, like Mimi, a theoretician about love. She was different from Mimi in that Mimi really intended to do everything for herself if others failed her. And maybe Mimi didn't even need others except as witnesses or accessories. Thea knew better than that. I had heard from various men, and especially from Einhorn, about women's fanaticism in love, how for them all life was knotted around this one thing whereas men found several other vital places of attachment and therefore were more like to avoid monomania. You could always get part of the truth from Einhorn.

"It's a *fact*," I said. "Oliver went crazy and tried to kill her today."

"What are you trying to give me! Whom could that poor idiot hurt? Besides, why do you have to be the one to protect her? How do you get into this?"

"Because," I said, impatient over logic, "she asked me to take her out of town. She's trying to get to Mexico City, and she can't get on the bus here. The police might try to pick her up too."

"Even so, where do you come in?"

"But don't you see? She asked me!"

"Did she just? Or did she ask because you wanted her to?"

"Now how would I do that?" I said.

"As if you didn't know what I was talking about! I've seen you with women. I know what you look like when a handsome woman or even not such a handsome woman passes by."

I said, "Well—" about to assert how normal that was. Then I wanted to say instead, "What about the men out East, that Navy officer and the others?" But I held this back even though it crawled into my throat with a bitter taste. Minutes counted now; I remembered, however, seeing the Mexican faces that listened to this wrangle as if it were the New Testament. "Why do you have to do this?" I said. "Can't you take my word for it she's in danger? Let me do something for a change. We can take up these other things later, in private."

"Do you have to rush like this because of Oliver? Can't you protect her from him here?"

"I told you he was dangerous. Look!" I was out of my mind, nearly, with impatience. "He's going to try to get away and he wants to drag her with him."

"Oh, she's going to ditch him and you're helping her."

"No!" I almost yelled, then dropped my voice low. "Don't you understand any part of what I'm trying to tell you? Why are you being so stubborn?"

"For God's sake, go then, if you have to go. What are you arguing with me for! Are you waiting for my permission? Because you won't get it. You're telling me something ridiculous. She doesn't have to go with him if she doesn't want to."

"Right, she doesn't, and I'm helping her to get away."

"You? You'll be glad if Oliver doesn't have her."

I threw myself on the crank, ramming it in the shaft.

"Augie, don't go! Listen, we're supposed to go to Chilpanzingo in the morning. Why don't we take her up to the house? He won't dare bother us up there."

"No, this is something I've decided to do. I promised."

"Why, you're ashamed to change your mind and do the right thing!"

"Maybe so," I said. "You may understand this better, but that won't stop me."

"Don't go! Don't!"

"Well," I said, turning to her, "suppose you come along. I'll drive her up to Cuernavaca and we'll be back in a few hours."

"No, I won't come along."

"Then I'll see you later."

"By a little flattery anyone can get what he wants from you, Augie. I've told you that before. Where does that put me? I came after you. I flattered you. But I can't outflatter everyone in the world."

She stabbed me hard with this, and suffered as she did so. I knew I'd bleed a long time from it. I grabbed and gave an inhuman twist to the crank. The kick of the motor tore at my arms, and I jumped to the wheel. In the headlights I saw Thea's dress; she was standing still and probably she was waiting to see what I would do. My real desire was to get out. But

already the car had gone a way over the cobbles and it seemed
to me that having just got it under way I couldn't check it.
That's so often what it is with machinery: be somewhat in
doubt and it carries the decision.

I took the turn for Cuernavaca, a climbing, steep road,
black, badly marked. We rose above the town, which sat like
embers in its circle, and I put on as much speed as I dared, for
enough people had seen us in the square so that Oliver would
quickly know. I thought if Stella could hire a taxi in Cuernavaca it would be better than the bus, for the bus made all
the one-horse stops and Oliver could easily catch up with it.

At a terrible rate for that dark road we climbed toward
Cuernavaca, even while, in the black air and orangy fragrance
which we burned through in our speed, the danger we were
escaping appeared smaller and slighter every minute; flying up
the mountain in the machine from that pipsqueak Oliver
began to seem what Thea had thought it was—foolish. This
silent Stella in the seat, who lit cigarettes with the dashboard
lighter in such apparent calm of mind, it was hard to think
how she could have taken seriously the ability of a man like
Oliver to do harm. Even if he had threatened her with his gun
it must have been in a kind of dither, and more than likely she
was escaping from his trouble not his threats.

"I see some lights in the road," she said.

They were flares; it was a detour. I went very slow over the
ruts of an old cart track until I came to a big arrow nailed
pointing upward. There were wheel marks in both directions.
Having detoured to the right, I bore left, and that was a mistake. We went up a narrowing, long way, I heard brush and
grass underneath but was scared to try to back down and
went on looking for a widening of the road where I could
maneuver a turn. I came to one I reckoned I could try, and I
twisted hard and raced the motor, for I dreaded to stall. The
clumsy wagon just failed to make the circle. Cautious, I eased
out the clutch, the gear in reverse, but the transmission was
poor; the clutch grabbed and the lurch killed the engine.
Which was just as well, there being an unusual softness under
the rear right wheel. When I went out I saw that it rested on
a tuft of grass right on the edge of a deep drop. I couldn't
measure the distance below, but we had been climbing a good

while, and it wouldn't have been any mere fifty feet. I was all over sweat, and I lightly opened the other door and said to Stella, low, "Quick!" which she understood, and she slipped out. Reaching through the window, I turned the wheels and drew the gearshift back to neutral position. The car rolled a few feet and stopped against the mountain wall. But the battery was dead now, and the crank wouldn't work.

She said, "Are we going to be stuck here all night?"

"It could have been even more permanent than that. And I told Thea I'd be back in a few hours," I said. Of course she had heard the whole conversation between Thea and me. This fact made an enormous difference. It was just as if, after that talk in the orange grove, Thea had given Stella and me a new introduction to each other. Was I so vain and nonsensical, and was Stella so unscrupulous? We didn't speak about it. Stella could, and did, act as though it was no use answering the accusations of an overwrought woman. As for me, I thought that if what Thea said of me was true, then the truth must be sticking out all over me, and if it was so plain there was nothing much to say. And after all the rush and anxious sweat and urgency, to be here on the mountain like the millipede with one bank of legs suddenly out of commission while the other tried to continue with haste, gave me an unpleasant sort of feeling inside.

"If there were a couple of men to pick up the front end and straighten us out we could get a start by rolling."

"What," she said, "roll with those lights?" The lights were just a feeble yellow. "Anyhow, where are you going to find two men to help you?"

Nevertheless I went to look for help and descended as far as the giant arrow pointing nowhere. Over the grass distances I couldn't be sure whether what I saw was stars or human lights, but I knew I better not try to find out now which they were. There'd be many a fall on terrain like this before I reached what possibly was a village. Or I might be trying to reach the southern heaven. And even to say "southern heaven" is to try to familiarize terrific convulsions of fire in the million light-year distances (and why, from space to space, does the occupancy have to be by fire?). There were falls, though, and also thorns and cactuses, from huge maguey to vicious leg-tearing pads; and animals too. No car came along the detour, and then it occurred to me that the next car that passed might be Oliver's. Was I waiting there for him to come and shoot at me with his pistol? I gave up and went back to the station wagon. There were some blankets and a shelter-half in the back. As I hunted them with the flashlight I thought how much dislike I bore to this machine and the false positions it had put me in. I spread the canvas shelter-half on the wet grass, and when I crouched and was nearly still great speed and motion continued to go through me. I worried about Thea; I knew she was bound to let me have it. She'd never excuse me for this.

And now Stella was lying close to me, for it was cold. Her smell was tender, from her hair and face powder—I suppose the mountain coldness made a difference in the odor. I felt her weight full, both soft and heavy, from her hips and breasts. And if before I vaguely thought how I'd be swayed, there wasn't much vagueness now.

I suppose if you pass the night with a woman in a deserted mountain place there's only one appropriate thing, according to the secret urging of the world. Or not so secret. And the woman, who has done so much to be dangerous in this same scheme, the more she comes of the world the less she knows how to vary from it. I thought that in the crisis that seems to have to occur when a man and a woman are thrown together nothing, nothing easy, can happen until first one difficulty is cleared and it is shown how the man is a man and the woman a woman; as if a life's trial had to be made, and the pretensions of the man and the woman satisfied. I say I thought, and so I did. A considerable number of things. But I was terribly hot for this woman. As, suddenly, with a breathless impulse toward me, she was for me too. Her tongue was in my mouth, my hands were drawing up her clothes. It made no difference what other thought beat on me, it beat from outside. As her things came off, as in the cold of night her shoulders, her breasts, and her humid heat I fell on maddened me, my voice came out of me strangely. She talked rapidly in my ear, she heaved her body, pressed my face, gathered up her breasts, and she gave herself like a prize. She did many things like a woman who had studied from men what it was that pleased them. This was in part innocent in her. It seemed an instant after blowing that, happily, she began to talk, every now and then kissing. It made her laugh that back at the party she had told me that I mistook her, and that I had apologized. I had known then that it had no more weight than a matchstick, that. The inevitability that brought us together on this mountain of wet grass was greater than the total of all other considerations. We had all known that, all three of us. After much making with sense, it's senselessness that you submit to. Thea foresaw that I'd do this. It annoyed me all the more with her, as though if she hadn't made the prediction it wouldn't have happened. And I thought savagely that if she hadn't put herself in the way and told me what to do there wouldn't have been this struggle with my pride. It was my unreasonable idea that she had tried to spoil everything for me. But I could bring forth a lot more reasons without reaching as high as the foot of the inevitability.

Between Stella and me only one true subject was possible now whether there was anything permanent between us. But I was thinking mostly of Thea. And as this couldn't be said, neither could any other genuine thing. Therefore we didn't talk of genuine things. She mentioned Thea once, saying that her standards were awfully high, it seemed. At last we were both silent, and then we slept, and that was more intimate than talk.

A similar night for me was, years after this, on a crowded ship from Palma de Mallorca to Barcelona. The cabins were full, and I slept on deck where there was a throng of what they call there the humble people, laborers in denim jumpers, whole families, babes at breast, young girls of delicate stomach vomiting in the sea, singers who pumped on the concertina, old people on the deck cargo—like dead, or musing, with awkward released feet and large bellies. A sad night, damp, with floating carbon flakes from the cheap fuel. The puny officers in white, stepping over the bodies on the boards. A young Texas girl shared my coat; she was frank to say she had sought out another American in the foreign crowd. So all night she lay close to me, and in the shrimp chill of dawn when the pink light of the rocking sea fell on us she reminded me powerfully of Stella.

That rising was in the Spanish commotion of the wet deck, and this other in the smoky white dawn sun and a freight-yard hush of mountains, like the silence after the crash of cars, here and there a skinny, armored cricket still trying out a trill. The gray-green cold came down from the rocks, the smoke from a village mixed with it. Such a smell of charcoal, the very smell of familiarity and welcome day to some, was the last tinge of foreignness to me. Stella stood rolled in the blanket and tried to look to the bottom of the cliff; the sight of that depth shriveled my stomach.

Some Indians, for a peso apiece, set the car straight. When we started to roll the engine caught, and we went on to Cuernavaca, where I hired a car to take her to Mexico, giving her all the dollars I had. She said she'd pay me through Wells Fargo, and there was all that talk about settling up indebtedness that's so hard to give a definite character. I didn't believe her, but money was the only subject we now could talk of. Gratitude wasn't all she felt, that's certain, but since she did have some gratitude to express, she stuck to that and let the rest go. She did say, however, "Someday, will you come see me?"

"Sure I will."

Waiting in the sun for the taxi, we were at the side of the market, by the flowers, and stood where the stones were slippery from the cast-off blooms, just the light greasiness of flowers underfoot. Facing us were the butchers' stalls, and on the hooks the tripes and lights and the carcasses were slung, on which the flies gave out nearly a roar and bounded like the first drops of cloudburst on a red wall. Under a chopping block squatted a naked kid and he slowly made a strange color of defecation. We went slowly around the broad steel gallery, the glass roof rising over the packed tinware, peppers, beef, bananas, pork, orchids, baskets, and this flash, rage, the chitin, electric loud tissue-sound of fond love, the wild loving hum of the bluebottles and green. As if a huge spool were revolving that caught up all threads from the sunlight.

The driver came around. She made sure again that I had written down the name of her theatrical agent who always knew where to find her. She kissed me, and her lips made an unknown sensation on the side of my face, so I asked myself what mistake might I be on the verge of making now. Whilst the cab moved slowly in the market crowd, I walked beside it and we pressed hands through the window. She said, "Thank you. You were a real friend."

"Good luck, Stella," I said. "*Better* luck . . ."

"I wouldn't let her be too rough on me if I were you," she told me.

I wasn't going to let her be rough, I thought as I went to face and to lie to Thea. I didn't really feel the sharpness of the lying I was prepared to do. I came back to her thinking I was now more faithful than before, so I believed I was going to maintain something more true than not. And I didn't expect to feel as bad as I did feel when I saw her in the garden, by a hedge that had turned out to have a red waxy berry. She wore the punctured hat and was ready to start for Chilpanzingo. I too was ready to go immediately, if she'd let me. I wanted her back in the worst way. But then I decided I'd better not go. My idea now was that I'd already given in too much to these strange activities; with the eagle, even, I should have called a halt, not seemed so unsurprised by every bizarre thing as if I had seen it before. But I was moving toward the future much too fast.

"Well! Here you come," she said harshly. "I didn't know whether to expect you. I thought you'd stay away. I think I'd have liked that better."

"All right," I said, "don't be so spoken in full. Just come to the point."

She did speak differently, next, and I was sorry I had asked her to. On a sort of cry, and with mouth trembling, she said, "We're washed up—washed up! It's all finished, Augie. We made a mistake. *I* made a mistake."

"Now don't rush like that. Wait, will you? One thing at a time. If what's bothering you is that Stella and I—"

"Spent the night together!"

"We had to. But because I got on the wrong road, that's why."

"Oh, please, stop that, don't say that! It just poisons me to hear you sound like that," she said with uncontrollable wretchedness. Her look was very sick.

"Why, it's true," I insisted. "What do you mean? You shouldn't be jealous like this. The car got stuck in the mountains."

"I could hardly get out of bed this morning. And now it's worse, it's worse. Don't tell me this story. I can't stand stories."

"Well," I said, looking down at the fresh-washed stones where the sun cooled all over, uneven, the green like velvet, "If you're bound to have such thoughts and be tortured by them, nobody can help that."

She said, "In a way I wish it were just my own trouble."

Somehow this made me stiffen toward her. "Well, it is your trouble," I said to her. "Suppose it was really what you think. It wouldn't be so hard to tell you after what you've told me about yourself, about the Navy man and so forth, while you were married to Smitty. You're quite a few up on me." We flushed, both of us, in each other's sight.

"I didn't think what I said to you would come back to me this way," she said unevenly, and this shiver of voice made me feel a chill, like briny thick ice on the shore in the first freezes, "or that there was a score to keep."

She looked very bad, with that more brilliant than friendly glance from her black eyes, her pallor very deep; her nostrils seemed as if they had accepted some of the sickness, smelled the poison she spoke of. And the animals and animal objects, the oxhide chairs, the straw-rustle snakes, the horned and shaggy heads, all that had seemed to have *raison d'être* got dull, useless, brutal, or to be a jumble, a clutter merely, when something was wrong with her. While she herself looked tired, tendony in the neck, pinched on the shoulders. She didn't even smell right. And up and down she was gripped by the most frightful jealousy; she wanted, and needed, to do me harm.

For some reason I thought this would pass presently. But at the same time I trembled too. I said, "You can't even imagine that nothing happened, can you? And you have to assume that because we were together all night we made love too."

"Well, maybe it is irrational," she said. "But whether it is or not, can you tell me it really didn't happen? Can you?"

I was about, slowly, to do that, because it was necessary— and I felt monstrous to be putting up a lying face not having even washed Stella's odor from me—but Thea stopped me. She said, "No, don't, you'll only repeat the same thing. I know. And don't ask me to imagine anything. I already have imagined everything. Don't expect me to be superhuman. I won't try. It's too painful already, and a lot more than I thought I could stand." She didn't have any outburst of tears, but just like a sudden darkness, just that silent, they appeared in her eyes.

That softened or melted all my hardness, as if by this quick heat. I said, "Let's quit this, Thea," and came toward her, but she moved away.

"You should have stayed with her."

"Listen—"

"I mean it. You can be tender with me now. In ten minutes you could be with her, and fifteen minutes later with some other tramp. There isn't that much of you to go around. How did you get mixed up with this girl? That's what I want to know."

"How? I met her with Oliver, through Moulton."

"Why didn't she ask your friend Moulton then? Why you? Because you flirted with her."

"No, because she picked me for someone sympathetic. She knew how I was with you, and she must have thought I'd understand a woman's situation faster than somebody else would."

"That's just the kind of easy lie you often tell. She picked you because you look so damn obliging and she figured she could do what she wanted with you."

"Oh no," I said, "you're wrong. She was just in a bad spot and I felt for her." But I remembered, of course, in the orange grove, that sensation of something that drew on me in a vital place and where I couldn't stop it. Apparently Thea knew something about this too, which amazed me. Back in Chicago she had predicted that I'd go for another woman who ran after me. If only she hadn't described me to myself so mercilessly hard though. There, however, in Chicago, I thought how pleased I was I didn't have to have secrets from her; now there was a dusky sort of fluctuation back from this, as if it were fatal to be without hidden things. "I really and truly wanted to help her," I said.

She cried, "What are you talking about—help! The man was picked up by the police just about as you were leaving."

"Who, Oliver?" It stunned me. "Arrested? I guess I shouldn't have been in such a hurry. But I was afraid he'd drag her with him. Because he did have a gun, and he hit Louie Fu, he was getting to be violent and I thought he'd force her—"

"That foolish, weak, poor drunk moron—force her? *That* girl? What did he force before? She didn't lie in bed at the point of a gun, did she? She's a whore! But it didn't take her very long to see what you were like, that you'd be afraid to fall beneath her expectations, not be the man she wanted you to be, that you'd play her game. You play everyone's."

"You're mad because I don't always play yours. Yes, I reckon she did understand me. She didn't tell me to do this. She asked me. She must have seen I was fed up with being told—"

This made her look with intensified sickness at me, as if a new gust of it had hit her; she held her lip an instant with her teeth. Then she said, "It wasn't a game. I see you took it that way. Well, it wasn't, it was genuine. As far as I could make it, it was. It may have looked like a game to you. I guess it would. Maybe you wouldn't have anything else."

"We're not talking about the same thing. Not the love. It's the other things you're so fantastic about."

"Me—so fantastic?" she said with dry mouth and laid her hand over her breast.

"Well, how can you think you're not—the eagle, the other things, the snakes, hunting every day?"

It gave her another hurt.

"What, were you just being indulgent with me? About the eagle? That didn't mean anything to you? All along you thought I was only fantastic?"

I felt what a terrible thing I had done to her by this, and so I tried to mitigate it. "Don't those things ever strike you as queer, even for a minute?" I said.

This made her throat tighten, and the tears, before, were nothing to this tightness. She said, "A lot of things look queer to me too. Some of them maybe much more than what I do seems to you. Loving you, that wasn't queer at all to me.

But now *you* start to seem queer, like many other things. Maybe I am peculiar, that I only know these strange ways of doing something. Instead of sticking to the ordinary way and doing something false. So"—and I was silent, recognizing the right on her side in this—"you made allowances for me." I could scarcely bear how she suffered. Sometimes I wasn't sure whether she could add the next word, her throat kept so many other sounds back, in abeyance. "I didn't ask you to— ever. Why didn't you say how you felt? You could have told me. I didn't want to seem fantastic to you."

"You yourself, you never were. No, you weren't."

"You don't tell anybody, I suppose. But to me you didn't have to behave as you do with anyone else. You could have done as you couldn't with anyone else. Isn't there one person in the whole world to whom you could? Do you tell anybody? Yes, I guess love would come in a queer form. You think the queerness is your excuse. But perhaps love would be strange and foreign to you no matter which way it happened, and maybe you just don't want it. In that case I made a mistake, because I thought you did. And you don't, do you?"

"What do you want to do to me, burn me down to the ground? It's just because you're so jealous and sore—"

"Yes, I am jealous. I feel very sick and disappointed, other- wise I probably wouldn't do this. I know you can't take it. But I'm disappointed. I'm not just jealous. When I came up to your room in Chicago you had a girl, and when you came to see me I didn't ask you first whether you loved her or not. I knew it couldn't amount to much. But even if it had been important I thought I had to try! I felt mostly alone, as if the world were full of things but empty of people. I know," she admitted, dismaying me deeper than ever, "I must be a little crazy." She said it in a husky and quiet tone. "I must be, I have to admit. But I thought if I could get through to one other person I could get through to more. So people wouldn't tire me, and so I wouldn't be afraid of them. Be- cause my feeling can't be people's fault, so much. *They* don't make it. Well, I believed it must be you who could do this for me. And you could. I was so happy to find you. I thought you knew all about what you could do and you were so lucky and so special. That's why it's not just jealousy. I didn't want

you to come back. I'm sorry you're here now. You're not special. You're like everybody else. You get tired easily. I don't
want to see you any more."

Now she bent her head. She was crying. The hat dropped
from her head and held by the cord. Gripped hard in my
chest like a sick squirrel trapped in a chimney, in the silky
shudder of smoke, was a terrible stuck feeling. I tried to come
near again, and she straightened, looked me in the face, and
cried, "I don't want you to do that! I don't want it; I can't
allow you to. I know you think this, that, or the other can always be overlooked, but I don't."

She walked past me to the door, where she stopped. "I'm
going to Chilpanzingo," she said. She had stopped crying.

"I'll come with you."

"No, you won't. There won't be any more games. I'm
going there alone."

"And what am I supposed to do?"

"Don't ask me. You figure that out yourself."

"I get it," I said.

I was in the room collecting my stuff, burning, with tears
and cries that couldn't find an outlet from suffocation, and
stones of pity heaped up in me, when I saw her descending to
the *zócalo* with a rifle, and Jacinto with baggage behind her.
She was leaving immediately. I wanted to yell to her, "Don't
go!" as she had called to me last night in the *zócalo*, and tell
her what a mistake she was making. But what I called her mistake was, in my own emotion, that she was abandoning me.
That was what made me tremble when I tried to call her. She
couldn't leave me. I ran through the house to holler from the
kitchen garden wall.

Something about me scared the cook; she grabbed up her
kid and beat it when she saw me. And suddenly I was as full
of rage as of grief, so that they choked me. I tore open the
garden door and ran pounding down toward the *zócalo*, but
the station wagon was no longer there. I turned back and
kicked open the gate of the house, looking for what to attack
and smash. Swooping and bursting, I tore up rocks in the garden and hurled them at the wall, knocking down the stucco.
I went into the living room and wrecked the oxhide chairs,
the glassware, tore off curtains and pictures. Next, finding

myself on the porch, I kicked to pieces the snake cases, over-turned them, and stood and watched the panic of the monsters as they flowed and fled, surged for cover. Every last box I booted over.

Then I grabbed my valise and got out. I pounded down into the *zócalo*, sobbing in my chest.

On Hilario's porch, there was Moulton. I saw only his face above the Carta Blanca shield. He looked down. Him, the pope of rubble.

"Hey, Bolingbroke, where's the girl? Oliver is in the jug. Come on up here, I want to talk to you."

"Why don't you go to hell!"

He didn't hear.

"Why are you carrying a valise?" he said.

I went away and roamed the town some more. In the market place I met Iggy and his little daughter.

"Hey, where did you come from? Oliver was arrested last night."

"Oh, fuck Oliver!"

"Please, Bolingbroke, don't talk that way in front of the kid."

"Don't call me Bolingbroke any more."

I went around with him though, as he led the kid by the hand. We looked at the stalls and finally he bought the kid a cornhusk dolly.

He talked about his troubles. Now she was through with Jepson, should he remarry his wife? I had nothing to say, but felt my eyes burn as I looked at him.

"So you helped Stella get away, huh?" he said. "I guess you did right. Why should she get it in the neck because of him? Wiley says in jail last night he was screaming about her running out on him."

Then he saw my valise for the first time and said, "Oh-oh, I'm sorry, man! Busted up, huh?"

I flinched, my face twisted, I made a dumb sign and then burst into tears.

Chapter XIX

THE SNAKES escaped—I presume to the mountains. I didn't go back to Casa Descuitada to find out. Iggy took me to a room in the villa where he stayed. For a time I didn't do anything, only lay in the small warm stone cell at the top of the house. You climbed the stairs till they gave out and then continued the rest of the way up a ladder. There I stretched out on the low bed and remained for days, sick. If Tertullian came to the window of heaven to rejoice in the sight of the damned, as he said he'd do, he might have seen my leg across his line of vision through the sunlight. That was how I felt.

Iggy came and kept me company. There was a low chair on which he sat for hours without saying a word, his chin drawn inward so that his neck was creased and swollen, and his trousers tied at the bottom with the strings of the *alpargatas* like those of a bicycle rider who doesn't want his cuffs to tangle in the chain. So he sat, his head sunk and his green eyes with inflamed lids. Now and then the church bell would sound, lurching back and forth as if someone were carrying water that was clear, all right, but in a squalid bucket, and stumbling and slipping on the stones. Iggy knew I was in a crisis and didn't want me to be alone. But if I tried to say anything he turned the edge of it back against me and accepted nothing of what I told him even after he had encouraged me to talk. Of course I told him everything, to the end of my breath, and then I felt as if he had covered my face with his hand and wouldn't let me say any more. So after this stifling had happened a few times I quit talking. I thought he came to be merciful and stayed to be sure I choked. He got some obscure revenge out of me at the same time that he pitied me.

Anyway, he sat by the dry handsome wall on which the sun fell in over the ledge where the pigeons landed with their red feet and fanned down dust and straw. Sometimes he would actually lay his cheek to the plaster.

I knew I had done wrong. And as I lay and thought of it I felt my eyes roll as if in search of an out. Something happened to my forgetting power, it was impaired. My mistakes and faults came from all sides and gnawed at me. They gnawed away, and I broke out in a sweat, and turned, or felt the vanity of turning.

I'd try again and say, "Iggy, what can I do to prove I love her?"

"I don't know what. Maybe you couldn't prove it because you don't."

"No, Iggy, how can you say that! Can't you see how it is?"

"Why did you go away with that broad then?"

"That was kind of a revolt or something. How should I know why! I didn't invent human beings, Iggy."

"You don't know the score yet, Boling. I'm sorry for you," he said from his wall, "honest I am. But this has got to happen to you before you get anywheres. You always had it too good. You got to get knocked over and crushed like this. If you don't you'll never understand how much you hurt her. You've got to find out about this and not be so larky."

"She's too angry. If she loved me she wouldn't be so angry. She needs some reason to be so angry."

"Well, you gave her it."

It was no use trying to argue with Iggy, so I lay silent and argued and pleaded in my mind with Thea instead, but I only kept losing more and more. Why had I done it? I had wounded her badly, I knew it. I could see it as clearly as I could see her saying, white, with a strained throat, "I am disappointed!" "Well, honey, listen," I wanted to tell her, "of course everybody is disappointed sometime or another. Why, you know that. Everybody gets damaged, and everybody does some damage. Especially in love. And I've done you this damage. But I love you, and you should forgive me so we can continue."

I ought to have taken my chances with the snakes in the hot mountains, creeping after them with nooses on the brown soil up there, instead of hanging around the dizzy town where things were even more dangerous.

It had hit her hard when I revealed what I thought of her hunting. But hadn't she also tried to carry me to the ground and crush me with the attack she made on me, saying how vain I was, how unreliable, how I was always looking at other women and had no conscience? And was it true, as she said, that love would appear strange to me no matter what form it took, even if there were no eagles and snakes?

I thought about it and was astonished at how much truth there actually was in this. Why, it was so! And I had always believed that where love was concerned I was on my mother's side, against the Grandma Lausches, the Mrs. Renlings, and the Lucy Magnuses.

If I didn't have money or profession or duties, wasn't it so that I could be free, and a sincere follower of love?

Me, love's servant? I wasn't at all! And suddenly my heart felt ugly, I was sick of myself. I thought that my aim of being simple was just a fraud, that I wasn't a bit goodhearted or affectionate, and I began to wish that Mexico from beyond the walls would come in and kill me and that I would be thrown in the bone dust and twisted, spiky crosses of the cemetery, for the insects and lizards.

Now I had started, and this terrible investigation had to go on. If this was how I was, it was certainly not how I appeared but must be my secret. So if I wanted to please, it was in order to mislead or show everyone, wasn't it, now? And this must be because I had an idea everyone was my better and had something I didn't have. But what did people seem to me anyhow, something fantastic? I didn't want to be what they made of me but wanted to please them. Kindly explain! An independent fate, and love too—what confusion!

I must be a monster to make such confusion.

But no, I couldn't be a monster and suffer both. That would be too unjust. I didn't believe it.

It wasn't right to think everyone else had more power of being. Why, look now, it was clear as anything that it wasn't so but merely imagination, exaggerating how you're regarded, misunderstanding how you're liked for what you're not, disliked for what you're not, both from error and laziness. The way must be not to care, but in that case you must know how really to care and understand what's pleasing or displeasing in yourself. But do you think every newcomer is concerned and is watching? No. And do you care that anyone should care in return? Not by a long shot. Because nobody anyhow can show what he is without a sense of exposure and shame, and can't care while preoccupied with this but must appear better and stronger than anyone else, mad! And meantime feels no real strength in himself, cheats and gets cheated, relies on cheating but believes abnormally in the strength of the strong. All this time nothing genuine is allowed to appear and nobody knows what's real. And that's disfigured, degenerate, dark mankind—mere humanity.

But then with everyone going around so capable and purposeful in his strong handsome case, can you let yourself limp in feeble and poor, some silly creature, laughing and harmless? No, you have to plot in your heart to come out differently. External life being so mighty, the instruments so huge and terrible, the performances so great, the thoughts so great and threatening, you produce a someone who can exist before it. You invent a man who can stand before the terrible appearances. This way he can't get justice and he can't give justice, but he can live. And this is what mere humanity always does. It's made up of these inventors or artists, millions and millions of them, each in his own way trying to recruit other people to play a supporting role and sustain him in his make-believe. The great chiefs and leaders recruit the greatest number, and that's what their power is. There's one image that gets out in front to lead the rest and can impose its claim to being genuine with more force than others, or one voice enlarged to thunder is heard above the others. Then a huge invention, which is the invention maybe of the world itself, and of nature, becomes the actual world—with cities, factories, public buildings, railroads, armies, dams, prisons, and movies —becomes the actuality. That's the struggle of humanity, to recruit others to your version of what's real. Then even the flowers and the moss on the stones become the moss and the flowers of a version.

I certainly looked like an ideal recruit. But the invented things never became real for me no matter how I urged myself to think they were.

My real fault was that I couldn't stay with my purest feelings. This was what tore the greatest hole in me. Maybe Thea couldn't stand many happy days in a row either, that did occur to me as a reason for her cooling off. Perhaps she had this trouble too, with her chosen thing. The year before, when

Mimi was in trouble, Kayo Obermark had said to me that this happened to everyone. Everyone got bitterness in his chosen thing. It might be in the end that the chosen thing in itself is bitterness, because to arrive at the chosen thing needs courage, because it's intense, and intensity is what the feeble humanity of us can't take for long. And also the chosen thing can't be one that we already have, since what we already have there isn't much use or respect for. Oh, this made me feel terrible contempt, the way I felt, riled and savage. The fucking slaves! I thought. The lousy cowards!

As for me personally, not much better than some of the worst, my invention and special thing was simplicity. I wanted simplicity and denied complexity, and in this I was guileful and suppressed many patents in my secret heart, and was as devising as anybody else. Or why would I long for simplicity?

Personality is unsafe in the first place. It's the types that are safe. So almost all make deformations on themselves so that the great terror will let them be. It isn't new. The timid tribespeople, they flatten down heads or pierce lips or noses, or hack off thumbs, or make themselves masks as terrible as the terror itself, or paint or tattoo. It's all to anticipate the terror which does not welcome your being.

Tell me, how many Jacobs are there who sleep on the stone and force it to be their pillow, or to go to the mat with angels and wrestle the great fear to win a right to exist? These brave are so few that they are made the fathers of a whole people.

While as for me, whoever would give me cover from this mighty free-running terror and wild cold of chaos I went to, and therefore to temporary embraces. It wasn't very courageous. That I was like many others in this was no consolation. If there were so many they must all suffer the same way I did.

Well, now that I knew of this I wanted another chance. I thought I must try to be brave again. So I decided I'd go and plead with her in Chilpanzingo, and say that though I was a weak man I could little by little alter if she'd bear with me.

As soon as I had decided this I felt much better. I went to the *peluquería* and had myself shaved. Then I ate lunch at Louie Fu's and one of his daughters pressed my pants for me. I was overwrought but primed with hopes too. I already saw how she'd whiten in the face as she denounced me, and her eyes darken and flash out at me. But also she'd throw her arms around me. Because she also needed me. And all her eccentric force, which came from doubt as to whether her desire could ever trust someone again, would stop and rest on me.

Imagining how this would be, I melted, my chest got hot, soft, sore, and yearning. I saw it already happening. It's always been like that with me, that fantasy went ahead of me and prepared the way. Or else, as it seems, the big heavy personal van, dark and cumbersome, can't start into strange terrain. But this imagination of mine, like the Roman army out in Spain or Gaul, makes streets and walls even if it's only camping, for the night.

While I sat in my shorts and waited for my pants, Louie's dog came out. Listless and fat, she smelled like old Winnie. She stood square before me and gazed. Not wanting to be stroked, she backed away with clicking claws when I reached out, and she showed little old teeth. Not that she was sore, but wanted to go back to her isolation. So she did, under the curtain with an extreme sigh. She was very old.

The bus, an old rural schoolbus from the States, arrived like the buckboard of olden times. I was already inside, holding my ticket, when Moulton came up and said through the window, "Come out, I want to talk to you."

"No, I won't."

"Come," he said earnestly. "It's important. You'd better."

Iggy said, "Whyn't you mind your own business, Wiley?"

Moulton's big brow and squash nose were covered with a white sweat. "Will it be better if he walks into something and gets knocked over?" he said.

I got out. "What do you mean, knocked over?" I asked.

Before Iggy could interfere, if he was about to try, Moulton clasped my hand next to his hard belly, drew my arm taut under his, and with burly haste he made me walk a few fast steps on the stones and rosy garbage, on my turned-over heels.

"Get onto yourself," he said. "Talavera was Thea's friend, old man. He's there with her in Chilpanzingo."

I tore loose. I was going to get my fingers into his neck and choke him to death.

"Ig," he yelled, "you better hold on to him!"

Iggy who was just behind us took hold of me.

"Let go!"

"Wait, you're not going to kill him right here with cops and everybody around. You better beat it, Wiley. He's pulling like a bull."

I wanted to smash Iggy to the ground too as he held my arm.

"Now wait, Boling. Find out first if it's true. Chrissake, use your head!"

Moulton was going backwards while I dragged Iggy on my arm.

"Don't be a foolish bastard, Boling," said Moulton. "It's true all right. You think I want trouble with you? I only did it to help, so you wouldn't get hurt. It's dangerous down there. Talavera will kill you."

"Look what a favor you done him!" said Iggy. "Look at his face!"

"Is it true he went down there with her, Iggy?" I said, stopping. I was so clawed and bit inside I could hardly get out this question.

"He was her boy friend here before," Iggy said. "A guy told me yesterday that Talavera took off for Chilpanzingo right after Thea."

"When was he—?"

"A few years ago. Why, he was living at Casa Descuitada, just about," said Moulton.

I couldn't any longer stay on my feet and slumped down against the bandstand. I covered my head with my hands and shivered, my face on my knees.

Moulton was severe toward me. "I'm surprised the way you take it, March," he said.

"How do you want him to take it? Stop layin' it on him," said Iggy.

"He acts like a kid and you encourage him," Moulton said. "This has happened to me, it's happened to you. It happened to Talavera when she showed up with Smitty and then with *him*."

"No, it didn't. Talavera knew she was married."

"What's the difference? Even if Talavera is a chorus-boy horse-rider he has his feelings. Well, shouldn't a man find out when this happens to him? Shouldn't I have found out? Shouldn't you have found out? This is one of those damn facts that have got to be known."

"But the guy still loves her. You got mad when somebody put the blocks to your wife, but not because you loved her."

"Well, does she love him?" said Moulton. "Then what was she doing in the mountains with Talavera after March got knocked on the dome and was laid up?"

"She was doing nothing in the mountains with him," I cried out, ragging again. "If he's in Chilpanzingo now, he's just in Chilpanzingo and not with Thea."

He stared at me, acting full of curiosity. He said, "Brother, I bet you see exactly what everybody else sees, but you just stick by your opinions. Why didn't she tell you he was her old boy friend? And what were they doing, just having a debate of yes or no, and she didn't get off her horse for him?"

"Nothing went on. Nothing! If you don't stop talking I'll ram one of these stones down your throat!"

But he was terribly roused too and bound to go on; he wasn't just trifling but intended something. His eyes were open large and fixed on me.

"Too bad, friend, but women have no judgment. They aren't just for happy young fellows like you. What do you want to bet her britches came down for him, and she didn't save all her sweet little things for you?"

I jumped at him. Iggy held me from the back, and I picked him off the ground and tried to get rid of him by dashing him against the bandstand, but he clung, and when I threw my weight backwards and crushed him so he'd let go, he gasped, "Christ, you lost your mind? I'm keepin' you outa trouble."

Moulton had already gotten away, down the busy street that led to the market. I yelled after him, "Okay, you filthy slob sonofabitch. You wait. I'll kill you!"

"Quit that, Boling, there's a cop with his eye on you."

An Indian policeman sat on the running board of a nearby car. He probably was used to drunken gringos wrangling and scrapping.

Iggy had forced me down on my knee; he still clutched my arms. "Can I let you loose now? You won't run after him?" I uttered a kind of sob and shook my head. He helped me to stand up. "Look at you, covered with muck. You'll have to change your clothes."

"No, I haven't got time."

"Come on to my room. I'll get this stuff off you at least with a brush."

"I'm not going to miss that bus."

"You mean to say you're going down there anyway? You must be cracked."

But I had decided I'd go. I washed my face at Louie's and got into the bus; my place was taken there, and all the early birds who had watched me by the bandstand appeared to have understood what it was about, that I was a poor *cabrón* who had lost his woman.

Iggy entered the bus with me. He said, "Never mind him. He tried to make her himself and propositioned her a dozen times. He was dying to get her. That's why he was interested in you and would come up to the villa. At Oliver's party he tried to make her again. It was why she left so fast."

It didn't matter so much; it was about like a burning match next to a four-alarm fire.

"Don't go getting into a fight there. You'd be nuts. Talavera will kill you. Maybe I should come and keep you out of trouble. You want me to?"

"Thanks. Just let me alone."

He didn't really want to come with me.

The old bus made a sudden noise, as of sewing machines in a loft. Through the fumes the cathedral seemed as if reflected in a river.

"Shoving off," said Iggy. "Remember," he warned me again as he got to the ground, "you're foolish to go. You're just asking for it."

As the bus rolled down from the town a peasant woman kindly shared her edge of the seat with me. When I sat down I felt it start to burst through me again. Oh, fire, fire! Spasms or cramps of jealous sickness, violent and burning. I held my face and felt that I might croak.

What did she do it for? Why did she take up with Talavera? To punish me? That was a way to punish somebody!

Why, she was guilty herself of what she accused me! Was I

looking over her shoulder at Stella? Well, she was looking over mine at Talavera and had revenge ready right away.

Where was that little cat we used to have in Chicago? All at once I wondered. Because one time when we had been away in Wisconsin for two days and came back at night this little thing was crying from hunger. Then Thea started to weep over it and put it inside her dress while we drove to Fulton Street market to feed it a whole fish. And where was this cat now? Left behind somewhere, nowhere special, and that was how permanent Thea's attachments were.

Then I thought that I had loved her so, it was a pleasure to me that the creases at the joints of our fingers were similar; so now with these fingers she would touch Talavera where she had touched me. And when I thought of her doing with another man what she had done with me, that she would forget herself the same, and praise him and kiss him, and kiss in the same places, gone out of her mind with tenderness, eyes wide, hugging his head, opening her legs, it just about annihilated me. I watched in my imagination and suffered horribly.

I had wanted to marry her, but there isn't any possession. No, no, wives don't own husbands, nor husbands wives, nor parents children. They go away, or they die. So the only possessing is of the moment. If you're able. And while any wish lives, it lives in the face of its negative. This is why we make the obstinate sign of possession. Like deeds, certificates, rings, pledges, and other permanent things.

We tore toward Chilpanzingo in the heat. First the brown stormy mountains, then badland rocks and green Florida feathers. As we rolled into the town someone jumped on the side of the bus for a free ride, grabbing my arm and digging his fingers into it hard. I fought and tore it free. In jumping off this joy-rider whacked the palm of my hand as I reached after him. It stung, and I was furious.

Here was the *zócalo*. White filthy walls sunk toward the ground and rat-gnawed Spanish charm moldered from the balconies, a horrible street like Seville rotting, and falling down to flowering garbage heaps.

I thought if I saw Talavera on the street I'd try to kill him. What with? I had a penknife. It wasn't dangerous enough. In the square I looked for a shop where I could buy a knife, but

I saw none. What I did see was a place that said "Café." It was a square black opening in a wall, as if dug free in the Syrian desert from thousand-years' burial. I went in with the object of stealing a knife off the counter. There weren't any knives there, only tiny spoons with braided necks in the sugar. A piece of white mosquito net hung down torn, like close, fine work done to no useful purpose.

Coming out of the café, I saw the station wagon parked in front of a New Orleans ironwork kind of a place from which there were pieces missing. Without thinking any more of knives, I ran there and went inside. No clerk was at the desk; there was only an old man who cleaned the sand of the path in the decayed patio. He told me Thea's room number. I had him go up and ask if she would see me. She herself called to me from a gap in the shutter. What did I want? I went up the stairs swiftly, and at the big wooden double doors of her room I said to her, "I have to talk to you."

She let me in, and when I entered I looked first for signs of him. There was the usual mess of clothes and equipment. I couldn't tell whether any of it belonged to him. But it wouldn't have made any difference. I was determined to go beyond any such things. "What do you want, Augie?" she said again. I looked at her. Her eyes were not as keen as usual and she looked ill; above, her brilliant black hair was slipping from its combs. She wore a silk coat or robe. Apparently she had just put it on. In heat like this she preferred to go naked in her room. When I wanted to recall how she was, naked, I found I could do it very well. She saw my eyes on her lower belly and her hand descended to hold the edge of the robe there. Seeing that colorful, round-fingered hand descend I bitterly felt how my privilege had ended and passed to another man. I wanted it back.

I said with my face flaming, "I came to ask if we could be together again."

"No, I don't think we can now."

"I hear Talavera is here with you. Is he?"

"Is it any business of yours?"

I took that for an affirmative and felt in great pain.

I said, "I suppose it isn't. But why did you have to take up with him right away? As soon as I had someone, you had to have someone. You're no better than I am. You kept him in reserve."

"I think the only reason you're here is that you heard about him," she said.

"No, I came to ask how about another chance. He doesn't make so much difference to me."

"No?" she said with that white warmth of the face she had. She gave a momentary smile of thought.

"I could forget about him if you still wanted me."

"You'd be bringing him up every other day, whenever we had any trouble."

"No, I wouldn't."

"I know that now you're dying with worry that he'll come in and you'll have a fight. But he's not here, so you can set your mind at rest."

"So he was here!"

She didn't answer. Had she sent him away? Maybe she had. At least that mixed hope and anxiety could end. Of course I had been afraid. But also I hoped I might have killed him. I'd have tried to. I already had thought this over. I pictured that he would have stabbed me.

She said, "You can't love me, thinking I'm with another man. You must want to murder the both of us. You must want to see him fall off a mountain ten thousand feet, and me in a coffin at my funeral."

I was silent, and while she stared at me, what a strange view I had of her in this moldery Hispanic room, the tropical sun in the gaps of the shutter—decay in the town, the spiky, twisted patch of grave iron on the slope, bleeding bougainvillaea bubbles, purple and tubercular on the walls, vines shrieky green, and the big lips and forehead of the mountains begging or singing; then the mess of the room itself, the rags and costly things which she used alike as they happened to come to hand, Kleenexes or silk underthings, dresses, cameras, cosmetics. She did things fast, hoping she did them right. Evidently she didn't believe what I had come to say. She didn't believe because she didn't feel, and didn't feel because of a broken connection.

"You don't have to decide now, Thea."

"No, well—I suppose not. I may feel differently about you

later, but I don't think I will. Right now I have no use for you. Especially when I think how you behave with other people. I wish you all the harm I can think of. I wish you were dead."

"And I still love you," I said. And it must have been evident, for I wasn't lying. I stood and was shaking. But she gave no answer.

"Don't you want to have it again the way it was?" I said. "I think I could do it right this time."

"How do you know you could?"

"Most people are probably in the same condition I'm in. But there must be a way to learn to do better."

"*Must* there?" she said. "I guess you would think so."

"Of course. How would the hope be there at all otherwise? How would I know what to want? How did you know?"

"What do you want to prove by me and what I know?" She said in a low voice, "I've been wrong a good many times— more than I want to discuss with you." She changed the subject. "Jacinto sent me a message about the snakes," she said. "If you had been around I'd have hit you with something."

But I sensed that this was one offense of mine that didn't displease her. I had an impression of a smile of halfway appreciation of it. But I couldn't take much hope from that, because smiling and abstraction, obstinacy, intention to hurt, alternated fast in her cloudy white nervousness, and I saw she was unable to gather together her feelings toward me. I couldn't expect an answer. Never. There wasn't any more connection.

In a waterless fishbowl covered with a straw *petate* I now saw a creature puffed up in scales, warty as a pickle, gray, with skinny gray wattles and tickle claws, breathing on its belly.

"You've started a new collection," I said.

"I caught this one yesterday. He's about the most interesting so far. But I'm not staying here. I'm going to Acapulco and then taking a plane for Vera Cruz, and then I'm going to Yucatán. I'm supposed to see where some rare flamingoes have migrated from Florida."

"Let me come with you."

"No."

That was how it was. Nothing as I had foreseen it.

Chapter XX

B ACK IN ACATLA I lay around. I hoped all the same to hear from Thea, and though it was useless I kept calling at the post office. Notified of nothing, I generally went, then, and drank tequila with beer chasers. I no longer played poker at Louie's and saw none of that gang. Jepson was picked up for vagrancy and sent back to the States, thus Iggy's wife wanted him back. The little kid knew what it was all about, and when I saw them out walking sensed how sharp she was already, at her age, and pitied her.

So on some of the golden afternoons by the dive where I sat on a bench in neglected pants and dirty shirt and with three days of bristles, I had the inclination to start out and say, "O you creatures still above the ground, what are you up to! Even happiness and beauty is like a movie." Many times I felt tears. Or again I'd be angry and want to holler. But while no other creature is reprimanded for its noise, for yelling, roaring, screaming, cawing, or braying, there is supposed to be more delicate relief for the human species. However, I'd go up one of the mountain roads where only an occasional Indian heard and wouldn't say what he thought of it, and there I'd speak my feelings aloud or I'd yell, and it made me feel better temporarily.

There was one companion I had for a few days, a Russian who had been dropped by the Cossack chorus after a fight. He still wore his serge tunic with white piping and all the spaces for bullets. He was very proud and nervous, he bit his nails. His scalp was bare and gave like a soft light on the handsome solemnity of his face, clean shaven at all times. His nose was straight, his mouth was held in with tender rancor, and he had black, continuous, illustrious brows. Damn, if he didn't look like a picture of the poet D'Annunzio that I once saw.

He drank and he was broke, and pretty soon he'd be picked up too, like Jepson. I had very little money left but I bought a bottle of tequila now and then, so he was attached to me.

Well, I felt about my relations with him somewhat as I did

about Iggy's little girl, pitying her for what she had to understand. At first I was sorry he was my companion. But then I liked him better. And as I wanted to tell someone about Thea, I confessed all to him. I told the whole story. I thought he'd sympathize with me. Those many deep hash marks of enlistment with grief that he had on his forehead were what made me think so.

"So you see how rough it's been," I said. "I'm not having it easy. I suffer a great deal. Part of the time I'm half dead."

"Wait," he told me, "you haven't seen anything yet."

This made me furious with him. All in a rush I said to him, "Why you lousy egotist!" I wanted to knock him down; I was drunk enough then to do it. "What do you mean, you runt! You cheesecloth Cossack you! After I've told you how I feel—"

But he wanted to carry the emphasis over to how he felt. He with his naked head and reddened nose and rancor of the mouth. But he wasn't such a bad wretch at that. It was actually only natural. Why, he too had a life. He sat there hopeless. He smelled like a bygone brand of footpowder there had once been in the house. But all the same he was *simpatico*.

"All right pal," I said. "That's true, you have had a bad time. You may never see Harbin again, or wherever you're from."

"Not Harbin, Paris," he said.

"Okay, you poor jerk, Paris. Let it be Paris then."

"I had an uncle in Moscow," he said, "who dressed himself like a woman and went to the church. And he scared everybody because he had a beard and looked very fierce. A policeman said to him, 'You look to me, sir, like a man and not a woman.' So he said, 'Do you know, you look to me like a woman and not a man.' And he went away. Everybody was scared of him."

"This is very fine, but how does it mean I haven't seen anything yet?"

"I mean you have been disappointed in love, but don't you know how many things there are to be disappointed in besides love? You are lucky to be still disappointed in love. Later it may be even more terrible. Don't you think my uncle must have been desperate to go in that dark church and frighten everybody? He had to use his powers. He felt he had only a few years more to live."

Well, I pretended not to understand because it suited me to make him out as ridiculous, but I knew very well what he was trying to get across. Not that life should end is so terrible in itself, but that it should end with so many disappointments in the essential. This is a fact.

Finally I had to stop going around with him. He took to pimping for Negra who was the madame of the *foco rojo*, and I decided to make a move. I sold my fancy equipment, like the riding boots and the life-saving Lake Huron jacket, to Louie Fu, and with the pesos I went to Mexico City. I gave up on waiting for Thea to forgive me. It was sad putting up at the Regina without her. The management and the chambermaids remembered her and the bird and saw I had come down in life; no station wagon, no bags, no wild beast, no happy joy and eating mangos in bed, etcetera. The assignation couples made noise at night, when this was no place for me. But it was cheap and so I closed my ears.

There was no dough from Stella at Wells Fargo. However, I had Sylvester's number at Coyoacán and could call him when flat broke. First I thought I'd try Manny Padilla's cousin. He was nothing like Manny, but scrawny, red-skinned, glittering his teeth and hungry, a fast man with a buck. He wanted to be my guide to the city, but Thea had already shown me it; he wanted to introduce me to Spanish literature and finally he put the touch on me for some dough. He said he was going to buy me a blanket with it, but he never showed up again.

I ached in my body for Thea though I knew she was by now unobtainable and absolutely removed from me by the difficulty of her mind and the peculiarity of my own character. So I knocked around the city thinking things over. I'd watch the mariachis and death-song fiddler-cripples or the flower-sellers and the bees feeding off the candystands. Whichever way you turned there was the snow of one of the volcanoes and the whole mountain floating in. If I could help it I wouldn't look in a mirror those days, being haggard and ill. At one time I felt that if Death came up and tapped me on the shoulder, saying, "Ready?" I'd think it over a minute and then say, "Okay." So in a way I died somewhat, and if there was anything I knew by now it was how impossible it is to live without something infinitely mighty and great. However, the city was beautiful—even the unsightliness, misery, and scrawls were rich—it was warm, and this kept me going. My heart would complain and I felt sick, but not continually in the utmost despair.

At last I got in touch with Sylvester. He came to see me and lent me some dough. He wasn't saying much at first. I understood that he couldn't talk about political and confidential things.

"You look starved and raggedy," he said. "If I didn't know you I'd say you were one of these Pan-American bums. You've got to clean yourself up."

I felt as if I were an object Caligula had dropped about a thousand feet to the earth. The air screamed. The colors were about like the colors of Jerusalem. However, getting up stunned, I wanted to be steadfast. Go and be steadfast though! Just like that! It's not a small order. Sylvester realized that I wanted to get myself reconstructed and not go to wrack. He gave me his grin with little dark lines, always amused at me.

"My luck has been very bad, Sylvester," I said.

"I see. I see. Well, do you want to stick around here until it changes or do you want to go back to Chicago?"

"What do you think? I don't know what I should do."

"Stick around. There's a sympathizer who'll put you up for a while if Frazer asks him."

"I'd be glad. I'd be very grateful, Sylvester. Who is this sympathizer?"

"He's a friend of the Old Man from away back. He'd put you up. I don't like to see you go around the way you are."

"Gee thanks, Sylvester. Thanks."

So then Frazer came around and took me over to be introduced to the sympathizer, whose name was Paslavitch. He was a friendly Yugoslavian who lived in a little villa out in Coyoacán. Beside his mouth were deep folds and inside them grew little shining bristles, as the geode or marvel of the rock world is full of tiny crystals. He was a very original kind of person. His head was onion-shaped and clipped close. In the garden where he was when we met the heat was trembling off the top of his dome.

He said, "You are very welcome. I am glad to have company. Maybe you will give me English lessons?"

"Sure he will," said Frazer. Frazer's looks had changed too. I never understood better why Mimi had called him "Preacher." With the pucker of thought between his eyes he did look like a minister. And also like an officer of the Confederate Army. He appeared to have grave weights on his mind and to be preoccupied with superior things.

He left me with this Paslavitch, then, and for some reason I felt I was put in deposit or reserve, but I was tired and didn't much care what he had in mind. Paslavitch showed me the rooms and the garden. I gazed at the birds, caged and free, the hummingbirds in the flowers and the spiny applauding of the cactuses. Lying in the grass or standing along the path were Mexican gods who gripped and clutched on themselves and cooled their hot teeth and tongues in the blue air.

Paslavitch was a kind, worried, meek, stubborn man who covered Mexico for the Yugoslav press. He considered himself a Bolshevik and old revolutionary but he was a *lacrimae rerum* type if I ever saw one; everything was forever touching him, and he had tears the way a pine has gum to give. He played Chopin on the piano, and when he executed a particular march he'd say to me, "Frederic Chopin wrote this during a storm when he was in Mallorca with George Sand. She was sailing on the Mediterranean. When she arrived he said, 'I thought you were drowned!'" Pressing on the pedals in his Mexican shoes, he made you think of Nero acting in a tragedy. Most of all this Paslavitch was in love with French culture and had a keen wish to teach me. In fact he had an obsession about teaching and was always saying, "Teach me about Chicago," "Teach me about General Ulysses S. Grant. I will teach you. I will tell you about Fontenelle's ham omelette. We will exchange."

He was very eager. "Fontenelle wanted to eat a ham omelette on a Friday but a terrible storm started, with thunder. So finally he threw the omelette out of the window and said to God, '*Seigneur! Tant de bruit pour une omelette.*'" It could be illuminating. He'd sway, with closed eyes and tight pronunciation. Or else he'd tell me, "Louis Thirteenth loved to play barber and would shave his gentlemen whether they wanted it or not. Also he enjoyed to imitate dying agonies, so he would make faces, and furthermore he would spend the wedding night in the same bed with young couples and was the last expression of feudal degeneracy."

Maybe he was, but Paslavitch loved him because he was French. He'd keep me after supper and repeat these conversations of Voltaire and Frederick the Great, de la Rochefoucauld and the Duchesse de Longueville, Diderot and a young actress, Chamfort and somebody else. I liked Paslavitch but sometimes it was heavy going, being his guest. I also had to go and play billiards with him at a club on the Calle de Uruguay. And to drink with him, when he felt like drinking. I did not want to do it in the afternoon because it reminded me too much of the tequila drinking I did in Acatla. But we'd sit and kill a few bottles of wine. Thousand soft moose-lashes of the copper forest sun passed through the trees; the garden was green while the woman's form of the volcano slept in the snow. I was a guest and guests have to go along with hosts. I paid my way by teaching him about the major leagues, etcetera.

Meanwhile I was building up my health somewhat, and then Frazer came around and sprung what he had been saving me for.

"You know that the GPU wants the Old Man's life," said Frazer.

I knew it. I had read in the papers about the machine-gun attack on his villa and Paslavitch had told me many other details.

"Well," said Frazer, "a man named Mink who is the chief of the Russian police has arrived in Mexico to take over the campaign against the Old Man."

"What a terrible thing! What can you do to protect him?"

"Well, the villa is being fortified, and we have a bodyguard. But the fortification isn't ready yet. The cops aren't enough to do the job. Stalin is out to get him because he's the conscience of the revolutionary world."

"Why are you telling me this, Frazer?"

"Here's the thing. There's a scheme being discussed. Maybe the Old Man will shake the GPU by traveling incognito around the country."

"What do you mean, incognito?"

"This is confidential, March. I mean that he should take off his beard and mustache, cut his hair, and pass as a tourist."

Well, I thought this mighty queer. As if Gandhi should go dressed in a Prince Albert. That this formerly so mighty and commanding man should have to alter and humble himself. Somehow, though I had seen and known lots of trouble, this struck me very hard.

I said, "Whose idea is this?"

"Why it's been discussed," said Frazer in his professional revolutionary way, meaning it wasn't any of my business. "I trust you, March, or I wouldn't have suggested you for a part in this."

"Why, where do I come in?" I said.

He said, "If the Old Man is going to travel incognito as a visitor to Mexico he's going to need a nephew from the States."

"Me, you mean?"

"You and a girl comrade as husband and wife. Would you do it?"

I saw myself driving around Mexico with this great person, tracked by secret agents. I felt too worn out to take it on.

"There wouldn't be any hanky-panky with the girl," said Frazer.

"I don't even understand what you mean. I'm trying to recover from the injury of a love affair."

Please God! I thought, keep me from being sucked into another one of those great currents where I can't be myself. Naturally I wanted to be of help, and rescue and peril attracted me. But I wasn't up to it at all, going up and down the mountains of Mexico through the bazaar of red nature and dizzy with deaths and noises.

"I'm telling you this because the Old Man is very moral."

Frazer spoke as though he too were very moral. Tell it to the marines! I thought.

"He won't do it anyhow," I said. "It's a loony idea."

"That's for the people who're protecting him to decide."

But to me it seemed his appearance was his trademark. His head was. Sooner than touch it he'd maybe let it be taken off him and kept just as it was for martyrdom. Kind of like St. John and Herod. And I had to stop and ask myself about martyrdom. Out in Russia was his enemy who didn't mind obliging him. He'd kill him. Death discredits. Survival is the whole success. The voice of the dead goes away. There isn't any memory. The power that's established fills the earth and destiny is whatever survives, so whatever is *is* right. That's what passed through my mind.

"You'd have to pack a gun. Does that scare you?"

"Me? Of course not," I said. "Not that part of it."

I reflected in my private mind that I must have holes in my head like a colander not to refuse. Was I so flattered by the chance to be with this giant historical personality, speeding around the mountains? The car would rush like mad. The wild beasts would flee. The terrible earth would turn around. And he would be silent to me on his thoughts of nations and destiny. The lost world would call after us with secret voice, and behind us there would be a team of international killers pursuing and waiting for their chance.

"Sometimes I wonder," I said, "if people who are going to tell the truth shouldn't make sure first that they can defend themselves."

"That's not a good point of view," said Frazer.

"No? Maybe. It's just a thought."

"Will you do it?"

"You feel I'm the right sort of guy for it?"

"We need somebody who looks very American."

"I guess I could spare some time," I said, "if it doesn't take too long."

"A few weeks, just to shake off Mink and his men."

He went away, and I was sitting in the garden where the lizards were tickling in the grass and there was a choke of gorgeous color by the birds along the hot walls. The gods stood or lay and persisted in their gray volcano illustrations of what the forces of life are. Paslavitch was playing Chopin upstairs. My next idea was how nothing was more dreadful than to be forced by another to feel his persuasion as to how horrible it is to exist, how deathly to hope, and taste the same despair. How of all the impositions this was the worst imposition. Not just to be as they make you but to feel as they dictate. If you didn't have the strongest alliance you surely would despair at last and your mouth would drink blood.

Paslavitch came out on his balcony in his blue bathrobe and asked meekly if I wanted a drink.

"Okay," I said. I was very worried about this whole scheme.

But it fell through, and when it did I was very glad. I had been in a clutch about it and lost sleep dreaming how we would chase from town to town all the way through Jalisco or out into the deserts. But the Old Man vetoed this. I wanted to send him a letter telling him how smart I thought he was, but then I thought it wouldn't be right for me to discuss secrets of his political activity. He must certainly have given a scream when they propositioned him on it.

Anyhow, I felt now that there was something about the effect of Mexico on me, that I couldn't hold my own against it any more and had better get back to the States. Paslavitch lent me two hundred pesos and I bought my ticket to Chicago. He was affected a lot by my going and told me many times in French that he would miss me. Likewise, I'm sure. He was a very decent guy. You don't meet so many such.

Chapter XXI

ON THE WAY back from Mexico to Chicago I took a side trip or pilgrimage out of East St. Louis and went toward Pinckneyville to see my brother George after many years. He was already a grown man, a large hulk insecure in his steps. Darkenings of brown in his fair skin under the eyes showed how after his own fashion he too made the struggle that we make if we consent to live. Just as though, the time for it coming round, we left what company we were in and went privately to take a few falls with our own select antagonist in his secret room, like inside a mountain or down in a huge root-cellar. This was how it was with George too.

Nevertheless he was a man of fine appearance, as he had been a beautiful child. Now as then his shirt still bagged out in that senseless style over his back, and his hair grew like chestnut burr the same as formerly, brown and gold, close bristles. I was kind of proud of him that he took his fate with dignity. They had made a shoemaker of him. He couldn't run one of those machines you see thumping under their fender in a repair shop with the screaming disks and circular brushes, and he wasn't equal to making shoes by hand, but he was good at heeling and soling. Down in the basement, under the veranda, was where he worked. It was a wide veranda, for the place was far enough downstate to be reckoned Southern, and the buildings were big, white, of wood. Vines gave green color to his dusty half-window below. I saw him bent over the last, taking nails out of his mouth and sending them through the leather.

"George!" I said, looking at the man he had grown to be. He knew me right away, and he stood up, happy, and exactly as in the old days said, "Hi, Aug! Hi, Aug!" in his nasal voice. This repetition of two words if it went on long enough led usually to howling. So I went up to him, as he didn't move toward me. "Well, how is it, old man?" I said to him. I pulled him to me with one arm and put my head on his shoulder. He wore a blue work shirt; he was big, white, and clean, except his hands. Eyes, nose, and small mouth of his undeveloped face were as they had always been, simple. I was moved that he couldn't know how much of a complaint he had against me for neglect, and no sooner saw me than was happy.

He hadn't had a visitor in three or four years, so they let me see him by special permission for the whole day.

"What do you remember, Georgie?" I asked him. "Grandma, and Mama, Simon, Winnie?" With his small smile he said these names after me, as in the song he used to sing when he trotted with the dog along the curl-wired fence, singing how everybody loved Mama. Within his moist mouth his teeth were white and good, though his eye-teeth were very sharp. I took him by the hand, which now was bigger than mine, and we went walking in the grounds.

It was the beginning of May and the oak leaves were shot out full, dark and healthy; worked through just as richly were the big dandelion blades and warm bottom-land-smelling air surrounded us. We walked along the wall, which at first was simply a wall to me. But then suddenly I was disturbed to think that he was a prisoner and never got outside, poor George. So without asking permission I took him off the grounds. He looked at his feet in the unfamiliar road to watch where they were going, for he was frightened. In a crossroads store I bought him a package of chocolate marshmallow cookies. He took them but wouldn't eat them, putting the package in his pocket. His eyes were now turning very uneasily, and I said, "Okay, George, we're going back right away." That calmed him.

When he heard the dinner bell go—which was like the clink of the church bell of mouse-town in a children's zoo—trained to answer right away, he went to the rambly green cafeteria. He left me here. I had to follow him. He picked up his tray, and with those disconnected others who scraped their tinware and fed, wagging their weak noggins, without talk or observation, we sat down and ate.

It must be as simple as the blue and white of pillow-ticking to lay plans to take care of creatures so, clothe them, feed them, put them in their dormitory. There is probably just nothing to it.

The rest of the trip I kept thinking that something should be done for Georgie, not to let him spend his entire life like that; also I thought how quick we were to latch on to the excuse to deal practically with any element, like jailbirds, orphans, cripples, the weak-brained or the old. And I decided that after I had visited Mama I'd go and talk to Simon about Georgie. I didn't have anything specific to propose. But I said to myself that Simon had money, therefore he ought to know what money could do. And anyway, as I was coming back to Chicago I thought of Simon. I wanted to see him.

I went from the one institution straight to the other in Chicago. But the two places were very different. Mama wasn't any longer right off the kitchen but established in almost an apartment with a Gulistan on the floor and drapes on the window. I had phoned that I was coming, and she waited for me down in front and rested on her white cane. While still at a distance I spoke to her, so she wouldn't be startled. She weaved her head to locate me and with her crying-out voice of painful joy called my name. From the top rims of her goggles, which were dull dark, the brows of her pink long face lifted as if she were trying to use her eyes too. She then kissed me and whispered to me. She felt my face and said, "You're skinny. Augie, why you're so skinny?" And then, a long figure herself, nearly as tall as I, she led me up to her room by the back entrance. An odor of boiling fish spouted up the stairs; that passed into my home-coming mood and made me feel the kitchen heat of old days, sitting with my mother.

On the dresser all my postcards from Mexico were set out, and there were photos of Simon and Charlotte also. To show the seeing people who came. But besides the supervisor and his wife, who hated Simon, who did come? Only once in a while Anna Coblin. Or Simon himself. He'd come in, see how fixed up she was in her bourgeois parlor, and be satisfied. She too realized that she was being treated in a satisfactory way. On her wrist was a silver bracelet, she wore high heels, she had a radio with a big chromium zigzag across the speaker. In fact when Grandma Lausch had put on her black Odessa best in the Nelson Home she was laying claim feebly to the style Mama here was living in. That was how the Lausch brothers had let the old lady down, failing to appreciate legitimacy and without any sense of standards. Yet it wasn't a light duty for Mama that she had to live up to what

Simon and Charlotte were doing for her. Simon was if anything even more difficult than Charlotte, I gathered. He was
very fussy. He opened her closet and inspected all her clothes
to see if they were cleaned or if any were missing from the
rack. I knew how Simon could be when he was doing something for your good and welfare; he could make things hot.

But maybe that spicy, sumptuous fish-gravy odor that belonged to the past made me too much of a critic of the present moment, exaggerating Mama's difficulties and imagining
that the Gulistan and the drapes were the softenings of a cage.
A blind woman, growing elderly, she had to live in a room,
some room, and therefore why not a comfortable room?
Moreover, it was perhaps my fault that I saw both Georgie
and Mama as prisoners, and was unhappy that I was tooting
freely around while they were confined.

"Augie, go see him," she said. "Don't be mad on Simon. I
told him *he* shouldn't be."

"I will, Ma, as soon as I find a room and begin to settle
down."

"What are you going to do?" she said.

"Oh—something. I hope something interesting."

"What? Do you make a living, Augie?"

"Well, here I am. What do you mean, Ma? I *am* living."

"Why are you so skinny? But the clothes are good—I felt
the material."

They ought to have been good. Thea had paid a fancy price
for them.

"Augie, don't wait too long to call Simon. He wants you
to. He told me I should tell you. He talks about you all the
time."

Simon did want to see me. As soon as he heard my voice
over the phone he said, "Augie! Where are you? Stay put. I'll
come and pick you up right away."

I was calling from a booth near my new place, which wasn't
far from the old, on the South Side. He lived in the vicinity
and was there within a few minutes in his black Cadillac, this
beautiful enamel shell coming so softly to the curb, inside like
jewelry. He beckoned and I got in. "I have to go right back,"
he said. "I left without a shirt; I just put on this coat and hat.
Well, let's look at you."

He said this, but actually didn't much look, despite his rush to get down. Of course he was driving, but just the touch of manicured hands on the valuable stones on the wheel—something like jade—did the trick. The thing pretty well ran itself. I thought he was sorry about the fight we had had over Lucy and Mimi. I wasn't angry any more but was looking ahead. Simon was heftier than before. The light raglan with its chestnut buttons came open on his hard bare belly. Also his face was larger, and rude, autocratic. The fat of it was not clear, as it is in some faces. Mrs. Klein, Jimmy's mother, had had a fat face, almost oriental, but there the fat illuminated something. However, I found out that I couldn't be critical of Simon when I saw him after a long interval. No matter what he had done or what he was up to now, the instant I saw him I loved him again. I couldn't help it. It came over me. I wanted to be brothers again. And why did he come running for me if he didn't want the same?

Well, now he wanted to know how rugged things had been for me, and I didn't have any intention of telling him. What was I up to in Mexico?

"I was in love with a girl."

"You were, uh? And what else?"

I didn't say anything about the bird or my failures and lessons. Maybe I should have. He criticized me anyway in his mind for my randomness and sentiment. So what did I stand to lose by telling him the facts? However, something haughty kept me. That was how brief the first warmth of love turned out to be. So he was judging me—what of it? Let him. Wasn't I busted down, creased, head-damaged, missing teeth, disappointed, and so forth? And couldn't I have said, "Well, all right, Simon, here I am." No, what I told him was that I had gone down to Mexico to work out something important.

Then he started to talk about himself. He had built up his business and sold it at a whopping profit. Since he didn't want to have to do with the Magnuses he had gone into other kinds of business and he was very lucky. He said, "I certainly do have the gold touch. After all, I did start in the Depression when everything was supposed to be over and done with." Then he described how he had bought an old hospital building at auction and turned it into a tenement. Inside of six months he had cleared fifty thousand bucks on this, and then had organized a management company and run the place for the new owners. He had a large interest in a Spanish cobalt mine now. They sold the stuff in Turkey, or some place in the Middle East. He also had a potato-chip concession in several railroad stations. In fact, Einhorn himself couldn't have dreamed up such deals, much less have made them pay off.

"How much do you think I'm worth now?"

"A hundred grand?"

He smiled. "Let yourself go a little," he said. "If I'm not a millionaire soon there's a hitch in my arithmetic."

It impressed me; who wouldn't be impressed? He couldn't help seeing this. Nevertheless, with his autocratic blue eyes darkening, he looked at me and asked, "Augie, you don't think you're superior to me because you have no money, do you?"

The question made me laugh, and maybe I laughed more than I should have. I said, "That's a strange thing to be asking. How can I? And if I can, why should you care?" Then I said, "I guess it's true that people fix it to come out better than those near to them. Why, sure I'd like to have money too."

I didn't say that I had to have a fate good enough, and that this came first.

My answer satisfied him. "You're wasting a lot of time," he said.

"I know it."

"You ought to quit stalling. You're not a boy. Even George is something, he's a shoemaker."

You know, I did admire Georgie for the way he took his fate. I wished I had one that was more evident, and that I could quit this pilgrimage of mine. I didn't feel I was better than Simon, not at all. If there had been real ease in me, he might have envied me. As it was, what was there to envy?

Bodily overbearing, his fashionable pointed shoe on the rubber pad of the accelerator, he drove over the streets. This proud car, it had heraldry, it was royal, and wasn't my brother like a prince of Detroit; full of force and darkness? Why, what was the matter with that, to be a power of the world of machinery? Wasn't it good enough? And to what should you go rather? I wasn't proud of myself, believe me, and my stubbornness about a "higher," independent fate. I was no wizard, for sure, nor gazetted as anything illustrious, nor billed to stand up to Apollyon with his horrible scales and bear's feet, nor slated to find the answer to all my shames like Jean-Jacques on the way to Vincennes sinking down with emotion of the conception that evil society is to blame for all that happened to warm, impulsive, loving me. There was no such first-rate thing that I could boast, and who was I, not to make up my mind and be so obstinate? The one thing I could say was that though I wanted this independent fate it wasn't merely for my own sake I wanted it.

Oh, but why get too earnest? Seriousness is only for a few, a gift or grace, and though all have it rough only the favorites can speak of it plain and sober.

"So when are you going to start what you're going to do?"

"I wish I knew. But it seems to be one of those things you can't rush."

"Well, people don't trust you if they don't know what you do, and you can't blame them."

He pulled up before his apartment, and he left the Cadillac triple-parked in the street for the doorman to worry about. Rising up swift and soundless in the elevator, we came to the ivory white door of his flat. As he opened it he was already yelling for the maid to cook some ham and eggs right away. He took on like a king, a Francis back from the hunt; he swelled, hollered, turned things round, not so much showing me the great rooms as dominating them typically. Well, there were vast rugs and table lamps as tall as life-sized dolls or female idols, walls that were all mahogany, drawers full of underwear and shirts, sliding doors that opened on racks of shoes, on rows of coats, cases of gloves, of socks, bottles of eau de cologne, little caskets, lights lining the corners, water hissing criss-cross in the showerstall. He took a shower. I went alone into the parlor; a huge China vase was there, and in secret I got up on a chair to lift the lid and look down, where I saw the reverse white bulge of the dragons and birds. The candy dishes were full of candy—I had some coconut balls and apricot marshmallows walking around while Simon took his shower. Then we went to eat, on a handsome marble-topped round table. The chairs were red leather. The metal circle that held up the marble was worked all around with peacocks and children's faces. The maid came from the blazing white of the kitchen with the ham and eggs and coffee. Simon's hand with its rings went out to test the heat of the cup. He behaved like some Italian Lord Moltocurante, jealous over the quality and exacting all he had coming.

I knew we had gone way up in the elevator but hadn't noticed to what floor. Now, after breakfast, when I strayed into one of the enormous carpeted rooms, dark as a Pullman when it sits with drawn blinds in the station, I drew a drape aside and saw we were on the twentieth story at least. I hadn't had a look at Chicago yet since my return. Well, here it was again, westward from this window, the gray snarled city with the hard black straps of rails, enormous industry cooking and its vapor shuddering to the air, the climb and fall of its stages in construction or demolition like mesas, and on these the different powers and sub-powers crouched and watched like sphinxes. Terrible dumbness covered it, like a judgment that would never find its word.

Simon came looking for me. He cried, "Hey, what the hell are you doing in a dark room, for Chrissake? Come on, you're going around with me today."

He wanted me to know what his life was like. And maybe he thought I'd run into something that would appeal to me, for my future's sake. "Wait a minute though," he said. "What kind of clown's suit are you wearing there? You can't go among people dressed like that."

"Listen, a friend of mine picked this out for me. Anyway, just feel the material. There's nothing wrong with this suit."

But his face was impatient, and he pulled the jacket from me and said, "Strip!" He dressed me in a double-breasted flannel, very elegant soft gray. It certainly was my fortune to be poor in style. From the skin out he reclothed me in swell linen and silk socks, new shoes, and called the maid to have my old suit cleaned and sent to me—it was sort of shiny on the elbows. The other stuff he ordered her to throw down the incinerator. So it plunged down into the fire. I wiped my face with the monogrammed handkerchief, now mine, and felt around with my toes in the narrow shoes, trying to accustom myself to them. To top it off he gave me fifty bucks. I made efforts to refuse this, but my tongue got in its own way. "Go! Stop mumbling," he said. "You have to have a little something in your pocket to live up to this outfit." He had a big gold money-clip and all the bills were new. "Now let's go. I have things to do at my office and Charlotte wants to be picked up at five. She's at the accountant's, going over some of the books." He called down for the Cadillac, and we drove away, stopping for scarcely anything in this lustrous hard shell with radio playing.

In his office Simon wore his hat like a Member of Parliament, and while he phoned his alligator-skin shoes knocked things off the desk. He was in on a deal to buy some macaroni in Brazil and sell it in Helsinki. Then he was interested in some mining machinery from Sudbury, Ontario, that was wanted by an Indo-Chinese company. The nephew of a Cabinet member came in with a proposition about waterproof material. And after him some sharp character interested Simon in distressed yard-goods from Muncie, Indiana. He bought it. Then he sold it as lining to a manufacturer of leather jackets. All this while he carried on over the phone and cursed and bullied, but that was just style, not anger, for he laughed often.

Then we drove to his club for lunch, arriving late. There was no service in the dining room. Simon went into the kitchen to bawl out the headwaiter. Seeing some pot roast on a platter he broke off a piece of bread and sopped the gravy, covering the meat with crumbs. The waiter hollered and Simon yelled back, furiously laughing in his face too, "Why don't you wait on people then, you jerk!"

Finally they fed us, and then Simon seemed to find the afternoon dragging.

We went into the cardroom where he forced his way into a poker game. I could tell he was hated, but no one could stand up to him. He said to some bald-headed guy, "Push over, Curly!" and sat in. "This is my brother," he said as if bidding them to look at me in the opulent gray flannel and button-down collar. I lounged just behind him in a leather chair.

Then he would turn and describe various people to me, pretending to lower his voice. "You see that guy in the blue, the one with the cigar, Augie? He's a lawyer but doesn't practice, only he keeps an office so he can say he's at the bar. He makes a living at cards. If nobody played with him he'd be on relief next week. Same with his wife. She plays in all the fancy hotels. And this other one, over there, that's Goonie. His father owns a sausage factory and he's a Harvard man. If I had a son like that I'd just as soon pour champagne on my dick as send him to college. The sonofabitch. I'd make him stuff *wurst*. He's a bachelor. He'll never have sons of his own, but he likes little boys, and last year he tried to pick up a sailor at the State and Lake and the kid gave him a shiner. Over there is Ruby Ruskin—he's a good fellow. He visits his old dad down in Joliet Penitentiary at least once a month. The old man took the rap for them both in an arson case."

Those players who weren't glaring or grinning appeared to be holding their breath, and I thought sure Simon would end by being clouted. Then he said, "Listen, you cruds, I want you to take a good look at my brother. He's a radical and he just got back from Mexico. Augie, tell them how soon the revolution's coming when they'll get sash weights tied on their necks and be thrown in the drainage canal."

He took a big pot—he must have won because the rest were too rattled to play their cards—and left the table with a swagger.

"They could drown you in a teaspoonful of water," I said. "Why do you want to make them hate you so?"

"Because I hate *them*. I want them to know it. What do I care if those jag-offs hate me? Why, they're all lice! I despise them!"

"Then why do you belong to their club?"

"Why not? I enjoy being a member of a club."

He played the Twenty-Six girl at a bar for smokes at the green baize board, socking down the leather dice cup, and won again. Putting some Havanas in my breast pocket, he said, "Let's visit a barbershop. You need it and I like it. God, I love barbershops!" We stopped at the Palmer House where they had those grand episcopal chairs. By the time we were finished with all the cutting, shaving, toweling, steaming, polishing, it was five o'clock, and on the run we got into the car and sped through illegal alley shortcuts out of the Loop. Charlotte was waiting in the street in her fur-trimmed suit, grimly handsome and immense. She was terribly put out at having had to wait, and right away she started, "Simon, where have you been? Do you know how late you are?"

"Shut up!" he said. "Here's my kid brother. You haven't seen him for two years and can't even say hello but have to start yacking first."

"How are you, Augie?" she said, more vigorous than friendly, turning her head upon her furs toward the back seat. "How did you like Mexico?"

"Oh, very much."

She looked to be at the peak of fashion, and with the straight rulings of brow and mouth would have seemed attractive if it wasn't so evident how tried in flesh and patience she was. Her devices for hiding impatience were in bad repair. Of course she observed that I was already dressed in a suit of Simon's. Not that she'd object to a thing like that, only she didn't miss it. When she talked to you she had a nagging, bidding way and was tough, a hard judge, and you a defendant. You had to watch what you said. But she anyhow arrived at the opinion that she wanted. In her fur-trimmed suit, large and handsome, she was like an officer of the court all right, even though her lips were painted and eyes mascaraed. And me, I was like some foxy pirate, *larron de mer*, only I wasn't really such a bold answerer.

One thing that disturbed her was that without having a cent I seemed perfectly at home with many of the satisfactions that the rich enjoy. Free of charge and trouble. It wasn't true, of course, but only another one of those appearances. However, she was particularly concerned that I didn't at least look more anxious.

At dinner I wanted to talk about Georgie with Simon, but he said, "Don't make any new problems. Don't make any new problems. He's fine. What do you want?"

"Why worry about your brother George when you haven't decided what to do with your own life?" said Charlotte. "It's very easy to turn into a bum."

Simon said, "Be quiet! Better a bum than your cousin Lucy's husband and your uncle's son-in-law. Let Augie alone. A bum is just what he doesn't want to be. What if it takes him a little longer to settle down?"

"You lost a tooth or two, didn't you?" said Charlotte.

"How did it happen? You look like hell—" She might have gone on but the bell rang and somebody who was admitted by the maid went down the passage into the living room. Charlotte became silent. Later I glanced in, and I saw a giant feminine figure sitting in the dark. I went to see who this Brobdingnag woman could be. Why, it was Charlotte's mother, Mrs. Magnus, sitting beside the China jug which didn't make her seem smaller, giant as it was. Even in the dark Mrs. Magnus's color, beautiful and healthful, and her braided hair and calm saddle nose and her size, touched my feeling.

"Why do you sit in the dark, Mrs. Magnus?" I said.

"I have to," she told me simply.

"But why do you have to?"

"Because my son-in-law doesn't want to see me."

"But what's the matter?" I asked Charlotte and Simon.

Charlotte said, "Simon bawled her out about the cheap clothes she wears."

"Because," said Simon, angry, "she comes here wearing nineteen-fifty dresses. A woman with half a million dollars! She looks like the ragman's horse."

Owing to me, Charlotte brought her mother in to sit at the table. We were eating cherries and drinking coffee. Charlotte laid off me, but Simon worked himself into a rage at Mrs. Magnus in her brown dress. He tried to read the paper and cut her—he hadn't said a word when she came in—but finally he said, and I could see the devil in him now, "Well, you lousy old miser, I see you still buy your clothes off the janitor's wife."

"Let her alone," said Charlotte sharply.

But suddenly Simon threw himself across the table, spilling the cherries and overturning coffee cups. He grabbed his mother-in-law's dress at the collar, thrust in his hand, and tore the cloth down to the waist. She screamed. There were her giant soft breasts wrapped in the pink band. What a great astonishment it was, all of a sudden to see them! She panted and covered the top nudity with her hands and turned away. However, her cries were also cries of laughter. How she loved Simon! He knew it too.

"Hide, hide!" he said, laughing.

"You crazy fool," cried Charlotte. She ran away on her high

heels to bring her mother a coat and came back laughing also. They were downright proud, I guess.

Simon wrote out a check and gave it to Mrs. Magnus. "Here," he said, "buy yourself something and don't come here looking like the scrubwoman." He went and kissed her on the braids, and she took his head and gave his kisses back two for one and with tremendous humor.

I went to see Einhorn, who was kind of white and peaky. Things were not too good with him. He had gone to the hospital and had a prostate operation while I was away. All the same he still had a fine presence, much as in the insurance literature and in the clippings and photos all over the place. In the midst of all these hung the portrait of the Commissioner —there was a man! What a fine, great head—with the famous obituary under it! Tillie was away on a holiday with the grandchild, and Mildred who was more than ever Einhorn's friend was in charge. In her stout orthopedic shoes she stood up at the office barrier, which was cut down from the old office across the way. She had a way about the eyes of making you go to war with her. Not me, thanks. Her hair was beginning to be gray. Einhorn's was snowy, which made his eyes blacker. He saw the double-breasted suit Simon had given me and said, "You certainly are doing fine, Augie." The house stunk. The books were falling off the shelves. The busts of great men were lost up near the ceiling. The black leather chairs on casters were aging well, but aging.

Einhorn made a powerful complaint against Mimi Villars, who was ruining his son.

Mimi was even more unkind when she spoke of him and what he had done to Arthur. "I'll tell you about that old man," she said. "He's a damned impresario for himself. Every time he goes to the toilet he wants to publish an article about it. I know everybody is vain, and that that's what makes the world go round. Maybe it isn't even vanity. Maybe it's like, with a bullet in your brain, you go on thinking of your nice hat. You go on thinking about the party you were invited to on Saturday, and so forth. But there ought to be a limit somewhere. If you can't help it, at least you should know that it isn't a good thing. All that old man wants is that Arthur should be a credit to him and bring him glory, but as for helping him worth a damn, no, he won't come across with a nickel. And parents who have money and won't give any to their children ought to have it all taken away. They ought to go and beg. I'd take and put the old man on the corner of State and Lake with a tin cup, that's what I'd do. And you know the grandfather left it all to Arthur. He knew better than to trust his son. Arthur has been trying to finish a book, which is a great book. I believe in it. You know he can't be expected to work while doing that."

Einhorn did have some money though she exaggerated his wealth. However, I didn't argue with her. I was down on Einhorn myself. Since the time when I came back from Buffalo and found the family wiped out, when he urged me to be hard on Simon, I didn't feel the old friendliness toward him. And, if you want to know, because he and Tillie had warned me in the old days not to expect anything, repeating how Arthur would come into all, I couldn't help feeling no one had been good enough for them and now they were not good enough for one another. Now maybe was my chance to pass them by.

"Of course," Mimi said with some of her old-time bitterness, "I have a pretty good job now, but last winter I was down with the flu and couldn't work. Not only that but Owens kicked us out because I couldn't pay the rent and a friend of ours on Dorchester took us in. But all Arthur and I had to sleep on was the sofa. Both of us on the sofa, and I had the flu. By morning he was so tired that when my friend went to work he got into her bed. So," she said with her universal-comedy laugh, "finally I said he should try to get a job. He said he'd try, and he got up one morning at eight and was back at ten. He said he had a job in the toy department at Wieboldt's and he was going to learn the details the next day. He left at nine that morning and was back at eleven. They had showed him, but before he started he wanted to clean up an important chapter about Kierkegaard—what do I know about it?

"So then he went away next day at half-past eight and was back at noon, fired, because the floorwalker told him to pick up a piece of paper and he said, 'Pick it up yourself, you dog. Your back isn't broken.'

"Then Arthur came down with the flu and I had to get up and give him the sofa. But," she said, "I love him. It's never dull with him. The worse our life gets, the more good I feel in love. And you?" she said, looking closely at me, how I had been browned by Mexico, aged by hard going and experience, finally thrown on those rocks by Bizcocho and eating cinders and ashes over Thea. Why, the way I came back I must have had something in common with a survivor of Crassus's army in the eastern desert, barely making it back from the massacre in tattered armor scales.

Well, people had warned me in the first place. Padilla, for instance, said, "Holy Christ, March, what did you have to go *there* for, with a broad like that and this bird! A girl who catches snakes, and God knows what else! What do you expect? No wonder you look like this. I hate like hell to be rubbing it in, but it seems to me you had it coming."

"Manny, what was I supposed to do? I fell in love with her."

"Is love supposed to ruin you? It seems to me you shouldn't destroy yourself out of life for purposes of love—or what good is it?"

"That's right, but I didn't love her as I ought to have. You see, I missed out. I should have been more pure, and stayed with it. There was something wrong with me."

"Old pal, let me tell you something," said Padilla. "You take too much blame on yourself, and the real reason is not such a good one. It's because you're too ambitious. You want too much, and therefore if you miss out you blame yourself too hard. But this is all a dream. The big investigation today is into how *bad* a guy can be, not how good he can be. You don't keep up with the times. You're going against history. Or at least you should admit how bad things are, which you don't do either. You should cut out this junketing around and go back to the university."

"I think I might do that. Only I'm still collecting my thoughts."

"Collect them meanwhile, in the evening. Can't you do two things at a time?"

And then Clem Tambow told me practically the same thing. He was getting his degree soon, and he looked very mature now with his heavy mustache and the cigar. He dressed like a poor man's press agent and his clothes smelled of cleaning fluid and the masculine odor. "Well, big boy, I see you're the same as when you left," he said. Now Clem and I liked each other very much, a splendid and goodhearted fellow, salt of the earth, ready with sympathy and appreciative of the general human plight. But I went on a toot with a rich woman, as he saw it, and if I was roughed up I had it coming to me. That was what he meant, for I wasn't at all the same as when I left.

"How is your campaign after a worth-while fate, Augie?" asked Clem, for he knew a lot about me, you see. Alas, why should he kid me so! I was only trying to do right, and I had broken my dome, lost teeth, got burned in my progress, a mighty slipshod campaigner. Lord, what a runner after good things, servant of love, embarker on schemes, recruit of sublime ideas, and good-time Charlie! Why, it was a crying matter, no fooling, to anyone who might know which side was up, that here was I trying to refuse to lead a disappointed life. A hell of a cause of sympathetic tears but also, as Clem saw, of haw-haws, as great jokes often are. So I looked desolated, and Clem laughed like anything. I couldn't feel sore at him.

You know why I struck people funny? I think it was because of the division of labor. Specialization was leaving the likes of me behind. I didn't know spot-welding, I didn't know traffic management, I couldn't remove an appendix, or anything like that. I discussed it with Clem, who was of like opinion. Clem was no slouch. He now said he was pushing ahead in the field of psychology and a lot was clear to him that was a mystery before. Oh, he still knocked himself. He said, "I bought all my fine notions at a fire sale," but he was growing more confident of his point of view. He made a big thing of my coming back, declaring that we were among the few true friends around. That was no lie. I had the warmest feelings toward him. Well, then, he came around and said we must go to the Oriental Theatre and have supper. Till his last penny, Clem had to treat, and then he didn't mind if you stood him to something. He liked to look well, though his face was often raging, wrinkled, or his laugh was enormous while his teeth were snaggly, his head huge, and the suit he wore was pros-

perous, solid, middle-aged, a banker's suit, but his shanks
were long, his shoes were wrecked, his socks old Argyles, he
wore a turtleneck sweater and stunk of cigars.

So we went to the Oriental. The stars crept in the blue
heavens there, like Arabian nights. We heard Milton Berle
singing "River, Stay Away from My Door," then floppy
dancers, as couch-dolls in velvet, followed by an act of little
dogs zipping across the stage in automobiles, and then a
troupe of girls playing bagpipes. First they performed "Annie
Laurie" and then went into classical numbers. They did the
"Liebestod" and "Valse Triste," and then came the feature,
which was so lousy we walked out and went to a restaurant.

Dignified again after his windy haw-haws in the wild
gallery, Clem ordered a big Chinese dinner—sweet and sour
pork, bamboo shoots, chicken chow mein with pineapple, egg
foo yung, and tea, rice, sherbet, almond cakes. We cleaned up
on this and meanwhile had a conversation.

"Now just suppose," he said, "we were on our way up the
Nile to the first cataract, sailing in a *dahabiyeh*. The green
fields and boys shying rocks at the heavy birds, and the splashing flowers, while we eat dates with aphrodisiacs in them and
beautiful Coptic girls come rowing up to the music of the la-
teen sails and so on. Going to Karnak to copy inscriptions.
How would that be?"

"Well, I just came back from one exotic place."

"Yes, but you jumped the gun. You weren't ready to go
yet. You won't take things step by step. That's why your trip
wasn't a success. Now if you were an Egyptologist you could
go on this trip up the Nile."

"Good, then I'll become one. All I need is about ten years'
preparation."

"Look at you, you look so bright and happy after supper
and your face is so pleasant, why, you might be the owner of
this building. Haw, haw! Oh, brother, you're swell!"

"The only thing is," said I, flattered and smiling, "why the
Nile?"

"For you? Something exceptional," said Clem. "When I
think of you I have to think in terms of something exceptional. On the level of achievement." He had picked up this
vocabulary at the university. One of his favorite words was

"reinforced," which meant to give food to a rat who has solved a problem, to encourage him. Meantime, with big red lips, scowling laughter, and territorial face, the great nose with its passages, he looked like a king. "Are you like one of the lousy crowd cheering the Coptics who row out to the boat? You are not. You are a distinguished personality. You are a man of feeling. Among us poor drips at the human masquerade you come like an angel."

I tried to tut-tut him, but he said, "Oh, keep your shirt on, I'm not finished yet. You may not like it so much before I finish."

"Well, don't build me up so, and you won't have to tear me down."

"We aren't in the same universe of discourse. This is not yet what St. Thomas calls my level of first intention. I didn't say I thought you were an angel; only us common-clay, step-by-step, unfortunate ordinary personnel see you arrive as for a ball, smiling and beaming. You have ambitions. But you're ambitious in general. You're not concrete enough. You have to be concrete. Now Napoleon was. Goethe was. You take this Professor Sayce who actually had this Nile deal. He knew everything along the banks for a thousand miles. Specific! Names and addresses. Dates. The whole mystery of life is in the specific data."

"What makes you so keen about Egypt suddenly?" I said. "And besides I know there's plenty that's wrong with me. Don't you worry."

"Why, of course, even though you're beaming you're full of anxiety. Don't I know it! I can see you pissing against the wind. What you need is some of Dr. Freud's medicine. It could do you a whole lot of good."

"As a matter of fact," I said, now somewhat disturbed, "I've been having plenty of peculiar dreams lately. Just listen. Last night, I dreamed that I was in my own house, somewhere—it was enough of a surprise to have a house of my own, much less dream what I dreamed. I was standing in my beautiful front room, entertaining a guest. And what do you think? I had two pianos. There were two grand pianos, as if ready for a concert. Then my guest, who had wonderful manners—and me too, regular society—he said, 'Isn't it unusual for somebody to own three grand pianos?' *Three!* I turned around, and God! if there wasn't another piano. And I had been trying to figure out how come I had two in my house, as I can't play any more than a bull can sew cushions. This seemed downright sinister. But even though I was thrown by it I didn't let on or show anything. I told this guy, 'Sure, of course there are three of them'; as if who could do with less? So I felt like a terrible faker."

"Oh, what a case! You'd be a regular conservatory for a scientific mind. You'd be the greatest collection of unknowns ever to lie on a couch. What I guess about you is that you have a nobility syndrome. You can't adjust to the reality situation. I can see it all over you. You want there should be Man, with capital M, with great stature. As we've been pals since boyhood, I know you and what you think. Remember how you used to come to the house every day? But I know what you want. O *paidea*! O King David! O Plutarch and Seneca! O chivalry, O Abbot Suger! O Strozzi Palace, O Weimar! O Don Giovanni, O lineaments of gratified desire! O godlike man! Tell me, pal, am I getting warm or not?"

"You are, yes you are," said I. We were in this woodwork bower, you see, of the Chinese restaurant, and all seemed right, good-tempered, friendly. When important thought doesn't have to be soliloquy, I know how valuable an occasion that is. Because to whom can you speak your full mind as to yourself?

"Go on, Clem, go on," I told him.

"I went to the Mottley School in the fourth grade. Mrs. Minsick was the teacher. She'd call you up to the front of the class and hand you a piece of chalk. 'Now, Dorabella, what flower are you going to smell?' Haw, haw! It was a riot. This little Dorabella Feingold would smell up until her pants showed and turn her eyes with ecstasy. She'd say, 'Sweetpea.' It was a regular drill. Inhale and exhale. Stephanie Kriezcki, she'd say, 'Violet, rose, nasturtium.'" He held the cigar by the stem and smelled with his inflated nose. "Just catch the picture of this lousy classroom, and all these poor punks full of sauerkraut and bread with pig's-feet, with immigrant blood and washday smells and kielbasa and home-brew beer. Where did they get off with this flora elegance? Why, hell! And then old lady Minsick would give a gold star to reinforce the good ones. She, with that kisser of hers with sharp teeth and tits that hung down to her belly, she'd hawk into the wastepaper basket. Well, the wild kids would say, 'Skunk cabbage, teach,' or, 'Wild schmooflowers,' or 'Dreck.' For this she'd grab you by the neck and rush you down to the principal. But these tough kids were right. Whoever saw any sweetpeas? Why, I'd fish through the sewer lid with a diaper pin because my wiseguy brother told me I'd catch goldfish."

"This is a sad story. But don't you see both kinds of kids were right? Some stood up for what they knew and some longed for what they didn't. What do you mean, that there are some kids or people for whom there can't be flowers? That couldn't be true."

"I knew you'd go for this chalk-smelling. You have a strong superego. You want to accept. But how do you know what you're accepting? You have to be nuts to take it come one come all. Nobody is going to thank you for trying. And you know you're going to ruin yourself ignoring the reality principle and trying to cheer up the dirty scene. You should accept the data of experience. Why don't you read some psychology? It did me a lot of good."

"Well, I'll borrow some of your books, since you think it's so important. Only you've got the whole thing wrong already. I'll put it to you as I see it. It can never be right to offer to die, and if that's what the data of experience tell you, then you must get along without them. I also understand what you're driving at about my not being concrete. It's as follows: In the world of today your individual man has to be willing to illustrate a more and more narrow and restricted point of existence. And I am not a specialist."

"Well, you tell me you can train birds."

Yes, so far that had been my only field of specialization.

And it's perfectly true, you have to be one of these spirits that get as if jumped into and driven far and powerfully by a social purpose. If somebody is needed to go and lie under the street, you be it. Or in a mine. Or work out joyrides in the carnival. Or invent names of new candy. Or electroplate babies' shoes. Or go around and put cardboard pictures of bims in barbershops or saloons. Or go die in one subdivided role or another, with one or two thoughts, these narrow, persistent ideas of your function.

I always believed that for what I wanted there wasn't much hope if you had to be a specialist, like a doctor or other expert. If so, as an expert, you'd be dealing with other experts. You wouldn't care for amateurs, for experts are like that about amateurs. And besides specialization means difficulty, or what's there to be a specialist about? I had Padilla's slogan of "Easy or not at all."

Mimi got a big laugh out of my Mexican experiences. "What a ball you've been having," she said. She made me feel unpleasant about Thea; and about Stella she said, "Guys like you make life easy for some women."

There hadn't been anything easy for anyone, but you couldn't tell Mimi that. Having gotten the story as she wanted it, she didn't listen to more, but with her push-faced vigor, her broad red mouth stretching and giving out with her helicon or hunting-horn voice, she let me have it almost the same as Clem. I'd better be cured of my attitudes. The reason why I didn't see things as they were was that I didn't want to; because I couldn't love them as they were. But the challenge was not to better them in your mind but to put every human weakness into the picture—the bad, the criminal, sick, envious, scavenging, wolfish, the living-on-the-dying. Start with that. Take the fact that people generally were full of loathing and it cost them an effort to look at one another. Mostly they wanted to be let alone. And they dug for unreality more than for treasure, unreality being their last great hope because then they could doubt that what they knew about themselves was true. Maybe she exaggerated her rake-the-heavens wrath and went beyond how she truly felt. However, there were blue marks of worry beneath her eyes these days.

When Arthur came around she talked about money and jobs. Four times out of five she changed the subject to that as soon as he showed up.

There was a certain job she kept after him to take. But he said, "Why, it's a farce!" And gently began to laugh in his dark way, crow-footed.

"The money's no farce."

"Oh, please, Mimi. Don't be absurd."

"There'd be practically no work connected with it."

However, he made it seem absolutely impossible. I began to think it was a job I might put in for myself, if qualified.

I met Arthur out walking and I asked him why he didn't want it.

It was a cool afternoon, and he was wearing cap and coat. He had lost much weight and was very bony, his shoulders up sharp, so that I was impressed with his resemblance to his uncle Dingbat and how he had subdued the same inheritance by a different life. He was of that same sharp skinny-chested build, with long face and a quick walk of inward-pointed toes. His shoes were tapered, as elegant as chivalry in the stirrups or the end of a lizard entering a crevice. But Arthur's health was poorer than Dingbat's and he had a swarthier color; his breath was strong with coffee and tobacco. He owned up to inferior teeth with his smile. Nevertheless he had all the charm of the Einhorns when he wanted to turn it on.

There was great style in his thinking. Sometimes I believed he was ready to say or consider anything. My personal preference was for useful thoughts. I mean thoughts that answered questions that moved you. Arthur said this was wrong; truth was truer when it had less to do with your needs. What personal need, for instance, is there in the investigation of the creep of light from the outermost stars which even at that unimaginable speed decays and breaks down because it grows so ancient in its travel? It fascinated me, this question.

However, about the job: there was a millionaire engaged in writing a book and he was looking for a research assistant.

"Do you think I'd fill the bill?"

"Of course you would, Augie. Are you interested?"

"Well, I need a job. Something that'll leave me the free time I want."

"I like the way you arrange your life. What do you intend to do with this free time?"

"I intend to use it." I didn't like the implication of this. Why should he need his time free and I be questioned?

"I'm just curious. Some people always appear to know what they're going to do, and others never. Of course I'm a poet, and relatively lucky. I've often thought, If I weren't a poet, what would I be? A politician? But just see how Lenin's life work turned out. A professor? That's much too tame. A painter? But nobody knows what painting's about any more. Whenever I write a dramatic poem I can't understand why the characters should ever want to be anything but poets themselves."

Well, this is how it was in Chicago when I came back. I stayed on the South Side. I got my case of books back from Arthur and I read in my room. The heat of June grew until the shady yards gave up the smell of the damp soil, of underground, and the city-Pluto kingdom of sewers and drains, and the mortar and roaring tar pots of roofers, the geraniums, lilies-of-the-valley, climbing roses, and sometimes the fiery devastation of the stockyards stink when the wind was strong. I read my books and almost each day wrote to Thea in care of Wells Fargo, but no answer came. One letter was forwarded from Mexico, and that one was from Stella. She was in New York. I never expected her to write such a good letter; I decided that I had underrated her. She said she couldn't pay me yet; she had to square herself with her union. But as soon as she landed a job she'd settle her debt.

Simon had given me some money so that I could take summer courses at the university. Now I thought I might like to be a schoolteacher and I was registered in several Education courses. I found it hard to sit in classes and read the textbooks. Simon was always ready to stand by me if I wanted to, though he himself didn't have much use for universities.

I was still after the job Arthur refused to take with the millionaire who wanted to write a book. This millionaire's name was Robey. He had studied with Frazer when Frazer was an instructor, and that was why Mimi knew him. He was tall and bent, he had a bad stammer, he wore a beard, he had been married four or five times—Mimi told me these facts. Arthur said the book was to be a survey or history of human happiness from the standpoint of the rich. I wasn't so sure that I wanted to do this but I didn't want Simon to keep on supporting me. I tried to fish a loan from Einhorn but he held it against me that I was an old friend of Mimi. He said, "I can't lend you anything. You realize that I have to support my grandchild. The extra burden is tough. And what if Arthur decides to bless my last years with another?" He was p.o.

So reluctantly I went to Arthur to ask him to phone Robey for me.

"This is a very strange fellow, Augie, he ought to amuse you."

"Oh hell, I don't want him to amuse me. I just want a job."

"Well, you'll have to try to understand him. He's very peculiar. He partly gets it from his mother. She thought she was the queen of Rockford, Illinois. She wore a crown. She had a throne. She expected everyone in town to bow to her."

"Does he live in Rockford now?"

"No, he has a mansion here on the South Side. When he was a student a chauffeur used to drive him to campus. For a long time he was mad on Great Books and he used to buy space in the want ads and put in quotations from Plato or Locke. Like, 'The unexamined life is not worth living.' He has a sister who's wacky too—Caroline. She think she's a Spaniard. But you have a gift of getting along with these temperaments. You were a jewel with my dad."

"I was kind of in love with him."

"Maybe you'll love Robey too."

"He sounds to me like another crank. I can't always be connected with ridiculous people. It's wrong."

But not long afterward, on a drizzly afternoon, I found myself face to face with this man Robey in his house on the lakefront. And what a face it was—what an appearance! Big, inflamed, reticent eyes, a reddish beard, red sullen lips, and across his nose a blotch; the night before, when he was drunk or sleepy, he had walked into the door of a taxi. His stutter was bad; when it really caught him he made a great effort, fixed his soul, and twisted his head while his eyes took on this discipline and almost hatred. At first I was astonished, and I was sorry for his sake when his teeth clicked or a snarl escaped. But I soon found out how fluent he could be in spite of it.

With those reticent, blood-flickered eyes of his he looked at me like someone who had to explain he was born to difficulty and hard luck, and he opened his lips before starting to speak, as if to separate the upper and lower hairs of the beard.

He said, "What about l-l-lunch?"

We had a rotten lunch—thin clam chowder, a smoked ham which he sliced himself, boiled potatoes, wax beans, and twice-heated coffee. It made me kind of sore that a million-aire should invite you to lunch and put on such a lousy feed.

He did the talking. Background first, he said. As his collaborator I'd have to have some personal knowledge of him. He started to tell me of his five marriages, taking his share of the blame for each divorce. But the marriages formed part of his education; therefore he had to evaluate them. I was disgusted. I took a sip of the coffee and let it flow back into the cup through my teeth, and made a face. But he didn't notice. He was on his third wife, terribly boring. The fourth gave him real insight into his character. I think he still carried the torch for her. As he was vibrating his neck over a troublesome word I interrupted. I was about to say, "What about some fresh coffee at least?" but I didn't have the heart. Instead I asked, "But can you give me an idea as to what my work will be?"

He became more tongue-free then. "I need advice," he said. "Help. I need to clear up some of my concepts, m-my thinking, n-n-need cl-clarity. This is *s-something*, this book."

"But what's it about?"

"It's not j-just a book—it's a guide, a p-p-program. I originated the idea b-but now it's too much for me. I need help." As he spoke of help he sounded frightened. "I discovered much too m-much. It was just an accident that it happened to be me, and now I'm stu-stuck with the responsibility."

We went into the salon to continue the conversation. His walk was belly-heavy, dragging, as if he had to remind himself not to step on his own dong.

It kept on drizzling; the lake looked like milk. Indoors, moony lamps glowed on the plush and Far East crimson and mahogany. There were Persian screens and Invalides horsehair helmets, busts of Pericles and Cicero and Athena, and who-else-not. And there was a portrait of his mother. Sure enough, she looked demented and wore a crown, a scepter in one hand and a rose in the other. The fog-cradled ore-boats from Duluth to Gary were moaning. Robey sat under a light, which showed the acne-exploded follicles under his beard.

He mightn't be very bright, Robey humbly started, but

what could he do? he couldn't escape ideas. None of us could escape ideas, and everybody was up against the same thing, namely, that there were hundreds of things to think about and to know. He had a duty to do his best at it. This was how he covered up his zeal, which I felt, however, powerfully trembling in the back.

This book, he went on, he wanted to call *The Needle's Eye.* Because there never had been a spiritual life for the rich if they didn't give up everything. But it wasn't any longer merely the rich who were headed for trouble. In the near future technology was going to create abundance and everyone would have enough of everything. There'd be inequality but not starvation or great need. People would eat. Well, when they ate, what then? The Eden of liberty, plenty, and love, the dream of the French Revolution coming to pass. But the French had been too optimistic and thought that when the decrepit old civilizations were busted nothing could stop us from entering the earthly paradise. But it wasn't so simple. We were facing the greatest crisis in history. And he didn't mean the war, then coming on. No, we'd find out if there was going to be this earthly paradise or not.

"B-bread's almost free now in America. What'll hap-happen when the struggle for bread is o-o. . . . Will goods free man or enslave him?"

You almost forgot to think about his goofy looks and about the lavish collection of screens, antiques, irons, Russian sleighs, hanks and tails of helmets, and mother-of-pearl boxes. All the same, even when he was in the top spheres he looked miserable, ready to weep tears. In the meantime the moldy ham taste kept coming up on me.

"M-machinery'll make an ocean of commodities. Dictators can't stop it. Man will accept death. Live without God. That's a b-brave project. End of an illusion. But with what values instead?"

"That's quite a deal," I said.

"But," he said, "that's toward the end of the b-book. I think we should start with Aristotle discussing how much of worldly goods you need before you can practice virtue."

"I haven't read much Aristotle."

"Well, that's one of the th-things you have to do. You'll be paid for it, never you worry. But I want this to be a solid piece of work and real scholarly. We're going to cover the Greeks and Romans, Middle Ages, Renaissance Italy, and I'm p-planning a chart, the Min-Minoans way high, Calvin down low, Sir Walter Raleigh, up; Carlyle, stinks; modern science, stand-still. Not even interested."

In the next half-hour he made sense only now and then; he seemed to tire, and he rambled, he blinked his fire-streaked eyes and coughed in his fist.

"N-now-now you tell me about yourself," he said. I didn't know where to begin and I damned him for asking me. But he wasn't listening. By the way he looked at his wristwatch I could tell he was wondering how soon he could be by himself again.

So I asked to be shown the can, and he pointed it out. When I came back he appeared to have recovered his interest in the book and wanted to discuss it some more. He said he was sure I was the man to help him. And he started to outline the whole thing for me. Part one, general statement. Part two, pagans. Three, Christians and so forth. Four, practical examples of the highest happiness. His excitement again rose. He took off a house slipper and laid it on a book or album that was on the coffee table and every now and then he put it on again. He was saying that Christianity originally was aimed at the lowly and slaves, and that was why crucifixion and nailing and all such punitive grandeur of martyrdom were necessary. But at the pole opposite, the happy pole, there ought to be an equal thickness. Joy without sin, love without darkness, gay prosperity. Not to be always spoiling things. O great age of generous love and time of a new man! Not the poor, dark, disfigured creature cramped by his falsehood, a liar from the cradle, flogged by poverty, smelling bad from cowardice, deeper than a latrine in jealousy, dead as a cabbage to feeling, a maggot to beauty, a shrimp to duty, spinning the same thread of cocoon preoccupation from his mouth. Without tears to weep or enough expendable breath to laugh; cruel, frigging, parasitic, sneaking, grousing, anxious, and slug-gardly. Drilled like a Prussian by the coarse hollering of sergeant fears. Robey poured it on me; he let it come down.

I thought, Oh, what a crazy bastard! What kind of screwloose millionaire have they sent me to? All the same my heart responded to this and these things went home. My bottommost thought was, God have mercy on us poor human saps! And this bottommost thought budded out with another: Even if God did have mercy, this was what He'd have mercy on.

Then Robey switched on me. He was a quick changer of mood.

The damn bourgeoisie, he said, should have been leaders and offered practical examples of happiness. But they were a historic failure. They fumbled it. A weak dominant class, because all they had known how to do was to imitate the flow of money around the world, fill in all the opportunities for profit, like water seeking its own level, and to imitate the machine. Robey didn't sound like himself now, not, that is, as earnest as before, but bookish. He scratched his foot and went on like a lecturer, and with his beard, which looked straw-stuck, he was just one more oddity of this room.

But I was still enough of an Einhorn worshiper to be taken with him. And I set aside some of my criticisms and said, "You were talking about the salary before. Could you be more definite?"

This made an unpleasant impression. "How m-much do you expect? Till I tell how you pan out, I c-can start you at a reasonable figure."

"What's reasonable?"

"Fifteen a week?"

"You must be making a mistake in your figure. Fifteen? I can get that much on relief and never lift a finger." It made me indignant.

"Eighteen then," he followed up fast.

"You try to get a plumber to fix your washbasin for less than half a buck an hour. Are you trying to hoax me or something? I don't think you're being serious."

"You ought to th-think of the ed-ed-ucation you'll be getting. And it isn't just a job but a cau-cau-cause." He was very disturbed. "Well, twenty bu-bucks and you can live upstairs rent free."

So he could lay hold of me and chew my ear whenever he felt like it, night and day? Not on his life. "No," I said, "thirty a week for thirty hours."

It hurt him to put out dough. I could see what a labor it was for his soul just to think about it.

Finally he said, "Okay, when you work out. Twenty-five to start."

"No, thirty, I told you."

He cried, "Why do you put me through this t-terrible haggle? It's really t-terrible. What the devil! It defeats the whole purpose." His look was positively full of hatred. But he hired me anyway.

From day to day he changed his plan. First he wanted to do the historical section and assigned me to read Max Weber, Tawney, and Marx. Next I had to drop all this to start research on a pamphlet on philanthropy. He hated all philanthropist millionaires and wanted to hit all the puritanical rich who looked so bad and felt so unhappy. He named some of his cousins among them, so I could see it was all a family affair. Even the big brazen Wall Street louse with his suckers full of blood did more good in the form of a devil than these rich men who were worried, he said, like everybody else. Simply worried. And he'd rave against them by the hour.

I was used to enthusiastic projects that would never leave the inventor's hangar. Like Einhorn's indexed Shakespeare back in the old days. And I really understood that Robey wanted from me what Einhorn had wanted, the very same thing, namely, a listener. He was on the telephone continually or sending the car for me or hunting for me in the library or waiting outside classrooms for me all the time.

The first few months he heaped readings on me. I never could have gotten through all those Greeks and Fathers and histories of Rome and the Eastern Empire and whatnot in years. I don't even know that anybody should want to wade through so much stuff. But it suited me fine to sit in the library amid a heap of books.

Twice a week we had official conferences. I'd come with my notebooks ready to answer his questions with quotations and paraphrases. It was all right when he was businesslike, but he had peculiar moods, when his voice straggled, he was in woe, his hair in spikes and his color bloodshot, tears or anger in his voice, and much too vexed and bothered to talk to me about Aristotle and theories of happiness and so forth. He sometimes gave me some real jolts and astonishments. As when, looking for him through the mansion one day, I found him standing on a kitchen chair, wrapped in his bathrobe, pumping Flit into a cupboard while hundreds of roaches rushed out practically clutching their heads and falling from the walls. What a moment that was! He wildly raised hell as he worked the spray gun, full of lust, and breathed as loudly as the spray itself while the animals landed as thick as beans or beat it, crazy, like an Oklahoma land rush, in every direction.

Caught by me like this, Robey tried to swallow down his emotions and to act as though he didn't hate the cockroaches or kill them with thrilling satisfaction. It was kind of too bad he couldn't admit it. Moreover, I knew I had barged in at the wrong moment and that he'd hold it against me. He wouldn't be able to help it.

He gave a bad twitch, as if I had touched him in the small of the back, and came down from the chair. "It's just too much. They're r-r-running away with the hou-hou—the house. I put a slice of bread in the toaster and a roach po-popped up toasted with the bread, so I couldn't t-take it any more."

All his rage, like an ember eating a hole through straw, suddenly was out, and he led me to the salon where in the sunlight was seen much busted-out stuffing and tears in buttonless royal green velvet and dust. He wiped the oily killer juice off on his gown, saying, "Did you work up that Italian Renaissance stuff for me about the p-princes and the h-humanists? How they suffered without God!" he said, looking off. "But they were godlike themse-selves. What courage! And terrible, t-t-too. But it had to happen, that m-man would dare."

In the autumn he lost his grip on himself. He went on giving me assignments and I collected my thirty bucks with a free conscience, but he didn't do any work.

I had often wondered what sort of women he went around with when unmarried, whether spiffy whores or ladies of his own set, or Back-of-the-Yards pickups, or nice little university girls, or what. I was surprised. He went for ordinary strippers from the Near North Side, from Clark Street, Broadway, Rush, and those parts, who were rough on him in their dealings.

And as if it were a just punishment he took it from them and even smiled. He tried to sell me on these girls, but I had taken up once more with Sophie Geratis. He mostly seemed to want me to come with him. Which I did a few times to North Side joints. One stripper insulted him about the beard; he bowed to this. Only his red eyes, which he didn't take off her—she was dressed now, wearing a gray tailored suit—were something scandalous. But he merely said pedantically, "In the old days of Elizabeth the barbers had lutes and guitars in the shop so the gentlemen waiting could sing and play. It was because the beards and the lovelocks took so long to fix."

On the same evening as he made this mild observation he went on a rampage and tore the meter off in a taxi. I was supposed to get out at Fifty-fifth Street but I worried lest the driver sock him for this and so took him home first.

But he gave me a rough time just the same. He was very sensitive and wanted my good opinion; however, he was extremely variable, humble one minute and making sure of his money's worth the next, and yelling or being sullen, sticking out his big red mouth in unhappiness or anger. I remember one day in particular. There were snow and sunshine all around, and it was fresh and beautiful, but he was in a nasty mood, prodding his hands knuckle to knuckle in the pigskin gloves. He bitched at me and kept on and on. So I said, "You don't want me to work for you. You want somebody who'll take this lousy nervousness from you." And I wrapped my old coat around me, which was a camel's hair going bald in places, and set off across the yard. He came after me to take it all back. In the thick powder of snow I had on overshoes, but he came on in his fine tan shoes which were slipper-like, saying, "Augie, let's not have a fight. For the love of God. Listen, I'm sorry." But I went on, good and mad. And that evening he phoned me and asked me to come and get him downtown. I could hear that things weren't right. He said he'd be at the Pump Room, than which few places were considered niftier in the city. When I got there and asked for him, two knickered footmen brought him out. He was drunk, mute, numb, and could scarcely budge a feature of his face or work his tongue.

Little by little he had come to depend on me. Somewhat

like Einhorn in the old days, he had found I wouldn't take advantage of him and that I was dependable. And with his peculiarity and confusion, downright Guiana jungle manifestations or freaks that the power of life will squeeze into sometimes, there nevertheless was something in him that drew me. Just that power, no doubt, tormenting his humanity and tormented in return. And while he was a bachelor and shared that mansion with his sister Caroline—well, she didn't do him much good. She was screwy. And when she found I had been in Mexico she took a shine to me, believing herself Spanish. She wrote me notes, such as, "*Eres muy Guapo.*" And now and then a telegram arrived, like, "*Amigo, que te vaya con toda suerte, Carolina.*" She was terribly scrambled, poor woman.

After all, I had taken care of my brother George. That ability or quality was with me yet, and sometimes people sensed it.

Sometimes I wished I could become a shoemaker too.

Chapter XXII

I N MY OLD ROOM up at Owens' which I finally got back I went along with the changes of the times, industrial, military, scientific. Personally I experienced steep variations myself, bad news, wasted expenditures, wicked dreams, wizard happenings like the appearance of animals in the heat of evenings to desert Fathers, still I am thankful to say that as I view it I was not harmed. The police couldn't have had any complaint against me, regardless of what the moralists might have had. The worse offenses were in my imagination, where such belong, while like a big and busy enterprise that tries to cover all it can, I also brooded in my higher mind over my course of life. I came to certain conclusions too, which were sometimes fragmentary—such as, The reason for solitude can only be reunion; or, Oh, it's very tiring to have your own opinions on everything—but other times were very full indeed, as will be shown in due course. I rambled around Chicago, my sociable self as always. But I was reverberating still from the plucks and pulls of Mexico. Thea didn't write, having disappeared for good to some blue shores of the ancient seas, probably on the trail of flamingos, with some new lover who would understand her no better than I did, and camping on a parapet with her guns and nooses, cameras, long-distance glasses. She'd pass into old age like this and never be any different.

I wasn't getting any younger myself, and my friends would make pleasantries about my appearance, which wasn't at all prosperous. I smiled minus a couple of teeth of the lower line and was somewhat smeared, or knocked, kissed by the rocky face of clasping experience. My hair grew upward, copious, covering my old mountain hunter's scars. Undeniably I had a touch of the green of cousin Five Properties' eyes in my own, and I went along whiffing a cigar and lacking any air of steady application to tasks, forgetful, elliptical, gleeful sometimes, but ah, more larky formerly than now. While I mused I often picked up objects off the street because they looked to me like coins; slugs, metals from bottletops, and tinfoil scraps buried, thus obviously hoping for a lucky break. Also I wished somebody would die and leave me everything. This was bad, for who could benefit me by dying that I shouldn't love and want to keep on earth? And what good did finding coins do, even if each was a quarter, in the consummation and final form of my life? Why, no good, friends, not the least bit.

It also gave amusement that I was after a teaching certificate for grade school, for I hardly looked to be the type, I suppose. Yet this I was persistent about. I loved the practice teaching. It moved me while I did it; it was no problem to be my natural self with the kids—as why, God help us, should it be with anyone? But let us not ask questions whose answers are among the world's well-kept secrets. In the classroom, or outside in the playground holleration, smelling pee in the hall, hearing the piano trimbles from the music room, among the busts, maps, and chalk-dust sunbeams, I was happy. I felt at home. I wanted to give the kids my best and tell them all I knew.

At this same school, teaching Latin and algebra, was my onetime neighbor, Kayo Obermark. Bushy, sloppy, and fat, he used to lie on his bed at Owens' when he had the room next to mine in his underpants, his thighs curl-haired and feet smelly, and stare at the wall with determined thought as he put out cigarettes behind him without looking in the grease of an old skillet in which he fried salami. He kept a milk bottle by the bed to do duty in, disliking trips to the bathroom.

Now the kids were springing like locusts around him while he walked in the schoolyard, sullen, like an emperor. His face was big, moody, white, unevenly scraped. Crumbled Kleenexes stuck to him; he smelled of a cold and sounded snotty. But he wasn't really sullen, this was just his dignity, and I was pleased that he was a teacher here.

He said, "I saw you drive up here in your car."

"It started this morning for a change." I did in fact own a ten-year-old Buick on which a very pleasant guy had gypped me like fury. It wouldn't start on cold mornings and was a trial to me. I put in two batteries on Padilla's advice but there was a fundamental defect in that the rods were bent. However, with a push it would go, and as it had a rumble seat and a long hood it looked powerful.

"Are you married yet?" said Kayo.

"No, I'm sorry to say."

"I have a son," he said proudly. "You better get on the ball. Don't you have anybody? Women are easy to get. It's your duty to have sons. There was an old philosopher caught by his disciple behind the Stoa with a woman, and he said, 'Mock not! I plant a man.' But I've been hearing all kinds of things about you, that you went to Mexico with a circus or carnival and that you were nearly assassinated too."

He was in quite a mood, and he walked me round the schoolyard several times, being extremely kind in his haughty way and quoting various poems in his tense tenor voice.

Perish strife, both from among gods and men,
And wrath which maketh even him that is considerate cruel,
Which getteth up in the heart of a man like smoke,
And the taste thereof is sweeter than drops of honey.

Les vrais voyageurs sont ceux-là seuls qui partent
Pour partir; cœurs légers, semblables aux ballons,
De leur fatalité jamais ils ne s'écartent,
Et, sans savoir pourquoi, disent toujours: Allons!

This last probably aimed at me and accused me of being too light of heart and ignorantly saying good-by. I seemed to have critics everywhere. However, for a cold day this had a very bright sun, the trains were passing in blackness over an embankment of yellow concrete, the kids were screaming and whirling over the whole vast play yard, around the flagpole and in and out of the portables, and I felt especially stirred.

"You *should* get married," said Kayo.

"I'd like to. I think about it often. As a matter of fact I dreamed last night that I was, but it wasn't so pleasant. I was very disturbed. It started out all right. I came home from work and there were gorgeous little birds by the window, and I smelled barbecue. My wife was very handsome, but her beautiful eyes were filled with tears and twice as big as normal. 'Lu, what's the matter?' I said. She said, 'The children were born unexpectedly this afternoon and I'm so ashamed I've hidden them.' 'But why? What's there to be ashamed of?'

'One of them is a calf,' she said, 'and the other is a bug of some kind.' 'I can't believe it. Where are they?' 'I didn't want the neighbors to see, so I put them behind the piano.' I felt terrible. But still they were our children and it wasn't right that they should be behind the piano, so I went to look. But there on a chair behind the upright, who should be sitting but my mother—who, as you know, is blind. I said, 'Mama, what are you sitting here for? Where are the children?' And she looked at me with sort of pity and said, 'Oh, my son, what are you doing? You must do right.' Then I started to sob. I felt full of tragedy, and I said, 'Isn't that what I want to do?'"

"Ah, you poor guy," said Kayo, sorry for me. "You're no worse than anybody else, don't you know that?"

"I really should simplify my existence. How much trouble is a person required to have? I mean, is it an assignment I have to carry out? It can't be, because the only good I ever knew of was done by people when they were happy. But to tell you the truth, Kayo, since you are the kind of guy who will understand it, my pride has always been hurt by my not being able to give an account of myself and always being manipulated. Reality comes from giving an account of yourself, and that's the worst of being helpless. Oh, I don't mean like the swimmer on the sea or the child on the grass, which is the innocent being in the great hand of Creation, but you can't lie down so innocent on objects made by man," I said to him. "In the world of nature you can trust, but in the world of artifacts you must beware. There you must *know*, and you can't keep so many things on your mind and be happy. 'Look on my works ye mighty and despair!' Well, never mind about Ozymandias now being just trunkless legs; in his day the humble had to live in his shadow, and so do we live under shadow, with acts of faith in functioning of inventions, as up in the stratosphere, down in the subway, crossing bridges, going through tunnels, rising and falling in elevators where our safety is given in keeping. Things done by man which overshadow us. And this is true also of meat on the table, heat in the pipes, print on the paper, sounds in the air, so that all matters are alike, of the same weight, of the same rank, the caldron of God's wrath on page one and Wieboldt's sale on page two. It is all external and the same. Well, then what makes your existence necessary, as it should be? These technical achievements which try to make you exist in their way?"

Kayo said, not much surprised by this, "What you are talking about is *moha*—a Navajo word, and also Sanskrit, meaning opposition of the finite. It is the Bronx cheer of the conditioning forces. Love is the only answer to *moha*, being infinite. I mean all the forms of love, eros, agape, libido, philia, and ecstasy. They are always the same but sometimes one quality dominates and sometimes another. Look, I'm glad we've had this chance to meet again. You seem to have become a much more serious fellow. Why don't you come and meet my wife? My mother-in-law lives with us and she's kind of a dull old woman who fusses about everything, but we can ignore her. She's a big help with the kid incidentally. But she's always giving me an earful about how my brother-in-law is doing so well for himself. He's a radio-repair man and a real fool. But come to dinner and we can have some conversation. I want to show you my kid too."

So I did go home with him; that was kind of Kayo. But his wife was unfriendly, highly suspicious. The child was very nice, for his age, of course, which was young. While I was there the brother-in-law came over; he was interested in the Buick, which fortunately was running well that night. He asked me questions, attracted by the rumble seat, and then drove it around and offered to buy it. I set a moderate price, taking some loss but never mentioning the bent rods, I am ashamed to say.

Well, he wanted to buy it right off, so we went to his house where he gave me a check for one hundred and eighty dollars on the Continental Illinois. But then he wouldn't let me get out of the house. Jokingly he said I should let him win back some of his money at poker. His wife played too. Obviously they were going to try to strip me. Kayo had to sit in on the game as well, so it would look friendly. It was really an attempted swindle. We sat at the circular table by the stove with a pot of coffee and condensed milk and played far into the night. The workbench with its busted radios was right there in the large kitchen. The husband got angry at the wife because she lost. If she had won they'd have won double, but since she lost he swore at her and she screamed at him. Kayo lost too. I was the only winner and would rather not have been. In fact I refunded Kayo's money on the way home. But then the brother-in-law stopped the check two days later, and I had to come and fetch the car, for it wouldn't run. There was an angry scene. And Kayo was very put out and wouldn't talk much to me at school for a time, though he eventually thawed out. I guess I really shouldn't have sold the car without telling of the bent rods.

Sophie Geratis, my friend of hotel-organizer days, was married now but wanted to divorce her husband and marry me. She told me he had a vice with other men and didn't pay attention to her at all. He gave her charge accounts and a car but he wanted her only as window dressing. His business was to sell a product to greenhouses, and this certain product was a monopoly, so his life was easy and he was chauffeured every day in his homburg hat and gloves around the hothouse belt of the city. Therefore Sophie spent a lot of time with me, fixing up my room at Owens' as it had never been fixed up before. She wondered that I would sleep on a pillow without a pillowcase, and she brought over several. "You're stingy," she told me. "You're not just sloppy, you appreciate good things." She was right. Sophie was very intelligent, never mind that she had been a chambermaid. About some things I was tight. When I went into a good bar or club I would feel my pocket and worry about the check. Naturally she knew this. "But also I know that you give your dough away if somebody touches you the right way. That's not good either. And there's that car of yours, but that's just plain dumbness. You were a knucklehead to buy it."

With her floating wide gaze, brown and slow, Sophie was very pretty. In addition to which, as I've said, she had gifts of the mind, though she was inclined to use them in a scornful way. She wouldn't use the fancy charge accounts her husband gave her. Wearing a hat of Polish flowers she had bought at Goldblatt's she would wash her things in my sink. She was in her slip and smoked a cigarette. The paradoxical part is that she was a very tender person, she was good to me, and not just because she needed me but somehow just the reverse, because I needed her. However, I wasn't prepared to marry.

"We'd get along fine if I fitted in more with your ambitions," she said. "I'm all right for bed, but not to marry. When that other girl came to fetch you, you dropped me in a second. You probably would be ashamed of me. You have the most use for me when you're feeling weak or low. I know you. Nothing is ever good enough for you to stick to. Your old man must have been some aristocrat bastard."

"I doubt it. My brother says he drove a truck for a laundry on Marshfield. I never thought that he was a hotshot. Besides, he found my mother working in a Wells Street loft."

"You don't really want me, do you?"

Well, she meant why wasn't I going to set my feet on a path of life and stop looking over the field. Why, there was nothing that I longed for more than that. Let it come! Let there be consummation, and superfluity be finished from the next drop of the pendulum onward! Let the necessity for the mystical great things of life, which, not satisfied, lives in us as the father of secret miseries, be fulfilled and have a chance to show it's not the devil himself. Did Sophie think I didn't want to have a wife, and sons and daughters, or be busy at my appropriate daily work? I stood up then and there and told her how entirely wrong she was about me.

"What are we waiting for?" she said, glad. "Let's start! I'll be a good wife to you, you know I will. I need to begin too."

Then I got red and embarrassed, and my tongue wouldn't move.

"See?" she said with sad frankness and wide, shadowed, rouged mouth while the electric light shone down on her clear bare shoulders. "I ain't good enough. Well, who is?"

I wasn't marrying just yet, that was what I said. But what Sophie had to tell me was what my Cossack pal also had meant, that time he hurt my pride. What he had really meant to say to me, as I sensed infallibly and right off, was that I couldn't be hurt enough by the fate of other people. He should have known, as he himself was wandering from here to there, and what should he be kicking around for, from Moscow to Turkestan, to Arabia, to Paris, Singapore? Nobody gets out of these pains like a pilgrim, looking at temples and docks and smoking cigarettes past the bone heaps of history and over many times digested soil, there where people stayed at home and caught it in the neck.

So Sophie's face, which was maturer now than the pretty face in the union office that I had first seen, was hurt. But she didn't quit me this time as when, after Thea knocked at the door, she suddenly had covered the backs of her thighs. By now she knew, I reckon, how much disappointment is in the taste of existence. But I didn't wish to marry her. She would have scolded me for my own good too much, I thought. So this one more soul I would fly by, that wanted something from me.

"You're waiting for that girl," she said with envy, wrongly.

I said, "No, I'll never see her again."

Nevertheless I was getting somewhere, you mustn't go entirely by appearances. I was coming to some particularly important conclusions. In fact I was lying on my couch in the state of grand summary one afternoon, still in my bathrobe and having called off all duties in the inspiration of the day, when Clem Tambow arrived, full of an idea of his own.

I don't believe Clem had many of the vices that lead to damnation, but such as they were they were very evident on this occasion—late rising, puffiness, double-breasted slovenliness of the kind that old gentleman La Bruyère thought so sordid, tobacco stink, lint, and cat hairs on him, kept up by dime-store purchase and cheap accommodation, as in aftershave lotion, Sta-comb, artificial silk socks, and so forth, besides his lordly self-abuse look. Be that as it might, he had been lying in bed too this solemn brown Chicago day and working also on a scheme.

He was going out into professional life. As soon as he got his psychology degree in the winter he aimed to get an office in one of the older skyscrapers on Dearborn near Jackson and set up as a vocational-guidance counselor.

"*You?*" I said. "You never did a day's work in your life!"

"That's what makes me so ideal," he answered, ready for me. "I'm relaxed. No bunk, Augie. You remember Benny Fry from the poolroom? He's cleaning up. He does marriage counseling too, and gives rabbit tests."

"If it's the same guy I'm thinking of, the one who wore the

elevator shoes, didn't they have him in court last month for a phony?"

"Yes, but we can do the same thing legitimately."

"I don't want to throw cold water," I said, still full of my own experience. "But how will you get clients?"

"Oh, that's no problem. Do people seem to you to know what they want? They beg you to tell them. So we'll be the experts they come to."

"Oh no, Clem. Not 'we.'"

"Augie, I want you to come into this with me. I don't like to go into things by myself. I'll give the aptitude test and you do the interviews. With the new Rogers nondirective technique you let them do the talking anyway. There's nothing to it. Listen here, you can't go on from one screwball job to another."

"I know, but Clem, something has just happened to me today."

"You're just being stubborn again," he said. "We can clean up in this racket."

"No, Clem. What could I do for these guys or women? I'd be ashamed to take their dough in this kind of an employment bureau."

"Oh, bushwah! You don't send guys out on jobs, you tell them what they're good for. This is modern activity. Modern activity is entirely different."

"Stop arguing," I said severely. "Can't you see something has happened to me too today?" Then he saw that I really was moved. I made a lengthy declaration, which I remember went somewhat as follows:

"I have a feeling," I said, "about the axial lines of life, with respect to which you must be straight or else your existence is merely clownery, hiding tragedy. I must have had a feeling since I was a kid about these axial lines which made me want to have my existence on them, and so I have said 'no' like a stubborn fellow to all my persuaders, just on the obstinacy of my memory of these lines, never entirely clear. But lately I have felt these thrilling lines again. When striving stops, there they are as a gift. I was lying on the couch here before and they suddenly went quivering right straight through me. Truth, love, peace, bounty, usefulness, harmony! And all

noise and grates, distortion, chatter, distraction, effort, superfluity, passed off like something unreal. And I believe that any
man at any time can come back to these axial lines, even if an
unfortunate bastard, if he will be quiet and wait it out. The
ambition of something special and outstanding I have always
had is only a boast that distorts this knowledge from its origin, which is the oldest knowledge, older than the Euphrates,
older than the Ganges. At any time life can come together
again and man be regenerated, and doesn't have to be a god
or public servant like Osiris who gets torn apart annually for
the sake of the common prosperity, but the man himself, finite and taped as he is, can still come where the axial lines are.
He will be brought into focus. He will live with true joy. Even
his pains will be joy if they are true, even his helplessness will
not take away his power, even wandering will not take him
away from himself, even the big social jokes and hoaxes need
not make him ridiculous, even disappointment after disappointment need not take away his love. Death will not be terrible to him if life is not. The embrace of other true people
will take away his dread of fast change and short life. And this
is not imaginary stuff, Clem, because I bring my entire life to
the test."

"You really are a persistent and obstinate type of a guy,"
said Clem.

"I thought if I knew more my problem would be simpli-
fied, and maybe I should complete my formal education. But
since I've been working for Robey I have reached the conclusion that I couldn't utilize even ten per cent of what I already
knew. I'll give you an example. I read about King Arthur's
Round Table when I was a kid, but what am I ever going to
do about it? My heart was touched by sacrifice and pure attempts, so what should I *do*? Or take the Gospels. How are
you supposed to put them to use? Why, they're not utilizable!
And then you go and pile on top of that more advice and information. Anything that just adds information that you can't
use is plain dangerous. Anyway, there's too much of everything of this kind, *that's* come home to me, too much history
and culture to keep track of, too many details, too much
news, too much example, too much influence, too many guys
who tell you to be as they are, and all this hugeness, abun-

dance, turbulence, Niagara Falls torrent. Which who is supposed to interpret? Me? I haven't got that much head to
master it all. I get carried away. It doesn't give my feelings
enough of a chance if I have to store up and become like an
encyclopedia. Why, just as a question of time spent in getting
prepared for life, look! a man could spend forty, fifty, sixty
years like that inside the walls of his own being. And all great
experience would only take place within the walls of his being.
And all high conversation would take place within those walls.
And all achievement would stay within those walls. And all
glamour too. And even hate, monstrousness, enviousness,
murder, would be inside them. This would be only a terrible,
hideous dream about existing. It's better to dig ditches and
hit other guys with your shovel than die in the walls."

"Well, come on, what are you trying to prove?"

"I don't want to prove a single thing, not a thing. Do you
think I have this kind of ambition to stand out and prove
something? Almost everybody I ever knew wanted to show in
some way how *he* held the world together. This only comes
from feeling the strain of holding yourself together, and it
gets exaggerated into the whole world from the hard labor
you put into it. But it doesn't take hard labor. Or at least
shouldn't. You don't do that. The world is held for you. So I
don't want to be representative or exemplary or head of my
generation or any model of manhood. All I want is something
of my own, and bethink myself. This is why I'm sounding off
now and am so excited. I want a place of my own. If it was
on Greenland's icy mountain, I'd take and go to Greenland,
and I'd never loan myself again to any other guy's scheme."

"So tell me before I die from impatience, what's this deal
of yours?"

"I aim to get myself a piece of property and settle down on
it. Right here in Illinois would suit me fine, though I
wouldn't object to Indiana or Wisconsin. Don't worry, I'm
not thinking about becoming a farmer, though I might do a
little farming, but what I'd like most is to get married and set
up a kind of home and teach school. I'll marry—of course my
wife would have to agree with me about this—and then I'd
get my mother out of the blind-home and my brother George
up from the South. I think Simon might give me some dough

to get a start. Oh, I don't expect to set up the Happy Isles. I don't consider myself any Prospero. I haven't got the build. I have no daughter. I never was a king, for instance. No, no, I'm not looking for any Pindar Hyperborean dwelling with the gods in ease a tearless life, never aging—"

"This is the most fantastic thing I ever heard come out of you yet. It's a scheme worthy of your mind. It makes me proud of you, kind of, though I'm also appalled when I think of the things you must think about when you look so calm and restful. But where are you going to get the kids for your school?"

"I thought maybe I could get accredited with the state or county, or whoever does it, as a foster-parent, and get kids from institutions. This way the board and keep would be taken care of, and we'd have these kids."

"Plus children of your own?"

"Of course. I'd love to have my own little children. I long for little children. And these kids from institutions who have had it rough—"

"And who might turn out to be little John Dillingers or Basil Bangharts or Tommy O'Connors. But I know what you're hoping. You think you'll love them so they'll turn into little Michelangelos and Tolstois, and you'll give them their chance in life and rescue them, so you'll be their saint and holy father. But if you make them so good, how will they get along in the world? They'll have to pass their whole life all alone."

"No, really, I could live with them. I'd be very happy. I'd fix up a shop for woodwork. Maybe I'd even learn how to repair my own car. My brother George could be the shoe-making instructor. Maybe I'd study languages so I could teach them. My mother could sit on the porch and the animals would come around her, by her shoes, the roosters and the cats. Maybe we could start a tree nursery."

"You do too want to be a king," said Clem. "You sonofa-bitch, you want to be the kind goddam king over these women and children and your half-wit brother. Your father ditched the family, and you did your share of ditching too, so now you want to make up for it."

"You can always find bad motives," I said. "There are always bad motives. So all I can say is I don't want to have them. I don't know about my unfortunate father—he seems to have done as most others, get in and then take off. Seemingly for liberty. Most likely for other trouble or suffering. But why should I want to cheat on a thing like this, when I'm looking for something lasting and durable and trying to get where those axial lines are? I realize this may not sound like such a great scheme to many people. But I know I can't have much of a chance to beat life at its greatest complication and *meshug-gah* power, so I want to start in lower down, and simpler."

"I wish you luck," he said. "But I don't think it ever can happen."

Well, now I had this sterling idea, my project. I was at the turning point. For a while I thought seriously that I might marry Sophie but that was in my hurry to make a start. When all of a sudden—wham! the war broke out on that terrible Sunday afternoon, and then there was nothing but war that you could think about. I got carried away immediately. Overnight I had no personal notions at all. Where had they gone to? They were on the bottom somewhere. It was just the war I cared about and I was on fire. How much are you required to care when such an event comes? Me, I cared like anything. At first I went off my rocker, I hated the enemy, I couldn't wait to go and fight. I was a madman in the movies and yelled and clapped in the newsreel. Well, what you terribly need you take when you get the chance, I reckon. After a while, if I thought of my great idea, I told myself that after the war I'd get a real start, but I couldn't do it while the whole earth was busy in this hell-making project, or man-eating Saturns were picking guys up left and right around me. I went around and made a speech to my pals, much to the amazement of people, about the universal ant heap the enemy would establish if they won, a fate nobody could escape then, mankind under one star of government, a human desert rolling up to monster pyramids of power. A few centuries after, and on this same earth's surface, under the same sun and moon, where there once had been men like gods there would be nothing but this bug-humanity that would make it-self as weird as the threatening universe outside and would imitate it by creating human mechanical regularity as invariable as physical laws. Obedience would be God, and freedom the Devil. There wouldn't any new Moses arise to lead an exodus, because amidst the new pyramids there wouldn't any new Moses be bred. Oh yes, I got up on my hindlegs like an orator and sounded off to everyone.

Then I went to volunteer, but it turned out that Bizcocho had ruptured me. The Army and Navy doctors had me cough for them and agreed that I had inguinal hernia. They recommended that I be operated on, which was free of charge.

So I went to County Hospital to have this done. I didn't mention it to Mama, never telling her of such things. Sophie said, "You're absolutely nuts, going under the knife while well and having an out from the draft." She took it personally. Her husband was being inducted, which was all the more reason for me to stick around, and if I was going to the hospital that meant I didn't want her. However, she saw me through. Clem also dropped around to see me in the ward, and so did Simon, but Sophie was there every visiting hour.

The operation was rough on me, and when it was done I couldn't stand straight for a long time and went slightly bent over.

The hospital was mobbed and was like Lent and Carnival battling. This was Harrison Street, where Mama and I used to come for her specs, and not far from where I had to go once to identify that dead coal heaver, the thundery gloom, bare stone brown, while the red cars lumbered and clanged. Every bed, window, separate frame of accommodation, every corner was filled, like the walls of Troy or the streets of Clermont when Peter the Hermit was preaching. Shruggers, hobblers, truss and harness wearers, crutch-dancers, wall inspectors, wheelchair people in bandage helmets, wound smells and drug flowers blossoming from gauze, from colorful horrors and out of the deep sinks. Not far the booby-hatch voices would scream, sing, and chirp and sound like the tropical bird collection of Lincoln Park. On warm days I went up to the roof and had a look at the city. Around was Chicago. In its repetition it exhausted your imagination of details and units, more units than the cells of the brain and bricks of Babel. The Ezekiel caldron of wrath, stoked with bones. In time the cal-

dron too would melt. A mysterious tremor, dust, vapor, ema-
nation of stupendous effort traveled with the air, over me on
top of the great establishment, so full as it was, and over the
clinics, clinks, factories, flophouses, morgue, skid row. As before the work of Egypt and Assyria, as before a sea, you're
nothing here. Nothing.

Simon came to see me and threw a bag of oranges on the
bed. He bawled me out that I hadn't gone to a private hospital. His temper was bad and nothing and nobody was
spared in his glare.

But they were letting me out, so why fuss? I was still
stooped, as if stitched in the wrong places, but they said it was
just temporary.

Well and good, I got back to the South Side and found that
Padilla had a girl staying in my room, his guest, and he moved
me into his own place. This was just a formality that the
young lady occupied my room, and sheer etiquette, because
he did too. He was never at home. Over at the university he
was working in the uranium project.

Where he lived was a little stale-air flat in a tenement. The
plaster stuck on the laths mostly by the force of the paint. The
neighbors were relief families, night owls who walked to the
window at 4 p.m. in their skivvies curiously to greet the day,
chicks, Filipinos neat and sharp, drunk old women and
gloomy guys. After a descent of many flights you came out of
this structure and crossed an entry of unusual architectural
fantasy, horizontally long, a Chinese hothouse where nothing
grew beneath the vermilion frames but sundry sticks, old *Tribune*s of the cats and dogs, trash. In the street, by cylinders of
garbage cans, you were just a step from a place of worship for
Buddhists that was formerly a church. Then a chop-suey joint.
Then a handbook behind, as usual, a dummy cigar store
where the shoppers were with racing forms, and the retired, or
precinct leaders, and heavy on their feet cigar chewers, and
cops. I wasn't feeling very keen while in this tenement. It took
me many long months to get better, and I was doing very
poorly. And about this time I got a letter from Thea, APO San
Francisco, telling me that she had married an Air Force captain. She felt she should tell me, but she maybe shouldn't
have, because the grief of it laid me up. My eyes sunk even

deeper than before, and my hands and feet were cold, and I lay in Padilla's dirty bed, feeling sick and broken up.

Naturally I couldn't be comforted by Sophie. It wasn't even the right thing to do, to accept comfort from her and not tell her the trouble. It was Clem I told how broken up I was.

"I know how it is. I had an affair with a copper's daughter and she did the same to me last year," he said. "She married some gambler and went to Florida. Anyway, you told me long ago it was over."

"It was," I said.

"But I see you Marches are a romantic family. I keep running into your brother with a blond doll. Even Einhorn has seen them. He was being carried piggyback from the Oriental Theatre, from Lou Holtz over to see *Juno and the Paycock*—he doesn't go out often, and when he does, as you know, he likes a full day. And while he was riding in his black cape on Louie Elimelek, the ex-welter, whom should he bump into but Simon and this broad. By his description the same broad. A *zaftige* piece too, in a mink stole."

"Poor Charlotte," I said, thinking at once of my sister-in-law.

"What's the matter with Charlotte? You mean that Charlotte doesn't understand about leading a double life? A woman with money and not know that? Double if not more? When it's practically the law of the land?"

So I had something more to think about during my convalescence, when I wanted to be gone from Chicago anyhow, to where world events were thick.

One day I was on the West Side. I had gone to take Mama for a walk in Douglas Park. It was good for us both, as I still dragged somewhat. Douglas Park in a cold sunlight, mossy, benches not well kept up in wartime, with elderly folks on them, newspapers, furs, stucco walls—paper sailing wild over the lagoon. Mama was beginning to have the aging stiffness and was somewhat bowlegged; she enjoyed the cold air though, and still had her calm smooth color of health.

I was taking her back to the Home when Simon's car drew up beside us. A woman, not Charlotte, was with him. I saw the fur stole and golden hair. Right away Simon, with smiles, wigwagged that Mama wasn't to be aware of her. Then he came out on the sidewalk and it seemed just plain not good enough for him, this West Side concrete so powerfully cracked and with grocers' and butchers' sawdust. He looked very good. From the shell cordovans to the ruby points of his cufflinks, the shirt white on white, most likely a Sulka tie, a Strook coat, everything handstitched and not intended just for cover like a Crusoe goatskin. I have to confess that, arriving like this, he was enviable to see.

Was he here to visit Mama? Or to point her out to the girl? To identify me for her he said, with pleasure, "Well, my *brother*! Isn't this a swell surprise! Why don't I ever see you? And, Mama, how are you?" An arm around each of us, he turned us to face the car, where the girl acknowledged us, friendly. "It's great the family's together," he said.

I wondered whether Mama felt him acting toward someone; maybe she did. But how would she in her innocence have known what to think about these two specially treated or gardened, enveloped in finery, pampered bodies that traveled on the Cadillac chassis and high cushions like a pair of carnival Romans cruising the Corso, this high-breasted girl and Simon?

He was making real dough now. A company he had invested in was manufacturing a gimmick for the Army. When he told me how the money poured in he always laughed, as if astonished himself, and said he hoped to catch up with my millionaire, Robey, and write a book himself. Then I'd be *his* helper. A crack I didn't like. Robey, by the way, was getting ready to go to Washington. He didn't seem able to explain why but just had to go.

Simon said, "I just stopped to find out if you were all right, Ma. I can't stay. And I'm taking Augie with me."

"Go, boys," she said. She wanted us to have business together.

We took her up the stone stairs and let her into the Home. When we were alone Simon said, and meant every word of it, "Before you start to think any different, I love this girl."

"You do? Since when?"

"Quite a while now."

"But who is she? Where does she come from?"

Smiling, he told me, "She left her husband the same night we met. It was at a night club in Detroit. I was there just two days on business. I danced with her and she said she'd never stay another day with this guy. I said, 'Come along,' and she's been with me ever since."

"Here, in Chicago?"

"Of course here—where do you think! Augie, I want you to know her. It's time you knew each other. She's alone a lot because—you can understand why. She knows all about you. Don't worry, I told her nothing but good things. All *right*!" he said, standing up straight over me with his advantage in height of an inch or two; the red was in his cheeks like a polish, or the color of effrontery. He answered my thought about Charlotte by saying, "I didn't think it would be so hard for you to understand how this is."

"No, it's not so hard."

"This has nothing to do with Charlotte. I don't tell Charlotte what to do. Let her go and do the same."

"Would she? Can she?"

"That's her problem if she can't. My problem—my problem is Renée here. And myself." For a second, as he said "myself," he looked grim and somehow in thought followed his soul past lots of dangers, downward. I couldn't see what there could be of such danger. I didn't yet understand. However, I was fascinated by him, by them both. "Renée, this is Augie," he said, turning me down the steps. It was a hard thing for me to get through my head, after I came to know her, that she could be so important to him.

Though slight, she certainly was stacked. You could see how her breasts went on with great richness under her clothes —*du monde au balcon* is the way they say it in the capital of sex—and her endowments went down into, and were visible through, her silk stockings. Extremely young, her face was made up to some thickness of gold tone, lips drawn to a forward point by thick rouge; her lashes and brows seemed to have gold dust sprinkled and rubbed into them; her hair, golden, appeared added to, like the hair of Versailles; her combs were gold, her glasses gold-trimmed, and she wore golden jewelry. I was about to say that she looked immature, but maybe that means that she didn't bear this gold freight with the fullest confidence; perhaps only some big woman could have done that. Not necessarily a physical giantess but a person whose capacity for adornment was really very great. One of that old sister-society whose pins and barrettes and little jars and combs from Assyria or Crete lie so curious with the wavy prongs and stained gold and green-gnawed bronze in museum cases—those sacred girls laid in the bed by the priests to wait for the secret night visit of Attis or whoever, the maidens who took part in the hot annual battles of gardens, amorous ditty singers, Syrians, Amorites, Moabites, and so on. The line continuing through *femmes galantes*, courts of love, Aquitaines, infantas, Medicis, courtesans, wild ladies, down to modern night clubs or first-class salons of luxury liners and the glamorous passengers for whom chefs plot their biggest soufflé, pastry-fish, and other surprises. This was what Renée was supposed to be, and in my opinion she wasn't entirely. You may think that for this all you have to do is surrender to instinct. As if that were so easy! For start that and how do you know which instincts are going to come out on top?

Renée seemed like a very suspicious girl to me. Along her nose, like a light, there was sort of a suspicion and uncertainness.

As soon as Simon had to step out of the car for a few minutes her first remark was, "I love your brother. The first minute I saw him I fell in love, and I'll love him till I die." She gave me her hand, in the glove, to take. "Believe me, Augie."

As this may have been true it was kind of a pity that she had to throw suspicion on it by extra effort. Games and games. Games within games. Even though, despite the games, somehow there remain things meant in earnest.

"I want us to know each other," she went on. "Maybe you don't realize it but Simon watches over you; you mean the world and all to him. You should hear how he talks about you! He says as soon as you really settle down to something you'll become a great man. And I only want you to consider me as a person who loves Simon and not judge me harshly."

"Why should I do that? Because of my sister-in-law?"

It made her stiffen, when I mentioned Charlotte. But then she saw I meant no harm.

Simon would speak of Charlotte all the time. It surprised

me. He said to his girl friend, "I want no trouble out of you about her. I respect her. I'll never leave her under any circumstances. In her way she's as close to me as anybody in the world." He was romantic about Charlotte too. And Renée had to bear it and know she could never have any exclusive claim on him. It didn't fail to occur to me that I had once done the same thing after my own style with Thea and Stella, covered myself from one by putting one in the way of the other, so I wouldn't be at the mercy of either. So neither one could do harm. Oh, I caught wise to this. You bet I knew it. It wasn't as Simon said. It wasn't even the common-sense consideration that he and Charlotte owned property jointly. I tried to explain this and warn him, but I only astonished him. However, before I tried I waited till I knew the situation well.

And how he and Renée did was as follows: Nearly every morning he picked her up at her apartment; she was waiting outside or in a restaurant nearby. She then drove him to his office, which she didn't enter though most of his employees knew her. Afterward she went off by herself to shop or to do his errands; or she read a magazine and waited till he'd be free. All day long she was with him or not far off, and then in the evening she drove him almost to his door and she went back home in a taxi. And during the day, every hour nearly, there were crises when they shouted and screamed at each other—she enlarged her eyes and arched and hardened her neck and he lost his head and sometimes tried to swat her while his skin wrinkled and teeth set with fury. He never had done anything about that broken front tooth, by which I saw in him still, this blond Germanic-looking ruddy businessman and investor, the schoolboy Grandma Lausch had sent to wait on tables in the resort hotel. The things he and Renée fought about were usually such as clothes, some gloves, a bottle of Chanel perfume, or the servant. She didn't need a servant was what he said, since she was never at home and could make the bed herself. What was the good of a woman sitting there? But Renée had to have whatever Charlotte had. She was completely posted on Charlotte, better than a sister, and often turned up at the same night club or had tickets to the same musical. Thus she knew how she looked and what she wore, and studied her. She demanded the same at least, and as long as it was for items like bags, dresses, lizard shoes, harlequin glasses, Ronson lighter, the demands could be pretty well satisfied. But the worst fight took place when she wanted a car of her own, like Charlotte's.

"Why, you beggar!" he said. "Charlotte has her own money, don't you realize that?"

"But not what you want. *I've* got that."

He roared, "Not you only! Don't fool yourself. Lots of women have it." And this was one of the few times when he minded my seeing him. Usually he didn't seem to care. And she, after her speech about wanting us to know each other better, assumed she had covered the ground by so saying and hardly ever spoke to me. "You see how your brother is?" she cried.

No, I didn't see how he was. Mainly what I saw was that he was all the time in a rage, open or disguised.

He'd break out and yell, "Why didn't you go to the doctor yesterday? How long are you going to neglect that cough? How do you know what you've got in your chest?" (Which made me glance toward that chest, approximately—like any living creature's, under the furs and the silk, under the brassiere, under the breasts, it was there.) "No, sir, you did *not* go. I checked on you. I phoned there, you liar! I bet you thought I feel too important to phone him about you or am afraid of it getting back to Charlotte." (She went to Charlotte's doctor; but he was the best doctor.) "Well, I did it. You never showed up there. You can't tell the truth. Never! I doubt if even in bed you ever do. Even when you say you love me you're conniving."

Well, this is an example of his rage in the form of solicitude.

I couldn't wait to recover from the hernia and go to the war. Let me get going! I thought. But I wasn't fit yet, and meantime I had a stopgap position with a business-machine company. This was a fancy, select job. I could only get into it on account of the manpower shortage. If I had stayed with the company I might have turned into a salesman-prince, traveling parlor car to St. Paul twice a month, seven good cigars to the trip and a dignified descent at the station, breathing winter steam and holding a portfolio. But no, I had to get into the service.

"Well, you horse's foot," said Simon, "I expected you to live to see middle age, but I guess you're too dumb to make it and want to get yourself wiped out. If you have to go and get shot up, and be in a cast and vomit blood, and lie in mud and eat potato peel, go! If you get on the casualty list it will do my business good. What a hell of a deal for Ma it is to have only one normal son! And me? It leaves me alone in the world. The idea of making a buck is my intelligent companion, my brother not."

But I went ahead anyway. Only I still wasn't acceptable to the Army or the Navy and so I signed with the Merchant Marine and was scheduled to leave for Sheepshead Bay to go into training there.

Next time I saw Simon I ran into him on Randolph Street and he didn't behave as usual. "Let's go in and have a bite," he said, for we were in front of Henrici's and they had a vat of out-of-season strawberries in the window. The waiters knew him but he hardly even answered when they spoke to him, instead of being proud, as would have been normal. When we sat down and he lifted off his hat, the whiteness of his face gave me a start.

I said, "What's the matter—what goes on?"

"Renée tried to commit suicide last night," he said. "She took sleeping pills. I got there as she was passing out, I shook her and slapped her, I made her walk, threw her in a cold bath until the doctor got there—and she's alive. She'll be all right."

"Was it a real attempt? Did she mean business?"

"The doctor said she wasn't really in danger. Maybe she didn't know how many pills to take."

"That doesn't sound likely to me."

"Me neither. She must have been faking. She is a counterfeiter. It wasn't the first time by a long shot." I got a glimpse of struggles that probably could never make sense. It afflicted me.

"People will act themselves into something at last though," he went on. "They get carried away." And he said, "If it's for pleasure you pay a steep price, okay. But suppose it's a price for no pleasure. Only trying to have it. Wanting pleasure. You pay for what you want, not always what you get. That's what a price means. Otherwise where's the price? The payment is in something you're liable to run short on."

"I wish I knew of anything I could do."

"You could shove me in front of a train," he said.

He began to tell me what had happened. Charlotte had found out about Renée. "I think she knew for a long time," he said, "but I guess she wanted to wait." It would have been surprising if Charlotte hadn't known. Information and thoughts about Simon were streaming through her mind all the time. Everybody knew him in the downtown district. The waiter who brought the strawberries in the pewter dishes said, "Here you are, Mr. March." Renée was with Simon all the time too, and they were continually playing with the chance of discovery. Why did she drive him almost to the door? One day after she left I picked up a gold comb from the floor of the car, and he said, "Damn her, she's too careless," and put it in his pocket. Now it couldn't be that during two years Charlotte hadn't found anything—no gold hairs, no hankies, no matches in the glove compartment from salons she didn't go to; or that she couldn't read in Simon's husbandly home-coming with hat and evening paper, kiss of the cheek or married joke on the backside, that only five minutes before, in only the time it took to park the car and ride up in the elevator, he had been with another woman. She certainly must have. I figure that for a while she'd have said to herself, "What I don't see with my own eyes won't hurt me"—this not quite deliberate blindness but the tight grasp of people who devise very deeply. Somebody wrestling a bear for dear life, and with forehead lost against the grizzly pelt, figuring anyway what to do next Sunday, whom to invite to dinner and how to fix the table.

But with Charlotte you never could tell. She perhaps understood that with a lot of noise she'd drive him to be rash, because of romantic honor, and she therefore was cautious with him.

Once she explained to me, "Your brother needs money, a whole lot of money. If he didn't have it to spend, as much as he needed, he'd die." This astounded me when I heard it—on a hot morning it was, in the sunny, barbaric-carpeted skyscraper living room and its vases, hot breezes that blew the plants, and she herself a large figure in a white satin coat and with a cigarette holder in her rouged mouth but looking as severe as any Magnus, any of her uncles or cousins. She was as good as telling me that she was saving Simon's life.

But he did need dough. Renée lived in the same style as Charlotte. He had a feeling that that was right; also he owed it to himself not to try to do things cheaply. When he and Charlotte went to Florida the girl came along a day or so later and stayed at as swanky a hotel. He didn't so much worry about the expenses. What poisoned his life by this time was the slavery of constant thought and arrangement-making. He went to defy his wife, and soon he found himself twice-married.

Poor Simon! I pitied him. I pitied my brother.

All along he had been telling me the affair would never be permanent. So? How short is temporary? Eventually his idea was Renée would marry some rich man. I was once present when they discussed it.

"This guy Karham at the club," he said. "He asked me about you after we ran into him. He wants to go out with you."

"I won't do it," she said.

"You will. Don't be a sap. We have to set you up. He's got a lot of dough. A bachelor. In the paving business."

"I don't care what he's got. He's an ugly old man. His mouth is full of bridges. What do you think I am! Leave me alone." She folded her arms, angry, holding her small biceps —it being warm summer she was in a sleeveless dress; she brought her knees together and looked fixedly through the windshield. You have to remember these conversations took place mostly in the car.

I told Simon afterward, "It's you she aims to marry."

"No, she only wants to stay with me. It suits her this way. She's got it better than a wife."

"Some conceit you've got, Simon. You mean to say she can't think up anything better than to ride around with you every day and read movie magazines while you make your calls?"

But what he was telling me at Henrici's now was that a few weeks before, Charlotte had come out and said the affair had gone far enough. It had to stop now. Fights broke out. But not because he disagreed with Charlotte. He knew he had to stop and told Renée, and what happened with her was even worse. She screamed, threatened to take him to court, and fainted. Next Simon's lawyer came into the picture. He called a meeting in his office to settle everything. Renée was told Charlotte wouldn't be there, but then Charlotte showed up. Renée cursed her. Charlotte slapped her. Simon slapped Renée too. Then they all cried, for which there seemed to be plenty of reason.

"Why did you have to slap her?"

"You should have heard what she was saying. You would have done the same," he said. "I got carried away."

Finally Renée agreed to go away to California provided she was paid off. And she did go. But now she was back again and said on the phone that she was pregnant. "I don't care," Simon told her. "You're a crook. You took the dough and went to California when you knew you'd be coming right back." After a silence she hung up. This was when he thought she would kill herself. And, sure enough, when he got to the hotel it was just after she had swallowed the pills.

She was in her fourth month of pregnancy.

"What'll I do?" he said.

"What's there to do? Nothing. There'll be a kid now. Who knows but that this is the way you and George and I happened to come into the world."

I comforted him the best I knew how.

Chapter XXIII

I F THE GREAT Andromeda galaxy had to depend on you to hold it up, where would it be now but fallen way to hell? Why, March, let the prophetic soul of the wide world dreaming on things to come (S. T. Coleridge) summon its giants and mobilizers, Caesars and Atlases. But you! you pitiful recruit, where do you come in? Go on, marry a loving wife and settle at March's farm and academy, and don't get in the way when the nations are furiously raging together. My friend, I said, speaking to myself, relax and knock off effort. The time is in the hands of mighty men to whom you are like the single item in the mind of the chief of a great Sears, Roebuck Company, and here come you, wishing to do right and not lead a disappointed life (sic!).

However, my conscience had already decided. I was committed and couldn't stay, and at last the hour struck. There was a windy, flattening rain that beat the smoke down, the whole city sodden and black, the pillars of La Salle Street Station weeping. Clem said to me, "Don't push your luck. Don't take a risk with the clap. Don't tell your secrets to anybody to satisfy their curiosity. Don't get married without a six-month engagement. If you get in dutch I can always spare you a few bucks."

I put in for the Purser's and Pharmacist's Mate's School, and they took my application. For a while I had a wrangle with a psychiatrist fellow. Why had I indicated with an X that I was a bed-wetter? I insisted my bed was always dry. "But here's the X opposite the question in the *Yes* column." Didn't he realize, I said, that in filling out twenty questionnaires and taking five examinations after thirty hours without sleep on the train a man might make a single slip? "But why *this* slip, not another?" he said cunningly. I began to hate him very much, sitting there on his cool white fanny while his lazy eyes arrived at unpleasant conclusions about me. I said, "Do you want me to confess that I do wet the bed even though it's not so? Or do you mean that I'd like to wet the bed?" He told me I had an aggressive character.

Anyway, before I could start at the school, they sent us away on a training cruise in Chesapeake Bay. We sailed up and down through flickering heat. The ship was a many-decked old contraption from McKinley's time. White, an iron, floury, adrift bakery, it wallowed wide and aimless all week. The white ferries with Dixie pillars passed us by, very elegant. Or the flattop whales that had planes like kids' jacks on the deck, and monstrous hair-stuffing smoke came from their sides. We did fire-fighting and abandon-ship drills eight or ten times a day. The boats crashed down from the davits; the trainees poured into them from manlines and cargo nets, rambunctious, mauling and horsing around, prodding with boat hooks, goosing and carrying on, screaming about female genitals. Then rowed. Hours and hours of rowing. The water curled like a huge bed of endive.

Between times you could bask on the fantail of this painted old vertical bakery, and crates, spoiled lettuces, oranges, turds, and little crabs followed on the stream or departed. The sky enamel, the sun with gold spindles. It makes me think of the picture of the fools with fish and cake and the boaters with soup-ladle oars in the painting of the old master Hieronymus B.—this idle craft with the excursion strummers, roast chicken trussed in a tree; death's head in the little twigs above. Other scenes too: eggs spitted on knives trotting with tiny feet; men inside oyster shells carried to a cannibal banquet. Herring, meat, and other belly-goods. But, all the same, human eyes were looking out. Up to no good, maybe, but how do you know? Or the rich kings at Bethlehem. Joseph by a fire of sticks. But off in the meadow, what goes on? A wolf bleeding at a knife wound eating the swineherd who struck him, and someone else dashing like mad for the goofy towers of the city, the potato-masher castles and the pots, double-boilers, and smokehouses of habitations.

We ate plenty: flapjacks, chops, ham, spuds, steak, chili con and rice, ice cream, pie. Everybody talked about the chow, discussed the menus, and remembered home recipes.

Saturday we put in at Baltimore where the tramps of the port were waiting on Clap Hill, and the denominations with printed verses. There was mail call. Simon had been turned down for service because of a bad ear. "A way out I could've used," he said. Clem wasn't doing well at his new business. There were two letters from Sophie Geratis, now with her husband at Camp Blanding. She said farewell but kept saying it in different letters. From Einhorn there was a mimeographed message to his friends in the service, full of corny sentiment and comedy. In a personal note he added that Dingbat was a soldier in New Guinea, driving a jeep, and that he himself was ailing.

And so, more weeks of captivity on this cruise, back and forth over the bay; the same endive waves and blare of public-address system, horseplay in the head, boat drills, brine, heavy meals, sun, hell-raising, and this continual whanging away on a few elements so as to deafen you.

At last we were returned to Sheepshead, and I started to study bookkeeping and ship's doctoring. The science part consoled me. As long as I could keep improving my mind, I figured, I was doing okay.

Sylvester was in New York. Also Stella Chesney, the girl I had helped escape in Mexico. Of course I went to see her first. On my first liberty I phoned her, and she said to come right over. So I bought a bottle of wine and the delicacies of the season and went; and of course I told myself I could use the dough she owed me and what not, but I ought to have known myself better than that.

What use was war without also love?

The place where she lived seemed to be among dress factories, silent on Saturday. As I climbed the stairs I was very excited. But I warned myself not to think we could take up where we had stopped at Cuernavaca. Oliver being in jail, chances were that there was someone else.

But there was the object of these wicked thoughts with a warm healthy face, looking innocent and happy to see me. What a beauty! My heart whanged without pity for me. I already saw myself humbled in the dust of love, the god Eros holding me down with his foot and forcing all kinds of impossible stuff on me.

She made the same impression on me that she had made the first time when I saw her on the little porch above the Carta Blanca beer shield with bulge-eyed Oliver and the two friends. Then I thought of her in the lace dress she wore in court the time Oliver socked Louie Fu. Then in the mountains under the tarpaulin when her dress and petticoat went up so fast. And there were those same legs above me. They were bare, I saw, by the white of the skylight and the reflection of the green carpet.

"Well, if it isn't a pleasure," she said and put out her hand. I was all dressed up in my brand-new government goods, and as I walked I felt upon me the skivvies and socks, new shoes and tight jumper and pants. To say nothing of the white cap and the embroidery of anchors on the sailor collar. "You didn't tell me you were drafted. What a surprise!"

"When I look, I'm surprised myself," I said.

But what I really thought of was whether to kiss her. It suddenly came back to me, to my cheek itself, what the sensation of her lips had been like in the hot market place. My face heated now. Finally I decided I'd better speak my mind, and I told her, "I can't decide whether it would be right to kiss you."

"Please! Don't create a problem." She laughed, meaning that I should. I put my lips on the side of her face, exactly as she had done to me, and I flushed instantaneous as electricity. She colored too, pleased that I had done it.

Was she not so simple and free of ulterior motives as she looked? Well, neither was I.

We sat down to talk. She wanted to know about me. "What do you do?" she asked. When not a rich young beauty's friend, nor an eagle-tamer nor poker player, was what she meant.

"I've had a hard time deciding just what I should do. But now I think I was cut out to be a teacher. I want to get a place of my own and have a family. I'm tired of knocking around."

"Oh, you like children? You'd make a good father."

I thought it was very nice of her to say so. I wanted to offer her everything I had, suddenly. Glorious constructions began to rise in my mind, golden and complicated. Maybe she would give up whatever life she was leading for my sake. If she had another man maybe she'd quit him. Maybe he'd be killed in an automobile accident. Maybe he'd go back to his wife and children. You perhaps know yourself what such vain imaginings can be. O ye charitable gods, don't hold it against me! My heart was beginning to bake. I couldn't see her straight; she dazed me.

She wore velvet houseshoes, with ties; her dark hair was piled three ways; she had on an orange skirt. Her eyes looked soft and gentle. I wondered if she could look so fresh without having a lover and bothered myself about it.

I should hope!—about the father part, I mean. And what did she do? Well, it was hard to get a clear account. She mentioned various things unfamiliar to me. Women's colleges, musical career, stage career, painting. From college there were books; from music, piano, etcetera; from the theater inscribed photos, also a sewing machine of spidery cast-iron, circa 1910, which I connected with costumes; her pictures were on the walls—flowers, oranges, bedsteads, nudes in the bath. She talked about getting on the radio and mentioned the USO and Stage-Door Canteen. I did my best to follow.

"You like my house?" she said.

It wasn't a house but a room, a parlor, high, long, and old-fashioned, with archduke moldings of musical instruments and pears. Plants, piano, a big decorative bed, fishes, a cat and dog. The dog was a heavy breather—he was getting on in years. The cat played around her ankles and scratched them; I quickly walloped him with a newspaper, but she didn't like that. He sat on her shoulder, and when she said, "Kiss, Ginger—kiss, kiss," he licked her face.

Over the way were dress factories. Scraps of material floated and waved from the wire window guards. Planes with powerful rotary noise cut the blue air clear from Britain to California. She served the wine I brought. I drank and my head gave a throb in its injured place. Then I became very heated and filled with amorous anxiety. But I thought, There's her pride to consider. I wanted to get away from her in Cuernavaca. Why should she believe I'm falling for her now? And maybe I shouldn't fall. What if she's the Cressida type, as Einhorn used to call Cissy F.?

"I still intend to pay you the money you were so kind as to lend me," she said.

"No, please, I didn't come for that."

"But you probably need it now."

"Why, I haven't even touched my last month's pay."

"My father sends me an allowance from Jamaica. That's where he is. Of course I can't live on it. I haven't done any too well recently." This was not a complaint but sounded as though soon she'd do better. "Oliver set me back. I depended on him. I thought I was in love with him. Did you love that girl you were with?"

"Yes," I said. I'm glad I didn't lie, I may say.

"She must have hated me like poison."

"She married a captain out in the Pacific."

"I'm sorry."

"Oh no, don't be. It's been over for quite a while."

"I felt in the wrong afterward. But you were the only person who would have helped me. And I never thought——"

"I'm glad I was able to help. As far as that goes, I came out way ahead."

"It's nice of you to say so. But you know—now that it's finished you won't care if I say it—I thought we were in the same boat. Everybody said how she——"

"Went hunting without me. I know." I hoped she wouldn't mention Talavera.

"You got into trouble without knowing it, the way I did. Maybe you deserved it though—like me. It served me right. I was on my way to Hollywood with him. Mexico was just a side trip; he was going to make a star of me. Wasn't that ridiculous?"

"No, it wasn't. You'd make a first-rate star. But how could Oliver do that to you when he knew he was going to jail?"

"He put it over easily because for a while I was in love."

It went to my head when she spoke that word.

I was constructing higher and higher, up to the top spheres, and simultaneously committing a dozen crimes to achieve my end. The cat scratched my hand as it swung by the chair. I thought I was going to have a nosebleed also, from passion. One minute I felt gross and swollen, and the next my soul was up there concertizing among her brilliant sister souls.

"Or worse than ridiculous," said she, pointedly.

Worse? Oh, how she paid her way, did she mean? She didn't have to say that. It pained me that she should feel such explanations necessary. I certainly was lucky to be seated; my legs wouldn't have kept me up.

"Why, what's the matter?" she said in her warmhearted voice.

I begged her not to make fun, please. I said, "When I was covered with bandages and playing poker at the Chinaman's, how could you think we were in the same boat?"

"I'm sure you remember how we looked at each other that day in the bar where they had that monkey thing."

"The kinkajou."

Crossing her hands in her lap and bringing her knees together around them—which I admired and wished she would, however, not do—she said, "Nobody should pretend to be always one hundred per cent honest. I wish I knew how to be seventy, sixty per cent."

I swore she must be one hundred and ten, two hundred. Then I said something I didn't expect myself. I said, "Nobody should be a mystery intentionally. Unintentionally is mysterious enough."

"I'll try not to be. With you, anyway."

She was sincere. I knew it. I saw how her throat suddenly grew full.

My body, which is maybe all I am, this effortful creature, felt subject to currents and helpless. I wanted to go and hug her by the legs, but I thought I'd better wait. For why should I assume it would be right? Because I felt like?

I said, "I suppose you see how I'm getting to feel about you. If I'm making a mistake, you'd better tell me."

"A mistake? Why do you say that?"

"Well, in the first place," I said, "I haven't been here long. You'll think I'm in too much of a hurry."

"And the second place? What makes you speak so slowly?"

Was I speaking in an unusual way? I didn't even know it. "In the second, I feel I did wrong in Cuernavaca by going back."

"Maybe you can do right this time," she said.

Then I dropped to the ground and hugged her legs. She bent to kiss me. I would have hurried, but her idea was to be slower. She said, "We'd better shut the animals in the kitchen." She collared the dog, I lifted up the cat from underneath, and we put them there. The kitchen door was fastened with a bent nail, having no knob or hook. Then she took the cover from the bed and we helped each other to undress.

"What are you saying to yourself?" she whispered when we lay down. I wasn't aware that I was saying anything. I was afraid she would bump her head against the wall and tried to cover it with my hands, which she then understood, and helped me. I was hungry and kissed her wherever my mouth could reach, till she kept my lip in her teeth and drew on me, drew on me. Nothing could be put over by effort any more, and there was nothing to try.

Was she a vain person, or injurious or cynical, it couldn't make any difference now. Or was I a foolish, uncorrected, blundering, provisional, unreliable man, this was taken away as of no account and couldn't have any sense or meaning. The real truth about one or the other was simpler than any such description.

I told her I loved her. It was true. I felt I had come to the end of my trouble and hankering, and it was conclusive. As we lay in bed kissing, whispering, and loving all weekend long, the air was strong and blue outside, the sun was splendid and sailed around handsome and haughty. We got up only to take the dog, Harry, to the roof. The cat walked on the covers over the bed and kneaded us with its paws. The only people we saw were two old guys playing pinochle on a cutting table of the dress factory over the way.

However, Monday morning I had to be back at the base. She woke me in the middle of the night and got me dressed and went down with me to the subway.

I kept asking, Would she marry me? She said, "You want all your troubles to be over all of a sudden and you're so anxious for it you may be making a mistake."

This was just before dawn, by the descent-into-hell stairs of the subway, just under the Eastern vault of wired glass, and the blackout light like a dumb posy on its thick iron. So by this blue illumination we were kissing with loving faces until it began to drizzle and her slippers got wet.

"Darling, go home," I said.

"Will you phone me?"

"Every chance I get. Do you love me?"

"Of course I love you."

Every time she said this I was so moved that happy gratitude poured over me down to my very feet while my backhair prickled. Like when you're swimming in the pleasure of the sea and feel some contact come up behind. All the deep breathes like silent concertinas and the shore is gay with stripes and bunting.

Finally I had to go down into the tunnel and take a train. I couldn't see her for five days. And meantime I didn't dare fall behind in the Purser's School or tangle with a master-at-arms and lose my next liberty. Every evening I went down by the sea where the phone booths were; and she was often out, having a busy life. I had a terrible fear that she had spent the weekend with me out of friendliness alone, or so that I would understand better what should have happened in the mountains that night. If this was so, I was sunk, for by now I was more in love than I could stand, as if some mineral had got into my veins and arteries and I ached, flesh and bones, the way you will on the verge of the grippe.

All week the freighters groaned in from the sea, while Coney Island was wrapped in gray or lilac fog and I sat with a suffering spirit of love in the phone booth after evening chow trying to do my lessons and waiting for her to answer. I was afraid I was too much of a latecomer and had nothing to expect. In which case I was ruined, because everything now depended on her.

On Saturday, in a fever, I got off the base as soon as the usual parade shenanigans were over. What a state I was in! When I rode over the bridge from Brooklyn suspended on those heaven-hung struts over the brick valleys, then the fiery flux of harbor water, the speedy gulls, the battleships open like vast radio sets in the yards, beast-horns of Hengist and Horsa, and then the tunnel again, I felt that if I had to continue to ride and ride I would certainly not last but would give out.

But there was no need to be scared, for Stella was waiting. She had been sick all week because I wasn't there, running a temperature, wondering did I love her. She cried when we were in bed, with her hands pressed on my back and her breasts against me. She said that when she saw me in front of the cathedral from the balcony of the bar where the Carta Blanca shield was hung she fell in love with me. She didn't even need the money she borrowed from me at Cuernavaca but took it as a means of keeping in touch. As for Oliver—

"What's it to me what happened with Oliver? It's none of my business," I said. "I want to get married."

Clem had urged me to be engaged for six months, in view of my personality and make-up. But this advice was good for people who were merely shopping, not for someone who had lived all his life with one great object.

"Of course," she said, "I want to get married if you love me."

I deeply assured her.

"If you still love me after lunch," she said, "ask me again."

She brought the lunch to me in bed, which was a bed she had bought at an auction, ivory colored and painted with wreaths and Arcadia roses. It came from Bavaria. Well, she served me here, and wouldn't even let me butter my own bread. As if I was the Elector, I got waited on hand and foot, and in turn I gave the animal staff ham trimmings and leftovers.

She felt obliged to tell me all she could about herself.

"I buy a ticket in the Irish Sweepstakes every year," she said.

I could see nothing objectionable in this.

"Also I'm a mystic, a Gurdjieff follower."

This was a new one on me. She showed me a picture of this old boy, a shaved head, deep eyes, and mustachios of the old school of Crimean fighter. I saw no special harm in him.

What else? She spent lots of money on clothes. This I could see; her closets were stuffed with dresses. But I didn't bother my head about it. Since she went along with me in my scheme for the foster home and academy, and she enthusiastically did, what difference could her wardrobe make? In fact, I was proud that she was so elegant. Also she owed money, she said.

"Why, darling, don't worry, we'll pay everybody. *C'est la moindre des choses*, as they say on the other side." When I was loved and sitting in a fine bed like this, I was just like royalty and disposed of all matters with a word.

We decided to get married as soon as I graduated from Sheepshead.

Chapter XXIV

I SEE BEFORE ME next a fellow named Mintouchian, who is an Armenian, of course. We are sitting together in a Turkish bath having a conversation, except that Mintouchian is doing most of the talking, explaining various facts of existence to me, by allegory mostly. The time is a week before Stella and I were married and I shipped out.

This Mintouchian was a monument of a person, with his head very abrupt at the back, as Armenian heads tend sometimes to be, but lionlike in front, with red cheekbones. He had legs on him like that statue of Clemenceau on the Champs Elysées where Clemenceau is striding against a wind and is thinking of bread and war, and the misery and grandeur, going on with last strength in his longjohns and gaiters.

Sitting together in this little white-tile room, Mintouchian and I were quite pals in spite of differences of age and income —Mintouchian was supposed to be loaded. He looked overpowering, and he had tones in his voice like the dumping of coal. This must have done him good in court, as he was a lawyer. He was a friend of a friend of Stella whose name was Agnes Kuttner. Agnes lived in big style in an apartment off Fifth Avenue near one of the Latin-American embassies, furnished in Empire, with tremendous mirrors and chandeliers, Chinese screens, alabaster birds of night, thick drapes, and all luxuries like that. She went around to auction rooms and bought up treasures of the Romanoffs and Hapsburgs; she herself came from Vienna. Mintouchian had set up a trust fund for her, so she wasn't at all in the business of antiques, and her apartment was his home away from home, as hotels sometimes falsely speak of themselves. His other home was also in New York, but his wife was an invalid. Every evening he went and had dinner with her, served by her nurse in the bedroom. But before this he had visited Agnes. Usually his chauffeur was driving him across Central Park at 7:45 for the meal with his wife.

The reason why I was with him in the bath this particular

afternoon was that Stella had gone shopping with Agnes for the wedding. These two, Agnes and Mintouchian, were the only people we ever saw when I got liberty from the base on weekends. He enjoyed taking us to Toots Shor's or the Diamond Horseshoe, I think, and other scarlet-and-gold-door places. The one time I tried to pick up the tab he pushed me away. I would have had to borrow from Stella to pay it. But Mintouchian was very openhanded, a grand good-time Charlie. Almost always in evening clothes of Rembrandt blackness, with his red-edged eyes and craggy head and ears, and as if smelling the sands and savannahs with his flat nose, but a smile of spin-on-the-music, spend-the-money; his teeth were long, and he was ever so slightly feline whiskered to go with his corrupt, intelligent wrinkles and expanding mouth. Amid the ladies he didn't let go with this smile, but now when he sat like a village headman of the south of Asia in his carnival colors towel, he did; and while conversing more man to man he was pinching himself under the eyes to make the bags disappear—his yellow toenails were lacquered with clear polish, except the small toes grievously buried in the lifeworn foot with its skinful of vessels. I wondered if he was really one of those hot-to-the-touch and perilous guys like Zaharoff or Juan March, or the Swedish Match King or Jake the Barber or Three-Finger Brown. Stella said he had money he hadn't even folded yet. He certainly was laying out plenty for Agnes, whom he had met in Cuba; he paid her husband a remittance to stay there. However, even though I found out that Mintouchian wasn't strictly honest, he was never a rogue's-gallery character. To get his legal education, as a matter of fact, he had played the organ in silent movies. But he was a crack lawyer now and had global business interests, and, moreover, he was a lettered person and reader. It was one of his curiosities to figure out historical happenings like the building of the Berlin-Baghdad Railway or the Battle of Tannenberg, and he furthermore knew a lot about the lives of Martyrs. He was another of those persons who persistently arise before me with life counsels and illumination throughout my entire earthly pilgrimage.

I couldn't figure out what he saw in Agnes, who was obviously the boss over him. Her eyes were deep brown, of an aristocratic favorite of cafés and carriages of Imperial days, although she must have been only a child in those times. And what's more, she had a slight depression on either side of her turned-up nose which made her look not exactly of an open nature. Nevertheless she was Stella's friend and Mintouchian loved her. This made me think of the deep wishes of elderly people, or desires unslayable short of total demolition by death.

"Death!" Mintouchian said it himself. He was describing how he was subject to strokes. He said, "I don't want to make you gloomy, so close to your wedding."

"Oh no, sir, you couldn't make me gloomy. I love Stella too much to consider it."

"Well, I won't say that I was as happy as you, but I was also very feeling when I got married. Maybe it came from playing the mood music, which I was then doing. For sea adventures I'd play 'Fingal's Cave.' For Rudolph Valentino, 'Orientale,' César Cui, Tchaikovsky's 'Sehnsucht.' Also 'Poet and Peasant.' *You* try to fight this stuff, when Milton Sills sees Conway Tearle didn't go down on the *Titanic*, or something. I was playing it all from my book on torts, boning up for the bar exam. But all the same, those were times of emotion. Or maybe you think this is guff?"

"No, why?"

"You think I'm a bandit, only you wouldn't say it on a bet. You fight your malice too much."

"Everybody says so. It's as if you were supposed to have low opinions. I'd never say I was angelic, but I respect as much as I can."

Mintouchian said, "In one day of practice I see more than you could imagine if it was a project. The Balzac *Comédie Humaine* is child's play in comparison. I wake up in the morning and have to ask myself, 'Now in the case of *Shiml* versus *Shiml*, who is screwing who? Who is going to be in worse shape in the end? The man who takes the child away from the living-in-sin mother? The lover who makes her give up the kid to avoid the publicity so it won't harm his business? The mother who does anything for the lover?' *Ribono shel Olam!*"

I was surprised by this phrase, which he explained as

follows: "My father was janitor of a synagogue, and I hung around the cellar. I had an uncle who was a colonel in the Boer War. Who is what? So if history casts a strange or even ridiculous light on us, we are still all serious, aren't we? We die anyway." He went back to the subject of his strokes. "Here several years ago I was sitting on the toilet figuring a big deal mentally when suddenly the Angel of Death plucked me by the nose. My mind turned black. I fell on my face. I think if my belly hadn't been in the way to break the force I might have been killed. As it was, the blood from my nose sprayed the door like seltzer. Which, in my vanity, I had shut. Then by and by the spark of life came back to me. My mind filled again with the typical thought and light of Mintouchian. Now, I reflected, you're Mintouchian again. As if I had an option. Do I have to come back Mintouchian, including the distressing parts? Yes, because to live is to be Mintouchian, my dear man. I went over all my secrets and found they were still in place. I still didn't know who was screwing whom, and I crept into my bed and shivered from the touch of death.

"But I was saying"—he gave me a genial smile with heart-felt squint and then he yawned and enjoyed the golden light— "how a guy struggles with malice. How life goes beyond the conscience of nice well-reared people. A good upbringing stops them from knowing what *they* think even. Because we all think the same, more or less. You love Stella—all right, don't you?"

"Like I never loved anyone before."

"That's swell. That's what I call answering like a man. When is your birthday?"

"In January."

"I'd have sworn to it. So is mine. I believe the highest types are born in January. It's barometric—you can look it up in Ellsworth Huntington. The parents make love in spring when the organism is healthiest and then the best specimens are conceived. If you want children you should plan to knock up your dear one in that season. Ancient wisdom is right. Now science comes lately and finds it out. But what I wanted to say about your bride, *even* she, is that she's no different from the rest of us except more gifted and beautiful. It is absolutely certain that she has thought of the future both with and without you.

I should worry, I should care,
I should marry a millionaire,
He should die and I should cry,
I should marry another guy.

But this has taken place in inner consciousness, which is outlaw and accepts no check. What of it? Life is possible anyhow.
Except that even legitimate and reasonable things have to
come through this Mongolia, or clear-light desert minus
trees. What do we respect more than commerce and industry?
But when Mr. Cecil Rhodes of the British Empire weeps
many tears because he can't do business with the blazing
stars, this is not decadence but inner consciousness speaking
over all the highest works of presumptuous man."

I was deeply wounded when he spoke of Stella in this way.
Where did he get off, this rude bastard, having her bump me
off in her inner consciousness? I burned with resentment.
"First you talk about ancient wisdom," I said, angry, "and
then you take a crack at love."

"Well, I'm a sonofabitch!" he said, getting up in the Turkish heat and rewrapping the towel. "I didn't mean to hurt any
feelings. Damn! If I did in this idle conversation to while away
time, please forgive me. I see you really are, *really*, in love. God
bless you for such noble feelings! You're going to ship out
soon too, and the danger as well as separation from the loved
one has stirred up natural emotions. But this little song of little
girls also is ancient wisdom. This is not a reason for cynicism,
but pride in the conquest of nature. The human mind has
bounded the exploding oceans of universal space; the head has
swallowed up the empyrean. But you shouldn't overlook also
how much secret thought and conniving goes on.

"Listen, since we're talking, let me give you a few examples
from my practice of what goes on in other parts of the soul.
A few years ago a client's wife reports she has lost a valuable
bracelet. Perfectly trustworthy woman, and mother of three,
a wealthy husband who has given her a hundred thousand
dollars' worth of property, only keeping the power of attor-
ney for himself. The bracelet is lost? Very well. It's just a
routine matter for the company. They investigate, come back
to the husband, and tell him, 'Your wife did not lose this

bracelet, she gave it to her lover who was broke.' Yoy, indignation! 'My wife, a lover? My respected spouse, mother of children, who shows me constant affection and proofs of loyalty? My dear wife, my beloved of years?' Nevertheless her can has been over a barrel, she has spread, or equivalent. This poor man. Heart-shattered! How could it be! Imagine his pain and bewilderment that she should have such a secret from him. What a failure of life when he worked so hard that there should be a certain, guaranteed reason that life might last longer than from Thursday to Saturday. If anything deserves tears this does. However, he mustn't take the word of the insurance investigator, so he comes to me and I get him a private eye. He comes back with the same facts, that this lover is a bum with a prison record for pimping and dealing in hot goods. They show the poor husband a photo, even, so he can describe this character. Thick nose, long sideburns. You know the type. Well, the poor fellow is going crazy. And now he finds that in the whole suburb where he lives he's the only one who didn't know about it. They're seen in the car, parked all over the vicinity. The woods, the bushes. It comes down on him like a busted house. 'Who is left among you that saw this house in her first glory? and how do ye see it now?'"

Oh, the poor guy. My heart broke for him.

"People start to tell him, 'Throw her out, man! Don't be a damn chump. This other guy has been ramming her and been her fancy-man at your expense.' So not able to stand it any more, he accuses her. Why, she denies everything. Every single thing. He brings out names, dates, places, therefore, and there's nothing she can say. All is true. Then she says, 'I won't leave this house and the children, they're mine.' He comes to me and asks advice. All the law is on his side. He can throw her in the street if he wants. But does he want? No!"

Like the wife of Hosea who fooled around, I thought: "Thou shall abide for me many days."

"And I'll tell you something else. She loved her husband too. That's how clouded the situation can be. She gave up the fancy pimp. And then the neighbors saw her and the husband in the movies holding hands and kissing like young lovers."

I was glad it had turned out like that, and they forgave each other. My heart gave a happy bound that they had made it.

I said, "You have to pity the wife also."

"You have to pity her more," said Mintouchian, "because she had to do the lying and lead the two lives. This secrecy is what the real burden is. You come home still panting or dripping or dizzy from an encounter. And what's here? Another world, another life; you are another self. You also know exactly what you are doing. Exactly as a druggist when he goes from one prescription to another. Just the right amount of atropine or arsenic. There'd better be. There'd better!" Mintouchian said with kind of personal barbarism or force of heart. He couldn't stop it up. "You come home. 'Hello, husband or wife.' 'What was in the office today?' 'Just the usual.' 'I see you changed the sheets.' 'I also sent out the insurance premium.' 'That's good.' So you are another person. Where are the words you spoke an hour before? Gone! Where is Central? Oh my dear friend, Central is listening in from Mongolia. Do you say a *double* life? It's secret over secret, mystery and then infinity sign stuck on to that. So who knows the ultimate and where is the hour of truth?

"Of course," he said, "this has got nothing to do with you." He grinned and tried to get brighter, but there was some sort of darkness at this time in the superilluminated little sweat room. He went on after this effort, as follows: "But just for the interest of it I give you another case. There was a rich couple I had before the war. Husband handsome, wife gorgeous. Connecticut, Yale, and so forth background. The husband goes to Italy on a business trip, meets an Italian lady and has an *affaire de cœur*, and then he indiscreetly corresponds with the lady after he comes back. The wife catches a letter of love he kept in his back pocket. Not only did he keep it, March, but where the words of the dear hand were faded by his perspiration he restored them with his own pen. Then the wife comes to me with blood in her eye. Now I know for a fact that while he was gone she had herself a ball with someone, a man friend. But now she wants the husband punished. Because she caught *him*! She wants to go to Italy with the husband, confront the Italian lady, and have the husband deny before them both he ever loved her. Otherwise, divorce. Naturally I can't tell the husband what to do, and he goes. Seven-thousand-mile trip to perform this necessary act.

They then come home, and what do you think? You're an intelligent man, you know what then."

"He finds out about her. Listen," I said, now smelling a rat, "how are these stories supposed to apply, just now, before my marriage? Are you saying that I should put the shoe on to see if it fits?" The thought made me boil.

"Hup! Now don't take it personally. I never said these stories applied to you. They probably apply only in general. Would I say anything against Miss Chesney? Not only is she Agnes's friend, but I wouldn't be a killjoy and interfere with genuine love, which I see all over you.

"You may be as interested as I was, though, in what a clever fellow once said to me about the connection of love and adultery. On any certain day, when you're happy, you know it can't last, but the weather will change, the health will be sickness, the year will end, and also life will end. In another place another day there'll be a different lover. The face you're kissing will change to some other face, and so will your face be replaced. It can't be helped, this guy said. Of course he was a lousy bastard himself and a counterfeit no-good mooch, and he was in and out of Bellevue, and women supported him all his life; he deserted his kid and nobody could depend on him. But love *is* adultery, he said, and expresses change. You make your peace with change. Another city, another woman, a different bed, but you're the same and so you must be flexible. You kiss the woman and you show how you love your fate, and you worship and adore the changes of life. You obey this law. Whether or not this bum was right, may God hate his soul! don't think you don't have to obey the laws of life."

My strange teacher, for he certainly was teaching, said further, "Erratic is nothing. Only system taps the will of the universe."

"I want to obey those laws," I said. "I'm not trying to get out from under. I never did try."

By now the sweat was running very fast down both our faces, and his carnival towel, which had fallen from his fat chest and armpits down to the everglades moss of his belly, was like the robe of a sage. I would never agree that love had to be adultery. Never! Why, imagine! Even if I had to admit that many lovers were adulterers, such as Paolo and Francesca or Anna Karenina, Grandma Lausch's favorite. Which led my mind toward suffering that got mixed with love. As eating the damaged fruit so as not to offend the gods, for whom pure joy is reserved.

He looked as if he were grinning, with great, bland, pouring-faced kindness, like a sage, prophet, or guru, a prince of experience with his jewel toes. I wanted him to give me wisdom.

"Why do you have to think that the thing that kills you is the thing that you stand for? Because you are the author of your death. What is the weapon? The nails and hammer of your character. What is the cross? Your own bones on which you gradually weaken. And the husband or the wife gets the other to do the deed. 'Kind spouse, you will make me my fate,' they might as well say, and tell them and show them how. The fish wills water, and the bird wills air, and you and me our dominant idea."

"Can you say what is your dominant idea, Mr. Mintouchian?"

He answered readily, "Secrets. Society makes us have some, of course. The brotherhood of man wants to let us out of them by the power of confession. But I must beget secrets. I will be known by secrets at my death, like St. Blas who was killed by wool combs and was made the patron saint of woolcombers.

"Complications, lies, lies, and lies!" he said. "Disguises, vaudevilles, multiple personalities, diseases, conversations. Even in a few minutes' conversation, do you realize how many times what you feel is converted before it comes out as what you say? Somebody tells you A. Your response is B. B you can't say, so you transform it, you put it through the coils of your breast. From DC to AC, increased four hundred volts, filtered. So instead of B there comes out gamma sub one. The longer the train of transformation, the worse the stink of gamma sub one. Mind you, I'm a great admirer of our species. I stand in awe of the genius of the race. But a large part of this genius is devoted to lying and seeming what you are not. We love when this man Ulysses comes back in disguise for his revenge. But suppose he forgot what he came back for and just sat around day in, day out in the disguise. This happens to many a frail spirit who forgets what the disguises are for, doesn't understand complexity, or how to return to simplicity. From telling different things to everyone, forgets what the case is originally and what he wants himself. How rare is simple thought and pureheartedness! Even a moment of pureheartedness I bow to, down to the ground. That's why I think well of you when you tell me you're in love. I appreciate this durability, and I'm a lover myself."

God bless Mintouchian! What a good man! He really paid attention, and I returned him love for love.

"You will understand, Mr. Mintouchian, if I tell you that I have always tried to become what I am. But it's a frightening thing. Because what if what I am by nature isn't good enough?" I was close to tears as I said it to him. "I suppose I better, anyway, give in and be it. I will never force the hand of fate to create a better Augie March, nor change the time to an age of gold."

"That's exactly right. You must take your chance on what you are. And you can't sit still. I know this double poser, that if you make a move you may lose but if you sit still you will decay. But what will you lose? You will not invent better than God or nature or turn yourself into the man who lacks no gift or development before you make the move. This is not given to us."

"That's right, and I'm grateful to you," I said. "I owe you much for this explanation."

This took place on the fifty-eighth story of a building in midtown Manhattan, behind sliding glass doors. No use being so blasé as not to mention it.

"It is better to die what you are than to live a stranger forever," he said.

After this he concentrated in silence for a while, as though he were counting drops from an invisible dropper. What were the drops of, of pure essence, or of gall?

"I think you will be interested in a matter that's bothered me the last few months." Gall. I saw that now. His large eyes grew heavy and sad.

"The reason why I told of a bracelet before," he said, "is that I have jewelry on my mind on account of a diamond ring that Mrs. Kuttner, Agnes, lost several months ago. She said she was mugged in Central Park while walking the dog in the evening. It happens of course that people are mugged."

"But why wear a diamond ring while walking a dog?"

"That is explained by the fact that we had a date. On her throat fingermarks. Good enough evidence, huh? Also, she was found lying on a path between the Met and the children's playground. The cops took her home. Pretty convincing, isn't it?"

"It sounds absolutely—"

"She collected the insurance of five thousand dollars. And now I tell you in strict confidence that she did it all herself."

"What?"

"Choked herself unconscious. The marks on her throat she made with her own fingers."

"How could she!"

"*She* could."

The vision of the Vienna beauty choking herself in the night park stupefied me. "How do you know?"

"Because one of her friends is keeping the ring for her."

"But what is she trying to put over?"

"That's the whole thing. I give her all the money she needs. Plus sending a check to her husband in Cuba. So what does she want this extra swindle for?"

"Maybe it's just social-security money, like? Have you provided for her?"

"She is very managing about property. That's my best hope. Provided? Of course. I gave her a house on the Island. But what if it isn't that? You get the pitch? She has secrets from me; she's double-lifing me."

"It might turn out to be something very ordinary, like a brother in trouble she doesn't want to tell you about. Or she's tired of just being handed money and wants to *make* money."

He was aware that I was trying to comfort him.

"There must be easier ways. No, what if it's to pay off somebody? Ah, law practice makes me very suspicious. But don't you see where I'm at?" Mintouchian asked me. "With my outlook?"

Sometimes on short acquaintance you can get very closely knitted to someone. And Mintouchian and I now were.

On this particular Saturday, Stella and Agnes not showing up because of a misunderstanding about the arrangements,

Mintouchian became very nervous as we waited in his office for them. Dinner hour with his wife was approaching, that was why. Finally he sent word by his chauffeur to Stella's apartment that we'd join them at half-past nine, and then took me home with him in a cab, across the park.

So I met Mrs. Mintouchian. I couldn't figure out her complaint. She was dressed in a quilted blue robe and her hair was gray. She was dignified, if not haughty; I felt her conduct like a kind of touching athletic prowess.

She gave me a very upstage reception.

"Harold, the martinis have to be mixed in the kitchen," she said to Mintouchian. So he went out, and as soon as he left she said, almost with violence, "Who are you, young man?"

"Me? I'm a client of Mr. Mintouchian. You see, I'm just about to get married."

"I don't expect you to tell me anything," she said. "I know that Harold has his secrets. I mean, he thinks he has. I really know all about him, because I think about him all the time. It isn't so hard if you spend all your time thinking about somebody. I don't have to leave this room."

I was astonished. I felt my eyes get wide.

I said, "I haven't known Mr. Mintouchian long, ma'am, but in my opinion he's a great man."

"Oh, you realize that? He is great, even if he's all too human."

It awed me that when this lion, Mintouchian, sobbed in the brakes of, he thought, most solitude, this invalid was standing listening behind him.

But then he came carrying the glasses and the conversation was finished.

Chapter XXV

As DRUGGED with love as I was, why, nothing could deter me from marriage. I'm not sure whether Mintouchian was trying to do that, but if he was he didn't stand a chance, because I wasn't hospitable to suspicions. However, he acted the part of a good friend. He arranged with the catering service for the wedding lunch and bought roses and gardenias for everybody. By City Hall the air was blue, and there seemed to be trembles of music. When we came down in the elevator I remembered how more than a year before I was standing on top of County Hospital, Chicago, and reflecting how of all our family, including old Grandma, Simon was the only one who had managed to stay out of an institution. But now I didn't have any more reason to envy him. Envy? Why, I thought I had it all over him, seeing I was married to a woman I loved and therefore I was advancing on the only true course of life. I told myself my brother was the kind of man who could only leave the world as he found it and hand on the fate he inherited to any children he might now have—I didn't for sure know whether he had any. Yes, this was how such people were subject to all the laws in the book, like the mountain peaks leaning toward their respective magnetic poles, or like crabs in the weeds or crystals in the caves. Whereas I, with the help of love, had gotten in on a much better thing and was giving this account of myself that reality comes from and was not just at the mercy. And here was the bride with me, her face was burning with happy excitement; she wanted what I wanted. In her time she had made mistakes, but all mistakes were now wiped out.

We came out on the steps. The doves were walking around, and Mintouchian had arranged for a photographer to be there and make a picture of the wedding party. He was very thoughtful and acted kind to everyone.

I had graduated from Sheepshead the day before and had my new rating in my pocket. My smile was changed, because they had given me some lower teeth gratis to replace the ones I lost in Mexico. I have to confess that in addition to passionate love and the pride of the day I had a bubble in me like the air bubble of the carpenter's level. But I was shaved and combed like a movie actor and dressed in the new high-pressure uniform, which lacked only service ribbons and stars. I would have liked some, and to have married a beauty as a hero of the service of his country. I promised myself that I would have been modest. However, you wouldn't have been able to tell how nervous I was, I think. It wasn't just because I had to ship out soon after the wedding that I was nervous, but also because Stella was bound the week after for Alaska and the Aleutians with a USO show. I didn't want her to go.

Of course I wouldn't say anything to spoil the occasion. We had pictures taken of the wedding party, which included also Agnes and Sylvester. I looked with changed eyes on Agnes since hearing of her self-strangulation. She was wearing a fine gray suit that showed off her hips, and a collar sweeping upward as if to keep you from seeing her throat.

Anyway, turkey, ham, champagne, cognac, fruit, and cake were set up on the buffet in Stella's apartment. It was very grand. Robey and Frazer had showed up in town together, and I invited them, so I was well represented. Frazer wore a major's uniform. Robey's beard was fuller and he had put on weight down in Washington. He sat by himself in a corner, clasping his knee in two hands and never saying anything. There was enough conversation without him.

After a few glasses of champagne Sylvester broke out in grins. He was a funny, melancholy guy, Sylvester. He wanted to be taken serious and straight, but gave himself away in his dark-lined grins, and the unthoughtful part of him fought its way out. In his double-breasted pinstriped business suit he sat by me. I held Stella around the waist and stroked her satin wedding dress.

"What a dish!" said Sylvester to me. "What you've fallen into! And when I think you used to work for me!"

This was when he had owned the Star Theatre on California Avenue, below that dentist who tormented Grandma. Sylvester was no kid; he was getting on. He said he was off politics now. I wanted to ask him about Mexico, but the wedding day was no time for that, so I passed the question over.

The man of the hour at this party was not myself so much as Frazer, in a way.

Frazer had just come back from the Orient. He was in the Intelligence and attached to a mission to Chungking.

He was talking to Agnes and Mintouchian about the East. I still admired Frazer a whole lot and looked up to him. He was a mighty attractive and ideal man. There was a lanky American elegance about him, in the ease of his long legs and his cropped-on-the-sides head which from chin to top showed the male molding on the strong side of haggardness; his gray eyes on the cool side of frankness. All the markings of his face were strong, with creases beginning to deepen from world pressure. And there was something else about him—as if he were in the barber's chair at the conclusion of shaving, the witch hazel drying, the fine Western shoes stuck out. He knew so much too. Suppose that you said something about D'Alembert or Isidore of Seville, Frazer would have been ready to discuss them. You couldn't find a subject that stumped him. He was going to become an important person. You could see how he was flying at the highest, from one peak of life to the next. And yet he looked relaxed. But the more ease and leisure he achieved the more distance and flashing there were; he talked about Thucydides or Marx and showed pictures of history-like visions. You got shivers on the back and thrills clear into the teeth. I was real proud to have such a friend come. He gave tone to the wedding and was a great success.

But as you listened to this brilliant educational discussion it was somewhat scary too; like catching hold of high voltage.

Declarations, resolutions, treaties, theories, congresses, bones of kings, Cromwells, Loyolas, Lenins and czars, hordes of India and China, famines, huddles, massacres, sacrifices, he mentioned. Great crowds of Benares and London, Rome, he made me see; Jerusalem against Titus, Hell when Ulysses visited, Paris when they butchered horses in the street. Dead Ur and Memphis. Atoms of near silence, the dead acts, that formed a collective roar. Macedonian sentinels. Subway moles. Mr. Kreindl shoving a cannon wheel with his buddies. Grandma and legendary Lausch in his armor cutaway having an argument in the Odessa railroad station the day the Japanese war broke out. My parents taking a walk by the Humboldt Park lagoon the day I was conceived. Flowery springtime.

And I thought there was altogether too much of this to live with. Better forget it, in part. The Ganges is there with its demons and lords; but you have a right also, and merely, to wash your feet and do your personal laundry in it. Or even if you had a good car it would take more than a lifetime to do a tour of all the Calvaries.

Whether I was all I might be troubled me as Frazer held forth, but much less than it would have done before my conversations with Clem about the axial lines and with Mintouchian in the Turkish bath. It gave me great comfort that Mintouchian was here. And in the end it was marriage-day tribute—all that happened. The champagne being at an end, the white meat eaten, the two pinochle players of the cutting table opposite putting on their jackets to depart, our company bowed out too. Farewell all, and many thanks.

"Isn't my friend Frazer smart?" I said.

"Yes, but you're my darling," said Stella and kissed me. So we went to the bridal bed.

Two days of honeymoon were all we had.

I had to ship from Boston. Stella went up on the train with me the night before. And separating of course was tough. I sent her back in the morning.

"Go, sweetheart."

"Augie, darling, good-by," she said from the platform of the train. Some people can't bear a train departure at any time, and how crushing these departures were in the stations during the war, as the cars moved away and left throngs behind, and the oil-spotted empty tracks and the mounting, multiplying ties. "Please," she said, "be careful about everything."

"Oh, I will," I promised her. "Don't worry about that. I love you too much to go and get sunk, on my first trip out. You take care too, out there in Alaska."

She made it sound as though it were somehow up to me, as though I could make my own safe way over the Atlantic waters of wartime. But I knew what she was trying to say.

"Radar has licked the submarines," I told her. "It says so in the papers."

This piece of news was improvised; it did a lot of good,

however, and I went on talking, so extremely salty you'd have taken me for an old sailor.

The conductor came to close the door, and I said, "Go on inside, honey, go on."

Till the last moment I saw her big eyes at the window. As she bent forward from the hips in her seat, the prettiness and grace of it was a killing thing to have to miss during months on the water.

So the train went and I was left in the crowd and felt low and bleak.

To add to it, the weather was gray and windy and the ship, the *Sam MacManus*, was old. Black machinery beside it, at the wharf, grim gimmicks on it, grease, darkness, blues, the day itself housed in iron. The ocean was waiting with grand and bitter provocations, as if it invited you to think how deep it was, how much colder than your blood or saltier, or to outguess it, to tell which were its feints or passes and which its real intentions, meaning business. It wasn't any apostle-crossed or Aeneas-stirred Mediterranean, the clement, silky, marvelous beauty-sparkle bath in which all the ancientest races were children. As we left the harbor, the North Atlantic, brute gray, heckled the ship with its strength, clanging, pushing, muttering; a hungry sizzle salted the bulkheads.

But next morning, in the sun and warmth, we were steaming south with all our might. I came on deck from an all-night bout of seasickness—the Mothersills pills, even, hadn't helped—and being torn by longing and worry about Alaska.

The middle-aged ship was busting through the water so as to make you feel great depth and the air was sweet, radiant. It was pellucid. Even the sooty *MacManus* in the flush, like a kitchen insect escaping into the garden at dawn. The bluey deck rattled underfoot with the chainlike drag of the rudder engine. A few confused resemblances: clouds or distant coast, birds or corpuscles, fled across my eyes.

I went to investigate my office and duties. Nothing much, in fact. Druggist and bookkeeper setup, as I've already said. Green old filing cases. Lockers of same color. A swivel chair and fair light to read by. I squared myself away for the voyage.

So there were several days of mechanical progress over the water, the horizon sea rising to grip after a cloud like a crab

after a butterfly, with armored totter, then falling and travail-
ing. Plus the sun's heat and the patriarch wake, spitting and
lacy.

In my privacy I read books and wrote an endless letter
chronicle to Stella which I hoped to send from Dakar, out to
Alaska. Of course there were guns and a radar ring to remind
you of danger, but the time was very pleasant.

Before long the word got around that I was a listener to
hard-luck stories, personal histories, gripes, and that I gave
advice, and by and by I had a daily clientele, almost like a fortuneteller. By golly, I could have taken fees! Clem knew what
he was talking about when he urged me to come into the advice business. Here I was doing it free of charge, and in dangerous conditions. Although all seemed tranquil enough. Of
an early evening, say, red and gold, with the deep blue tense
surface, the full-up ocean, and some guy came darkening between me and the light, as if to a session of spiritual guidance. I can't claim it annoyed me. It gave me a chance to
learn secrets, and also to sound off on the problems of life. I
was on fine terms practically with everyone. Even the union
delegate, when he saw I didn't intend to be hard-nosed and
difficult about the company's interests. And the Old Man—
he did correspondence courses in philosophy at a bunch of
universities, it was his hobby, and was forever writing out
assignments—he took to me too, though he didn't approve
of my leniency.

Anyway, I became ship's confidant. Though not all the confidences gave hope to the soul.

More than one guy dropped in to sound me out on a
black-market proposition or fast buck on foreign soil.

One planned to become a hairdresser after the war, he told
me, because then he'd have his hands on the head of every
broad in Kenosha.

One who had washed out of paratroop school and still
wore his Fort Benning boots told me frankly when the matter of his beneficiary came up that he had three legal wives in
different parts of Pennsylvania and New Jersey.

Some wanted diagnosis, as if I were a professional head-
feeler and not the humble understudy's understudy of the
cult of Asclepius the Maritime Commission had made me.

"You think I maybe have an inferiority complex, do you think?" one of them asked me.

Indeed I saw many ravages, but I never said.

Beside-itself humanity, hurrying, hurrying, with liquid eyes.

"Suppose you was the guy in a fix like this . . ."

"There was this certain friend of mine . . ."

"He said, 'You support the old man for a while and see how you like it.'"

"He ran away for a Carnie."

"Now this girl, who was a cripple in one leg, she worked in the paint lab of the stove factory."

"He was a Rumania-box type of swindler, where you put in a buck and it comes out a fiver."

"If he floated down the river with a hard-on he expected them to raise the bridges for him, that's how he was an egotist."

"I said, 'You listen here to me, fart-blossom, you chiseler . . .'"

"Though I knew she was so sweet and we had the kids, the time just came when I couldn't keep the multiplication table out of my head, and then I knew, 'Bitches is all you deserve and should be with. Let them rob you and kick you around. That's okay!'"

Lasciar le donne? Pazzo! Lasciar le donne!

"I was trying to have one night with this girl before I shipped out. We both worked in the shipping department. But I couldn't swing it. So for weeks I was carrying a safety in my pocket and couldn't get to use it. One time it was all set and then my wife's grandmother died. I had to go fetch grandfather to the funeral. He couldn't understand what it was all about. We sat in the chapel where the organ played. He said, 'Why, that's the music the old dog died to,' and made one joke after another. Then he recognized her in the coffin, and he said, excited, 'Why, there's Mother! I saw her yesterday in the A and P. What's she doing here? Mother, why, Mother!' And then he understood and bust into tears. Oh, he cried. Me too. All of us. Me with the safety still in my pocket. What do you think? Everybody is some kind of tricker. Even me.

"Then my wife and kid took me to the station. I still hadn't made it with that girl and probably she forgot all about it and started with another guy. My little daughter said, 'Daddy, I got to take a pisst.' She'd heard the boys talk. We had to laugh. But then, good-by. My heart weighed a ton. So long, honey. She was cryin' away by the train window, and I felt the same. And meantime that safety was in my vest pocket. I didn't throw it away."

This man's face was flat, slender, rosy, bony-nosed, gray-eyed, and his mouth was small.

I passed out advice in moderate amounts; nobody is perfect. I advocated love, especially.

Some terribly strange personalities came forward.

Griswold, for instance, one of the stewards. A former undertaker and also zoot-suiter and cat. A light Negro, extremely handsome and grand, short beard full of graceful glitters, hair rich and oiled; a burn on his cheek gleamed with Unguentine. His pants flowed voluminous and stripy down to a two-strap shoe. He smoked tea for his quiet recreation and studied grammar in a number of languages for kicks. Griswold handed me the following poem of his own writing:

How much, you ask me, do I suffer.
Now, baby, listen, I am not a good bluffer.
My ambitions and aspirations don't leave me no rest;
I am born with a high mind and aim for the best.

His knee went up and down rapidly while I read this, and his eyes were dark and anxious.

If I dwell on these individual members of the crew it's in the nature of a memorial. For on the fifteenth day out, when we were off the Canaries, the *Sam MacManus* was sent down by a torpedo.

It happened while I was hearing one of these unofficial confiteors, in fact. It was night, and we must have been making twelve knots, when suddenly there came a crushing great blow on the side; we were flung down. There were bucklings and crashes and then the inside stun of an explosion. We rushed for the outer deck, fast. Already hairs of fire came up through the busted plates, and the superstructure was lighted clear by the flames. Patches of water also burned close by, and the bright water approached. Hungry yells and steam blasts, plunges; the huge rafts swooped over the side, released, and the boats crashed from the davits. We scrambled up to the boats, this guy and I, and started to wind one out. It hung caught and crooked. I shouted to him to jump in and see what was fouling. He didn't seem to get this, his eyes looking wildly at me. "Get in there!" I yelled, weirdly hoarse with the terror. Then I hopped in myself to free the boat, whereupon, the winch letting go, unbraked, the boat slammed fast and hard on the water, knocking me overboard. My thought when I went under was that the ship would suck me with it as it sank. The fear squeezed and milked the strength out of my arms and legs, but I tried to fight, hearing grunts and Orpheus pulls of string from the deep bottom, and then all the consciousness there was to me seemed a hairlash in the crushing water universe.

I came up wanting to howl but unable to; my jaws tore open only to breathe. And where was the lifeboat? Well, there were boats and rafts here and there in the water-fires. I was spitting, vomiting up sea, weeping, and straining to get distance from the flaming ship from which, in the white of the fire, men were still jumping.

I made for a boat that floated a hundred yards or so off. I labored after it in terror lest it pull away. However, I saw no oars out. I couldn't have hollered after; my voice seemed to have gone. But it only drifted, and I made it. I grabbed the painter and called to whoever might be lying inside, for I was too beat to get in. But the boat was vacant. Then the *Mac-Manus* went down. The sudden quench of the white light was how I knew it. Fire still burned all over the surface, but the current was carrying fast. I saw a loaded raft in the torn light of flames. Then I had another go at climbing into the boat. I worked my way to the middle, where the gunwale was lower. From that position I saw a guy who held on to the stern, poor bastard. I yelled to him, thrilled, glad, but his head hung back. I frantically swam behind him to see what was wrong.

"You hurt?" I asked.

"No, bushed," he muttered.

"Come, I'll boost you over and then you give me a hand. We've got to see if we can pick up any other guys."

We had to wait until he had the strength to try. Finally I gave him a hand-stirrup, and he made it.

I waited for his assistance but it didn't come. He let me trail for I don't know how long. I hollered and cried, cursed, rocked the boat. No soap. At last I threw a leg over the side and toiled and dragged myself astride the gunwale. He was sitting on a thwart, there, hands between his knees. Furious, I drove my fist down on his sodden back. He lurched but otherwise didn't move, only turned up a pair of animal-in-the-headlights eyes. "Le' me drown, you sonofabitch? I'll bash your brains out!" I yelled. He didn't answer, only covered me with his cold eyes and his face twitched.

"Grab an oar and let's go pick up survivors," I said.

But there was only one oar to grab. The rest were gone.

There was nothing to do but sit and drift. I gazed and called over the water in case there should be someone carried out this way. But there wasn't anybody. The fires were receding and going out. I half expected the sub to surface and take stock, and I half wanted it to. It was around, all right, beating it down in the sea. What did I think that I'd get a chance to holler and give them a piece of my mind? No, they went away, no doubt, continuing their supper perhaps, or playing cards. And by the time night fell completely there wasn't the light of boat of raft to be seen anywhere.

I sat and waited for daylight, when I hoped there'd something show on the horizon.

Nothing showed. At dawn we were in a haze like the swelter of an old-fashioned laundry Monday, with the sun a burning copper-bottom, and through this air distortion and diffused color you couldn't see fifty yards. We sighted some wreckage but no boats. The sea was empty. I was awed by the death of those guys and the disappearance of the survivors, swept away. Down in the engine room they couldn't have had much of a chance.

Glum and bitter, I started to take stock. There were smudgepots and flares for signaling, and there was no food or water problem for the time being, since there were only two of us. But who was it that fate had billeted on me? This guy sitting on the thwart whom I had beaten last night, as far as my strength permitted, what trouble would I have with him?

He was the ship's carpenter and handyman, and from one point of view I was in luck, having no manual skill or ingenuity myself. He rigged up a kind of sail by stepping up the oar; and he claimed we couldn't be more than two hundred miles west of the Canaries, and that if we had any luck at all we'd sail right into them. He told me that every day he'd gone and looked at the charts, and so he knew exactly where we were and what the currents were doing. He figured it out with great satisfaction and self-confidence, and he seemed absolutely untroubled. About my beating and cursing him, not a single word.

He was of broad, stocky build, carrying a judicious big ball of a head, cut close. Many of his bristles were white, but not with age; he had a dark mustache that followed the corners of his mouth calmly downward. His eyes were blue and he wore specs. A pair of bleached-at-the-knees overalls dried slowly on his wide calves.

I took a flier of imagination at his past and saw him at age ten reading *Popular Mechanics.*

Even as I sized him up, he did me, of course.

"You're Mr. March, the purser," he said at last. He commanded, when he wanted to, a very cultured deep voice.

"That's right," said I, surprised by the sudden viola tone.

"Basteshaw, ship's carpenter. By the way, aren't you a Chicagoan too?"

Basteshaw, after all, was a name I had heard before. "Wasn't your dad in the real-estate business? Around Einhorn's, back in the twenties, there was a man named Basteshaw."

"He dabbled in real estate. He was in the produce business. Basteshaw the Soupngreens King."

"That's not what Commissioner Einhorn called him."

"What was that?"

It was too late now to back out, and so I said, "He nicknamed him Butcher-Paper."

Basteshaw laughed. He had broad teeth. "That's great!" he said.

Imagine! Over this trouble, solitude, danger, heartbreak of the disaster, there blows suddenly home-town familiarity, and even a faux pas about the nickname.

He didn't respect his old father. I didn't approve of that.

Respect? Why, it came out how he downright hated him. He was glad he was dead. I'm willing to believe old Basteshaw was a tyrant, a miser, a terrible man. Nevertheless he was the fellow's father.

In beauty or doom colors, according to what was in your heart, the sea and skies made their cycles of day and night, the jeweled water gadding universally, the night-glittering fury setting in. The days were sultry. We sat under the crust of the canvas, in the patch of shade. There was scarcely any wind for the first few days, which was lucky.

I tried to master my anxious mind, which kept asking whether I'd ever see Stella again, or my mother, my brothers, Einhorn, Clem. I kept the smudgepot and flares by me, dry. Our chances of being picked up were not bad in these parts. It wasn't as though we had gone down in the extreme south where there wasn't much shipping then.

As the heat fanned over you, you sometimes heard the actual salt in the water, like rustling, or like a brittle snow when it starts to melt.

Basteshaw was forever watching me through those goggles. Even during a nap he seemed to watch, his head backed off, studious, vigilant. Cousin Anna Coblin didn't look more persistently into mirrors. There he sat, with his thick chest interposed, ponderous. He was built like a horse, this Basteshaw. As if hoofs, not hands, were on his knees. If he had hit back at me that first night there'd have been real trouble. But then we were both too weak to fight. And now he seemed to have forgotten all about it. His poise was that of a human fortress, and you could never catch him off balance. He often laughed. But while the sounds of his laughter went out into the spaces of the sea his eyes, blue and small, never lost sight of me through the goggles.

"One thing I'm glad of," he said, "is that I didn't meet my end by drowning. Not yet, anyway. I'd rather die of hunger, exposure, anything else. My dad, you see, drowned in the lake."

"Did he?" Ah, then, farewell Butcher-Paper. This was when I learned of his death.

"At Montrose Beach during his vacation. Busy men often die on their holiday, as if they had no time for it during the business week. Relaxation kills them. He had a heart attack."

"But I thought he drowned?"

"He fell in the water and was drowned. Early in the morning. He was sitting on the pier, reading the *Trib*. He always got up before dawn from years in the market. The coronary was slight and wouldn't have been fatal. It was the water in his lungs."

Basteshaw, I discovered, loved medical and all scientific conversation of any sort.

"The guards found him when they came on duty. The afternoon papers carried a story of foul play. There was a wad of money in his pocket, big thick rings on his fingers. That infuriated me. I went down to Brisbane Street to give them a piece of my mind. I thought it was scandalous. Trading on people's emotions like that. There was poor Ma, horrified. Murder? I forced them to print a retraction."

I know those small paragraphs of retraction on page thirty, in tiny print.

However, Basteshaw announced it with real pride. He put on his old man's best Borsalino hat, he told me, and he took the Cadillac out of the garage and smashed it up. He drove it into a wall on purpose. For the old man never would let him have it and kept it like a Swiss watch. The late Butcher-Paper had had a thing about breakage. When he had a violent fit and was about to smash something, Mrs. Basteshaw would cry, "Aaron, Aaron, the drawer!" Old pie tins were kept in a kitchen drawer for him that he could fling and stamp on. No matter how enraged, he always used these pie tins, not good china.

Basteshaw laughed as he told this, but I was sad for the old man.

"The car couldn't be used in the funeral because it was in smithereens. That made it a Viking funeral, after a fashion. After he was planted my next move"—I flinched in advance— "was to break off with my cousin Lee. The old man made me get engaged to her on the ground that I trifled with her affections. After he mixed in I never intended to marry her."

"Trifle? What did he mean?"

"That I was in the sack with her. But I swore I'd never give the old man the satisfaction."

"You might have been in love with her, old man or no old man."

He gave me a sharp glance. I didn't know what sort of person I was dealing with.

"She had pulmonary phthisis, and people like that are frequently highly stimulated. Increased temperatures often act on the erogenous zones spectacularly," said he in his lecturer's tone.

"But was she in love with you?"

"Birds with their higher temperature also lead a more intense emotional life. I see from the way you speak of love that you don't know a thing about psychology or biology. She needed me and therefore loved me. If another guy had been around she would have loved him. Suppose I had never been born, does that mean she wouldn't have loved anyone? If the old man hadn't interfered I might have married her, but he was pro so I was contra. Besides, she was dying. So I told her I couldn't possibly marry her. Why string her along?"

Brute!

Pig!

Snake!

Murderer!

He had hastened her death. I couldn't bear the look of him for a while.

"Within a year she died. Toward the end her face was absolutely mealy, poor girl. She was quite pretty originally."

"Why don't you shut up!"

He was surprised at me. "Why, what's eating you?" he said.

"Listen, drop dead!"

He would have let me drown too, or be eaten by sharks.

Nevertheless the conversation was resumed by and by. Under the circumstances, what else?

So now Basteshaw told me about another relative, an aunt. She slept for fifteen years. And then one day suddenly arose and went about the house as if nothing had happened. "She dropped off when I was ten years old. She woke up when I was twenty-five, and she knew me right as soon as she saw me. She wasn't even surprised."

I'll bet.

"One day my uncle Mort was coming home from work—this was out in Ravenswood. You know how they build the bungalows there? He was going around to the back, between two houses, and as he passed the bedroom he saw her hand reach out to pull the window blind. He recognized the hand by the wedding band, and he came close to filling his pants. He stumbled in, and sure enough, she had cooked supper and it was on the table. She said, 'Go wash!'"

"Incredible! Could it really happen? Why, it's a regular sleeping-beauty story. Was it sleeping sickness?"

"If she had been a beauty she wouldn't have slept so long. My own diagnosis is some form of narcolepsy. Etiology purely mental. It may account for Lazarus. For Miss Usher of the House of Usher and many others. Only my aunt's case is extremely illuminating. Deep secrets of life. Deeper than this ocean. To hold tight is the wish of every neurotic character. While she slept she ruled. In some part of her mind she knew what was going on, as evidenced by the fact that she could resume life after fifteen years with accuracy. She knew where things were, and she was not surprised by the changes. She had the power achieved by those who lie still."

I had to think of Einhorn in his wheel chair, lecturing me about strength.

"While battles rage, planes fly, machinery produces, money changes hands, Eskimos hunt, kidnapers sweep the roads—that person is safe who by lying in bed can make the world come to him, or to her. My Aunt Ettl's whole life was a preparation for this miracle."

"It's something, all right," I said.

"You bet your sweet life. It's of the utmost significance too. Do you remember how the great Sherlock Holmes doped things out in his room on Baker Street? But compared to his brother Mycroft he was no place. That Mycroft! There was a brain, March! He never budged from his club, and he was a real mastermind and knew everything. So when Sherlock was stumped he came to Mycroft, who gave him the answer. You know the reason? Because Mycroft sat tighter than Sherlock. Sitting tight is power. The king sits on his prat, and the common folks are on their feet. Pascal says people get in trouble because they can't stay in their rooms. The next poet laureate of England—I figure—prays God to teach us to sit still. You know that famous painting of the gypsy Arab traveler sleeping with his mandolin and the lion gazing on him? That doesn't mean the lion respects his repose. No, it means the Arab's immobility controls the lion. This is magic. Passivity plus power. Listen to me, March, that old Rip van Winkle conked out on purpose."

"Who took care of your aunt all that time?"

"A Polack woman—Wadjka. And let me say that after the miracle was over my uncle was in a hell of a spot. Because he had arranged his life around my sleeping aunt. She slept, and he had his card parties and his honeybunch. After she woke we all pitied him."

"As far as compassion goes," I said, "what about some for your aunt? She put in all that time, a chunk of her life like that. Like a long prison term practically."

A smile began to draw Basteshaw's mustache.

"I once was bugs on the history of art," he said. "Instead of being on the hustle in the summer, as my old man wanted, I'd slip away to the Newberry library where I'd be the only lad among eight or ten nuns at a reading table. I picked up a book by Ghiberti once, anyhow, and it made a great impression on me. He told about a German goldsmith of the Duke of Anjou who was the equal of the great sculptors of Greece. At the end of his life he had to stand by and watch his masterpieces melted down for bullion. His labor all in vain. He prayed on his knees, 'O Lord, creator of all, let me not follow after false gods.' Then he went into a monastery, this holy man, where he cashed in his chips and checked out for good."

O blight! That the firm world should give out at the end of life. Blasted! But he had God to fall back on. And what if there had been no God for him? What if the truth should be even more terrible and furious?

"So what was Aunt Ettl's sickness but a work of art? And just like this poor German fellow, she had to be prepared for failure. That's what they mean by the ruins of time—

> Or go to Rome, which is the sepulcher.

I suppose you know Shelley—

> Go thou to Rome—at once the Paradise,
> The grave, the city, and the wilderness.

So works of art *aren't* eternal. So beauty *is* perishable. Didn't this saintly German wake up many mornings inspired, with joy in his heart? What more can you ask? He couldn't be both happy and sure of being right for eternity. You have to take your chance that being happy is also being right."

I was with him there; I nodded with answering intelligence. I had a better opinion of him. There was something to him, after all. He had some nobility of heart and was a good guy in some mysterious respects. Though what a mixture!

Meanwhile the boat sauntered through glassy stabs of light and wheewhocked on the steep drink.

And then I had to bring to mind how many times, thinking myself right, I had been wrong.

And wrong again.

And wrong again.

And again.

And how long would I be right now?

But I had great confidence in my love of Stella and her love of me.

And then again, perhaps all matters of right and wrong would finish soon, as we might not survive.

Points and crosses of diamond dazzled from the slopey blue ever-full waters. Fish and monsters did their business within. Some of our drowned were near, maybe, and passed beneath us.

Now he talked of his aunt Ettl as an artist and sounded pompous. Here it wasn't so many days ago that he was scarcely able to fiddle his legs, and shrunk down to nothing with fright, and now look at him, astride his mental powers, sweating and round-headed, sitting there so sturdy.

"Why does an educated fellow like you ship out as carpenter?" I said, asking the question that had puzzled me for some time.

And then it came out that he was a biologist or biochemist; or psycho-biophysicist, which he liked best of all. Six universities had canned him for his strange ideas and refused to look at his experimental results. With all this scientific training he wasn't going to be an infantry man. So he shipped, and this was his fifth voyage. At sea he could keep up his scientific work.

Why did I always have to fall among theoreticians!

He started in to tell me of this work of his, beginning with a survey of his life.

"You know how there are things every child wants to be. For instance, when I was twelve I was very fast on the ice and could have become a skating champion. But I lost interest. Then I became a stamp expert. I lost interest in that too. Next a socialist, and that didn't last. I took up the bassoon and I quit. So I went through a large number of interests and nothing suited me. Then when I was in college I caught an extreme desire to be—or to have been—a Renaissance cardinal. That was the one thing I'd have loved. A wicked one, smoking with life, neighing and plunging. Yeah, boy! I'd put my mother in a nunnery. I'd keep my father in a gunny sack. I'd commission Michelangelo to go beyond the Farnese and the Strozzi. Spontaneous, I'd have been. Vigorous. Without embarrassment. Happy as a god. Ah, well, what can you do, impose your ideas on life? Everybody wants to be the most desirable kind of man.

"And how does it start? Well, go back to when I was a kid in the municipal swimming pool. A thousand naked little bastards screaming, punching, pushing, kicking. The lifeguards whistle and holler and punish you, the cops on duty squash you in the ribs with their thumbs and call you snot-nose. Shivery little rat. Lips blue, blood thin, scared, your little balls tight, your little thing shriveled. Skinny you. The shoving multitude bears down, and you're nothing, a meaningless name, and not just obscure in eternity but right now. The fate of the meanest your fate. Death! But no, there must be some distinction. The soul cries out against this namelessness. And then it exaggerates. It tells you, 'You were meant to astonish the world. You, Hymie Basteshaw, *Stupor mundi!* My boy, brace up. You have been called, and you will be chosen. So start looking the part. The generations of man will venerate you as long as calendars exist!' This is neurotic, I know—excuse the jargon—but to be not neurotic is to adjust to what they call the reality situation. But the reality situation is what I have described. A billion souls boiling with anger at a doom of insignificance. Reality is also these private hopes the imagination invents. Hopes, the indispensable evils of Pandora's Box. Assurance of a fate worth suffering for. In other words, desiring to be cast in the mold of true manhood. But who is cast in this mold? Nobody knows.

"I did my best to be as much of a Renaissance cardinal as one can under modern conditions.

"After much effort to live up to a glorious standard there came fatigue, wan hope, and boredom. I experienced extreme boredom. I saw others experiencing it too, many denying, by the way, that any such thing existed. And finally I decided that I would make boredom my subject matter. That I'd study it. That I'd become the world's leading authority on it. March, that was a red-letter day for humanity. What a field! What a domain! Titanic! Promethean! I trembled before it. I was inspired. I couldn't sleep. Ideas came in the night and I wrote them down, volumes of them. Strange that no one had gone after this systematically. Oh, melancholy, yes, but not modern boredom.

"I did a fair amount of research in literature and among modern thinkers. The first conclusions were obvious. Boredom starts with useless effort. You have shortcomings and aren't what you should be? Boredom is the conviction that you can't change. You begin to worry about loss of variety in your character and the uncomplimentary comparison with others in your secret mind, and this makes you feel your own tiresomeness. On your social side boredom is a manifestation of the power of society. The stronger society is, the more it expects you to hold yourself in readiness to perform your social duties, the greater your availability, the smaller your significance. On Monday you are justifying yourself by your work. But on Sunday, how are you justified? Hideous Sunday, enemy of humanity. Sunday you're on your own—free. Free for what? Free to discover what's in your heart, what you feel toward your wife, children, friends, and pastimes. The spirit of man, enslaved, sobs in the silence of boredom, the bitter antagonist. Boredom therefore can arise from the cessation of habitual functions, even though these may be boring too. It is also the shriek of unused capacities, the doom of serving no great end or design, or contributing to no master force. The obedience that is not willingly given because nobody knows how to request it. The harmony that is not accomplished. This lies behind boredom. But you see the endless vistas."

Did I! I was stupefied. I watched him climb around like an alpinist of the mountains of his own brain, sturdy, and with his calm goggles and his blue glances of certitude.

"And I wanted to approach it scientifically," he went on. "So my first project was to study the physiology of boredom. I looked into the muscular fatigue experiments of Jacobson and others and that led me into biochemistry. I knocked out my M.A. in record time, I may add, in cell chemistry. Keeping rat tissues alive *in vitro*, after Harrison and the technique improved by Carrel. This drew me on to von Wettstein, Leo Loeb, and so forth. How come the simple cells wish for immortality whereas the complex organisms get bored? The cells have the will to persist in their essence . . ."

There ensued certain descriptions which I don't command the physical chemistry to repeat, the kinesis of enzymes and so forth. But the upshot of this was, that as he investigated the irritability of protoplasm he discovered some of the secrets of life. "I'm sure you'll find it hard to believe what happened next. Nobody else has believed it."

"You didn't create life!"

"In all humility, that's exactly what I did. Six universities have thrown me out for claiming it."

"Why, it's crazy! Are you sure that's what you did?"

He said stiffly, "I'm a serious person. My whole existence has been intensely serious. I don't intend to jeopardize my own sanity by making wild claims. I get the same results time after time—protoplasm."

"You must be genius."

He didn't offer to deny this.

He'd better be one. If he wasn't a genius I was in this boat with a maniac.

"I stumbled on this," he said. "I am not God."

"But couldn't they see you had done it?"

"I couldn't get them to. And then the first cells I made lacked two essential powers, the regenerative and the reproductive, and were sterile and fragile forms. But in the last two years I've made a special study of biological organizers. I've been in embryology, and I've made some further discoveries."

He had to take a swig of water, for he had talked himself

onto dry spittle. Huge-headed, huge-chested, stalwart, calm, he was like an enormous case of the finest capacities. Like one of those Egyptian mummy cases that follow the outlines of the bodies they enclose. And also his resemblance to a horse continued very strong.

"But still you haven't explained what a man of your ability was doing as ship's carpenter on the *MacManus*."

"Continuing my experiments."

"You mean there was some of that protoplasm aboard?"

"As a matter of fact, there was."

"And it's floating in the ocean now?"

"I'm sure it is."

"And what's going to happen?"

"I don't know. It's one of my later forms, a great advance over that earlier, perishable form."

"What if a new chain of evolution begins?"

"Exactly. What if?"

"Something terrible maybe. Damn you guys, you don't care how you fiddle with nature!" I said, feeling extremely angry. "Somebody is going to burn up the atmosphere one day or kill us all with a gas."

He conceded that it was not impossible.

"Why should one man have the power to damage all nature or pollute the entire world?" I asked him.

"I don't think there's much chance of that," he said. And then he wouldn't continue the conversation but fell into fascinated thought.

Often Basteshaw seemed to be thinking over my head, and he would be in a strange humor in which you could see him make him an observation, both grim and amusing to himself. It made me wonder what he was up to. And for long spells, though he patrolled me still from the side of his eyes and knew my every move, he sometimes sat as heavy as a piece of foundry brass. I became very uneasy.

A couple of days went by and not a single remark was spoken. This was a strange thing, first to be overwhelmed with talk and then to be utterly isolated. Speak of boredom! Why, I began to feel as stiff as the boat itself. But I took some of the blame for this. I said to myself, "You have only this one person, one soul to deal with here—what's the matter, can't you do better? It's enough like yours, this soul, as one lion is pretty nearly all the lions, and there are just the two here, and some of the last things of all could be said. You're not doing so good, if you want to know the truth."

I had a very strange dream on the boat's bottom that night, which was this, that a flatfooted, in gym shoes, pug-nosed old woman panhandled me. I laughed at her. "Why, you old guzzler, I can hear the beer cans clinking in your shopping bag!" "No, them ain't beer cans," she said, "it's my window-washer stuff, my squeegee and Bon Ami and such, and for the love of God, must I wash my forty-fifty windows every day of my life? Give us something, won't you?" "Okay, okay," I said, me the bighearted, grinning. Among other things it made me feel good to see the West Side of Chicago again. I put my hand in my pocket, and I meant to give her only chickenfeed. Being not downright stingy, but a little close on some days, to tell the truth. But to my own surprise, instead of giving her the price of a beer I gave her one coin of each kind—half a buck, a quarter, a dime, a jitney, and a penny. All these were lined up in my palm, ninety-one cents, and I dropped them in her hand. The same instant I was sorry, for it was far too much. But then I began to feel clean proud of myself. And Ugly Face, she thanked me; she was almost like a dwarf, with a wide behind. "Well, there's a few windows free," I said. "I haven't got one I can call my own." "Come," said she warmly, "and let me treat you to a beer." "No, thanks, mother, I've got to go. Thanks all the same." I felt kindness in the depth of my breast. In kindness, I touched her on the crown of her old head and a great thrill passed through me from it. "Why, old woman," I said, "you've got the hair of an angel!" "Why shouldn't I have," she said gently, "like other daughters of men?"

My bosom was full of stormy surprises and dark bursts of happiness.

"God send you truth," said the window-washer dwarf. She went toward the shadow and the cool of the beer cavern.

I gave a long sigh and unwillingly woke. The stars were restless and fevery. Basteshaw was asleep in a sitting position, transversely. I regretted he wasn't awake so I could immediately start to talk to him.

But instead of bosom fraternity, what took place next day was a battle.

Basteshaw claimed we must be close to land; he said he had seen land birds and also seaweed and floating branches. I didn't believe him. Also, the color of the water was changing, he said, and was a yellower green. It didn't seem so to me. He pulled his scientific authority on me. Because, he said, after all, he was a scientist; he had seen the charts and studied the currents and made the calculations and watched all the signs, so there couldn't be any two ways about it. But the reason I resisted believing him was that I was afraid to encourage my joy and increase the heaviness of the opposite if he should be wrong.

However, the trouble didn't start until I thought I saw a ship on the west horizon. I began to shout and leap and wave my shirt. I was frantic. And then I rushed to put a smudge-pot into the water. I had taken good care of the signaling equipment and had read the instructions for using it fifty times if I'd read them once. So now with sweaty hands and anxiety-crippled fingers I started to get the pot ready.

Then Basteshaw, with that calm of voice that was his specialty and made me doubt I heard right, said, "What do you want to make signals for?"

Damn! The guy didn't want to be saved! He wanted to pass up a chance of rescue!

I turned my back on him and lowered the pot on the water. The black smoke began to rise against the pure color of the air. I went on flagging my shirt. I could almost feel Stella's arms slip round my waist and her face touch my shoulder. And meantime my heart filled with black murder at this lunatic Basteshaw, who sat in the stern with crossed arms. It was maddening to see him.

But now there wasn't anything on the horizon, and I had to think my imagination had pulled a stunt on me. I was deeply graveled and felt my fatigue and weakness for the first time; with just that clong of hope departing that I had been afraid of, and sunken darkness.

"I'm sorry to tell you you were hallucinated," he said, while I was covered with weak sweat.

"Why, you blind bastard, there is a ship out there, just over the horizon!"

"My vision is corrected to twenty-twenty," he said. It was just that kind of pedantry that made me hate him wildly.

"You damn four-eyed fool, what makes you want to croak out here? Do you think you have a built-in compass? Maybe you believe you can navigate, but don't expect me to have the same sublime confidence. I'm not passing up any chances."

"Now take it easy. Nobody's going to croak. I had a careful look at the course a few hours before we went down and I know we're close to land. We must be, we've been going due east. We're going to land on Spanish territory and be interned. Don't *you* be a damn fool. Haven't you had enough war yet? But for dumb luck you'd have been burned alive or become shark food. Now," he said, getting severe, "listen attentively. I don't like to chew my cabbage twice. I've been figuring this, and I believe luck is on our side. I'm going to land in the Canaries and be interned. For the rest of the war I'll just stay there and do my research. Which they wouldn't exempt me for at home though I went to Washington with an appeal. Now. I have plenty of money in the States; my old man left me close to a hundred grand and we can work here. I'll teach you. You're a pretty smart fellow, though you have all kinds of cockeyed ideas about yourself. In a year you'll know more than a Ph.D. in biochemistry. Think of the opportunity you've fallen into. To understand the birth of life and be in on the profoundest secrets. Wiser than the Sphinx. You'll gaze on the riddle of the universe with comprehension!"

He went on with his oratory. I was frightened and awed. Not just by the storming of his mind, great as that was, but by the appearance once more of the sign of the recruit under which I had been born.

"I say to you this is a great chance for you, not simply to rise to eminence, not just to give your intellectual powers the very highest development, but to assist in making a historic contribution to the happiness of mankind. These experiments with cells, March, will give the clue to the origin of boredom in the higher organisms. To what used to be called the sin of acedia. The old fellows were right, for it is a sin. Blindness to life, secession, unreceptivity, a dull wall of anxious, overprotected flesh, ignorant of the subtlety of God or Nature and unfeeling toward its beauty. March, when liberated from this boredom, every man will be a poet and every woman a saint. Love will fill the world. Injustice will go, and slavery, blood-shed, cruelty. They will belong to the past, and, seeing all these horrors of past times, all mankind will sit down and weep at the memory of them, the memory of blood and the horrible life of monads, at misunderstanding and murderous rages and carnage of innocents. The breasts and bowels will melt at this vision of the past. And then a new brotherhood of man will begin. The prisons and madhouses will be muse-ums. Like the pyramids and the ruins of Maya, they will com-memorate an erroneous development of human genius. Real freedom will manifest itself, not based on politics and revolu-tions, which never gave it anyhow, because it's not a gift but a possession of the man who is not bored. March, this is what my experiments are leading toward. I am going to create a serum—a serum like a new River Jordan. With respect to which I will be a Moses. And you Joshua. To lead an Israel consisting of the entire human race across it. And this is why I don't want to go back to the States."

I was wrought up, choked. The very air that passed over me was as if from the mouth of prophecy. Meantime the pot went on diffusing smoke. He was watching it like an enemy.

"I'm not passing up any chance to be saved. I don't want to be interned. I've just gotten married. So even if I was sure you knew what you were talking about I'd still say no."

"You think I don't know what I'm talking about?"

I should have been more tactful. He saw that that was ex-actly what I thought.

"I'm offering you a great course of life," he said. "Worth taking a risk for."

"I already have a course of life."

"Indeed?" he said.

"Yes, and I'm dead against doing things to the entire hu-man race. I don't want any more done to me, and I don't want to tamper with anyone else. No one will be a poet or saint because you fool with him. When you come right down to it, I've had trouble enough becoming what I already am, by nature. I don't want to go to the Canaries with you. I need my wife."

He sat with his big arms crossed and his face devoid of expression while the smudgepot sent silky, oily curls into the sea freshness of morning. The early red was still on the water from the east fringe of the sky. I kept glancing toward the horizon.

"I assure you I don't think your answer is frivolous," he said. "I think it is sincere, but it is minor. Life has a much greater scale. I'm sure you will agree with me later on, after we have worked and discussed, in the islands. Which I understand are charming."

"We may be passing a hundred miles to the north or the south and never see those islands at all," I said. "You want to put it over on me that you're such a great scientist you can steer by the power of your brain. Well, go ahead, but I'm getting rescued if I can."

"It is my conviction that we may see land at any time," he said. "So why don't you extinguish that smudge?"

"No, I won't!" I shouted. "No, and that's final!" The fellow was really out of his mind. But even then, in anger, I thought, what if he really was a genius too, and I was lacking in faith.

He said quietly, "Okay."

I turned to give my full attention to the horizon, when suddenly a heavy blow descended on me and knocked me flat. He had clobbered me with the oar. He was getting ready to hit me again, with the loom this time, having hit me with the blade before. That Moses, Savior and Messiah! He raised up on his heavy legs. More of a look of a task to be done than lust was on his face. I tried to roll away from this blow and I yelled, "For Chrissake, don't kill me!"

Then I made a rush for him, and the minute I got my hands on him I felt I'd kill him if I could, that much rage was in me. I wanted to strangle him. He dropped the oar and gripped me round the ribs. The way he grabbed me I couldn't use my arms. I butted and kicked while he put on more pressure, till I couldn't breathe.

He was a maniac.

And a murderer.

Two demented land creatures struggling on the vast water, head to head, putting out all the strength they had. I would certainly have killed him then if I'd been able. But he was the stronger man. He threw his immense weight on me, he was heavy as brass, and I fell over a thwart with my face on the cleats of the bottom.

I made ready for the end.

The powers of the universe should take me back as they had sent me forth.

Death!

But he didn't mean to murder me. He was tearing my clothes off and binding me with them. He twisted the shirt into bonds for my wrists. My pants he tied my legs with. Then he tore off my skivvies to wipe the blood from my face and the sweat from his. He yanked the painter off and reinforced my bonds.

Then he doused the smudgepot, and he stepped up the oar again with its piece of canvas and sat looking eastward for the shore he was so sure of while I lay naked and gasping, still on my side as he had left me.

Later he picked me up and set me down under the tarpaulin because the sun was burning on me. When he laid hands on me I flinched and heaved. "Anything busted?" he said, doctorlike, and felt my person, my ribs and shoulders. I cursed him till my throat was raw.

When it came time to eat he fed me; and he said, "Better let me know when you have to go to bathroom, otherwise there'll be a problem."

I said, "If you untie me, I give my word of honor I won't send any signals."

"I can't take chances with you," he said. "This is too important."

Once in a while he'd chafe the arms and legs to help my circulation.

I begged him now. I said, "I'll get gangrene."

But no, he told me; I had made my choice. Besides, he said, we'd hit those happy isles soon. Late in the afternoon he declared he could smell the land breeze. He also said, "It's getting hotter," and took to shading his eyes. And when evening came on he stretched out. He did it with heaviness, and, while I watched and wished him the worst, stretched out those doughty big legs and that bowl of tireless contemplations from which the instructions had come to lam me and leave me tied for the night, and which might direct him to do worse yet.

The moon shone, a damp fell, and the boat crept; it scarcely budged on the water. I wore out my wrists trying to pull free, and then I thought that if I could crawl that far I might find a corner of the metal locker on which I could saw myself free. I turned on my back and began to work toward it, using my heels. Basteshaw didn't wake. He lay like that great painted mummy case, his feet cocked out and his head like stone.

He had made a big welt on my back, and this I scraped as I crawled, and I had to stop and take it out on my lip with my teeth. It didn't seem any use. Terrible deep sorrow came on me, and I wept to myself. So as not to wake him.

It took me half the night to reach the locker and work my hands loose. But finally the shirt tore off and I flaked away at the painter, soaking it to make it expand. At last it came off. I crouched there and licked my raw wrists. My back was flaming from the beating it had taken, but there was one cool place in my body, which was where I kept murder in my heart toward Basteshaw. I crept over to him; I didn't stand up because he might wake and see me standing in the moonlight. I had my choice now of pushing him in the water, of strangling him, of beating him with the oar as he had done me, of breaking his bones and seeing his blood.

I decided as the first step to tie him and take off his goggles. Then we'd see.

Well, as I stood poised over him on my toes, full of revenge, holding the painter, I felt heat rising off him. I lightly touched his cheek. The guy was burning up with fever. I listened to his heart. Some kind of gunnery seemed to be going on there, hollow and terrible.

I was gypped of revenge. For as a matter of course I took care of him. I cut a hole in a piece of canvas to make myself a poncho, my other clothes being ripped to tatters, and I sat up with him all night.

Like Henry Ware of the Kentucky border and the great chief of the Ohio, Timmendiquas. He might have stabbed Timmendiquas but he let him go.

I felt sorrow and pity for him too. I realized how much he was barren of, or trying to be barren of in order to become the man of his ideas. Didn't he, even if mainly from his head rather than from his heart, want to bring about redemption and rescue the whole brotherhood of man from suffering?

He was off his rocker all the next day. It would have been the end of him if I hadn't sighted and signaled a British tanker late that day. It would have been the end of me too, for it turned out that we were way past the Canaries and somewhere off the Rio de Oro. This scientist Basteshaw! Why, he was cuckoo! Why, we'd both have rotted in that African sea, and the boat would have rotted, and there would have been nothing but death and mad ideas to the last. Or he'd have murdered and eaten me, still calm and utterly reasonable, and gone on steering to his goal.

Anyway, they dragged us aboard, both in a bad way. Naples was the first port this Limey ship made. There the authorities stuck us in a hospital. And it was a few weeks before I was afoot again, and I met Basteshaw in the corridor in a bathrobe, coming along slowly. He seemed himself again, confident and proud-headed. But he was decidedly cool to me. I could see he was blaming me for frustrating his great plan. Now he'd have to ship again. No Canaries. His research, so essential to human survival itself—that was no small thing to postpone.

"Do you realize," I said, driving it home, still indignant at what might have happened, "that you missed, you great navigator? I might never have seen my wife again if I had listened to you."

He heard me out and meanwhile took my measure. He said, "The power of an individual to act through his intellect on the reason of mankind is smaller now than ever."

"Go ahead! Save mankind!" I said. "But don't forget if you had your way you'd be dead now."

He wouldn't talk to me after that, and I didn't care. We snubbed each other in the corridor. All I thought about was Stella anyhow.

It was six months before I saw New York again, for they found one reason after another to detain me at the hospital.

So it was a night in September when the taxi let me off at Stella's door, which now also was mine, and she came running down the stairs to me.

Chapter XXVI

IF I COULD have come back and started to lead a happy, peaceful life I think very few people would have the right to complain that I wasn't ready yet or hadn't paid the admission price that's set by whoever sets prices. Guys like the broken-down Cossack of the Mexican mountains and other spokesmen would at least have to agree that I had a breather coming. Nevertheless I had almost none. It probably is too much to ask.

I said when I started to make the record that I would be plain and heed the knocks as they came, and also that a man's character was his fate. Well, then it is obvious that this fate, or what he settles for, is also his character. And since I never have had any place of rest, it should follow that I have trouble being still, and furthermore my hope is based upon getting to be still so that the axial lines can be found. When striving stops, the truth comes as a gift—bounty, harmony, love, and so forth. Maybe I can't take these very things I want.

Once I said to Mintouchian when we were discussing this, "Wherever I stay it has always been on somebody's hospitality. First on old Grandma—it was really her house. Then those people in Evanston, the Renlings, then this Casa Descuitada in Mexico, and with Mr. Paslavitch the Yugoslavian."

"Some people, if they didn't make it hard for themselves, might fall asleep," said Mintouchian. "Even the Son of Man made it hard so He would have enough in common with our race to be its God."

"I had this idea of an academy foster-home or something like that."

"It could never work. Excuse me, but it's a ridiculous idea. Of course some ridiculous ideas do work, but yours wouldn't, having so many children to take care of. You're not the type, and Stella even less."

"Oh, I know it was a goofy idea that I should educate children. Who am I to educate anybody? It wasn't so much education as love. That was the idea. What I wanted was to have somebody living with *me* for a change, instead of the other way around."

*

I always denied that I was the only creature of my kind. But how seldom two imaginations coincide! That's because they are ambitious imaginations, both. If they meant to be satisfied, then they would coincide.

I saw one thing and Stella another when we thought about matters like this academy and foster-home. What I had in my mind was this private green place like one of those Walden or Innisfree wattle jobs under the kind sun, surrounded by velvet woods and bright gardens and Elysium lawns sown with Lincoln Park grass seed. However, we are meant to be carried away by the complex and hear the simple like the far horn of Roland when he and Oliver are being wiped out by the Saracens. I told Stella I was keen about beekeeping. Hell, I thought, I had got along with an eagle, why not get along with different winged creatures and there be honey instead? So she bought me a book on beekeeping and I took it out with me on my second voyage. But I already knew what she thought the academy would look like: a beaten-up frame house of dead-drunk jerry-builders under dusty laborious trees, laundry boiling in the yard, pinched chickens of misfortune, rioting kids, my blind mother wearing my old shoes and George cobblering, me with a crate of bees in the woods.

At first Stella said it was a lovely idea, but what else was she going to say in the emotions of reunion when I told her how the ship went down, and the rest. She cried, holding on to me, and her tears fell on my chest, almost spurted. "Oh, Augie," she said, "the things that happen to you! Poor Augie!" We were in bed. I saw her round smooth back by the Italian mirror, a big circular one that hung over the mantel. "Well, to hell with this war and falling in the water and all of that," I said. "I want to get this place where we can have a settled life."

"Oh yes," she said. But at that time what else could she say?

However, I didn't have the least idea of how to go about it. And of course it was only one of those bubble-headed dreams of people who haven't yet realized what they're like nor what they're intended for.

Pretty soon I understood that I would mostly do as she wanted because it was I who loved her most. What it was that

she wanted wasn't clear for a time. You see, there was all the
immenso giubbilo of homecoming and being saved from the
sea and this Basteshaw, a romantic survivor and escapee; it
was appropriate there should be cries of Thanksgiving as if
written down by Franz Joseph Haydn and sung by the Schola
Cantorum, and so on. And after all Stella did love me, and we
had a honeymoon still to catch up on. So if sometimes I saw
she was preoccupied I considered that probably her preoccupations were with me. That was the intelligent thing to consider. Yet it wasn't really I who absorbed her most. What do
you think it is, to drag people from their preoccupations,
where they do their habitual toil! At first you wouldn't think
anything in such a connection with a woman who looks as she
does, with those endowments, not light but solid, her body
rising toward a delicate head with feathery dark bangs.
Around some people the space is their space, and when you
want to approach them it has to be across their territory so
that how you are to behave to them is mainly under their
control, and then it is always astonishing to learn that they
suffer, and perhaps worse than others, from their predomi-
nant ideas. Now my foster-home and academy dream was not
a preoccupation but one of those featherhead millenarian notions or summer butterflies. You should never try to cook
such butterflies in lard. So to speak. Other preoccupations are
my fate, or what fills life and thought. Among them, preoccupation with Stella, so that what happens to her happens, by
necessity, to me too.

Guys may very likely think, Why hell! What's this talk
about fates? and will feel it all comes to me from another day,
and a mistaken day, when there were fewer people in the
world and there was more room between them so that they
grew not like wild grass but like trees in a park, well set apart
and developing year by year in the rosy light. Now instead of
such comparison you think, Let's see it instead not even as
the grass but as a band of particles, a universal shawl of them,
and these particles may have functions but certainly lack fates.
And there's even an attitude of mind which finds it almost
disgusting to be a person and not a function. Nevertheless I
stand by my idea of a fate. For which a function is a substitution of a deeper despair.

Not long ago I was in Florence, Italy. Stella and I are in Europe now and have been since the end of the war. She wanted to come for professional reasons, and I'm in a kind of business I'll soon tell about. Anyway, I was in Florence; I travel all over; a few days before I had been in Sicily where it was warm. Here it was freezing when I arrived; when I came out of the station the mountain stars were barking. The wind called the Tramontana was pouring in. In the morning when I woke, in the Hotel Porta Rossa, just behind the Arno, I felt cold. The maid brought coffee, which warmed me some. Some light shell of old metal in a church tower rung in the swift glossy rush of the free-sight mountain air. I washed with hot water, splashing the wooden floor. It was a comfort on an icy day to go out in a rubbed body, wrapped in a warm coat.

I asked the clerk, "What's a good thing to see that I can go out and see in an hour? I have an appointment at noon."

I knew this was a very American question, but it happened to be the truth.

I won't conceal what the appointment was about. I was acting for Mintouchian in a piece of business and had to contact a man who was arranging to obtain an Italian import license for us so we could unload Army surplus goods bought cheap in Germany. Vitamin pills especially, and other pharmaceutical goods. Mintouchian knew all about this type of speculation and we were making a lot of dough. There was this Florentine uncle of a Rome bigshot I had to pay off, and he was one of these civilized personalities with about five motives to my one. However, I have got the hang of dealing with them by now, and when in doubt I talk to Mintouchian on the transatlantic phone and he tells me what to do.

The clerk at the Porta Rossa said, "You can see the gold doors of the Baptistery with the sculptures of Ghiberti."

I recollected that that lunatic Basteshaw had spoken of this Ghiberti and so I followed the man's directions to the Piazza del Duomo.

Horses were shivering from the cutting wind. Down the cold alleys flames tore from the salamander cans of the people selling chestnuts far in the stone angles of walls and cobblestones.

There were not many people by the Baptistery, due to this cold, only a few huddlers with teary eyes who offered souvenirs for sale and were flapping packs of postcards hinged together. I went and looked into the gold panels telling the entire history of humankind. As I stared and these gold heads of our supposedly common fathers and mothers burned in the sun while they told once and for all what they were, an old lady came up to explain what they represented, and she began to tell me the story of Joseph, of Jacob wrestling with the Angel, about the flight from Egypt and about the Twelve Apostles. She got everything balled up, for they're not well up on the Bible in Latin countries. And I wanted to be let alone and moved away, but she followed. She carried a stick down which her pocketbook was sliding by the handle and she wore a veil. At last I looked at her face beneath the veil, this aged face of a great lady covered by mange spots and with tarry blemishes on her lips. The fur of her coat was used up and the bald hide broken and crustlike. What she had to say to me was, "Now I'll tell you about these gates. You're an American, aren't you? I'll help you, because you'll never understand things like these without help. I knew many Americans during the war."

"You're not an Italian, are you?" I said. She had a German sort of accent.

"I'm a Piedmontese," she answered. "Many people tell me I don't speak English like an Italian. I'm not a Nazi, if that's what you're driving at. I'd tell you my name if you knew something about distinguished names, but you probably don't, so why should I pronounce it?"

"You're absolutely right. You shouldn't have to tell strangers your name."

I walked on, with my face stung by the Tramontana, and applied myself again to the sculptures of the gate.

She was after me again on her sprawl feet, but quick.

"I don't want a guide," I said, and I took some dough out of my pocket and gave her a hundred lire.

"What is this?" she said.

"What do you mean? It's money."

"*What* are you giving me? Do you know I have to stay in a convent in the mountains with the nuns and that they put me in a room with fourteen other women? All sorts of women? I have to sleep with fourteen other people. And I have to walk into the city because the Sisters won't give us the bus fare."

"Do they want you to stay up there?"

"The nuns are not very intelligent," she said. She wasn't able to stay up there and do dull tasks and escaped into town. She was full of rebellion. But her bones were showing through, her teeth were mixed up, her veil didn't quite hide the quavery hairs of her chin and mouth, this unfunny joke on former lady smoothness.

I wanted to look at the doors and thought, Why can't they let you alone in this country?

"This is Isaac going to his own sacrifice," she said.

I looked, and doubted if that could be right. I said to her, "I don't want a guide. I understand how it is, but what do you want me to do? People are coming up to me all the time. So why don't you please take this money and—" I was beginning to be in pain over it.

"People! But I am not other people. You should realize that. I am—" and she was voice-stopped, she was so angry. "This is happening to *me*!" she said. She seemed to crowd her heart with her elbow and came up close and started it again, that queer begging and demanding.

O destroying laws!

What was the matter, hadn't this thing taken long enough, wasn't it gradual enough? I mean, the wrinkles coming, the gray choking out the black, the skin slackening and sinews getting stringy? Did she still have fresh in her mind the villa she had lost, the husband or lovers, the children, the carpets and piano, the servants and money? What was the matter that she still was as if in the first pain of a deep fall?

I gave her another hundred lire.

"Give me five hundred and I'll show you the cathedral and I'll take you to Santa Maria Novella. It's not far, and you won't know anything if someone doesn't tell you."

"As a matter of fact, I have to meet a man right away on business. Thanks just the same."

I took off. I might as well have, since Ghiberti didn't have much of a spell over me anyhow just then.

This ancient lady was right too, and there always is a *me* it happens to. Death is going to take the boundaries away from us, that we should no more be persons. That's what death is about. When that is what life also wants to be about, how can you feel except rebellious?

Yes, Europe is where Stella and I went after I made three other voyages in the war.

I have written out these memoirs of mine since, as a traveling man, traveling by myself, I have lots of time on my hands. For a couple of months last year I had to be in Rome. It was summer, and the place broke out in red flowers, hot and sleepy. All the southern cities are sleep cities in summer, and daytime sleep makes me heavy and tasteless to myself. To wake up in the afternoon I would drink coffee and smoke cigars, and by the time I came to myself after the siesta it was well-nigh evening. You have dinner, and it's soft nerveless green night with quiet gas mantles in the street going on incandescent and making a long throbbing scratch in the utter night. Time to sleep again, so you go and subside thickly on the bed.

Therefore I got into the habit of going every afternoon to the Café Valadier in the Borghese Gardens on top of the Pincio, with the whole cumulous Rome underneath, where I sat at a table and declared that I was an American, Chicago born, and all these other events and notions. Said not in order to be so highly significant but probably because human beings have the power to say and ought to employ it at the proper time. When finally you're done speaking you're dumb forever after, and when you're through stirring you go still, but this is no reason to decline to speak and stir or to be what you are.

I try most of the time to be in Paris because that's where Stella works. She's with a film company that does international movies. We have an apartment on Rue François Ier, a pretty fancy section near the Hôtel Georges V. It's the ornamental and luxury quarter, but the joint Stella and I rented was terrible. It belonged to an old Britisher and his French wife. They took off for Mentone to live off the high rent they soaked us, and here all winter the rain and fog never let up. I'd pass days trying to get used to this moldy though fancied-up apartment, somewhat obstinate, seeing that it was now my place. But there was no getting anywhere with the carpets and chairs, the lamps that looked as if grown on Coney Island, cat-house pictures, alabaster owls with electric eyes, books of Ouida and Marie Corelli in leather binding, smelling like spit. The old crook of a Britisher who was the *locataire* had something he called a study, which was a sort of closet with a nasty piece of carpet, a set of Larousse's encyclopedia from way back, and a green table. The drawers of this green felt table were full of pieces of paper covered with figures on conversion of pounds and francs, dollars, pesetas, schillings, marks, escudos, piasters, and even rubles. This old man, Ryehurst, practically dead, sat here in a suit like for burial, purple flannel without lapels or buttons or buttonholes, and he calculated about money and wrote letters to the papers on the Fall of France and how to get the peasants' gold out of hiding, or which passes to Italy were the best for motorists. In his youth he had broken the speed record from Turin to London. There was a photo of him in his racer. A little Irish terrier sat in the cockpit with him.

The front rooms were bad enough, but the dining room was too much for me. Stella would leave early to be on the lot, and even though there was a *bonne à tout faire* to fix my breakfast I couldn't always bring myself to sit down at the yellow red-embroidered Turkestan cloth for my coffee.

So I would go out to a little café for breakfast, and here one day I ran into my old friend Hooker Frazer. At this café, the Roseraie, which was a jazzy kind of place, there were round tables, wicker chairs, palms in brass tubs, candy-striped fiber carpet, red and white awnings, steam of a huge coffee machine of hundreds of gimmicks, cakes in cellophane, and all that kind of stuff. After I set up the coal stoves—this maid, Jacqueline, was very nice but she didn't know a thing about getting coal to catch; I was an expert from way back—I'd go to breakfast. Thus one morning I was ordering coffee at the Roseraie. Old folks in slippers, as if in their own lace-veined parlors, walked in the street, with horsemeat and strawberries, etcetera, coming from the market on Place de l'Alma. All at once Frazer came by. I hadn't seen him since my wedding day.

"Frazer, hey!"

"Augie!"

"What brings you to Paris, old pal?"

"How are you? Same healthy color as always, and smiling away! Why, I'm working with the World Educational Fund. I think I've seen everyone I ever knew here during this past year. But what a surprise to run across you, Augie, in the City of Man!"

He was feeling very grand, the place inspired him, and he sat down and gave me a sort of talk—pretty amazing!—about Paris and how nothing like it existed, the capital of the hope that Man could be free without the help of gods, clear of mind, civilized, wise, pleasant, and all of that. For a minute I felt rather insulted that he should laugh when he asked me what I was doing here. It might be incongruous, but if it was for Man why shouldn't it be for me too? If it wasn't, perhaps that wasn't one hundred per cent my fault. Which Man was it the City of? Some version again. It's always some version or other.

But who could complain of this pert, pretty Paris when it revolved like a merry-go-round—the gold bridge-horses, the Greek Tuileries heroes and stone beauties, the overloaded Opéra, the racy show windows and dapper colors, the may-pole obelisk, the all-colors ice-cream, the gaudy package of the world.

I don't suppose Frazer meant to hurt my feelings; he was merely surprised to see me here.

"I've been over since the end of the war," I said.

"Is that so? What doing?"

"I'm connected in business with that Armenian lawyer you met at my wedding. Remember?"

"Oh, of course, you're married. Is your wife here with you?"

"Naturally. She works in pictures. Maybe you've seen her in *Les Orphelines*. It's about displaced persons."

"No, as a matter of fact I don't see many movies. But I'm not surprised to hear she's an actress. She's very beautiful, you know. How are things working out?"

"I love her," I said.

As if that was an answer! But how can you blame me if I was unwilling to say more to Frazer? Suppose I started to explain that she loved me too, but loved me in the same way that Paris is the City of Man, or with what she brought to it, given her preoccupations—love being the victory of love over preoccupations, or what Mintouchian called dominant ideas that afternoon in the Turkish bath. I wasn't going to go into all this with Frazer. When I took it up with Stella, and once in a while I did, or tried to, I seemed to sound like a fanatic, and maybe sounded to her as other people had to me, sounding off about their idea that they were trying to sell or to recruit you for. This made her a mirror, like, where I could see my own obstinacy of yore and how it must have looked when I balked. She was right when we took cover in the garden of the Japanese villa in Acatla and she observed that we were very similar. So we are.

However, even if I am not the honestest type in the world I don't want to lie more than is average. Stella does. Of course you can call it lying or you can call it protection of your vision. I think I prefer the second description. Stella looks happy and firm and wants me to look the same. She sits down by the bird-breasted stove in the salon, on the chair the old English gent Ryehurst warned me—having damages in mind—was a genuine Chippendale, and she's calm, intelligent, forceful, vital, tremendously handsome, and this is how she wants to put herself across. It's the vision. Naturally it often takes me a while to know where we're really at. She talks about happenings at the studio and laughs with her clear, bosomy voice about the jokes of the day. And what have I been doing? Well, perhaps I had a meeting with a person who used to be in Dachau and did some business with him in dental supplies from Germany. That took an hour or two. After which I may have gone to the cold halls of the Louvre and visited in the Dutch School, or noticed how the Seine smelled like medicine, or went into a café and wrote a letter, and so passed the day.

She sits and listens with crossed legs under the batik house-wrap she wears, with her heavy three-way-piled hair and cigarette at her mouth and refuses me—for the time being, anyway—the most important things I ask of her.

It's really kind of tremendous how it all takes place. You'd never guess how much labor goes into it. Only some time ago it occurred to me how great an amount. She came back from the studio and went to take a bath, and from the bath she called out to me, "Darling, please bring me a towel." I took

one of those towel robes that I had bought at the Bon
Marché department store and came along with it. The little
bathroom was in twilight. In the *chauffe-eau* machine, the
brass box with teeth of gas burning, the green metal dropped
crumbs inside from the thousand-candle blaze. Her body
with its warm woman's smell was covered with water starting
in a calm line over her breasts. The glass of the medicine chest
shone like a deep blue place in the wall, as if a window to the
evening sea and not the ashy fog of Paris. I sat down with the
robe over my shoulder and felt very much at peace. For a
change the apartment seemed clean and was warm; the abominations were gone into the background, the stoves drew well
and they shone. Jacqueline was cooking dinner and it smelled
of gravy. I felt settled and easy, my chest free and my fingers
comfortable and open. And now here's the thing. It takes a
time like this for you to find out how sore your heart has
been, and moreover, all the while you thought you were
going around idle terribly hard work was taking place. Hard,
hard work, excavation and digging, mining, moling through
tunnels, heaving, pushing, moving rock, working, working,
working, working, working, panting, hauling, hoisting. And
none of this work is seen from the outside. It's internally
done. It happens because you are powerless and unable to get
anywhere, to obtain justice or have requital, and therefore in
yourself you labor, you wage and combat, settle scores, remember insults, fight, reply, deny, blab, denounce, triumph,
outwit, overcome, vindicate, cry, persist, absolve, die and rise
again. All by yourself! Where is everybody? Inside your breast
and skin, the entire cast.

Lying in the bath, Stella was performing labor. It was obvious to me. And generally I was doing hard work too. And
what for?

Everybody gives me a line about Paris being a place of ease
and mentions *calme, ordre, luxe, et volupté*, and yet there is
this toil being done. Every precious personality framed dra-
matically and doing the indispensable work. If Stella weren't
bound to do her hardest work we wouldn't be in this city of
calm and luxury, so called. The clothes, the night clubs and
entertainment, the supposed play of the studio and the friendship of the artists—who strike me as being characters of pretty

high stomach, like our buddy Alain du Niveau—there's nothing easy in it. I'll tell you about this du Niveau. He's what the Parisians call a *noceur*, meaning that it's always the wedding night for him or that he plays musical beds. That's just about the least of it.

Anyway, I would have preferred to stay in the States and have children. Instead I'm in the bondage of strangeness for a time still. It's only temporary. We'll get out of it.

I said that Stella lied more than average, unfortunately. She told me a number of things that weren't so; she forgot to tell me others that were so. For instance, she said she was getting money from her dad in Jamaica. There was no such party in Jamaica. She had never gone to college either. And she had never cared anything about Oliver. He wasn't the important man. The important one was a big operator whose name was Cumberland. It wasn't she who first told me about him. I found out from someone else that there was such a man. And then she told me that this Cumberland was a crook. Of morals, that is; in business he was not only respectable but great. In fact he was one of these powerful characters whose pictures don't even get into the papers because they're too strong to be named. And gradually this man, with whom she had taken up while still a high-school girl, built up to be about like Jupiter-Ammon, with an eye like that new telescope out at the Mount Palomar observatory, about as wicked as Tiberius, a czar and mastermind. To tell the truth, I'm good and tired of all these big personalities, destiny molders, and heavy-water brains, Machiavellis and wizard evildoers, big-wheels and imposers-upon, absolutists. After Basteshaw clobbered me I took an oath of unsusceptibility. But this oath is probably a mice-and-man matter, for here the specter of one of this breed was over me. Brother! You never are through, you just think you are!

The first I heard about this Cumberland was from Alain du Niveau, who was in New York during the war, in the movie industry. Mintouchian knew him, and Agnes. He was originally a friend of Agnes. When we met he told me he was a descendant of the Duc de Saint-Simon. I'm always a sucker for lineage, but this du Niveau didn't really look very good. He had blue whiskyish eyes in his tight-packed heavy face with its color of bad good-health. Although he probably meant no harm by it he had a very insolent expression. Thin and sandy, his hair was combed like a British officer's, neat and bleak. His shoes were fleece-lined; his long overcoat was all beautiful suede, down to the ankles; his body was thick. He was a chaser and wolf after girls on the subway. He'd tell you himself how he picked up women, and as he described it these poor weak birdies when he got them alone were like confronted by a fiery god, etcetera.

When he mentioned Cumberland to me we were in the lobby of the Paramount Theatre waiting for Stella. Oliver's name came up, and du Niveau said, "He's still in jail."

"Did you know the guy?" I said.

"Yes. And what a comedown for her after Cumberland. I knew him too."

"Who?"

He didn't realize what he had said. He hardly ever did. I felt as if I had been trapped in a shaft by a sudden fall of dirt. Terrible despair, rage, jealousy, burst out in me.

"Who? What Cumberland?"

Then he looked at me and realized that for some reason my eyes were burning and I was in pain. I think he was very surprised and tried to remove himself with dignity from this trouble.

Actually I had been aware for some time of something peculiar that would sooner or later have to be explained. People were dunning Stella constantly. There was trouble about a car. She didn't own a car. And there was litigation about an apartment uptown. What sort of apartment had she had uptown? And as it would have been inhuman not to mention it, I guess, she had told me about a seventy-five-hundred-dollar mink coat she had had to sell, and a diamond necklace. Business envelopes came in the mail which she wouldn't open. There's something about those business envelopes with the transparent oblong address part that my soul runs away from.

And then, was I supposed to overlook what Mintouchian had said to me in the Turkish bath? How could I?

"Who is this Cumberland?" I said.

Just then Stella came down from the ladies' lounge and I took her arm and hurried her out to a cab. We tore back to the apartment and I blew my top. "I should have known there was something dishonest!" I yelled at her. "Who is this Cumberland?"

"Augie! Don't carry on," she said, pale. "I should have told you. But what difference does it make? It proves that I love you and didn't want to lose you by telling you."

"He was the one that gave you the coat?"

"Yes, darling. But I married you, not him."

"And the car?"

"It was a present, honey. But, sweetheart, it's you I love."

"And all the things in the house?"

"The furniture? Why, it's just stuff. It's only you that matters."

Gradually she calmed me.

"When was the last time you saw him?"

"I haven't had a thing to do with him for two years."

"I can't stand these fellows being brought up," I said. "I can't take it. There shouldn't be these secret things jumping out."

"But after all," she cried, "it was rougher on me. I was the one that actually suffered from him. All you suffer from is hearing about it."

Now that the subject was open it became very hard to put an end to. She wanted to talk about it. To prove that I had no reason to be jealous she had to tell me every last thing that had happened, and I couldn't stop her—a gallant, active flashing temperament like that, you see, you can't control her easily.

"What a dog!" she said. "What a coward! He didn't have a single human feeling. He mainly wanted me to help him entertain his business friends and show off because he was ashamed of his wife."

It didn't absolutely square with her attitude toward the things she had enjoyed, like the summer house in New Jersey, the charge accounts, and the Mercedes-Benz automobile, which was an extremely hardheaded attitude. She was very well informed about the tax situation and the insurance and so on. Of course it's nothing against a woman that she should understand these things. Why shouldn't she understand them? But I was afraid I'd have to give up on an ideal explanation of her past life. Oh well, there didn't have to be one necessarily.

"He wouldn't let me be independent. If he found out I had a savings account he made me spend the money. He thought I should be helpless. Once the president of a lumber company whom I knew was going to open a big gambling joint on Long Island and offered me fifteen thousand a year to be hostess. Cumberland was furious about it when he heard."

"He found out everything?"

"He hired detectives. You have a lot to learn about such people. He'd rent the moon if he had any use for it."

"I already have learned all I want to learn."

"Oh, Augie! Please, honey, remember that you made mistakes too. You went to smuggle immigrants from Canada. You stole. A lot of people led you astray also."

Okay, but why couldn't she be satisfied that I loved her and stop this talk? What did she mean, about the lumberman? Had she really intended to become a hostess? I would meditate over all this and sit there feeling terrible. The very arms of the chair seemed about to stab me through the sides, and the playful flowery Bavarian bed and the knickknacks and stuffed orioles, and all were a drag on me. Was I going to be wrong *again*? It was the thought I had in the boat when I was adrift with Basteshaw that I had been wrong again and again.

Nevertheless I believed we would make it, finally. I don't want to give a false impression of one hundred per cent desperation. It is not like that. I don't know who this saint was who woke up, lifted his face, opened his mouth, and reported on his secret dream that blessedness covers the whole Creation but covers it thicker in some places than in others. Whoever he was, it's my great weakness to respond to such dreams. This is the *amor fati*, that's what it is, or mysterious adoration of what occurs.

There is a certain amount of simple-mindedness in Stella as well as deception, a sort of naïve seriousness. She cries very sincerely and with utmost warmth. But it's not a simple matter to get her to change her mind on any matter. I've tried, for instance, to get her to wear her nails shorter; she grows them very long, and when they tear they tear into the quick and she starts to cry. Then I say, "Good heavens, why do you

984 THE ADVENTURES OF AUGIE MARCH

let them grow like that!" and take the scissors and trim them, which she submits to. However, she only lets them grow long again. Or, in the case of the cat, Ginger, who's very spoiled and wakes you up at night by turning over lamps and dishes so that you'll feed him, I only made myself look foolish arguing that he ought to be shut in the kitchen at night. I couldn't get anywhere.

She'd repeat continually how she had wanted to be independent.

"Naturally. Who doesn't want that?"

"No, I mean I wanted to do something that was my own idea. It wasn't just a matter of money." He *oppressed* her, that was what, practically with wrung hands, she had to put across to me. "Every time he promised to let me do something he'd go back on his word. So finally I made a break and went to California. I knew someone there who once offered me a screen test. I took a wonderful test and got a part in a musical. But when the picture was released all my lines were cut out. I looked like such a fool, just smiling and getting ready to say something, and I never said it. After the preview I was sick. He used his influence to make the producer do it. I sent him a wire and told him I was through for good. Next day I had an attack of appendicitis and went to the hospital, and in about twenty-four hours he showed up by my bedside. I said to him, 'What excuse did you give your wife for this trip!' I was done with him forever."

I always wince when I hear husbands and wives talking to each other about past marriages and affairs. I'm unusually sensitive in this respect.

Of course I knew this was Stella's hard work. She wasn't done suffering from it, not by a long shot. She had to harrow his memory over and over, and in so doing she dug me up considerably too.

"All right, Stella, now, please," I said at last.

"All right *what?*" she said, angry. "Am I supposed not to talk about it at all, ever?"

"But you talk about it all the time, and you talk about him more than anyone else."

"Because I hate him. I'm still in debt because of all these obligations that were his fault."

"We'll get rid of them."

"How?"

"I don't know yet. I'll take it up with Mintouchian."

She didn't want me to do that. She was seriously opposed, but I went to see him all the same.

He already knew all about Cumberland, which isn't in the least surprising. We talked it over in his office on Fifth Avenue. "Since you bring it up," he said, "excuse me, but she's been a nuisance to him. He was unfair to her, but he's an older fellow now and the whole thing is over. It's difficult for his family. His son is now head of the firm and he says she won't get anywhere by threatening them. She wouldn't have much coming legally."

"Threatening? What threat? You mean to say she's bothering him? Why, she told me she hasn't had anything to do with him for two years!"

"Well, she hasn't told you the truth—strictly speaking."

I was overthrown by this; I was very ashamed. How are you supposed to proceed? If you don't defend yourself you can get murdered, and if you do defend yourself you're liable to die of that too.

"I'm afraid she's impatient to go to law," said Mintouchian. "She's very restless."

I said to Stella, "You've got to quit this. There isn't going to be any lawsuit. You always know where this man is and what he's doing. You haven't told me the truth. It has to stop immediately. I have to ship again in a week and I don't want to be mulling it over for months and months. If you won't promise to stop I can't come back."

She gave in. She cried with bitterness that I threatened her, but she promised. She has a warm, easily coloring face, Stella. When she starts to cry the pink of it begins to darken and darkens up into her eyes, which seemed so amorous the first time I saw them in Acatla. Her features rise very slightly from the surface of her face, as if she had a Javanese or Sumatran inheritance. I sat both hurt and comforted as she wept. Crying is further stubbornness with some women, but with Stella it's the truthful moment. She knew she shouldn't talk so much about the old man, she confessed, and try to make him take all the blame.

So I sailed in a better frame of mind, and this was when she bought me a book on bee culture. I studied it with devotion and learned a lot about bees and honey, which I knew, however, wouldn't likely be of any practical use.

Of course the whole movie enterprise is to show Cumberland that she could make the grade independently. She doesn't have any terrific talent for acting, but that's how it appears to go. People don't do what they have a talent for but what the preoccupation leads to. If they're good at auto-repairing they have to sing Don Giovanni; if they can sing they have to be architects; and if they have a gift for architecture they wish to become school superintendents or abstract painters or anything else. *Anything!* It's a spite. It's having to prove full and ultimate self-sufficiency or some such monster dream that you don't need anyone else to do these things for you.

Well, Stella is in du Niveau's film company, and I am in illicit dealing—to discriminate against myself, more than half the business of Europe being the same. It is indeed cockeyed. But there is nothing I can do about it. It must be clear, however, that I am a person of hope, and now my hopes have settled themselves upon children and a settled life. I haven't been able to convince Stella as yet. Therefore while I knock around on *rapides* over falling horizons, over Alps, in steam and haste, or blast the air in my black Citroën, smoking cigars and watching the road through polaroid glasses, it's unborn children I pore over far oftener than business deals.

I wonder if it's a phase, or what, but sometimes I feel I already am a father.

Recently in Rome a whore tried to pick me up on the Via Veneto. The circumstances were peculiar; I am a tall man and the girl who propositioned me was very small, plump, and dressed in second- or third-year mourning. A sad face. "Come with me," she said. Now let me not be a liar and say I was not in the least drawn. You always are, somewhat. However, it cost no great effort to refuse, and when I said no, she looked deeply wounded, personally, and said, "What's the matter, am I not good enough for you?" I said, "Oh, of course, *signorina*, but I'm married. I have children. *Io ho bambini.*" So she was overwhelmed entirely and said, "I'm very sorry, I didn't know you had children," and she was about to cry over this error. To have been perfectly fair I should have explained this to her, that it was hokum and that I just had an impulse. But let me say that I am aware where this deception of *bambini* came from. It came from that picture of Stella's that I mentioned to Frazer, *Les Orphelines.* I had to see it several times, in the course of events, and one part of it made a deep impression on me once in the cutting room, this boarded, insulated, burlap-deadened room where it stunk of Gauloise cigarettes and high-grade perfume. The scene was one in which Stella pleaded with an Italian doctor for a woman and her baby. They had coached her on the Italian lines and so she cried out, "*Ma Maria, ed il bambino. Il bambino!*" And the doctor, who couldn't offer help, shrugged and said, "*Che posso fare! Che posso fare!*"

I saw this run over and over and was full of sorrow, almost provoked to an outburst of tears and ripe to exclaim to Stella, "Here, here, if you want something to cry out about! Right here! What do you need theoretical people for and these ghosts of emotions never of this world anyway?" The grief was about to drop down from my eyes.

It's supposed to be easier to suffer for hypothetical people too, for Hecubas. It ought to be easier than for the ones you yourself hurt, for you can see their enemies or persecutors better than you can see yourself balking someone of life or doing him wrong.

Be that as it may, this was why I imagined I already had the *bambini.*

Simon and Charlotte came to Paris and put up at the Crillon. I wished that they had brought Mama too, although it would have been probably lost on her. Something big would have to be done for her one of these days, I thought; I'd have to decide what was appropriate, and I could now swing it by myself, having the money. It satisfied Simon that I was now in business. Charlotte thought better of me also, though she wanted to know more particulars. Some chance she had of getting them out of me! I took them around to the Tour d'Argent and the Lapin Agile and Casino de Paris, The Rose Rouge and other gaiety haunts, and picked up the tab. This made Simon say proudly to Charlotte, "Well, what do you think now? My kid brother has turned out to be a regular man of the world."

Stella and I smiled across the Rose Rouge table.

Charlotte, this solid and suspecting woman in her early thirties, handsome, immovable in her opinions, was full of grudges. Whatever she had against Simon she formerly would take out on me. Now that I looked a little more substantial than I used to and seemed to have a few right ideas anyhow, she could complain about him to me. I was eager to know the score. The first week or so there was not much I could find out, because we were on the town. Du Niveau helped a lot; he made a big hit with them because of being a genuine aristocrat and the deference of flunkies to him in restaurants and night clubs and haute-couture joints. Stella helped too. "What a dish!" said Simon. "She's good for you also; she'll keep you on your toes." He meant that to provide for a beautiful woman is stabilizing; it makes a man earn money. "The only thing," said Simon, "is why you keep her in such a pigpen."

"It's hard to find apartments in this section of Paris near the Champs Elysées. Besides we're not at home much, either of us. But I aim to get a villa out at St. Cloud if we have to settle here."

"If you have to? You sound as if you didn't want to."

"Oh—it's all the same to me where I live."

Of all places, we were in the Petit Palais at a picture exhibition from the Pinacothek of Munich. These grand masterpieces were sitting on the walls. Du Niveau was along, massive, in his red suede coat and highly polished pointy shoes. Simon and he admired each other's clothes. Stella and Charlotte were wearing mink stoles, Simon a double-breasted plaid and crocodile shoes, and I a camel's-hair coat, so that we looked appropriately gorgeous to pass in one of those Italian portrait crowds of gold and jewels.

Du Niveau said, "I love pictures, but I can't stand religious subjects."

Nobody was thinking much about painting, unless it was Stella who sometimes paints. I can't explain how come we were there. Maybe nothing better was open just then.

Simon and I dropped behind for a while and I asked him, "Whatever happened to Renée?"

A heavy red color crowded his blond face—he had become very stout. He said, "Why do you have to ask me here, for the love of God!"

"We can talk, Simon. They won't overhear anything. Did she have a kid?"

"No, no, it was just a bluff. There wasn't any kid."

"But you said—"

"Never mind what I said. You asked me, and I'm telling you."

I didn't know whether or not to believe him, he was in such a rush to get rid of the subject. And how touchy he was! He didn't want to be talked about.

But at lunch, when Stella and du Niveau had gone back to the studio, Charlotte opened up. She was sitting upright in her mink and in a velour hat which suited her face because she has a very downy skin which was covered with high color. Evidently Simon's trouble with Renée had been all over the Chicago papers, and she took it for granted that I had read about it. No, I hadn't heard a thing. I was completely surprised. Simon kept his mouth shut during this, and perhaps it tormented him that I might add something which Charlotte didn't happen to know. Not me; I was silent too and didn't ask any questions. Renée had sued him and made a scandal. She claimed she had a child by him. She might have accused three other men, said Charlotte, and Charlotte knew what she was talking about you can be sure; she was a well-informed woman. If the case hadn't been thrown out of court right away she was ready with plenty of evidence. "I'd have given her a case!" she said. "The little whore!" Simon wasn't having anything to do with either of us during this conversation. He sat at the table but, as it were, we didn't have his company. "Every minute she was with him she was collecting evidence," said Charlotte. "They never stopped at a place but what she didn't take a pack of matches and write the date inside. She even had his cigar butts for evidence. And all the time it was supposed to be love. What did she love you for?" said Charlotte with a terrible sudden outburst. "Your fat belly? Your scar on your forehead? Your bald spot? It was the money. It never was anything except money." I wanted to duck as this came down; my shoulders flinched. Down it burned and beat on us. Simon nevertheless didn't seem much disturbed, only thoughtful, and continued drawing at his cigar. At no time did he answer anything. Maybe he thought that as he himself had wanted money he couldn't condemn Renée for wanting it, but he didn't say.

"Then she'd phone me and say, 'You can't have children, you should let him go, he wants a family.' 'Go on, take him away if you can,' I said to her. 'You know you can't get him because you're nothing but a little tramp. You and he are both no good.' But she got out a summons for him, and when they tried to serve it I phoned him and told him he'd better get out of town. He wouldn't leave without me. 'What've you got to be afraid of?' I said. 'It isn't your kid. It's three other guys'.' I happened to have the flu then and was supposed to stay in bed, but when he wouldn't leave alone I had to come to the airport to meet him, and it was a rainstorm. Finally we took off, and we had to make an emergency landing in Nebraska. And he said, 'I might as well get knocked off. I've wasted my life anyhow.' And what did I do, if he wasted his life? What was I there for? What was in it for me? As soon as it got bad he came running to me for protection, and I protected him. If he didn't have such an abnormal idea about being happy in the first place it wouldn't have happened. Who told him he had any business to expect all that? What right has anybody? There is no such right," she said.

In the back the musicians were smoothing their bows away over their instruments.

"Now she's married. She married one of those guys and disappeared with him somewhere . . ."

I wanted Charlotte to stop. It now was too much, flying in the rainstorm and about wasted lives, while he looked more and more indifferent, which he could do only by making himself abstract like this. I started to cough. I had a long coughing fit. Shall I explain why? Because many years ago when I was a kid and went to have my tonsils out I began to cry when the ether mask was put on me. A nurse said, "Is he crying, a big boy like that?" And another answered, "Why, no, he's brave. He's not crying, he's coughing." And when I heard that I started to cough in earnest. This is the kind of coughing it was, of great distress. It stopped the conversation. The maître d'hôtel came to see what was the matter and gave me a glass of water.

Lord! How much of this did Simon have to hear? If she didn't stop she'd turn him into stone. He'd have turned into stone long ago if it hadn't been for these Renées. What are you supposed to do, lay down your life? That's what she wanted from him and what she meant by "right." Sheer murder. If she meant that you have to die anyway and might as well do it sooner than later, it's criminal murder.

He was ashamed, stony with shame. His secrets were being told. His secrets! What did they amount to? You'd think they were as towering as the Himalayas. But all they were about was his mismanaged effort to live. To live and not die. And this was what he had to be ashamed of.

"You'd better do something for that cold," said Charlotte severely.

I love my brother very much. I never meet him again without the utmost love filling me up. He has it too, though we both seem to fight it.

"It sounds like the old whooping cough you used to have," Simon said and looked toward me once again.

Just then I thought that the worst of it for him was not to have the child.

I couldn't spend much time with Simon in Paris. Mintouchian cabled me to go to Bruges and look up a guy there who had a big nylon deal on his mind, and so I started out. I had Jacqueline the maid with me as passenger. She has folks in Normandy and was going to pay them a Christmas visit, and as she was bringing a couple of suitcases full of presents I gave her a lift.

Jacqueline was referred to Stella by du Niveau. When he first knew her she was a waitress in Vichy just after the French defeat and he was on his way out of the country. They must have become friends, and it is hard to conceive because she looks so grotesque. Though this was some time back and then she might have been seeing the last of her best days. At the outer corners Jacqueline's eyes sink down queerly. She has a large, crooked Norman nose, fair hair not in very good health, veiny temples, a long chin and a disciplinarian mouth that lipstick doesn't do a great deal to change. She is highly painted and has a sweet odor of cosmetics and cleaning fluid. Her manner is very busy. She pounds the floor very rapidly and hard as she walks, but she is a person of sweet temper, though gossipy and with all kinds of incomprehensible social ambitions. In addition to doing housework she also is employed as an *ouvreuse*, or usherette, in a movie, which is more of du Niveau's influence. Therefore she has a lot of social history to relate of the movie and the tough night life after closing time when she stops at the Coupole for a cup of coffee. She is always being offered violence, like holdup and rape, Arabs hitting her or trying to force their way into her room at night. Her hips are big and legs varicose for all that she moves so briskly, and this with her sharp face and breasts that have gone out of shape; and yet what is it that dismisses a person from desirability? I'm not the one to say. She has unkillable pride in her sensuality and adventurous spirit, and if she has these outrageous colors and parrot bite, what about it?

It was a big holiday deal when we started out. She removed some stains from my camel's-hair coat with tea, which she claimed was just the thing, and then I carried her jammed cardboard valises with their tin locks down and stowed them in the trunk of the Citroën.

It was cold; a hard cold with snowflakes. We circled the Etoile and roared off toward Rouen. I should have gone by way of Amiens, but it wasn't too much of a detour for her sake. She's a kind, grateful, and by and large docile woman. So we went at this hungry speed through Rouen and then bore north toward the channel. She was telling of Vichy in the good old days and of the celebrities she knew there. It was her cunning way of getting the conversation round to du Niveau, for she never missed a chance to discuss him with me, and what she really wanted was to warn me to be on guard, that he was unscrupulous. Not that she wasn't grateful, you understand, but she also was beholden to me and she hinted at various crimes he was guilty of. I realized that she was simply romancing about him. He represented some great ideal to her which her spirit was hungry for.

We were getting close to her destination, and I wasn't too sorry, even though it was a sad, dark day and I'd have to continue to Bruges alone. The ride by way of Dunkerque and Ostend is a terribly melancholy one through ruins and along the grim Channel water.

Only a few kilometers from her uncle's farm the Citroën's engine began to miss and finally we stalled. I picked up the hood, but a lot I know about motors. Besides, it was freezing. So we started to walk toward the farm across the fields. She was going to send her nephew to town for a mechanic when we got there. But we had a good long way to hike, three or four miles across the fields, which were brown, turfy and stiff, these fields where battles of the Hundred Years' War had been fought, where the bones of the killed English were bleached and sent back to be buried in churches, where wolves and crows had cleaned up. The cold, after a time, made you gasp. The tears were cutting tracks over Jacqueline's face, which was flaming through the make-up. I was stung and numb too, hand and foot.

"Our stomachs may freeze," she said to me after we had gone about a mile. "It is very dangerous."

"Stomach? How can the stomach freeze?"

"It can. You can be ailing for life if that happens."

"What do you do to prevent it?" I said.

"The thing to do is sing," she said, desperate in her thin Paris shoes and trying to stretch her cotton muffler over the back of her head. And she started singing some night-club song. The cold blackbirds flapped out of the woods of rusty oaks and even they must have been too cold for noise because I heard no grating from them. Only Jacqueline's poor voice which didn't appear to get far over the thin snowy pockets and furrows. "You must absolutely try to sing," she said. "Otherwise you can never be sure. Something may happen." And because I didn't want to argue with her about medical superstitions and be so right or superior wising her up about modern science I decided, finally, what the hell! I might as well sing too. The only thing I could think to sing was "La Cucaracha." I kept up La Cucaracha for a mile or two and felt more chilled than helped. Then she said, after we had both worn ourselves out trying to breathe in the harsh wind and keep up the song cure, "That wasn't French that you were singing, was it?"

I said it was a Mexican song.

At which she exclaimed, "Ah, the dream of my life is to go to Mexico!"

The dream of her life? What, not Saigon? Not Hollywood? Not Bogotá? Not Aleppo? I gave a double-take at her water-sparkling eyes and freezing, wavering, mascara-lined, goblin, earnest and disciplinarian, membranous, and yet gorgeous face, with its fairy soot of pink and that red snare of her mouth; yet feminine; yet mischievous; yet still hopefully and obstinately seductive. What would she be doing in Mexico? I tried to picture her there. How queer it was! I started to laugh loudly. And what was I doing here in the fields of Normandy? How about that?

"Have you thought of something funny, M'sieu March?" she said as she hurried with me, swinging her arms in her short jacket of leg-of-mutton sleeves.

"Very funny!"

Then she pointed. "*Vous voyez les chiens?*" The dogs of the farm had leaped a brook and were dashing for us on the brown coat of the turf, yelling and yapping. "Don't you worry about them," she said, picking up a branch. "They know me well." Sure enough they did. They bounded into the air and licked her face.

The trouble was with the spark plugs, which were soon repaired, and I cut out for Dunkerque and Ostend. Where the British were so punished the town is ruined. Quonset huts stand there on the ruins. The back of the ancient water was like wolf gray. Then on the long sand the waves crashed white; they spit themselves to pieces. I saw this specter of white anger coming from the savage gray and meanwhile shot northward, in a great hurry to get to Bruges and out of this line of white which was like eternity opening up right beside destructions of the modern world, hoary and grumbling. I thought if I could beat the dark to Bruges I'd see the green canals and ancient palaces. On a day like this I could use the comfort of it, when it was so raw. I was still chilled from the hike across the fields, but, thinking of Jacqueline and Mexico, I got to grinning again. That's the *animal ridens* in me, the laughing creature, forever rising up. What's so laughable, that a Jacqueline, for instance, as hard used as that by rough forces, will still refuse to lead a disappointed life? Or is the laugh at nature—including eternity—that it thinks it can win over us and the power of hope? Nah, nah! I think. It never will. But that probably is the joke, on one or the other, and laughing is an enigma that includes both. Look at me, going everywhere! Why, I am a sort of Columbus of those near-at-hand and believe you can come to them in this immediate *terra incognita* that spreads out in every gaze. I may well be a flop at this line of endeavor. Columbus too thought he was a flop, probably, when they sent him back in chains. Which didn't prove there was no America.

CHRONOLOGY

NOTE ON THE TEXTS

NOTES

Chronology

1915   Born Solomon Bellows in Lachine, Quebec, on June 10, fourth child of Abram Bellows and Lescha Gordin, Russian–Jewish immigrants from St. Petersburg. (The family name was changed from "Belo" on arriving in Canada in 1913. Abram Bellows was an importer of dry goods, baker, and junk-dealer. One sister, Zelda, nine years older than Bellow, and two brothers Movscha, seven years older, and Samuel, four years older, were born in Russia.)

1918   Family moves to Saint Dominique Street, in a poor area of Montreal. (Bellow will later write: "The Jewish slums of Montreal during my childhood, just after the First World War, were not too far removed from the ghettos of Poland and Russia. Life in such places was anything but ordinary.") Parents speak Russian and Yiddish; their children speak English and Yiddish at home; French is spoken on the street. Bellow later claims the Armistice parade as one of his earliest memories.

1923   Falls ill with peritonitis and pneumonia, and spends six months in Royal Victoria Hospital, Montreal, where he reads, and is deeply affected by, the New Testament Gospels. Father becomes a bootlegger helping to smuggle liquor into the United States.

1924   Father goes to Chicago to work for cousin's bakery. In July, the rest of family is smuggled across the border to join him. They live on the east side of Humboldt Park. Bellow takes up violin. Attends Lafayette School and Columbus Elementary School. His main source for books is the Budlong branch of Chicago Public Library on North Avenue.

1930   Graduates from Sabin Junior High School. Enters Tuley High School, where he befriends Isaac Rosenfeld, Oscar Tarcov, and Sam Freifeld, all aspiring writers.

1931   Family moves to a more prosperous area of Chicago on the west side of Humboldt Park.

1933 Graduates from Tuley in January. Mother dies of breast cancer in February. Moves out of home in fall, and takes room in a boarding house near the University of Chicago, where he is now enrolled along with his classmate Isaac Rosenfeld.

1934 Father remarries; he is now the successful owner of the Carroll Coal Company.

1935 During the winter the driver of one of the Carroll Company's trucks is killed. Without insurance, father is forced to pay costs, and can no longer afford $100-per-quarter fees of University of Chicago. Bellow is forced to leave university and returns home; in fall transfers to Northwestern University, where he takes dual major in English and anthropology, the latter under Melville J. Herskovits.

1936 First published piece, "Pets of the North Shore," a whimsical sketch about dogs and their owners, appears in *The Daily Northwestern*. Literary editor of university paper rejects one of his short stories. Wins third prize in "Campus in Print" story competition; story appears under a newly adopted name, Saul Bellow: "I wanted to break with everybody, even my own family, so I chose the other name, which was a legitimate name, and belonged to me."

1937 Becomes associate editor of *The Beacon*, a monthly journal, to which he contributes many pieces. Receives B.A. from Northwestern with honors in anthropology and sociology; goes on to graduate fellowship in Department of Sociology and Anthropology at University of Wisconsin, Madison, where Isaac Rosenfeld is a Ph.D. candidate. Works on a thesis on culture of French Canadians, but is soon discouraged ("Every time I worked on my thesis, it turned out to be a story"). Leaves before the end of the year.

1938 Returns to Chicago, where he marries Anita Goshkin. Works in his brother Maurice's coalyard, but is fired for absenteeism. Takes a part-time job in the fall teaching anthropology and English composition at Pestalozzi-Freobel Teachers College on South Michigan Avenue. His assigned reading list (which he will substantially retain through decades of teaching) includes Lawrence, Dostoevsky, Dreiser, and Flaubert. Works on the Federal Writers' Project, part of the New Deal Works Progress Administration; his job is to compile sketches of contemporary American authors.

1940   Travels to Mexico in summer; reads Lawrence's *Mornings in Mexico* and Stendhal. Arrives in Mexico City on August 21, to find that Trotsky had been assassinated the day before; views body at morgue. Stories rejected by *The Saturday Evening Post* and *The Kenyon Review*.

1941   *Partisan Review* (May–June) publishes short story "Two Morning Monologues." Works on a novel entitled "The Very Dark Trees"; after being rejected by several publishers, it is accepted by William Roth of the Colt Press for $150.

1942   Visits New York, where Isaac Rosenfeld is studying at NYU. Meets Alfred Kazin; spends time with poet Delmore Schwartz. Draft board defers him until end of term at Pestalozzi Teachers College; in June defers him again until mid-July. William Roth, now enlisted, cancels publication of "The Very Dark Trees," sending Bellow consolatory $50. Bellow burns manuscript.

1943   Applies unsuccessfully for a Guggenheim fellowship. During summer, rejected for job at *Time* by Whittaker Chambers, editor of the magazine's books and arts pages. Works as editor on *Encyclopedia Britannica*'s "Syntopicon," a two-volume supplement to the "Great Books of the Western World" project. "Notes of a Dangling Man" appears in *Partisan Review* (September–October).

1944   Novel *Dangling Man* published in March by Vanguard Press. Edmund Wilson describes it in *The New Yorker* as "one of the most honest pieces of testimony on the psychology of a whole generation who have grown up during the depression and the war." The book sells a total of 1,506 copies. Son Gregory born in April. Draft board again defers Bellow, who has been diagnosed with inguinal hernia. Studio executive at MGM, seeing author photograph in newspaper, offers to make him a Hollywood star, playing "the guy who loses the girl to the George Raft type or the Errol Flynn type."

1945   Volunteers in April for the Merchant Marine, and is as-
            signed to the Atlantic district headquarters in Sheepshead
            Bay, Brooklyn. Moves to New York in September. Lives on
            Pineapple Street, Brooklyn Heights, writing book reviews
            and reading for publishers; works on novel *The Victim.*

1946   A second Guggenheim application is rejected. In the fall,
            becomes assistant professor at the University of Minne-
            sota, Minneapolis; meets Robert Penn Warren, who is at
            work on *All the King's Men.*

1947   Travels to Europe in July, visiting Paris, Madrid, and
            Granada. Writes "Spanish Letter" for *Partisan Review.* Re-
            turns to Minneapolis in September. *The Victim* is published
            in November by Vanguard Press and sells 2,257 copies.

1948–49   Receives Guggenheim fellowship after third application.
            With the Foundation's $2,500 and a $3,000 advance for his
            next novel from his new publisher, Viking, travels in the fall
            to Paris, where he will live for the next two years. Meets
            Georges Bataille, Maurice Merleau-Ponty, and Albert Ca-
            mus at the home of his Chicago friend Harold Kaplan.
            Other Paris friends include Herbert Gold, Mary McCarthy,
            Lionel Abel, and William Phillips. Works on a third novel,
            "The Crab and the Butterfly," about two invalids in a
            Chicago hospital. Abandons novel in progress in October
            1949 and begins *The Adventures of Augie March.* (Writes
            later: "The book just came to me. All I had to do was be
            there with buckets to catch it.") "From the Life of Augie
            March" appears in November *Partisan Review.* Visits Lon-
            don in December; meets Cyril Connolly, Henry Green,
            and Stephen Spender.

1950   In summer, gives lectures at Salzburg Seminar in Ameri-
            can Studies. Visits Venice, Florence, and Rome, where he
            works for six weeks on *Augie March* in the Borghese Gar-
            dens. Meets Alberto Moravia and Ignazio Silone. Returns
            to New York in October; takes a modest apartment in
            Forest Hills, Queens.

1951   Becomes interested in sexual and emotional therapy of
            Wilhelm Reich. Begins Reichian therapy with Dr. Chester
            Raphael; spends hours sitting in "orgone box," supposed
            to concentrate "orgone energy." Hired as part-time assis-

tant professor at NYU. Applies unsuccessfully for a renewal of Guggenheim fellowship; borrows $500 from Viking. *Commentary* publishes his story "Looking for Mr. Green." Departs for Salzburg Seminar in December, stopping en route in Paris. Reads passages of *Augie March* to his Salzburg students.

1952   Returns to New York in mid-February. Travels west to lecture at universities of Washington and Oregon. Spends time with Theodore Roethke and Dylan Thomas in Seattle. A dramatization of *The Victim* opens off-Broadway in May. Receives a $1,000 grant from the American Academy of Arts and Letters. Spends summer at Yaddo writers' colony in Saratoga Springs, New York. Translates Isaac Bashevis Singer's story "Gimpel the Fool" from the Yiddish (Singer's first appearance in English). In fall, takes creative-writing job at Princeton as Delmore Schwartz's assistant, where he meets John Berryman and wife, Eileen Simpson. Meets Sondra Tschacbasov. Suffers severe case of pneumonia in December. An excerpt from *Augie March* appears in *The New Yorker*.

1953   In September, takes one-year job at Bard College, in Annandale-on-Hudson, New York. At Bard, befriends Keith Botsford and Jack Ludwig. His temporary landlord is Chanler Chapman, later a model for the hero of *Henderson the Rain King*. *The Adventures of Augie March* is published in September. Gives interview to *New York Times*. In December, receives royalty check for $2,000. Takes temporary apartment on Riverside Drive in New York, where he spends weekends.

1954   Wins National Book Award for *Adventures of Augie March*. Writes "How I Wrote Augie March's Story" in *New York Times* in January: "The book was writing itself very rapidly. I was coming to be strangely independent of place. Chicago itself had grown exotic to me." Separates from Anita Goshkin. Leaves Bard in June; spends summer in Wellfleet, Massachusetts, where friends include Mary McCarthy, Harry Levin, and Alfred Kazin. Applies for another grant from the Guggenheim Foundation. Works on "Memoirs of a Bootlegger's Son," a fictional portrait of Bellows family in Montreal, portions of which will later be incorporated into *Herzog*.

1955   Father dies of an aneurysm in May. The Guggenheim
        Foundation grants him a second fellowship. In August
        visits small towns in Illinois for *Holiday* travel piece. Spends
        next eight months in Reno, Nevada, while waiting for
        divorce.

1956   Marries Sondra Tschacbasov in Reno in February. Works
        on novel *Henderson the Rain King*. Visited in April by
        Arthur Miller and Marilyn Monroe. Finishes novella *Seize
        the Day*, which appears in the summer issue of *Partisan
        Review*. In July, childhood friend Isaac Rosenfeld dies of
        heart attack in Chicago, aged 38. Buys house in Tivoli,
        New York, with the help of $8,000 legacy from father.
        Spends the fall at Yaddo, where he becomes friends with
        John Cheever. *Seize the Day* is published in November.

1957   Second son, Adam, is born in January. Takes temporary
        appointment for the spring semester at the University of
        Minnesota, where he spends time with John Berryman; in
        Bellow's absence, Ralph Ellison moves into Tivoli house.
        Meets 23-year-old Philip Roth in Chicago. Spends the fall
        in Chicago, teaching at Northwestern. In "The Univer-
        sity as Villain," published in *The Nation* in November, ac-
        cuses English departments of being full of "discouraged
        people who stand dully upon a brilliant plane, in charge
        of masterpieces but not themselves inspired."

1958   Finishes early draft of *Henderson the Rain King* in March.
        Dictates the novel's revisions for six weeks to secretary in
        Tivoli house. In fall, returns to teach at University of
        Minnesota. Enters therapy with a clinical psychologist.

1959   *Henderson the Rain King* is published in February. Re-
        ceives $16,000 grant from the Ford Foundation. Returns
        to Tivoli for summer. Works on play *The Last Analysis*.
        Separates from Sondra Tschacbasov in November. Stays
        briefly at Yaddo and then in Herbert Gold's New York
        apartment before going to Europe for a lecture tour of
        Poland and Yugoslavia at the invitation of the State
        Department.

1960   *The Noble Savage*, a journal co-edited by Bellow, Jack
        Ludwig, and Keith Botsford, appears in February (five

numbers will be published); contributors include Harold Rosenberg, Ralph Ellison, and John Berryman. In March, visits Italy, Israel, and England. Returns from Europe in March; enters therapy with sexologist Dr. Albert Ellis. Spends summer at Tivoli. Divorce becomes final in June. In "The Sealed Treasure," essay published in the July *TLS*, argues against modern Flaubertian aestheticism, and its "disappointment with its human material," in favor of an American novel that might more optimistically search for the "sealed treasure" of ordinary inner life.

1961   Teaches spring term at the University of Puerto Rico. Marries Susan Glassman in November. Spends fall at the University of Chicago, where he has temporary teaching appointment.

1962   Works steadily on novel *Herzog*. Made honorary Doctor of Letters, Northwestern University. Attends White House dinner for André Malraux in May. An excerpt from *The Last Analysis* appears in the summer issue of *Partisan Review*. Accepts five-year appointment as professor at the Committee on Social Thought of the University of Chicago, and moves into Hyde Park apartment. (Will stay at University of Chicago for thirty years.) John Steinbeck, who has just been awarded the Nobel Prize for Literature, inscribes copy of Nobel lecture to Bellow: "You're next."

1963   Old school friend Oscar Tarcov dies, aged 48. Made honorary Doctor of Letters, Bard College. "Some Notes on Recent American Fiction" is published in *Encounter* in November.

1964   Third son, Daniel, born in March. Spends July and August on Martha's Vineyard, finishing *Herzog* and *The Last Analysis*. *Herzog* is published in September, and reaches top of the best-seller list in October. *The Last Analysis* opens on Broadway the same month; closes within a month. Donates manuscripts of *Augie March* and *Henderson the Rain King* to University of Chicago. Pat Covici, Viking editor and dedicatee of *Herzog*, dies of heart attack in October.

1965   Now increasingly wealthy from *Herzog* sales, gives the
        Tivoli house to Bard. *Herzog* wins the National Book
        Award in March. Attends festival of the arts at White
        House in June, at which he reads from *Herzog*. (Festival
        is controversial because of Vietnam War, and Edmund
        Wilson and Robert Lowell return their invitations.) Is
        interviewed at length for *Paris Review*. Spends summer
        on Martha's Vineyard.

1966   Receives the Prix Internationale de Litterature (Formen-
        tor Prize). Delivers keynote address at PEN Congress in
        New York in June, declaring: "We have at present a large
        literary community and something we can call, *faute de
        mieux*, a literary culture, in my opinion a very bad one."
        Under the Weather, a trilogy of one-act plays, opens at the
        Fortune Theatre in London in the summer; opens in Oc-
        tober in New York, where it closes in less than two weeks.
        Lectures in the fall at the American Embassy in London;
        travels to Holland and Poland. By the end of the year,
        marriage has ended. Moves out of Chicago apartment.
        Begins work on novel *Mr. Sammler's Planet*.

1967   Travels to Israel to cover Six-Day War for *Newsday* in
        June, writing a series of four articles. Spends summer in
        rented house in East Hampton, where he sees Saul Stein-
        berg and Harold Rosenberg. Essay "Skepticism and the
        Depth of Life" published in anthology *The Arts & the
        Public*.

1968   Becomes Chevalier des Arts et Lettres in January. B'nai
        Brith confers Jewish Heritage Award for Excellence in
        Literature. Gives talk in the spring at San Francisco State
        College, where he is heckled by novelist Floyd Salas, a
        faculty member; incorporates detailed description of the
        incident into his new novel. Spends September at Villa
        Serbelloni, Rockefeller Foundation villa on Lake Como.
        A collection of stories, *Mosby's Memoirs*, is published in
        October. Travels to London in December to see his pub-
        lisher George Weidenfeld.

1969   Continues to work on *Mr. Sammler's Planet*, describing it
        as "a dramatic essay of some sort, wrung from me by the
        crazy Sixties." In March, enters analysis with Heinz Kohut.

1970   *Mr. Sammler's Planet* is published. On his first trip to
        Africa in February, visits Nairobi and Addis Ababa.
        In April delivers lecture at Purdue University entitled
        "Culture Now: Some Animadversions, Some Laughs," in
        which he attacks 1960s avant-gardism in the arts. Receives
        honorary degree in May from New York University.
        Spends June in Israel, attending symposium at Tel Aviv
        U.S. Cultural Center and a banquet in Jerusalem where
        Elie Wiesel and Golda Meir speak. Becomes chairman of
        Committee on Social Thought (will retain position until
        1975). In December, *Anon*, a new journal, again co-edited
        with Keith Botsford, appears for only one issue.

1971   Wins third National Book Award for *Mr. Sammler's
        Planet*. A revival of *The Last Analysis* opens off-Broadway
        in June; closes August 1. Travels to London in fall to
        serve as judge for Booker Prize for fiction; visits Lisbon,
        Turin, and Dublin. John Berryman writes to him: "Let's
        join forces, large and small, as in the winter beginning of
        1953 in Princeton, with the Bradstreet blazing and Augie
        fleecing away. We're promising."

1972   John Berryman commits suicide in January. Visits Japan
        in April and Europe in August. Delivers lecture "Litera-
        ture in the Age of Technology" at the Smithsonian in
        November.

1973   In April, stays for several weeks at Monks House, Rodmell
        (former home of Virginia and Leonard Woolf), where he
        works on novel *Humboldt's Gift*. Receives honorary de-
        grees from Harvard and Yale. Begins attending meetings
        of the Chicago Anthroposophical Society.

1974   Marries Alexandra Ionescu Tulcea, a professor of mathe-
        matics at Northwestern, in November.

1975   Attends White House dinner in January for British Prime
        Minister Harold Wilson. Delivers proofs of *Humboldt's
        Gift* in June, and travels to London, where he meets
        Owen Barfield, English scholar of Rudolf Steiner's
        anthroposophical thought, with whom he will carry on a
        long correspondence. Spends time at Costa del Sol home

of his British publisher Barley Alison. *Humboldt's Gift* is published in August. In October, begins three-month sabbatical in Israel, where, for a projected nonfiction book, he interviews A. B. Yehoshua, Amos Oz, Abba Eban, Jerusalem mayor Teddy Kollek, and Prime Minister Yitzhak Rabin. Louis Simpson attacks *Humboldt's Gift* in *The New York Times* in December, claiming that the novel's fictionalized portrait of Delmore Schwartz denigrates American poets.

1976　　　Visits Stanford, where he renews friendship with John Cheever. Receives Pulitzer Prize in May for *Humboldt's Gift* (prize is mocked in the novel as "the pullet surprise, a dummy newspaper publicity award given by crooks and illiterates—for the birds"). Excerpt from *To Jerusalem and Back* appears in *The New Yorker* in July. First District Court of Chicago rules that Bellow has misled Susan Glassman about his stated income, and orders him to pay her legal costs of $200,000. *To Jerusalem and Back* is published in October. In the same month Bellow wins the Nobel Prize, following a unanimous decision of the committee. In his Stockholm speech in December, argues against the anti-humanism of the *nouveau roman*, and reasserts his belief that fiction must not "give up the connection of literature with the main human enterprise."

1977　　　Gives Jefferson Lecture in the Humanities in March. Works on the "Chicago Book," a work of reportage that will later become novel *The Dean's December*. In September, is held in contempt of court by Cook County judge and sentenced to ten days in jail for failing to pay increased alimony to Susan Glassman; sentence is appealed and later voided, and Bellow is never jailed. Spends academic year in Boston, where both he and Alexandra Tulcea teach at Brandeis.

1978　　　Attends memorial service in July for Harold Rosenberg, along with Dwight Macdonald, Saul Steinberg, and Mary McCarthy. Leaves Viking, his publisher of thirty years, for Harper & Row, with large advance for "nonfiction book about Chicago." Travels to Romania in December, where he attends funeral of his mother-in-law, a former minister of health.

1979   Work in progress shifts from nonfiction "Chicago Book" to *The Dean's December*, which will include Romanian scenes. Rents summer house in West Halifax, Vermont.

1981   Visits London in spring, and in October attends Tuley High School's fiftieth reunion for classes of 1931 and 1932. Continues to work on *The Dean's December*.

1982   Spends spring semester as guest lecturer at the University of Victoria, British Columbia. *The Dean's December* is published in February to mixed reviews. In June, attends John Cheever's funeral; tells mourners, "Our friendship, a sort of hydroponic plant, flourished in the air." In September, visits London and Paris, where he appears on Bernard Pivot's literary television show *Apostrophes*.

1984   At work on short stories; "What Kind of Day Did You Have?" (a fictionalized portrait of Harold Rosenberg) appears in *Vanity Fair* in February. Collection of stories, *Him with His Foot in His Mouth*, is published in May. Lachine Public Library is renamed after Bellow; he attends building's commemoration on June 10, his birthday, and gives a speech in both French and English: "The human soul has its own way to declare its own freedom and to develop itself in its own way, and it is not true to say: 'Show me where you came from and I'll tell you what you are.'" Visits his birthplace at 130 Eighth Avenue.

1985   Anita Goshkin, first wife, dies in March, followed by his two brothers, Maurice, in May, and Sam, in June. His marriage to Alexandra Tulcea begins to break up. Delivers lecture at the Ethical Culture Society in New York, in which he quips that he meant *Herzog* "as an attack on higher education in America."

1986   In January attends rancorous PEN Congress in New York, where he falls into heated argument with Günter Grass about poverty and the spiritual life in America. Leaves Harper & Row in November for William Morrow.

1987   *The Closing of the American Mind*, by Chicago colleague and friend Allan Bloom, is published in March, with an introduction by Bellow, and becomes a best seller. Has an emotional reunion with Isaac Rosenfeld's son in New York. In April, travels to Israel for a conference on his work at University of Haifa, at which Allan Bloom, Martin Amis, A. B. Yehoshua, and Amos Oz give lectures. Interviewed by *New York Times* about Allan Bloom and controversies over multiculturalism, remarks: "Who is the Tolstoy of the Zulus, the Proust of the Papuans? I'd be glad to read him." Novel *More Die of Heartbreak* appears in June. Spends summer in Vermont.

1989   Returns to Viking with *A Theft*, a novella published in March as a paperback original. In May, sells manuscript of *Mr. Sammler's Planet* to New York Public Library for $66,000. Marries Janis Freedman in August. Takes teaching job at Boston University for fall semester. Has house built near Brattleboro, Vermont, which subsequently becomes summer home. Novella *The Bellarosa Connection* is published in December.

1990   Friends and relatives, including his three sons, Philip Roth, and Saul Steinberg, gather for 75th birthday party in West Dover, Vermont. In October, Mayor Richard M. Daley gives belated birthday party at the Art Institute in Chicago. Receives medal in November from the National Book Foundation for "distinguished contribution to American letters." Allan Bloom falls ill.

1991   *Something to Remember Me By*, a collection of three long stories also including *A Theft* and *The Bellarosa Connection*, is published in fall. Reads title story at Harvard in October to celebrate inauguration of new university president Neil Rudenstine. Travels to Florence in November to give a talk about Mozart at the Teatro Comunale.

1992   Allan Bloom, visited every day by Bellow in his last months, dies in October, probably from complications from HIV; Bellow delivers eulogy at memorial service. Visits Paris, where he sees old Chicago friend H. J. Kaplan.

1993   Becomes University Professor at Boston University in the fall.

1994   Collected essays published as *It All Adds Up*. Ralph Ellison dies. Writes op-ed piece for *New York Times* in March entitled "Papuans and Zulus," an attempt to revise his earlier controversial comments, and praises *Chaka* by Thomas Mofolo, a Zulu novel which he had read as a student, as "a profoundly, unbearably tragic book." Contracts ciguatera poisoning in April from eating contaminated shellfish in St. Martin; suffers heart failure and double pneumonia, and spends three weeks in coma, close to death. Recovers very slowly.

1995 Short story "By the St. Lawrence" appears in *Esquire* (July). At end of year, returns to Chicago, and speaks to a crowd of a thousand in Mandel Hall on "Literature in a Democracy." Begins *News from the Republic of Letters*, a literary journal, with Keith Botsford as co-editor.

1996 In February, ends twenty-five year relationship with literary agent Harriet Wasserman, and engages Andrew Wylie as his new agent. Susan Glassman dies in December, aged 63.

1997 *The Actual*, a novella, published in April. Attends ceremony in July at National Portrait Gallery, Washington, D.C., for unveiling of portrait. Harriet Wasserman publishes *Handsome Is*, a memoir of her relationship with Bellow.

1999 Works on novel *Ravelstein*, a fictionalized account of his friendship with Allan Bloom. Daughter, Naomi Rose, born in December.

2000 *Ravelstein* is published to warm reviews and controversy stemming from its treatment of Bloom's homosexuality and Bellow's statement in an interview that Bloom's death was AIDS-related (claim is challenged by some, and Bellow revises novel's galleys to omit references to HIV and AIDS in published version).

2001 *Collected Stories* published in March, with a preface by Janis Bellow.

Note on the Texts

This volume contains the first three novels published by Saul Bellow: *Dangling Man* (1944), *The Victim* (1947), and *The Adventures of Augie March* (1953).

In 1942, shortly after Bellow's draft board informed him that it was deferring his enlistment in the army, he began writing a novel entitled "Notes of a Dangling Man." In the summer of 1943 he submitted it to James Henle of the Vanguard Press, who had become interested in Bellow's work after reading "The Very Dark Trees," an unpublished novel that Bellow destroyed in 1942. Not long after receiving the typescript Henle wrote that he was "deeply impressed" with *Dangling Man*, the final title of the book, and two weeks later Bellow signed a contract with the publisher. *Dangling Man* was published by the Vanguard Press on March 23, 1944. This edition was published in London by John Lehmann two years later. The text of the 1944 Vanguard Press edition of *Dangling Man* is printed here.

On his application for a Guggenheim fellowship submitted in October 1945, Bellow wrote that he was working on *The Victim*, "a novel whose theme is guilt." He worked on it throughout 1946 and submitted a complete draft to James Henle in January 1947. He spent the following spring revising *The Victim*, and was reviewing proofs as he traveled to Europe by ship in July. *The Victim* was published by the Vanguard Press on November 6, 1947; John Lehmann published a new edition in England the following year. A stage version adapted by Leonard Lesley opened in New York in May 1952. This volume prints the text of the 1947 Vanguard Press edition of *The Victim*.

In the spring of 1948, Bellow was approached by Monroe Engel of the Viking Press, which hoped to publish his third novel. His contract with Vanguard gave that firm an option on his next book, but Bellow successfully negotiated a release from this contract and signed an agreement with Viking. After moving in the fall of 1948 to Paris, where he lived for the next two years, he began work on a novel about two invalids in adjoining beds in a Chicago hospital ward. Eventually he abandoned this novel and began another, writing to Engel on October 24, 1949: "I've dived into something else I had started. On this, I've for some reason been able to work much faster than I've ever been able to work before. I do one fairly long chapter a week, and I expect to have the length of a book in first draft by Christmas. By the length of a book, I mean something like

100,000 words, not by any means the full length of what I plan." An excerpt from *The Adventures of Augie March* appeared in *Partisan Review* in November 1949; other excerpts were subsequently published in *Hudson Review*, *Harper's Bazaar*, and *The New Yorker*. Bellow finished the novel late in 1952, and it was published in September 1953 by Viking Press. This edition was published in England by Weidenfeld & Nicholson in 1954. The text of the 1953 Viking Press edition of *The Adventures of Augie March* is printed here.

This volume presents the texts of the original printings chosen for inclusion here, but it does not attempt to reproduce nontextual features of their typographic design. The texts are presented without change, except for the correction of typographical errors. Spelling, punctuation, and capitalization are often expressive features and are not altered, even when inconsistent or irregular. The following is a list of typographical errors corrected, cited by page and line number: 17.29, such; 27.29, "strangers—"; 50.40, might; 67.19, "Oh,"I; 104.24, said.; 104.35, are"; 185.11, said.; 205.24, too.; 213.2, up.; 235.17, he; 335.36, Never."; 363.30, hamered; 402.21, *codo-duello*; 591.40, Einhorn?; 614.40, Reynold's; 615.19, shortweighed; 786.37, Navarro; 823.18, Mexico, but; 856.28, drowned!'.

Notes

In the notes below, the reference numbers denote page and line of this volume (the line count includes headings). No note is made for material included in standard desk-reference books. Biblical quotations are keyed to the King James Version. Quotations from Shakespeare are keyed to *The Riverside Shakespeare*, ed. G. Blakemore Evans (Boston: Houghton Mifflin, 1974). For references to other studies, and further biographical background than is contained in the Chronology, see: Gloria L. Cronin and Blaine H. Hall, *Saul Bellow: An Annotated Bibliography, Second Edition* (New York: Garland Publishing, 1987); James Atlas, *Bellow: A Biography* (New York: Random House, 2000).

DANGLING MAN

6.10   *Pepé le Moko*] French film (1936), directed by Julien Duvivier, in which Jean Gabin portrays a gangster who hides out in the casbah in Algiers.

8.16–18   Mr. Five-by-five . . . five feet wide] From "Mister Five by Five" (1941), song by Gene De Paul and Don Raye.

10.20   *Radix malorum est*] Is the root of evil.

16.36–37   "United Front from Below."] Slogan adopted by the Communist International in 1928 when it denounced the leadership of Social Democratic parties and unions as "Social Fascists" and called upon their members to join the Communist movement. The slogan was dropped in 1935 when the Comintern adopted a new "Popular Front" strategy.

18.22   *tout comprendre c'est tout pardonner*] To understand everything is to forgive everything.

26.16   "nasty, brutish, short."] Cf. Thomas Hobbes, *Leviathan*, Book One, chapter 13.

30.23–24   *Science and Health*] Religious treatise (1875) by Mary Baker Eddy (1821–1910), expounding the tenets of Christian Science.

30.26–27   like Johnson's . . . over Berkeley] See James Boswell, *The Life of Samuel Johnson*: "I observed that though we are satisfied his doctrine is not true, it is impossible to refute it. I never shall forget the alacrity with which Johnson answered, striking his foot with mighty force against a large stone, till he rebounded from it, 'I refute it *thus*.'"

41.39–42.4   "Because the daughters . . . parts."] See Isaiah 3:16–17.

48.16   Cugat] Xaviar Cugat (1900–90), Spanish-born band leader who helped popularize Cuban dance music in the United States; his hits included "The Lady in Red" and "The Breeze and I."

54.10–11   *Er ist schön . . . Mephisto war auch schön*] He is beautiful . . . Mephistopheles was beautiful too.

58.16   *A basso*] Down with.

58.28   Catalina] A twin-engined flying boat.

62.13–14   *Anti-Duhring . . . Gotha Program*] Essay (1878) by Friedrich Engels; polemical letter (written 1875, published 1891) by Karl Marx.

65.28   General Bergonzoli] General Annibale Bergonzoli surrendered with the Italian XXIII Corps at Bardia, Libya, to Australian troops on January 5, 1941.

75.3–5   Dinner in the diner . . . choochoo] From "Chattanooga Choo Choo," written by Mack Gordon and Harry Warren and recorded by the Glenn Miller Orchestra (1941).

75.7   bronze Laocoön] A reproduction of the central figure of the Laocoön group, a Hellenistic sculpture from Rhodes depicting the Trojan priest Laocoön and his sons entwined in the coils of a serpent; they were punished for warning the Trojans against the wooden horse of the Greeks.

80.40   *Vae victis!*] Woe to the vanquished! (See Livy, Book 5, chapter 48.)

87.1–2   Bucharest . . . from hooks in a slaughterhouse.] The murders were committed by the fascist Iron Guard during the pogrom in Bucharest, January 20–23, 1941.

90.19–21   "Pause, now, and . . . from *King John*] Cf. *The Merchant of Venice*, II.vii.24–25; cf. *Hamlet*, I.i.76; cf. *King John*, IV.i.40.

92.10–11   *un (personnage) composé . . . de déraison*] A person composed of high and low, of good sense and irrationality.

94.2–4   *Magda . . . Cyrano*] *Magda*, English version of Hermann Sudermann's play *Heimat* (1893); *Desire Under the Elms* (1924), play by Eugene O'Neill; *Juno and the Paycock* (1924), play by Sean O'Casey; *Cyrano de Bergerac* (1897), play by Edmond Rostand.

95.5   Federal productions] The Federal Theatre Project (1935–39) was established under the Works Progress Administration.

97.37   *Tu As Raison Aussi*] You are also right.

115.1–2   *c'est plus fort que moi*] It's stronger than me.

120.1   *Man and Superman*] Play (1905) by George Bernard Shaw.

124.28   *Sacre du Vin Temps*] Pun on Igor Stravinsky's *Le Sacre du Printemps*.

THE VICTIM

170.9   *Schicker.*]   Yiddish for "drunk."

195.1   God was no respecter of persons]   Cf. Acts 10:34–35.

203.39–40   sons of Belial]   I Samuel 2:12.

204.1   Noah lies drunk]   Cf. Genesis 9:21–25.

215.27   Krueger the match king's]   Ivar Krueger, Swedish manufacturer who attempted to secure dominance over European production of household matches; after his suicide in 1932, he was found to have defrauded investors of millions.

226.1   Karloff]   Boris Karloff (1887–1969), actor whose many films included *Frankenstein* (1931), *The Mask of Fu Manchu* (1932), and *The Black Cat* (1934).

244.18–19   Nazimova . . . *The Three Sisters*]   The Russian actress Alla Nazimova (1879–1948); *The Three Sisters* (1901), play by Anton Chekhov.

246.5   who said . . . John Bull's chest?]   The Scottish historian Thomas Carlyle (1795–1881).

246.23   *Der . . . Mann!*]   "The old Jew, he is the man!" Remark reputedly made by Bismarck about Disraeli at the Berlin Congress of 1878.

248.8   George Arliss]   Arliss (1868–1946) made his stage debut in 1886; his stage portrayal of Benjamin Disraeli was followed by film versions in 1921 and 1929.

249.25   *Narischer mensch!*]   Foolish man!

293.10   *Brujo*]   Sorcerer.

301.21   a flat tamed piece]   See *Troilus and Cressida*, IV.i.63.

301.26   *Grosser philosoph.*]   Big philosopher.

347.29–30   Oh, Death!" . . . I had thee least in mind.]   See the early 16th-century morality play *Everyman*, line 119.

347.35–36   The funeral baked meats . . . feast.]   See *Hamlet*, I.ii.180–81.

350.14   Black Friday]   The stock market crash of October 25, 1929.

354.38   the Protocols]   *Protocols of the Elders of Zion*, fraudulent document forged by Russian police officials exposing a purported plot of Jews and Freemasons to subvert Christian civilization and create a world state; published in Russia in 1902, it was translated into German, English, French, Polish and other languages in the 1920s.

THE ADVENTURES OF AUGIE MARCH

384.28   *Tom Brown's Schooldays*]   Novel (1857) by Thomas Hughes based on his boyhood experiences at Rugby School under the tutelage of Thomas Arnold.

390.17   *ehrlich*]   Honest; sincere.

390.38   *junge*]   Young man.

392.11   *Eugene Onegin*]   Narrative poem (1828) by Alexander Pushkin.

392.14   *roman*]   Novel.

393.39–394.1   Natty Bumppo . . . good news from Ratisbon]   Natty Bumppo, protagonist of James Fenimore Cooper's Leatherstocking novels; Quentin Durward, Scottish youth in the service of France's Louis XI in Sir Walter Scott's novel *Quentin Durward* (1823); Tom Brown, hero of Thomas Hughes' *Tom Brown's Schooldays*; George Rogers Clark captured the British frontier post at Kaskaskia, Illinois, on July 4, 1778; Ratisbon (Regensburg) was the site of a French victory in the Napoleonic Wars on April 23, 1809.

394.3   Sandow]   Eugene Sandow (1867–1925), professional strongman and propagandist for physical culture.

394.38   *accoucherka*]   Midwife.

397.2   Vronsky . . . Des Grieux]   Male protagonists of, respectively, Leo Tolstoy's *Anna Karenina* (1874–76) and Abbé Prevost's *Manon Lescaut* (1731).

400.6–7   impediment of Moses . . . the coal]   According to Jewish legend, the infant Moses was tested by advisers of Pharaoh who were convinced he would grow up to overthrow the dynasty; given the choice of reaching for a gem or a lump of hot coal, he was guided by an angel toward the coal. When he burned his hand, he put it to his mouth, thus causing his speech impediment.

400.11   When the Frost Is on the Punkin']   Poem by James Whitcomb Riley (1849–1916).

400.30   Ophelia's brook]   See *Hamlet*, IV.vii.166–183.

404.6   *Tu l'as voulu, Georges Dandin*]   "You asked for it, Georges Dandin." Cf. Molière, *Georges Dandin* (1668), Act I, Scene 9: "Vous l'avez voulu, Georges Dandin, vous l'avez voulu." The line is addressed by the protagonist to himself.

405.22   time when O'Bannion was knocked off]   Dion O'Banion, a major Chicago bootlegger, was shot to death in his flower shop on November 10, 1924.

405.34   Belshazzar's Feast]   In Daniel, chapter 5, Daniel interprets writing that appears on the wall during a feast, predicting the murder of Belshazzar, king of Babylon, and the fall of his kingdom.

410.10–11   fair Briseis . . . Achilles racked up his spear]   See *Iliad*, Book One.

412.3–4   Isaac sporting with Rebecca . . . rape of Dinah by Shechem] Genesis 24:61–67 and Genesis 34:1–2.

414.4–5   Chevalier Bayard]   Pierre Terrail, Seigneur de Bayard (c. 1473–1524), French knight and soldier.

414.5   Cincinnatus at the plow]   According to Roman tradition, Lucius Quinctius Cincinnatus (c. 5th century B.C.) left his plowing to help the Roman army against the invading Aequi; made dictator, he preferred to return to his farm after the war ended.

414.33   *meshant*]   *Mechant:* naughty.

419.35   John Gilbert]   Silent movie actor (1895–1936) who co-starred with Greta Garbo in films including *Flesh and the Devil* (1927) and *A Woman of Affairs* (1928).

420.10–12   Julius Rosenwald . . . always to Negroes,]   The Julius Rosenwald Fund, founded in 1913 by the president of Sears Roebuck, was a major source of private support for black education.

423.17   *Gedenk, Augie, wenn ich bin todt!*]   Remember, Augie, when I'm dead!

425.8–9   Sophie Tucker . . . "Red Hot Mama,"]   The Russian-born entertainer Sophie Tucker (1889–1966) was billed as "The Last of the Red Hot Mamas."

425.25   *Bardelys the Magnificent*]   Adventure film (1926) set in the 16th century, directed by King Vidor.

432.2–3   Roger Touhy . . . Dillinger]   Roger Touhy led a major bootlegging and gambling organization in northwest Cook County from the 1920s until his arrest on kidnapping charges in 1933. O'Connor and Banghart were gunmen who worked for Touhy. Bankrobber John Dillinger was killed by the FBI in 1934 as he left a movie theater in Chicago.

437.29   Jake the Barber]   John "Jake the Barber" Factor, a confidence man and swindler with close ties to the Chicago underworld.

437.33   Johnny Torrio]   A leading Chicago gangster and mentor of Al Capone. Torrio retired from the Chicago underworld after being badly wounded in an ambush on January 24, 1925.

439.39–440.3   Similar to Elisha's bear . . . falling off the wagon.]   See II Kings 2:23–24 and II Samuel 6:6–7.

452.11   Château Thierry]   In early June 1918, American troops helped stop a major German offensive in heavy fighting around Château Thierry, a town on the Marine River 40 miles east of Paris.

453.1–4   Ani-ka, hula wicki-wicki . . . Waikiki] Based on "On the Beach at Waikiki" (1915), song by G. H. Stoner and Henry Kailimai.

455.33   Big Bill Thompson] William Hale Thompson (1867–1944) was mayor of Chicago, 1915–23 and 1927–31; he became notorious for the free rein he gave the city's gangsters during the Prohibition era.

457.20–23   "'Dear Kate . . . That's Henry Fifth] Cf. Shakespeare, *Henry V*, V.ii.244–47.

460.29   Couéism] Technique of psychotherapy through autosuggestion developed by Émile Coué (1857–1926); his methods included the repetition of the phrase "Every day, and in every way, I am becoming better and better."

460.30   Fletcherism] The health recommendations of the nutritionist Horace Fletcher (1849–1919) included "Fletcherizing," the practice of eating only when hungry and chewing food thoroughly, preferably until liquified.

460.31   Henry George] George (1839–1897), an American economist and author of *Progress and Poverty* (1879), maintained that a single tax on land would cover the costs of government.

461.23–24   Katzenjammers . . . Somebody's Stenog] The "Katzenjam-mer Kids" was a long-running popular comic strip by Rudolph Birks which first appeared in 1897 in the New York *Sunday Journal*. Alfred E. Hayward's comic strip "Somebody's Stenog" ran from 1918 to 1938.

461.39–462.1   "Not like the slave scourged to his quarry"] See William Cullen Bryant, "Thanatopsis," lines 77–78: "Thou go not, like the quarry-slave at night, Scourged to his dungeon. . . ."

462.2–3   Whittier: "Prince . . . Republican,"] "The Barefoot Boy" (1855), lines 11–12.

462.3–4   "Build thee more stately mansions, O my soul!"] Oliver Wendell Holmes, "The Chambered Nautilus" (1858), line 29.

462.28   cripple Hephaestus who made ingenious machines] Hephaestus, the Greek god of fire and smith of the gods, was lame from birth; he made, among many extraordinary things, the shield of Achilles and the thunderbolts of Zeus.

463.2   Moses had faltering speech] See Exodus 4:10.

464.39   Sarah and the son of Hagar] See Genesis 21:9–21.

466.28–29   What a piece of work . . . with gold] See *Hamlet*, II.ii.300–8.

466.29   *gescheft*] Business.

467.11   Sardanapalus] In Byron's verse drama *Sardanapalus* (1821), the ancient Mesopotamian ruler Sardanapalus, besieged by the Medes, surrounds himself with luxurious pleasures in the midst of his seraglio before perishing on the funeral pyre he has prepared for himself.

467.29 chain-mail English kings . . . Brutus] According to medieval tradition, the English kings were descended from Brutus, great-grandson of Aeneas.

468.4 *Homo Sum!*] "I am a man!" See Terence's play *Heauton Timoroumenos* (The Self-Tormentor): Homo sum; humani nihil a me alienum puto (I am a man; I count nothing human as alien to me).

470.28–29 Coué theory] See note 460.29.

470.29 *It Can Be Done*] Weekly CBS radio show of the 1930s, hosted by the popular poet Edgar A. Guest.

474.23 *integer vitae*] An upright man. See Horace, *Odes,* I, 22.

474.25 tricky Tybalt] Juliet's cousin, slain by Romeo in retaliation for his killing of Mercutio in *Romeo and Juliet.*

475.30 *lettres de cachet*] Letters sealed with the king's seal that sentenced accused persons without trial.

475.39–40 a picture of Aristotle . . . some nasty whore] Based on an episode in the 13th-century Norman poet Henri d'Andeli's verse tale *Lai d'Aristote*, the image of Aristotle on all fours being ridden by a young woman was frequently depicted during the Middle Ages.

475.40–476.1 Pythagoras who got killed . . . cut his wrists;] It was Archimedes who, distracted as he drew a diagram, was killed by a Roman soldier following the fall of Syracuse in 212 B.C. Seneca was ordered to commit suicide by the emperor Nero, c. A.D. 65.

476.22–23 gentle Sir Cedric . . . an apple tree.] In the 1939 film *On Borrowed Time*, Cedric Hardwicke (1893–1964) plays Mr. Brink, an emissary of Death whose mission is deferred when he is confined to the top of an apple tree.

477.25–26 not sent in your ephod before Eli to start service in the temple] See I Samuel 2:28.

479.20 Willard fight] Jack Dempsey won the heavyweight boxing championship by defeating Jess Willard in three rounds in Toledo, Ohio, on July 4, 1919.

481.3 *sursum corda*] "Let us lift up our hearts," Lamentations 3:41 (Vulgate).

485.6–7 the set of Harvard Classics] A 50-volume series edited by Charles W. Eliot, president of Harvard, published in 1910; it was sometimes referred to as "Dr. Eliot's Five-Foot Shelf."

486.27 *The Voyage of the Beagle*] Account (1839) by Charles Darwin of his five-year voyage in South America and the Pacific as naturalist of the H.M.S. *Beagle.*

494.18–19   Leporello]   Don Giovanni's servant, in Mozart's 1787 opera.

495.23–24   smiting the sledded Polack on the ice]   See *Hamlet*, I.i.63.

495.24   Belisarius]   General (c. 505–65) of the Byzantine emperor Justinian (483–565).

495.38   gold-watch-consulting Plugsons]   See Thomas Carlyle, *Past and Present* (1843), in which Plugson of Undershot typifies the new breed of businessmen focused on the "cash nexus."

495.40   the horsemen of St. John]   See Revelation 6:1–8.

497.29   Haldeman-Julius blue books]   E. Haldeman-Julius (1889–1951) of Girard, Kansas, was publisher and editor, beginning in 1919, of a series of inexpensive "Little Blue Books" which ultimately included almost two thousand titles.

499.1–2   Achilles among the maidens]   Achilles' mother, Thetis, dressed him as a girl and hid him among women in Scyros, in an attempt to prevent the doom she foresaw for him in the Trojan War.

500.25   murderer of the Strelitzes and of his own son]   In 1698 Peter the Great brutally suppressed a rebellion of the military units known as the *streltsi*; Peter's son Alexis, convicted on false charges of treason, was tortured to death in 1718.

503.2   old tale of Croesus]   See Herodotus's *History*, Book One.

503.28–29   Insull's watered and pyramided utilities]   The enormous public-utilities empire of the English-born financier Samuel Insull (1859–1938) collapsed in 1932; Insull fled the country but was extradited in 1934 on fraud and embezzlement charges, of which he was acquitted.

507.38–39   Jackson . . . the duelist's bullet]   After being wounded in the chest in a duel fought on May 30, 1806, Andrew Jackson shot and killed his opponent, Charles Dickinson.

527.28   Gordon or Chartist riots]   In June 1780 an anti-Catholic mass demonstration organized by Lord George Gordon resulted in a week of rioting in London during which at least 285 people were killed. The Chartist mass movement for political reform in Britain led to several outbreaks of rioting in Britain in 1839 and 1840.

531.36   Almanach de Gotha]   A publication containing the genealogies of royal houses of Europe and their descendants, first published in 1763.

531.40–532.2   Queen Carlotta . . . Napoleon the Third]   Charlotte (1840–1927), a Belgian princess, was the wife of Maximilian (1832–67), Austrian archduke and emperor of Mexico (1864–67) until his overthrow and execution after Napoleon III withdrew French troops from the country.

532.24 Teapot Dome Scandal] Corruption scandal involving the leasing of government oil reserves during the Harding administration.

542.15 *Inter pares*] Among equals.

572.36 CCC] Civilian Conservation Corps.

582.23–24 "September Morn."] Painting (1912) by French salon artist Paul Emile Chabas (1869–1937); it was widely reproduced, and was banned in some American cities.

582.27–28 Napoleon from the mud of the Arcole] Napoleon defeated the Austrians at Arcole in northern Italy on November 17, 1796.

583.8–9 Tobit, the day the angel visited] See Tobit 5.

590.37–38 Cressida going over to the Greek camp] During the Trojan War, Cressida pledged fidelity to her lover Troilus shortly before being offered to the Greeks in exchange for the return of three Trojan princes; she broke her vow soon after the exchange, giving tokens of Troilus's pledge to her Greek lover Diomed.

594.34 *au pied du mur*] At the foot of the wall.

595.14–15 Xenophon's Ten Thousand in Persia] A mercenary Greek army stranded in 401 B.C. north of Babylon following the death of their commander, Cyrus the Younger; their retreat through hostile territory is recounted in Xenophon's *Anabasis.*

595.24 St. Valentine's Day Massacre] The murder on February 14, 1929, of seven members of the Moran gang by gunmen working for Al Capone took place in a garage at 2122 North Clark Street.

598.4 Dr. Eliot's Five-Foot Shelf] See note 485.6–7.

602.34 Baths of Caracalla] Large hot baths in Rome, begun in A.D. 212 by emperor Aurelius Antoninus Bassianus (A.D. 188–217), called Caracalla.

617.38–39 Christ Church or Magdalen] Colleges at Oxford University.

618.24 *Esprit des Lois*] *The Spirit of the Laws* (1748) by Charles-Louis de Montesquieu.

621.6 *The Island of Dr. Moreau*] *Island of Lost Souls* (1932), starring Charles Laughton, was based on H. G. Wells's novel *The Island of Dr. Moreau* (1896).

621.15 Cachin] The French Communist politician and newspaper editor Marcel Cachin (1869–1958).

632.37–38 Valley of Ezekiel slain] See Ezekiel 37:1–10.

644.2 San Juan Hill] The hill, outside of Santiago, Cuba, was captured from the Spanish by American troops, including Theodore Roosevelt's "Rough Riders" regiment of volunteer cavalry, on July 1, 1898.

645.5   *piva*] Beer.

645.35   Newgate] Notorious London prison; it became a general term for prisons.

646.15   Masaniello's head] Tomasso Aniello (1620–47), a Neapolitan fisherman, led protests against taxes levied as tribute to Spain; he was assassinated after encouraging wider insurrection.

646.15–16   hang great admirals . . . Lord Nelson] In 1799 British admiral Horatio Nelson had Francesco Caracciolo, the naval commander of the French-backed Neapolitan republic, hanged after he was court-martialed by Neapolitan officers onboard a British warship. The execution was widely denounced as a violation of the terms under which Caracciolo had surrendered.

648.14   Pasiphaë] A byword for a lustful woman. The wife of Cretan King Minos, Pasiphaë was made by Poseidon to fall in love with a bull; the result of their union was the Minotaur.

650.18   Unsex me here!] See *Macbeth*, I.v.41.

650.28   "My Blue Heaven"] Song (1927) by George Whiting and Walter Donaldson.

650.28–29   "A Faded Summer's Love,"] "A Faded Summer Love" (1931), song by Phil Baxter.

653.19   Balaam] See Numbers 22:22–34.

656.5   *ottimati*] Dignitaries.

656.23–24   *Ich kann nicht anders—so help me God!*] See Martin Luther's speech to the Diet at Worms, April 18, 1521: "Here I stand; I cannot do otherwise. God help me. Amen."

663.3–4   Father Coughlin . . . the money-changers] Father Charles Coughlin (1891–1979), a Catholic priest and popular radio broadcaster during the 1930s, initially supported the New Deal but then turned against Franklin Roosevelt and in 1938 began making anti-Semitic and pro-fascist statements in his broadcasts.

668.15   Steelkilt] See "The Town-Ho's Story" in Melville's *Moby-Dick* (1851).

669.18   Hesperides apples] Golden apples given to Hera as a wedding present were guarded by the Hesperides in a garden at the western edge of the ocean.

675.6   Cesar Romero] Actor (b. 1907) whose films included *The Thin Man* (1934) and *The Devil Is a Woman* (1935).

688.1   *The Enneads*] Collection of mystical treatises by Plotinus (A.D. 205–70).

704.15–16   the schismatics in the sixth bulge of hell]   See Dante, *Inferno*, canto IX.

710.6–7   What Christ . . . "Woman."]   See John 2:4.

711.24   WPA]   Works Progress Administration.

714.12   *garde-manger*]   Larder.

723.36   working woman's Thesmophoria]   Athenian festival restricted to women; it provided the basis for Aristophanes' comedy *Thesmophoriazusae*.

730.25–26   one of his favorite poets]   Arthur Rimbaud (1854–91).

734.34–35   one of the painted attackers of Schenectady]   The English settlement at Schenectady, New York, was destroyed by French and Indian raiders in 1690.

738.7–8   the overseer killed by Moses]   Cf. Exodus 2:11–12.

739.7–8   Republic Steel . . . Decoration Day Massacre]   Ten strikers were killed and 90 wounded by police at a Republic Steel plant in Chicago on May 30, 1937.

749.35   Dan and Julie Mannix]   The Philadelphia writer Daniel Mannix published an article in *The Saturday Evening Post* detailing the trip he and his wife, Julie, made to Mexico in 1940 with an eagle trained to hunt iguanas.

750.4   the Trianon]   A palace built at Versailles in 1687.

750.5   Hagenbeck]   Karl Hagenbeck (1844–1913) was a German animal trader and trainer who established the first open-air zoological park near Hamburg in 1907.

753.22   son of a Hagar]   See Genesis 21:9–21.

754.21   Acheron]   River in Greece which, in the *Odyssey* and elsewhere, is depicted as leading to the entrance to Hades.

758.5   Danaë]   Imprisoned in a tower by her father Acrisius, Danaë was visited by Jove in the form of a shower of gold; Perseus was born from their union.

758.5–6   Flora the Belle Romaine]   See François Villon, "La Ballade des Femmes du Temps Jadis" in *Le Testament* (1461).

759.39–760.3   Rousseau . . . tears from their cheeks]   See Jean-Jacques Rousseau, *The Confessions*.

762.19   Palamons and Emilies]   Cf. Geoffrey Chaucer, "The Knight's Tale" in *The Canterbury Tales*.

764.29   high-flying eagles of Bombay]   The Bombay Hook National Wildlife Refuge in Delaware, established in 1937 as a bird sanctuary.

764.32   Colonel Julian the Black Eagle of Harlem] Hubert Julian, an African-American aviator who flew across the Atlantic in 1929 and the United States in 1931. His military rank was awarded him by Emperor Haile Selassie of Ethiopia in 1930.

764.33   ravens of Noah and Elijah] See Genesis 8:7 and I Kings 17:6.

772.28–29   licentious old Cyprian one] Venus.

776.2–4   And strange it is . . . Our most persisted deeds.] See *Antony and Cleopatra*, V.i.30–32.

779.34   *alpargatas*] Hemp sandals.

786.37   Ramon Novarro] Movie actor (1899–1968) best known for his starring role in *Ben-Hur* (1925).

790.17–18   beasts that embraced Odysseus . . . Circe's yard.] See *Odyssey*, Book 10.

792.5–6   *Tres cosas . . . amor*] There are three things in life / Health, money, and love.

792.7–8   Claudia Muzio . . . *Jewels of the Madonna.*] Murzo (1889–1936) and Galli-Curci (1882–1963), Italian sopranos; *Jewels of the Madonna*, opera (1911) by Ermanno Wolf-Ferrari.

795.10–13   "*Están cazando . . . Culebras,*"] "They're hunting." "What?" "Snakes."

797.31–32   "*Es el amo del águila!*"] "It's the master of the eagle!"

802.20   *foco rojo*] Brothel.

809.24   *La Forza del Destino*] Opera (1862) by Giuseppe Verdi.

811.13   *limosnita*] Small alms.

814.25   *en seguida*] Right away.

851.29   *petate*] Sleeping mat.

856.21–22   *lacrimae rerum*] The sadness of things.

857.25–28   the GPU . . . attack on his villa] Trotsky's villa near Mexico City was attacked early on May 24, 1940, by about 20 Mexican and Spanish Communists, led by the painter David Alfredo Siqueiros, who sprayed the building with gun fire. Trotsky survived the assault by hiding under his bed. The attack was organized by the foreign intelligence service of Soviet state security, which was known from 1922 to 1934 as the GPU.

858.39–40   St. John and Herod] See Matthew 14:1–12.

867.3   Apollyon] Malevolent dragon in John Bunyan's *The Pilgrim's Progress* (1678).

877.11   "Liebestod" . . . "Valse Triste,"]   Compositions respectively by Franz Liszt and Jan Sibelius.

878.21   Professor Sayce]   Archibald Henry Sayce (1845–1933), philologist and archeologist whose books included *Monuments of the Hittites* (1881), *Ancient Empires of the East* (1884), and *Archaeology of Cuneiform Inscriptions* (1907).

879.19   lineaments of gratified desire]   See William Blake, "The Question Answer'd": "What is it men in women do require? / The lineaments of gratified desire. / What is it women do in men require? / The lineaments of gratified desire."

892.11   *Eres muy Guapo.*]   You are very handsome.

892.12–13   *Amigo, que . . . Carolina.*]   Friend, go with good luck, Carolina.

895.13–16   Perish strife . . . honey.]   See *Iliad*, Book 18.

895.17–20   *Les vrais voyageurs . . . Allons!*]   Charles Baudelaire, "Le Voyage," stanza 5.

896.29–30   'Look on my works ye mighty and despair!']   Percy Bysshe Shelley, "Ozymandias," line 11.

896.40   Wieboldt's]   Chicago department store; its flagship store was located on Milwaukee Avenue on Chicago's Northwest Side.

904.20–21   John Dillingers . . . Tommy O'Connors.]   See note 432.2–3.

906.29–30   streets of Clermont . . . preaching]   Peter the Hermit (c. 1050–1115), a wandering preacher of northern France, played a major role in promulgating the First Crusade.

908.15   *Juno and the Paycock*]   Play (1924) by Sean O'Casey.

910.29   *du monde au balcon*]   Crowded in the balcony.

918.4–5   let the prophetic soul . . . (S. T. Coleridge)]   See Shakespeare's Sonnet 33, lines 1–2; the lines are cited by Samuel Taylor Coleridge in chapter 15 of *Biographia Literaria* (1817).

919.22   Hieronymus B.]   Hieronymus Bosch.

922.17   Stage-Door Canteen]   A New York club for service personnel run by show-business people during World War II. Similar canteens also operated in several other cities.

926.32–33   Hengist and Horsa]   According to legend, leaders of the first Saxons to settle in England in the fifth century A.D.

927.24   Gurdjieff]   Georgei Ivanovitch Gurdjieff (1877–1949), occultist, founder of the Institute for the Harmonious Development of Man (1912) in Moscow, and of a school at Fontainebleau (1922); his students included P. D. Ouspensky, A. R. Orage, Hart Crane, and Katherine Mansfield.

927.35–36   *C'est la moindre des choses*]   It's the least of things.

929.22–24   Zaharoff . . . Three-Finger Brown]   Sir Basil Zaharoff (1850–1936), munitions magnate and financier widely suspected of political intrigue and war profiteering; Juan March (1884–1962), Spanish financier who helped fund the Nationalist rebellion against the Spanish Republic in 1936; Ivar Krueger, known as the "Swedish Match King," who after his suicide in 1932 was found to have defrauded investors of millions; John "Jake the Barber" Factor, gangster associated with the Capone organization in Chicago; Gaetano (Thomas) Lucchese (1899–1967), a New York gangster who had three fingers on one hand and was known as "Three-Finger Brown" after the three-fingered baseball pitcher Mordecai Brown (1876–1948).

930.17–19   'Fingal's Cave.' . . . 'Poet and Peasant.']   *The Hebrides, or Fingal's Cave*, overture (1832) by Felix Mendelssohn; *Orientale*, composition (1894) originally written for violin and piano by Russian composer César Cui (1835–1918); *Nur we die Sehnsucht kennt*, song (1869) by Pyotr Tchaikovsky; *Poet and Peasant*, overture (1846) by Austrian composer Franz von Suppé (1819–95).

930.19–20   Milton Sills . . . Conway Tearle]   Milton Sills (1882–1930), actor whose films included *Souls for Sale* (1922), *Flaming Youth* (1923), and *The Unguarded Hour* (1925); Conway Tearle (1878–1938), actor whose films included *The Eternal Flame* (1922), *School for Wives* (1925), and *Altars of Desire* (1927).

930.38–39   *Ribono shel Olam!*]   Master of the universe!

931.32   Ellsworth Huntington.]   American geographer and explorer (1876–1947) whose books included *Civilization and Climate* (1915).

933.21–22   'Who is left . . . now?']   Haggai 2:3.

933.33–34   wife of Hosea . . . days.]   See Hosea 3:3, in which Hosea says to the adulteress he has bought as his wife: "Thou shalt abide for me many days; thou shalt not play the harlot, and thou shalt not be for another man: so will I also be for thee."

942.31–32   Hell when Ulysses visited]   See *Odyssey*, Book 11.

946.24   *Lasciar le donne? Pazzo!*]   "Give up women? Crazy!" From Act II of *Don Giovanni*, opera (1787) by Mozart.

954.37–38   The next poet laureate . . . sit still.]   See T. S. Eliot, "Ash Wednesday," section VI.

954.39–40   famous painting . . . the lion gazing on him?]   *The Sleeping Gypsy* (1897) by Henri Rousseau (1844–1910).

955.34–37   Or go to Rome, . . . the wilderness]   From Percy Bysshe Shelley, *Adonais: an Elegy on the Death of John Keats* (1821), stanzas 48 and 49.

967.35–36   Like Henry Ware . . . Timmendiquas]   Characters in the popular Young Trailers series of novels by Joseph A. Altsheler (1862–1919), including *The Scouts of the Valley* (1911).

970.7–8   one of those Walden or Inisfree wattle jobs]   See Henry David Thoreau, *Walden* (1854), and W. B. Yeats, "The Lake Isle of Innisfree."

970.11–13   far horn of Roland . . . Saracens]   In the medieval French poem *La Chanson de Roland*, the mortally wounded Roland sounds his horn as a warning to Charlemagne.

971.2   *immenso giubbilo*]   Great rejoicing.

971.5–6   Schola Cantorum]   Music school founded in Paris in 1895 by the composers Vincent d'Indy, Charles Bordes, and Alexandre Guilmant as an alternative to the Paris Conservatory.

976.2   Ouida and Marie Corelli]   Ouida (pen name of Marie Louise de la Ramée, 1839–1908) was the author of *Under Two Flags* (1867) and *Moths* (1880); the novels of Marie Corelli (1855–1924) included *The Soul of Lilith* (1892) and *The Sorrows of Satan* (1895).

976.3   *locataire*]   Owner.

976.20   *bonne à tout faire*]   Maid of all work.

979.3   *chauffe-eau*]   Water-heating.

979.34   *calme, ordre, luxe, et volupté*]   See Baudelaire, "L'Invitation au Voyage," from *Les fleurs de mal* (1857).

980.24   Jupiter-Ammon]   Ammon was an Egyptian god identified with Jupiter by the Romans.

983.32   *amor fati*]   Love of fate: a key term of the philosophical writings of Friedrich Nietzsche.

987.13–14   "*Ma Maria, ed . . . posso fare!*"]   "But Maria, and the child. The child!". . . "What can I do! What can I do!"

987.23   for Hecubas]   See *Hamlet*, II.ii.558–60.

Library of Congress Cataloging-in-Publication Data

Bellow, Saul.
[Novels. Selections]
 Novels, 1944–1953 / Saul Bellow.
        p.   cm. — (The Library of America; 141)
Contents: Dangling man — The victim — The adventures of Augie March.
ISBN 1–931082–38–3 (alk. paper)
I. Title. II. Dangling man. III. The victim.
IV. The adventures of Augie March. V. Library of America ; 141.

PS3503.E4488A6   2003
813°.52—dc21   2003040144

THE LIBRARY OF AMERICA SERIES

The Library of America fosters appreciation and pride in America's literary heritage by publishing, and keeping permanently in print, authoritative editions of America's best and most significant writing. An independent nonprofit organization, it was founded in 1979 with seed money from the National Endowment for the Humanities and the Ford Foundation.

*This book is set in 10 point Linotron Galliard,
a face designed for photocomposition by Matthew Carter
and based on the sixteenth-century face Granjon. The paper
is acid-free Domtar Literary Opaque and meets the requirements
for permanence of the American National Standards Institute. The
binding material is Brillianta, a woven rayon cloth made by
Van Heek-Scholco Textielfabrieken, Holland. The composition is by The Clarinda Company. Printing and
binding by R.R.Donnelley & Sons Company.
Designed by Bruce Campbell.*